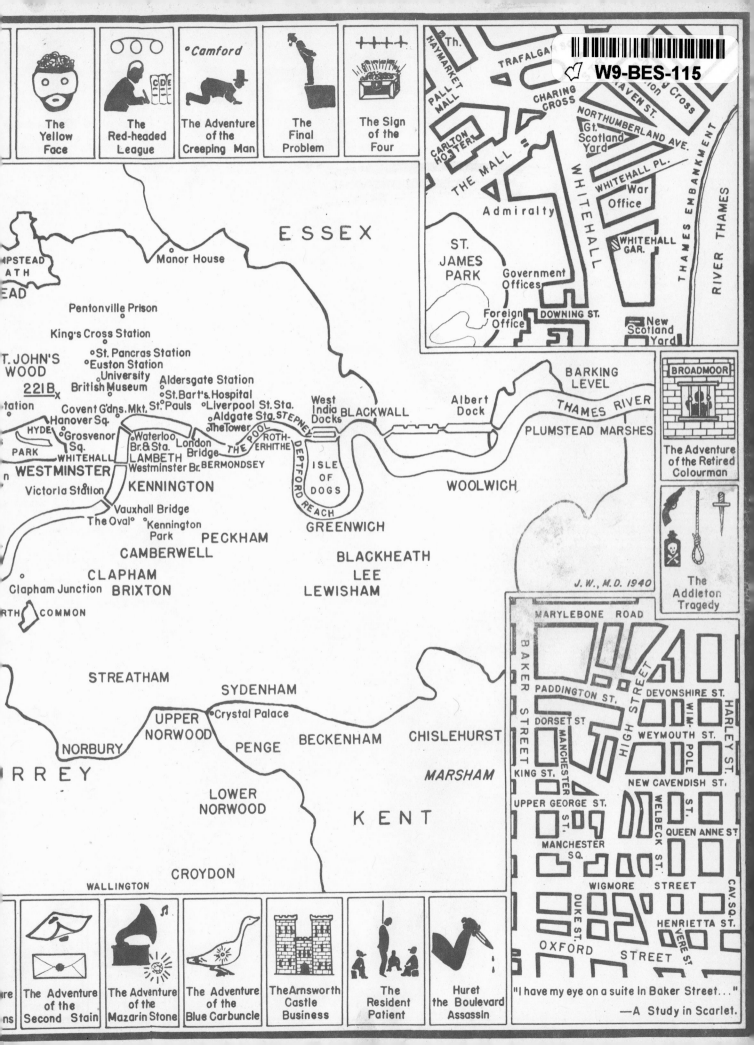

The Yellow Face

The Red-headed League

The Adventure of the Creeping Man

°Camford

The Final Problem

The Sign of the Four

BROADMOOR

The Adventure of the Retired Colourman

The Addleton Tragedy

ESSEX

Manor House

HAYMARKET
Th.
TRAFALGAR
PALL MALL
THE MALL
CARLTON HO. TER.
CHARING CROSS
NORTHUMBERLAND AVE.
Gt. Scotland Yard
WHITEHALL
WHITEHALL PL.
War Office
WHITEHALL GAR.
THAMES EMBANKMENT
RIVER THAMES
Admiralty
ST. JAMES PARK
Government Offices
Foreign Office
DOWNING ST.
New Scotland Yard

MPSTEAD ATH
EAD

Pentonville Prison

King's Cross Station
St. Pancras Station
Euston Station
University
British Museum
Aldersgate Station
St. Bart's Hospital
Liverpool St. Sta.
Aldgate Sta.
The Tower
St. Pauls
Covent G'dns. Mkt.

T. JOHN'S WOOD
221B
station

West India Docks
BLACKWALL
STEPNEY
ROTH-ERHITHE
BARKING LEVEL
THAMES RIVER
Albert Dock
PLUMSTEAD MARSHES

Hanover Sq.
HYDE PARK
Grosvenor Sq.
WHITEHALL
WESTMINSTER
Victoria Station

Waterloo Br. & Sta.
London Bridge
LAMBETH
Westminster Br.
BERMONDSEY
THE POOL
DEPTFORD REACH
ISLE OF DOGS
GREENWICH
WOOLWICH

KENNINGTON
Vauxhall Bridge
The Oval
Kennington Park
PECKHAM
CAMBERWELL
BLACKHEATH
LEE
LEWISHAM

CLAPHAM
Clapham Junction
BRIXTON
RTH COMMON

STREATHAM

SYDENHAM
Crystal Palace
UPPER NORWOOD
NORBURY
PENGE
BECKENHAM
CHISLEHURST

RREY

LOWER NORWOOD
MARSHAM
KENT

MARYLEBONE ROAD
BAKER STREET
PADDINGTON ST.
DORSET ST.
HIGH STREET
DEVONSHIRE ST.
WIM-POLE
HARLEY ST.
WEYMOUTH ST.
MANCHESTER ST.
KING ST.
NEW CAVENDISH ST.
UPPER GEORGE ST.
WELBECK ST.
QUEEN ANNE ST.
MANCHESTER SQ.
WIGMORE STREET
DUKE ST.
HENRIETTA ST.
OXFORD STREET
VERE ST.
CAV. SQ.

CROYDON
WALLINGTON

J. W., M.D. 1940

"I have my eye on a suite in Baker Street..."
—A Study in Scarlet

The Adventure of the Second Stain

The Adventure of the Mazarin Stone

The Adventure of the Blue Carbuncle

The Arnsworth Castle Business

The Resident Patient

Huret the Boulevard Assassin

SIR ARTHUR CONAN DOYLE

The creator of Sherlock Holmes and John H. Watson, M.D., from a pastel portrait by Henry Gates, 1933, after an oil painting by the same artist, 1927. The original hangs in the National Portrait Gallery, London, a presentation by Sir Arthur's daughter, Lady Bromet.

The
ANNOTATED
Sherlock Holmes

The ANNOTATED Sherlock Holmes

VOLUME I

THE FOUR NOVELS AND THE
FIFTY-SIX SHORT STORIES COMPLETE

BY SIR ARTHUR CONAN DOYLE

Edited, with an Introduction, Notes, and Bibliography by

WILLIAM S. BARING-GOULD

*Illustrated with Maps, Diagrams, Coats-of-Arms, Photographs,
and Drawings by Charles Doyle, Howard K. Elcock, D. H.
Friston, A. Gilbert, James Grieg, George Hutchinson, William
H. Hyde, Charles Raymond Macauley, Sidney Paget, Frederic
Dorr Steele, Arthur Twidle, Frank Wiles, and Numerous Others*

 *Clarkson N. Potter, Inc./Publisher* NEW YORK

DISTRIBUTED BY CROWN PUBLISHERS, INC.

Table of Contents

I trust that the younger public may find these romances of interest, and that here and there one of the older generation may recapture an ancient thrill.

ARTHUR CONAN DOYLE
Written in June, 1929, for his Preface to
The Complete Sherlock Holmes Long Stories

The enthusiast likes to dream of the great omnibus volume in which the whole Sherlockian codex would be annotated from end to end for a new generation.

CHRISTOPHER MORLEY
Written *circa* November, 1943, for his Introduction to *Sherlock Holmes and Dr. Watson: A Textbook of Friendship*

The
ANNOTATED
Sherlock Holmes

I. TWO DOCTORS AND A DETECTIVE:

SIR ARTHUR CONAN DOYLE,
JOHN H. WATSON, M.D., AND
MR. SHERLOCK HOLMES OF BAKER STREET

. . . the most famous and best beloved
physician in literature . . .—VINCENT STARRETT
Introduction to the Limited Edition Club's
The Adventures of Sherlock Holmes

. . . the most convincing, the most brilliant,
the most congenial and well-loved
of all detectives of fiction.—A. E. Murch,
The Development of the Detective Novel

STEEL TRUE
BLADE STRAIGHT
ARTHUR CONAN DOYLE
KNIGHT
PATRIOT, PHYSICIAN & MAN OF LETTERS

—His Epitaph

"I HEAR OF SHERLOCK EVERYWHERE SINCE YOU BECAME HIS CHRONICLER"

[Mycroft Holmes to John H. Watson, M.D., "The Greek Interpreter"]

"It is possible that there are some, who will read this, who have never read *The Valley of Fear*," said Mr. Anthony Boucher, introducing that last of the Sherlock Holmes novels to Limited Editions Club subscribers in 1952. "It is probable that there are others who have not read it recently and remember no details. . . . If you belong to either of these groups, . . . forego, at least for the time being, the rest of this introduction . . ."

We echo Mr. Boucher. If you have never read a Sherlock Holmes story, or if you have not read one for a long time—advance immediately to the opening story in this book and continue, perhaps, until you have reached the end of the volume. Then, if you have a mind to, kindly return to this introduction.

• • •

And now that we are both well acquainted with Mr. Sherlock Holmes and Dr. John H. Watson, let us settle down to a leisurely discussion of the detective, the doctor, and the man who created them both; the tributes that have been paid to all three; and some of the major problems raised by the "Sacred Writings," or Saga, or Canon.**1**

"Dr. Watson, Mr. Sherlock Holmes," said young Stamford, introducing them. And having performed his catalytic task, he disappeared from the Saga forever.**2**

Holmes had solved problems before his meeting with Watson; he was to handle, solo, at least one case ("The Adventure of the Lion's Mane") after the partnership was dissolved by his retirement in late 1903; but the adventures we remember best are those in which the detective and the doctor both played a part, and which Watson then recounted as part of his long series of reminiscences.

Watson's handwriting was the despair of typesetters. And it seems curious that this should have been so: as Professor Remsen Ten Eyck Schenck has pointed out ("Holmes, Cryptanalysis and the Dancing Men"), "A large part of Watson's professional activity . . . lay in writing and compounding prescriptions. In this connection, the importance of accuracy had been most thoroughly drilled into him: if he should confuse berberine and bebeerine, grams with grains, ounces with drachms (the symbols for these two differ only slightly), it could easily cost a patient's life."

1 Or Conan.

2 Unless, turned forger, he was also that Archie Stamford whom Holmes, in "The Adventure of the Solitary Cyclist," referred to as having been captured near Farnham, on the borders of Surrey.

3 Writing as he often did of events in the very recent past, Watson had to be exceedingly careful that he did not land himself, or Holmes, or both, in serious legal trouble. In a defense of Watson as a writer, Mr. Humfrey Michell has said that: "Actually, he was the most painstaking and accurate of chroniclers, whose elaborate notes and memoranda on each case were models of laborious compilation; in fact they constituted the official records of Holmes' professional practice, in which accuracy was necessarily beyond all other considerations. When he set out to tell the stories to the public, it was another matter, and, with considerable ingenuity by confusing dates and places, he was able to throw the inquisitive so completely off the scent that identification becomes impossible."

4 "We are thus forced to the conclusion, unwilling though we may be to admit it, that Watson did at least sometimes alter his data or embellish them, to strengthen the story in some way."—Nathan L. Bengis, "Take a Bow, Dr. Watson."

"Watson loved to dramatize and romanticize his reports; and if accuracy of facts suffered, so be it."—Hyman Parker, "Birdy Edwards and the Scowrers Reconsidered."

PICARDY PLACE, EDINBURGH

Where, on May 22, 1859, Sir Arthur Conan Doyle was born. Photograph by Morris Rosenblum, *The Baker Street Journal*, December, 1963.

He seems seldom to have checked proof against his original manuscript; a flagrant example is "The Adventure of Wisteria Lodge," in which Watson let "1892" stand as the year of the adventure (in 1892, Watson supposedly thought Holmes dead and buried beneath the waters of the Reichenbach Fall in Switzerland).

His memory was often faulty. To take but one instance: in "The Adventure of the Veiled Lodger," Holmes asks Watson, "Have you no recollection of the Abbas Parva tragedy?" "None, Holmes." "And yet you were with me then."

He had a disregard for time-sequence relationships and an apparently complete lack of "time-sense." "With one shining exception ["The Adventure of the Devil's Foot"]," the late Professor Jay Finley Christ wrote ("An Adventure in the Lower Criticism; Part I: Doctor Watson and the Calendar"), "whenever a reminiscence gives us (whether specifically or deducibly) the *year* of action, together with the *month*, the *day of the month*, and the *day of the week*, we are led into confusion, frustration and high glee (?)."

Too, Victorian discreetness—and his own native shrewdness **3**—frequently made it necessary for him to veil a name, a place, a date, the exact nature of an event. His writings are studded with phrases like "due suppression," "any details which would help the reader to identify the college or the criminal would be injudicious and offensive," "a carefully guarded account," "somewhat vague in certain details," "my reticence," "I am obliged to be particularly careful to avoid any indiscretion," "no confidence will be abused."

Add to this the fact that Watson was a master storyteller, and that no small part of his skill as a writer was his ability to communicate to the reader the full drama of a situation. To do so, as he himself admits, sometimes required "a little editing." How revealing is his statement in "The Adventure of the Illustrious Client": "Then [Holmes] told the story, which I would repeat in this way . . ."**4**

And we can all be thankful that Dr. Watson wrote as he did: half the fun in reading and rereading the Saga is that of catching him out—as generations of his admirers have been discovering for more than three-quarters of a century now.

Of course, the truth of the matter is that Watson wrote as he did because his creator—and the creator of Holmes and young Stamford—was also a master storyteller who was sometimes discourteous to his "facts" for the sake of his story.

"In short stories it has always seemed to me that so long as you produce your dramatic effect, accuracy of detail matters little," Conan Doyle once said. "I have never striven for it and have made some bad mistakes in consequence. What matter if I hold my readers?"

What matter indeed? And hold his readers he did.

Arthur Conan Doyle, the author of the Sherlock Holmes stories (and of many other writings, fictional and nonfictional, which he held to be far more important works) was born at Picardy Place, Edinburgh, on May 22, 1859. He was the son of Charles Doyle, a civil servant and spare-time painter of Irish descent, and his wife Mary Foley Doyle, also of Irish parentage.

On both sides, the line was distinguished: Mrs. Doyle could trace her ancestry back to the ancient house of Percy-Louvain, three times allied by marriage with princesses of the Plantagenet line.

As for the Doyles, they came originally from Pont d'Oilly near Rouen, in Normandy. They took part in the conquest of Ireland, and in 1333, Alexander d'Oilly was granted lands in County Wexford by King Edward III. A Roman Catholic family, the Doyles of the 17th and 18th centuries were gradually evicted from their lands. At the beginning of the last century, John, Sir Arthur's grandfather, left Ireland to settle in London. There, under the initials "HB," he soon became the leading political caricaturist of his day. He was the first but by no means the last of his family to enter the *Dictionary of National Biography*. Three of his sons won the same recognition: James, as a historian and genealogist; Henry, as an artist and Director of the National Gallery, Dublin; Richard, also an artist and a friend of men like Dickens and Thackeray (we shall have more to say of "Dicky" Doyle later).**5**

Conan Doyle's schooling began at the age of seven and continued, when he was nine, at Hodder, the preparatory school of Stonyhurst College, which he attended until he was sixteen. A year of schooling at Feldkirch in Austria was followed by his return to Edinburgh in the summer of 1876. Edinburgh University had a well-deserved reputation for the fine medical training available there, and it was soon decided that young Arthur should become a doctor. He entered the University in October, 1876, and commenced what he later called a "long weary grind at botany, chemistry, anatomy,

5 For the growing number of people who take an interest in heraldry, here is the blazoning of the Doyle family coat-of-arms: Quarterly, 1st grand quarter: argent, within a bordure counter-compony or and sable, 3 bucks' heads gules, erased, and attired or, arranged 2 & 1, for DOYLE. 2nd grand quarter: argent, a fess between 3 trefoils sable, within a bordure of the last, for FOLEY. 3rd grand quarter: quarterly, sable and erminois; in the 1st quarter a sword in bend sinister argent, pommel and hilt or, encircled by a wreath of the last; in the 4th a cinquefoil of the 3rd; in the center chief, pendent from a crimson ribbon, bordered blue, a representation of the golden cross and clasps presented to Maj.-Gen. Pack by H.M. George III, in testimony of his royal approbation of the signal valor displayed by the said Maj.-Gen. Pack in diverse actions with the enemy in the Peninsula of Spain, for PACK. 4th grand quarter: quarterly, 1st & 4th, or, a lion rampant azure between 3 trefoils vert; 2nd & 3rd, azure, 3 fusils in fess or between 2 silver trefoils in pale, all within a border compony gules and argent, for PERCY. Crest: out of a ducal coronet, a buck's head gules, attired or. Moto: *Fortitudine Vincit.*

"... DURING MY LAST YEARS AT THE UNIVERSITY ..."
(THE MUSGRAVE RITUAL)

Arthur Conan Doyle as a student at Edinburgh. From *Introducing Mr. Sherlock Holmes.*

"... OUR OWN BLAZONINGS AND CHARGES ..."
(THE MUSGRAVE RITUAL)

Sir Arthur Conan Doyle's bookplate, showing the family coat-of-arms. *The Baker Street Journal,* September, 1962.

... PICKED UP A HOUSE CALLED BUSH VILLA ...

From *Murder for Pleasure*, by Howard Haycraft.

6 In the period with which we are concerned, the British shilling was worth slightly less than a quarter in U.S. currency, making the British pound of twenty shillings worth approximately five American dollars. These figures will be convenient, if not strictly accurate, to use in our Introduction and Notes, but the reader need not remember them: we will translate pence, shillings, and pounds into pennies, quarters, and dollars as we go along.

7 There seems little doubt that "Dr. Cullingworth" in Conan Doyle's autobiographical novel, *The Stark Munro Letters*, represents the eccentric Dr. Budd.

8 When the income-tax paper arrived that year, Conan Doyle filled it up to show he was not liable. The authorities returned the form with the words, "Most unsatisfactory" scrawled across it. Conan Doyle wrote, "I entirely agree"—and sent the form back to the authorities.

9 One of which, published anonymously, was acclaimed by the critics as the work of Robert Louis Stevenson.

physiology, and a whole list of compulsory subjects, many of which have a very indirect bearing upon the art of curing."

Trying to help his family in vacation times (Charles Doyle fathered six other children), he worked as a medical assistant to doctors in Sheffield; Ruyton-of-the-eleven-towns, a tiny place in Shropshire; and Aston, Birmingham, where he was assistant to Dr. Reginald Ratcliffe Hoare at Clifton House, Aston Road North, a site now marked by a plaque (as is the birthplace of Sir Arthur Conan Doyle in Edinburgh).

It was here that Conan Doyle's first short story, "The Mystery of Sassassa Valley," was written and sold for £3 3s. ($15.75) **6** to *Chamber's Journal*, where it was published in the issue of October, 1879.

In February of 1880, Conan Doyle accepted a job as surgeon on a whaling ship, the *Hope*, and spent seven months in the Arctic. In the latter part of 1880 he returned to Aston where he remained until early in 1881 as assistant to Dr. Hoare, after which he resumed his studies for the degree of Bachelor of Medicine, which he took in August, 1881, as he said, "with fair but not notable distinction."

A voyage to Africa as medical officer on the ship *Mayumba* followed; then he went into partnership, at Plymouth, with an explosive friend he had made at Edinburgh, Dr. George Budd.**7** Through no fault of Conan Doyle's, there was friction between him and Budd, and he decided to leave. He arrived at Southsea, a suburb of Portsmouth, on an afternoon in July, 1882, picked up a house called Bush Villa (later renamed Doyle House by the owners; destroyed in the Blitz in 1941) at a rental of £40 ($200) a year plus another £10 ($50) in taxes, hung up his carefully burnished brass plate, and embarked on a practice that was neither very exacting nor very rewarding: he made £154 ($770) the first year,**8** £250 ($1,250) the second, never more than £300 ($1,500).

It may be asked here why a man who was born a patrician should have been so poor and without influence at the very outset of his professional career; the scion of a family which, though far from wealthy, could yet afford to entertain the Prime Minister, Sir Walter Scott, Cardinal Newman, and other celebrated men at their dinner table. The answer lies in the fact that Conan Doyle, who had left the Catholic faith, considered it dishonorable to use his letters of introduction to the Duke of Norfolk, the Bishop of Southsea, and other Catholic notables.

Soon young Arthur Conan Doyle was engaged to Louise Hawkins, the daughter of one of his patients; she became his first wife on August 6, 1885, a month after Conan Doyle had taken his doctorate.

Meantime, between 1878 and 1883, Conan Doyle had written and sold a few short stories**9** and had completed two novels, *The Narrative of John Smith*, lost in the post and never recovered, and *The Firm of Girdlestone*, which was then still making a dreary round of the publishers.

Now, in the March of 1886, with time on his hands and creditors at his door, young Dr. Conan Doyle—he was then only twenty-six—turned his mind to the writing of a detective story.

•   •   •

Our friend, Mr. Michael Harrison, thinks that the plot of *A Study in Scarlet* may have suggested itself to Conan Doyle by the real-life disappearance, in London, of a German baker, Urban Napoleon Stanger, whose name is echoed in the "Stangerson" of the story.[10] A private detective named Wendel Scherer had been called in to find the missing man, but he failed to do so, and the baker's manager, Franz Felix Stumm, was charged with the murder.

Conan Doyle set out to create a private detective who would *not* fail in such an assignment because he would have developed "habits of observation and inference into a system,"[11] and he thought at once of one of his former teachers at the University, Joseph Bell, M.D., F.R.C.S., consulting surgeon to the Royal Infirmary and Royal Hospital for Sick Children, member of University Court, Edinburgh University; born in Edinburgh in 1837, he died in 1911.

A "thin, wiry, dark" man, "with a high-nosed acute face, penetrating gray eyes, angular shoulders" and a "high discordant" voice, Dr. Bell "would sit in his receiving room with a face like a Red Indian, and diagnose the people as they came in, before they even opened their mouths. He would tell them their symptoms, and even give them details of their past life; and hardly ever would he make a mistake."

Of the many anecdotes told of Dr. Joseph Bell, here is one of the lesser-known (from the *Lancet*, issue of August 1, 1956):

> A woman with a small child was shown in. Joe Bell said good morning to her and she said good morning in reply. "What sort of a crossing di' ye have fra' Burntisland?" "It was guid." "And had ye a guid walk up Inverleith Row?" "Yes." "And what did ye do with th' other wain?" "I left him with my sister in Leith." "And would ye still be working at the linoleum factory?" "Yes, I am." "You see, gentlemen, when she said good morning to me I noted her Fife accent, and, as you know, the nearest town in Fife is Burntisland. You noticed the red clay on the edges of the soles of her shoes, and the only such clay within twenty miles of Edinburgh is in the Botanical Gardens. Inverleigh Row borders the gardens and is her nearest way here from Leith. You observed that the coat she carried over her arm is too big for the child who is with her, and therefore she set out from home with two children. Finally she has a dermatitis on the fingers of the right hand which is peculiar to workers in the linoleum factory at Burntisland."

Here is how Conan Doyle himself wrote about this period in his life, in his autobiography, *Memories and Adventures:*[12]

> I felt now that I was capable of something fresher and crisper and more workmanlike [than many of the detective stories that had been written up to that time]. Gaboriau had rather attracted me by the neat dovetailing of his plots, and Poe's masterful detective, M. Dupin, had from boyhood been one of my heroes. But could I

10 See Mr. Harrison's *London by Gaslight* and his standard guide to the London (and England) of Holmes and Watson, *In the Footsteps of Sherlock Holmes.*

11 As Mr. J. L. Hitchings was one of the first to point out (in "Sherlock Holmes, the Logician"), Holmes throughout the Canon is wont to refer to his entire process of reasoning as "the science of deduction." His usual method, however, is to make brilliant inferences from minute details he has observed—and this, strictly speaking, is *induction*— that is, reasoning from the particular to the general—rather than *deduction*—reasoning from the general to the particular. In "The Adventure of the Six Napoleons," Holmes refers to his reasoning as *inductive*, but in fact it is perhaps more *deductive* in this adventure than in any other.

12 "How"—Ellery Queen asked in his Introduction to *The Misadventures of Sherlock Holmes*— "how could [he] have resisted the overwhelming temptation to call his autobiography *Adventures and Memoirs*"?

YOUNG DR. ARTHUR CONAN DOYLE

As he looked in the Southsea days, from *Murder for Pleasure*, by Howard Haycraft.

DR. JOSEPH BELL OF EDINBURGH

An early photograph of the "fabulous original" upon whom Conan Doyle based Sherlock Holmes. From *Murder for Pleasure*, by Howard Haycraft.

bring an addition of my own? I thought of my old teacher Joe Bell, of his eagle face, of his curious ways, of his eerie trick of spotting details. If he were a detective he would surely reduce this fascinating business to something nearer an exact science. I would try if I could get this effect. It was surely possible in real life, so why should I not make it plausible in fiction? It is all very well to say that a man is clever, but the reader wants to see examples of it—such examples as Bell gave us every day in the wards.

Again, in a letter to Dr. Bell dated May 4, 1892, Conan Doyle wrote:

It is most certainly to you that I owe Sherlock Holmes, and though in the stories I have the advantage of being able to place [the detective] in all sorts of dramatic positions, I do not think that his analytical work is in the least an exaggeration of some effects which I have seen you produce in the out-patient ward. Round the centre of deduction and inference and observation which I have heard you inculcate I have tried to build up a man who pushed the thing as far as it would go—further occasionally—and I am so glad that the result has satisfied you, who are the critic with the most right to be severe.

Dr. Conan Doyle dedicated *The Adventures of Sherlock Holmes* to Dr. Joseph Bell, and Dr. Joseph Bell contributed a note on "Mr. Sherlock Holmes" (originally published in the *Bookman* of London) to the fourth English edition of *A Study in Scarlet* (London: Ward, Lock & Bowden, 1893).**13**

This, then, was the *inception*.

But here let us try to be quite clear:

Bell himself states that Conan Doyle has made a great deal out of very little and proceeds to give the credit for Sherlock Holmes' genius to Conan Doyle's own gifts and training.

"You are yourself Sherlock Holmes and well you know it," he wrote to Conan Doyle.

Bell, undoubtedly, was the model for the consulting detective, Sherlock Holmes. But Bell was *not* Sherlock Holmes as we best know him. Save for his remarkable gift of deduction, Bell was never once able, in real-life crime cases, to show that he possessed any Holmesian powers; Conan Doyle, on the other hand, as we shall see, played a part in the investigation of many real-life crimes; certainly he was consulted by Sir Bernard Spilsbury, H. Ashton-Wolfe, and other criminologists and police officials.

Let us compare the character of Holmes with the character of his creator:

Holmes, like Conan Doyle, was partial toward old dressing gowns, clay pipes, keeping documents and lacking the time to arrange them, a habit of working with a magnifying glass on his desk and a pistol in the drawer. "Holmes' ancestors, like Conan Doyle's, were country squires," Professor Pierre Weil Nordon of the University of Paris**14** has written in *Sir Arthur Conan Doyle*, a handsome volume issued in 1959

13 It is perhaps worth noting that Sherlock Holmes' resemblance to Dr. Joseph Bell did not go unremarked by at least one of Conan Doyle's avid readers. From Vailima, Apia, Samoa, Robert Louis Stevenson wrote to Conan Doyle on April 5, 1893: ". . . can this be *our old friend Joe Bell?*"

14 Professor Nordon, after almost a decade of research and writing, has now completed a definitive biography of Sir Arthur Conan Doyle. At this writing, it has already been published in France and England, and a U.S. edition is forthcoming.

as a centenary memorial to the author, "the author's grand-mother, Marianna Conan, was of French descent and Holmes' own grandmother was the sister of the French artist, Horace Vernet; Holmes' bank was the same as Conan Doyle's; he was offered a knighthood in the same year and in the same month as Conan Doyle was knighted;15 both evince a special interest in Winwood Reade, or in the origin of the Cornish dialect; both loathe suffragettes; both wish with the same eagerness the establishment of a close alliance between all English-speaking countries. Finally . . . Conan Doyle, like Holmes, was treated by criminologists as one of their colleagues, and was honoured by them when they gave his name to police laboratories."

The story of Conan Doyle's ingenuity in transmitting news of the first World War to British prisoners in Germany is well known: this he did by sending books in which he had put needle-pricks under various printed letters so as to spell out the desired messages, but beginning always with the third chapter in the belief that the German censors would examine the earlier chapters more carefully.

We have said that Conan Doyle interested himself in many real-life crimes: he investigated the Mrs. Rome case (result unknown); he looked into the missing Dane case (solved); he went to the scene of the killing in the Thorne murder. A statement from a journalist, now in the Conan Doyle archives, attests that it was Conan Doyle who put the police on the trail of that infamous murderer Smith in the celebrated "Brides-in-the-Bath" case.

As examples of Conan Doyle's interest in fair play and justice, however, the best-known cases are those of George Edalji and Oscar Slater.16

That Conan Doyle had a gift of his own for making quick and accurate deductions has been demonstrated in "Some Recollections of Sir Arthur Conan Doyle." Here Dr. Harold Gordon tells how Conan Doyle once

> stopped at the crib of a young baby, about two and a half years old. The child's mother was watching at the lad's side. Almost without hesitation, Sir Arthur turned to the mother and said, kindly but with authority, "You must stop painting the child's crib." Sure enough, the child was in with lead poisoning. We were aware of the diagnosis, but asked how he had arrived at the right conclusion so quickly. He smiled as he answered, "The child looked pale but well-fed. He was listless and his wrist dropped as he tried to hold a toy. The mother was neatly dressed, but she had specks of white paint on the fingers of her right hand. Children like to sharpen their teeth on the rails of a crib—so lead poisoning seemed a likely diagnosis."

Now, the name "Sherlock Holmes" did not come to Conan Doyle's mind in a flash of inspiration; he had to labor over it.

In *Memories and Adventures* he wrote: "What should I call the fellow? . . . One rebelled against the elementary art which gives some inkling of character in the name, and creates Mr. Sharps or Mr. Ferrets. First it was Sher*ringford* Holmes [our italics] . . ."

DR. JOSEPH BELL IN LATER LIFE

From *The Private Life of Sherlock Holmes*, by Vincent Starrett.

15 "How ridiculous that the author should only have been Knighted," the late Christopher Morley once commented. "He should have been Sainted."

16 George Edalji was sentenced in 1903 to seven years' penal servitude for horse-maiming. In 1906 Conan Doyle heard of this rather obscure case and, after exhaustive investigations lasting nearly a year, began a series of newspaper articles analyzing the incredibly weak evidence of the prosecution and making public "this blot upon the record of English justice." In consequence of Conan Doyle's endeavor, Edalji was released but denied compensation. In 1909, Oscar Slater was sentenced to death in Edinburgh for a brutal murder in Glasgow. This sentence was commuted to penal servitude for life. An unceasing battle was fought to prove Slater's innocence. Approached by Slater's lawyer, Conan Doyle took up this case of miscarriage of justice. It was not, however, until 1927 that Conan Doyle finally secured the release of Slater. The reader interested in knowing more about these cases is recommended to the three excellent accounts given by John Dickson Carr (in *The Life of Sir Arthur Conan Doyle*); Michael and Mollie Hardwick (in *The Man Who Was Sherlock Holmes*); and Vincent Starrett (in *The Private Life of Sherlock Holmes*).

17 The name Sherlock, as Mr. Duncan Mac-Dougald, Jr., has reported in "Some Onomatological Notes on 'Sherlock Holmes' and Other Names in the Sacred Writings," comes from the Irish *scorlóz*—Shearlock or Sherloch, which is derived from *searlóz*—Scurloch, Shirlock, or Sherloch, which in turn is the Gaelic version of the Anglo-Saxon *scortlog*, literally "short-lock," that is, one with shorn locks. Mr. MacDougald also notes that, according to Patrick Woulfe, *Irish Names and Surnames*, Dublin, 1923, the Sherlock family, "which, to judge from the name, is of Anglo-Saxon origin, had settled in Ireland before the beginning of the thirteenth century, and soon became very widespread, being found in Dublin, Meath, Louth, Wexford, Waterford, Tipperary, etc."

Sherlockian scholars, on the other hand, have speculated that Holmes was perhaps named for the famous Bishop Thomas Sherlock, 1678–1761, or his father, William Sherlock, 1641–1707, who became dean of St. Paul's and the author of *A Practical Discourse Concerning Death*. "There can be little doubt," Christopher Morley once wrote, "that the detective's full name was either Thomas Sherlock Holmes or William Sherlock Holmes."

But was even this the detective's *full* name? We know that Holmes took "Escott"—S (for Sherlock) Scott?—as his alias in "The Adventure of Charles Augustus Milverton," and this has led to the suggestion that the detective's *full* name was Thomas (or William) Sherlock Scott Holmes.

18 Sherlockians owe much of their information about Dr. James Watson to the researches of Dr. Maurice Campbell and his report of those researches to the Sherlock Holmes Society of London at their "Bruce-Partington Night Dinner," held on January 4, 1956.

19 The "middle-sized" will not pass without comment by that eminent Irregular, Mr. Elliot Kimball. In "The Stature of John H. Watson" he has demonstrated that "the amiable doctor was *five feet* and *ten inches* tall . . ."

20 In "The Adventure of the Red Circle," Holmes himself describes Watson's moustache as "modest."

21 He later repurchased the rights to the *Study*. Adrian M. Conan Doyle's recollection is that he paid £5,000 for them—two hundred times what he had originally been paid for the *Study*.

But Mr. Vincent Starrett first published in this country—in *The Private Life of Sherlock Holmes*—a page from an old notebook of Conan Doyle's on which the name Sherr*inford* Holmes—no *g*—is clearly to be seen.

Let us delve a little more deeply into the sources of the ultimate name—*Sherlock Holmes*.

The Holmes: As a student, Conan Doyle had gone without lunches to buy Oliver Wendell Holmes' *Autocrat, Poet*, and *Professor at the Breakfast Table* (as well as many other books). And Holmes (Oliver Wendell, Senior) was very much in the news in that May of 1886—he was making a famous and much-publicized visit to England. "Never have I so known and loved a man whom I had never seen," Conan Doyle wrote later. "It was one of the ambitions of my lifetime to look into his face, but by the irony of Fate I arrived in his native city just in time to lay a wreath on his newly turned grave."

The Sherlock: Mr. John Dickson Carr in his brilliant *Life of Sir Arthur Conan Doyle* tells us that the author hit on the Irish name of Sherlock**17** "entirely at random." But the Sherlocks *were* landowners in the very part of Ireland where the Doyle family had once held its estates—County Wicklow—and Conan Doyle, a student of heraldry, may well have seen the name in family papers. Again, Conan Doyle in a newspaper interview unearthed by Mr. Vincent Starrett was once quoted as saying that "years ago I made thirty runs [at cricket] against a bowler by the name of Sherlock, and I always had a kindly feeling for the name." We may take this quip for the little it is worth.

Now young Dr. Doyle needed a narrator for his story—a man who, mentally and physically, would provide a contrast with Holmes. Originally designated "Ormond Sacker," a name Conan Doyle speedily, and rightly, dropped as sounding much too dandified, "John H. Watson, M.D., late of the Army Medical Department," owes his surname to Conan Doyle's friend and fellow-member of the Southsea Literary and Scientific Society, *James* Elmwood Watson, M.D., Edinburgh, 1863. House physician at the Edinburgh Royal, then a physician to the British Consulate at Newchwung, Manchuria, Dr. James Watson had come to practice in Southsea in 1883.**18**

But here again other influences seem to have helped in molding the character. Watson only once in his own reminiscences allows a physical description of himself to creep in—in "The Adventure of Charles Augustus Milverton" he is "a middle-sized,**19** strongly built man—square jaw, thick neck, moustache . . ."**20**—and this is a very accurate description of Alfred Wood, in World War I, Major Alfred Wood, an associate of Conan Doyle's since 1885 who later served as secretary to the author until the Major's retirement in 1927.

And just as Conan Doyle in so many ways resembled Sherlock Holmes, so there are some remarkable parallels to be found in the lives of Conan Doyle and Dr. John H. Watson, though Conan Doyle was seven years the younger. Both started their medicine when they were seventeen, both studied at Edinburgh University, both received their M.D. degree when they were twenty-six (Conan Doyle at Edinburgh, Watson at the University of London). Conan Doyle had considered joining the army just as Watson did, but chose to go as a ship's surgeon instead. Both arrived at Plymouth by sea, Watson on November 26, 1880, Conan Doyle after a shorter voyage in July, 1882. Conan Doyle married in 1885 and Watson (your editor believes) married for the first time in 1886; both married again, Conan Doyle once, Watson perhaps twice.

And so at last, with his characters firmly fixed in his mind, Conan Doyle set furiously to work on the story he called at first *A Tangled Skein;* a month later, on a Sunday in late April, 1886, Mrs. Doyle was able to write to her husband's sister Lottie: "Arthur has written another book, a little novel about 200 pages long, called *A Study in Scarlet . . .*"

After several rejections it arrived, in October, 1886, on the desk of the chief editor of Ward, Lock & Co., Professor G. T. Bettany, who gave the manuscript to his wife to judge. She herself was a writer, and she was enthusiastic about the *Study:* "This man is a born novelist. It will be a great success!" But Messrs. Ward, Lock & Co. could not publish the manuscript for at least a year and they could give Conan Doyle only £25 ($125) for the copyright. The author objected to both the delay and the offer, and wrote to ask for a percentage of the sales. This was rejected, and Conan Doyle at last accepted the £25.**21**

"DR. WATSON, I PRESUME?"

Major Alfred Wood, for forty years secretary to Sir Arthur Conan Doyle. From *Sir Arthur Conan Doyle 1959 Centenary Memorial Volume.*

CONAN DOYLE'S NOTES FOR A STUDY IN SCARLET

A photostat of this page hangs in the museum of the Sherlock Holmes Tavern in Northumberland Street, London. The original of the page is a part of the Doyle Archives, in the possession of Mr. Adrian M. Conan Doyle. From *The Private Life of Sherlock Holmes,* by Vincent Starrett.

FRONT WRAPPER OF THE RARE FIRST EDITION OF
A STUDY IN SCARLET

The illustration, by an unknown artist, may be the first pictorial representation of Sherlock Holmes, although the late James Montgomery, certainly one of the foremost authorities on the iconography of the Canon, wrote that he could not support this connection. From *The Private Life of Sherlock Holmes,* by Vincent Starrett.

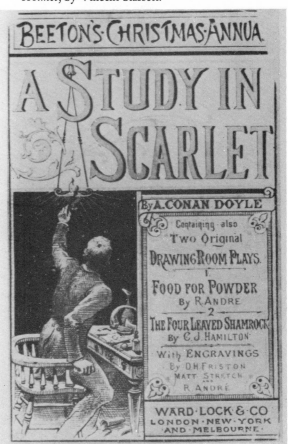

It was published, with four engravings, three of which show the initials D.H.F. (D. H. Friston),**22** in late November or early December, 1887, in the twenty-eighth issue of *Beeton's Christmas Annual*, a publication which had been founded in 1860 by Samuel Orchart Beeton and his wife Isabella Mary Beeton. The price: one shilling. "That lurid paperback," Mr. Vincent Starrett has written, "is today one of the rarest books of modern times—a keystone sought by discriminating collectors in every corner of the earth." A copy was last reported to have sold at more than $1,000— and it is noteworthy that, in spite of advertising and inquiries in the *London Times*, no copy of *Beeton's* could be found for the Sherlock Holmes Exhibition held during the Festival of Britain until a public-spirited citizen turned up with a copy he had acquired *for sixpence* at a London stall. Fortunately for collectors, the Baker Street Irregulars, Inc., and the Sherlock Holmes Society of London jointly published, in 1960, a complete and perfect facsimile edition of 168 pages —with multicolored cover, full contents including advertisements intact. Its price, then, to subscribers was $7, otherwise $10; today, it, too, is a collector's item.

The late Dorothy L. Sayers has said that *A Study in Scarlet* was "flung like a bombshell into the field of detective fiction,"**23** but Biographer Carr wrote: "And nothing happened. It was unlikely that any critic would trouble, at Christmas-time, to review an annual; and none did."

The indefatigable Vincent Starrett has nonetheless discovered one critic who *did* review the *Study*—in the *Graphic* for December 10, 1887:

> It is not at all a bad imitation but it would never have been written but for Poe, Gaboriau and R. L. Stevenson. . . . Those who like detective stories and have not read the great originals will find the tale full of interest. It hangs together well and finishes ingeniously.

And the equally indefatigable Dr. Julian Wolff has discovered a September 1, 1888, review of the *Study* in its first book appearance—also in the *Graphic*, but the *Graphic* in a considerably kinder mood:

> Nobody who cares for detective stories should pass over *A Study in Scarlet*. . . . The author has equalled the best of his predecessors. . . . He has actually succeeded in inventing a brand new detective. . . . The plot

A STUDY IN SCARLET, THE INCREDIBLY RARE FIRST SEPARATE PUBLICATION OF THE FIRST SHERLOCK HOLMES STORY (1888)

From *The Baker Street Journal*, January, 1946

JAMES GREIG'S COVER ILLUSTRATION FOR THE STUDY IN SCARLET SUPPLEMENT TO THE WINDSOR MAGAZINE FOR CHRISTMAS, 1895

is . . . daringly constructed. . . . There is no trace of vulgarity or slovenliness, too often characteristic of detective stories. . . . Besides being exceptionally ingenious, it may be read with pleasure by those [who] do not care for such things in a general way.

In any case, *Beeton's Christmas Annual* for Christmas, 1887, was a sellout. Early in 1888, Ward, Lock proposed a new edition in which the novel should appear by itself. "Though the author could [then] gain no penny out of it," Carr writes, "it was suggested that the new edition should be illustrated by his father, Charles Doyle. Ill and aged as he was, Charles Doyle produced six black-and-white drawings; and it must have brought tears to the old man's eyes when he learned his work was still wanted in London."

This edition of *A Study in Scarlet* in its original condition is by far the most difficult of all the Sherlock Holmes books for the collector to obtain; the location of only about four copies of each of the two printings is known.

The first American edition was published in Philadelphia by the J. B. Lippincott Company on March 1, 1890. An edition with a frontispiece and 39 other illustrations by George Hutchinson (11 of which were also included in the Lippincott edition of 1893) was published by Ward, Lock, Bowden & Co., London, in 1891. The previously mentioned note on "Mr. Sherlock Holmes" by Dr. Joseph Bell was included in the fourth English edition (London: Ward, Lock & Bowden, Ltd., 1893). And still another edition—this one with seven illustrations by James Greig—was issued as a supplement to the *Windsor Magazine* for Christmas, 1895.

Now, one reader of *A Study in Scarlet* was a Mr. Stoddard, the American editor of *Lippincott's Magazine*, which was published simultaneously in Philadelphia by J. B. Lippincott and in London by Ward, Lock. He wanted another Sherlock Holmes adventure to publish complete in a single issue, and he (or his representative: the record is not clear on this point) invited Conan Doyle and Oscar Wilde to dine at a London restaurant. Though Conan Doyle was then hard at work on his historical novel, *The White Company*, he promised *Lippincott's* another Sherlock Holmes adventure, and Wilde for his part agreed to write the short novel we know today as *The Picture of Dorian Gray*.

Conan Doyle paid a generous tribute to Wilde's artistry in *Memories and Adventures*. (Some critics, rather fancifully, have even thought that they could detect Wildean echoes in *The Sign of the Four*.) But Conan Doyle evidently did not recognize that Wilde, like Sherlock Holmes, could sometimes be guilty of a little leg-pulling. When Wilde urged Conan Doyle to see one of his plays—"Ah, you must go. It is wonderful. It is genius"—Conan Doyle rather heavily recorded in his diary that he thought Wilde must be mad.

The Sign of the Four; or, The Problem of the Sholtos, appeared in both the English and American *Lippincott's* for February, 1890, with a frontispiece by an unknown artist. Single copies of the issue, in either the London or the Philadelphia edition, are rarer than single copies of the *Strand Magazine* of 1891, but by no means as rare as *Beeton's*. (The

22 The fourth illustration is inscribed in very small letters W. M. H. Quick, "but available information has not yet determined conclusively whether that was the signature of the engraver or of a second artist," the late James Montgomery wrote in *A Study in Pictures*. "Certainly the illustration . . . is identical in style and execution with the three bearing the initials 'D.H.F.'"

23 Introduction to *Great Short Stories of Detection, Mystery and Horror*, titled, in the United States, *The Omnibus of Crime*.

THE COVER OF LIPPINCOTT'S MAGAZINE FOR FEBRUARY, 1890

This was the first publication of the second Sherlock Holmes story, *The Sign of the Four*.

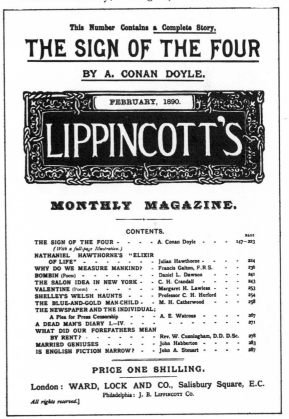

"WHAT HE HAD NOW WAS NO LONGER A PUPPET . . ."

This caricature by Sir Bernard Partridge originally appeared in *Punch* in 1926.

24 The earliest known book publication of *The Sign of the Four* in America was a piracy—by the *Once a Week Library* (New York: P. F. Collier), issue of March 15, 1891. The first authorized American book edition was published in Philadelphia by the J. B. Lippincott Company in 1893.

25 In America the first series of short stories was published, simultaneously with their appearance in the *Strand*, in a large number of daily newspapers, serviced by the newly formed McClure's Syndicate—"no small item," says Howard Haycraft in *Murder for Pleasure*, "in Holmes' early and wide American renown."

26 The first twelve short stories were published in book form by George Newnes of London in 1892, in an edition that included 104 illustrations drawn for the *Strand Magazine* by Sidney Paget. The first American edition of *The Adventures of Sherlock Holmes*, with a frontispiece and 15 other illustrations by Paget, was published by Harper & Brothers of New York that same year. In 1902 Newnes published a "Souvenir" edition that contained a frontispiece and 20 other illustrations by Paget, all from the 1892 edition, and in 1958 the Folio Society of London published a handsome edition with 12 illustrations by Paul Hogarth.

London issue is far harder to come by than the Philadelphia issue.) Just as bound *Strand*s are easier to find than single copies, so are bound *Lippincott's*.

When Spencer Blackett published the adventure in book form (with a frontispiece by Charles Kerr) in the spring of 1890—as *The Sign of Four*, which Conan Doyle always preferred to call it—"it faded away with scarcely more critical attention than had attended *A Study in Scarlet*."**24**

Said the critic of the London *Athenaeum* (December 6, 1890):

> A detective story is usually lively reading, but we cannot pretend to think that *The Sign of Four* is up to the level of the writer's best work. It is a curious medley, and full of horrors; and surely those who play at hide and seek with the fatal treasure are a curious company. The wooden-legged convict and his fiendish misshapen little mate, the ghastly twins, the genial prizefighters, the detectives wise and foolish, and the gentle girl whose lover tells the tale, twist in and out together in a mazy dance, culminating in that mad and terrible rush down the river which ends the mystery and the treasure. Dr. Doyle's admirers will read the little volume through eagerly enough, but they will hardly care to pick it up again.

No, the bombshell that was Holmes was not to explode until Conan Doyle conceived the then brand new (in England) idea of *writing a series of short stories around one central character*. His agent, A. P. Watt, sent the first of the series—"A Scandal in Bohemia"—to the acting editor of the *Strand Magazine*, "the shrewd, bespectacled, heavily moustached" Greenhough Smith, who liked the story and encouraged Conan Doyle to write a series of six, for which he agreed to pay an average of £35 ($175) each.

The speed with which Conan Doyle could work is shown by his diary: on Friday, April 10, 1891, a week after sending off "A Scandal in Bohemia," he noted: "Finished 'A Case of Identity.'" On Monday the 20th he sent off "The Red-Headed League." On the 27th he posted "The Boscombe Valley Mystery." After that he wrote "The Five Orange Pips," but it was not mailed until Monday, May 18th, because he was prostrated by an attack of influenza.

When "A Scandal in Bohemia" appeared in the July, 1891, issue of the *Strand*,**25** Holmes at last did blaze into popularity, and by October 14th of that year Conan Doyle could write to his mother that his publishers were "imploring him to continue Holmes."

He raised his price to £50 ($250) a story "irrespective of length" and a letter by return post agreed to his terms for six more adventures. He at once began work on the seventh in the series—"The Adventure of the Blue Carbuncle"—and by November 11th he was able to report to his mother that he had completed all but one of the additional half-dozen.**26**

"I think," Conan Doyle added casually, "of slaying Holmes in the last and winding him up for good. He takes my mind from better things."

"You won't!" his mother raged. "You can't. You *mustn't*."

So he ended the twelve adventures with that of "The Copper Beeches," based on an idea suggested to him by his mother. Sherlock Holmes' life—for the time being, at least—had been saved by "the Ma'am."

"They"—the editors of the *Strand*—"have been bothering me for more Sherlock Holmes tales," Conan Doyle wrote to his mother in February, 1892. "Under pressure I offered to do a dozen for a thousand pounds, but I sincerely hope they won't accept it now."

A thousand pounds—$5,000—was a very large payment in 1892, but accept it the *Strand* did, and "Silver Blaze," the first of the new series, duly appeared in the December, 1892, issue of the magazine.**27**

Early in the next year—but let Conan Doyle tell it himself: "I went with my wife for a short holiday in Switzerland, in the course of which we saw the wonderful falls of Reichenbach, a terrible place, and one that I thought would make a worthy tomb for Sherlock, even if I buried my banking account along with him . . ."**28**

Back home, Conan Doyle on April 6th again wrote to his mother: "I am in the middle of the last Holmes story, after which the gentleman vanishes, never to return. I am weary of his name."

"What he had now was no longer a puppet," John Dickson Carr wrote; "it was an Old Man of the Brain locked round him with a windpipe-grip."

And so, "with a happy sigh of relief," he sat down to write the story he had hopefully titled "The Final Problem."

"Killed Holmes," he noted laconically in his diary a short time later . . .

•   •   •

Sherlock Holmes dead?

The amazed readers of the *Strand Magazine* (and of *Mc-Clure's Magazine* in America) could scarcely believe their eyes. Conan Doyle heard of many who wept, of sober City men who even went to their work wearing mourning bands. He himself wrote:

> I was amazed at the concern expressed by the public. They say a man is never properly appreciated until he is dead, and the general protest against my summary execution of Holmes taught me how many and how numerous were his friends. "You Brute!" was the beginning of the letter of remonstrance which one lady sent me, and I expect she spoke for others beside herself. . . . I fear I was utterly callous myself, and only glad to have a chance of opening out into new fields of imagination, for the temptation of high prices made it difficult to get one's thoughts away from Holmes.

"There will be only a temporary interval in the Sherlock Holmes stories," the editors of the *Strand* rather hysterically hastened to assure their readers. "A new series will commence in an early number. Meanwhile, powerful detective stories will be contributed by other eminent writers."

"LIFE'S DARKEST MOMENT"

One of the late H. T. Webster's well-remembered cartoons.

27 In America, its first appearance was in the February 25, 1893, issue of *Harper's Weekly*. Eleven of the twelve short stories in this series (the exception is "The Cardboard Box") were first published in book form as *The Memoirs of Sherlock Holmes* by George Newnes of London in 1894. All twelve stories were included in the first American edition, published by Harper & Brothers of New York two months later in the year. At Conan Doyle's insistence, however, this edition was withdrawn from circulation and a second American edition, omitting "The Cardboard Box," was printed and distributed. Conan Doyle had grave thoughts about the propriety of "The Cardboard Box," with its outspoken—for those days—admission that there could be sex without marriage. With changing manners and morals, Conan Doyle relented and allowed the story to be printed in book form at last as part of his 1917 collection, *His Last Bow*.

28 Another result of the visit to Switzerland was Conan Doyle's poem, "An Alpine Walk," first published in the *Independent* for December 14, 1893; reprinted in the *Baker Street Journal*, Vol. XII, No. 3, New Series, July, 1962, p. 134.

29 Conan Doyle received, *for the American rights alone*, $5,000 a story for the thirteen stories that make up *The Return of Sherlock Holmes*. This is believed to be the highest price per story ever paid to an author up to that time.

"THE RE-APPEARANCE OF SHERLOCK HOLMES"

How the *Strand Magazine*, in its issue of October, 1901, promoted the public's reaction to the opening installments of *The Hound of the Baskervilles*.

But Dr. Conan Doyle stood firm—though "readers implored him, editors cajoled him, agents worried him, publishers tried to bribe him, some people even threatened him."

"I couldn't revive him if I would, at least not for years," Conan Doyle wrote to a friend, "for I have had such an overdose of him that I feel towards him as I do towards *pâté-de-foie-gras*, of which I once ate too much, so that the name of it gives me a sickly feeling to this day."

Not for eight years, not until 1901, would he publish a new Sherlock Holmes story, and then he was careful to date it *before* the Affair Reichenbach; *The Hound of the Baskervilles* was a *reminiscence*, not a *resurrection*, of Sherlock Holmes.

It was nonetheless a tremendous success.

The circulation of the *Strand* soared 30,000 copies an issue with the number in which the first installment of the *Hound* appeared (August, 1901); the magazine could not print enough copies fast enough to meet the demand; long queues formed in Southampton Street to buy them straight from the presses. George Newnes of London brought it out in book form in 1902, with 16 of Sidney Paget's 60 *Strand* illustrations, in the largest edition so far accorded a Sherlock Holmes book, and McClure, Phillips & Company of New York issued it in the same year in America, with eight of Paget's illustrations. On both sides of the Atlantic, Holmes enthusiasts greeted the volume with raptures.

Conan Doyle began to weaken somewhat in his decision never to resuscitate Holmes.

In an interview quoted in *Harper's Weekly* for August 31, 1901, he is reported to have said:

"I know that my friend Dr. Watson is a most trustworthy man, and I gave the utmost credit to his story of the dreadful affair in Switzerland. He may have been mistaken, of course. It may not have been Mr. Holmes who fell from the ledge at all, or the whole affair might be the result of hallucination . . ."

His final surrender came in October, 1903, with the publication of "The Adventure of the Empty House."**29**

The Return of Sherlock Holmes ended with "The Adventure of the Second Stain," published in the *Strand Magazine* for December, 1904, and *Collier's Magazine* for January 28, 1905. The thirteen stories that made up the series were first published in book form by George Newnes of London in 1905, with 16 illustrations by Sidney Paget. The first American edition, by McClure, Phillips & Company of New York, with a frontispiece and 12 interior illustrations by Charles Raymond Macauley, was published the same year. (The Newnes edition is now extremely hard to find—and it is growing less modestly priced with every passing year.)

"And yet," says Howard Haycraft . . .

And yet the reception of the new tales was not entirely unmixed. Doyle enjoyed relating a homely incident that expressed the popular mind neatly. "I think, sir," he quoted a Cornish boatman as saying to him, "when Holmes fell over that cliff he may not have killed himself, but he was never quite the same man afterwards."

The Return of Sherlock Holmes was followed by the novel, *The Valley of Fear,***30** and by two more collections of Sherlock Holmes short stories, *His Last Bow* (London: John Murray, 1917; New York: George H. Doran Company, 1917) and *The Case-Book of Sherlock Holmes* (London: John Murray, 1927; New York: George H. Doran Company, 1927).

The sixtieth, and last, of the Sherlock Holmes adventures, "Shoscombe Old Place," was published in March, 1927.

We should mention here, however, that Conan Doyle wrote two short stories in which Sherlock Holmes *may* be present, though offstage. The first, "The Man With the Watches," appeared in the *Strand Magazine* for July, 1898; here "a well-known criminal investigator" writes a letter to the press which purportedly appeared in the *Daily Gazette* in March of 1892. A month later, in its issue of August, 1898, the *Strand* published an account of "The Lost Special," in which Conan Doyle quoted a letter which appeared, it is said, on July 3, 1890, in the *London Times*, "over the signature of an amateur reasoner of some celebrity at that date." The extract begins: "It is one of the elementary principles of practical reasoning that when the impossible has been eliminated the residuum, *however improbable*, must contain the truth"—and this, as we shall see, was the favorite axiom of Mr. Sherlock Holmes.**31**

We should also mention that the August, 1948, issue of *Cosmopolitan Magazine* carried what was billed on the cover as "The Last Adventure of SHERLOCK HOLMES . . . A hitherto unpublished story by Sir Arthur Conan Doyle." This was the story titled "The Man Who Was Wanted," with two splendid illustrations by Robert Fawcett. In fact, the story was written by a retired English architect who had fallen upon hard times, Arthur Whitaker, who sent the story to Conan Doyle. "Create your own characters," Conan Doyle replied, but typically he sent Whitaker a check for £10 which was gratefully received. Conan Doyle then tossed "The Man Who was Wanted" into his wastebasket. Rescued by Lady Conan Doyle and filed among the author's papers, it was found years after the death of Lady and Sir Arthur Conan Doyle. The Doyle Estate, under the natural impression that it was indeed "a hitherto unpublished story by Sir Arthur Conan Doyle," sold it in good faith to the Hearst Magazines. It also appeared in three installments in the *Sunday Dispatch* of London, Manchester, and Edinburgh, issues of January 2, 9, and 16, 1949, with ten tiny illustrations about the size of a postage stamp and one larger illustration of Holmes the width of a column—no mention of the artist's name.

"And so, reader, Farewell to Sherlock Holmes," Conan Doyle wrote. "I thank you for your constancy and can but hope that some return has been made in the shape of that distraction from the worries of life and stimulating change of thought which can only be found in the fairy kingdom of romance."

Still, publishers continued to hope that Conan Doyle would write more about Sherlock Holmes. George Doran, in his *Chronicles of Barabbas* (1935) writes: "It occurred to me that since Doyle declined to write further Sherlock

30 *The Valley of Fear* was serialized in the United States in ten weekly installments from September 20, 1914, to November 22, 1914, inclusive, by the Associated Sunday Newspapers, Inc., a syndicated publication which formed a Sunday magazine supplement to various newspapers throughout the country. The series was illustrated by 12 drawings by Arthur I. Keller. This constitutes the first complete appearance of the story anywhere, since its monthly serialization in the *Strand Magazine* did not begin until the September, 1914, issue and did not end until May, 1915. There it was embellished with 31 illustrations by Frank Wiles. In book form also, the American edition, with seven illustrations by Arthur I. Keller, published by the George H. Doran Company of New York on March 1, 1915, constitutes the true first edition. The English edition, with a frontispiece by Frank Wiles, was first published by Smith, Elder & Co. of London on June 15, 1915 (dates taken from the *Publisher's Weekly* and the *Publisher's Circular*, respectively, by Professor David A. Randall for his article, "*The Valley of Fear* Bibliographically Considered").

31 The late Edgar W. Smith, in 1942, proposed that both these tales should be "subsumed" into the Holmesian Canon. It was pointed out at the time that the letter in the *Gazette* must have been the work of Mycroft Holmes, Sherlock being in Tibet at the time. It was also suggested that "The Lost Special" was material which Dr. Watson proposed to amplify into the case he once referred to as concerning "the papers of Ex-President Murillo."

32 After the death of a son in World War I, Conan Doyle had become deeply immersed in spiritualistic phenomena; indeed, he became a world leader in the movement.

"HIS GREATEST ADVENTURE"

Editorial comment on the death of Sir Arthur Conan Doyle, *New York World*, July 7, 1930.

Holmes adventures in anything like their old form, a biography of Dr. Watson . . . might provide him with a perfectly legitimate vehicle for further cases." Conan Doyle conceded that this was the best idea he had heard about for a revival of Holmes, but felt at the time "he could not take himself away from his psychic work."**32**

Early in 1930, Conan Doyle set forth on a lecture tour of the Continent from which he returned suffering from angina pectoris, the result of overstrain. "I am quite prepared to go or stay," he told a friend, "for I know that life and love go on forever."

At his home in Crowborough, Sussex, at half-past nine on the morning of July 7, 1930, Sir Arthur Conan Doyle died.

He lies today in the churchyard at Minstead in the heart of the New Forest—that same New Forest which provided the background for so many of the scenes in his book *The White Company*, that same New Forest for whose glades Watson yearned on a blazing hot day in August when Baker Street was "like an oven."

As this is written, a fitting memorial to Sir Arthur Conan Doyle is being prepared by his son Adrian. The eleventh-century Château de Lucens, Lucens, Switzerland, will house his papers, letters, documents, pressbooks, and other memorabilia—"probably the most complete biographical records of any literary figure in the past hundred years." Here, too, will be the third and finest of "the Sherlock Holmes Rooms" —a reproduction of the old sitting room where Holmes and Watson so often sat and talked while "the storm grew louder and louder, and the wind cried and sobbed like a child in the chimney."

CHÂTEAU DE LUCENS, LUCENS, SWITZERLAND

The new home of the Doyle Collection and the third and finest Sherlock Holmes Room. Photograph courtesy of Mr. Adrian M. Conan Doyle.

6 Two additional Solar Pons adventures, jointly agented by Mr. Derleth and Mr. Mack Reynolds, appear in *The Science-Fictional Sherlock Holmes*: "The Adventure of the Snitch in Time" and "The Adventure of the Ball of Nostradamus." The Solar Pons books have all been published by one of Mr. Derleth's own three publishing houses: Mycroft & Moran of Sauk City, Wisconsin. For the fourth volume the late Robert R. Pattrick prepared "A Chronology of Solar Pons"; for the fifth, Mr. Michael Harrison, author of *In the Footnotes of Sherlock Holmes*, contributed a monograph on Dr. Lyndon Parker, Pons' Watson.

Mystery Magazine. The author is Robert L. Fish, under his own name and a slightly disguised pseudonym the writer of a first-rate series of detective-intrigue-suspense-crime novels. We concur with Mr. Anthony Boucher, who has said that "It seems to me at least possible that Robert L. Fish is writing the very best Holmesian parodies in all the long history of the Misadventures." Mr. Fish's detective is Schlock Homes (of Bagle Street); his friend and companion in adventure is Dr. Watney.

Novel-length pastiches—beginning with *A Taste for Honey* (New York: Vanguard, 1941)—have been written by Mr. H. F. Heard; the name Sherlock Holmes is never mentioned, but they do concern a detective who calls himself "Mr. Mycroft" and keeps bees on the Sussex Downs.

In volume, however, the king of the pastiche writers is certainly Mr. August Derleth of Sauk City, Wisconsin. He wrote his first adventure of "Solar Pons"—"The Adventure of the Black Narcissus"—in the early autumn of 1928, when he was in his junior year at the University of Wisconsin, and it was published by Harold Hersey in the February, 1929, issue of *Dragnet Magazine*. In the September issue of the same magazine, Solar Pons appeared for a second time in "The Adventure of the Broken Chessman," and in 1945 he made his bow in his first book collection, *The Adventures of Solar Pons*. At this writing, there are four major collections of Solar Pons short stories—comprising, in all, 56 adventures from that of "The Frightened Baronet" to that of "The Innkeeper's Clerk"—*The Adventures*, *The Memoirs*, *The Return*, *The Reminiscences*, and *The Casebook of Solar Pons*.**6**

As Mr. Vincent Starrett wrote in introducing the first Pontian collection, Pons is "a clever impersonator, with a twinkle in his eye, which tells us that he is not Sherlock Holmes, and knows that *we* know it, but that he hopes we will like him anyway for what he symbolizes"—and, Mr. Anthony Boucher has added, "for what he *is* as well."

Few admirers of Sherlock Holmes and Dr. John H. Watson could ask for anything more.

"HE IS NOW TRANSLATING MY SMALL WORKS INTO FRENCH"

[*Sherlock Holmes to John H. Watson, M.D.*, The Sign of the Four]

It must not be thought that it was only in England and America that Sherlock Holmes was known and loved.

In France and Germany, the translated Canon enjoyed a great vogue.

Holland saw numerous translations of Holmes' exploits, many illustrated with the *Strand Magazine* drawings of Sidney Paget.

In prerevolutionary Russia, Sherlock Holmes had been a hero since individual stories from the Saga began to appear at the turn of the century; the works of Sir Arthur Conan Doyle, complete up to the time, were published in Russia in 1909.

In Spain and Latin America, the popularity of the great detective owed much to translations but even more to a lengthy series of pastiches called the *Memorias íntimes de Sherlock Holmes*.

One of the treasures of your editor's own collection is a copy of *The Hound of the Baskervilles* in Japanese.

That genial Sherlockian, Mr. Irving Fenton, has in fact devoted a good part of his long lifetime to collecting the adventures of Sherlock Holmes in foreign editions.

In short, as the late Elmer Davis wrote in "The Real Sherlock Holmes," "there can be few languages if any that do not know [Sherlock Holmes]. If you want to brush up on your Arabic, or your Swedish, or your Polish, or your Croatian, with the aid of a pony, you need go no farther than the New York Public Library to read the history of Sherlock Holmes in those tongues."

And Mr. Adrian M. Conan Doyle, the author's son, has stated in a letter which appeared in the *Daily Telegraph*, October 8, 1955, that in the previous year "our sales in all languages . . . totalled 500,000 copies. This has amounted to about 10 million copies over the past few years. The Russians owe us an equivalent of £500,000 in unpaid royalties. It should be added, however, that the Russian publishing figures include *The Lost World*, which seems to be as popular in Russia as Sherlock Holmes."

HOLMES IN RUSSIA, HOLMES IN HOLLAND

(*Above*) An edition of "The Adventure of the the Six Napoleons" published for the Little Library of the *Journal of the Red Army Soldier*. From *The Sherlock Holmes Journal*, Winter, 1956. (*Below*) A recent edition in Dutch of "The Adventure of the Naval Treaty" and "The Adventure of Charles Augustus Milverton." From *The Sherlock Holmes Journal*, Winter, 1961.

1 "The Adventure of the Two Collaborators" may be read in Ellery Queen's collection, *The Misadventures of Sherlock Holmes; it was also reprinted in the *Baker Street Journal*, Vol. VII, No. 4, New Series, October, 1957, pp. 221B–24.

2 "The Field Bazaar" first appeared in the *Student*, Edinburgh, November 20, 1896. Its first separate appearance was in a private edition for the Sherlock Holmes Society's annual dinner, London, 1939, printed by Mr. A. G. Macdonell in an edition limited to 100 copies. Its first appearance in an anthology was in *221B: Studies in Sherlock Holmes*. Its second separate appearance, with an introduction by the late Edgar W. Smith, was by the Pamphlet House: Summit, N.J., 1947; limited to 250 copies.

3 "How Watson Learned the Trick" made its first appearance in the *Book of the Queen's Doll's House Library;* London: Methuen & Co., Ltd., Vol. II, pp. 92–94, edited by E. V. Lucas in 1924. Its first separate appearance was in a private edition by Robert J. Bayer and Vincent Starrett; Chicago: Camden House, 1947; limited to 60 copies. It made a magazine appearance in the *Baker Street Journal*, Vol. I, No. 2, New Series, April, 1951, with a special note by Edgar W. Smith. It was also included in Mr. Smith's anthology, the *Incunabular Sherlock Holmes*, in 1958.

In 1958, the Doyle Estate reported that it was drawing royalties in 72 currencies; and Mr. Adrian M. Conan Doyle has also stated (in a letter to *The New York Times*, reported on May 20, 1962), that the present translation of his father's works (Sherlock Holmes and others) "now can be met in forty-one languages, including Eskimo, Esperanto, Basuto, Afrikaans and shorthand. The works have been published in thirty-eight countries."

"It has been stated, and I think correctly, that the Sherlock Holmes books sales are second only to the Bible," Mr. Conan Doyle had written earlier.

"More significant of [Holmes'] stature than the translations" (we are again quoting Mr. Davis) "are the parodies, the burlesques, the apocryphal additions to his history. The best of the burlesques were by Bret Harte and John Kendrick Bangs, the indubitably worst by Mark Twain; Mr. Starrett lists many others, unfortunately omitting O. Henry's tale of the success of Shamrock Jolnes in finding the missing scrubwoman. Of the foreign imitations, some, such as [Maurice] Leblanc's *Arsène Lupin vs. Herlock Sholmes*, were apparently authorized, or at least condoned . . ."

Conan Doyle himself thought that by far the best of the parodies was "The Adventure of the Two Collaborators," written by Sir James M. Barrie after the play *Jane Annie*, on which he had collaborated with Conan Doyle in 1893, had proved a dismal failure.**1** But Holmes enthusiasts will perhaps prefer the two parodies of the Sherlock Holmes stories that were written by Conan Doyle himself. The first of these, "The Field Bazaar," takes the form of the familiar and well-loved Holmes-Watson breakfast scene.**2** The second, "How Watson Learned the Trick," written in the third person, again takes the form of a breakfast-table conversation.**3**

The pick of the short parodies and pastiches, written up to 1944, have been collected by Ellery Queen in the previously mentioned anthology, *The Misadventures of Sherlock Holmes*. Elsewhere (in his introduction to August Derleth's *The Memoirs of Solar Pons*) Ellery Queen has written:

> . . . more has been written about Sherlock Holmes than about any other character in fiction, and more has been written about Holmes *by others* than by [Conan Doyle] himself. The numerous pastiches, parodies, and burlesques of Sherlock Holmes have given birth to a whole mythogenesis of reasonable and unreasonable facsimiles, both of the character and the name. As a general rule, the writers of pastiches have retained the sacred and inviolate form—Sherlock Holmes—and rightfully, because a pastiche is a serious and sincere imitation in the exact manner of the original. But writers of parodies and burlesques, which are humorous or satirical take-offs, have had no such reverent scruples. They usually strive for the weirdest possible distortions, and it must be admitted that many highly ingenious travesties of the name have been conceived. Fortunately or unfortunately the name Sherlock Holmes is peculiarly susceptible to the twistings and misshapings of burlesque-minded idolators.

Here is a by-no-means complete list of these "twistings and misshapings":

Sherlock Abodes	Stately Homes
Fetlock Bones	(of England)
Haricot Bones	Purlock Hone
Thinlock Bones	Sheerluck Hums
Warlock Bones	Hemlock Jones
Oilcock Combs	Sherlaw Kombs
Herlock Domes	Sheerluck Ohms
Picklock Holes	Holmlock Shears
Hemlock Holmes	Kerlock Shomes
Loufork Holmes	Herlock Soames
Padlock Homes	Sheerluck Soames

And here is what "burlesque-minded idolators" have done to poor Watson:

Dawson	Whatsup
Potson	Whatson
Watsoname	Watts Ion
Goswell	Warsaw
Spotson	Watts
Watsis	

In science fiction, Sherlock Holmes even has a Martian counterpart in Syaloch, of the "Street of Those Who Prepare Nourishment in Ovens."**4**

Of the pastiches—the serious and sincere imitations in the manner of the original—Edgar W. Smith has written (in his introduction to August Derleth's *The Return of Solar Pons*):

> There is no Sherlockian worthy of his salt who has not, at least once in his life, taken Dr. Watson's pen in hand and given himself to the production of a veritable adventure. . . . The writing of a pastiche is compulsive and inevitable; it is, the psychologists would say, a wholesome manifestation of the urge that is in us all to return to the times and places we have loved and lost, an evidence, specifically, of our happily unrepressed desire to make ourselves at one with the Master of Baker Street and all his works—and to do this not only receptively, but creatively as well . . .

At the top of the list of the many pastiches that have been written by detective-story writers, famous literary figures, humorists, devotees, and others, we must certainly place Mr. Vincent Starrett's "The Adventure of the Unique Hamlet."**5**

Next on the list should go *The Exploits of Sherlock Holmes*, a series of twelve "simulacra" written by Adrian M. Conan Doyle and John Dickson Carr. Of these, six were written by Mr. Doyle, two by Mr. Carr, and four were collaborations. The first of the stories, "The Adventure of the Seven Clocks," appeared in *Life*'s issue of December 29, 1952; the others began to appear in *Collier's Magazine* with its issue of May 23, 1953, superbly illustrated by the same Robert Fawcett who had provided two drawings for Arthur Whitaker's "The Man Who Was Wanted" in *Cosmopolitan*.

A word, too, should be said here about a remarkable series of parodies which has been appearing since February, 1960, with "The Adventure of the Ascot Tie," in *Ellery Queen's*

SHERLOCK HOLMES IN CARICATURE

A drawing by Peter Newell to illustrate John Kendrick Bangs' *The Pursuit of the House-Boat* (Harper & Brothers): *The stranger drew forth a bundle of business cards.*

4 See Poul Anderson's "The Martian Crown Jewels" in *The Science-Fictional Sherlock Holmes*, edited by Norman Metcalf. For an idea of how the far, far future may view Sherlock Holmes, see Anthony Boucher's "The Greatest Tertian" in the same volume.

5 The first edition, privately printed in 1920, was limited to 200 copies. It was originally planned that 100 copies were to be printed for Mr. Starrett and 100 copies for Mr. Walter M. Hill, with each man's name to appear on the title page of his respective copies in this format: "FOR THE FRIENDS OF [NAME INSERTED]." Due to an oversight on the part of the printer, only 10 copies with Mr. Starrett's name inserted were delivered, and 190 with Mr. Hill's name inserted. The volume is a great rarity, and those who would like to read "The Adventure of the Unique Hamlet" are advised that they may come by it easier in *The Misadventures of Sherlock Holmes; 221B*; or the revised and expanded edition of Mr. Starrett's *The Private Life of Sherlock Holmes*.

"I ... HAVE EVEN CONTRIBUTED TO THE LITERATURE OF THE SUBJECT"

[Sherlock Holmes, "The Red-Headed League"]

With the death of Sir Arthur Conan Doyle and the realization that no more Sherlock Holmes stories would come from his hand, the writings *about* Sherlock Holmes—"the Writings about the Writings"—began to take a somewhat more serious turn.

The reader has only to turn to the "References" listed at the end of this collection—a by-no-means complete list—to see how extensive this curious branch of literature has become.

One of the earliest of the critics, commentators, glossators, and chronologists was certainly "F. S.";**1** in an "open letter" to Dr. Watson, published in the *Cambridge Review* for January 23, 1902, he put many searching questions concerning the various dates mentioned in *The Hound of the Baskervilles*.

In that same year, 1902, Arthur Bartlett Maurice wrote two short pieces of editorial comment, "Some Inconsistencies of Sherlock Holmes" and "More Sherlock Holmes Theories" for the New York *Bookman* (also reprinted in *The Incunabular Sherlock Holmes*).

Two years later, in 1904, the English critic, essayist, historian, poet, and translator, Andrew Lang, 1844–1912, was reading "The Adventure of the Three Students" and subjecting it to careful analysis in *Longman's Magazine*.**2**

But a place of honor as the cornerstone work in any collection of Sherlockiana must certainly go to Father, later Monsignor, Ronald A. Knox for his "Studies in the Literature of Sherlock Holmes," a paper first read, in 1911, to the Gryphon Club of Trinity College, Oxford. "This new frolic in criticism was welcome at once," the late Christopher Morley recalled later; "those who were students at Oxford in that ancient day remember how Mr. Knox was invited round from college to college to re-read his agreeable lampoon; it was first printed [in 1912] in a journal of undergraduate highbrows (*The Blue Book*) then appropriately edited by W. H. L. Watson."

Before continuing our review of these critical landmarks, let us for a moment consider "the rule of the game," as the late Dorothy L. Sayers expressed it in *Unpopular Opinions*: "The rule of the game is that it must be played as solemnly as a county cricket match at Lord's; the slightest touch of extravagance or burlesque ruins the atmosphere."

We are dealing here, you see, with something entirely different from the parodies, burlesques, and pastiches about which we wrote in our preceding chapter: we are dealing with a highly specialized form of literary criticism.

1 "F. S." was Frank Sidgwick, 1879–1939, who later went into the book business (Sidgwick and Jackson) and published the poems of Rupert Brooke. His "open letter," with many other examples of early Sherlockiana, hard to come by elsewhere, has been reprinted in *The Incunabular Sherlock Holmes*.

2 See the interesting article by Mr. Roger Lancelyn Green, "Dr. Watson's First Critic," listed in our References.

3 English Sherlockians like to call themselves Holmesians; American Holmesians like to call themselves Sherlockians.

And there is no denying that, in recent years, some of "the Writings about the Writings" have threatened to "ruin the atmosphere." Mr. S. C. Roberts (later Sir Sydney Roberts) in England and Mr. Vincent Starrett in America have both felt called upon to issue warnings to overzealous Sherlockians and Holmesians:**3** "One of the temptations that besets the investigator of the life and work of Sherlock Holmes," Roberts wrote in the first issue of *The Sherlock Holmes Journal,* "is the temptation to seek always after novelty. . . . Like the Athenians of the time of St. Paul, Holmesian enthusiasts are always eager for some new thing. Freshness of conjecture or of conclusion is of course attractive to all of us, but we have to remember that a straining after novelty for its own sake does not advance the purposes of sound scholarship. Still less does it accord with the principles and methods of Holmes himself, of the man who called always for data, and prescribed deduction in place of guess-work."

We have tried, in the Notes which accompany the stories that follow, to give ear to Sir Sydney's warning: the "scholarship" revealed in them, if fantastic at times, is, we hope, in most cases sound.

The publication of *Essays in Satire,* including "Studies in the Literature of Sherlock Holmes," in 1928 had two important results. First, the late Sir Desmond MacCarthy, 1877–1952, broadcast over the B.B.C. an important talk on Dr. Watson, one of the "Miniature Biographies" series, which was published in *The Listener,* December 11, 1929.

Second, Sir Sydney Roberts, then Mr. S. C. Roberts, composed "A Note on the Watson Problem" which was published by the University Press of Cambridge, England, in an edition limited to 100 copies.

This was followed, in 1931, by Roberts' *Doctor Watson: Prolegomena to a Biographical Problem,* described by the late Elmer Davis, in "The Real Sherlock Holmes," as "the fullest and best, but not yet definitive, biography of this enigmatic figure—perhaps the most typical of late-Victorian middleclass Englishmen, behind whose commonplace and stodgy front research reveals depths of psychological complexity still unplumbed."

In the following year, 1932, the late Harold Wilmerding Bell, 1885–1947, an American archeologist of note, produced the first attempt to date each of the Sherlock Holmes cases, recorded and unrecorded, in *Sherlock Holmes and Dr. Watson: The Chronology of Their Adventures,* a handsome, blue-green volume, published by Constable & Co., Ltd., of London, in a limited edition of 500 copies, priced at 15 shillings a copy. A copy of the original edition is very hard to find today, but twenty-one years after its first publication, a paperbound but page-by-page facsimile edition was printed from the original plates by the Baker Street Irregulars, Inc., 1953. Said the late Edgar W. Smith in his introduction to that volume: "[Bell] was a pioneer, working through a forest that had not, when he wrote, felt any but the most tentative of axes, and the trail he cut is all the more pleasant because it does, admittedly, have a few bad turnings."

October of that same year, 1932, saw the publication of *Sherlock Holmes: Fact or Fiction?* by the erudite and always delightful Mr. T. S. Blakeney. A chronology of sorts, it is also much more than that: its chapters on "Mr. Sherlock Holmes," "Holmes and Scotland Yard," and "The Literature of Sherlock Holmes" (plus its valuable appendices) throw a brilliant light on both Sherlock and the Saga. It, too, is a hard book to find in its original printing, and it, too, has been reproduced in page-by-page facsimile from the original plates by the Baker Street Irregulars, Inc. (1954).

Only two years later, in 1934, Bell edited the first of the Sherlockian anthologies, *Baker Street Studies*, "plumbing the depths of the Canon through eight different borings, with its list of collaborators chosen from among the foremost Sherlockian scholars of their—or any other—day." (The words are again those of Edgar Smith, in his introduction to the facsimile edition of *Baker Street Studies* published in 1955 by the Baker Street Irregulars.)

In that same year, 1934, The Macmillan Company published *The Private Life of Sherlock Holmes;* it is an authoritative, mellow, and wholly charming presentation of the life and times of the Master Detective by the greatest living Sherlockian, Mr. Vincent Starrett of Chicago.

Meantime, in 1930, Christopher Morley had written his enduring introduction to the Doubleday omnibus, *The Complete Sherlock Holmes;* ten years later, in 1940, came the first American anthology, edited by Vincent Starrett: *221B: Studies in Sherlock Holmes* was published originally by Macmillan; it too has been reprinted, in 1956, by the Baker Street Irregulars, Inc., in a paperbound facsimile edition.

March 31, 1944, was a particularly notable day in Sherlockian annals—it marked the publication of no less than three new books of Sherlockiana: Christopher Morley's *Sherlock Holmes and Dr. Watson: A Textbook of Friendship*, the first annotated collection (five stories); Ellery Queen's *The Misadventures of Sherlock Holmes*, the first collection of parodies and pastiches; and Edgar W. Smith's *Profile by Gaslight: An Irregular Reader About the Private Life of Sherlock Holmes*, an especially rich collection of verse, essays, and other commentaries.

Not until 1947 did the third Sherlockian chronology appear: *An Irregular Chronology of Sherlock Holmes of Baker Street*, by the late Professor (of the University of Chicago) Jay Finley Christ was published by the Fanlight House of Ann Arbor, Michigan, in an edition limited to 175 copies; it is one of the most scholarly and almost certainly the most daring of the (now) seven chronologies.

It was followed, in 1951, by the late Gavin Brend's *My Dear Holmes, A Study in Sherlock*, and, in 1953, by the late Dr. Ernest Bloomfield Zeisler's *Baker Street Chronology: Commentaries on the Sacred Writings of Dr. John H. Watson.* In 1955 came your editor's own attempt to date (by day of the week, date of the month and year) all of Holmes' cases, recorded and unrecorded, *The Chronological Holmes;* and the Reverend Henry T. Folsom has since (1964) produced a revised edition of his *Through the Years at Baker Street: A Chronology of Sherlock Holmes*, bringing to seven the number of full-length chronologies.4

Today, Sherlock Holmes is the only fictional character

4 Other commentators—Mr. Svend Petersen, the late Robert R. Pattrick, the late Edgar W. Smith and others—have produced briefer chronological tables and listings, and these we will have cause to refer to in the Notes to the stories which follow.

5 *Sherlock Holmes of Baker Street: A Life of the World's First Consulting Detective*, by William S. Baring-Gould; New York: Clarkson N. Potter, Inc., 1962; as *Sherlock Holmes: A Biography* in England; London: Rupert Hart-Davis, Ltd., 1962; also published in French and German editions.

who has ever been the subject of a full-length "biography."[5] There is also a Sherlockian Concordance (by Professor Christ), a Sherlockian Repertory (by Mr. Smith), a Sherlockian Glossary (by Magistrate S. Tupper Bigelow of Toronto), two Sherlockian Encyclopedias (one by Michael and Mollie Hardwick, the other by Orlando Park), two Sherlockian Iconographies (one by the late James Montgomery, the other by Mr. Walter Klinefelter), a Baker Street Song Book (by the late Harvey Officer), a Sherlockian Almanac (by Mr. Svend Petersen), a Sherlockian Gazetteer (also by Mr. Smith), a Sherlockian Atlas (by Dr. Julian Wolff) and a Practical Handbook of Sherlockian Heraldry (also by Dr. Wolff).

One is reminded of the remark made by the late Christopher Morley as he once compared the list of contributors to *The Baker Street Journal* with the list of subscribers to that publication.

"Never," said Morley wryly, "never has so much been written by so many for so few."

"YOU WOULD HAVE MADE AN ACTOR,
AND A RARE ONE"

[*Inspector Athelney Jones to Mr. Sherlock Holmes*, The Sign of the Four]

On the night of October 23, 1899, Sherlock Holmes in the flesh—all six feet of him—stepped onto the stage of the Star Theatre in Buffalo, New York.**1**

Some skeptics have since claimed that Holmes was impersonated on that occasion—and for many nights thereafter—by a distinguished contemporary actor named William Gillette,**2** and there seems little doubt that Gillette *did* write the four-act drama called, simply and classically, *Sherlock Holmes*, "being a hitherto unpublished episode in the career of the great detective, and showing his connection with The Strange Case of Miss [Alice] Faulkner."

Mr. John Dickson Carr, in his *Life of Sir Arthur Conan Doyle*, tells us that Conan Doyle in 1897 wrote a play about Sherlock Holmes but was unable to get it accepted by any suitable actor-manager. Eventually the American producer Charles Frohman was granted permission to have Gillette rewrite the play; the actor is said to have done so in four weeks, working basically from three of Conan Doyle's stories, the two short stories, "A Scandal in Bohemia" and "The Final Problem" and the novel, *A Study in Scarlet*. Amazingly enough, Gillette up to that time had never read a Sherlock Holmes story.

Now he read them all—all that had been written up to that time—steeping himself in the great detective's character and achievements. One thing bothered him—what liberties might he take with Conan Doyle's famous character? At last he wrote to Conan Doyle: "May I marry Holmes?" "Marry him or murder him or do anything else you like with him," Conan Doyle is reported to have replied.

In the summer of 1899 Gillette visited England to submit the finished script to Conan Doyle, and it must have surprised the creator of Sherlock Holmes, attired, we may imagine, in a highly conservative top hat and frock coat, to see Gillette descend from the train: the actor had donned a deerstalker hat and a long caped overcoat as a suitable costume for that first meeting.

Sherlock Holmes opened in New York City two weeks after its premiere performance in Buffalo—at the Garrick Theatre on November 6, 1899.

"I can think of no more perfect realisation of a fictional character on the stage," the famous artist, Frederic Dorr Steele, who was later to illustrate so many of the Sherlock

1 Bruce McRae played Watson in the production, and the part of Professor Moriarty was taken by George Wessells.

2 William Hooker Gillette was born on July 23, 1853, the youngest of six children. He made his professional debut on September 13, 1875, at Boston's old Globe Theatre in a play called *Faint Heart*, and first appeared on the London stage at the Adelphi Theatre as Lewis Dumont in *Secret Service*.

WILLIAM GILLETTE AS SHERLOCK HOLMES

The dauntless figure that faced Professor James Moriarty in Gillette's melodrama of 1899, from *Catalogue of the Collection in The Sherlock Holmes Tavern.*

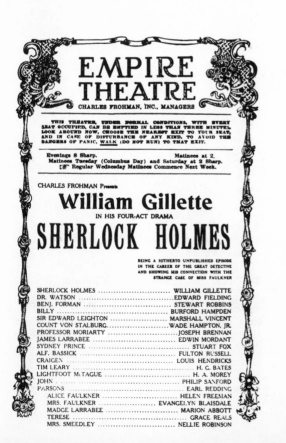

Holmes short stories for *Collier's Magazine*, wrote many years later in "Sherlock Holmes in Pictures." "Gillette's quiet, but incisive, histrionic method exactly fitted such a part as Sherlock Holmes."

But the *New York Herald Tribune* declared that "the play has no lasting value whatever, unless it be the value of an occasional melodramatic incident; it is trivial at the beginning and feeble at the end"—a strange verdict indeed considering that the engagement at the Garrick continued until June 16, 1900, with capacity audiences at practically every performance.

After a series of performances at the Hollis Theatre in Boston starting on February 18, 1901, the play went on a most successful United States tour. It opened then in England at the Shakespeare Theatre in Liverpool on September 2, 1901, and played for the first time in London at the famous Lyceum Theatre (see *The Sign of the Four*), opening on September 9, 1901. There it scored a tremendous success, drawing capacity attendance until April 11, 1902. The play then toured the provinces as far north as Edinburgh.

Gillette in his time also wrote a sketch, "The Painful Predicament of Sherlock Holmes" (the "painful predicament" was that Holmes had a female client—played by Miss Ethel Barrymore—so voluble that the detective was unable to utter a single word during the entire length of the scene). "The Painful Predicament" was given as a benefit performance for Joseph Jefferson Holland at the Metropolitan Opera House in New York City on the afternoon of Friday, May 24, 1905. The parody was performed on at least three other occasions —in New York at the Criterion Theatre on April 14, 1905; in London at the Duke of York's Theatre on October 3, 1905; and as a curtain raiser to Gillette's play *Clarice* in Boston at the Colonial Theatre on Christmas Eve, 1905. Casting about in London for a Cockney boy who might act the part of Billy the Page, Gillette finally settled upon a little, frightened, underfed, sixteen-year-old named Charles Spencer Chaplin. (Charlie also played Billy for almost two years— well before 1905—when the English actor H. A. Saintsbury went on tour in Gillette's play, *Sherlock Holmes*.)

William Gillette was not the first actor to portray the great detective—that honor should apparently go to John Webb, who played Holmes in Glasgow, in a play by Charles Rogers, as early as May, 1894. But Gillette, after 1902, made almost a career in itself of playing Holmes. In 1916 he appeared as Holmes in a seven-reel motion picture produced by Essanay with Ernest Maupain as Professor Moriarty and Edward Fielding as Watson; this was Gillette's only venture within the medium of the screen.

Sherlock Holmes, the play, was revived or continued in 1904–05, 1910–11, 1915–16, 1929 (Springfield, Mass.) and 1931–32 (Boston). Gillette played the role for the last time in Princeton, New Jersey, on May 12, 1932; he died in Hartford, Connecticut, on April 29, 1937, at the age of eighty-

"CHARLES FROHMAN PRESENTS . . ."

The cast listing from the program of one of the later productions of Gillette's play, *Sherlock Holmes*, the Empire Theatre, New York City.

three, and today lies buried in the family plot at Farmington, Connecticut.

If William Gillette's *Sherlock Holmes* takes all honors as the most famous translation of Conan Doyle's most celebrated character to the medium of the stage, second place must certainly go to Conan Doyle's own dramatization of his famous short story, "The Adventure of the Speckled Band."

After his play, *The House of Temperley*, closed in May, 1910, Conan Doyle was left with the Royal Adelphi Theatre on his hands. Once more he turned to Holmes and wrote the play version of *The Speckled Band*, it is said, in two weeks. It opened on June 4, 1910, and the Sherlockian magic worked again: it was a box-office success from the start and ran for 169 continuous performances. The play, although keeping to the main plot of the story, has many variations,3 some of the most interesting of which we will consider in our Notes to "The Adventure of the Speckled Band."

The previously mentioned H. A. Saintsbury played Holmes and the English actor Lyn Harding turned in a spectacular performance as the villainous "Dr. Rylott" (the Dr. *Roylott* of the story). A rock boa essayed the taxing role of "the speckled band." *The Speckled Band* was later filmed (in 1930–31) by the British and Dominion Film Company with Raymond Massey in the role of Holmes; Lyn Harding recreated his role as Rylott-Roylott; Harding also appeared as Holmes' archenemy, Professor James Moriarty, in two British-made motion pictures starring Arthur Wontner as Holmes.

Conan Doyle, in 1921, also wrote a one-act play about Holmes, "The Crown Diamond: An Evening with Sherlock Holmes," about which we shall have more to say later (see Chapter 73: ". . . It Is Undoubtedly Queer . . .").

To date, 21 serious plays have been based on the adventures of Sherlock Holmes: in 1903, for example, came the (unauthorized) drama, *Sherlock Holmes, Private Detective*, and 1905 saw a production called *The Bank of England: An Adventure in the Life of Sherlock Holmes*. Twenty-seven years later, in 1932, a somewhat startled London audience saw another Holmes play, *The Holmeses of Baker Street*, in which Sherlock appeared as a widower of over sixty—with a grown-up daughter named *Shirley*.

As Holmes was parodied in print, so was he satirized on the stage, and not only by Gillette in "The Painful Predicament": there was a burlesque called *Sheerluck Jones, or Why D'Gillette Him Off?*, with Clarence Blakiston in the title role; it appeared at Terry's Theatre in the Strand only a month after Gillette's *Sherlock Holmes* had opened at the Lyceum. This was followed, in January, 1902, by a turn in which "Sherlock Holmes" took the stage in many of London's music halls.4

Conan Doyle also authorized a play in four acts, *The Return of Sherlock Holmes*. Written originally by J. E. Harold Terry and Arthur Rose, *The Return* was later revised by Rose and Ernest Dudley and presented at the New Theatre, Bromley, on January 19, 1953. The original version, first produced at the Princess Theatre in 1923, ran for over 130 performances with the memorable Eille Norwood in the role of Holmes.5

LYN HARDING AS DR. GRIMESBY ROYLOTT, RAYMOND MASSEY AS SHERLOCK HOLMES

A scene from *The Speckled Band*, produced by the British and Dominion Film Company in 1931.

3 It has been published by Samuel French, London and New York, 1912.

4 A Holmes-Watson play in the interesting form of a puppet show—"The Case of the Elusive Train," by Charles Eames—was first presented by IBM at the New York World's Fair in the summer of 1964. The script has been published in the *Baker Street Journal*, Vol. XIV, No. 4, New Series, December, 1964, pp. 196–98.

5 Neither the original nor the revised version of *The Return of Sherlock Holmes* was ever published, but typed copies of the manuscript are held by a few lucky collectors.

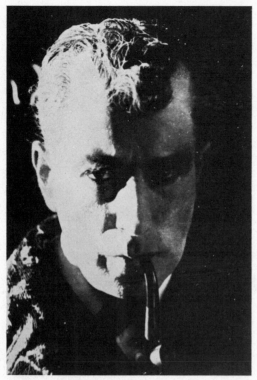

EILLE NORWOOD

This noted figure of the silent film in Britain as he appeared as Sherlock Holmes in *The Sign of the Four* for Stoll Productions, 1922.

Eille Norwood—his real name was Anthony Edward Brett; he chose his stage name because he once had a girl friend named Eille who lived in Norwood—was born October 11, 1861, at York, attended St. John's College, Cambridge, received an M.A. degree there, and married the actress Ruth Mackay. He played *Raffles* on tour and acted prior to his entry into films with such distinguished actors as H. B. Irving and Arthur Bourchier. He died in London on Christmas Eve, 1948, at the age of eighty-seven.

Norwood played Holmes not only in *The Return* but also on the screen in no less than 47 film adventures produced by the Stoll Film Company, starting as long ago as 1920. Conan Doyle had a very high opinion of Norwood's performances. In *Memories and Adventures*, the creator of Sherlock Holmes wrote: "Norwood has that rare quality which can only be described as glamour, which compels you to watch an actor eagerly even when he is doing nothing. He has the brooding eye which excites expectation and he has also a quite unrivaled power of disguise."

Still another English actor who made a name for himself in the role of Holmes was Arthur Wontner, 1875–1960. In the considered opinion of Mr. Vincent Starrett, "No better Sherlock Holmes than Arthur Wontner is likely to be seen and heard in pictures in our time. . . . His detective is the veritable fathomer of Baker Street in person."

Wontner was first chosen to play Holmes in December of 1930. With only an extremely limited budget, a modest film adaptation of "The Final Problem" and "The Adventure of the Empty House" was made in "a tin hut film studio" at Twickenham. The film was released in 1931 under the title of *The Sleeping Cardinal* (in England) and *Sherlock Holmes' Fatal Hour* (in America). It was an immediate success and, in America, made film history for the time by running for over a month on Broadway—then an almost unprecedented event for a British film.

The following year Mr. Wontner again impersonated Holmes in an adaptation of "The Adventure of Charles Augustus Milverton" called *The Missing Rembrandt*. Later in the same year, 1932, he appeared in *The Sign of the Four*,

ARTHUR WONTNER AS SHERLOCK HOLMES

(*Left*) In *The Missing Rembrandt* (1932) with Minnie Rayner as Mrs. Hudson, Ian Fleming as Dr. Watson. (*Right*) with Ian Fleming as Watson in *The Triumph of Sherlock Holmes* (1935).

and in 1935 he made an excellent version of *The Valley of Fear* under the title of *The Triumph of Sherlock Holmes*. Finally, in 1937, came his last bow as a screen Holmes in *Silver Blaze*. (In 1951, however, he again appeared as Holmes on television in connection with the Sherlock Holmes Exhibition at the Festival of Britain.)

Still another film Holmes (in Britain) was Peter Cushing, who turned in a notable performance in the Hammer production of *The Hound of the Baskervilles*, which opened at the London Pavilion on Friday, March 7, 1959. It was the seventh film *Hound* and the *121st* Holmes film. (In 1945 a copy of a German version of the *Hound* was found in Hitler's private film library at Berchtesgaden.)

Perhaps the earliest Holmes film of all was *Sherlock Holmes Baffled*, produced in 1903. Between 1908 and 1912 the Nordisk Film Company of Denmark made a long series of Holmes films, first with the Danish actor Holger Madsen, then with the German actor Alvin Neuss as Holmes. Italian, German, and French film companies were also quick to see the screen potentialities in Holmes.

In America, too, Holmes has had a long and distinguished film history, beginning in 1922 with his portrayal by John Barrymore, with Roland Young as Watson and Gustav von Seyffertitz as Moriarty. The most novel feature of the film —called *Sherlock Holmes* in the United States and *Moriarty* in England—was a prologue dealing with the youth and college career of Sherlock Holmes.

Clive Brook was another prominent film actor who played Holmes in America: in 1929, in the first talking Holmes film, made by Paramount, *The Return of Sherlock Holmes*, and again in 1933 in a sequel made for Fox Pictures. (A curious claim to distinction can be made by Reginald Owen, who is probably the only actor who has played both Holmes and Watson on the screen; in 1933 he was Watson to Clive Brook's Holmes, then, later in the same year, he was cast as Holmes in a film version of *A Study in Scarlet*.)

But there is little doubt that this country's best known Holmes today is Basil Rathbone, who first played the role in 1929 in 20th Century-Fox's *The Hound of the Baskervilles*. The late Nigel Bruce also made his debut as Dr. Watson in this same motion picture. Rathbone and Bruce were to repeat their portrayals in thirteen later films made for Universal between 1942 and 1946. The first three films rather unhappily showed a patriotic Holmes in World War II saving a secret bombsight from the Nazis, rescuing a vital document from a spy ring, and silencing a subversive radio station.

But this is not said to detract from Rathbone's characterization. As Mr. Anthony Howlett, the former Chairman of the Sherlock Holmes Society of London and an outstanding authority on the Holmes of stage and screen, has said: "The physical resemblance of Rathbone to the Sidney Paget illustrations [in the old *Strand Magazine*] was quite striking and, next to Arthur Wontner, probably no one has been so happily cast."

To turn to another medium, the radio adventures of Mr. Sherlock Holmes of Baker Street are still recalled with

GERMAN ACTOR ALWIN NEUSS AS THE GREAT DETECTIVE

From one of the early Holmes films between 1908 and 1912 by the Nordisk Film Company of Denmark, probably *The Murder in Baker Street*.

THE FILM HOLMES IN AMERICA

(*Above*) John Barrymore, with Gustav von Seyffertitz as Moriarty. (*Below*) Clive Brook as Sherlock Holmes.

"THE GAME IS AFOOT!"

Basil Rathbone as Sherlock Holmes and Nigel Bruce as Dr. Watson in an ingeniously photographed scene from Universal's *The House of Fear.*

MR. CARLETON HOBBS

The Sherlock Holmes of the British Broadcasting Corporation.

pleasure by more than one generation of listeners. Basil Rathbone, Sir John Gielgud, and the late Sir Cedric Hardwicke are only three of the many fine actors who have appeared as Holmes on radio; in England there is also Mr. Carleton Hobbs, who has portrayed Holmes in a long series of radio plays (in one of which, "The Greek Interpreter," he played both Sherlock Holmes and Sherlock's brother Mycroft, in conversation together).

A series of 39 Holmes films for television, produced in Europe under the direction of Sheldon Reynolds, premiered in the New York City area on October 18, 1954. Ronald Howard, son of the late Leslie Howard, starred as Holmes, and H. Marion Crawford portrayed Watson as the sturdy fellow he really was.

On phonograph records also Holmes has left his mark: there is *Sherlock Holmes Explained by His Creator Sir Arthur Conan Doyle and Presented in Action by William Gillette* (issued in 1939 by the Gramophone Company, Limited, in Great Britain and by the National Vocarium in the United States; Conan Doyle's part was recorded in 1928, Gillette's in 1936). There is the Decca recording (No. K4164) which features Sir John Gielgud as Holmes, Sir Ralph Richardson as Watson and Orson Welles as Moriarty in dramatizations of "The Final Problem," the first meeting of Holmes and Watson and "The Adventure of Charles Augustus Milverton." And there are two series of "Talking Books" of Holmes adventures, issued by the Listening Library of New York City, the first narrated by John Brewster, the second by Basil Rathbone.

Sherlock Holmes—to the amusement (and distress) of some of his admirers—has even appeared in *ballet.* "The Great Detective," written by Margaret Dale to music by Richard Arnell, had its premiere performance at the Sadler Wells Ballet Theatre in London on January 21, 1953.

And there was more to come, as Fritz Weaver made his bow as Sherlock Holmes in the first musical comedy ever produced about the adventures of the world's greatest detective. *Baker Street,* with Inga Swenson as Irene Adler and Martin Gabel as Professor Moriarty, opened in Boston on Christmas Eve, 1964, and had its first New York performance on Tuesday, February 16, 1965.

FRITZ WEAVER AS SHERLOCK HOLMES

In the Alexander H. Cohen production of *Baker Street,* "a musical adventure of Sherlock Holmes," at the Brodway Theatre, New York City, 1965.

5

"YOUR PICTURES ARE NOT UNLIKE YOU, SIR, IF I MAY SAY SO"

["Killer" Evans, alias John Garrideb, to Mr. Sherlock Holmes,
"The Adventure of the Three Garridebs"]

Conan Doyle—and Holmes enthusiasts everywhere—were fortunate that the editors of the *Strand Magazine* in England and *Collier's Magazine* in the United States were able to find two such superb artists as Sidney Paget and Frederic Dorr Steele to illustrate the great majority of the Sherlock Holmes stories.

Ironically, Sidney Paget was commissioned in error; the *Strand*'s editors were under the mistaken impression that they were writing to his artist-brother, Walter Paget, who had made the drawings for Sir H. Rider Haggard's *King Solomon's Mines* and *She*, but was perhaps best known for his illustrations for *Robinson Crusoe* and *Treasure Island*.[1]

Sidney Edward Paget was born on October 4, 1860, in London. He was the fifth son of the late Robert Paget, vestry clerk of Clerkenwell, was educated at a City school, and early developed a taste for drawing. On leaving school he studied from the antique at the British Museum for two years, after which he went to Heatherley's School of Art, in Norman Street, London, to study painting. Successful as an exhibitor (he showed two pictures at the Academy when he was only eighteen years old), he took a studio and began painting portraits and small pictures, at the same time illustrating books and papers, chiefly war subjects of Egypt and the Sudan. At twenty-one he entered the Royal Academy Schools for a term of six years, during which he carried off several important prizes.

Starting with "A Scandal in Bohemia" in the *Strand Magazine* for July, 1891, Paget produced a total of 357 drawings to illustrate *The Adventures, The Memoirs, The Hound of the Baskervilles*, and *The Return of Sherlock Holmes*, ending with "The Adventure of the Second Stain" in December, 1904.

Although brother "Wal" Paget had lost by misadventure the commission to illustrate the stories, he nonetheless made a major contribution to the picture many of us have of Holmes today: Walter Paget served as his brother Sidney's model for the great detective. So, too, did Paget take as his model for Dr. Watson another face familiar and convenient to him—that of his friend, Alfred Morris Butler, a well-known architect of the time.

1 After his brother Sidney's death, Walter Paget did illustrate a single Sherlock Holmes short story —"The Adventure of the Dying Detective" in the December, 1913, issue of the *Strand*.

"... WHAT PHIZ DID FOR PICKWICK, PAGET DID FOR
SHERLOCK HOLMES"

A *Strand Magazine* photograph of the English
artist who produced 357 Sherlock Holmes drawings.

2 Cuneo also illustrated the "Raffles" stories by
E. W. Hornung, Conan Doyle's brother-in-law,
when the Amateur Cracksman took over from the
Master Detective in the pages of *Collier's Magazine*,
whose editors had announced "The Second Stain"
as the "last" adventure of Sherlock Holmes. It was
Hornung who once said: "Though he might be
more humble, there's no police like Holmes."

3 "A curious and interesting point arises here,"
the artist's daughter, Winifred Paget, wrote in
"Full Circle." "If Holmes disappeared in April,
1891, and was not seen again until 1894, how did
he manage to send the cigarette case to my father
in 1893? Surely this is important evidence to support the theory that Holmes was not in Tibet or
Persia during those years but probably wandering
much nearer home in one of his many disguises
[see Chapter 46: "You May Have Heard of the
Remarkable Explorations of a Norwegian Named
Sigerson . . ."]. The cigarette case could, I suppose, have been despatched by Mycroft Holmes
acting on his brother's instructions . . ."

4 Steele himself always defended Paget: if his
earlier pictures seem imperfect to our eye, the
American artist pointed out, "it is partly because
of the crude woodcut reproductions." Those of
us who have seen the originals of Paget's illustrations heartily agree that his early work, at least,
lost much in the publishing.

Conan Doyle's own favorite illustrator was Cyrus Cuneo,
who never illustrated a Holmes adventure but did illustrate
many of Conan Doyle's other works;**2** Conan Doyle complained that Paget had made Holmes far handsomer than his
creator had ever intended him to be. But Conan Doyle was
honest enough to admit that this was probably a good thing:
it attracted a greater female readership to the stories in the
Strand.

Indeed, there is evidence that Conan Doyle was much impressed by Paget's work and considered him essential to the
success of each new venture; when the author wrote Greenhough Smith, the editor of the *Strand*, that he was contemplating putting Holmes into a real "creeper" to be called
The Hound of the Baskervilles, Conan Doyle specifically
asked for Paget as illustrator "in the event that Smith should
find the story acceptable."

With the disappearance of Holmes in "The Final Problem," the busy Paget apparently had time for the first time
to pursue the woman of his choice and eventually to marry
her on June 1, 1893. On the morning of his wedding day he
received a silver cigarette case bearing the inscription: "From
Sherlock Holmes 1893." The case became one of Paget's most
treasured possessions.**3**

Of Paget's work, the late James Montgomery has written
(*A Study in Pictures*):

> It would be impossible to overestimate the influence
> that he exerted upon the hearts and minds of the count-
> less thousands who based their conception then—as they
> still continue to do after sixty years—on his interpreta-
> tion of Holmes, Watson, and the golden time "where it
> is always 1895." From that day to this no characterization,
> no other mood has been accepted by English readers,
> and when his untimely death in 1908 necessarily shifted
> his mantle to other shoulders, the artists who followed
> him—several of greater skill and reputation—were com-
> pelled to subordinate themselves to the Paget style in all
> essential particulars. It has been truly said that what
> Phiz did for Pickwick, Paget did for Sherlock Holmes.

And now to America:

The late Elmer Davis wrote that Holmes in *The Return*
was "better than ever; for here in *Collier's* appeared, for the
first time in print, what has become the classic, final and
unalterable portrait of Sherlock Holmes. I say, for the first
time in print; it had long been familiar on the stage. For it
was William Gillette in a deerstalker cap who so unmistakably was Sherlock Holmes that, when Frederic Dorr Steele
[1874–1944] came to illustrate the stories in *The Return*, he
had to do no more than draw a picture of Gillette; and instantly all previous likenesses set down by Paget and Hyde
and Friston and the rest became merely collectors' items."

This is more than a little hard on Paget,**4** but many other
students of the Saga have certainly paid high tribute to
Steele's skill as an illustrator. Mr. Vincent Starrett has waxed
rhapsodic about Steele in his essay on Canonical illustrators
in *The Private Life of Sherlock Holmes*; "No one can touch
Steele in making you feel what is going on behind the door,"

the novelist Arthur Somers Roche once said; and the late Edmund Pearson went so far as to call Steele's drawings "the most interesting decorations of all time" in "Sherlock Holmes Among the Illustrators." "Countless other Americans," Montgomery wrote, "cannot possibly imagine any other portrayal of Holmes, Watson, and the adventures the two experienced, their whole love and enthusiasm for the tales being built on a recollection of and an association with the Steele illustrations . . ."**5**

Born in a lumber camp near Marquette, Michigan, but a New Yorker since boyhood, Frederic Dorr Steele studied at the National Academy of Design and the Art Students League, where he later taught drawing. He took his first job, on the old *Harper's Weekly*, for $15 a week "and glory," but soon graduated into free-lance work, illustrating the stories of such writers as Richard Harding Davis, Rudyard Kipling, O. Henry, and Mark Twain. Known primarily as an illustrator, Steele worked in nearly every medium except oil, and his drawings ranged from delicate pen work to bold poster designs in color. While vacationing at Monhegan, Maine, one summer, he developed an interest in cartography and a considerable skill as an etcher; he often asserted afterward that his "favorite drawing" was a large-scale map of Monhegan which, with characteristic patience, he spent twenty-four years perfecting.

Steele also had an enormous talent for caricature, which he exercised mercilessly upon fellow members of the Players Club, of which he was forty years a member. His membership in the Players acquainted him with most of the principal actors and actresses of the New York stage, many of whom—Katharine Cornell, Judith Anderson, Tallulah Bankhead, Helen Hayes, Maurice Evans, Josephine Hull, Walter Huston, Frank Craven, Bobby Clark, Ethel Waters, Paul Lukas, among others—he portrayed over fifteen years in the drama section of the *New York Herald Tribune*. He stood, according to one art critic, "in the first rank of American illustrators." Already represented in private collections and at the Carnegie Institute of Pittsburgh at the time of his death, Steele was also the first living illustrator to be exhibited at the Library of Congress.

"I did not need to be told to make my Sherlock look like Gillette," the artist wrote in "Sherlock Holmes in Pictures." "The thing was inevitable. I kept him in mind and even copied or adapted parts of a few of the stage photographs. At that time I had never seen the play, and it was not until 1929 that Mr. Gillette actually became my model in the flesh . . ."

Steele's original model for Sherlock Holmes was an Englishman named Robert King. Later, the artist "fell back on that standby of the studios, Frank B. Wilson," and his two sons. Later still, Steele's Sherlocks were drawn from "the fine frame and crag-like head" of a model named S. B. Doughty.

We have previously mentioned some of the many other artists who have illustrated the Canon in books and magazines; in Notes to come, we will have occasion to mention and to comment upon many others.

But no discussion of Holmes in art would be complete without some reference to the Holmes of the Sunday supplements and the daily "comic-strip" pages.

5 Montgomery himself, as we have seen, vastly preferred Paget as an illustrator to Steele; he deplored the American artist's frequent lack of accuracy in depicting scenes in *The Return* and many later adventures.

FREDERIC DORR STEELE

The artist shown at the first one-man show of his drawings, held at the Contemporary Arts Gallery in 1935. Photo by Steffen, *New York Herald Tribune*.

WILLIAM GILLETTE AS SKETCHED FROM LIFE BY FREDERIC DORR STEELE IN 1929

"MEANWHILE AT 221-B BAKER STREET . . ."

The Sherlock Holmes of the "comic strip" pages, as written by Edith Meiser and drawn by Frank Giacoia.

SHERLOCK HOLMES IN ADVERTISING

"The Press, Watson, is a most valuable institution, if you only know how to use it."

Now *there's* a tobacco you could smoke all day without burning your tongue.

Amazing, Holmes!

Elementary, my dear Watson—it's

Grand Cut

Never burns the tongue of old or young   2 oz 8/2

The late Sidney Smith, creator of "The Gumps," produced between 1911 and 1914 a series of color comics called "Sherlock Holmes, Jr." Years later, an adaptation of the stories by Edith Meiser, strikingly illustrated by Frank Giacoia, appeared in many United States newspapers. In this medium also Holmes was parodied—as "Hawkshaw, the Detective," for example, who appeared in the late 1910's and early 1920's in a comic strip drawn by Gus Mager, with a Dr. Watson who was called simply "Colonel."

All of us are familiar, too, with the Holmes who has appeared so often in newspaper and magazine advertising.

The late Judge Kenneth G. Brill, of St. Paul, Minnesota, made it his hobby to amass Holmesian advertisements; reviewing the collection after Judge Brill's death, Dean E. W. Zierbath of the University of Minnesota reported: "A spot check reveals some 67 references which I consider major, and 23 which might, because of the incomplete nature of the Holmesian reference, be regarded as minor. The majority of these are from the press or popular journals of the United States, but several Canadian and a few British examples are included."

Holmes seems to be every bit as popular in advertising today as he was at the turn of the century. Cocking an eye at such messages as that for Grand Cut Tobacco (see illustration) we feel he might well say—as he *did* say in "The Adventure of the Six Napoleons"—"The Press, Watson, is a most valuable institution, if you only know how to use it."

THE "THREE HOURS FOR LUNCH" CLUB IN SESSION

According to Mr. Robert Keith Leavitt, the historian of the Baker Street Irregulars, this drawing by George Ennis shows (*top row, left to right*) Franklin Abbot, Christ Cella, Frank V. Morley, "Torino" (a Cella waiter), Hulbert Footner, Mrs. Cella and (*front row*) Robert Keith Leavitt, Frank C. Henry, William S. Hall, Christopher Morley, Don Marquis, and Émile Gauvreau. From *The Baker Street Journal*, September, 1961.

6

"A SINGULAR SET OF PEOPLE, WATSON . . ."

[Sherlock Holmes, "The Adventure of Wisteria Lodge"]

The late Christopher Morley, 1890–1957, like the great Dr. Sam Johnson, had a flair for founding congenial clubs—among them a more or less stag affair called the Three Hours for Lunch Club and a slightly more coeducational dinner society, the *Grillparzer Sittenpolizei Verein*, or Grillparzer Morals-Police Association.

From these grew the Baker Street Irregulars.

The time was ripe for such a sodality—"even whisky-and-sodality," as Morley once said: William Gillette's recent revivals of his play *Sherlock Holmes* had met with great success, and the Doubleday omnibus, *The Complete Sherlock Holmes*, was enjoying wide circulation. Then came S. C. Roberts' brilliant little biography of *Doctor Watson* and Vincent Starrett's admirable *The Private Life of Sherlock Holmes*—the latter reviewed (December 2, 1933) in *The Saturday Review of Literature* (now the *Saturday Review*) by the late political commentator and essayist Elmer Davis, 1890–1958, in a stunning piece that Davis afterward revised into the form of an essay "On the Emotional Geology of Baker Street."

It was all but inevitable that the first meeting of what was to become the Baker Street Irregulars should be held. And held it was, on January 6, 1934, when a group of enthusiasts —drawn mostly from the members of the Three Hours for Lunch Club and GSV—met at the old Hotel Duane on Madison Avenue, New York City.

The name the Baker Street Irregulars, as an organization outside the pages of Sir Arthur Conan Doyle, seems to have appeared in print for the first time in Morley's "Bowling Green" column in the *SRL* for January 27, 1934. According to the "Bowling Green," the "secretary" of the BSI, William S. Hall, had allowed him—Morley—to "look over the minutes of the first meeting of the club." Among other business it appears that the matter of an official toast was discussed. It was agreed that the first health must always be drunk to "*The* Woman" (Irene Adler of "A Scandal in Bohemia"). Suggestions for succeeding sentiments were "Mrs. Hudson," "Mycroft," "The Second Mrs. Watson," "The Game Is Afoot!" and "The Second Most Dangerous Man in London."

By February 3, 1934, Morley was printing Holmesian correspondence under the heading of "The Baker Street Irregulars," and on February 17th he ran two significant items. The first was a letter from Mr. Vincent Starrett, a masterly presentation of the problem of the Moriarty brothers, both named James. The second was the document that constitutes

CROSSWORD 221 B (*Baker Street Irregular*)   Mycroft Holmes

ACROSS

1. A treatise on this, written at the age of twenty-one, had a European vogue and earned its author a professorship. (2 words, 8, 7)
8. It was of course to see these that Holmes enquired the way from Saxe-Coburg Square to the Strand (2 words, 10, 5)
11. How the pips were set (2)
13. Not an Eley's No. 2 (which is an excellent argument with a gentleman who can twist steel pokers into knots) but the weapon in the tragedy of Birlstone (3)
14. What was done on the opposite wall in bullet-pocks by the patriotic Holmes (2)
15. What Watson recognized when he put his hand on Bartholomew Sholto's leg (5)
18. Where Watson met young Stamford, who introduced him to Sherlock Holmes (3)
20. A kind of pet, over which Dr. Grimesby Roylott hurled the local blacksmith (4)
21. Holmes should have said this before being so sure of catching the murderers of John Openshaw (2)
22. The kind of Pedro whence came the tiger (3)
23. Though he knew the methods, Watson sometimes found it difficult to do this (3)
25. Patron saint of old Mr. Farquhar's affliction and perhaps of Abe Slaney's men (5)
27. Perhaps a measure of Holmes's chemicals (2)
28. In short, Watson (2)
29. 〳〵 (2)
30. Curious that he did nothing in the nighttime (2)
31. This would obviously not describe the empty house opposite 221b Baker Street (3)
34. It seems likely that Watson's elder brother suffered from this disease (2)
35. Though you might have taken this at Lodge 29, Chicago, nevertheless, you had to pass a test as well at Lodge 341, Vermissa (4)
37. The *Star* of Savannah (4)
40. Mrs. Barclay's reproach (in The Crooked Man, of course) suggests the parable of this (3)
41. Scrawled in blood-red letters across the bare plaster at No. 3, Lauriston Gardens (5)
43. Holmes found this, because he was looking for it in the mud (5)
44. Suggests Jonathan Small's leg (3)
45. The brother who left Watson no choice but to relate The Final Problem (2 words, 5, 13)

DOWN

1. A country district in the west of England where "Cooee" was a common signal (2 words, 8, 6)
2. Charles Augustus Milverton dealt with no niggard hand; therefore this would not describe him (4)
3. The kind of practice indulged by Mr. Williamson, the solitary cyclist's unfrocked clergyman—"there was a man of that name in orders, whose career has been a singularly dark one." (3)
4. There is comparatively as much sense in Hafiz. Indeed, it's a case of identity. (3 words, 2, 2, 6)
5. Caused the rift in the beryl coronet (3)
6. Many of Holmes's opponents had cause to (3)
7. Begins: 'Whose was it?' 'His who is gone.' 'Who shall have it?' 'He who will come.' (2 words, 8, 6)
9. of four (4)
10. The number of Napoleons plus the number of Randall gang (4)
12. One of the five sent 'S.H. for J.O.' (3)
16. To save the dying detective trouble, Mr. Culverton Smith was kind enough to give the signal by turning this up (3)
17. The blundering constable who failed to gain his sergeant's stripes in the Lauriston Gardens Mystery (5)
19. There was a giant one of Sumatra; yet it was unwritten (4)
23. How Watson felt after the Final Problem (3)
24. He was epollicate (8)
26. Initials of the second most dangerous man in London (2)
32. Though Miss Mary Sutherland's boots were not unlike, they were really odd ones; the one having this slightly decorated, and the other plain (3)
33. You may forgive the plural form of these tobaccos, since Holmes smoked so much of them (5)
36. Behind this Black Jack of Ballarat waited and smoked an Indian cigar, of the variety which are rolled in Rotterdam (4)
38 and 39. The best I can make of these is the Latin for the sufferers of the epidemic which pleased Holmes so extremely that he said 'A long shot, Watson, a very long shot,' and pinched the Doctor's arm (4)
42. One of the two in the cardboard box (3)
44. Initials of the street in which Mycroft lodged (2)

Problem (2 words, 5, 8)

. . . THE CLOSEST THING THE BSI EVER HAD TO . . .
AN EXAMINATION

The crossword puzzle by Frank V. Morley, first published in *The Saturday Review of Literature*, May 3, 1934.

the Constitution and Buy—*Buy*, not *By*—Laws of the Baker Street Irregulars, the work of Elmer Davis.

It is worth quoting here in full:

CONSTITUTION
ARTICLE I

The name of this society shall be the Baker Street Irregulars.

ARTICLE II

Its purpose shall be the study of the Sacred Writings.

ARTICLE III

All persons shall be eligible for membership who pass an examination in the Sacred Writings set by officers of the society, and who are considered otherwise suitable.

ARTICLE IV

The officers shall be: a Gasogene, a Tantalus, and a Commissionaire.

The duties of the Gasogene shall be those commonly performed by a President.

The duties of the Tantalus shall be those commonly performed by a Secretary.

The duties of the Commissionaire shall be to telephone down for ice, White Rock, and whatever else may be required and available; to conduct all negotiations with waiters; and to assess the members pro rata for the cost of same.

BUY-LAWS

1. An annual meeting shall be held on January 6, at which the canonical toasts shall be drunk; after which the members shall drink at will.

2. The current round shall be bought by any member who fails to identify, by title of story and context, any quotation from the Sacred Writings submitted by any other member.

Qualification A. If two or more members fail so to identify, a round shall be bought by each of those so failing.

Qualification B. If the submitter of the quotation, upon challenge, fails to identify it correctly, he shall buy the round.

3. Special meetings may be called at any time or place by any one of three members, two of whom shall constitute a quorum.

Qualification A. If said two people are of opposite sexes, they shall use care in selecting the place of meeting, to avoid misinterpretation (or interpretation either, for that matter).

4. All other business shall be left for the monthly meeting.

5. There shall be no monthly meeting.

The Constitution refers to "an examination in the Sacred Writings" as a prerequisite for membership, but the closest thing the BSI ever had to such an examination was a crossword puzzle, concocted by a bored Frank V. Morley in the smokeroom of a Cunard liner during a dull Atlantic crossing. It was published—as by "Mycroft Holmes"—in the "Bowling Green" of May 3, 1934, with this challenge from Christopher

Morley: ". . . I will delay printing the solution of the cross-word for two weeks, to give our clients plenty of time to consider it. All those who send me correct solutions—but they must be correct in every detail—will automatically become members of the Baker Street Irregulars."

Fifteen perfect solutions were received, and Morley on May 29, 1934, wrote a letter to successful contestants of the male gender who had got their entries onto his desk before the deadline:[1]

"The first formal meeting of the Baker Street Irregulars will be at 144 East 45th Street [then the site of Christ Cella's Restaurant] on Tuesday, June 5th at 6:30 P.M. . . . The proprietor has set aside a room for us upstairs which we can use as permanent headquarters . . ."[2]

Of those invited, only eight were able to attend: in the order in which they were seated, they were Morley himself (the Gasogene), Malcolm Johnson, Allan Price, Harvey Officer, Earle Walbridge, Robert Keith Leavitt, Frank Henry, and William S. Hall.[3]

The next recorded meeting took place on Friday, December 7, 1934—"a sort of jump-the-gun Anniversary [of the birth of Sherlock Holmes] Dinner," Morley called it; the second Annual Dinner was held, less irregularly, on the night of January 6, 1936, a Monday. (Since then, however, the Annual Dinner of the Baker Street Irregulars has always been held on the Friday which falls closest to January 6th, unless that Friday is in too close conflict with the festivities attending the New Year.)

Records of the early Dinners are fragmentary, at best, but it seems that 18 or 20 Irregulars turned up for the 1934 Dinner, among them William Gillette, Frederic Dorr Steele, H. W. Bell, Gene Tunney, and Vincent Starrett. Also present was Alexander Woollcott; never a member of the BSI, Woollcott attended the first Dinner of the society as the guest of Vincent Starrett, whose hospitality he returned by writing a mocking piece about the Irregulars for the December 29, 1934, issue of *The New Yorker*.

[1] The letter also went to certain of Morley's cronies in the Three Hours for Lunch Club who had made no attempt to solve the puzzle—the late Don Marquis, for example.

[2] Morley later recalled that in addition to the meeting room there were "two retiring rooms, which we persuaded Christ Cella to label as Sherlock and Irene. This puzzled some customers, but was effective for segregation."

[3] Until his death in 1961, Earle Walbridge was the only member of the BSI who had attended *every* meeting.

BYPLAY BEFORE THE 1947 DINNER OF THE BAKER STREET IRREGULARS

This dinner was held at the old Murray Hill Hotel in New York City on January 3rd. *Left to right:* Fred Dannay (one half of "Ellery Queen"), the late Elmer Davis, William S. Hall as Sherlock Holmes, the late Christopher Morley, and Rex Stout of Nero Wolfe and Archie Goodwin fame.

"The happiest achievement of the BSI," Morley recalled later, "was when it attracted the attention of our devoted Edgar Smith. . . . He wrote in a vein of decorous modesty asking if he could be put on the waiting list and offered to undergo any sort of inquest of suitability. It was plain from the first that here was *the* Man. . . . Mr. Edgar Smith's affectionate zeal, his delight in keeping orderly records and his access to mimeographic, parchment-engrossing and secretarial resources, all these were irresistible."

The late Edgar W. Smith, 1894–1960, joined the BSI in 1938—the same year in which he was made a Vice-President of the General Motors Overseas Operations and Director of that company's Institutional Relations. (He subsequently, before his retirement, had responsibility for public and personnel relations as well as for research in international trade and public affairs.)

It was Edgar Smith who launched the *Baker Street Journal* as a quarterly publication in January, 1946, and it was Edgar Smith who served as its editor until his death. "There were those who were sure it could not possibly last for long," he recalled in later years, "because practically everything that might ever be said upon the subject of Sherlock Holmes had already been said." But thirteen fat issues of the old *Journal* were published, containing an aggregate of 1,700-odd closely printed pages, all devoted exclusively to the life and times of Sherlock Holmes. The *Journal* suspended publication for a time (the last issue of the old *Journal* was dated January, 1949)4 but in January, 1951, a new series of *Journals* began to issue, and the saga of the Saga continues to this day.

Although by the Certificate of Investiture, members of the BSI are entitled to "go everywhere, see everything, overhear everyone," they cannot do all these things in all places at the same time. And so it was inevitable that Scion Societies should spring up from Toronto, Ontario, to New Orleans, Louisiana; from Boston, Massachusetts, to Los Angeles, California.

The first to be formed was the Five Orange Pips of Westchester County. Founded in 1935 by Richard W. Clarke, its membership grew to ten, but deaths in recent years have reduced its present membership to the original number, five. By far the most erudite of the Scion Societies, the Five Orange Pips holds elaborate formal dinners at irregular intervals; its members have also written and published *The Best of the Pips* (1955), by all odds one of the handsomest of the many volumes of Sherlockian commentary sponsored by the Scions.

The honor of being the first Scion Society to be formed beyond the boundaries of the greater New York area goes to the Speckled Band of Boston, founded April 26, 1940, by the late James Keddie, Sr. It, too, has published handsome volumes: *The Second Cab* (1957) and *The Third Cab* (1960).

Indeed, there is today hardly a city of any size in the United States where a member of the BSI cannot find a Scion Society whose members share his interest in things Holmesian.

There are the Hounds of the Baskerville (*sic*) of Chicago, founded 1943; the Scowrers of San Francisco, founded 1944, the only Scion Society which can boast a female auxiliary,

THE CERTIFICATE OF INVESTITURE IN THE BAKER STREET IRREGULARS

The name of the member, with the title of the Sherlock Holmes adventure, recorded or unrecorded, which he will henceforth represent, is inserted at the top of the Certificate; at the lower left is affixed a Victorian shilling.

4 Dr. Julian Wolff, who is now Commissionaire of the BSI and editor of the *Journal*, has always referred to the three issues unpublished in 1949 as "The Missing Three-Quarters."

the Molly Maguires; the Greek Interpreters of East Lansing, Michigan, founded 1945; the Amateur Mendicant Society of Detroit, founded January, 1946; the Dancing Men of Providence and the Scandalous Bohemians of Akron, both founded February, 1946; the Six Napoleons of Baltimore, founded September, 1946; the Illustrious Clients of Indianapolis, founded October, 1946; the Creeping Men of Cleveland, founded April, 1947; the Sons of the Copper Beeches of Philadelphia, founded December, 1947; the Musgrave Ritualists of New York and the Norwegian Explorers of Minneapolis and St. Paul, both founded January, 1948; the Priory Scholars of Pittsburgh, founded October, 1948; the Red Circle of Washington, D.C., founded 1951; the Old Soldiers of Baker Street (the Old SOBs), founded 1952.

Affiliated with the BSI, and invading the bonds of Empire in one case at least, are the Red-Headed League of Sydney, Australia; the Baritsu Chapter of Tokyo, Japan; the Boulevard Assassins of Paris; the Sherlock Holmes Klubben i Danmark; and the Crew of the S.S. *Friesland* of Amsterdam, Holland.

To this far-from-complete list, yearly growing, should be added the William Gillette Memorial Luncheon and the Martha Hudson Breakfast, organized to take care of the other two meals of the day on which is annually held the BSI Dinner.

Meantime, as early as May 12, 1934, Christopher Morley was able to announce in the "Bowling Green" that "Mr. A. G. Macdonell writes that the English Sherlock Holmes Society has organized and sends greetings to our own Baker Street Irregulars. The SHS is to hold its first dinner on June 6th [1934] at a restaurant [Canuto's, since vanished] in Baker Street. 'June 6th being Derby Day,' says Mr. Macdonell, 'it was felt that "Silver Blaze" might well be discussed.' "

This Society would seem to have perished with the death of its first and only President, the Reverend Dick Sheppard; its Chairman was the late Ivar Gunn, whose widow, Margaret Gunn, is now the Honourable Co-Secretary of the reconstituted Sherlock Holmes Society of London.

Writing in the *Sherlock Holmes Journal* ("For a World Now Prepared"), Mr. Colin Prestige has stated that "the actual decision to form [this later] society was . . . taken on the evening of Tuesday, February 20, 1951. On that day Anthony D. Howlett, Professor (then Dr.) W. T. Williams and I had met [C. T.] Thorne at Marylebone to discuss certain ideas concerning the [Sherlock Holmes Exhibition at the Festival of Britain]. . . . As a result of this friendly evening, Jack Thorne convened a meeting for Friday, March 16, inviting a number of Holmesians to meet in the Marylebone Children's Library. . . . There were present R. Ivar Gunn, James E. Holroyd, Anthony D. Howlett, Owen T. C. Jones (of Toronto), Winifred Paget, Colin Prestige, C. T. Thorne, W. T. Williams and Patricia Coulson (Mrs. Wynne-Jones). Studying these careful minutes, it is instructive to note how faithfully the Society has kept to the tentative proposals then discussed: a *Journal*, preferably printed, was felt to be essential; it was thought meetings should be four times a year, spread over the winter months (in fact, there are usually five or six each year); it was agreed to exhibit old Holmes films;

and it was agreed that qualifications for membership should be interest rather than learning. Finally, it was determined to call a full-scale meeting for Wednesday, April 17, to decide whether or not to form a society."

So far as Mr. Prestige's excellent memory serves, the following were present at this historic meeting (prewar members are denoted with asterisks): *Ivor Black, *Maurice Campbell, *R. Ivar Gunn, Michael Hall, James E. Holroyd, Anthony D. Howlett, *Sir Gerald Kelly, Ian M. Leslie, Ed Lewis, Winifred Paget, Freda Pearce, Colin Prestige, C. T. Thorne, Guy Warrack, Michael Weight, W. T. Williams, and Patricia Wynne-Jones.

Today, the Society lists 290 members, exclusive of its ten officers.

Like the BSI, the Sherlock Holmes Society of London has its Scion Societies, among them the Reigate Squires, the Inner Brotherhood of the Four, the Abbey Grangers of Chislehurst, and the very active Milvertonians of Hampstead. Affiliated with the Society is at least one Continental Scion, the King of Scandinavia's Own Sherlockians (there is also the Society of the Solitary Cyclists of Sweden, founded January 9, 1964).

And, like the BSI, the Sherlock Holmes Society of London publishes a *Journal*, first issued in May, 1952, with James Edward Holroyd and Philip Dalton as coeditors. It was then a mimeographed, staple-bound little publication of 40 pages —a far cry from the printed, handsomely illustrated *Journal* of today, now under the editorship of the Marquess of Donegall, which is currently mailed twice a year to its subscribers.

"There have been, of course, occasional hard-minded observers who thought it silly for a group of grown men to dally so intently over a literature of entertainment for which even its own author had only moderate regard," Christopher Morley once wrote. "Let me repeat what I have said before, that no printed body of modern social history . . . either by purpose or accident contains a richer pandect of the efficient impulses of its age. It has shown itself keen forecast in many ways, and some of its allusions may yet again be painfully timely. I wouldn't be surprised at any moment to see Afghanistan, or the *Orontes*, or the Coptic Patriarchs, or the dynamics of an asteroid, reappear in the news."

7

"YOUR MERITS SHOULD BE PUBLICLY RECOGNIZED"

[John H. Watson, M.D., to Mr. Sherlock Holmes, A Study in Scarlet]

We have mentioned the Sherlock Holmes Exhibition which was held at Abbey House on Baker Street, London, N.W. 1, May 22nd to September 22nd in 1951 as part of the Festival of Britain. The conception was first debated by the Councillors of the Borough of Marylebone as long ago as October, 1950, as a fitting tribute to "their most distinguished resident." Approved, a sum running to several thousand pounds was appropriated, and the project was triumphantly carried out, to the great delight of the thousands of enthusiasts who flocked to the Exhibition.

Certainly the most heartwarming and ingenious display of this entire Exhibition was the reproduction of the sitting room at 221B. The experts who did the exhaustive research were headed by Mr. C. T. Thorne, then a librarian of the St. Marylebone Borough; Professor W. T. Williams was the chief scientific adviser; and the room itself was the work of Michael Weight, a talented stage designer.

Fifty-four thousand people had seen the Exhibition when it closed in London; it then opened a six-and-a-half-weeks run at the Plaza Art Galleries in New York City on July 2, 1952, on the first leg of what was to be an international tour. The original room was almost entirely broken up on its return from New York, but Mrs. Adrian M. Conan Doyle reconstructed it for the Sherlock Holmes Inn from exhibits and material supplied by her husband. The reconstructed room was moved to the Inn on December 12, 1957, where it may be seen today; many other items from the Exhibition are on display in the ground-floor barrooms. **1**

1 The first public Sherlockian room in the United States, the Irregulars' Room in Sage's Restaurant, Chicago, was opened on February 26, 1964.

SITTING ROOM, 221B BAKER STREET, RECONSTRUCTED FOR THE 1951 SHERLOCK HOLMES EXHIBITION BY MICHAEL WEIGHT

The drawing is by Ronald Searle and originally appeared in *Punch*.

CATALOGUE COVER OF SHERLOCK HOLMES EXHIBITION, 1951

Drawing of Holmes by Bruce Angrave.

But the best and most accurate reconstruction of Mr. Sherlock Holmes' sitting room rests at this writing in the vaults of the castle of Lucens. Mrs. Adrian M. Conan Doyle, actively assisted by Mr. Thorne, has worked for months past to create the Room; Thorne pronounces it the best of the three.

No more impressive tribute to Sherlock Holmes has ever been paid than this remarkable Exhibition. But we may note many others:

Item: The late President of the United States, Franklin Delano Roosevelt, chose to call the cabins at his weekend retreat where the Secret Service men sheltered "221B Baker Street."[2]

Item: The London County Council in recent years has renamed the street once called York Mews South; it is now *Sherlock* Mews.

Item: The Diorama Room at Madame Tussaud's famous wax museum now features a remarkable reconstruction of the chase on the moor in *The Hound of the Baskervilles;* that it should do so was first suggested by Mr. Humphrey Morton of the Milvertonians of Hampstead.

Item: As part of the celebration of the Conan Doyle Centenary in May, 1959, a handsome bookcase was placed on permanent loan to the St. Marylebone Council to encourage the building up of a comprehensive collection of Holmesian texts and higher criticism.

Item: No. 8, one of a group of twenty electric locomotives of the Metropolitan Railway named for Great Britain's Great Men from John Lyon (No. 1) to Christopher Wren (No. 20) was designated "The Sherlock Holmes." The nameplate, unhappily, had to be melted down for scrap metal during the dark days of World War II, but on Monday, October 5, 1953, the name was restored to one of the Metropolitan Line electric locomotives hauling passenger trains on the Aylesbury line between Baker Street and Rickmansworth. (It was returned to the Sherlock Holmes Society, its donor, however, on November 14, 1962, when the Metropolitan Line was modernized and the locomotive put out to pension; London Transport then arranged an impressive luncheon ceremony.)

Item: It was Old Irregular Tom Stix who conceived the idea of inaugurating the Silver Blaze Purse as a regular feature of the Eastern racing season. His conception saw realization in 1952, on the 18th of April, when the Silver Blaze Purse was run for the first time as the sixth (feature) race at Jamaica, Long Island, with a $5,000 purse for three-year-olds which had never won three races other than maiden or claiming 122 pounds; the distance was one mile and a sixteenth; there were eight entries of whom Quick Step was the winner. Today, Silver Blaze Handicaps or similarly named races are more or less annual features of the racing season not only in New York but also in Toronto, Ontario (where the Sherlockian Plate was first run at Woodbine in 1961); in Chicago (first run at Arlington Park on August 5, 1960); in San Francisco (first run at the Bay Meadows Track in San Mateo on October 20, 1961); and at Aalborg in Denmark (first run on September 29, 1963).

Still, first place after the Sherlock Holmes Exhibition should probably go to the series of memorials which have been installed at sites of Holmesian interest by devoted mem-

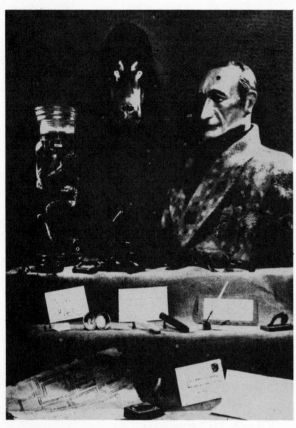

RELICS OF FAMOUS HOLMES CASES IN THE COLLECTION OF THE SHERLOCK HOLMES TAVERN

2 Only the Baker Street Irregulars knew, while he lived, that President Roosevelt was a free and accepted member of their order. After his death a collection of his letters to Edgar Smith, commenting shrewdly on many aspects of the Canon, was published by the society.

bers of the BSI and the Sherlock Holmes Society of London.

The first of these memorials was the inspiration of Mr. W. T. Rabe, organizer during World War II of the Old Soldiers of Baker Street. Mr. Rabe was instrumental in securing the erection of a plaque at the Rosslei Inn, in Meiringen, Switzerland, in the immediate vicinity of the Reichenbach Falls. The plaque was erected in November, 1952, and reads as follows:

TO THIS VALLEY IN MAY, 1891, CAME DR. WATSON AND SHERLOCK HOLMES AND HERE HOLMES BESTED THE INFAMOUS PROF. MORIARTY IN MORTAL COMBAT: THOUGH HOLMES WAS THOUGHT TO HAVE PERISHED, HE ESCAPED AND RETURNED TO LONDON IN 1894. HE HAS SINCE RETIRED TO SUSSEX AND BEE-KEEPING.

On January 3, 1953, a second plaque—a circular bronze with white enamel lettering—was erected in Piccadilly on the north wall of the Criterion building. It reads:

THIS PLAQUE
COMMEMORATES THE
HISTORIC MEETING EARLY
IN 1881 AT THE ORIGINAL
CRITERION LONG BAR
OF DR. STAMFORD AND
DR. JOHN H. WATSON
WHICH LED TO THE INTRODUCTION
OF DR. WATSON TO
MR. SHERLOCK HOLMES

Beneath it is a small plaque inscribed:

ERECTED BY THE BARITSU CHAPTER
OF THE
BAKER STREET IRREGULARS, TOKYO

A third plaque of handsome bronze was erected on January 21, 1954, at St. Bartholomew's Hospital, in the curator's room adjoining the pathological laboratory, facing the door and above the fireplace:

AT THIS PLACE NEW YEAR'S DAY, 1881
WERE SPOKEN THESE DEATHLESS WORDS
"YOU HAVE BEEN
IN AFGHANISTAN, I PERCEIVE"
BY
MR. SHERLOCK HOLMES
IN GREETING TO
JOHN H. WATSON, M.D.
AT THEIR FIRST MEETING
THE BAKER STREET IRREGULARS—1953
BY THE AMATEUR MENDICANTS AT THE CAUCUS CLUB.

Still a fourth plaque was erected in June, 1957, at the Reichenbach Falls itself.**3**

SHERLOCK MEWS, LONDON, W. 1—FORMERLY YORK MEWS SOUTH

3 Since complete agreement cannot yet be reached on the true site of No. 221B, there is still no plaque on any house in Baker Street. We recall a meeting of the BSI at which two opposing groups argued hotly for their respective sites. Growing weary of the bickering, the late Earle Walbridge stalked to the bar with a muttered, "A plaque on both your houses."

ACROSS THIS "DREADFUL CAULDRON" OCCURRED
THE CULMINATING EVENT IN THE CAREER OF
SHERLOCK HOLMES, THE WORLD'S GREATEST
DETECTIVE, WHEN ON MAY 4, 1891 HE
VANQUISHED PROF. MORIARTY
THE NAPOLEON OF CRIME
ERECTED BY THE NORWEGIAN EXPLORERS
OF MINNESOTA AND THE SHERLOCK HOLMES
SOCIETY OF LONDON 25 JUNE 1957

Regrettably, there has not yet been erected on Baker Street the great statue of Holmes mentioned by Opal, Lady Portsock, writing in the year 1988, as described by Monsignor Ronald A. Knox in his *Memories of the Future*. When it *is* erected, its sponsors might well consider a life-sized duplication of the statuette, some 17 inches tall, commissioned by Mr. Luther Leon Norris of Culver City, California, and executed by the well-known sculptor, Luques Whitmore, a student of the great George Stanley, creator of the Hollywood Oscar.

Until that statue is one of London's noted landmarks, we present an illustration of the Norris-Whitmore Holmes.

THE NORRIS-WHITMORE HOLMES

The friends of Mr. Sherlock Holmes hope that a life-size reproduction of this statuette will someday stand in Portman Square, looking north up Baker Street.

TWO PLAQUES THAT HONOR HOLMES

(*Left*) The plaque at St. Bartholomew's Hospital, erected January 21, 1954, by the Amateur Mendicants Society of Detroit. (*Right*) The plaque at the Reichenbach Falls, erected June 25, 1947, by the Norwegian Explorers of Minneapolis and St. Paul and the Sherlock Holmes Society of London.

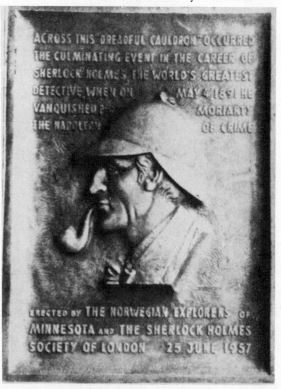

8

"THE BEST AND THE WISEST MAN
WHOM I HAVE EVER KNOWN"

[John H. Watson, M.D., of Sherlock Holmes, "The Final Problem"]

And now let us turn from the Sherlock Holmes of fiction to the Sherlock Holmes so many of us would like to think of as *fact:*

William (or Thomas) Sherlock Scott Holmes was born on the 6th of January, 1854, at the farmstead of Mycroft, near Sigerside, in the North Riding**1** of Yorkshire.

Every one of these statements will be disputed by your editor's fellow Sherlockians and Holmesians, and this is no doubt how it should be.

The year of Holmes' birth, for example:

The speculations of scholars have placed this important event variously in the years 1852, 1853, 1854, 1855, 1857–58, and even in 1867.

The last year above is that given by Mr. Douglas M. Hoffecker in "Forgive Us, Oh Lord!" Mr. Hoffecker holds that when Holmes, in "The *Gloria Scott*," visited Donnithrope on "the fixed date" of 1885 he was eighteen years old, and was therefore born in 1867.

It is true that eighteen is the average age of students entering either Oxford or Cambridge, so most Sherlockians base their conclusions as to the year of Holmes' birth on (1) the date they assign to the adventure of "The *Gloria Scott*"; (2) the college year in which they believe this adventure to have taken place (that is, was Holmes at the time a first- or a second-year man?).

But there is a difficulty in this line of reasoning: Holmes must certainly have been a precocious youngster. He may even have been a child prodigy. Are we justified, then, in assuming that he was indeed eighteen, and not two or even three years younger, when he first entered a university?

There are, however, two other Canonical clues to the Master's age:

First, Holmes described himself as a "middle-aged" man in June, 1889 ("The Boscombe Valley Mystery"). ". . . while many are reluctant to admit it," the late A. Carson Simpson wrote in "It Must Have Been Two Other Fellows," "[thirty-five] has been accepted as middle age for many centuries. It is the halfway point of the Biblical 'threescore years and ten'; [Holmes] would have passed 'the middle of the pathway of our life,' as Dante puts it in the first line of the *Inferno*." If Holmes was, indeed, thirty-five in 1889, it follows that he was born in the year 1854.

1 Yorkshire folk will tell you that a *riding* measured the distance that a Saxon overlord could go riding in a day, but the true meaning is not so picturesque. A riding is only a thriding, or thirding, a division into three parts. There is, of course, no *South* Riding of Yorkshire. The three are the North, the East, and the West.

SHERLOCK HOLMES OF BAKER STREET

A portrait by Sidney Paget. The late James Montgomery wrote (*A Study in Pictures*): "Possibly the most satisfactory Paget portrait of Holmes is one that never appeared with any of the stories, but is reputed to have been rescued from a scrap basket by the artist's wife after he had torn it in half and discarded it." This wonderful character study of the Master in contemplative mood was first published in the *Cornhill Magazine* for Summer, 1951, reprinted in *The Baker Street Journal* for October, 1953, and distributed as a Christmas card in 1953 by the Sherlock Holmes Society of London. The original was on display at the Exhibitions in London (1951) and New York (1952).

Second, we are told that Holmes appeared to be a man of sixty in 1914 in his character of Altamont ("His Last Bow"). Again we reach 1854—but here we must register a violent dissent by the late Dr. Ernest Bloomfield Zeisler. Dr. Zeisler has pointed out that part of Holmes' disguise in this role was a goatee that might have made him look older than he actually was. "In *The Sign of the Four*," Dr. Zeisler wrote in *Baker Street Chronology*, "[Holmes] appears as an 'aged' man, clad in seafaring garb. In 'A Scandal in Bohemia' he appears once as a 'drunken-looking groom, ill-kempt and side-whiskered, with an inflamed face and disreputable clothes' and another time as an 'amiable and simpleminded Nonconformist clergyman.' In 'The Adventure of the Beryl Coronet' he is 'a loafer,' in 'The Adventure of the Empty House' he is 'an elderly deformed man carrying books,' and in 'The Adventure of Charles Augustus Milverton' [he appears as] a 'rakish young workman with a goatee.' It has not occurred to anyone to conclude from these descriptions that the Master actually was an aged man, a groom, a clergyman, a loafer, an elderly deformed man, or a young workman."

We see now why there is so much disagreement as to the year of Holmes' birth.

"We reach 1852 as the year . . . ," Mr. T. S. Blakeney wrote. "We are probably safe in thinking that an earlier date is inadmissible; but, on the other hand, 1853 is possible."

"While his birth certificate cannot be traced, it is generally accepted by commentators that Sherlock Holmes was born either late in 1852 or early in 1853," Mr. O. F. Grazebrook wrote in his *Studies in Sherlock Holmes, I*.

"1853 (late 1852 or early 1854): Birth of Sherlock Holmes," the late Dorothy L. Sayers stated in "Holmes' College Career."

"It would seem that the most likely year for [Holmes'] birth would be 1853," was the verdict of the late Gavin Brend.

Dr. Rufus S. Tucker also favored 1853 in his "Genealogical Notes on Holmes," and made an "Ancestry of Sherlock Holmes, of London," in which he said: "Born January 6, 1853."

In "Oxford or Cambridge or Both?" Mr. N. P. Metcalfe concurred with Dr. Tucker.

"We may deduce by the normal methods of arithmetic that [Holmes] was born in 1854, though arguments have been advanced in favor of 1852 or 1853," Mr. S. C. Roberts wrote in "The Personality of Sherlock Holmes."

"[Holmes] was probably born in 1855, or late in 1854," the late H. W. Bell decided.

"There is not enough evidence on which to date the Master's birth any more accurately than the interval 1857–59, with the probabilities favoring 1857 or 1858," was Dr. Zeisler's final verdict.

It would appear that Holmes could not have been born much before 1853 or much later than 1857; the Baker Street Irregulars have discussed the problem at length and have decided that they prefer 1854. Let us leave it at that.

For the "January 6th" we have the evidence of *The Valley of Fear*. That interesting case began on January 7th (1888) and we are told that Holmes on the morning of that day

2 Miss Revill had something to say about Watson also: his Sun is badly menaced, and the Grand Tine shows that he had a very susceptible heart and a tendency for burying wives because Saturn and Uranus in Taurus tangle with the Moon Wife.

"leaned upon his hand, with his untasted breakfast before him . . ." "Surely it is clear," Mr. Nathan L. Bengis wrote in "What Was the Month?", "that there had been some small jollification the night before in celebration of the Master's birthday, and that his lack of appetite was the result of a hangover?"

Again, Holmes quotes Shakespeare often, but *Twelfth Night* is the only such play that Holmes quotes *twice*. Twelfth Night is January 6th; Holmes, then, was especially fond of that play because January 6th was his own birthdate.

The ancient art of astrology provides a further clue: In the March, 1964, issue of the British astrology magazine *Prediction*, Miss Joan Revill has noted that in the early hours of January 6, 1854, Scorpio had just reached the ascendant. "Scorpio fits [Holmes] like a glove . . . impassive features . . . relentless, courageous prober of mysteries, dabbler in poisons and chemicals . . ." It seems that the Master got a bit of Virgo, too: "painstaking attention to details, finer shades of analysis and deduction, man of concentrated habits." Uranus came in also and made Holmes something of an eccentric, but *not* slovenly. Watching the agony column is a Third House activity, and Venus in Pisces would explain why he was so much attracted to Irene Adler, *the* woman.**2**

Opposed to the January school of thought, however, is the June school, represented by Messrs. Russell McLauchlin and Rolfe Boswell, who base their case on the emerald tiepin presented to Holmes by Queen Victoria for his successful solution to the theft of the Bruce-Partington submarine plans.

"If the Widow of Windsor took it into her dear, old head to give somebody a precious stone," Mr. McLauchlin wrote ("On the Dating of the Master's Birth"), "there is only one plan of selection that would have occurred to her. She would, of course, choose his birthstone. There is some question about birthstones, to be sure. There are ancient and modern theories. According to the former, the emerald is the birthstone for May. By more modern reckoning, it is the birthstone for June. Which system, so to speak, did Queen Victoria play?"

To this, Mr. Boswell has responded ("A Rare Day in June") that "the Queen, as her subjects well knew, was a stickler for the proprieties. In her day, the agate was first choice for May's birthstone, while the emerald held pride of place for June. . . . On balancing probabilities, it is apparent that the Master was born in June. Can that Rare Day be pinpointed? The reply is in the positive. . . . Sherlock Holmes was born on Saturday, June 17, 1854 [June 17th is Mr. Boswell's date for "The Red-Headed League"]."

But Mr. Bengis has struck a telling counterblow for the January school in "What Was the Month?": ". . . the only thing we can be sure of . . . is not that the gem was an emerald, but that it was green. Now the first choice for January . . . was the garnet. Further research has revealed that there is a somewhat rare variety of garnet, emerald green in color, called uvarovite. If the gem in the tiepin was uvarovite, it was still a garnet and therefore still a January stone, even though it looked like an emerald [to Watson]."

Mr. Michael Harrison has recently expressed the view that

Holmes may have been connected with the peerage of both Ireland and Great Britain (in his monograph, "The Blue Blood of the Holmeses"). The Irish peerage in question was that of Holmes of Kilmallock, an Irish barony created in the first year of King George III. This became extinct when Thomas, first Baron Holmes, died on July 21, 1764, leaving no male heirs. It was revived, however, on March 4, 1798, when his nephew Leonard Troughear (who had assumed the name of Holmes by Royal License) became Baron Holmes by a King's Letter of October 25, 1797. He died about May, 1804, again without leaving a male heir. But his elder daughter Elizabeth by her second husband, Sir Henry Worsley, did leave a son and heir who adopted the additional patronymic of Holmes, becoming Sir Henry Worsley Holmes, Baronet.

Sherlock Holmes himself, however, tells us only that his ancestors were "country squires, who appear to have led much the same life as is natural to their class" ("The Greek Interpreter").

"Clearly Holmes must have belonged to an old county family," Mr. S. C. Roberts wrote in "The Personality of Sherlock Holmes." "But whether it was the Shropshire Holmses or the Lincolnshire branch we do not know."

On the other hand, we have the authority of Conan Doyle himself that Holmes may have come from Surrey: in the Holmes-Watson parody, "How Watson Learned the Trick," Holmes, reading the cricket page of his newspaper, gives "a loud exclamation of interest" on finding that "Surrey was holding its own against Kent."

"Although a man may have only 'small experience of cricket clubs' (as Holmes admits in [Conan Doyle's other Holmes-Watson parody] 'The Field Bazaar') it is not unusual for him to follow his home county side with interest, even enthusiasm," Mr. Peter Richard wrote in "Completing the Canon." "It therefore would seem probable that Holmes' birthplace was in Surrey—possible, in fact, that his ancestors, being country squires and Reigate being in Surrey, that they were indeed the original Reigate Squires!"

This view has received enthusiastic endorsement from Mr.

THREE COATS OF ARMS OF MR. SHERLOCK HOLMES

The Holmes arms according to Mr. Rolfe Boswell ("A Connecticut Yankee in Support of Sir Arthur"): Argent a fess sable with three caltrops in the chief proper. A small crescent, symbol of a second son, is charged upon the fess to distinguish Sherlock from his elder brother Mycroft. Crest: a sinister hand proper encrusted with icicles grasping a banner gules, thereon a golden bee and the watchword EXCELSIOR in silver letters. Motto: We can but try.

The Holmes arms according to Mr. Belden Wigglesworth ("The Coat of Arms of Sherlock Holmes"): Quarterly, sable first and fourth, a cat-a-mountain argent, salient, armed and langued. Second party per bend sinister; first argent, a beehive with bees, diversely volant, sable; second azure, three millstones argent. Argent third, three fleurs-de-lis sable, their tips or. Crest: a fox proper passant-regardant. Motto: *Je pense, alors je suis* ("I think, therefore I am").

The Holmes arms according to Mr. William S. Hall ("The True and Proper Coat of Arms"): Argent, three buglehorns, sable. Crest: a lion rampant. Motto: *Justim et tenacem propositi* ("Just and firm of purpose").

MYCROFT, SIGERSIDE, NORTH RIDING

The lonely farm on the Yorkshire moors where Sherlock Holmes was born on January 6, 1854. From *Sherlock Holmes: A Biography*, by William S. Baring-Gould.

3 Against this view, however, we must in all fairness point out that Holmes *twice* (once in "The *Gloria Scott*" and again in "The Adventure of the Priory School") displays an ignorance of the North of England that would seem to have come only from a Southerner.

4 Mr. O. F. Grazebrook noted in "Oxford or Cambridge" that "a French strain . . . was also to be found in Lord Peter Wimsey's pedigree. It is perhaps the special advantage of French blood to give logic to the mind, and provide careers for private investigators."

We may also note here that Sir Arthur Conan Doyle was an ardent Francophile, and that his son, Adrian M. Conan Doyle, tells us that there is little doubt that Holmes' Vernet connection may be traced to a painting by Vernet given to Conan Doyle some time before he wrote *A Study in Scarlet* by his uncle Henry Doyle, Director of the National Gallery in Dublin. "With the painting are two letters from Richard Doyle, Henry's brother, on the subject of Vernet's artistic merit."

C. O. Merriman of the Sherlock Holmes Society of London. In "Birthplace of Holmes," Mr. Merriman noted, first, that Reigate is in the Vale of Holmesdale; second, that at least six of Holmes' cases were directly connected with Surrey and still more were in neighboring counties; third, that Holmes after his exertions against the machinations of Baron Maupertuis ("The Reigate Squires") would be likely to seek a rest cure in the pleasant countryside and soothing quiet of his own hometown.

Still a third view, to which your editor subscribes, holds that Holmes was a Yorkshire man, born in the North Riding.**3**

As the erudite Dr. Tucker wrote in his "Genealogical Notes on Holmes": "It has, I believe, not previously been pointed out that the name [of Holmes' brother] Mycroft is a clue to the origin of the family. Could any parent have inflicted so ugly a name on a helpless infant except for the strongest of family reasons? Obviously as the oldest son he was doomed to bear the name of the family estate. The North Riding of Yorkshire contains several manors by the name of 'Croft' or some compound of 'croft,' an old Saxon word that means an enclosed field. The founder of the Holmes line, in order to distinguish *his* 'croft' from the others, called it Mycroft, and Sherlock's older brother suffered the consequences . . ."

Christopher Morley was another strong supporter of the Yorkshire school of thought. "A study of the place-names of the Holdernesse region [in Yorkshire, between the North Sea and the Humber] assures me that the . . . squirearchy from which Sherlock . . . descended was certainly in this neighborhood," he wrote. "There, more than anywhere in England, one finds all possible variations of the ancient word *holm* [meaning an islet in a river or lake or near the mainland]."

Elsewhere Mr. Morley pinpointed his choice of Holmes' birthplace, declaring that it is still marked on the map as the Holmes Hall, "about 2½ miles east of the village of Croft on Tees, in the North Riding of Yorkshire. Lat. 54.29 N., Long. 1.30 W. . . ."

But of course we must not forget that there was also a *French* strain in Holmes' ancestry; he tells us, again in "The Greek Interpreter," that his grandmother was "the sister of Vernet, the French artist."**4**

In his scholarly essay, "Zero Wolf Meets Sherlock Holmes," Mr. Ben Wolf has traced the history of the Vernets for us:

The founder of the House of Vernet was named Antoine. He was born at Avignon, in 1689, and he died there in 1753. As he sired 22 children, one assumes that he did not have much free time for travel. Apparently, he did not have much leisure for painting, either, as Bryant's *Dictionary of Painters and Engravers* records only a single study, "Flowers and Birds," in the possession of the Musée Calvet, in Avignon.

Of his 22 offspring, four were to become painters. . . . Obviously, the distracted father of this enormous brood ran out of names at a point. Two of his four painting sons shared the name of Antoine. The other two, however, were named Claude Joseph and François Gabriel. . . .

Of the four painter sons, Claude Joseph, who was born also in Avignon in 1714, appears to have had the most active career. At the age of 17, a patron sent him to Rome to study. On the voyage he witnessed a violent storm and, according to tradition, lashed himself to the mast of the ship in order that he might accurately observe the effects for future painting. Both the ship and Vernet survived the ordeal, and in Rome he began by depicting his memories of the stormy sea. During his sojourn in the Eternal City—and doubtless as a result of his studies—he turned to the ruins and landscapes and costumes of Rome, adopting a style reminiscent of Salvator Rosa. He fell in love with the daughter of the Pope's Naval Commandant and, in due course, they were married.

During Claude Joseph's stay in Rome he had been shipping canvases back to France. They were much admired—one of his admirers being no less than Mme. de Pompadour. At her behest, he settled in Paris. He was admitted to the Académie and was commissioned by Louis XV to paint a set of 20 pictures of French seaports. His career seems to have proceeded swimmingly, but his last years were embittered by the madness and death of his wife. Incidentally, his own death could not have been staged more brilliantly, insofar as its setting was concerned. He died in the Louvre on 3 December 1789. . . .

Issue of this union was Antoine Charles Horace, known as Carle, who was born at Bordeaux,**5** in 1758. We are told that he drew horses when quite a child and studied painting principally with his father. At 21 he received the Second Prize of the Academy of Painting, and three years later the Grand Prize of Rome.

While in Italy he apparently raised considerable hell in the oat-sowing field, was overcome by remorse and almost became a monk, but his father managed to get him back to France. Although during the French Revolution his sympathies were at first with the People's Cause, his feelings in their behalf were somewhat dimmed by the fact that he received a musket-ball . . . through his hand during an uprising in Paris.

His earlier works had been classic in style. This period was followed by military subjects, and his canvas, "Morning of Austerlitz," earned the Legion of Honour in 1808. He died in 1836.

Charles Horace (or Carle) had a son named Émile Jean Horace. . . . The son was an ardent Bonapartist and remained one, even after the Restoration, which displeased the Bourbons to an understandable degree. Émile, however, was apparently possessed of footwork the equal of his brushwork. He was restored to favour in France and managed, possibly by absenting himself during changes in administration (*via* short sojourns in other European courts), to adjust himself to a succession of regimes. Filled with patriotism and facility, his canvases can be seen in great quantity at Versailles . . .

Robert Lefèvre pinx.   Fremy del. et Sculp.

SHERLOCK HOLMES' GREAT-UNCLE: ÉMILE JEAN HORACE
VERNET, CALLED HORACE VERNET, 1789–1863

5 "Here we have an association with the south of France," Christopher Morley wrote in "Was Sherlock Holmes an American?" "which [Holmes] acknowledges by his interest in Montpellier ["The Adventure of the Empty House," "The Disappearance of Lady Frances Carfax"], where he probably had French kindred. . . . It is significant that though he declined a knighthood in Britain ["The Adventure of the Three Garridebs"] he was willing to accept the Legion of Honour in France ["The Adventure of the Golden Pince-Nez"]. . . ."

The weight of Sherlockian authority holds that Holmes' grandmother was the daughter of Antoine Charles Horace, called Carle, and the sister of Émile Jean Horace, called Horace; she was presumably born about the year 1787.

Let us look a little more closely at Horace Vernet, Sherlock Holmes' greatuncle:

. . . from the pen of Mendelssohn the musician [Mr. O. F. Grazebrook wrote in *Oxford or Cambridge*] . . . we learn that gifted with extensive powers of perception, and a most astonishing memory, [Horace] Vernet was of so methodical and orderly a character that his mind was like a well-stocked bureau. Vernet had but to open a drawer in it and find what he needed. ("A man should keep his little brain attic stocked with all the furniture that he is likely to use, and the rest he can put away in the lumber room of his library, where he can get it if he wants it."—Sherlock Holmes, "The Five Orange Pips").

It was related of Holmes' great uncle that a single glance at a model was sufficient to tell him all that was necessary for the most minute detail of appearance. It is obvious, therefore, that some of these traits, these excellencies of Horace Vernet, were passed on in the family genes and are in themselves sufficient to account for many, if not all, of Sherlock Holmes' distinctive abilities. . . .

Horace Vernet's first picture was exhibited in the Salon of 1812; amid a host of other masterpieces, there is one, painted in 1822, which has a special interest for all students of Holmes literature. In that picture, the artist has painted himself in his studio, surrounded by men *boxing* and *fencing* (is it remarkable that Holmes was expert in both?) in the midst of a medley of clients, visitors, horses, *dogs* and models, and an assembly as variegated and fascinating as the clients, yet unborn, who were to throng and to climb the immortal stairs of Baker Street.

L'ATELIER OF HORACE VERNET

From *Oxford or Cambridge,* by O. F. Grazebrook.

But the question remains: was Mlle. Vernet Holmes' *paternal* or *maternal* grandmother? Did she marry a Holmes, and bear Sherlock's father? Or did she marry a man with another name, and so bear the child who was to become the mother of Sherlock Holmes?

Mr. Rolfe Boswell speaks for the paternal school of thought in "A Connecticut Yankee in Support of Sir Arthur": "Some time between 1806 and 1808, Dr. Lathrop Holmes [of Woodstock, Connecticut, U.S.A.] appears to have married a daughter of . . . Carle Vernet. By the former Mlle. Vernet, Dr. Holmes was the father of at least one child, a son. . . . Sherlock was Oliver [Wendell Holmes] Senior's first cousin once removed, since he was the grandson of Dr. Lathrop Holmes, [who was in fact] Oliver's uncle; and, thus, Mr. Justice Holmes' second cousin."

On the other hand, Mr. Vincent Starrett has written in his *Private Life of Sherlock Holmes:* "[Holmes'] grandmother—but on which side? The mother's, one suspects, since in general his ancestors were English country squires."

And Mr. Ian Mackay, in "Knowledge of Politics—Feeble?", has written that "there was a revolutionary strain on the distaff side in Holmes . . ."

Of his mother and father, Holmes tells us nothing—a fact that led the late President of the United States, Franklin Roosevelt, to speculate that Holmes was a foundling. In one of the letters in *A Baker Street Folio*, Mr. Roosevelt wrote (to Mr. Belden Wigglesworth of the Speckled Band of Boston): "Being a foundling his one great failure was his inability after long search to find his parents."[6]

Dr. Tucker, speaking guardedly of President Roosevelt's original surmise in his "Genealogical Notes," wrote: "A noted authority—in fact the ultimate personification of authority in every field but this—has recently expressed the opinion that Holmes was a foundling. We cannot reject such an opinion offhand, but it is not a bar against further inquiry. This same personage has been known to use words in a Pickwickian sense. Moreover, to the scion of eight generations of Hudson Valley patroons a man whose ancestors were merely English country squires would naturally appear to be, comparatively speaking, a foundling."

We may perhaps surmise that Holmes' mother's Christian name was Violet: it is noteworthy that this name belonged to five ladies[7] whom Holmes later treated with more than his ordinary courtesy.

What was her surname before she became a Holmes?

She was a Miss Sherlock, Rolfe Boswell surmised ("A Connecticut Yankee in Support of Sir Arthur"); but Dr. Tucker thought it far more likely that Sherlock was the maiden name of Holmes' *paternal* grandmother. Mr. Elliot Kimball, on the other hand, writing in "The First Man Who Beat Holmes," has stated unequivocally that Holmes' maternal grandfather, he who married Mlle. Vernet and fathered Holmes' mother, was Sir Edward Sherrinford, in September of 1860 seventy-two years old.

On still another hand, Professor Jacques Barzun has argued ("How Holmes Came to Play the Violin") that Holmes' *mother*, rather than his grandmother, was a Vernet, and unmarried: "Holmes was obviously brought up in a retired way by his mother *alone*."

As for Holmes *père*, we may be reasonably sure that he was named Sigurd or Siger Holmes, since Sherlock later took as his alias the name *Sigerson*, a Norwegian form of Sigurdson.

Holmes had, as we know, at least one brother: Mycroft Holmes, seven years Sherlock's senior, and born, therefore, in 1847.

But if Mycroft and Sherlock came from a line of country squires, as Sherlock said they did, why did not Mycroft, as the elder brother, inherit the family estate?

One possible explanation has been put forward by Messrs. J. H. and Humfrey Michell in "Sherlock Holmes the Chemist." Here it is suggested that Holmes' father had perhaps "been speculating in stocks and had been ruined. . . . Mycroft . . . is forced to take a humble position in the Civil Service, and Sherlock, his brilliant career at Cambridge cut short, retires to Montague Street to earn his bread and butter as a consulting detective."

[6] In a later letter, however, addressed to the late Edgar W. Smith, Mr. Roosevelt recanted and said: "On further study I am inclined to revise my former estimate that Holmes was a foundling. Actually he was born an American and was brought up by his father or a foster father in the underground world, thus learning all the tricks of the trade in the highly developed American art of crime."

[7] Miss Hunter in "The Adventure of the Copper Beeches," Miss Smith in "The Adventure of the Solitary Cyclist," Miss de Merville in "The Adventure of the Illustrious Client," Miss Westbury in "The Adventure of the Bruce-Partington Plans" and Miss Stonor in the *play* version of "The Adventure of the Speckled Band."

Another possible explanation has been advanced by Mr. R. S. Colborne ("Orphans of the Storm?"): "In writings on the origin and early life of Holmes, it does not appear to have been realized that Mycroft and Sherlock must have been sons of a second marriage. In the stable Victorian era, the landed squirearchy, from which Holmes and his brother stemmed, must have had another heir, and the fact that Sherlock Holmes seemed to have retained no connection with his family clearly points to a second marriage. Holmes senior probably lost his first wife and remarried in the late 1840's. He himself apparently died about 1864, when Sherlock was 10 years old, and the assumption of the squirearchy by the eldest son of the first marriage was the main reason for Sherlock's mother taking him and Mycroft away to start a new home . . ."

A third possible explanation is that there was a *third* brother, senior to Mycroft. "Watson had known Holmes for . . . years before he learned that his friend had even one brother, so the existence of another is not impossible," Mr. Anthony Boucher pointed out in "Was the Later Holmes an Imposter?" Dr. Tucker thought that this brother might have been named Gerard, but there is also the distinct possibility that the first Holmes son was named Sherrinford; after all, we know that Sherrinford was, in one sense at least, an elder Holmes than Sherlock.

Professor Jacques Barzun has suggested ("How Holmes Came to Play the Violin") that the Dr. Verner to whom Holmes alluded as his cousin when he bought Watson's practice ("The Adventure of the Norwood Builder") was very possibly a third brother, and Christopher Morley held that Sherlock and Mycroft had a brother younger than either of them whose name was Raffles Holmes. More recently, Mr. Jerry Neal Williamson has put forth the alarming suggestion ("'There Was Something Very Strange'") that Professor James Moriarty, the Napoleon of Crime, was really a Holmes brother, in age between Sherlock and Mycroft.

Dr. Tucker wrote that "Holmes never mentioned . . . his . . . father . . . because he died when Sherlock was too young to have formed any impression of him," and Mr. Michael Harrison (*In the Footsteps of Sherlock Holmes*) has also made out a very good case for Sherlock and Mycroft having been orphaned at a fairly early age.

In any case, Holmes is as reticent about his boyhood and his early schooling as he is about his parentage. But Mr. Bernard Davies has written ("Was Holmes a Londoner?") that Holmes' "obvious lack of the normal public school background displayed by Watson and his all-round proficiency in the arts of self-defense rather than team sports strongly suggests an education by a tutor."

This is also the view of Mr. S. C. Roberts ("The Personality of Sherlock Holmes"): ". . . it is perhaps legitimate to conjecture that, being temperamentally unfitted for the normal activities of public school life, either [Holmes] was privately educated from early boyhood or after a short period at a public school he was so miserable that his parents removed him to the care of a private tutor."

Your editor's own researches have convinced him that travel on the Continent accounted for much of Holmes' early life (as it did for another well-known Victorian, a clergyman and author, who entered Cambridge speaking six languages although he had never had a day of the British schooling usual in those times for sons of the landed gentry).

In *Sherlock Holmes of Baker Street* we have reported on these travels:

> . . . Siger Holmes led his entire family aboard the steamship *Lerdo* on July 7, 1855. They were bound for Bordeaux, across the Bay of Biscay. From Bordeaux they traveled to Pau, and there they wintered, taking a flat in the Grande Place. . . .
>
> They stayed at Pau until the May of 1858, until Sherlock was four. Then the whole family removed to Montpellier . . .

After a brief return to England:

> In October, 1860, [the Holmes family] crossed to Rotterdam. Two months later this wandering family, these genteel gypsies, pitched tent in Cologne.
>
> The Rhine in that winter of 1860–61 was frozen over, and the whole family had several months of peace during which Siger Holmes continued his studies. But when the ice began to break and whirl down the stream, the restless Yorkshireman got out his carriage and was off again. . . .
>
> Darmstadt, Karlsruhe, Stuttgart, Mannheim, Munich, Heidelberg—the carriage covered thousands of kilometers over bad roads, in all weathers and temperatures, the baggage piled on top, the family jostling within.
>
> Heidelberg to Berne, Berne to Lucerne, Lucerne to Thun by October—on and on the rumbling carriage rolled, beyond the cities, into villages and towns and wild corners of Europe where few English families had ever been before, where few for many years were to follow. They visited Italy, they traveled to the Tyrol and to Salzburg, they went to Vienna and thence to Dresden. They arrived in Saxony, and later stayed for a long time at Mannheim.
>
> The journey lasted almost four long years, and had a lifelong influence on young Master Sherlock Holmes. He developed an enviably intimate knowledge of Europe. He became to some extent a European, that civilized being whom the Western world has not yet succeeded in turning out in quantity. Unaware of a boy's ordinary interests, always in the company of his brothers and his parents . . . the whole bent of his character was formed at this time.
>
> It was a highly unusual childhood, but Sherlock Holmes was a highly unusual boy, destined to become a highly unusual man. . . .

Again, in 1868, it was Pau again for the Holmes family:

> Siger, Violet, and Sherlock Holmes sailed in September, 1868, from Plymouth to St. Malo, taking a leisurely month over the rolling miles southward, resolutely halt-

ing wherever they chanced to be each Sunday to attend the church that meant so much in the life of Sherlock's mother.

They arrived at Pau in October, 1868, thus beginning the last Continental visit Sherlock Holmes was ever to make with his parents.

From it, Sherlock was to get two benefits that would stand him in good stead for many years to come. To "toughen" the boy, Siger Holmes himself volunteered to teach him boxing. The father also had the son enrolled in the most celebrated fencing school in Europe, the salon of Maître Alphonse Bencin. . . .

Watson's annals make one other fact about Holmes' childhood clear: whether with a parent or parents or perhaps with some solid, bourgeois relations, he almost certainly must have spent at least some years in South London, in one of those districts later engulfed in the giant boroughs of Lambeth, Wandsworth, and Camberwell.

The evidence is in Chapter III of *The Sign of the Four*, where Holmes, although displaying an intimate knowledge of South London, calls *two of the streets by names long out of date.***8**

"Brixton, Kennington, Vauxhall, Stockwell," Mr. Davies wrote in "Was Holmes a Londoner?"—"somewhere in this region stood a house which Holmes called home; one of those solid, middle-class villas that abounded in these once pleasant suburbs of the 'sixties. If it still stands it will be a little faded now, perhaps, just a number in a long, dreary highway. But Holmes would have known it before it had a number . . ."

We come now to "The *Gloria Scott*" and "The Musgrave Ritual," and a consideration of Holmes, the university undergraduate.

How long was he a student? At what university or universities?

Let us marshal the evidence given to us in these two early adventures:

1. "The *Gloria Scott*" was the first case in which Holmes was ever engaged.**9** He had already formed "habits of observation and inference" "into a system, although I had not yet appreciated the part they were to play in my life." The senior Trevor's recommendation, he tells us, was "the very first thing which ever made me feel that a profession might be made out of what had up to that time been the merest hobby."

2. Holmes speaks of "the two years that I was at college" —and tells us that during these two years "the only friend I made" was young Victor Trevor. "I was never a very sociable fellow, Watson, always rather fond of moping in my rooms and working out my own little methods of thought, so that I never mixed much with the men of my year. Bar fencing and boxing I had few athletic tastes, and then my line of study was quite distinct from that of the other fellows, so that we had no points of contact at all. Trevor was the only man I knew, and that only through the accident of his bull-terrier freezing on to my ankle one morning as I went down to chapel." "Finally he [young Trevor] invited

---

8 He refers to Stockwell Place, which became Stockwell *Road* in 1872, and Robert Street, which was displaced by *Robsart* Street in 1880. The late Gavin Brend ("Was Sherlock Holmes at Westminster?") took this as evidence that Holmes had been a day boy at Westminster. But the editors of the *Sherlock Holmes Journal* pointed out that Mr. Brend's argument applied as well to "the Greycoat School, formerly in Artillery Row, or even the local school round the corner in Great Peter Street. If the latter, there would be special significance in [Holmes'] panegyric on Board Schools in 'The Naval Treaty.'"

9 It is a strange tale—so strange that the late H. W. Bell considered Holmes to be "the dupe of a terrified but astute man nearly forty years his senior."

me down to his father's place in Donnithorpe, in Norfolk, and I accepted his hospitality for a month of the long vacation."

3. During Holmes' "last years at the university there was a good deal of talk there about myself and my methods" ("The Musgrave Ritual").

4. After Holmes came up to London, he had rooms in Montague Street, just round the corner from the British Museum. "There I waited, filling in my too abundant leisure time by studying all those branches of science which might make me more efficient." "You can hardly realize how difficult I found it at first, and how long I had to wait before I succeeded in making any headway." There were "months of inaction."

5. At last "cases came in my way" now and again, "principally through the introduction of old fellow students."

6. "The third of these cases was that of the Musgrave Ritual and it is to the interest which was aroused by that singular chain of events, and the large issues which proved to be at stake, that I made my first stride toward the position which I now hold."

7. Reginald Musgrave had been in the same college as Holmes and Holmes had "some slight acquaintance with him." But Holmes had seen nothing of Musgrave "for four years" until he walked into Holmes' rooms in Montague Street one morning.

8. Holmes' early cases (other than "The Musgrave Ritual") were "not all successes" but there were "some pretty little problems among them."

9. By the time of his first meeting with Watson Holmes had "established a considerable, though not a very lucrative, connection."

It should be abundantly clear by now that Holmes in these two adventures is talking about *two entirely different academic experiences.*[10]

For consider:

1. Holmes speaks of "the two years that I was at college" and his "last years at the university." In England, as Dr. Ernest Bloomfield Zeisler noted, "a college is part of a university, but not every university student is in a college, at least, not in all universities." This, by itself, then, could mean that Holmes was at a university for *at least three* years, *two* of which he had spent in a college of that university.

2. But Reginald Musgrave had been in the *same* college as Holmes, and Holmes had "some slight acquaintance with him." Thus the college attended by Holmes and Musgrave *cannot be* the college attended for two years by Holmes and young Trevor, for at the latter college Trevor was the *"only* friend I made" and the *"only* man I knew."

3. In addition, as Miss Dorothy L. Sayers shrewdly pointed out ("Holmes' College Career"), Holmes and Musgrave must have been men of the *same year* as well as men of the *same college,* for if Musgrave were senior to Holmes, his reserved and somewhat exclusive manner would have precluded him from associating with an underclassman; if he were junior to Holmes, it would have precluded him from "sucking up" to an upperclassman.[11] But at the college

10 The late Elmer Davis would seem to have been the first to suggest that Holmes may have been a student at *both* Oxford and Cambridge (in December, 1933, in "The Real Sherlock Holmes" in *The Saturday Review of Literature*). Your editor was to elaborate on this view in 1955, in his *Chronological Holmes;* in December, 1956, Mr. N. P. Metcalfe treated the whole question at length in his splendid essay, "Oxford or Cambridge or Both?" Other commentators unhappily seem loath to accept this perceptive view, insisting that Holmes attended *one* or *another* of the two universities. As Mr. Davis wrote (in his Introduction to *The Return of Sherlock Holmes*): ". . . the question which of [these] ancient institutions of learning had the honor of educating, or at least housing for some years, Sherlock Holmes [is] a question chiefly of interest because graduates of each seem to want to wish him on the other. Dorothy Sayers and Monsignor Knox, both of Oxford, hold that he must have been a Cambridge man. . . . But S. C. Roberts, who is not only of Cambridge but at this writing [1952] *is* Cambridge—the Vice-Chancellor, the active head, of that university—says that Holmes must have been an Oxford man."

11 Mr. Melcalfe bears this out: ". . . men up at [a] University strictly stick to their own year (a rule only relaxed during and after the two world wars when the age of entry was anything from 18 to about 26 years)."

attended by Holmes and young Trevor, Holmes "*never* mixed much with the men of my year."

4. Our conclusion that Holmes attended two universities is further borne out by the early cases that came his way "principally through the introduction of old fellow students." A man who has "*no points of contact at all*" with his fellow students is not likely to be recommended by them later.

5. Our conclusion is further borne out by Musgrave's statement that Holmes "used to amaze us" with his powers in college and Holmes' statement that during his "last years at the university there was a good deal of talk there about myself and my methods." These years can hardly have been a part of the "two years . . . at college" when Holmes "was *never* a very sociable fellow" and was "*always* rather fond of moping in my rooms."

Holmes, then, was at *one* university for *two* years, during *both* of which he was in a college of that university; he was at *another* university for *at least three* years, during *at least one* of which he was in a college of that university.

We can now be fairly sure that what Holmes *really* said to Watson in telling him about the adventure of "The *Gloria Scott*" was: "the two years that I was at X college," perhaps adding, "at *A* university."

It is not, of course, the normal procedure for a man to attend one university for two years and another for at least three.**12** We must ask ourselves why Holmes did this. The answer leaps to the eye: following his second year at University *A* he had had an experience that convinced him that the course of study he was able to follow at his present university was not sufficient to equip him for the career he had determined upon at that time, and that he consequently must transfer to a university with more suitable facilities. *This experience can only have been* the adventure of "The *Gloria Scott*," for Holmes makes it very clear that old Trevor's recommendation was "the *very first thing* which ever made me feel that a *profession* might be made out of what had up to then been the merest *hobby*."

Holmes, then, must have enrolled at University *B* in the Michaelmas term following the long vacation during which "The *Gloria Scott*" adventure took place. At University *B*, as we have seen, he lived a very different life than he had lived at University *A*—further evidence that "The *Gloria Scott*" was in every way a major turning point in his life.

Holmes, although changing universities, would still speak of himself as a man of such-and-such a year—and Reginald Musgrave, as we have seen, was a man of this same year at University *B*. He was therefore a *third-year* man at that university when Holmes first knew him. We have every reason to believe that Musgrave, unlike Holmes, spent the normal number of years at University *B*. Since, in the 1870's, a three-year rather than the present four-year course of study, was the norm, Musgrave must have gone down in the year following the Michaelmas term in which Holmes first met him.

"Four years later"—at the time of "The Musgrave Ritual" —Holmes saw Musgrave again for the first time since Musgrave went down.

Between "The Musgrave Ritual" and his meeting with Watson, Holmes had established his considerable but not

12 But Holmes was by no means *unique* in attending *both* universities: as Mr. Davis pointed out in "The Real Sherlock Holmes": ". . . it is at least possible that Holmes may have been one of that small but distinguished company, including King Edward VII and Charles Stuart Calverley, who were both Oxford and Cambridge men."

very lucrative connection. Certainly we must allow a year, and probably longer, for him to do this. *Three* years is too long a period, however; Holmes tells us that it was to "the interest aroused by that singular chain of events" (The Musgrave Ritual) . . . that I made my first stride toward the position which I now hold," and Holmes after *three* years of striding would certainly have been able to afford rooms on his own, without seeking for a Watson to share the expenses with him. Thus "The Musgrave Ritual" took place in 1879, or, possibly, late in 1878.

"The Musgrave Ritual" had come after "months of inaction." "You can hardly realize how long I had to wait." Holmes must have waited in Montague Street for at least a year, perhaps as long as two. Thus Holmes took the rooms in Montague Street no earlier than 1876, no later than 1877.

Since he had not seen Musgrave for "four years," we see that Musgrave must have gone down in 1874 or 1875.

Holmes was a man of the same year as Musgrave, so *his* normal year to go down would also have been 1874 or 1875 (we know, however, that he spent two additional years at University *B*). He must therefore have enrolled at University *B* after the long vacation of 1873 or 1874—the long vacation of "The *Gloria Scott*."

What can we learn from "The *Gloria Scott*" that will help us to date the case more exactly? Holmes says:

1. There was "excellent wild-duck shooting in the fens" at the time of his visit to Donnithorpe. Professor Christ was the first to note that under the Act of 1872, the duck season *did not open* until August 1st. Holmes' visit must therefore have included a period after that date.

2. "At last I became so convinced that I was causing [old Trevor] uneasiness that I drew my visit to a close." It is clear, then, that Holmes did not stay at Donnithorpe for the full month for which he was invited. Since he says "at last" it is probable that he left at the end of about three weeks.

3. He tells us that "All this occurred during the first month of the long vacation."

4. "I went up to my London rooms, where I spent seven weeks working out a few experiments in organic chemistry. One day, however, when the autumn was far advanced and the vacation was drawing to a close, I received a telegram from my friend imploring me to return to Donnithorpe . . ." Popularly, in Great Britain, "autumn" comprises the months of August, September, and October. Holmes must therefore have been called back to Donnithorpe late in September, which means, in turn, that he drew his first visit to a close in the first week of August. Since he had spent about three weeks there, he must have arrived at Donnithorpe around the middle of July.

In the 1870's, old Trevor, "a man of some wealth and consideration, a J. P., and a landed proprietor," would certainly not have sent his only son to one of the lesser universities; as Miss Sayers said, he would want young Trevor to have all the advantages he himself had missed.

Young Trevor and Holmes were therefore students at one of England's two great universities—Oxford or Cambridge.**13**

In the years under consideration, the long vacation fell as

13 We should note here, however, that the Reverend Stephen Adams has suggested ("Holmes: A Student of London?") King's College at the University of London; Mr. G. W. Welch has suggested ("Which University?") Manchester University; and Mr. O. F. Grazebrook (*Oxford or Cambridge*) speaks of "a body of Medical opinion in [Birmingham] . . . who claimed that Sherlock Holmes had been educated at Queen's College in the town of Birmingham." Mr. Grazebrook, however, would have none of this: "At [the time of "The *Gloria Scott*" and "The Musgrave Ritual"], any reference to a University implied without any reservation at all either Oxford or Cambridge. Today, the mention of Universities available to students would make any such reference somewhat vague, but there can be no doubt at all that any consideration of which University, must be confined to one of these two."

follows at each of these universities:

	Oxford	Cambridge
1873	July 5–October 10	June 20–October 1
1874	July 11–October 10	June 26–October 1

One quickly sees that the Cambridge vacations will not begin to fit Holmes' description:

1. Neither provides a legal period for duck-hunting "during the first month of the long vacation."

2. Holmes would have received young Trevor's wire *c.* August 31st (1873) or September 6th (1874). At neither time was the autumn "far advanced"—and the vacation could hardly be said to be "drawing to a close"; the beginning of the Michaelmas was still about a month away.

The Oxford vacation of 1874, on the other hand, fits Holmes' description exactly:

1. His invitation to Donnithorpe for the first month of the long vacation would be for the month July 12–August 11th approximately, an invitation that would provide almost two weeks of legal duck-shooting in the fens.

2. He would have left Donnithorpe close to August 4th.

3. "Seven weeks working out a few experiments in organic chemistry" would bring us to September 22nd—at which time the autumn *was* "far advanced" and the beginning of the Michaelmas term was only a little over two weeks away.

We may conclude that:

1. "The *Gloria Scott*" took place in the long vacation of 1874.

2. Holmes enrolled at University *B* at the beginning of the Michaelmas term of 1874.

3. Musgrave went down in 1875.[14]

4. Since, as we have shown, Holmes continued to study at University *B* for two more years, he went to London and took rooms in Montague Street in 1877.

5. Reginald Musgrave visited him there in 1879, "four years" after Holmes had last seen him.[15]

We see, then, that Holmes was a student at Oxford University from the autumn of 1872 to the start of the long vacation in 1874. We know, further, that Holmes was a student at another of England's great universities from the autumn of 1874 to late in 1877 (during at least one of which he was in a college of that university). As Mr. Brend pointed out in *My Dear Holmes*, Musgrave, he of the "grey archways and mullioned windows and all the venerable wreckage of a feudal keep," certainly does not sound like the sort of undergraduate "whom one would expect to find at one of the lesser Universities in the seventies," and we are fully justified in designating University *B* as Cambridge.[16]

We must now deal briefly with an argument that has been raised to show that the university of "The *Gloria Scott*" could not have been Oxford:

Holmes as a first-year man at Oxford in 1872 would live *in college*, since students at that university reside in college for two years, moving into lodgings in the town only at the beginning of their third year of residence. At Cambridge, on the other hand, first-year men and second-year men are usually accommodated with lodgings in town.

---

14 Miss Sayers suggested that the month was March or December—March if he were taking a classical or mathematical tripos, December if he were taking a tripos in law and history.

15 In our notes to "The Musgrave Ritual" we will show that the exact date in the year 1879 may be determined.

16 While Mr. Metcalfe and your editor are in full agreement that Holmes attended *both* universities, Mr. Metcalfe holds that Holmes attended, first, Cambridge (October, 1871, to late September, 1873 or 1874), then Oxford (October, 1873 or 1874 to 1875 or 1876).

Holmes, as we know, was bitten by Victor Trevor's bull-terrier on his way to chapel. Since dogs are not allowed within the grounds at either university, it has been said that Holmes was going *from* his lodgings *to* chapel when he was bitten by the dog; he was therefore bitten outside the university grounds; he was therefore going *from* his lodgings *to* the university; he was therefore a student at Cambridge, where first- and second-year men go *from* lodgings *to* chapel at their college.

But this argument has been hotly contested.

Mr. S. C. Roberts has pointed out that Holmes may have stepped into the street to buy a newspaper before going to chapel. Mr. Metcalfe has suggested that Holmes' college may have been one of those at Oxford which has buildings on both sides of the road. Mr. Brend has asked: "Could not the dog have been smuggled into the college for the purpose of some practical joke? Alternatively, from the standpoint of the dog, could not the event happen both outside and inside the college? Why should it not have been frightened or hurt out in the street with the result that before it could be stopped it ran through the gate and fastened on to the unfortunate Holmes?" Indeed, Trevor's dog may have broken loose from its tethering in the college porch—for, despite the rules, this seems to have been an Oxford custom. Mr. Max Beerbohm has indicated this in *Zuleika Dobson:* "In the porch of the College there were, as usual, some chained-up dogs." And Mr. Roger Lancelyn Green has added, in a letter to the *Sherlock Holmes Journal,* that there were certainly in-college dogs at least at University College, Oxford, in the 1870's.

Again, Holmes may well have been bitten *off* the university grounds on his way to a chapel *in town.* If this perhaps seems out of character, it must be remembered that Holmes in later days was far from being an irreligious man: he knew his Bible well, and drew much inspiration therefrom.

We see that the dog cannot be allowed to stand as evidence for or against either university.

"Common consent amongst those who favor Oxford points to Christ Church as the most likely [college for Holmes to have attended]," Mr. Metcalfe wrote in "Oxford or Cambridge or Both?", and your editor most heartily agrees. As to Cambridge, Christopher Morley thought it likely that Peterhouse was Holmes' college, but Miss Sayers opted for Sidney Sussex because she found a *T. S. Holmes* at that college in the appropriate years. (Unhappily for Miss Sayers' theory, *this* Holmes later became the Chancellor of Wells Cathedral, as Mr. S. C. Roberts pointed out.) Your editor's own view is that Holmes entered Gonville and Caius College, famous for its associations with medicine and with the natural sciences.

It is possible—indeed it is highly probable—that Holmes spent as much time as he could afford in these early years in travel on the Continent and perhaps in America. Mr. A. N. Griffith ("Some Observations on Sherlock Holmes

THE COATS OF ARMS OF HOLMES' UNIVERSITIES

(*Left*) Oxford: Azure, an open book proper, leathered gules, garnished and having on the dexter side seven seals or, between three open crowns of the last. (*Right*) Cambridge: Gules, a cross ermine between four lions passant gardant or, and upon the cross a closed book, gules, edged, clasped and garnished gold.

CHRIST CHURCH COLLEGE, OXFORD

As it looked when Sherlock Holmes was an undergraduate there in 1872.

and Dr. Watson at Bart's") has found reason to believe that Holmes was in Strasbourg during the Franco-Prussian War of 1870–1871, and Mr. A. Carson Simpson (*I'm Off for Philadelphia in the Morning*) has postulated a visit to the City of Brotherly Love in the fall of 1873. Miss Dorothy L. Sayers ("Holmes' College Career") suggested that Holmes "in all probability . . . passed the year 1875 at a German university, with vacation trips to France and Italy, returning to England in December to take his B.A. and then proceeding (perhaps after a short holiday at home) to London . . ."

Mr. Charles B. Stephens ("The Birlstone Hoax") has advanced the interesting speculation that Holmes in 1875 "was one of the participants in the drama just beginning to unfold in Vermissa Valley, Pennsylvania, U.S.A. [*The Valley of Fear*]. . . . He resolved to go to America to study the techniques of criminal detection then being so successfully applied by the Pinkertons. Their work would appeal to him, because they were and still are 'private' detectives in the professional sense in which Holmes wished to apply his talents. No doubt he contacted the great Allan Pinkerton himself, and sought employment as an operative in order to learn at first hand the secrets of successful detection. We can well imagine that the ability and enthusiasm of the pupil commended him favorably to the tutor, so that when Pinkerton came to plan his strategy for capturing the Scowrers, he chose young Holmes for the role of Captain Marvin."

"My own thought"—Christopher Morley wrote in "Was Sherlock Holmes an American?"—"is that the opening of the Johns Hopkins University in Baltimore in 1876, and the extraordinary and informal opportunities offered there for graduate study, tempted [Holmes] across the water. . . . The great Centennial Exposition in Philadelphia (1876) was surely worth a visit; there he observed the mark of the Pennsylvania Small Arms Company (*The Valley of Fear*). During his year or so in the States he traveled widely. He met Wilson Hargreave who later became important in the New York Police Department—('The Adventure of the Dancing Men'), perhaps in connection with the case of Vanderbilt and the Yeggman, a record of which he kept in his scrapbook ('The Adventure of the Sussex Vampire'). He went to Chicago, where he made his first acquaintance with organized gangsterism ('My knowledge of the crooks of Chicago,' *v.* 'The Adventure of the Dancing Men'). I suggest that perhaps he visited his kinsmen the Sherlocks in Iowa —e.g. in Des Moines, where a younger member of the family, Mr. C. C. Sherlock, has since written so ably on rural topics (C. C. Sherlock: *Care and Management of Rabbits*, 1920; *The Modern Hen*, 1922; *Bulb Gardening*, 1922; *v. Who's Who in America*). Iowa is a great apiarian state (undoubtedly from the Sherlock side came the interest in roses, beekeeping, etc.). He must have gone to Topeka (otherwise how could he know there was no such person as Dr. Lysander Starr—'The Adventure of the Three Garridebs'); and of course he made pilgrimage to Cambridge, Mass., to pay respect to the great doctor, poet, and essayist. From Oliver Wendell Holmes, Jr., then a rising lawyer in Boston, he heard firsthand stories of the Civil War, which fired his interest in 'that gallant struggle' ('The Cardboard Box')."**17**

17 Your editor's own researches have led him to believe that it was in November, 1879, that Holmes sailed for America, not as a student but as an actor with the Sasanoff Shakespearian Company. His eight-months-long tour of the United States ended in August, 1880, when he embarked for his trip back to England.

Our date for the beginning of Holmes' practice—July, 1877 —is fully borne out by Watson's statement at the beginning of "The Adventure of the Veiled Lodger" that Holmes "was in active practice for twenty-three years . . ."

Holmes' last datable case while in active practice was "The Adventure of the Creeping Man," in which he was engaged in September, 1903, and we are told by Watson that this was "one of the very last cases handled by Holmes before he retired from practice."

Some considerable time before the publication of "The Adventure of the Second Stain" in December, 1904, he had definitely retired and was keeping bees on the Sussex Downs, so it is fair to assume that his withdrawal to private life occurred *circa* October, 1903.

As Mr. H. W. Bell wrote, dead reckoning would oblige us to place the beginning of Holmes' career twenty-three years earlier—that is, late in 1880. But we learn ("The Final Problem" and "The Adventure of the Empty House") that there was a hiatus of three years—the Great Hiatus of May, 1891, to April, 1894—during which Holmes was presumed dead. Three years, then, must be prefixed to the autumn of 1880; and thus the latter half of 1877 is established as the beginning of the practice.

"The Musgrave Ritual" was the third of the cases that came Holmes' way after he took up his practice in Montague Street, and earnest research has enabled two distinguished Sherlockian scholars to identify the two earlier cases.

"As the student will discover by reading the *Proceedings* of the [British] Rifle Association for 1877, 1880 and 1881," Mr. Robert Keith Leavitt wrote in "Annie Oakley in Baker Street," "there was a scandal in that organization in the years 1877 and 1878 concerning alleged cheating by collusion between shooters and scorers during the course of rifle matches, and it became so notorious that the Association went to the trouble and expense of retaining counsel and agents to collect 'voluminous evidence against persons suspected of fraud at the matches.' "

Consulting the *Proceedings* for 1879, Mr. Leavitt found, in the records of one of the biggest matches, the Alexander, of the preceding year, 1878, that ninth place with a prize of £10 was won by *Corporal Holmes of the 19th North Yorkshires*. In the same year, the same Holmes had taken forty-eighth place in the match called the St. George's for a prize of £6.

Note that Corporal Holmes' unit was the 19th North Yorkshires, recall that Sherlock Holmes was born in the North Riding of Yorkshire. Obviously, Sherlock Holmes was the agent retained to gather the evidence of fraud. Naturally, he would have gathered that evidence in the guise of a competitor.

"This scandal, known as 'The Mullineaux Case,' " Mr. Leavitt concluded triumphantly, "occupied Holmes over three months [according to the *Proceedings*] but was handled by him with such competence and discretion that [as in so many of his later cases] legal proceedings were avoided and the details never became public, though as late as 1880 members of the Association who were in the know were clamoring for information—and being shut up for their pains."

THE ONLY KNOWN PHOTOGRAPH OF
MR. SHERLOCK HOLMES

Taken in Cettigne (Cetinj), Montenegro, in June, 1891, this priceless memento is reproduced from William S. Baring-Gould's *Sherlock Holmes: A Biography*.

If Holmes' first case, in the Montague Street days, was perhaps somewhat prosaic, his second case of the time was exotic enough to delight the most romantic writer.

We shall see that Holmes, in the spring of the year 1887, was able to be of service to one who called himself Wilhelm Gottsreich Sigismond von Ormstein, Grand-Duke of Cassel-Falstein and hereditary King of Bohemia.

But was 1887 Holmes' *first* meeting with this mysterious personage?

Not at all, the late Edgar W. Smith suggested in "A Scandal in Identity."

"I shall not lament the loss of my incognito, for it enables me to thank you with the more authority."

These words, Mr. Smith wrote, might well have been addressed to Sherlock Holmes by "the hereditary King of Bohemia" in that spring of 1887. But they were not. "They were . . . addressed in 1878 to a certain Brackenbury Rich, a dashing lieutenant in Her Majesty's forces who had greatly distinguished himself in one of the lesser Indian hill wars, by one who called himself Prince Florizel. And as authority for their utterance we have the testimony not of John H. Watson, M.D. . . . but of Robert Louis Stevenson, who chronicled in his *New Arabian Nights*, the doings of this royal blade.

"Yet we cannot doubt," Mr. Smith continued, "on the strength of the evidence available in the two accounts, that Gottsreich and Florizel were one being and the same. However carefully the two narrators may have tried to give their heroes individuality, the likeness of their propensities, their characters, their very persons, shines with the clarity of a beacon through the pages in which their deeds are told. . . .

"We know, of course, to whom the embattled Gottsreich turned when blackmail reared its ugly head and ruin loomed upon the horizon. . . . But we are not told who it was, [nine] years earlier, who had engineered the escape of Florizel from the equally imminent, but purely physical terrors of the Suicide Club. 'All has been managed by the simplest means,' the faithful Colonel Geraldine reported. 'I arranged this afternoon with a celebrated detective. Secrecy has been promised and paid for.' Who could have merited the trust of Florizel's entourage in this previous hour of royal need? Who could have been brought to share the sacred confidence of this differently dangerous escapade? Who, indeed, but that same Great Man who was to serve the smitten Gottsreich so discreetly and so well in [the year 1887]?"

It is probable that it was during the period between "The Musgrave Ritual" and Holmes' meeting with Watson that he solved the Tarleton murders, the case of Vamberry, the wine merchant, that of the old Russian woman, the singular affair of the aluminium crutch, and that of Ricoletti of the club foot and his abominable wife ("The Musgrave Ritual").

Not all of the "pretty little problems" that were presented to Holmes during these early years were successes, however, and it is likely that it was also during this period that he was beaten three times by men ("The Five Orange Pips").

But now, for the time being, let us leave Sherlock Holmes of Baker Street and meet the other half of the Great Partnership that was so shortly to begin . . .

9

"GOOD OLD WATSON!"

[Sherlock Holmes, "His Last Bow"]

His name, we know, was *John* H. Watson, although his first wife, on one occasion, at least ("The Man with the Twisted Lip"), *did* call him James.

It is a name which is particularly fitting—the commonest of all masculine names, not only in English, but also in many European languages. It is a contraction of Johannes, which is derived from the Hebrew Johanan, from *Jah*—God—plus *chaanach*—grace.

Watson is "the son of Watt," the last word being a diminutive of Walter, from the Old High German Waldhar, from *vald*—rule—and *harja*—folk. But here, regrettably, we must note that "there is some evidence for a Scots strain in Watson"**1**—and *wat*, in Scottish, means "given to drinking." One interpretation of the name Watson might therefore be "the son of one given to drinking." A brother of Watson's, as we learn in *The Sign of the Four*, was a drunkard, and Watson himself was drinking at the Criterion bar when he met young Stamford, who introduced him to Holmes (*A Study in Scarlet*).

But what, we may ask, does that *H*. stand for?

Mr. S. C. Roberts early suggested (*Doctor Watson*) that Watson's mother was "a devout woman with Tractarian leanings" and that she caused her child to be baptized John *Henry* after the great Cardinal Newman.

To this, the late H. W. Bell objected (*Sherlock Holmes and Dr. Watson: The Chronology of Their Adventures*) that "Newman had become a Catholic in 1845, seven years before the date which Mr. Roberts proposes for Watson's birth [1852]. If Mrs. Watson had indeed the 'Tractarian leanings' with which Mr. Roberts credits her, she would hardly have named her son after the illustrious convert."

"Might it not be possible, though, that the Watsons, father and mother, were Tractarians who followed Newman along the path to Rome?", Mr. Gordon Sewell wrote in "Holmes and Watson in the South Country." "I think of Watson senior as a High Church parson in a North Hampshire village. He, too, had ridden on horseback through the parishes dropping tracts about fasting and baptism in the doors of neighbouring rectories. And then came the great crisis of Newman's change of allegiance. The Reverend Mr. Watson and his wife also make their submission. In that case young John Henry—like Sir Arthur Conan Doyle—would have been brought up a Catholic."

1 "Sturdily and essentially English as [John H. Watson] was, he may well, like most English people, have had a Scottish ancestor in his family tree. The English are probably the only people in the world who actually make a boast of mongrel ancestry. The words 'hundred per cent English' are never heard on true English lips, for the English know well enough that their crossbreeding is their strength."—Dorothy L. Sayers, "Dr. Watson's Christian Name."

But the late Dorothy L. Sayers was as vehement as Mr. Bell in totally rejecting the Newman theory. "If there were, in Dr. Watson's character, the slightest trace of Tractarian sympathies, or even of strong anti-Tractarian sympathies, the suggestion might carry some weight, for no one could be brought up in an atmosphere of Tractarian fervour without reacting to it in one way or another. But Watson's religious views remain completely colourless."

Miss Sayers, as we have seen, held that there was a Scots strain in Watson: "It may not be mere coincidence that led Holmes (a shrewd student of national character) to select the adjective 'pawky' for the vein of humour which Watson displayed in the adventure of *The Valley of Fear* and which took his distinguished friend a little aback. Watson's mother may have been a Scot—not, I think, a Highland woman, but a native of Eastern Scotland. The true Highlander is a Celt —quick-tempered, poetical and humourless—everything that Watson was not. Dourness and pawkiness belong to the Aberdeen side of the country" ("Dr. Watson's Christian Name").

"There is only one plain conclusion to be drawn from the facts," Miss Sayers concluded. "Only one name will reconcile the appellation 'James' with the initial letter 'H.' The doctor's full name was 'John Hamish Watson.'"

Hamish, Miss Sayers pointed out, is the Scottish form of "James," and "it is [not] at all unusual for a wife to call her husband by his second name, in preference to his first. . . . 'Hamish' seemed to [Mrs. John H. Watson] perhaps a little highfalutin. By playfully re-Englishing it to 'James' she found for her husband a pet name which was his own name as well."

"This proposal," Mr. Bliss Austin wrote in "What Son Was Watson?", "though entitled to consideration, is nevertheless open to serious objection. . . . I am told that in *good* Gaelic the equivalent of James is Seumas, which hasn't an *H* in it; finally, the whole notion seems a bit too hamish."

The late Christopher Morley agreed that Watson's middle name was *Henry*—not for Cardinal Newman, he maintained, but for Henry Ward Beecher, whose unframed portrait stood on top of Watson's books in the old sitting room at 221B Baker Street ("The Cardboard Box").

But there have been many other suggestions:

1. *Holmes.* Watson "was the Master's first cousin," Mr. Will Oursler wrote in "His French Cousin."

2. *Hubert.* "As revealed by incontestably-sound research on the present writer's part," Mr. Elliot Kimsball wrote in "The Stature of John H. Watson."

3. *Hudson.* "Mrs. Hudson [the landlady at 221 Baker Street] was Watson's grand aunt. . . . And in fact it was he who really engineered [the meeting with Holmes], because he wanted to live in the chambers his aunty had to let, and he could not afford the price she asked. She was a business woman . . . and would give no discount because of being a relative," Mrs. Crighton Sellars wrote in "A Visit with Sherlock Holmes."

4. *Huffham.* "It is probable that [Watson's mother] was an admirer of [Charles John Huffham] Dickens. It is more probable that she desired to name her son after a popular

A PORTRAIT OF JOHN H. WATSON, M.D., IN HIS PRIME
(ABOUT 1887)

The drawing is by Harry Eckman of the Amateur Mendicant Society of Detroit, a scion society of the Baker Street Irregulars.

literary figure of the day who was an intimate friend of her husband's relations [*David Copperfield* was dedicated to the Watsons: the Honourable Richard and Mrs. Watson of Rockingham Castle]," Miss Jane Throckmorton wrote in "'H.' Stands for—?".

Sherlockian scholars are generally but not unanimously agreed that John H. Watson was born in the year 1852. They arrive at this date by reasoning backwards from 1878, the year in which he received his doctor's degree at the University of London.**2**

But here we must register an objection from Dr. Vernon Pennell ("A Résumé of the Medical Life of John H. Watson, M.D., Late of the Army Medical Department"). "S. C. Roberts has pointed out, with a thin veil of anonymity, that [1878] was the same year as the M.D. taken by the late Sir Charters Symonds, F.R.C.S.—with a considerable weight of probability that Watson was born in the same year. Against this, however, we must allow that there is nothing in Watson's after life to suggest undue brilliance. He was certainly *not* a Charters Symonds—a truly brilliant alumnus of London University—and it is not unjust to suspect that on one or two occasions, in some part of his curriculum, he failed to satisfy the examiners and that he was probably a few years older than Symonds rather than younger. We cannot more accurately assess the years of Watson's birth than mention it was, in all probability, in the early '50s."

Mr. William Smith, writing in "'You Have Been in Gettysburg, I Perceive,'" has advanced an even earlier date: Watson, he says, was born in 1842. "In 1861, aged nineteen, Watson is to be discovered in Philadelphia, having saved sufficient funds from several years labor at odd jobs (see Conan Doyle's astonishing 'J. Habakuk Jephson's Statement' for a full, though slightly inaccurately detailed, sketch of a disguised Watson in his American days, complete with the ubiquitous Murray)**3** to matriculate at the School of Medicine of the University of Pennsylvania. . . .

"One fine morning, strolling past the Customs House, he observed that one Colonel John J. Murphy was raising a three-year regiment, the Twenty-Ninth Pennsylvania Volunteers. To one with burning Abolishionist convictions, the appeal of the recruiting posters and the flights of Murphy's Irish oratory must have proved irresistible, for, on the rolls of Company I, we can find the name of John Watson, enlisted July 1, 1861. This regiment was mustered into the Army on July 10, 1861, and subsequently saw action against Jackson in the Valley campaign, at Antietam and at Fredricksburg in 1862, and at Chancellorsville and Gettysburg in 1863. Its history after that crucial battle, though gallant, is hardly of interest to Sherlockians, for it was at Gettysburg, on July 3, 1863, that John Watson was injured, lost track of, and presumed to be dead. . . . Private John Murray of Company C, Twenty-Ninth Pennsylvania Volunteers, must have seen Watson fall, and managed to get him to safety in the town of Gettysburg that afternoon during the confusion caused by Longstreet's artillery barrage . . ."

Watson's birthday has been placed on July 7th by some commentators, who note that in *The Sign of the Four* the good doctor celebrated, on the opening day of the case, by

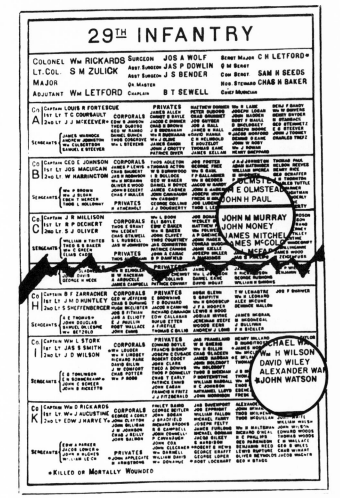

ROSTER OF THE TWENTY-NINTH PENNSYLVANIA VOLUNTEERS

Showing the names of John M. Murray as a member of C Company and John Watson as a member of I Company.

2 "1852 is generally accepted as John H. Watson's year of birth from the fact that he graduated in medicine in 1878 . . ."—Dr. W. S. Bristowe, "The Mystery of the Third Continent." "Mr. Roberts has plausibly suggested that Watson was probably born in 1852."—H. W. Bell, *Sherlock Holmes and Dr. Watson: The Chronology of Their Adventures.*

3 Murray, as we learn in *A Study in Scarlet*, was the orderly who saved Watson's life at the fatal battle of Maiwand. In "J. Habakuk Jephson's Statement," first published in the January, 1884, issue of the *Cornhill Magazine*, three years before *A Study in Scarlet*, it is also "Murray" who saves the life of the hero—this time at the battle of Antietam.

THE COAT OF ARMS OF JOHN H. WATSON, M.D.,
ACCORDING TO MR. WILLIAM S. HALL

Or, on a chief vert, an ermine passant, proper. Crest: an ermine passant, proper, vulned on the shoulder, gules. Motto: *Mea gloria fides* ("Fidelity is my glory").

taking Beaune with his lunch. But most chronologists now hold that the opening day of *The Sign of the Four* was not July 7th but September 18th.

Watson's birthplace is unknown, but data can be found in his reminiscences which have led to much controversy.

Mr. T. S. Blakeney, for example, has speculated somewhat tentatively ("The Apocryphal Ancestry of Dr. Watson") that Watson was born in the neighborhood of Abingdon, Berkshire, in 1854 or 1855 (not later than 1858), the son of John Fairford Watson, the second, M.D., and Henrietta Rivers, whom Watson *père* married not later than 1852.

On the other hand, the "incontestably-sound research" of Mr. Elliott Kimball has demonstrated ("The Watsons of Northumberland") that Watson was the youngest son of Hubert Anselm Watson, a Northumberland squire of the last century resident at the ancestral Manor of Norham, four miles west-northwest of Mitford, a village in the beautiful valley of the Wansbeck west of Morpeth, some seventeen miles due north of Newcastle-on-Tyne. Watson Senior's first wife, Mr. Kimball has declared, was Guinevere Bowcliff or Bowcliffe, a Northumberland lass, who bore him two sons: Hubert Anselm Junior, born March 19, 1846, and a brother Harold Hubert, born May 11, 1848. The first Mrs. Watson died on December 14, 1849, and Hubert Watson Senior remarried on June 2, 1851; his second wife was Janet Anne Dexter, descendant of an old Sussex family. Janet Anne became the mother of a boy, John Hubert, on July 7, 1852. Her untimely and lamented death occurred on March 16, 1853. Hubert Anselm Watson Senior died on February 3, 1869.

Mr. S. C. Roberts would place Watson's birthplace in Hampshire on somewhat slender evidence: Watson yearned for the glades of the New Forest or the shingle of Southsea on a sultry summer's day in Baker Street ("The Cardboard Box"), and he expressed admiration for the beauty of the countryside stretching toward Aldershot when he was traveling to Winchester with Holmes in "The Adventure of the Copper Beeches." But his knowledge of Hampshire and his admiration for this lovely county may well have been acquired in several other ways.

As Dr. W. S. Bristowe has written ("The Mystery of the Third Continent"): "If this kind of evidence in favour of Hampshire is to be admitted, it should be pointed out that a stronger case can be presented for considering Sussex as his county. On one occasion Watson speaks almost like a guide book about the early Saxon history of the Forest Row neighbourhood ["The Adventure of Black Peter"]. Whilst on another his knowledge of the villages and houses in the district south of Horsham is so intimate as to suggest past residence there ["The Adventure of the Sussex Vampire"]. . . . Even here we should notice that he does not say 'I was born in that country, Holmes,' as we might have expected if his birthplace was in the district."

Although but little is known about John H. Watson's early days or how he was brought up, certain facts stand out clearly.

For example, it seems certain that he spent a portion of his boyhood in Australia: as he and Miss Morstan stood, "her hand in mine" like two children in the grounds of Pondi-cherry Lodge (*The Sign of the Four*) and surveyed the great rubbish heaps which cumbered those grounds, Watson said: "I have seen something of the sort on the side of a hill near Ballarat, where the prospectors had been at work." "Of the influence of this Australian upbringing on the character of Doctor Watson we have abundant evidence," Mr. Roberts wrote in *Doctor Watson;* "his sturdy common sense, his coolness, his adaptability to rough conditions on Dartmoor or elsewhere are marks of that tightening of moral and physical fibre which comes from the hard schooling of colonial life."**4**

The presumption is that Watson *père* was attracted to Australia by the discovery of gold at Ballarat in 1851. In Australia he married, and in Australia John H. Watson and his elder brother were born.**5**

On the other hand, Watson *père* may have been attracted to Australia, not for its goldfields, but for the railroading then going on there. In "A Chronometric Excogitation," the late A. Carson Simpson wrote:

It is true that the goldrush in and around Ballarat began in 1851 and rivalled in intensity the days of the '49ers in California, but three months was reckoned a speedy voyage for the fastest clipper-ships to the gold diggings, and the new and infrequent steam service of the Peninsular & Oriental Steam Navigation Co. saved little time. It is hardly likely that the younger Watson would have been taken on such a long journey before he was, say, three years old, which would be in 1855. By then, the goldrush had been going for four years, the fever had abated somewhat, and the rich claims had almost all been pre-empted. Despite the Doctor's known propensity for speculating on shares and taking an occasional flyer on the ponies, somehow Sir Sydney [Roberts'] suggestion about the father does not ring true. . . .

[Watson's father] was just such a man as would be chosen by one of the Australian Colonies for an important post in its expanding railway empire. [He played an important part, no doubt, in the completion of the Sydney Railway, which opened on September 26, 1855. Not the first railway in Australia, it was the first of any length, running 22 miles southwestwardly from Sydney to Liverpool.] It seems likely that sometime—probably late, for it left him with a lasting impression—in the period between 1855 and 1865 (when John H. Watson returned to England for his further schooling), his father took him to Ballarat in the course of a construction survey of the Melbourne-Adelaide line.

This hypothesis . . . enables us to paint a picture of [Watson's father as] a boy born during the Napoleonic Wars, say in 1810. He went to work young, as was usual in those days. He was fifteen years old when real rail-roading began in 1825, with George Stephenson driving his own locomotive (the "No. 1") at the head of a train on the Stockton & Darlington Railway. The perspica-cious, up-and-coming lad saw his opportunity and got into this rapidly-growing business. He learned, as one

4 Still, if Watson spent his early boyhood in Australia, it is curious that he does not comment upon the fact on many occasions when he had a fitting opportunity to do so: with Holy Peters, "one of the most unscrupulous rascals that Australia has evolved . . ." ("The Disappearance of Lady Frances Carfax"); with the beautiful and unhappily married Mary Fraser of Adelaide ("The Adventure of the Abbey Grange"); with the call of "Cooee" and the dying reference to a (Balla)rat in "The Boscombe Valley Mystery"; and especially in the case of the convict Trevor, who made his fortune in the gold diggings ("The *Gloria Scott*").

5 There may well have been one or more brothers: Holmes in *The Sign of the Four* speaks once of Watson's *eldest* brother, implying that John may have been the third or even later child in the family.

had to do in those days, by experience, and profited by it to such an extent that, at the age of thirty (in 1840), he could afford to buy a fifty-guinea watch.**6** Undoubtedly he continued to rise in his chosen profession, and, by the time he was forty-five (in 1855) was a railroader of recognized ability and experience. . . . The father came back to England when the future Doctor returned for his schooling, or shortly thereafter, and was an important figure in the engineering department of the Great Western Railway until his death or retirement [which accounts for Watson's ability to get a number of patients from among the officials at Paddington Station so soon after his establishing his practice in Paddington; see "The Adventure of the Engineer's Thumb"].

Mrs. Jennifer Chorley ("Some Diggings Down Under") has given us a very different picture of Watson's father. Him she has identified with William Watson, that same William Watson who, in 1861, as a member of the Gardiner gang of bushrangers attacked the Brennan Station on the Billabong with Henry Keene and Michael Lawler. Watson, unhappily, was the chief villain, but all three were captured and sentenced to death at Goulburn. "I don't care if it's tomorrow," William Watson was reported to have said. "Well, goodbye."

"This dreadful tragedy," Mrs. Chorley wrote, "must have killed Mrs. Watson. The two little boys, one about ten and the other a few years older, must have been sent back to England as orphans to be brought up by an aged relative. . . . No doubt Watson's brother inherited his father's weaknesses, nor is it surprising that, with such a history, 'he threw away his chances.' "

Although it is probable that Watson's mother—whom he never mentions—did die when the boy was very young, we would prefer to think that Watson's father, then a well-to-do man, returned to England with young John, perhaps leaving his older boy or boys in Australia.**7**

However, Dr. W. S. Bristowe has noted the intense feelings which Henry Ward Beecher's life aroused "in Watson's usually stolid imagination" ("The Cardboard Box") and he has suggested that both Watson's father and elder or eldest brother became converts to Beecher's cause soon after their return to England from Australia. Did Beecher's amazing eloquence in behalf of the Northern cause during the Civil War "lead Watson's father to cross the Atlantic in 1863 with his elder son leaving Watson at school in England in the care of his mother (if she was still alive) or more probably of a guardian in Sussex?" Dr. Bristowe has asked. "If we suppose that Watson's father was a casualty . . . we can at once begin to see why Watson had such a deep personal interest in Beecher as to install his portrait in Baker Street.**8** He would feel 'passionate indignation' against those Englishmen who opposed his father's hero during his mission in 1863. The campaign on which his father and brother had embarked would have caused his eyes to shine and his hands to clench as he thought of it. And then, as his mind turned to the consequences on the Watson family his face would have saddened just as Holmes described."

6 The meager Canonical information that we have about Watson's father comes from the incident in *The Sign of the Four* in which Holmes makes certin deductions about Watson's brother from this watch, inherited by the brother from the father.

7 When he reached London after his service in the Second Afghan War, John H. Watson stated that he had neither kith nor kin *in England*.

8 Mr. Robert Keith Leavitt has presented a very different view of Watson's interest in Beecher in his essay on "The Preposterously Paired Performances of the Preacher's Portrait." When Holmes made his deductions from the "H. W." initials on the back of the watch, the detective, Mr. Leavitt contends, intentionally or unintentionally overlooked the traces of a third initial—a "B."—and deduced "in one blinding flash the true identity of Watson's father."

The school to which Watson was sent is never mentioned but it would seem that it must have been one of the better known public schools from the fact that Watson's friend "Tadpole" Phelps of "The Naval Treaty" was "extremely well-connected," a nephew of Lord Holdhurst, and that it prepared Phelps for a scholarship to Cambridge.

"Our choice is greatly narrowed," Dr. Bristowe wrote, "when we remember that Watson played [rugby] for Blackheath ["The Adventure of the Sussex Vampire"] in later years which provides us with the reasonable assumption that it was one of the few public schools where rugby football was played in those days. When we also find that [Watson] decided to pursue the profession of an army surgeon and was for a time attached to a Berkshire regiment [*A Study in Scarlet*] we may think it not unlikely that Wellington College was the school selected for him. Wellington fills our requirements in being a well-known public school in Berkshire not too far distant from his home where rugby football was played and where the strong army influence induced him to join the service."

But Mr. Frederick Bryan-Brown has written (in "Sherlockian Schools and Schoolmasters") that: "I am not convinced that [Watson's school] must have been one of the leading schools because of Percy Phelps and his uncle and his university scholarship. Lord Holdhurst still had many calls even when Phelps was a prospering civil servant, and in earlier years would not have been able to spend too much on the education of his nephew. On the balance of probability I feel that Watson was a doctor's son (medicine, like art, is often in the blood). Holdhurst's sister had presumably married beneath her and yet not to money. What would be more likely than a brilliant, overworked, underpaid medical practitioner for her husband? A school was founded in the 1850's to cater for the sons of doctors and its rugby club was established by 1870. So I submit as something to be shot at, the hypothesis that Epsom College was Watson's school. . . . If a circle is drawn . . . at a radius of ten-plus miles with Reigate as its centre we get the area of Watson's youth, near enough to London for him to be at home there and yet not so far that he would be prevented by loyalty from referring to its cesspool-like qualities."

In any case, Watson's old school number—presumably the number of his locker in the bootroom—was thirty-one ("The Adventure of the Retired Colourman").

Most of what we know about Watson's medical training and military career comes to us from the doctor himself, in the opening pages of his first published reminiscence, *A Study in Scarlet*.

He tells us, first, that in the year 1878 he took his degree of Doctor of Medicine of the University of London.

This, to begin with, is a specialist's degree, taken only by a select few either in "pure" medicine or, perhaps, in pathology, public health, psychology, or midwifery. To qualify for it, Watson would first have had to take a Bachelor's degree of M.B. or B.S. or a diploma of M.R.C.S. or L.R.C.P. "Watson *might* have qualified for the M.B. as late as '77 or as early as '72," Dr. Pennell wrote, "for there were three alternative methods of procedure for the acquisition of an M.D. and each of these modes of entry could be modified according to whether or not the candidate was placed in the 'First Division' at the Second Examination. The delay might be two, three or even five years."

Watson would also have to have taken a B.S.—a Baccalaureate of Surgery—which could not be taken until one year after taking the M.B. and attendance at a course of instruction in operative surgery. It is extremely unlikely that Watson omitted to take the B.S., for he *was* a surgeon: he must have been to have held the post of House Surgeon at St. Bartholomew's Hospital, because only a House Surgeon would have a "dresser" (a surgeon's assistant) under him, as was young Stamford to Watson. "It seems not unlikely," Dr. Pennell continued, "that Watson commenced his medical studies about the age of eighteen [that is, in 1870], took five or five and a half years at least to satisfy the examiners of his sufficient knowledge of Medicine and Surgery to acquire the M.B., B.S. (Lond.). A further period of two years in hospital after qualifications, during which time he held the post of House Surgeon, seems reasonable, for in the '70s and '80s it was not uncommon for the junior staff appointments of House Surgeon or House Physician to be held for a period of one or two years rather than the six months' tenure of the present day. Indeed, Dr. Mortimer of Grimpen, is shown in Dr. Watson's *Medical Directory* [*The Hound of the Baskervilles*] to have been H.S. at Charing Cross Hospital from '82 to '84."

Although Dr. Pennell assumes that Watson took his degree of Bachelor of Medicine and his Baccalaureate of Surgery at the University of London, the honor of awarding him with those degrees should go, we think, to the University of Edinburgh.**9**

The evidence for this is Conan Doyle himself, who wrote, in "The Field Bazaar" (it is Holmes speaking to Watson here): "I saw upon [the envelope] the same shield-shaped device which I have observed upon your old college cricket cap. It was clear, then, that the request came from Edinburgh University—or from some club connected with the University."

Doubts that Watson was, in fact, a *Doctor* of Medicine have been cast by many commentators—not the least of them Conan Doyle, in the very essay mentioned above; here he has Holmes say: ". . . I began by glancing at the address, and I could tell . . . that it was an unofficial communication. This I gathered from the use of the word 'Doctor' upon the address, to which as a Bachelor of Medicine, you have no legal claim."

Add to this the statement that Holmes, admittedly in a fretful mood, made to Watson in "The Adventure of the Dying Detective": "After all, you are only a general practitioner with very limited experience and mediocre qualifications," and we are led to the conclusion that Watson was *not* a Doctor of Medicine but a Bachelor of Medicine with a Baccalaureate of Surgery. He might nonetheless be called "Doctor," but by courtesy only. The aforementioned James Mortimer, a man of precise mind, punctiliously disclaimed the title on the grounds that he possessed only the humble (or, as Holmes would say, mediocre) qualifications of a

9 Mr. Elliot Kimball agrees ("The Admirable Murray"); "Watson was a student at Edinburgh from 1870 to 1872."

Member of the Royal College of Surgeons; nevertheless, he is known from start to finish as *Dr.* Mortimer.

Watson tells us, next, that after taking the degree of "Doctor" of Medicine of the University of London, he proceeded to Netley to go through the course prescribed for surgeons in the army.

In all scholarly earnestness, we must ask here why a rising young physician whose medical career had opened, most promisingly, with the appointment of House Surgeon at St. Bartholomew's Hospital, should a few years later have decided to become an Assistant Surgeon in the British Army.

The late Elmer Davis, writing "On the Emotional Geology of Baker Street," suggested that Watson must have fallen insanely in love with some actress or singer who presently tired of him. It was Watson's continued pursuit of her—"undissuadable, shameless, ridiculous, and above all unconcealed"—that cost the house man at Bart's his position and his career.

But perhaps we are maligning Watson. As Dr. Reginald Fitz has written in "A Belated Eulogy: To John H. Watson, M.D.," the newspapers at the time "were bitter over the indignities that were being heaped upon the British Lion along the Indian Frontier, and the Russian Bear seemed always to be snarling. A good deal of recruiting was being done in London with fine promise of adventure and excitement to anyone with spirit. Therefore, Dr. Watson, good sport that he was, naturally joined the Colours as soon as he could. . . ."

It is likely, however, that Watson had done some traveling before entering the service. Dr. Vernon Pennell has suggested that "It is not unlikely that this versatile, if rather pedestrian practitioner, may have spent a year or more as a ship's surgeon after taking his Qualifying Examinations (the M.B. and the B.S.) and in that capacity he visited Australia, for a second time, and India for the first." And Mr. Elliot Kimball has written (*Dr. John H. Watson at Netley*): "Watson left the University of London at the close of the academic year in late June of 1878. He was at the end of a long road of study which had extended from 1872 to 1878. . . . It was more or less in desperation that Dr. Watson turned to an army career, qualified as a candidate for Netley, and went abroad, again, for the summer of 1879. . . . The course he took began in October, 1879, and was terminated in March, 1880."

Netley is near Southampton, and it was in the Royal Victoria Military Hospital there that Watson would have taken his training. This would have consisted of courses in pathology, military surgery, medicine, and hygiene; his instructors, as Mr. Kimball demonstrated in *Dr. Watson at Netley*, would have been Surgeon-General Sir Thomas Longmore in surgery; Surgeon-General W. Campbell Maclean in medicine; Surgeon-Major F.S.B.F. de Chaumont in hygiene; and Sir William Aikens in pathology.

Whether Watson was Hampshire-born or Australian-born or neither, he would certainly have had an opportunity at this time to explore the southern parts of the county, and so, years later, to be able to think nostalgically of the cool glades of the New Forest and the shingle (beach) at Southsea.

Having passed his examination, Watson was duly attached to the Fifth Northumberland Fusiliers as Assistant Surgeon. This, Dr. Pennell has written, is "a somewhat ambiguous reference to the Fifth Regiment of Foot. The Northumberland Fusiliers are rightly proud of their titles 'The Fighting Fifth' and 'The Fifth Fusiliers.' Watson's nomenclature might possibly lead one to suppose that there were five or more *battalions* to this illustrious regiment—a most unlikely cadre at the time of the Afghan Wars, and an early example of Watson's inexactitude." (We may notice in passing that Fusiliers are infantry soldiers who formerly carried a fusil, or flintlock, but the name is still borne by some of the British infantry.)

Watson tells us that the Northumberland Fusiliers were in India at this time (in fact, they were); he necessarily had to travel there to join his regiment. Before he could do so, he states, the Second Afghan War had broken out.

"The Second Afghan War began in November, 1868," Mr. Kimball wrote in *Dr. Watson at Netley*, "but consisted in little more than piddling skirmishes until the spring of 1880. Indeed, there were two protracted lulls, during each of which it was anticipated that a negotiated peace would be declared. It was in the spring of 1880 that Ayub Khan recruited and assembled a powerful force which he put in the field with the intent to drive the British from Afghanistan. Actually the *first* battle of the Second Afghan War was Maiwand (July 27, 1880). When Watson wrote of war having broken out, he meant that Ayub Khan was in the field with an army, and that hostilities of major proportions were about to develop."

In his study of Watson's military career, "Watson, Come Here; I Want You: in Afghanistan," Professor Richard D. Lesh has written:

On landing at Bombay, Watson learned that his corps had advanced over the passes and was deep in the enemy's country. It is safe to assume that he then took, with numerous other officers who found themselves in the same position, a coastal steamer and disembarked at Karachi, the northern port of supply for the War. Here there were three choices up the Indus Valley toward the southwest passes. Assistant Surgeon Watson most certainly took the troop train by Indus Valley Railway to Sukkur, as the river steamers and camel caravans were much too tedious and were reserved for heavy cargo. A new railway ran from the Indus through Jacobabad to Sibi, a distance of 159 miles. Here Watson was attached to one of the numerous camel and horse caravans supplying troops beyond the passes.

It is most certain that Watson travelled to Dadar, close by, and entered that rocky arid defile known as Bolan Pass on his way to Quetta, 88 miles away. Here for the first time the caravan undoubtedly met the enemy in the form of murderous Ghazi raiders who would strike swiftly the lightly guarded encampments, terrorising the native baggage escorts and stealing horses and camels. The main command of the western sector of the Afghan operations was at Quetta (where the British

Army in 1851 officially recorded temperatures of 140° F.), and it was here that Watson caught up with the Fifth Northumberland Fusiliers and began his duties. Dysentery and enteric fever (typhoid) were responsible for far more deaths among the troops than enemy action, and the temperatures were so unbearable that troop movements were almost impossible. The tents were like ovens all night. Heat exhaustion and dehydration were deadly. On one recorded patrol of 25 men travelling 40 miles in two days' journey, 14 men perished of the heat.

But to the north at [Kandahar—Watson's Candahar], if the temperatures were less severe, the situation was more critical, and for this reason Assistant Surgeon Watson was ordered to duty with the Berkshires . . . at the post hospital at Kandahar, some 155 miles into Afghan territory and under sporadic harassment by the fanatic Ghazis and Pathans. . . .

Watson himself tells us that he was "removed" from his brigade—a word which has caused raised eyebrows among some commentators. "In British usage," Christopher Morley wrote, "the verb *seconded*, meaning transfer of an officer from his own regiment to some other outfit—or possibly promoted to staff duty—is always pronounced as in French: se*conded* (like absconded). Then, methought, poor Watson was se*conded* . . . from his Northumberland Fusiliers. . . .**10** But when I look it up, it says 'I was removed from my brigade.' That *removed* has to me a somewhat sinister sound? It doesn't sound *pukka* military talk at all, and seems to suggest less than promotion."

"Presumably," the late Dr. Ernest Bloomfield Zeisler commented in *Baker Street Chronology*, "there was some reason for [Watson's] removal, and this reason may well have been why he was not honoured or promoted [during the Afghan campaign]. . . . What could the reason have been? He was not courtmartialed or jailed or expelled from the Army; hence he had not been guilty of insubordination, disloyalty or desertion. We know from his subsequent career that he was not a coward, a drunkard or a quarreler. There remains one possible explanation: Watson had contracted a venereal disease, either syphilis or gonorrhea, both of which were always common in and about military establishments in those days. What presumably occurred is that Watson was laid up with acute gonorrhea while his brigade moved on; after several weeks of discomfort he was ready to return to duty but had to join another outfit because his own had gone ahead. For this reason he was not honoured or promoted even after being wounded in battle."

Whatever one may think of this, we must acknowledge that Dr. Watson *was* "removed" from his brigade and attached to the Berkshires, or, to give them their full title, Princess Charlotte of Wales' Royal Berkshire Regiment, composed of the 49th and 66th Foot. It was the 66th Foot to which Dr. Watson was attached, for it was this unit, commanded by Brigadier-General Burrows, which fought at the Battle of Maiwand.

In tracing Dr. Watson's military career, we should note here that the Fifth Northumberland Fusiliers is an establishment of the *Bengal* Army, and the Berkshires is an estab-

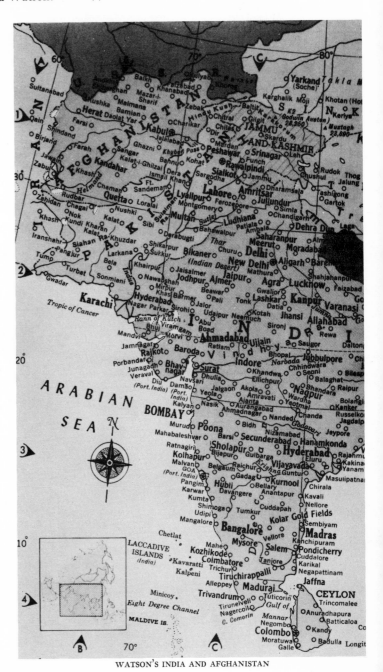

WATSON'S INDIA AND AFGHANISTAN

10 In "Dr. Watson and the British Army," Mrs. Crighton Sellars has observed that it is interesting to muse on the fact that had Watson "not been detached from the Fusiliers at Candahar . . . we might never have had the Sherlock Holmes stories; for the Fusiliers were not sent to Maiwand, and had Watson stayed with them he would not have acquired [the wound or wounds] which invalided him home and out of the service, and he would never have met Sherlock Holmes."

lishment of the *Bombay* Army. In neither case did Watson belong to the *Indian* Army, as he later wrote that he did in "The Problem of Thor Bridge."

On July 4, 1880, a British force of some 2,453 men and a large baggage escort left for the Helmand River near Girishk to take a stand against the advancing armies under Ayub Khan. The six companies of the Berkshires 66th Foot, Watson among them, were commanded by the valiant Lt.-Col. James Galbraith, who was to fall at Maiwand. Burrows' Berkshires were outflanked as Ayub Khan's main body of troops crossed the Helmand some thirty miles farther north than anticipated, at a point which is usually unfordable. Burrows was forced to retreat toward Kandahar and regroup for a stand in a desert valley just south of the village of Maiwand, which lies some fifty miles to the northwest of Kandahar.

On the morning of Tuesday, July 27, 1880, at nine o'clock, the "fatal battle of Maiwand" began. It was indeed a fatal battle, with an estimated 2,734 British soldiers engaged, of whom 934 were killed and 175 wounded. The 66th Foot lost ten officers and 275 men killed, two officers and 33 men wounded. When six o'clock came, a forlorn column of weary and dejected men were retreating to Kandahar, hopelessly beaten by an overwhelming enemy.

And the "murderous Ghazis,"[11] as Watson called them, poured a continuous fire on those retreating. The official report says that the majority of the casualties were caused by men falling from heat and exhaustion—the season was the hottest of the year; it was 105° F. in the shade—and the flight to Kandahar had to be undertaken after marching and fighting without food or water for twenty-four hours. Ayub Khan suffered severe casualties also, and could not pursue the remnants of the brigade more than five miles.

And what of Watson?

He was, he tells us, one of the wounded; he had been struck on the shoulder—we later learn, from Holmes, that it was his *left* shoulder—by a Jezail bullet,[12] which shattered the bone and grazed the subclavian artery.

Watson would have fallen into the hands of the murderous Ghazis had it not been for the devotion and courage shown by Murray, his orderly,[13] who threw him across a packhorse and succeeded in bringing him safely to the British lines.

Watson was extremely fortunate—for, as Rudyard Kipling wrote, in "The Young British Soldier":

> When you're wounded and left on Afghanistan's plains,
> And the women come out to cut up what remains,
> Just roll to your rifle and blow out your brains
>   An' go to your Gawd like a soldier . . .

But Watson's "British lines" are a little mysterious: there *were no* British lines between Maiwand and Kandahar. Watson "must have been misinformed on this point," Mr. N. P. Metcalfe wrote in "The Date of the *Study in Scarlet*." ". . . he was in no fit state to act as a military correspondent and, anyway, probably relied on the information of his orderly, Murray. It was definitely a case of *sauve qui peut*."

11 Among Moslems, a Ghazi is a warrior champion, especially in the destruction of infidels.

12 "According to the best authorities, the rifle or musket from which this bullet is fired is long and heavy with a crooked stock and used with a forked rest. It is of native manufacture and is patterned after the British Lee-Enfield rifle. Bannerman's complete catalogue of military weapons does not list the Jezail rifle as such, although numerous India matchlock guns are featured. The bullets are often slugs made from nails or odd scraps of metal including silver, and may produce infected wounds."—Dr. Roland Hammond, "The Surgeon Probes Doctor Watson's Wound."

13 A noncommissioned officer or soldier who attends a superior officer to carry out his orders or to render other services.

There *were* two companies of the Berkshires under Major Ready who were stationed on detachment at Khelat-i-Ghilzai, some seventy miles northeast of Kandahar on the Kabul road. While these did not share in the defeat, they, like the man who took part in the battle, were cooped up in Kandahar from July 27th until General Roberts' relief force appeared before the town on August 31st, and General Phayre's from Quetta, 137 miles away, arrived on September 6th. The month's siege at Kandahar was rigorous and morale was low —yet Watson never mentions it.

It seems safe to conclude that he was never there. He tells us, certainly, that he was removed, with a great train of wounded sufferers, to the base hospital at Peshawar (which Watson spells Peshawur), the most distant command of the Afghan Operations in the extreme Northeast, a distance of some 480 miles.**14**

Whether Watson reached Peshawar via Kabul or via Quetta is a point debated by commentators; as is the route taken. In any case, Watson, we think, would have reached the base hospital at Peshawar by the end of August, 1880.

Here he rallied, and had already improved so far as to be able to walk about the wards, when he was struck down by "enteric fever, that curse of our Indian possessions."

"I am told by Dr. Louis A. Hauser, of the staff of the New York Hospital, that the term 'enteric fever,' which is now obsolete, was used at the time of the Afghan wars to describe intestinal fevers generally, including the fever now designated as typhoid," the late Edgar W. Smith wrote in "The Long Road from Maiwand." "The bacillus typhosus was not isolated by Eberth of Germany until the year 1880, but Dr. Hauser feels, despite the lack of facilities for accurate diagnosis available in India at the time, that Watson's malady was certainly typhoid, and he believes, from the references made, that it might have laid him low for three months."

But the length of Watson's bout with "enteric fever"— he tells us that his life was despaired of "for months"—is another matter of controversy.

As Mr. Metcalfe wrote, in "The Date of the *Study in Scarlet*," "With respect to Dr. Hauser, I feel that the opinion of a medical man who has himself experienced this disease [Dr. Maurice Campbell] is to be preferred. It is as follows: 'The duration of enteric fever (nowadays called typhoid) is three weeks—though, of course, the attack may vary from subject to subject and depend on the severity or mildness of the onset. After his hectic experiences . . . Watson's months of despair were probably only weeks; his remark that his life was despaired of for months should not be taken literally. That is not a reasonable statement about any ordinary complications of typhoid where the risk is generally over during a much shorter period. There is nothing so indeterminable as a long stay in a base hospital as anyone who has experienced it can vouch.'"

When at last Watson came to himself, he was so weak and emaciated that a medical board determined that not a day should be lost in sending him back to England.

He had, then, a rather long journey to take—by rail about a thousand miles from Peshawar to the port of Karachi, and then for about 600 miles by boat from Karachi to Bombay.

14 Mr. Samuel F. Howard has suggested ("More About Maiwand") that Watson would be sent, not to Peshawar, but to Multan, but Mr. T. S. Blakeney ("Some Disjecta Membra") doubts this: "Multan is a notoriously hot place and most unsuitable for wounded."

15 Named after the ancient name of Syria's principal river, now called El Asi or Nahr El-Ashy.

16 It was always Christopher Morley's belief that "the very day" was January 1, 1881—"a day when Watson would naturally be making resolutions for a more frugal life. . . . Also the fact of its being a Holiday would account for Holmes being *the only student working in the laboratory*."

JOHN H. WATSON, M.D., AT THE TIME OF HIS MEETING WITH SHERLOCK HOLMES

From *Sherlock Holmes: A Biography*, by William S. Baring-Gould.

From Bombay he was dispatched in the troopship *Orontes* **15** —and here, thanks to the researches of Mr. Metcalfe ("The Date of the *Study in Scarlet*"), we are able to determine the exact date. Mr. Metcalfe, scanning the Naval and Military Intelligence column of the *London Times* from July, 1880, to December, 1881, has revealed that "a ship called the *Orontes* was pressed into special service in July, 1880, and troops for Afghanistan and India were embarked on her on August 3rd. She sailed from Portsmouth to Queenstown, the Mediterranean and Bombay on August 4th. The journey was scheduled to take twenty-eight days, but she actually arrived in Bombay on September 1st. On October 31st, she left Bombay for Portsmouth, calling at Malta on November 16th, and arriving at Portsmouth on Friday afternoon, November 26th, *bringing home the first troops from Afghanistan, including eighteen invalids*."

This corresponds almost precisely with Watson's statement that he "landed a month later on Portsmouth jetty."

In Portsmouth "there are Sheer Jetty, Pitch House Jetty, South Jetty, etc.," Christopher Morley wrote, "but obviously where JHW landed was *Troopship Jetty* marked large as life on the map [in Muirhead's *Guide to England*]. . . . I can almost see the *Orontes* unloading . . . at the south end of the Royal Dock Yard, close to the Royal Naval College."

The wounded off the *Orontes* were sent to Netley, but Watson was not among them. Rather he "gravitated" to London, "that great cesspool into which all the loungers and idlers of the Empire are irresistibly drained."

"Gravitated" is a curious word for Watson to have used —by fast train, it takes only an hour and three-quarters to make the 74-mile run from Portsmouth to London—and we may perhaps assume that Watson at this time acquired some of that knowledge of Hampshire and Sussex which he displayed later.

In London Watson stayed for "some" time at a private hotel in the Strand. It was the Craven Hotel, Christopher Morley thought—and Mr. Michael Harrison has asked (*In the Footsteps of Sherlock Holmes*): "Could it have been Horrex's, at the corner of Norfolk Street, or Osmond's, at 87, Strand, or Scott's Private, at 13 Cecil Street?"

He led there, he tells us, "a comfortless, meaningless existence," and so alarming did the state of his finances become that he soon realized that he must make a complete alteration in his style of living. On the very day that he came to this conclusion, he was standing at the Criterion Bar, where he met young Stamford. **16**

Stamford, as we know, introduced Watson to Holmes. The two met "next day" and inspected the rooms at No. 221 Baker Street. "That very evening" Watson moved his things round from the hotel, and Sherlock Holmes followed him "on the following morning." The Great Partnership was about to begin.

10

"HE IS THE NAPOLEON OF CRIME, WATSON"

[Sherlock Holmes of Professor James Moriarty, "The Final Problem"]

Before considering the home of Holmes (and Watson)—its location, physical features and furnishings—we should look briefly at the most deep-dyed of all the villains with whom Mr. Sherlock Holmes of Baker Street ever had to contend.

He was a man extremely tall and thin, with rounded shoulders. He had gray hair above a forehead that domed out in a curve, and below that forehead his eyes, puckered and blinking, were deeply sunken into his pale, white head. He had a solemn way of talking, and the total impression he created was one of dignity and asceticism, somewhat marred by one unpleasant mannerism: his face, protruded forward, was forever oscillating from side to side in a curiously reptilian fashion.

"This man is a scholar," you and I would have said on meeting him, and we would have been right.

He was also the most dangerous man in the London of the 1880's, the greatest schemer of his time, the organizer of every devilry, the controlling brain of the underworld of what was then and still is one of the world's greatest cities.

He was Professor James Moriarty.

Note well the "James." We cannot doubt that "James" *was* his Christian name (if anything could be said to be Christian about so monstrous an individual), for we are given this on the authority of the man who knew him best and hated him most: Sherlock Holmes himself.

And yet, side by side with this, we have the authority of the man who knew *Holmes* best and loved him most, his companion and biographer, John H. Watson, M.D., that Professor Moriarty had a brother who followed a military career and rose to the rank of colonel. And the first name of this brother, we are told, *was James also.*

There was a third brother, less successful in life than Professor James and Colonel James: he was a stationmaster in the west of England. We are never told his name, but we must assume that it, too, was James—for, as Mr. Vincent Starrett long ago pointed out: "Two brothers named James would appear a trifle silly; but if there were three, one might well suppose some sort of sinister pattern . . ."

Mr. Elliot Kimball has written (in "The Watsons of Northumberland") that "There is nothing particularly extraordinary about the matter. Onomatologists (or nomenologists) have long been familiar with the fact that brothers of the

THE YOUTHFUL JAMES MORIARTY

(*Above*) At the age of eight. (*Below*) At the age of twenty-one. Photographs from *Sherlock Holmes: A Biography,* by William S. Baring-Gould.

1 As Mr. Duncan MacDougald, Jr., has shown ("Some Onomatological Notes on 'Sherlock Holmes' and Other Names in the Sacred Writings"), the name Moriarty comes from the Irish *o'muiriĉerzaiz*—O Morierty, O Murtagh, Moriarty, from *muir*, "sea," plus the aspirated form of *ceart*, "right, true," plus the personal suffix *ach*.

2 Mr. Smith suggested 1846 for Moriarty's birth, and Professor H. W. Starr ("A Submersible Subterfuge or Proof Impositive") has opted for 1830: "Is it not likely that the portrait of Captain Nemo in [Jules Verne's] *Twenty Thousand Leagues Under the Sea* is a portrayal of a sinister figure well known to us—Professor James Moriarty?"

3 In "A Treatise on the Binomial Theorem," Mr. Poul Anderson has written: "The theorem itself is simply the expansion of the binomial $(a + b)$ raised to the nth power, where n is any number:

$$(a+b)^n = a^n + na^{n-1}b + \frac{n(n-1)}{1.2}a^{n-2}b^2$$
$$+ \frac{\ldots n(n-1)\ldots(n-r+1)}{r!}a^{n-r}b^r \ldots$$
$$b + \ldots + b^n$$

It vexed mathematicians for many centuries. The Hindus and the Arabs knew something of it. Newton discovered it about 1665, and an exposition is found in a letter dated 1676, but no real proof is given. Bernoulli and Euler sought the proof, but it remained for the Norwegian Niels Henrik Abel, 1802–1829, to demonstrate it rigorously for all n. This having been done before Moriarty's time, what remained for him? . . . It seems probable . . . that [he] was working on the basic idea of number itself, and that he developed a general binomial theorem applicable to other algebras than the one we know. If he could do this at the three-cornered age of 21, it is obvious that in his case, as in the Master's, genius flowered early."

same sibship not infrequently bore the same given name in earlier days. One staunch adherent of the Stuarts, who sired fourteen (14) sons named them all Charles; individuality in a cognominal sense, or with respect to the first given name, was not possible for the fourteen; but such identifications depended upon the second given name, *e.g.*, Charles Edward, Charles James, Charles Francis. Instances in which three or four brothers (or sisters) of the same sibship had the identical first given name are by no means uncommon. . . ."

Still, in the "sinister pattern" established by Moriarty *mère* and Moriarty *père* in the naming of their offspring, we like to think that we may have found the key to the aberrant personality that Professor Moriarty was later to become: he suffered psychologically as a child, we think, from a loss of identity in the Moriarty household, a loss that was to warp and twist what otherwise would have been a genius to admire, an intellect to esteem.

The Moriartys were of Irish extraction;**1** they were resident, we may suppose, in that part of the west of England where the youngest brother was later employed as a stationmaster. (The late Edgar W. Smith, in his "Prolegomena to a Memoir of Professor Moriarty," "suggested Liverpool on the basis that it "would qualify technically as the west of England" and "there are more Irishmen to the square foot [there] than in any other area on earth outside of Ireland, with the possible exception of Boston, Massachusetts.") We have reason to believe that Moriarty I, the later professor, was some ten years older than his archenemy Holmes. Holmes, we know, was born on January 6, 1854; Moriarty, then, was most probably born in 1844, although the latter part of 1843 is a distinct possibility.**2** He must have had an excellent education: in 1865, when he was only twenty-one, this remarkable youth wrote a treatise on the binomial theorem**3** which had a European vogue and won him the Chair of Mathematics at one of the lesser English universities at an annual salary of seven hundred pounds ($3,500).

One envies his students; Professor Moriarty must have been a marvelous instructor. Who can forget how, in *The Valley of Fear*, he was able to entrance Inspector MacDonald of Scotland Yard with such a lucid explanation of the nature of the eclipse, using as his props only a globe and a reflector lantern? (He "made it all clear in a minute," the Inspector exclaimed.)

COAT OF ARMS OF JAMES MORIARTY, SC.D., ACCORDING TO MR. WILLIAM S. HALL

Argent, an eagle displayed, sable. Crest: an arm embowed in armour, holding a dagger, and the bladed environed with a serpent. Motto: *Aspera me juvant*—"Peril delights me."

But a treatise on the binomial theorem was child's play to the man who later wrote *The Dynamics of an Asteroid*. This *magnum opus* ascended to such rarefied heights of pure mathematics that it was all but incomprehensible to the scientific critics of the day. "The magnitude of his achievement," Mr. Anderson wrote ("A Treatise on the Binomial Theorem") "can be appreciated by reflecting that there are nine known major planets, all influencing the asteroid simultaneously, and that no general solution has yet been found even for the three-body problem. (Given the positions, masses, and velocities of three bodies acting under gravitation, find their orbits for all past time and all time to come.)" And the late Edgar Smith observed that Professor Einstein's Theory of Special Relativity, first published (*Ann. d. Physik*) in June, 1905, bore the "imitative title" *Zur Elektrodynamic Körper* (On the Electrodynamics of Moving Bodies).

Indeed, there seems little reason to doubt that Moriarty did anticipate Einstein in the construction of the formula $E = mc^2$. If, however, it was in fact Moriarty who first perceived the awful potentialities of atomic fission and fusion, and so paved the way for the atomic and the hydrogen bomb, we must also credit him with having laid much of the theoretical groundwork for man-made satellites and the space station now under consideration.

Despite his growing fame as one of the foremost abstract thinkers the world has ever known, dark rumors about Moriarty began to circulate through the little university town, and he was forced to resign his position. In the latter part of the 1870's or early in the 1880's he came to London, where he set himself up as an army coach. Not a very lucrative profession, one would have said. And yet he was somehow able to indulge his sincere love for and his vast appreciation of fine art: on his study wall there hung a painting by Jean-Baptiste Greuze; it showed a sweet young woman with her head on her hands, peeping at the observer sideways. Moriarty may have paid as much as £4,000 ($20,000) for it, for Holmes referred to another painting by Greuze, his *Jeune Fille à l'Agneau* which, in 1865, had fetched that magnificent sum.**4**

Too, as we later learn, Professor Moriarty was able to pay a stipend of £6,000 ($30,000) a year to his right-hand man, the *second* most dangerous man in London, the cheater at cards, the hunter of big game, and the authority on air guns as lethal weapons: the notorious Colonel Sebastian Moran.

The money—so much of it that Moriarty was compelled to keep at least six bank accounts—came, of course, from crime: from forgery cases, robberies, murders, and lesser atrocities. Not that there was ever anything to connect the ostensible "army coach" with a single illegal action. Dear me—Professor Moriarty's favorite expression—dear me, no.

Moriarty did little himself; he only planned. But his agents were numerous and splendidly organized. Was there a paper to be abstracted, a house to be rifled, a man to be removed —the word was passed to the Professor, and the matter was seen to. The agent might be caught. But the deep organizing power, which forever stood in the way of the law and threw a shield over the wrongdoer, was never caught—never so much as suspected. Moriarty pervaded London, and no one had ever heard of him.

PROFESSOR JAMES MORIARTY

As portrayed by Mr. Martin Gabel in Alexander H. Cohen's production of *Baker Street*, "a musical adventure of Sherlock Holmes."

4 In *The Private Life of Sherlock Holmes*, Mr. Vincent Starrett has suggested that Conan Doyle may have modeled Professor Moriarty on "Adam North, who stole the famous Gainsborough, in 1876, and hid it for a quarter of a century, but even that master criminal might have taken lessons from the Moriarty of Holmes and Watson, a figure of colossal resource and malevolence."

EX-PROFESSOR JAMES MORIARTY, SC.D.

As he looked at the time of his first meeting with Mr. Sherlock Holmes. From Edgar W. Smith, "Prolegomena to a Memoir of Professor Moriarty."

No one, that is, except Sherlock Holmes. Often it was only the smallest trace, the faintest indication, and yet it was enough to tell the master detective that the great malignant brain was there, as the gentlest tremors at the edge of the web remind one of the foul spider which lurks at its center. "Petty thefts, wanton assaults, purposeless outrage," Holmes once said, "—to the man who held the clue all could be worked into one connected whole."

The duel came to its climax in the early months of 1891. "You crossed my path on the 4th of January," Moriarty snarled at Holmes. "On the 23rd you incommoded me; by the middle of February I was seriously inconvenienced by you; at the end of March I was absolutely hampered in my plans; and now, at the close of April, I find myself placed in such a position through your continual persecution that I am in positive danger of losing my liberty. The situation is becoming an impossible one."

Little over a week later, it is said, Moriarty lay twisted and broken and dead at the foot of the Reichenbach Falls near the little village of Meiringen in Switzerland.

"London," Mr. Sherlock Holmes was to complain some years after, "has become a singularly uninteresting city since the death of the late lamented Professor Moriarty."

But was Moriarty in truth "the late lamented?"

For four long years, as we shall see, Watson and the world thought that Holmes also lay dead beneath the dark and swirling waters of the Reichenbach; but Holmes in 1894 was very much alive and once again "free to devote his life to examining those interesting little problems which the complex life of London so plentifully presents."

Why not Moriarty?

His body was never recovered; that much is certain. And the suspicion will not rest that Moriarty, like Holmes, survived and carried on.

He could hardly be alive today—after all, he would be at least 120 years of age. But anyone familiar with the history of evil in the world since 1894 has little difficulty in seeing that Professor Moriarty was taking advantage of a long period of social unrest to consolidate and expand his undisputed position as the Napoleon of crime . . .

11

"I HAVE MY EYE ON A SUITE IN BAKER STREET"

[*Sherlock Holmes*, A Study in Scarlet]

Early in this century a party of French schoolboys were visiting London. Asked what historic sight they chose to see first, they answered with one voice: "The house where Sherlock Holmes lives!"

221 Baker Street—it is one of the most famous addresses in all literature, and we have a right, as the late Christopher Morley once said, "to be interested in all details."

But we had better settle, first, the question of whether or not Conan Doyle had any particular house in mind as the home of Holmes and Watson. If he did, he declined to admit it: "But that is a point which for excellent reasons," he observed in his autobiography, "I will not decide."**1**

Indeed, Conan Doyle once went so far as to declare to an interviewer that, to the best of his memory, he had *never been* in Baker Street in his life, but here, almost certainly Conan Doyle was guilty of a bit of leg-pulling: there exists a photograph of the author taken by a photographer's studio, Messrs. Elliott and Fry, in Baker Street.

The "B" in 221B need not concern us long: it probably stood for *bis*, literally meaning *twice*, which was a frequent English identification for a subsidiary address. Christopher Morley cited Leonard Merrick's story *Conrad in Quest of His Youth* (1903) where one of his chorus girls gives her address as:

> Miss Tattie Lascelles
> c/o Madame Hermiance,
> 42 bis, Great Titchfield Street, W.

1 Years later, however, in his memoirs, *Back View*, Sir Harold Morris, Q.C., wrote that his father, Sir Malcolm, had suggested the Morris home on Baker Street to Conan Doyle as a suitable house for the detective and the doctor. Its *present* number is, not 221, but *21;* in Holmes' and Watson's day, its number was 77. Unhappily, it fails to answer a number of the qualifications we will outline for No. "221."

BAKER STREET ABOUT 1890

Portman Mansions, now Portman Street, is on the right. The picture shows the flat-fronted houses which were the standard type in Baker Street. Despite rebuilding, many of the old houses still remain. From The London Electrotype Agency, Ltd.

2 This house no longer exists. Along with its neighbors it was demolished to make room for the head offices of the Abbey National Building Society. It is now no more than a part of the site of Abbey House.

3 Baker Street was named for Sir Edward Baker, *c.* 1763–1825, a neighbor of the Portmans in Dorsetshire, who assisted Mr. Portman in developing his London estate. While Holmes was unquestionably its most famous resident, there were others: Mme. Tussaud at No. 59 (formerly No. 58); Edward Bulwer Lytton at No. 68 (formerly No. 31); William Pitt at No. 120 (formerly 14 York Place); Mrs. Sarah Siddons at No. 27 Upper Baker Street (a house that no longer exists); Arnold Bennett at Chiltern Court Mansions (over the Baker Street Station of the Underground).

4 This fact led Mr. Harrison to surmise that Watson, to get an imaginary number, divided the non-existent 43 by 2 and got 21½. But both No. 21 and No. 21½ already existed. So Watson prefixed 21½ —or 21B—with his divisor, 2, and got 221B Baker Street.

BAKER STREET AS IT WAS IN 1881

From *The Baker Street Journal*, December, 1964.

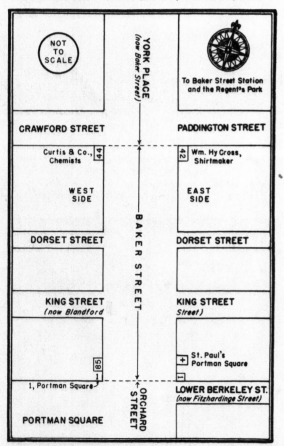

Mme. Hermiance ran a laundry on the ground floor, and Miss Tattie had rooms one flight up—on the English *first,* American *second* floor—just as Holmes and Watson did.

Let us begin our reexamination of the problem of the proper location of No. 221 by noting that the rooms shared for so many years by Holmes and Watson were positively *not* in the house which, until the 1930's, bore the number 221.**2**

Nor, in Holmes' and Watson's day, could *any* house in Baker Street proper have possibly been numbered 221.**3**

The facts are these:

1. Baker Street in 1881 was barely a quarter of a mile long. It consisted of some eighty generously proportioned, four-story buildings. At the southern end, the street passed along one side of Portman Square and continued to the south as Orchard Street, a name which it still bears. Northward, past the crossing of Crawford Street, on the west, and Paddington Street, on the east, it was called *York Place,* and beyond the crossing at Marylebone Road it was called *Upper Baker Street.* As Mr. Michael Harrison wrote, in "Why '221B'?", "The east side . . . ran from No. 1, at the corner of Lower Berkeley (now Fitzhardinge) Street, to No. 42. . . . The street numbers ran consecutively. On the opposite side of the road—the west side—the numbers ran, without a break, from No. 44 . . . at the corner of Crawford Street, to No. 85, which was the building immediately before the big Georgian house at the corner of Portman Square [No. 1, Portman Square]." The numbers in Baker Street proper ended, then, at 85, and there was no No. 43, Baker Street.**4**

2. On January 1, 1921, York Place was incorporated with Baker Street.

3. In 1930 Upper Baker Street was merged with Baker Street, and the entire street was renumbered on the west, or left going north, side—this, as we shall see, is the side that concerns us—from 185 to 247. *For the first time there was a No. 221 Baker Street.*

Had the quarters of 1881 been in the vicinity of the present Abbey House, then Holmes would have had to *anticipate* that Upper Baker Street, where he lived, would some day be merged with Baker Street proper, and that his house, after renumbering, would become 221—which is precisely what he *did* do, if we are to accept the suggestion put forward by Mr. A. L. Shearn in "The Street and the Detective": "It is the writer's considered opinion that notwithstanding other claims, Sherlock Holmes' real address was none other than this house which later became known as 221 Baker Street."

If, however, we choose to disregard this suggestion, we must ask what house in Baker Street proper, or beyond, Watson in 1881 masked as No. "221."

Our single most important piece of Canonical evidence here is the route followed by Holmes and Watson in "The Adventure of the Empty House"—from Cavendish Square into Manchester Street and so to Blandford Street, then down a narrow passage.

Now, *this narrow passage must be one of two:* Kendall Mews, leading south, or Blandford Mews, leading north.

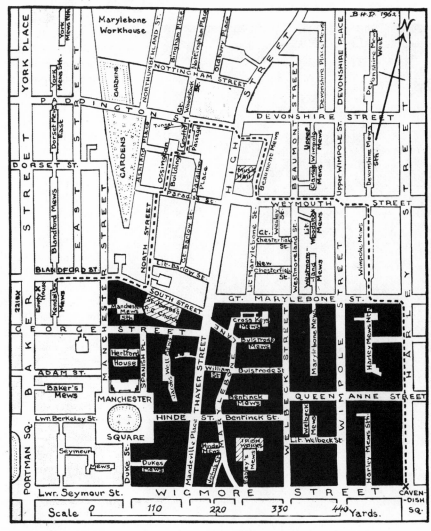

The text reads: "down a narrow passage." This would seem to indicate that Holmes and Watson turned *south* into Kendall Mews (had they gone north, Watson might better have said "up a narrow passage")—and this in turn would mean that 221 Baker Street, which stood opposite "Camden House"—"the empty house"—was on the *west* side of Baker Street, between George Street on the south and King (west)-Blandford (east) streets on the north, among the present Nos. 19–35.

Despite Watson's "down a narrow passage," let us for the moment, however, leave this segment of Baker Street proper and assume (as the late Gavin Brend, among others, did) that Holmes and Watson turned *north* into Blandford Mews. 221 Baker Street would then be on the *west* side of Baker Street, between King-Blandford streets on the south and Dorset Street on the north, among the present Nos. 37–67:

No. 49. "Reliable local authority has informed us that No. 49 is accepted in that district as being upon the site," Mr. T. S. Blakeney wrote in *Sherlock Holmes: Fact or Fiction?*

No. 61. "As between [the numbers 59, 61, and 63] there is little to choose and we are not justified in eliminating any of them, but if anything, the advantage is slightly in favor of No. 61," Mr. Brend wrote in *My Dear Holmes.***5**

On Mr. Bernard Davies' map, black-shaded blocks are those lying directly between Cavendish Square and Manchester Street, with *no* routes by ways of mews, etc. Unshaded blocks are those nearest to Cavendish Square which, in sequence, could have formed part of the journey taken by Holmes and Watson in "The Adventure of the Empty House." The suggested route from Cavendish Square to No. 34 Baker Street is shown by the bold dotted lines. From *The Sherlock Holmes Journal*, Winter, 1962.

5 Mr. Blakeney's No. 49 went down in the blitz, and Mr. Brend's No. 61 (which existed when he wrote his book) has now been demolished to make way for a large block of offices.

NO. 109 BAKER STREET

As photographed by Mr. D. Martin Dakin of The
Sherlock Holmes Society of London; the original
is in color.

6 Dr. Briggs' identification of 221 Baker Street
with the present No. 111 was first published in
"Sherlock Holmes," by Frederic Dorr Steele, in
Sherlock Holmes Farewell Appearances of William Gillette, 1929–1930; New York: Al. Greenstone, 1929, pp. 4–5, and illustrations, p. 7. No. 111
Baker Street was blitzed during World War II and
was rebuilt as a block of offices.

No. 66. This house, we are told, once satisfied Mr. Vincent
Starrett's "occult sense of rightness" as the dwelling place of
Sherlock Holmes. But this number would be on the *east*, or
right side going north, of Baker Street, and could therefore
not have been opposite "Camden House," also on the east
side.

Nos. 59–67A. "If one were to retrace the route followed
[in "The Adventure of the Empty House"] one would be
in the block of Nos. 59–67A," the late Paul McPharlin wrote
in "221B Baker Street: Certain Physical Details."

We must now note that Holmes and Watson, turning north
into Blandford Mews, *might* have continued along the route
sketched by the late H. W. Bell in his *Sherlock Holmes and
Dr. Watson: The Chronology of Their Adventures.* In this
case "Holmes and Watson must have gone the length of
Blandford Mews, crossed Dorset Street, kept on through
Kenrick Place [then known as Dorchester Mews East], and
at Paddington Street have turned to the right into East
Street, and then to the left into Portman Mansions [now
Portman Street], in order to reach York Mews North, in the
rear of Camden House. (York Mews South—known since
1936 as Sherlock Mews, W. 1—which is entered from Paddington Street oposite the north end of Kenrick Place [Dorchester Mews East], is a blind alley, having no communication with York Mews South.)" 221 would then be on the
west side of Baker Street, between Dorset Street on the
south and the Marylebone Road on the north.

No. 109. "Necessarily one of half a dozen houses on the
opposite side of the road [the western side] must be number
221B. . . . The present numbers 109 or 111 single themselves
out as likely, being the central houses in the block. Our own
choice is 109," Mr. Ernest H. Short wrote. And Mr. James
Edward Holroyd is another who has proved to his own
satisfaction that the present No. 109 was 221 Baker Street.

No. 111. "Spending a part of his summer vacation in London a few years ago, Dr. Gray Chandler Briggs of St. Louis,
the well-known roentologist, mapped Baker Street from end
to end. . . . Like Holmes himself, he had turned into a narrow
alley and passed through a wooden gate into a yard, to find
himself at the back door which admitted the detective. Looking in, he saw the long, straight hall extending through the
house to a front door of solid wood, above which was a fanshaped transom. Conclusive, all of it, for already over the
door in front he had read the surviving placard—*Camden
House.* . . . The deduction that followed this discovery was,
obviously, elementary. Since Camden House stood opposite
the famous lodgings, the rooms of Sherlock Holmes in Baker
Street were, of necessity, those upon the second story of the
building numbered 111." So wrote Mr. Vincent Starrett in
his *Private Life of Sherlock Holmes.***6**

It now seems clear beyond all possible doubt that 221 was
on the *west* side of Baker Street, despite Watson's statement
in "The Cardboard Box" that the sunlight, which must have
been *morning* sunlight, glared on the yellowed brickwork
of the opposite house.

But the question remains: was 221 (1) south of King-Blandford streets; (2) between King-Blandford streets and Dorset Street; or (3) north of Dorset Street?

A strong point in favor of the North-of-Dorset-Street school of thought is the fact, as noted by Dr. Briggs, that, until recent years, No. 118 Baker Street was indeed Camden House—Camden House School, a well-known preparatory school, now removed to neighboring Gloucester Place.

Against the North-of-Dorset-Street point of view, however, there is the fact, noted above, that, at the time of Holmes' adventures, the modern Nos. 109 and 111 *were not in Baker Street at all, but in York Place.*

Against the North-of-Dorset-Street view there is also the evidence of:

1. "The Red-Headed League." " 'You [Watson] walked briskly across [Hyde Park] from your home [in Kensington] to meet me [Holmes] at ten for that dramatic end to the plans of the Red-Headed League. You left on the stroke of 9:15, and I doubt if there is a man alive who could have reached No. 111 Baker Street on foot in that time."—James T. Hyslop, "The Master Adds a Postscript."

2. "The Adventure of the Blue Carbuncle." Assuming, as most commentators have, that Commissionaire Peterson lived at or very near 221 Baker Street,**7** identifying No. 221 as the modern No. 111 "would place us on the left-hand side [of Baker Street] going north, somewhere between York Street and Marylebone, or well towards the mainline railway station at Marylebone. But that theory becomes untenable when you consider the route which our good Commissionnaire Peterson took to get home after his Christmas jollification. . . . One glance at the map will convince you that no man in his right mind would try to reach 111 by such a route, but that it was, on the other hand, a natural direction for a man bound for any point in Baker Street between Blandford and the Oxford Street end."—James T. Hyslop, "The Master Adds a Postscript." In this same adventure, Watson tells us that his footfalls and Holmes' "rang out crisply and loudly as we swung through the doctors' quarter, Wimpole Street, Harley Street, and so through Wigmore Street into Oxford Street." "It is as clear as day," Mr. Hyslop continued, "that [the] path was that of men who lived in the southern part of Baker Street."

3. "The Adventure of the Beryl Coronet." "A further objection to . . . No. 111," Mr. Brend wrote in *My Dear Holmes,* "is that [it is] much too close to Baker Street Underground Station. . . . A passenger from the Underground [would not] take a cab to visit Holmes. He would no sooner have got into the cab then he would have to get out again."

Let us now summarize our evidence so far: the evidence of "The Adventure of the Empty House," "The Red-Headed League," "The Adventure of the Blue Carbuncle," and "The Adventure of the Beryl Coronet" would all seem to indicate that 221 Baker Street was a house on the west (or left going north) side of Baker Street, *below* Dorset Street.

NO. 111 BAKER STREET

The site of "221" according to Dr. Gray Chandler Briggs. No. 111 was demolished in the blitz.

7 "I am assuming that Peterson lived at 221B though I am not sure this is correct. Holmes gives him orders to carry out and he rushes into the room unannounced when his wife discovers the carbuncle. It looks as if he lived there . . ."—Gavin Brend, "The Route of the Blue Carbuncle." "The fact that Peterson was able to produce the Blue Carbuncle without leaving his post indicates clearly that Mrs. Peterson and the oven which was to receive the famous bird were very near at hand."—James T. Hyslop, "The Master Adds a Postscript."

And now let us return to Kendall Mews and consider the situation if Holmes and Watson had turned *south* into it, as we believe they did. 221 Baker Street would then stand on the west side of Baker Street between George Street and King-Blandford streets, among the present Nos. 19–35.

Of *No. 19*, Mr. Hyslop has written: ". . . I think it is clear that our rooms were in South Baker Street, and yet if I can trust your estimate of distances we were at least 200 yards from the Oxford Street end. Personally, I would put it a little less than that. My estimate would be that our quarters were somewhere between George Street and Blandford Street on the left-hand (west) side going north . . . [probably] No. 19, first house after George Street, on the left-hand side going north."

Dr. Maurice Campbell in *Sherlock Holmes and Dr. Watson: A Medical Digression*, suggested *No. 27*, and Sir Harold Morris, as we have seen, has made a case for *No. 21* Baker Street.

And now let us consider *No. 31*.

This is the choice of Mr. Bernard Davies—a choice with which your editor most heartily concurs—and the evidence for it is to be found in Mr. Davies' remarkable study, "The Back Yards of Baker Street."

"BAKER STREET IN 1894 FROM PORTMAN MANSIONS TO GEORGE STREET"

On Mr. Bernard Davies' map, small black triangles indicate front doors; black blobs with lines indicate street lamps. The map is based on Ordnance Survey 5-foot plans, sheet VII/51, 1st Edition, 1872 (east side only); resurveyed 1893–1894; 2nd edition, 1895. Modern numbering inserted. From *The Sherlock Holmes Journal*, Winter, 1959.

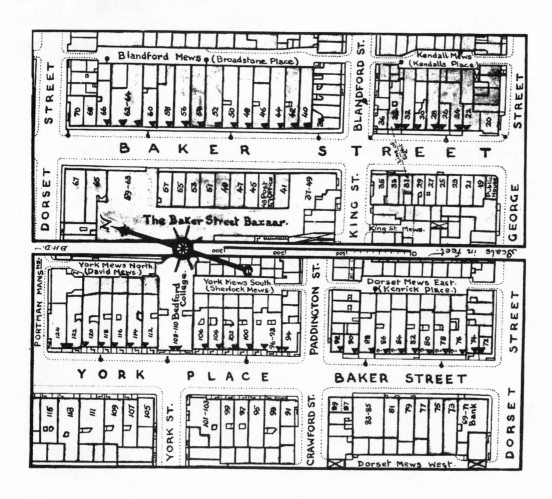

Mr. Davies searched first for "the Empty House," basing his hunt principally on the information contained in that adventure. The requirements are:

A. BACK

1. It must have had a mews or similar passage behind it giving access to the rear premises.

2. It must have possessed a backyard abutting on to the mews. As the back door opened into this yard the latter must have been *an open space in the rear*, and not a small enclosed court or air well within the building.

3. Holmes and Watson passed "through a wooden gate" from the mews into the yard; therefore there was no mews property intervening.

B. FRONT

4. Its front door and entrance hall must have been on the *south* side (that is, on the *right* side when viewed from the street), because "Holmes turned suddenly to the right" into the front room when approaching from the rear, impossible if the hall was on the north.

5. There was no streetlamp outside it in 1894. "There was no lamp near . . ."

Mr. Davies concluded that the house best answering these specifications was *the present No. 34, the former No. 15 Baker Street.*

Mr. Davies then searched for 221 itself, basing that search on these specifications:

A. BACK

1. It must have possessed a back yard large enough to contain a plane tree at the time of "The Problem of Thor Bridge" (1900). The tree may not have been very large, but the October wind "whirling the last remaining leaves" from its branches suggests that it was of reasonable height and foliage. The yard, therefore, was fairly spacious and open to the wind. Both factors, together with the phrase "behind our house," rule out a narrow well or court within the building. •

B. FRONT

2. Here there are numerous points, but none of any practical use:

a. "Two large windows" in the sitting room (*A Study in Scarlet*). Very few Baker Street houses are only two window-widths across, but we cannot be certain how far across the frontage the room extended at that period.

b. One was a "bow window" ("The Adventure of the Beryl Coronet," "The Adventure of the Mazarin Stone"). "This is dubious," Mr. Davies wrote, "and may be a literary fancy."

c. At least three stories high, as Watson slept on the floor above the sitting room ("The Problem of Thor Bridge," "The Adventure of the Speckled Band" and many other references). All the original buildings have at least three floors, and most have four.

d. The front door possessed a semicircular fanlight ("The Adventure of the Blue Carbuncle"). This, in some form, was practically universal.

NO. 31 BAKER STREET TODAY

The site of "221," according to Mr. Bernard Davies. From *Sherlock Holmes: A Biography*, by William S. Baring-Gould.

8 Your editor is basing much of this description of No. 221 on a visit to No. 31 Baker Street which he had the pleasure of making in October, 1963, in company with Mr. Bernard Davies and Mr. Anthony Howlett, then Chairman of the Sherlock Holmes Society of London.

9 Holmes, in "The Naval Treaty," says: "Her cuisine is a little limited, but she has as good an idea of breakfast as a Scotchwoman."

e. The main staircase had seventeen steps up to the first landing ("A Scandal in Bohemia"). "My own researches," Mr. Davies wrote, "confirm those of Dr. W. S. Bristowe. All existing examples have about twenty, some more."

"a and b are so doubtful," Mr. Davies continued, "c and d so universal, while e is so in conflict with all the known facts that it is advisable to ignore the front elevation and rely solely on Point 1."

With "uncanny precision," this reliance led Mr. Davies to the identification of *the present No. 31, the former No. 72,* as No. "221."

"The clinching argument," Mr. Davies concluded, "is, of course, as plain as a pikestaff. No. 31 and No. 34 are opposite each other. Not dead opposite, it is true, but near enough for the sight-line to be no more than fifteen or twenty degrees off. . . . Here, and nowhere else, could that famous vigil have been kept opposite that bright window in the gloom on which 'the shadow of a man who was seated on a chair within was thrown in hard, black outline—a perfect reproduction of Holmes.' Our half-mile search of Baker Street could come to no more happy and reassuring end."

And now that we have found our way to No. 221 Baker Street, let us enter through the front door with its semicircular fanlight that Watson called so "well-remembered" ("A Scandal in Bohemia").**8**

Ahead of us, down a short and narrow passage, is a door leading to the stairs to the basement floor. In Mrs. Hudson's time, this floor was lighted, to some extent, by area windows, now paved over. It would accommodate the kitchen, a storeroom, a corner for the page boy, perhaps a waiting room for callers, although, for this last, we have only the doubtful authority of "The Adventure of the Mazarin Stone."

We picture it as a warm and cheerful place, even though it was underground and generally lit by artificial light. It would be furnished with deal tables and a dresser, chairs for meals, and perhaps a couple of Windsor armchairs for Mrs. Hudson's leisure moments with her "cronies." There would be a huge range fitted with ovens and boilers, and it would consume enormous quantities of coal, stored in a shed in the backyard. Batteries of iron or copper saucepans would reflect its flames, and with them would hang frying pans, skillets, skimmers, and sieves of varying finenesses. In the early days, Mrs. Hudson would have done all the cooking,**9** but we are told in "The Problem of Thor Bridge" that 221 Baker Street had a *new* cook, and a new cook implies that there must have been an *old* one, perhaps hired by Mrs. Hudson when Holmes' payments for her lodgings became "princely" in 1887 ("The Adventure of the Dying Detective"). She would expect to be supplied with numerous fancy molds for puddings, jellies, and aspics, as well as with preserving pans, bread tins, milk bowls, and many other utensils.

Returning to the ground floor passage, we would find, to our right on entering, a shop or office, the former dining room and pantry. The presence of Commissionaire Peterson, in "The Adventure of the Blue Carbuncle," suggests an office rather than a shop. To our left are two flights of steps, seventeen in all, leading to the first floor. At the head of the staircase we shall find (perhaps) two doors: the first we pass leads into Holmes' bedroom (if, again, we may trust "The Adventure of the Mazarin Stone"); the second is the door to the famous sitting room. At the west end of this passageway another flight of stairs climbs to the English *second*, American *third* floor.

Entering the sitting room, we see it as Watson first saw it on that day in late 1880 or early 1881: it is a "large airy" room, perhaps about thirty feet long, twenty-five feet wide, and ten feet high, "cheerfully furnished and illuminated by two broad [and, we can believe, low-silled] windows."

Mr. Michael Harrison has written (*In the Footsteps of Sherlock Holmes*) that "the reference to broad windows is curious: for all the windows of the Baker Street houses are of the same width: it is in their *height* that they vary."

And these windows are curious in more than their breadth; it is curious, for example, that Watson should speak of *two* windows, for Baker Street houses of this kind, as we have seen, almost uniformly boast *three* broad windows looking out into Baker Street (certainly No. 31 does).

Perhaps what Watson *meant* to say is that the sitting room had two broad windows flanking a third window, *a bow window*, for he mentions "the bow window" on more than one occasion.

And let us pause here for a moment to try to remove some of the confusion that exists in the minds of many of us between *bow* windows and *bay* windows, for they are two very different things. (No house in Baker Street had or has a *bay* window, but *bow* windows, in Holmes' and Watson's day, were rather plentiful.)

Mr. Ronald R. Weaver has made the distinction between these two "interesting details of the late Gothic school of architecture" remarkably clear in his essay, "Bow Window in Baker Street," in which he says: "The bay window is a structural affair, composed of plane or curved sections, projecting from the building elevation proper, with flat or curved glass conforming to the structural sections of the bay. But the bow window is merely a curved or rounded glass, set in a suitable frame. It can be incorporated in a bay, but it does not require such a structure. On the contrary, it is—or was—far more commonly installed in plane elevations, thereby affording an enlarged view. It was quite fashionable in the Victorian era, but its popularity waned because it was relatively fragile, and difficult and expensive to replace. The window in question, as appears by the Canon, was specifically a bow window. Therefore, no further time need be lost in looking for a bay, or evidence that such a device once existed, or has been removed, anywhere in Baker Street."

Mr. Weaver suggested that the bow window was shattered in the very first adventure shared by Holmes and Watson —*A Study in Scarlet*—during the frenzied efforts by which Mr. Jefferson Hope attempted to escape the clutches of Messrs. Holmes, Lestrade, Gregson, and Watson.

It was certainly replaced with another window of the bow type, for Holmes, at the time of *The Hound of the Baskervilles*, first spied Dr. Mortimer on his doorstep from "the recess of the window." Again, in "The Adventure of the

Beryl Coronet," Watson stood in the bow window and watched the unhappy Mr. Holder stagger down Baker Street.

It is probable that the bow window was shattered again by the firemen who put out the conflagration in 221B set off by the Moriarty gang in April, 1891—and it may have been shattered for a third time in April, 1894, by the expanding air gun bullet fired by Colonel Sebastian Moran ("The Adventure of the Empty House").**10**

Facing east, as they did, these windows would of course receive the morning sun ("Holmes held up the paper so that the sunlight shone full upon it"—"The Adventure of the Dancing Men"). They were equipped with blinds, and—although Watson does not mention it—they were probably hung with white Nottingham lace curtains between the blinds and the heavier serge, damask, or velvet drapes.

The floor of the room would be wide boards of good old English oak, painted or stained a dark brown, and covered, no doubt, with a well-worn carpet leaving bare only a foot or so around the edge of the room.

The wallpaper, like the carpet, would be heavily patterned in damask or floral designs. Dark reds, greens, and blues were the favorite colors, and these were repeated in the long thick drapes at the windows.

One wall would be marred, of course, by the patriotic "V. R." (Victoria Regina) punctured out by Holmes with a "hair-trigger revolver and a box of Boxer cartridges" ("The Musgrave Ritual"). This, as Mr. Robert Keith Leavitt has convincingly demonstrated in "Annie Oakley in Baker Street," would be the *script* V. R., with crown, and the wall that it disfigured, or adorned, would be the *south* wall, opposite the fireplace, which was centered in the north wall of the room.

We know, from "The Adventure of the Noble Bachelor" and later references, that a clock hung someplace on a wall.

Gas fixtures would be strategically placed on the walls to provide illumination ("Our gas was lit"—"The Adventure of the Copper Beeches"). But gas, in Holmes' and Watson's day, was not laid on casually; it was expensive, and was confined to the main rooms. Oil lamps would be used, both for economy and for additional lighting. These gave a soft, clear light, very restful to the eyes, but they involved a good deal of work in cleaning and filling. It is probable that a hanging lamp for mineral oil and candles was suspended from the center of the ceiling. At 221, as in most Victorian homes, a row of candlesticks would be placed on a hall table every night, and as each person retired, he would take one with him, and by its small light undress and go to bed.

There was, of course, no central heating at 221 Baker Street in Holmes' and Watson's day, so the fireplace with its cheery blaze of sea coals would be the sitting-room's only source of warmth and its chief attraction on a cold winter's day.**11** "Generally, . . . one thinks the life of the detective went on around the fireplace," Mr. Vincent Starrett wrote in *The Private Life of Sherlock Holmes*. "It follows that everything he might require would be within his reach; certainly it would be so by evening, on any day that he remained at home."

10 It is true that "The Adventure of the Mazarin Stone" would seem to indicate that the bow window was indeed a *bay* window, but this case, as we shall see, can hardly be taken as evidence for the true structural details of the 221B sitting room.

11 No fewer than 27 of the 60 adventures include mention of a fire.

THE ROOM'S FURNISHINGS, seen in picture at left, are itemized numerically above: **1**—The bust with which Holmes drew the fire of Colonel Sebastian Moran, "the second most dangerous man in London" (*The Adventure of the Empty House*). **2**—Holmes's "low-powered microscope" (*The Adventure of Shoscombe Old Place*). **3**—Bookshelf containing among other things Clark Russell's "fine sea stories" of which Watson was so fond. **4**—Portrait of Irene Adler, who was always "*the woman*" (*A Scandal in Bohemia*). **5**—Holmes's dark lantern (*The Red-Headed League*). **6**—The desk and chair Conan Doyle used in writing the Holmes stories. **7**—Tray with tea, half-eaten toast and boardinghouse china typical of the period. **8**—Watson's chair. **9**—Holmes's velvet-lined chair. **10**—The "acid-stained, deal-topped table" in "the chemical corner." **11**—The skin of the "swamp-adder" (*The Adventure of the Speckled Band*). **12**—Holmes's stick rack, on which is the cane he used to lash the Speckled Band. **13**—Watson's Afghanistan trophies. **14**—Code employed by Abe Slaney in *The Adventure of the Dancing Men*. **15**—The box containing Holmes's relics from *The Musgrave Ritual*. **16**—Holmes's "unanswered correspondence transfixed by a jack-knife into the very centre of his wooden mantelpiece." **17**—His tobacco, kept in the toe of a Persian slipper. **18**—The coal scuttle that held his cigars.

THE SITTING ROOM AT 221B BAKER STREET

With a key to the furnishings, from *Life*.

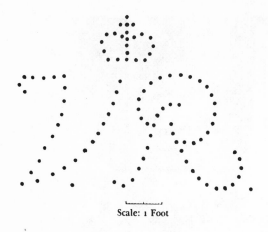

Scale: 1 Foot

THE SCRIPT V. R., WITH CROWN

This drawing, done to scale, of the script with which Holmes adorned the south wall of the sitting room at 221B Baker Street, was made by Mr. Robert Keith Leavitt to illustrate his essay, "Annie Oakley in Baker Street." From *Profile by Gaslight,* edited by Edgar W. Smith.

12 The cigars may have been Holmes', but the coal scuttle may well have been Watson's, if he was of Scots descent and a student, for a time, at the Medical College at the University of Edinburgh. As the late James Keddie, Sr., wrote in "Gasogene, Coal Box, Persian Slipper": "In Edinburgh the coal box was an ornament, and in it were stored such details of fireside comfort as slippers, unread magazines, and so forth. Why not cigars?" Scottish Sir James M. Barrie, in fact, kept both his cigars and his telephone in his coal scuttle. The scuttle is usually pictured as a metal vessel, but Mr. Frank A. Waters has suggested ("The Rooms in Baker Street") that it "was a square box made of wood."

13 The famous reconstruction of the Baker Street sitting room created for the Sherlock Holmes Exhibition during the Festival of Britain places Holmes' chemical corner, with its acid-stained, deal-topped table and its formidable array of bottles, retorts, and test tubes, in the northeast corner of the room; we feel, however, that there is better evidence for placing it in the *northwest* corner, with a tall stool in front of it. "Scientific charts" hung above it; one of them, surely, was a periodic table of the elements.

The fireplace was black marble, we think, with a mantel of wood. Holmes' unanswered correspondence was transfixed by a jackknife into the very center of this mantel; in one corner stood his cocaine bottle, and "all the plugs and dottles left from his smokes of the day before [were] carefully dried and collected on the corner of the mantlepiece" —"The Adventure of the Engineer's Thumb." A looking glass hung above it, as we know from "The Adventure of the Beryl Coronet."

Before the fireplace, we must place a bearskin hearthrug ("The Adventure of the Priory School"). The coal scuttle, containing Holmes' cigars,**12** stood to the left of the fireplace, we think, and the poker and the other fireplace instruments in their customary place to the right of the fire.

Handy, too, would be the Persian slipper stuffed with shag tobacco. It most probably hung by means of a ring to a hook on the wall to the left of the fireplace. This, too, was in all likelihood a custom introduced to Holmes by his good friend Watson via Edinburgh. Says Keddie Senior: "[In Edinburgh] even unto this day single Persian slippers may be purchased for the self-same purpose. . . . The slippers so far as I know were never sold in pairs. They were made of soft Persian leather and were without heels. The tobacco was stuffed into the forward, or toe part of the slipper." The Persian slipper could not have made a very good humidor, however; the tobacco would surely dry out and become covered with dust, in spite of the rate at which Holmes consumed it.

The bellpull, which Watson on one occasion at least, rang rather petulantly, would presumably hang in a convenient place, perhaps just to the right of the fireplace.

To each side of the fireplace stood an armchair—one Holmes', the other Watson's. We would prefer to give the *west* armchair, low and velvet-lined, to Holmes. This would allow him to sit adjacent to his coat-scuttle humidor and convenient to his chemicals.**13**

Watson in the east armchair would be well placed to "put the pearls in the safe and get out the papers of the Conk-Singleton forgery" ("The Adventure of the Six Napoleons"), as well as for maneuverings with the poker ("The Adventure of the Three Gables").

To the far right of the fireplace stood a breakfront bookcase ("The Adventure of the Noble Bachelor," "The Adventure of the Sussex Vampire"). (The safe was no doubt in the bottom of this bookcase.) Here Holmes kept his maps and his many reference books (*Whitaker's Almanack,* an American encyclopedia, the *Continental Gazetteer,* a *Crockford,* and a *Bradshaw*), his toxicology collection, soil analyses, chemistry texts, anatomical guides, factual writings about the misdeeds of criminals and fictional writings about the triumphs of detectives, volumes on singlestick playing, boxing and swordsmanship, law books. Here, too, we would find Hafiz and Horace, Tacitus, Flaubert and George Sand, Thoreau, Goethe, Carlyle, Meredith and Winwood Reade. Certainly a place of honor would be given to Holmes' own monographs. On the lowest, tallest shelves, we imagine, stood the commonplace books, all neatly lettered on their buckram backs in the precise and clerkly hand of Sherlock Holmes.

The major pieces furnishing the room—what Watson in "The Adventure of the Noble Bachelor" calls "our humble lodging-house mahogany"—would be for the most part heavily carved, highly polished early Victorian. Some of them, perhaps, were of rosewood.

Opposite the fireplace, against the south wall, beneath Holmes' patriotic "V. R.," would stand that piece of furniture variously referred to as a couch, sofa, or settee. It was done, we think, in a worn and faded green, and it was covered with several large cushions, which Holmes sometimes threw upon the floor to sit upon. Holmes' violin, when it did not stand in its accustomed place in the corner of the room, frequently lay carelessly upon the sofa. Handy to the sofa stood a small table (the "side-table" of "The Resident Patient"), marred, no doubt, by cigarette burns, and upon this table stood the pipe rack.

To one side of the sofa stood Holmes' desk, and, on the other side, Watson's. Holmes kept his desk locked (at least he did in 1883, as we know from "The Adventure of the Speckled Band"), and he kept his "small case-book" in one of its drawers. Sherlock's diary ("The Adventure of the Blanched Soldier") was probably kept in that same locked desk, although the "case-book" and the "diary" may be one and the same volume.

Another very important piece of furniture was the sideboard. The late Paul McPharlin ("221B Baker Street: Certain Physical Details") has placed it, correctly we think, against the west wall, relying on a quotation from J. C. Loudon's *Encyclopaedia of Architecture and Furniture* which says that a sideboard "is placed at the ends of drawing rooms. . . . The panels in the back are of looking glass; and the doors of the two pedestals have panels filled in with fluted silk. . . . The tops . . . are frequently formed of statuary marble, and the supports and the upper shelf of finest rosewood. . . . On the bottom board, in front of the lower glass, are placed vases for holding flowers, and a number of other ornaments."

Holmes and Watson kept their sideboard littered with tumblers, cigar boxes, odds and ends of cold food, and, of course, the spirit case and the gasogene.

The spirit case, or tantalus, was a metal stand with a rod rising from its center, to whose top were attached arms which embraced the necks of two or more decanters, locking about them with a small padlock.

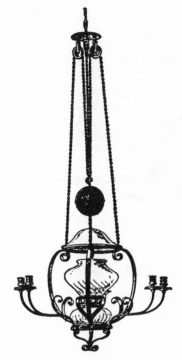

. . . A HANGING LAMP FOR MINERAL OIL AND CANDLES WAS SUSPENDED FROM THE CENTER OF THE CEILING

From *A History of Everyday Things in England*, Vol. IV.

TO EACH SIDE OF THE FIREPLACE STOOD AN ARMCHAIR . . .

From *The Baker Street Journal*, April, 1947.

. . . THAT PIECE OF FURNITURE VARIOUSLY REFERRED TO AS A COUCH, SOFA, OR SETTEE

TO ONE SIDE OF THE SOFA
STOOD HOLMES' DESK . . .

THE GASOGENE

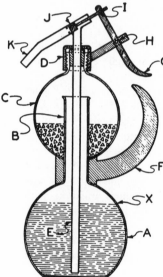

ANOTHER VERY IMPORTANT
PIECE OF FURNITURE WAS THE SIDEBOARD

Construction: This airtight system consists of a glass flask (A) with a long neck (B), and a small glass globe (C) mounted upon the flask. At the top of (C) is a removable screw-cap (D). Attached to the screw-cap are two tubes, (K) extending outside the globe and (E) extending nearly to the bottom of flask (A); also attached to the screw-cap is a valve (J) controlled by the lever-system (G), (H), and (I). A handle is provided in (F). (A) and (C) are usually enclosed in a stiff metal network, to prevent breakage, either by pressure or by accidental dropping or contact with other objects, should the "hand of the potter shake."
Operation: Globe (A) is filled with beverage water. In (C) is deposited a small quantity of chemical tablets or salts. The screw-cap (D) is closed. The whole device is tipped so that water from (A) will run into (C) until (C) is about one-third full. The device is then brought back to a vertical position. The chemical action of the water upon the crystals in (C) produces carbonic acid gas (carbon dioxide) which builds up a pressure in (C) and is driven down through (B) into the water in (A). The operator grasps handle (F) and presses upon lever (G), holding some vessel under tube (K). The depression of (G) causes the levers (G) to pivot at (H) and pull at (I), thus opening the valve (J) and permitting water charged with gas to be ejected by pressure through the tube (E) into tube (K) and so into the vessel held below (K). Release of pressure upon (F) allows an internal spring to close (J) (not shown), closing the system.

THE WORKINGS OF THE GASOGENE

The late Professor Jay Finley Christ's drawing from *The Baker Street Journal*, January, 1946.

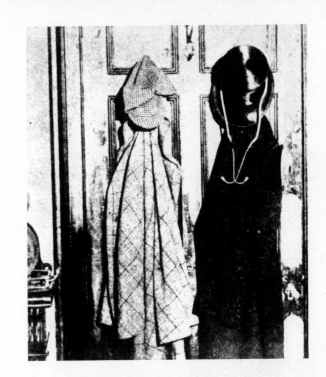

HERE HUNG HOLMES' DEERSTALKER AND CAPE-BACKED OVERCOAT, WATSON'S TOP HAT AND BOWLER, HIS STETHOSCOPE AND HIS GREATCOAT.

The stethoscope is perhaps a little out-of-period (see notes to "A Scandal in Bohemia").

The gasogene, we are told by the late James Keddie, Sr., is "a glass vessel shaped like a figure 8—the upper part being crowned with a handle and nozzle like a common, or beer-garden, siphon for swizzling soda-water into your whisky. The gasogene was loaded in its upper chamber with acid crystals and sodas and whatnot to generate gas, which passed into the lower chamber which was three parts filled with water. The gas generated in the upper chamber aerated the water in the lower chamber, and after a proper period had elapsed the gasogene simply became the siphon of every afternoon use. These contrivances had a habit of exploding, and I well remember a room in my father's house in which the wall paper was bejewelled with fine fragments of glass which had been embedded in it by such an explosion. The whole contrivance was enclosed in a wire netting, presumably to hold the fragments together when the burst came, but the smaller and more deadly pieces of glass shrapnel easily penetrated the mesh and anything within several feet of it."[14]

To the left of the sideboard, as we face it, is the door to Holmes' bedroom; to *its* left is the door to the passageway. Whether this hall door hinged to the left or to the right is something of a problem, as Mr. James Edward Holroyd pointed out in his delightful book, *Baker Street Byways:* "Perhaps it achieves its greatest individuality in 'A Case of Identity' in which it consecutively opened inwards, hinged left; inwards, hinged right; outwards, hinged left!" On the roomside of this door were the pegs for coats and hats. Here hung Holmes' deerstalker and cape-backed overcoat, Watson's tophat and bowler, his stethoscope and his greatcoat. Between the doors, we think, stood the cane rack, mentioned in "The Red-Headed League."

In the center of the room was a table, the drop-leaf kind to save room, we imagine, on the white cloth of which the china and silver glimmered in the lamplight ("The Adventure of the Cooper Beeches"). On it stood a student lamp which burned low until Holmes and Watson got back from an adventure and turned it up ("The Adventure of Charles Augustus Milverton").

We will have to scatter around the room one or more wooden chairs, one of which was once used as a study rack for a seedy hat ("The Adventure of the Blue Carbuncle"). There was also a basket chair, which Dr. Julian Wolff ("I Have My Eye on a Suite in Baker Street") and Mr. Paul McPharlin agreed should go to the east of the center table.[15] We also must agree with this: Lady Hilda Trelawney Hope had to "manoeuvre" to reach the basket chair and so place the light at her back ("The Adventure of the Second Stain").

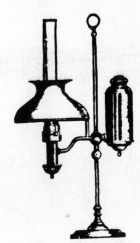

. . . A STUDENT LAMP WHICH BURNED LOW UNTIL HOLMES AND WATSON GOT BACK FROM AN ADVENTURE AND TURNED IT UP.

[14] A modern gasogene plays a key role in Mr. John Dickson Carr's fine Dr. Gideon Fell short story, "The Locked Room."

[15] "Few Americans," Christopher Morley wrote in "The Blue Carbuncle, or, the Season of Forgiveness," "know what is a basket chair (Minty's Varsity Chair) invented (at Oxford?) to help students fall asleep beside the fireplace." This suggests that the basket chair may have been contributed to the Baker Street menage by Holmes, as a relic of his student days.

. . . A FRAMED PORTRAIT OF GENERAL GORDON AND AN
UNFRAMED PICTURE OF HENRY WARD BEECHER.

16 Mr. James Edward Holroyd has called attention to an article in the January, 1893, issue of the *Strand Magazine* in which it is stated that a Mr. Ed Clifford "was the only English artist General Gordon ever sat to." If Watson's "newly-framed picture" showed "Chinese" Gordon, then, it was most probably a reproduction of Mr. Clifford's painting.

The frequently mentioned visitor's chair—"the vacant chair upon which a newcomer must sit" ("The Five Orange Pips")—was probably a low, velvet-covered, brass-nail-edged, antimacassar-protected seat, calculated to ease the innocent and terrify the guilty; it faced the light, and must therefore have stood to the west of the center table.

We know that a stool stood at Holmes' chemical table, but we may be sure that at least one of the chairs was also equipped with a footstool, for Holmes "squatted down upon a stool" in the adventure of "The Musgrave Ritual."

We must also provide the room with a small bookcase for Watson's "medical shelf" (*The Hound of the Baskervilles*). Prominent on the shelf would be his own works: a small brochure with the somewhat fantastic title of *A Study in Scarlet* and that other volume called *The Sign of the Four* are specifically mentioned in the annals (*The Sign of the Four*, "The Cardboard Box"). Watson also kept a scrapbook into which he pasted clippings about Holmes' cases (*The Sign of the Four*) and a notebook in which he jotted his none-too-accurate observations ("The Adventure of Wisteria Lodge"). But the good doctor had other interests: on stormy evenings he liked to read one of Clark Russell's fine sea stories ("The Five Orange Pips"); at other times Henri Murger's *Vie de Bohème* attracted him (*A Study in Scarlet*), and he would often sit up late nodding over a yellow-backed novel ("The Boscombe Valley Mystery").

Watson's books, we are told in "The Cardboard Box," stood beneath a framed portrait of General Gordon and an unframed picture of Henry Ward Beecher. The framed portrait is generally accepted as having been a picture of Charles George ("Chinese") Gordon, the hero of Khartoum, 1833–1885, but Watson's thoughts when he looked at it soon turned to the Civil War, and this raises the question—might the picture have been that of John Brown Gordon, 1832–1904, Confederate general, senator, and Governor of Georgia? **16**

Finally it may be observed that a telephone had been installed by 1898 ("The Adventure of the Retired Colourman") although the use of it, particularly by Watson, seems to have been half-hearted and Holmes himself remained largely faithful to his telegrams.

"That the chamber was perennially untidy is one of the soundest of our certainties," Mr. Vincent Starrett wrote in "The Singular Adventures of Martha Hudson." "One fancies Watson as making shift to keep the place in order, but there is a clear record of his despair. The principal duties of the maid, then, upstairs, it may be ventured, was making up the beds." Mr. Starrett, as always, is quite correct: fresh editions of every paper were supplied by the news agent, we are told in "Silver Blaze," and Watson writes in "The Musgrave Ritual" that "month after month [Holmes'] papers accumulated, until every corner of the room was stacked with bundles of manuscript." Holmes' female clients, in the gowns of the 1880's and 1890's, must often have found it difficult to steer their way about the overcrowded room without knocking something over; fortunately for them, the art of graceful walking was included in the education of most young women.

We know, by many references, that Holmes' bedroom connected with the sitting room ("He went to his bedroom, from which he returned presently pulling a large tin box behind him"—"The Musgrave Ritual"; "Sherlock Holmes sprang to his feet . . . and rushed into his room"—*A Study in Scarlet*; "With a nod he vanished into the bedroom"—"A Scandal in Bohemia"; "he sprang to his feet and passed into his bedroom"—"The Adventure of Charles Augustus Milverton").

There are, however, two puzzling references in "The Adventure of the Beryl Coronet": here Holmes "hurried to his chamber and was down again in a few minutes" and later in the same afternoon "hastened upstairs" from the sitting room. "In spite of these apparently unambiguous statements," Mr. G. B. Newton wrote in "This Desirable Residence," "the theory that Holmes had even temporarily betaken himself to the top floor is I feel untenable. It is noticeable that while on other occasions Watson deliberately alluded to Holmes' 'bedroom' this time he refers to his 'chamber'—the word bedroom is not mentioned. It is also noticeable that Holmes used it for the purpose of getting into and out of one of his disguises. By this time he must have accumulated a considerable variety of disguises and other impedimenta and may well have used one of the [lumber] rooms upstairs as a kind of dressing room and store for this purpose. The use of the word 'chamber' may be a little odd but Watson who was pedantic enough to refer to one of his own works, *A Study in Scarlet*, as a 'brochure' was quite capable of applying the term chamber to almost any sort of apartment. We remain convinced that Holmes was firmly rooted to his first-floor bedroom throughout his years at Baker Street."

The bedroom, as we know, had two doors, one opening into the sitting room, the second into the first-floor passageway, but it is difficult, indeed impossible, to see how a door from the bedroom could possibly lead behind the curtain of the bow window, as we are told that it did in "The Adventure of the Marazin Stone." We must really regard this "adventure" as apocryphal.

Our best description of Holmes' bedroom comes to us in "The Adventure of the Dying Detective."**17** Here we learn that the bedroom, like the sitting room, had a fireplace, with a clock on the mantel and a litter of "pipes, tobacco pouches, penknives, revolver cartridges and other debris." Its "every wall" was adorned with the pictures of famous criminals. There was a "closet," more probably a wardrobe of oak or mahogany, out of which came many of Holmes' varied disguises. The bed was a large one, and had a high, solid head, for the portly Watson was able to squeeze behind it to later confront a chagrined Culverton Smith. There was a large tin box in the corner, which Holmes once dragged into the sitting room ("The Musgrave Ritual"). If we are to credit "The Adventure of the Mazarin Stone," it contained, in 1903, at least, a gramophone.

Its other furnishings were probably sparse. We would add a bedside table, complete with candlestick, a marble-topped washstand with a jug and basin of plain or flowered china, a chest of drawers and dressing mirror, a simple chair. These are the minimum requirements of an English bedroom.

. . . A WARDROBE OF OAK OR MAHOGANY, OUT OF WHICH CAME MANY OF HOLMES' VARIED DISGUISES.

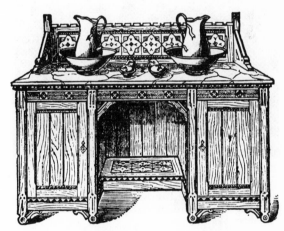

. . . A MARBLE-TOPPED WASHSTAND WITH A JUG AND BASIN OF PLAIN OR FLOWERED CHINA . . .

17 Dr. Wolff disagrees; he believes the room described in "The Adventure of the Dying Detective" to be "the sitting-room converted to a sick room." Our view would seem to be borne out however, by Watson's statement that he heard "the opening and the closing of the bedroom door."

There has hitherto been some discussion as to whether or not a bathroom opened off Holmes' bedroom (or any other bedroom at 221 Baker Street). In "A Scandal in Bohemia" Watson tells us that Holmes returned to the Baker Street sitting room in the character of "a drunken groom, ill-kempt and side-whiskered with an inflamed face and disreputable clothes." "With a nod he vanished into the bedroom, whence he emerged in five minutes tweed-suited and respectable, as of old." But Holmes of course used his washstand to remove his makeup, not a bathroom: bathrooms, with hot water laid on, were not common until the very end of the nineteenth century. Where a room was reserved for bathing alone, it was usually an ordinary small room converted for the purpose, containing a fireplace, a wood-rimmed metal bath, and sometimes a shower bath of a sort. The water was heated by the kitchen fire. When Holmes or Watson took a bath (we know that Watson took one in *The Sign of the Four*) he would have done so in his bedroom, in a hip bath with a high back, or in a flat shallow pan of metal painted to look like wood. This was kept, when not in use, in the maid's closet or under the bed. When wanted it was set before the fire, with large towels spread under it to protect the carpet from splashes. It was filled with hot water brought up from the basement in metal cans, and in it the bather sat soaking and warming himself in comfort, without having to worry about keeping others waiting if he dallied too long. A screen, or covered towel horse, behind the bather protected him from draughts; and, when he was ready to get out, there were towels already warming before the fire in which to wrap himself. Other essential facilities for comfort and sanitation were provided by commodes, kept usually in the washstand.

And now let us climb the stairs to the English *second*, American *third*, floor of the house. Here we will find Watson's bedroom**18** (at the back) and Mrs. Hudson's bedroom (at the front). (The maid, we think, slept on the top floor, with the two lumber rooms.) It will be remembered that Watson in *A Study in Scarlet* heard both the landlady and the maid preceding him up to bed when he was awaiting Holmes' return one night in the sitting room.

Watson's bedroom has four ascertainable features: a view of a plane tree ("The Problem of Thor Bridge"), a shaving mirror ("The Boscombe Valley Mystery"), a clock on the mantel, and therefore a fireplace ("The Adventure of the Speckled Band") and, of course a bed ("The Adventure of the Speckled Band," "The Adventure of the Abbey Grange"). Surely it was always very neat and tidy, as became an ex-army officer.

Watson's bedroom was also the "spare" bedroom. It was available to Percy Phelps at the time of "The Naval Treaty," for Watson was not then living at 221 Baker Street. Some years later, however, when Watson was back in residence ("The Adventure of the Golden Pince-Nez"), Inspector Stanley Hopkins of Scotland Yard had to make do on the sofa in the sitting room, drawn up before the fire.

This, then, was 221 Baker Street. For Holmes and Watson, in every way, it was indeed "a most desirable residence."

WATSON'S BEDROOM

The only known illustration showing this room is the work of the Dutch draughtsman and cartoonist L. J. Jordaan, executed in 1909 for a Holmes-Watson pastiche.

18 By many references: "Sherlock Holmes was already at breakfast when I came down" ("The Five Orange Pips"); "I . . . was ready in a few minutes to accompany my friend down to the sitting-room" ("The Adventure of the Speckled Band"); "When I came down to breakfast in the morning" ("The Adventure of the Beryl Coronet"); "I descended to breakfast" ("The Problem of Thor Bridge").

12

WHAT IS IT THAT WE LOVE IN SHERLOCK HOLMES?

"What is it that we love in Sherlock Holmes?"

The late Edgar W. Smith asked, and answered, that question in an editorial first published in the *Baker Street Journal*'s second issue.

"We love the times in which he lived, of course," Edgar wrote, "the half-remembered, half-forgotten times of snug Victorian illusion, of gaslit comfort and contentment, of perfect dignity and grace. The world was poised precariously in balance, and rude disturbances were coming with the years; but those who moved upon the scene were very sure that all was well: that nothing ever would be any worse nor ever could be any better. There was no threat to righteousness and justice and the cause of peace on earth except from such as Moriarty and the lesser villains in his train. The cycle of events had come full turn, and the times were ripe for living—and for being lost. It is because their loss was suffered before they had been fully lived that they are times to which our hearts and longings cling.

"And we love the place in which the Master moved and had his being: the England of those times, fat with the fruits of her achievements, but strong and daring still with the spirit of imperial adventure. The seas were pounding, then as now, upon her coasts; the winds swept in across the moors, and fog came down on London. It was a stout and pleasant land, full of the flavor of the age; and it is small wonder that we who claim it in our thoughts should look to Baker Street as its epitome. For there the cabs rolled up before a certain door, and hurried steps were heard upon the stair, and England and her times had rendezvous within a hallowed room, at once familiar and mysterious. . . .

"But there is more than time and space and the yearning for things gone by to account for what we feel toward Sherlock Holmes. Not only there and then, but here and now, he stands before us as a symbol—a symbol, if you please, of all that we are not, but ever would be. His figure is sufficiently remote to make our secret aspirations for transference seem unshameful, yet close enough to give them plausibility. We see him as the fine expression of our urge to trample evil and to set aright the wrongs with which the world is plagued. He is Galahad and Socrates, bringing high adventure to our dull existences and calm, judicial logic to our biased minds. He is the success of all our failures; the bold escape from our imprisonment.

EDGAR W. SMITH, 1894–1960

From the Sherlockian Hall of Fame.

"Or, if this be too complex a psychological basis to account for our devotion, let it be said, more simply, that he is the personification of something in us that we have lost, or never had. For it is not Sherlock Holmes who sits in Baker Street, comfortable, competent and self-assured; it is ourselves who are there, full of a tremendous capacity for wisdom, complacent in the presence of our humble Watson, conscious of a warm well-being and a timeless, imperishable content. The easy chair in the room is drawn up to the hearthstone of our very hearts—it is *our* tobacco in the Persian slipper, and *our* violin lying so carelessly across the knees—it is *we* who hear the pounding on the stairs and the knock upon the door. The swirling fog without and the acrid smoke within bite deep indeed, for we taste them even now. And the time and place and all the great events are near and dear to us not because our memories call them forth in pure nostalgia, but because they are a part of us today.

"That is the Sherlock Holmes we love—the Holmes implicit and eternal in ourselves."

It is to the memory of Edgar Wadsworth Smith, April 1, 1894–September 17, 1960—one of "the best and the wisest" men it has ever been our great good fortune to know—that this edition of his favorite reading is dedicated.

WILLIAM S. BARING-GOULD

Stonycroft
East Woods Road
Pound Ridge, New York

II. THE EARLY HOLMES

[July and September, 1874, and Thursday, October 2, 1879]

"These are the records of your early work,
then?" I asked. "I have often wished
that I had notes of those cases."

"Yes, my boy; these were all done prematurely,
before my biographer had come to glorify me."

—*"The Musgrave Ritual"*

. . . IN THE COUNTRY OF THE BROADS

Photograph by J. Allan Cash, F.I.B.P., F.R.P.S., for *The Fens*, by
Alan Bloom, London: Robert Hale, Ltd., 1953.

13

THE *GLORIA SCOTT*

[Sunday, July 12, to Tuesday, August 4, and Tuesday, September 22, 1874]

" I HAVE some papers here," said my friend, Sherlock Holmes, as we sat one winter's night on **1** either side of the fire, " which I really think, Watson, it would be worth your while to glance over. These are the documents in the extraordinary case of the *Gloria Scott*, and this is the message which struck Justice of the Peace Trevor dead with horror when he read it."

He had picked from a drawer a little tarnished cylinder, and, undoing the tape, he handed me a short note scrawled upon a half sheet of slate-grey paper.

" The supply of game for London is going steadily up," it ran. " Head-keeper Hudson, we believe, has been now told to receive all orders for fly-paper, and for preservation of your hen pheasant's life."

As I glanced up from reading this enigmatical message I saw Holmes chuckling at the expression upon my face.

" You look a little bewildered," said he.

" I cannot see how such a message as this could inspire horror. It seems to me to be rather grotesque than otherwise."

" Very likely. Yet the fact remains that the reader, who was a fine, robust old man, was knocked clean down by it, as if it had been the butt-end of a pistol."

" You arouse my curiosity," said I. " But why did you say just now that there were very particular reasons why I should study this case ? "

" Because it was the first in which I was ever engaged." **2**

I had often endeavoured to elicit from my companion what had first turned his mind in the direction of criminal research, but I had never caught him before in a communicative humour. Now he sat forward in his armchair, and spread out the documents upon his knees. Then he lit his pipe and sat for some time smoking and **3** turning them over.

" You never heard me talk of Victor Trevor ? " he asked. " He was the only friend I made during the two years that I was at college. I was never a very sociable fellow, Watson, always rather fond of moping in my rooms and working out my own little methods of thought, so that I never mixed much with the men of my year. Bar

1 *one winter's night.* The winter of 1887–1888 suggests itself: after Watson's return to Baker Street, following the death of his first wife (see our Chapter 21, "Now, Watson, the Fair Sex Is Your Department"). It would be like Holmes to try to distract the doctor's mind from his grief by telling him about these early exploits—"The Musgrave Ritual" as well as "The *Gloria Scott*." The late H. W. Bell, on the other hand, cast his vote for the winter of 1886–1887, and Mr. George W. Welch concurred with Mr. Bell in his essay on "The Terai Planter."

2 *the first in which I was ever engaged.*" Neither Holmes nor Watson dates the adventure of "The *Gloria Scott*" for us, but we suggest that it fell into two stages: *Sunday, July 12, to Tuesday, August 4, and Tuesday, September 22, 1874.* Sayers (with a leaning toward 1873) would date it in 1872. Blakeney, Brend, Davies, Folsom, and Harrison would date it 1873—as would Metcalfe (with a leaning toward 1874). Bell and Smith would date the adventure in 1875; Andrew, Christ, Pattrick, Petersen and Zeisler in 1876.

3 *Then he lit his pipe.* In his scholarly monograph on Holmes and tobacco ("No Fire Without Some Smoke"), Mr. John L. Hicks has written that: "No one can seriously doubt that the Master preferred a pipe to cigars and cigarettes. He smokes a pipe in thirty-five of the sixty cases in the Canon, probably does in three others, and in still another talks about his pipe without, as far as the reader knows, actually lighting it. He smokes nothing but a pipe in twenty-nine or, if one includes the doubtful instances, thirty-two. He indulges in cigars definitely in eight tales and probably in one other, and in cigarettes definitely in nine and probably in one other. In only ten cases does he smoke cigars and/or cigarettes but not a pipe. In eleven tales there is no mention of smoking by Holmes, but there is no reason to believe that the great man stopped the habit at any time, especially since these cases are scattered throughout his career. Holmes very likely smoked a pipe during the adventures recorded in the eleven tales in which there is no reference to smoking, as well as during those of the ten in which Watson names cigars and cigarettes. . . . Briar, clay and cherry-wood pipes are . . . the only ones mentioned in the Sacred Writings. . . . Most admirers of Sherlock Holmes have believed that his favorite pipe was made of clay . . . but the evidence supports the theory that Holmes liked a briar pipe better than any other kind."

It will be noted that neither Holmes nor Watson ever mentioned a pipe with a *curved* stem; indeed, Mr. John Dickson Carr has stated that the curved pipe was unknown in England until the time of the Boer War (1889). Why, then has the curved pipe—a calabash or a meerschaum, for example—become a Holmesian trademark? Because Gillette, in playing the role of Holmes, found it difficult to speak his lines with a *straight* pipe between his lips; because Steele worked from photographs of Gillette as Holmes in drawing his famous illustrations for *Collier's Magazine*. (In Paget's illustrations for the *Strand*, all of Holmes' pipes had straight stems—as Professor Christ pointed out in his essay, "The Pipe and the Cap.")

Holmes must also have been a snuff-taker, else there would have been little reason for the King of Bohemia to present him with a snuffbox ("A Case of Identity").

4 *Bar fencing and boxing.* Conan Doyle himself never missed an opportunity to box with anyone who cared to take him on. He also played first-class cricket, represented his county at football, reached the third round of the Amateur Billiards Championship, was a member of the British motor-racing team in the Prince Henry Tour of 1911, and helped introduce skiing to Switzerland. In 1909, Conan Doyle received, but declined, an invitation to referee the forthcoming World Heavy-weight Championship fight between Jim Jeffries and the Negro contender, Jack Johnson.

Those who believe, as your editor does, that the university of "The *Gloria Scott*" was Oxford have pointed to the fact that there was an excellent school of boxing there, according to Mr. E. B. Mitchell, the *Badminton Library*'s authority on boxing and sparring in 1889.

5 *Norfolk.* Norfolk—a land of fens and broad and swampy, lush meadowlands and flat, fertile farms —is said to be the richest county in England, and is certainly one that has changed the least since Holmes visited it in 1874 and again in 1898 ("The Adventure of the Dancing Men"). Norfolk is a maritime county in the *east* of England, yet Holmes later calls Norfolk "the north." Christopher Morley once commented that this was like calling Montreal "the west," and Mr. (later Sir) Paul H. Gore-Booth wrote in "The Journeys of Sherlock Holmes" that: "No normal Briton refers to Norfolk as 'the north.' " This is not an isolated

4 fencing and boxing I had few athletic tastes, and then my line of study was quite distinct from that of the other fellows, so that we had no points of contact at all. Trevor was the only man I knew, and that only through the accident of his bull-terrier freezing on to my ankle one morning as I went down to chapel.

" It was a prosaic way of forming a friendship, but it was effective. I was laid by the heels for ten days, and Trevor used to come in to inquire after me. At first it was only a minute's chat, but soon his visits lengthened, and before the end of the term we were close friends. He was a hearty, full-blooded fellow, full of spirit and energy, the very opposite to me in most respects ; but we found we had some subjects in common, and it was a bond of union when I learned that he was as friendless as I. Finally, he invited me down to his father's place at **5** Donnithorpe, in Norfolk, and I accepted his hospitality **6** for a month of the long vacation.

" Old Trevor was evidently a man of some wealth and **7** consideration, a J.P. and a landed proprietor. Donni- **8** thorpe is a little hamlet just to the north of Langmere, in **9** the country of the Broads. The house was an old-fashioned, wide-spread, oak-beamed, brick building, with a fine lime-lined avenue leading up to it. There was excellent wild-duck shooting in the fens, remarkably good **10-11** fishing, a small but select library, taken over, as I understood, from a former occupant, and a tolerable cook, so that it would be a fastidious man who could not put in a pleasant month there.

" Trevor senior was a widower, and my friend was his only son. There had been a daughter, I heard, but she **12** had died of diphtheria while on a visit to Birmingham. The father interested me extremely. He was a man of little culture, but with a considerable amount of rude strength both physically and mentally. He knew hardly any books, but he had travelled far, had seen much of the world, and had remembered all that he had learned. In person he was a thick-set, burly man, with a shock of grizzled hair, a brown, weather-beaten face, and blue eyes

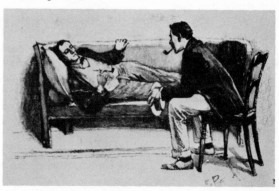

". . . TREVOR USED TO COME IN TO INQUIRE AFTER ME."

Illustration by Sidney Paget for the *Strand Magazine*, April, 1893.

which were keen to the verge of fierceness.   Yet he had a reputation for kindness and charity on the country-side, and was noted for the leniency of his sentences from the bench.

" One evening, shortly after my arrival, we were sitting over a glass of port after dinner, when young Trevor **13** began to talk about those habits of observation and inference which I had already formed into a system, although I had not yet appreciated the part which they were to play in my life.   The old man evidently thought that his son was exaggerating in his description of one or two trivial feats which I had performed.

" ' Come now, Mr. Holmes,' said he, laughing good-humouredly, ' I'm an excellent subject, if you can deduce anything from me.'

" ' I fear there is not very much,' I answered. ' I might suggest that you have gone about in fear of some personal attack within the last twelve months.'

" The laugh faded from his lips, and he stared at me in great surprise.

" ' Well, that's true enough,' said he. ' You know, Victor,' turning to his son, ' when we broke up that poaching gang, they swore to knife us ; and Sir Edward **14** Hoby has actually been attacked.   I've always been on my guard since then, though I have no idea how you know it.'

" ' You have a very handsome stick,' I answered. ' By the inscription, I observed that you had not had it more than a year.   But you have taken some pains to bore the head of it and pour melted lead into the hole, so as to make it a formidable weapon.   I argued that you would not take such precautions unless you had some danger to fear.'

" ' Anything else ? ' he asked, smiling.

" ' You have boxed a good deal in your youth.'

" ' Right again.   How did you know it ?   Is my nose knocked a little out of the straight ? '

" ' No,' said I. ' It is your ears.   They have the peculiar flattening and thickening which marks the boxing **15** man.'

" ' Anything else ? '

" ' You have done a great deal of digging, by your callosities.' **16**

" ' Made all my money at the gold-fields.'

" ' You have been in New Zealand.'

" ' Right again.'

" ' You have visited Japan.'

" ' Quite true.'

" ' And you have been most intimately associated with someone whose initials were J. A., and whom you afterwards were eager to entirely forget.'

" Mr. Trevor stood slowly up, fixed his large blue eyes on me with a strange, wild stare, and then pitched forward on his face among the nutshells which strewed the cloth, in a dead faint.

" You can imagine, Watson, how shocked both his son and I were.   His attack did not last long, however, for when we undid his collar and sprinkled the water from one of the finger-glasses over his face, he gave a gasp or two and sat up.

instance (see "The Adventure of the Priory School"), and we can only conclude, with Sir Paul, that, for Holmes, "the north began some 120 miles from London in a generally northerly direction."

6 *the long vacation*. What we in America would call the summer vacation; in England, a period, roughly from July 1st to October 1st, during which a university is formally closed.

7 *a J.P.* Holmes has already told us that Trevor Senior was a *Justice of the Peace*—a subordinate magistrate appointed (first in 1327) to keep the peace in a specified district. In Great Britain and the United States his principal duties are to administer summary justice in minor cases, to commit for trial in a superior court on cause shown, and, in Great Britain, to grant licenses and act, if a county justice, as judge at quarter sessions.

8 *a little hamlet just to the north of Langmere*. Neither "Donnithorpe" nor "Langmere" is to be found on the map, but Mr. N. P. Metcalfe suggests (in "Oxford or Cambridge or Both?") that *Fordham*, later mentioned as the name of the doctor, "is also the name of a village near Downham Market in the fen country" and therefore may be helpful in identifying the true site of Squire Trevor's home.

9 *the Broads*. Generally, in England, broads are pieces of fresh water, formed by the broadening out of a river, or a marshy territory, with plentiful waterways.

10 *remarkably good fishing*. We see Holmes as a fisherman again in "The Adventure of Shoscombe Old Place."

11 *a small but select library*. An early example of Holmes' consuming interest in books. "I am an omniverous reader," he tells us in "The Adventure of the Lion's Mane." In Baker Street he would spend many happy hours "buried among his old books" ("A Scandal in Bohemia"). This makes nonsense of Watson's early judgment, in *A Study in Scarlet*, that Holmes' knowledge of literature was "nil." It is of course possible to argue, as Mr. Bell pointed out in *Sherlock Holmes and Dr. Watson: The Chronology of Their Adventures*, "that Holmes' knowledge of literature in 1881 was in fact 'nil' [and that] it was Watson's influence and example that affected the change. But this is to take seriously Holmes' jocular reference to Watson as a man of letters ('The Adventure of Wisteria Lodge'); it is ascribing too much influence to a man whose preference ran to yellow-backed novels ('The Boscombe Valley Mystery') and the sea stories of Clark Russell ('The Five Orange Pips')." In fairness to Watson, however, it should be noted that it was he who tagged *A Study in Scarlet* with an apt quotation from Horace.

12 *but she had died of diptheria while on a visit to Birmingham.* "I should never marry myself, lest I bias my judgment," Holmes says in *The Sign of the Four*. But many distinguished commentators hold that Holmes *was* married, or at least had fallen deeply in love, at an early age:

Dr. Richard Asher in "Holmes and the Fair Sex": "From [Holmes' often later-expressed] attitude to women I think it is probable that early in his life he had an unfortunate love affair."

The late Elmer Davis in "The Real Sherlock Holmes": "Must we not suppose that in youth [Holmes] was strongly attracted to some blameless nitwit, perhaps the daughter of a neighboring country family; and that the discovery, happily not too belated, of her stupidity sickened him not only of her, but of an emotion which such a woman—even such a woman—could inspire?"

And Mr. S. C. Roberts, reflecting on the "curious sentence" given us here, has written ("Sherlock Holmes and the Fair Sex"): "Assuming, for the moment, that Trevor's sister was in fact alive at the time of [Holmes' meeting with Victor Trevor, and] assuming, further, that Holmes' specific, and yet wholly superfluous reference, conceals an indication of some closer interest than is conveyed in the bald sentence in the narrative . . . , are we not justified in the conjecture, to put it no higher, that Holmes was in fact attracted to Miss Trevor and that his hopes and affections were rudely shattered by the ravages of diptheria in Birmingham in the seventies?"

Miss Esther Longfellow ("The Distaff Side of Baker Street") scouts the conjecture that Holmes had any special interest in Miss Trevor, but she, too, believes that Holmes "was once married—at an early age—emerging shortly as a widower and that slightly cynical but undisillusioned man we know."

(See also "The Adventure of the Illustrious Client," Note 17.)

13 *a glass of port.* Holmes washed his supper down with a long draught of water in "The Five Orange Pips," but the attentive reader will have to look long and hard to find any other instance when he drank this liquid. "We may presume that Holmes used [water] for washing purposes, and perhaps, to a limited extent, for his chemical studies," Mr. Jørgen Cold wrote in "What Did Sherlock Holmes Drink?", but Holmes obviously preferred something a little stronger than water to drink whenever he could get it. Holmes, like many Englishmen, had a special fondness for port: he served it to his guests before the chase down the Thames in *The Sign of the Four* and he spoke highly (for Holmes) of the quality of the port served at the "Chequers" in "The Adventure of the Creeping Man."

14 *that poaching gang.* Under English law, it is unlawful to take game (poach), especially at night, on the lands of another; as a Justice of the Peace,

" 'Ah boys !' said he, forcing a smile. 'I hope I haven't frightened you. Strong as I look, there is a weak place in my heart, and it does not take much to knock me over. I don't know how you manage this, Mr. Holmes, but it seems to me that all the detectives of fact and of fancy would be children in your hands. That's your line of life, sir, and you may take the word of a man who has seen something of the world.'

"And that recommendation, with the exaggerated estimate of my ability with which he prefaced it, was, if you will believe me, Watson, the very first thing which ever made me feel that a profession might be made out of what had up to that time been the merest hobby. At the moment, however, I was too much concerned at the sudden illness of my host to think of anything else.

" 'I hope that I have said nothing to pain you,' said I.

" 'Well, you certainly touched upon rather a tender point. Might I ask how you know and how much you know ?' He spoke now in a half-jesting fashion, but a look of terror still lurked at the back of his eyes.

" 'It is simplicity itself,' said I. 'When you bared your arm to draw that fish into the boat, I saw that **17** " J. A." had been tattooed in the bend of the elbow. The letters were still legible, but it was perfectly clear from their blurred appearance, and from the staining of the skin round them, that efforts had been made to obliterate them. It was obvious, then, that those initials had once been very familiar to you, and that you had afterwards wished to forget them.'

" 'What an eye you have !' he cried, with a sigh of relief. 'It is just as you say. But we won't talk of it. Of all ghosts the ghosts of our old loves are the worst. Come into the billiard-room and have a quiet cigar.'

" From that day, amid all his cordiality, there was always a touch of suspicion in Mr. Trevor's manner towards me. Even his son remarked it. 'You've given the governor such a turn,' said he, 'that he'll never be sure again of what you know and what you don't know.' He did not mean to show it, I am sure, but it was so strongly in his mind that it peeped out at every action. At last I became so convinced that I was causing him uneasiness that I drew my visit to a close. On the very day, however, before I left, an incident occurred which proved in the sequel to be of importance.

" We were sitting out upon the lawn on garden chairs, the three of us, basking in the sun and admiring the view across the Broads, when the maid came out to say that there was a man at the door who wanted to see Mr. Trevor.

" 'What is his name ?' asked my host.

" 'He would not give any.'

" 'What does he want, then ?'

" 'He says that you know him, and that he only wants a moment's conversation.'

" 'Show him round here.' An instant afterwards there appeared a little weazened fellow, with a cringing manner and a shambling style of walking. He wore an open jacket, with a splotch of tar on the sleeve, a red and

"... FIXED HIS LARGE BLUE EYES ON ME WITH A STRANGE, WILD STARE ..."

Illustration by William H. Hyde for *Harper's Weekly*, April 15, 1893. Of Hyde's illustrations, the late James Montgomery wrote (*A Study in Pictures*): "[They] are striking in their effect. Hyde chose to depict some of the most dramatic moments of the stories, but seemed to have a strange aversion to Holmes himself. In all his twenty-one pictures the Master is portrayed only five times, and in two of these he is seated in a chair with his back turned toward us. . . . Holmes [in this illustration] is shown as a mere stripling—almost too immature to make his amazingly deductive powers believable, and certainly far too young to be the college chum of the sophisticated Victor seated at his left. Of all recorded pictorial representations of the Master this is assuredly the earliest of his tender years."

black check shirt, dungaree trousers, and heavy boots badly worn. His face was thin and brown and crafty, with a perpetual smile upon it, which showed an irregular line of yellow teeth, and his crinkled hands were half closed in a way that is distinctive of sailors. As he came slouching across the lawn I heard Mr. Trevor make a sort of hiccoughing noise in his throat, and, jumping out of his chair, he ran into the house. He was back in a moment, and I smelt a strong reek of brandy as he passed me.

" ' Well, my man,' said he, ' what can I do for you ? '

" The sailor stood looking at him with puckered eyes, and with the same loose-lipped smile upon his face.

" ' You don't know me ? ' he asked.

" ' Why, dear me, it is surely Hudson ! ' said Mr. **18** Trevor, in a tone of surprise.

" ' Hudson it is, sir,' said the seaman. ' Why, it's thirty year and more since I saw you last. Here you are in your house, and me still picking my salt meat out of the harness cask.' **19**

" ' Tut, you will find that I have not forgotten old times,' cried Mr. Trevor, and, walking towards the sailor, he said something in a low voice. ' Go into the kitchen,' he continued out loud, ' and you will get food and drink. I have no doubt that I shall find you a situation.'

" ' Thank you, sir,' said the seaman, touching his forelock. ' I'm just off a two-yearer in an eight-knot tramp, **20** short handed at that, and I wants a rest. I thought I'd get it either with Mr. Beddoes or with you.'

Trevor senior would be bound to put down the practice within his jurisdiction. But as Mr. Welch, in "The Terai Planter," has asked: "Why should [Trevor senior's] treatment of 'poachers' lead to vows of vengeance? He was noted for the leniency of his sentences upon other wrongdoers."

15 *which marks the boxing man.*' But the late H. T. Webster pointed out ("Observations of Sherlock Holmes As an Athlete and Sportsman") that "in his early days, Holmes knew so little about wrestling that he was unaware that wrestlers as well as boxers have cauliflower ears . . ." Holmes was later to write two short monographs on the subject of the human ear ("The Cardboard Box").

16 *by your callosities.*' And Holmes was later to write "a curious little work" upon the influence of a trade upon the form of the hand (*The Sign of the Four*).

17 *tattooed in the bend of the elbow.* Holmes was later to write upon the subject of tattoo marks also ("The Red-Headed League").

18 *it is surely Hudson!*' "It has never been pointed out," Christopher Morley wrote in "Was Sherlock Holmes an American?", "that Holmes never admitted to Watson why he chose Mrs. Hudson's lodgings. She was the widow of the ruffian Hudson who blackmailed old Mr. Trevor—and so more than ever 'a long-suffering woman.' " And Mr. Manly Wade Wellman has added ("The Great Man's Great Son"): "It is the careless habit of many to consider [Mrs. Hudson] a widow, but Watson never says so. Yet Mr. Hudson was plainly not living at 221B Baker Street. This adds up to estrangement, and a good thing, too; for [he] was worthy of no woman, least of all of his wondrous wife. We know that once he lounged, a weazened, mocking, yellow-fanged blackmailer, around the beautiful home of Squire Trevor in Donnithorpe." (Mr. Wellman even went so far as to suggest that the Hudson of "The *Gloria Scott*" was also the Morse Hudson of "The Adventure of the Six Napoleons"—then an art dealer in the Kennington Road.) This view has been denied, however, and by Mrs. Hudson herself: "I never saw that bad Hudson and I certainly never wanted to. A convict indeed! My Hudson was a respectable tradesman, I'd have you know, in a very small way in Peckham, and he died when I was barely 25 years old" (Miss Zasu Pitts, in "Mrs. Hudson Speaks").

19 *the harness cask.*' A cask or tub with a rimmed cover used on board ship for keeping salt meats for current consumption.

20 *a two-yearer in an eight-knot tramp.* A two-year service on a freight-carrying vessel running on no regular line or timetable, with a maximum speed of eight knots.

Illustration by Sidney Paget for the *Strand Magazine*, April, 1893. Note that Holmes seems to be wearing a *light blue* ribbon on his straw hat. This would indicate that he was, at the time of "The *Gloria Scott*," a student at Cambridge rather than Oxford—a point first noted by Christopher Morley in "Was Sherlock Holmes an American?"

21 *my London rooms*. There is nothing to prevent an undergraduate who has the means to do so from taking rooms in London in order to pursue a course of study during the long vacation, as the late Dorothy L. Sayers pointed out in "Holmes' College Career." It would take means: to maintain such a *pied-à-terre* in town, Holmes must have been fairly well off at this time, as the Messrs. J. H. and Humfrey Michell pointed out in "Sherlock Holmes the Chemist." It is very much to be doubted that these "London rooms" are the same as those in Montague Street which Holmes mentions in "The Musgrave Ritual." True, he speaks of the Montague Street rooms as those which he took when he "first" came up to London, but he undoubtedly meant the "first" in that case to be followed by "to establish myself in my career after I had completed my formal education."

22 *a few experiments in organic chemistry*. "What was Holmes' particular interest in chemical research?" the Michells asked in "Sherlock Holmes the Chemist." "It is not hard to answer that question, and we may say unhesitatingly—the coal tar derivatives [which Holmes studied in Montpellier during the period of the Great Hiatus; see "The Adventure of the Empty House"]." The Michells believe that Holmes went to London to be near the works recently established at Harrow by the brilliant chemist W. H. Perkin. Until 1856 nearly all dyes were made from plants or mosses, but in that year Perkin, only eighteen years old at the time, and an assistant at the Royal College of Chemistry in London, made a remarkable discovery. Experimenting with artificial quinine, he produced a dirty black powder that did not seem to be of any particular interest. He washed and liquefied it, however, and the totally unexpected result was a strong mauve dye. This was the beginning of aniline dyes, produced from coal tar. Perkin borrowed money from his father to set up

" 'Ah!' cried Mr. Trevor, 'you know where Mr. Beddoes is?'

" 'Bless you, sir, I know where all my old friends are,' said the fellow, with a sinister smile, and slouched off after the maid to the kitchen.   Mr. Trevor mumbled something to us about having been shipmates with the man when he was going back to the diggings, and then, leaving us on the lawn, he went indoors.   An hour later, when we entered the house we found him stretched dead drunk upon the dining-room sofa.   The whole incident left a most ugly impression upon my mind, and I was not sorry next day to leave Donnithorpe behind me, for I felt that my presence must be a source of embarrassment to my friend.

" All this occurred during the first month of the long **21** vacation.   I went up to my London rooms, where I spent seven weeks working out a few experiments in organic **22** chemistry.   One day, however, when the autumn was far advanced and the vacation drawing to a close, I received a telegram from my friend imploring me to return to Donnithorpe, and saying that he was in great need of my advice and assistance.   Of course I dropped everything and set out for the north once more.

" He met me with the dog-cart at the station, and I **23** saw at a glance that the last two months had been very trying ones for him.   He had grown thin and careworn, and had lost the loud, cheery manner for which he had been remarkable.

" 'The governor is dying,' were the first words he said.

" 'Impossible!' I cried.   'What is the matter?'

" 'Apoplexy. Nervous shock. He's been on the verge all day.   I doubt if we shall find him alive.'

" I was, as you may think, Watson, horrified at this unexpected news.

" 'What has caused it?' I asked.

" 'Ah, that is the point.   Jump in, and we can talk it over while we drive.   You remember that fellow who came upon the evening before you left us?'

" 'Perfectly.'

" 'Do you know who it was that we let into the house that day?'

" 'I have no idea.'

" 'It was the Devil, Holmes!' he cried.

" I stared at him in astonishment.

" 'Yes; it was the Devil himself.   We have not had a peaceful hour since—not one.   The governor has never held up his head from that evening, and now the life has been crushed out of him, and his heart broken all through this accursed Hudson.'

" 'What power had he, then?'

" ' Ah, that is what I would give so much to know. The kindly, charitable, good old governor ! How could he have fallen into the clutches of such a ruffian ? But I am so glad that you have come, Holmes. I trust very much to your judgment and discretion, and I know that you will advise me for the best.'

" We were dashing along the smooth, white country road, with the long stretch of Broads in front of us glimmering in the red light of the setting sun. From a grove upon our left I could already see the high chimneys and the flag-staff which marked the squire's dwelling.

" ' My father made the fellow gardener,' said my companion, ' and then, as that did not satisfy him, he was promoted to be butler. The house seemed to be at his mercy, and he wandered about and did what he chose in it. The maids complained of his drunken habits and his vile language. The dad raised their wages all round to recompense them for the annoyance. The fellow would take the boat and my father's best gun and treat himself to little shooting parties. And all this with such a sneering, leering, insolent face, that I would have knocked him down twenty times over if he had been a man of my own age. I tell you, Holmes, I have had to keep a tight hold upon myself all this time, and now I am asking myself whether, if I had let myself go a little more, I might not have been a wiser man.

" ' Well, matters went from bad to worse with us, and this animal, Hudson, became more and more intrusive, until at last, on his making some insolent reply to my father in my presence one day, I took him by the shoulder and turned him out of the room. He slunk away with a livid face, and two venomous eyes which uttered more threats than his tongue could do. I don't know what passed between the poor dad and him after that, but the dad came to me next day and asked me whether I would mind apologizing to Hudson. I refused, as you can imagine, and asked my father how he could allow such a wretch to take such liberties with himself and his household.

" ' " Ah, my boy," said he, " it is all very well to talk, but you don't know how I am placed. But you shall know, Victor. I'll see that you shall know, come what may ! You wouldn't believe harm of your poor old father, would you, lad ? " He was very much moved, and shut himself up in the study all day, where I could see through the window that he was writing busily.

" ' That evening there came what seemed to be a grand release, for Hudson told us that he was going to leave us. He walked into the dining-room as we sat after dinner and announced his intention in the thick voice of a half-drunken man.

" ' " I've had enough of Norfolk," said he, " I'll run down to Mr. Beddoes, in Hampshire. He'll be as glad **24** to see me as you were, I dare say."

" ' " You're not going away in an unkind spirit, Hudson, I hope ? " said my father, with a tameness which made my blood boil.

" ' " I've not had my 'pology," said he, sulkily, glancing in my direction.

his factory, and in a very short time the new purples became the rage. Gowns, gloves, hats, feathers, ribbons were all purple; one writer in 1859 declared that "We shall soon have purple omnibuses and purple houses." Later experiments produced greens, blues, magentas, and other shades, and the coal-tar industry was firmly established. At first the new shades were much harsher than those made from the old vegetable dyes and, as a result, the fashionable Victorian lady went about in crude, startling colors that would be considered in very bad taste today.

23 *the last two months.* Holmes has already told us that *seven weeks* elapsed between his first and second visit to Donnithorpe. These seven weeks embraced the latter part of August and the early part of September—Holmes' "two months."

24 *Hampshire.* Or Hants, but officially Southampton since 1888. Hampshire is an undulating region in the South of England devoted to sheep raising and dairy farming, but it also has shipbuilding and a large maritime trade.

"HE MET ME WITH THE DOG-CART AT THE STATION."

The dog-cart shown above was not a cart drawn by a large dog, as some might think, but a sportsman's vehicle: a two-wheeled, one-horse cart with two seats back to back, the rear seat being so constructed that it could be shut to form a box for carrying a dog.

25 *bearing the Fordingbridge postmark.* Holmes' second visit to Donnithorpe could not have been made upon a Monday, because the letter to Trevor senior had been delivered—by post—on the preceding day.

" ' " I'VE NOT HAD MY 'POLOGY," SAID HE, SULKILY.' "

Illustration by Sidney Paget for the *Strand Magazine*, April, 1893.

" ' " Victor, you will acknowledge that you have used this worthy fellow rather roughly ? " said the dad, turning to me.

" ' " On the contrary, I think that we have both shown extraordinary patience towards him," I answered.

" ' " Oh, you do, do you ? " he snarled. ' Very good, mate. We'll see about that ! " He slouched out of the room, and half an hour afterwards left the house, leaving my father in a state of pitiable nervousness. Night after night I heard him pacing his room, and it was just as he was recovering his confidence that the blow did at last fall.'

" ' And how ? ' I asked, eagerly.

" ' In a most extraordinary fashion. A letter arrived for my father yesterday evening, bearing the Fording-**25** bridge postmark. My father read it, clapped both his hands to his head, and began running round the room in little circles like a man who has been driven out of his senses. When I at last drew him down on to the sofa, his mouth and eyelids were all puckered on one side, and I saw that he had a stroke. Dr. Fordham came over at once, and we put him to bed ; but the paralysis has spread, he has shown no sign of returning consciousness, and I think that we shall hardly find him alive.'

" ' You horrify me, Trevor ! ' I cried. ' What, then, could have been in this letter to cause so dreadful a result ? '

" ' Nothing. There lies the inexplicable part of it. The message was absurd and trivial. Ah, my God, it is as I feared ! '

" As he spoke we came round the curve of the avenue, and saw in the fading light that every blind in the house had been drawn down. As we dashed up to the door, my friend's face convulsed with grief, a gentleman in black emerged from it.

" ' When did it happen, doctor ? ' asked Trevor.

" ' Almost immediately after you left.'

" ' Did he recover consciousness ? '

" ' For an instant before the end.'

" ' Any message for me ? '

" ' Only that the papers were in the back drawer of the Japanese cabinet.'

" My friend ascended with the doctor to the chamber of death, while I remained in the study, turning the whole matter over and over in my head, and feeling as sombre as ever I had done in my life. What was the past of this Trevor : pugilist, traveller, and gold-digger ? and how had he placed himself in the power of this acid-faced seaman ? Why, too, should he faint at an allusion to the half-effaced initials upon his arm, and die of fright when he had a letter from Fordingbridge ? Then I remembered that Fordingbridge was in Hampshire, and that this Mr. Beddoes, whom the seaman had gone to visit, and presumably to blackmail, had also been mentioned as living in Hampshire. The letter, then, might either come from Hudson, the seaman, saying that he had betrayed the guilty secret which appeared to exist, or it might come from Beddoes, warning an old confederate that such a betrayal was imminent. So far it seemed clear enough. But, then, how could the letter be trivial and grotesque as described by the son ? He must have mis-read it. If so, it must have been one of those ingenious secret codes which mean one thing while they seem to **26** mean another. I must see this letter. If there were a hidden meaning in it, I was confident that I could pluck it forth. For an hour I sat pondering over it in the gloom, until at last a weeping maid brought in a lamp, and close at her heels came my friend Trevor, pale but composed, with these very papers which lie upon my knee held in his grasp. He sat down opposite to me, drew the lamp to the edge of the table, and handed me a short note scribbled, as you see, upon a single sheet of grey paper. 'The supply of game for London is going steadily up,' it ran. 'Head-keeper Hudson, we believe, has been now told to receive all orders for fly-paper and for preservation of your hen pheasant's life.'

" I dare say my face looked as bewildered as yours did just now when first I read this message. Then I re-read it very carefully. It was evidently as I had thought, and some second meaning must be buried in this strange com-bination of words. Or could it be that there was a pre-arranged significance to such phrases as ' fly-paper ' and ' hen pheasant ' ? Such a meaning would be arbitrary, and could not be deduced in any way. And yet I was loath to believe that this was the case, and the presence of the word ' Hudson ' seemed to show that the subject of the message was as I had guessed, and that it was from Bed-does rather than the sailor. I tried it backwards, but the combination, ' Life pheasant's hen,' was not encouraging. Then I tried alternate words, but neither ' The of for ' nor ' supply game London ' promised to throw any light upon it. Then in an instant the key of the riddle was in my hands, and I saw that every third word beginning with the first would give a message which might well drive old Trevor to despair.

" It was short and terse, the warning, as I now read it to my companion :

" ' The game is up. Hudson has told all. Fly for your life.'

" Victor Trevor sank his face into his shaking hands. ' It must be that, I suppose,' said he. ' This is worse than death, for it means disgrace as well. But what is the meaning of these " head-keepers " and "hen pheasants "? '

' It means nothing to the message, but it might mean a good deal to us if we had no other means of discovering the sender. You see that he has begun by writing, " The . . . game . . . is," and so on. Afterwards he had, to fulfil the prearranged cipher, to fill in any two words in each space. He would naturally use the first words which came to his mind, and if there were so many which **27** referred to sport among them, you may be tolerably sure that he is either an ardent shot or interested in breeding. Do you know anything of this Beddoes ? '

" ' Why, now that you mention it,' said he, ' I remem-ber that my poor father used to have an invitation from him to shoot over his preserves every autumn.'

" ' Then it is undoubtedly from him that the note

26 *one of those ingenious secret codes.* Holmes was later to write "a trifling monograph" upon the subject of secret writings, in which he analyzed 160 separate ciphers ("The Adventure of the Danc-ing Men"). But we should point out here that Bed-does' message was more properly a *cipher* than a *code*, which is a form of secret writing in which one word is made to stand for another word (or phrase).

27 *the first words which came to his mind.* Holmes has here anticipated the word-association tests of modern psychology.

"THEN IN AN INSTANT THE KEY OF THE RIDDLE WAS IN MY HANDS . . ."

Illustration by Sidney Paget for the *Strand Maga-zine*, April, 1893.

THE BARQUE *Gloria Scott*

Actually, the barque *Macquarie*, built in 1875. The photograph, by Hughes & Son, Ltd., is from *Sailing Ships and Their Story*, by E. Keble Chatterton, London: Sidgwick & Jackson, Ltd., 1909. A barque is officially a three-masted vessel with the foremast and mainmast square-rigged, the mizzenmast fore-and-aft rigged. Mr. Richard W. Clarke, in his extensive research "On the Nomenclature of Watson's Ships" was forced to conclude that the *Gloria Scott*, the *Norah Creina* of "The Resident Patient," and the *Sophy Anderson* of "The Five Orange Pips" were all "former childhood sweethearts whom Watson endeavored to honor in his sentimental way; hoping, no doubt, that their eyes would see the printed page where their names appeared."

28 *Falmouth*. The great port and fishing town in Cornwall.

comes,' said I. 'It only remains for us to find out what this secret was which the sailor Hudson seems to have held over the heads of these two wealthy and respected men.'

" ' Alas, Holmes, I fear that it is one of sin and shame !' cried my friend. ' But from you I shall have no secrets. Here is the statement which was drawn up by my father when he knew that the danger from Hudson had become imminent. I found it in the Japanese cabinet, as he told the doctor. Take it and read it to me, for I have neither the strength nor the courage to do it myself.'

" These are the very papers, Watson, which he handed to me, and I will read them to you as I read them in the old study that night to him. They are endorsed outside as you see : ' Some particulars of the voyage of the barque

28 *Gloria Scott*, from her leaving Falmouth on the 8th October, 1855, to her destruction in N. lat. 15° 20', W. long. 25° 14', on November 6th.' It is in the form of a letter, and runs in this way :

" My dear, dear son,—Now that approaching disgrace begins to darken the closing years of my life, I can write with all truth and honesty that it is not the terror of the law, it is not the loss of my position in the county, nor is it my fall in the eyes of all who have known me, which cuts me to the heart ; but it is the thought that you should come to blush for me—you who love me, and who have seldom, I hope, had reason to do other than respect me. But if the blow falls which is for ever hanging over me, then I should wish you to read this that you may know straight from me how far I have been to blame. On the other hand, if all should go well (which may kind God Almighty grant !), then if by any chance this paper should be still undestroyed, and should fall into your hands, I conjure you by all you hold sacred, by the memory of your dear mother, and by the love which has been between us, to hurl it into the fire, and to never

29 give one thought to it again.

" If, then, your eye goes on to read this line, I know that I shall already have been exposed and dragged from my home, or, as is more likely—for you know that my heart is weak—be lying with my tongue sealed for ever in death. In either case the time for suppression is past, and every word which I tell you is the naked truth ; and this I swear as I hope for mercy.

" My name, dear lad, is not Trevor. I was James Armitage in my younger days, and you can understand now the shock that it was to me a few weeks ago when your college friend addressed me in words which seemed to imply that he had surmised my secret. As Armitage it was that I entered a London banking house, and as Armitage I was convicted of breaking my country's laws,

30 and was sentenced to transportation. Do not think very harshly of me, laddie. It was a debt of honour, so-called, which I had to pay, and I used money which was not my own to do it, in the certainty that I could replace it before there could be any possibility of its being missed. But the most dreadful ill-luck pursued me. The money which I had reckoned upon never came to hand, and a premature examination of accounts exposed my deficit. The case might have been dealt leniently with, but the laws were more harshly administered thirty years ago than now, and on my twenty-third birthday I found myself chained as a felon with thirty-seven other convicts in the 'tween-decks of the barque *Gloria Scott*, bound for Australia.

" It was the year '55, when the Crimean War was at its height, and the old convict ships had been largely used as **31** transports in the Black Sea. The Government was compelled therefore to use smaller and less suitable vessels for sending out their prisoners. The *Gloria Scott* had been in the Chinese tea trade, but she was an old-fashioned, heavy-bowed, broad-beamed craft, and the new clippers **32** had cut her out. She was a 500-ton boat, and besides her thirty-eight gaol-birds, she carried twenty-six of a crew, eighteen soldiers, a captain, three mates, a doctor, a chaplain, and four warders. Nearly a hundred souls were in her, all told, when we set sail from Falmouth.

" The partitions between the cells of the convicts, instead of being of thick oak, as is usual in convict ships, were quite thin and frail. The man next to me upon the aft side was one whom I had particularly noticed when we were led down to the quay. He was a young man with a clear, hairless face, a long thin nose, and rather nutcracker jaws. He carried his head very jauntily in the air, had a swaggering style of walking, and was above all else remarkable for his extraordinary height. I don't think any of our heads would come up to his shoulder, and I am sure that he could not have measured less than six and a half feet. It was strange among so many sad and weary faces to see one which was full of energy and resolution. The sight of it was to me like a fire in a snowstorm. I was glad then to find that he was my neighbour, and gladder still when, in the dead of the night, I heard a whisper close to my ear, and found that he had managed to cut an opening in the board which separated us.

" ' Halloa, chummy ! ' said he, ' what's your name, and what are you here for ? '

" I answered him, and asked in turn who I was talking with.

" ' I'm Jack Prendergast,' said he, and, by God, you'll learn to bless my name before you've done with me ! '

" I remembered hearing of his case, for it was one which had made an immense sensation throughout the country, some time before my own arrest. He was a man of good family and of great ability, but of incurably vicious habits, who had, by an ingenious system of fraud, obtained huge sums of money from the leading London merchants.

" ' Ah, ah ! You remember my case ? ' said he, proudly.

" ' Very well indeed.'

" ' Then maybe you remember something queer about it ? '

" ' What was that, then ? '

" ' I'd had nearly a quarter of a million, hadn't I ? ' **33**

" ' So it was said.'

" ' But none was recovered, eh ? '

" ' No.'

29 *and to never give one thought to it again.* As Mr. Welch has observed in "The Terai Planter," "The literary style is better than one would have expected from a man of little culture, who knew hardly any books."

30 *sentenced to transportation.* In criminal law, the sending away of a convict to a remote place to be held there as a measure of punishment.

31 *when the Crimean War was at its height.* The Crimean War began in 1854 and ended with the Treaty of Paris in February of 1856, and was actually at its height in 1855. But if 1855 was "thirty years ago" we should have to date "The *Gloria Scott*" in *1885*, and this, from what we know of Holmes' later history, is ridiculous. We must either: (1) discard "the year '55, when the Crimean War was at its height"; or (2) revise the "thirty years."

Most commentators prefer to do the former, and for three good reasons:

1. Hudson's "thirty year and more" (since he last saw Trevor senior) is in undesigned coincidence with Trevor's own "thirty years ago."

2. Trevor senior was "a fine, robust old man" at the time of his meeting with Holmes; he had completed his twenty-third year (he tells us) at the time of the sailing from Falmouth. This substantiates the passing of thirty years.

3. If we accept Trevor senior's "thirty years ago" we can believe that he had returned to England "more than twenty years" ago, married, and had a son who was a contemporary of Holmes (that is, born around 1854). If, on the other hand, we accept Trevor senior's "year '55," we must suppose, with the late Clifton R. Andrew ("Who Is Who, and When, in 'The *Gloria Scott*' ") "that Victor Trevor was *not a natural son* of Old Man Trevor, but instead was a stepson . . ."

The complexities of dating this adventure have been cogently summed up by Mr. T. S. Blakeney in "More Disjecta Membra": "All sound critics, I think, agree that 1855 is impossible for [Holmes' adventure at Donnithorpe]; suggestions have been made, therefore, to put the date of the sailing back to 1845 and in this connection particular weight has attached to Professor Christ's note [in *An Irregular Chronology*] quoting the *Encyclopaedia Britannica* (11th edn.), that transportation of criminals [to Australia] was suspended in 1846. The most authoritative recent study of criminal transportation is Charles Bateson's *The Convict Ships: 1787–1868*, and it may be seen there that the *Britannica's* statement . . . is incorrect. Transportation to New South Wales, the main penal settlement, was abolished by Order-in-Council on May 22, 1840, but towards the end of 1844 it was proposed that 'exiles' (prisoners who had served a probationary period in England) might go out to the Port Philip district (which was only separated from N.S.W. on July 1, 1851). In 1848 Earl Grey revoked the Order-in-Council abolishing transportation to

N.S.W., but protests followed and in April, 1851, his revocation was rescinded. In 1853 transportation to Tasmania was abolished, but not until 1868 in Western Australia. It will thus be seen that 1846 did not see the end of the transportation system; although very few convicts reached N.S.W. after 1840, Trevor could have been going to Tasmania or W. Australia. It does not, to my thinking, in any way effect the need to alter old Trevor's sailing date from 1855 to 1845, but, since one's aim in all these matters is to emulate Holmes himself, in having a passion for exact knowledge, it is perhaps as well to draw attention to the true facts concerning the duration of the convict transportation system."

32 *the new clippers*. Fast sailing vessels—full-rigged ships of a type developed by American builders about 1840, characterized by fine lines, an overhanging bow, tall raking masts and a large sail area; ships, usually, of about 1,500 tons. Since Trevor senior calls the clippers "new" this is another indication that the *Gloria Scott* sailed from Falmouth in 1845 rather than 1855.

33 *nearly a quarter of a million*. Some $1,250,000 —a fantastic sum for 1845 (or 1855, either).

34 *the dibbs*. Correctly, *dibs*—slang for money.

"'I'M JACK PRENDERGAST,' SAID HE."

Illustration by Sidney Paget for the *Strand Magazine*, April, 1893.

"'Well, where d'ye suppose the balance is?' he asked.
"'I have no idea,' said I.
"'Right between my finger and thumb,' he cried. 'By God, I've got more pounds to my name than you have hairs on your head. And if you've money, my son, and know how to handle it and spread it, you can do *anything*! Now, you don't think it likely that a man who could do anything is going to wear his breeches out sitting in the stinking hold of a rat-gutted, beetle-ridden, mouldy old coffin of a China coaster? No, sir, such a man will look after himself, and will look after his chums. You may lay to that! You hold on to him, and you may kiss the Book that he'll haul you through.'
"That was his style of talk, and at first I thought it meant nothing, but after a while, when he had tested me and sworn me in with all possible solemnity, he let me understand that there really was a plot to gain command of the vessel. A dozen of the prisoners had hatched it before they came aboard; Prendergast was the leader, and his money was the motive power.
"'I'd a partner,' said he, 'a rare good man, as true as a stock to a barrel. He's got the dibbs, he has, and where do you think he is at this moment? Why, he's the chaplain of this ship—the chaplain, no less! He came aboard with a black coat and his papers right, and money enough in his box to buy the thing right up from keel to maintruck. The crew are his, body and soul. He could buy 'em at so much a gross with a cash discount, and he did it before ever they signed on. He's got two of the warders and Mercer the second mate, and he'd get the captain himself if he thought him worth it.'
"'What are we to do, then?' I asked.

ONE OF "THE NEW CLIPPERS"

Shown here is the American clipper *Red Jacket*, internationally famous in her day for swift Atlantic crossings. In 1854, she did 413 miles in a day. This means that a sailing ship was driven for a day and a night at an average speed of about 18½ knots, a speed that steamers did not reach for another thirty years. The photo is from *The Sailing Ship: Six Thousand Years of History*, by Romola and R. C. Anderson, New York: Robert M. McBride & Company, 1947.

" ' What do you think ? ' said he. ' We'll make the coats of some of these soldiers redder than ever the tailor did.'

" ' But they are armed,' said I.

" ' And so shall we be, my boy. There's a brace of pistols for every mother's son of us, and if we can't carry this ship, with the crew at our back, it's time we were all sent to a young Misses' boarding school. You speak to your mate on the left to-night, and see if he is to be trusted.'

" I did so, and found my other neighbour to be a young fellow in much the same position as myself, whose crime had been forgery. His name was Evans, but he afterwards changed it, like myself, and he is now a rich and prosperous man in the South of England. He was ready enough to join the conspiracy, as the only means of saving ourselves, and before we had crossed the Bay there were **35** only two of the prisoners who were not in the secret. One of these was of weak mind, and we did not dare to trust him, and the other was suffering from jaundice, and could not be of any use to us.

" From the beginning there was really nothing to prevent us taking possession of the ship. The crew were a set of ruffians, specially picked for the job. The sham chaplain came into our cells to exhort us, carrying a black bag, supposed to be full of tracts ; and so often did he come that by the third day we had each stowed away at the foot of our bed a file, a brace of pistols, a pound of powder, and twenty slugs. Two of the warders were agents of Prendergast, and the second mate was his right-hand man. The captain, the two mates, two warders, Lieutenant Martin, his eighteen soldiers, and the doctor were all that we had against us. Yet, safe as it was, we determined to neglect no precaution, and to make our attack suddenly at night. It came, however, more quickly than we expected, and in this way :

" One evening, about the third week after our start, the **36** doctor had come down to see one of the prisoners, who was ill, and, putting his hand down on the bottom of his bunk, he felt the outline of the pistols. If he had been silent he might have blown the whole thing ; but he was a nervous little chap, so he gave a cry of surprise and turned so pale, that the man knew what was up in an instant and seized him. He was gagged before he could give the alarm, and tied down upon the bed. He had unlocked the door that led to the deck, and we were through it in a rush. The two sentries were shot down, and so was a corporal who came running to see what was the matter. There were two more soldiers at the door of the state-room, and their muskets seemed not to be loaded, for they never fired upon us, and they were shot while trying to fix their bayonets. Then we rushed on into the captain's cabin, but as we pushed open the door there was an explosion from within, and there he lay with his head on the chart of the Atlantic, which was pinned upon the table, while the chaplain stood, with a smoking pistol in his hand, at his elbow. The two mates had both been seized by the crew, and the whole business seemed to be settled.

35 *the Bay.* The Bay of Biscay.

36 *about the third week after our start.* "This," Dr. Ernest Bloomfield Zeisler noted in his *Baker Street Chronology*, "would make it October 29th at the very latest, yet previously old Trevor wrote that the ship was destroyed on November 6th, which is the beginning of the *fifth* week after she sailed."

". . . WHILE THE CHAPLAIN STOOD, WITH A SMOKING PISTOL IN HIS HAND . . ."

Illustration by William H. Hyde for *Harper's Weekly*, April 15, 1893. Paget illustrated the same scene for the *Strand Magazine*, as did Arthur Twidle for the 1903 "Author's Edition" of *The Memoirs of Sherlock Holmes*, London: Smith, Elder.

"... WE PULLED HIM ABOARD THE BOAT ..."

Illustration by Sidney Paget for the *Strand Magazine*, April, 1893.

"The state-room was next the cabin, and we flocked in there and flopped down on the settees all speaking together, for we were just mad with the feeling that we were free once more. There were lockers all round, and Wilson, the sham chaplain, knocked one of them in, and pulled out a dozen of brown sherry. We cracked off the necks of the bottles, poured the stuff out into tumblers, and were just tossing them off, when in an instant, without warning, there came the roar of muskets in our ears, and the saloon was so full of smoke that we could not see across the table. When it cleared away again the place was a shambles. Wilson and eight others were wriggling on the top of each other on the floor, and the blood and brown sherry on that table turn me sick now when I think of it. We were so cowed by the sight that I think we should have given the job up if it had not been for Prendergast. He bellowed like a bull and rushed for the door with all that were left alive at his heels. Out we ran, and there on the poop were the lieutenant and ten of his men. The swing skylights above the saloon table had been a bit open, and they had fired on us through the slit. We got on them before they could load, and they stood to it like men, but we had the upper hand of them, and in five minutes it was all over. My God! was there ever a slaughter-house like that ship? Prendergast was like a raging devil, and he picked the soldiers up as if they had been children and threw them overboard, alive or dead. There was one sergeant that was horribly wounded, and yet kept on swimming for a surprising time, until some-one in mercy blew out his brains. When the fighting was over there was no one left of our enemies except just the warders, the mates, and the doctor.

"It was over them that the great quarrel arose. There were many of us who were glad enough to win back our freedom, and yet who had no wish to have murder on our souls. It was one thing to knock the soldiers over with their muskets in their hands, and it was another to stand by while men were being killed in cold blood. Eight of us, five convicts and three sailors, said that we would not see it done. But there was no moving Prendergast and those who were with him. Our only chance of safety lay in making a clean job of it, said he, and he would not leave a tongue with power to wag in a witness-box. It nearly came to our sharing the fate of the prisoners, but at last he said that if we wished we might take a boat and go   We jumped at the offer, for we were already sick of these bloodthirsty doings, and we saw that there would be worse before it was done. We were given a suit of sailor's togs each, a barrel of water, two casks, one of **37** junk and one of biscuits, and a compass. Prendergast threw us over a chart, told us that we were shipwrecked mariners whose ship had foundered in lat. 15° N. and long. 25° W., and then cut the painter and let us go.

"And now I come to the most surprising part of my story, my dear son. The seamen had hauled the foreyard aback during the rising, but now as we left them they brought it square again, and, as there was a light wind from the north and east, the barque began to draw slowly away from us. Our boat lay, rising and falling, upon the

37 *junk.* Hard salted beef supplied to ships.

long, smooth rollers, and Evans and I, who were the most educated of the party, were sitting in the sheets working out our position and planning what coast we should make for. It was a nice question, for the Cape de Verds was about 500 miles to the north of us, and the African coast about 700 miles to the east. On the whole, as the wind **38** was coming round to north, we thought that Sierra Leone might be best, and turned our head in that direction, the barque being at that time nearly hull down on our starboard quarter. Suddenly as we looked at her we saw a dense black cloud of smoke shoot up from her, which hung like a monstrous tree upon the skyline. A few seconds later a roar like thunder burst upon our ears, and as the smoke thinned away there was no sign left of the *Gloria Scott*. In an instant we swept the boat's head round again, and pulled with all our strength for the place where the haze, still trailing over the water, marked the scene of this catastrophe.

" It was a long hour before we reached it, and at first we feared that we had come too late to save anyone. A splintered boat and a number of crates and fragments of spars rising and falling on the waves showed us where the vessel had foundered, but there was no sign of life, and we had turned away in despair when we heard a cry for help, and saw at some distance a piece of wreckage with a man lying stretched across it. When we pulled him aboard the boat he proved to be a young seaman of the name of Hudson, who was so burned and exhausted that he could give us no account of what had happened until the following morning.

" It seemed that after we had left, Prendergast and his gang had proceeded to put to death the five remaining prisoners : the two warders had been shot and thrown overboard, and so also had the third mate. Prendergast then descended into the 'tween-decks, and with his own hands cut the throat of the unfortunate surgeon. There only remained the first mate, who was a bold and active man. When he saw the convict approaching him with the bloody knife in his hand, he kicked off his bonds, which he had somehow contrived to loosen, and rushing down the deck he plunged into the afterhold.

" A dozen convicts who descended with their pistols in search of him found him with a match-box in his hand seated beside an open powder barrel, which was one of a hundred carried on board, and swearing that he would blow all hands up if he were in any way molested. An instant later the explosion occurred, though Hudson thought it was caused by the misdirected bullet of one of the convicts rather than the mate's match. Be the cause what it may, it was the end of the *Gloria Scott*, and of the rabble who held command of her.

" Such, in a few words, my dear boy, is the history of this terrible business in which I was involved. Next day we were picked up by the brig *Hotspur*, bound for Australia, whose captain found no difficulty in believing that we were the survivors of a passenger ship which had foundered. The transport ship, *Gloria Scott*, was set **39** down by the Admiralty as being lost at sea, and no word

38 *about 700 miles to the east.* Here Dr. Zeisler caught Trevor senior in another error: "The Cape Verde Islands lie between 14 degrees 47 minutes and 17 degrees 13 minutes North latitude, and are nowhere more than some 140 miles north of the position given for the shipwreck [N. Lat. 15° 20', W. Long. 25° 14']; and the westernmost point of the Cape Verde Islands is not more than 150 miles west of the African coast. Hence Trevor was mistaken in either his position or his distance."

39 *a passenger ship which had foundered.* ". . . is it conceivable that the captain of the *Hotspur* should not have closely questioned the nine castaways, in order to obtain a full account of the shipwreck, the name and destination of the ship, and all the many details which he would have had to embody in his report to the authorities?" the late H. W. Bell asked in *Sherlock Holmes and Dr. Watson: The Chronology of Their Adventures*. "It is certain that sooner or later he would have detected sufficient inconsistencies in their various accounts to arouse his suspicions, and to cause him to clap them all in irons until arrival at Sydney, where a full investigation would have had its inevitable sequel."

"... THE BRIG *Hotspur* ..."

Shown here is H.M.S. *Martin*, a training brig (a two-masted, square-rigged vessel) launched in 1836. The photo is from *Sailing Ships and Their Story*, by E. Keble Chatterton; London: Sidgwick & Jackson, Ltd., 1909.

40 *and we bought country estates.* "Another inconsistency," Mr. Bell continued, "is [Trevor senior's] statement that he, though an escaped convict, 'came back' to England, where he became a Justice of the Peace. This would have been to tempt Providence by needlessly multiplying the chances of discovery. It is far more probable that he was a colonial, that his misdeeds were committed in the Eastern seas (he admitted to Holmes an acquaintance with New Zealand and Japan) and that he fled to England in order to put the greatest possible distance between himself and the theatre of his crimes."

41 *Sweet Lord, have mercy on our souls!'* "The note at the end of the confession mentions the arrival of Beddoes' letter," Mr. Welch wrote in "The Terai Planter." "But the combined evidence of Victor and the doctor is that Mr. Trevor had a stroke immediately on reading this letter and never recovered consciousness, save for an instant before the end. It was *impossible* for him to have written the postscript and to have placed the papers in the Japanese cabinet." In Mr. Welch's view, Trevor senior was *not* dead but a living partner in a conspiracy that involved both Dr. Fordham and Victor Trevor. (See "A Scandal in Bohemia," Note 7.)

42 *"That was the narrative which I read that night.* "It is obvious," Mr. Bell concluded, "that Trevor's yarn is the fabric of his imagination . . . [and] we have now to consider the motive for this elaborate and mendacious history. A man does not confess, even posthumously, to a devoted son a false account of embezzlement, transportation and mutiny, unless he is trying desperately to conceal some far more heinous crime. What it was, we cannot, of course, know for certain; but it was sinister enough to induce him to submit to insolence and blackmail at Hudson's hands rather than let his son have any inkling of its true nature, and to lead him to invent a substitute account sufficiently lurid to prevent Victor from making further inquiries. Bearing in mind the fact that he was 'a man of little culture,' we are safe in assuming that he would not have departed from the circle of his own experiences in devising a false tale. Therefore, out of many engaging possibilities, the most probable is privacy, coupled with the murder of all on board and the scuttling of the ship —a theory which comes perilously close to his own story. If, then, we imagine Trevor, together with 'Beddoes' and Hudson, as the surviving criminals of such an enterprise, we may assume that the two friends marooned Hudson, or 'double-crossed' him in some way, and appropriated his share of the loot. The information, after so many years, that he was alive and out for revenge, would be ample reason for Trevor to have 'gone about in fear of some personal attack.' "

43 *the Terai.* A swampy lowland belt in India north of the Ganges River at the foot of the Himalayan Mountains.

has ever leaked out as to her true fate.   After an excellent voyage the *Hotspur* landed us at Sydney, where Evans and I changed our names and made our way to the diggings, where among the crowds who were gathered from all nations, we had no difficulty in losing our former identities.

    " The rest I need not relate.   We prospered, we travelled, we came back as rich colonials to England, and

40 we bought country estates.   For more than twenty years we have led peaceful and useful lives, and we hoped that our past was for ever buried.   Imagine, then, my feelings when in the seaman who came to us I recognized instantly the man who had been picked off the wreck !   He had tracked us down somehow, and had set himself to live upon our fears.   You will understand now how it was that I strove to keep peace with him, and you will in some measure sympathize with me in the fears which fill me, now that he has gone from me to his other victim with threats upon his tongue.

    " Underneath is written, in a hand so shaky as to be hardly legible, ' Beddoes writes in cipher to say that H.

41 has told all.   Sweet Lord, have mercy on our souls ! '

42   " That was the narrative which I read that night to young Trevor, and I think, Watson, that under the circumstances it was a dramatic one.   The good fellow was

43 heartbroken at it, and went out to the Terai tea planting, where I hear that he is doing well.   As to the sailor and Beddoes, neither of them was ever heard of again after that day on which the letter of warning was written. They both disappeared utterly and completely.   No complaint had been lodged with the police, so that Beddoes had mistaken a threat for a deed.   Hudson had been seen lurking about, and it was believed by the police that he had done away with Beddoes, and had fled.   For myself, I believe that the truth was exactly the opposite.   I think it is most probable that Beddoes, pushed to desperation, and believing himself to have been already betrayed, had revenged himself upon Hudson, and had fled from the country with as much money as he could lay his hands on.   Those are the facts of the case, Doctor, and if they are of any use to your collection, I am sure that they are very heartily at your service."

14

THE MUSGRAVE RITUAL

[Thursday, October 2, 1879]

AN anomaly which often struck me in the character of my friend Sherlock Holmes was that, although in his methods of thought he was the neatest and most methodical of mankind, and although also he affected a certain quiet primness of dress, he was none the less in his personal habits one of the most untidy men that ever drove a fellow-lodger to distraction. Not that I am in the least conventional in that respect myself. The rough-and-tumble work in Afghanistan, coming on the top of a natural Bohemianism of disposition, has made me rather more lax than befits a medical man. But with me there is a limit, and when I find a man who keeps his cigars in the coal-scuttle, his tobacco in the toe-end of a Persian slipper, and his unanswered correspondence transfixed by a jack-knife into the very centre of his wooden mantelpiece, then I begin to give myself virtuous airs. I have always held, too, that pistol practice should distinctly be an open-air pastime ; and when Holmes in one of his queer humours would sit in an arm-chair, with his hair-trigger and a **1** hundred Boxer cartridges, and proceed to adorn the **2** opposite wall with a patriotic V.R. done in bullet-pocks, **3** I felt strongly that neither the atmosphere nor the appearance of our room was improved by it. **4**

"... WITH HIS HAIR-TRIGGER ..."

"The 'hair-trigger' pistol," Mr. Robert Keith Leavitt wrote in "Annie Oakley in Baker Street," "is an inherently dangerous weapon, prohibited in match shooting, impractical for sport and impractical in the extreme for detecting operations. Almost certainly this one was a single-shot 'salon' pistol of Continental make. [Captain Hugh B. C.] Pollard, the English authority [in his *The Book of the Pistol*, New York: Robert McBride & Co., 1917, from which the illustration above is taken] calls these 'wonderfully complicated . . . [but] so delicate . . . as to [be] practically worthless for ordinary use. . . . For trick work, like shooting the pips off the ace of clubs, they are invaluable.' No shooting with this weapon could conceivably improve practical proficiency in the use of the standard handgun."

1 *would sit in an arm-chair.* ". . . a position," Mr. Robert Keith Leavitt wrote in "Annie Oakley in Baker Street," "from which one may rarely or never expect to shoot with deadly intent. [Holmes] undertook a job of Spencerian nicety which almost certainly necessitated doubling his knees, resting his pistol hand on the right knee and supporting that hand by grasping its wrist with the left hand, the left forearm resting on the left knee. This position would be necessary for precision in explosive calligraphy but useful for little else." Mr. Leavitt's thesis, as we shall have several occasions to note, is that Holmes, a good shot with a rifle, was a poor shot at best with a handgun, and relied much more on Watson's marksmanship with such a weapon than he did on his own.

2 *Boxer cartridges.* ". . . the name Boxer," Leavitt wrote, "was used in England as a generic name for *any center-fire* cartridge—a form of ammunition perfected by Colonel Boxer, R.A., in 1867."

3 *a patriotic V.R.* For Victoria Regina, as previously noted. The late Christopher Morley held that Holmes shot the V.R. into the wall in 1887 to celebrate the Queen's Golden Jubilee on June 21st of that year ("Dr. Watson's Secret"), but other commentators are not agreed that Watson was sharing rooms with Holmes at that time.

4 *was improved by it.* Mr. Leavitt has written that of all Watson's understatements, this is the classic: ". . . center-fire cartridges cannot be made in small calibres or very low power. And in the nineteenth century the smallest center-fire—or Boxer—cartridge was cal. .310, slightly smaller than the modern .32, which packs 100 foot-pounds of muzzle energy. . . . Long before Holmes had finished, the room—*and the entire house*—would have been filled with gritty, white plaster-dust, and the end result after all hundred cartridges had been expended, would have been a vast area chipped away in a shallow concave and glowering out redly over a room littered ankle-deep in chunks of plaster and great ugly shards of what had once been good English brick." On the other hand, the authors of the *Catalogue of the Sherlock Holmes*

Exhibition held at Abbey House in 1951 felt that Dr. Watson applied the term "Boxer" loosely, and that the ammunition used by Holmes consisted of "rimfire" cartridges which would make little noise and accomplish little damage. Today the only survivor of the rimfire system is the .22 calibre cartridge.

5 *somewhere in these incoherent memoirs.* In *A Study in Scarlet.*

6 *his commonplace book.* Armine D. Mackenzie has suggested ("The Case of the Illustrious Predecessor") that Holmes "was perhaps the first special librarian of which there is record." It seems clear from the Canon that Holmes kept *three* permanent files. First in importance was his casebook, or diary, containing only the records of his own cases. Independent of these were the commonplace books and the index of biographies. Into the commonplace books Holmes pasted press cuttings about any incidents arresting his attention, including items from the agony column ("Bleat, unmitigated bleat!" he once called them, but they proved very useful to him in "The Adventure of the Red Circle.") Holmes' ceaseless gathering and filing of new cuttings would make the commonplace books awkward if not impossible to keep in alphabetical order, and this necessitated the index of biographies, an alphabetical cross-reference showing where to find items in the commonplace volumes. "Consequently," the late H. W. Bell wrote in *Sherlock Holmes and Dr. Watson: The Chronology of Their Adventures,* "when 'Morgan the poisoner, and Merridew of abominable memory' are quoted from the index ["The Adventure of the Empty House"], and when the long list of cases under the letter V ["The Adventure of the Sussex Vamprie"] are read out . . . , we cannot be sure if they refer to incidents in Holmes' own practice or not."

7 *Vamberry, the wine merchant.* A pastiche stemming from this reference of Holmes, Mr. A. Lloyd-Taylor's "The Wine Merchant," appeared in the *Sherlock Holmes Journal* in two parts—issues of Winter, 1959, and Spring, 1960.

8 *the singular affair of the aluminium crutch.* Or *crotch?* Why should a metal so rare and costly in those days have been used in making such a simple device as a crutch when wood would have done as well? It occurred to Mr. Rolfe Boswell that some other definition of the noun *crutch* might offer a more logical explanation. A dictionary published in England calls a crutch "a support . . . fork, crotch." And Mr. Boswell noted that "a 'support' worn at the 'crotch' sometimes *is* made of aluminium." A pastiche stemming from this reference of Holmes', "The Affair of the Aluminium Crutch," by H. Bedford-Jones, appeared originally in the *Palm Springs News,* February-March, 1936, and was reprinted in the *Baker Street Journal,* Vol. I, No. 1, Old Series, January, 1946.

Our chambers were always full of chemicals and of criminal relics, which had a way of wandering into unlikely positions, and of turning up in the butter-dish, or in even less desirable places. But his papers were my great crux. He had a horror of destroying documents, especially those which were connected with his past cases, and yet it was only once in every year or two that he would muster energy to docket and arrange them, for as I **5** have mentioned somewhere in these incoherent memoirs, the outbursts of passionate energy when he performed the remarkable feats with which his name is associated were followed by reactions of lethargy, during which he would lie about with his violin and his books, hardly moving, save from the sofa to the table. Thus month after month his papers accumulated, until every corner of the room was stacked with bundles of manuscript which were on no account to be burned, and which could not be put away save by their owner.

One winter's night, as we sat together by the fire, I ventured to suggest to him that as he had finished pasting **6** extracts into his commonplace book he might employ the next two hours in making our room a little more habitable. He could not deny the justice of my request, so with a rather rueful face he went off to his bedroom, from which he returned presently pulling a large tin box behind him. This he placed in the middle of the floor, and squatting down upon a stool in front of it he threw back the lid. I could see that it was already a third full of bundles of paper tied up with red tape into separate packages.

" There are cases enough here, Watson," said he, looking at me with mischievous eyes. " I think that if you knew all that I had in this box you would ask me to pull some out instead of putting others in."

" These are the records of your early work, then ? " I asked. " I have often wished that I had notes of those cases."

" Yes, my boy ; these were all done prematurely, before my biographer had come to glorify me." He lifted bundle after bundle in a tender, caressing sort of way. " They are not all successes, Watson," said he, " but there are some pretty little problems among them. Here's the record of the Tarleton murders, and the case of Vamberry, **7** the wine merchant, and the adventure of the old Russian **8** woman, and the singular affair of the aluminium crutch, as well as a full account of Ricoletti of the club foot and **9** his abominable wife. And here—ah, now ! this really is **10** something a little *recherché.*"

He dived his arm down to the bottom of the chest, and brought up a small wooden box, with a sliding lid, such as children's toys are kept in. From within he produced a crumpled piece of paper, an old-fashioned brass key, a peg of wood with a ball of string attached to it, and three rusty old discs of metal.

" Well, my boy, what do you make of this lot ? " he asked, smiling at my expression.

" It is a curious collection."

" Very curious, and the story that hangs round it will strike you as being more curious still."

" These relics have a history, then ? "

"IT IS A CURIOUS COLLECTION."

Illustration by Sidney Paget for the *Strand Maga-zine*, May, 1893.

" So much so that they *are* history."

" What do you mean by that ? "

Sherlock Holmes picked them up one by one, and laid them along the edge of the table.   Then he re-seated himself in his chair, and looked them over with a gleam of satisfaction in his eyes.

" These," said he, " are all that I have left to remind me of the episode of the Musgrave Ritual."

I had heard him mention the case more than once, though I had never been able to gather the details.

" I should be so glad," said I, " if you would give me an account of it."

" And leave the litter as it is ? " he cried, mischievously. " Your tidiness won't bear much strain, after all, Watson. But I should be glad that you should add this case to your annals, for there are points in it which make it quite unique in the criminal records of this or, I believe, of any other country.   A collection of my trifling achievements would certainly be incomplete which contained no account of this very singular business.

" You may remember how the affair of the *Gloria Scott*, and my conversation with the unhappy man whose fate I told you of, first turned my attention in the direction of the profession which has become my life's work. You see me now when my name has become known far and wide, and when I am generally recognized both by the public and by the official force as being a final court of appeal in doubtful cases.   Even when you knew me first, at the time of the affair which you have commemorated in ' A Study in Scarlet,' I had already established a **11** considerable, though not a very lucrative, connection. You can hardly realize, then, how difficult I found it at first, and how long I had to wait before I succeeded in **12** making any headway.

" When I first came up to London I had rooms in Montague Street, just round the corner from the British **13** Museum, and there I waited, filling in my too abundant **14** leisure time by studying all those branches of science

9 *Ricoletti of the club foot and his abominable wife.* "The truth may be—in part, at any rate— that Holmes' acid humor was responsible for many of the tantalizing references to cases still unre-corded by his Boswell," Mr. Vincent Starrett wrote in *The Private Life of Sherlock Holmes.* "His in-tentional mystification of that humble collaborator is frequently manifest in Watson's pages; what more likely than that the detective, in quizzical temper, whispered hints of extraordinary problems that actually had never come before him?"

10 *recherché.*" French: sought out with care; choice, hence of rare quality, elegance, or attrac-tiveness, peculiar and refined in kind; also far-fetched. When Holmes uses French words and phrases, as he so often does, we must remember that his grandmother was French.

11 *the affair which you have commemorated in 'A Study in Scarlet.'* Holmes has called Watson his "biographer"; and he has spoken of Watson's "annals" and "A collection of my trifling achieve-ments"; now he says that Watson has "commemo-rated" the affair of *A Study in Scarlet.* It would seem that the "winter's night" on which Holmes told Watson the story of "The Musgrave Ritual" must therefore have been after December, 1887, when *A Study in Scarlet* was published in *Beeton's Christmas Annual.* This would seem to confirm our suggestion that the winter was that of 1887– 1888 (see "The *Gloria Scott,*" Note 1), although the winter of 1888–1889 is a distinct possibility. Mr. Bell, on the other hand, held that "Holmes had read [*A Study in Scarlet*] in manuscript."

12 *how long I had to wait.* Holmes, as we have seen, began his career as a consulting detective late in the year 1877. Most commentators and chronologists (Bell, Blakeney, Brend, Elie, Fol-som, Hill, Harrison, Petersen, Roberts, Sayers, and Smith among them) believe that he waited a year for the adventure of "The Musgrave Ritual"; three (Baring-Gould, Pattrick, and Zeisler) believe that he waited two years; one (Christ) holds that he waited two and a half years, which (as the late Gavin Brend wrote in *My Dear Holmes*) may well be taken "as the extreme limit of [Holmes'] patience." We suggest that the adventure of "The Musgrave Ritual" took place on *Thursday, Octo-ber 2, 1879.*

Holmes must have had some income upon which to live during this trying period, and Mr. Fred-erick Bryan-Brown has suggested (in "Sherlockian Schools and Schoolmasters") that Holmes perhaps in his Montague Street (see below) days may have augmented whatever family income he may have had by teaching: "The public schools were begin-ning to take Science masters as a novelty and I suggest that Holmes went round the corner to Gower Street where, free thinker that he was, he gained employment at University College School; here later (1890/91) went as a pupil another great medico-legal expert, Sir Bernard Spilsbury."

13 *Montague Street.* "Bedford House, a family seat of the Russell family, was demolished in 1800 and Montague Street was formed on the gardens of the mansion between 1803 and 1805," Mr. William H. Gill wrote in his essay on "Some Notable Sherlockian Buildings." "Holmes seems to have been attracted to the quiet and simple architecture of the late Georgian period for both [the rooms in Montague Street and 221B Baker Street] were in houses of this kind. Montague Street was not quite as fashionable as Baker Street, but the logical and unadorned houses must have appealed to Holmes' austere mind."

It is interesting to note here that Dr. Conan Doyle, when *he* first came up to London, had lodgings at 23 Montague *Place*, close to Baker Street, with a consulting room at 2 Devonshire Place. (Miss Violet Hunter, of "The Adventure of the Copper Beeches," also lived in Montague *Place*.)

"It is reasonable to suppose that, for a single room, with service—which included bringing up the hot-water and coals—but without meals, Sherlock Holmes paid between 10 s. [$2.50] and 15 s. [$3.75] a week," Mr. Michael Harrison wrote (*In the Footsteps of Sherlock Holmes*).

14 *the British Museum.* The British Museum, Augustus J. C. Hare wrote in his *Walks in London*, Vol. II, "was built on the site of Montague House, 1823–1847, from designs by Sir Robert Smirke, continued under his brother Sydney. Otherwise handsome, it is dwarfed and spoilt by having no suitable base. Its collections originated in the purchase of those of Sir Hans Sloane [of whom we shall hear in "The Adventure of the Three Garridebs"] in 1753. The most important gifts have been those of the Royal Library by George II, and of George III's library by George IV; the most important purchases those of Sir William Hamilton's collections, the Townley, Phigalian, and Elgin Marbles, Dr. Burney's MSS, and the Landsdowne and Arundel MSS."

These collections would have been invaluable to Holmes in preparing the monographs which many Sherlockian scholars believe that he wrote at this time:

"Those long hours in the rooms at Montague Street would have been admirable for literary enterprise, and it seems highly likely that many of them were thus employed" (Vincent Starrett: *The Private Life of Sherlock Holmes*).

"It cannot fail to be the earnest conviction of anyone who ponders deeply the problems presented by Holmes the author that not only were the technical writings the direct outgrowth of the special and out-of-the-ordinary studies which he undertook in preparation for his life's work while still at college, and which he continued after he came up to London, but that the composition of the major ones . . . was a *fait accompli* when the Baker Street menage became a reality" (Walter Klinefelter: "The Writings of Mr. Sherlock Holmes").

15 which might make me more efficient. Now and again cases came in my way, principally through the introduction of old fellow-students, for during my last years at the university there was a good deal of talk there about myself and my methods. The third of these cases was that of the Musgrave Ritual, and it is to the interest which was aroused by that singular chain of events, and the large issues which proved to be at stake, that I trace my first stride towards the position which I now hold.

" Reginald Musgrave had been in the same college as myself, and I had some slight acquaintance with him. He was not generally popular among the undergraduates, though it always seemed to me that what was set down as pride was really an attempt to cover extreme natural diffidence. In appearance he was a man of an exceedingly aristocratic type, thin, high-nosed, and large-eyed, with languid and yet courtly manners. He was indeed a scion of one of the very oldest families in the kingdom, though

16 his branch was a cadet one which had separated from the Northern Musgraves some time in the sixteenth century,

17 and had established itself in Western Sussex, where the manor house of Hurlstone is perhaps the oldest inhabited building in the county. Something of his birthplace seemed to cling to the man, and I never looked at his pale, keen face, or the poise of his head, without associating him with grey archways and mullioned windows and all the venerable wreckage of a feudal keep. Now and again we drifted into talk, and I can remember that more than once he expressed a keen interest in my methods of observation and inference.

" For four years I had seen nothing of him, until one morning he walked into my room in Montague Street. He had changed little, was dressed like a young man of fashion—he was always a bit of a dandy—and preserved the same quiet, suave manner which had formerly distinguished him.

" ' How has all gone with you, Musgrave ? ' I asked, after we had cordially shaken hands.

" ' You probably heard of my poor father's death,' said he. ' He was carried off about two years ago. Since then I have, of course, had the Hurlstone estates to manage, and as I am member for my district as well, my life has been a busy one ; but I understand, Holmes, that you are turning to practical ends those powers with which you used to amaze us.'

" ' Yes,' said I, ' I have taken to living by my wits.'

" ' I am delighted to hear it, for your advice at present would be exceedingly valuable to me. We have had some very strange doings at Hurlstone, and the police have been able to throw no light upon the matter. It is really the most extraordinary and inexplicable business.'

" You can imagine with what eagerness I listened to him, Watson, for the very chance for which I had been panting during all those months of inaction seemed to have come within my reach. In my inmost heart I believed that I could succeed where others failed, and now I had the opportunity to test myself.

" ' Pray let me have the details,' I cried.

" Reginald Musgrave sat down opposite to me, and lit the cigarette which I had pushed towards him.

"... I HAD ROOMS IN MONTAGUE STREET ..."

In which house did Sherlock Holmes lodge during his early days in London? "For years," Mr. James Edward Holroyd wrote, "I lived within five minutes' walk of [Montague Street]. In it there is a very pleasant private hotel called The Whitehall. I have always supposed that Sherlock chose this address for his first quarters since it would remind him of Brother Mycroft." Reliable local authority, however, states that Holmes' rooms were probably on the top floor having the fifth and sixth or ninth and tenth windows in the London County Council photograph shown above (from *Sherlock Holmes: A Biography*, by William S. Baring-Gould).

15 *all those branches of science which might make me more efficient.* Both Mrs. Winifred M. Christie ("Sherlock Holmes and Graphology") and Mr. Martin J. Swanson ("Graphologists in the Canon") have stated their conviction that graphology was one of those branches of science which Holmes studied at this time. Graphology, the study of handwriting as a medium expressive of the writer's personality and character, was of more interest to the French than to the English in the nineteenth century, and one of its greatest exponents was Crépieux-Jamin, whose *magnum opus* was *L'Écriture et la Caractère*, published in 1888. By far the most concentrated graphological analysis in the Saga appears in "The Reigate Squires," which took place in 1887, a year *before* Crépieux-Jamin published *L'Écriture*; Holmes was a pioneer always.

16 *a cadet one.* A younger branch of the Musgrave family.

17 *Western Sussex.* Sussex, a maritime county in the South of England, is divided into Sussex East and Sussex West for administrative purposes. It is almost entirely an agricultural and pastoral region. Holmes adventured often in Sussex (*The Valley of Fear*, "The Adventure of Black Peter," "The Adventure of the Sussex Vampire") and chose its South Downs for his bee farm when the time came for retirement ("The Adventure of the Lion's Mane").

THE READING ROOM OF THE BRITISH MUSEUM

Where Holmes in 1877 studied the literature of crime and met Karl Marx (according to your editor's biography, *Sherlock Holmes of Baker Street*).

"... HE WAS A MAN OF AN EXCEEDINGLY ARISTOCRATIC TYPE, THIN, HIGH-NOSED, AND LARGE-EYED, WITH LANGUID AND YET COURTLY MANNERS."

Portrait of Reginald Musgrave by Sidney Paget for the *Strand Magazine*, May, 1893.

"'... BEGAN TO STUDY IT WITH MINUTE ATTENTION.'"

Illustration by William H. Hyde for *Harper's Weekly*, May 13, 1893.

"... THE MANOR HOUSE OF HURLSTONE IS PERHAPS THE OLDEST INHABITED BUILDING IN THE COUNTY"

In fact, this is the manor house of *West Hoathly*, Sussex. The photograph, by Will F. Taylor of Reigate, is from *Sussex*, by Esther Meynell, London: Robert Hale, Limited, 1947.

18 *I preserve*. To keep up and reserve for personal or special use; as, to preserve game or fish by raising and protecting it.

19 *a Don Juan*. Legendary hero of many literary works, supposedly based on the life of Don Juan Tehorio of Seville. Don Juan seduces a girl, then kills her father. He invites a statue of the father to a feast; it comes, seizes the libertine, and drags him to hell. Don Juan is the subject of Mozart's opera *Don Giovanni*, a ballet by Gluck, a poem by Byron; also used by Tellez (Tirso de Malina), T. Corneille, Goldini, Molière, Balzac, Robert Browning, and George Bernard Shaw.

" 'You must know,' said he, 'that though I am a bachelor I have to keep up a considerable staff of servants at Hurlstone, for it is a rambling old place, and takes a **18** good deal of looking after. I preserve, too, and in the pheasant months I usually have a house-party, so that it would not do to be short-handed. Altogether there are eight maids, the cook, the butler, two footmen, and a boy. The garden and the stables, of course, have a separate staff.

" 'Of these servants the one who had been longest in our service was Brunton, the butler. He was a young schoolmaster out of place when he was first taken up by my father, but he was a man of great energy and character, and he soon became quite invaluable in the household. He was a well-grown, handsome man, with a splendid forehead, and though he has been with us for twenty years he cannot be more than forty now. With his personal advantages and his extraordinary gifts, for he can speak several languages and play nearly every musical instrument, it is wonderful that he should have been satisfied so long in such a position, but I suppose that he was comfortable and lacked energy to make any change. The butler of Hurlstone is always a thing that is remembered by all who visit us.

" 'But this paragon has one fault. He is a bit of a Don **19** Juan, and you can imagine that for a man like him it is not a very difficult part to play in a quiet country district.

" 'When he was married it was all right, but since he has been a widower we have had no end of trouble with him. A few months ago we were in hopes that he was about to settle down again, for he became engaged to Rachel Howells, our second housemaid, but he has thrown her over since then and taken up with Janet Tregellis, the daughter of the head gamekeeper. Rachel, who is a very good girl, but of an excitable Welsh temperament, had a sharp touch of brain fever, and goes about the house now —or did until yesterday—like a black-eyed shadow of her former self. That was our first drama at Hurlstone, but a second one came to drive it from our minds, and it was prefaced by the disgrace and dismissal of butler Brunton.

" ' This is how it came about. I have said that the man was intelligent, and this very intelligence has caused his ruin, for it seems to have led to an insatiable curiosity about things which did not in the least concern him. I had no idea of the lengths to which this would carry him until the merest accident opened my eyes to it.

" ' I have said that the house is a rambling one. One night last week—on Thursday night, to be more exact—I found that I could not sleep, having foolishly taken a cup of strong *café noir* after my dinner. After struggling **20** against it until two in the morning I felt that it was quite hopeless, so I rose and lit the candle with the intention of continuing a novel which I was reading. The book, however, had been left in the billiard-room, so I pulled on my dressing-gown and started off to get it.

" ' In order to reach the billiard-room I had to descend a flight of stairs, and then to cross the head of the passage which led to the library and the gun-room. You can imagine my surprise when as I looked down this corridor I saw a glimmer of light coming from the open door of the library. I had myself extinguished the lamp and closed the door before coming to bed. Naturally, my first thought was of burglars. The corridors at Hurlstone have their walls largely decorated with trophies of old weapons. From one of these I picked a battle-axe, and then, leaving my candle behind me, I crept on tiptoe down the passage and peeped in at the open door.

" ' Brunton, the butler. was in the library. He was sitting, fully dressed, in an easy chair, with a slip of paper, which looked like a map, upon his knee, and his forehead sunk forward upon his hand in deep thought. I stood, dumb with astonishment, watching him from the darkness. A small taper on the edge of the table shed a feeble light, which sufficed to show me that he was fully dressed. Suddenly, as I looked, he rose from his chair, and walking over to a bureau at the side, he unlocked it and drew out one of the drawers. From this he took a paper, and, returning to his seat, he flattened it out beside the taper on the edge of the table, and began to study it with minute attention. My indignation at this calm examination of our family documents overcame me so far that I took a step forward, and Brunton looking up saw me standing in the doorway. He sprang to his feet, his face turned livid with fear, and he thrust into his breast the chart-like paper which he had been originally studying.

" ' " So ! " said I, " this is how you repay the trust which we have reposed in you ! You will leave my service to-morrow."

" ' He bowed with the look of a man who is utterly crushed, and slunk past me without a word. The taper was still on the table, and by its light I glanced to see what the paper was which Brunton had taken from the

20 café noir. Black coffee—coffee without milk or cream.

" ' HE SPRANG TO HIS FEET, HIS FACE TURNED LIVID WITH FEAR . . .' "

Illustration by Sidney Paget for the *Strand Magazine*, May, 1893.

" ' . . . OUR OWN BLAZONINGS AND CHARGES . . .' "

"The Musgraves," Dr. Julian Wolff wrote in his *Practical Handbook of Sherlockian Heraldry*, "are an ancient and loyal family. . . . Many prominent supporters of the Royalist side in the Civil Wars bore this honored name. [The arms are:] Azure, six annulets or, three, two and one."

bureau. To my surprise it was nothing of any importance at all, but simply a copy of the questions and answers in the singular old observance called the Musgrave Ritual. It is a sort of ceremony peculiar to our family, which each Musgrave for centuries past has gone through upon his coming of age—a thing of private interest, and perhaps of some little importance to the archæologist, like our own blazonings and charges, but of no practical use whatever.

" ' " We had better come back to the paper afterwards," said I.

" ' " If you think it really necessary," he answered, with some hesitation.

" ' To continue my statement, however, I re-locked the bureau, using the key which Brunton had left, and I had turned to go, when I was surprised to find that the butler had returned and was standing before me.

" ' " Mr. Musgrave, sir," he cried, in a voice which was hoarse with emotion, " I can't bear disgrace, sir. I've always been proud above my station in life, and disgrace would kill me. My blood will be on your head, sir—it will, indeed—if you drive me to despair. If you cannot keep me after what has passed, then for God's sake let me give you notice and leave in a month, as if of my own free will. I could stand that, Mr. Musgrave, but not to be cast out before all the folk that I know so well."

" ' " You don't deserve much consideration, Brunton," I answered. " Your conduct has been most infamous. However, as you have been a long time in the family, I have no wish to bring public disgrace upon you. A month, however, is too long. Take yourself away in a week, and give what reason you like for going."

" ' " Only a week, sir ? " he cried in a despairing voice. " A fortnight—say at least a fortnight."

" ' " A week," I repeated, " and you may consider yourself to have been very leniently dealt with."

" ' He crept away, his face sunk upon his breast, like a broken man, while I put out the light and returned to my room.

" ' For two days after this Brunton was most assiduous in his attention to his duties. I made no allusion to what had passed, and waited with some curiosity to see how he would cover his disgrace. On the third morning, however, he did not appear, as was his custom, after breakfast to receive my instructions for the day. As I left the dining-room I happened to meet Rachel Howells, the maid. I have told you that she had only recently recovered from an illness, and was looking so wretchedly pale and wan that I remonstrated with her for being at work.

" ' " You should be in bed," I said. " Come back to your duties when you are stronger."

" ' She looked at me with so strange an expression that I began to suspect that her brain was affected.

" ' " I am strong enough, Mr. Musgrave," said she.

" ' " We will see what the doctor says," I answered. " You must stop work now, and when you go downstairs just say that I wish to see Brunton."

" ' " The butler is gone," said she.

" ' " Gone ! Gone where ? "

" ' " He is gone.   No one has seen him.   He is not in his room.   Oh, yes, he is gone—he is gone ! "   She fell back against the wall with shriek after shriek of laughter, while I, horrified at this sudden hysterical attack, rushed to the bell to summon help.   The girl was taken to her room, still screaming and sobbing, while I made inquiries about Brunton.   There was no doubt about it that he had disappeared.   His bed had not been slept in ; he had been seen by no one since he had retired to his room the night before ; and yet it was difficult to see how he could have left the house, as both windows and doors were found to be fastened in the morning.   His clothes, his watch, and even his money were in his room—but the black suit which he usually wore was missing.   His slippers, too, were gone, but his boots were left behind.   Where, then, could butler Brunton have gone in the night, and what could have become of him now ?

" ' Of course we searched the house from cellar to garret, but there was no trace of him.   It is as I have said a labyrinth of an old house, especially the original wing, which is now practically uninhabited, but we ransacked every room and attic without discovering the least sign of the missing man.   It was incredible to me that he could have gone away leaving all his property behind him, and yet where could he be ?   I called in the local police, but without success. Rain had fallen on the night before, and we examined the lawn and the paths all round the house, but in vain.   Matters were in this state when a new development quite drew our attention away from the original mystery.

" ' For two days Rachel Howells had been so ill, sometimes delirious, sometimes hysterical, that a nurse had been employed to sit up with her at night.   On the third night after Brunton's disappearance, the nurse, finding her patient sleeping nicely, had dropped into a nap in the arm-chair, when she woke in the early morning to find the bed empty, the window open, and no signs of the invalid.   I was instantly aroused, and with the two footmen started off at once in search of the missing girl. It was not difficult to tell the direction which she had taken, for, starting from under her window, we could follow her footmarks easily across the lawn to the edge of the mere, where they vanished, close to the gravel path which leads out of the grounds.   The lake there is 8 feet deep, and you can imagine our feelings when we saw that the trail of the poor demented girl came to an end at the edge of it.

" ' Of course, we had the drags at once, and set to work to recover the remains ; but no trace of the body could we find.   On the other hand, we brought to the surface an object of a most unexpected kind.   It was a linen bag, which contained within it a mass of old rusted and discoloured metal and several dull-coloured pieces of pebble or glass.   This strange find was all that we could get from the mere, and although we made every possible search and inquiry yesterday, we know nothing of the fate either of Rachel Howells or Richard Brunton.   The county police are at their wits' end, and I have come up to you as a last resource.'

" You can imagine, Watson, with what eagerness I

21

21 *as a last resource.*' "When Musgrave comes to consult Holmes, he tells him that 'last week—on Thursday night' he discovered Brunton, the butler, in the library examining family documents. He dismissed the man from his service with a week's notice. 'For two days after this' [Friday and Saturday] he was 'most assiduous in his attention to his duties.' 'On the third morning [Sunday] he did not appear.' . . . Holmes, as appears from his narrative, was consulted on the following Thursday." —H. W. Bell, *Sherlock Holmes and Dr. Watson: The Chronology of Their Adventures.*

22 " '*The sixth from the first.*' " It must be pointed out here that when "The Musgrave Ritual" was first published in the *Strand Magazine*, the Ritual consisted of *seven* couplets only—"What was the month?" "The sixth from the first"—was omitted. But when the story was included in the Newnes volume of *The Memoirs* in 1894, the eighth couplet was added. Somehow this suppressed time-clue—essential to anyone attempting to discover the whereabouts of the treasure by following the directions in the Ritual—had slipped back in, and all subsequent English editions retained it. Not so the American editions; perhaps their editors were worried that readers might not understand the complications of the month that was "The sixth from the first."

For, as Mr. Bell wrote, ". . . the chief problem in the dating of this case is to determine the season in which it happened. In the 'Ritual' of the Musgraves itself there is a fundamental ambiguity: the month specified . . . might have been reckoned either from March 25th, the legal beginning of the year in England from the fourteenth century until 1752, or from January 1st, as was common among historians during the period of the Stuarts."

We will now turn the matter over to Dr. Zeisler, who wrote (in *Baker Street Chronology*): "If January is counted as the first month, then the sixth month from this is . . . July, and if one reckons from March 25th then the sixth month from the first is the month from September 25th to October 24th. The Ritual, as we learn later, was written in the time of Charles II by one of his staunch adherents, who would probably date things not in the manner of the historians but in the usual legal manner of the time, so that there is, perhaps, a small probability in favor of the autumn date over the summer date, but too slight to be of much use. . . . But the Ritual was not written later than 1660. In 1752 the Gregorian calendar was adopted in England, and this entailed skipping eleven days, so that we must add eleven days to the above dates. Hence the intervals under consideration are July 12th to August 11th and October 6th to November 4th."

Dr. Zeisler further pointed out that Brunton, when told by Musgrave to leave in a week, begged for "a fortnight." "Thus at the time he was caught he must have calculated that six days later, namely the Thursday of the story, would be too early to satisfy the requirements of the Ritual, so that we can be sure that the day of the story was *not later than* July 12th or October 6th, respectively; or, if we allow the required day to be later in the month we conclude that the day of the story was not later than August 11th or November 4th, according to whether it was summer or autumn. Since two weeks would have satisfied Brunton we can likewise conclude that seven days after the story would have reached or passed the required day, so that the day of the story is *not before* July 5th or September 29th. Hence the day of the story is one of the intervals July 5th to August 11th and

listened to this extraordinary sequence of events, and endeavoured to piece them together, and to devise some common thread upon which they might all hang.

"The butler was gone. The maid was gone. The maid had loved the butler, but had afterwards had cause to hate him. She was of Welsh blood, fiery and passionate. She had been terribly excited immediately after his disappearance. She had flung into the lake a bag containing some curious contents. These were all factors which had to be taken into consideration, and yet none of them got quite to the heart of the matter. What was the starting-point of this chain of events? There lay the end of this tangled line.

" ' I must see that paper, Musgrave,' said I, ' which this butler of yours thought it worth his while to consult, even at the risk of the loss of his place.'

" ' It is rather an absurd business, this Ritual of ours,' he answered, ' but it has at least the saving grace of antiquity to excuse it. I have a copy of the questions and answers here, if you care to run your eye over them.'

"He handed me the very paper which I have here, Watson, and this is the strange catechism to which each Musgrave had to submit when he came to man's estate. I will read you the questions and answers as they stand:
" ' Whose was it?
" ' His who is gone.
" ' Who shall have it?
" ' He who will come.
" ' What was the month?
22 " ' The sixth from the first.
" ' Where was the sun?
" ' Over the oak.
" ' Where was the shadow?
" ' Under the elm.
" ' How was it stepped?
" ' North by ten and by ten, east by five and by five, south by two and by two, west by one and by one, and so under.
" ' What shall we give for it?
" ' All that is ours.
" ' Why should we give it?
23 " ' For the sake of the trust.
" ' The original has no date, but is in the spelling of the middle of the seventeenth century,' remarked Musgrave. ' I am afraid, however, that it can be of little help to you in solving this mystery.'

" ' At least,' said I, ' it gives us another mystery, and one which is even more interesting than the first. It may be that the solution of the one may prove to be the solution of the other. You will excuse me, Musgrave, if I say that your butler appears to me to have been a very clever man, and to have had a clearer insight than ten generations of his masters.'

" ' I hardly follow you,' said Musgrave. ' The paper seems to me of no practical importance.'

" ' But to me it seems immensely practical, and I fancy that Brunton took the same view. He had probably seen it before that night on which you caught him.'

" ' It is very possible. We took no pains to hide it.'

" ' He simply wished, I should imagine, to refresh his memory upon that last occasion. He had, as I understand, some sort of map or chart which he was comparing with the manuscript, and which he thrust into his pocket when you appeared ? '

" ' That is true. But what could he have to do with this old family custom of ours, and what does this rigmarole mean ? '

" ' I don't think that we should have much difficulty in determining that,' said I. ' With your permission we will take the first train down to Sussex and go a little more deeply into the matter upon the spot.'

" The same afternoon saw us both at Hurlstone. Possibly you have seen pictures and read descriptions of the famous old building, so I will confine my account of it to saying that it is built in the shape of an **L**, the long arm being the more modern portion, and the shorter the ancient nucleus from which the other has developed Over the low, heavy-lintelled door, in the centre of this old part, is chiselled the date 1607, but experts are agreed that the beams and stonework are really much older than this. The enormously thick walls and tiny windows **24** of this part had in the last century driven the family into building the new wing, and the old one was used now as a storehouse and a cellar when it was used at all. A splendid park, with fine old timber, surrounded the house, and the lake, to which my client had referred, lay close to the avenue, about two hundred yards from the building.

" I was already firmly convinced, Watson, that there were not three separate mysteries here, but one only, and that if I could read the Musgrave Ritual aright, I should hold in my hand the clue which would lead me to the truth concerning both the butler Brunton, and the maid Howells. To that, then, I turned all my energies. Why should this servant be so anxious to master this old formula ? Evidently because he saw something in it which had escaped all those generations of country squires, and from which he expected some personal advantage. What was it, then, and how had it affected his fate ?

" It was perfectly obvious to me on reading the Ritual that the measurements must refer to some spot to which the rest of the document alluded, and that if we could find that spot we should be in a fair way towards knowing what the secret was which the old Musgraves had thought it necessary to embalm in so curious a fashion. There were two guides given us to start with, an oak and an elm. As to the oak, there could be no question at all. Right in front of the house, upon the left-hand side of the drive, there stood a patriarch among oaks, one of the most magnificent trees that I have ever seen.

" ' That was there when your Ritual was drawn up ? ' said I, as we drove past it.

" ' It was there at the Norman Conquest, in all probability,' he answered. ' It has a girth of 23 feet.'

" Here was one of my fixed points secured.

" ' Have you any old elms ? ' I asked.

" ' There used to be a very old one over yonder, but it was struck by lightning ten years ago, and we cut down the stump.'

September 29th to November 4th, and is most probably one of the intervals July 5th to July 12th and September 29th to October 6th."

23 " '*For the sake of the trust.*' The late T. S. Eliot's adaption of these lines in *Murder in the Cathedral* has led some commentators to speculate that Mr. Eliot and Dr. Conan Doyle were using a common source. This was not the case, as Mr. Eliot himself declared in a letter to Mr. Nathan L. Bengis quoted in the *Times Literary Supplement*, London, September 28, 1951: "My use of the Musgrave Ritual was deliberate and wholly conscious."

24 *The enormously thick walls.* "Walls six feet thick are common on rammed-earth cottages of the period; enormously thick walls might easily be ten feet or more through," Poul and Karen Anderson wrote in "The Curious Behavior of the Ritual in the Daytime."

" 'IT HAS A GIRTH OF 23 FEET.' "

Illustration by Sidney Paget for the *Strand Magazine*, May, 1893.

25 *It was 64 feet.'* "The Ritual had been prepared between the two Charleses—in the 1650s," the late Professor Jay Finley Christ wrote in "Musgrave Mathematics." "The oak was an enormous one which had stood at the time of the Conquest; and the elm was a sizeable tree in Musgrave's youth. It puts more than moderate strain upon my credulity, to consider that neither of these two trees grew a foot or so in height during two hundred years or more. Every foot of growth for either of them would have thrown the reckoning out by some eighteen inches!"

To this, Dr. Zeisler replied: "Professor Christ is mistaken as to the oak, for its growth would not have affected things since its only role was to give direction. But he is certainly correct as to the elm; its growth would have thrown things off very definitely. . . . The only possible explanation is that . . . the elm in this case had reached its maximum height before 1650, and the author of the Ritual had had an opportunity to learn that it was no longer growing in height."

26 *when the sun was just clear of the oak."* "What made it clear *where* the observer was to stand in order to see the sun over the oak?" Professor Christ asked in "Musgrave Mathematics." "Holmes seems to have stood just where the elm had been, but why? The compiler of the Ritual could not have stood there when the tree was in place."

27 *It was 9 feet in length.* If a rod of six feet threw a shadow of nine feet in Lat. 51° N. (for Sussex), then the sun was practically due west and 33.7° above the horizon and the time could not have been later than 4:20 P.M. But Professor Christ long ago demonstrated (*An Irregular Chronology*) that all these conditions are met with "during only about a week during the year. The week must run from just before to just after the summer solstice [June 21st]." But what does this make of the Ritual's "sixth month from the first"? And what of Holmes' remark (which must have been made not later than about 3:30 P.M.) that "It [the sun] was low in the heavens?" Dr. Zeisler, in his "elaborate analysis" of the problems engendered by this adventure concluded (*Baker Street Chronology*) that the sun *could* have been due west but "it could also have been either north or south of west . . ."

28 *almost to the wall of the house.* This, as we shall see, was the *west* wall of the "ancient nucleus."

29 *having first taken the cardinal points by my pocket compass.* "Now comes the strangest part of Holmes' exploit," Mr. A. D. Galbraith wrote in "The Real Moriarty." "The directions were taken with his pocket compass. But when the ancestral Musgrave buried the treasure, a perfect compass pointed almost true north, while when Holmes and Brunton found the hiding-place it pointed about 20° west of north. Thus the only way they could both come to the right spot would be to have com-

" ' You can see where it used to be ? '

" ' Oh, yes.'

" ' There are no other elms ? '

" ' No old ones, but plenty of beeches.'

" ' I should like to see where it grew.'

" We had driven up in a dog-cart, and my client led me away at once, without our entering the house, to the scar on the lawn where the elm had stood. It was nearly midway between the oak and the house. My investigation seemed to be progressing.

" ' I suppose it is impossible to find out how high the elm was ? ' I asked.

25 " ' I can give you it at once. It was 64 feet.'

" ' How do you come to know it ? ' I asked in surprise.

" ' When my old tutor used to give me an exercise in trigonometry it always took the shape of measuring heights. When I was a lad I worked out every tree and building on the estate.'

" This was an unexpected piece of luck. My data were coming more quickly than I could have reasonably hoped.

" ' Tell me,' I asked, ' did your butler ever ask you such a question ? '

" Reginald Musgrave looked at me in astonishment. ' Now that you call it to my mind,' he answered, ' Brunton *did* ask me about the height of the tree some months ago, in connection with some little argument with the groom.'

" This was excellent news, Watson, for it showed me that I was on the right road. I looked up at the sun. It was low in the heavens, and I calculated that in less than an hour it would lie just above the topmost branches of the old oak. One condition mentioned in the Ritual would then be fulfilled. And the shadow of the elm must mean the further end of the shadow, otherwise the trunk would have been chosen as the guide. I had then to find where the far end of the shadow would fall when the **26** sun was just clear of the oak."

" That must have been difficult, Holmes, when the elm was no longer there."

" Well, at least, I knew that if Brunton could do it, I could also. Besides, there was no real difficulty. I went with Musgrave to his study and whittled myself this peg, to which I tied this long string, with a knot at each yard. Then I took two lengths of a fishing-rod, which came to just 6 feet, and I went back with my client to where the elm had been. The sun was just grazing the top of the oak. I fastened the rod on end, marked out the direction of the shadow, and measured it. **27** It was 9 feet in length.

" Of course, the calculation was now a simple one. If a rod of 6 feet threw a shadow of 9 feet, a tree of 64 feet would throw one of 96 feet, and the line of one would of course be the line of the other. I measured out the distance, which brought me almost to the wall of the **28** house, and I thrust a peg into the spot. You can imagine my exultation, Watson, when within 2 inches of my peg I saw a conical depression in the ground. I knew that it was the mark made by Brunton in his measurements, and that I was still upon his trail.

" From this starting-point I proceeded to step, having first taken the cardinal points by my pocket compass. **29** Ten steps with each foot took me along parallel with the wall of the house, and again I marked my spot with a peg. Then I carefully paced off five to the east and two to the south. It brought me to the very threshold of the old door. Two steps to the west meant now that I was to go two paces down the stone-flagged passage, and this was the place indicated by the Ritual. ·

" Never have I felt such a cold chill of disappointment, Watson. For a moment it seemed to me that there must be some radical mistake in my calculations. The setting **30** sun shone full upon the passage floor, and I could see **31** that the old foot-worn grey stones, with which it was paved, were firmly cemented together, and had certainly not been moved for many a long year. Brunton had not been at work here. I tapped upon the floor, but it sounded the same all over, and there was no sign of any crack or crevice. But fortunately Musgrave, who had begun to appreciate the meaning of my proceedings, and who was now as excited as myself, took out his manuscript to check my calculations.

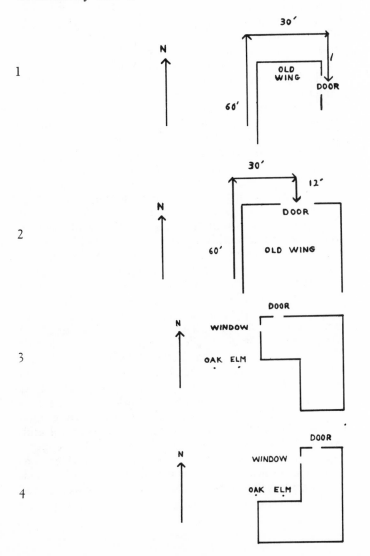

passes with the same error, which is hard to believe; and to have this error and the error in old Sir Ralph Musgrave's compass combine to compensate for the change of 20° in declination is incredible."

30 *some radical mistake in my calculations*. We may note here that the problem of "the emplacement of Hurlstone" is one that has long concerned Sherlockian scholars. Authoritative English references give the length of a pace as 30 inches (in quick time; double time is 33 inches). But was it a "pace" that Holmes used? Yes, for although he mentions the number of "steps" involved, and although the Ritual itself asks, "How was it stepped?", the fact remains that Holmes is precise in pointing out: "Then I carefully *paced* off . . ."

From the outside, it is possible to come to a threshold in the center of a wall from any one of three points of the compass. So, at first glance, there appear to be two possibilities here. First, that the old door might have been in the center of the *east* wall of the "ancient nucleus," thus:

Second, that the old door might have been in the center of the *north* wall, thus:

The apparent dilemma dissolves itself when one translates the pacings of the courses into linear distances, thus: 20 paces = 50 feet, 10 paces = 25 feet, 4 paces = 10 feet, 2 paces = 5 feet. Under the first drawing above, the width of the "ancient nucleus" could be little more than 30 feet at best. "A box sixty by thirty feet seems rather modest for 'one of the oldest families in the kingdom,' " Poul and Karen Anderson wrote in "The Curious Behavior of the Ritual in the Daytime." "When we consider one more fact, it becomes impossible. For the walls of this section are described as 'enormously thick.' "

Having eliminated the impossible, we must therefore conclude that Holmes was brought to the "very threshold" of a door in the center of the *north* wall of the older portion of the house.

The "emplacement of Hurlstone" must therefore have been this:

Or this:

The first plan clearly puts the oak too far to the west of Hurlstone—the old *or* the new portion —for the always precise Holmes to have said that it stood "right in front of the house."

We therefore suggest that the second plan represents the true emplacement—cramped as it still is, it is somewhat *less* cramped. There are, of course, other solutions, some of them involving plans in which the house must take the shape of an *inverted* L, which we do not feel is allowable. (Dr. Zeisler, indeed, was forced to conclude that the "stone-flagged passage" was *exterior* to the "ancient nucleus.") As Professor Christ justly concluded: "Certainly the place was not designed for the story . . ."

31 *The setting sun shone full upon the passage floor.* Since, as we have seen, the time must now be not later than about 4:30 P.M., Holmes' the *setting* sun must be modified to the *settling* sun, whatever the month of this adventure. But here is another indication that the sun of that day *was* shining from a direction practically due west. As Mr. Bell put it in *Sherlock Holmes and Dr. Watson: The Chronology of Their Adventures:* ". . . we are told that this old wing of the house had 'enormously thick walls and tiny windows'; therefore, unless the . . . sun had been shining straight through one such tiny window . . . in the west wall, its light could not possibly have reached the pavement. We have seen that the house faced the cardinal points; hence the sun must have been setting due west, and the season, consequently, was late September [or, in our view, early October]." And he added in a note: "In June, when the sun sets in the north-west, the light would have been lost in the deep window-embrasure, or would, at the farthest, have illuminated a small portion of the south wall of the passage."

". . . AND THIS WAS THE PLACE INDICATED BY THE RITUAL"

Illustration by Sidney Paget for the *Strand Magazine*, May, 1893.

" ' And under,' he cried : ' you have omitted the " and under." '

" I had thought that it meant that we were to dig, but now, of course, I saw at once that I was wrong. ' There is a cellar under this, then ? ' I cried.

" ' Yes, and as old as the house. Down here, through this door.'

" We went down a winding stone stair, and my companion, striking a match, lit a large lantern which stood on **32** a barrel in the corner. In an instant it was obvious that we had at last come upon the true place, and that we had not been the only people to visit the spot recently.

" It had been used for the storage of wood, but the billets, which had evidently been littered over the floor, were now piled at the sides so as to leave a clear space in the middle. In this space lay a large and heavy flagstone, with a rusted iron ring in the centre, to which a thick shepherd's check muffler was attached.

" ' By Jove ! ' cried my client, ' that's Brunton's muffler. I have seen it on him, and could swear to it. What has the villain been doing here ? '

" At my suggestion a couple of the county police were summoned to be present, and I then endeavoured to raise the stone by pulling on the cravat. I could only move it slightly, and it was with the aid of one of the constables that I succeeded at last in carrying it to one side. A black hole yawned beneath, into which we all peered, while Musgrave, kneeling at the side, pushed down the lantern.

" A small chamber about 7 feet deep and 4 feet square lay open to us. At one side of this was a squat, brass-bound, wooden box, the lid of which was hinged upwards, with this curious, old-fashioned key projecting from the lock. It was furred outside by a thick layer of dust, and damp and worms had eaten through the wood so that a crop of living fungi was growing on the inside of it. Several discs of metal—old coins apparently—such as I hold here, were scattered over the bottom of the box, but it contained nothing else.

" At the moment, however, we had not thought for the old chest, for our eyes were riveted upon that which crouched beside it. It was the figure of a man, clad in a suit of black, who squatted down upon his hams with his forehead sunk upon the edge of the box and his two arms thrown out on each side of it. The attitude had drawn all the stagnant blood to his face, and no man could have recognized that distorted, liver-coloured countenance ; but his height, his dress, and his hair were all sufficient to show my client, when we had drawn the body up, that it was indeed his missing butler. He had been dead some days, but there was no wound or bruise upon his person to show how he had met his dreadful end. When his body had been carried from the cellar we found ourselves still confronted with a problem which was almost as formidable as that with which we had started.

" I confess that so far, Watson, I had been disappointed in my investigation. I had reckoned upon solving the matter when once I had found the place referred to in the Ritual ; but now I was there, and was apparently as far as ever from knowing what it was which the family had concealed with such elaborate precautions. It is true that I had thrown a light upon the fate of Brunton, but now I had to ascertain how that fate had come upon him, and what part had been played in the matter by the woman who had disappeared. I sat down upon a keg in the corner and thought the whole matter carefully over.

" You know my methods in such cases, Watson : I put myself in the man's place, and having first gauged his intelligence, I try to imagine how I should myself have proceeded under the same circumstances. In this case the matter was simplified by Brunton's intelligence being quite first rate, so that it was unnecessary to make any allowance for personal equation, as the astronomers have dubbed it. He knew that something valuable was concealed. He had spotted the place. He found that the stone which covered it was just too heavy for a man to move unaided. What would he do next ? He could not get help from outside, even if he had someone whom he could trust, without the unbarring of doors, and considerable risk of detection. It was better, if he could, to have his helpmate inside the house. But whom could he ask ? This girl had been devoted to him. A man always finds it hard to realize that he may have finally lost a woman's love, however badly he may have treated her. He would try by a few attentions to make his peace with the girl Howells, and then would engage her as his accomplice. Together they would come at night to the cellar, and their united force would suffice to raise the stone. So far I could follow their actions as if I had actually seen them.

" But for two of them, and one a woman, it must have been heavy work, the raising of that stone. A burly Sussex policeman and I had found it no light job. What would they do to assist them ? Probably what I should have done myself. I rose and examined carefully the different billets of wood which were scattered round the floor. Almost at once I came upon what I expected. One piece, about 3 feet in length, had a marked indentation at one end, while several were flattened at the sides as if they had been compressed by some considerable weight. Evidently as they had dragged the stone up they had thrust the chunks of wood into the chink, until at last, when the opening was large enough to crawl through, they would hold it open by a billet placed lengthwise, which might very well become indented at the lower end, since the whole weight of the stone would press it down on to the edge of the other slab. So far I was still on safe ground.

" And now, how was I to proceed to reconstruct this midnight drama ? Clearly only one could get into the hole, and that one was Brunton. The girl must have waited above. Brunton then unlocked the box, handed up the contents, presumably—since they were not to be

32 *lit a large lantern which stood on a barrel in the corner.* But Musgrave earlier stated that the house had been thoroughly searched from cellar to garret. "If so," Mr. H. B. Williams asked in "Pleasure in Pictures," "why was this particular place missed? Musgrave knew it was there. He led Holmes to it and lit a match to light the lantern which he knew was standing on the barrel in the corner. Yet, familiar as he was with the cellar, the story would lead us to believe that it was missed in the search of the house. Incredible."

"IT WAS THE FIGURE OF A MAN . . ."

Illustration by Sidney Paget for the *Strand Magazine,* May, 1893.

"... STILL CLUTCHING AT HER TREASURE-TROVE ..."

Illustration by William H. Hyde for *Harper's Weekly*, May 13, 1893.

found—and then—and then what happened ?

" What smouldering fire of vengeance had suddenly sprung into flame in this passionate Celtic woman's soul when she saw the man who had wronged her—wronged her perhaps far more than we suspected—in her power ? Was it a chance that the wood had slipped and that the stone had shut Brunton into what had become his sepulchre ? Had she only been guilty of silence as to his fate ? Or had some sudden blow from her hand dashed the support away and sent the slab crashing down into its place. Be that as it might, I seemed to see that woman's figure, still clutching at her treasure-trove, and flying wildly up the winding stair with her ears ringing perhaps with the muffled screams from behind her, and with the drumming of frenzied hands against the slab of stone which was choking her faithless lover's life out.

" Here was the secret of her blanched face, her shaken nerves, her peals of hysterical laughter on the next morning. But what had been in the box ? What had she done with that ? Of course, it must have been the old metal and pebbles which my client had dragged from the mere. She had thrown them in there at the first opportunity, to remove the last trace of her crime.

" For twenty minutes I had sat motionless thinking the matter out. Musgrave still stood with a very pale face swinging his lantern and peering down into the hole.

" ' These are coins of Charles I,' said he, holding out the few which had been left in the box. ' You see we were right in fixing our date for the Ritual.'

" ' We may find something else of Charles I,' I cried, as the probable meaning of the first two questions of the Ritual broke suddenly upon me. ' Let me see the contents of the bag you fished from the mere.'

" We ascended to his study, and he laid the *débris* before me. I could understand his regarding it as of small importance when I looked at it, for the metal was almost black, and the stones lustreless and dull. I rubbed one of them on my sleeve, however, and it glowed afterwards like a spark, in the dark hollow of my hand. The metal-work was in the form of a double-ring, but it had been bent and twisted out of its original shape.

" ' You must bear in mind,' said I, ' that the Royal party made head in England even after the death of the King, and that when they at last fled they probably left many of their most precious possessions buried behind them, with the intention of returning for them in more peaceful times.'

" ' My ancestor, Sir Ralph Musgrave, was a prominent Cavalier, and the right-hand man of Charles II in his wanderings,' said my friend.

" ' Ah, indeed ! ' I answered. ' Well, now, I think that really should give us the last link that we wanted. I must congratulate you on coming into possession, though in rather a tragic manner, of a relic which is of great intrinsic value, but even of greater importance as an historical curiosity.'

" 'THESE ARE COINS OF CHARLES I . . .' "

Charles I Gold of England: 22 n.d. angel, Tower mint. 23 1644 triple unite, Oxford mint. 24 n.d. unite, Truro mint. 25 n.d. crown, Tower mint. *Charles I Gold of Scotland:* 26 n.d. unit. 27 n.d. double-crown. 28 n.d. half-crown. The illustrations are from *Numismatics in the Canon,* Part II: "A Very Treasury of Coin of Divers Realms," by the late A. Carson Simpson. Mr. Simpson noted that Watson, "in describing the coins as 'rusty,' showed either a lamentable lack of precision or else a remarkable ability to forget the chemistry he had been compelled to study to get his M.D. Although laymen occasionally use the word 'rust' in its secondary sense of 'corrosion,' yet, at the time Watson was in the University of London and presumably received at least an elementary training in chemistry, usage confined it to hydrous ferric oxide. Despite the turbulent times in which Charles I lived, he had never been reduced to striking *iron* coins."

" 'THE CROWN!' "

The "battered and shapeless diadem," here shown restored, has been identified by Mr. Nathan L. Bengis ("Whose Was It? An Examination into the Crowning Lapse of Sherlockian Scholarship") as the ancient Crown of St. Edward, about which the few details that are known tally perfectly with those given in the story. "The 1649 inventory [of British regalia] described the crown of St. Edward (listed as King Alfred's Crown) as being of 'gould wyer worke, sett with slight stones.' This seems to signify a filigree frame, which could easily be bent out of shape, as was the crown found at Hurlstone. The 'gould' was probably a base metal gilded to resemble gold. . . . Such a metalwork, after defacement, would tarnish in over two centuries to the ugly 'almost black' described in the Canon. The 'slight stones' would be discolored in time, so that eventually they would lose their lustre and would have to be rubbed, as was done by Sherlock Holmes, for them to glow again. . . . It is now plain that when Sherlock Holmes spoke of the crown as having 'once encircled the brows of the royal Stuarts,' he was speaking the literal truth: the crown of St. Edward was indeed worn once, and once only, by James I and Charles I, on the occasion of their respective coronations."

33 *the moon was shining brightly in the sky*. Professor Christ, who dated this case in June, commented ("Musgrave Mathematics"): "Amazing, Holmes! In that latitude, there is no real night at all for a month either way from the summer solstice, twilight can hardly be said to close in, and the nights are scarcely bright enough to permit the moon to shine brightly. She depends for her apparent brightness largely upon contrast with a dark sky."

Dr. Zeisler, who dated the case in October, concluded (*Baker Street Chronology*): "Hence we know that on that day the moon set *after* the sun. . . . [On Thursday, October 2, 1879—a date with which your editor concurs] the sun was at altitude 33.7° at 1:05 P.M., the moon was only two days past full and would have been shining brightly in the sky at 6:00 P.M., although it would have risen only eleven minutes before and twilight would have begun only twenty-five minutes earlier."

34 *before they were allowed to retain it*. "The most amazing feature of the whole story," Mr. Bengis wrote in "Whose Was It?", "is not that this relic survived, but that Reginald Musgrave was allowed by the British Government to retain it. . . . Whatever was paid could not have represented the minutest fraction of its worth as a unique historic treasure. . . . The crown was a public possession, and therefore no more negotiable than London Bridge."

Auctorial Note: For the March, 1927, issue of the *Strand Magazine*, Sir Arthur Conan Doyle was asked to draw up a list of his own favorite Sherlock Holmes short stories, excluding those in *The Case-Book*, which had not then been collected in book form. Sir Arthur chose twelve, of which he ranked "The Musgrave Ritual" No. 11.

" ' What is it, then ? ' he gasped in astonishment.

" ' It is nothing less than the ancient crown of the Kings of England.'

" ' The crown ! '

" ' Precisely. Consider what the Ritual says. How does it run ? " Whose was it ? " " His who is gone." That was after the execution of Charles. Then, " Who shall have it ? " " He who will come." That was Charles II, whose advent was already foreseen. There can, I think, be no doubt that this battered and shapeless diadem once encircled the brows of the Royal Stuarts.'

" ' And how came it in the pond ? '

" ' Ah, that is a question which will take some time to answer,' and with that I sketched out the whole long chain of surmise and of proof which I had constructed. The twilight had closed in and the moon was shining **33** brightly in the sky before my narrative was finished.

" ' And how was it, then, that Charles did not get his crown when he returned ? ' asked Musgrave, pushing back the relic into its linen bag.

" ' Ah, there you lay your finger upon the one point which we shall probably never be able to clear up. It is likely that the Musgrave who held the secret died in the interval, and by some oversight left this guide to his descendant without explaining the meaning of it. From that day to this it has been handed down from father to son, until at last it came within reach of a man who tore its secret out of it and lost his life in the venture.'

" And that's the story of the Musgrave Ritual, Watson. They have the crown down at Hurlstone—though they had some legal bother, and a considerable sum to pay **34** before they were allowed to retain it. I am sure that if you mentioned my name they would be happy to show it to you. Of the woman nothing was ever heard, and the probability is that she got away out of England, and carried herself, and the memory of her crime, to some land beyond the seas."

III. THE PARTNERSHIP,
TO DR. WATSON'S FIRST MARRIAGE

[Early January, 1881, to November, 1886]

"Get your hat, said he.

"You wish me to come?"

"Yes, if you have nothing better to do."

—*A Study in Scarlet*

. . . TOOK MY DEGREE OF DOCTOR OF MEDICINE OF THE UNIVERSITY OF LONDON . . .

The University of London, in Watson's day housed in a new (1870) build-
ing which had been erected for the University at Burlington Gardens, was
chiefly founded by the exertions of Lord Brougham for the purpose of
providing education in literature, science, and the arts at moderate cost.
The foundation stone of the building now known as University College, in
Gower Street, shown here, was laid on April 30, 1827, by the Duke of
Sussex, and the building was opened on October 1, 1828. It was designed by
William Wilkins, R.A., the architect of the National Gallery, and built
under the direction of J. Gandy Deering, A.R.A. Today it has many affiliated colleges, institutions, and schools, such as the London School of Politics
and Political Science. Its medical colleges include St. Bartholomew's, Guy's
and Westminster hospitals. Watson, an admirer of General Charles George
Gordon ("The Cardboard Box"), would be pleased to know that among
the manuscripts owned by the library of the University of London is a
signed dispatch in Arabic sent by General Gordon from Khartoum on June
22, 1884. The engraving above is from a copy of T. H. Shepherd's *The
World's Metropolis*, 1857, in the Cambridge University Library.

15

A STUDY IN SCARLET

[Friday, March 4, to Monday, March 7, 1881]

(Being a reprint from the Reminiscences of JOHN H. WATSON, M.D., *Late of the Army Medical Department.)* **1**

I   ♦   MR SHERLOCK HOLMES

In the year 1878 I took my degree of Doctor of Medicine of the University of London, and proceeded to Netley to go through the course prescribed for surgeons in the army. Having completed my studies there, I was duly attached to the Fifth Northumberland Fusiliers as Assistant Surgeon. The regiment was stationed in India at the time, and before I could join it, the second Afghan war had broken out. On landing at Bombay, I learned that my corps had advanced through the passes, and was already deep in the enemy's country. I followed, however, with many other officers who were in the same situation as myself, and succeeded in reaching Candahar in safety, where I found my regiment, and at once entered upon my new duties.

The campaign brought honours and promotion to many, but for me it had nothing but misfortune and disaster. I was removed from my brigade and attached to the Berkshires, with whom I served at the fatal battle of Maiwand. There I was struck on the shoulder by a Jezail bullet, which shattered the bone and grazed the subclavian artery. I should have fallen into the hands of the murderous Ghazis had it not been for the devotion and courage shown by Murray, my orderly, who threw me across a packhorse, and succeeded in bringing me safely to the British lines.

Worn with pain, and weak from the prolonged hardships which I had undergone, I was removed, with a great train of wounded sufferers, to the base hospital at Peshawur. Here I rallied, and had already improved so far as to be able to walk about the wards, and even to bask a little upon the verandah, when I was struck down by enteric fever, that curse of our Indian possessions. For months my life was despaired of, and when at last I came to myself and became convalescent, I was so weak and emaciated that a medical board determined that not a day should be lost in sending me back to England. I was despatched, accordingly, in the troopship *Orontes,* and landed a month later on Portsmouth jetty, with my health irretrievably ruined, but with permission from a paternal government to spend the next nine months in attempting to improve it.

1 (Being a reprint...) "Visualize, if you will, this volume for what it must be," the late Edgar W. Smith wrote in "A Bibliographical Note." "It is a fine, sturdy product, surely, nicely bound and neatly printed, and probably privately published along about the year 1885. Along with his account of the first adventure he shared with his room-mate, we would find in it an assortment of the doctor's earlier writings: something, of course, about his experiences with women extending over many nations and three separate continents [*The Sign of the Four*], and a more detailed report of the things he saw in India, including, we must hope, a definitive account of how and where his wound-stripe or stripes came to be won. There was much he had to say: he was only 33 when he wrote, but, being the man he was, there was enough for him to call what he set down his 'Reminiscences.' "

Most students, however, feel that this edition of the "Reminiscences" never saw print: "In . . . recent years," Mr. John Ball, Jr., wrote in "The Second Collaboration," "intensive research has been put forth to locate every available edition [of Dr. Watson's published records], but no known copy of the *original* publication of the 'Reminiscences' referred to has ever been found. Since even a very limited edition would have left some traces for future researchers to uncover, the possibility presents itself that no such edition did, in fact, exist."

"How did Watson meet Dr. Doyle?" Mr. Bliss Austin asked in *A Baker Street Christmas Stocking* for 1962. He suggests that Conan Doyle himself may have shed some light on the question when he wrote in his autobiography: "My pleasant recollection of those days from 1880 to 1893 lay in my first introduction, as a more or less rising author, to the literary life of London." "He then goes on," Mr. Austin wrote, "to list a number of writers whom he met including 'Rudyard Kipling, James Stephen Phillips, Watson . . .' and a whole list of others. So he met Watson in literary circles! But what had Watson written to gain admission to such a select group? Obviously, his reminiscences of which *A Study in Scarlet* is an admitted reprint."

2 *an income of eleven shillings and sixpence a day.* Worth, in American currency in those days, about $2.87. It "may not seem a princely sum in this inflated era," Mr. L. S. Holstein wrote in "Bull Pups and Literary Agents," "but one should remember the time was the 1880's, when, in this country, the laboring day was twelve hours and the pay commonly one dollar, worth 100 cents."

"Eleven shillings sixpence a day was better than two hundred pounds a year and I am told that Hart's *Army List for the British Army* (1891) states that the full pay of an army surgeon was about two hundred pounds a year. Surely, then, this was no starvation income," Mr. Bliss Austin wrote in *A Baker Street Christmas Stocking* for 1962.

On the other hand, Mr. Michael Harrison has noted (*In the Footsteps of Sherlock Holmes*) that "for a man wishing to keep above the level of the working-class, the world of 1881 was not a cheap one." If Watson was staying at one of the smaller hotels off the Strand he would have had to pay probably 7/6 (about $1.87) for "bed and breakfast," which would leave him only four shillings ($1.00) a day for all other expenses. He might possibly get a single bedroom *en pension*, that is, at a boardinghouse rate, for 10/6 ($2.62) a day, but this would leave him only a shilling (25¢) a day for tobacco and extras.

It is very much to be doubted that Watson survived for long on his pension alone. From 1887 on, he would enjoy the proceeds of his accounts of the Sherlock Holmes cases, even if he shared those proceeds with his collaborator, Dr. Conan Doyle. Indeed, it has even been suggested that some of Watson's experiences before his meeting with Holmes may have furnished Dr. Conan Doyle with material for stories sold to the *Strand Magazine*, the *Cornhill Magazine*, and other English publications.

In addition, Mr. T. S. Blakeney has suggested (*Sherlock Holmes: Fact or Fiction?*) that Watson's father, "who could leave his eldest son a 50-guinea watch and (so Holmes deduced) probably other financial advantages, may not have overlooked the decidedly more respectable younger son. Watson may have inherited a bit of money, in addition to his 11/6 a day pension. He had to have *some* ready money to buy his practice after marrying Miss Morstan. Perhaps he got one of her pearls to sell. As these six splendid pearls (plus the remainder of the chaplet, which was in Thaddeus [Sholto's] possession) were Miss Morstan's property, I should think she might well have got a jeweler to reset the pearls in the chap-

. . . STAYED FOR SOME TIME AT A PRIVATE HOTEL IN THE STRAND . . .

An ancient highway, the Strand: from the earliest days it connected London and Westminster; it is mentioned in documents that survive from pre-Norman Conquest times. Today it is a vast thoroughfare crowded with traffic—and so it was in Holmes' and Watson's day. But the name which the street bears reminds us that it began as little more than a country lane following the *strand*, the shore, of the Thames. In 1740 a Mr. Bathoe established London's first circulating library in the Strand, and about the same time it was the proper thing for ladies of fashion to visit Messrs. Twining's shop to sample a delicate china cup of that comparatively rare beverage, tea. Many of the taverns and coffeehouses in the Strand became meeting places for literary personalities; it followed that many publishers and booksellers set up their businesses there. The entertainment world also became centered there; in Holmes' and Watson's day most London theatres, including the Adelphi and the Gaiety, stood in or near the Strand. If we wish to know how it may have looked to Dr. Watson, we have the description by Augustus J. C. Hare in *Walks in London*: "If we could linger, as we might in the early morning, when there would be no great traffic to hinder us, we should see that, even now, the great street is far from unpicturesque. The houses, projecting, receding, still ornamented here and there with bow-windows, sometimes with a little sculpture or pargetting work, present a very broken outline to the sky; and, at the end, in the blue haze which is so beautiful on a fine day in London, rises the Flemish-looking steeple of St. Mary-le-Strand with the light streaming through its open pillars." The photograph, by London Transport Executive, is from Michael Harrison's *In the Footsteps of Sherlock Holmes*.

I had neither kith nor kin in England, and was therefore as free as air—or as free as an income of eleven shillings and sixpence a day will permit a man to be. Under such circum- **2** stances I naturally gravitated to London, that great cesspool into which all the loungers and idlers of the Empire are irresistibly drained. There I stayed for some time at a private hotel in the Strand, leading a comfortless, meaningless exis- tence, and spending such money as I had, considerably more freely than I ought. So alarming did the state of my finances become, that I soon realized that I must either leave the metropolis and rusticate somewhere in the country, or that I must make a complete alteration in my style of living. Choos- **3** ing the latter alternative, I began by making up my mind to leave the hotel, and to take up my quarters in some less pre- tentious and less expensive domicile.

On the very day that I had come to this conclusion, I was standing at the Criterion Bar, when someone tapped me on the shoulder, and turning round I recognized young Stam- ford, who had been a dresser under me at Barts. The sight of a friendly face in the great wilderness of London is a pleasant thing indeed to a lonely man. In old days Stamford had never been a particular crony of mine, but now I hailed him with enthusiasm, and he, in his turn, appeared to be delighted to see me. In the exuberance of my joy, I asked him to lunch with me at the Holborn, and we started off together in a hansom.

let and sell the latter at Christie's. She'd have made some thousands for certain—perhaps five figures. I fancy Watson, by his marriage, made his finan- cial condition a much easier one . . ."

The late Christopher Morley thought that Mary Morstan may have contributed to Watson's in- come after their marriage in another way: he sug- gested that Mary's skill with the needle enabled her to set up an expensive dressmaking shop ("Watson à la Mode").

3 *a complete alteration in my style of living.* Mr. John Ball, Jr., has suggested ("The Second Col- laboration") that Watson and Conan Doyle prob-

. . . I WAS STANDING AT THE CRITERION BAR, WHEN SOMEONE TAPPED ME ON THE SHOULDER . . .

The Criterion Restaurant, designed by Thomas Verity, built in 1873 at a cost of £80,000, including the internal equipment, was then eight years old. Still with us, it "occupies about half the block ly- ing within a rectangle formed by Haymarket, Jermyn Street, Piccadilly Circus, and Lower Re- gent Street. . . . Its white façade, capped by its two Second Empire truncated-pyramid roof towers [is] every bit as much of a landmark as aluminum Eros on his bronze fountain" (Michael Harrison, *In the Footsteps of Sherlock Holmes*). It stands on the site of the White Bear Inn, which was for- merly one of the busiest coaching houses trading with the west and southwest of England. Dr. Wat- son frequented the establishment, we suppose, be- cause the original proprietors were two Australians, Spiers and Pond. Or it may have been because the Criterion attracted the pretty society women of the period; it was also a great gathering place for racing men. It is regrettable to add that the site of the Criterion's original Long Bar is now occupied by one of the many *milk* bars in the great Forte chain. The illustration shown here was used by the Sherlock Holmes Society of London for its 1954 Christmas card.

... I ASKED HIM TO LUNCH WITH ME AT THE HOLBORN ...

The Holborn Restaurant, now demolished, stood at the west corner of Kingsway and High Holborn. Originally the Holborn Casino, it was the largest and best conducted dance hall in London during the seventies of the last century. "It was an example of Victorian classicism at its worst," Mr. William H. Gill wrote in "Some Notable Sherlockian Buildings," "with heavy Portland stone ashlar front, much superfluous ornament, and three floors covered with hideously proportioned windows. No doubt the fact that it had been recently patronised by Royalty [H.R.H. the Prince of Wales, later King Edward VII], impressed the young Watson and his companion." Dr. Watson took young Stamford to the Holborn, rather than lunching at the Criterion, because the Holborn was considerably cheaper. But despite the doctor's desire to economize, he generously stood Stamford to wine with his lunch. "There was a vintage Richebourg," Mr. Michael Harrison wrote (*In the Footsteps of Sherlock Holmes*), "on the wine list at 4s. 6d. [$1.12] a bottle—the Romanée, vintage 1865, at 10s. [$2.50] was a little past its prime; though the Nuits, vintage 1875, at 7s. 6d. [$1.87], was excellent. Let us assume that Watson compromised with his 'enthusiasm' and ordered a bottle at about five shillings [$1.25]. With what he would have called a 'pre-prandial' sherry, as well as coffee and cigars . . . he would have spent a pound [$5.00]." The Holborn described itself in an advertisement of 1880 as "one of the sights and one of the comforts of London." It combined, it said, the "attractions of the chief Parisian establishments with the quiet and order essential to English custom." Apart from luncheon it offered a *table d'hôte* dinner "at separate tables every evening from 5:30 to 8:30 in the Grand Salon, the Prince's Salon and the Duke's Salon." It included "two soups, two kinds of fish, two entrées, joints, sweets, cheese (in variety), salad, etc., with ices and dessert." The price was 3s. 6d. (about 87¢). "This favourite dinner is accompanied by a selection of high-class instrumental music." The woodcut shown here, from *The Builder*, reproduced in Michael Harrison's *In the Footsteps of Sherlock Holmes*, shows the restaurant before the addition of the wing at the corner of Little Queen Street, now Kingsway. The building on the right of the picture survives as a branch of Lloyd's Bank.

St. Bartholomew's Hospital—popularly known as Barts—lies within an irregular triangle formed by Newgate Street on the south, Giltspur Street on the west, and King Edward Street on the east. Tradition has it that the hospital was founded by Rahere, a sort of King's jester to Henry I. Rahere, on his deathbed, vowed that if he should by some miracle recover he would atone for his sins by dedicating a religious foundation. Rahere did recover, persuaded Henry to make him a grant of land, and there, in 1123, he built a hospital and a priory, both named for the saint who had appeared to him in a vision during his illness. Doctors other than John H. Watson who served Bart's in their time included Dr. Harvey, the personal physician to Charles I, who discovered the circulation of the blood; Percival Pott, who gave his name to the "Pott's fracture"; and John Abernethy, the brilliant surgeon whose lectures were so well attended that the lecture hall had to be enlarged to accommodate his listeners. Abernethy's brusqueness and independence were legendary; it is just as well that Watson did not call him in during "The Adventure of the Dying Detective" —he was adept at recognizing malingerers and treated them with withering scorn. Shown here is the Library and Museum of Bart's as it looked when Holmes was a research student and met Watson there. The etching, by Hulton, is from Michael Harrison's *In the Footsteps of Sherlock Holmes*.

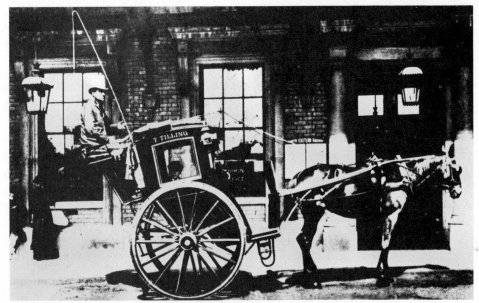

. . . AND WE STARTED OFF TOGETHER IN A HANSOM.

"The gondolas of London" was the felicitous title conferred upon the hansom cabs by the great Benjamin Disraeli. Named for Joseph Aloysius Hansom, 1803–1882, redesigned by John Chapman, a rival carriage maker, made fashionable by Forder, whose luxurious hansom, constructed especially for the Prince of Wales, carried off first prize at the Carriage Exhibition of 1872, the hansom cab was in all probability the fastest vehicle devised up to that time for negotiating the narrow and congested streets of London at high speeds. The top-hatted driver sat high up at the back of the hansom, with the reins passing through a support on the front of the roof. The front of the hansom was open, except for two folding doors which came about halfway up and protected the traveler's feet and legs against the weather. To ride in this type of cab, with its brightly polished lamps and brasswork, its jingling harness and smartly trotting horse, was a highly pleasant experience, as both Holmes and Watson knew well. In their day there were more than 8,000 of the cabs circulating through London; in 1933, their centennial year, there were only three hansom cabs left in the entire city. The minimum hansom cab fare for one or two passengers was a shilling (25¢) for two miles and sixpence (12½¢) a mile over that, but a cabman was not obliged to drive over six miles even if he could charge more when he got beyond the "Four Mile Radius"—a circle drawn with Charing Cross as the center. As Kipling wrote in his poem, "Et Dona Ferentes":

In extended observation of the ways and works of man
From the Four Mile Radius roughly to the plains of
Hindustan.

ably met at this time: "Despite the lack of immediate funds and the limitation of few friendships from which to draw strength and encouragement, Dr. Watson could not and did not fail to give some thought to the matter of setting up in practice. At about the same time, another physician, in closely parallel circumstances, found that he too had a need for gainful professional employment. It is not recorded at what time or under what circumstances the two young doctors met, but meet they unmistakably did. It may have been at a medical lecture, in the physicians' section of the public library, at a medical supply house where they had gone separately to ascertain the cost of the equipment needed to outfit a modest office. Wherever it was, a friendship and a collaboration was formed which was to enrich the world. For, great as was the association between Dr. Watson and Sherlock Holmes, of nearly equal importance to posterity was the second collaboration between Dr. Watson and the other physician who was also destined for immortal fame, Dr. Arthur Conan Doyle."

4 *looked rather strangely at me over his wine-glass.* "Had he some kind of intuition that he was to be one of the great liason-officers of literary history, that he was shortly to bring about a meeting comparable in its far-reaching influences with that other meeting arranged by Tom Davies in Russell Street, Covent Garden, more than a hundred years before?", Mr. S. C. Roberts asked in *Doctor Watson.* Mr. Roberts here refers to Thomas Davies, English actor and bookseller 1712–1785. Davies was a friend of Dr. Sam Johnson's; Johnson first met Boswell at Davies' home in 1763.

5 *well up in anatomy.* "Accurate, but unsystematic," was Watson's later judgment of Holmes' knowledge of anatomy.

"I'VE FOUND IT! I'VE FOUND IT," HE SHOUTED TO MY
COMPANION . . .

Illustration by George Hutchinson for the London, 1891, Ward, Lock, Bowden & Co. edition of *A Study in Scarlet.* Hutchinson, the late James Montgomery wrote in *A Study in Pictures,* "taxes our romantic illusions to the utmost by his almost diabolically unattractive representations."

'Whatever have you been doing with yourself, Watson?' he asked in undisguised wonder, as we rattled through the crowded London streets. 'You are as thin as a lath and as brown as a nut.'

I gave him a short sketch of my adventures, and had hardly concluded it by the time that we reached our destination.

'Poor devil!' he said commiseratingly, after he had listened to my misfortunes. 'What are you up to now?'

'Looking for lodgings,' I answered. 'Trying to solve the problem as to whether it is possible to get comfortable rooms at a reasonable price.'

'That's a strange thing,' remarked my companion, 'you are the second man today that has used that expression to me.'

'And who was the first?' I asked.

'A fellow who is working at the chemical laboratory up at the hospital. He was bemoaning himself this morning because he could not get someone to go halves with him in some nice rooms which he had found, and which were too much for his purse.'

'By Jove!' I cried; 'if he really wants someone to share the rooms and the expense, I am the very man for him. I should prefer having a partner to being alone.'

Young Stamford looked rather strangely at me over his **4** wine-glass. 'You don't know Sherlock Holmes yet,' he said; 'perhaps you would not care for him as a constant companion.'

'Why, what is there against him?'

'Oh, I didn't say there was anything against him. He is a little queer in his ideas—an enthusiast in some branches of science. As far as I know he is a decent fellow enough.'

'A medical student, I suppose?' said I.

'No—I have no idea what he intends to go in for. I believe **5** he is well up in anatomy, and he is a first-class chemist; but, as far as I know, he has never taken out any systematic medical classes. His studies are very desultory and eccentric,

but he has amassed a lot of out-of-the-way knowledge which would astonish his professors.'

'Did you never ask him what he was going in for?' I asked.

'No; he is not a man that it is easy to draw out, though he can be communicative enough when the fancy seizes him.'

'I should like to meet him,' I said. 'If I am to lodge with anyone, I should prefer a man of studious and quiet habits. I am not strong enough yet to stand much noise or excitement. I had enough of both in Afghanistan to last me for the remainder of my natural existence. How could I meet this friend of yours?'

'He is sure to be at the laboratory,' returned my companion. 'He either avoids the place for weeks, or else he works there from morning till night. If you like, we will drive round together after luncheon.'

'Certainly,' I answered, and the conversation drifted away into other channels.

As we made our way to the hospital after leaving the Holborn, Stamford gave me a few more particulars about the gentleman whom I proposed to take as a fellow-lodger.

'You mustn't blame me if you don't get on with him,' he said; 'I know nothing more of him than I have learned from meeting him occasionally in the laboratory. You proposed this arrangement, so you must not hold me responsible.'

'If we don't get on it will be easy to part company,' I answered. 'It seems to me, Stamford,' I added, looking hard at my companion, 'that you have some reason for washing your hands of the matter. Is this fellow's temper so formidable, or what is it? Don't be mealy-mouthed about it.'

'It is not easy to express the inexpressible,' he answered with a laugh. 'Holmes is a little too scientific for my tastes—it approaches to cold-bloodedness. I could imagine his giving a friend a little pinch of the latest vegetable alkaloid, not out **6** of malevolence, you understand, but simply out of a spirit of inquiry in order to have an accurate idea of the effects. To do him justice, I think that he would take it himself with the same readiness. He appears to have a passion for definite and exact knowledge.'

'Very right too.'

'Yes, but it may be pushed to excess. When it comes to beating the subjects in the dissecting-rooms with a stick, it is certainly taking rather a bizarre shape.'

'Beating the subjects!'

'Yes, to verify how far bruises may be produced after death. I saw him at it with my own eyes.'

'And yet you say he is not a medical student?'

'No. Heaven knows what the objects of his studies are. But here we are, and you must form your own impressions about him.' As he spoke, we turned down a narrow lane and passed **7** through a small side-door, which opened into a wing of the great hospital. It was familiar ground to me, and I needed no guiding as we ascended the bleak stone staircase and made our way down the long corridor with its vista of whitewashed wall and dun-coloured doors. Near the farther end a low arched passage branched away from it and led to the chemical laboratory.

This was a lofty chamber, lined and littered with countless bottles. Broad, low tables were scattered about, which bristled with retorts, test-tubes, and little Bunsen lamps, with their **8**

6 *the latest vegetable alkaloid.* The first alkaloid, impure nicotine, was prepared by Derosne in 1803; by 1840 practically all the more important alkaloids (veratrine, strychnine, piperine, caffeine, quinine, bernerine, conine, stropine, codeine, aconite, and colchicene) had been isolated. Vegetable alkaloids are those which are obtained from plants, as distinguished from those that are extracted from viscera and stomach contents—the "animal" alkaloids. "The chemist," says the *Encyclopaedia Britannica*, "looks upon the alkaloids as fascinating problems for the exercise of his technique and imagination. He has devoted much attention to devising methods for their detection, isolation and purification; and he has displayed considerable ingenuity in splitting their intimate structures as will provide a basis for producing them at will in his laboratory."

7 *we turned down a narrow lane.* In entering Bart's, "Watson must have passed under the great Renaissance gateway designed by James Gibbs (the best of Wren's pupils) in 1702, whilst the bulk of the great hospital was built by the same architect in 1730," Mr. William H. Gill wrote in "Some Notable Sherlockian Buildings." "From the description given in *A Study in Scarlet* the simplicity of the laboratory points to it being a part of Gibbs' work, and it is pleasing to think that the two immortal friends first met in a room designed by one of Britain's greatest architects."

8 *little Bunsen lamps.* Named for their inventor, Robert Wilhelm Eberhard Bunsen (1811–1899), German chemist and discoverer, Professor of Heidelberg University. The Bunsen lamp consists typically of a straight tube, four or five inches long, with small holes for the entrance of air at the bottom. Illuminating gas being also admitted at the bottom, a mixture of gas and air is formed which burns at the top with a feebly luminous but intensely hot blue flame.

9 *There was only one student in the room.* Writing in the *St. Bartholomew's Hospital Journal*, Mr. A. N. Griffith noted ("Some Observations on Sherlock Holmes and Dr. Watson at Bart's") that "Augustus Mattiesson was the lecturer in chemistry at Bart's from 1870 onwards. Sir Norman Moore recalls that he had two private pupils; one was Moore himself, the other he does not name though he does give us some information about him. He had been in Strasbourg during the Franco-Prussian War, . . . when a shell passed through his house. Mattiesson was interested in opium and together they investigated its alkaloids. He was a constant and eager experimenter. The likeness between this student and Holmes becomes more and more apparent, and we may, in fact, conclude that they were the same person. If this be accepted, his position at Bart's is accounted for, his absence from Britain during the Franco-Prussian War explained [see "The Adventure of the Noble Bachelor," Note 28] as is his useful knowledge of German, for it will be remembered he was happy to quote Goethe quite glibly."

10 *The proportion of blood cannot be more than one in a million.* "Holmes . . . made a gross error in estimating to Watson . . . the concentration of his blood solution: one drop of blood in a litre of water . . . actually cannot be less than one in 30,000," Professor Remsen Ten Eyck Schenck wrote in "Baker Street Fables."

11 *a brownish dust was precipitated to the bottom of the glass jar.* "This can be neither of the known methods for the detection of blood, since the outmoded guaiac reaction gives a blue coloration and the usual benzedrine test a blue-green," Professor Schenck wrote. "Holmes' discovery would certainly be in universal use today were it valid, and it must therefore be concluded that his belief in its specificity for haemoglobin was unfounded. Presumably he discovered on further study that a similar result was obtained with other common substances, or else that it was not due to haemoglobin at all, but rather to some other ingredient present in the blood, but not peculiar to it."

". . . it is surely as valid to reason that this research finally resulted in the present-day haemochromogen test as it is to state that it is no test at all," Mr. L. S. Holstein reported in "'7. Knowledge of Chemistry—Profound.'" "Forensic chemistry has made great strides in the past two generations. That 'dull mahogany colour' that Watson observed may be the nineteenth century version of the pinkish cast of the haemochromogen crystals."

12 *The old guaiacum test.* "The guaiacum or lignum vitae tree is native to the West Indies and northern South America," Christopher Morley wrote in *Sherlock Holmes and Dr. Watson: A Textbook of Friendship.* "Both bark and resin

blue flickering flames. There was only one student in the **9** room, who was bending over a distant table absorbed in his work. At the sound of our steps he glanced round and sprang to his feet with a cry of pleasure. 'I've found it! I've found it,' he shouted to my companion, running towards us with a test-tube in his hand. 'I have found a reagent which is precipitated by hæmoglobin, and by nothing else.' Had he discovered a gold mine, greater delight could not have shone upon his features.

'Dr Watson, Mr Sherlock Holmes,' said Stamford, introducing us.

'How are you?' he said cordially, gripping my hand with a strength for which I should hardly have given him credit. 'You have been in Afghanistan, I perceive.'

'How on earth did you know that?' I asked in astonishment.

'Never mind,' said he, chuckling to himself. 'The question now is about hæmoglobin. No doubt you see the significance of this discovery of mine?'

'It is interesting, chemically, no doubt,' I answered, 'but practically——'

'Why, man, it is the most practical medico-legal discovery for years. Don't you see that it gives us an infallible test for blood stains. Come over here now!' He seized me by the coat-sleeve in his eagerness, and drew me over to the table at which he had been working. 'Let us have some fresh blood,' he said, digging a long bodkin into his finger, and drawing off the resulting drop of blood in a chemical pipette. 'Now, I add this small quantity of blood to a litre of water. You perceive that the resulting mixture has the appearance of pure water. The proportion of blood cannot be more than one in a **10** million. I have no doubt, however, that we shall be able to obtain the characteristic reaction.' As he spoke, he threw into the vessel a few white crystals, and then added some drops of a transparent fluid. In an instant the contents assumed a dull mahogany colour, and a brownish dust was precipitated to **11** the bottom of the glass jar.

'Ha! ha!' he cried, clapping his hands, and looking as delighted as a child with a new toy. 'What do you think of that?'

'It seems to be a very delicate test,' I remarked.

12 'Beautiful! beautiful! The old guaiacum test was very clumsy and uncertain. So is the microscopic examination for blood corpuscles. The latter is valueless if the stains are a few hours old. Now, this appears to act as well whether the blood is old or new. Had this test been invented, there are hundreds of men now walking the earth who would long ago have paid the penalty of their crimes.'

'Indeed!' I murmured.

'Criminal cases are continually hinging upon that one point. A man is suspected of a crime months perhaps after it has been committed. His linen or clothes are examined and brownish stains discovered upon them. Are they blood stains, or mud stains, or rust stains, or fruit stains, or what are they? That is a question which has puzzled many an expert, and why? Because there was no reliable test. Now we have the Sherlock Holmes test, and there will no longer be any difficulty.'

His eyes fairly glittered as he spoke, and he put his hand

over his heart and bowed as if to some applauding crowd conjured up by his imagination.

'You are to be congratulated,' I remarked, considerably surprised at his enthusiasm.

'There was the case of Von Bischoff at Frankfort last year. **13** He would certainly have been hung had this test been in existence. Then there was Mason of Bradford, and the notorious **14** Muller, and Lefevre of Montpellier, and Samson of New **15** Orleans. I could name a score of cases in which it would have been decisive.'

'You seem to be a walking calendar of crime,' said Stamford with a laugh. 'You might start a paper on those lines. Call it the "Police News of the Past."'

'Very interesting reading it might be made, too,' remarked Sherlock Holmes, sticking a small piece of plaster over the prick on his finger. 'I have to be careful,' he continued, turning to me with a smile, 'for I dabble with poisons a good deal.' He held out his hand as he spoke, and I noticed that it was all mottled over with similar pieces of plaster, and discoloured with strong acids.

'We came here on business,' said Stamford, sitting down on a high three-legged stool, and pushing another one in my direction with his foot. 'My friend here wants to take diggings; and as you were complaining that you could get no **16** one to go halves with you, I thought that I had better bring you together.'

Sherlock Holmes seemed delighted at the idea of sharing his rooms with me. 'I have my eye on a suite in Baker Street,' he said, 'which would suit us down to the ground. You don't mind the smell of strong tobacco, I hope?'

'I always smoke "ship's" myself,' I answered. **17**

'That's good enough. I generally have chemicals about, and occasionally do experiments. Would that annoy you?'

'By no means.'

'Let me see—what are my other shortcomings. I get in the dumps at times, and don't open my mouth for days on end. You must not think I am sulky when I do that. Just let me alone, and I'll soon be right. What have you to confess now? It's just as well for two fellows to know the worst of one another before they begin to live together.'

I laughed at this cross-examination. 'I keep a bull pup,' I **18** said, 'and I object to row, because my nerves are shaken, and I get up at all sorts of ungodly hours, and I am extremely lazy. I have another set of vices when I'm well, but those are the **19** principal ones at present.'

'Do you include violin playing in your category of rows?' he asked, anxiously.

'It depends on the player,' I answered. 'A well-played violin is a treat for the gods—a badly-played one——'

'Oh, that's all right,' he cried, with a merry laugh. 'I think **20** we may consider the thing as settled—that is, if the rooms are agreeable to you.'

'When shall we see them?'

'Call for me here at noon tomorrow, and we'll go together and settle everything,' he answered.

'All right—noon exactly,' said I, shaking his hand.

We left him working among his chemicals, and we walked together towards my hotel.

have been much used in pharmacy. In testing for the presence of blood a tincture of 1 part resin to 6 parts alcohol was used. This was added to a smaller quantity of the liquid under examination, and shaken together with a few drops of hydrogen peroxide in ether. The ether dissolves the resin, and if haemoglobin is present the mixture turns bright blue."

In *The Shadow of the Wolf*, by the late R. Austin Freeman, we read this description of the process: ". . . He poured a quantity of the tincture [of guaiacum] on the middle of the stained area. The pool of liquid rapidly spread considerably beyond the limits of the stain, growing paler as it extended. Then Thorndyke cautiously dropped small quantities of ozonic ether at various points around the stained area, and watched closely as the two liquids mingled in the fabric of the sail. Gradually the ether spread towards the stain, and, first at one point and then at another, approached and finally crossed the wavy grey line; and at each point the same change occurred: first the faint grey line turned into a strong blue line, and then the colour extended to the enclosed space until the entire area of the stain stood out in a conspicuous blue patch. 'You understand the meaning of this,' said Thorndyke. 'This is a bloodstain.'"

According to Mr. P. M. Stone in his essay, "The Other Friendship: A Speculation," Holmes and Thorndyke knew each other well. "It seems a pity that they did not know each other's methods better," the late Edgar W. Smith once commented.

13 *last year.* This direct quotation from Holmes might be of great value to researchers in dating *A Study in Scarlet* once for all, but scholars have so far failed to determine the year in which Von Bischoff was tried and (presumably) acquitted.

14 *Bradford.* In Yorkshire—a center of the worsted-milling industry.

15 *Montpellier.* An indication of Holmes' lifelong interest in the south of France.

16 *diggings.* English slang for lodgings.

17 *'I always smoke "ship's" myself.'* Miss Sherry Keen ("Ship's or 'ship's'?") has noted that both *A Dictionary of Slang and Unconventional English* by Eric Partridge and *Soldier and Sailor, Words and Phrases* by Fraser and Gibbons refer to "ship's" as a "naval tobacco." "Ship's" with Watson was evidently a passing fancy, picked up from the sailors aboard the *Orontes*, for in "The Crooked Man" Holmes says to Watson: "Hum! you still smoke the Arcadia mixture of your bachelor days, then!"

18 *'I keep a bull pup.'* It is never heard of again. We must remember that Holmes in his college days had been bitten in the ankle by a bull terrier (Victor Trevor's) and Watson's bull pup may have found the same target irresistible. "Watson, that dog must go!" However, many Sherlockians —both dog-lovers and caniphobes—have pondered the problem of the bull pup, and other suggestions include these: 1) Mrs. Hudson objected to the animal, perhaps because she had an ancient terrier of her own; 2) The pup was accidentally killed by Watson, who stumbled while carrying the animal up the seventeen stairs to the sitting room; 3) The pup was a victim of one of Holmes' chemical experiments; 4) The dog, unable to stand the Baker Street menage, deserted. "The real mystery, it seems to me," Mr. L. S. Holstein wrote in "Bull Pups and Literary Agents," "is why Watson should have had a bull pup in the first place, no matter how great a dog-lover he may have been. He was a man without a home, up to the time of taking residence at 221B, and without means to feed an extra mouth even though that be only a dog's mouth. And can you imagine that the 'private hotel in the Strand' allowed him to keep a dog?"

19 *I have another set of vices when I'm well.* Watson perhaps refers here to his experience of women, his propensity for gambling, or his occasional intemperance.

20 *with a merry laugh.* "It is curious, and momentarily disconcerting, to find that Dr. Watson asserts in 'The Adventure of the Sussex Vampire,' that a dry chuckle was Mr. Holmes' 'nearest approach to a laugh,'" Dean Theodore C. Blegen wrote in "These Were Hidden Fires, Indeed!" (And in "The Adventure of the Mazarin Stone," Watson wrote of Holmes that he "seldom laughed.") "In case after case," Dean Blegen continued, "the doctor has reported roars and explosions and even paroxysms of laughter by Mr. Holmes. I think we must, unhappily, assume another little lapse of memory on Dr. Watson's part . . ."

Indeed, Mr. A. G. Cooper, in "Holmesian Humour," has uncovered 292 examples, and Messrs. Charles E. and Edward S. Lauterbach, in their extensive researches, have shown that "Holmes smiled 103 times, laughed 65 times, joked 58 times, chuckled 31 times, and expressed humor in other ways 59 times—a total of 316 responses to humorous situations or statements" ("The Man Who Seldom Laughed").

21 *"The proper study of mankind is man."* Watson quotes from *An Essay on Man,* Ep. ii, 1.2, by Alexander Pope, 1688-1744.

22 *so moderate did the terms seem.* "It is likely that Holmes and Watson shared an 'all-in' rent of between £3 [$15] and £4 [$20] a week—probably nearer the latter than the former," Mr. Michael Harrison wrote in *In the Footsteps of*

'By the way,' I asked suddenly, stopping and turning upon Stamford, 'how the deuce did he know that I had come from Afghanistan?'

My companion smiled an enigmatical smile. 'That's just his little peculiarity,' he said. 'A good many people have wanted to know how he finds things out.'

'Oh! a mystery is it?' I cried, rubbing my hands. 'This is very piquant. I am much obliged to you for bringing us to- **21** gether. "The proper study of mankind is man," you know.'

'You must study him, then,' Stamford said, as he bade me good-bye. 'You'll find him a knotty problem, though. I'll wager he learns more about you than you about him. Good-bye.'

'Good-bye,' I answered, and strolled on to my hotel, considerably interested in my new acquaintance.

◆

2 ◆ THE SCIENCE OF DEDUCTION
◆

We met next day as he had arranged, and inspected the rooms at No. 221B, Baker Street, of which he had spoken at our meeting. They consisted of a couple of comfortable bedrooms and a single large airy sitting-room, cheerfully furnished, and illuminated by two broad windows. So desirable in every way **22** were the apartments, and so moderate did the terms seem

UPON MY QUOTING THOMAS CARLYLE . . .

This is the portrait of Carlyle by Sir John Millais which hangs in the National Portrait Gallery, London.

when divided between us, that the bargain was concluded upon the spot, and we at once entered into possession. That very evening I moved my things round from the hotel, and on the following morning Sherlock Holmes followed me with several boxes and portmanteaus. For a day or two we were busily employed in unpacking and laying out our property to the best advantage. That done, we gradually began to settle down and to accommodate ourselves to our new surroundings.

Holmes was certainly not a difficult man to live with. He was quiet in his ways, and his habits were regular. It was rare for him to be up after ten at night, and he had invariably breakfasted and gone out before I rose in the morning. Some- **23** times he spent his day at the chemical laboratory, sometimes in the dissecting rooms, and occasionally in long walks, which appeared to take him into the lowest portions of the city. **24** Nothing could exceed his energy when the working fit was upon him; but now and again a reaction would seize him, and for days on end he would lie upon the sofa in the sitting-room, hardly uttering a word or moving a muscle from morning to night. On these occasions I have noticed such a dreamy, vacant expression in his eyes, that I might have suspected him of being addicted to the use of some narcotic, had not the temperance and cleanliness of his whole life forbidden such a notion. **25**

As the weeks went by, my interest in him and my curiosity **26** as to his aims in life gradually deepened and increased. His very person and appearance were such as to strike the attention of the most casual observer. In height he was rather over six feet, and so excessively lean that he seemed to be considerably taller. His eyes were sharp and piercing, save during **27** those intervals of torpor to which I have alluded; and his thin, hawk-like nose gave his whole expression an air of alertness and decision. His chin, too, had the prominence and squareness which mark the man of determination. His hands were **28** invariably blotted with ink and stained with chemicals, yet he was possessed of extraordinary delicacy of touch, as I frequently had occasion to observe when I watched him manipulating his fragile philosophical instruments.

The reader may set me down as a hopeless busybody, when I confess how much this man stimulated my curiosity, and how often I endeavoured to break through the reticence which he showed on all that concerned himself. Before pronouncing judgment, however, be it remembered how objectless was my life, and how little there was to engage my attention. My health forbade me from venturing out unless the weather was exceptionally genial, and I had no friends who would call upon me and break the monotony of my daily existence. Under these circumstances, I eagerly hailed the little mystery which hung around my companion, and spent much of my time in endeavouring to unravel it.

He was not studying medicine. He had himself, in reply to a question, confirmed Stamford's opinion upon that point. Neither did he appear to have pursued any course of reading which might fit him for a degree in science or any other recognized portal which would give him an entrance into the learned world. Yet his zeal for certain studies was remark- **29** able, and within eccentric limits his knowledge was so extra-

Sherlock Holmes. "Let us assume that Holmes and Watson were sharing a rent of some £200 [$1,000] a year, which might have included laundry, as well as food; but . . . it is unlikely that illuminating-gas was included in the 'all-in' terms, which may explain the references, frequent throughout Watson's writings, to the oil-lamps at 221B."

23 *before I rose in the morning.* Watson has already told us that he got up "at all sorts of ungodly hours." (Perhaps this is what he means when he writes, in "The Adventure of the Speckled Band," that "I was myself regular in my habits.") But he also tells us—again in "The Adventure of the Speckled Band"—that Holmes "was a late riser as a rule." And in *The Hound of the Baskervilles,* Watson tells us that Holmes "was usually very late in the mornings." Watson, then, must have been a slug-a-bed indeed—a view confirmed by the late breakfast he is having in "The Boscombe Valley Mystery."

24 *the lowest portions of the city.* Since Holmes was "a man who seldom took exercise for exercise's sake" ("The Yellow Face"), these "long walks" were obviously taken in connection with cases which Holmes was handling at the time.

25 *forbidden such a notion.* This is an amazingly shrewd observation on Watson's part. Holmes' tremendous exertions in the spring of 1887—six years after Watson made this statement—left him a very sick man. At that time, to Watson's deep distress, Holmes turned for solace to cocaine. Holmes tells us himself (*The Sign of the Four*) that he found its influence so transcendently stimulating and clarifying to the mind as to make him careless of the ravages inevitable upon his body and soul. By September, 1888, he was indulging in doses of 7 percent cocaine solution three times a day. It is pleasant to be able to record that Watson over the years was gradually able to cure Holmes completely of the habit. By the end of 1896 ("The Adventure of the Missing Three-Quarter") Holmes under ordinary conditions no longer craved this artificial stimulation.

We have stated here the majority view, but there are others: Dr. Charles Goodman, for example, believes that Holmes first took to cocaine neither from weakness nor from boredom but from toothache; he was, as Dr. Goodman has convincingly established ("The Dental Holmes") a chronic sufferer from pyorrhea.

Dr. George F. McCleary has examined the evidence and has arrived at the conclusion that Holmes was never a drug addict, but that he did succeed in deceiving the innocent Watson, and, in fact, took a certain delight in doing so: "All we know of Holmes' alleged addiction can be explained if we assume that he did not actually take the drug, but mystified Watson into believing that he did."

With this view Mr. Michael Harrison is in

strong disagreement (*In the Footsteps of Sherlock Holmes*): ". . . that Holmes had a serious addiction, all Watson's descriptions of Holmes' nervous activity makes clear: the restlessness, the ability to work for days without adequate sleep, and even without rest at all; the abrupt changes of mood; and the equally abrupt collapse into a somnolence not far (if at all) removed from a torpor bordering on coma: these, to those who have studied the effects of drug-addiction, are the unmistakable evidence of heavy and prolonged indulgence in some powerful narcotic."

A middle-road position has been expressed by **Dr. Eugene F. Carey** ("Holmes, Watson and Cocaine"), who has called Holmes "a judicious user" —a view shared by the late Edgar W. Smith ("Up from the Needle"): ". . . he was never a slave to the vice in the clinical sense of the term, for . . . he was always able to cast off the spell, and to find inspiration in the exhilaration of the chase."

26 *As the weeks went by.* Since the case described in *A Study in Scarlet* took place, as we shall see, in March, this is an indication that the partnership was formed early in the year or very late in the preceding year.

27 *His eyes were sharp and piercing.* They were gray eyes, as we are told later on numerous occasions.

28 *which mark the man of determination.* ". . . there seems little doubt that Holmes must have been enormously attractive to women," Dr. Richard Asher wrote in "Holmes and the Fair Sex." "His teeth may have detracted slightly from this impressive appearance for with his excessive consumption of shag they must have been heavily tobacco-stained and moreover we know that the left canine tooth had been knocked out by Mathews in the waiting-room at Charing Cross ["The Adventure of the Empty House"]; but perhaps he wore a denture."

29 *an entrance into the learned world.* We know to the contrary that Holmes was two years at Oxford and three years at Cambridge. But whether or not he was ever admitted to a degree or degrees is a point still debated by commentators.

30 *and what he had done.* "We do not know the circumstances in which this remark was made, but probably it was at a time when Holmes wanted to give his whole attention to a case as yet unsolved, and simply could not be bothered to be drawn into a discussion about Carlyle or anything else," the late Gavin Brend wrote in *My Dear Holmes.*

"The truth of the matter . . . is that Holmes was irritated by Watson's ill-concealed curiosity and took the occasion to cut him short, or that Holmes was guying his roommate . . .", Mr. Whitfield J. Bell, Jr., wrote in "Holmes and History."

ordinarily ample and minute that his observations have fairly astounded me. Surely no man would work so hard or attain such precise information unless he had some definite end in view. Desultory readers are seldom remarkable for the exactness of their learning. No man burdens his mind with small matters unless he has some very good reason for doing so.

His ignorance was as remarkable as his knowledge. Of contemporary literature, philosophy and politics he appeared to know next to nothing. Upon my quoting Thomas Carlyle, he inquired in the naïvest way who he might be and what he **30** had done. My surprise reached a climax, however, when I found incidentally that he was ignorant of the Copernican **31** Theory and of the composition of the Solar System. That any civilized human being in this nineteenth century should not be aware that the earth travelled round the sun appeared to be **32** to me such an extraordinary fact that I could hardly realize it.

'You appear to be astonished,' he said, smiling at my expression of surprise. 'Now that I do know it I shall do my best to forget it.'

'To forget it!'

'You see,' he explained, 'I consider that a man's brain originally is like a little empty attic, and you have to stock it with such furniture as you choose. A fool takes in all the lumber of every sort that he comes across, so that the knowledge which might be useful to him gets crowded out, or at best is jumbled up with a lot of other things, so that he has a difficulty in laying his hands upon it. Now the skilled workman is very careful indeed as to what he takes into his brain-attic. He will have nothing but the tools which may help him in doing his work, but of these he has a large assortment, and all in the most perfect order. It is a mistake to think that that little room has elastic walls and can distend to any extent. Depend upon it there comes a time when for every addition of knowledge you forget something that you knew before. It is of the highest importance, therefore, not to have **33** useless facts elbowing out the useful ones.'

'But the Solar System!' I protested.

'What the deuce is it to me?' he interrupted impatiently: 'you say that we go round the sun. If we went round the moon it would not make a pennyworth of difference to me or to my work.'

(continued on page 156)

The latter is the more popular view among commentators: "Holmes was gently pulling Watson's leg," Christopher Morley wrote, "for shortly thereafter he glibly quotes Carlyle's most famous apothegm."

"I suspect that at that period Watson was far too ready to take Holmes' remarks *au pied de la lettre*," Mr. S. C. Roberts wrote in "The Personality of Sherlock Holmes."

Watson was later to learn that Holmes had, indeed, a very well-developed sense of mischief: in "The Problem of Thor Bridge," Holmes looked into Watson's eyes "with the peculiarly mischievous glance which was characteristic of his more imp-like moods," and on many other occasions Watson was sharply aware of Holmes' "mischievous twinkle."

But why, Christopher Morley asked, should Watson have raised the topic of Carlyle at all? "Because Carlyle died on February 4, 1881! Watson of course had read all the published obituaries, and they were undoubtedly still fresh in his mind, including the one referred to by George Gissing who wrote (in London, February 11, '81) that 'I have just risen from the memoir of Carlyle in the *Times*.' Obviously, Carlyle's recent death was the occasion for the mention Watson made of [the great Scottish author, historian and essayist, 1795–1881]."

31 *the Copernican Theory*. Nicholas Copernicus, Polish astronomer, 1473–1543, founded the system on which modern astronomy is based. In his famous treatise *De revolutionibus orbium coelestium*, published in 1543, he described the sun as the center of the solar system, with the earth revolving around it.

32 *I could hardly realize it*. More leg-pulling on Holmes' part. In "The Musgrave Ritual" he spoke of "any allowance for personal equation, as the astronomers have dubbed it." In "The Adventure of the Bruce-Partington Plans" he compares his brother Mycroft's visit to a planet leaving its orbit, and in "The Greek Interpreter" during a "desultory" chat "after tea on a summer evening" he discusses "the causes of the change in the obliquity of the ecliptic."

33 *useless facts elbowing out the useful ones*.' Holmes did not live up to his preaching here. He later extols "the oblique uses of knowledge" for their good results (*The Valley of Fear*), and of such knowledge he had more than the average stock, as he himself tells us in "The Adventure of the Lion's Mane."

34 SHERLOCK HOLMES—*his limits*. "A list of Watson's own points might, at this juncture, have been headed by the specification: 1. Knowledge of Sherlock Holmes.—Nil," said the late Edgar W. Smith.

35 *2. Knowledge of Philosophy.—Nil*. But in his preface to *His Last Bow*, Watson speaks of Holmes, in retirement, as dividing his time between philosophy and agriculture.

36 *4. Knowledge of Politics.—Feeble.* As Mr. T. S. Blakeney wrote in *Sherlock Holmes: Fact or Fiction?*, "it is hard to believe that Holmes, who had so close a grip on realities, could ever have taken much interest in the pettiness of party politics, nor could so strong an individualist have anything but contempt for the equalitarian ideals of much modern sociological theory."

But Mr. S. C. Roberts has written ("The Personality of Sherlock Holmes"): ". . . it is perfectly true that the clash of political opinions and of political parties does not seem to have aroused great interest in Holmes' mind. But, fundamentally, there can be no doubt that Holmes believed in democracy and progress. . . . It would be difficult to find a more concise expression of the confident aspirations of late Victorian liberalism [than Holmes' remarks on Board schools in "The Naval Treaty"]."

And Mr. Whitfield J. Bell, Jr., in "Holmes and History," has added that "Holmes' knowledge of politics was anything but weak or partial. Of the hurly-burly of the machines, the petty trade for office and advantage, it is perhaps true that Holmes knew little. But of politics on the highest level, in the grand manner, particularly international politics, no one was better informed . . ."

37 *and poisons generally*. "It is probably safe to assume, therefore, that Holmes . . . owned several important works in those fields," Miss Madeleine B. Stern wrote in her impressive study, "Sherlock Holmes: Rare Book Collector." "His toxicology collection probably included Santes Ardoyno's *Opus de Venenis*, though more likely in the Basle 1562 second edition than in the incunable first edition. To this he may well have added such fine volumes as Mercuriale's *De Venenis* (Frankfurt, 1584) and Codronchi's *De Morbis Veneficiia* (Milan, 1618). The nineteenth century produced many informative toxicologies which Holmes doubtless purchased from time to time. He was not likely to have passed up Sir Robert Christison's *Treatise on Poisons* (Edinburgh, 1829), since Christison had taught medical jurisprudence at Edinburgh and had performed the autopsy on one of the victims in the trial of Burke and Hare. Another treatise, published the same year, Morgan and Addison's *Essay on the Operation of Poisonous Agents upon the Living Body* was very possibly added to the Holmes collection, since it was the first book in English on the actions of poisons in the human body. Dragendorff, who introduced methods for the detection of poisons in the human body, was more likely represented on the Holmes shelf by his *Die Gerichtlichchemische Ermitter-*

I was on the point of asking him what that work might be, but something in his manner showed me that the question would be an unwelcome one. I pondered over our short conversation, however, and endeavoured to draw my deductions from it. He said that he would acquire no knowledge which did not bear upon his object. Therefore all the knowledge which he possessed was such as would be useful to him. I enumerated in my own mind all the various points upon which he had shown me that he was exceptionally well-informed. I even took a pencil and jotted them down. I could not help smiling at the document when I had completed it. It ran in this way:

		SHERLOCK HOLMES—his limits.
34		1. Knowledge of Literature.—Nil.
35		2. „ „ Philosophy.—Nil.
		3. „ „ Astronomy.—Nil.
36		4. „ „ Politics.—Feeble.
37		5. „ „ Botany.—Variable. Well up in belladonna, opium, and poisons generally. Knows nothing of practical gardening.
38		6. „ „ Geology.—Practical, but limited. Tells at a glance different soils from each other. After walks has shown me splashes upon his trousers, and told me by their colour and consistence in what part of London he had received them.
39		7. „ „ Chemistry.—Profound.
40		8. „ „ Anatomy.—Accurate, but unsystematic.
41		9. „ „ Sensational Literature.—Immense. He appears to know every detail of every horror perpetrated in the century.
		10. Plays the violin well.
42-43		11. Is an expert singlestick player, boxer, and swordsman.
44		12. Has a good practical knowledge of British law.

ling von Giften (St. Petersburg, 1868). On the specific subject of opium, Holmes may have acquired Hartmann's *Discursis Qvidam de Opio* (London, 1753), and, of course, a first edition of De Quincey. It is likely that Holmes also owned a copy of the London, 1867, edition of De Quincey's *Confessions of an English Opium-Eater* —an edition to which are added Analects from John Paul Richter. Among the analects is one on 'The Grandeur of Man in His Littleness,' a concept to which Holmes referred during his work on *The Sign of the Four*. On the subject of belladonna, Holmes surely purchased Kilmer's treatise, *Belladonna: A Study of Its History*, *Action and Uses in Medicine*, when it appeared in 1894."

38 *Tells at a glance different soils from each other.* "Holmes' geological interest in soils . . . marks him out as a forerunner in this field," Miss Stern continued. "Most soil analyses appeared later than that date, except, for example, Bergman's *Specimen Academicum, Caussas Sterilitatis Agorum Exponens* (Upsala, 1754) which Holmes likely acquired. When the works of Sir John Bennett Lawes (*The Nitrogen as Nitric Acid in the Soils and Subsoils of . . . Rothamsted*, London, 1883) and Charles Barnard (*Talks About the Soil in Its Relation to Plants and Business*, New York, 1894) emerged . . . Holmes almost certainly added them to his library."

39 7. *Knowledge of Chemistry.—Profound.* Watson later misquoted himself as having said here "chemistry eccentric" ("The Five Orange Pips").

"Who can question, then," Miss Stern asked, "that . . . [Holmes] acquired Giovanni Batista della Porta's *De Distillatione* (Rome, 1608) with its splendid woodcuts of chemical apparatus, or Lavoisier's *Traité Élémentaire de Chimie* (Paris, 1789), *Lectures on the Elements of Chemistry* (Edinburgh, 1803) by Joseph Black, founder of quantitative analysis and pneumatic chemistry, or a first edition of Davy's *Elements of Chemical Philosophy* (London, 1812)."

40 8. *Knowledge of Anatomy.—Accurate, but unsystematic.* "It is difficult . . . to do more than suggest one or two titles that may have appeared on Holmes' shelf." (We are again quoting Miss Stern.) "Bidloo's *Anatomia* (Amsterdam, 1685) probably bore a Holmes *ex libris*, and it is even possible that the detector may have invested in one or two incunables, such as Mondino de' Luzzi's *Anothomia* (Pavia, 1478), the first book devoted solely to anatomy. It is difficult to be sure of this, however, though there is little doubt that Holmes acquired later works in the field, notably Sir Charles Bell's *System of Dissections* (Edinburgh, 1798–1803)."

41 9. *Knowledge of Sensational Literature.—Immense.* "This category comprises more or less factual writings about the misdeeds of real criminals," Professor Clarke Olney wrote in "The Literacy of Sherlock Holmes." "Sherlock makes frequent use of his unique knowledge of the classic cases in the annals of crime, from Jonathan Wild, to whom Holmes compares Professor Moriarty [*The Valley of Fear*], to Thomas Griffiths Wainewright, the poisoner ["The Adventure of the Illustrious Client"], and insists that such knowledge is invaluable to the practicing detective. It should surprise no one, therefore, that Holmes shows himself equally familiar with the exploits and methods of the fictional detectives M. Dupin of Poe and M. Lecoq of Gaboriau."

Miss Stern adds: "Though Holmes probably owned *The Newgate Calendar . . . from . . . 1700 to the Present Time* (London, 1773) as well as the later *Newgate Calendar: Containing the Lives . . . of . . . Housebreakers, Highwaymen, etc.*, by an Old-Bailey Barrister (London, 1840?), it must be admitted that his 'immense' knowledge of the field was based primarily upon his own commonplace books, in which, from time to time, he placed cuttings on crime, pasted extracts, and made out his ever useful indexes."

42 *singlestick player.* "A singlestick is about 34″ long," Mr. Ralph A. Ashton wrote in "The Secret Weapons of 221B Baker Street." "It is usually made of hickory or oak. . . . [It] has a basket guard to protect the user's hand from the onslaughts of his opponent. . . . The singlestick is essentially a slashing, whacking, battering, beating and clubbing sort of weapon, designed to train sabre-fighters in the gentle art of carving the casques of men. The *coup d'honneur* in singlestick play is a broken head. . . . Singlestick play [should not be confused with] the French cane-fencing, which is specifically designed to teach one the art of self-defense with a walking-stick."

"It is doubtful if Holmes engaged in any singlestick competition after his early days in London," the late H. T. Webster wrote in "Observations of Sherlock Holmes as an Athlete and Sportsman," "but his youthful practice with it made the cane ["The Adventure of the Speckled Band"] or hunting crop an unusually formidable weapon in his hands. Watson declared that the latter was Holmes' favorite weapon ["The Adventure of the Six Napoleons"]. . . . Holmes therefore kept his hunting-crop in his rooms ["A Case of Identity"]. On one occasion, at least ["The Red-Headed League"], he found it effective protection against a man armed with a pistol."

43 *boxer, and swordsman.* We know that boxing and fencing were Holmes' only sports in his days at Oxford ("The *Gloria Scott*"). There is no Canonical report of Holmes with sword in hand, however, and it seems safe to assume that he seldom or never touched a foil or épée after his early acquaintanceship with Watson.

Miss Stern has added: "On singlestick and swordmanship [Holmes] may have owned the *Practise* (London, 1595) of Saviolo, L'Abbat's *Art of Fencing* (Dublin, 1734) and, more than likely, *Anti-Pugilism, or the Science of Defense Exemplified in Short and Easy Lessons, for the Practice of the Broad Sword and Single Stick . . . By a Highland Officer* (London, 1790) with four copperplates by Cruikshank. On boxing, he may well have purchased the Mercurialis, *De Arte Gymnastica* (Venice, 1573) with its boxing cuts, Whitehead's *Gymnasiad* (London, 1744), the first publication dealing exclusively with boxing in English, *The Art of Boxing* (1789) by the champion, Daniel Mendoza, and other lesser works on the Queensberry rules and *la boxe française*."

44 *a good practical knowledge of British law.* So much so that Mr. Albert P. Blaustein ("Sherlock Holmes as a Lawyer") holds that Holmes *was* a lawyer.

The late Fletcher Pratt added ("Very Little Murder") that "when the record of Mr. Holmes' cases is examined, we find that in every single case where an actual crime was committed . . . he obtained legal proof full enough to satisfy any jury; witness evidence plus circumstantial evidence, and in many cases . . . a confession in addition. . . . This demonstrates conclusively that Holmes' knowledge of the law was . . . profound."

Miss Stern has noted that "it is fairly safe . . . to suppose that [Holmes] owned Fitzherbert's *Great Abridgement of the Law* (London, 1516), the first serious attempt to systematize the law of England, as well as Littleton's *Tenures in English* (London, 1583) and a copy of the first edition of Blackstone's *Commentaries* (Oxford, 1765–1769)."

45 *Mendelssohn's Lieder.* The *Lieder ohne Wortes,* or "Songs Without Words," of Jakob Ludwig Felix Mendelssohn-Bartholdy, 1809–1847.

46 *fantastic and cheerful.* "I submit," the late Harvey Officer, composer of the *Baker Street Suite* for violin and piano, in five movements, wrote in "Sherlock Holmes and Music," "that you can do sonorous or melancholy chords or fantastic and cheerful chords on a piano with a certain degree of carelessness, but I defy any violinist to produce such chords on a violin that is lying carelessly across his knees. Chords on a violin are always a *tour de force.* They are not natural to the instrument. They can only be played when the violin is held strongly in its accustomed position, and even then they are not the violin's most expressive sounds. It is pre-eminently the instrument of melody, not of harmony."

"I suggest that Holmes, as he sat in his chair, placed the tail piece of the violin against his middle, holding his left arm under it and the fingers of that arm on the fingerboard in the usual way," William Braid White, Mus. Doc., wrote in "Sherlock Holmes and the Equal Temperament." "This would bring the violin to a position nearly at right angles to his body as he sat in the chair, leaving his right arm and hand free to use the bow, and the left arm and hand, as before remarked, equally free for the fingerboard."

Mr. Rolfe Boswell ("Quick, Watson, the Fiddle!") could not bring himself to agree with Dr. White's suggestion. Holmes' instrument, he thought, was not the violin at all but the "violin's darklinger congener"—the viola.

In any case, both Dr. White and Mr. Guy Warrack (*Sherlock Holmes and Music*) agree that when Holmes produced these chords he was reminding himself, and perhaps practicing, the famous *Chaconne* (at any rate, the introductory parts of it) from Johann Sebastian Bach's *D Minor Sonata* for violin alone.

47 *the trial upon my patience.* Mr. Emanuel Berg ("For It's Greatly to Their Credit") has taken Watson's wording here to indicate that the "series of favourite airs" were the work of William Schwenck Gilbert, 1836–1911, and Arthur Seymour Sullivan, 1842–1900, from *Trial by Jury* (produced March 25, 1875) to *Patience* (although *Patience* was not produced until April 23, 1881).

Mr. Warrack has suggested that Mendelssohn's *Auf Flugen des Gesanges* "might well have been [another] favourite with" Watson. "Only two versions were available [on the recordings of that time]," Mr. Anthony Boucher has noted in "The Records of Baker Street," "one by the soprano Irene Abendroth (7″ black G & T, Dresden, 1902, 43181) and one by tenor Marian Alma (10″ Berliner, Berlin, 1901, 42164 or 42167). But we can well imagine his satisfaction with the sturdy and popular English numbers—*Hearts of Oak, Robin Adair, The Lost Chord*—recorded by such native singers as Perceval Allen, Andrew Black, William

When I had got so far in my list I threw it into the fire in despair. 'If I can only find what the fellow is driving at by reconciling all these accomplishments, and discovering a calling which needs them all,' I said to myself, 'I may as well give up the attempt at once.'

I see that I have alluded above to his powers upon the violin. These were very remarkable, but as eccentric as all his other accomplishments. That he could play pieces, and difficult pieces, I knew well, because at my request he has played **45** me some of Mendelssohn's Lieder, and other favourites. When left to himself, however, he would seldom produce any music or attempt any recognized air. Leaning back in his arm-chair of an evening, he would close his eyes and scrape carelessly at the fiddle which was thrown across his knee. Sometimes the chords were sonorous and melancholy. Occasionally **46** they were fantastic and cheerful. Clearly they reflected the thoughts which possessed him, but whether the music aided those thoughts, or whether the playing was simply the result of a whim or fancy, was more than I could determine. I might have rebelled against these exasperating solos had it not been that he usually terminated them by playing in quick succession a whole series of my favourite airs as a slight compensa- **47** tion for the trial upon my patience.

During the first week or so we had no callers, and I had begun to think that my companion was as friendless a man as I was myself. Presently, however, I found that he had many acquaintances, and those in the most different classes of society. There was one little sallow, rat-faced, dark-eyed **48** fellow, who was introduced to me as Mr Lestrade, and who came three or four times in a single week. One morning a young girl called, fashionably dressed, and stayed for half an hour or more. The same afternoon brought a grey-headed, seedy visitor, looking like a Jew pedlar, who appeared to me to be much excited, and who was closely followed by a slip-shod elderly woman. On another occasion an old white-haired

PRESENTLY, HOWEVER, I FOUND THAT HE HAD MANY ACQUAINTANCES . . .

Illustration by C. Coulston for *Stories of Sherlock Holmes,* Vol. I, New York and London: Harper & Brothers, 1904. Coulston, if we have correctly deciphered the name, is not mentioned in either of the two iconographies that have so far been published on Holmes.

gentleman had an interview with my companion; and on another, a railway porter in his velveteen uniform. When **49** any of these nondescript individuals put in an appearance, Sherlock Holmes used to beg for the use of the sitting-room, and I would retire to my bedroom. He always apologized to me for putting me to this inconvenience. 'I have to use this room as a place of business,' he said, 'and these people are my clients.' Again I had an opportunity of asking him a point-blank question, and again my delicacy prevented me from forcing another man to confide in me. I imagined at the time that he had some strong reason for not alluding to it, but he soon dispelled the idea by coming round to the subject of his own accord.

It was upon the 4th of March, as I have good reason to **50** remember, that I rose somewhat earlier than usual, and found that Sherlock Holmes had not yet finished his breakfast. The landlady had become so accustomed to my late habits that **51** my place had not been laid nor my coffee prepared. With the unreasonable petulance of mankind I rang the bell and gave a curt intimation that I was ready. Then I picked up a maga-zine from the table and attempted to while away the time **52** with it, while my companion munched silently at his toast. **53** One of the articles had a pencil mark at the heading, and I naturally began to run my eye through it.

Its somewhat ambitious title was *The Book of Life,* and it attempted to show how much an observant man might learn by an accurate and systematic examination of all that came in his way. It struck me as being a remarkable mixture of shrewdness and of absurdity. The reasoning was close and intense, but the deductions appeared to me to be far-fetched and exaggerated. The writer claimed by a momentary ex-pression, a twitch of a muscle or a glance of an eye, to fathom a man's inmost thoughts. Deceit, according to him, was an impossibility in the case of one trained to observation and analysis. His conclusions were as infallible as so many proposi-tions of Euclid. So startling would his results appear to the **54** uninitiated that until they learned the processes by which he had arrived at them they might well consider him as a necro-mancer.

'From a drop of water,' said the writer, 'a logician could infer the possibility of an Atlantic or a Niagara without having seen or heard of one or the other. So all life is a great chain, the nature of which is known whenever we are shown a single link of it. Like all other arts, the Science of Deduction and Analysis is one which can only be acquired by long and patient study, nor is life long enough to allow any mortal to attain the highest possible perfection in it. Before turning to those moral and mental aspects of the matter which present the greatest difficulties, let the inquirer begin by mastering more elementary problems. Let him on meeting a fellow-mortal, learn at a glance to distinguish the history of the man, and the trade or profession to which he belongs. Puerile as such an exercise may seem, it sharpens the faculties of obser-vation, and teaches one where to look and what to look for. By a man's finger-nails, by his coat-sleeve, by his boot, by his trouser-knees, by the callosities of his forefinger and thumb, by his expression, by his shirt-cuffs—by each of these things a man's calling is plainly revealed. That all united should fail to enlighten the competent inquirer in any case is almost in-conceivable.'

Green, John Harrison, Esther Palliser and William Paull—to say nothing of one Herbert Goddard, which was the psuedonym wisely chosen for such purposes by the suspiciously foreign-sounding Emilio do Gogorza (who also recorded for the Spanish as Carlos Francisco and for the French as M. Fernand)."

48 *one little sallow, rat-faced, dark-eyed fellow.* Mr. Lestrade—*Inspector* Lestrade, as we shortly learn, and Inspector G. Lestrade as he later signed himself in a letter to Holmes ("The Cardboard Box") had been, we are soon told, a Scotland Yard Inspector for twenty years and was to be a Scot-land Yard Inspector twenty years later. As the late Gavin Brend wrote in "The Man from the Yard":

> A life of ease I am much afraid
> Was denied to Inspector G. Lestrade.
> With the *Study in Scarlet* in '81
> You'd think that his job had just begun.
> But nevertheless the fact appears
> He'd already put in some twenty years.
> And yet if the Garrideb case be true
> He was still at the Yard in 1902.
> I feel it must be exceedingly hard
> To spend forty years at Scotland Yard.

But it has never been clear just how this "little sallow, rat-faced, dark-eyed fellow"—clearly be-low the regulation height—ever got into the police in the first place. Watson mellowed in his attitude toward Lestrade as the years went on: in "The Adventure of the Second Stain" and "The Card-board Box" he is using the terms "bulldog features" and "wiry, dapper and ferret-like" to describe Lestrade, and in *The Hound of the Baskervilles,* Lestrade is "a small, wiry, bulldog of a man." The outstanding study to date of Inspector G. Lestrade is that by Mr. L. S. Holstein. In "Inspector G. Lestrade" he has written: "We find [Lestrade] active in twelve of Dr. Watson's writings, as well as a reference to him in the text of 'The Adven-ture of the Three Garridebs.' . . . His Christian name is unknown to us. . . . One can speculate on the denotation of that tantalizing 'G.' from George to Gouverneur without success. There is no clue, and without a shred of evidence I lean toward Gustave as a name that fits the subject. [Sponsors of a French origin for Lestrade might identify G. also with Giles or Gracchus, as Mr. Eliot Kimball pointed out in his "Origin and Evolution of G. Lestrade: I—Onomatological Considerations."] If we make the generous assumption that he joined the Metropolitan Police at the age of twenty-one, he would have been on the high side of forty at the time of the Drebber affair, and we know he was still active in [1902]. We may draw the con-clusion from all this that Lestrade was Holmes' senior by some ten or twelve years [born, that is, in 1844–1846], and served on the force more than forty years. At the outset, he may have pounded a beat . . . but because of his lack of stature, it is more likely that he came up through the records bureau, and not as a constable."

49 *a railway porter in his velveteen uniform.* As Mr. Robert Keith Leavitt observed in "Nummi in Arca or The Fiscal Holmes," ". . . Holmes very soon outgrew his dependence upon [clients like these], though he continued (be it said to his credit) to interest himself in such cases all through his years of affluence."

50 *the 4th of March.* A Friday in 1881. That it *was* 1881 has again been indicated by the late Christopher Morley. In "Was Sherlock Holmes an American?", he wrote: "Why . . . does Watson write, 'It was upon the 4th of March, as I have good reason to remember,' . . . And why was Holmes still at the breakfast table? It was the 4th of March, 1881, and Holmes was absorbed in reading the news dispatches about the inauguration, to take place that day, of President Garfield."

51 *The landlady.* This is the famous Mrs. Hudson, although we are not told her name in this adventure. She was Mrs. *Martha* Hudson if, as most commentators think, Mrs. Hudson and the housekeeper who served Holmes after his retirement to the Sussex Downs were one and the same. "A young widow, one imagines her to have been, who took up commercial housekeeping when the experiment of marriage was in some way tragically ended," Mr. Vincent Starrett wrote in his scholarly study of "The Singular Adventures of Martha Hudson." "But no whisper of her life before that day in 1881, when Holmes first called upon her, has ever been revealed. The notion persists that she had been unhappy; she kept so very still about it all." Some students take the fact that she had a "stately tread," as we soon learn, to mean that Mrs. Hudson was corpulent. "But stately, too, is the tread of many a queenly artist's model and showgirl," Mr. Manly Wade Wellman wrote in "The Great Man's Great Son." "Mrs. Hudson was opulently made, no more than five feet four inches tall, fair and rosy, with wide eyes of deepest blue. Connoisseurs of the eighties would, and probably did, call her a demm'd fine figure of a woman."

52 *a magazine.* It was the *Cornhill Magazine*, the late Edgar W. Smith thought. It was "unquestionably" the *Fortnightly*, in the late Christopher Morley's opinion.

53 *munched silently at his toast.* How Holmes accomplished this minor miracle is not known.

54 *Euclid.* The Greek mathematician often called "the father of geometry." He was born in and resided in Alexandria, Egypt, about 350–300 B.C. Euclid was famous for his *Elements*, a collection of theorems and problems which formed the basis of geometry until "modern mathematics" were introduced into the curricula.

55 *a third-class carriage.* Throughout the Canon, both Holmes and Watson travel first class, as did

'What ineffable twaddle!' I cried, slapping the magazine down on the table; 'I never read such rubbish in my life.'

'What is it?' asked Sherlock Holmes.

'Why, this article,' I said, pointing at it with my egg-spoon as I sat down to my breakfast. 'I see that you have read it since you have marked it. I don't deny that it is smartly written. It irritates me though. It is evidently the theory of some armchair lounger who evolves all these neat little paradoxes in the seclusion of his own study. It is not practical. I should **55** like to see him clapped down in a third-class carriage on the **56** Underground, and asked to give the trades of all his fellow-**57** travellers. I would lay a thousand to one against him.'

'You would lose your money,' Holmes remarked calmly. 'As for the article, I wrote it myself.'

'You!'

'Yes; I have a turn both for observation and for deduction. The theories which I have expressed there, and which appear to you to be so chimerical, are really extremely practical—so practical that I depend upon them for my bread and cheese.'

'And how?' I asked involuntarily.

'Well, I have a trade of my own. I suppose I am the only one in the world. I'm a consulting detective, if you can understand what that is. Here in London we have lots of Government detectives and lots of private ones. When these fellows are at fault, they come to me, and I manage to put them on the right scent. They lay all the evidence before me, and I am generally able, by the help of my knowledge of the history of crime, to set them straight. There is a strong family resem-**58** blance about misdeeds, and if you have all the details of a thousand at your finger ends, it is odd if you can't unravel **59** the thousand and first. Lestrade is a well-known detective. He got himself into a fog recently over a forgery case, and that was what brought him here.'

'And these other people?'

'They are mostly sent on by private inquiry agencies. They are all people who are in trouble about something, and want a little enlightening. I listen to their story, they listen to my comments, and then I pocket my fee.'

'But do you mean to say,' I said, 'that without leaving your room you can unravel some knot which other men can make nothing of, although they have seen every detail for themselves?'

'Quite so. I have a kind of intuition that way. Now and again a case turns up which is a little more complex. Then I have to bustle about and see things with my own eyes. You see I have a lot of special knowledge which I apply to the problem, and which facilitates matters wonderfully. Those rules of deduction laid down in that article which aroused your scorn are invaluable to me in practical work. Observation with me is second nature. You appeared to be surprised when I told you, on our first meeting, that you had come from Afghanistan.'

'You were told, no doubt.'

'Nothing of the sort. I *knew* you came from Afghanistan. From long habit the train of thoughts ran so swiftly through my mind that I arrived at the conclusion without being conscious of intermediate steps. There were such steps, however. The train of reasoning ran, "Here is a gentleman of a medical type, but with the air of a military man. Clearly an

NEW SCOTLAND YARD

The illustration is from *The Baker Street Journal*, Vol. III, No. 1, Old Series, January, 1948, p. 36.

most men in their position in those days, and we know Watson's opinion of the Retired Colourman who insisted on traveling third class.

56 *on the Underground.* It was the City Solicitor, Charles Pearson, who first proposed to relieve the terrible congestion that made the narrow London streets all but impassable at times by encircling the metropolis with a tunnel-railroad, with frequent stations, which would connect with all the railway termini taking visitors in and out of the city. Despite long and bitter opposition to a "Sewer Railway" (*Punch*'s term), the first of London's "subways," the Metropolitan Railway Company, began operations, using coal-burning steam locomotives, on January 9, 1863, between Bishop's Road, Paddington, and Farringdon Street. On the opening day over 30,000 people traveled over the line, and from nine o'clock in the morning until past midday it was impossible to obtain a seat in the City-bound trains at any of the intermediate stations. The carriages were then mere open trucks (*see illustration*). In the evening the returning crowds from Farringdon Street were equally great. In the following year the number of passengers carried amounted to nearly 9.5 million, or more than three times the population of London at that time; as early as 1877 the Underground was carrying 56 million passengers a year. A second London Underground, the Metropolitan District Railway, followed the shallow design and used the steam locomotives of the first line, but the City and South London Railway, opened in 1890, was placed in tubes ranging from 48 to 105 feet beneath the surface, and began operations with electric locomotives that at least did away with the "fearsome mixture of coal smoke, sulphur, carbon dioxide and carbonic acid" that had formed the atmosphere of the Undergrounds up to that time.

57 *I would lay a thousand to one against him.'* An early indication that Watson was a man who relished gambling and betting.

BAKER STREET STATION ON THE DAY THE METROPOLITAN RAILWAY BEGAN OPERATIONS, JANUARY 9, 1863

Mr. Gladstone is seated in the truck in the foreground. The illustration is from G. M. Trevelyan's *Illustrated English Social History*, *Vol. IV, The Nineteenth Century*, London and New York: Longmans, Green and Co., Ltd., 1942 and 1944.

58 *There is a strong family resemblance about misdeeds.* Later in *A Study in Scarlet*, Holmes says: "There is nothing new under the sun. It has all been done before." And in *The Valley of Fear* he says: "Everything comes in circles, even Professor Moriarty." "These remarks," Mr. T. S. Blakeney wrote in *Sherlock Holmes: Fact or Fiction?*, "suffice to show us why Holmes laid such stress on accumulating that knowledge of sensational literature . . . that so impressed Watson and Stamford. If you had all the details of a thousand cases at your fingerends, it was odd, said Holmes, if you could not unravel the thousand and first. Many times he impresses this point upon his listeners—to Lestrade, to Gregson, to Inspector MacDonald; and M. François le Villard was quick to acknowledge his indebtedness to the same faculty [*The Sign of the Four*]."

59 *Lestrade is a well-known detective.* Of the sixty cases recorded in the Canon, forty involve the official police. Of these, Lestrade, as we have seen, is mentioned or takes some part in thirteen. Gregson appears in four, Hopkins in four, Bradstreet in three, and others in seventeen.

60 *Clearly in Afghanistan."* ". . . for all Holmes knew, Watson could have been, not in Afghanistan, but in South Africa, where also the British Army had just concluded a sizeable colonial war, that of 1879–1880 against the Zulus," Mr. Samuel F. Howard wrote in "More About Maiwand." "Either Holmes had other data that he did not explain to Watson (or Watson did not pass on to us), or he was guilty of sheer guesswork. I prefer to believe he observed some other detail in Watson's appearance that he did not bother to repeat to Watson . . ."

61 *Dupin.* Ratiocinative hero of "The Murders in the Rue Morgue" (1841), "The Purloined Letter" (1845) and "The Mystery of Marie Rogêt" (1842). "Dupin, C. Auguste, poet and amateur of the arts and of deduction; b. circa 1820. Unmarried. Came of good family but suffered financial reverses. . . . Hobbies: Reading; living by candlelight during the day and wandering abroad at night. Residence: 33 Rue Donât, Faubourg St. Germain, Paris."— Kenneth Macgowan, *Sleuths: Twenty-three Great Detectives of Fiction and Their Best Stories*; New York: Harcourt, Brace & Company, 1931.

62 *Dupin was a very inferior fellow.* It is Holmes, not Conan Doyle, who is being less than gracious here. Conan Doyle once said that if he had to name the few books which had really influenced his own life, he would put Poe's stories second only to Macaulay's essays. He considered Poe to be "the supreme original short story writer," and he stressed the debt that all later writers of detective fiction owe to "those admirable stories of M. Dupin, so wonderful in their dramatic force, their reticence, their quick dramatic point" (*Through the Magic Door*). Speaking at a dinner sponsored

army doctor, then. He has just come from the tropics, for his face is dark, and that is not the natural tint of his skin, for his wrists are fair. He has undergone hardship and sickness, as his haggard face says clearly. His left arm has been injured. He holds it in a stiff and unnatural manner. Where in the tropics could an English army doctor have seen much hard-**60** ship and got his arm wounded? Clearly in Afghanistan." The whole train of thought did not occupy a second. I then remarked that you came from Afghanistan, and you were astonished.'

'It is simple enough as you explain it,' I said, smiling. 'You **61** remind me of Edgar Allen Poe's Dupin. I had no idea that such individuals did exist outside of stories.'

Sherlock Holmes rose and lit his pipe. 'No doubt you think that you are complimenting me in comparing me to Dupin,' he observed. 'Now, in my opinion, Dupin was **62** a very inferior fellow. That trick of his of breaking in on his friends' thoughts with an apropos remark after a quarter of an hour's silence is really very showy and superficial. He had some analytical genius, no doubt; but he was by no means such a phenomenon as Poe appeared to imagine.'

63 'Have you read Gaboriau's works?' I asked. 'Does Lecoq come up to your idea of a detective?'

Sherlock Holmes sniffed sardonically. 'Lecoq was a miserable bungler,' he said, in an angry voice; 'he had only one thing to recommend him, and that was his energy. That book made me positively ill. The question was how to identify an unknown prisoner. I could have done it in twenty-four hours. Lecoq took six months or so. It might be made a text-book for detectives to teach them what to avoid.'

I felt rather indignant at having two characters whom I had admired treated in this cavalier style. I walked over to the window, and stood looking out into the busy street. 'This fellow may be very clever,' I said to myself, 'but he is certainly very conceited.'

64 'There are no crimes and no criminals in these days,' he said, querulously. 'What is the use of having brains in our profession. I know well that I have it in me to make my name famous. No man lives or has ever lived who has brought the same amount of study and of natural talent to the detection of crime which I have done. And what is the result? There is no crime to detect, or, at most, some bungling villainy with a **65** motive so transparent that even a Scotland Yard official can see through it.'

I was still annoyed at his bumptious style of conversation. I thought it best to change the topic.

'I wonder what that fellow is looking for?' I asked, pointing to a stalwart, plainly-dressed individual who was walking slowly down the other side of the street, looking anxiously at the numbers. He had a large blue envelope in his hand, and was evidently the bearer of a message.

'You mean the retired sergeant of Marines,' said Sherlock Holmes.

'Brag and bounce!' thought I to myself. 'He knows that I cannot verify his guess.'

The thought had hardly passed through my mind when the man whom we were watching caught sight of the number on our door, and ran rapidly across the roadway. We heard a loud knock, a deep voice below, and heavy steps ascending the stair.

'For Mr Sherlock Holmes,' he said, stepping into the room and handing my friend the letter.

Here was an opportunity of taking the conceit out of him. He little thought of this when he made that random shot. 'May I ask, my lad,' I said, in the blandest voice, 'what your trade may be?'

'Commissionaire, sir,' he said, gruffly. 'Uniform away for **66** repairs.'

'And you were?' I asked, with a slightly malicious glance at my companion.

'A sergeant, sir, Royal Marine Light Infantry, sir. No **67** answer? Right, sir.'

He clicked his heels together, raised his hand in a salute, and was gone.

---

by the Authors' Club on March 1, 1909, to honor the centenary of Poe's birth, Conan Doyle said: ". . . his tales were one of the great landmarks and starting points in the literature of the last century for French as well as for English writers. For those tales have been so pregnant with suggestion, so stimulating to the minds of others, that it may be said of many of them that each is a root from which a whole literature has developed. . . . His original and inventive brain was always . . . opening up pioneer tracks for other men to explore. Where was the detective story until Poe breathed the breath of life into it?" Even Holmes seems to have changed his mind about Dupin later, if we take it for granted that he meant Dupin when he spoke to Watson about a "close reasoner" in Poe's passage to Watson and implies that Watson was the detractor—"inclined to treat the matter as a mere *tour-de-force* of the author" ("The Cardboard Box"). "Watson must have been a patient man to have endured this turn-about on Holmes' part," Mr. Morris Rosenblum commented in "Foreign Language Quotations in the Canon."

63 *Gaboriau's works?'* The works of the French novelist Émile Gaboriau, 1833–1873, whose detective stories about M. Lecoq include five books: *L'Affaire Lerouge* (1866), *Le Dossier 113* (1867), *Le Crime d'Orcival* (1868), *Monsieur Lecoq* (1869) and *Les Esclaves de Paris* (1869). "Through the jostling throng of *banquiers véreux*, Monsieur Lecoq, simple agent of the Sûreté, comes stepping, fresh as a bridegroom, *un beau gars*, *à l'oeil clair*, *à l'air resolu*, or, as casual visitors saw him in his careful disguise, a sober personage of distinguished appearance, with his gold spectacles, his white tie, his *mince redingote*. Against a canvas of tiresome puppets he stands out as a living figure."—Valentine Williams, "Gaboriau: Father of Detective Novels."

64 *'There are no crimes and no criminals in these days.'* Compare Holmes' observations in *The Sign*

of the Four and "The Adventure of Wisteria Lodge": "Crime is commonplace, existence is commonplace, and no qualities save those which are commonplace have any function upon earth"; "Life is commonplace, the papers are sterile; audacity and romance seem to have passed forever from the criminal world." "We clearly see from these observations," Mr. T. S. Blakeney wrote in *Sherlock Holmes: Fact or Fiction?*, "that the artist [in Holmes] has outstripped the social worker. Mr. Thomas Burke, we think, has been known to regret the good old, bad old days of Limehouse; so Holmes, too, could lament the lack of a first-class criminal. 'What we want,' he might have said with H. B. Irving, 'is a good bloody murder.' (Compare Holmes' almost bloodthirsty remarks to Watson at the opening of 'The Adventure of the Bruce-Partington Plans.') More than once we catch a wistful tone in his reference to the dear departed Professor Moriarty—see 'The Adventure of the Norwood Builder' and the tinge of hope that inspired his suggestion that Dr. Leslie Armstrong ["The Adventure of the Missing Three-Quarter"] might fill the gap left by the professor's death."

65 *Scotland Yard.* "Scotland Yard" is the popular name for the London Metropolitan Police force established in 1829 by Sir Robert Peel at No. 4 Whitehall Place—called "Scotland Yard" because the spot marked the site of a palace where, in Saxon times and later, the Kings of Scotland resided when they came to London to do homage to the Kings of England for fiefs held by them as vassals to the English crown—Cumberland, Huntingdon, and other places. Old Scotland Yard was housed in "a handsome building of three floors, of mellow London brick with Portland Stone dressings" (William H. Gill, "Some Notable Sherlockian Buildings"). "Former occupants, before the arrival of the police . . . , were the Royal Surveyors-General, including such illustrious names as Inigo Jones, Sir Christopher Wren, and Sir John Vanbrugh. The vast increase in population of the Outer Ring of the Metropolis between 1880 and 1900 made it imperative for the police to erect a new Headquarters. The architect selected was Norman Shaw who attempted to bring Scottish architecture to the English capital. The New Scotland Yard opened in 1891 [*see illustration*] was built on the actual foundations of a defunct National Opera House, designed by Francis Fowler in 1875. Its foundation stone was actually laid by the Duke of Edinburgh in 1878, but the new Opera House never climbed above its foundations. These may still be seen under New Scotland Yard, and Shaw erected his fierce Scottish baronial castle over them, built of dour granite, quarried by Dartmoor convicts." There is, at New Scotland Yard, a "Black Museum" which includes such exhibits as the false arm, dark spectacles and folding ladder of Holmes' "old friend," Charles Peace (see "The Adventure of the Illustrious Client").

66 *'Commissionaire.* A (normally) uniformed messenger employed by the Corps of Commissionaires founded in 1859 by Captain Sir Edward Walter for the employment of pensioned soldiers, sailors, and (now) airmen. Said the Langham Hotel's *Guide to London* in its 1881 edition: "Among the excellent features of London may be numbered the Corps of Commissionaires, composed of retired veterans, most of whom are decorated . . . who for a consideration will run a message, chaperone a young lady, attend an old one, fetch or carry a love-letter, tend the baby, and do a variety of things handily and surely, at the rate of sixpence an hour. . . . They are to be seen everywhere, in a uniform as gorgeous as a major-general's, and are always respectable and trustworthy."

67 *Royal Marine Light Infantry.* Unlike the Americans, who rate their Marines as part of the Navy, the British rate theirs as part of the Army. The British Marines grew out of the Trained Bands of London, and as such they enjoy a unique privilege: they are allowed to march through London with drums beating and colors flying.

3 • THE LAURISTON GARDENS MYSTERY

I confess that I was considerably startled by this fresh proof of the practical nature of my companion's theories. My respect for his powers of analysis increased wondrously. There still remained some lurking suspicion in my mind, however, that the whole thing was a prearranged episode, intended to dazzle me, though what earthly object he could have in taking me in was past my comprehension. When I looked at him, he had finished reading the note, and his eyes had assumed the vacant, lack-lustre expression which showed mental abstraction.

'How in the world did you deduce that?' I asked.

'Deduce what?' said he petulantly.

'Why, that he was a retired sergeant of Marines.'

'I have no time for trifles,' he answered, brusquely; then with a smile, 'Excuse my rudeness. You broke the thread of my thoughts; but perhaps it is as well. So you actually were not able to see that that man was a sergeant of Marines?'

'No, indeed.'

'It was easier to know it than to explain why I know it. If you were asked to prove that two and two made four, you might find some difficulty, and yet you are quite sure of the fact. Even across the street I could see a great blue anchor tattooed on the back of the fellow's hand. That smacked of the sea. He had a military carriage, however, and regulation side whiskers. There we have the marine. He was a man with some amount of self-importance and a certain air of command. You must have observed the way in which he held his head and swung his cane. A steady, respectable, middle-aged

man, too, on the face of him—all facts which led me to believe that he had been a sergeant.'

'Wonderful!' I ejaculated.

'Commonplace,' said Holmes, though I thought from his expression that he was pleased at my evident surprise and admiration. 'I said just now that there were no criminals. It appears that I am wrong—look at this!' He threw me over the note which the commissionaire had brought.

'Why,' I cried, as I cast my eye over it, 'this is terrible!'

'It does seem to be a little out of the common,' he remarked, calmly. 'Would you mind reading it to me aloud?'   **68**

This is the letter which I read to him:

MY DEAR MR SHERLOCK HOLMES,

There has been a bad business during the night at 3, Lauriston Gardens, off the Brixton Road. Our man on the beat saw a light there about two in the morning, and as the house was an empty one, suspected that something was amiss. He found the door open, and in the front room, which is bare of furniture, discovered the body of a gentleman, well dressed, and having cards in his pocket bearing the name of 'Enoch J. Drebber, Cleveland, Ohio, U.S.A.' There had been no robbery, nor is there any evidence as to how the man met his death. There are marks of blood in the room, but there is no wound upon his person. We are at a loss as to how he came into the empty house; indeed the whole affair is a puzzler. If you can come round to the house any time before twelve, you will find me there. I have left everything *in statu quo* until I hear from you. If you are unable to come, I shall **69** give you fuller details, and would esteem it a great kindness if you would favour me with your opinion.

Yours faithfully,

TOBIAS GREGSON.

'Gregson is the smartest of the Scotland Yarders,' my friend **70** remarked; 'he and Lestrade are the pick of a bad lot. They are both quick and energetic, but conventional—shockingly so. They have their knives into one another, too. They are as jealous as a pair of professional beauties. There will be some fun over this case if they are both put upon the scent.'   **71**

I was amazed at the calm way in which he rippled on. 'Surely there is not a moment to be lost,' I cried; 'shall I go and order you a cab?'   **72**

'I'm not sure about whether I shall go. I am the most incurably lazy devil that ever stood in shoe leather—that is, when the fit is on me, for I can be spry enough at times.'

'Why, it is just such a chance as you have been longing for.'

"... OFF THE BRIXTON ROAD."

The Brixton Road is, today, the Oxford Street of South London and contains some of the largest and finest shops to be found in that area. In Holmes' and Watson's day it was lined, on its east side, with shabby houses which have now been replaced with rows of quite handsome new buildings. (Mrs. Maggie Oakshott of "The Adventure of the Blue Carbuncle" bred geese in a garden back of No. 117 Brixton Road.) The photograph, from the Tate Central Library, is from Michael Harrison's *In the Footsteps of Sherlock Holmes*. It shows the Brixton Road in the winter of 1883, two years after the affair of *A Study in Scarlet*.

68 '*Would you mind reading it to me aloud?*' In *A Study in Scarlet* we see Holmes and Watson looking down from the second (American usage) story of their sitting room across wide Baker Street. Holmes pinpoints a stranger as a sergeant of Marines, partly from the tattoo of a blue anchor on the back of the fellow's hand. Now, says Mr. Jerry Neal Williamson, in "'And Especially Your Eyes,'" "only a man with tremendous 'long vision' could recognize at such a distance what might have been dirt, a scar, a birthmark, a shadow or a mole. Immediately after this remarkable evidence of Holmes' uncanny distance clarity the sleuth threw Watson a note brought him by the commissionaire, saying 'Would you mind reading it to me aloud?'" Holmes, Mr. Williamson deduces, was farsighted: "he suffered from hypermetropia. . . . The basic handicap of a hypermetropic individual can be quickly summed up. This person sees things at a distance with perception and clarity, while he finds it difficult to read clearly anything inches and sometimes feet from his eyes. It is the opposite of myopia; and it assuredly describes Sherlock Holmes." Mr. Williamson, we cannot help but feel, is correct; again and again, as we shall see, Holmes asks Watson (or another) "Would you read it to me aloud?"

69 in statu quo *until I hear from you.* Now this, as Mr. John Ball, Jr., has noted in "Early Days in Baker Street," is a remarkable deference to Holmes, the young amateur, by "the smartest of the Scotland Yarders," explicable only if Gregson recognized Holmes as his superior in both ability and rank. In Mr. Ball's view, Holmes from the start was a private agent in Her Majesty's Government, probably with the classification of a Queen's Messenger, "a unique and highly restricted office. Queen's (or King's) Messenger may go anywhere in the British Empire on official business, and have extraordinary authority in the field. They can, if necessary, command the services of a cruiser; they are diplomatic couriers *par excellence*, to whom are entrusted missions and specialized duties of the highest importance." (The King's Messengers of Charles II play an important role in Mr. John Dickson Carr's recent—1964—historical detective story, *Most Secret*.)

Mr. Robert Keith Leavitt has another view ("Nummi in Arca or The Fiscal Holmes"): "It is demonstrable that Holmes had no official commission from Scotland Yard to act in any of the affairs of record in the Canon. What, then, *was* the nature of Holmes' relation with the Inspectors from the Yard? Clearly this: he was a private detective engaged by each of them privately. For what purpose? For the enhancement of the Inspectors' professional reputations. And how was he paid? He was paid from the private pockets of his Inspector clients."

70 *the smartest of the Scotland Yarders.'* ". . . the only case that Gregson truly worked and collaborated with Holmes on was *A Study in Scarlet*," the late Clifton R. Andrew wrote in "That Scotland Yarder, Gregson—What a Help (?) He Was" (although Gregson appears or is mentioned in four other cases: *The Sign of the Four*, "The Greek Interpreter," "The Adventure of Wisteria Lodge," and "The Adventure of the Red Circle").

71 *if they are both put upon the scent.*' ". . . the experiment was never repeated," the late Gavin Brend wrote in *My Dear Holmes*. "Henceforward Lestrade and Gregson went their separate ways and we never again find them both appearing in the same case."

72 '*shall I go and order you a cab?*' Watson would not have had far to go: the cab rank in Baker Street was at the corner of Dorset Street, a trifle over a block, although a long block, away.

73 *an unofficial personage.*' ". . . on at least two occasions . . . Holmes disclaimed any official connections," Mr. John Ball, Jr., noted in "Early Days in Baker Street." "We must discount these claims to non-official status, for he believed firmly in saying, at all times, whatever was necessary to suit the purpose of the moment. He is certainly not the first confidential agent in history to deny the true source of his employment."

74 *a dun-coloured veil.* Here is another indication that the year of *A Study in Scarlet* was indeed 1881. Weather reports from the *Times* of London show that Friday, March 4, 1881 was "wet and unsettled," and the forecast was for "dull and cold, rain or snow." Saturday, March 4, 1882, on the other hand, was "cloudy" but "generally fine."

75 *the difference between a Stradivarius and an Amati.* The Amati of Cremona were a family of violin-makers which began with Andrew Amati, *fl.* 1535–1580, and reached its peak with Niccolo Amati, 1596–1684. Their pupil Antonio Stradivari or Antonius Stradivarius, 1644–1737, produced at least 1,116 instruments, including violas, cellos, viols, guitars and mandolins, between 1666 and 1737, the finest after 1700. Holmes' own violin, as we learn in "The Cardboard Box," was a Stradivarius. Mr. Guy Warrack in *Sherlock Holmes and Music* has asked why Holmes on this occasion did not mention the *third* great family of Cremonese luthiers—that of Giuseppe Antonio Guarneri (1683–1745).

76 *It biases the judgment.*' Compare: "It is a capital offense to theorize in advance of the facts" —"The Adventure of the Second Stain." "I make a point of never having any prejudices and of following docilely wherever fact may lead me"— "The Reigate Squires." "We approached the case with an absolutely blank mind, which is always an advantage"—"The Cardboard Box." "It is an error to argue in front of your data. You find yourself insensibly twisting them round to fit your theories" —"The Adventure of Wisteria Lodge." "One

'My dear fellow, what does it matter to me? Supposing I unravel the whole matter, you may be sure that Gregson, Lestrade, and Co. will pocket all the credit. That comes of **73** being an unofficial personage.'

'But he begs you to help him.'

'Yes. He knows that I am his superior, and acknowledges it to me; but he would cut his tongue out before he would own it to any third person. However, we may as well go and have a look. I shall work it out on my own hook. I may have a laugh at them, if I have nothing else. Come on!'

He hustled on his overcoat, and bustled about in a way that showed that an energetic fit had superseded the apathetic one.

'Get your hat,' he said.

'You wish me to come?'

'Yes, if you have nothing better to do.' A minute later we were both in a hansom, driving furiously for the Brixton Road.

74   It was a foggy, cloudy morning, and a dun-coloured veil hung over the house-tops, looking like the reflection of the mud-coloured streets beneath. My companion was in the best of spirits, and prattled away about Cremona fiddles, and the **75** difference between a Stradivarius and an Amati. As for myself, I was silent, for the dull weather and the melancholy business upon which we were engaged, depressed my spirits.

'You don't seem to give much thought to the matter in hand,' I said at last, interrupting Holmes' musical disquisition.

'No data yet,' he answered. 'It is a capital mistake to theor- **76** ize before you have all the evidence. It biases the judgment.'

'You will have your data soon,' I remarked, pointing with my finger; 'this is the Brixton Road, and that is the house, if I am not very much mistaken.'

'So it is. Stop, driver, stop!' We were still a hundred yards or so from it, but he insisted upon our alighting, and we finished our journey upon foot.

Number 3, Lauriston Gardens, wore an ill-omened and minatory look. It was one of four which stood back some little way from the street, two being occupied and two empty. The latter looked out with three tiers of vacant melancholy windows, which were blank and dreary, save that here and there a 'To Let' card had developed like a cataract upon the bleared panes. A small garden sprinkled over with a scattered eruption of sickly plants separated each of these houses from the street, and was traversed by a narrow pathway, yellowish in colour, and consisting apparently of a mixture of clay and of gravel. The whole place was very sloppy from the rain which had fallen through the night. The garden was bounded by a three-foot brick wall with a fringe of wood rails upon **77** the top and against this wall was leaning a stalwart police constable, surrounded by a small knot of loafers, who craned their necks and strained their eyes in the vain hope of catching some glimpse of the proceedings within.

I had imagined that Sherlock Holmes would at once have hurried into the house and plunged into a study of the mystery. Nothing appeared to be further from his intention. With an air of nonchalance which, under the circumstances, seemed to me to border upon affectation, he lounged up and down the pavement, and gazed vacantly at the ground, the sky, the opposite houses and the line of railings. Having finished his scrutiny, he proceeded slowly down the path, or rather down the fringe of grass which flanked the path, keeping his eyes riveted upon the ground. Twice he stopped, and once I saw him smile, and heard him utter an exclamation of satisfaction. There were many marks of footsteps upon the **78** wet clayey soil; but since the police had been coming and going over it, I was unable to see how my companion could hope to learn anything from it. Still I had had such extraordinary evidence of the quickness of his perceptive faculties, that I had no doubt that he could see a great deal which was hidden from me.

At the door of the house we were met by a tall, white-faced, flaxen-haired man, with a note-book in his hand, who rushed forward and wrung my companion's hand with effusion. 'It is indeed kind of you to come,' he said, 'I have had everything left untouched.'

'Except that!' my friend answered, pointing at the pathway. 'If a herd of buffaloes had passed along there could not **79** be a greater mess. No doubt, however, you had drawn your own conclusions, Gregson, before you permitted this.'

'I have had so much to do inside the house,' the detective said evasively. 'My colleague, Mr Lestrade, is here. I had relied upon him to look after this.'

Holmes glanced at me and raised his eyebrows sardonically. 'With two such men as yourself and Lestrade upon the ground there will not be much for a third party to find out,' he said.

Gregson rubbed his hands in a self-satisfied way. 'I think we have done all that can be done,' he answered; 'it's a queer case though, and I knew your taste for such things.'

'You did not come here in a cab?' asked Sherlock Holmes.

'No, sir.'

'Nor Lestrade?'

'No, sir.'

'Then let us go and look at the room.' With which inconsequent remark he strode on into the house, followed by Gregson, whose features expressed his astonishment.

A short passage, bare-planked and dusty, led to the kitchen and offices. Two doors opened out of it to the left and to the right. One of these had obviously been closed for many weeks. The other belonged to the dining-room, which was the apartment in which the mysterious affair had occurred. Holmes walked in, and I followed him with that subdued feeling at my heart which the presence of death inspires.

It was a large square room, looking all the larger from the absence of all furniture. A vulgar flaring paper adorned the walls, but it was blotched in places with mildew, and here and there great strips had become detached and hung down, exposing the yellow plaster beneath. Opposite the door was a showy fireplace, surmounted by a mantelpiece of imitation white marble. On one corner of this was stuck the stump of a red wax candle. The solitary window was so dirty that the light was hazy and uncertain, giving a dull grey tinge to everything, which was intensified by the thick layer of dust which coated the whole apartment.

All these details I observed afterwards. At present my attention was centred upon the single, grim, motionless figure which lay stretched upon the boards, with vacant, sightless eyes staring up at the discoloured ceiling. It was that of a

forms provisional theories and waits for time or fuller knowledge to explode them. A bad habit"— "The Adventure of the Sussex Vampire." "If I had not taken things for granted, if I had examined everything with the care which I would have shown had we approached the case *de novo* and had no cut-and-dried story to warp my mind, would I not then have found something more definite to go upon?"—"The Adventure of the Abbey Grange." "These abundant references," Mr. T. S. Blakeney wrote in *Sherlock Holmes: Fact or Fiction?*, ". . . show how keenly Holmes appreciated the liability to form one's suspicions on insufficient evidence. He was not, however, entirely immune from the tendency himself, for both in *The Sign of the Four* and 'The Adventure of the Missing Three-Quarter' he had to reform his theories, and in 'The Yellow Face' his conclusions were definitely wrong."

77 *with a fringe of wood rails upon the top.* Was "Number 3, Lauriston Gardens" *off* the Brixton Road, as Gregson said in his letter, or was it actually *in* the Brixton Road? Conflicting clues are to be found in *A Study in Scarlet*, and commentators are not agreed on their interpretation.

Both the late H. W. Bell ("Three Identifications") and Mr. Michael Harrison (*In the Footsteps of Sherlock Holmes*) have taken the view that the row of four houses was actually *in* the Brixton Road, and yet in a sense *off* it, being set back some distance from the pavement. "And in fact," Mr. Bell wrote, "there is no such group of four houses in any of the streets intersecting the Road. Furthermore, though there are in that thoroughfare itself several pairs of houses, a few groups of three and five, and many more extensive, there is only one which consists precisely of four. These four houses, it is pleasant to observe, correspond with almost perfect accuracy to Watson's description. They are three storeys in height, and are set back about thirty feet from the pavement, from which one mounts a few steps to the pathway leading to the front door. The gardens are bounded by a three-foot brick wall, upon which, however, the old wooden railing has been replaced by a more durable affair in iron. . . . They are numbered from 314 to 320. Since Watson specified No. 3, we may suppose that No. 318, the third in the row, was the scene of the death of Enoch J. Drebber."

"The nearest street bearing the name 'Lauriston,' is Lauriston Road, which leads off the South Side, Wimbledon Common;" Mr. Harrison wrote, "and not by any stretch of the topographical imagination can this be described as 'off the Brixton Road.' . . . 'Lauriston Gardens' was one of those small blocks of houses, set back from Brixton Road behind a wall, and with a small 'carriage drive,' which are still to be seen. . . . There is a block of five houses—numbered 152 to 160, Brixton Road, inclusive—which almost perfectly fit the description that Watson gives us of 'Lauriston Gardens.'"

On the other hand, Mr. Colin Prestige ("South London Adventures") is convinced that ". . . the area known as Myatt's Fields [*see sketch map*] immediately stands out as being the most probable location. . . . The streets which enclose the Fields vary in name; that on the east side is Knatchbull Road, and [a number of factors] would support the theory that No. 3, Lauriston Gardens was one of the houses along the northern stretch of Knatchbull Road. . . ."

78 *marks of footsteps.* Footprints—which Holmes and Watson always preferred to call "footsteps"—were clues of the utmost importance not only in *A Study in Scarlet* but also in *The Sign of the Four*, "The Resident Patient," *The Hound of the Baskervilles*, "The Adventure of the Beryl Coronet," and "The Adventure of the Golden Pince-Nez."

79 *a herd of buffaloes.* The late Christopher Morley always maintained that Holmes' use of this expression (he used it again in "The Boscombe Valley Mystery") was one of many indications that he had spent some time in America prior to his meeting with Watson.

80 *There is nothing new under the sun.* Holmes draws on Ecclesiastes, 1, 9: "There is no new thing under the sun." "But this generalization was not the glib and shallow schoolboy's 'History repeats itself,'" Mr. Whitfield J. Bell, Jr., wrote in "Holmes and History"; "nor was it dogma that nothing might contravene. Holmes had a feeling for the rhythms of human life, and he was always ready to admit the unusual and the unique. But history was serviceable to Holmes and had meaning to him because he saw that the wheel comes round, that power corrupts and tyranny must fail . . ."

man about forty-three or forty-four years of age, middle-sized, broad-shouldered, with crisp curling black hair, and a short, stubbly beard. He was dressed in a heavy broadcloth frock coat and waistcoat, with light-coloured trousers, and immaculate collar and cuffs. A top hat, well brushed and trim, was placed upon the floor beside him. His hands were clenched and his arms thrown abroad, while his lower limbs were interlocked, as though his death struggle had been a grievous one. On his rigid face there stood an expression of horror, and, as it seemed to me, of hatred, such as I have never seen upon human features. This malignant and terrible contortion, combined with the low forehead, blunt nose, and prognathous jaw, gave the dead man a singularly simous and ape-like appearance, which was increased by his writhing, unnatural posture. I have seen death in many forms, but never has it appeared to me in a more fearsome aspect than in that dark, grimy apartment, which looked out upon one of the main arteries of suburban London.

Lestrade, lean and ferret-like as ever, was standing by the doorway, and greeted my companion and myself.

'This case will make a stir, sir,' he remarked. 'It beats anything I have seen, and I am no chicken.'

'There is no clue?' said Gregson.

'None at all,' chimed in Lestrade.

Sherlock Holmes approached the body, and, kneeling down, examined it intently. 'You are sure that there is no wound?' he asked, pointing to numerous gouts and splashes of blood which lay all round.

'Positive!' cried both detectives.

'Then, of course, this blood belongs to a second individual—presumably the murderer, if murder has been committed. It reminds me of the circumstances attendant on the death of Van Jansen, in Utrecht, in the year '34. Do you remember the case, Gregson?'

'No, sir.'

'Read it up—you really should. There is nothing new **80** under the sun. It has all been done before.'

As he spoke, his nimble fingers were flying here, there, and everywhere, feeling, pressing, unbuttoning, examining, while his eyes wore the same far-away expression which I have already remarked upon. So swiftly was the examination made, that one would hardly have guessed the minuteness with which it was conducted. Finally, he sniffed the dead man's lips, and then glanced at the soles of his patent leather boots.

'He has not been moved at all?' he asked.

'No more than was necessary for the purposes of our examination.'

'You can take him to the mortuary now,' he said. 'There is nothing more to be learned.'

Gregson had a stretcher and four men at hand. At his call they entered the room, and the stranger was lifted and carried out. As they raised him, a ring tinkled down and rolled across the floor. Lestrade grabbed it up and stared at it with mystified eyes.

EAST OF THE BRIXTON ROAD

Mr. Colin Prestige's sketch map, from *The Sherlock Holmes Journal*, June, 1953, showing the White Hart, Holland Grove, Myatt's Fields and the Knatchbull Road. Also shown is No. 117 Brixton Road where Mrs. Maggie Oakshott bred geese ("The Adventure of the Blue Carbuncle").

'There's been a woman here,' he cried. 'It's a woman's wedding-ring.'

He held it out, as he spoke, upon the palm of his hand. We all gathered round him and gazed at it. There could be no doubt that that circlet of plain gold had once adorned the finger of a bride.

'This complicates matters,' said Gregson. 'Heaven knows, they were complicated enough before.'

'You're sure it doesn't simplify them?' observed Holmes. 'There's nothing to be learned by staring at it. What did you find in his pockets?'

'We have it all here,' said Gregson, pointing to a litter of objects upon one of the bottom steps of the stairs. 'A gold watch, No. 97163 by Barraud, of London. Gold Albert chain, **81** very heavy and solid. Gold ring, with masonic device. Gold pin—bull-dog's head, with rubies as eyes. Russian leather card-case, with cards of Enoch J. Drebber of Cleveland, corresponding with the E. J. D. upon the linen. No purse, but loose money to the extent of seven pounds thirteen. Pocket **82** edition of Boccaccio's *Decameron*, with name of Joseph **83** Stangerson upon the fly-leaf. Two letters—one addressed to E. J. Drebber and one to Joseph Stangerson.'

'At what address?'

'American Exchange, Strand—to be left till called for. They are both from the Guion Steamship Company, and refer to the sailing of their boats from Liverpool. It is clear that this unfortunate man was about to return to New York.'   **84**

81 *Gold Albert chain.* A watch chain made up of heavy links, named for Albert, Prince Consort of Queen Victoria, 1819–1861.

82 *seven pounds thirteen.* About $38.25.

83 *Boccaccio's* Decameron. Although the *Decameron* is the chief work of Giovanni Boccaccio, 1313–1375, he also wrote a biography of Dante, prose romances, and a verse satire on women, the *Corbaccio*.

84 *was about to return to New York.'* As Mr. N. P. Metcalfe pointed out ("The Date of the *Study in Scarlet*"), this again suggests 1881. Drebber's plan was to sail on the *Abyssinia* of the Guion Line, which in 1881 arrived at Queenstown from Liverpool en route to New York on March 6th.

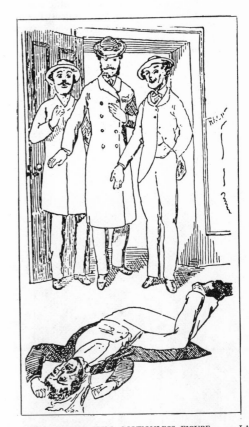

. . . THE SINGLE, GRIM, MOTIONLESS FIGURE . . . LAY
STRETCHED UPON THE BOARDS . . .

One of the six drawings done by Charles Doyle, Conan Doyle's father, for *A Study in Scarlet*, London: Ward, Lock & Co., 1888. The late James Montgomery noted in *A Study in Pictures* that it shows a *bearded* Holmes and a Gregson with their coats buttoning from right to left instead of in the usual direction, although the letters of the word RACHE are in positive position.

AS HE SPOKE, HIS NIMBLE FINGERS WERE FLYING HERE,
THERE, AND EVERYWHERE . . .

Illustration by D. H. Friston for *Beeton's Christmas Annual*, December, 1887. True to form, Lestrade and Gregson stand beside the body during this examination, but seemingly pay little heed to activities so far beyond their comprehension.

Named for an American, S. B. Guion, the company did a large transatlantic business from the 1860's to the 1880's. Their *Atlantic* was the first ship to cross the Atlantic in less than a week. ". . . to judge by its advertising cards, [one of which is shown at right] was the last word in transatlantic travel at the time," the late James Montgomery wrote in *Shots from the Canon*. "'The provisions supplied,' says a card, 'are abundant and excellent in quality, and are served and cooked by the company's stewards.' 'Bear in mind,' says another, 'that the Guion Line has not lost a single English, Welsh, Scotch or Irish passenger for the last 25 years.' These advantages evidently proved strong arguments to Drebber and Stangerson, who not only enjoyed the good things of life but also required a maximum degree of personal safety at all times to allay their constant jitters, brought on by an inward sense of guilt. They must have reasoned, not illogically, that if the steamship line had such a remarkable record in preserving its English, Welsh, Scotch and Irish passengers it was prepared to do the same thing for any Americans who might entrust themselves to its capable care."

'Have you made any inquiries as to this man Stangerson?'

'I did it at once, sir,' said Gregson. 'I have had advertisements sent to all the newspapers, and one of my men has gone to the American Exchange, but he has not returned yet.'

'Have you sent to Cleveland?'

'We telegraphed this morning.'

'How did you word your inquiries?'

'We simply detailed the circumstances, and said that we should be glad of any information which could help us.'

'You did not ask for particulars on any point which appeared to you to be crucial?'

'I asked about Stangerson.'

'Nothing else? Is there no circumstance on which this whole case appears to hinge? Will you not telegraph again?'

'I have said all I have to say,' said Gregson, in an offended voice.

Sherlock Holmes chuckled to himself, and appeared to be about to make some remark, when Lestrade, who had been in the front room while we were holding this conversation in the hall, reappeared upon the scene, rubbing his hands in a pompous and self-satisfied manner.

'Mr Gregson,' he said, 'I have just made a discovery of the highest importance, and one which would have been overlooked had I not made a careful examination of the walls.'

The little man's eyes sparkled as he spoke, and he was evidently in a state of suppressed exultation at having scored a point against his colleague.

'Come here,' he said, bustling back into the room, the atmosphere of which felt clearer since the removal of its ghastly inmate. 'Now, stand there!'

He struck a match on his boot and held it up against the wall.

'Look at that!' he said, triumphantly.

I have remarked that the paper had fallen away in parts. In this particular corner of the room a large piece had peeled off, leaving a yellow square of coarse plastering. Across this bare space there was scrawled in blood-red letters a single word—

RACHE.

HE STRUCK A MATCH ON HIS BOOT AND HELD IT UP
AGAINST THE WALL.

Illustration by George Hutchinson for the London, 1891, Ward, Lock, Bowden & Co. edition of *A Study in Scarlet*.

'What do you think of that?' cried the detective, with the air of a showman exhibiting his show. 'This was overlooked because it was in the darkest corner of the room, and no one thought of looking there. The murderer has written it with his or her own blood. See this smear where it has trickled down the wall! That disposes of the idea of suicide anyhow. Why was that corner chosen to write it on? I will tell you. See that candle on the mantelpiece. It was lit at the time, and if it was lit this corner would be the brightest instead of the darkest portion of the wall.'

'And what does it mean now that you *have* found it?' asked Gregson in a depreciatory voice.

'Mean? Why, it means that the writer was going to put the female name Rachel, but was disturbed before he or she had time to finish. You mark my words, when this case comes to be cleared up, you will find that a woman named Rachel has something to do with it. It's all very well for you to laugh, Mr Sherlock Holmes. You may be very smart and clever, but the old hound is the best, when all is said and done.' **85**

'I really beg your pardon!' said my companion, who had ruffled the little man's temper by bursting into an explosion of laughter. 'You certainly have the credit of being the first of us to find this out and, as you say, it bears every mark of having been written by the other participant in last night's mystery. I have not had time to examine this room yet, but with your permission I shall do so now.'

As he spoke, he whipped a tape measure and a large round magnifying glass from his pocket. With these two implements **86** he trotted noiselessly about the room, sometimes stopping, occasionally kneeling, and once lying flat upon his face. So engrossed was he with his occupation that he appeared to have forgotten our presence, for he chattered away to himself under his breath the whole time, keeping up a running fire of exclamations, groans, whistles, and little cries suggestive of encouragement and of hope. As I watched him I was irresistibly reminded of a pure-blooded, well-trained foxhound as it dashes backwards and forwards through the covert, whining in its eagerness, until it comes across the lost scent. For twenty minutes or more he continued his researches, measuring with the most exact care the distance between marks which were entirely invisible to me, and occasionally applying his tape to the walls in an equally incomprehensible manner. In one place he gathered up very carefully a little pile of grey dust from the floor, and packed it away in an envelope. Finally he examined with his glass the word upon the wall, going over every letter of it with the most minute exactness. This done, he appeared to be satisfied, for he replaced his tape and his glass in his pocket.

'They say that genius is an infinite capacity for taking pains,' he remarked with a smile. 'It's a very bad definition, **87** but it does apply to detective work.'

Gregson and Lestrade had watched the manœuvres of their amateur companion with considerable curiosity and some contempt. They evidently failed to appreciate the fact, which I had begun to realize, that Sherlock Holmes' smallest actions were all directed towards some definite and practical end.

'What do you think of it, sir?' they both asked.

85 *the old hound is the best, when all is said and done.'* Less than a page later in Watson's account Lestrade changes his tune to "What do you think of it, sir?" "Watson failed to note this, as well as the liberties extended to Holmes which no responsible officer would give to an outsider, especially one who did not hold his complete respect," Mr. John Ball, Jr., wrote in "Early Days in Baker Street."

86 *a large round magnifying glass.* "The 'lens' is in use by Holmes in sixteen stories, with a full twenty-five references," Mr. Jerry Neal Williamson wrote in "Sherlock's Murder Bag."

87 *genius is an infinite capacity for taking pains.* This is the apothegm often attributed to Carlyle, in his *Life of Frederick the Great*, Book IV, Chapter 3: "Genius . . . which is the transcendent capacity for taking trouble first of all."

FINALLY HE EXAMINED WITH HIS GLASS THE WORD UPON THE WALL . . .

If we agree that the cover of *Beeton's Christmas Annual* for December, 1887, was not intended to be the first depiction of Mr. Sherlock Holmes, this frontispiece by D. H. Friston must be accorded that honor. It shows us Holmes as an unfamiliar figure in belted cape-coat and sideburns—and Watson as a walrus-mustached, doglike figure in a top hat. The other two grotesques are, of course, from left to right, Inspectors Lestrade and Gregson. Sometime between the first text illustration and this frontispiece, Gregson has seen fit to change his hat.

88 *Kennington Park Gate*.' Kennington Park, at the junction of Camberwell New Road, was originally a common, but was enclosed by iron railings in 1853 and converted into an ornamental park. About the same time the old Kennington turnpike gate, which stood near this spot, was removed. Audley Court, at "Kennington Park Gate," was presumably near the site of the old turnpike gate.

89 '*There has been murder done*. It is interesting to note, as an examination by the late Fletcher Pratt ("Very Little Murder") has shown, "that in the course of a long and brilliant career, Holmes was called upon to investigate only eight cases of murder. . . . In fifteen [of the sixty recorded cases], or one-quarter of the total, *no crime took place*."

90 *a Trichinopoly cigar*. A cigar made from the dark tobacco grown near Trichinopoly in the Madras district of India. The Trichinopoly was usually a "pierced" cigar, open at both ends, and was often sold with a straw inserted through this opening to keep it clear until smoking.

91 '*"Rache" is the German for "revenge.*" "Rache is [also] an old word meaning 'hunting dog,' and it could have been scribbled on the wall by Gregson (or Lestrade) to confuse his rival," the late Professor Jay Finley Christ pointed out in "Sherlock and the Canons."

92 *Parthian shot*. A concluding retort, so called because the ancient calvary of Parthia used to shoot backward as they fled.

'It would be robbing you of the credit of the case if I was to presume to help you,' remarked my friend. 'You are doing so well now that it would be a pity for anyone to interfere.' There was a world of sarcasm in his voice as he spoke. 'If you will let me know how your investigations go,' he continued, 'I shall be happy to give you any help I can. In the meantime I should like to speak to the constable who found the body. Can you give me his name and address?'

Lestrade glanced at his note-book. 'John Rance,' he said. 'He is off duty now. You will find him at 46, Audley Court, **88** Kennington Park Gate.'

Holmes took a note of the address.

'Come along, Doctor,' he said; 'we shall go and look him up. I'll tell you one thing which may help you in the case,' he continued, turning to the two detectives. 'There has been **89** murder done, and the murderer was a man. He was more than six feet high, was in the prime of life, had small feet for his height, wore coarse, square-toed boots and smoked a Trichi-**90** nopoly cigar. He came here with his victim in a four-wheeled cab, which was drawn by a horse with three old shoes and one new one on his off fore-leg. In all probability the murderer had a florid face, and the finger-nails of his right hand were remarkably long. These are only a few indications, but they may assist you.'

Lestrade and Gregson glanced at each other with an incredulous smile.

'If this man was murdered, how was it done?' asked the former.

'Poison,' said Sherlock Holmes curtly, and strode off. 'One other thing, Lestrade,' he added, turning round at the door: **91** '"Rache" is the German for "revenge"; so don't lose your time looking for Miss Rachel.'

92   With which Parthian shot he walked away, leaving the two rivals open-mouthed behind him.

"HE CAME HERE WITH HIS VICTIM IN A FOUR-WHEELED CAB . . ."

Victorian cabs were of two kinds, the four-wheeler, or "growler," which carried four passengers but was slower than the other cab, the smart, two-wheeled hansom. It may have been called a "growler" because of its rumble and creak, or perhaps because of the cabby's habit of protesting an insufficient tip. The bowler, or billycock, hat was *de riguer* with the drivers of growlers. The photograph is from Michael Harrison's *In the Footsteps of Sherlock Holmes*.

4 • WHAT JOHN RANCE HAD TO TELL

It was one o'clock when we left No. 3, Lauriston Gardens. Sherlock Holmes led me to the nearest telegraph office, **93** whence he dispatched a long telegram. He then hailed a cab, **94** and ordered the driver to take us to the address given us by Lestrade.

'There is nothing like first-hand evidence,' he remarked; **95** 'as a matter of fact, my mind is entirely made up upon the case, but still we may as well learn all that is to be learned.'

'You amaze me, Holmes,' said I. 'Surely you are not as sure as you pretend to be of all those particulars which you gave.'

'There's no room for a mistake,' he answered. 'The very first thing which I observed on arriving there was that a cab had made two ruts with its wheels close to the kerb. Now, up to last night, we have had no rain for a week, so that those **96** wheels which left such a deep impression must have been there during the night. There were the marks of the horse's hoofs, too, the outline of one of which was far more clearly cut than that of the other three, showing that that was a new shoe. Since the cab was there after the rain began, and was not there at any time during the morning—I have Gregson's word for that—it follows that it must have been there during the night, and, therefore, that it brought those two individuals to the house.'

'That seems simple enough,' said I; 'but how about the other man's height?'

'Why, the height of a man, in nine cases out of ten, can be told from the length of his stride. It is a simple calculation **97** enough, though there is no use my boring you with figures. I had this fellow's stride both on the clay outside and on the dust within. Then I had a way of checking my calculation. When a man writes on a wall, his instinct leads him to write about the level of his own eyes. Now that writing was just over six feet from the ground. It was child's play.'

'And his age?' I asked.

'Well, if a man can stride four and a half feet without the smallest effort, he can't be quite in the sere and yellow. That was the breadth of a puddle on the garden walk which he had evidently walked across. Patent-leather boots had gone round, and Square-toes had hopped over. There is no mystery about it at all. I am simply applying to ordinary life a few of those precepts of observation and deduction which I advocated in that article. Is there anything else that puzzles you?'

'The finger-nails and the Trichinopoly,' I suggested.

'The writing on the wall was done with a man's fore-finger dipped in blood. My glass allowed me to observe that the plaster was slightly scratched in doing it, which would not have been the case if the man's nail had been trimmed. I gathered up some scattered ash from the floor. It was dark in colour and flakey—such an ash as is only made by a Trichinopoly. I have made a special study of cigar ashes—in fact, I have written a monograph upon the subject. I flatter **98** myself that I can distinguish at a glance the ash of any known brand either of cigar or of tobacco. It is just in such details **99** that the skilled detective differs from the Gregson and Lestrade type.'

'And the florid face?' I asked.

---

93 *the nearest telegraph office.* In support of his identification of No. 318, Brixton Road, as "No. 3, Lauriston Gardens," the late H. W. Bell noted that about sixty yards up the road from No. 318, and on the same, or western side, there was a post-office, where, in England, telegrams may be dispatched, as late as 1896.

94 *dispatched a long telegram.* Despite its length, it would not have cost Holmes too much: in those days, a telegram could be sent for a shilling (25¢) anywhere in the United Kingdom for the first twenty words, not counting the names and addresses of the sender and the receiver. London and its suburbs had about 300 telegraph offices. The telegram, even after the introduction of the telephone, remained Holmes' favorite means of communication. He was no doubt mindful of the fact that, in the summer of 1846, it was the magnetic telegraph that made it possible to catch a thief who, running across the platform at Cambridge and leaping on a train, had been picked up by the police on reaching London. The *Daily News*, the first daily newspaper, edited by Charles Dickens, added the striking detail that the warning message from Cambridge had taken less than half a minute to speed to London.

95 *'There is nothing like first-hand evidence.'* "This truism was carefully borne in mind by Holmes—he was at all times prepared to hear the true facts of a case retold to him," Mr. T. S. Blakeney wrote in *Sherlock Holmes: Fact or Fiction?* "Equally he is found ready to relate the points of a problem to a listener, for, as he says, 'nothing clears up a case so much as stating it to another person ('Silver Blaze'). We find him adopting the same practice in 'The Adventure of the Abbey Grange,' 'The Man with the Twisted Lip' and 'The Adventure of Wisteria Lodge.'"

96 *we have had no rain for a week.* There was considerable rain in the week preceding Saturday, March 4, 1882—but in the week preceding Friday, March 4, 1881, it rained only once: a meager .01 inches fell on Sunday, February 27th—too little, surely, to discredit Holmes' statement. It seems safe to say, then, that his part in the case began on *Friday, March 4, 1881*, and not on Saturday, March 4, 1882, as has been contended by a number of commentators, notably the late Edgar W. Smith ("The Long Road from Maiwand").

97 *can be told from the length of his stride.* ". . . is not the length of a man's pace largely a matter of idiosyncracy—something which is not, at any rate materially, dependent upon stature?" Mr. J. B. Mackenzie asked in "Sherlock Holmes' Plots and Strategy." "Do not very many tall men take comparatively short steps, and a good number, of less inches, cover more ground with each? Have we not, besides, experience to testify that the upper and lower halves of the human body are often largely disproportioned?"

98 *I have written a monograph upon the subject.* Holmes probably drew on "Redi's *Esperienze intorno a Diverse Cose Naturali* (Florence 1686), containing the first scientific tests with nicotine, as well as the Philone de Conversationibus' *Venus Rebutee* (Cologne, 1722), an account of the various kinds of tobacco raised in Virginia and Germany with a description of the types of ash produced by each," Miss Madeleine B. Stern wrote in "Sherlock Holmes: Rare Book Collector." "His tobacco collection was not complete without Tiedmann's *Geschichte des Tabaka* (1856) dealing with various smoking mixtures and cake tobacco, cigars, cigarettes and snuff, nor—though it was not directly related to his studies—could Holmes have resisted the purchase of *Medical Reports, of the Effects of Tobacco* (1788) by Thomas Fowler, who wrote also on the effects of arsenic. It is interesting to note that Holmes' article, written by 1881, probably influenced Gaetano Casoria, whose treatise, *Sulla Combustibilitá alcune Varietá de Tobacchi*, with a chemical analysis of the ash of various tobaccos, appeared the following year."

Holmes did not at this time disclose the actual title of his monograph (*Upon the Distinction Between the Ashes of the Various Tobaccos: An Enumeration of 140 Forms of Cigar, Cigarette, and Pipe Tobacco, with Coloured Plates Illustrating the Difference in the Ash*). That remained unknown until his biographer gave to the world the story called *The Sign of the Four*. "Referred to again by its author . . . during his investigation of the murder of Charles McCarthy in Boscombe Valley," Mr. Walter Klinefelter wrote in "The Writings of Sherlock Holmes," the monograph "is the only one of Holmes' works which Watson quotes the detective as mentioning more than once in the Canon. Consequently, it may be inferred that he took more than a little pride in its authorship, probably considering it his most important contribution to what may be termed the minutiae of scientific detection. . . . It is known from Holmes' own statement (*The Sign of the Four*) that . . . François le Villard of the French detective service was [then] translating the work into his native language." Mr. Klinefelter added that a Philadelphia tobacconist once wrote to Conan Doyle to ask where he might obtain a copy of the monograph. "Rather funny, isn't it?" the author commented.

99 *I can distinguish at a glance the ash of any known brand.* "It is not generally considered possible, however, to distinguish one tobacco ash from another, particularly as ash varies according to the rate at which the tobacco is smoked," wrote the editors of the Catalogue of the Sherlock Holmes Exhibition.

100 *'My head is in a whirl.'* But let us note that having said this, Watson immediately comes out with a string of seven quite apposite questions.

'Ah, that was a more daring shot, though I have no doubt that I was right. You must not ask me that at the present state of the affair.'

100   I passed my hand over my brow. 'My head is in a whirl,' I remarked; 'the more one thinks of it the more mysterious it grows. How came these two men—if there were two men—into an empty house? What has become of the cabman who drove them? How could one man compel another to take poison? Where did the blood come from? What was the object of the murderer, since robbery had no part in it? How came the woman's ring there? Above all, why should the second man write up the German word RACHE before decamping? I confess that I cannot see any possible way of reconciling all these facts.'

My companion smiled approvingly.

'You sum up the difficulties of the situation succinctly and well,' he said. 'There is much that is still obscure, though I have quite made up my mind on the main facts. As to poor Lestrade's discovery, it was simply a blind intended to put the police upon a wrong track, by suggesting Socialism and **101** secret societies. It was not done by a German. The A, if you noticed, was printed somewhat after the German fashion. Now, a real German invariably prints in the Latin character, so that we may safely say that this was not written by one, but by a clumsy imitator who overdid his part. It was simply a ruse to divert inquiry into a wrong channel. I'm not going to tell you much more of the case, Doctor. You know a conjuror gets no credit when once he has explained his trick; and if I show you too much of my method of working, you will come to the conclusion that I am a very ordinary individual after all.'

'I shall never do that,' I answered; 'you have brought detection as near an exact science as it ever will be brought in this world.'

My companion flushed up with pleasure at my words, and the earnest way in which I uttered them. I had already observed that he was as sensitive to flattery on the score of his art as any girl could be of her beauty.

'I'll tell you one other thing,' he said. 'Patent-leathers and Square-toes came in the same cab, and they walked down the pathway together as friendly as possible—arm-in-arm, in all probability. When they got inside, they walked up and down the room—or rather, Patent-leathers stood still while Square-toes walked up and down. I could read all that in the dust; and I could read that as he walked he grew more and more excited. That is shown by the increased length of his strides. He was talking all the while, and working himself up, no doubt, into a fury. Then the tragedy occurred. I've told you all I know myself now, for the rest is mere surmise and conjecture. We have a good working basis, however, on which to **102** start. We must hurry up, for I want to go to Hallé's concert to **103-104** hear Norman Neruda this afternoon.'

This conversation had occurred while our cab had been threading its way through a long succession of dingy streets and dreary byways. In the dingiest and dreariest of them our driver suddenly came to a stand. 'That's Audley Court in there,' he said, pointing to a narrow slit in the line of dead-coloured brick. 'You'll find me here when you come back.'

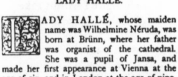

LADY HALLÉ.

LADY HALLÉ, whose maiden name was Wilhelmine Néruda, was born at Brünn, where her father was organist of the cathedral. She was a pupil of Jansa, and made her first appearance at Vienna at the age of six, and in London at the age of nine. After this she returned to the Continent, and in 1864 she married Ludwig Norman, a

Swedish musician. Since 1869 she has been in England every winter, playing especially at the concerts of Sir Charles Hallé, whom she married in 1888.

"HER ATTACK AND HER BOWING ARE SPLENDID."

Lady Hallé (the former Mme. Norman-Neruda) as she was depicted in the *Strand Magazine* in 1890 in "Celebrities Then and Now," a feature which appeared for many months in the pages of the *Strand*.

Audley Court was not an attractive locality. The narrow passage led us into a quadrangle paved with flags and lined by sordid dwellings. We picked our way among groups of dirty children, and through lines of discoloured linen, until we came to Number 46, the door of which was decorated with a small slip of brass on which the name Rance was engraved. On inquiry we found that the constable was in bed, and we were shown into a little front parlour to await his coming.

101 *Socialism and secret societies.* At this time, as the late Christopher Morley wrote in *Sherlock Holmes and Dr. Watson: A Textbook of Friendship*, "Socialists were sometimes (and perhaps unfairly) associated in the public mind with other groups who believed in violent action as a protest against the inequalities of civilization. There were a number of dynamite outrages in London in the eighties, which suggested the theme of Robert Louis Stevenson's humorous satire, *The Dynamiter*." An excellent account of the dynamite outrages will be found in Mr. Michael Harrison's *In the Footsteps of Sherlock Holmes*.

102 *Hallé's concert.* "During the last third of the nineteenth century," Mr. Paul S. Clarkson wrote in his stimulating essay, "'In the Beginning . . .'", "there was one annual series of London events as certain as the seasons or the months, viz., Charles Hallé's Popular Concerts. Beginning in 1861, they were repeated year after year during the late fall and winter with as much regularity and with as faithful a following, as the performances of the Boston Symphony and the New York Philharmonic Orchestras in this country and century. Born Karl Hallé in Westphalia, in 1819, this great pianist and director came to England in 1843. He began as a player and producer of chamber music recitals in London, but soon was conducting symphony orchestras and operatic performances, notably at Manchester, but also at Bristol, Liverpool, Edinburgh, Glasgow, Belfast, Dublin, and many other cities. It was Hallé who introduced Berlioz's instrumental and operatic compositions to England, as well as a great deal of Chopin. In recognition of his many contributions to the popularizing of fine music in the British Isles for nearly a half century, Hallé was knighted by Queen Victoria in 1888. The great symphony orchestra which he organized at Manchester in 1858 continued after his death in 1895, and to this day gives concerts and makes records of classical music in the grand tradition."

103 *to hear Norman Neruda.* "From the beginning," Mr. Clarkson continued, "Hallé procured the best instrumental soloists of the day, from the Continent as well as from England, to play for his concerts. Among these was the great violin virtuoso, 'the female Paganini' of her own—or perhaps of any—day—the brilliant, the beloved of the concert platform, the incomparable Mme. Norman-Neruda [unlike Watson, she always used the hyphen]. She was born in Brunn, in Moravia, in 1839, one of a long line and numerous family of fine musicians. Trained by the great Jansa, when seven years old she gave her first public recital, in Vienna. Even at that tender age, she excited as much amazement as admiration, in her rendering of a Bach sonata, for the strength of her bowing, the purity of her catilena, and the beauty of her execution, despite her small, childish hands. Holmes was far from being the first critic—or the last—to observe that 'her attack and her bowing are splendid.' She was christened Wilhelmina, which she shortened and Anglicized to Wilma for her engagements in London. She married a Swedish musician, Ludwig Norman, from whom she derived the first half of her hyphenated *nom de salle de concert*. Three years after his death, she married (in 1888) Hallé, with whom she had been closely associated on the concert stage for nearly twenty years, and was thenceforth, of course, usually referred to as Lady Hallé. In 1901, 'a certain gracious lady' conferred upon her the title 'Violinist to the Queen.' Beyond their love of great music, and their playing the violin, Mme. Norman-Neruda and Sherlock Holmes had another unusual and distinguished factor in common: each was the owner of a violin made by the great Cremonese, Antonio Stradivari. Norman-Neruda's was the famous 'Ernst Violin,' made in the master's 'Golden Period' (in 1709) which had had a most interesting and romantic history. It was purchased and presented to her, in 1876, by the Duke of Saxe-Coburg-Gotha (formerly the Duke of Edinburgh), and the Earls of Dudley and Hardwicke, as a token of their esteem. Thereafter, she played this great instrument with its 'ripe, woody, and yet sparkling quality' of tone, at all her concerts, including those on her American tour in 1899."

104 *this afternoon.*' The first of many indications that Watson, for one reason or another, is becoming hopelessly confused in the sequence of events he is recounting to us in *A Study in Scarlet*. By Watson's account, Holmes attended Hallé's concert on the afternoon of Friday, March 4, 1881. But this he could not possibly have done. As Mr. Clarkson pointed out: "Upon examining the actual records of the concert platform in London for this entire period, we shall find that the afternoon of *Saturday, March 5, 1881*, is the only date that historically meets all of [the] specifications. Hallé's 'Popular Concerts' were a biweekly feature of London's winter music season. They were given every year at St. James's Hall from about the first of December to the first of March—and always and only on Monday nights and on Saturday afternoons. Holmes' attendance 'this afternoon' fixes the day of the week to a Saturday, and no other possible day."

105 *the White Hart*. Identified by the late H. W. Bell as the Old White Horse on the Brixton Road. But Mr. Colin Prestige, in "South London Adventures," has written that there is only one White Hart in the district: '. . . although the present White Hart has only been in existence since 1938, it replaces an earlier 'pub' of the same name of considerable antiquity, which was on the same site until demolished for rebuilding in the 1930s." The site (*see sketch map*) is at the junction of Loughborough Road and Lilford Road.

106 *Holland Grove. See sketch map.* The "Henrietta Street" which follows is not now identifiable.

He appeared presently, looking a little irritable at being disturbed in his slumbers. 'I made my report at the office,' he said.

Holmes took a half-sovereign from his pocket and played with it pensively. 'We thought that we should like to hear it all from your own lips,' he said.

'I shall be most happy to tell you anything I can,' the constable answered, with his eyes upon the little golden disk.

'Just let us hear it all in your own way as it occurred.'

Rance sat down on the horsehair sofa, and knitted his brows as though determined not to omit anything in his narrative.

'I'll tell it ye from the beginning,' he said. 'My time is from ten at night to six in the morning. At eleven there was a fight **105** at the White Hart; but bar that all was quiet enough on the beat. At one o'clock it began to rain, and I met Harry Mur- **106** cher—him who has the Holland Grove beat—and we stood together at the corner of Henrietta Street a-talkin'. Presently —maybe about two or a little after—I thought I would take a look round and see that all was right down the Brixton Road. It was precious dirty and lonely. Not a soul did I meet all the way down, though a cab or two went past me. I was a-strollin' down, thinkin' between ourselves how uncommon **107** handy a four of gin hot would be, when suddenly the glint of a light caught me eye in the window of that same house. Now, I knew that them two houses in Lauriston Gardens was empty on account of him that owns them who won't have the drains seed to, though the very last tenant what lived in one of them died o' typhoid fever. I was knocked all in a heap, therefore, at seeing a light in the window; and I suspected as something was wrong. When I got to the door——'

'You stopped, and then walked back to the garden gate,' my companion interrupted. 'What did you do that for?'

Rance gave a violent jump, and stared at Sherlock Holmes with the utmost amazement upon his features.

'Why, that's true, sir,' he said; 'though how you come to know it, Heaven only knows. Ye see when I got up to the door, it was so still and so lonesome, that I thought I'd be none the worse for someone with me. I ain't afeard of anything on this side o' the grave; but I thought that maybe it was him that died o' the typhoid inspecting the drains what killed him. The thought gave me a kind o' turn, and I walked back to the gate to see if I could see Murcher's lantern, but there wasn't no sign of him nor of anyone else.'

'There was no one in the street?'

'Not a livin' soul, sir, nor as much as a dog. Then I pulled myself together and went back and pushed the door open. All was quiet inside, so I went into the room where the light was a-burnin'. There was a candle flickerin' on the mantelpiece— a red wax one—and by its light I saw——'

'Yes, I know all that you saw. You walked round the room several times, and you knelt down by the body, and then you walked through and tried the kitchen door, and then——'

John Rance sprang to his feet with a frightened face and **108** suspicion in his eyes. 'Where was you hid to see all that?' he cried. 'It seems to me that you knows a deal more than you should.'

Holmes laughed and threw his card across the table to the constable. 'Don't get arresting me for the murder,' he said. 'I am one of the hounds and not the wolf; Mr Gregson or Mr Lestrade will answer for that. Go on, though. What did you do next?'

Rance resumed his seat, without, however, losing his mystified expression. 'I went back to the gate and sounded my whistle. That brought Murcher and two more to the spot.'

'Was the street empty then?'

'Well, it was, as far as anybody that could be of any good goes.'

'What do you mean?'

The constable's features broadened into a grin. 'I've seen many a drunk chap in my time,' he said, 'but never anyone so cryin' drunk as that cove. He was at the gate when I came out, a-leanin' up ag'in the railings, and a-singin' at the pitch o' his lungs about Columbine's New-fangled Banner, or some such stuff. He couldn't stand, far less help.'

'What sort of a man was he?' asked Sherlock Holmes.

John Rance appeared to be somewhat irritated at this digression. 'He was an uncommon drunk sort o' man,' he said. 'He'd ha' found hisself in the station if we hadn't been so took up.'

'His face—his dress—didn't you notice them?' Holmes broke in impatiently.

'I should think I did notice them, seeing that I had to prop him up—me and Murcher between us. He was a long chap, with a red face, the lower part muffled round——'

'That will do,' cried Holmes. 'What became of him?'

'We'd enough to do without lookin' after him,' the policeman said, in an aggrieved voice. 'I'll wager he found his way home all right.'

'How was he dressed?'

'A brown overcoat.'

'Had he a whip in his hand?'

'A whip—no.'

'He must have left it behind,' muttered my companion. 'You didn't happen to see or hear a cab after that?'

'No.'

'There's a half-sovereign for you,' my companion said, standing up and taking his hat. 'I am afraid, Rance, that you will never rise in the force. That head of yours should be for use as well as ornament. You might have gained your sergeant's stripes last night. The man whom you held in your hands is the man who holds the clue of this mystery, and whom we are seeking. There is no use of arguing about it now; I tell you that it is so. Come along, Doctor.'

We started off for the cab together, leaving our informant incredulous, but obviously uncomfortable.

'The blundering fool!' Holmes said, bitterly, as we drove back to our lodgings. 'Just to think of his having such an incomparable bit of good luck, and not taking advantage of it.'

'I am rather in the dark still. It is true that the description of this man tallies with your idea of the second party in this mystery. But why should he come back to the house after leaving it? That is not the way of criminals.'

'The ring, man, the ring: that was what he came back for. If we have no other way of catching him, we can always bait our line with the ring. I shall have him, Doctor—I'll lay you

HOLMES TOOK A HALF-SOVEREIGN FROM HIS POCKET . . .

The half-sovereign was valued at 10 shillings, or approximately $2.50 in U.S. currency at that time. This piece, the late A. Carson Simpson wrote in *Numismatics in the Canon* (Part I: "Full Thirty Thousand Marks of English Coin"), "has many forerunners under varied names, including the rosenoble of Edward IV and the ryal of Henry VII. It was first named a half-sovereign by Henry VIII and a half-pound by Elizabeth I. The Stuarts and the Commonwealth called it a double-crown; the angel was also revalued at 10/–. It gave way to the half-guinea until George III's 1816 reform and was last struck regularly in London in 1915, but later in colonial mints. There are a number of Canonical references to the half-sovereign. . . . A characteristic one is Watson's: 'I took our mongrel accordingly and left him, together with a half-sovereign, at the old naturalist's in Pinchin Lane' (*The Sign of the Four*). Other references: 'A Scandal in Bohemia' (twice); *The Hound of the Baskervilles*; 'The Adventure of Black Peter' (twice)."

107 *a four of gin hot.* Fourpence (8¢) worth of gin with hot water and lemon.

108 *'Where was you hid to see all that?'* That Holmes was indeed on the spot at the time of the murder—disguised as the cab horse "with three old shoes and one new one on his off fore-leg"— was the astounding theory put forward by the late Robert S. Morgan in his volume *Spotlight on a Simple Case*, a *tour de force* that must be read to be believed.

109 *a little art jargon.* An early indication of Holmes' more than casual interest in art. In his day paintings were frequently called "A Study in Such and Such a Color." For instance, Whistler's "Nocturne in Green and Gold," or the Portrait of his Mother, often alluded to as "A Study in Black and Gray."

110 *Chopin's.* Frédéric François Chopin, 1810–1849, Polish composer and pianist. His highly romantic music, almost all for solo piano, includes piano concertos, mazurkas, polonaises, nocturnes, waltzes, preludes, etudes, scherzos, ballades, and sonatas.

111 *Tra-la-la-lira-lira-lay.'* "The principal, and for all practical purposes insuperable, difficulty [in identifying that little thing of Chopin's] lies in the fact . . . that Chopin *never composed one single piece for the solo violin,*" Mr. Paul S. Clarkson wrote in "In the Beginning. . . ." "Indeed, 'four times only did Chopin write for stringed instruments, and all four of the pieces contain parts for the cello. Only once did he add violin: in the (G minor) Trio . . .' Of course, any piano piece ever written can be 'arranged' for the violin, as everyone knows. But, as anyone also knows, concert violinists rarely, if ever, perform piano pieces. And no one will be surprised to hear that a search of all reported concert programs, for a period of several years prior to the occasion of Holmes'. . . question, discloses not one Chopin opus played by Mme. Norman-Neruda." Mr. Clarkson therefore suggested that Holmes, at a previous concert (June 4, 1880) heard Charles Hallé play Chopin's Nocturne in E (Op. 62, No. 2), and the Barcarolle in F sharp (Op. 60), also by Chopin, but also heard Mme. Norman-Neruda play her favorite Handel's D major sonata. It was the sonata he was thinking of, but he mistakenly attributed its composition to Chopin.

This is an ingenious suggestion, but it is only one of many ingenious suggestions put forward by Sherlockian scholars. As Dr. Julian Wolff wrote ("Just What Was That Little Thing of Chopin's?"): "The great interest in this question is evidenced by the amount of research that has been done and the number of papers published." Here is a list of the important literature on the subject and the conclusions reached by various authors, arranged in chronological order:

1) Warrack, Guy: *Sherlock Holmes and Music.* F minor Nocturne (Nocturne for piano, No. 15 in F minor).

2) Montgomery, James: "Chopin in Baker Street." Etude in E major, Opus 10 (Etude in E major for Piano, Op. 10, No. 3).

3) Zeisler, Dr. Ernest Bloomfield: "Tra-la-lira-lira-lay." Valse in E minor, No. 14 (Op. Posth.).

4) Thiman, Eric H., Mus. D.: "Tra-la-la-lira-lira-lay." Mazurka in E flat minor, Op. 6, No. 4.

5) Christie, Winifred M.: "Some Reflections on

two to one that I have him. I must thank you for it all. I might not have gone but for you, and so have missed the finest study I ever came across: a study in scarlet, eh? Why shouldn't we **109** use a little art jargon. There's the scarlet thread of murder running through the colourless skein of life, and our duty is to unravel it, and isolate it, and expose every inch of it. And now for lunch, and then for Norman Neruda. Her attack and **110** her bowing are splendid. What's that little thing of Chopin's **111** she plays so magnificently: Tra-la-la-lira-lira-lay.'

Leaning back in the cab, this amateur bloodhound carolled away like a lark while I meditated upon the manysidedness of the human mind.

♦

5 ♦ OUR ADVERTISEMENT BRINGS A VISITOR
♦

Our morning's exertions had been too much for my weak health, and I was tired out in the afternoon. After Holmes' departure for the concert, I lay down upon the sofa and endeavoured to get a couple of hours' sleep. It was a useless attempt. My mind had been too much excited by all that had occurred, and the strangest fancies and surmises crowded into it. Every time that I closed my eyes I saw before me the distorted, baboon-like countenance of the murdered man. So sinister was the impression which that face had produced upon me that I found it difficult to feel anything but gratitude for him who had removed its owner from the world. If ever human features bespoke vice of the most malignant type, they were certainly those of Enoch J. Drebber, of Cleveland. Still I recognized that justice must be done, and that the depravity of the victim was no condonement in the eyes of the law.

The more I thought of it the more extraordinary did my companion's hypothesis, that the man had been poisoned, appear. I remembered how he had sniffed his lips, and had no doubt that he had detected something which had given rise to the idea. Then, again, if not poison, what had caused the man's death, since there was neither wound nor marks of strangulation? But, on the other hand, whose blood was that which lay so thickly upon the floor? There were no signs of a struggle, nor had the victim any weapon with which he might have wounded an antagonist. As long as all these questions were unsolved, I felt that sleep would be no easy matter, either for Holmes or myself. His quiet, self-confident manner convinced me that he had already formed a theory which explained all the facts, though what it was I could not for an instant conjecture.

He was very late in returning—so late that I knew that the concert could not have detained him all the time. Dinner was on the table before he appeared.

'It was magnificent,' he said, as he took his seat. 'Do you remember what Darwin says about music? He claims that the power of producing and appreciating it existed among the **112** human race long before the power of speech was arrived at. Perhaps that is why we are so subtly influenced by it. There are vague memories in our souls of those misty centuries when the world was in its childhood.'

'That's rather a broad idea,' I remarked.

'One's ideas must be as broad as Nature if they are to interpret Nature,' he answered. 'What's the matter? You're **113** not looking quite yourself. This Brixton Road affair has upset you.'

'To tell the truth, it has,' I said. 'I ought to be more case-hardened after my Afghan experiences. I saw my own comrades hacked to pieces at Maiwand without losing my nerve.'

'I can understand. There is a mystery about this which stimulates the imagination; where there is no imagination there is no horror. Have you seen the evening paper?'   **114**

'No.'

'It gives a fairly good account of the affair. It does not mention the fact that when the man was raised up a woman's wedding ring fell upon the floor. It is just as well it does not.'

'Why?'

'Look at this advertisement,' he answered. 'I had one sent to every paper this morning immediately after the affair.'   **115**

He threw the paper across to me and I glanced at the place indicated. It was the first announcement in the 'Found' column. 'In Brixton Road, this morning,' it ran, 'a plain gold wedding ring, found in the roadway between the White Hart Tavern and Holland Grove. Apply Dr Watson, 221B, Baker Street, between eight and nine this evening.'

'Excuse my using your name,' he said. 'If I used my own, some of these dunderheads would recognize it, and want to meddle in the affair.'

'That is all right,' I answered. 'But supposing any one applies, I have no ring.'

'Oh yes, you have,' said he, handing me one. 'This will do very well. It is almost a facsimile.'

'And who do you expect will answer this advertisement?'

'Why, the man in the brown coat—our florid friend with the square toes. If he does not come himself, he will send an accomplice.'

'Would he not consider it as too dangerous?'

'Not at all. If my view of the case is correct, and I have every reason to believe that it is, this man would rather risk anything than lose the ring. According to my notion he dropped it while stooping over Drebber's body, and did not miss it at the time. After leaving the house he discovered his loss and hurried back, but found the police already in possession, owing to his own folly in leaving the candle burning. He had to pretend to be drunk in order to allay the suspicions which might have been aroused by his appearance at the gate. Now put yourself in that man's place. On thinking the matter over, it must have occurred to him that it was possible that he had lost the ring in the road after leaving the house. What would he do then? He would eagerly look out for the evening papers in the hope of seeing it among the articles found. His eye, of course, would light upon this. He would be overjoyed. Why should he fear a trap? There would be no reason in his eyes why the finding of the ring should be connected with the murder. He would come. He will come. You shall see him within an hour!'

'And then?' I asked.

'Oh, you can leave me to deal with him then. Have you any arms?'

'I have my old service revolver and a few cartridges.'   **116**

That Little Thing of Chopin's." Study in A minor, Op. 25, No. 11.

6) Harrison, Michael: *In the Footsteps of Sherlock Holmes.* The Impromptu in C sharp minor.

7) Smith, William: "That Little Thing of Chopin's." Fourth Polonaise, in C minor.

Dr. Wolff himself offered "the timid suggestion that . . . Watson was not quoting Holmes (or Chopin) at all, but was merely misquoting Tennyson (*The Lady of Shalott*): 'From the bank and from the river / He flash'd into the crystal mirror, / "Tirra lirra," by the river / Sang Sir Lancelot.' "

112 *long before the power of speech was arrived at.* Holmes is apparently referring to some comments made in *The Descent of Man* by Charles Robert Darwin, 1809–1882, the English naturalist, traveler, and philosopher who promulgated the theory of organic evolution by natural selection in his *Origin of Species* (1859).

113 *if they are to interpret Nature.'* "As an instance of an idea of Holmes' as broad as Nature, we may select his theory 'that the individual represents in his development the whole procession of his ancestors,' ["The Adventure of the Empty House"]," Mr. T. S. Blakeney commented in *Sherlock Holmes: Fact or Fiction?*

114 *Have you seen the evening paper?'* "Close at hand," Miss Madeleine B. Stern wrote in "Sherlock Holmes: Rare Book Collector," "—at 36 Baker Street—[Holmes] found the news-dealer, James Ellis Hawkins, who could dispatch the latest editions of the London papers to Holmes' rooms."

115 *immediately after the affair.'* But when? If Holmes sent the advertisement to the papers at the same time that he dispatched his "long telegram," it was then after one o'clock in the afternoon, and it would have been unusually smart of him to be able to send off a personal to the evening papers so late in the day and get it into that afternoon's editions. It would seem, certainly, that Watson has somehow lost a day, and that we have now arrived at the afternoon of Saturday, March 5, 1881, after Holmes' return from the concert.

116 *my old service revolver.* This weapon, Mr. Robert Keith Leavitt wrote in "Annie Oakley in Baker Street," "was the Adams 6-shot cal. .450 breech-loader, with a good honest 6″ barrel, standard in the British Army in the second Afghan War. Its somewhat scanted front sight (a decided advantage for carrying in the pocket but difficult to use in a dim light) was more than offset by the length of the barrel with ample sighting radius. It was precisely the weapon for such a shot as that at Tonga in *The Sign of the Four*."

The editors of the Catalogue of the Sherlock Holmes Exhibition thought it more likely that this revolver was "a .442/450 Solid Frame Webley

Double Action. While slower to load and reload than a modern self-ejecting revolver, these sturdy weapons were not superseded for many years. The self-ejector was not wholly adopted until 1885, and indeed the practice of quick ejection and quick reloading was only necessary in military-type weapons."

On at least ten occasions, Holmes asked Watson to take his revolver on a dangerous mission, or in the face of danger, to draw it, and Mr. Leavitt has concluded that "this fact in itself proves conclusively that Watson was much the better pistol shot of the two. There was every reason why he should have been. He put in a considerable stretch as an army surgeon—a post in which, as Miss Helen Simpson has pointed out ["Medical Career and Capacities of Dr. J. H. Watson"], his duties were light. In his leisure the methodical Watson obviously spent a great deal of time in pistol practice."

117 *I picked up at a stall yesterday.* "These are the words of a bibliophile," Mr. Whitfield J. Bell, Jr., wrote in "Holmes and History." "It was as a bibliophile, in fact, a collector of obscure volumes, that Holmes disguised himself on his return from France in 1894 ["The Adventure of the Empty House"]."

And Miss Madeleine B. Stern has added ("Sherlock Holmes: Rare Book Collector"): "It is supremely tempting . . . to ask ourselves where Holmes obtained his many fine books. . . . His favorite book dealer was almost undoubtedly Albert B. Clementson, who plied his trade at 73 Church Street, Kensington, and who suggested [the disguise used by Holmes in "The Adventure of the Empty House"]. . . . There were other dealers, scores of them, into whose musty shops Holmes surely ventured as he passed through the winding lanes and alleys of his London. The Strand was full of shops, where books towered to the ceiling and spilled over onto the floors as Holmes browsed among them, his expert's eye glancing at a calf or vellum back. Nevington Butts could always give him a field day, and who can doubt that he would walk through Camden passage without a visit to Mrs. Susannah Kettle, or through Church Street, Paddington, without a glance at Uriah Maggs' stock? For medical works, he could journey to Wardour Street, where Richard Kimpton plied a specialized trade, and everywhere—in Farringdon Street and New Oxford Street, on Praed Street and Drury Lane—he could, and did, wander through the dimly-lighted cellars and the intriguing anterooms of one bookseller after another. There was Framjee Feroza on Camberwell Road; there was William Wright on St. Martin's Lane; there was Mrs. Robenah Boyle on White Horse Street in Stepney—there were dozens upon dozens of dealers from whom he could buy the earliest on opium or the latest on belladonna. For a French treatise, he might patronize Madame Celine Subtil in Prince's Buildings, Coventry Street. . . . Some from whom he bought,

'You had better clean it and load it. He will be a desperate man; and though I shall take him unawares, it is as well to be ready for anything.'

I went to my bedroom and followed his advice. When I returned with the pistol, the table had been cleared, and Holmes was engaged in his favourite occupation of scraping upon his violin.

'The plot thickens,' he said, as I entered; 'I have just had an answer to my American telegram. My view of the case is the correct one.'

'And that is?' I asked eagerly.

'My fiddle would be the better for new strings,' he remarked. 'Put your pistol in your pocket. When the fellow comes, speak to him in an ordinary way. Leave the rest to me. Don't frighten him by looking at him too hard.'

'It is eight o'clock now,' I said, glancing at my watch.

'Yes. He will probably be here in a few minutes. Open the door slightly. That will do. Now put the key on the inside. Thank you! This is a queer old book I picked up at a stall

117-118 yesterday—*De Jure inter Gentes*—published in Latin at Liege in the Lowlands, in 1642. Charles's head was still firm on his shoulders when this little brown-backed volume was struck off.'

'Who is the printer?'

119 'Philippe de Croy, whoever he may have been. On the fly-leaf, in very faded ink, is written "Ex libris Gulielmi Whyte." I wonder who William Whyte was. Some pragmatical seventeenth-century lawyer, I suppose. His writing has a legal

120 twist about it. Here comes our man, I think.'

As he spoke there was a sharp ring at the bell. Sherlock Holmes rose softly and moved his chair in the direction of the

121 door. We heard the servant pass along the hall, and the sharp click of the latch as she opened it.

"MORE THAN ONCE . . . A GOOD FRIEND IN NEED"

So wrote Watson of his old service revolver in "The Problem of Thor Bridge." Identified by Mr. Robert Keith Leavitt as the Adams .450, shown above, Watson's old service revolver was standard in the British Army during the doctor's term of service. Though a good shot with this piece, Watson later replaced it with a more compact gun for pocket wear.

'Does Dr Watson live here?' asked a clear but rather harsh voice. We could not hear the servant's reply, but the door closed, and someone began to ascend the stairs. The footfall was an uncertain and shuffling one. A look of surprise passed over the face of my companion as he listened to it. It came slowly along the passage, and there was a feeble tap at the door.

'Come in,' I cried.

At my summons, instead of the man of violence whom we expected, a very old and wrinkled woman hobbled into the apartment. She appeared to be dazzled by the sudden blaze of light, and after dropping a curtsy, she stood blinking at us with her bleared eyes and fumbling in her pocket with nervous, shaky fingers. I glanced at my companion, and his face had assumed such a disconsolate expression that it was all I could do to keep my countenance.

The old crone drew out an evening paper, and pointed at our advertisement. 'It's this as has brought me, good gentlemen,' she said, dropping another curtsy; 'a gold wedding ring in the Brixton Road. It belongs to my girl Sally, as was married only this time twelve-month, which her husband is steward aboard a Union boat, and what he'd say if he come **122** 'ome and found her without her ring is more than I can think, he being short enough at the best o' times, but more especially when he has the drink. If it please you, she went to the circus **123** last night along with——'

'Is that her ring?' I asked.

'The Lord be thanked!' cried the old woman; 'Sally will be a glad woman this night. That's the ring.'

'And what may your address be?' I inquired, taking up a pencil.

'13, Duncan Street, Houndsditch. A weary way from here.' **124**

'The Brixton Road does not lie between any circus and Houndsditch,' said Sherlock Holmes sharply.

The old woman faced round and looked keenly at him from her little red-rimmed eyes. 'The gentleman asked me for *my* address,' she said. 'Sally lives in lodgings at 3, Mayfield Place, Peckham.'   **125**

'And your name is——?'

'My name is Sawyer—hers is Dennis, which Tom Dennis married her—and a smart, clean lad, too, as long as he's at sea, and no steward in the company more thought of; but when on shore, what with the women and what with liquor shops——'

'Here is your ring, Mrs Sawyer,' I interrupted, in obedience to a sign from my companion; 'it clearly belongs to your daughter, and I am glad to be able to restore it to the rightful owner.'

With many mumbled blessings and protestations of gratitude the old crone packed it away in her pocket, and shuffled off down the stairs. Sherlock Holmes sprang to his feet the moment that she was gone and rushed into his room. He returned in a few seconds enveloped in an ulster and a cravat. 'I'll follow her,' he said, hurriedly; 'she must be an accomplice, and will lead me to him. Wait up for me.' The hall door had hardly slammed behind our visitor before Holmes had descended the stair. Looking through the window I could see her walking feebly along the other side, while her pursuer dogged her some little distance behind. 'Either his whole

or tried to buy, still flourish: George Harding, Henry Stevens & Son, Bumpus, Quaritch, Francis Edwards. Most of them have vanished, and with them have gone the records of Holmes' purchases."

118 De Jure inter Gentes. A volume titled *De Jure Naturae et Getium* was written in 1672 by Samuel Profendorf, born in Saxony in 1632. "Can this have been the work picked up by Holmes?" Mr. Morris Rosenblum asked in "Some Latin Byways in the Canon." "Could he or Watson's printer have been careless about the title and date?" (Mr. Rosenblum also suggested that the volume might have been "a curious edition of Hugo Grotius' celebrated *De Jure Belli et Pacis,* first printed in Paris in 1625 and based largely on the Roman *jus gentium*.)

On the other hand, Miss Madeleine B. Stern has suggested ("Sherlock Holmes: Rare Book Collector") that this volume was actually "one of the most extraordinary volumes in the Holmes treasure room!—a book unique both for its contents and its imprint. The *De Jure inter Gentes,* though published anonymously, was really written by Richard Zouche (1590–1661), the English civilian. Prior to Holmes' 'find,' the first edition was thought to have been printed in Oxford in 1650 under the title: *Juris et Judicii fecialis, sive Juris inter gentes,* and it was the second part of the title that suggested to Bentham the felicitous phrase, 'international law.' The anonymous edition, bearing the title *De Jure inter Gentes,* is rare enough when it carries the Leyden 1651 imprint. But Holmes' copy antedates even the so-called first edition of 1650, and hence is a find of extraordinary magnitude, one of the most desirable books in any legal collection."

119 '*Philippe de Croy, whoever he may have been.* "According to the *Grand Dictionnaire Universal, Larousse,* the name Cröuy, or Croy, belonged to one of the most ancient families of Europe, which claimed descent from the kings of Hungary," Mr. Morris Rosenblum wrote in "Some Latin Byways in the Canon." "A Philippe de Croy (1526–1595), the third Duke of Aerschot, went to Spain on military and diplomatic missions and attended the wedding of the son of Marguerite of Parme. Another Philippe de Croy, the first Duke of Solre, was sent to Madrid by the Estates-General to congratulate Philip II on the marriage of the Infanta in 1598, and made other missions later. These two Philippe de Croys were from the Lowlands and lived within about fifty years of the date mentioned by Holmes, but neither seems to have established a printing house. The De Croy family produced hundreds of notables, among whom were two cardinals, five bishops, many generals, scores of knights, artists and writers—but no printers!"

120 *His writing has a legal twist about it.* "As if he did not know that the copy had belonged to the English divine, William White, 1604–1678, who had fathered several interesting Latin works under the pseudonym of 'Gulielmus Phalerius.'" —Madeline B. Stern, "Sherlock Holmes: Rare Book Collector."

121 *the servant.* "Servants' wages were then very low, and almost everyone could afford to employ at least a maid," Marjorie and C. H. B. Quennell wrote in *A History of Everyday Things in England, Vol. IV, 1851 to 1914.* "In middle-class households there were usually two or three, and in larger houses many more, as well as men-servants. This made the work lighter for the individual but there was always a great deal to be done. Labour-saving devices were practically unknown, and houses were not designed to make the daily round easier. Much time was taken up in carrying coal and food upstairs; stone-paved halls and long passages, kitchens, sculleries and front-door steps needed continual scrubbing. The heavy furniture, often elaborately carved, required constant polishing, and two or three substantial meals had to be prepared and served every day."

"The morning after James Openshaw's visit to 221B in the matter of the Five Orange Pips, Watson comes down to find Holmes already at breakfast," the late Robert R. Pattrick wrote in "The

theory is incorrect,' I thought to myself, 'or else he will be led now to the heart of the mystery.' There was no need for him to ask me to wait up for him, for I felt that sleep was impossible until I heard the result of his adventure.

It was close upon nine when he set out. I had no idea how long he might be, but I sat stolidly puffing at my pipe and **126** skipping over the pages of Henri Murger's *Vie de Bohème.* Ten o'clock passed, and I heard the footsteps of the maid as they pattered off to bed. Eleven, and the more stately tread of the landlady passed my door, bound for the same destination. It was close upon twelve before I heard the sharp sound of his latch-key. The instant he entered I saw by his face that he had not been successful. Amusement and chagrin seemed to be struggling for the mastery, until the former suddenly carried the day, and he burst into a hearty laugh.

'I wouldn't have the Scotland Yarders know it for the world,' he cried, dropping into his chair; 'I have chaffed them so much that they would never have let me hear the end of it. I can afford to laugh, because I know that I will be even with them in the long run.'

'What is it then?' I asked.

'Oh, I don't mind telling a story against myself. That creature had gone a little way when she began to limp and show every sign of being footsore. Presently she came to a halt, and hailed a four-wheeler which was passing. I managed to be close to her so as to hear the address, but I need not

A VERY OLD AND WRINKLED WOMAN HOBBLED INTO THE APARTMENT . . . AND POINTED AT OUR ADVERTISEMENT.

How two different artists saw much the same scene: *left,* James Greig in an illustration for a supplement to the *Windsor Magazine,* Christmas, 1895. *right,* George Hutchinson in an illustration for the London, 1891, Ward, Lock, Bowden & Co. edition of *A Study in Scarlet.* (Charles Doyle, Conan Doyle's father, depicted the same situation in the 1888 Ward, Lock & Co. edition.) Of Greig's work, the late James Montgomery wrote (*A Study in Pictures*) that it was "possibly a little more urbane but still very much in the same undistinguished style as [the illustrations] of George Hutchinson . . ."

have been so anxious, for she sang it out loud enough to be heard at the other side of the street, "Drive to 13, Duncan Street, Houndsditch," she cried. This begins to look genuine, I thought, and having seen her safely inside, I perched myself behind. That's an art which every detective should be an expert at. Well, away we rattled, and never drew rein until we reached the street in question. I hopped off before we came to the door, and strolled down the street in an easy lounging way. I saw the cab pull up. The driver jumped down, and I saw him open the door and stand expectantly. Nothing came out though. When I reached him, he was groping about frantically in the empty cab, and giving vent to the finest assorted collection of oaths that ever I listened to. There was no sign or trace of his passenger, and I fear it will be some time before he gets his fare. On inquiring at Number 13 we found that the house belonged to a respectable paper-hanger, named Keswick, and that no one of the name either of Sawyer or Dennis had ever been heard of there.'

'You don't mean to say,' I cried, in amazement, 'that that tottering, feeble old woman was able to get out of the cab while it was in motion, without either you or the driver seeing her?'

'Old woman be damned!' said Sherlock Holmes, sharply. **127** 'We were the old women to be so taken in. It must have been a young man, and an active one, too, besides being an incomparable actor. The get-up was inimitable. He saw that he was **128** followed, no doubt, and used this means of giving me the slip. It shows that the man we are after is not as lonely as I imagined he was, but has friends who are ready to risk something for him. Now, Doctor, you are looking done-up. Take my advice and turn in.'

I was certainly feeling very weary, so I obeyed his injunction. I left Holmes seated in front of the smouldering fire, and long into the watches of the night, I heard the low, melancholy wailings of his violin, and knew that he was still ponder- **129** ing over the strange problem which he had set himself to unravel.

Case of the Superfluous Landlady." " 'Just ring the bell,' says Holmes, 'and the maid will bring up your coffee.' The only other time Watson mentions the maid is in 1895, during the case of 'The Bruce-Partington Plans.' "

122 *a Union boat.* A steamer of the old Union line, which ran to South Africa. This company and the Castle Line were merged in 1900 to form the famous Union-Castle Line.

123 *the circus.* A favorite with Mid- and Late Victorians of all classes. The best-known circus of the period was "Lord George" Sanger's. His Grand National Ampitheatre stood on the Westminster Bridge Road.

124 *Houndsditch.* The name derives from the old fosse which once encircled this quarter of the City and formed a depository for dead dogs.

125 *Peckham.* Formerly a village, Peckham increased greatly in population between 1820 and 1840 and has now become more or less joined to the metropolis as part of the borough of Camberwell.

126 *Vie de Bohème.* This 1848 collection of the sketches of Henri Murger, 1822–1861, onetime secretary to Count Aleksei Tolstoi, describes the fortunes and misfortunes, the loves, studies, amusements, and sufferings of a group of impecunious students, artists, and men of letters, of whom Rudolphe represents Murger himself. The sketches form the basis of Puccini's opera *La Bohème* (1898). The late Christopher Morley wrote (*Sherlock Holmes and Dr. Watson: A Textbook of Friendship*) that Watson was presumably "trying to improve his rather simple French by reading some of Holmes' books," but Mr. Benjamin Grosbayne ("Sherlock Holmes—Musician") thought "the not-so-sly implications" are that Watson "read wicked French books in the original so easily that he could skip about and . . . that he wants us to realize what a gay old dog he really is 'neath his respectable exterior."

127 *'Old woman be damned!'* Although we will read of many other occasions on which Holmes cursed, swore, or raved, this is the one instance on record on which we are told what he said.

128 *The get-up was inimitable.* "Much has been written on Sherlock Holmes' adeptness in the art of disguise," Mr. Nathan L. Bengis wrote in "Sherlock Stays After School." "It should be pointed out, however, that in at least two instances he was himself completely foiled by the disguise of others. . . . It almost staggers belief that Holmes would not have seen through the blatantly obvious disguise [employed here]."

129 *the low, melancholy wailings of his violin.* "This sounds as if the music might have been Bach's *Aria for the G String* or Paganini's 'Moses' Variations, also for the fourth string," Mr. Benjamin Grosbayne wrote in "Sherlock Holmes—Musician." "It may also have been improvisation, just as Nicolò Paganini, whom Holmes so admired ["The Cardboard Box"], used to thrill audiences extemporaneously. . . . From the many descriptions of Holmes' style of violin playing . . . it is easy to see that Holmes consciously or subconsciously patterned his own style after that of [this] most glamorous violinist of all time."

130 *The papers next day*. Saturday, by Watson's account. If this is correct, it is still another blow at dating the case 1882: if it began on Saturday, March 4, 1882, papers would not have been published "next day," a Sunday. Nor, as we learn later, could the stable boy have seen Hope leaving Stangerson's room and thought it "early for a carpenter to be at work."

131 *leaders*. Editorials.

132 *The* Daily Telegraph. "The supposed comment by the three great newspapers is acute parody based on the style and predilections of each," the late Christopher Morley wrote in *Sherlock Holmes and Dr. Watson: A Textbook of Friendship*. "The *Telegraph*, then edited by the flamboyant G. A. Sala, was a popular journal of lively tone. The *Standard* was conservative and genteel. The *Daily News* was Liberal in sympathies." We may suppose that the *Times* (mentioned nine times in the Canon) was Holmes' favorite newspaper, and the *Telegraph* (seven mentions) was Watson's.

133 *the Vehmgericht*. A system of secret courts that grew up in Germany in the Middle Ages to execute punishment or revenge.

134 *aqua tofana*. A secret poison attributed to a Sicilian woman called Tofana.

135 *Carbonari*. A secret society of Italian patriots in the early nineteenth century, called Carbonari (charcoal burners) because its members met in the forests in the guise of woodcutters and charcoal burners.

136 *the Marchioness de Brinvilliers*. The French poisoner of the seventeenth century. Her gruesome career plays an extraordinary part in John Dickson Carr's brilliant detective story, *The Burning Court*.

137 *the principles of Malthus*. Thomas Robert Malthus, 1766–1834, English clergyman and writer on political economy. Malthus held "that population unchecked goes on doubling itself every twenty-five years—or increases in geometrical ratio. The rate according to which the productions of the earth increase must be totally of a different nature from the ratio of the increase in population. . . . Therefore, considering the present average state of the earth, the means of subsistence, under circumstances the most favorable to human industry, could not possibly be made to increase faster than in an arithmetical ratio. . . . The power of propagation being in every period so much superior, the increase of the human species can only be kept down to the level of the means of subsistence by the constant operation of the strong law of necessity, acting as a check upon the greater power" (*Essay on Population*).

138 *the Ratcliff Highway murders*. "These were the gruesome crimes described by De Quincey in

6 : TOBIAS GREGSON SHOWS
: WHAT HE CAN DO

130 The papers next day were full of the 'Brixton Mystery,' as they termed it. Each had a long account of the affair, and
131 some had leaders upon it in addition. There was some information in them which was new to me. I still retain in my scrap-book numerous clippings and extracts upon the case. Here is a condensation of a few of them:

132   The *Daily Telegraph* remarked that in the history of crime there had seldom been a tragedy which presented stranger features. The German name of the victim, the absence of all other motive, and the sinister inscription on the wall, all pointed to its perpetration by political refugees and revolutionists. The Socialists had many branches in America, and the deceased had, no doubt, infringed their unwritten laws, and been tracked down by them. After alluding airily to the
133-134 Vehmgericht, aqua tofana, Carbonari, the Marchioness de
135 136 Brinvilliers, the Darwinian theory, the principles of Malthus,
137 138 and the Ratcliff Highway murders, the article concluded by admonishing the Government and advocating a closer watch over foreigners in England.

The *Standard* commented upon the fact that lawless outrages of the sort usually occurred under a Liberal Administra-
139 tion. They arose from the unsettling of the minds of the masses, and the consequent weakening of all authority. The deceased was an American gentleman who had been residing for some weeks in the Metropolis. He had stayed at the boarding-house of Madame Charpentier, in Torquay Ter-
140 race, Camberwell. He was accompanied in his travels by his private secretary, Mr Joseph Stangerson. The two bade adieu
141 to their landlady upon Tuesday, the 4th inst., and departed
142 to Euston Station with the avowed intention of catching the Liverpool express. They were afterwards seen together upon the platform. Nothing more is known of them until Mr Drebber's body was, as recorded, discovered in an empty house in the Brixton Road, many miles from Euston. How he came there, or how he met his fate, are questions which are still involved in mystery. Nothing is known of the whereabouts of Stangerson. We are glad to learn that Mr Lestrade and Mr Gregson, of Scotland Yard, are both engaged upon the case, and it is confidently anticipated that these well-known officers will speedily throw light upon the matter.

The *Daily News* observed that there was no doubt as to the crime being a political one. The despotism and hatred of Liberalism which animated the Continental Governments had had the effect of driving to our shores a number of men who might have made excellent citizens were they not soured by the recollection of all that they had undergone. Among these men there was a stringent code of honour, any infringement of which was punished by death. Every effort should be made to find the secretary, Stangerson, and to ascertain some particulars of the habits of the deceased. A great step had been gained by the discovery of the address of the house at which he had boarded—a result which was entirely due to the acuteness and energy of Mr Gregson of Scotland Yard.

Sherlock Holmes and I read these notices over together at breakfast, and they appeared to afford him considerable amusement.

'I told you that, whatever happened, Lestrade and Gregson would be sure to score.'

'That depends on how it turns out.'

'Oh, bless you, it doesn't matter in the least. If the man is caught, it will be *on account* of their exertions; if he escapes, is will be *in spite* of their exertions. It's heads I win and tails you lose. Whatever they do, they will have followers. "Un sot trouve toujours un plus sot qui l'admire." ' **143**

'What on earth is this?' I cried, for at this moment there came the pattering of many steps in the hall and on the stairs, accompanied by audible expressions of disgust upon the part of our landlady.

'It's the Baker Street division of the detective police force,' said my companion gravely; and as he spoke there rushed into the room half a dozen of the dirtiest and most ragged street arabs that ever I clapped eyes on.

' 'Tention!' cried Holmes, in a sharp tone, and the six dirty little scoundrels stood in a line like so many disreputable statuettes. 'In future you shall send up Wiggins alone to report, and the rest of you must wait in the street. Have you found it, Wiggins?'

'No, sir, we hain't,' said one of the youths.

'I hardly expected you would. You must keep on until you do. Here are your wages.' He handed each of them a shilling. 'Now, off you go, and come back with a better report next time.' **144**

He waved his hand, and they scampered away downstairs like so many rats, and we heard their shrill voices next moment in the street.

'There's more work to be got out of one of those little beggars than out of a dozen of the force,' Holmes remarked. 'The mere sight of an official-looking person seals men's lips. These youngsters, however, go everywhere, and hear everything. They are as sharp as needles, too; all they want is organization.'

'Is it on this Brixton case that you are employing them?' I asked.

'Yes; there is a point which I wish to ascertain. It is merely a matter of time. Hullo! we are going to hear some news now with a vengeance! Here is Gregson coming down the road with beatitude written upon every feature of his face. Bound for us, I know. Yes, he is stopping. There he is!'

There was a violent peal at the bell, and in a few seconds the fair-haired detective came up the stairs, three steps at a time, and burst into our sitting-room.

'My dear fellow,' he cried, wringing Holmes' unresponsive hand, 'congratulate me! I have made the whole thing as clear as day.'

A shade of anxiety seemed to me to cross my companion's expressive face.

'Do you mean that you are on the right track?' he asked.

'The right track! Why, sir, we have the man under lock and key.'

'And his name is?'

'Arthur Charpentier, sub-lieutenant in Her Majesty's Navy,' cried Gregson pompously, rubbing his fat hands and inflating his chest.

Sherlock Holmes gave a sigh of relief and relaxed into a smile.

his masterpiece, 'Murder Considered As One of the Fine Arts,' " the late Christopher Morley wrote in *Sherlock Holmes and Dr. Watson: A Textbook in Friendship*. "The Ratcliff Highway, in the region of the docks, acquired such a sinister repute that its name was later changed to St. George's Street. As recently as 1910 a London guidebook said of it 'here is Jamrach's emporium of wild beasts, that have been known to escape into the streets, and of a Saturday night might not find themselves altogether without kindred society!' "

139 *a Liberal Administration.* The Liberal party in Britain (Lord John Russell is credited with the name) grew out of the Whig party. Its policies were free trade, religious liberty, abolition of slavery, and extension of the franchise.

140 *Camberwell.* "Camberwell, across the Thames in South London, was an unusual lodging place for well-to-do tourists—unless possibly they chose to be near the Crystal Palace, still very famous in those days [it was demolished about 1940 so that its great iron girders could be used for military material]," Christopher Morley wrote in *Sherlock Holmes and Dr. Watson: A Textbook of Friendship*. "Black's *London Guide* (1910) described Camberwell as 'an extremely prosaic suburb,' but it was always romantic to Dr. Watson, for reasons you will discover in *The Sign of the Four*. It has also a charming connotation in the name of a beautiful and rare butterfly, the Camberwell Beauty."

141 *Tuesday, the 4th inst.* The *Standard* was clearly wrong in calling the 4th, a Friday in 1881, a Tuesday, as virtually all commentators agree. The only Marches in this entire period in which the 4th fell on a Tuesday were 1879 (much too early) and 1884 (even more too late).

142 *Euston Station.* Originally designed as the terminus of the London and Birmingham Railway, now the principal terminus of the British Railways Midland Region, Euston was the first of the larger railroad stations to be erected in London (it occupies an area of twelve acres). Compared to the newer Waterloo and Victoria Stations, Euston today is shabby, inconvenient, and straggling. It was at Euston Station on November 1, 1848, that Messrs. W. H. Smith opened the first of the hundreds of bookstalls which have now made that firm a national institution.

143 *"Un sot trouve toujours un plus sot qui l'admire."* ' This is the end line (232) of Canto I of *L'Art Poétique* by Nicolas Boileau Despréaux, 1636–1711, and is translated as: "A fool can always find a greater fool to admire him." Mr. Dean W. Dickensheet, in his study of "Sherlock Holmes—Linguist," has shown that Holmes was fluent in English, idiomatic American, French, German, Italian, Norwegian, and Gaelic. He had some knowledge of Russian, Swedish, Dutch, and prob-

"IT'S THE BAKER STREET DIVISION OF THE DETECTIVE
POLICE FORCE."

Illustration by George Hutchinson for *A Study in
Scarlet;* London: Ward, Lock, Bowden & Co., 1891.

'Take a seat, and try one of these cigars,' he said. 'We are
anxious to know how you managed it. Will you have some
145 whisky and water?'

'I don't mind if I do,' the detective answered. 'The tremendous exertions which I have gone through during the last day
146 or two have worn me out. Not so much bodily exertion, you
understand, as the strain upon the mind. You will appreciate
that, Mr Sherlock Holmes, for we are both brain-workers.'

'You do me too much honour,' said Holmes, gravely. 'Let
us hear how you arrived at this most gratifying result.'

The detective seated himself in the arm-chair, and puffed
complacently at his cigar. Then suddenly he slapped his thigh
in a paroxysm of amusement.

. . . THE SIX DIRTY LITTLE SCOUNDRELS STOOD IN A LINE
LIKE SO MANY DISREPUTABLE STATUETTES.

The first representation of the Baker Street Irregulars—one of the six drawings done by Charles
Doyle, Conan Doyle's father, for *A Study in Scarlet;* London: Ward, Lock & Co., 1888. It "has the
urchins saluting with their left hands, although the
quill pen is on the right of the writing block, as it
should be, and Holmes is gesturing with his right
forefinger," the late James Montgomery wrote in
A Study in Pictures. "Watson buttons his vest in
the wrong direction but one of the Irregulars
fastens his the other way, so nothing can be proved
there. And how one shudders at the figures of
Holmes and Watson—the former now clean shaven
and smiling vapidly in an ill-fitting toupee—the
latter bearded like a Saxon chieftain!"

'The fun of it is,' he cried, 'that that fool Lestrade, who thinks himself so smart, has gone off upon the wrong track altogether. He is after the secretary Stangerson, who had no more to do with the crime than the babe unborn. I have no doubt that he has caught him by this time.'

The idea tickled Gregson so much that he laughed until he choked.

'And how did you get your clue?'

'Ah, I'll tell you all about it. Of course, Doctor Watson, this is strictly between ourselves. The first difficulty which we had to contend with was the finding of this American's antecedents. Some people would have waited until their advertisements were answered, or until parties came forward and volunteered information. That is not Tobias Gregson's way of going to work. You remember the hat beside the dead man?'

'Yes,' said Holmes; 'by John Underwood and Sons, 129, Camberwell Road.' **147**

Gregson looked quite crestfallen.

'I had no idea that you noticed that,' he said. 'Have you been there?'

'No.'

'Ha!' cried Gregson, in a relieved voice; 'you should never neglect a chance, however small it may seem.'

'To a great mind, nothing is little,' remarked Holmes, **148** sententiously.

'Well, I went to Underwood, and asked him if he had sold a hat of that size and description. He looked over his books, and came on it at once. He had sent the hat to a Mr Drebber, residing at Charpentier's Boarding Establishment, Torquay Terrace. Thus I got at his address.'

'Smart—very smart!' murmured Sherlock Holmes.

'I next called upon Madame Charpentier,' continued the detective. 'I found her very pale and distressed. Her daughter was in the room, too—an uncommonly fine girl she is, too; she was looking red about the eyes and her lips trembled as I spoke to her. That didn't escape my notice. I began to smell a rat. You know the feeling, Mr Sherlock Holmes, when you come upon the right scent—a kind of thrill in your nerves. "Have you heard of the mysterious death of your late boarder Mr Enoch J. Drebber, of Cleveland?" I asked.

'The mother nodded. She didn't seem able to get out a word. The daughter burst into tears. I felt more than ever that these people knew something of the matter.

' "At what o'clock did Mr Drebber leave your house for the train?" I asked.

' "At eight o'clock," she said, gulping in her throat to keep down her agitation. "His secretary, Mr Stangerson, said that there were two trains—one at 9.15 and one at 11. He was to catch the first."

' "And was that the last which you saw of him?"

'A terrible change came over the woman's face as I asked the question. Her features turned perfectly livid. It was some seconds before she could get out the single word "Yes"—and when it did come it was in a husky, unnatural tone.

'There was silence for a moment, and then the daughter spoke in a calm, clear voice.

' "No good can ever come of falsehood, mother," she said. "Let us be frank with this gentleman. We *did* see Mr Drebber again."

ably Chinese. His travels after Reichenbach required a knowledge of Arabic, but the languages of the Tibeto-Burman group, as well as any other Asian or African tongue, were spoken through interpreters. He had a superior knowledge of Latin and was capable of making comparative studies of ancient Cornish and Chaldean. He knew some Greek, some Persian, and had at least some knowledge of the philological antecedents of English, French, and German.

144 *come back with a better report next time.'* Holmes "loved children—how else could he have commanded the sworn services of Wiggins and those other invaluable urchins, the Baker Street Irregulars, or have kept the worship of Billy the page ["The Adventure of the Mazarin Stone"]?" —Manly Wade Wellman, "The Great Man's Great Son."

145 *whisky and water?'* Holmes and Watson drank plain water with their whisky in the early, less affluent days; the gasogene ("A Scandal in Bohemia") was a later sophistication. Mr. Michael Harrison has noted (*In the Footsteps of Sherlock Holmes*) that Irish whiskey was more widely drunk than Scotch whisky in Holmes' and Watson's day, and could be dearer. Watson does not seem to distinguish between Irish and Scotch, but he does invariably use the Scotch spelling *whisky*.

146 *during the last day or two.* If Gregson arrived at Baker Street on Saturday, as Watson tells us he did, he perhaps would not have referred to his exertions "during the last day or two." But the late Dr. Ernest Bloomfield Zeisler argued ("A Chronological Study in Scarlet") that Gregson "had been working on the case from about 3:00 A.M. of Friday until at least noon on Saturday; nine hours longer than a day and quite long enough to warrant calling it 'a day or so'; had it been a few hours more it should have been called 'two days' or 'almost two days.' "

147 *Camberwell Road.* Opened in 1820 from Kennington Common to Camberwell Green, the new road saved nearly two miles and a half in the distance from Westminster into Kent.

148 *'To a great mind, nothing is little.'* Compare: "It is of course a trifle, but there is nothing so important as trifles"—"The Man with the Twisted Lip." "It has long been a maxim of mine that the little things are infinitely the most important"—"A Case of Identity." "You know my method. It is founded upon the observance of trifles"—"The Boscombe Valley Mystery." "I dare call nothing trivial when I reflect that some of my most classic cases have had the least promising commencement"—"The Adventure of the Six Napoleons." "Holmes has, as Watson remarked, an extraordinary gift for minutiae [*The Sign of the Four*]," Mr. T. S. Blakeney commented in *Sherlock Holmes: Fact or Fiction?*

HE HANDED EACH OF THEM A SHILLING.

11 above is the 1824 shilling of George IV; *11a* the 1817 shilling of George III, reverse only; *11b* the 1821 shilling of George IV, reverse only; *11c* the 1893 shilling of Victoria, reverse only; *11d* the 1902 shilling of Edward VII, reverse only. The shilling, as we have seen, was worth slightly less than *25¢* in U.S. currency in Holmes' and Watson's day. As the late A. Carson Simpson wrote in *Numismatics in the Canon*, Part I: "The shilling of 12d. traces back to the testoon (the 'tester' of *A Midsummer Night's Dream*) of Henry VII (*circa* 1505), which derives its name from the Italian testone—literally a coin which bears the head (testa) of the ruler. It was, in fact, the first English silver coin which carried a true portrait—as distinct from the medieval conventional representation—of the monarch. Under Henry VIII, the name shilling (after the Anglo-Saxon money of account) began to come into use and was soon adopted generally. This denomination has been coined by all rulers since then except Mary Tudor, though, in the period of the silver bullion shortage during the reign of George III, there were several gaps over ten years in length. There are more Canonical references to the shilling than to any other coin. . . . Nine types of shilling were probably in circulation during the appropriate period."

149 *fourteen pounds a week*. About $70.

' "God forgive you!" cried Madame Charpentier, throwing up her hands, and sinking back in her chair. "You have murdered your brother."

' "Arthur would rather that we spoke the truth," the girl answered firmly.

' "You had best tell me all about it now," I said. "Half-confidences are worse than none. Besides, you do not know how much we know of it."

' "On your head be it, Alice!" cried her mother; and then, turning to me, "I will tell you all, sir. Do not imagine that my agitation on behalf of my son arises from any fear lest he should have had a hand in this terrible affair. He is utterly innocent of it. My dread is, however, that in your eyes and in the eyes of others he may appear to be compromised. That, however, is surely impossible. His high character, his profession, his antecedents would all forbid it."

' "Your best way is to make a clean breast of the facts," I answered. "Depend upon it, if your son is innocent he will be none the worse."

' "Perhaps, Alice, you had better leave us together," she said, and her daughter withdrew. "Now, sir," she continued, "I had no intention of telling you all this, but since my poor daughter has disclosed it I have no alternative. Having once decided to speak, I will tell you all without omitting any particular."

' "It is your wisest course," said I.

' "Mr Drebber has been with us nearly three weeks. He and his secretary, Mr Stangerson, had been travelling on the Continent. I noticed a 'Copenhagen' label upon each of their trunks, showing that that had been their last stopping-place. Stangerson was a quiet, reserved man, but his employer, I am sorry to say, was far otherwise. He was coarse in his habits and brutish in his ways. The very night of his arrival he became very much the worse for drink, and, indeed, after twelve o'clock in the day he could hardly ever be said to be sober. His manners towards the maid-servants were disgustingly free and familiar. Worst of all, he speedily assumed the same attitude towards my daughter, Alice, and spoke to her more than once in a way which, fortunately, she is too innocent to understand. On one occasion he actually seized her in his arms and embraced her—an outrage which caused his own secretary to reproach him for his unmanly conduct."

' "But why did you stand all this?" I asked. "I suppose that you can get rid of your boarders when you wish."

'Madame Charpentier blushed at my pertinent question. "Would to God that I had given him notice on the very day that he came," she said. "But it was a sore temptation. They **149** were paying a pound a day each—fourteen pounds a week, and this is the slack season. I am a widow, and my boy in the Navy has cost me much. I grudged to lose the money. I acted for the best. This last was too much, however, and I gave him notice to leave on account of it. That was the reason of his going."

' "Well?"

' "My heart grew light when I saw him drive away. My son is on leave just now, but I did not tell him anything of all this, for his temper is violent, and he is passionately fond of his sister. When I closed the door behind them a load seemed to be lifted from my mind. Alas, in less than an hour there was a ring at the bell, and I learned that **Mr Drebber** had returned. He was much excited, and evidently the worse for drink. He forced his way into the room, where I was sitting with my daughter, and made some incoherent remark about having missed his train. He then turned to Alice, and before my very face proposed to her that she should fly with him. 'You are of age,' he said, 'and there is no law to stop you. I have money enough and to spare. Never mind the old girl here, but come along with me now straight away. You shall live like a princess.' Poor Alice was so frightened that she shrank away from him, but he caught her by the wrist and endeavoured to draw her towards the door. I screamed, and at that moment my son Arthur came into the room. What happened then I do not know. I heard oaths and the confused sounds of a scuffle. I was too terrified to raise my head. When I did look up I saw Arthur standing in the doorway laughing, with a stick in his hand. 'I don't think that fine fellow will trouble us again,' he said. 'I will just go after him and see what he does with himself.' With those words he took his hat and started off down the street. The next morning we heard of Mr Drebber's mysterious death." **150**

'This statement came from Madame Charpentier's lips with many gasps and pauses. At times she spoke so low that I could hardly catch the words. I made shorthand notes of all that she **151** said, however, so that there should be no possibility of a mistake.'

'It's quite exciting,' said Sherlock Holmes, with a yawn. 'What happened next?'

'When Madame Charpentier paused,' the detective continued, 'I saw that the whole case hung upon one point. Fixing her with my eye in a way which I always found effective with women, I asked her at what hour her son returned.

' "I do not know," she answered.

' "Not know?"

' "No; he has a latch-key, and he let himself in."

' "After you went to bed?"

' "Yes."

' "When did you go to bed?"

' "About eleven."

' "So your son was gone at least two hours?"

' "Yes."

' "Possibly four or five?"

' "Yes."

' "What was he doing during that time?"

' "I do not know," she answered, turning white to her very lips.

'Of course after that there was nothing more to be done. I found out where Lieutenant Charpentier was, took two officers with me, and arrested him. When I touched him on the shoulder and warned him to come quietly with us, he answered us as bold as brass, "I suppose you are arresting me for being concerned in the death of that scoundrel Drebber," he said. We had said nothing to him about it, so that his alluding to it had a most suspicious aspect.'

'Very,' said Holmes.

'He still carried the heavy stick which the mother described him as having when he followed Drebber. It was a stout oak cudgel.'

'What is your theory, then?'

'Well, my theory is that he followed Drebber as far as the

150 *The next morning we heard of Mr. Drebber's mysterious death."* Mme. Charpentier would not, on the Friday afternoon, have referred to the morning of that day as 'the next morning," but as "this morning"—an indication that Gregson called on her, not on Friday, but on the following Saturday morning.

151 *I made shorthand notes.* Gregson (and later, Lestrade) probably followed the Pitman Method since the Gregg system did not come into vogue until about 1888. We may note here that an edition of *The Sign of the Four* was issued in Pitman's shorthand in 1898, and proved so popular that Gregg put the same book into shorthand in 1918.

Brixton Road. When there, a fresh altercation arose between them, in the course of which Drebber received a blow from the stick, in the pit of the stomach perhaps, which killed him without leaving any mark. The night was so wet that no one was about, so Charpentier dragged the body of his victim into the empty house. As to the candle, and the blood, and the writing on the wall, and the ring, they may all be so many tricks to throw the police on to the wrong scent.'

'Well done!' said Holmes in an encouraging voice. 'Really, Gregson, you are getting along. We shall make something of you yet.'

'I flatter myself that I have managed it rather neatly,' the detective answered proudly. 'The young man volunteered a statement, in which he said that after following Drebber some time, the latter perceived him, and took a cab in order to get away from him. On his way home he met an old shipmate, and took a long walk with him. On being asked where this old shipmate lived, he was unable to give any satisfactory reply. I think the whole case fits together uncommonly well. What amuses me is to think of Lestrade, who had started off upon the wrong scent. I am afraid he won't make much of it. Why, by Jove, here's the very man himself!'

It was indeed Lestrade, who had ascended the stairs while we were talking, and who now entered the room. The assurance and jauntiness which generally marked his demeanour and dress were, however, wanting. His face was disturbed and troubled, while his clothes were disarranged and untidy. He had evidently come with the intention of consulting with Sherlock Holmes, for on perceiving his colleague he appeared to be embarrassed and put out. He stood in the centre of the room, fumbling nervously with his hat and uncertain what to do. 'This is a most extraordinary case,' he said at last—'a most incomprehensible affair.'

'Ah, you find it so, Mr Lestrade!' cried Gregson, triumphantly. 'I thought you would come to that conclusion. Have you managed to land the secretary, Mr Joseph Stangerson?'

'The secretary, Mr Joseph Stangerson,' said Lestrade, gravely, 'was murdered at Halliday's Private Hotel about six o'clock this morning.'

7 • LIGHT IN THE DARKNESS

The intelligence with which Lestrade greeted us was so momentous and so unexpected that we were all three fairly dumbfounded. Gregson sprang out of his chair and upset the remainder of his whisky and water. I stared in silence at Sherlock Holmes, whose lips were compressed and his brows drawn down over his eyes.

'Stangerson too!' he muttered. 'The plot thickens.'

'It was quite thick enough before,' grumbled Lestrade, taking a chair. 'I seem to have dropped into a sort of council of war.'

'Are you—are you sure of this piece of intelligence?' stammered Gregson.

'I have just come from his room,' said Lestrade. 'I was the first to discover what had occurred.'

'We have been hearing Gregson's view of the matter,' Holmes observed. 'Would you mind letting us know what you have seen and done?'

'I have no objection,' Lestrade answered, seating himself. 'I freely confess that I was of the opinion that Stangerson was concerned in the death of Drebber. This fresh development has shown me that I was completely mistaken. Full of the one idea, I set myself to find out what had become of the secretary. They had been seen together at Euston Station about half-past eight on the evening of the third. At two in the morning **152** Drebber had been found in the Brixton Road. The question which confronted me was to find out how Stangerson had been employed between 8.30 and the time of the crime, and what had become of him afterwards. I telegraphed to Liverpool, giving a description of the man, and warning them to keep a watch upon the American boats. I then set to work calling upon all the hotels and lodging-houses in the vicinity of Euston. You see, I argued that if Drebber and his companion had become separated, the natural course for the latter would be to put up somewhere in the vicinity for the night, and then to hang about the station again next morning.'

'They would be likely to agree on some meeting place beforehand,' remarked Holmes.

'So it proved. I spent the whole of yesterday evening in making inquiries entirely without avail. This morning I began very early, and at eight o'clock I reached Halliday's Private Hotel, in Little George Street. On my inquiry as to whether a Mr Stangerson was living there, they at once answered me in the affirmative.

' "No doubt you are the gentleman whom he was expecting," they said. "He has been waiting for a gentleman for two days."

' "Where is he now?" I asked.

' "He is upstairs in bed. He wished to be called at nine."

' "I will go up and see him at once," I said.

'It seemed to me that my sudden appearance might shake his nerves and lead him to say something unguarded. The Boots volunteered to show me the room: it was on the second **153** floor, and there was a small corridor leading up to it. The Boots pointed out the door to me, and was about to go downstairs again when I saw something that made me feel sickish, in spite of my twenty years' experience. From under the door there curled a little red ribbon of blood, which had meandered across the passage and formed a little pool along the skirting at the other side. I gave a cry, which brought the Boots back. He nearly fainted when he saw it. The door was locked on the inside, but we put our shoulders to it, and knocked it in. The window of the room was open, and beside the window, all huddled up, lay the body of a man in his nightdress. He was quite dead, and had been for some time, for his limbs were rigid and cold. When we turned him over, the Boots recognized him at once as being the same gentleman who had engaged the room under the name of Joseph Stangerson. The cause of death was a deep stab in the left

152 *on the evening of the third.* Corroborating Watson's statement that it was "upon the 4th of March" that Holmes was brought into the case.

153 *The Boots.* A servant at an inn or hotel who blackened boots and did minor offices for the guests.

154 *the mews*. Stableyard, or a back lane or alley leading to the stables.

155 *eighty odd pounds*. Some $400.

156 *a small chip ointment box*. A box made of thin wood.

side, which must have penetrated the heart. And now comes the strangest part of the affair. What do you suppose was above the murdered man?'

I felt a creeping of the flesh, and a presentiment of coming horror, even before Sherlock Holmes answered.

'The word RACHE, written in letters of blood,' he said.

'That was it,' said Lestrade, in an awestruck voice; and we were all silent for awhile.

There was something so methodical and so incomprehensible about the deeds of this unknown assassin, that it imparted a fresh ghastliness to his crimes. My nerves, which were steady enough on the field of battle, tingled as I thought of it.

'The man was seen,' continued Lestrade. 'A milk boy, passing on his way to the dairy, happened to walk down the lane **154** which leads from the mews at the back of the hotel. He noticed that a ladder, which usually lay there, was raised against one of the windows of the second floor, which was wide open. After passing, he looked back and saw a man descend the ladder. He came down so quietly and openly that the boy imagined him to be some carpenter or joiner at work in the hotel. He took no particular notice of him, beyond thinking in his own mind that it was early for him to be at work. He has an impression that the man was tall, had a reddish face, and was dressed in a long, brownish coat. He must have stayed in the room some little time after the murder, for we found blood-stained water in the basin, where he had washed his hands, and marks on the sheets where he had deliberately wiped his knife.'

I glanced at Holmes on hearing the description of the murderer which tallied so exactly with his own. There was, however, no trace of exultation or satisfaction upon his face.

'Did you find nothing in the room which could furnish a clue to the murderer?' he asked.

'Nothing. Stangerson had Drebber's purse in his pocket, but it seems that this was usual, as he did all the paying. There **155** was eighty odd pounds in it, but nothing had been taken. Whatever the motives of these extraordinary crimes, robbery is certainly not one of them. There were no papers or memoranda in the murdered man's pocket, except a single telegram, dated from Cleveland about a month ago, and containing the words, "J. H. is in Europe." There was no name appended to this message.'

'And there was nothing else?' Holmes asked.

'Nothing of any importance. The man's novel, with which he had read himself to sleep, was lying upon the bed, and his pipe was on a chair beside him. There was a glass of water on **156** the table, and on the window-sill a small chip ointment box containing a couple of pills.'

Sherlock Holmes sprang from his chair with an exclamation of delight.

'The last link,' he cried, exultantly. 'My case is complete.'

The two detectives stared at him in amazement.

'I have now in my hands,' my companion said, confidently, 'all the threads which have formed such a tangle. There are, of course, details to be filled in, but I am as certain of all the main facts, from the time that Drebber parted from Stangerson at the station, up to the discovery of the body of the latter, as if I had seen them with my own eyes. I will give you a proof of my knowledge. Could you lay your hand upon those pills?'

'I have them,' said Lestrade, producing a small white box; 'I took them and the purse and the telegram, intending to have them put in a place of safety at the Police Station. It was the merest chance my taking these pills, for I am bound to say that I do not attach any importance to them.'

'Give them here,' said Holmes. 'Now, Doctor,' turning to me, 'are those ordinary pills?'

They certainly were not. They were of a pearly grey colour, small, round, and almost transparent against the light. 'From their lightness and transparency, I should imagine that they are soluble in water,' I remarked.

'Precisely so,' answered Holmes. 'Now would you mind going down and fetching that poor little devil of a terrier which has been bad so long, and which the landlady wanted you to put out of its pain yesterday.'

I went downstairs and carried the dog upstairs in my arms. Its laboured breathing and glazing eye showed that it was not far from its end. Indeed, its snow-white muzzle proclaimed that it had already exceeded the usual term of canine existence. I placed it upon a cushion on the rug.

'I will now cut one of these pills in two,' said Holmes, and drawing his penknife he suited the action to the word. 'One half we return into the box for future purposes. The other half I will place in this wine glass, in which is a teaspoonful of water. You perceive that our friend, the Doctor, is right, and that it readily dissolves.'

'This may be very interesting,' said Lestrade, in the injured tone of one who suspects that he is being laughed at; 'I cannot see, however, what it has to do with the death of Mr Joseph Stangerson.'

'Patience, my friend, patience! You will find in time that it has everything to do with it. I shall now add a little milk to make the mixture palatable, and on presenting it to the dog we find that he laps it up readily enough.'

As he spoke he turned the contents of the wine glass into a saucer and placed it in front of the terrier, who speedily licked it dry. Sherlock Holmes' earnest demeanour had so far convinced us that we all sat in silence, watching the animal intently, and expecting some startling effect. None such appeared, however. The dog continued to lie stretched upon the cushion, breathing in a laboured way, but apparently neither the better nor the worse for its draught.

Holmes had taken out his watch, and as minute followed minute without result, an expression of the utmost chagrin and disappointment appeared upon his features. He gnawed his lip, drummed his fingers upon the table, and showed every other symptom of acute impatience. So great was his emotion that I felt sincerely sorry for him, while the two detectives smiled derisively, by no means displeased at this check which he had met.

'It can't be a coincidence,' he cried, at last springing from his chair and pacing wildly up and down the room; 'it is impossible that it should be a mere coincidence. The very pills which I suspected in the case of Drebber are actually found after the death of Stangerson. And yet they are inert. What can it mean? Surely my whole chain of reasoning cannot have

157 *proves to be capable of bearing some other interpretation.* Compare: "One should always look for a possible alternative and provide against it. It is the first rule of criminal investigation"—"The Adventure of Black Peter." "When you follow two separate trains of thought, you will find some point of intersection which should approximate to the truth"—"The Disappearance of Lady Frances Carfax." "One drawback of an active mind is that one can always conceive alternative explanations, which would make our scent a false one"—"The Problem of Thor Bridge."

158 *no new or special features from which deductions may be drawn.* Compare: "Singularity is almost invariably a clue. The more featureless and commonplace a crime is, the more difficult it is to bring home"—"The Boscombe Valley Mystery." "The more bizarre a thing is the less mysterious it proves to be"—"The Red-Headed League."

159 *outré.* French: exaggerated, excessive, unusual.

THE UNFORTUNATE CREATURE'S TONGUE SEEMED HARDLY TO HAVE BEEN MOISTENED IN IT BEFORE IT GAVE A CONVULSIVE SHUDDER IN EVERY LIMB, AND LAY AS RIGID AND LIFELESS AS IF IT HAD BEEN STRUCK BY LIGHTNING.

Illustration by George Hutchinson for *A Study in Scarlet*; London: Ward, Lock, Bowden & Co., 1891.

been false. It is impossible! And yet this wretched dog is none the worse. Ah, I have it! I have it!' With a perfect shriek of delight he rushed to the box, cut the other pill in two, dissolved it, added milk, and presented it to the terrier. The unfortunate creature's tongue seemed hardly to have been moistened in it before it gave a convulsive shiver in every limb, and lay as rigid and lifeless as if it had been struck by lightning.

Sherlock Holmes drew a long breath, and wiped the perspiration from his forehead. 'I should have more faith,' he said; 'I ought to know by this time that when a fact appears to be opposed to a long train of deductions it invariably **157** proves to be capable of bearing some other interpretation. Of the two pills in that box, one was of the most deadly poison, and the other was entirely harmless. I ought to have known that before ever I saw the box at all.'

This last statement appeared to me to be so startling that I could hardly believe that he was in his sober senses. There was the dead dog, however, to prove that his conjecture had been correct. It seemed to me that the mists in my own mind were gradually clearing away, and I began to have a dim, vague perception of the truth.

'All this seems strange to you,' continued Holmes, 'because you failed at the beginning of the inquiry to grasp the importance of the single real clue which was presented to you. I had the good fortune to seize upon that, and everything which has occurred since then has served to confirm my original supposition, and, indeed, was the logical sequence of it. Hence things which have perplexed you and made the case more obscure have served to enlighten me and to strengthen my conclusions. It is a mistake to confound strangeness with mystery. The most commonplace crime is often the most mysterious, because it presents no new or **158** special features from which deductions may be drawn. This murder would have been infinitely more difficult to unravel had the body of the victim been simply found lying in the **159** roadway without any of those *outré* and sensational accompaniments which have rendered it remarkable. These strange details, far from making the case more difficult, have really had the effect of making it less so.'

Mr Gregson, who had listened to this address with considerable impatience, could contain himself no longer. 'Look here, Mr Sherlock Holmes,' he said, 'we are all ready to acknowledge that you are a smart man, and that you have your own methods of working. We want something more than mere theory and preaching now, though. It is a case of taking the man. I have made my case out, and it seems I was wrong. Young Charpentier could not have been engaged in this second affair. Lestrade went after his man, Stangerson, and it appears that he was wrong too. You have thrown out hints here, and hints there, and seem to know more than we do, but the time has come when we feel that we have a right to ask you straight how much you do know of the business. Can you name the man who did it?'

'I cannot help feeling that Gregson is right, sir,' remarked Lestrade. 'We have both tried, and we have both failed. You have remarked more than once since I have been in the room that you had all the evidence which you require. Surely you will not withhold it any longer.'

'Any delay in arresting the assassin,' I observed, 'might give him time to perpetrate some fresh atrocity.'

Thus pressed by us all, Holmes showed signs of irresolution. He continued to walk up and down the room with his head sunk on his chest and his brows drawn down, as was his habit when lost in thought.

'There will be no more murders,' he said at last, stopping abruptly and facing us. 'You can put that consideration out of the question. You have asked me if I know the name of the assassin. I do. The mere knowing of his name is a small thing, however, compared with the power of laying our hands upon him. This I expect very shortly to do. I have good hopes of managing it through my own arrangements; but it is a thing which needs delicate handling, for we have a shrewd and desperate man to deal with, who is supported, as I have had occasion to prove, by another who is as clever as himself. As long as this man has no idea that anyone can have a clue there is some chance of securing him; but if he had the slightest suspicion, he would change his name, and vanish in an instant among the four million inhabitants of this great city. With-**160** out meaning to hurt either of your feelings, I am bound to say that I consider these men to be more than a match for the official force, and that is why I have not asked your assistance. If I fail, I shall, of course, incur all the blame due to this omission; but that I am prepared for. At present I am ready to promise that the instant that I can communicate with you without endangering my own combinations, I shall do so.'

Gregson and Lestrade seemed to be far from satisfied by this assurance, or by the depreciating allusion to the detective police. The former had flushed up to the roots of his flaxen hair, while the other's beady eyes glistened with curiosity and resentment. Neither of them had time to speak, however, before there was a tap at the door, and the spokesman of the street Arabs, young Wiggins, introduced his insignificant and unsavoury person.

'Please, sir,' he said, touching his forelock, 'I have the cab downstairs.'

'Good boy,' said Holmes, blandly. 'Why don't you introduce this pattern at Scotland Yard?' he continued, taking a pair of steel handcuffs from a drawer. 'See how beautifully the spring works. They fasten in an instant.' **161**

'The old pattern is good enough,' remarked Lestrade, 'if we can only find the man to put them on.'

'Very good, very good,' said Holmes, smiling. 'The cabman may as well help me with my boxes. Just ask him to step up, Wiggins.'

I was surprised to find my companion speaking as though he were about to set out on a journey, since he had not said anything to me about it. There was a small portmanteau in the room, and this he pulled out and began to strap. He was busily engaged at it when the cabman entered the room.

'Just give me a help with this buckle, cabman,' he said, kneeling over his task, and never turning his head.

The fellow came forward with a somewhat sullen, defiant air, and put down his hands to assist. At that instant there was a sharp click, the jangling of metal, and Sherlock Holmes sprang to his feet again.

'Gentlemen,' he cried, with flashing eyes, 'let me introduce you to Mr Jefferson Hope, the murderer of Enoch Drebber and of Joseph Stangerson.'

160 *the four million inhabitants of this great city.* "In 1881, the Registrar-General's figures gave the population of London as close upon four millions, but even three years earlier, when the official population figure had been but 3,577,304, it was estimated that the people living within the Metropolitan Police district—the actual dwellers—totalled some four-and-a-half millions."—Michael Harrison, *In the Footsteps of Sherlock Holmes.*

161 *They fasten in an instant.'* "Cognoscenti will recall that Holmes advocated use of automatically-locking handcuffs as early as 1881 in the capture of Jefferson Hope. . . . A student of police methods has suggested that such handcuffs were not available prior to 1896. The issue is delegated to the specialist for resolution. Mr. Holmes may have pioneered in this field, and in that event the darbies used in 1881 represent the only mechanical invention by Holmes known to this writer."—Elliot Kimball, "Origin and Evolution of G. Lestrade: 2—A Matter of Mancinism."

... LESTRADE, AND HOLMES SPRANG UPON HIM LIKE SO
MANY STAGHOUNDS.

Illustration by George Hutchinson for *A Study in
Scarlet*; London: Ward, Lock, Bowden & Co., 1891.

The whole thing occurred in a moment—so quickly that I had no time to realize it. I have a vivid recollection of that instant, of Holmes' triumphant expression and the ring of his voice, of the cabman's dazed, savage face, as he glared at the glittering handcuffs, which had appeared as if by magic upon his wrists. For a second or two we might have been a group of statues. Then with an inarticulate roar of fury, the prisoner wrenched himself free from Holmes' grasp, and hurled himself through the window. Woodwork and glass gave way before him; but before he got quite through, Gregson, Lestrade, and Holmes sprang upon him like so many staghounds. He was dragged back into the room, and then commenced a terrific conflict. So powerful and so fierce was he that the four of us were shaken off again and again. He appeared to have the convulsive strength of a man in an epileptic fit. His face and hands were terribly mangled by his passage through the glass, but the loss of blood had no effect in diminishing his resistance. It was not until Lestrade succeeded in getting his hand inside his neckcloth and half-strangling him that we made him realize that his struggles were of no avail; and even then we felt no security until we had pinioned his feet as well as his hands. That done, we rose to our feet breathless and panting.

'We have his cab,' said Sherlock Holmes. 'It will serve to take him to Scotland Yard. And now, gentlemen,' he continued, with a pleasant smile, 'we have reached the end of our little mystery. You are very welcome to put any questions that you like to me now, and there is no danger that I will refuse to answer them.'

PART II

The Country of the Saints

8 ✦ ON THE GREAT ALKALI PLAIN

In the central portion of the great North American Continent there lies an arid and repulsive desert, which for many a long year served as a barrier against the advance of civilization. From the Sierra Nevada to Nebraska, and from the Yellowstone River in the north to the Colorado upon the south, is a region of desolation and silence. Nor is Nature always in one mood throughout this grim district. It comprises snow-capped and lofty mountains, and dark and gloomy valleys. There are swift-flowing rivers which dash through jagged cañons; and there are enormous plains, which in winter are white with snow, and in summer are grey with the saline alkali dust. They all preserve, however, the common characteristics of barrenness, inhospitality and misery.

There are no inhabitants of this land of despair. A band of Pawnees or of Blackfeet may occasionally traverse it in order to reach other hunting-grounds, but the hardiest of the braves are glad to lose sight of those awesome plains, and to find themselves once more upon their prairies. The coyote skulks among the scrub, the buzzard flaps heavily through the air, and the clumsy grizzly bear lumbers through the dark ravines, and picks up such sustenance as it can amongst the rocks. These are the sole dwellers in the wilderness.

In the whole world there can be no more dreary view than that from the northern slope of the Sierra Blanco. As far as the eye can reach stretches the great flat plain-land, all dusted over with patches of alkali, and intersected by clumps of the dwarfish chaparral bushes. On the extreme verge of the horizon lie a long chain of mountain peaks with their rugged summits flecked with snow. In this great stretch of country there is no sign of life, nor of anything appertaining to life. There is no bird in the steel-blue heaven, no movement upon the dull, grey earth—above all, there is absolute silence. Listen as one may, there is no shadow of a sound in all that mighty wilderness; nothing but silence—complete and heart-subduing silence.

It has been said there is nothing appertaining to life upon the broad plain. That is hardly true. Looking down from the Sierra Blanco, one sees a pathway traced out across the desert, which winds away and is lost in the extreme distance. It is rutted with wheels and trodden down by the feet of many adventurers. Here and there there are scattered white objects which glisten in the sun, and stand out against the dull deposit of alkali. Approach, and examine them! They are bones: some large and coarse, others smaller and more delicate. The former have belonged to oxen, and the latter to men. For fifteen hundred miles one may trace this ghastly caravan route by these scattered remains of those who had fallen by the wayside.

Looking down on this very scene, there stood upon the fourth of May, eighteen hundred and forty-seven, a solitary traveller. His appearance was such that he might have been the very genius or demon of the region. An observer would have found it difficult to say whether he was nearer to forty or to sixty. His face was lean and haggard, and the brown parchment-like skin was drawn tightly over the projecting bones; his long, brown hair and beard were all flecked and dashed with white; his eyes were sunken in his head, and burned with an unnatural lustre; while the hand which grasped his rifle was hardly more fleshy than that of a skeleton. As he stood, he leaned upon his weapon for support, and yet his tall figure and the massive framework of his bones suggested a wiry and vigorous constitution. His gaunt face, however, and his clothes, which hung so baggily over his shrivelled limbs, proclaimed what it was that gave him that senile and decrepit appearance. The man was dying—dying from hunger and from thirst.

He had toiled painfully down the ravine, and on to this little elevation, in the vain hope of seeing some signs of water. Now the great salt plain stretched before his eyes, and the distant belt of savage mountains, without a sign anywhere of plant or tree, which might indicate the presence of moisture. In all that broad landscape there was no gleam of hope. North and east, and west he looked with wild, questioning eyes, and then he realized that his wanderings had come to an end, and that there, on that barren crag, he was about to die. 'Why not here, as well as in a feather bed, twenty years hence,' he muttered, as he seated himself in the shelter of a boulder.

Before sitting down, he had deposited upon the ground his useless rifle, and also a large bundle tied up in a grey shawl, which he had carried slung over his right shoulder. It appeared to be somewhat too heavy for his strength, for in lowering it, it came down on the ground with some little violence. Instantly there broke from the grey parcel a little moaning cry, and from it there protruded a small, scared face, with very bright brown eyes, and two little speckled, dimpled fists.

'You've hurt me!' said a childish voice reproachfully.

'Have I, though,' the man answered penitently; 'I didn't go for to do it.' As he spoke he unwrapped the grey shawl and extricated a pretty little girl of about five years of age, whose dainty shoes and smart, pink frock with its little linen apron, all bespoke a mother's care. The child was pale and wan, but her healthy arms and legs showed that she had suffered less than her companion.

'How is it now?' he answered anxiously, for she was still rubbing the towsy golden curls which covered the back of her head.

'Kiss it and make it well,' she said, with perfect gravity, showing the injured part up to him. 'That's what mother used to do. Where's mother?'

'Mother's gone. I guess you'll see her before long.'

'Gone, eh!' said the little girl. 'Funny, she didn't say goodbye; she 'most always did if she was just goin' over to auntie's for tea, and now she's been away three days. Say, it's awful dry, ain't it? Ain't there no water nor nothing to eat?'

'No, there ain't nothing, dearie. You'll just need to be patient awhile, and then you'll be all right. Put your head up ag'in me like that, and then you'll feel bullier. It ain't easy to talk when your lips is like leather, but I guess I'd best let you know how the cards lie. What's that you've got?'

'Pretty things! fine things!' cried the little girl enthusiastically, holding up two glittering fragments of mica. 'When we goes back to home I'll give them to brother Bob.'

'You'll see prettier things than them soon,' said the man confidently. 'You just wait a bit. I was going to tell you though —you remember when we left the river?'

'Oh, yes.'

'Well, we reckoned we'd strike another river soon, d'ye see. But there was somethin' wrong; compasses, or map, or somethin', and it didn't turn up. Water ran out. Just except a little drop for the likes of you, and—and——'

'And you couldn't wash yourself,' interrupted his companion gravely, staring up at his grimy visage.

'No, nor drink. And Mr Bender, he was the fust to go, and then Indian Pete, and then Mrs McGregor, and then Johnny Hones, and then, dearie, your mother.'

'Then mother's a deader too,' cried the little girl, dropping her face in her pinafore and sobbing bitterly.

'Yes, they all went except you and me. Then I thought there was some chance of water in this direction, so I heaved you over my shoulder and we tramped it together. It don't seem as though we've improved matters. There's an almighty small chance for us now!'

'Do you mean that we are going to die too?' asked the child, checking her sobs, and raising her tear-stained face.

'I guess that's about the size of it.'

'Why didn't you say so before?' she said, laughing gleefully. 'You gave me such a fright. Why, of course, now as long as we die we'll be with mother again.'

'Yes, you will, dearie.'

'And you too. I'll tell her how awful good you've been. I'll bet she meets us at the door of heaven with a big pitcher of water, and a lot of buckwheat cakes, hot, and toasted on both sides, like Bob and me was fond of. How long will it be first?'

'I don't know—not very long.' The man's eyes were fixed upon the northern horizon. In the blue vault of the heaven there had appeared three little specks which increased in size every moment, so rapidly did they approach. They speedily resolved themselves into three large brown birds, which circled over the heads of the two wanderers, and then settled upon some rocks which overlooked them. They were buzzards, the vultures of the west, whose coming is the forerunner of death.

'Cocks and hens,' cried the little girl gleefully, pointing at their ill-omened forms, and clapping her hands to make them rise. 'Say, did God make this country?'

'In course He did,' said her companion, rather startled by this unexpected question.

'He made the country down in Illinois, and He made the Missouri,' the little girl continued. 'I guess somebody else made the country in these parts. It's not nearly so well done. They forgot the water and the trees.'

'What would ye think of offering up prayer?' the man asked diffidently.

'It ain't night yet,' she answered.

'It don't matter. It ain't quite regular, but He won't mind that, you bet. You say over them ones that you used to say every night in the wagon when we was on the Plains.'

'Why don't you say some yourself?' the child asked with wondering eyes.

'I disremember them,' he answered. 'I hain't said none since I was half the height o' that gun. I guess it's never too late. You say them out, and I'll stand by and come in on the choruses.'

'Then you'll need to kneel down, and me too,' she said, laying the shawl out for that purpose. 'You've got to put your hands up like this. It makes you feel kind of good.'

It was a strange sight, had there been anything but the buzzards to see it. Side by side on the narrow shawl knelt the two wanderers, the little prattling child and the reckless, hardened adventurer. Her chubby face and his haggard, angular visage were both turned up to the cloudless heaven in heartfelt entreaty to that dread Being with whom they were face to face, while the two voices—the one thin and clear, the other deep and harsh—united in the entreaty for mercy and forgiveness. The prayer finished, they resumed their seat in the shadow of the boulder until the child fell asleep, nestling upon the broad breast of her protector. He watched over her slumber for some time, but Nature proved to be too strong for him. For three days and three nights he had allowed himself neither rest nor repose. Slowly the eyelids drooped over the tired eyes, and the head sunk lower and lower upon the breast, until the man's grizzled beard was mixed with the gold

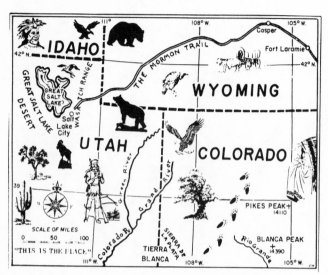

DR. JULIAN WOLFF'S MAP OF THE MORMON TRAIL

Dr. Wolff adds a word as the editor of *The Baker Street Journal*: "1. Present-day state boundaries are shown on the map. 2. There is a 'Sierra Blanca' but it is located in New Mexico, almost three hundred miles south of Blanca Peak in Colorado, shown here. 3. On older maps (*e.g.* 'Colton's Territories of New Mexico & Utah,' 1855) the Colorado River is shown as the Grand River above its junction with the Green River. 4. On Plate CXX ('Territory and Military Department of Utah, 1860') of the *Atlas to Accompany the Official Records of the Union and Confederate Armies*, Washington: Government Printing Office, 1891–1895, mountains called Sierra de la Plata are shown in the location indicated. Whether Plata (silver) could be confused with Blanco (white) is a point that might be discussed. Also, there is a locality labelled *Tierra Blanca*. However, all of these are far south of the Mormon Trail, and as far as our story is concerned, the Rio Grande and the Sierra Blanco must have been two other places. '. . . there was somethin' wrong; compasses, or map, or somethin'. . . .' "

tresses of his companion, and both slept the same deep and dreamless slumber.

Had the wanderer remained awake for another half-hour a strange sight would have met his eyes. Far away on the extreme verge of the alkali plain there rose up a little spray of dust, very slight at first, and hardly to be distinguished from the mists of the distance, but gradually growing higher and broader until it formed a solid, well-defined cloud. This cloud continued to increase in size until it became evident that it could only be raised by a great multitude of moving creatures. In more fertile spots the observer would have come to the conclusion that one of those great herds of bisons which graze upon the prairie land was approaching him. This was obviously impossible in these arid wilds. As the whirl of dust drew nearer to the solitary bluff upon which the two castaways were reposing, the canvas-covered tilts of wagons and the figures of armed horsemen began to show up through the haze, and the apparition revealed itself as being a great caravan upon its journey for the West. But what a caravan! When the head of it had reached the base of the mountains, the rear was not yet visible on the horizon. Right across the enormous plain stretched the straggling array, wagons and carts, men on horseback, and men on foot. Innumerable women who staggered along under burdens, and children who toddled beside the wagons or peeped out from under the white coverings. This was evidently no ordinary party of immigrants, but rather some nomad people who had been compelled from stress of circumstances to seek themselves a new country. There rose through the clear air a confused clattering and rumbling from this great mass of humanity, with the creaking of wheels and the neighing of horses. Loud as it was, it was not sufficient to rouse the two tired wayfarers above them.

At the head of the column there rode a score or more of grave, ironfaced men, clad in sombre, homespun garments and armed with rifles. On reaching the base of the bluff they halted, and held a short council among themselves.

'The wells are to the right, my brothers,' said one, a hard-lipped, clean-shaven man with grizzly hair.

'To the right of the Sierra Blanco—so we shall reach the Rio Grande,' said another.

'Fear not for water,' cried a third. 'He who could draw it from the rocks will not now abandon His chosen people.'

'Amen! amen!' responded the whole party.

They were about to resume their journey when one of the youngest and keenest-eyed uttered an exclamation and pointed up at the rugged crag above them. From its summit there fluttered a little wisp of pink, showing up hard and bright against the grey rocks behind. At the sight there was a general reining up of horses and unslinging of guns, while fresh horsemen came galloping up to reinforce the vanguard. The word 'Redskins' was on every lip.

'There can't be any number of Injuns here,' said the elderly man who appeared to be in command. 'We have passed the Pawnees, and there are no other tribes until we cross the great mountains.'

'Shall I go forward and see, Brother Stangerson,' asked one of the band.

'And I,' 'and I,' cried a dozen voices.

'Leave your horses below and we will await you here,' the

elder answered. In a moment the young fellows had dismounted, fastened their horses, and were ascending the precipitous slope which led up to the object which had excited their curiosity. They advanced rapidly and noiselessly, with the confidence and dexterity of practised scouts. The watchers from the plain below could see them flit from rock to rock until their figures stood out against the skyline. The young man who had first given the alarm was leading them. Suddenly his followers saw him throw up his hands, as though overcome with astonishment, and on joining him they were affected in the same way by the sight which met their eyes.

On the little plateau which crowned the barren hills there stood a single giant boulder, and against this boulder there lay a tall man, long-bearded and hard-featured, but of an excessive thinness. His placid face and regular breathing showed that he was fast asleep. Beside him lay a little child, with her round, white arms encircling his brown, sinewy neck, and her golden-haired head resting upon the breast of his velveteen tunic. Her rosy lips were parted, showing the regular line of snow-white teeth within, and a playful smile played over her infantile features. Her plump little white legs, terminating in white socks and neat shoes with shining buckles, offered a strange contrast to the long, shrivelled members of her companion. On the ledge of rock above this strange couple there stood three solemn buzzards, who, at the sight of the new-comers, uttered raucous screams of disappointment and flapped sullenly away.

The cries of the foul birds awoke the two sleepers, who stared about them in bewilderment. The man staggered to his feet and looked down upon the plain which had been so desolate when sleep had overtaken him, and which was now traversed by this enormous body of men and of beasts. His face assumed an expression of incredulity as he gazed, and he passed his bony hand over his eyes. 'This is what they call delirium, I guess,' he muttered. The child stood beside him, holding on to the skirt of his coat, and said nothing, but looked all around her with the wondering, questioning gaze of childhood.

The rescuing party were speedily able to convince the two castaways that their appearance was no delusion. One of them seized the little girl and hoisted her upon his shoulder, while two others supported her gaunt companion, and assisted him towards the wagons.

'My name is John Ferrier,' the wanderer explained; 'me and that little un are all that's left o' twenty-one people. The rest is all dead o' thirst and hunger away down in the south.'

'Is she your child?' asked someone.

'I guess she is now,' the other cried, defiantly; 'she's mine 'cause I saved her. No man will take her from me. She's Lucy Ferrier from this day on. Who are you, though?' he continued, glancing with curiosity at his stalwart, sunburned rescuers; 'there seems to be a powerful lot of ye.'

'Nigh upon ten thousand,' said one of the young men; 'we **162** are the persecuted children of God—the chosen of the Angel Merona.'

'I never heard tell on him,' said the wanderer. 'He appears to have chosen a fair crowd of ye.'

'Do not jest at that which is sacred,' said the other sternly.

162 *'Nigh upon ten thousand.'* "It is interesting to note that in Brigham Young's own record of the great journey to the Great Salt Lake Valley in 1847, he mentioned that he arrived with 143 men, 3 women and 2 children."—Rev. Otis R. Rice, "Clergymen in the Canon."

ONE OF THEM SEIZED THE LITTLE GIRL AND HOISTED HER UPON HIS SHOULDER . . .

Illustration for *Beeton's Christmas Annual*, December, 1887. The picture is signed by W. M. R. Quick, but, as the late James Montgomery wrote (*A Study in Pictures*), "available informtaion has not yet determined conclusively whether that was the signature of the engraver or of a second artist. Certainly the illustration . . . is identical in style and execution with the three bearing the initials 'D. H. F.'"

163 *Joseph Smith*. It was in 1823, at Palmyra, New York, that a vision revealed the hiding place of the golden tablets to Joseph Smith, 1805–1844. Smith founded his first church in 1830, but the hostility of neighbors drove him to Kirtland, Ohio, and later to Nauvoo, Illinois. Trouble with non-Mormons led to his arrest on charges of treason. On July 27, 1844, he and his brother Hyrum were murdered by a mob at Carthage, Illinois.

164 *Brigham Young*. After Joseph Smith's assassination, Brigham Young, 1801–1877, became the dominant figure in Mormonism. He led the great migration west in 1846–1847, and directed the settlement at Salt Lake City. He seems to have been married in all to 27 wives, but he was a stern moralist as well as a brilliant leader.

'We are of those who believe in those sacred writings, drawn in Egyptian letters on plates of beaten gold, which were **163** handed unto the holy Joseph Smith at Palmyra. We have come from Nauvoo, in the State of Illinois, where we had founded our temple. We have come to seek a refuge from the violent man and from the godless, even though it be the heart of the desert.'

The name of Nauvoo evidently recalled recollections to John Ferrier. 'I see,' he said; 'you are the Mormons.'

'We are the Mormons,' answered his companions with one voice.

'And where are you going?'

'We do not know. The hand of God is leading us under the person of our Prophet. You must come before him. He shall say what is to be done with you.'

They had reached the base of the hill by this time, and were surrounded by crowds of the pilgrims—pale-faced, meek-looking women; strong, laughing children; and anxious, earnest-eyed men. Many were the cries of astonishment and of commiseration which arose from them when they perceived the youth of one of the strangers and the destitution of the other. Their escort did not halt, however, but pushed on, followed by a great crowd of Mormons, until they reached a wagon, which was conspicuous for its great size and for the gaudiness and smartness of its appearance. Six horses were yoked to it, whereas the others were furnished with two, or, at most, four apiece. Beside the driver there sat a man who could not have been more than thirty years of age, but whose massive head and resolute expression marked him as a leader. He was reading a brown-backed volume, but as the crowd approached he laid it aside, and listened attentively to an account of the episode. Then he turned to the two castaways.

'If we take you with us,' he said, in solemn words, 'it can only be as believers in our own creed. We shall have no wolves in our fold. Better far that your bones should bleach in this wilderness than that you should prove to be that little speck of decay which in time corrupts the whole fruit. Will you come with us on these terms?'

'Guess I'll come with you on any terms,' said Ferrier, with such emphasis that the grave Elders could not restrain a smile. The leader alone retained his stern, impressive expression.

'Take him, Brother Stangerson,' he said, 'give him food and drink, and the child likewise. Let it be your task also to teach him our holy creed. We have delayed long enough. Forward! On, on to Zion!'

'On, on to Zion!' cried the crowd of Mormons, and the words rippled down the long caravan, passing from mouth to mouth until they died away in a dull murmur in the far distance. With a cracking of whips and a creaking of wheels the great wagons got into motion, and soon the whole caravan was winding along once more. The Elder to whose care the two waifs had been committed led them to his wagon, where a meal was already awaiting them.

'You shall remain here,' he said. 'In a few days you will have recovered from your fatigues. In the meantime, remember **164** that now and for ever you are of our religion. Brigham Young has said it, and he has spoken with the voice of Joseph Smith, which is the voice of God.'

9 • THE FLOWER OF UTAH

This is not the place to commemorate the trials and privations endured by the immigrant Mormons before they came to their final haven. From the shores of the Mississippi to the western slopes of the Rocky Mountains they had struggled on with a constancy almost unparalleled in history. The savage man, and the savage beast, hunger, thirst, fatigue, and disease —every impediment which Nature could place in the way— had all been overcome with Anglo-Saxon tenacity. Yet the long journey and the accumulated terrors had shaken the hearts of the stoutest among them. There was not one who did not sink upon his knees in heartfelt prayer when they saw the broad valley of Utah bathed in the sunlight beneath them, and learned from the lips of their leader that this was the promised land, and that these virgin acres were to be theirs for evermore.

Young speedily proved himself to be a skilful administrator as well as a resolute chief. Maps were drawn and charts prepared, in which the future city was sketched out. All around farms were apportioned and allotted in proportion to the standing of each individual. The tradesman was put to his trade and the artisan to his calling. In the town streets and squares sprang up as if by magic. In the country there was draining and hedging, planting and clearing, until the next summer saw the whole country golden with the wheat crop. Everything prospered in the strange settlement. Above all, the great temple which they had erected in the centre of the city grew ever taller and larger. From the first blush of dawn until the closing of the twilight, the clatter of the hammer and the rasp of the saw were never absent from the monument which the immigrants erected to Him who had led them safe through many dangers.

The two castaways, John Ferrier and the little girl, who had shared his fortunes and had been adopted as his daughter, accompanied the Mormons to the end of their great pilgrimage. Little Lucy Ferrier was borne along pleasantly enough in Elder Stangerson's wagon, a retreat which she shared with the Mormon's three wives and with his son, a headstrong, forward boy of twelve. Having rallied, with the elasticity of childhood, from the shock caused by her mother's death, she soon became a pet with the women, and reconciled herself to this new life in her moving canvas-covered home. In the meantime Ferrier, having recovered from his privations, distinguished himself as a useful guide and an indefatigable hunter. So rapidly did he gain the esteem of his new companions, that when they reached the end of their wanderings, it was unanimously agreed that he should be provided with as large and as fertile a tract of land as any of the settlers, with the exception of Young himself, and of Stangerson, Kemball, Johnston, and Drebber, who were the four principal Elders.

On the farm thus acquired John Ferrier built himself a substantial log-house, which received so many additions in succeeding years that it grew into a roomy villa. He was a man of a practical turn of mind, keen in his dealings and skilful with his hands. His iron constitution enabled him to work morning and evening at improving and tilling his lands.

Hence it came about that his farm and all that belonged to him prospered exceedingly. In three years he was better off than his neighbours, in six he was well-to-do, in nine he was rich, and in twelve there were not half a dozen men in the whole of Salt Lake City who could compare with him. From the great inland sea to the distant Wahsatch Mountains there was no name better known than that of John Ferrier.

There was one way and only one in which he offended the susceptibilities of his co-religionists. No argument or persuasion could ever induce him to set up a female establishment after the manner of his companions. He never gave reasons for this persistent refusal, but contented himself by resolutely and inflexibly adhering to his determination. There were some who accused him of lukewarmness in his adopted religion, and others who put it down to greed of wealth and reluctance to incur expense. Others, again, spoke of some early love affair, and of a fair-haired girl who had pined away on the shores of the Atlantic. Whatever the reason, Ferrier remained strictly celibate. In every other respect he conformed to the religion of the young settlement, and gained the name of being an orthodox and straight-walking man.

Lucy Ferrier grew up within the log-house, and assisted her adopted father in all his undertakings. The keen air of the mountains and the balsamic odour of the pine trees took the place of nurse and mother to the young girl. As year succeeded to year she grew taller and stronger, her cheek more ruddy and her step more elastic. Many a wayfarer upon the high road which ran by Ferrier's farm felt long-forgotten thoughts revive in their minds as they watched her lithe, girlish figure tripping through the wheatfields, or met her mounted upon her father's mustang, and managing it with all the ease and grace of a true child of the West. So the bud blossomed into a flower, and the year which saw her father the richest of the farmers left her as fair a specimen of American girlhood as could be found in the whole Pacific slope.

It was not the father, however, who first discovered that the child had developed into the woman. It seldom is in such cases. That mysterious change is too subtle and too gradual to be measured by dates. Least of all does the maiden herself know it until the tone of a voice or the touch of a hand sets her heart thrilling within her, and she learns, with a mixture of pride and of fear, that a new and a larger nature has awoke within her. There are few who cannot recall that day and remember the one little incident which heralded the dawn of a new life. In the case of Lucy Ferrier the occasion was serious enough in itself, apart from its future influence on her destiny and that of many besides.

It was a warm June morning, and the Latter Day Saints were as busy as the bees whose hive they have chosen for their emblem. In the fields and in the streets rose the same hum of human industry. Down the dusty high roads defiled long streams of heavily laden mules, all heading to the west, for the gold fever had broken out in California, and the overland route lay through the city of the Elect. There, too, were droves of sheep and bullocks coming in from the outlying pasture lands, and trains of tired immigrants, men and horses equally weary of their interminable journey. Through all this motley assemblage, threading her way with the skill of an accomplished rider, there galloped Lucy Ferrier, her fair face flushed with the exercise and her long chestnut hair floating out behind her. She had a commission from her father in the city, and was dashing in as she had done many a time before, with all the fearlessness of youth, thinking only of her task and how it was to be performed. The travel-stained adventurers gazed after her in astonishment, and even the unemotional Indians, journeying in with their pelties, relaxed their accustomed stoicism as they marvelled at the beauty of the pale-faced maiden.

She had reached the outskirts of the city when she found the road blocked by a great drove of cattle, driven by a half-dozen wild-looking herdsmen from the plains. In her impatience she endeavoured to pass this obstacle by pushing her horse into what appeared to be a gap. Scarcely had she got fairly into it, however, before the beasts closed in behind her, and she found herself completely imbedded in the moving stream of fierce-eyed, long-horned bullocks. Accustomed as she was to deal with cattle, she was not alarmed at her situation, but took advantage of every opportunity to urge her horse on, in the hopes of pushing her way through the cavalcade. Unfortunately the horns of one of the creatures, either by accident or design, came in violent contact with the flank of the mustang, and excited it to madness. In an instant it reared up upon its hind legs with a snort of rage, and pranced and tossed in a way that would have unseated any but a skilful rider. The situation was full of peril. Every plunge of the excited horse brought it against the horns again, and goaded it to fresh madness. It was all that the girl could do to keep herself in the saddle, yet a slip would mean a terrible death under the hoofs of the unwieldy and terrified animals. Unaccustomed to sudden emergencies, her head began to swim, and her grip upon the bridle to relax. Choked by the rising cloud of dust and by the steam from the struggling creatures, she might have abandoned her efforts in despair, but for a kindly voice at her elbow which assured her of assistance. At the same moment a sinewy, brown hand caught the frightened horse by the curb, and forcing a way through the drove, soon brought her to the outskirts.

'You're not hurt, I hope, miss,' said her preserver respectfully.

She looked up at his dark, fierce face, and laughed saucily. 'I'm awful frightened,' she said, naïvely; 'whoever would have thought that Poncho would have been so scared by a lot of cows?'

'Thank God you kept your seat,' the other said earnestly. He was a tall, savage-looking young fellow, mounted on a powerful roan horse, and clad in the rough dress of a hunter, with a long rifle slung over his shoulders. 'I guess you are the daughter of John Ferrier,' he remarked; 'I saw you ride down from his house. When you see him, ask him if he remembers the Jefferson Hopes of St Louis. If he's the same Ferrier, my father and he were pretty thick.'

'Hadn't you better come and ask yourself?' she asked, demurely.

The young fellow seemed pleased at the suggestion, and his dark eyes sparkled with pleasure. 'I'll do so,' he said; 'we've been in the mountains for two months, and are not over and

. . . A SINEWY, BROWN HAND CAUGHT THE FRIGHTENED HORSE BY THE CURB . . .

Illustration by George Hutchinson for *A Study in Scarlet*; London: Ward, Lock, Bowden & Co., 1891.

above in visiting condition. He must take us as he finds us.'

'He has a good deal to thank you for, and so have I,' she answered, 'he's awful fond of me. If those cows had jumped on me he'd have never got over it.'

'Neither would I,' said her companion.

'You! Well, I don't see that it would make much matter to you, anyhow. You ain't even a friend of ours.'

The young hunter's dark face grew so gloomy over this remark that Lucy Ferrier laughed aloud.

'There, I didn't mean that,' she said; 'of course, you are a friend now. You must come and see us. Now I must push along, or father won't trust me with his business any more. Good-bye!'

'Good-bye,' he answered, raising his broad sombrero, and bending over her little hand. She wheeled her mustang round, gave it a cut with her riding-whip, and darted away down the broad road in a rolling cloud of dust.

Young Jefferson Hope rode on with his companions, gloomy and taciturn. He and they had been among the Nevada Mountains prospecting for silver, and were returning to Salt Lake City in the hope of raising capital enough to work some lodes which they had discovered. He had been as keen as any of them upon the business until this sudden incident had drawn his thoughts into another channel. The sight of the fair young girl, as frank and wholesome as the Sierra breezes, had stirred his volcanic, untamed heart to its very depths. When she had vanished from his sight, he realized that a crisis had come in his life, and that neither silver speculations nor any other questions could ever be of such importance to him as this new and all-absorbing one. The love which had sprung up in his heart was not the sudden, changeable fancy of a boy, but rather the wild, fierce passion of a man of strong will and imperious temper. He had been accustomed to succeed in all that he undertook. He swore in his heart that he would not fail in this if human effort and human perseverance could render him successful.

He called on John Ferrier that night, and many times again, until his face was a familiar one at the farm-house. John, cooped up in the valley, and absorbed in his work, had had little chance of learning the news of the outside world during the last twelve years. All this Jefferson Hope was able to tell him, and in a style which interested Lucy as well as her father. He had been a pioneer in California, and could narrate many a strange tale of fortunes made and fortunes lost in those wild, halcyon days. He had been a scout, too, and a trapper, a silver explorer, and a ranchman. Wherever stirring adventures were to be had, Jefferson Hope had been there in search of them. He soon became a favourite with the old farmer, who spoke eloquently of his virtues. On such occasions, Lucy was silent, but her blushing cheek and her bright, happy eyes showed only too clearly that her young heart was no longer her own. Her honest father may not have observed these symptoms, but they were assuredly not thrown away upon the man who had won her affections.

One summer evening he came galloping down the road and pulled up at the gate. She was at the doorway, and came down to meet him. He threw the bridle over the fence and strode up the pathway.

'I am off, Lucy,' he said, taking her two hands in his, and

gazing tenderly down into her face; 'I won't ask you to come with me now, but will you be ready to come when I am here again?'

'And when will that be?' she asked, blushing and laughing.

'A couple of months at the outside. I will come and claim you then, my darling. There's no one who can stand between us.'

'And how about father?' she asked.

'He has given his consent, provided we get these mines working all right. I have no fear on that head.'

'Oh, well; of course, if you and father have arranged it all, there's no more to be said,' she whispered, with her cheek against his broad breast.

'Thank God!' he said hoarsely, stooping and kissing her. 'It is settled, then. The longer I stay, the harder it will be to go. They are waiting for me at the cañon. Good-bye, my own darling—good-bye. In two months you shall see me.'

He tore himself from her as he spoke, and, flinging himself upon his horse, galloped furiously away, never even looking round, as though afraid that his resolution might fail him if he took one glance at what he was leaving. She stood at the gate, gazing after him until he vanished from her sight. Then she walked back into the house, the happiest girl in all Utah.

10 ❖ JOHN FERRIER TALKS
❖ WITH THE PROPHET

Three weeks had passed since Jefferson Hope and his comrades had departed from Salt Lake City. John Ferrier's heart was sore within him when he thought of the young man's return, and of the impending loss of his adopted child. Yet her bright and happy face reconciled him to the arrangement more than any argument could have done. He had always determined, deep down in his resolute heart, that nothing would ever induce him to allow his daughter to wed a Mormon. Such a marriage he regarded as no marriage at all, but as a shame and a disgrace. Whatever he might think of the Mormon doctrines, upon that one point he was inflexible. He had to seal his mouth on the subject, however, for to express an unorthodox opinion was a dangerous matter in those days in the Land of the Saints.

Yes, a dangerous matter—so dangerous that even the most saintly dared only whisper their religious opinions with bated breath, lest something which fell from their lips might be misconstrued, and bring down a swift retribution upon them. The victims of persecution had now turned persecutors on their own account, and persecutors of the most terrible description. Not the Inquisition of Seville, nor the German Vehmgericht, nor the Secret Societies of Italy, were ever able to put a more formidable machinery in motion than that which cast a cloud over the State of Utah.

Its invisibility, and the mystery which was attached to it, made this organization doubly terrible. It appeared to be

165 *a sinister and an ill-omened one.* As Mr. Michael Harrison has pointed out (*In the Footsteps of Sherlock Holmes*), the British reading public of 1887 was quite willing to believe these slanders on the Mormons. Mid-Victorian England was convinced that the Mormons "stole English servant-girls, to spirit them out of the country and to make them White Slaves in a Mormon harem." "There were riots over the Mormons," Mr. Harrison wrote, "especially when the servant-girls [compared] their lot below-stairs with the prospects offered of life in a state which has never known unemployment . . ."

omniscient and omnipotent, and yet was neither seen nor heard. The man who held out against the Church vanished away, and none knew whither he had gone or what had befallen him. His wife and his children awaited him at home, but no father ever returned to tell them how he had fared at the hands of his secret judges. A rash word or a hasty act was followed by annihilation, and yet none knew what the nature might be of this terrible power which was suspended over them. No wonder that men went about in fear and trembling, and that even in the heart of the wilderness they dared not whisper the doubts which oppressed them.

At first this vague and terrible power was exercised only upon the recalcitrants who, having embraced the Mormon faith, wished afterwards to pervert or to abandon it. Soon, however, it took a wider range. The supply of adult women was running short, and polygamy without a female population on which to draw was a barren doctrine indeed. Strange rumours began to be bandied about—rumours of murdered immigrants and rifled camps in regions where Indians had never been seen. Fresh women appeared in the harems of the Elders—women who pined and wept, and bore upon their faces the traces of an unextinguishable horror. Belated wanderers upon the mountains spoke of gangs of armed men, masked, stealthy, and noiseless, who flitted by them in the darkness. These tales and rumours took substance and shape, and were corroborated and re-corroborated, until they resolved themselves into a definite name. To this day, in the lonely ranches of the West, the name of the Danite Band, or **165** the Avenging Angels, is a sinister and an ill-omened one.

Fuller knowledge of the organization which produced such terrible results served to increase rather than to lessen the horror which it inspired in the minds of men. None knew who belonged to this ruthless society. The names of the participators in the deeds of blood and violence done under the name of religion were kept profoundly secret. The very friend to whom you communicated your misgivings as to the Prophet and his mission might be one of those who would come forth at night with fire and sword to exact a terrible reparation. Hence every man feared his neighbour, and none spoke of the things which were nearest his heart.

One fine morning John Ferrier was about to set out to his wheat-fields, when he heard the click of the latch, and, looking through the window, saw a stout, sandy-haired middle-aged man coming up the pathway. His heart leapt to his mouth, for this was none other than the great Brigham Young himself. Full of trepidation—for he knew that such a visit boded him little good—Ferrier ran to the door to greet the Mormon chief. The latter, however, received his salutations coldly, and followed him with a stern face into the sitting-room.

'Brother Ferrier,' he said, taking a seat, and eyeing the farmer keenly from under his light-coloured eyelashes, 'the true believers have been good friends to you. We picked you up when you were starving in the desert, we shared our food with you, led you safe to the Chosen Valley, gave you a goodly share of land, and allowed you to wax rich under our protection. Is not this so?'

'It is so,' answered John Ferrier.

'In return for all this we asked but one condition: that was, that you should embrace the true faith, and conform in every way to its usages. This you promised to do, and this, if common report says truly, you have neglected.'

'And how have I neglected it?' asked Ferrier, throwing out his hands in expostulation. 'Have I not given to the common fund? Have I not attended at the Temple? Have I not——?'

'Where are your wives?' asked Young, looking round him. 'Call them in, that I may greet them.'

'It is true that I have not married,' Ferrier answered. 'But women were few, and there were many who had better claims than I. I was not a lonely man: I had my daughter to attend to my wants.'

'It is of that daughter that I would speak to you,' said the leader of the Mormons. 'She has grown to be the flower of Utah, and has found favour in the eyes of many who are high in the land.'

John Ferrier groaned internally.

'There are stories of her which I would fain disbelieve—stories that she is sealed to some Gentile. This must be the gossip of idle tongues.

'What is the thirteenth rule in the code of the sainted Joseph Smith? "Let every maiden of the true faith marry one of the elect; for if she wed a Gentile, she commits a grievous sin." This being so, it is impossible that you, who profess the holy creed, should suffer your daughter to violate it.'

John Ferrier made no answer, but he played nervously with his riding-whip.

'Upon this one point your whole faith shall be tested—so it has been decided in the Sacred Council of Four. The girl is young, and we would not have her wed grey hairs, neither would we deprive her of all choice. We Elders have many heifers, but our children must also be provided. Stangerson **166** has a son, and Drebber has a son, and either of them would gladly welcome your daughter to their house. Let her choose between them. They are young and rich, and of the true faith. What say you to that?'

Ferrier remained silent for some little time with his brows knitted.

'You will give us time,' he said at last. 'My daughter is very young—she is scarce of an age to marry.'

'She shall have a month to choose,' said Young, rising from his seat. 'At the end of that time she shall give her answer.'

He was passing through the door, when he turned, with flushed face and flashing eyes. 'It were better for you, John Ferrier,' he thundered, 'that you and she were now lying blanched skeletons upon the Sierra Blanco, than that you should put your weak wills against the orders of the Holy Four!'

With a threatening gesture of his hand, he turned from the door, and Ferrier heard his heavy steps scrunching along the shingly path.

He was still sitting with his elbow upon his knee, consider-

166 *We Elders have many heifers.* "Heber C. Kemball, in one of his sermons, alludes to his hundred wives under this endearing epithet," Conan Doyle noted here.

ing how he should broach the matter to his daughter, when a soft hand was laid upon his, and looking up, he saw her standing beside him. One glance at her pale, frightened face showed him that she had heard what had passed.

'I could not help it,' she said, in answer to his look. 'His voice rang through the house. Oh, father, father, what shall we do?'

'Don't you scare yourself,' he answered, drawing her to him, and passing his broad, rough hand caressingly over her chestnut hair. 'We'll fix it up somehow or another. You don't find your fancy kind o' lessening for this chap, do you?'

A sob and a squeeze of his hand was her only answer.

'No; of course not. I shouldn't care to hear you say you did. He's a likely lad, and he's a Christian, which is more than these folk here, in spite o' all their praying and preaching. There's a party starting for Nevada tomorrow, and I'll manage to send him a message letting him know the hole we are in. If I know anything o' that young man, he'll be back here with a speed that would whip electro-telegraphs.'

Lucy laughed through her tears at her father's description.

'When he comes, he will advise us for the best. But it is for you that I am frightened, dear. One hears—one hears such dreadful stories about those who oppose the Prophet: something terrible always happens to them.'

'But we haven't opposed him yet,' her father answered. 'It will be time to look out for squalls when we do. We have a clear month before us; at the end of that, I guess we had best shin out of Utah.'

'Leave Utah!'

'That's about the size of it.'

'But the farm?'

'We will raise as much as we can in money, and let the rest go. To tell the truth, Lucy, it isn't the first time I have thought of doing it. I don't care about knuckling under to any man, as these folk do to their darned Prophet. I'm a free-born American, and it's all new to me. Guess I'm too old to learn. If he comes browsing about this farm, he might chance to run up against a charge of buck-shot travelling in the opposite direction.'

'But they won't let us leave,' his daughter objected.

'Wait till Jefferson comes, and we'll soon manage that. In the meantime, don't you fret yourself, my dearie, and don't get your eyes swelled up, else he'll be walking into me when he sees you. There's nothing to be afeard about, and there's no danger at all.'

John Ferrier uttered these consoling remarks in a very confident tone, but she could not help observing that he paid unusual care to the fastening of the doors that night, and that he carefully cleaned and loaded the rusty old shot-gun which hung upon the wall of his bedroom.

II ◆ A FLIGHT FOR LIFE

On the morning which followed his interview with the Mormon Prophet, John Ferrier went in to Salt Lake City, and having found his acquaintance, who was bound for the Nevada Mountains, he entrusted him with his message to Jefferson Hope. In it he told the young man of the imminent danger which threatened them, and how necessary it was that he should return. Having done thus he felt easier in his mind, and returned home with a lighter heart.

As he approached his farm, he was surprised to see a horse hitched to each of the posts of the gate. Still more surprised was he on entering to find two young men in possession of his sitting-room. One, with a long, pale face, was leaning back in the rocking-chair, with his feet cocked up upon the stove. The other, a bull-necked youth with coarse, bloated features, was standing in front of the window with his hands in his pockets whistling a popular hymn. Both of them nodded to Ferrier as he entered, and the one in the rocking-chair commenced the conversation.

'Maybe you don't know us,' he said. 'This here is the son of Elder Drebber, and I'm Joseph Stangerson, who travelled with you in the desert when the Lord stretched out His hand and gathered you into the true fold.'

'As He will all the nations in His own good time,' said the other in a nasal voice; 'He grindeth slowly but exceeding small.'

John Ferrier bowed coldly. He had guessed who his visitors were.

'We have come,' continued Stangerson, 'at the advice of our fathers to solicit the hand of your daughter for whichever of us may seem good to you and to her. As I have but four wives and Brother Drebber here has seven, it appears to me that my claim is the stronger one.'

'Nay, nay, Brother Stangerson,' cried the other; 'the question is not how many wives we have, but how many we can keep. My father has now given over his mills to me, and I am the richer man.'

'But my prospects are better,' said the other, warmly. 'When the Lord removes my father, I shall have his tanning yard and his leather factory. Then I am your elder, and am higher in the Church.'

'It will be for the maiden to decide,' rejoined young Drebber, smirking at his own reflection in the glass. 'We will leave it all to her decision.'

During this dialogue John Ferrier had stood fuming in the doorway, hardly able to keep his riding-whip from the backs of his two visitors.

'Look here,' he said at last, striding up to them, 'when my daughter summons you, you can come, but until then I don't want to see your faces again.'

The two young Mormons stared at him in amazement. In their eyes this competition between them for the maiden's hand was the highest of honours both to her and her father.

'There are two ways out of the room,' cried Ferrier; 'there is the door, and there is the window. Which do you care to use?'

His brown face looked so savage, and his gaunt hands so

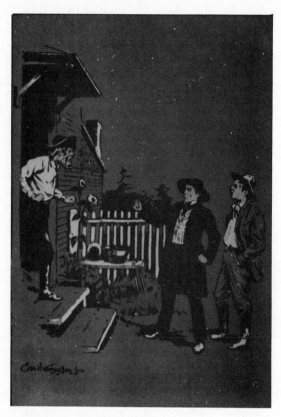

"YOU SHALL SMART FOR THIS!" STANGERSON CRIED,
WHITE WITH RAGE.

Illustration by George Hutchinson for *A Study in Scarlet*; London: Ward, Lock, Bowden & Co., 1891.

threatening, that his visitors sprang to their feet and beat a hurried retreat. The old farmer followed them to the door.

'Let me know when you have settled which it is to be,' he said, sardonically.

'You shall smart for this!' Stangerson cried, white with rage. 'You have defied the Prophet and the Council of Four. You shall rue it to the end of your days.'

'The hand of the Lord shall be heavy upon you,' cried young Drebber; 'He will arise and smite you!'

'Then I'll start the smiting,' exclaimed Ferrier, furiously, and would have rushed upstairs for his gun had not Lucy seized him by the arm and restrained him. Before he could escape from her, the clatter of horses' hoofs told him that they were beyond his reach.

'The young canting rascals!' he exclaimed, wiping the perspiration from his forehead; 'I would sooner see you in your grave, my girl, than the wife of either of them.'

'And so should I, father,' she answered, with spirit; 'but Jefferson will soon be here.'

'Yes. It will not be long before he comes. The sooner the better, for we do not know what their next move may be.'

It was, indeed, high time that someone capable of giving advice and help should come to the aid of the sturdy old farmer and his adopted daughter. In the whole history of the settlement there had never been such a case of rank disobedience to the authority of the Elders. If minor errors were punished so sternly, what would be the fate of this arch rebel. Ferrier knew that his wealth and position would be of no avail to him. Others as well known and as rich as himself had been spirited away before now, and their goods given over to the Church. He was a brave man, but he trembled at the vague, shadowy terrors which hung over him. Any known danger he could face with a firm lip, but this suspense was unnerving. He concealed his fears from his daughter, however, and affected to make light of the whole matter, though she, with the keen eye of love, saw plainly that he was ill at ease.

He expected that he would receive some message or remonstrance from Young as to his conduct, and he was not mistaken, though it came in an unlooked-for manner. Upon rising next morning he found, to his surprise, a small square of paper pinned on to the coverlet of his bed just over his chest. On it was printed in bold, straggling letters:

'Twenty-nine days are given you for amendment, and then——'

The dash was more fear-inspiring than any threat could have been. How this warning came into his room puzzled John Ferrier sorely, for his servants slept in an outhouse, and the doors and windows had all been secured. He crumpled the paper up and said nothing to his daughter, but the incident struck a chill into his heart. The twenty-nine days were evidently the balance of the month which Young had promised. What strength or courage could avail against an enemy armed with such mysterious powers? The hand which fastened that pin, might have struck him to the heart, and he could never have known who had slain him.

Still more shaken was he next morning. They had sat down to their breakfast, when Lucy with a cry of surprise pointed upwards. In the centre of the ceiling was scrawled, with a

burned stick apparently, the number 28. To his daughter it
was unintelligible, and he did not enlighten her. That night
he sat up with his gun and kept watch and ward. He saw and
he heard nothing, and yet in the morning a great 27 had been
painted upon the outside of his door.

Thus day followed day; and as sure as morning came he
found that his unseen enemies had kept their register, and
had marked up in some conspicuous position how many days
were still left to him out of the month of grace. Sometimes
the fatal numbers appeared upon the walls, sometimes upon
the floors, occasionally they were on small placards stuck upon
the garden gate or the railings. With all his vigilance John
Ferrier could not discover whence these daily warnings proceeded. A horror which was almost superstitious came upon
him at the sight of them. He became haggard and restless, and
his eyes had the troubled look of some hunted creature. He
had but one hope in life now, and that was for the arrival of
the young hunter from Nevada.

Twenty had changed to fifteen, and fifteen to ten, but
there was no news of the absentee. One by one the numbers
dwindled down, and still there came no sign of him. Whenever a horseman clattered down the road, or a driver shouted
at his team, the old farmer hurried to the gate, thinking that
help had arrived at last. At last, when he saw five give way to
four and that again to three, he lost heart, and abandoned all
hope of escape. Singlehanded, and with his limited knowledge of the mountains which surrounded the settlement, he
knew that he was powerless. The more-frequented roads were
strictly watched and guarded, and none could pass along
them without an order from the Council. Turn which way he
would, there appeared to be no avoiding the blow which hung
over him. Yet the old man never wavered in his resolution to
part with life itself before he consented to what he regarded
as his daughter's dishonour.

He was sitting alone one evening pondering deeply over
his troubles, and searching vainly for some way out of them.
That morning had shown the figure 2 upon the wall of his
house, and the next day would be the last of the allotted time.
What was to happen then? All manner of vague and terrible
fancies filled his imagination. And his daughter—what was
to become of her after he was gone? Was there no escape from
the invisible network which was drawn all round them? He
sank his head upon the table and sobbed at the thought of his
own impotence.

What was that? In the silence he heard a gentle scratching
sound—low, but very distinct in the quiet of the night. It
came from the door of the house. Ferrier crept out into the
hall and listened intently. There was a pause for a few
moments, and then the low, insidious sound was repeated.
Someone was evidently tapping very gently upon one of the
panels of the door. Was it some midnight assassin who had
come to carry out the murderous orders of the secret tribunal?
Or was it some agent who was marking up that the last day
of grace had arrived. John Ferrier felt that instant death
would be better than the suspense which shook his nerves and
chilled his heart. Springing forward, he drew the bolt and
threw the door open.

Outside all was calm and quiet. The night was fine, and
the stars were twinkling brightly overhead. The little front

garden lay before the farmer's eyes bounded by the fence and gate, but neither there nor on the road was any human being to be seen. With a sigh of relief Ferrier looked to right and to left, until, happening to glance straight down at his own feet, he saw to his astonishment a man lying flat upon his face upon the ground, with arms and legs all asprawl.

So unnerved was he at the sight that he leaned up against the wall with his hand to his throat to stifle his inclination to call out. His first thought was that the prostrate figure was that of some wounded or dying man, but as he watched it he saw it writhe along the ground and into the hall with the rapidity and noiselessness of a serpent. Once within the house the man sprang to his feet, closed the door, and revealed to the astonished farmer the fierce face and resolute expression of Jefferson Hope.

'Good God!' gasped John Ferrier. 'How you scared me. Whatever made you come in like that.'

'Give me food,' the other said, hoarsely. 'I have had no time for bit or sup for eight-and-forty hours.' He flung himself upon the cold meat and bread which were still lying upon the table from his host's supper, and devoured it voraciously. 'Does Lucy bear up well?' he asked, when he had satisfied his hunger.

'Yes. She does not know the danger,' her father answered.

'That is well. The house is watched on every side. That is why I crawled my way up to it. They may be darned sharp, but they're not quite sharp enough to catch a Washoe hunter.'

John Ferrier felt a different man now that he realized that he had a devoted ally. He seized the young man's leathery hand and wrung it cordially. 'You're a man to be proud of,' he said. 'There are not many who would come to share our danger and our troubles.'

'You've hit it there, pard,' the young hunter answered. 'I have a respect for you, but if you were alone in this business I'd think twice before I put my head into such a hornet's nest. It's Lucy that brings me here, and before harm comes on her I guess there will be one less o' the Hope family in Utah.'

'What are we to do?'

'Tomorrow is your last day, and unless you act tonight you are lost. I have a mule and two horses waiting in the Eagle Ravine. How much money have you?'

167 'Two thousand dollars in gold and five in notes.'

'That will do. I have as much more to add to it. We must push for Carson City through the mountains. You had best wake Lucy. It is as well that the servants do not sleep in the house.'

While Ferrier was absent, preparing his daughter for the approaching journey, Jefferson Hope packed all the eatables that he could find into a small parcel, and filled a stoneware jar with water, for he knew by experience that the mountain wells were few and far between. He had hardly completed his arrangements before the farmer returned with his daughter all dressed and ready for a start. The greeting between the lovers was warm, but brief, for minutes were precious, and there was much to be done.

'We must make our start at once,' said Jefferson Hope, speaking in a low but resolute voice, like one who realizes the greatness of the peril, but has steeled his heart to meet it. 'The

. . . AS HE WATCHED IT HE SAW IT WRITHE ALONG THE GROUND AND INTO THE HALL . . .

Illustration by D. H. Friston for *Beeton's Christmas Annual*, December, 1887. George Hutchinson illustrated much the same scene for the London, 1891, Ward, Lock, Bowden & Co. edition of *A Study in Scarlet*, and J. Watson Davis for *Tales of Sherlock Holmes*, published by A. L. Burt Company, New York, in 1906.

167 '*Two thousand dollars in gold and five in notes.*' Mr. A. Carson Simpson, in his study of *Numismatics in the Canon* (Part II: "A Very Treasury of Coin of Divers Realms") has conjectured that part of this hoard was made up of privately issued gold pieces—really tokens—used at that time in the Far West—coins often referred to as "pioneer" or "territorial" gold. Most of these were probably produced in California. Some would be undated, but most would bear dates from 1849 to 1855. The denominations were generally $5, $10, $20; Ferrier may also have had some of the large, showy $50 pieces. Almost certainly his hoard also included gold pieces struck by the Mormons themselves; they were first issued in 1849 in denominations of $2.50, $5, $10, and $20.

front and back entrances are watched, but with caution we may get away through the side window and across the fields. Once on the road we are only two miles from the Ravine where the horses are waiting. By daybreak we should be halfway through the mountains.'

'What if we are stopped?' asked Ferrier.

Hope slapped the revolver butt which protruded from the front of his tunic. 'If they are too many for us, we shall take two or three of them with us,' he said with a sinister smile.

The lights inside the house had all been extinguished, and from the darkened window Ferrier peered over the fields which had been his own, and which he was now about to abandon for ever. He had long nerved himself to the sacrifice, however, and the thought of the honour and happiness of his daughter outweighed any regret at his ruined fortunes. All looked so peaceful and happy, the rustling trees and the broad, silent stretch of grainland, that it was difficult to realize that the spirit of murder lurked through it all. Yet the white face and set expression of the young hunter showed that in his approach to the house he had seen enough to satisfy him upon that head.

Ferrier carried the bag of gold and notes, Jefferson Hope had the scanty provisions and water, while Lucy had a small bundle containing a few of her more valued possessions. Opening the window very slowly and carefully, they waited until a dark cloud had somewhat obscured the night, and then one by one passed through into the little garden. With bated breath and crouching figures they stumbled across it, and gained the shelter of the hedge, which they skirted until they came to the gap which opened into the cornfield. They had just reached this point when the young man seized his two companions and dragged them down into the shadow, where they lay silent and trembling.

It was as well that his prairie training had given Jefferson Hope the ears of a lynx. He and his friends had hardly crouched down before the melancholy hooting of a mountain owl was heard within a few yards of them, which was immediately answered by another hoot at a small distance. At the same moment a vague, shadowy figure emerged from the gap for which they had been making, and uttered the plaintive signal cry again, on which a second man appeared out of the obscurity.

'Tomorrow at midnight,' said the first, who appeared to be in authority. 'When the whip-poor-will calls three times.'

'It is well,' returned the other. 'Shall I tell Brother Drebber?'

'Pass it on to him, and from him to the others. Nine to seven!'

'Seven to five!' repeated the other; and the two figures flitted away in different directions. Their concluding words had evidently been some form of sign and countersign. The instant that their footsteps had died away in the distance, Jefferson Hope sprang to his feet, and helping his companions through the gap, led the way across the fields at the top of his speed, supporting and half-carrying the girl when her strength appeared to fail her.

'Hurry on! hurry on!' he gasped from time to time. 'We are through the line of sentinels. Everything depends on speed. Hurry on!'

Once on the high road, they made rapid progress. Only once did they meet anyone, and then they managed to slip into a field, and so avoid recognition. Before reaching the town the hunter branched away into a rugged and narrow footpath which led to the mountains. Two dark, jagged peaks loomed above them through the darkness, and the defile which led between them was the Eagle Cañon in which the horses were awaiting them. With unerring instinct Jefferson Hope picked his way among the great boulders and along the bed of a dried-up watercourse, until he came to the retired corner screened with rocks, where the faithful animals had been picketed. The girl was placed upon the mule, and old Ferrier upon one of the horses, with his money-bag, while Jefferson Hope led the other along the precipitous and dangerous path.

It was a bewildering route for anyone who was not accustomed to face Nature in her wildest moods. On the one side a great crag towered up a thousand feet or more, black, stern, and menacing, with long basaltic columns upon its rugged surface like the ribs of some petrified monster. On the other hand a wild chaos of boulders and debris made all advance impossible. Between the two ran the irregular track, so narrow in places that they had to travel in Indian file, and so rough that only practised riders could have traversed it at all. Yet, in spite of all dangers and difficulties, the hearts of the fugitives were light within them, for every step increased the distance between them and the terrible despotism from which they were flying.

They soon had a proof, however, that they were still within the jurisdiction of the Saints. They had reached the very wildest and most desolate portion of the pass when the girl gave a startled cry, and pointed upwards. On a rock which overlooked the track, showing out dark and plain against the sky, there stood a solitary sentinel. He saw them as soon as they perceived him, and his military challenge of 'Who goes there?' rang through the silent ravine.

'Travellers for Nevada,' said Jefferson Hope, with his hand upon the rifle which hung by his saddle.

They could see the lonely watcher fingering his gun, and peering down at them as if dissatisfied at their reply.

'By whose permission?' he asked.

'The Holy Four,' answered Ferrier. His Mormon experiences had taught him that that was the highest authority to which he could refer.

'Nine to seven,' cried the sentinel.

'Seven to five,' returned Jefferson Hope promptly, remembering the countersign which he had heard in the garden.

'Pass, and the Lord go with you,' said the voice from above. Beyond his post the path broadened out, and the horses were able to break into a trot. Looking back, they could see the solitary watcher leaning upon his gun, and knew that they had passed the outlying post of the Chosen People, and that freedom lay before them.

12 ◆ THE AVENGING ANGELS

All night their course lay through intricate defiles and over irregular and rock-strewn paths. More than once they lost their way, but Hope's intimate knowledge of the mountains enabled them to regain the track once more. When morning broke, a scene of marvellous though savage beauty lay before them. In every direction the great snow-capped peaks hemmed them in, peeping over each other's shoulders to the far horizon. So steep were the rocky banks on either side of them that the larch and the pine seemed to be suspended over their heads, and to need only a gust of wind to come hurtling down upon them. Nor was the fear entirely an illusion, for the barren valley was thickly strewn with trees and boulders which had fallen in a similar manner. Even as they passed a great rock came thundering down with a hoarse rattle which woke the echoes in the silent gorges, and startled the weary horses into a gallop.

As the sun rose slowly above the eastern horizon the caps of the great mountains lit up one after the other, like lamps at a festival, until they were all ruddy and glowing. The magnificent spectacle cheered the hearts of the three fugitives and gave them fresh energy. At a wild torrent which swept out of a ravine they called a halt and watered their horses, while they partook of a hasty breakfast. Lucy and her father would fain have rested longer, but Jefferson Hope was inexorable. 'They will be upon our track by this time,' he said. 'Everything depends upon our speed. Once safe in Carson, we may rest for the remainder of our lives.'

During the whole of that day they struggled on through the defiles, and by evening they calculated that they were more than thirty miles from their enemies. At night-time they chose the base of a beetling crag, where the rocks offered some protection from the chill wind, and there, huddled together for warmth, they enjoyed a few hours' sleep. Before daybreak, however, they were up and on their way once more. They had seen no signs of any pursuers, and Jefferson Hope began to think that they were fairly out of the reach of the terrible organization whose enmity they had incurred. He little knew how far that iron grasp could reach, or how soon it was to close upon them and crush them.

About the middle of the second day of their flight their scanty store of provisions began to run out. This gave the hunter little uneasiness, however, for there was game to be had among the mountains, and he had frequently before had to depend upon his rifle for the needs of life. Choosing a sheltered nook, he piled together a few dried branches and made a blazing fire, at which his companions might warm themselves, for they were now nearly five thousand feet above the sea level, and the air was bitter and keen. Having tethered the horses, and bade Lucy adieu, he threw his gun over his shoulder, and set out in search of whatever chance might throw in his way. Looking back, he saw the old man and the young girl crouching over the blazing fire, while the three animals stood motionless in the background. Then the intervening rocks hid them from his view.

He walked for a couple of miles through one ravine after another without success, though, from the marks upon the

168 *the moon had not yet risen*. The night, we shortly learn, was that of August 4, 1860. Commenting on Dr. Watson's recurring difficulties with the moon ("An Adventure in the Lower Criticism, Part II: Dr. Watson and the Moon"), the late Professor Jay Finley Christ noted that "When Hope returned to his camp, it was 'dark,' because 'the moon had not yet risen.' The moon had been full on August 1st; on the 4th, the sun set at 7:41 and the moon rose at 8:21 P. M. Twilight ended officially at 9:00 P. M., according to the *American Almanac*. Perhaps it *was* dark in the canyons."

THE INSCRIPTION UPON THE PAPER WAS BRIEF, BUT TO THE POINT . . .

Illustration by George Hutchinson for *A Study in Scarlet*, London: Ward, Lock, Bowden & Co., 1891.

bark of the trees, and other indications, he judged that there were numerous bears in the vicinity. At last, after two or three hours' fruitless search, he was thinking of turning back in despair, when casting his eyes upwards he saw a sight which sent a thrill of pleasure through his heart. On the edge of a jutting pinnacle, three or four hundred feet above him, there stood a creature somewhat resembling a sheep in appearance, but armed with a pair of gigantic horns. The big-horn—for so it is called—was acting, probably, as a guardian over a flock which were invisible to the hunter; but fortunately it was heading in the opposite direction, and had not perceived him. Lying on his face, he rested his rifle upon a rock, and took a long and steady aim before drawing the trigger. The animal sprang into the air, tottered for a moment upon the edge of the precipice, and then came crashing down into the valley beneath.

The creature was too unwieldy to lift, so the hunter contented himself with cutting away one haunch and part of the flank. With this trophy over his shoulder, he hastened to retrace his steps, for the evening was already drawing in. He had hardly started, however, before he realized the difficulty which faced him. In his eagerness he had wandered far past the ravines which were known to him, and it was no easy matter to pick out the path which he had taken. The valley in which he found himself divided and subdivided into many gorges, which were so like each other that it was impossible to distinguish one from the other. He followed one for a mile or more until he came to a mountain torrent which he was sure that he had never seen before. Convinced that he had taken the wrong turn, he tried another, but with the same result. Night was coming on rapidly, and it was almost dark before he at last found himself in a defile which was familiar to him. Even then it was no easy matter to keep to the right track, for **168** the moon had not yet risen, and the high cliffs on either side made the obscurity more profound. Weighed down with his burden, and weary from his exertions, he stumbled along, keeping up his heart by the reflection that every step brought him nearer to Lucy, and that he carried with him enough to ensure them food for the remainder of their journey.

He had now come to the mouth of the very defile in which he had left them. Even in the darkness he could recognize the outline of the cliffs which bounded it. They must, he reflected, be awaiting him anxiously, for he had been absent nearly five hours. In the gladness of his heart he put his hands to his mouth and made the glen re-echo to a loud halloo as a signal that he was coming. He paused and listened for an answer. None came save his own cry, which clattered up the dreary, silent ravines, and was borne back to his ears in countless repetitions. Again he shouted, even louder than before, and again no whisper came back from the friends whom he had left such a short time ago. A vague, nameless dread came over him, and he hurried onwards frantically, dropping the precious food in his agitation.

When he turned the corner, he came full in sight of the spot where the fire had been lit. There was still a glowing pile of wood ashes there, but it had evidently not been tended since his departure. The same dead silence still reigned all round. With his fears all changed to convictions, he hurried on. There was no living creature near the remains of the fire:

animals, man, maiden, all were gone. It was only too clear
that some sudden and terrible disaster had occurred during
his absence—a disaster which had embraced them all, and
yet had left no traces behind it.

Bewildered and stunned by this blow, Jefferson Hope felt
his head spin round, and had to lean upon his rifle to save
himself from falling. He was essentially a man of action, however, and speedily recovered from his temporary impotence.
Seizing a half-consumed piece of wood from the smouldering
fire, he blew it into a flame, and proceeded with its help to
examine the little camp. The ground was all stamped down
by the feet of horses, showing that a large party of mounted
men had overtaken the fugitives, and the direction of their
tracks proved that they had afterwards turned back to Salt
Lake City. Had they carried back both of his companions with
them? Jefferson Hope had almost persuaded himself that they
must have done so, when his eye fell upon an object which
made every nerve of his body tingle within him. A little way
on one side of the camp was a low-lying heap of reddish soil,
which had assuredly not been there before. There was no mis-
taking it for anything but a newly dug grave. As the young
hunter approached it, he perceived that a stick had been
planted on it, with a sheet of paper stuck in the cleft fork of
it. The inscription upon the paper was brief, but to the point:

JOHN FERRIER,

FORMERLY OF SALT LAKE CITY.

Died August 4th, 1860.

The sturdy old man, whom he had left so short a time before,
was gone, then, and this was all his epitaph. Jefferson Hope
looked wildly round to see if there was a second grave, but
there was no sign of one. Lucy had been carried back by their
terrible pursuers to fulfil her original destiny, by becoming
one of the harem of the Elder's son. As the young fellow
realized the certainty of her fate, and his own powerlessness
to prevent it, he wished that he, too, was lying with the old
farmer in his last silent resting-place.

Again, however, his active spirit shook off the lethargy
which springs from despair. If there was nothing else left
to him, he could at least devote his life to revenge. With
indomitable patience and perseverance, Jefferson Hope possessed also a power of sustained vindictiveness, which he may
have learned from the Indians amongst whom he had lived.
As he stood by the desolate fire, he felt that the only one
thing which could assuage his grief would be thorough and
complete retribution, brought by his own hand upon his
enemies. His strong will and untiring energy should, he determined, be devoted to that one end. With a grim, white face,
he retraced his steps to where he had dropped the food, and
having stirred up the smouldering fire, he cooked enough to
last him for a few days. This he made up into a bundle, and,
tired as he was, he set himself to walk back through the mountains upon the track of the Avenging Angels.

For five days he toiled footsore and weary through the
defiles which he had already traversed on horseback. At night
he flung himself down among the rocks, and snatched a few
hours of sleep; but before daybreak he was always well on his

way. On the sixth day, he reached the Eagle Cañon, from which they had commenced their ill-fated flight. Thence he could look down upon the home of the Saints. Worn and exhausted, he leaned upon his rifle and shook his gaunt hand fiercely at the silent, widespread city beneath him. As he looked at it, he observed that there were flags in some of the principal streets, and other signs of festivity. He was still speculating as to what this might mean when he heard the clatter of horses' hoofs, and saw a mounted man riding towards him. As he approached, he recognized him as a Mormon named Cowper, to whom he had rendered services at different times. He therefore accosted him when he got up to him, with the object of finding out what Lucy Ferrier's fate had been.

'I am Jefferson Hope,' he said. 'You remember me.'

The Mormon looked at him with undisguised astonishment—indeed, it was difficult to recognize in this tattered, unkempt wanderer, with ghastly white face and fierce, wild eyes, the spruce young hunter of former days. Having, however, at last satisfied himself as to his identity, the man's surprise changed to consternation.

'You are mad to come here,' he cried. 'It is as much as my own life is worth to be seen talking with you. There is a warrant against you from the Holy Four for assisting the Ferriers away.'

'I don't fear them, or their warrant,' Hope said, earnestly. 'You must know something of this matter, Cowper. I conjure you by everything you hold dear to answer a few questions. We have always been friends. For God's sake, don't refuse to answer me.'

'What is it?' the Mormon asked uneasily. 'Be quick. The very rocks have ears and the trees eyes.'

'What has become of Lucy Ferrier?'

'She was married yesterday to young Drebber. Hold up, man, hold up; you have no life left in you.'

'Don't mind me,' said Hope faintly. He was white to the very lips, and had sunk down on the stone against which he had been leaning. 'Married you say?'

'Married yesterday—that's what those flags are for on the Endowment House. There was some words between young Drebber and young Stangerson as to which was to have her. They'd both been in the party that followed them, and Stangerson had shot her father, which seemed to give him the best claim; but when they argued it out in council, Drebber's party was the stronger, so the Prophet gave her over to him. No one won't have her very long though, for I saw death in her face yesterday. She is more like a ghost than a woman. Are you off, then?'

'Yes, I am off,' said Jefferson Hope, who had risen from his seat. His face might have been chiselled out of marble, so hard and set was its expression, while its eyes glowed with a baleful light.

'Where are you going?'

'Never mind,' he answered; and, slinging his weapon over his shoulder, strode off down the gorge and so away into the heart of the mountains to the haunts of the wild beasts. Amongst them all there was none so fierce and so dangerous as himself.

The prediction of the Mormon was only too well fulfilled.

Whether it was the terrible death of her father or the effects of the hateful marriage into which she had been forced, poor Lucy never held up her head again, but pined away and died within a month. Her sottish husband, who had married her principally for the sake of John Ferrier's property, did not affect any great grief at his bereavement; but his other wives mourned over her, and sat up with her the night before the burial, as is the Mormon custom. They were grouped round the bier in the early hours of the morning, when, to their inexpressible fear and astonishment, the door was flung open, and a savage-looking, weather-beaten man in tattered garments strode into the room. Without a glance or a word to the cowering women, he walked up to the white, silent figure which had once contained the pure soul of Lucy Ferrier. Stooping over her, he pressed his lips reverently to her cold forehead, and then, snatching up her hand, he took the wedding-ring from her finger. 'She shall not be buried in that,' he cried with a fierce snarl, and before an alarm could be raised sprang down the stairs and was gone. So strange and so brief was the episode that the watchers might have found it hard to believe it themselves or persuade other people of it, had it not been for the undeniable fact that the circlet of gold which marked her as having been a bride had disappeared.

For some months Jefferson Hope lingered among the mountains, leading a strange, wild life, and nursing in his heart the fierce desire for vengeance which possessed him. Tales were told in the city of the weird figure which was seen prowling about the suburbs, and which haunted the lonely mountain gorges. Once a bullet whistled through Stangerson's window and flattened itself upon the wall within a foot of him. On another occasion, as Drebber passed under a cliff a great boulder crashed down on him, and he only escaped a terrible death by throwing himself upon his face. The two young Mormons were not long in discovering the reason of these attempts upon their lives and led repeated expeditions into the mountains in the hope of capturing or killing their enemy, but always without success. Then they adopted the precaution of never going out alone or after nightfall, and of having their houses guarded. After a time they were able to relax these measures, for nothing was either heard or seen of their opponent, and they hoped that time had cooled his vindictiveness.

Far from doing so, it had, if anything, augmented it. The hunter's mind was of a hard, unyielding nature, and the predominant idea of revenge had taken such complete possession of it that there was no room for any other emotion. He was, however, above all things, practical. He soon realized that even his iron constitution could not stand the incessant strain which he was putting upon it. Exposure and want of wholesome food were wearing him out. If he died like a dog among the mountains, what was to become of his revenge then? And yet such a death was sure to overtake him if he persisted. He felt that that was to play his enemy's game, so he reluctantly returned to the old Nevada mines, there to recruit his health and to amass money enough to allow him to pursue his object without privation.

His intention had been to be absent a year at the most, but a combination of unforeseen circumstances prevented his leaving the mines for nearly five. At the end of that time, however, his memory of his wrongs and his craving for revenge were quite as keen as on that memorable night when he had stood by John Ferrier's grave. Disguised, and under an assumed name, he returned to Salt Lake City, careless what became of his own life as long as he obtained what he knew to be justice. There he found evil tidings awaiting him. There had been a schism among the Chosen People a few months before, some of the younger members of the Church having rebelled against the authority of the Elders, and the result had been the secession of a certain number of the malcontents, who had left Utah and become Gentiles. Among these had been Drebber and Stangerson; and no one knew whither they had gone. Rumour reported that Drebber had managed to convert a large part of his property into money, and that he had departed a wealthy man, while his companion, Stangerson, was comparatively poor. There was no clue at all, however, as to their whereabouts.

Many a man, however vindictive, would have abandoned all thought of revenge in the face of such a difficulty, but Jefferson Hope never faltered for a moment. With the small competence he possessed, eked out by such employment as he could pick up, he travelled from town to town through the United States in quest of his enemies. Year passed into year, his black hair turned grizzled, but still he wandered on, a human bloodhound, with his mind wholly set upon the one object to which he had devoted his life. At last his perseverance was rewarded. It was but a glance of a face in a window, but that one glance told him that Cleveland in Ohio possessed the men whom he was in pursuit of. He returned to his miserable lodgings with his plan of vengeance all arranged. It chanced, however, that Drebber, looking from his window, had recognized the vagrant in the street, and had read murder in his eyes. He hurried before a justice of the peace, accompanied by Stangerson, who had become his private secretary, and represented to him that they were in danger of their lives from the jealousy and hatred of an old rival. That evening Jefferson Hope was taken into custody, and not being able to find sureties, was detained for some weeks. When at last he was liberated it was only to find that Drebber's house was deserted, and that he and his secretary had departed for Europe.

Again the avenger had been foiled, and again his concentrated hatred urged him to continue the pursuit. Funds were wanting, however, and for some time he had to return to work, saving every dollar for his approaching journey. At last, having collected enough to keep life in him, he departed for Europe, and tracked his enemies from city to city, working his way in any menial capacity, but never overtaking the fugitives. When he reached St Petersburg, they had departed for Paris; and when he followed them there, he learned that they had just set off for Copenhagen. At the Danish capital he was again a few days late, for they had journeyed on to London, where he at last succeeded in running them to earth. As to what occurred there, we cannot do better than quote the old hunter's own account, as duly recorded in Dr Watson's Journal, to which we are already under such obligations.

13 : A CONTINUATION OF THE
     : REMINISCENCES OF JOHN WATSON, M.D.

Our prisoner's furious resistance did not apparently indicate any ferocity in his disposition towards ourselves, for on finding himself powerless, he smiled in an affable manner, and expressed his hopes that he had not hurt any of us in the scuffle. 'I guess you're going to take me to the police station,' he remarked to Sherlock Holmes. 'My cab's at the door. If you'll loose my legs I'll walk down to it. I'm not so light to lift as I used to be.'

Gregson and Lestrade exchanged glances, as if they thought this proposition rather a bold one; but Holmes at once took the prisoner at his word, and loosened the towel which we had bound round his ankles. He rose and stretched his legs, as though to assure himself that they were free once more. I remember that I thought to myself, as I eyed him, that I had seldom seen a more powerfully built man; and his dark, sunburned face bore an expression of determination and energy which was as formidable as his personal strength.

'If there's a vacant place for a chief of the police, I reckon you are the man for it,' he said, gazing with undisguised admiration at my fellow-lodger. 'The way you kept on my trail was a caution.'

'You had better come with me,' said Holmes to the two detectives.

'I can drive you,' said Lestrade.

'Good! and Gregson can come inside with me. You, too, Doctor. You have taken an interest in the case, and may as well stick to us.'

I assented gladly, and we all descended together. Our prisoner made no attempt at escape, but stepped calmly into the cab which had been his, and we followed him. Lestrade mounted the box, whipped up the horse, and brought us in a very short time to our destination. We were ushered into a small chamber, where a police inspector noted down our prisoner's name and the names of the men with whose murder he had been charged. The official was a white-faced, unemotional man, who went through his duties in a dull, mechanical way. 'The prisoner will be put before the magistrates in the course of the week,' he said; 'in the meantime, Mr Jefferson Hope, have you anything that you wish to say? I must warn you that your words will be taken down, and may be used against you.'

'I've got a good deal to say,' our prisoner said slowly. 'I want to tell you gentlemen all about it.'

'Hadn't you better reserve that for your trial?' asked the inspector.

'I may never be tried,' he answered. 'You needn't look startled. It isn't suicide I am thinking of. Are you a doctor?' He turned his fierce, dark eyes upon me as he asked this last question.

'Yes, I am,' I answered.

'Then put your hand here,' he said, with a smile, motioning with his manacled wrists towards his chest.

I did so; and became at once conscious of an extraordinary throbbing and commotion which was going on inside. The walls of his chest seemed to thrill and quiver as a frail build-

169 *a dull humming and buzzing noise.* "Objections have been made to [Watson's] description of Jefferson Hope's aortic aneurism as being somewhat too sensational," Miss Helen Simpson wrote in "Medical Career and Capacities of Dr. J. H. Watson." "But it must be remembered that Watson was speaking as a doctor, to whom the implications of any considerable variation from the normal heartbeat were at once apparent; [his] phrases therefore must not be taken as his impression of actual sounds, but of sounds whose significance as danger signals he could only convey by some exaggeration in speech."

170 *over-exposure and under-feeding.* Watson's "discretion veils the fact that this kind of aneurism is generally a consequence of syphilis," Miss Simpson wrote. The late Dr. Ernest Bloomfield Zeisler concurred: "Though under-feeding had nothing to do with it, over-exposure most certainly did, namely over-exposure to the spirochete, though this is not what [Hope] meant to imply. Watson, however, was a well-trained physician and certainly knew what every junior medical student knew, namely that except in very rare cases when it is due to trauma—which was not involved here—aneurysm of the thoracic area is always due to syphilis."

ing would do inside when some powerful engine was at work. In the silence of the room I could hear a dull humming and
169 buzzing noise which proceeded from the same source.

'Why,' I cried, 'you have an aortic aneurism!'

'That's what they call it,' he said, placidly. 'I went to a doctor last week about it, and he told me that it is bound to burst before many days passed. It has been getting worse for
170 years. I got it from over-exposure and under-feeding among the Salt Lake Mountains. I've done my work now, and I don't care how soon I go, but I should like to leave some account of the business behind me. I don't want to be remembered as a common cut-throat.'

The inspector and the two detectives had a hurried discussion as to the advisability of allowing him to tell his story.

'Do you consider, Doctor, that there is immediate danger?' the former asked.

'Most certainly there is,' I answered.

'In that case it is clearly our duty, in the interests of justice, to take his statement,' said the inspector. 'You are at liberty, sir, to give your account, which I again warn you will be taken down.'

'I'll sit down, with your leave,' the prisoner said, suiting the action to the word. 'This aneurism of mine makes me easily tired, and the tussle we had half an hour ago has not mended matters. I'm on the brink of the grave, and I am not likely to lie to you. Every word I say is the absolute truth, and how you use it is a matter of no consequence to me.'

With these words, Jefferson Hope leaned back in his chair and began the following remarkable statement. He spoke in a calm and methodical manner, as though the events which he narrated were commonplace enough. I can vouch for the accuracy of the subjoined account, for I have had access to Lestrade's note-book, in which the prisoner's words were taken down exactly as they were uttered.

'It don't much matter to you why I hated these men,' he said; 'it's enough that they were guilty of the death of two human beings—a father and a daughter—and that they had, therefore, forfeited their own lives. After the lapse of time that has passed since their crime, it was impossible for me to secure a conviction against them in any court. I knew of their guilt, though, and I determined that I should be judge, jury and executioner all rolled into one. You'd have done the same, if you have any manhood in you, if you had been in my place.

'That girl that I spoke of was to have married me twenty years ago. She was forced into marrying that same Drebber, and broke her heart over it. I took the marriage ring from her dead finger, and I vowed that his dying eyes should rest upon that very ring, and that his last thoughts should be of the crime for which he was punished. I have carried it about with me, and have followed him and his accomplice over two continents until I caught them. They thought to tire me out, but they could not do it. If I die tomorrow, as is likely enough, I die knowing that my work in this world is done, and well done. They have perished, and by my hand. There is nothing left for me to hope for, or to desire.

'They were rich and I was poor, so that it was no easy matter for me to follow them. When I got to London my pocket was about empty, and I found that I must turn my hand to something for my living. Driving and riding are as natural to me as walking, so I applied at a cab-owner's office, and soon got employment. I was to bring a certain sum a week to the owner, and whatever was over that I might keep for myself. There was seldom much over, but I managed to scrape along somehow. The hardest job was to learn my way about, for I reckon that of all the mazes that ever were contrived, this city is the most confusing. I had a map beside me, though, and when once I had spotted the principal hotels and stations, I got on pretty well.

'It was some time before I found out where my two gentlemen were living; but I inquired and inquired until at last I dropped across them. They were at a boarding-house at Camberwell, over on the other side of the river. When once I found them out, I knew that I had them at my mercy. I had grown my beard, and there was no chance of their recognizing me. I would dog them and follow them until I saw my opportunity. I was determined that they should not escape me again.

'They were very near doing it for all that. Go where they would about London, I was always at their heels. Sometimes I followed them on my cab, and sometimes on foot, but the former was the best, for then they could not get away from me. It was only early in the morning or late at night that I could earn anything, so that I began to get behindhand with my employer. I did not mind that, however, as long as I could lay my hand upon the men I wanted.

'They were very cunning, though. They must have thought that there was some chance of their being followed, for they would never go out alone, and never after nightfall. During two weeks I drove behind them every day, and never once saw them separate. Drebber himself was drunk half the time, but Stangerson was not to be caught napping. I watched them late and early, but never saw the ghost of a chance; but I was not discouraged, for something told me that the hour had almost come. My only fear was that this thing in my chest might burst a little too soon and leave my work undone.

'At last, one evening I was driving up and down Torquay Terrace, as the street was called in which they boarded, when I saw a cab drive up to their door. Presently some luggage was brought out and after a time Drebber and Stangerson followed it, and drove off. I whipped up my horse and kept within sight of them, feeling very ill at ease, for I feared that they were going to shift their quarters. At Euston Station they got out, and I left a boy to hold my horse and followed them on to the platform. I heard them ask for the Liverpool train, and the guard answer that one had just gone, and there would not be another for some hours. Stangerson seemed to be put out at that, but Drebber was rather pleased than otherwise. I got so close to them in the bustle that I could hear every word that passed between them. Drebber said that he had a little business of his own to do, and that if the other would wait for him he would soon rejoin him. His companion remonstrated with him, and reminded him that they had resolved to stick together. Drebber answered that the matter was a delicate one, and that he must go alone. I could not catch what Stangerson said to that, but the other burst out swearing, and reminded him that he was nothing more than his paid servant, and that he must not presume to dictate to him.

171 *Waterloo Bridge.* Waterloo Bridge, first called Strand Bridge, was "the noble work of George Rennie, built 1811–1817 and opened on the second anniversary of the Battle of Waterloo," Augustus J. C. Hare wrote in *Walks in London*, Vol. I. "It is built of granite, and has nine arches, one hundred and twenty inches span and thirty-five high. Canova considered it 'the noblest bridge in the world—worth a visit from the remotest corners of the earth'; and Dupin describes it as 'a colossal monument worthy of Sesostris and the Caesars.'" The bridge of today is not the bridge that Holmes and Watson knew; in 1924, it was reported that one of the main arches had become weakened, and work on the present bridge began in 1937; on May 4, 1939, the cornerstone was laid.

172 *My mouth gets dry with the talking.'* Wrote Dr. Vernon Pennell in his "Resumé of the Medical Life of John H. Watson, M.D., Late of the Army Medical Department": "Although the criminal had just engaged in a battle royal with Holmes, Gregson, Lestrade and Watson himself, and had all but defeated them in his efforts to escape; though his wrists, hands and face were severely cut, the loss of blood heavy, and half strangled by Lestrade, he suffered no shortness of breath or other distress and only complained of a dryness of the throat after talking, which called for a glass of water. Indeed the only people short of breath were his captors who 'rose to their feet breathless and panting.' As Watson pronounced him *in extremis* and likely to die at any moment, one wonders why the violent struggle had not already precipitated the aneurismal burst which took place later in the comparative quietude of the prison cell, the night after his capture."

On that the secretary gave it up as a bad job, and simply bargained with him that if he missed the last train he should rejoin him at Halliday's Private Hotel; to which Drebber answered that he would be back on the platform before eleven, and made his way out of the station.

'The moment for which I had waited so long had at last come. I had my enemies within my power. Together they could protect each other, but singly they were at my mercy. I did not act, however, with undue precipitation. My plans were already formed. There is no satisfaction in vengeance unless the offender has time to realize who it is that strikes him, and why retribution has come upon him. I had my plans arranged by which I should have the opportunity of making the man who had wronged me understand that his old sin had found him out. It chanced that some days before a gentleman who had been engaged in looking over some houses in the Brixton Road had dropped the key of one of them in my carriage. It was claimed that same evening, and returned; but in the interval I had taken a moulding of it, and had a duplicate constructed. By means of this I had access to at least one spot in this great city where I could rely upon being free from interruption. How to get Drebber to that house was the difficult problem which I had now to solve.

'He walked down the road and went into one or two liquor shops, staying for nearly half an hour in the last of them. When he came out, he staggered in his walk, and was evidently pretty well on. There was a hansom just in front of me, and he hailed it. I followed it so close that the nose of my horse was within a yard of his driver the whole way. We rattled **171** across Waterloo Bridge and through miles of streets, until, to my astonishment, we found ourselves back in the terrace in which he had boarded. I could not imagine what his intention was in returning there; but I went on and pulled up my cab a hundred yards or so from the house. He entered it, and his hansom drove away. Give me a glass of water, if you **172** please. My mouth gets dry with the talking.'

I handed him the glass, and he drank it down.

'That's better,' he said. 'Well, I waited for a quarter of an hour, or more, when suddenly there came a noise like people struggling inside the house. Next moment the door was flung open and two men appeared, one of whom was Drebber, and the other was a young chap whom I had never seen before. This fellow had Drebber by the collar, and when they came to the head of the steps he gave him a shove and a kick which sent him half across the road. "You hound!" he cried, shaking his stick at him; "I'll teach you to insult an honest girl!" He was so hot that I think he would have thrashed Drebber with his cudgel, only that the cur staggered away down the road as fast as his legs would carry him. He ran as far as the corner, and then, seeing my cab, he hailed me and jumped in. "Drive me to Halliday's Private Hotel," said he.

'When I had him fairly inside my cab, my heart jumped so with joy that I feared lest at this last moment my aneurism might go wrong. I drove along slowly, weighing in my own mind what it was best to do. I might take him right out into the country, and there in some deserted lane have my last interview with him. I had almost decided upon this, when he solved the problem for me. The craze for drink had seized him again, and he ordered me to pull up outside a gin palace. He went in, leaving word that I should wait for him. There he remained until closing time, and when he came out he was so far gone that I knew the game was in my own hands.

'Don't imagine that I intended to kill him in cold blood. It would only have been rigid justice if I had done so, but I could not bring myself to do it. I had long determined that he should have a show for his life if he chose to take advantage of it. Among the many billets which I have filled in America during my wandering life, I was once janitor and sweeper-out of the laboratory at York College. One day the professor was **173** lecturing on poisons, and he showed his students some alkaloid, as he called it, which he had extracted from some South American arrow poison, and which was so powerful that the **174** least grain meant instant death. I spotted the bottle in which this preparation was kept, and when they were all gone, I helped myself to a little of it. I was a fairly good dispenser, so I worked this alkaloid into small, soluble pills, and each pill I put in a box with a similar pill made without the poison. I determined at the time that when I had my chance my gentlemen should each have a draw out of one of these boxes, while I ate the pill that remained. It would be quite as deadly and a good deal less noisy than firing across a handkerchief. From that day I had always my pill boxes about with me, and the time had now come when I was to use them.

'It was nearer one than twelve, and a wild, bleak night, blowing hard and raining in torrents. Dismal as it was outside, I was glad within—so glad that I could have shouted out from pure exultation. If any of you gentlemen have ever pined for a thing, and longed for it during twenty long years, and then suddenly found it within your reach, you would understand my feelings. I lit a cigar, and puffed at it to steady my nerves, but my hands were trembling and my temples throbbing with excitement. As I drove, I could see old John Ferrier and sweet Lucy looking at me out of the darkness and smiling at me, just as plain as I see you all in this room. All the way they were ahead of me, one on each side of the horse, until I pulled up at the house in the Brixton Road.

'There was not a soul to be seen, nor a sound to be heard, except the dripping of the rain. When I looked in at the window, I found Drebber all huddled together in a drunken sleep. I shook him by the arm. "It's time to get out," I said.

' "All right, cabby," said he.

'I suppose he thought we had come to the hotel that he had mentioned, for he got out without another word, and followed me down the garden. I had to walk beside him to keep him steady, for he was still a little top-heavy. When we came to the door, I opened it, and led him into the front room. I give you my word that all the way, the father and the daughter were walking in front of us.

' "It's infernally dark," said he, stamping about.

' "We'll soon have a light," I said, striking a match and putting it to a wax candle which I had brought with me. "Now, Enoch Drebber," I continued, turning to him, and holding the light to my own face, "who am I?"

'He gazed at me with bleared, drunken eyes for a moment, and then I saw horror spring up in them, and convulse his whole features, which showed me that he knew me. He staggered back with a livid face, and I saw the perspiration break out upon his brow, while his teeth chattered in his head. At

173 *York College.* There is a York College in Nebraska, but it was not founded until 1890. Hope probably meant the old medical college of New York University.

174 *some South American arrow poison.* Hope presumably thought that he was using curare. But Mr. J. Raymond Hendrickson has written ("De Re Pharmaca") that "the alkaloid employed by Hope could have been what he believed it to be is denied by every detail of Drebber's *ante-mortem* and *post-mortem* appearance . . ." He suggests that the poison which killed Drebber was nicotine.

On the other hand, F. A. Allen, M.P.S., has written ("Devilish Drugs," Part I) that the poison "was evidently one of the erythrina alkaloids. . . . Let us suggest that an odorous and more potent alkaloid than . . . erythroidine, from the seeds of *E. corraloides*, awaits discovery by the explorer."

Again, Dr. George B. Koelle has written ("The Poisons of the Canon") that Hope must have confused a "South American arrow poison" with a "South African ordeal poison"—physostigmine or eserine. "This is highly potent, readily absorbed when taken by mouth, and the victim remains conscious nearly to the time of death; all these facts are consistent with Hope's account and Holmes' deductions."

HE COWERED AWAY WITH WILD CRIES AND PRAYERS
FOR MERCY . . .

Illustration by George Hutchinson for *A Study in
Scarlet*, London: Ward, Lock, Bowden & Co., 1891.
The scene is a favorite with Canonical artists:
Arthur Twidle chose it for the single illustration
he made for *A Study in Scarlet* for the "Author's
Edition" published by John Murray, London, in
1903. Of Twidle's work the late James Montgomery wrote (*A Study in Pictures*): "Here at
last one finds art work on a par with the story.
. . . A superbly menacing Hope, with drawn dagger and pill box thrust forward toward the cringing Mormon, makes us fairly creep with horror at
the awful retribution about to be exacted in the
dilapidated room of the deserted house." J. Watson Davis later (1906) illustrated the same scene
for the A. L. Burt Company's edition of *Tales of
Sherlock Holmes*.

the sight I leaned my back against the door and laughed loud
and long. I had always known that vengeance would be sweet,
but I had never hoped for the contentment of soul which now
possessed me.

' "You dog!" I said; "I have hunted you from Salt Lake City
to St Petersburg, and you have always escaped me. Now, at
last, your wanderings have come to an end, for either you
or I shall never see tomorrow's sun rise." He shrank still
farther away as I spoke, and I could see on his face that he
thought I was mad. So I was for the time. The pulses in my
temples beat like sledge-hammers, and I believe I would have
had a fit of some sort if the blood had not gushed from my
nose and relieved me.

' "What do you think of Lucy Ferrier now?" I cried, locking the door, and shaking the key in his face. "Punishment has
been slow in coming, but it has overtaken you at last." I saw
his coward lips tremble as I spoke. He would have begged for
his life, but he knew well that it was useless.

' "Would you murder me?" he stammered.

' "There is no murder," I answered. "Who talks of murdering a mad dog? What mercy had you upon my poor darling,
when you dragged her from her slaughtered father, and bore
her away to your accursed and shameless harem."

' "It was not I who killed her father," he cried.

' "But it was you who broke her innocent heart," I shrieked,
thrusting the box before him. "Let the high God judge between us. Choose and eat. There is death in one and life in
the other. I shall take what you leave. Let us see if there is
justice upon the earth, or if we are ruled by chance."

'He cowered away with wild cries and prayers for mercy,
but I drew my knife and held it to his throat until he had
obeyed me. Then I swallowed the other, and we stood facing
one another in silence for a minute or more, waiting to see
which was to live and which was to die. Shall I ever forget the
look which came over his face when the first warning pangs
told him that the poison was in his system? I laughed as I saw
it, and held Lucy's marriage ring in front of his eyes. It was
but for a moment, for the action of the alkaloid is rapid. A
spasm of pain contorted his features; he threw his hands out
in front of him, staggered, and then, with a hoarse cry, fell
heavily upon the floor. I turned him over with my foot, and
placed my hand upon his heart. There was no movement. He
was dead!

'The blood had been streaming from my nose, but I had
taken no notice of it. I don't know what it was that put it into
my head to write upon the wall with it. Perhaps it was some
mischievous idea of setting the police upon a wrong track, for
I felt light-hearted and cheerful. I remembered a German
being found in New York with RACHE written up above
him, and it was argued at the time in the newspapers that the
secret societies must have done it. I guessed that what puzzled
the New Yorkers would puzzle the Londoners, so I dipped my
finger in my own blood and printed it on a convenient place
on the wall. Then I walked down to my cab and found that
there was nobody about, and that the night was still very wild.
I had driven some distance when I put my hand into the
pocket in which I usually kept Lucy's ring, and found that
it was not there. I was thunderstruck at this, for it was the
only memento that I had of her. Thinking that I might have

dropped it when I stooped over Drebber's body, I drove back, and leaving my cab in a side street, I went boldly up to the house—for I was ready to dare anything rather than lose the ring. When I arrived there, I walked right into the arms of a police-officer who was coming out, and only managed to disarm his suspicions by pretending to be hopelessly drunk.

'That was how Enoch Drebber came to his end. All I had to do then was to do as much for Stangerson, and so pay off John Ferrier's debt. I knew that he was staying at Halliday's Private Hotel, and I hung about all day, but he never came out. I fancy that he suspected something when Drebber failed to put in an appearance. He was cunning, was Stangerson, and always on his guard. If he thought he could keep me off by staying indoors he was very much mistaken. I soon found out which was the window of his bedroom, and early next **175** morning I took advantage of some ladders which were lying in the lane behind the hotel, and so made my way into his room in the grey of the dawn. I woke him up and told him that the hour had come when he was to answer for the life he had taken so long before. I described Drebber's death to him, and I gave him the same choice of the poisoned pills. Instead of grasping at the chance of safety which that offered him, he sprang from his bed and flew at my throat. In self-defence I stabbed him to the heart. It would have been the same in any case, for Providence would never have allowed his guilty hand to pick out anything but the poison.

'I have little more to say, and it's as well, for I am about done up. I went on cabbing it for a day or so intending to **176** keep at it until I could save enough to take me back to America. I was standing in the yard when a ragged youngster

175 *early next morning.* A curious phrase for Hope to use, if he confessed on the afternoon of the same day on which he had murdered Stangerson, as Watson tells us he did. It is suggested that while Hope must have murdered Stangerson on the morning of Saturday, March 5th, it was not until Sunday, March 6th, that his capture took place.

176 *I went on cabbing it for a day or so.* The late Professor Christ wrote: "That he could not possibly have done, for it was only on the same morning [Watson tells us] that Stangerson was done in."

In contrast, your editor has accepted Hope's statement as correct, and has inferred that it was made *after* Saturday, that is, on Sunday, March 6th: it will be recalled that Watson took down Hope's words "exactly as they were uttered from Lestrade's notebook."

To this, the late Dr. Zeisler replied: "Hope had not left his cab for forty-eight hours or so from the Thursday afternoon until his capture, except long enough to settle his accounts first with Drebber and then with Stangerson. He had been waiting nearly twenty-one years to wreak vengeance on these two, and had lately greatly feared that his aneurysm would rupture before he could be successful. His tremendous excitement, and the exaltation of the past few days, together with his lack of rest, could very easily account for his confusing one event with another, for he had in fact been cabbing it for a full thirty-six hours since Drebber's death. It was this same confusion which led him on the evening of his capture to refer to that very morning as 'next morning,' meaning the morning following the day on which he 'hung about' Stangerson's hotel; he would otherwise have called it 'this morning.' "

... I DIPPED MY FINGER IN MY OWN BLOOD AND PRINTED IT ON A CONVENIENT PLACE ON THE WALL.

Cover illustration by a unknown artist for a German-language edition of *A Study in Scarlet* published in Milwaukee, Wisconsin. Its discoverer, Mr. H. B. Williams, has stated that the publisher was the Milwaukee *Herold*, one of that city's old German-language newspapers.

177 *I went round suspecting no harm.* The late Clifton R. Andrew ("A Difficulty in *A Study in Scarlet*") and Mr. C. B. H. Vaill ("A Study in Intellects") have both called attention to this remarkable statement. Says Mr. Vaill: "Since Hope had by this time completed his second murder, it would be reasonable to suppose that his caution would be increased. But no; the fact that he was singled out of all the cabbies in London; by name, and directed to call at the very address which had proven to be a trap only a short time before, did not arouse even the 'slightest suspicion' which Holmes feared. Jefferson Hope waltzed right downtown into the new-style spring handcuffs, and that was that."

Mr. Larry Van Gelder has suggested one answer to the problem: Hope deliberately committed suicide. Aware, as he must have been, who Holmes was and where he lived, he knowingly walked into the "trap" and put up the struggle he did simply in order to "agitate his aneurism." "This theory," the late Edgar W. Smith commented, "seems much more plausible, it must be admitted, than the incredible system of events in which Watson would have us believe."

178 *blasé.* French: wearied or worn out by surfeit.

179 *My friend volunteered to go and see.* "Hope was a stranger in London and could have little, if any, knowledge of Sherlock Holmes or potential danger at 221B Baker Street," the late Robert R. Pattrick wrote in "Moriarty Was There." "He was, moreover, a murderer. Yet he claimed to have a friend sufficiently loyal to risk entering this possible police trap. And who, conveniently, was an expert in impersonation. Obviously, the true answer can only be—Moriarty. For a fee, of course. The agent escaped, and Hope would not give evidence. But the significance of the agent was not lost on Holmes. He had even warned Gregson and Lestrade: 'We have a shrewd and desperate man to deal with, who is supported, as I have had occasion to prove, by another who is as clever as himself. . . . I am bound to say that I consider these men to be more than a match for the official force.'"

asked if there was a cabby there called Jefferson Hope, and said that his cab was wanted by a gentleman at 221B, Baker **177** Street. I went round suspecting no harm, and the next thing I knew, this young man here had the bracelets on my wrists, and as neatly snackled as ever I saw in my life. That's the whole of my story, gentlemen. You may consider me to be a murderer; but I hold that I am just as much an officer of justice as you are.'

So thrilling had the man's narrative been and his manner was so impressive that we had sat silent and absorbed. Even **178** the professional detectives, *blasé* as they were in every detail of crime, appeared to be keenly interested in the man's story. When he finished, we sat for some minutes in a stillness which was only broken by the scratching of Lestrade's pencil as he gave the finishing touches to his shorthand account.

'There is only one point on which I should like a little more information,' Sherlock Holmes said at last. 'Who was your accomplice who came for the ring which I advertised?'

The prisoner winked at my friend jocosely. 'I can tell my own secrets,' he said, 'but I don't get other people into trouble. I saw your advertisement, and I thought it might be a plant, or it might be the ring which I wanted. My friend volunteered **179** to go and see. I think you'll own he did it smartly.'

'Not a doubt of that,' said Holmes, heartily.

'Now, gentlemen,' the inspector remarked, gravely, 'the forms of the law must be complied with. On Thursday the prisoner will be brought before the magistrates, and your attendance will be required. Until then I will be responsible for him.' He rang the bell as he spoke, and Jefferson Hope was led off by a couple of warders, while my friend and I made our way out of the station and took a cab back to Baker Street.

14 ❖ THE CONCLUSION

We had all been warned to appear before the magistrates upon the Thursday; but when the Thursday came there was no occasion for our testimony. A higher Judge had taken the matter in hand, and Jefferson Hope had been summoned before a tribunal where strict justice would be meted out to him. On the very night after his capture the aneurism burst, and he was found in the morning stretched upon the floor of the cell, with a placid smile upon his face, as though he had been able in his dying moments to look back upon a useful life, and on work well done.

'Gregson and Lestrade will be wild about his death,' Holmes remarked, as we chatted it over next evening. 'Where will their grand advertisement be now?'

'I don't see that they had very much to do with his capture,' I answered.

'What you do in this world is a matter of no consequence,' returned my companion, bitterly. 'The question is, what can you make people believe that you have done. Never mind,' he continued, more brightly, after a pause. 'I would not have missed the investigation for anything. There has been no better case within my recollection. Simple as it was, there were several most instructive points about it.'

'Simple!' I ejaculated.

'Well, really, it can hardly be described as otherwise,' said Sherlock Holmes, smiling at my surprise. 'The proof of its intrinsic simplicity is, that without any help save a few very ordinary deductions I was able to lay my hand upon the criminal within three days.'   **180**

'That is true,' said I.

'I have already explained to you that what is out of the common is usually a guide rather than a hindrance. In solving a problem of this sort, the grand thing is to be able to reason backwards. That is a very useful accomplishment, and a very easy one, but people do not practise it much. In the everyday affairs of life it is more useful to reason forwards, and so the other comes to be neglected. There are fifty who can reason synthetically for one who can reason analytically.'

'I confess,' said I, 'that I do not quite follow you.'

'I hardly expected that you would. Let me see if I can make it clearer. Most people, if you describe a train of events to them, will tell you what the result would be. They can put those events together in their minds, and argue from them that something will come to pass. There are few people, however, who, if you told them a result, would be able to evolve from their own inner consciousness what the steps were which led up to that result. This power is what I mean when I talk of reasoning backwards, or analytically.'

'I understand,' said I.

'Now this was a case in which you were given the result and had to find everything else for yourself. Now let me endeavour to show you the different steps in my reasoning. To begin at the beginning. I approached the house, as you know, on foot, and with my mind entirely free from all impressions. I naturally began by examining the roadway, and there, as I have already explained to you, I saw clearly the marks of a cab, which, I ascertained by inquiry, must have been there during the night. I satisfied myself that it was a cab and not a private carriage by the narrow gauge of the wheels. The ordinary London growler is considerably less wide than a gentleman's brougham.

180 *I was able to lay my hand upon the criminal within three days.'* As your editor has written elsewhere (*The Chronological Holmes*): "Surely Holmes would have made no such statement if he had in truth captured Hope within the two days allotted to him by Watson."

To this, Dr. Zeisler replied ("A Chronological Study in Scarlet:)" "It might be considered frivolous to point out that within two days actually is within three days. But it seems evident that the Master really said 'Within two days' and that the printed text is in error. This may have arisen in either of two ways: first, due to the fact that when Watson wrote his chronicle some six years after the events he himself was confused by the rapidity with which they had occurred; it is not strange if they seemed in retrospect to have occupied most of three days instead of two days; secondly, it is possible, of course, that Watson wrote '2' in his manuscript, and that the typesetter read '3'—for Watson's calligraphy was not quite perfect."

". . . A GENTLEMAN'S BROUGHAM."

The brougham, named for Henry, Lord Brougham, British lawyer, orator, writer, and statesman, 1778–1868, was a closed, four-wheeled vehicle with its two front wheels turning short on a pivot. The illustration, by John Leech, is from *A History of Everyday Things in England, Vol. IV, 1851 to 1914*, by Marjorie and C. H. B. Quennell.

181 *as the art of tracing footsteps*. Probably Holmes by this time had written his monograph "upon the tracing of footsteps, with some remarks upon the use of plaster of Paris as a preserver of impresses," of which he speaks in *The Sign of the Four*.

'This was the first point gained. I then walked slowly down the garden path, which happened to be composed of a clay soil, peculiarly suitable for taking impressions. No doubt it appeared to you to be a mere trampled line of slush, but to my trained eyes every mark upon its surface had a meaning. There is no branch of detective science which is so important

181 and so much neglected as the art of tracing footsteps. Happily, I have always laid great stress upon it, and much practice has made it second nature to me. I saw the heavy footmarks of the constables, but I saw also the track of the two men who had first passed through the garden. It was easy to tell that they had been before the others, because in places their marks had been entirely obliterated by the others coming upon the top of them. In this way my second link was formed, which told me that the nocturnal visitors were two in number, one remarkable for his height (as I calculated from the length of his stride) and the other fashionably dressed, to judge from the small and elegant impression left by his boots.

'On entering the house this last inference was confirmed. My well-booted man lay before me. The tall one, then, had done the murder, if murder there was. There was no wound upon the dead man's person, but the agitated expression upon his face assured me that he had foreseen his fate before it came upon him. Men who die from heart disease, or any sudden natural cause, never by any chance exhibit agitation upon their features. Having sniffed the dead man's lips, I detected a slightly sour smell, and I came to the conclusion that he had had poison forced upon him. Again, I argued that it had been forced upon him from the hatred and fear expressed upon his face. By the method of exclusion, I had arrived at this result, for no other hypothesis would meet the facts. Do not imagine that it was a very unheard-of idea. The forcible administration of poison is by no means a new thing in criminal annals. The cases of Dolsky in Odessa, and of Leturier in Montpellier, will occur at once to any toxicologist.

'And now came the great question as to the reason why. Robbery had not been the object of the murder, for nothing was taken. Was it politics, then, or was it a woman? That was the question which confronted me. I was inclined from the first to the latter supposition. Political assassins are only too glad to do their work and to fly. This murder had, on the contrary, been done most deliberately, and the perpetrator had left his tracks all over the room, showing that he had been there all the time. It must have been a private wrong, and not a political one, which called for such a methodical revenge. When the inscription was discovered upon the wall, I was more inclined than ever to my opinion. The thing was too evidently a blind. When the ring was found, however, it settled the question. Clearly the murderer had used it to remind his victim of some dead or absent woman. It was at this point that I asked Gregson whether he had inquired in his telegram to Cleveland as to any particular point in Mr Drebber's former career. He answered, you remember, in the negative.

'I then proceeded to make a careful examination of the room, which confirmed me in my opinion as to the murderer's height, and furnished me with the additional details as to the Trichinopoly cigar and the length of his nails. I had already come to the conclusion, since there were no signs of a struggle, that the blood which covered the floor had burst from the murderer's nose in his excitement. I could perceive that the track of blood coincided with the track of his feet. It is seldom that any man, unless he is very full-blooded, breaks out in this way through emotion, so I hazarded the opinion that the criminal was probably a robust and ruddy-faced man. Events proved that I had judged correctly.

'Having left the house, I proceeded to do what Gregson had neglected. I telegraphed to the head of the police at Cleveland, limiting my inquiry to the circumstances connected with the marriage of Enoch Drebber. The answer was conclusive. It told me that Drebber had already applied for the protection of the law against an old rival in love, named Jefferson Hope, and that this same Hope was at present in Europe. I knew now that I held the clue to the mystery in my hand, and all that remained was to secure the murderer.

'I had already determined in my own mind that the man who had walked into the house with Drebber was none other than the man who had driven the cab. The marks in the road showed me that the horse had wandered on in a way which would have been impossible had there been anyone in charge of it. Where, then, could the driver be, unless he were inside the house? Again, it is absurd to suppose that any sane man would carry out a deliberate crime under the very eyes, as it were, of a third person, who was sure to betray him. Lastly, supposing one man wished to dog another through London, what better means could he adopt than to turn cabdriver? All these considerations led me to the irresistible conclusion that Jefferson Hope was to be found among the jarveys of the **182** Metropolis.

'If he had been one, there was no reason to believe that he had ceased to be. On the contrary from his point of view, any sudden change would be likely to draw attention to himself. He would probably, for a time at least, continue to perform his duties. There was no reason to suppose that he was going under an assumed name. Why should he change his name in a country where no one knew his original one? I therefore organized my street arab detective corps, and sent them systematically to every cab proprietor in London until they ferreted out the man that I wanted. How well they succeeded, and how quickly I took advantage of it, are still fresh in your recollection. The murder of Stangerson was an incident which was entirely unexpected, but which could hardly, in any case, have been prevented. Through it, as you know, I came into possession of the pills, the existence of which I had already surmised. You see, the whole thing is a chain of logical sequences without a break or flaw.'

'It is wonderful!' I cried. 'Your merits should be publicly recognized. You should publish an account of the case. If you won't, I will for you.'

'You may do what you like, Doctor,' he answered. 'See here!' he continued, handing a paper over to me, 'look at this!'

It was the *Echo* for the day, and the paragraph to which **183** he pointed was devoted to the case in question.

'The public,' it said, 'have lost a sensational treat through the sudden death of the man Hope, who was suspected of the murder of Mr Enoch Drebber and of Mr Joseph Stangerson. The details of the case will probably be never known now,

"YOU MAY DO WHAT YOU LIKE, DOCTOR," HE ANSWERED.

"But this promise was long in its fulfillment," the late Edgar W. Smith wrote in "Dr. Watson and the Great Censorship." "The permission Holmes had so cavalierly given was withdrawn, we must believe, before Watson could act on it, and the facts, for all their drama and momentousness, were not revealed [until December, 1887]." The illustration, by George Hutchinson, is from *A Study in Scarlet*, London: Ward, Lock, Bowden & Co., 1891.

182 *the jarveys*. Cockney slang for coachmen or cabdrivers. The term perhaps comes from the name of Saint Gervase, whose emblem was the whip.

183 *It was the* Echo *for the day*. As your editor has written elsewhere (*The Chronological Holmes*): "Watson tells us that Hope died on the night of his capture, and that the next evening he and Holmes discussed the case. By Watson's account, this discussion would have come on the Sunday. This it could not have done, because Watson speaks of the *Echo* for the day."

Dr. Zeisler agreed that this discussion must have been on the Monday evening, "from which it follows that Hope died during the night of Sunday-

Monday." The difficulty here lies in the interpretation which one places upon Watson's statement that Hope died "on the very night after his capture." Your editor has taken this to mean that Hope was captured on Sunday, March 6, 1881, and died on that night; Dr. Zeisler took it to mean that Hope was captured on Saturday, March 5, 1881, and died on the night of the following day, Sunday, March 6—"the very night *after* [the day of] his capture."

"Clearly," your editor concluded, "what happened was this: Watson, eager to make his first account of a Holmes case as dramatic as possible, and to cast all possible credit on the Master and his methods, *telescoped the events of two days into one.*"

This Dr. Zeisler considered "absolutely impossible, and for three reasons: 1) There was surely no need to make the case more dramatic than it was in any case, or to try to cast more credit on the Master and his methods than they would have deserved even if the case had lasted one day longer than it did; 2) if . . . Watson wished to make it appear that a three-day case had lasted only two days, would he, after elaborate distortions, have nullified his efforts by quoting the Master as saying that he had captured Hope 'within three days'? Surely, he would have been most careful at this very point to have altered it to 'two days.' 3) When Holmes glanced over Watson's chronicle—as he tells us he did in Chapter I of *The Sign of the Four*, he noticed the error but perhaps did not wish Watson to think that his criticisms were in any way dictated by vanity, and he considered a correction unnecessary inasmuch as careful reading would show that he had solved the case in two days."

184 *contemplar in arca." ' Contemplar* is incorrect; the word should be *contemplor.* Watson here quotes a foreign author for the one and only time in the Saga; he draws upon the *First Satire* of the First Book (lines 66 and 67) of Horace, translated by Christopher Morely as "The Public hisses at me, but I'm pleased with myself in private when I look at the money in my box"; by Morris Rosenblum as "The People hiss at me but I applaud myself in my own home as I gaze fondly at the coins in my strongbox"; by Professor John B. Wolf as "People hiss at me, but I am satisfied with myself; I stay home and contemplate the money in my strongbox." Watson errs in calling the speaker "the Roman miser." As Mr. Rosenblum pointed out: "Every schoolboy knows . . . that Horace does not speak of a Roman miser but of a rich man in Athens."

Auctorial Note: In the competition conducted by the *Observer*, in which its readers were asked to vote on their favorite Sherlock Holmes stories, including both the short stories *and* the novels, *A Study in Scarlet* was given fourth place, falling just behind "The Adventure of the Speckled Band," *The Hound of the Baskervilles* and *The Sign of the Four*.

though we are informed upon good authority that the crime was the result of an old-standing and romantic feud, in which love and Mormonism bore a part. It seems that both the victims belonged, in their younger days, to the Latter Day Saints, and Hope, the deceased prisoner, hails also from Salt Lake City. If the case has had no other effect, it, at least, brings out in the most striking manner the efficiency of our detective police force, and will serve as a lesson to all foreigners that they will do wisely to settle their feuds at home, and not to carry them on to British soil. It is an open secret that the credit of this smart capture belongs entirely to the well-known Scotland Yard officials, Messrs Lestrade and Gregson. The man was apprehended, it appears, in the rooms of a certain Mr Sherlock Holmes, who has himself, as an amateur, shown some talent in the detective line, and who, with such instructors, may hope in time to attain to some degree of their skill. It is expected that a testimonial of some sort will be presented to the two officers as a fitting recognition of their services.'

'Didn't I tell you so when we started?' cried Sherlock Holmes with a laugh. 'That's the result of all our Study in Scarlet: to get them a testimonial!'

'Never mind,' I answered; 'I have all the facts in my journal, and the public shall know them. In the meantime you must make yourself contented by the consciousness of success, like the Roman miser—

184
' "Populus me sibilat, at mihi plaudo
Ipse domi simul ac nummos contemplar in arca." ' '

16

"AS TO YOUR DATES, THAT IS THE BIGGEST MYSTIFICATION OF ALL"

[John H. Watson, M.D., to Sherlock Holmes,
"The Adventure of the Creeping Man"]

"Mr. Sherlock Holmes was in active practice for twenty-three years, and . . . during seventeen of these I was allowed to co-operate with him and to keep notes of his doings."

So Watson wrote in the opening lines of "The Adventure of the Veiled Lodger."

Ten of these seventeen years occupy the period from March, 1881 (*A Study in Scarlet*), to May, 1891 ("The Final Problem"). The partnership was reconstituted shortly after April, 1894 ("The Adventure of the Empty House"), and it came to an end with Holmes' retirement in the autumn of 1903—a period of nine years and six months, or a total of *nineteen and a half* years.

There were, then, two and a half years during the period of "the partnership" in which Watson did *not* "co-operate with" Holmes or "keep notes of his doings."

We know that Watson was living at Baker Street in late 1895 ("The Adventure of the Bruce-Partington Plans"); but he does *not* seem to be living there in October, 1896 ("The Adventure of the Veiled Lodger"). There is a presumption, amounting almost to a certainty, that late 1895–late 1896 is one of our "missing years."

Another possibility is the year May, 1901 ("The Adventure of the Priory School") to May, 1902 ("The Adventure of Shoscombe Old Place")—a period of twelve months during which there is no indication whatsoever that Watson was "allowed to co-operate with Holmes and to keep notes of his doings."

Even including this, however, would leave us with a period of *at least six months* to account for.

Here we may note a third remarkable fact: Watson recorded no Holmes case which took place between *A Study in Scarlet* (March, 1881) and "The Adventure of the Speckled Band" (April, 1883)—nor any case which took place between "The Adventure of the Speckled Band" and "The Resident Patient" (October, 1886)—*more than three years later.*

The Reverend Henry T. Folsom has suggested ("Seventeen Out of Twenty-Three") that Watson was on *sick leave* from the Army until shortly after March, 1881; he reported *back to duty* in the summer of 1881, serving his second hitch with the Army from summer, 1881, to spring, 1883.

Mr. S. C. Roberts, on the other hand, holds (*Doctor Watson*) that Watson spent a portion of the early days of the partnership in civilian travel. "In later years," Mr. Roberts wrote, "Watson refers to 'an experience of women which extends over many nations and three separate continents' [*The Sign of the Four*]. The three continents are clearly Europe, India, and Australia. In Australia he had been but a boy; in India he can have seen few women except the staff nurses at Peshawar. It is conceivable, though not likely, that he revisited Australia at this time. It is much more probable that Watson spent some time on the Continent and that, in particular, he visited such resorts as contained the additional attraction of a casino."

India, we may agree, is "clearly" one of Watson's "three separate continents." As the late Dr. Ernest Bloomfield Zeisler pointed out in *Baker Street Chronology:* "Throughout the Sacred Writings there are numerous evidences that Watson was inordinately susceptible to ladies and that in general he was successful with them; the Master says as much, and Watson's many palpitating descriptions of attractive young women and their silhouettes point in the same direction. It is quite likely that Watson found it physiologically impossible to be entirely deprived of women for as long as eighteen months of war."

Europe, also, we may clearly allow Mr. Roberts, remembering Watson's long residence in England during many, if not all, of the years between *A Study in Scarlet* and his boast of "three separate continents" in *The Sign of the Four*.

About *Australia,* however, even Mr. Roberts does not seem too happy; and Dr. W. S. Bristowe (in "The Mystery of the Third Continent") is really quite devastating: "The assumption is usually made that [the third continent] was Australia where [Watson] certainly spent some of his childhood days, but as he and 'Tadpole' Phelps were 'little boys' at school together in England, . . . I cannot believe that Watson was so precocious as to have had 'experience of women' in any man-of-the-world sense before leaving Australia at thirteen or younger to go to school in England."

Africa? Here Dr. Bristowe has written: ". . . it may be advisable to discount any claim which might be based on the hour or two [Watson] could have spent ashore at Port Said on his way to India. During the homeward journey, of course, he would have been too much of an invalid to take any interest."

And now let us consider the case for *America.*

Again, it is Dr. Bristowe who has summed up the case so cogently:

We know that Watson had notes of hundreds of cases from which only sixty were selected for publication, one by Holmes himself and others perhaps by Sir Arthur Conan Doyle. Of those selected by Watson it is remarkable to find about one in every five had some connection with America or Americans. Surely this is no coincidence. It shows a personal interest in America which is well illustrated by the special zest with which he describes the American scene in both *A Study in Scarlet* and *The Valley of Fear*. . . . My conclusion that America was the third continent to which Watson was referring now receives dramatic confirmation from a source whose authenticity can scarcely be doubted. It is well known that Sir Arthur Conan Doyle was closely associated with Watson and described him as his friend in 1908 [in the *Strand Magazine*] so anything from his pen must be treated with the highest respect. We have learned from Mr. J[ohn] Dickson Carr of some unpublished notes about Watson which were written by Sir Arthur Conan Doyle in 1889 under the title of *Angels of Darkness* (*The Life of Sir Arthur Conan Doyle*). Many details are withheld but we are allowed to know that Watson not only visited America but stayed on long enough in San Francisco to practice medicine there.

As we have seen, Dr. Bristowe has also held that both Watson's father and elder brother came to America to fight in the Civil War: it was to visit his dying brother that Watson came to America late in 1883 or early in 1884. His visit, Dr. Bristowe has suggested, "taxed" his resources beyond their limit with the result that he was forced to go into practice for a time in order to keep himself and to pay for the return passage to England." **1**

Other authorities, while agreeing that America was indeed the third continent, hold that Watson's visit there was made at a time other than 1884–1885.

Mr. William Smith, as we have already seem, has placed Watson in America in the 1860's, himself a participant in the American Civil War.

Mr. Robert Keith Leavitt, on the other hand, has held that Watson's visit to America was made in the year 1874, four years before Watson took his medical degree. "Obviously, the young man was making the Grand Tour." ("The Preposterously Paired Performances of the Preacher's Portrait.")

And Dr. Winthrop Weatherbee has written (in "The Third Continent"):

> It will be recalled that, as a small boy, Watson attended an English school, where one of his classmates was "Tadpole" Phelps ["The Naval Treaty"]. Phelps, however, was in the fifth form when Watson was in the third, and it is not unreasonable to suppose that it was shortly after this time that the decline of the Watson family fortunes necessitated [an] emigration from England. When we recall Watson's old school-number [31 —see "The Adventure of the Retired Colourman"] everything falls into place. The only city in the northern part of the United States large enough at that time to support such an aggregation of schools was New York, where, to interpret what he said, Watson must have attended P.S. No. 31. . . .

If we are agreed that Watson, at some time prior to the adventure of *The Sign of the Four* (September, 1888) visited America, we have resolved the mystery of the three continents—but the mystery of the missing years that disrupted the partnership between 1881–1894 and 1894–1903 still calls for investigation.

1 We shall have occasion to refer to this American visit again in Chapter 21, "Now, Watson, the Fair Sex Is Your Department," in which we shall consider the wives of Watson.

2 The late Dorothy L. Sayers, in "Dr. Watson, Widower," expressed her doubts that there was any break in the partnership at this time. She accounted for the missing years by suggesting an interruption between August, 1898, and July, 1900. "It was during this period (October, 1899) that the War broke out in the Transvaal, and it would be natural that Watson (that spirited old warhorse) should hear his country's call and hasten to place his services, in some capacity, at the disposal of his Government."

3 The reader must remember that it was not until September, 1903, with the first publication of "The Adventure of the Empty House," that Watson was allowed to reveal to the world that Holmes was not dead.

There is now general but by no means universal agreement that there were three breaks in the partnership, chronologically as follows:

1. A period between April, 1883 ("The Adventure of the Speckled Band"), and October, 1886 ("The Resident Patient"), during which Watson traveled, presumably to America.

2. A period between November, 1895 ("The Adventure of the Bruce-Partington Plans"), and October, 1896 ("The Adventure of the Veiled Lodger").**2**

3. A period between May, 1901 ("The Adventure of the Priory School"), and May, 1902 ("The Adventure of Shoscombe Old Place").

For an explanation of this third break, we cannot do better than to quote the words of the late Edgar W. Smith, in "Dr. Watson and the Great Censorship." After Holmes' Return in 1894

> the game was everywhere afoot. Great Sherlock strode the stage in majesty and dominance, and evil-doers cringed and slunk away. But for all the world might know, as far as John H. Watson was concerned, his friend lay crushed and broken still at the bottom of the Reichenbach Falls. **3**
>
> Back in 1890, before his disappearance, Holmes had told Watson quite bluntly that he had "degraded what should have been a course of lectures into a series of tales" ("The Adventure of the Copper Beeches"). . . . He accused him of recounting his stories "wrong end foremost" ("The Adventure of Wisteria Lodge"). And he said later, with even heavier sarcasm, "You slur over work of the utmost finesse and delicacy, in order to dwell upon sensational details which may excite, but cannot possibly instruct, the reader" ("The Adventure of the Abbey Grange"). No Wonder Watson felt impelled to hold his peace.
>
> We shall never learn what it was that broke the spell of silence—whether it was some new and urgent economic need, or an irresistible excess of enthusiasm, or sheer perverse defiance of the wishes of his friend—but the fact remains that in August, 1901, Watson threw caution to the winds and gave the world another tale of Sherlock Holmes. The *Strand Magazine* for that month carried the first instalment of an old and almost forgotten adventure, which was to run until April, 1902, under the title of *The Hound of the Baskervilles*. While this story was appearing, Watson was relegated arbitrarily to Holmes' outer limbo, for he shows no knowledge whatsoever of any of the Master's cases during the whole period in which the *Hound* was running.

About the cause of the 1895–1896 break, however, there is considerable difference of opinion.

The late H. W. Bell, as we shall see, when we come to consider "The Fair Sex" as Watson's department, suggested a quick marriage in 1896 lasting somewhat less than a year, but this suggestion has not survived careful examination.

Mr. Elliot Kimball, in "The Missing Year," has suggested a less legitimate liaison: in November of 1895, Mr. Kimball states, Watson met a blue-eyed blonde; an *affaire de cœur* persisted for a twelve-month. "Watson was no longer willing to temporize; hole-in-the-corner assignations were both distressing and ignoble; the Baker Street scene offered no scope for erotic exercises; wherefore, Watson cut the painter, took rooms, and departed from 221B, like a matured fledgling from the nest."

The late Gavin Brend advanced evidence pointing to a temporary estrangement between Holmes and Watson caused partly by Watson's excessive gambling on horses and partly by Watson's persistent nagging of Holmes about the drug habit, especially annoying to the detective because he knew he had permanently freed himself from the habit.

Mr. William D. Jenkins has recently (1964) put forward an extremely novel and interesting suggestion, for which the reader is referred to "The Adventure of the Solitary Cyclist," Note 3.

On the other hand, we may also recall here Holmes' marked reluctance to confide fully in Watson when he was engaged in matters of Government importance ("One has to be discreet when one talks of high matters of State").[4] We should also recall that Holmes' last recorded case in 1895 was "The Adventure of the Bruce-Partington Plans," at the conclusion of which he spent a day at Windsor and returned to Baker Street with a remarkably fine emerald tiepin. If "high matters of State" should call for investigation a short time later in the year 1895 or early in 1896, is it thinkable that those in high places in Britain would call on the services of any other investigator?

It is not, and we conclude that almost certainly Sherlock Holmes conducted a supremely important investigation for the British Crown in 1895–1896—and Watson, unfortunately for all of us, had to be left behind.

In this connection, we have two very interesting suggestions, the first of which has been put forward by Mr. L. A. Morrow in his essay, "A Diplomatic Secret": Mr. Morrow notes that in 1896 Guglielmo Marconi, the inventor of wireless, went to England armed with a letter to Sir William Preece, Engineer-in-Chief of the British Post Office, and a promise of help from his cousin Jameson Davis, a man "in considerable practice as an engineer in London." Mr. Davis afterward recalled how Marconi's "instruments were broken by the customs authorities, as they were not understood and were thought to be dangerous. New instruments had to be procured and these we ordered to Marconi's specifications." Finally, Marconi was ready to demonstrate his wireless in England and to try to get capital together for future expanded experimental work. Quoting *Marconi, the Man and His Wireless*, by Orrin E. Dunlap, Jr.; The Macmillan Company, New York, 1937, Mr. Morrow continues:

"Britain was interested in this thing called wireless and was anxious to get to the root of it." The British Government must have been more than a little annoyed at the customs authorities who had broken Marconi's instruments. We can imagine Mycroft, who occasionally *was*

[4] See Dr. Felix Morley's illuminating remarks on this subject in "The Adventure of the Bruce-Partington Plans," Note 4.

5 It will be recalled that Holmes visited Poldhu in the March of 1897, at the time of "The Adventure of the Devil's Foot."

the British Government, saying decisively, "You must drop everything, Sherlock! Marconi must be protected not only from petty government officials but from crackpots who would interfere with his experiments. And you must find a good location on the coast for a high-powered transmitting station, too. Leave no stone unturned! This young Italian genius may be able to transmit clear across the Atlantic if he has a proper spot for his aerial." . . . Of course the assignment was carried out with Holmes' usual efficiency. There is no record of any more broken instruments nor of interference to experiments. On the contrary, successful tests were conducted at several locations . . . and in July of 1897 Marconi's company was incorporated with a capitalisation of £100,000. It is not difficult to guess the name of at least one of the original subscribers. . . .

Holmes' suggested site for the transmitting station was at Poldhu, in Cornwall:**5** In July of 1900 Marconi "went to the barren southwest tip of England and selected Poldhu . . . as the site for a pioneer transmitter, 199 times more powerful than any station ever built."

Our second suggestion concerning Holmes' activities in the missing year 1895–1896 comes from Dr. John D. Clark. In "A Chemist's View of Canonical Chemistry," Dr. Clark writes:

It has been remarked by many Sherlockian scholars that there is no record of Holmes' activities from the latter part of 1895 until October, 1896. Where the Canon offers no clue there is probably a good reason for the lack: " 'The dog did nothing in the night-time.' 'That was the curious incident' . . ." Under these circumstances, it is imperative that the student search somewhere else than in the field of criminology if he is to find traces of the activities of Mr. Sherlock Holmes.

The traces are there, and it is a remarkable fact that they have not already been pointed out. For in the year 1896 there appeared a series of papers which changed the history of the world—and may yet terminate it. And the *style* of the research they record is the style of Mr. Sherlock Holmes.

In 1895, M. Antoine Henri Becquerel (1852–1908), the third of a line of distinguished French scientists, was appointed to the chair of physics at the École Polytechnique in Paris. He immediately turned his attention to the fascinating question of the nature and properties of the X-rays, which had been discovered by W. K. Roentgen (1845–1923) less than a year previously. It is inconceivable that Holmes could have been unaware of this discovery. Nor is it unreasonable to believe that he, with his close connections with the scientific life of France, would have had any difficulty in obtaining entrance to the laboratories of the École Polytechnique, and to that of M. Becquerel. (After all, security and "need to know" had not yet been invented.) And it can hardly be doubted that once he had gained entrance to the laboratory, he would profoundly influence the course of the investigations conducted therein.

For consider what happened in the laboratory of M. Becquerel. It was known that X-rays were a peculiarly penetrating type of radiation, and that they produced a phosphorent effect when they impinged upon glass. Reasoning by analogy (frequently a dangerous procedure), several scientists thought that substances phosphorescent in ordinary light might themselves be emitting a penetrating radiation. M. Becquerel, testing this hypothesis, placed a certain phosphorescent material on top of an unexposed photographic plate wrapped in black paper, left it to its own devices for some days, and then developed the plate. Sure enough, the developed plate showed a faint image of the phosphorescent sample.

In the subsequent course of the investigation the methods of Holmes are so conspicuously present that it is impossible to conceive of his physical absence from the scene. For consider what happened next. Other phosphorescent materials were tried. Negative results. Conclusion: The phosphorescence of the original compound had nothing to do with its effect on the photographic plate. Then other, *non*-phosphorescent compounds containing the same elements as the original sample were tried. Positive results. Ergo—one particular element produced a penetrating radiation. Did others? The investigator (or more properly, and probably, investigators) tried compounds of every element they could lay their hands on. No results. "'. . . when all other contingencies fail, whatever remains, however, improbable, must be the truth.'" One element, and one element alone, of the dozens available to the investigators, spontaneously emitted a penetrating radiation, similar to X-rays.

The name of that element was uranium.

Holmes returned to London in October, 1896, when the papers reporting the discovery of radioactivity were either in print or in preparation. The basic discovery had been made, and he left its exploitation and development to others. Why he permitted no mention of his name in connection with the discovery is a fascinating question, but when, in 1903, M. Becquerel and M. Pierre Curie shared the Nobel Prize in chemistry, Holmes must have received the news with somewhat mixed feelings.

Perhaps he was just a little too far-sighted to wish his name to be associated with the most shattering discovery since the domestication of fire. If he could foresee even a little of the consequences, his early retirement to the Sussex Downs was not unreasonable. He wanted to enjoy them while they were still there.

Holmes was a distinguished forensic chemist. But it is only fair to remind the world that as a chemist he was something more. From Baker Street to the École Polytechnique to the Rutherford Laboratories at Cambridge, and on to Almagordo—the trace is there for anyone to see.

"REVERIES"

Wyndham Robinson pictures Holmes, in a nostalgic mood, meditating on some of the early Sidney Paget drawings.

17

THE ADVENTURE OF THE SPECKLED BAND

[Friday, April 6, 1883]

IN glancing over my notes of the seventy odd cases in which I have during the last eight years studied the **1** methods of my friend Sherlock Holmes, I find many tragic, some comic, a large number merely strange, but none commonplace ; for, working as he did rather for the love of his art than for the acquirement of wealth, he refused to associate himself with any investigation which did not tend towards the unusual, and even the fantastic. Of all these varied cases, however, I cannot recall any which presented more singular features than that which was associated with the well-known Surrey family of the **2** Roylotts of Stoke Moran. The events in question occurred in the early days of my association with Holmes, when we were sharing rooms as bachelors, in Baker Street. It is possible that I might have placed them upon record before, but a promise of secrecy was made at the time, from which I have only been freed during the last month by the untimely death of the lady to whom the pledge was given. It is perhaps as well that the facts should now come to light, for I have reasons to know there are widespread rumours as to the death of Dr. Grimesby Roylott which tend to make the matter even more terrible than the truth.

It was early in April, in the year '83, that I woke one **3** morning to find Sherlock Holmes standing, fully dressed, **4** by the side of my bed. He was a late riser as a rule, and, as the clock on the mantelpiece showed me that it was only a quarter past seven, I blinked up at him in some surprise, and perhaps just a little resentment, for I was myself regular in my habits.

" Very sorry to knock you up, Watson," said he, " but it's the common lot this morning. Mrs. Hudson has been knocked up, she retorted upon me, and I on you."

" What is it, then ? A fire ? "

" No, a client. It seems that a young lady has arrived in a considerable state of excitement, who insists upon seeing me. She is waiting now in the sitting-room. Now, when young ladies wander about the metropolis at this hour of the morning, and knock sleepy people up out of their beds, I presume that it is something very pressing which they have to communicate. Should it prove to be an interesting case, you would, I am sure, wish to follow it from the outset. I thought at any rate that I should call **5** you, and give you the chance."

1 *the last eight years*. The Reverend Henry T. Folsom has suggested ("Seventeen Out of Twenty-Three") that "The Adventure of the Speckled Band" must have been written after May, 1891, "because the wording of the first paragragh indicates that Holmes is thought to be *already* dead at the time of writing: '. . . for, working as he *did* . . . he *refused* to associate himself with any investigation . . .' Note the use of tenses—the simple and apparently tragic past tense." This interpretation would mean that Watson shared "seventy odd cases" with Holmes between 1883, the year of "The Adventure of the Speckled Band," and 1891. Mr. Frank A. Waters has estimated ("Upon the Probable Number of Cases of Mr. Sherlock Holmes") that the detective by the time of his retirement in late October, 1903, had handled some 1,700 cases.

2 *Surrey*. One of the "Home Counties" around London, Surrey is chiefly an agricultural county with some dairying and sheep raising. Here are Croyden (airport), Wimbledon (tennis matches), Epsom (horse racing) and Kew (botanical gardens). King John signed the Magna Carta at Runnymede in Surrey in the year 1215. Holmes found Surrey criminally fertile: it was the scene, not only of "The Adventure of the Speckled Band," but also of "The Reigate Squires," "The Naval Treaty," the adventures of the "Solitary Cyclist" and "Wisteria Lodge."

3 *It was early in April, in the year '83*. No Sherlockian chronologist in the long list that includes Baring-Gould, Bell, Blakeney, Brend, Christ, Folsom, Pattrick, Petersen, Smith, and Zeisler has so far disagreed with Dr. Watson, although your editor cannot agree with the consensus that the day of the adventure was Wednesday, April 4th.

4 *fully dressed*. "Holmes was fully dressed when he awakened Watson at 7:15 on a morning in April, '83," Mr. James Edward Holroyd commented in his column, "The Egg Spoon." "But if the visit of Miss Stoner was as urgent as he appeared to think, why waste valuable minutes getting into his own clothes before rousing Watson? Why not have slipped on one of his many dressing gowns? Or if

Masterly modesty forbade him to appear before a lady so scantily garbed, why not have asked Mrs. Hudson to call the doctor immediately?"

5 *you would, I am sure, wish to follow it.* We see that Watson in the past two years has firmly established himself as Holmes' comrade in detection.

6 *Leatherhead.* A small town on the river Mole with a narrow main street and several old inns, notably the Swan and the Running Horse. Its industries include tanning, brewing, and the manufacture of bricks and tiles.

7 *Waterloo.* The largest and finest railway terminal in Great Britain, Waterloo and its approaches cover the great part of the land enclosed by York Road, Waterloo Road, Lambeth Lower Marsh, and Westminster Bridge Road. The original terminus of the former London and South Western Railway was situated at Nine Elms, Vauxhall, at great inconvenience to London passengers who had to continue into the metropolis by bus, steamboat, or cab. In consequence, in 1848, the Railway extended their line to Waterloo at a cost of £800,000, most of it spent for the six bridges that had to be constructed along the two miles of new line. The present station, which was rebuilt between 1900 and 1921, covers two and a quarter acres, has twenty-one platforms and a normal service of 1,200 trains a day. It was formally opened by Queen Mary on March 21, 1922.

SHE RAISED HER VEIL AS SHE SPOKE, AND WE COULD SEE THAT SHE WAS INDEED IN A PITIABLE STATE OF AGITATION . . .

Illustration by Sidney Paget for the *Strand Magazine*, February, 1892.

"My dear fellow, I would not miss it for anything."

I had no keener pleasure than in following Holmes in his professional investigations, and in admiring the rapid deductions, as swift as intuitions, and yet always founded on a logical basis, with which he unravelled the problems which were submitted to him. I rapidly threw on my clothes, and was ready in a few minutes to accompany my friend down to the sitting-room. A lady dressed in black and heavily veiled, who had been sitting in the window, rose as we entered.

"Good morning, madam," said Holmes cheerily. "My name is Sherlock Holmes. This is my intimate friend and associate, Dr. Watson, before whom you can speak as freely as before myself. Ha, I am glad to see that Mrs. Hudson has had the good sense to light the fire. Pray draw up to it, and I shall order you a cup of hot coffee, for I observe that you are shivering."

"It is not cold which makes me shiver," said the woman in a low voice, changing her seat as requested.

"What then?"

"It is fear, Mr. Holmes. It is terror." She raised her veil as she spoke, and we could see that she was indeed in a pitiable state of agitation, her face all drawn and grey, with restless, frightened eyes, like those of some hunted animal. Her features and figure were those of a woman of thirty, but her hair was shot with premature grey, and her expression was weary and haggard. Sherlock Holmes ran her over with one of his quick, all-comprehensive glances.

"You must not fear," said he soothingly, bending forward and patting her forearm. "We shall soon set matters right, I have no doubt. You have come in by train this morning, I see."

"You know me, then?"

"No, but I observe the second half of a return ticket in the palm of your left glove. You must have started early, and yet you had a good drive in a dog-cart, along heavy roads, before you reached the station."

The lady gave a violent start, and stared in bewilderment at my companion.

"There is no mystery, my dear madam," said he, smiling. "The left arm of your jacket is spattered with mud in no less than seven places. The marks are perfectly fresh. There is no vehicle save a dog-cart which throws up mud in that way, and then only when you sit on the left-hand side of the driver."

"Whatever your reasons may be, you are perfectly correct," said she. "I started from home before six, **6** reached Leatherhead at twenty past, and came in by the **7** first train to Waterloo. Sir, I can stand this strain no longer, I shall go mad if it continues. I have no one to turn to—none, save only one, who cares for me, and he, poor fellow, can be of little aid. I have heard of you, Mr. Holmes; I have heard of you from Mrs. Farintosh, whom you helped in the hour of her sore need. It was from her that I had your address. Oh, sir, do you not think you could help me too, and at least throw a little light through the dense darkness which surrounds me? At present it is out of my power to reward you for your services, but in a month or two I shall be married, with the control of my own income, and then at least you shall not find me ungrateful."

Holmes turned to his desk, and unlocking it, drew out a small case-book which he consulted.

" Farintosh," said he. " Ah, yes, I recall the case ; it was concerned with an opal tiara. I think it was before your time, Watson. I can only say, madam, that I shall **8** be happy to devote the same care to your case as I did to that of your friend. As to reward, my profession is its reward ; but you are at liberty to defray whatever expenses I may be put to, at the time which suits you best. And **9** now I beg that you will lay before us everything that may help us in forming an opinion upon the matter."

" Alas ! " replied our visitor. " The very horror of my situation lies in the fact that my fears are so vague, and my suspicions depend so entirely upon small points, which might seem trivial to another, that even he to whom of all others I have a right to look for help and advice looks upon all that I tell him about it as the fancies of a nervous woman. He does not say so, but I can read it from his soothing answers and averted eyes. But I have heard, Mr. Holmes, that you can see deeply into the manifold wickedness of the human heart. You may advise me how to walk amid the dangers which encompass me."

" I am all attention, madam."

" My name is Helen Stoner, and I am living with my stepfather, who is the last survivor of one of the oldest Saxon families in England, the Roylotts of Stoke Moran, on the western border of Surrey."   **10**

Holmes nodded his head. " The name is familiar to me," said he.

" The family was at one time among the richest in England, and the estate extended over the borders into Berkshire in the north, and Hampshire in the west. In **11-12** the last century, however, four successive heirs were of a dissolute and wasteful disposition, and the family ruin was eventually completed by a gambler, in the days of the Regency. Nothing was left save a few acres of ground **13** and the two-hundred-year-old house, which is itself crushed under a heavy mortgage. The last squire dragged out his existence there, living the horrible life of an aristocratic pauper ; but his only son, my stepfather, seeing that he must adapt himself to the new conditions, obtained an advance from a relative, which enabled him to take a medical degree, and went out to Calcutta, where, by his professional skill and his force of character, he established a large practice. In a fit of anger, however, caused by some robberies which had been perpetrated in the house, he beat his native butler to death, and narrowly escaped a capital sentence. As it was, he suffered a long term of imprisonment, and afterwards returned to England a morose and disappointed man.

" When Dr. Roylott was in India he married my mother, Mrs. Stoner, the young widow of Major-General Stoner, of the Bengal Artillery. My sister Julia and I were twins, **14** and we were only two years old at the time of my mother's re-marriage. She had a considerable sum of money, not less than a thousand a year, and this she bequeathed to

8 *I think it was before your time, Watson.* Mr. Howard Collins has asked ("Ex Libris Sherlock Holmes"): "But if [the case of Mrs. Farintosh] was before Watson's time, how did [Helen Stoner] get the Baker Street address?" And he has answered himself by saying: "Elementary! The case was begun before Holmes and Watson met, and the bill was rendered after the case was completed, by which time Holmes had moved to Baker Street." If Holmes rendered his bills on the first of the month, the case can thus be dated the first week in January, 1881.

9 *to defray whatever expenses I may be put to.* Holmes has come a long way in the two years which have passed since he depended for his bread and cheese on the clients to whose stories he listened, commented, and then pocketed his fee (*A Study in Scarlet*). As Mr. Thayer Cumings has noted ("Concerning Mr. Holmes' Fees"), Holmes "could afford to dine on 'oysters, a brace of grouse and something a little choice in white wine.' He could afford three shots of cocaine a day for many months at a time ('a seven per cent solution'). He could afford to go at will to the opera, or to Hallé's concert hall to hear Madame Norman-Neruda, and always to travel in the railway carriage first-class. He could afford to buy a Stradivarius. He could even afford a villa whenever he wanted one, or to travel abroad for as long as three years, and as far away as Tibet and Persia . . ." The fees which he must have collected to be able to afford these luxuries, Mr. Cumings thinks, "came from those cases for which we have not yet been prepared. . . . It must have been . . . [the] fascinating day-to-day *unrecorded* adventures which provided him with the wherewithal to live—and live to the hilt —the wonderful life he lived. *Lives*."

10 *on the western border of Surrey.* ". . . though no map, today or of 1883, will show the name 'Stoke Moran,' a little consideration of the clues will make it certain that Watson, under the name 'Stoke Moran,' has rather clumsily sought to conceal the identity of Stoke D'Abernon, a village some three miles (in a direct line) from the now populous town of Leatherhead," Mr. Michael Harrison wrote (*In the Footsteps of Sherlock Holmes*). The Roylott house—now demolished—Mr. Harrison has placed between the still-existing Slyfield House and Woodlands Park.

However: Miss Stoner has said that she "started from home before six, reached Leatherhead at twenty past, and came in by the first train to Waterloo." She reached Baker Street about seven, for Holmes, fully dressed, "knocked up" Watson at "only a quarter past seven." Reviewing this data Mr. Roger T. Clapp has pointed out (in "The Curious Problem of the Railway Timetables") that an examination of a Bradshaw of the period and the *A B C Railway Guide*, an equally reliable publication dating back to 1853, "discloses the singular fact that Helen Stoner could not have left Leatherhead in the morning in time to reach Baker Street by seven. The earliest train from Leatherhead to Waterloo left at 7:22, arriving at 8:11. Even if, allowing for a minor inaccuracy by Watson, she had actually taken the earlier train at 7:13 for London Bridge she still could not have arrived in the city before eight. . . . Helen Stoner undoubtedly did take a 6:20 train to London but not from Leatherhead since wherever Stoke Moran actually was it was not twenty minutes by dog-cart from Leatherhead. . . . If, for example, [Stoke Moran] was some twenty minutes by dog-cart from Clapham Junction then Helen Stoner could have easily caught the 6:25 to Waterloo arriving there at 6:39 and in ample time to get to Baker Street by seven."

11 *Berkshire*. Or Berks, an inland county in the Thames River basin. Largely agricultural, Berkshire has dairying and hog raising. At Windsor is the famous royal castle at which a certain gracious lady rewarded Holmes with an emerald tiepin. It was to Berkshire that Holmes and Watson went to solve the mystery of "Shoscombe Old Place."

12 *Hampshire*. In size the seventh of the English counties, Hampshire is packed with history. Romans, Saxons, Danes, and Normans landed there. Winchester was the first capital of a united England, and for a short period the capital, too, of a Scandinavian Empire. Many battles have been fought within its borders, and in the Puritan victory in Cheriton Wood which, so Clarendon recorded, "broke all the measures and altered the whole scheme of the king's counsels," the Civil War came to its end. It remains one of the most rural of the counties near London. Hampshire provided Holmes and Watson with two adventures, those of "The Copper Beeches" and "Thor Bridge."

13 *the Regency*. The last nine years, 1811–1820, of the reign of George III when, due to his periodic insanity, the government was conducted in the name of the Prince of Wales, later George IV. There was in truth a gay and dissolute group around the prince regent, of which the Roylott heir may well have been one.

14 *My sister Julia and I were twins*. It is interesting to note that in Conan Doyle's original manuscript, Helen Stoner is Helen Roylott, and Dr. Roylott is her father. In the 1910 play version, Helen and Julia appear as Enid and Violet Stonor (not Stoner). This last adds another bloom to the author's curious collection of Violets.

15 *Crewe*. An important railway junction in the county of Cheshire.

"LAST WEEK HE HURLED THE LOCAL BLACKSMITH OVER A PARAPET INTO A STREAM . . ."

Illustration by Sidney Paget for the *Strand Magazine*, February, 1892.

Dr. Roylott entirely whilst we resided with him, with a provision that a certain annual sum should be allowed to each of us in the event of our marriage.   Shortly after our return to England my mother died—she was killed eight years ago in a railway accident near Crewe.   Dr. Roylott then abandoned his attempts to establish himself in practice in London, and took us to live with him in the ancestral house at Stoke Moran.   The money which my mother had left was enough for all our wants, and there seemed no obstacle to our happiness.

" But a terrible change came over our stepfather about this time.   Instead of making friends and exchanging visits with our neighbours, who had at first been overjoyed to see a Roylott of Stoke Moran back in the old family seat, he shut himself up in his house, and seldom came out save to indulge in ferocious quarrels with whoever might cross his path.   Violence of temper approaching to mania has been hereditary in the men of the family, and in my stepfather's case it had, I believe, been intensified by his long residence in the tropics. A series of disgraceful brawls took place, two of which ended in the police-court, until at last he became the terror of the village, and the folks would fly at his approach, for he is a man of immense strength, and absolutely uncontrollable in his anger.

" Last week he hurled the local blacksmith over a parapet into a stream and it was only by paying over all the money that I could gather together that I was able to avert another public exposure.   He had no friends at all save the wandering gipsies, and he would give these vagabonds leave to encamp upon the few acres of bramble-covered land which represent the family estate, and would accept

in return the hospitality of their tents, wandering away with them sometimes for weeks on end. He has a passion also for Indian animals, which are sent over to him by a correspondent, and he has at this moment a cheetah and a baboon, which wander freely over his grounds, and are **16** feared by the villagers almost as much as their master.

" You can imagine from what I say that my poor sister Julia and I had no great pleasure in our lives. No servant would stay with us, and for a long time we did all the work of the house. She was but thirty at the time of her death, and yet her hair had already begun to whiten, even as mine has."

" Your sister is dead, then ? "

" She died just two years ago, and it is of her death that I wish to speak to you. You can understand that, living the life which I have described, we were little likely to see anyone of our own age and position. We had, however, an aunt, my mother's maiden sister, Miss Honoria West- phail, who lives near Harrow, and we were occasionally **17** allowed to pay short visits at this lady's house. Julia went there at Christmas two years ago, and met there a half-pay **18** Major of Marines, to whom she became engaged. My stepfather learned of the engagement when my sister returned, and offered no objection to the marriage ; but within a fortnight of the day which had been fixed for the wedding, the terrible event occurred which has deprived me of my only companion."

Sherlock Holmes had been leaning back in his chair with his eyes closed, and his head sunk in a cushion, but he half opened his lids now, and glanced across at his visitor.

" Pray be precise as to details," said he.

" It is easy for me to be so, for every event of that dreadful time is seared into my memory. The manor house is, as I have already said, very old, and only one wing is now inhabited. The bedrooms in this wing are on the ground floor, the sitting-rooms being in the central block of the buildings. Of these bedrooms, the first is Dr. Roylott's, the second my sister's, and the third my own. There is no communication between them, but they all open out into the same corridor. Do I make myself plain ? "

" Perfectly so."

" The windows of the three rooms open out upon the lawn. That fatal night Dr. Roylott had gone to his room early, though we knew that he had not retired to rest, for my sister was troubled by the smell of the strong Indian cigars which it was his custom to smoke. She left her room, therefore, and came into mine, where she sat for some time, chatting about her approaching wedding. At eleven o'clock she rose to leave me, but she paused at the door and looked back.

" ' Tell me, Helen,' said she, ' have you ever heard any-one whistle in the dead of the night ? '

" ' Never,' said I.

" ' I suppose that you could not possibly whistle your-self in your sleep ? '

" ' Certainly not. But why ? '

" ' Because during the last few nights I have always, about three in the morning, heard a low clear whistle. I

16 *a cheetah and a baboon.* "I don't know what kind of a watch-dog a baboon develops into," Mr. James Edward Holroyd wrote in "The Egg Spoon," "but to judge from this extract from *African Hunter* by J. A. Hunter (London: Hamish, Hamilton, 1954), Holmes and Watson had little to fear from the other half of the partnership: 'The cheetah is a long-legged cat, very gentle, and once much in demand among the Indian rajahs who domesticated them and kept them to hunt antelope, much as greyhounds are kept to course hares. Cheetahs are so good-natured that even an adult animal can easily be tamed. I do not believe that in the entire history of Africa there has been a single case of a cheetah attacking a human being.' It is of course possible that the Stoke Moran cheetah, having been sent from India, was a more intractable species than the one described above; just as, in reverse, the African elephant is less amenable to training than his Indian counterpart."

Despite Miss Stoner's "Indian animals," the pos-sibility exists that *both* the cheetah and the baboon came from Africa: apart from the small black baboon (*Cynopithecus niger* of the Celebes), as the editors of the Catalogue of the Sherlock Holmes Exhibition pointed out, baboons are confined to Africa and Arabia.

17 *Harrow.* In Middlesex, the home of the famous public school.

18 *half-pay.* The reduced pay of an army or navy officer when he is not on active service.

am a light sleeper, and it has awakened me. I cannot tell where it came from—perhaps from the next room, perhaps from the lawn. I thought that I would just ask you whether you had heard it.'

" ' No, I have not. It must be those wretched gipsies in the plantation.'

" ' Very likely. And yet if it were on the lawn I wonder that you did not hear it also.'

" ' Ah, but I sleep more heavily than you.'

" ' Well, it is of no great consequence, at any rate,' she smiled back at me, closed my door, and a few moments later I heard her key turn in the lock."

" Indeed," said Holmes. " Was it your custom always to lock yourselves in at night ? "

" Always."

" And why ? "

" I think that I mentioned to you that the Doctor kept a cheetah and a baboon. We had no feeling of security unless our doors were locked."

" Quite so. Pray proceed with your statement."

" I could not sleep that night. A vague feeling of impending misfortune impressed me. My sister and I, you will recollect, were twins, and you know how subtle are the links which bind two souls which are so closely allied. It was a wild night. The wind was howling outside, and the rain was beating and splashing against the windows. Suddenly, amidst all the hubbub of the gale, there burst forth the wild scream of a terrified woman. I knew that it was my sister's voice. I sprang from my bed, wrapped a shawl round me, and rushed into the corridor. As I opened my door I seemed to hear a low whistle, such as my sister described, and a few moments later a clanging sound, as if a mass of metal had fallen. As I ran down the passage my sister's door was unlocked, and revolved slowly upon its hinges. I stared at it horror-stricken, not knowing what was about to issue from it. By the light of the corridor lamp I saw my sister appear at the opening, her face blanched with terror, her hands groping for help, her whole figure swaying to and fro like that of a drunkard. I ran to her and threw my arms round her, but at that moment her knees seemed to give way and she fell to the ground. She writhed as one who is in terrible pain, and her limbs were dreadfully convulsed. At first I thought that she had not recognized me, but as I bent over her she suddenly shrieked out in a voice which I shall never forget, ' O, my God ! Helen ! It was the band ! The speckled band ! ' There was something else which she would fain have said, and she stabbed with her finger into the air in the direction of the Doctor's room, but a fresh convulsion seized her and choked her words. I rushed out, calling loudly for my stepfather, and I met him hastening from his room in his dressing-gown. When he reached my sister's side she was unconscious, and though he poured brandy down her throat, and sent for medical aid from the village, all efforts were in vain, for she slowly sank and died without having recovered her consciousness. Such was the dreadful end of my beloved sister."

" One moment," said Holmes ; " are you sure about this whistle and metallic sound ? Could you swear to it ? "

" That was what the county coroner asked me at the

". . . I SAW MY SISTER APPEAR IN THE OPENING, HER
FACE BLANCHED WITH TERROR . . ."

Illustration by Sidney Paget for the *Strand Magazine*, February, 1892.

19

inquiry. It is my strong impression that I heard it, and yet among the crash of the gale, and the creaking of an old house, I may possibly have been deceived."

" Was your sister dressed ? "

" No, she was in her nightdress. In her right hand was found the charred stump of a match, and in her left a matchbox." **20**

" Showing that she had struck a light and looked about her when the alarm took place. That is important. And what conclusions did the coroner come to ? "

" He investigated the case with great care, for Dr. Roylott's conduct had long been notorious in the county, but he was unable to find any satisfactory cause of death. My evidence showed that the door had been fastened upon the inner side, and the windows were blocked by old-fashioned shutters with broad iron bars, which were secured every night. The walls were carefully sounded, and were shown to be quite solid all round, and the flooring was also thoroughly examined, with the same result. The chimney is wide, but is barred up by four large staples. It is certain, therefore, that my sister was quite alone when she met her end. Besides, there were no marks of any violence upon her."

" How about poison ? "

" The doctors examined her for it, but without success."

" What do you think that this unfortunate lady died of, then ? "

" It is my belief that she died of pure fear and nervous shock, though what it was which frightened her I cannot imagine."

" Were there gipsies in the plantation at the time ? "

" Yes, there are nearly always some there."

" Ah, and what did you gather from this allusion to a band—a speckled band ? "

" Sometimes I have thought that it was merely the wild talk of delirium, sometimes that it may have referred to some band of people, perhaps to these very gipsies in the plantation. I do not know whether the spotted handkerchiefs which so many of them wear over their heads might have suggested the strange adjective which she used."

Holmes shook his head like a man who is far from being satisfied.

" These are very deep waters," said he ; " pray go on with your narrative."

" Two years have passed since then, and my life has been until lately lonelier than ever. A month ago, however, a dear friend, whom I have known for many years, has done me the honour to ask my hand in marriage. His name is Armitage—Percy Armitage—the second son of Mr. Armitage, of Crane Water, near Reading. My step- **21** father has offered no opposition to the match, and we are to be married in the course of the spring. Two days ago some repairs were started in the west wing of the building, **22** and my bedroom wall has been pierced, so that I have had to move into the chamber in which my sister died, and to sleep in the very bed in which she slept. Imagine, then, my thrill of terror when last night, as I lay awake, thinking over her terrible fate, I suddenly heard in the silence of the night the low whistle which had been the herald of her own death. I sprang up and lit the lamp, but nothing was to

19 *he poured brandy down her throat.* In many later cases, we shall see that Dr. Watson also uses brandy as his almost universal specific. "It is still held by many physicians and pharmacologists as well that brandy or whisky are useful therapeutic agents in emergencies," Dr. Edward J. Van Liere wrote in "Dr. Watson's Universal Specific." "Dr. Torald Sellman, dean of American pharmacologists, in his textbook, *A Manual of Pharmacology*, W. B. Saunders Co., Philadelphia, 1946 6th ed., p. 704, writes: 'Its temporary usefulness as a quickly acting stimulant can scarcely be doubted in the various forms of sudden circulatory collapse—syncope, exhaustion, hemorrhage, traumatic shock . . .' He attributes its effect to reflex stimulation and on this account its action is brief. He writes further: 'alcohol acts mainly as a temporary emergency remedy, to tide the patient over the immediate danger.' He suggests a dose of 25 cc. of whisky or brandy (roughly an ounce) and that it should be repeated every 10 to 15 minutes according to effect."

20 *and in her left a matchbox."* Just how the unfortunate Julia Stoner's hands could be "groping for help" with a match in her right hand and a matchbox in her left, we will leave to the reader to decide.

21 *Reading.* The county town of Berkshire, 36 miles southwest of London by Great Western Railway, a railway junction and agricultural center with famous nursery gardens. Oscar Wilde, who so much impressed Conan Doyle at their first meeting, wrote *The Ballad of Reading Gaol* while in prison there.

22 *some repairs were started in the west wing.* The repairs would not have been started on a Sunday, so the day on which Miss Stoner called on Holmes was not a Tuesday.

23 *as soon as it was daylight.* Miss Stoner has told us that she left Stoke Moran before 6:00 A.M. If it became daylight shortly before 6:00 A.M., the time of the year would have been early April, corroborating Watson.

24 *the crackling fire.* We will find several references in the Canon to "the crackling fire." (See, for example, "The Adventure of the Blue Carbuncle.") They are hard to understand. Holmes and Watson burned soft coal, surely, and soft coal may crack but seldom if ever crackles.

25 *upon some most important business.* The day was therefore a weekday.

be seen in the room.   I was too shaken to go to bed again,
23 however, so I dressed, and as soon as it was daylight I slipped down, got a dog-cart at the Crown Inn, which is opposite, and drove to Leatherhead, from whence I have come on this morning, with the one object of seeing you and asking your advice.'

"You have done wisely," said my friend.   "But have you told me all?"

"Yes, all."

"Miss Stoner, you have not.   You are screening your stepfather."

"Why, what do you mean?"

For answer Holmes pushed back the frill of black lace which fringed the hand that lay upon our visitor's knee. Five little livid spots, the marks of four fingers and a thumb, were printed upon the white wrist.

"You have been cruelly used," said Holmes.

The lady coloured deeply, and covered over her injured wrist.   "He is a hard man," she said, "and perhaps he hardly knows his own strength."

There was a long silence, during which Holmes leaned
24 his chin upon his hands and stared into the crackling fire.

"This is very deep business," he said at last.   "There are a thousand details which I should desire to know before I decide upon our course of action.   Yet we have not a moment to lose.   If we were to come to Stoke Moran to-day, would it be possible for us to see over these rooms without the knowledge of your stepfather?"

"As it happens, he spoke of coming into town to-day
25 upon some most important business.   It is probable that he will be away all day, and that there would be nothing to disturb you.   We have a housekeeper now, but she is old and foolish, and I could easily get her out of the way."

"Excellent.   You are not averse to this trip, Watson?"

"By no means."

"Then we shall both come.   What are you going to do yourself?"

"I have one or two things which I would wish to do now that I am in town.   But I shall return by the twelve o'clock train, so as to be there in time for your coming."

"And you may expect us early in the afternoon.   I have myself some small business matters to attend to. Will you not wait and breakfast?"

"No, I must go.   My heart is lightened already since I have confided my trouble to you.   I shall look forward to seeing you again this afternoon."   She dropped her thick black veil over her face, and glided from the room.

"And what do you think of it all, Watson?" asked Sherlock Holmes, leaning back in his chair.

"It seems to me to be a most dark and sinister business."

"Dark enough and sinister enough."

"Yet if the lady is correct in saying that the flooring and walls are sound, and that the door, window, and chimney are impassable, then her sister must have been undoubtedly alone when she met her mysterious end."

"What becomes, then, of these nocturnal whistles, and what of the very peculiar words of the dying woman?"

"I cannot think."

"When you combine the ideas of whistles at night, the

presence of a band of gipsies who are on intimate terms with this old doctor, the fact that we have every reason to believe that the doctor has an interest in preventing his stepdaughter's marriage, the dying allusion to a band, and finally, the fact that Miss Helen Stoner heard a metallic clang, which might have been caused by one of those metal bars which secured the shutters falling back into their place, I think there is good ground to think that the mystery may be cleared along those lines."

" But what, then, did the gipsies do ? "

" I cannot imagine."

" I see many objections to any such a theory."

" And so do I. It is precisely for that reason that we are going to Stoke Moran this day. I want to see whether the objections are fatal, or if they may be explained away. But what, in the name of the devil ! "

The ejaculation had been drawn from my companion by the fact that our door had been suddenly dashed open, and that a huge man framed himself in the aperture. His costume was a peculiar mixture of the professional and of the agricultural, having a black top-hat, a long frock-coat, and a pair of high gaiters, with a hunting-crop swinging in his hand. So tall was he that his hat actually brushed the cross-bar of the doorway, and his breadth seemed to span it across from side to side. A large face, seared with a thousand wrinkles, burned yellow with the sun, and marked with every evil passion, was turned from one to the other of us, while his deep-set, bile-shot eyes, and the high thin fleshless nose, gave him somewhat the resemblance to a fierce old bird of prey.

" Which of you is Holmes ? " asked this apparition.

" My name, sir, but you have the advantage of me," said my companion quietly.

" I am Dr. Grimesby Roylott, of Stoke Moran."

" Indeed, Doctor," said Holmes blandly. " Pray take a seat."

" I will do nothing of the kind. My stepdaughter has been here. I have traced her. What has she been saying to you ? "

" It is a little cold for the time of the year," said Holmes.

" What has she been saying to you ? " screamed the old man furiously.

" But I have heard that the crocuses promise well," continued my companion imperturbably.

" Ha ! You put me off, do you ? " said our new visitor, taking a step forward, and shaking his hunting-crop. " I know you, you scoundrel ! I have heard of you before. You are Holmes the meddler."

My friend smiled.

" Holmes the busybody ! "

His smile broadened.

" Holmes the Scotland Yard jack-in-office."

Holmes chuckled heartily. " Your conversation is most entertaining," said he. " When you go out close the door, for there is a decided draught."

" I will go when I have had my say. Don't you dare to meddle with my affairs. I know that Miss Stoner has been here—I traced her ! I am a dangerous man to fall foul of ! See here." He stepped swiftly forward, seized

. . . A HUGE MAN FRAMED HIMSELF IN THE APERTURE.

Illustration by Sidney Paget for the *Strand Magazine*, February, 1892.

HE STEPPED SWIFTLY FORWARD, SEIZED THE POKER, AND BENT IT INTO A CURVE WITH HIS HUGE BROWN HANDS.

Illustration by Joseph Camana for *Cases of Sherlock Holmes*, St. Louis: Webster Publishing Co., 1947.

26 *Doctors' Commons.* Originally, the common table and dining hall of the Association or College of Doctors of Civil Law in London; later, the building near St. Paul's Churchyard, occupied by this corporation, in which there were ecclesiastical and admiralty courts and offices having jurisdiction over marriage licenses, divorces, registrations of wills, etc. The building was taken down in 1867; Holmes, in 1883, would have visited *Somerset House*, to which, in 1874, the wills previously registered at Doctors' Commons were transferred (a charge of one shilling is, and was, made for showing wills or registered copies thereof—an item for Holmes' expense account to Helen Stoner).

27 *an income of £250.* Worth, at the time, about $1,250 U.S. The total income, once amounting to about $5,000, had fallen to not more than $3,750.

28 *a trap.* Colloquial English for a one-horse, two-wheeled carriage on springs.

"... AN EXCELLENT ARGUMENT WITH GENTLEMEN WHO CAN TWIST STEEL POKERS INTO KNOTS."

This is not Watson's old service revolver, but a pistol acquired by him after his move to Baker Street. Actually, the gun was a *Webley's No. 2,* .320 bore, described in the Catalogue of the Sherlock Holmes Exhibition as "a small, heavy, but relatively effective weapon. . . . Essentially a pocket pistol it takes up little room but would be adequate for dealing with the most determined criminal. It was the smallest really practicable weapon of its time. . . . The Eley cartridges of the time were sold in boxes labeled to say which weapon they fitted; and [Holmes'] 'Eley No. 2' is probably a confusion arising out of a box marked in large letters 'Eley' and, in smaller letters, 'for the Webley Pistol, No. 2.' Moreover, some Webley pistols were marketed with 'Eley .320' on the barrel to prevent confusion with the Smith and Wesson .32, which was not the same as the British or Continental, .320, or the similar .32 Colt."

the poker, and bent it into a curve with his huge brown hands.

"See that you keep yourself out of my grip," he snarled, and hurling the twisted poker into the fireplace, he strode out of the room.

"He seems a very amiable person," said Holmes, laughing. "I am not quite so bulky, but if he had remained I might have shown him that my grip was not much more feeble than his own." As he spoke he picked up the steel poker, and with a sudden effort straightened it out again.

"Fancy his having the insolence to confound me with the official detective force! This incident gives zest to our investigation, however, and I only trust that our little friend will not suffer from her imprudence in allowing this brute to trace her. And now, Watson, we shall order breakfast, and afterwards I shall walk down to Doctors' **26** Commons, where I hope to get some data which may help us in this matter."

It was nearly one o'clock when Sherlock Holmes returned from his excursion. He held in his hand a sheet of blue paper, scrawled over with notes and figures.

"I have seen the will of the deceased wife," said he. "To determine its exact meaning I have been obliged to work out the present prices of the investments with which it is concerned. The total income, which at the time of the wife's death was little short of £1,100, is now through the fall in agricultural prices not more than £750. Each **27** daughter can claim an income of £250, in case of marriage. It is evident, therefore, that if both girls had married this beauty would have had a mere pittance, while even one of them would cripple him to a serious extent. My morning's work has not been wasted, since it has proved that he has the very strongest motives for standing in the way of anything of the sort. And now, Watson, this is too serious for dawdling, especially as the old man is aware that we are interesting ourselves in his affairs, so if you are ready we shall call a cab and drive to Waterloo. I should be very much obliged if you would slip your revolver into your pocket. An Eley's No. 2 is an excellent argument with gentlemen who can twist steel pokers into knots. That and a tooth-brush are, I think, all that we need."

At Waterloo we were fortunate in catching a train for **28** Leatherhead, where we hired a trap at the station inn, and drove for four or five miles through the lovely Surrey **29** lanes. It was a perfect day, with a bright sun and a few fleecy clouds in the heavens. The trees and wayside hedges were just throwing out their first green shoots, and the air was full of the pleasant smell of the moist earth. To me at least there was a strange contrast between the sweet promise of the spring and this sinister quest upon which we were engaged. My companion sat in front of the trap, his arms folded, his hat pulled down over his eyes, and his chin sunk upon his breast, buried in the deepest thought. Suddenly, however, he started, tapped me on the shoulder, and pointed over the meadows.

"Look there!" said he.

A heavily timbered park stretched up in a gentle slope, thickening into a grove at the highest point. From amidst the branches there jutted out the grey gables and high roof-tree of a very old mansion.

" Stoke Moran ? " said he.

" Yes, sir, that be the house of Dr. Grimesby Roylott," remarked the driver.

" There is some building going on there," said Holmes ; " that is where we are going."

" There's the village," said the driver, pointing to a cluster of roofs some distance to the left ; " but if you want to get to the house, you'll find it shorter to go over this stile, and so by the footpath over the fields. There it is, where the lady is walking."

" And the lady, I fancy, is Miss Stoner," observed Holmes, shading his eyes. " Yes, I think we had better do as you suggest."

We got off, paid our fare, and the trap rattled back on its way to Leatherhead.

" I thought it as well," said Holmes, as we climbed the stile, " that this fellow should think we had come here as architects, or on some definite business. It may stop his gossip. Good afternoon, Miss Stoner. You see that we have been as good as our word."

Our client of the morning had hurried forward to meet us with a face which spoke her joy. " I have been waiting so eagerly for you," she cried, shaking hands with us warmly. " All has turned out splendidly. Dr. Roylott has gone to town, and it is unlikely that he will be back before evening."

" We have had the pleasure of making the Doctor's acquaintance," said Holmes, and in a few words he sketched out what had occurred. Miss Stoner turned white to the lips as she listened.

" Good heavens ! " she cried, " he has followed me, then."

" So it appears."

" He is so cunning that I never know when I am safe from him. What will he say when he returns ? "

" He must guard himself, for he may find that there is someone more cunning than himself upon his track. You must lock yourself from him to-night. If he is violent, we shall take you away to your aunt's at Harrow. Now, we must make the best use of our time, so kindly take us at once to the rooms which we are to examine."

The building was of grey, lichen-blotched stone, with a high central portion, and two curving wings, like the claws of a crab, thrown out on each side. In one of these wings the windows were broken, and blocked with wooden boards, while the roof was partly caved in, a picture of ruin. The central portion was in little better repair, but the right-hand block was comparatively modern, and the blinds in the windows, with the blue smoke curling up from the chimneys, showed that this was where the family resided. Some scaffolding had been erected against the end wall, and the stonework had been broken into, but there were no signs of any workmen at the moment of our visit. Holmes walked slowly up and down the ill-trimmed lawn, and examined with deep attention the outsides of the windows.

" This, I take it, belongs to the room in which you used

29 *It was a perfect day*. The day of the case was a bright, sunny day, and Wednesday, April 4, 1883, was a day on which the sun shone for only two hours and two minutes. The sun shone for nine hours and eight minutes on Monday, April 2, 1883, but we doubt that the repairs on the west wing would have been started on a Saturday. In your editor's opinion, the day was *Friday, April 6, 1883*, a day on which the sun shone for nine hours and two minutes. Early April is again corroborated by Watson's "first green shoots" and "sweet promise of the spring."

WE GOT OFF, PAID OUR FARE . . .

Illustration by Sidney Paget for the *Strand Magazine*, February, 1892.

30 *Wilton carpet.* A cut-pile Brussels carpet or rug first manufactured in the Wiltshire town of Wilton.

"WHERE DOES THAT BELL COMMUNICATE WITH?"
HE ASKED AT LAST . . .

A modern conception of Sherlock Holmes by Tom Gill, for the Simon and Schuster "Golden Picture Classic," *Sherlock Holmes,* 1957.

to sleep, the centre one to your sister's, and the one next to the main building to Dr. Roylott's chamber?"

" Exactly so. But I am now sleeping in the middle one."

" Pending the alterations, as I understand. By the way, there does not seem to be any very pressing need for repairs at that end wall."

" There were none. I believe that it was an excuse to move me from my room."

" Ah! that is suggestive. Now, on the other side of this narrow wing runs the corridor from which these three rooms open. There are windows in it, of course?"

" Yes, but very small ones. Too narrow for anyone to pass through."

" As you both locked your doors at night, your rooms were unapproachable from that side. Now, would you have the kindness to go into your room, and to bar your shutters."

Miss Stoner did so, and Holmes, after a careful examination through the open window, endeavoured in every way to force the shutter open, but without success. There was no slit through which a knife could be passed to raise the bar. Then with his lens he tested the hinges, but they were of solid iron, built firmly into the massive masonry. " Hum!" said he, scratching his chin in some perplexity, " my theory certainly presents some difficulties. No one could pass these shutters if they were bolted. Well, we shall see if the inside throws any light upon the matter."

A small side-door led into the whitewashed corridor from which the three bedrooms opened. Holmes refused to examine the third chamber, so we passed at once to the second, that in which Miss Stoner was now sleeping, and in which her sister had met her fate. It was a homely little room, with a low ceiling and a gaping fireplace, after the fashion of old country houses. A brown chest of drawers stood in one corner, a narrow white-counterpaned bed in another, and a dressing-table on the left-hand side of the window. These articles, with two small wicker-work chairs, made up all the furniture in the room, save **30** for a square of Wilton carpet in the centre. The boards round and the panelling of the walls were brown, worm-eaten oak, so old and discoloured that it may have dated from the original building of the house. Holmes drew one of the chairs into a corner and sat silent, while his eyes travelled round and round and up and down, taking in every detail of the apartment.

" Where does that bell communicate with?" he asked at last, pointing to a thick bell-rope which hung down beside the bed, the tassel actually lying upon the pillow.

" It goes to the housekeeper's room."

" It looks newer than the other things?"

" Yes, it was only put there a couple of years ago."

" Your sister asked for it, I suppose?"

" No, I never heard of her using it. We used always to get what we wanted for ourselves."

" Indeed, it seemed unnecessary to put so nice a bell-pull there. You will excuse me for a few minutes while I satisfy myself as to this floor." He threw himself down upon his face with his lens in his hand, and crawled swiftly backwards and forwards, examining minutely the cracks between the boards. Then he did the same with the woodwork with which the chamber was panelled. Finally he walked over to the bed and spent some time in staring at it, and in running his eye up and down the wall. Finally he took the bell-rope in his hand and gave it a brisk tug.

" Why, it's a dummy," said he.

" Won't it ring ? "

" No, it is not even attached to a wire. This is very interesting. You can see now that it is fastened to a hook just above where the little opening of the ventilator is."

" How very absurd ! I never noticed that before."

" Very strange ! " muttered Holmes, pulling at the rope. " There are one or two very singular points about this room. For example, what a fool a builder must be to open a ventilator in another room, when, with the same trouble, he might have communicated with the outside air ! "

" That is also quite modern," said the lady.

" Done about the same time as the bell-rope," remarked Holmes.

" Yes, there were several little changes carried out about that time."

" They seem to have been of a most interesting character—dummy bell-ropes, and ventilators which do not ventilate. With your permission, Miss Stoner, we shall now carry our researches into the inner apartment."

Dr. Grimesby Roylott's chamber was larger than that of his stepdaughter, but was as plainly furnished. A camp bed, a small wooden shelf full of books, mostly of a technical character, an arm-chair beside the bed, a plain wooden chair against the wall, a round table, and a large iron safe were the principal things which met the eye. Holmes walked slowly round and examined each and all of them with the keenest interest.

" What's in here ? " he asked, tapping the safe.

" My stepfather's business papers."

" Oh ! you have seen inside, then ? "

" Only once, some years ago. I remember that it was full of papers."

" There isn't a cat in it, for example ? "

" No. What a strange idea ! "

" Well, look at this ! " He took up a small saucer of milk which stood on the top of it.

" No ; we don't keep a cat. But there is a cheetah and a baboon."

" Ah, yes, of course ! Well, a cheetah is just a big cat, and yet a saucer of milk does not go very far in satisfying its wants, I daresay. There is one point which I should wish to determine." He squatted down in front of the wooden chair, and examined the seat of it with the greatest attention.

" Thank you. That is quite settled," said he, rising and putting his lens in his pocket. " Hullo ! here is something interesting ! "

The object which had caught his eye was a small dog lash hung on one corner of the bed. The lash, however, was curled upon itself, and tied so as to make a loop of whipcord.

" What do you make of that, Watson ? "

" It's a common enough lash. But I don't know why it should be tied."

" That is not quite so common, is it ? Ah, me ! it's a wicked world, and when a clever man turns his brain to

"WELL, LOOK AT THIS!" HE TOOK UP A SMALL SAUCER OF MILK . . .

Illustration by Sidney Paget for the *Strand Magazine*, February, 1892.

"GOOD-BYE, AND BE BRAVE . . ."

Illustration by Sidney Paget for the *Strand Magazine*, February, 1892.

crime it is the worst of all. I think that I have seen enough now, Miss Stoner, and, with your permission, we shall walk out upon the lawn."

I had never seen my friend's face so grim, or his brow so dark, as it was when we turned from the scene of this investigation. We had walked several times up and down the lawn, neither Miss Stoner nor myself liking to break in upon his thoughts before he roused himself from his reverie.

" It is very essential, Miss Stoner," said he, " that you should absolutely follow my advice in every respect."

" I shall most certainly do so."

" The matter is too serious for any hesitation. Your life may depend upon your compliance."

" I assure you that I am in your hands."

" In the first place, both my friend and I must spend the night in your room."

Both Miss Stoner and I gazed at him in astonishment.

" Yes, it must be so. Let me explain. I believe that that is the village inn over there ? "

" Yes, that is the ' Crown.' "

" Very good. Your windows would be visible from there ? "

" Certainly."

" You must confine yourself to your room, on pretence of a headache, when your stepfather comes back. Then when you hear him retire for the night, you must open the shutters of your window, undo the hasp, put your lamp there as a signal to us, and then withdraw with everything which you are likely to want into the room which you used to occupy. I have no doubt that, in spite of the repairs, you could manage there for one night."

" Oh, yes, easily."

" The rest you will leave in our hands."

" But what will you do ? "

" We shall spend the night in your room, and we shall investigate the cause of this noise which has disturbed you."

" I believe, Mr. Holmes, that you have already made up your mind," said Miss Stoner, laying her hand upon my companion's sleeve.

" Perhaps I have."

" Then for pity's sake tell me what was the cause of my sister's death."

" I should prefer to have clearer proofs before I speak."

" You can at least tell me whether my own thought is correct, and if she died from some sudden fright."

" No, I do not think so. I think that there was probably some more tangible cause. And now, Miss Stoner, we must leave you, for if Dr. Roylott returned and saw us, our journey would be in vain. Good-bye, and be brave, for if you will do what I have told you, you may rest assured that we shall soon drive away the dangers that threaten you."

Sherlock Holmes and I had no difficulty in engaging a bedroom and sitting-room at the Crown Inn. They were on the upper floor, and from our window we could command a view of the avenue gate, and of the inhabited wing of Stoke Moran Manor House. At dusk we saw Dr. Grimesby Roylott drive past, his huge form looming up beside the little figure of the lad who drove him. The boy had some slight difficulty in undoing the heavy iron gates, and we heard the hoarse roar of the Doctor's voice, and saw the fury with which he shook his clenched fists at him. The trap drove on, and a few minutes later we saw a sudden light spring up among the trees as the lamp was lit in one of the sitting-rooms.

" Do you know, Watson," said Holmes, as we sat together in the gathering darkness, " I have really some scruples as to taking you to-night. There is a distinct element of danger."

" Can I be of assistance ? "

" Your presence might be invaluable."

" Then I shall certainly come."

" It is very kind of you."

" You speak of danger. You have evidently seen more in these rooms than was visible to me."

" No, but I fancy that I may have deduced a little more. I imagine that you saw all that I did."

" I saw nothing remarkable save the bell-rope, and what purpose that could answer I confess is more than I can imagine."

" You saw the ventilator, too ? "

" Yes, but I do not think that it is such a very unusual thing to have a small opening between two rooms. It was so small that a rat could hardly pass through."

" I knew that we should find a ventilator before ever we came to Stoke Moran."

" My dear Holmes ! "

" Oh, yes, I did. You remember in her statement she said that her sister could smell Dr. Roylott's cigar. Now, of course that suggests at once that there must be a communication between the two rooms. It could only be a small one, or it would have been remarked upon at the coroner's inquiry. I deduced a ventilator."

" But what harm can there be in that ? "

" Well, there is at least a curious coincidence of dates. A ventilator is made, a cord is hung, and a lady who sleeps in the bed dies. Does not that strike you ? "

" I cannot as yet see any connection."

" Did you observe anything very peculiar about that bed ? "

" No."

" It was clamped to the floor. Did you ever see a bed fastened like that before ? "

" I cannot say that I have."

" The lady could not move her bed. It must always be in the same relative position to the ventilator and to the rope—for so we may call it, since it was clearly never meant for a bell-pull."

" Holmes," I cried, " I seem to see dimly what you are hitting at. We are only just in time to prevent some subtle and horrible crime."

" Subtle enough and horrible enough. When a doctor does go wrong he is the first of criminals. He has nerve and he has knowledge. Palmer and Pritchard were among the heads of their profession. This man strikes even deeper, but I think, Watson, that we shall be able to strike deeper still. But we shall have horrors enough before the night is over : for goodness' sake let us have a quiet pipe, and turn our minds for a few hours to something more cheerful."

"WHEN A DOCTOR DOES GO WRONG HE IS THE FIRST OF CRIMINALS."

At left, William Palmer, executed in 1856 for the murder of a friend by poison. At right, that "benevolent monster," Edward William Pritchard, a Glasgow practitioner who was hanged in 1865 for poisoning his wife and mother-in-law. Excellent accounts of Palmer and Pritchard, both by Harold Eaton, will be found in *The Fifty Most Amazing Crimes of the Last 100 Years*, edited by J. M. Parrish and John R. Crossland, London: Odhams Press, Ltd., 1936, from which these sketches are taken.

31 *we were out on the dark road.* "This, too, checks with early April," the late Professor Jay Finley Christ wrote in *An Irregular Chronology*, "for in that month in 1883, the moon was not visible in the evening until the 13th."

About nine o'clock the light among the trees was extinguished, and all was dark in the direction of the Manor House. Two hours passed slowly away, and then, suddenly, just at the stroke of eleven, a single bright light shone out right in front of us.

"That is our signal," said Holmes, springing to his feet; "it comes from the middle window."

As we passed out he exchanged a few words with the landlord, explaining that we were going on a late visit to an acquaintance, and that it was possible that we might spend the night there. A moment later we were out on **31** the dark road, a chill wind blowing in our faces, and one yellow light twinkling in front of us through the gloom to guide us on our sombre errand.

There was little difficulty in entering the grounds, for unrepaired breaches gaped in the old park wall. Making our way among the trees, we reached the lawn, crossed it, and were about to enter through the window, when out from a clump of laurel bushes there darted what seemed to be a hideous and distorted child, who threw itself on the grass with writhing limbs, and then ran swiftly across the lawn into the darkness.

"My God!" I whispered, ' did you see it ? '

Holmes was for the moment as startled as I. His hand closed like a vice upon my wrist in his agitation. Then he broke into a low laugh, and put his lips to my ear.

"It is a nice household," he murmured, " that is the baboon."

I had forgotten the strange pets which the Doctor affected. There was a cheetah, too ; perhaps we might find it upon our shoulders at any moment. I confess that I felt easier in my mind when, after following Holmes' example and slipping off my shoes, I found myself inside the bedroom. My companion noiselessly closed the shutters, moved the lamp on to the table, and cast his eyes round the room. All was as we had seen it in the day-time. Then creeping up to me and making a trumpet of his hand, he whispered into my ear again so gently that it was all that I could do to distinguish the words :

"The least sound would be fatal to our plans."

I nodded to show that I had heard.

"We must sit without a light. He would see it through the ventilator."

I nodded again.

"Do not go to sleep ; your very life may depend upon it. Have your pistol ready in case we should need it. I will sit on the side of the bed, and you in that chair."

I took out my revolver and laid it on the corner of the table.

Holmes had brought up a long thin cane, and this he placed upon the bed beside him. By it he laid the box of matches and the stump of a candle. Then he turned down the lamp and we were left in darkness.

How shall I ever forget that dreadful vigil ? I could not hear a sound, not even the drawing of a breath, and yet I knew that my companion sat open-eyed, within a few feet of me, in the same state of nervous tension in which I was myself. The shutters cut off the least ray of light, and we waited in absolute darkness. From outside came the occasional cry of a night-bird, and once at our very window a long drawn, cat-like whine, which told us that the cheetah was indeed at liberty. Far away we could hear the deep tones of the parish clock, which boomed out every quarter of an hour. How long they seemed, those quarters ! Twelve o'clock, and one, and two, and three, and still we sat waiting silently for whatever might befall.

Suddenly there was the momentary gleam of a light up in the direction of the ventilator, which vanished immediately, but was succeeded by a strong smell of burning oil and heated metal. Someone in the next room had lit a dark lantern. I heard a gentle sound of movement, and then all was silent once more, though the smell grew stronger. For half an hour I sat with straining ears. Then suddenly another sound became audible—a very gentle, soothing sound, like that of a small jet of steam escaping continually from a kettle. The instant that we heard it, Holmes sprang from the bed, struck a match, and lashed furiously with his cane at the bell-pull.

" You see it, Watson ? " he yelled. " You see it ? "

But I saw nothing. At the moment when Holmes **32** struck the light I heard a low, clear whistle, but the sudden glare flashing into my weary eyes made it impossible for me to tell what it was at which my friend lashed so savagely. I could, however, see that his face was deadly pale, and filled with horror and loathing.

He had ceased to strike, and was gazing up at the ventilator, when suddenly there broke from the silence of the night the most horrible cry to which I have ever listened. It swelled up louder and louder, a hoarse yell of pain and fear and anger all mingled in the one dreadful shriek. They say that away down in the village, and even in the distant parsonage, that cry raised the sleepers from their beds. It struck cold to our hearts, and I stood gazing at Holmes, and he at me, until the last echoes of it had died away into the silence from which it rose.

32 *But I saw nothing.* We know that Watson's eyesight was phenomenally acute, for we are told in *The Hound of the Baskervilles* that he was able to discern a boy's figure at a distance of "several miles" with the naked eye. However, Dr. Vernon Pennell has deduced from Watson's statement here that Watson suffered as a minor defect a deficiency of Vitamin A that resulted in night blindness ("A Résumé of the Medical Life of John H. Watson, M.D., Late of the Army Medical Department").

HOLMES . . . LASHED FURIOUSLY WITH HIS CANE AT THE BELL-PULL.

Illustration by Sidney Paget for the *Strand Magazine*, February, 1892.

SOMEONE IN THE NEXT ROOM HAD LIT A DARK LANTERN.

The predecessor of the modern electric flashlight. "A dark lantern's principal use, and the way it differed from an ordinary hand lantern, was in respect that it could be darkened while lit, by a mechanism of its own," Mr. Melvin Cross wrote in "The Lantern of Sherlock Holmes." "The light could be shut off without extinguishing the flame, thereby rendering the user invisible at will to anyone foreign to his purpose. It was used in a crude form centuries ago for military purposes. Until within the past few years it was used to flash signals, a spring being attached to the shutter, and sold under the name of Boat Signal Lantern. . . . The construction of the various pieces used in the dark-lantern seems to be about the same in general principles; that is, the main body is cylindrical in form, with door and a pointed top, which latter is fluted and acts to let the heated air out. The door has a round projection extending directly away from the body, and here the lens is held. The door also gives access to the burner for lighting and adjustment. On the back are the carrying devices: generally near the bottom and in the front, is a small knob. This is pushed around in a slot to adjust the shade, which latter also acts as a reflector. When the light is on full, the reflector has been moved between the burner and the lens—a rather ingenious arrangement." Other references to dark lanterns and pocket lanterns—there are some twenty-two in all throughout the Canon—occur in *A Study in Scarlet, The Sign of the Four,* "The Greek Interpreter," "The Adventure of the Empty House," "The Adventure of Charles Augustus Milverton," "The Adventure of the Six Napoleons," "The Adventure of Wisteria Lodge," "The Adventure of the Red Circle," "The Adventure of the Bruce-Partington Plans" and "The Adventure of Shoscombe Old Place." Shown here, at top, are three small lanterns, compared in size with a pencil. The two right-hand pieces are pocket lanterns, complete with handles and vertical slides. At bottom, a lantern is shown with the shade open, half closed and closed. When the shutter is open (*left*) it is behind the burner and acts as a reflector. All lanterns are from the collection of Mr. Melvin Cross.

"What can it mean?" I gasped.

"It means that it is all over," Holmes answered. "And perhaps, after all, it is for the best. Take your pistol, and we shall enter Dr. Roylott's room."

With a grave face he lit the lamp, and led the way down the corridor. Twice he struck at the chamber door without any reply from within. Then he turned the handle and entered, I at his heels, with the cocked pistol in my hand.

It was a singular sight which met our eyes. On the table stood a dark lantern with the shutter half open, throwing a brilliant beam of light upon the iron safe, the door of which was ajar. Beside this table, on the wooden chair, sat Dr. Grimesby Roylott, clad in a long grey dressing-gown, his bare ankles protruding beneath, and his feet thrust into red heelless Turkish slippers. Across his lap lay the short stock with the long lash which we had noticed during the day. His chin was cocked upwards, and his eyes were fixed in a dreadful rigid stare at the corner of the ceiling. Round his brow he had a peculiar yellow band, with brownish speckles, which seemed to be bound tightly round his head. As we entered he made neither sound nor motion.

"The band! the speckled band!" whispered Holmes.

I took a step forward. In an instant his strange headgear began to move, and there reared itself from among his hair the squat diamond-shaped head and puffed neck of a loathsome serpent.

"It is a swamp adder!" cried Holmes—"the deadliest snake in India. He has died within ten seconds of being bitten. Violence does, in truth, recoil upon the violent, and the schemer falls into the pit which he digs for another. **33** Let us thrust this creature back into its den, and we can then remove Miss Stoner to some place of shelter, and let the county police know what has happened."

As he spoke he drew the dog whip swiftly from the dead man's lap, and throwing the noose round the reptile's neck, he drew it from its horrid perch, and, carrying it at arm's length, threw it into the iron safe, which he closed upon it.

Such are the true facts of the death of Dr. Grimesby Roylott, of Stoke Moran. It is not necessary that I should prolong a narrative which has already run to too great a length, by telling how we broke the sad news to the terrified girl, how we conveyed her by the morning train to the care of her good aunt at Harrow, of how the slow process of official inquiry came to the conclusion that the Doctor met his fate while indiscreetly playing with a dangerous pet. The little which I had yet to learn of the case was told me by Sherlock Holmes as we travelled back next day.

"I had," said he, "come to an entirely erroneous conclusion, which shows, my dear Watson, how dangerous it always is to reason from insufficient data. The presence of the gipsies, and the use of the word 'band,' which was used by the poor girl, no doubt, to explain the appearance which she had caught a horrid glimpse of by

ROUND HIS BROW HE HAD A PECULIAR YELLOW BAND, WITH BROWNISH SPECKLES, WHICH SEEMED TO BE BOUND TIGHTLY ROUND HIS HEAD.

Illustration by Joseph Camana for *Cases of Sherlock Holmes*; St. Louis: Webster Publishing Co., 1947. Sidney Paget illustrated the same scene for the *Strand Magazine*, February, 1892.

33 *the schemer falls into the pit which he digs for another.* Holmes again demonstrates his familiarity with Holy Writ: "He that diggeth a pit shall fall into it; and whoso breaketh an hedge, a serpent shall bite him" (Ecclesiastes, 1:2).

the light of her match, were sufficient to put me upon an entirely wrong scent. I can only claim the merit that I instantly reconsidered my position when, however, it became clear to me that whatever danger threatened an occupant of the room could not come either from the window or the door. My attention was speedily drawn, as I have already remarked to you, to this ventilator, and to the bell-rope which hung down to the bed. The discovery that this was a dummy, and that the bed was clamped to the floor, instantly gave rise to the suspicion that the rope was there as a bridge for something passing through the hole, and coming to the bed. The idea of a snake instantly occurred to me, and when I coupled it with my knowledge that the Doctor was furnished with a supply of creatures from India, I felt that I was probably on the right track. The idea of using a form of poison which could not possibly be discovered by any chemical test was just such a one as would occur to a clever and ruthless man who had had an Eastern training. The rapidity with which such a poison would take effect would also, from his point of view, be an advantage. It would be a sharp-eyed coroner indeed who could distinguish the two little dark punctures which would show where the poison fangs had done their work. Then I thought of the whistle. Of course, he must recall the snake before the morning light revealed it to the victim. He had trained it, probably by the use of the milk which we saw, to return to him when summoned. He would put it through the ventilator at the hour that he thought best, with the certainty that it would crawl down the rope, and land on the bed. It might or might not bite the occupant, perhaps she might escape every night for a week, but sooner or later she must fall a victim.

" I had come to these conclusions before ever I had entered his room. An inspection of his chair showed me that he had been in the habit of standing on it, which, of course, would be necessary in order that he should reach the ventilator. The sight of the safe, the saucer of milk, and the loop of whipcord were enough to finally dispel any doubts which may have remained. The metallic clang heard by Miss Stoner was obviously caused by her father hastily closing the door of his safe upon its terrible occupant. Having once made up my mind, you know the steps which I took in order to put the matter to the proof. I heard the creature hiss, as I have no doubt that you did also, and I instantly lit the light and attacked it."

" With the result of driving it through the ventilator."

" And also with the result of causing it to turn upon its master at the other side. Some of the blows of my cane came home, and roused its snakish temper, so that it flew upon the first person it saw. In this way I am no doubt indirectly responsible for Dr. Grimesby Roylott's death, and I cannot say that it is likely to weigh very heavily upon my conscience."

Auctorial and Bibliographical Note: There has been some discussion among the members of the Conan Doyle Literary Society that Sir Arthur's sister Connie (Mrs. E. W. Hornung) may have given him the idea upon which he based "The Adventure of the Speckled Band." In any case, of all the short stories (excluding those in the *Case-Book*), it was Sir Arthur's favorite: he placed it first on the "twelve best" list he drew up for the March, 1927, issue of the *Strand*. Of all the adventures, the short stories and the novels, it also ranked first with the readers of the *Observer*. The original manuscript, consisting of 33 folio pages, two in the hand of a secretary but containing corrections by Conan Doyle, was auctioned in London on March 26, 1934, bringing £82. It was later sold by Scribner's to a Chicago dealer. Its present location is unknown.

18

"IT IS ... THE DEADLIEST SNAKE IN INDIA"

[An Afterword to "The Adventure of the Speckled Band"]

Holmes called the speckled band "a swamp adder"—a name not now in common use, as the editors of the Catalogue of the Sherlock Holmes Exhibition noted: "It may be an obsolete vernacular name from some early work of natural history now forgotten; or it may be a purely local name, acquired by Holmes from one of his cosmopolitan acquaintances, in which case it is unlikely to appear in any standard work of reference. The identity of the snake must therefore be deduced from such information as we possess on its appearance and behaviour."

Let us therefore consider the data describing Dr. Roylott's messenger of death, as Watson has recorded it for us:

1. The snake, according to Holmes, was "Indian." "There is a wide-spread belief" (the editors of the Catalogue of the Exhibition continued) "that [the puff adder, *Bitis Arietans*] was the snake intended. The fact that it is African in origin does not disqualify it, since there is only circumstantial evidence that the snake was Indian. . . . However, the lethargic nature of this snake, its relatively slow-acting venom, and its striking markings (which could not reasonably be described, even by Julia Stoner immediately after being bitten, as speckled) seem to rule it out. Apart from the sea-snakes (*Hydrophiidae*) of the Indian coasts, whose flat oar-like tails would seem to preclude them from negotiating bell-ropes, there are no truly aquatic venomous snakes in India. Holmes' use of the term 'swamp' adder' has caused some investigators to suggest the damp-loving river-jack vipers of the African rain-forests (*Bitis nasicornis* and *B. gabonica*); but these must be ruled out for precisely the same reasons as the puff adder."

2. Its fangs left "two little dark punctures" in its victims. "The only snakes that kill by poison fangs in India are divided . . . into two families—the *Elapidae* and the *Viperidie*," Mr. Douglas Lawson wrote in "The Speckled Band—What Was It?" "One of the major differences between these families is the difference in poison fangs. In *Elapidae* the relatively short fangs lie in the front of the jaw, and, on contact, eject poison into the victim—*but not in killing amounts*. After the ejection of the poison, the series of frontal teeth and four half-jaws pull the drugged victim closer to its attacker, and the poison fangs, embedded repeatedly, eject new quantities of poison at each contact. The result to an observer is that a victim of *Elapidae*'s poison has a series of marks where the poison fangs have embedded themselves again and again. In *Viperidie*, the poison fangs are much larger, and when not in use lie in the roof of the mouth at the back of the head. When the viper attacks, these poison fangs extend beyond the mouth and make the first contact with the victim; and only one contact. . . . Thus a victim poisoned by *Viperidie* has only two puncture marks, and this was what Holmes and Watson found when they examined the body of Dr. Roylott. We have therefore established that Dr. Roylott's messenger of death was an Indian viper."

3. In color it was yellow with brown specks. "Of the numerous viper families throughout the world," Mr. Lawson continued, "there are but two poisonous varieties in India . . . the Russell's Viper and *Echis Carinata* [the saw-scaled viper]. Of these two snakes, the most prolific and the most featured in Indian snake-lore is the Russell's Viper—consider the popularity of its names: Tic Polonga, Daboia Russelli, Daboia Elegans, Chain Viper, Ullo Borra, Siahchunder Amata —and Russell's Viper. In contrast, *Echis Carinata* has only one pseudonym." In Mr. Lawson's view, the death of Julia Stoner was caused by a young Russell's Viper, the death of Dr. Roylott by the *Echis Carinata*. Certainly the markings of the *Echis Carinata* would seem to correspond more closely than those of the Russell's Viper to the snake described by Watson: *Echis Carinata* has been described (by the late Dr. Raymond Lee Ditmars, in his *Snakes of the World*; New York: The Macmillan Company, 1931) as: "The body is browning-gray with three longitudinal series of whitish black-edged spots," whereas the Russell's Viper is described as a pale brown body, with three longitudinal series of black rings, centered with a chocolate brown and ringed in a frame of white and yellow.

4. Its hiss was "gentle" and "soothing, like that of a small jet of steam escaping from a tea-kettle." "The Russell's Viper is silent until thoroughly aroused," Mr. Lawson continued, "and then hisses violently on both the outgo and intake of its breath. The hissing of a Tic Polonga would have boomed on the Doctor's eardrums. Therefore, the Doctor did *not* hear the hissing of a Russell's Viper. However, the ophidologists agree on one snake that answers the description as though it were a tape recording: *Echis Carinata* probably does not hiss at all, but in any excitement, he emits a sibilant sound by the constant rubbing together of his scales as he coils and twists his lithe body, and the sound to the listener is 'that of steam escaping from a tea-kettle.' "

5. It was perhaps three feet in length. "The average length of a Russell's Viper is a strong four to five feet," Mr. Lawson continued. "Since the circumference of Dr. Roylott's head probably was not more than 27 inches, it would seem that a Russell's Viper must have encircled the head twice, still allowing room to park its neck in the Roylott scalp. Surely Dr. Watson would not have described such a voluminous headpiece as a 'speckled band.' What, then, could he have seen? The *Echis Carinata*, attaining a length of two to three feet, and a very much thinner snake than its bigger counterpart, would have answered photographically to Dr. Watson's description."

6. Its bite caused death "within ten seconds" (in the case *of Dr. Roylott*). The bite of *no* snake would kill in so short a time as ten seconds; either Dr. Roylott was still alive when Holmes and Watson entered his room or the doctor had died of a heart attack and the snake embedded its fangs in a dead man (Mr. Lawson's theory). We may add here that both the Russell's Viper and *Echis Carinata* carry "haemotoxic" venom, which acts on the blood system—much slower to kill than "neurotoxic" venom, which acts on the nervous system.

7. *But Dr. Roylott's death "within ten seconds" is inconsistent with the death of Julia Stoner, who "slowly sank and died . . ."* "There had presumably been no change of snake," wrote the editors of the Catalogue of the Sherlock Holmes Exhibition, but both Mr. Lawson (as we have seen) and Mr. Rolfe Boswell ("Dr. Roylott's Wily Fillip") disagree with this verdict. In Mr. Boswell's view, Julia Stoner was bitten by a bamboo viper, Dr. Roylott by a Russell's Viper.

8. *It had a "squat, diamond-shaped head."* This is true to a greater or a lesser degree of practically all snakes.

9. *It had a "puffed neck."* This would seem to rule out both the Russell's Viper and *Echis Carinata*; the only snake that might answer to this description would be *Naja naja*, the cobra, which, indeed the editors of the Catalogue of the Sherlock Holmes Exhibition finally decided "the speckled band" to have been.

10. *The snake, we are told, is recalled to the doctor's room by a whistle.* But "how could this be when it is well known that snakes are quite deaf?", Mr. Laurence M. Klauber asked in "The Truth About the Speckled Band." "It is true that they are extraordinarily sensitive to vibrations of the substratum upon which they rest, so they often appear to hear sounds of sufficient magnitude to affect such a vibrator as a box in which they may be kept; but this could not be the case with a snake clinging tenuously to a flimsy bell-rope."

11. *"He had trained it, probably by the use of the milk which we saw."* Experts have said that no snake drinks milk from choice, though it may do so if it is thirsty enough and water is not available. "The creature lives on milk," Mr. Klauber wrote, "not a natural food of any snake and one that it will accept only rarely as a substitute for water, if the latter be unobtainable."

12. *The speckled band, we are told, "would crawl down the rope" "with . . . certainty."* Whether any snake would crawl down—and then up—a rope with certainty under these or similar conditions is another point debated by experts. Mr. Raymond Massey, who played the role of Holmes in a motion picture version of "The Adventure of the Speckled Band," stated in a letter to Mr. Nathan L. Bengis that the snake used "climbed down the bell-rope with a realism which I think satisfied the most rabid Holmes fan." On the other hand, Mr. Klauber has written: ". . . while admitting that a snake might slide down a bell-rope, it could certainly not climb up one, particularly with the lower end swinging loose above the fatal bed. For snakes do not climb as many think—by twining themselves around an object; they climb by wedging their bodies into any crannies and interstices, taking advantage of every irregularity or protusion upon which a loop of the body may be hooked. It is

by this method that they progress rapidly upon the rough bark of branching trees or the tangled skein of a vine."

It would seem, regretfully, that *no known species of snake fully satisfies all the requirements of "the speckled band."*

But if the "terrible occupant" of Dr. Roylott's safe was *not* a snake, what could it have been? In the opinion of Mr. Klauber, the creature was a horrible hybrid bred by Dr. Roylott—a sinister combination of the Mexican Gila monster (*Heloderma horridum*) and the spectacled or Indian cobra, now known as *Naja naja naja*. Such a creature would unite the intelligence and agility of the lizard with the inimical disposition of the snake. It would have fangs in the upper jaw inherited from one parent, and in the lower jaw from the other, and a venom incomparably strengthened by hybridization, "thus assuring the almost instant demise of any victim. Here we have an animal that would feed on the batter that was mistaken for milk, for so does its parent, the Gila monster; one with ears like any lizard, wherewith to hear a whistle; and one whose legs and claws permitted it to run up a bell-rope as easily as down. . . . Here was a reptile that would be handled with a noose on a dog switch; whereas any snake handler would have used a stick terminated with a hook. And, above all, when we combine the cobra and the heloderm the result is certain to assume the likeness of a speckled band."

.   .   .

FOR THREE HOURS WE STROLLED ABOUT TOGETHER . . .

Illustration by Sidney Paget for the *Strand Magazine*, August, 1893.

19

THE RESIDENT PATIENT

[Wednesday, October 6, to Thursday, October 7, 1886]

IN glancing over the somewhat incoherent series of memoirs with which I have endeavoured to illustrate a few of the mental peculiarities of my friend, Mr. Sherlock Holmes, I have been struck by the difficulty which I have experienced in picking out examples which shall in every way answer my purpose. For in those cases in which Holmes has performed some *tour-de-force* of **1** analytical reasoning, and has demonstrated the value of his peculiar methods of investigation, the facts themselves have often been so slight or so commonplace that I could not feel justified in laying them before the public. On the other hand, it has frequently happened that he has been concerned in some research where the facts have been of the most remarkable and dramatic character, but where the share which he has himself taken in determining their causes has been less pronounced than I, as his biographer, could wish. The small matter which I have chronicled under the heading of " A Study in Scarlet," and that other later one connected with the **2** loss of the *Gloria Scott*, may serve as examples of this Scylla and Charybdis which are for ever threatening his **3** historian. It may be that, in the business of which I am now about to write, the part which my friend played is not sufficiently accentuated ; and yet the whole train of circumstances is so remarkable that I cannot bring myself to omit it entirely from this series.

It had been a close, rainy day in October. " Unhealthy weather, Watson," said my friend. But the evening has brought a breeze with it. What do you say to a ramble through London ? " **4**

I was weary of our little sitting-room, and gladly **5** acquiesced. For three hours we strolled about together, watching the ever-changing kaleidoscope of life as it ebbs and flows through Fleet Street and the Strand. Holmes' **6** characteristic talk, with its keen observance of detail and subtle power of inference, held me amused and enthralled.

It was ten o'clock before we reached Baker Street again. A brougham was waiting at our door.

" Hum ! A doctor's—general practitioner, I perceive," said Holmes. " Not been long in practice, but has had a good deal to do. Come to consult us, I fancy ! Lucky we came back ! "

I was sufficiently conversant with Holmes' methods to

1 tour-de-force. French: a feat of remarkable skill or strength.

2 *that other later one*. Watson is of course speaking in terms of the time of publication, not of occurrence.

3 *Scylla and Charybdis*. Scylla was a sea-monster with six heads, twelve feet, and a voice like the yelp of a dog. It lived in a cave by the sea, whence it thrust out its heads to snatch seamen from passing ships (Homer's *Odyssey*, Book XII, 1, 73). Opposite Scylla dwelt Charybdis, another sea monster. In later classical times these Homeric monsters were localized in the Gulf of Messina, Scylla as the rock on the Italian and Charybdis as a whirlpool on the Sicilian side.

4 *What do you say to a ramble through London?"* When "The Resident Patient" first saw publication in the *Strand Magazine* for August, 1893, this paragraph appeared as two paragraphs which read:

> I cannot be sure of the exact date, for some of my memoranda upon the matter have been mislaid, but it must have been towards the end of the first year during which Holmes and I shared chambers in Baker Street. It was boisterous October weather, and we had both remained indoors all day, I because I feared with my shaken health to face the keen autumn wind, while he was deep in some of those abstruse chemical investigations which absorbed him utterly as long as he was engaged upon them. Towards evening, however, the breaking of a test-tube brought his research to a premature ending, and he sprang up from his chair with an exclamation of impatience and a clouded brow.
>
> "A day's work ruined, Watson," said he, striding across to the window. "Ha! the stars are out and the wind has fallen. What do you say to a ramble through London?"

This, as we shall see, is a manifestly inaccurate version, which is why the two paragraphs became one when Watson's account of the case of "The Resident Patient" appeared in *Sherlock Holmes:*

The Complete Short Stories (London: John Murray, 1928).

Quite obviously, as the late Mr. H. W. Bell indicated in *Sherlock Holmes and Dr. Watson: The Chronology of Their Adventures*, the missing memoranda must eventually have been discovered; Watson undoubtedly consulted them before the publication of the first complete collection of his shorter chronicles, checked the fact that the month was indeed October, and removed from the text the paragraph about "the end of the first year during which Holmes and I shared chambers in Baker Street."

5 *I was weary of our little sitting-room.* Your editor believes that the adventure of "The Resident Patient" took place only a few weeks before Dr. Watson married for the first time. His approaching nuptials may well have accounted for the statement that he was "weary" of the sitting room at 221B at this time.

6 *Fleet Street.* "Fleet Street . . . takes its name from the once rapid and clear, but now fearfully polluted river Fleet, which has its source far away in the breezy heights of Hampstead, and flows through the valley where Farringdon Street now is, in which it once turned the mills which are still commemorated in Turnmill Street. . . . [Fleet Street has] always been considered as the chief approach to the City," Augustus J. C. Hare wrote in *Walks in London*, Vol. I. Fleet Street today is the center of the newspaper industry, and is equally famous for its many fine taverns.

7 *to be able to follow his reasoning.* Despite his constant self-disparagement, Watson made many deductions, some of them brilliant, on his own. Here he analyzes, in acceptable Sherlockian style, the physician with the unusual Resident Patient. In "A Scandal in Bohemia," Watson makes several pertinent deductions from the King's notepaper before the Master adds his own. Watson easily connects the Five Orange Pips with a seafaring man with no other indication than the postmarks. In *The Sign of the Four* he is able to deduce, with only a little prompting from the sleuth, that the murderer entered through the roof, *improbable as that was*. In *The Hound of the Baskervilles* his reconstruction of Dr. James Mortimer from his walking stick is shrewd if not altogther accurate. He later makes an accurate analysis of Mr. McCarthy's fatal injuries at Boscombe Valley.

"Another instance is found in the opening pages of "The Adventure of Wisteria Lodge,' where Watson, from but one glance at Scott Eccles, gives us a string of accurate inferences worthy of Holmes himself," Mr. Nathan L. Bengis wrote in "Take a Bow, Dr. Watson." "So, too, Dr. Watson's interview with Mrs. Laura Lyons in *The Hound of the Baskervilles* is handled by him throughout with such admirable aplomb as to indicate that he would make an excellent prosecuting attorney if he had been inclined that way."

7 be able to follow his reasoning, and to see that the nature and state of the various medical instruments in the wicker basket which hung in the lamp-light inside the brougham had given him the data for his swift deduction. The light in our window above showed that this late visit was indeed intended for us. With some curiosity as to what could have sent a brother medico to us at such an hour, I followed Holmes into our sanctum.

A pale, taper-faced man with sandy whiskers rose up from a chair by the fire as we entered. His age may not have been more than three- or four-and-thirty, but his haggard expression and unhealthy hue told of a life which had sapped his strength and robbed him of his youth. His manner was nervous and shy, like that of a sensitive gentleman, and the thin white hand which he laid on the mantelpiece as he rose was that of an artist rather than of a surgeon. His dress was quiet and sombre, a black frock-coat, dark trousers, and a touch of colour about his necktie.

" Good evening, Doctor," said Holmes, cheerily ; " I am glad to see that you have only been waiting a very few minutes."

" You spoke to my coachman, then ? "

" No, it was the candle on the side-table that told me. Pray resume your seat and let me know how I can serve you."

" My name is Doctor Percy Trevelyan," said our visitor, **8** " and I live at 403 Brook Street."

" Are you not the author of a monograph upon obscure nervous lesions ? " I asked.

His pale cheeks flushed with pleasure at hearing that his work was known to me.

" I so seldom hear of the work that I thought it was **9** quite dead," said he. " My publishers give me a most discouraging account of its sale. You are yourself, I presume, a medical man ? "

" A retired Army surgeon."

" My own hobby has always been nervous disease. I should wish to make it an absolute speciality, but, of course, a man must take what he can get at first. This, however, is beside the question, Mr. Sherlock Holmes, and I quite appreciate how valuable your time is. The fact is that a very singular train of events has occurred recently at my house in Brook Street, and to-night they came to such a head that I felt it was quite impossible for me to wait another hour before asking for your advice and assistance."

Sherlock Holmes sat down and lit his pipe. " You are very welcome to both," said he. " Pray let me have a detailed account of what the circumstances are which have disturbed you."

" One or two of them are so trivial," said Dr. Trevelyan, " that really I am almost ashamed to mention them. But the matter is so inexplicable, and the recent turn which it has taken is so elaborate, that I shall lay it all before you, and you shall judge what is essential and what is not.

" I am compelled, to begin with, to say something of my own college career. I am a London University man, you know, and I am sure you will not think that I am unduly singing my own praises if I say that my student career was considered by my professors to be a very promising one. After I had graduated I continued to devote myself to research, occupying a minor position in King's College Hospital, and I was fortunate enough to **10** excite considerable interest by my research into the pathology of catalepsy, and finally to win the Bruce Pinkerton prize and medal by the monograph on nervous **11** lesions to which your friend has just alluded. I should not go too far if I were to say that there was a general impression at that time that a distinguished career lay before me.

"But the one great stumbling-block lay in my want of capital. As you will readily understand, a specialist who aims high is compelled to start in one of a dozen streets in the Cavendish Square quarter, all of which entail **12** enormous rents and furnishing expenses. Besides this preliminary outlay, he must be prepared to keep himself for some years, and to hire a presentable carriage and horse. To do this was quite beyond my power, and I could only hope that by economy I might in ten years' time save enough to enable me to put up my plate. Suddenly, however, an unexpected incident opened up quite a new prospect to me.

"This was a visit from a gentleman of the name of Blessington, who was a complete stranger to me. He came up into my room one morning, and plunged into business in an instant.

"'You are the same Percy Trevelyan who has had so distinguished a career and won a great prize lately?' said he. I bowed.

"'Answer me frankly,' he continued, 'for you will find it to your interest to do so. You have all the cleverness which makes a successful man. Have you the tact?'

"I could not help smiling at the abruptness of the question.

"'I trust that I have my share,' I said.

"'Any bad habits? Not drawn towards drink, eh?'

"'Really, sir!' I cried.

"'Quite right! That's all right! But I was bound to ask. With all these qualities why are you not in practice?'

"I shrugged my shoulders.

"'Come, come!' said he, in his bustling way. 'It's the old story. More in your brains than in your pocket, eh? What would you say if I were to start you in Brook Street?'

"I stared at him in astonishment.

"'Oh, it's for my sake, not for yours,' he cried. 'I'll be perfectly frank with you, and if it suits you it will suit me very well. I have a few thousands to invest, d'ye see, and I think I'll sink them in you.'

"'But why?' I gasped.

"'Well, it's just like any other speculation, and safer than most.'

"I STARED AT HIM IN ASTONISHMENT."

Illustration by Sidney Paget for the *Strand Magazine*, August, 1893.

"Indeed," Mr. Ed S. Woodhead concludes ("In Defense of Dr. Watson") "there is hardly a case that does not supply further evidence of Watson's perspicacity; but the best testimony of all is the fact that, although after each of his expeditions in search of details for Holmes he is taunted for his omissions, he is nevertheless sent out again on the same errands, time after time. And when Holmes in less sarcastic moods (when the evidence brought in by Watson is evaluated and the case grows less baffling?) he describes Watson's investigations as 'invaluable.' Probably Watson's best case was at Baskerville Hall where Holmes says, 'Our researches have evidently been running on parallel lines,' and his letters from that place of mystery are masterpieces."

8 *Brook Street.* ". . . so called from the Tye Bourne whose course it marks," Augustus J. C. Hare wrote in *Walks in London*, Vol. II. "No. 57, four doors from Bond Street, was the house of George Frederick Handel, the famous composer, who used to give rehearsals of his oratorios there." Brook Street today contains some elegant shops as well as the world-famous Claridge's Hotel, at the south corner of Davies Street; this hotel, formerly Mivart's, was opened in 1808.

9 *I thought it was quite dead."* Your editor believes that Watson planned shortly to resume an active role in medicine. His knowledge of Dr. Trevelyan's obscure monograph would indicate that he was "boning up." Watson at this time perhaps thought of becoming a psychiatrist, since the work was on "nervous lesions." Watson in many later cases displays his keen interest in the treatment and cure of mental diseases.

10 *King's College Hospital.* Founded at Clare Market in 1839 in connection with King's College, King's College Hospital in Holmes' and Watson's day stood in Portugal Street, named in honor of Catherine of Braganza. The Hospital and its surroundings were built over the burial ground of St.

Clement Danes, where Nathaniel Lee, the bombastic dramatist, 1657–1692, author of *Sophonisba* and *Gloriana*, was buried, having been killed in a drunken street brawl. Here also was a monument to "Honest Joe Miller," the "Father of Jokes," 1684–1738.

11 *the Bruce Pinkerton prize*. "In spite of considerable research we have been unable to discover any connection between this gentleman and Bruce-Partington, the inventor of the submarine," the late Gavin Brend wrote in *My Dear Holmes*.

12 *the Cavendish Square quarter*. "Cavendish Square, laid out in 1717, takes its name (with the neighbouring Henrietta Street and Holles Street) from Lady Henrietta Cavendish Holles, who married, in 1713, Edward Harley, second Earl of Oxford. . . . At No. 24 lived and painted George Romney, always called by Sir Joshua Reynolds, whom he had the honour of rivalling, 'the man of Cavendish Square.' Princess Amelia, daughter of George II, lived in the large house at the corner of Harley Street. . . . There is little more worth noticing in the frightful district north of Oxford Street, which, with the exception of [Manchester Square and Cavendish Square] *generally* marks the limits of fashionable society."—Augustus J. C. Hare, *Walks in London*, Vol. II.

13 *Lady Day*. March 25th. Lady Day is a day observed in honor of the Virgin Mary, commemorating some occasion in her life; specifically, the Feast of the Annunciation.

14 *the West End*. The west side of London—basically the City of Westminster, as opposed to the east end of London, the business and financial district including the ancient City of London.

"'What am I to do, then?'

"'I'll tell you. I'll take the house, furnish it, pay the maids, and run the whole place. All you have to do is to wear out your chair in the consulting-room. I'll let you have pocket-money and everything. Then you hand over to me three-quarters of what you earn, and you keep the other quarter for yourself.'

"This was the strange proposal, Mr. Holmes, with which the man Blessington approached me. I won't weary you with the account of how we bargained and negotiated. It ended in my moving into the house next **13** Lady Day, and starting in practice on very much the same conditions as he had suggested. He came himself to live with me in the character of a resident patient. His heart was weak, it appears, and he needed constant medical supervision. He turned the two best rooms on the first floor into a sitting-room and bedroom for himself. He was a man of singular habits, shunning company and very seldom going out. His life was irregular, but in one respect he was regularity itself. Every evening at the same hour he walked into the consulting-room, examined the books, put down five and threepence for every guinea that I had earned, and carried the rest off to the strong box in his own room.

"I may say with confidence that he never had occasion to regret his speculation. From the first it was a success. A few good cases and the reputation which I had won in the hospital brought me rapidly to the front, and during the last year or two I have made him a rich man.

"So much, Mr. Holmes, for my past history and my relations with Mr. Blessington. It only remains for me now to tell you what has occurred to bring me here to-night.

"Some weeks ago Mr. Blessington came down to me in, as it seemed to me, a state of considerable agitation. He spoke of some burglary which, he said, had been committed in the West End, and he appeared, I remember, to be quite unnecessarily excited about it, declaring that a day should not pass before we should add stronger bolts to our windows and doors. For a week he continued to be in a peculiar state of restlessness, peering continually out of the windows, and ceasing to take the short walk which had usually been the prelude to his dinner. From his manner it struck me that he was in mortal dread of

"... PUT DOWN FIVE AND THREEPENCE FOR EVERY GUINEA THAT I HAD EARNED ..."

Five shillings and threepence meant that Blessington put down the then equivalent of approximately $1.31 for every $5.25 Trevelyan earned. The guinea, be it noted, equals 21 shillings. It is a unit of currency so aristocratic that there exists today no coin or banknote for it. (The guinea was last coined in 1813, and shown in the illustration above is an 1813 guinea of George III. The coin took its name from the Guinea Coast, later the Crown Colony of the Gold Coast of Africa, a very important source of gold exploited by the Royal African Company.) To this day, professional men in Britain state the fee for their services in guineas (see, in this connection the "receipted bill for thirteen guineas, paid by Mr. Godfrey Staunton last month to Dr. Leslie Armstrong"—"The Adventure of the Missing Three-Quarter.") The guinea is also the usual unit used in pricing expensive luxuries (see, in this connection, "Silver Blaze," in which Mme. Lesurier of Bond Street charges 22 guineas for a costume). Shown below is a threepence of 1859.

something or somebody, but when I questioned him upon the point he became so offensive that I was compelled to drop the subject. Gradually as time passed his fears appeared to die away, and he had renewed his former habits, when a fresh event reduced him to the pitiable state of prostration in which he now lies.

"What happened was this. Two days ago I received the letter which I now read to you. Neither address nor **15** date is attached to it.

"'A Russian nobleman who is now resident in England,' it runs, 'would be glad to avail himself of the professional assistance of Dr. Percy Trevelyan. He has been for some years a victim to cataleptic attacks, on which, as is well known, Dr. Trevelyan is an authority. He proposes to call at about a quarter-past six to-morrow evening, if Dr. Trevelyan will make it convenient to be **16** at home.'

"This letter interested me deeply, because the chief difficulty in the study of catalepsy is the rareness of the disease. You may believe, then, that I was in my consulting-room when at the appointed hour, the page showed in the patient.

"He was an elderly man, thin, demure, and commonplace—by no means the conception one forms of a Russian nobleman. I was much more struck by the appearance of his companion. This was a tall young man, surprisingly handsome, with a dark, fierce face, and the limbs and chest of a Hercules. He had his hand under **17** the other's arm as they entered, and helped him to a chair with a tenderness which one would hardly have expected from his appearance.

"'You will excuse my coming in, Doctor,' said he to me, speaking English with a slight lisp. 'This is my father, and his health is a matter of the most overwhelming importance to me.'

"I was touched by this filial anxiety. 'You would, perhaps, care to remain during the consultation?' said I.

"'Not for the world,' he cried, with a gesture of horror. 'It is more painful to me than I can express. If I were to see my father in one of those dreadful seizures, I am convinced that I should never survive it. My own nervous system is an exceptionally sensitive one. With your permission I will remain in the waiting-room while you go into my father's case.'

"To this, of course, I assented, and the young man withdrew. The patient and I then plunged into a discussion of his case, of which I took exhaustive notes. He was not remarkable for intelligence, and his answers were frequently obscure, which I attributed to his limited acquaintance with our language. Suddenly, however, as I sat writing he ceased to give any answer at all to my inquiries, and on my turning towards him I was shocked to see that he was sitting bolt upright in his chair, staring at me with a perfectly blank and rigid face. He was again in the grip of his mysterious malady.

"My first feeling, as I have just said, was one of pity and horror. My second, I fear, was rather one of professional satisfaction. I made notes of my patient's pulse and temperature, tested the rigidity of his muscles, and

15 *Two days ago I received the letter*. The day on which the case began was therefore not a Tuesday.

16 *to-morrow evening*. The appointment would not have been made for a Sunday; the day on which the case began was therefore not a Monday.

17 *a Hercules*. Watson was later to compare the King of Bohemia to this most popular hero in the Greek and Roman legends, famous for his extraordinary strength and courage.

"HE HAD HIS HAND UNDER THE OTHER'S ARM AS THEY ENTERED, AND HELPED HIM TO A CHAIR . . ."

Illustration by Sidney Paget for the *Strand Magazine*, August, 1893.

". . . I WAS SHOCKED TO SEE THAT HE WAS SITTING BOLT UPRIGHT IN HIS CHAIR, STARING AT ME WITH A PERFECTLY BLANK AND RIGID FACE."

Illustration by William H. Hyde for *Harper's Weekly*, August 12, 1893.

18 *at the very same hour this evening.* The day on which the case began was therefore not a Sunday.

". . . HE BURST INTO MY CONSULTING-ROOM LIKE A MAN WHO IS MAD WITH PANIC."

Illustration by Sidney Paget for the *Strand Magazine*, August, 1893.

examined his reflexes. There was nothing markedly abnormal in any of these conditions, which harmonized with my former experiences. I had obtained good results in such cases by the inhalation of nitrite of amyl, and the present seemed an admirable opportunity of testing its virtues. The bottle was downstairs in my laboratory, so, leaving my patient seated in his chair, I ran down to get it. There was some little delay in finding it—five minutes, let us say—and then I returned. Imagine my amazement to find the room empty and the patient gone!

"Of course, my first act was to run into the waiting-room. The son had gone also. The hall door had been closed, but not shut. My page who admits patients is a new boy, and by no means quick. He waits downstairs, and runs up to show patients out when I ring the consulting-room bell. He had heard nothing, and the affair remained a complete mystery. Mr. Blessington came in from his walk shortly afterwards, but I did not say anything to him upon the subject, for to tell the truth, I have got in the way of late of holding as little communication with him as possible.

"Well, I never thought that I should see anything more of the Russian and his son, so you can imagine my **18** amazement when at the very same hour this evening they both came marching into my consulting-room, just as they had done before.

"'I feel that I owe you a great many apologies for my abrupt departure yesterday, Doctor,' said my patient.

"'I confess that I was very much surprised at it,' said I.

"'Well, the fact is,' he remarked, 'that when I recover from these attacks my mind is always very clouded as to all that has gone before. I woke up in a strange room, as it seemed to me, and made my way out into the street in a sort of dazed way when you were absent.'

"'And I,' said the son, 'seeing my father pass the door of the waiting-room, naturally thought that the consultation had come to an end. It was not until we had reached home that I began to realize the true state of affairs.'

"'Well,' said I, laughing, 'there is no harm done, except that you puzzled me terribly; so if you, sir, would kindly step into the waiting-room, I shall be happy to continue our consultation, which was brought to so abrupt an ending.'

"For half an hour or so I discussed the old gentleman's symptoms with him, and then, having prescribed for him, I saw him go off on the arm of his son.

"I have told you that Mr. Blessington generally chose this hour of the day for his exercise. He came in shortly afterwards and passed upstairs. An instant later I heard him running down, and he burst into my consulting-room like a man who is mad with panic.

"'Who has been in my room?' he cried.

"'No one,' said I.

"'It's a lie!' he yelled. 'Come up and look.'

"I passed over the grossness of his language, as he seemed half out of his mind with fear. When I went upstairs with him he pointed to several footprints upon the light carpet.

" ' D'you mean to say those are mine ? ' he cried.

" They were certainly very much larger than any which he could have made, and were evidently quite fresh. It rained hard this afternoon, as you know, and my patients **19** were the only people who called. It must have been the case, then, that the man in the waiting-room had for some unknown reason, while I was busy with the other, ascended to the room of my resident patient. Nothing had been touched or taken, but there were the footprints to prove that the intrusion was an undoubted fact.

" Mr. Blessington seemed more excited over the matter than I should have thought possible, though, of course, it was enough to disturb anybody's peace of mind. He actually sat crying in an arm-chair, and I could hardly get him to speak coherently. It was his suggestion that I should come round to you, and of course I at once saw the propriety of it, for certainly the incident is a very singular one, though he appears to completely overrate its importance. If you would only come back with me in my brougham, you would at least be able to soothe him, though I can hardly hope that you will be able to explain this remarkable occurrence."

Sherlock Holmes had listened to this long narrative with an intentness which showed me that his interest was keenly aroused. His face was as impassive as ever, but his lids had drooped more heavily over his eyes, and his smoke had curled up more thickly from his pipe to emphasize each curious episode in the doctor's tale. As our visitor concluded Holmes sprang up without a word, handed me my hat, picked up his own from the table, and followed Dr. Trevelyan to the door. Within a quarter of an hour we had been dropped at the door of the physician's residence in Brook Street, one of those sombre, flat-faced houses which one associates with a West End practice. A small page admitted us, and we began at once to ascend the broad, well-carpeted stair.

But a singular interruption brought us to a standstill. The light at the top was suddenly whisked out, and from the darkness came a reedy, quavering voice.

" I have a pistol," it cried ; " I give you my word that I'll fire if you come any nearer."

" This really grows outrageous, Mr. Blessington," cried Dr. Trevelyan.

" Oh, then it is you, Doctor ? " said the voice, with a great heave of relief. " But those other gentlemen, are they what they pretend to be ? "

We were conscious of a long scrutiny out of the darkness.

" Yes, yes, it's all right," said the voice at last. " You can come up, and I am sorry if my precautions have annoyed you."

He re-lit the stair gas as he spoke, and we saw before us a singular-looking man, whose appearance, as well as his voice, testified to his jangled nerves. He was very fat, but had apparently at some time been much fatter, so that the skin hung about his face in loose pouches, like the cheeks of a bloodhound. He was of a sickly colour, and his thin, sandy hair seemed to bristle up with the

19 *It rained hard this afternoon.* In October, 1886, your editor's month and year for "The Resident Patient," the two rainiest days were the 12th, a Tuesday, and therefore not the day, and the 15th—a Friday. The 15th would be acceptable except for Watson's earlier adjective "close"—on Friday, the 15th of October, 1886, the wind achieved a pressure of 16.5 pounds. The *third* rainiest day in October, 1886, was Wednesday, October 6th—and the wind pressure on that day was only two pounds. We will attempt to justify our choice of the year 1886 later.

IN HIS HAND HE HELD A PISTOL . . .

Illustration by Sidney Paget for the *Strand Magazine*, August, 1893.

20 *Oxford Street*. Slightly over a mile in length, Oxford Street today is one of the finest thoroughfares in London and the most popular shopping street in the British Empire. In Holmes' and Watson's day, however, it was a rather shabby thoroughfare, lined with third-rate houses. Hare wrote of it: "Though Oxford Street was the high-road to the University, it derives its name from Edward Harley, Earl of Oxford, owner of the manor of Tyburn. It was formerly called the Tyburn Road, and, in 1729, was only enclosed by houses on its northern side. . . . Oxford Street leads to the north-eastern corner of Hyde Park, which is entered at Cumberland Gate by the Marble Arch —one of our national follies—a despicable caricature of the Arch of Constantine, originally erected by Nash at a cost of £75,000, as an approach to Buckingham Palace, and removed hither (when the palace was enlarged in 1851) at a cost of £4,340."

21 *Harley Street*. Then as now a street inhabited largely by consulting physicians and specialists. Hare wrote of it: "We may take Harley Street as a fair example of [its] dreary neighbourhood, with the grim rows of expressionless uniform houses, between which and 'unexceptionable society' Dickens draws such a vivid portrait in *Little Dorrit*. Taine shows it to us from a Frenchman's point of view. 'From Regent's Park to Piccadilly a funereal vista of broad interminable streets. The footway is macadamized and black. The monotonous rows of buildings are of blackened brick; the windowpanes flash in black shadows. Each house is divided from the street by its railings and area. Scarcely a shop, certainly not a pretty one: no plate-glass fronts, no prints. How sad we should find it! Nothing to catch or amuse the eye. Lounging is out of the question. One must work at home, or hurry by under an umbrella to one's office or club. (*Notes sur l'Angleterre*.)"

intensity of his emotion. In his hand he held a pistol, but he thrust it into his pocket as we advanced.

" Good evening, Mr. Holmes," said he ; " I am sure I am very much obliged to you for coming round. No one ever needed your advice more than I do. I suppose that Dr. Trevelyan has told you of this most unwarrantable intrusion into my rooms ? "

" Quite so," said Holmes. " Who are these two men, Mr. Blessington, and why do they wish to molest you ? "

" Well, well," said the resident patient, in a nervous fashion, " of course it is hard to say that. You can hardly expect me to answer that, Mr. Holmes."

" Do you mean that you don't know ? "

" Come in here, if you please. Just have the kindness to step in here."

He led the way into his bedroom, which was large and comfortably furnished.

" You see that ? " said he, pointing to a big black box at the end of his bed. " I have never been a very rich man, Mr. Holmes—never made but one investment in my life, as Dr. Trevelyan would tell you. But I don't believe in bankers. I would never trust a banker, Mr. Holmes. Between ourselves, what little I have is in that box, so you can understand what it means to me when unknown people force themselves into my rooms."

Holmes looked at Blessington in his questioning way, and shook his head.

" I cannot possibly advise you if you try to deceive me," said he.

" But I have told you everything."

Holmes turned on his heel with a gesture of disgust. " Good night, Dr. Trevelyan," said he.

" And no advice for me ? " cried Blessington, in a breaking voice.

" My advice to you, sir, is to speak the truth."

A minute later we were in the street and walking for **20** home. We had crossed Oxford Street, and were half-way **21** down Harley Street before I could get a word from my companion.

" Sorry to bring you out on such a fool's errand, Watson," he said, at last. " It is an interesting case, too, at the bottom of it."

" I can make little of it," I confessed.

" Well, it is quite evident that there are two men— more, perhaps, but at least two—who are determined for some reason to get at this fellow Blessington. I have no doubt in my mind that both on the first and on the second occasion that young man penetrated to Blessington's room, while his confederate, by an ingenious device, kept the doctor from interfering."

" And the catalepsy ! "

" A fraudulent imitation, Watson, though I should hardly dare to hint as much to our specialist. It is a very easy complaint to imitate. I have done it myself."

" And then ? "

" By the purest chance Blessington was out on each occasion. Their reason for choosing so unusual an hour for a consultation was obviously to ensure that there should be no other patient in the waiting-room. It just happened, however, that this hour coincided with Blessington's constitutional, which seems to show that they were not very well acquainted with his daily routine. Of course if they had been merely after plunder they would at least have made some attempt to search for it. Besides, I can read in a man's eye when it is his own skin that he is frightened for. It is inconceivable that this fellow could have made two such vindictive enemies as these appear to be without knowing of it. I hold it, therefore, to be certain that he does know who these men are, and that for reasons of his own he suppresses it. It is just possible that to-morrow may find him in a more communicative mood."

" Is there not one alternative," I suggested, " grotesquely improbable, no doubt, but still just conceivable ? Might the whole story of the cataleptic Russian and his son be a concoction of Dr. Trevelyan's, who has, for his own purposes, been in Blessington's rooms ? "

I saw in the gaslight that Holmes wore an amused smile at this brilliant departure of mine.

" My dear fellow," said he, " it was one of the first solutions which occurred to me, but I was soon able to corroborate the doctor's tale. This young man has left prints upon the stair carpet which made it quite superfluous for me to ask to see those which he had made in the room. When I tell you that his shoes were squaretoed, instead of being pointed like Blessington's, and were quite an inch and a third longer than the doctor's, you will acknowledge that there can be no doubt as to his individuality. But we may sleep on it now, for I shall be surprised if we do not hear something further from Brook Street in the morning."

Sherlock Holmes' prophecy was soon fulfilled, and in a dramatic fashion. At half-past seven next morning, in the first dim glimmer of daylight, I found him standing **22** by my bedside in his dressing-gown.

" There's a brougham waiting for us, Watson," said he.

" What's the matter, then ? "

" The Brook Street business."

" Any fresh news ? "

" Tragic, but ambiguous," said he pulling up the blind. " Look at this—a sheet from a notebook with ' For God's sake, come at once—P. T.' scrawled upon it in pencil. Our friend the doctor was hard put to it when he wrote this. Come along, my dear fellow, for it's an urgent call."

In a quarter of an hour or so we were back at the physician's house. He came running out to meet us with a face of horror.

" Oh, such a business ! " he cried, with his hands to his temples.

" What, then ? "

" Blessington has committed suicide ! "

Holmes whistled.

" Yes, he hanged himself during the night ! "

We had entered, and the doctor had preceded us into what was evidently his waiting-room.

" I really hardly know what I am doing," he cried. " The police are already upstairs. It has shaken me most dreadfully."

22 *in the first dim glimmer of daylight.* Daybreak in England in October is shortly after 4:00 A.M. on the first of the month and about 5:00 A.M. on the thirty-first. "The first dim glimmer of daylight" must be discarded as a clue to the dating of "The Resident Patient," if the month is indeed October and the hour of Watson's awakening 7:30 A.M. "The morning might have been a cloudy one," the late Professor Jay Finley Christ wrote. ". . . Watson still had a slight nocturnal film over his eyes when he first woke up," was the verdict of the late Dr. Ernest Bloomfield Zeisler.

23 *When the maid entered about seven.* Trevelyan of course sent for Holmes at once. This confirms Watson's statement that Holmes awakened him "At half-past seven" in the morning.

HOLMES OPENED IT AND SMELLED THE SINGLE CIGAR
WHICH IT CONTAINED.

Illustration by Sidney Paget for the *Strand Magazine*, August, 1893.

" When did you find it out ? "

" He has a cup of tea taken in to him early every **23** morning. When the maid entered about seven, there the unfortunate fellow was hanging in the middle of the room. He had tied his cord to the hook on which the heavy lamp used to hang, and he had jumped off from the top of the very box that he showed us yesterday."

Holmes stood for a moment in deep thought.

" With your permission," said he at last, " I should like to go upstairs and look into the matter." We both ascended, followed by the doctor.

It was a dreadful sight which met us as we entered the bedroom door. I have spoken of the impression of flabbiness which this man Blessington conveyed. As he dangled from the hook it was exaggerated and intensified until he was scarce human in his appearance. The neck was drawn out like a plucked chicken's, making the rest of him seem the more obese and unnatural by the contrast. He was clad only in his long night-dress, and his swollen ankles and ungainly feet protruded starkly from beneath it. Beside him stood a smart-looking police inspector, who was taking notes in a pocket-book.

" Ah, Mr. Holmes," said he, as my friend entered. " I am delighted to see you."

" Good morning, Lanner," answered Holmes. " You won't think me an intruder, I am sure. Have you heard of the events which led up to this affair ? "

" Yes, I heard something of them."

" Have you formed any opinion ? "

" As far as I can see, the man has been driven out of his senses by fright. The bed has been well slept in, you see. There's his impression deep enough. It's about five in the morning, you know, that suicides are most common. That would be about his time for hanging himself. It seems to have been a very deliberate affair."

" I should say that he has been dead about three hours, judging by the rigidity of the muscles," said I.

" Noticed anything peculiar about the room ? " asked Holmes.

" Found a screwdriver and some screws on the wash-hand stand. Seems to have smoked heavily during the night, too. Here are four cigar-ends that I picked out of the fire-place."

" Hum ! " said Holmes. " Have you got his cigar-holder ? "

" No, I have seen none."

" His cigar-case, then ? "

" Yes, it was in his coat pocket."

Holmes opened it and smelled the single cigar which it contained.

" Oh, this is a Havana, and these others are cigars of the peculiar sort which are imported by the Dutch from their East Indian colonies. They are usually wrapped in straw, you know, and are thinner for their length than any other brand." He picked up the four ends and examined them with his pocket lens.

" Two of these have been smoked from a holder and two without," said he. " Two have been cut by a not very sharp knife, and two have had the ends bitten off by a set of excellent teeth. This is no suicide, Mr. Lanner. It is a very deeply planned and cold-blooded murder."

" Impossible ! " cried the Inspector.

" And why ? "

" Why should anyone murder a man in so clumsy a fashion as by hanging him ? "

" That is what we have to find out."

" How could they get in ? "

" Through the front door."

" It was barred in the morning."

" Then it was barred after them."

" How do you know ? "

" I saw their traces. Excuse me a moment, and I may be able to give you some further information about it."

He went over to the door, and turning the lock he examined it in his methodical fashion. Then he took out the key, which was on the inside, and inspected that also. The bed, the carpet, the chairs, the mantelpiece, the dead body, and the rope were each in turn examined, until at last he professed himself satisfied, and with my aid and that of the Inspector cut down the wretched object, and **24** laid it reverently under a sheet.

" How about this rope ? " he asked.

" It is cut off this," said Dr. Trevelyan, drawing a large coil from under the bed. " He was morbidly nervous of fire, and always kept this beside him, so that he might escape by the window in case the stairs were burning."

" That must have saved them trouble," said Holmes, thoughtfully. " Yes, the actual facts are very plain, and I shall be surprised if by the afternoon I cannot give you the reasons for them as well. I will take this photograph of Blessington which I see upon the mantelpiece, as it may help me in my inquiries."

" But you have told us nothing," cried the doctor.

" Oh, there can be no doubt as to the sequence of events," said Holmes. " There were three of them in it : the young man, the old man, and a third to whose identity I have no clue. The first two, I need hardly remark, are the same who masqueraded as the Russian Count and his son, so we can give a very full description of them. They were admitted by a confederate inside the house. If I might offer you a word of advice, Inspector, it would be to arrest the page, who, as I understand has only recently come into your service, Doctor."

" The young imp cannot be found," said Dr. Trevelyan ; " the maid and the cook have just been searching for him."

Holmes shrugged his shoulders.

" He has played a not unimportant part in this drama," **25** said he. " The three men having ascended the stair, which they did on tiptoe, the elder man first, the younger man second, and the unknown man in the rear——"

" My dear Holmes ! " I ejaculated.

" Oh, there could be no question as to the superimposing of the footmarks. I had the advantage of learning which was which last night. They ascended then to Mr. Blessington's room, the door of which they found to be locked. With the help of a wire, however, they forced

24 *cut down the wretched object.* "Surely the first act of a doctor, or indeed of anyone else, would be to cut [Blessington] down and to endeavour immediately to restore his respiration before it was too late," the late Gavin Brend wrote in *My Dear Holmes.* "Instead the body is allowed to remain hanging while Holmes first questions Inspector Lanner and then examines the cigar-ends, the lock, the key, the bed, the carpet, the chairs, the mantelpiece, the body and the rope. Only after all this has been done is the body cut down."

25 *"He has played a not unimportant part in this drama."* The late Page Heldenbrand has written ("On an Obscure Nervous Page") that "... we must blow the whistle on Holmes when he insists that the page was [a confederate] because 1) he had not grown old and gray in Trevelyan's service, and 2) having heard of Blessington's ... unnatural demise, he succumbed to youthful panic and vacated the premises. The very facts of the case eliminate the probability of the page's guilt. For if the 'Russian nobleman' and his 'son' had planted an ally inside the house, he would only have been needed to report on Blessington's movements. And Holmes himself pointed out that 'they were not very well acquainted with his daily routine'; indeed, their two calls upon Dr. Trevelyan coincided with Blessington's usual pre-dinner constitutional. Subsequently, of course, the door-opening confederate became necessary; but the page was no more qualified for the job than were the cook, the maid(s) and Dr. Percy Trevelyan. ... [The] deduction that flight from the scene of the crime indicates guilt [is] one that is worthy of Lestrade."

round the key. Even without the lens, you will perceive, by the scratches on this ward, where the pressure was applied.

" On entering the room, their first proceeding must have been to gag Mr. Blessington. He may have been asleep, or he may have been so paralysed with terror as to have been unable to cry out. These walls are thick, and it is conceivable that his shriek, if he had time to utter one, was unheard.

" Having secured him, it is evident to me that a consultation of some sort was held. Probably it was something in the nature of a judicial proceeding. It must have lasted for some time, for it was then that these cigars were smoked. The older man sat in that wicker chair : it was he who used the cigar-holder. The younger man sat over yonder ; he knocked his ash off against the chest of drawers. The third fellow paced up and down. Blessington, I think, sat upright in the bed, but of that I cannot be absolutely certain.

" Well, it ended by their taking Blessington and hanging him. The matter was so pre-arranged that it is my belief that they brought with them some sort of block or pulley which might serve as a gallows. That screwdriver and those screws were, as I conceive, for fixing it up. Seeing the hook, however, they naturally saved themselves the trouble. Having finished their work they made off, and the door was barred behind them by their confederate."

We had all listened with the deepest interest to this sketch of the night's doings, which Holmes had deduced from signs so subtle and minute, that even when he had pointed them out to us, we could scarcely follow him in his reasonings. The Inspector hurried away on the instant to make inquiries about the page, while Holmes and I returned to Baker Street for breakfast.

" I'll be back by three," said he when we had finished our meal. " Both the Inspector and the doctor will meet me here at that hour, and I hope by that time to have cleared up any little obscurity which the case may still present."

"BLESSINGTON, I THINK, SAT UPRIGHT IN THE BED . . ."

Illustration by William H. Hyde for *Harper's Weekly*, August 12, 1893.

Our visitors arrived at the appointed time, but it was a quarter to four before my friend put in an appearance. From his expression as he entered, however, I could see that all had gone well with him.

" Any news, Inspector ? "

" We have got the boy, sir."

" Excellent, and I have got the men."

" You have got them ! " we cried all three.

" Well, at least I have got their identity. This so-called Blessington is, as I expected, well known at headquarters, and so are his assailants. Their names are Biddle, Hayward, and Moffat."

" The Worthingdon bank gang," cried the Inspector.

" Precisely," said Holmes.

" Then Blessington must have been Sutton ? "

" Exactly," said Holmes.

" Why, that makes it as clear as crystal," said the Inspector.

But Trevelyan and I looked at each other in bewilderment.

" You must surely remember the great Worthingdon bank business," said Holmes ; " five men were in it, these four and a fifth called Cartwright. Tobin, the caretaker, was murdered, and the thieves got away with seven thousand pounds. This was in 1875. They were **26** all five arrested, but the evidence against them was by no means conclusive. This Blessington or Sutton, who was the worst of the gang, turned informer. On his evidence Cartwright was hanged, and the other three got fifteen years apiece. When they got out the other day, which was some years before their full term, they set **27** themselves, as you perceive, to hunt down the traitor and to avenge the death of their comrade upon him. Twice they tried to get at him and failed ; a third time, you see, it came off. Is there anything further which I can explain, Dr. Trevelyan ? "

" I think you have made it all remarkably clear," said the doctor. " No doubt the day on which he was so perturbed was the day when he read of their release in the newspapers."

26 *seven thousand pounds.* About $35,000.

27 *some years before their full term.* English justice in the seventies was no less swift than English justice today; we are justified in assuming that no time was lost in trying and sentencing the thieves who had "got away with seven thousand pounds." We do not know in what month the robbery occurred, but the men must have been sentenced in either 1875 or 1876. 1890, then, 1891 at the latest, would have been the year for their release had they served their full term. In those days, as the late Professor Jay Finley Christ pointed out in *An Irregular Chronology*, the penal laws of England provided a maximum remission of three years and 197 days from a sentence of fifteen years, for good behavior. We may be sure that Biddle, Hayward and Moffat, counting the days until they could petition for release and settle their score with Sutton, would comport themselves as model prisoners, in order to secure the maximum remission. The date of their release would therefore fall in the approximate period July, 1886, to June, 1887. The adventure of "The Resident Patient" took place, as we know, in the month of October; we may now with some confidence date it exactly to *Wednesday, October 6 and Thursday, October 7, 1886.*

"YOU HAVE GOT THEM !" WE CRIED ALL THREE.

Illustration by Sidney Paget for the *Strand Magazine*, August, 1893.

28 Norah Creina. "Creina" is an Irish term of endearment, and the phrase Watson employed is to be found in Thomas Moore's poem, "Lesbia Hath a Beaming Eye": "Beauty lies in many eyes; but love in yours, / my Nora creina."

29 *lost some years ago with all hands.* "Dr. Watson was in error," Professor Alan Lang Strout wrote in *The Saturday Review of Literature,* "for, only a year before [Watson wrote his account of "The Resident Patient"] the *Norah Creina* carried Mr. Dodd safely into Honolulu: see R. L. Stevenson's *The Wrecker,* which appeared serially in *Scribner's Magazine* in 1891 and as a book in 1892."

" Quite so. His talk about a burglary was the merest blind."

" But why could he not tell you this ? "

" Well, my dear sir, knowing the vindictive character of his old associates, he was trying to hide his own identity from everybody as long as he could. His secret was a shameful one, and he could not bring himself to divulge it. However, wretch as he was, he was still living under the shield of British law, and I have no doubt, Inspector, that you will see that, though that shield may fail to guard, the sword of justice is still there to avenge."

Such were the singular circumstances in connection with the resident patient and the Brook Street doctor. From that night nothing has been seen of the three murderers by the police, and it is surmised at Scotland Yard that they were among the passengers of the ill-fated **28** steamer *Norah Creina,* which was lost some years ago **29** with all hands upon the Portuguese coast, some leagues to the north of Oporto. The proceedings against the page broke down for want of evidence, and the " Brook Street Mystery," as it was called, has never, until now, been fully dealt with in any public print.

· · ·

". . . ONE OF THOSE UNWELCOME SOCIAL SUMMONSES WHICH CALL UPON A MAN EITHER TO BE BORED OR TO LIE."

Holmes' remark, says Dr. Richard Asher in "Holmes and the Fair Sex," "sounds more like Oscar Wilde than Sherlock Holmes and shows not only that Holmes was much in demand at the highest social functions and attended them often enough to be bored." (See also "A Scandal in Bohemia," Note 5.) The illustration, by George du Maurier, is from a copy of *Society Pictures from Punch* (1891) in the British Museum.

20

THE ADVENTURE OF THE NOBLE BACHELOR

[Friday, October 8, 1886]

THE Lord St. Simon marriage, and its curious termination, have long since ceased to be a subject of interest in those exalted circles in which the unfortunate bridegroom moves. Fresh scandals have eclipsed it, and their more piquant details have drawn the gossips away from this four-year-old drama. **1** As I have reason to believe, however, that the full facts have never been revealed to the general public, and as my friend Sherlock Holmes had a considerable share in clearing the matter up, I feel that no memoir of him would be complete without some little sketch of this remarkable episode.

It was a few weeks before my own marriage, during **2** the days when I was still sharing rooms with Holmes in Baker Street, that he came home from an afternoon stroll to find a letter on the table waiting for him. I had remained indoors all day, for the weather had taken a sudden turn to rain, with high autumnal winds, and the jezail bullet which I had brought back in one of my limbs as a **3** relic of my Afghan campaign, throbbed with dull persistency. With my body in one easy chair and my legs upon another, I had surrounded myself with a cloud of newspapers, until at last, saturated with the news of the day, I **4** tossed them all aside and lay listless, watching the huge crest and monogram upon the envelope upon the table, and wondering lazily who my friend's noble correspondent could be.

"Here is a very fashionable epistle," I remarked as he entered. "Your morning letters, if I remember right, were from a fishmonger and a tide-waiter." **5**

"Yes, my correspondence has certainly the charm of variety," he answered, smiling, "and the humbler are usually the more interesting. This looks like one of those unwelcome social summonses which call upon a man either to be bored or to lie."

He broke the seal, and glanced over the contents.

"Oh, come, it may prove to be something of interest after all."

"Not social, then?"

"No, distinctly professional."

"And from a noble client?"

1 *this four-year-old drama.* Since Watson's account of the adventure appeared in the *Strand Magazine* for April, 1892, the case must have taken place before April, 1888, at the latest, and probably a good many months earlier, since Watson's "four-year-old drama" must be dated from the *writing* rather than the *publishing* of his account.

2 *a few weeks before my own marriage.* Generally accepted by other commentators to mean Watson's marriage to Mary Morstan, whom he met during the adventure of *The Sign of the Four*, and therefore dated by them to 1887 (Andrew, Bell, Brend, Harrison, Hoff, Morley, and Newton) or 1888 (Blakeney, Christ, Folsom, Knox, Pattrick, Petersen, Smith, White, and Zeisler). On the other hand, your editor holds that Watson here refers to the marriage he celebrated *circa* November 1, 1886—two-and-a-half years before his marriage, *circa* May 1, 1889, to Mary Morstan (see "Now, Watson, the Fair Sex Is Your Department").

HE BROKE THE SEAL, AND GLANCED OVER THE CONTENTS.

Illustration by Sidney Paget for the *Strand Magazine*, April, 1892.

3 *in one of my limbs.* A curious but perhaps a not-too-impossible way to refer to a shoulder wound which left Watson with a left arm which he held "in a stiff and unnatural manner" (see "Your Hand Stole Towards Your Old Wound . . .").

4 *saturated with the news of the day.* The day was not a Sunday, for papers would not have been published on a Sunday, nor would Holmes have received letters by the morning post on that day.

5 *a tide-waiter."* "All my life I have wondered just what was a 'tide-waiter'," the late Christopher Morley wrote. "Lo and behold the other day I was reading some of Robert Burns' letters (in *Autograph Poems and Letters of Robert Burns in the Collection of R. B. Adam,* privately printed, Buffalo, 1922). In August, 1795, he wrote to Mrs. Riddell discussing the possibilities of a protégé of hers getting a job as a tide-waiter. The context makes it abundantly plain that it meant a customs officer—one who waited for ships to come in with the tide. He wrote: 'I think there is little doubt but that your interest, if judicially directed, may procure a tide-waiter's place for your protégé, Shaw; but, alas, that is doing little for him! Fifteen pounds per an: is the salary; and the perquisites, in some lucky stations, may be ten more. . . . The appointment is not in the Excise; but in the Customs.'"

6 *the interest of his case.* Compare, from "The Adventure of the Copper Beeches": "To the man who loves art for its own sake, it is frequently in its least important and lowliest manifestations that the keenest pleasure is to be derived." Wrote Mr. T. S. Blakeney in *Sherlock Holmes: Fact or Fiction?*: "It is certainly true that Holmes, though no apostle of equality, and despite the fact that his services were sought by the rulers of many lands, was free from all taint of snobbishness, as evidenced by his epigrammatic comment on Lord St. Simon's fashionably-addressed letter."

7 *the agony column.* "Department of personal advertisements in newspapers, first made famous in the *Times* of London," the late Christopher Morley wrote in *Sherlock Holmes and Dr. Watson: A Textbook of Friendship.* "All such columns exhibit a weird or comic mixture of human perplexities, hence the appropriate nickname. An extraordinarily interesting and amusing little book is *The Agony Column of 'The Times,' 1800–1870,* edited by Alice Clay, London: Chatto & Windus, 1881. The late Earl Derr Biggers, creator of the detective Charlie Chan, said of this book, 'If I owned it I would never need to invent another plot.'"

8 *Lord St. Simon.* Holmes' repeated reference to "Lord St. Simon" is a curious solecism; as the *second* son of the Duke of Balmoral, the noble bachelor was "Lord Robert St. Simon," not "Lord St. Simon." In some editions of the Sacred Writ-

"One of the highest in England."

"My dear fellow, I congratulate you."

"I assure you, Watson, without affectation, that the status of my client is a matter of less moment to me than **6** the interest of his case. It is just possible, however, that that also may not be wanting in this new investigation. You have been reading the papers diligently of late, have you not?"

"It looks like it," said I ruefully, pointing to a huge bundle in the corner. "I have had nothing else to do."

"It is fortunate, for you will perhaps be able to post me up. I read nothing except the criminal news and the **7** agony column. The latter is always instructive. But if you have followed recent events so closely you must have **8** read about Lord St. Simon and his wedding?"

"Oh, yes, with the deepest interest."

"That is well. The letter which I hold in my hand is from Lord St. Simon. I will read it to you, and in return you must turn over these papers and let me have whatever bears upon the matter. This is what he says:

9 "'MY DEAR MR. SHERLOCK HOLMES,—Lord Backwater tells me that I may place implicit reliance upon your judgment and discretion. I have determined, therefore, to call upon you, and to consult you in reference to the very painful event which has occurred in connection with my wedding. Mr. Lestrade, of Scotland Yard, is acting already in the matter, but he assures me that he sees no objection to your co-operation, and that he even thinks that it might be of some assistance. I will call at four o'clock in the afternoon, and should you have any other engagement at that time, I hope you will postpone it, as this is a matter of paramount importance.—Yours faithfully,

'ROBERT ST. SIMON.'

10   It is dated from Grosvenor Mansions, written with a quill pen, and the noble lord has had the misfortune to get a smear of ink upon the outer side of his right little finger," remarked Holmes, as he folded up the epistle.

"He says four o'clock. It is three now. He will be here in an hour."

"Then I have just time, with your assistance, to get clear upon the subject. Turn over those papers, and arrange the extracts in their order of time, while I take a glance as to who our client is." He picked a red-covered **11** volume from a line of books of reference beside the mantelpiece. "Here he is," said he, sitting down and flattening it out upon his knee. "'Robert Walsingham de Vere St. Simon, second son of the Duke of Balmoral'—Hum! 'Arms: Azure, three caltrops in chief over a fess sable. **12** Born in 1846.' He's forty-one years of age, which is mature for marriage. Was Under-Secretary for the Colonies in a late Administration. The Duke, his father, was at one time Secretary for Foreign Affairs. They inherit Plantagenet blood by direct descent, and Tudor on the distaff side. Ha! Well, there is nothing very instructive in all this. I think I must turn to you, Watson, for something more solid."

" 'ARMS: AZURE, THREE CALTROPS IN CHIEF OVER A FESS SABLE.' "

Caltrops, we read in Mr. Rolfe Boswell's "A Connecticut Yankee in Support of Sir Arthur," "are four-spiked iron balls scattered on the ground in medieval warfare to impede the enemy's advance. 'I think they have strewn the highways with caltrops,' Beaumont and Fletcher recount in *Love's Pilgrimage*, 'no horse dares pass them.' The caltrop's four short, but strong, spikes, or gads, were conjoined in such a manner that, when thrown on the ground, one spike always would be erect. . . . The use of caltrops was revived by the New England colonists against the Indians."

The arms of the noble bachelor, as Watson has given them to us, commit a heraldic solecism. "It is a fundamental law of heraldry that metal should never be charged on metal, nor color on color," Mr. Boswell continued. "Caltrops normally would be depicted sable (black). Since the fess already has been blazoned as *sable*, therefore the field of the shield contains the falsity in blazonry. Since azure (blue) patently is in error, therefore the metal whose initial is also an *a* is the correct background for the . . . shield, namely argent (silver). In the preferred blazonry now used by twentieth-century heralds, the arms . . . become: 'Silver a fess sable with three caltrops in the chief proper.' That is, in their natural color, which would be iron-grey." (It is Mr. Boswell's theory that Holmes substituted *his own arms* for those of the noble bachelor in this description to Watson. He would add to the arms as described in the preferred blazonry "a small crescent, symbol of a second son . . . charged upon the fess to distinguish Sherlock from his elder brother, Mycroft.")

The heraldic use of color upon color or metal upon metal has been defended by Dr. Wolff in his *Practical Handbook of Sherlockian Heraldry*: ". . . not the best heraldry, but it is seen. The best example is found in the arms of the Kingdom of Jerusalem: argent a cross potent between four plain crosses or. Less known, but more spectacular, is the purple chief on a green field in the arms of Thackeray."

Dr. Wolff holds that Holmes substituted, not his own coat of arms, but that of James Boswell of Auchinleck, given by Robson as "az. on a fesse sa. three cinquefoils of the first.' Azure and a fess sable!" ("It is not an anti-climax," Dr. Wolff has added, "that the Boswell arms are really argent, not azure, with a fess sable. From what other work [than Robson] could [Holmes] have picked up his misinformation?")

Above, left: The coat of arms of Lord Robert St. Simon, according to Sherlock Holmes: Azure, three caltrops in chief over a fess sable. *Right:* The coat of arms substituted by Holmes for that of Lord Robert St. Simon, according to Dr. Julian Wolff. They are those of James Boswell of Auchinleck as they (mistakenly) appear in Robson: Azure on a fess sable three cinquefoils of the first.

ings he signs his note to Holmes (improperly) "St. Simon." In others, he signs himself (properly) "Robert St. Simon"—"just as the second son of the Duke of Denver signs himself 'Peter Wimsey,' and neither 'Wimsey' nor 'Lord Wimsey,' " Dr. William Braid White wrote in "Dr. Watson and the Peerage."

9 *Lord Backwater.* We hear of Lord Backwater again in 1890 (your editor's date): his horse, Desborough, ran against Silver Blaze in the Wessex Cup (or Plate). Other commentators have interpreted this reference to mean that "Silver Blaze" *preceded* "The Adventure of the Noble Bachelor." If it did not, however, there must have been another occasion on which Lord Backwater learned that one might place implicit reliance upon Holmes' judgment and discretion.

10 *Grosvenor Mansions.* On Victoria Street, at the corner of Palace Street. Begun in 1858, building operations were afterwards suspended, and the unfinished structure remained an eyesore for several years, after which it was purchased by the Freehold Investment Company and completed as a block of flats which were at first rented at £300 a year. The building, seven stories high, now consists principally of offices and shops.

11 *a red-covered volume.* Possibly a *Who's Who,* possibly a Burke's *Peerage,* possibly a Debrett, possibly a Doyle's *Official Baronage.* But Dr. Julian Wolff, in his *Practical Handbook of Sherlockian Heraldry,* has advanced a cogent reason for believing that it may also have been Thomas Robson's *The British Herald, or Cabinet of Armorial Bearings*—one of the three volumes of this work printed in Sunderland for the author in 1830.

12 *He's forty-one years of age.* Thus, on whatever day in 1846 Lord Robert may have been born —from January 1st to December 31st—he would have been closer to forty-one than to forty or forty-two between July 1, 1886, and June 30, 1888, and the case must fall within that period.

"THEY INHERIT PLANTAGENET BLOOD BY DIRECT DESCENT, AND TUDOR ON THE DISTAFF SIDE."

As Mr. Rolfe Boswell has pointed out ("A Connecticut Yankee in Support of Sir Arthur") "England's only ducal house which can fulfill this requirement is that of the Somersets, Dukes of Beaufort. . . . In quoting from his 'red-covered volume,' which Holmes takes care not to show Watson, 'flattening it out upon his knee,' the Master changes the surname Somerset to *St. Simon*, and makes his client 'second son of the *Duke of Balmoral*,' swiftly substituting a royal castle in Scotland . . . for the erstwhile royal castle in Anjou from which the Somersets take their title of Beaufort." Dr. Wolff has added: "The Duke of Beaufort . . . had an unmarried son who was born in 1847, not far from Watson's 1846—truly a noble bachelor! Those who choose to believe that Robert de Vere St. Simon was the son of the Duke of Beaufort may even derive some additional assurance from the coincidence that the present heir is H. Robert deVere Somerset." *Left:* the coat of arms of the Somersets, Dukes of Beaufort. It is blazoned: France and England quarterly within a bordure compony argent and azure. Crest: A portcullis or, nailed azure, chains gold. Supporters: Dexter, a panther argent, flames issuing from his mouth and ears proper, plain collared and chained or, and semé of torteaux, hurts and pomels alternately. Sinister, a wyvern vert, in the mouth a sinister hand couped at the wrist gules.

" I have very little difficulty in finding what I want," said I, " for the facts are quite recent, and the matter struck me as remarkable. I feared to refer them to you, however, as I knew that you had an inquiry on hand, and that you disliked the intrusion of other matters."

" Oh, you mean the little problem of the Grosvenor 13 Square furniture van. That is quite cleared up now—though, indeed, it was obvious from the first. Pray give me the results of your newspaper selections."

" Here is the first notice which I can find. It is in the personal column of the *Morning Post*, and dates, as you see, some weeks back. ' A marriage has been arranged,' it says, ' and will, if rumour is correct, very shortly take place, between Lord Robert St. Simon, second son of the Duke of Balmoral, and Miss Hatty Doran, the only daughter of Aloysius Doran, Esq., of San Francisco, Cal., U.S.A.' That is all."

" Terse and to the point," remarked Holmes, stretching his long, thin legs towards the fire.

" There was a paragraph amplifying this in one of the society papers of the same week. Ah, here it is. ' There will soon be a call for protection in the marriage market, for the present free-trade principle appears to tell heavily against our home product. One by one the management of the noble houses of Great Britain is passing into the hands of our fair cousins from across the Atlantic. An important addition has been made during the last week to the list of prizes which have been borne away by these charming invaders. Lord St. Simon, who has shown himself for over twenty years proof against the little god's arrows, has now definitely announced his approaching marriage with Miss Hatty Doran, the fascinating daughter of a Californian millionaire. Miss Doran, whose graceful figure and striking face attracted much attention at the 14 Westbury House festivities, is an only child, and it is currently reported that her dowry will run to considerably over the six figures, with expectancies for the future. As

13 *Grosvenor Square.* Grosvenor Square, six acres in extent, takes its name from Sir Robert Grosvenor (d. 1732). Built between 1720 and 1730, it contained, in Holmes' and Watson's day, many large houses which have now given way to blocks of flats. Hare wrote of it: "For a century and a half . . . the most fashionable place of residence in London. . . . The old ironwork and flambeau extinguishers before many of the doors in Grosvenor Square deserve notice. In the [eighteenth] century the nobility were proud of their flambeau, and it is remarkable that the aristocratic Square refused to adopt the use of gas till compelled to do so by force of public opinion in 1842. . . . Grosvenor Square is crossed by the two great arteries Grosvenor Street and Brook Street."

The late Clifton R. Andrew's "The Little Problem of the Grosvenor Square Furniture Van," a pastiche stemming from this reference of Holmes', appeared in the Freeport, Ohio, *Press* August 30-September 6, 1945.

14 *the Westbury House.* Today there is a Westbury Hotel in London, but the Westbury *House* is not now identifiable.

it is an open secret that the Duke of Balmoral has been compelled to sell his pictures within the last few years, and as Lord St. Simon has no property of his own, save the small estate of Birchmoor, it is obvious that the Californian heiress is not the only gainer by an alliance which will enable her to make the easy and common transition from a Republican lady to a British title.' "

" Anything else ? " asked Holmes, yawning.

" Oh yes ; plenty. Then there is another note in the *Morning Post* to say that the marriage would be an absolutely quiet one, that it would be at St. George's, Hanover Square, that only half a dozen intimate friends would be **15** invited, and that the party would return to the furnished house at Lancaster Gate which has been taken by Mr. **16** Aloysius Doran.   Two days later—that is, on Wednesday last—there is a curt announcement that the wedding had taken place, and that the honeymoon would be passed at Lord Backwater's place, near Petersfield.   Those are all **17** the notices which appeared before the disappearance of the bride."

" Before the what ? " asked Holmes, with a start.

" The vanishing of the lady."

" When did she vanish, then ? "

" At the wedding breakfast."

" Indeed.   This is more interesting than it promised to be ; quite dramatic, in fact."

" Yes ; it struck me as being a little out of the common."   **18**

" They often vanish before the ceremony, and occasionally during the honeymoon ; but I cannot call to mind anything quite so prompt as this.   Pray let me have the details."

" I warn you that they are very incomplete."

" Perhaps we may make them less so."

" Such as they are, they are set forth in a single article of a morning newspaper of yesterday, which I will read to you.   It is headed ' Singular Occurrence at a Fashionable Wedding ' :

" ' The family of Lord Robert St. Simon has been thrown into the greatest consternation by the strange and painful episodes which have taken place in connection with his wedding.   The ceremony, as shortly announced in the papers of yesterday, occurred on the previous morning ; but it is only now that it has been possible to confirm **19** the strange rumours which have been so persistently floating about.   In spite of the attempts of the friends to hush the matter up, so much public attention has now been drawn to it that no good purpose can be served by affecting to disregard what is a common subject for conversation.

" ' The ceremony, which was performed at St. George's, Hanover Square, was a very quiet one, no one being present save the father of the bride, Mr. Aloysius Doran, the Duchess of Balmoral, Lord Backwater, Lord Eustace and Lady Clara St. Simon (the younger brother and sister of the bridegroom), and Lady Alicia Whittington.   The whole party proceeded afterwards to the house of Mr. Aloysius Doran, at Lancaster Gate, where breakfast had been prepared.   It appears that some little

15 *St. George's; Hanover Square.* This church did enjoy an almost complete monopoly on marriages in high life. Built by John James in 1724, named in honor of George I, its marriage registers were a perfect library of the autographs of illustrious persons, among which the bold signature of "Wellington" appeared frequently. At the beginning of the nineteenth century from 1,100 to 1,200 couples were sometimes united there in a year. Nelson's Lady Hamilton was married at St. George's on September 6, 1791. This being the case, it is astonishing, as the Reverend Otis R. Rice has pointed out in "Clergymen in the Canon," "that the solemnization of the marriage [in this adventure] was left to the vicar or even one of his curates. For one of his noble and social rank St. Simon could be expected to do better than that. Why not an Archbishop? Or at least the Bishop of London? Or some other bishop who was conveniently kicking about? Was there some strange or sinister reason (apart from the bride's lowly station) which necessitated calling upon a mere priest to officiate? Is there the sad possibility that, in the exigencies of life in a mining camp and later in the arduous work of clipping coupons, neither Hatty nor her father found time to have her baptized? Perish the thought! The fact remains, however, that the officiating 'clergyman' in the tale . . . did not have his name mentioned in the press notice; a *most* unusual omission. Nor was he invited to the wedding breakfast. Here is another example of a questionable cleric encountered in the pages of the Writings."

Hanover Square, Augustus J. C. Hare tells us, "received its name instead of that of Oxford Square, as was first intended, in the days of the early popularity of George I. The square was built about 1731, when the place for executions was removed from Tyburn, lest the inhabitants of 'the new square' should be annoyed by them."

16 *Lancaster Gate.* Then a long and impressive range of balconied buildings, completed in 1866, in a well-to-do residential quarter north of Hyde Park.

17 *Petersfield.* A market town in Hampshire.

18 *It struck me as being a little out of the common."* An excellent early example of Watson's "pawky" sense of humor (*The Valley of Fear*).

19 *occurred on the previous morning.* The case took a day of Holmes' time—a Friday. This is certain from the newspaper accounts: 1) On "Wednesday last" there had appeared "a curt announcement that the wedding had taken place"; 2) the morning paper of "yesterday" had reported that "the ceremony, as shortly announced in the papers of yesterday [the Wednesday], occurred on the previous morning . . ." (the Tuesday); 3) since the morning paper of "yesterday" was therefore the morning paper of Thursday, it follows that the case opened (and closed) on a Friday.

" '. . . SHE WAS EJECTED BY THE BUTLER AND THE FOOTMAN.' "

Illustration by Sidney Paget for the *Strand Magazine*, April, 1892.

20 *a* danseuse. French: a female professional dancer; a ballet girl.

21 *our page-boy.* The Baker Street page boy is mentioned or makes an appearance in eight other adventures: "A Case of Identity" (October, 1887); *The Valley of Fear* (January, 1888); "The Yellow Face" (April, 1888); "The Greek Interpreter" (September, 1888); "The Naval Treaty" (August, 1889); "The Problem of Thor Bridge" (October, 1900); "The Adventure of Shoscombe Old Place" (May, 1902); and "The Adventure of the Mazarin Stone" (Summer, 1903).

In both *The Valley of Fear* and "The Adventure of the Mazarin Stone" we are told his given name—Billy. It is clear that a page boy was employed throughout most of the late eighties. But this cannot be the "young" page boy of the 1900–1903 period; either both boys were named Billy, or Billy was a generic name applied by Holmes and Watson to all the Baker Street page boys.

"It is possible," Mr. Vincent Starrett wrote in "The Singular Adventures of Martha Hudson,"

trouble had been caused by a woman, whose name has not been ascertained, who endeavoured to force her way into the house after the bridal party, alleging that she had some claim upon Lord St. Simon. It was only after a painful and prolonged scene that she was ejected by the butler and the footman. The bride, who had fortunately entered the house before this unpleasant interruption, had sat down to breakfast with the rest, when she complained of a sudden indisposition, and retired to her room. Her prolonged absence having caused some comment, her father followed her; but learned from her maid that she had only come up to her chamber for an instant, caught up an ulster and bonnet, and hurried down to the passage. One of the footmen declared that he had seen a lady leave the house thus apparelled; but had refused to credit that it was his mistress, believing her to be with the company. On ascertaining that his daughter had disappeared, Mr. Aloysius Doran, in conjunction with the bridegroom, instantly put themselves into communication with the police, and very energetic inquiries are being made, which will probably result in a speedy clearing up of this very singular business. Up to a late hour last night, however, nothing had transpired as to the whereabouts of the missing lady. There are rumours of foul play in the matter, and it is said that the police have caused the arrest of the woman who had caused the original disturbance, in the belief that, from jealousy or some other motive, she may have been concerned in the strange disappearance of the bride.' "

" And is that all ? "

" Only one little item in another of the morning papers, but it is a suggestive one."

" And it is ? "

" That Miss Flora Millar, the lady who had caused the disturbance, has actually been arrested. It appears that **20** she was formerly a *danseuse* at the Allegro, and that she had known the bridegroom for some years. There are no further particulars, and the whole case is in your hands now—so far as it has been set forth in the public press."

" And an exceedingly interesting case it appears to be. I would not have missed it for worlds. But there is a ring at the bell, Watson, and as the clock makes it a few minutes after four, I have no doubt that this will prove to be our noble client. Do not dream of going, Watson, for I very much prefer having a witness, if only as a check to my own memory."

21 " Lord Robert St. Simon," announced our page-boy, throwing open the door. A gentleman entered, with a pleasant, cultured face, high-nosed and pale, with something perhaps of petulance about the mouth, and with the steady, well-opened eye of a man whose pleasant lot it had ever been to command and to be obeyed. His manner was brisk, and yet his general appearance gave an undue impression of age, for he had a slight forward stoop, and a little bend of the knees as he walked. His hair, too, as he swept off his curly brimmed hat, was grizzled round the edges, and thin upon the top. As to his dress, it was careful to the verge of foppishness, with high collar, black frock-coat, white waistcoat, yellow gloves, patent-leather shoes, and light-coloured gaiters. **22** He advanced slowly into the room, turning his head from left to right, and swinging in his right hand the cord which held his golden eye-glasses.

"Good day, Lord St. Simon," said Holmes, rising and bowing. "Pray take the basket chair. This is my friend and colleague, Dr. Watson. Draw up a little to the fire, and we shall talk this matter over."

". . . SWINGING IN HIS RIGHT HAND THE CORD WHICH HELD HIS GOLDEN EYEGLASSES."

Portrait of Lord Robert St. Simon by Sidney Paget for the *Strand Magazine*, April, 1892.

"A most painful matter to me, as you can most readily imagine, Mr. Holmes. I have been cut to the quick. I understand you have already managed several delicate cases of this sort, sir, though I presume that they were hardly from the same class of society."

"No, I am descending."

"I beg pardon?"

"My last client of the sort was a king."

"Oh, really! I had no idea. And which king?"

"The King of Scandinavia." **23**

"What! Had he lost his wife?"

"You can understand," said Holmes suavely, "that I extend to the affairs of my other clients the same secrecy which I promise to you in yours."

"that [the page] was employed some months after the advent of the detective and the doctor, at a time when the increasing number of visitors, calling upon Mr. Sherlock Holmes, too frequently snatched the maid and Mrs. Hudson from their necessary household duties. Just conceivably he was a bit of swank on the part of Mrs. Hudson, who may well have looked forward to a time when she could afford a page, like other more prosperous landladies."

"If Billy's functions were confined to announcing visitors and running errands he must have had an extremely cushy time of it," Mr. G. B. Newton commented in "Billy the Page." "Even if he also valeted Holmes and Watson his duties would hardly have been onerous. On general grounds therefore it seems more likely that he was employed by Mrs. Hudson for general work in the house and that any references to 'our page-boy' were merely avuncular."

22 *gaiters.* Watson in later stories drops this old-fashioned word and modernizes his writing by calling these objects of male wearing apparel *spats.* Spats were one of the trademarks of the "Knut" of turn-of-the-century and later London —the well-to-do young Englishmen who made a career out of their clubs. It was on the "Knuts" that P. G. Wodehouse based (and never changed) the characters of Bertie Wooster, Bingo Little, and all the other "Eggs, Beans and Crumpets" of that memorable institution, "the Drones Club."

23 "*The King of Scandinavia.*" "Scandinavia is the peninsula on which Norway and Sweden are situated," Mr. Svend Petersen wrote in "When the Game Was Not Afoot." "At the time of the adventures in which the King of Scandinavia figures, that ruler was Oscar II, 1829–1907, who reigned over both nations from 1872 to 1905, Norway severing her personal connection with Sweden in the latter year."

It was to the second daughter of the King of Scandinavia, Clotilde Lothman von Saxe-Meningen, that the King of Bohemia was to be married ("A Scandal in Bohemia"), and commentators have surmised that it was perhaps to arrange this delicate business that Holmes was retained by the King of Scandinavia shortly before "The Adventure of the Noble Bachelor" (but, if so, the King of Bohemia certainly knew nothing about it).

Again, in late 1890 or early 1891, Holmes was to be of assistance to the Royal Family of Scandinavia ("The Final Problem").

In the light of the fact that Norway did not sever her connection with Sweden until 1905, it is quite possible that Holmes' visit to Norway in July, 1895 ("The Adventure of Black Peter") was also connected with a mission for Oscar II. It has been said that His Holiness, Pope Leo XIII, was the only client who *twice* commissioned Holmes (see *The Hound of the Baskervilles,* "The Adventure of Black Peter") but we learn here that this was not the case.

" Of course ! Very right ! very right ! I'm sure I beg pardon. As to my own case, I am ready to give you any information which may assist you in forming an opinion."

" Thank you. I have already learned all that is in the public prints, nothing more. I presume that I may take it as correct—this article, for example, as to the disappearance of the bride."

Lord St. Simon glanced over it. " Yes, it is correct, as far as it goes."

" But it needs a great deal of supplementing before anyone could offer an opinion. I think that I may arrive at my facts most directly by questioning you."

" Pray do so."

" When did you first meet Miss Hatty Doran ? "

" In San Francisco, a year ago."

" You were travelling in the States ? "

" Yes."

" Did you become engaged then ? "

" No."

" But you were on a friendly footing ? "

" I was amused by her society, and she could see that I was amused."

" Her father is very rich ? "

" He is said to be the richest man on the Pacific Slope."

" And how did he make his money ? "

" In mining. He had nothing a few years ago. Then he struck gold, invested it, and came up by leaps and bounds."

" Now, what is your own impression as to the young lady's—your wife's character ? "

The nobleman swung his glasses a little faster and stared down into the fire. " You see, Mr. Holmes," said he, " my wife was twenty before her father became a rich man. During that time she ran free in a mining camp, and wandered through woods or mountains, so that her education has come from nature rather than from the schoolmaster. She is what we call in England a tomboy, with a strong nature, wild and free, unfettered by any sort of traditions. She is impetuous—volcanic, I was about to say. She is swift in making up her mind, and fearless in carrying out her resolutions. On the other hand, I would not have given her the name which I have the honour to bear " (he gave a little stately cough) " had I not thought her to be at bottom a noble woman. I believe she is capable of heroic self-sacrifice, and that anything dishonourable would be repugnant to her."

" Have you her photograph ? "

" I brought this with me." He opened a locket, and showed us the full face of a very lovely woman. It was not a photograph, but an ivory miniature, and the artist had brought out the full effect of the lustrous black hair, the large dark eyes, and the exquisite mouth. Holmes gazed long and earnestly at it. Then he closed the locket and handed it back to Lord St. Simon.

" The young lady came to London, then, and you renewed your acquaintance ? "

" Yes, her father brought her over for this last London season. I met her several times, became engaged to her, and have now married her."

" She brought, I understand, a considerable dowry."

" A fair dowry.   Not more than is usual in my family."

" And this, of course, remains to you, since the marriage is a *fait accompli* ? " **24**

" I really have made no inquiries on the subject."

" Very naturally not.   Did you see Miss Doran on the day before the wedding ? "

" Yes."

" Was she in good spirits ? '

" Never better.   She kept talking of what we should do in our future lives."

" Indeed.   That is very interesting.   And on the morning of the wedding ? "

" She was as bright as possible—at least, until after the ceremony."

" And did you observe any change in her then ? "

" Well, to tell the truth, I saw then the first signs that I had ever seen that her temper was just a little sharp.   The incident, however, was too trivial to relate, and can have no possible bearing upon the case."

" Pray let us have it, for all that."

" Oh, it is childish.   She dropped her bouquet as we went towards the vestry.   She was passing the front pew at the time, and it fell over into the pew.   There was a moment's delay, but the gentleman in the pew handed it up to her again, and it did not appear to be the worse for the fall.   Yet, when I spoke to her of the matter, she answered me abruptly ; and in the carriage, on our way home, she seemed absurdly agitated over this trifling cause."

" Indeed.   You say that there was a gentleman in the pew.   Some of the general public were present, then ? "

" Oh, yes.   It is impossible to exclude them when the church is open."

" This gentleman was not one of your wife's friends ? "

" No, no ; I call him a gentleman by courtesy, but he was quite a common-looking person.   I hardly noticed his appearance.   But really I think that we are wandering rather far from the point."

" Lady St. Simon, then, returned from the wedding in a less cheerful frame of mind than she had gone to it.   What did she do on re-entering her father's house ? "

" I saw her in conversation with her maid."

" And who is her maid ? "

" Alice is her name.   She is an American, and came from California with her."

" A confidential servant ? "

" A little too much so.   It seemed to me that her mistress allowed her to take great liberties.   Still, of course, in America they look upon these things in a different way."

" How long did she speak to this Alice ? "

" Oh, a few minutes.   I had something else to think of."

" You did not overhear what they said ? "

" Lady St. Simon said something about ' jumping a claim.'   She was accustomed to use slang of the kind.   I have no idea what she meant."

" American slang is very expressive sometimes.   And what did your wife do when she had finished speaking to her maid ? "

24 *a* fait accompli?" French: a thing accomplished and supposedly irrevocable.

". . . BUT THE GENTLEMAN IN THE PEW HANDED IT UP TO HER AGAIN . . ."

Illustration by Sidney Paget for the *Strand Magazine*, April, 1892.

25 *"But this maid Alice, as I understand, deposes.* Holmes' use of the word "deposes" is another example of his practical knowledge of the law.

"... SHE WAS AFTERWARDS SEEN WALKING INTO HYDE PARK ..."

"Hyde Park (open to carriages, not to cabs), the principal recreation ground of London, takes its name from the manor of Hyde, which belonged to the Abbey of Westminster," Augustus J. C. Hare wrote in *Walks in London*, Vol. II. "The first park was enclosed by Henry VIII, and the French Ambassador hunted there in 1550. In the time of Charles I, the park was thrown open to the public, but it was sold under the Commonwealth, when Evelyn complained that 'every coach was made to pay a shilling, and horse sixpence, by the sordid fellow who had purchas'd it of the State as they were call'd.' ... Hyde Park has been much used of late years for radical meetings, and on Sundays numerous open-air congregations on the turf near the Marble Arch make the air resound with 'revival' melodies, and recall the days of Wesley and Whitefield." The photograph is from *The Baker Street Journal*, Vol. II, No. 1, Old Series, January, 1947.

" She walked into the breakfast-room."

" On your arm ? "

" No, alone. She was very independent in little matters like that. Then, after we had sat down for ten minutes or so, she rose hurriedly, muttered some words of apology, and left the room. She never came back."

25 " But this maid Alice, as I understand, deposes that she went to her room, covered her bride's dress with a long ulster, put on a bonnet, and went out."

" Quite so. And she was afterwards seen walking into Hyde Park in company with Flora Millar, a woman who is now in custody, and who had already made a disturbance at Mr. Doran's house that morning."

" Ah, yes. I should like a few particulars as to this young lady, and your relations to her."

Lord St. Simon shrugged his shoulders, and raised his eyebrows. " We have been on a friendly footing for some years—I may say on a *very* friendly footing. She used to be at the Allegro. I have not treated her ungenerously, and she has no just cause of complaint against me, but you know what women are, Mr. Holmes. Flora was a dear little thing, but exceedingly hot-headed, and devotedly attached to me. She wrote me dreadful letters when she heard that I was to be married, and to tell the truth the reason why I had the marriage celebrated so quietly was that I feared lest there might be a scandal in the church. She came to Mr. Doran's door just after we returned, and she endeavoured to push her way in, uttering very abusive expressions towards my wife, and even threatening her, but I had foreseen the possibility of something of the sort, and I had given instructions to the servants, who soon pushed her out again. She was quiet when she saw that there was no good in making a row."

" Did your wife hear all this ? "

" No, thank goodness, she did not."

" And she was seen walking with this very woman afterwards ? "

" Yes.   That is what Mr. Lestrade, of Scotland Yard, looks upon as so serious.   It is thought that Flora decoyed my wife out, and laid some terrible trap for her."

" Well, it is a possible supposition."

" You think so, too ? "

" I did not say a probable one.   But you do not yourself look upon this as likely ? "

" I do not think Flora would hurt a fly."

" Still, jealousy is a strange transformer of characters. Pray what is your own theory as to what took place ? "

" Well, really, I came to seek a theory, not to propound one.   I have given you all the facts.   Since you ask me, however, I may say that it has occurred to me as possible that the excitement of this affair, the consciousness that she had made so immense a social stride, had the effect of causing some little nervous disturbance in my wife."

" In short, that she had become suddenly deranged ? "

" Well, really, when I consider that she has turned her back—I will not say upon me, but upon so much that many have aspired to without success—I can hardly explain it in any other fashion."

" Well, certainly that is also a conceivable hypothesis," said Holmes, smiling.   " And now, Lord St. Simon, I think that I have nearly all my data.   May I ask whether you were seated at the breakfast-table so that you could see out of the window ? "

" We could see the other side of the road, and the Park."

" Quite so.   Then I do not think that I need detain you any longer.   I shall communicate with you."

" Should you be fortunate enough to solve this problem," said our client, rising.

" I have solved it."

" Eh ?   What was that ? "

" I say that I have solved it."

" Where, then, is my wife ? "

" That is a detail which I shall speedily supply."

Lord St. Simon shook his head.   " I am afraid that it will take wiser heads than yours or mine," he remarked, and bowing in a stately, old-fashioned manner, he departed.

" It is very good of Lord St. Simon to honour my head by putting it on a level with his own," said Sherlock Holmes, laughing.   " I think that I shall have a whisky and soda and a cigar after all this cross-questioning.   I had formed my conclusions as to the case before our client came into the room."

" My dear Holmes ! "

" I have notes of several similar cases, though none, as I remarked before, which were quite as prompt.   My whole examination served to turn my conjecture into a certainty. Circumstantial evidence is occasionally very convincing, **26** as when you find a trout in the milk, to quote Thoreau's example." **27**

" But I have heard all that you have heard."

" Without, however, the knowledge of pre-existing cases which serves me so well.   There was a parallel instance in Aberdeen some years back, and something on very much the same lines at Munich the year after the

26 *"Circumstantial evidence is occasionally very convincing.* Holmes had conflicting views on circumstantial evidence. In "The Boscombe Valley Mystery," he calls it "a very tricky thing." And in "The Problem of Thor Bridge," he says: "When once your point of view is changed, the very thing which was so damning becomes a clue to the truth."

27 *to quote Thoreau's example.* Holmes quotes Henry David Thoreau, 1817–1862, the American poet, naturalist, and essayist. As Miss Madeleine B. Stern wrote in "Sherlock Holmes: Rare Book Collector," this is "a clear enough sign that [Holmes] may have owned a copy of Thoreau's *Miscellanies* (Boston, 1863), to which Emerson has added a biographical sketch including sentences from the unpublished writings. Among the sentences was . . . the remark on circumstantial evidence, actually taken from the as yet unpublished *Journals* of Thoreau."

28 *the year after the Franco-Prussian War.* The war ended on January 28, 1871. Some commentators have surmised from Holmes' manner of speaking here that he may have had first-hand knowledge of one or both of these cases, attained, in the case of the affair at Munich, during a stay on the Continent in the years 1870–1871.

29 *a pea-jacket.* A short overcoat worn by sailors. *Pea* has nothing to do with its color; rather it comes from an old Dutch word, *pie* or *pij*, meaning coat. The pea-jacket was, on occasion, a favored garment with Holmes as well as Lestrade; the Master dons one in both "The Red-Headed League" and *The Sign of the Four*.

28 Franco-Prussian War. It is one of these cases—but hallo, here is Lestrade ! Good afternoon, Lestrade ! You will find an extra tumbler upon the sideboard, and there are cigars in the box."

29   The official detective was attired in a pea-jacket and cravat, which gave him a decidedly nautical appearance, and he carried a black canvas bag in his hand. With a short greeting he seated himself, and lit the cigar which had been offered to him.

"What's up, then ? " asked Holmes, with a twinkle in his eye. "You look dissatisfied."

" And I feel dissatisfied. It is this infernal St. Simon marriage case. I can make neither head nor tail of the business."

" Really ! You surprise me."

" Who ever heard of such a mixed affair ? Every clue seems to slip through my fingers. I have been at work upon it all day."

" And very wet it seems to have made you," said Holmes, laying his hand upon the arm of the pea-jacket.

" Yes, I have been dragging the Serpentine."

" In Heaven's name, what for ? "

" In search of the body of Lady St. Simon."

Sherlock Holmes leaned back in his chair and laughed heartily.

". . . I HAVE BEEN DRAGGING THE SERPENTINE."

"A little to the north of Rotten Row [in Hyde Park]," Augustus J. C. Hare wrote in *Walks in London*, Vol. II, "is the Serpentine, an artificial lake of fifty acres, much frequented for bathing in summer and for skating in winter. There is a delightful drive along its northern bank. Near this are the oldest trees in the Park, some of them oaks said to have been planted by Charles II." The photograph, by J. Allen Cash, is from *The First Country Life Picture Book of London*, London: Country Life, Ltd., 1951.

" Have you dragged the basin of the Trafalgar Square fountain ? " he asked.

" Why ? What do you mean ? "

" Because you have just as good a chance of finding this lady in the one as in the other."

Lestrade shot an angry glance at my companion. " I suppose you know all about it," he snarled.

" Well, I have only just heard the facts, but my mind is made up."

" Oh, indeed ! Then you think that the Serpentine plays no part in the matter ? "

" I think it very unlikely."

" Then perhaps you will kindly explain how it is that we found this in it ? " He opened his bag as he spoke, and tumbled on to the floor a wedding dress of watered silk, a pair of white satin shoes, and a bride's wreath and veil, all discoloured and soaked in water. " There," said he, putting a new wedding-ring upon the top of the pile. " There is a little nut for you to crack, Master Holmes."

" Oh, indeed," said my friend, blowing blue rings into the air. " You dragged them from the Serpentine ? "

" No. They were found floating near the margin by a park-keeper. They were identified as her clothes, and it seemed to me that if the clothes were there the body would not be far off."

" By the same brilliant reasoning, every man's body is to be found in the neighbourhood of his wardrobe. And pray what did you hope to arrive at through this ? "

" At some evidence implicating Flora Millar in the disappearance."

" I am afraid you will find it difficult."

"THERE," HE SAID, PUTTING A NEW WEDDING-RING UPON THE TOP OF THE PILE.

Illustration by Sidney Paget for the *Strand Magazine*, April, 1892.

"HAVE YOU DRAGGED THE BASIN OF THE TRAFALGAR SQUARE FOUNTAIN?"...

Augustus J. C. Hare, in his *Walks in London*, Vol. II, calls this famous square "a dreary expanse of granite with two granite fountains, intended to commemorate the last victory of Nelson. Its northern side is occupied by the miserable buildings of the National Gallery; its eastern and western sides by a hideous hotel and a frightful club. Where the noble Jacobian screen of Northumberland House . . . once drew the eye away from these abominations by its dignity and beauty, a view of the funnel-roof of Charing Cross Railway Station forms a poor substitute for the time-honoured palace of the Percy's! In the centre of the square is a Corinthian pillar of Devonshire granite, 145 feet in height, by W. Railton, erected in 1843. It supports a statue of Nelson by E. H. Bailey, R.A., a very poor work, which, however, does not much signify, as it can only be properly seen from the top of the Duke of York's column, which no one ascends. . . . On the east side of Trafalgar Square is its one ornament. Here, on a noble basement, approached by a broad flight of steps, rises the beautiful portico of the Church of St. Martin in the Fields." The photograph, by G. F. Allen, is from *The First Country Life Picture Book of London*, London: Country Life, Ltd., 1951.

30 " '*Oct. 4th.* There is no reason to doubt the month: Watson has earlier spoken of "high autumnal winds." More important, Holmes says, at the end of the case: "The only problem we have still to solve is now to while away these bleak autumnal evenings."

31 *glass sherry 8d.*' The room cost $2.00, the breakfast and lunch some 62½¢ each, the cocktail 25¢, the sherry, 16¢. We are later told that the bill was rendered by "one of the most expensive hotels" in London. *Eheu fugaces!*

32 *a couple of brace of cold woodcock.* "This admirable bird," Mr. Vincent Starrett wrote in "The Singular Adventures of Martha Hudson," "would appear to have been a favorite with Holmes. . . . [A] woodcock [was served] during the excitements of the detective's search for the Blue Carbuncle."

33 *a pheasant.* "The means of preparing woodcock and pheasant, when they are to be served cold, approach each other very closely, and the difference is only perceptible to a delicate palate," the late Fletcher Pratt wrote in "The Gastronomic Holmes." "Holmes was subtly flattering his guests by assuming that although they were Americans, they would know enough about the *haute cuisine* to be able to express an intelligent choice between the cold woodcock and the cold pheasant; that they would savor the fine distinction between the two and perhaps take a slice of each. . . . I think there can be little doubt about how the woodcock and the pheasant were served. At least one of them must have been *à la buloz* and the *chaud-froid.* There are only two possible recipes, the Bohemian, in which the bird appears in aspic in the center of a block of ice—which was impossible because the supper had to wait from 5:00 until after 9:00—and the recipe *à la croix de Berny,* which involves *pâté* and would therefore have been in conflict with the *pâté* already on the table in the pie. Therefore, the pheasant almost undoubtedly appeared in aspic, sliced and decorated with truffles coated with a sauce and served on a low bed of semolina. The woodcock would be gently poached, their skins removed, and the birds themselves coated with *chaud-froid* sauce and aspic, surrounded by cockscombs and mushrooms."

34 *a pâté-de-foie-gras pie.* "I have hunted through the works of culinary experts of Victoria's reign; I have found pigeon pies and pork pies and game pies, Christmas pies and venison pies and beef pies; nowhere a *pâté-de-foie-gras* pie," Miss Marie F. Rodell complained in "Living on Baker Street." To this the erudite Morris Rosenblum replied: "Miss Rodell conjectures that Watson either used the words carelessly, or that the pie was a secret concoction of the trade, or finally that Watson himself was the inventor of the pie. It is time to call a halt to the constant practice of imputing a faulty memory to Watson, especially when a little

" Are you indeed, now ? " cried Lestrade, with some bitterness. " I am afraid, Holmes, that you are not very practical with your deductions and your inferences. You have made two blunders in as many minutes. This dress does implicate Miss Flora Millar."

" And how ? "

" In the dress is a pocket. In the pocket is a card-case. In the card-case is a note. And here is the very note." He slapped it down upon the table in front of him. " Listen to this. ' You will see me when all is ready. Come at once. F. H. M.' Now my theory all along has been that Lady St. Simon was decoyed away by Flora Millar, and that she, with confederates no doubt, was responsible for her disappearance. Here, signed with her initials, is the very note which was no doubt quietly slipped into her hand at the door, and which lured her within their reach."

" Very good, Lestrade," said Holmes, laughing. " You really are very fine indeed. Let me see it." He took up the paper in a listless way, but his attention instantly became riveted, and he gave a little cry of satisfaction. " This is indeed important," said he.

" Ha, you find it so ? "

" Extremely so. I congratulate you warmly."

Lestrade rose in his triumph and bent his head to look. " Why," he shrieked, " you're looking on the wrong side."

" On the contrary, this is the right side."

" The right side ? You're mad ! Here is the note written in pencil over here."

" And over here is what appears to be a fragment of a hotel bill, which interests me deeply."

30 " There's nothing in it. I looked at it before," said
31 Lestrade. " ' Oct. 4th, rooms 8s., breakfast 2s. 6d., cocktail 1s., lunch 2s. 6d., glass sherry 8d.' I see nothing in that."

" Very likely not. It is most important all the same. As to the note, it is important also, or at least the initials are, so I congratulate you again."

" I've wasted time enough," said Lestrade, rising, " I believe in hard work, and not in sitting by the fire spinning fine theories. Good day, Mr Holmes, and we shall see which gets to the bottom of the matter first." He gathered up the garments, thrust them into the bag, and made for the door.

" Just one hint to you, Lestrade," drawled Holmes, before his rival vanished ; " I will tell you the true solution of the matter. Lady St. Simon is a myth. There is not, and there never has been, any such person."

Lestrade looked sadly at my companion. Then he turned to me, tapped his forehead three times, shook his head solemnly, and hurried away.

He had hardly shut the door behind him, when Holmes rose and put on his overcoat. " There is something in what the fellow says about outdoor work," he remarked, " so I think, Watson, that I must leave you to your papers for a little."

It was after five o'clock when Sherlock Holmes left me, but I had no time to be lonely, for within an hour there arrived a confectioner's man with a very large flat box. This he unpacked with the help of a youth whom he had brought with him, and presently, to my very great astonishment, a quite epicurean little cold supper began to be laid out upon our humble lodging-house mahogany. There were a couple of brace of cold woodcock, a pheas- **32** ant, a *pâté-de-foie-gras* pie, with a group of ancient and **33-34** cobwebby bottles. Having laid out all these luxuries, **35** my two visitors vanished away, like the genii of the Arabian Nights, with no explanation save that the things had been paid for, and were ordered to this address.

Just before nine o'clock Sherlock Holmes stepped briskly into the room. His features were gravely set, but there was a light in his eye which made me think that he had not been disappointed in his conclusions.

" They have laid the supper, then," he said, rubbing his hands.

" You seem to expect company. They have laid for **36** five."

" Yes, I fancy we may have some company dropping in," said he. " I am surprised that Lord St. Simon has not already arrived. Ha ! I fancy that I hear his step now upon the stairs."

It was indeed our visitor of the morning who came bustling in, dangling his glasses more vigorously than ever, and with a very perturbed expression upon his aristocratic features.

" My messenger reached you, then ? " asked Holmes.

" Yes, and I must confess that the contents startled me beyond measure. Have you good authority for what you say ? "

" The best possible."

Lord St. Simon sank into a chair, and passed his hand over his forehead.

" What will the Duke say," he murmured, " when he hears that one of the family has been subjected to such a humiliation ? "

" It is the purest accident. I cannot allow that there is any humiliation."

" Ah, you look on these things from another standpoint."

" I fail to see that anyone is to blame. I can hardly see how the lady could have acted otherwise, though her abrupt method of doing it was undoubtedly to be regretted. Having no mother, she had no one to advise her at such a crisis."

" It was a slight, sir, a public slight," said Lord St. Simon, tapping his fingers upon the table.

" You must make allowance for this poor girl, placed in so unprecedented a position."

" I will make no allowance. I am very angry indeed, and I have been shamefully used."

" I think I heard a ring," said Holmes. " Yes, there are steps on the landing. If I cannot persuade you to take a lenient view of the matter, Lord St. Simon, I have brought an advocate here who may be more successful." He opened the door and ushered in a lady and gentleman. " Lord St. Simon," said he, " allow me to introduce you to Mr. and Mrs. Francis Hay Moulton. The lady, I **37** think, you have already met."

At the sight of these new-comers our client had sprung from his seat, and stood very erect, with his eyes cast down and his hand thrust into the breast of his frock-coat,

additional research can clear his memory! The standard dictionaries reveal that the term '*pâté-de-foie-gras pie*' was used before Watson's time. Since *pâté-de-foie-gras* was the leading product of Strasburg in Alsace, the confection was also called a Strasburg pie. *The Oxford English Dictionary* has the following entries and illustrative quotations: '*Pâté-de-foie-gras*, pie or pasty of goose liver.' From Thackeray's *Yellowplush Papers* comes the quotation: 'He sent me out . . . for wot's called a Strasburg-pie—in French, a "patty defau graw." ' From H. S. Leigh's *Carols of Cockayne* (1869): 'Turtle and salmon and Strasbourg pie.' Culinary details about this pie can be found in Cassell's *Dictionary of Cookery* published in London and New York. No date of publication is given, but the copy which I consulted in the New York Public Library is stamped, 'Astor Library, September 30, 1864.' Copies were therefore available in the days of Holmes and Watson!"

35 *a group of ancient and cobwebby bottles.* "It is easy to presume that the dusty bottles were an aristocratic Burgundy matching the purpose and were no doubt a *Clos-Vougeot* or a similar brand," Mr. Jørgen Cold wrote in "What Did Sherlock Holmes Drink?"

If so, we may be sure it was a white *Clos-Vougeot* and not a red, for, as the late Fletcher Pratt wrote in "The Gastronomic Holmes": "Surely, with his fine taste in wines, Holmes would never have served reds beside pheasant and woodcock; and I am not aware of a white that could stand enough age to become cobwebby without also becoming vinegar. I can only suggest that he was once more exercising his delicate taste and immense knowledge by providing a Portugese rosé, which as a wired wine can stand much longer storage and, indeed, improves by it. The fact that there was not one, but a number of the ancient and cobwebby bottles, is very significant; quite clearly and very properly, Holmes expected to continue whatever drinking was done after the meal from the contents of these bottles. A Portugese rosé would serve this purpose admirably."

"It was definitely to the Bordeaux and the Burgundies that Holmes' natural tastes were inclined," the late Edgar W. Smith noted in "Up from the Needle." "Surprisingly, for an Englishman of his generation, he seems to have shunned the hocks completely. Nowhere are the vintages of the Moselle and the Rhineland given mention in the tales, and we are led to wonder if, forseeing the part he was to play in the Great War, he did not take it upon himself to set up a sort of individual boycott before the fact."

Holmes' wines probably came from the excellent wine-merchant's shop at No. 16 Baker Street, at the corner of Blandford Street. This shop, Mr. Michael Harrison tells us in *In the Footsteps of Sherlock Holmes*, belonged to the still-existing firm of H. Dolamore & Co.

"THE LADY, I THINK, YOU HAVE ALREADY MET."

Illustration by Sidney Paget for the *Strand Magazine*, April, 1892.

36 *They have laid for five."* "There is food enough for four but not for five, although five places were laid," the late Fletcher Pratt noted in "The Gastronomic Holmes." "One woodcock or half a pheasant is exactly a portion, and since the *pâté* pie would be required as a garnish, it was evidently not intended to serve the fifth eater. That is, Holmes must have deduced that Lord St. Simon would not remain to share the repast; a point which Watson completely missed."

37 *Mr. and Mrs. Francis Hay Moulton.* Mr. Robert Keith Leavitt has suggested ("The Preposterously Paired Performances of the Preacher's Portrait") that Mr. Francis Hay Moulton is possibly identifiable with that Francis H. Moulton, a friend of Theodore Tilton, who acted as a go-between in Tilton's 1871 negotiations with Henry Ward Beecher and became a star witness at the Tilton-Beecher trial in 1874.

a picture of offended dignity. The lady had taken a quick step forward and had held out her hand to him, but he still refused to raise his eyes. It was as well for his resolution, perhaps, for her pleading face was one which it was hard to resist.

"You're angry, Robert," said she. "Well, I guess you have every cause to be."

"Pray make no apology to me," said Lord St. Simon bitterly.

"Oh, yes, I know that I treated you real bad, and that I should have spoken to you before I went; but I was kind of rattled, and from the time when I saw Frank here again, I just didn't know what I was doing or saying. I only wonder that I didn't fall down and do a faint right there before the altar."

"Perhaps, Mrs. Moulton, you would like my friend and me to leave the room while you explain this matter?"

"If I may give an opinion," remarked the strange gentleman, "we've had just a little too much secrecy over this business already. For my part, I should like all Europe and America to hear the rights of it." He was a small, wiry, sunburned man, with a sharp face and alert manner.

"Then I'll tell our story right away," said the lady. "Frank here and I met in '81, in McQuire's camp, near the Rockies, where Pa was working a claim. We were engaged to each other, Frank and I; but then one day father struck a rich pocket, and made a pile, while poor Frank here had a claim that petered out and came to nothing. The richer Pa grew, the poorer was Frank; so at last Pa wouldn't hear of our engagement lasting any longer, and he took me away to 'Frisco. Frank wouldn't throw up his hand, though; so he followed me there, and he saw me without Pa knowing anything about it. It would only have made him mad to know, so we just fixed it all up for ourselves. Frank said that he would go and make his pile, too, and never come back to claim me until he had as much as Pa. So then I promised to wait for him to the end of time, and pledged myself not to marry anyone else while he lived. 'Why shouldn't we be married right away, then,' said he, and then I will feel sure of you; and I won't claim to be your husband until I come back.' Well, we talked it over, and he had fixed it all up so nicely, with a clergyman all ready in waiting, that we just did it right there; and then Frank went off to seek his fortune and I went back to Pa.

"The next that I heard of Frank was that he was in Montana, and then he went prospecting into Arizona, and then I heard of him from New Mexico. After that came a long newspaper story about how a miners' camp had been attacked by Apache Indians, and there was my Frank's name among the killed. I fainted dead away, and I was very sick for months after. Pa thought I had a decline, and took me to half the doctors in 'Frisco. Not a word of news came for a year or more, so that I never doubted that Frank was really dead. Then Lord St. Simon came to 'Frisco, and we came to London, and a marriage was arranged, and Pa was very pleased, but I felt all the time that no man on this earth would ever take the place in my heart that had been given to my poor Frank.

" Still, if I had married Lord St. Simon, of course I'd have done my duty by him. We can't command our love, but we can our actions. I went to the altar with him with the intention that I would make him just as good a wife as it was in me to be. But you may imagine what I felt when, just as I came to the altar rails, I glanced back and saw Frank standing looking at me out of the first pew. I thought it was his ghost at first ; but, when I looked again, there he was still, with a kind of question in his eyes as if to ask me whether I were glad or sorry to see him. I wonder I didn't drop. I know that everything was turning round, and the words of the clergyman were just like the buzz of a bee in my ear. I didn't know what to do. Should I stop the service and make a scene in the church ? I glanced at him again, and he seemed to know what I was thinking, for he raised his fingers to his lips to tell me to be still. Then I saw him scribble on a piece of paper, and I knew he was writing me a note. As I passed his pew on the way out I dropped my bouquet over to him, and he slipped the note into my hand when he returned me the flowers. It was only a line asking me to join him when he made the sign to me to do so. Of course I never doubted for a moment that my first duty now was to him, and I determined to do just whatever he might direct.

" When I got back I told my maid, who had known him in California, and had always been his friend. I ordered her to say nothing, but to get a few things packed and my ulster ready. I know I ought to have spoken to Lord St. Simon, but it was dreadful hard before his mother and all those great people. I just made up my mind to run away, and explain afterwards. I hadn't been at the table ten minutes before I saw Frank out of the window at the other side of the road. He beckoned to me, and then began walking into the Park. I slipped out, put on my things, and followed him. Some woman came talking something or other about Lord St. Simon to me—seemed to me from the little I heard as if he had a little secret of his own before marriage also—but I managed to get away from her, and soon overtook Frank. We got into a cab together, and away we drove to some lodgings he had taken in Gordon Square, and that was my true **38** wedding after all those years of waiting. Frank had been a prisoner among the Apaches, had escaped, came on to 'Frisco, found that I had given him up for dead and had gone to England, followed me there, and had come upon me at last on the very morning of my second wedding."

" I saw it in a paper," explained the American. " It gave the name and the church, but not where the lady lived."

" Then we had a talk as to what we should do, and Frank was all for openness, but I was so ashamed of it all that I felt as if I would like to vanish away and never see any of them again, just sending a line to Pa, perhaps, to show him that I was alive. It was awful to me to think of all those lords and ladies sitting round that breakfast-table, and waiting for me to come back. So Frank took my wedding clothes and things, and made a bundle of

38 *Gordon Square.* "From the north-west angle of Bedford Square we may proceed, through Woburn Square, to Gordon Square, containing the modern Catholic Apostolic (Irvingite) Church, a handsome building in the early English style, by Brandon and Ritchie," Augustus J. C. Hare wrote in *Walks in London*, Vol. II.

"SOME WOMAN CAME TALKING SOMETHING OR OTHER ABOUT LORD ST. SIMON TO ME . . ."

Illustration by Sidney Paget for the *Strand Magazine*, April, 1892.

"I THINK THAT, WITH YOUR PERMISSION, I WILL NOW
WISH YOU ALL A VERY GOOD NIGHT."

Illustration by Sidney Paget for the *Strand Magazine*, April, 1892.

them so that I should not be traced, and dropped them away somewhere where no one should find them. It is likely that we should have gone on to Paris to-morrow, only that this good gentleman, Mr. Holmes, came round to us this evening, though how he found us is more than I can think, and he showed us very clearly and kindly that I was wrong and that Frank was right, and that we should put ourselves in the wrong if we were so secret. Then he offered to give us a chance of talking to Lord St. Simon alone, and so we came right away round to his rooms at once. Now, Robert, you have heard all, and I am very sorry if I have given you pain, and I hope that you do not think very meanly of me."

Lord St. Simon had by no means relaxed his rigid attitude, but had listened with a frowning brow and a compressed lip to this long narrative.

"Excuse me," he said, "but it is not my custom to discuss my most intimate personal affairs in this public manner."

"Then you won't forgive me? You won't shake hands before I go?"

"Oh, certainly, if it would give you any pleasure." He put out his hand and coldly grasped that which she extended to him.

"I had hoped," suggested Holmes, "that you would have joined us in a friendly supper."

"I think that there you ask a little too much," responded his lordship. "I may be forced to acquiesce in these recent developments, but I can hardly be expected to make merry over them. I think that, with your permission, I will now wish you all a very good night." He included us all in a sweeping bow, and stalked out of the room.

"Then I trust that you at least will honour me with your company," said Sherlock Holmes. "It is always a joy to me to meet an American, Mr. Moulton, for I am one of those who believe that the folly of a monarch and the blundering of a Minister in fargone years will not prevent our children from being some day citizens of the same world-wide country under a flag which shall be a quartering of the Union Jack with the Stars and Stripes."

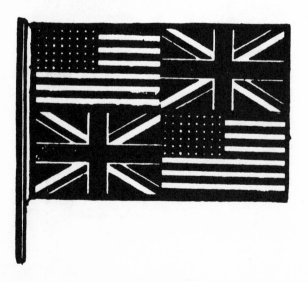

". . . A FLAG WHICH SHALL BE A QUARTERING OF THE UNION JACK WITH
THE STARS AND STRIPES."

"Holmes was in advance of his time in holding these views, and more recent historians of the War of Independence and its causes tend to spread the responsibility and blame over others beside George III and his Minister," Mr. T. S. Blakeney wrote in *Sherlock Holmes: Fact or Fiction?* "But the idea of an Anglo-American union has not been lost from view, and found favour in the sight of the late Lord Fisher, among others."

"One may reasonably surmise," Dr. Felix Morley wrote in "The Significance of the Second Stain," "that the two unfilled quarters of this banner were in Holmes' mind dedicated to other important democracies, probably France and the Netherlands, as the working basis of that federation of 'Union Now,' so persuasively urged today by my good friend Clarence Streit."

But Dr. Julian Wolff (*Practical Handbook of Sherlockian Heraldry*) has suggested that "when Holmes expressed a hope to have the two great nations live under this flag, as a loyal Englishman he gave precedence to the Union Jack. However, it is assumed by equally loyal Americans that there will be two forms of the flag. The one for use in the United States ought to have the Stars and Stripes in the first and fourth quarters and the Union Jack in the second and third. There is a precedent for this in the Queen's arms for Scotland: Quarterly, 1 and 4, Scotland; 2, England; 3, Ireland."

" The case has been an interesting one," remarked Holmes, when our visitors had left, " because it serves to show very clearly how simple the explanation may be of an affair which at first sight seems to be almost inexplicable. Nothing could be more inexplicable. Nothing could be more natural than the sequence of events as narrated by this lady, and nothing stranger than the result when viewed, for instance, by Mr. Lestrade of Scotland Yard."

" You were not yourself at fault, then ? "

" From the first, two facts were very obvious to me, the one that the lady had been quite willing to undergo the wedding ceremony, the other that she had repented of it within a few minutes of returning home. Obviously something had occurred during the morning, then, to cause her to change her mind. What could that something be ? She could not have spoken to anyone when she was out, for she had been in the company of the bridegroom. Had she seen someone, then ? If she had, it must be someone from America, because she had spent so short a time in this country that she could hardly have allowed anyone to acquire so deep an influence over her that the mere sight of him would induce her to change her plans so completely. You see we have already arrived, by a process of exclusion, at the idea that she might have seen an American. Then who could this American be, and why should he possess so much influence over her ? It might be a lover ; it might be a husband. Her young womanhood had, I knew, been spent in rough scenes, and under strange conditions. So far had I got before I ever heard Lord St. Simon's narrative. When he told us of a man in a pew, of the change in the bride's manner, of so transparent a device of obtaining a note as the dropping of a bouquet, of her resort to her confidential maid, and of her very significant allusion to claim-jumping, which in miners' parlance means taking possession of that which another person has a prior claim to, the whole situation became absolutely clear. She had gone off with a man, and the man was either a lover or was a previous husband, the chances being in favour of the latter."

" And how in the world did you find them ? "

" It might have been difficult, but friend Lestrade held information in his hands the value of which he did not himself know. The initials were of course of the highest importance, but more valuable still was it to know that within a week he had settled his bill at one of the most **39** select London hotels."

" How did you deduce the select ? "

" By the select prices. Eight shillings for a bed and eightpence for a glass of sherry, pointed to one of the most expensive hotels. There are not many in London which charge at that rate. In the second one which I visited in Northumberland Avenue, I learned by an inspection of the book that Francis H. Moulton, an American gentleman, had left only the day before, and on looking over the **40** entries against him, I came upon the very items which I had seen in the duplicate bill. His letters were to be forwarded to 226 Gordon Square, so thither I travelled, and being fortunate enough to find the loving couple at home,

39 *within a week he had settled his bill.* Dated, as we have seen, October 4th. Since Moulton had the receipted bill in his possession on Tuesday, the day of the wedding, he had obviously paid it that morning or earlier. It would seem clear that he paid it on the preceding day, Monday: the "curt announcement" on Wednesday that "the wedding had taken place" (on Tuesday) had appeared "two days later" than a note in the *Morning Post* (and no doubt in other newspapers) that the marriage was about to take place. These notes would therefore have appeared on Monday. Moulton saw an announcement of the wedding-to be that "gave the name of the church, but not where the lady lived." From the above, he must have seen this announcement on Monday (but not in the *Morning Post*, which told where the lady lived). A man of action, he would immediately pay his hotel bill and set out to find the lodgings in Gordon Square to which he took Hatty Doran after she had left her wedding breakfast so precipitously on the Tuesday. Moulton attended the wedding (on Tuesday), scribbled his note on the back of the duplicate of the hotel bill he had paid the day before, departed with Hatty to the lodgings in Gordon Square he had located the day before. October 4, 1886, *was* a Monday. We can now say with some confidence that "The Adventure of the Noble Bachelor" took place on *Friday, October 8, 1886.*

40 *had left only the day before.* Since Moulton had no place to go at the time of paying his hotel bill, he presumably left the bulk of the luggage he had brought from America in his hotel room, and therefore did not *check out* of the hotel; he simply settled his bill to that date. On Thursday, then, Moulton returned to the hotel, collected his luggage, and gave up his room.

I ventured to give them some paternal advice, and to point out to them that it would be better in every way that they should make their position a little clearer, both to the general public and to Lord St. Simon in particular. I invited them to meet him here, and, as you see, I made him keep the appointment."

" But with no very good results," I remarked. " His conduct was certainly not very gracious."

" Ah ! Watson," said Holmes, smiling, " perhaps you would not be very gracious either, if, after all the trouble of wooing and wedding, you found yourself deprived in an instant of wife and of fortune. I think that we may judge Lord St. Simon very mercifully, and thank our stars that we are never likely to find ourselves in the same position. Draw your chair up, and hand me my violin, for the only problem which we have still to solve is how to while away these bleak autumnal evenings."

Auctorial Note: Conan Doyle's own opinion of "The Adventure of the Noble Bachelor" was a low one. In a letter to a friend he put the story "about the bottom of the list."

"IN THE SECOND ONE WHICH I VISITED IN NORTHUMBERLAND AVENUE . . ."

This exceedingly handsome thoroughfare leads southeast of Charing Cross to the Embankment. Constructed across the grounds of Northumberland House at a total cost of £650,000, the avenue was opened to the public on March 18, 1876. It is rich in Sherlockian associations: the Turkish baths used by Holmes and Watson were in Northumberland Avenue, as was the hotel at which Sir Henry Baskerville was a guest (now the Sherlock Holmes Tavern). It is quite reasonable to suppose that this was the same hotel at which Mr. Francis Hay Moulton stayed. The hotels frequented by wealthy Orientals for whom Mr. Melas acted as guide ("The Greek Interpreter") were also located in Northumberland Avenue. The photograph below, from *Baker Street By-Ways*, by Mr. James Edward Holroyd, shows Northumberland Avenue looking toward Trafalgar Square. The Turkish baths used by Holmes and Watson were on the right-hand corner. The solitary hansom cab is stationed in front of what is now the Sherlock Holmes Tavern.

21

THE ADVENTURE OF THE SECOND STAIN

[*Tuesday, October 12, to Friday, October 15, 1886*]

I HAD intended the " Adventure of the Abbey Grange " to be the last of those exploits of my friend, Mr. Sherlock Holmes, which I should ever communicate to the public. This resolution of mine was not due to **1** any lack of material, since I have notes of many hundreds of cases to which I have never alluded, nor was it caused by any waning interest on the part of my readers in the singular personality and unique methods of this remarkable man. The real reason lay in the reluctance which Mr. Holmes has shown to the continued publication of his experiences. So long as he was in actual professional practice the records of his successes were of some practical value to him ; but since he has definitely retired from **2** London and betaken himself to study and bee-farming on the Sussex Downs, notoriety has become hateful to him, and he has peremptorily requested that his wishes in this matter should be strictly observed. It was only upon my **3** representing to him that I had given a promise that " The Adventure of the Second Stain " should be published when the time was ripe, and pointed out to him **4** that it was only appropriate that this long series of episodes should culminate in the most important international case which he has ever been called upon to handle, that I at last succeeded in obtaining his consent that a carefully guarded account of the incident should at last be laid before the public. If in telling the story I seem to be somewhat vague in certain details the public will readily understand that there is an excellent reason for my reticence.

It was, then, in a year, and even in a decade, that shall be nameless, that upon one Tuesday morning in autumn **5** we found two visitors of European fame within the walls of our humble room in Baker Street. The one, austere, **6** high-nosed, eagle-eyed, and dominant, was none other than the illustrious Lord Bellinger, twice Premier of Britain. The other, dark, clear-cut, and elegant, hardly yet of middle age, and endowed with every beauty of body and of mind, was the Right Honourable Trelawney Hope, Secretary for European Affairs, and the most **7**

1 *which I should ever communicate to the public.* "The Adventure of the Abbey Grange" was first published in the *Strand Magazine* for September, 1904. Three months later—in the *Strand* for December, 1904, our present adventure appeared for the first time. This was just two months after Holmes had retired from London and betaken himself to study and bee farming on the Sussex Downs.

2 *the records of his successes were of some practical value to him.* Mr. Roger T. Clapp has asked: "How . . . did Holmes secure the cases that were his meat and drink? . . . It was not the custom in those days for professional men to advertise, even to the limited extent modern professional ethics permit. So far as is known no newspapers or periodicals of the period carried Holmes' professional card. Further, in most, if not all, cases the press reports of the successful solution of a crime invariably gave all the credit to the professional police. In fact on many occasions Holmes deliberately permitted the police to take full credit —a shrewd business move this as it ensured continual reference of cases to him by his official friends. Pondering this problem he hit upon the idea . . . of having Watson advertise his abilities by publishing stories of his cases. That this was his underlying plan is quite clearly evidenced by his repeated—although subtle—suggestions that Watson select for his published stories those cases which best illustrated Holmes' deductive powers and resources, his constant references to his researches to indicate to prospective clients his unique technical equipment and his frequent complaints that Watson was sacrificing technical detail which would reflect Holmes' brilliance for the purely dramatic aspects of his cases. The next problem was to sell this idea to Watson. . . . Holmes utilized the since standard method of so subtly implanting the idea in Watson's mind that the Doctor would think it was his own. In the early days Holmes was careful to betray little interest in Watson's stories, even deprecating them at times. Essentially he gave the impression that if

The Premiers of Britain during the years when Holmes was in active practice were: Disraeli, 1874 (for the second time; he had succeeded Derby in 1867); Gladstone, 1880; Salisbury, 1885; Gladstone, 1886; Salisbury, 1886; Gladstone, 1892; Rosebery, 1894; Salisbury, 1895; Balfour, 1902. Since Watson was not with Holmes in 1874, when Disraeli was serving his second term as Premier, the Premier of "The Adventure of the Second Stain" must be either Gladstone or Salisbury. As the late Gavin Brend wrote in *My Dear Holmes:* "To decide between [Mr. Gladstone and Lord Salisbury] is no easy matter. Lord Bellinger is described as 'austere, high-nosed, eagle-eyed, and dominant.' This sounds far more like a description of [Gladstone] than of Lord Salisbury, but for this very reason we think we must choose the latter. Let us not forget Watson's statement that in certain details he is being deliberately vague. . . . He will . . . disguise his Prime Minister. The above pen-picture can hardly be described as a disguise of Gladstone. . . . We think . . . that the case occurred during Lord Salisbury's second period [as Prime Minister] from 1886 to 1892." Your editor is in complete agreement. Shown (*left*), then, is the coat of arms of "Lord Bellinger": Barry of ten, argent and azure, over all, six escutcheons, sable, three, two and one, each charged with a lion rampant of the first; a crescent for difference.

His arms, shown above, are blazoned: Argent, three cross crosslets in bend, sable.

Watson wanted to do that sort of thing it was all right with him. Later, possibly, when Watson's interest seemed to be flagging, Holmes would encourage him to write more, even suggesting cases . . ." We may add to Mr. Clapp's analysis the fact that Watson says (in *The Sign of the Four*) that *A Study in Scarlet* was written *especially to please* Holmes.

3 *should be strictly observed.* "The facts flatly contradict this assertion," the late Edgar W. Smith wrote in "Dr. Watson and the Great Censorship." "Actually, Holmes had scarcely had time to unpack his belongings in the comfort of his farmstead when the issue of the *Strand Magazine* for October, 1903, came out upon the stands with Watson's epochal 'Adventure of the Empty House,' in which he told an astounded, and no doubt bewildered world, that the Great Detective had not, after all, died in Switzerland in 1891, but that he had returned to his beloved London in 1894, and then and there had solved the murder

rising statesman in the country. They sat side by side upon our paper-littered settee, and it was easy to see from their worn and anxious faces that it was business of the most pressing importance which had brought them. The Premier's thin, blue-veined hands were clasped tightly over the ivory head of his umbrella, and his gaunt, ascetic face looked gloomily from Holmes to me. The European Secretary pulled nervously at his moustache and fidgeted with the seals of his watch-chain.

" When I discovered my loss, Mr. Holmes, which was at eight o'clock this morning, I at once informed the Prime Minister. It was at his suggestion that we have both come to you."

" Have you informed the police ? "

" No, sir," said the Prime Minister, with the quick, decisive manner for which he was famous. " We have not done so, nor is it possible that we should do so. To inform the police must, in the long run, mean to inform the public. This is what we particularly desire to avoid."

" And why, sir ? "

" Because the document in question is of such immense importance that its publication might very easily—I might almost say probably—lead to European complications of the utmost moment. It is not too much to say that peace or war may hang upon the issue. Unless its recovery can be attended with the utmost secrecy, then it may as well not be recovered at all, for all that is aimed at by those who have taken it is that its contents should be generally known."

"I understand. Now, Mr. Trelawney Hope, 1 should be much obliged if you would tell me exactly the circumstances under which this document disappeared."

"That can be done in a very few words, Mr. Holmes. The letter—for it was a letter from a foreign potentate— 8 was received six days ago. It was of such importance that I have never left it in my safe, but I have taken it across each evening to my house in Whitehall Terrace, 9 and kept it in my bedroom in a locked dispatch-box. It was there last night. Of that I am certain. I actually opened the box while I was dressing for dinner, and saw the document inside. This morning it was gone. The dispatch-box had stood beside the glass upon my dressing-table all night. I am a light sleeper, and so is my wife. We are both prepared to swear that no one could have entered the room during the night. And yet I repeat that the paper is gone."

"What time did you dine?"

"Half-past seven."

"How long was it before you went to bed?"

"My wife had gone to the theatre. I waited up for her. It was half-past eleven before we went to our room."

"Then for four hours the dispatch-box had lain unguarded?"

"No one is ever permitted to enter that room save the housemaid in the morning, and my valet, or my wife's maid, during the rest of the day. They are both trusty servants who have been with us for some time. Besides, neither of them could possibly have known that there was anything more valuable than the ordinary departmental papers in my dispatch-box."

"Who did know of the existence of that letter?"

"No one in the house."

"Surely your wife knew?"

"No, sir; I had said nothing to my wife until I missed the paper this morning."

THEY SAT SIDE BY SIDE UPON OUR PAPER-LITTERED SETTEE . . .

Illustration by Sidney Paget for the *Strand Magazine*, December, 1904.

of the Honourable Ronald Adair. It is difficult to believe that this was really news to the hundreds of people who had come in contact with the Master in the course of the dozens of cases he had handled since his tardily acknowledged resurrection, or to the many thousands of others who had heard of these cases, and, inevitably, of him. But the stolid and obedient Watson, after first repressing the story of his friend's demise for two years and eight months, had sought—operating under what he termed a 'positive prohibition'—to repress for nine years and six months the fact of his Return. And now, as Holmes himself looked on from the perspective of retirement, he gave the story to the world as news."

4 *when the time was ripe.* As we shall see, when we come to the adventure of "The Naval Treaty," Watson there refers to *an* "Adventure of the Second Stain" which he says took place in "the July which immediately succeeded my marriage." Of this adventure he wrote: "The new century will have come, however, before the story can be safely told." Whether or not this can be construed as "a promise" to publish the adventure "when the time was ripe" is a point debated by commentators.

5 *one Tuesday morning.* Note that this "Adventure of the Second Stain" began on a *Tuesday* morning.

6 *our humble room in Baker Street.* Chronologists who hold that this case and "The Adventure of the Second Stain" mentioned in "The Naval Treaty" are one and the same (as do Christ, Pattrick, Petersen and Zeisler) must explain: 1) Watson's "autumn" (instead of July); 2) the fact that he is apparently quite unmarried and living in Baker Street during the entire period of *this* adventure.

7 *Secretary for European Affairs.* Watson has said that the Right Honourable Trelawney Hope was "hardly of middle age," but *no* Foreign Secretary (Watson's "Secretary for European Affairs") throughout our period was that young a man. Still, as Mr. Brend wrote, "the case must . . . have occurred in the autumn of a year when the offices of Prime Minister and Foreign Secretary were held by two different men. But only the first year [of Lord Salisbury's second period as Prime Minister], 1886, meets this requirement. For Lord Iddesleigh, the first Foreign Secretary, died in January, 1887, and thereafter Lord Salisbury acted in both capacities. We can therefore decide that the case of 'The Second Stain' took place in the autumn of 1886." Again, your editor most heartily concurs.

To add to the "historicity" of Watson's account, we have the extremely valuable testimony of Dr. Felix Morley, who writes, in "The Significance of the Second Stain":

In the spring of 1886 Mr. Gladstone's Home Rule Bill was defeated and the subsequent general election swept Lord Salisbury, disguised by Watson as Lord Bellinger, into his second premiership. Salisbury promptly named Lord Iddesleigh, formerly Sir Stafford Northcote, as his Foreign Secretary. . . . Towards the close of that year—1886—occurred a series of startling Ministerial changes for which English historians have heretofore never been able fully to account. On Christmas Eve, Lord Randolph Churchill resigned, almost without explanation, as Chancellor of the Exchequer. Mr. W. H. Smith . . . followed suit by surrendering the War Office. Lord Iddesleigh was then literally ousted from the post of Foreign Secretary, which the Prime Minister himself assumed on January 4, 1887. Eight days later, as J. A. R. Marriot tells us (*England Since Waterloo*, p. 519) "the country was shocked to learn that he [Lord Iddesleigh] had died suddenly in the ante-room of the Premier's official residence at 10 Downing Street." Thus closed, "amid circumstances almost tragic, a life of high utility and complete blamelessness." How tragic the circumstances were the reader of "The Adventure of the Second Stain" can fully realize. While Holmes was able to restore the purloined letter he could not, evidently, prevent reports of Lord Iddesleigh's reckless carelessness with state papers from coming to the attention of the Cabinet. One recalls that Lady Hilda Trelawney Hope by her own admission "could not understand the consequences" in a matter of politics. I am on delicate ground, but it may be stated as a general rule that a lady who has twice been indiscreet is not unlikely to err a third time. Lady Hilda must have mentioned, perhaps before the butler, Jacobs, how Holmes had restored the letter which seemed to her so relatively unimportant. At any rate a new light is thrown on the unexplained resignation from Lord Salisbury's Cabinet and the sudden, "almost tragic" death of his Foreign Secretary.

8 *a foreign potentate.* Messrs. Bell, Blakeney, and Grazebrook have all suggested that the "foreign potentate" who sent the ill-advised letter must have been Kaiser Wilhelm II, and that "The Adventure of the Second Stain" must therefore be subsequent to June, 1888, when he ascended the throne. But Mr. Anthony Boucher has written: "The apparent reference to Wilhelm II which causes [these commentators] to date the published episode after his ascension to the throne in 1888 . . . is not to be taken too seriously in view of Watson's warning that this is a 'carefully guarded account . . . somewhat vague in certain details.'"

9 *Whitehall Terrace.* ". . . since there is not today —nor was sixty and more years ago—a 'Whitehall Terrace' to be found on a London map, it is evident that Watson means either 'Whitehall Gardens' or 'Richmond Terrace'—the latter, a block of 1791 houses being (though threatened) still standing," Mr. Michael Harrison wrote (*In the Footsteps of Sherlock Holmes*). "That 'Whitehall Terrace' is almost certainly meant for Richmond Terrace [is indicated by Trelawney Hope when

The Premier nodded approvingly.

" I have long known, sir, how high is your sense of public duty," said he. " I am convinced that in the case of a secret of this importance it would rise superior to the most intimate domestic ties."

The European Secretary bowed.

" You do me no more than justice, sir. Until this morning I have never breathed one word to my wife upon this matter."

" Could she have guessed ? "

" No, Mr. Holmes, she could not have guessed—nor could anyone have guessed."

" Have you lost any documents before ? "

" No, sir."

" Who is there in England who did know of the existence of this letter ? "

" Each member of the Cabinet was informed of it yesterday ; but the pledge of secrecy which attends every Cabinet meeting was increased by the solemn warning which was given by the Prime Minister. Good heavens, to think that within a few hours I should myself have lost it ! " His handsome face was distorted with a spasm of despair, and his hands tore at his hair. For a moment we caught a glimpse of the natural man— impulsive, ardent, keenly sensitive. The next the aristocratic mask was replaced, and the gentle voice had returned. " Besides the members of the Cabinet there are two, or possibly three, departmental officials who know of the letter. No one else in England, Mr. Holmes, I assure you."

" But abroad ? "

" I believe that no one abroad has seen it save the man who wrote it. I am well convinced that his ministers —that the usual official channels have not been employed."

Holmes considered for some little time.

" Now, sir, I must ask you more particularly what this document is, and why its disappearance should have such momentous consequences ? "

The two statesmen exchanged a quick glance, and the Premier's shaggy eyebrows gathered in a frown.

" Mr. Holmes, the envelope is a long, thin one of pale blue colour. There is a seal of red wax stamped with a crouching lion. It is addressed in large, bold handwriting to——"

" I fear," said Holmes, " that, interesting and indeed essential as these details are, my inquiries must go more to the root of things. What *was* the letter ? "

" That is a State secret of the utmost importance, and I fear that I cannot tell you, nor do I see that it is necessary. If by the aid of the powers which you are said to possess you can find such an envelope as I describe with its enclosure, you will have deserved well of your country, and earned any reward which it lies in our power to bestow."

Sherlock Holmes rose with a smile.

" You are two of the most busy men in the country," said he, " and in my own small way I have also a good many calls upon me. I regret exceedingly that I cannot help you in this matter, and any continuation of this interview would be a waste of time."

The Premier sprang to his feet with that quick, fierce gleam of his deep-set eyes before which a Cabinet had cowered. "I am not accustomed——" he began, but mastered his anger and resumed his seat. For a minute or more we all sat in silence. Then the old statesman shrugged his shoulders.

"We must accept your terms, Mr. Holmes. No doubt you are right, and it is unreasonable for us to expect you to act unless we give you our entire confidence."

"I agree with you, sir," said the younger statesman.

"Then I will tell you, relying entirely upon your honour and that of your colleague, Dr. Watson. I may appeal to your patriotism also, for I could not imagine a greater misfortune for the country than that this affair should come out."

"You may safely trust us."

"The letter, then, is from a certain foreign potentate who has been ruffled by some recent colonial developments of this country. It has been written hurriedly and upon his own responsibility entirely. Inquiries have shown that his ministers know nothing of the matter. At the same time it is couched in so unfortunate a manner, and certain phrases in it are of so provocative a character, that its publication would undoubtedly lead to a most dangerous state of feeling in this country. There would be such a ferment, sir, that I do not hesitate to say that within a week of the publication of that letter this country would be involved in a great war."

Holmes wrote a name upon a slip of paper and handed it to the Premier.

"Exactly. It was he. And it is this letter—this letter which may well mean the expenditure of a thousand millions and the lives of a hundred thousand men—which has become lost in this unaccountable fashion."

"Have you informed the sender?"

"Yes, sir, a cipher telegram has been despatched."

"Perhaps he desires the publication of the letter."

"No, sir, we have strong reason to believe that he already understands that he has acted in an indiscreet and hot-headed manner. It would be a greater blow to him and to his country than to us if this letter were to come out."

"If this is so, whose interest is it that the letter should come out? Why should anyone desire to steal it or to publish it?"

"There, Mr. Holmes, you take me into regions of high international politics. But if you consider the European situation you will have no difficulty in perceiving the motive. The whole of Europe is an armed camp. There is a double league which makes a fair balance of military power. Great Britain holds the scales. If Britain were driven into war with one confederacy, it would assure the supremacy of the other confederacy, whether they joined in the war or not. Do you follow?"

he speaks of the letter he has "taken . . . across" each evening from the Foreign Office to his home]."

10 *stamped with a crouching lion.* This would have been a curious device for Kaiser Wilhelm II to have stamped in the red wax which sealed the letter. Had it been a double-headed eagle, on the other hand . . .

THE PREMIER SPRANG TO HIS FEET . . .

Illustration by Sidney Paget for the *Strand Magazine,* December, 1904.

" Very clearly. It is then the interest of the enemies of this potentate to secure and publish this letter, so as to make a breach between his country and ours ? "

" Yes, sir."

" And to whom would this document be sent if it fell into the hands of an enemy ? "

" To any of the great Chancelleries of Europe. It is probably speeding on its way thither at the present instant as fast as steam can take it."

Mr. Trelawney Hope dropped his head on his chest and groaned aloud. The Premier placed his hand kindly upon his shoulder.

" It is your misfortune, my dear fellow. No one can blame you. There is no precaution which you have neglected. Now, Mr. Holmes, you are in full possession of the facts. What course do you recommend ? "

Holmes shook his head mournfully.

" You think, sir, that unless this document is recovered there will be war ? "

" I think it is very probable."

" Then, sir, prepare for war."

" That is a hard saying, Mr. Holmes."

" Consider the facts, sir. It is inconceivable that it was taken after eleven-thirty at night, since I understand that Mr. Hope and his wife were both in the room from that hour until the loss was found out. It was taken, then, yesterday evening between seven-thirty and eleven-thirty, probably near the earlier hour, since whoever took it evidently knew that it was there, and would naturally secure it as early as possible. Now, sir, if a document of this importance were taken at that hour, where can it be now ? No one has any reason to retain it. It has been passed rapidly on to those who need it. What chance have we now to overtake or even to trace it ? It is beyond our reach."

The Prime Minister rose from the settee.

" What you say is perfectly logical, Mr. Holmes. I feel that the matter is indeed out of our hands."

" Let us presume, for argument's sake, that the document was taken by the maid or by the valet——"

" They are both old and tried servants."

" I understand you to say that your room is on the second floor, that there is no entrance from without, and that from within no one could go up unobserved. It must, then, be somebody in the house who has taken it. To whom would the thief take it ? To one of several international spies and secret agents, whose names are tolerably familiar to me. There are three who may be said to be the heads of their profession. I will begin my research by going round and finding if each of them is at his post. If one is missing—especially if he has disappeared since last night—we will have some indication as to where the document has gone."

" Why should he be missing ? " asked the European Secretary. " He would take the letter to an Embassy in London, as likely as not."

" I fancy not. These agents work independently, and their relations with the Embassies are often strained."

The Prime Minister nodded his acquiescence.

" I believe you are right, Mr. Holmes. He would take

"The penny," the late A. Carson Simpson wrote (*Numismatics in the Canon*, Part I), "is the oldest British coin-denomination still in use. As its abbreviation 'd.' suggests, it is the lineal descendant of the Roman denarius, which, like the earlier British penny, was a silver coin. The silver penny survives only in Maundy Money. It became a copper coin in the late nineteenth century, and bronze in 1860. There are many Canonical references to the penny, which Holmes once referred to as a 'modest sum' (*The Valley of Fear*), but perhaps the most interesting one is that [given here] in which he threatened the happiness of every Englishman and which is, perhaps, his only statement lending itself to a Marxian interpretation."

so valuable a prize to headquarters with his own hands. I think that your course of action is an excellent one. Meanwhile, Hope, we cannot neglect our other duties on account of this one misfortune. Should there be any fresh developments during the day we shall communicate with you, and you will no doubt let us know the results of your own inquiries."

The two statesmen bowed and walked gravely from the room.

When our illustrious visitors had departed, Holmes lit his pipe in silence, and sat for some time lost in the deepest thought. I had opened the morning paper and was immersed in a sensational crime which had occurred in London the night before, when my friend gave an exclamation, sprang to his feet, and laid his pipe down upon the mantelpiece.

"Yes," said he, "there is no better way of approaching it. The situation is desperate, but not hopeless. Even now, if we could be sure which of them has taken it, it is just possible that it has not yet passed out of his hands. After all, it is a question of money with these fellows, and I have the British Treasury behind me. If it's on the market I'll buy it—if it means another penny on the income tax. It is conceivable that the fellow might hold it back to see what bids come from this side before he tries his luck on the other. There are only those three capable of playing so bold a game ; there are Oberstein, La Rothiere, and Eduardo Lucas. I will see each of **11** them."

I glanced at my morning paper.

" Is that Eduardo Lucas of Godolphin Street ? "   **12**

" Yes."

" You will not see him."

" Why not ? "

" He was murdered in his house last night."

My friend has so often astonished me in the course of our adventures that it was with a sense of exultation that I realized how completely I had astonished him. He stared in amazement, and then snatched the paper from my hands. This was the paragraph which I had been engaged in reading when he rose from his chair :

11 *Oberstein, La Rothiere, and Eduardo Lucas.* ". . . the first two reappear, with Oberstein as a principal character, in "The Adventure of the Bruce-Partington Plans," Dr. Felix Morley wrote in "The Significance of the Second Stain." "The date of [that] case is placed meticulously in the third week in November, 1895. . . . ["The Adventure of the Second Stain"], therefore, took place prior to November, 1895. We know it could not have been later because before the end of that month Oberstein was caught, with the missing Bruce-Partington submarine plans in his possession, and 'was safely engulfed for fifteen years in a British prison.' "

In consequence of the above line of reasoning, Messrs. Andrew, Bell, and Blakeney have all dated "The Adventure of the Second Stain" to 1894. It is curious, however, that the names of the spies in London were "tolerably familiar" to Holmes at the time of *this* adventure, whereas he had to get Brother Mycroft to jog his memory, at least as to their addresses, at the time of "The Bruce-Partington Plans." This is perhaps an indication that there was a lapse of some years, rather than a lapse of months, between the two adventures.

12 *Godolphin Street?"* We are shortly told that it was "one of the old-fashioned and secluded rows of eighteenth century houses which lie between the river and the Abbey, almost in the shadow of the great tower of the Houses of Parliament"— although it appears on no London map.

. . . BETWEEN THE RIVER AND THE ABBEY . . .

Westminster Abbey, here shown in a photograph by Acme, is a national shrine and one of England's finest Gothic buildings, the scene of the coronation of all English kings and queens since William I. It is the burial place of many kings and distinguished citizens, and a Poet's Corner in the south transept contains tombs of the great English poets. The present church was built mainly between the thirteenth and the fifteenth century.

13   MURDER IN WESTMINSTER.

A crime of a mysterious character was committed last night at 16 Godolphin Street, one of the old-fashioned and secluded rows of eighteenth-century houses which lie between the river and the Abbey, almost in the shadow of the great tower of the Houses of Parliament. This small but select mansion has been inhabited for some years by Mr. Eduardo Lucas, well known in society circles both on account of his charming personality and because he has the well-deserved reputation of being one of the best amateur tenors in the country. Mr. Lucas is an unmarried man, thirty-four years of age, and his establishment consists of Mrs. Pringle, an elderly housekeeper, and of Mitton, his valet. The former retires early and sleeps at the top of the house. The valet was out for the evening, visiting a

14 friend at Hammersmith. From ten o'clock onwards Mr. Lucas had the house to himself. What occurred during that time has not yet transpired, but at a quarter to twelve Police-constable Barrett, passing along Godolphin Street, observed that the door of No. 16 was ajar. He knocked, but received no answer. Perceiving a light in the front room he advanced into the passage and again knocked, but without reply. He then pushed open the door and entered. The room was in a state of wild disorder, the furniture being all swept to one side, and one chair lying on its back in the centre. Beside this chair, and still grasping one of its legs, lay the unfortunate tenant of the house. He had been stabbed to the heart, and must have died instantly. The knife with which the crime had been committed was a curved Indian dagger, plucked down from a trophy of Oriental arms which adorned one of the walls. Robbery does not appear to have been the motive of the crime, for there had been no attempt to remove the valuable contents of the room. Mr. Eduardo Lucas was so well known and popular that his violent and mysterious fate will arouse painful interest and intense sympathy in a widespread circle of friends.

"Well, Watson, what do you make of this?" asked Holmes, after a long pause.

"It is an amazing coincidence."

"A coincidence! Here is one of three men whom we had named as possible actors in this drama, and he meets a violent death during the very hours when we know that that drama was being enacted. The odds are enormous against its being coincidence. No figures could express them. No, my dear Watson, the two events are connected—*must* be connected. It is for us to find the

15 connection."

. . . ALMOST IN THE SHADOW OF THE GREAT TOWER OF THE HOUSES OF PARLIAMENT.

The present structure, shown left in a photograph by G. F. Allen for *The Second Country Life Picture Book of London*, London: Country Life, Ltd., 1953, was built in 1840–1859, from designs of Sir Charles Barry, R.A., in the Tudor style of Henry VIII. It is one of the largest Gothic buildings in the world. The "great tower of the Houses" is the Clock Tower, housing the world-famous "Big Ben." Three hundred and twenty feet high, the Clock Tower occupies nearly the same site as the ancient clock tower of Edward I, where the ancient Great Tom for four hundred years sounded the hours to the judges of England.

" But now the official police must know all."

" Not at all. They know all they see at Godolphin Street. They know—and shall know—nothing of Whitehall Terrace. Only *we* know of both events, and can trace the relation between them. There is one obvious point which would, in any case, have turned my suspicions against Lucas. Godolphin Street, Westminster, is only a few minutes' walk from Whitehall Terrace. The other secret agents whom I have named live in the extreme West End. It was easier, therefore, for Lucas than for the others to establish a connection or receive a message from the European Secretary's household—a small thing, and yet where events are compressed into a few hours it may prove essential. Halloa ! what have we here ? "

Mrs. Hudson had appeared with a lady's card upon her salver. Holmes glanced at it, raised his eyebrows, and handed it over to me.

" Ask Lady Hilda Trelawney Hope if she will be kind enough to step up," said he.

A moment later our modest apartment, already so distinguished that morning, was further honoured by the entrance of the most lovely woman in London. I had often heard of the beauty of the youngest daughter of the Duke of Belminster, but no description of it, and no contemplation of colourless photographs, had prepared me for the subtle, delicate charm and the beautiful colouring of that exquisite head. And yet as we saw it that autumn morning it was not its beauty which would be the first thing to impress the observer. The cheek was lovely, but it was paled with emotion ; the eyes were bright, but it was the brightness of fever ; the sensitive mouth was tight and drawn in an effort after self-command. Terror—not beauty—was what sprang first to **16** the eye as our fair visitor stood framed for an instant in the open door.

" Has my husband been here, Mr. Holmes ? "

" Yes, madam, he has been here."

" Mr. Holmes, I implore you not to tell him that I came here." Holmes bowed coldly and motioned the lady to a chair.

" Your ladyship places me in a very delicate position. I beg that you will sit down and tell me what you desire ; but I fear that I cannot make any unconditional promise."

She swept across the room and seated herself with her back to the window. It was a queenly presence—tall, graceful, and intensely womanly.

" Mr. Holmes," she said—and her white-gloved hands clasped and unclasped as she spoke—" I will speak frankly to you in the hope that it may induce you to speak frankly in return. There is complete confidence between my husband and me on all matters save one. That one is politics. On this his lips are sealed. He tells me nothing. Now, I am aware that there was a most deplorable occurrence in our house last night. I know that a paper has disappeared. But because the matter is political my husband refuses to take me into his complete confidence. Now it is essential—essential, I say—that I should thoroughly understand it. You are the only other person, save these politicians, who knows the true facts.

"NO, MY DEAR WATSON, THE TWO EVENTS ARE
CONNECTED—*must* BE CONNECTED."

Illustration by Sidney Paget for the *Strand Magazine*, December, 1904.

13 *WESTMINSTER*. The borough of West London in which are located Westminster Abbey, the Houses of Parliament, Buckingham Palace, Saint James's Palace, and Downing Street with its famous No. 10.

14 *Hammersmith*. Borough of West London in which is located the home of St. Paul's School for boys, founded in 1509, attended by Milton and Pepys.

15 *It is for us to find the connection*." "Holmes on more than one occasion warned against jumping to conclusions and theorizing without data," Mr. Nathan L. Bengis wrote in "Sherlock Stays After School." "Yet there are a number of occasions where he himself jumped at a conclusion which turned out to have no foundation in fact. In [the present] case, wonderful to relate, Watson was actually right, but allowed himself to be shouted down."

16 *in an effort after self-command*. "The doctor's pronounced susceptibility to . . . Lady Hilda Trelawney Hope is strongly indicative of the psychology of a man ripe and ready for marriage," Dr. Felix Morley wrote in "The Significance of the Second Stain." "It certainly does not suggest the reaction of one recently deprived of a very congenial mate. The authentic stamp of a bachelor ripe for the plucking is also evident in Watson's undisguised admiration for a comely female who is convicted by the facts of the story of being, to put it plainly, a perfect boob."

17 "*Now, Watson, the fair sex is your depart-ment.*" "To a newly-married man," Dr. Felix Morley continued in "The Significance of the Second Stain," "even more to a recent widower, such a remark would have verged on ribaldry, and would therefore have been impossible to one of Holmes' innate delicacy of feeling."

SHE LOOKED BACK AT US FROM THE DOOR . . .

Illustration by Sidney Paget for the *Strand Magazine*, December, 1904.

I beg you, then, Mr. Holmes, to tell me exactly what has happened and what it will lead to. Tell me all, Mr. Holmes. Let no regard for your client's interests keep you silent, for I assure you that his interests, if he would only see it, would be best served by taking me into his complete confidence. What was this paper that was stolen ? "

" Madam, what you ask me is really impossible."

She groaned and sank her face in her hands.

" You must see that this is so, madam. If your husband thinks fit to keep you in the dark over this matter, is it for me, who have only learned the true facts under the pledge of professional secrecy, to tell what he has withheld ? It is not fair to ask it. It is him whom you must ask."

" I have asked him. I come to you as a last resource. But without your telling me anything definite, Mr. Holmes, you may do a great service if you would enlighten me on one point."

" What is it, madam ? "

" Is my husband's political career likely to suffer through this incident ? "

" Well, madam, unless it is set right it may certainly have a very unfortunate effect."

" Ah ! " She drew in her breath sharply as one whose doubts are resolved.

" One more question, Mr. Holmes. From an expression which my husband dropped in the first shock of this disaster I understood that terrible public consequences might arise from the loss of this document."

" If he said so, I certainly cannot deny it."

" Of what nature are they ? "

" Nay, madam, there again you ask me more than I can possibly answer."

" Then I will take up no more of your time. I cannot blame you, Mr. Holmes, for having refused to speak more freely, and you on your side will not, I am sure, think the worse of me because I desire, even against his will, to share my husband's anxieties. Once more I beg that you will say nothing of my visit." She looked back at us from the door, and I had a last impression of that beautiful, haunted face, the startled eyes, and the drawn mouth. Then she was gone.

17   " Now, Watson, the fair sex is your department," said Holmes, with a smile, when the dwindling *frou-frou* of skirts had ended in the slam of the door. " What was the fair lady's game ? What did she really want ? "

" Surely her own statement is clear and her anxiety very natural."

" Hum ! Think of her appearance, Watson, her manner, her suppressed excitement, her restlessness, her tenacity in asking questions. Remember that she comes of a caste who do not lightly show emotion."

" She was certainly much moved."

" Remember also the curious earnestness with which she assured us that it was best for her husband that she should know all. What did she mean by that ? And you must have observed, Watson, how she manœuvred to have the light at her back. She did not wish us to read her expression."

"Yes ; she chose the one chair in the room." **18**

"And yet the motives of women are so inscrutable. You remember the woman at Margate whom I suspected **19** for the same reason. No powder on her nose—that proved to be the correct solution. How can you build on such a quicksand ? Their most trivial action may mean volumes, or their most extraordinary conduct may depend upon a hairpin or a curling-tongs. Good morning, Watson."

"You are off ? "

"Yes ; I will while away the morning at Godolphin Street with our friends of the regular establishment. With Eduardo Lucas lies the solution of our problem, though I must admit that I have not an inkling as to what form it may take. It is a capital mistake to theorize in advance of the facts. Do you stay on guard, my good Watson, and receive any fresh visitors. I'll join you at lunch if I am able."

All that day and the next and the next Holmes was in a **20** mood which his friends would call taciturn, and others morose. He ran out and ran in, smoked incessantly, played snatches on his violin, sank into reveries, devoured sandwiches at irregular hours, and hardly answered the casual questions which I put to him. It was evident to me that things were not going well with him or his quest. He would say nothing of the case, and it was from the papers that I learned the particulars of the inquest, and the arrest with the subsequent release of John Mitton, the valet of the deceased. The coroner's jury brought in the obvious " Wilful murder," but the parties remained as unknown as ever. No motive was suggested. The room was full of articles of value, but none had been taken. The dead man's papers had not been tampered with. They were carefully examined, and showed that he was a keen student of international politics, an indefatigable gossip, a remarkable linguist, and an untiring letter-writer. He had been on intimate terms with the leading politicians of several countries. But nothing sensational was discovered among the documents which filled his drawers. As to his relations with women, they appeared to have been promiscuous but superficial. He had many acquaintances among them, but few friends, and no one whom he loved. His habits were regular, his conduct inoffensive. His death was an absolute mystery, and likely to remain so.

As to the arrest of John Mitton, the valet, it was a counsel of despair as an alternative to absolute inaction. But no case could be sustained against him. He had visited friends in Hammersmith that night. The *alibi* was complete. It is true that he started home at an hour which should have brought him to Westminster before the time when the crime was discovered, but his own explanation that he had walked part of the way seemed probable enough in view of the fineness of the night. He had **21** actually arrived at twelve o'clock, and appeared to be overwhelmed by the unexpected tragedy. He had always been on good terms with his master. Several of the

18 *the one chair in the room."* Watson of course means the one chair in the room that would have put the light at her back. Thus Lady Hilda Trelawney Hope sat in *the basket chair*—the one chair in the sitting-room at 221B that, according to the highest authorities, would place a visitor's back to the light.

19 *Margate.* Municipal borough on the Isle of Thanet in Kent—a seaport and a popular summer resort.

20 *All that day and the next and the next.* Since (Watson has told us) "that day" was a Tuesday, "the next" was Wednesday and "the next" after that a Thursday. The case ended "Upon the fourth day"—and therefore upon a Friday.

21 *in view of the fineness of the night.* Watson, as we shall see, married for the first time *circa* November 1, 1886; "The Adventure of the Second Stain" must therefore have taken place late in September or during the month of October, 1886. The dates (as we have seen) were not Tuesday, October 5th to Friday, October 8th, however; in that period Holmes was solving both the adventure of "The Resident Patient" and "The Adventure of the Noble Bachelor." The possible dates would therefore seem to be: 1) Tuesday, September 28th, to Friday, October 1st; 2) Tuesday, October 12th, to Friday, October 15th; 3) Tuesday, October 19th, to Friday, October 22nd; 4) Tuesday, October 26th, to Friday, October 29th. The Monday night preceding the opening of the case had been a fine one. A meteorological examination of the four corresponding Mondays shows that *only one was without rain:* Monday, October 11th. We may therefore with some confidence date "The Adventure of the Second Stain" to *Tuesday, October 12 to Friday, October 15, 1886.*

dead man's possessions—notably a small case of razors —had been found in the valet's boxes, but he explained that they had been presents from the deceased, and the housekeeper was able to corroborate the story. Mitton had been in Lucas's employment for three years. It was noticeable that Lucas did not take Mitton on the Continent with him. Sometimes he visited Paris for three months on end, but Mitton was left in charge of the Godolphin Street house. As to the housekeeper, she had heard nothing on the night of the crime. If her master had a visitor, he had himself admitted him.

So for three mornings the mystery remained, so far as I could follow it in the papers. If Holmes knew more he kept his own counsel, but, as he told me that Inspector Lestrade had taken him into his confidence in the case. I knew that he was in close touch with every development. Upon the fourth day there appeared a long telegram from Paris which seemed to solve the whole question.

A discovery has just been made by the Parisian police (said the *Daily Telegraph*) which raises the veil which hung round the tragic fate of Mr. Eduardo Lucas, who met his death by violence last Monday night at Godolphin Street, Westminster. Our readers will remember that the deceased gentleman was found stabbed in his room, and that some suspicion attached to his valet, but that the case broke down on an *alibi*. Yesterday a lady, who has been known as Mme. Henri Fournaye, occupying a small villa in the Rue Austerlitz, was reported to the authorities by her servants as being insane. An examination showed that she had indeed developed mania of a dangerous and permanent form. On inquiry the police have discovered that Mme. Henri Fournaye only returned from a journey to London on Tuesday last, and there is evidence to connect her with the crime at Westminster. A comparison of photographs has proved conclusively that M. Henri Fournaye and Eduardo Lucas were really one and the same person, and that the deceased had for some reason lived a double life in London and Paris. Mme. Fournaye, who is of creole origin, is of an extremely excitable nature, and has suffered in the past from attacks of jealousy which have amounted to frenzy. It is conjectured that it was in one of these that she committed the terrible crime which has caused such a sensation in London. Her movements upon the Monday night have not yet been traced, but it is undoubted that a woman answering to her description attracted much attention at Charing Cross Station on Tuesday morning by the wildness of her appearance and the violence of her gestures. It is probable, therefore, that the crime was either committed when insane, or that its immediate effect was to drive the unhappy woman out of her mind. At present she is unable to give any coherent account of the past, and the doctors hold out no hopes of the re-establishment of her reason. There is evidence that a woman, who might have been Mme. Fournaye, was seen for some hours on Monday night watching the house in Godolphin Street.

" What do you think of that, Holmes ? " I had read the account aloud to him, while he finished his breakfast.

" My dear Watson," said he, as he rose from the table and paced up and down the room, " you are most long-suffering, but if I have told you nothing in the last three days it is because there is nothing to tell. Even now this report from Paris does not help us much."

" Surely it is final as regards the man's death."

" The man's death is a mere incident—a trivial episode

" . . . ATTRACTED MUCH ATTENTION AT CHARING CROSS STATION . . ."

The station was opened to the public on January 11, 1864, as the London terminus of the South-Eastern Railway. The etching, from the *Century Magazine*, December, 1888, is the work of Joseph Pennell.

—in comparison with our real task, which is to trace this document and save a European catastrophe. Only one important thing has happened in the last three days, and that is that nothing has happened. I get reports almost **22** hourly from the Government, and it is certain that nowhere in Europe is there any sign of trouble. Now, if this letter were loose—no, it *can't* be loose—but if it isn't loose, where can it be ? Who has it ? Why is it held back ? That's the question that beats in my brain like a hammer. Was it, indeed, a coincidence that Lucas should meet his death on the night when the letter disappeared ? Did the letter ever reach him ? If so, why is it not among his papers ? Did this mad wife of his carry it off with her ? If so, is it in her house in Paris ? How could I search for it without the French police having their suspicions aroused ? It is a case, my dear Watson, where the law is as dangerous to us as the criminals are. Every man's hand is against us, and yet the interests at stake are colossal. Should I bring it to a successful conclusion, it will certainly represent the crowning glory of my career. Ah, here is my latest from the front ! " He glanced hurriedly at the note which had been handed in. " Halloa ! Lestrade seems to have observed something of interest. Put on your hat, Watson, and we will stroll down together to Westminster."

It was my first visit to the scene of the crime—a high, dingy, narrow-chested house, prim, formal, and solid, like the century which gave it birth. Lestrade's bulldog features gazed out at us from the front window, and he greeted us warmly when a big constable had opened the door and let us in. The room into which we were shown was that in which the crime had been committed, but no trace of it now remained, save an ugly, irregular stain upon the carpet. This carpet was a small square drugget in the centre of the room, surrounded by a broad expanse of beautiful, old-fashioned, wood flooring in square blocks highly polished. Over the fireplace was a magnificent trophy of weapons, one of which had been used on that tragic night. In the window was a sumptuous writing-desk, and every detail of the apartment, the pictures, the rugs, and the hangings, all pointed to a taste which was luxurious to the verge of effeminacy.

" Seen the Paris news ? " asked Lestrade.

Holmes nodded.

" Our French friends seem to have touched the spot this time. No doubt it's just as they say. She knocked at the door—surprise visit, I guess, for he kept his life in watertight compartments. He let her in—couldn't keep her in the street. She told him how she had traced him, reproached him, one thing led to another, and then with that dagger so handy the end soon came. It wasn't all done in an instant, though, for these chairs were all swept over yonder, and he had one in his hand as if he had tried to hold her off with it. We've got it all as clear as if we had seen it."

Holmes raised his eyebrows.

" And yet you have sent for me ? "

" Ah, yes, that's another matter—a mere trifle, but the

22 *and that is that nothing has happened.* "As an illustration of the vital importance of negative evidence this is almost comparable with the classic and curious instance in 'Silver Blaze,' of the dog that 'did nothing in the night-time,' " Dr. Felix Morley wrote in "The Significance of the Second Stain." "In 'The Adventure of the Second Stain,' however, Holmes failed to make an equally brilliant—and obvious—deduction."

HE TOOK THE CORNER OF THE CARPET IN HIS HAND . . .

Illustration by Sidney Paget for the *Strand Magazine*, December, 1904.

"WHAT DO YOU MAKE OF THAT, MR. HOLMES?"

Illustration by Frederic Dorr Steele for the cover of *Collier's Magazine*, January 28, 1905.

sort of thing you take an interest in—queer, you know, and what you might call freakish. It has nothing to do with the main fact—can't have, on the face of it."

"What is it, then?"

"Well, you know after a crime of this sort we are very careful to keep things in their position. Nothing has been moved. Officer in charge here day and night. This morning, as the man was buried and the investigation over—so far as this room is concerned—we thought we could tidy up a bit. This carpet. You see, it is not fastened down; only just laid there. We had occasion to raise it. We found——"

"Yes? You found——"

Holmes' face grew tense with anxiety.

"Well, I'm sure you would never guess in a hundred years what we did find. You see that stain on the carpet? Well, a great deal must have soaked through, must it not?"

"Undoubtedly it must."

"Well, you will be surprised to hear that there is no stain on the white woodwork to correspond."

"No stain! But there must——"

"Yes; so you would say. But the fact remains that there isn't."

He took the corner of the carpet in his hand and, turning it over, he showed that it was indeed as he said.

"But the under side is as stained as the upper. It must have left a mark."

Lestrade chuckled with delight at having puzzled the famous expert.

"Now I'll show you the explanation. There *is* a second stain, but it does not correspond with the other. See for yourself." As he spoke he turned over another portion of the carpet, and there, sure enough, was a great crimson spill upon the square white facing of the old-fashioned floor. "What do you make of that, Mr. Holmes?"

"Why, it is simple enough. The two stains did correspond, but the carpet has been turned round. As it was square and unfastened, it was easily done."

"The official police don't need you, Mr. Holmes, to tell them that the carpet must have been turned round. That's clear enough, for the stains lie above each other—if you lay it over this way. But what I want to know is, who shifted the carpet, and why?"

I could see from Holmes' rigid face that he was vibrating with inward excitement.

"Look here, Lestrade!" said he. "Has that constable in the passage been in charge of the place all the time?"

"Yes, he has."

"Well, take my advice. Examine him carefully. Don't do it before us. We'll wait here. You take him into the back room. You'll be more likely to get a confession out of him alone. Ask him how he dare to admit people and leave them alone in this room. Don't ask him if he has done it. Take it for granted. Tell him you *know* someone has been here. Press him. Tell him that a full confession is his only chance of forgiveness. Do exactly what I tell you!"

"By George, if he knows I'll have it out of him!" cried Lestrade. He darted into the hall, and a few moments later his bullying voice sounded from the back room.

"Now, Watson, now!" cried Holmes, with frenzied eagerness. All the demoniacal force of the man masked behind that listless manner burst out in a paroxysm of energy. He tore the drugget from the floor, and in an instant was down on his hands and knees clawing at each of the squares of wood beneath it. One turned sideways as he dug his nails into the edge of it. It hinged back like the lid of a box. A small black cavity opened beneath it. Holmes plunged his eager hand into it, and drew it out with a bitter snarl of anger and disappointment. It was empty.

"Quick, Watson, quick! Get it back again!" The **23** wooden lid was replaced, and the drugget had only just been drawn straight, when Lestrade's voice was heard in the passage. He found Holmes leaning languidly against the mantelpiece, resigned and patient, endeavouring to conceal his irrepressible yawns.

"Sorry to keep you waiting, Mr. Holmes. I can see that you are bored to death with the whole affair. Well, he has confessed all right. Come in here, Mac-Pherson. Let these gentlemen hear of your most inexcusable conduct."

The big constable, very hot and penitent, sidled into the room.

"I meant no harm, sir, I'm sure. The young woman came to the door last evening—mistook the house, she did. And then we got talking. It's lonesome, when you're on duty here all day."

"Well, what happened then?"

23 *"Quick, Watson, quick!* "Holmes was not addicated to the use of the word 'Quick,'" Mr. C. B. H. Vaill wrote in "Quick, Watson, the Needle!" "He could never have said (and in the Canon never once does say), 'Quick, Watson, the needle!'"

IT HINGED BACK LIKE THE LID OF A BOX

Illustration by Sidney Paget for the *Strand Magazine*, December, 1904.

HE FOUND HOLMES LEANING LANGUIDLY AGAINST THE MANTELPIECE . . .

Illustration by Charles Raymond Macauley for *The Return of Sherlock Holmes*, New York: McClure, Phillips and Company, 1905. This book, the late James Montgomery wrote in *A Study in Pictures*, "had an enormous vogue, and as a result Macauley's illustrations were seen by millions, but in the light of Steele's tremendous popularity they exerted no permanent influence upon the conception of American Sherlockians, and are now almost completely forgotten."

24 *Queer Street.* An imaginary street or place of abode for queer people, especially for people who have become, or are likely to become, entangled in difficulties of any kind.

" She wanted to see where the crime was done—had read about it in the papers, she said. She was a very respectable, well-spoken young woman, sir, and I saw no harm in letting her have a peep. When she saw that mark on the carpet, down she dropped on the floor, and lay as if she were dead. I ran to the back and got some water, but I could not bring her to. Then I went round the corner to the ' Ivy Plant ' for some brandy, and by the time I had brought it back the young woman had recovered and was off—ashamed of herself, I dare say, and dared not face me."

" How about moving that drugget ? "

" Well, sir, it was a bit rumpled, certainly, when I came back. You see, she fell on it, and it lies on a polished floor with nothing to keep it in place. I straightened it out afterwards."

" It's a lesson to you that you can't deceive me, Constable MacPherson," said Lestrade, with dignity. " No doubt you thought that your breach of duty could never be discovered, and yet a mere glance at that drugget was enough to convince me that someone had been admitted to the room. It's lucky for you, my man, that nothing **24** is missing, or you would find yourself in Queer Street. I'm sorry to have to call you down over such a petty business, Mr. Holmes, but I thought the point of the second stain not corresponding with the first would interest you."

" Certainly it was most interesting. Has this woman only been here once, constable ? "

" Yes, sir, only once."

" Who was she ? "

" Don't know the name, sir. Was answering an advertisement about typewriting, and came to the wrong number—very pleasant, genteel young woman, sir."

" Tall ? Handsome ? "

" Yes, sir ; she was a well-grown young woman. I suppose you might say she was handsome. Perhaps some would say she was very handsome. ' Oh, officer, do let me have a peep ! ' says she. She had pretty, coaxing ways, as you might say, and I thought there was no harm in letting her just put her head through the door."

" How was she dressed ? "

" Quiet, sir—a long mantle down to her feet."

" What time was it ? "

" It was just growing dusk at the time. They were lighting the lamps as I came back with the brandy."

" Very good," said Holmes. " Come, Watson, I think that we have more important work elsewhere."

As we left the house Lestrade remained in the front room, while the repentant constable opened the door to let us out. Holmes turned on the step and held up something in his hand. The constable stared intently.

" Good Lord, sir ! " he cried, with amazement on his face. Holmes put his finger on his lips, replaced his hand in his breast-pocket, and burst out laughing as we turned down the street. " Excellent ! " said he. " Come, friend Watson, the curtain rings up for the last act. You will be relieved to hear that there will be no war, that the Right Honourable Trelawney Hope will suffer no setback in his brilliant career, that the indiscreet Sovereign will receive no punishment for his indiscretion, that the Prime Minister will have no European complication to deal with, and that with a little tact and management upon our part nobody will be a penny the worse for what might have been a very ugly accident."

My mind filled with admiration for this extraordinary man.

" You have solved it ! " I cried.

" Hardly that, Watson.   There are some points which are as dark as ever.   But we have so much that it will be our own fault if we cannot get the rest.   We will go straight to Whitehall Terrace and bring the matter to a head."

When we arrived at the residence of the European Secretary it was for Lady Hilda Trelawney Hope that Sherlock Holmes inquired.   We were shown into the morning-room.

" Mr. Holmes ! " said the lady, and her face was pink with indignation, " this is surely most unfair and ungenerous upon your part.   I desired, as I have explained, to keep my visit to you a secret, lest my husband should think that I was intruding into his affairs.   And yet you compromise me by coming here, and so showing that there are business relations between us."

" Unfortunately, madam, I had no possible alternative. I have been commissioned to recover this immensely important paper.   I must therefore ask you, madam, to be kind enough to place it in my hands."

The lady sprang to her feet, with the colour all dashed in an instant from her beautiful face.   Her eyes glazed —she tottered—I thought that she would faint.   Then with a grand effort she rallied from the shock, and a supreme astonishment and indignation chased every other expression from her features.

" You—you insult me, Mr. Holmes."

" Come, come, madam, it is useless.   Give up the letter."

She darted to the bell.

" The butler shall show you out."

" Do not ring, Lady Hilda.   If you do, then all my earnest efforts to avoid a scandal will be frustrated. Give up the letter, and all will be set right.   If you will work with me, I can arrange everything.   If you work against me, I must expose you."

She stood grandly defiant, a queenly figure, her eyes fixed upon his as if she would read his very soul.   Her hand was on the bell, but she had forborne to ring it.

" You are trying to frighten me.   It is not a very manly thing, Mr. Holmes, to come here and browbeat a woman. You say that you know something.   What is it that you know ? "

" Pray sit down, madam.   You will hurt yourself there if you fall.   I will not speak until you sit down.   Thank you."

" I give you five minutes, Mr. Holmes."

" One is enough, Lady Hilda.   I know of your visit to Eduardo Lucas, and of your giving him this document, of your ingenious return to the room last night, and of the

"YOU—YOU INSULT ME, MR. HOLMES."

Illustration by Sidney Paget for the *Strand Magazine*, December, 1904.

manner in which you took the letter from the hiding-place under the carpet."

She stared at him with an ashen face, and gulped twice before she could speak.

" You are mad, Mr. Holmes—you are mad ! " she cried at last.

He drew a small piece of cardboard from his pocket. It was the face of a woman cut out of a portrait.

" I have carried this because I thought it might be useful," said he. " The policeman has recognized it."

She gave a gasp, and her head dropped back in her chair.

" Come, Lady Hilda. You have the letter. The matter may still be adjusted. I have no desire to bring trouble to you. My duty ends when I have returned the lost letter to your husband. Take my advice and be frank with me ; it is your only chance."

Her courage was admirable. Even now she would not own defeat.

" I tell you again, Mr. Holmes, that you are under some absurd illusion."

Holmes rose from his chair.

" I am sorry for you, Lady Hilda. I have done my best for you ; I can see that it is all in vain."

He rang the bell. The butler entered.

" Is Mr. Trelawney Hope at home ? "

" He will be home, sir, at a quarter to one.'

Holmes glanced at his watch.

" Still a quarter of an hour," said he. " Very good, I shall wait."

The butler had hardly closed the door behind him when Lady Hilda was down on her knees at Holmes' feet, her hands outstretched, her beautiful face upturned and wet with her tears.

" Oh, spare me, Mr. Holmes ! Spare me ! " she pleaded, in a frenzy of supplication. " For Heaven's sake don't tell him ! I love him so ! I would not bring one shadow on his life, and this I know would break his noble heart."

Holmes raised the lady. " I am thankful, madam, that you have come to your senses even at this last moment ! There is not an instant to lose. Where is the letter ? "

She darted across to a writing-desk, unlocked it, and drew out a long blue envelope.

" Here it is, Mr. Holmes. Would to Heaven I had never seen it ! "

" How can we return it ? " Holmes muttered. " Quick, quick, we must think of some way ! Where is the dis-patch-box ? "

" Still in his bedroom."

" What a stroke of luck ! Quick, madam, bring it here."

A moment later she had appeared with a red flat box in her hand.

" How did you open it before ? You have a duplicate key ? Yes, of course you have. Open it ! "

From out of her bosom Lady Hilda had drawn a small key. The box flew open. It was stuffed with papers. Holmes thrust the blue envelope deep down into the heart of them, between the leaves of some other document. The box was shut, locked, and returned to his bedroom.

" Now we are ready for him," said Holmes ; " we have still ten minutes. I am going far to screen you, Lady Hilda. In return you will spend the time in telling me frankly the real meaning of this extraordinary affair."

" Mr. Holmes, I will tell you everything," cried the lady. " Oh, Mr. Holmes, I would cut off my right hand before I gave him a moment of sorrow ! There is no woman in all London who loves her husband as I do, and yet if he knew how I have acted—how I have been compelled to act—he would never forgive me. For his own honour stands so high that he could not forget or pardon a lapse in another. Help me, Mr. Holmes ! My happiness, his happiness, our very lives are at stake ! "

" Quick, madam, the time grows short ! "

" It was a letter of mine, Mr. Holmes, an indiscreet letter written before my marriage—a foolish letter, a letter of an impulsive, loving girl. I meant no harm, and yet he would have thought it criminal. Had he read that letter his confidence would have been for ever destroyed. It is years since I wrote it. I had thought that the whole matter was forgotten. Then at last I heard from this man, Lucas, that it had passed into his hands, and that he would lay it before my husband. I implored his mercy. He said that he would return my letter if I would return him a certain document which he described in my husband's dispatch-box. He had some spy in the office who had told him of its existence. He assured me that no harm could come to my husband. Put yourself in my position, Mr. Holmes ! What was I to do ? "

" Take your husband into your confidence."

" I could not, Mr. Holmes, I could not ! On the one side seemed certain ruin ; on the other, terrible as it seemed to take my husband's papers, still in a matter of politics I could not understand the consequences, while in a matter of love and trust they were only too clear to me. I did it, Mr. Holmes ! I took an impression of his key ; this man Lucas furnished a duplicate. I opened his dispatch-box, took the paper, and conveyed it to Godolphin Street."

" What happened there, madam ? "

" I tapped at the door, as agreed. Lucas opened it. I followed him into his room, leaving the hall door ajar behind me, for I feared to be alone with the man. I remembered that there was a woman outside as I entered. Our business was soon done. He had my letter on his desk ; I handed him the document. He gave me the letter. At this instant there was a sound at the door. There were steps in the passage. Lucas quickly turned back the drugget, thrust the document into some hiding-place there, and covered it over.

" What happened after that is like some fearful dream. I have a vision of a dark, frantic face, of a woman's voice, which screamed in French, ' My waiting is not in vain. At last, at last I have found you with her ! ' There was a savage struggle. I saw him with a chair in his hand, a knife gleamed in hers. I rushed from the horrible scene, ran from the house, and only next morning in the paper did I learn the dreadful result. That night I was happy, for I had my letter, and I had not seen yet what the future would bring.

" It was next morning that I realized that I had only exchanged one trouble for another. My husband's anguish at the loss of his paper went to my heart. I could hardly prevent myself from there and then kneeling down at his feet and telling him what I had done. But that again would mean a confession of the past. I came to you that morning in order to understand the full enormity of my offence. From the instant that I grasped it my whole mind was turned to the one thought of getting back my husband's paper. It must still be where Lucas had placed it, for it was concealed before this dreadful woman entered the room. If it had not been for her coming, I should not have known where his hiding-place was. How was I to get into the room ? For two days I watched the place, but the door was never left open. Last night I made a last attempt. What I did and how I succeeded, you have already learned. I brought the paper back with me, and thought of destroying it, since I could see no way of returning it without confessing my guilt to my husband. Heavens, I hear his step upon the stair ! "

The European Secretary burst excitedly into the room.

" Any news, Mr. Holmes, any news ? " he cried.

" I have some hopes."

" Ah, thank Heaven ! " His face became radiant. " The Prime Minister is lunching with me. May he share your hopes ? He has nerves of steel, and yet I know that he has hardly slept since this terrible event. Jacobs, will you ask the Prime Minister to come up ? As to you, dear, I fear that this is a matter of politics. We will join you in a few minutes in the dining-room."

The Prime Minister's manner was subdued, but I could see by the gleam of his eyes and the twitchings of his bony hands that he shared the excitement of his young colleague.

" I understand that you have something to report, Mr. Holmes ? "

" Purely negative as yet," my friend answered. " I have inquired at every point where it might be, and I am sure that there is no danger to be apprehended."

" But that is not enough, Mr. Holmes. We cannot live for ever on such a volcano. We must have something definite."

" I am in hopes of getting it. That is why I am here. The more I think of the matter the more convinced I am that the letter has never left this house."

" Mr. Holmes ! "

" If it had it would certainly have been public by now."

" But why should anyone take it in order to keep it in this house ? "

" I am not convinced that anyone did take it."

" Then how could it leave the dispatch-box ? "

" I am not convinced that it ever did leave the dispatch-box."

" Mr. Holmes, this joking is very ill-timed. You have my assurance that it left the box."

" Have you examined the box since Tuesday morning ? "

" No ; it was not necessary."

" You may conceivably have overlooked it."

" Impossible, I say."

" But I am not convinced of it ; I have known such things happen. I presume there are other papers there. Well, it may have got mixed with them."

" It was on the top."

" Someone may have shaken the box and displaced it."

" No, no ; I had everything out."

" Surely it is easily decided, Hope ! " said the Premier. " Let us have the dispatch-box brought in."

The Secretary rang the bell.

" Jacobs, bring down my dispatch-box. This is a farcical waste of time, but still, if nothing else will satisfy you, it shall be done. Thank you, Jacobs ; put it here. I have always had the key on my watch-chain. Here are the papers, you see. Letter from Lord Merrow, report from Sir Charles Hardy, memorandum from Belgrade, note on the Russo-German grain taxes, letter from Madrid, note from Lord Flowers—good heavens ! what is this ? Lord Bellinger ! Lord Bellinger ! "

The Premier snatched the blue envelope from his hand.

" Yes, it is it—and the letter intact. Hope, I congratulate you ! "

" Thank you ! Thank you ! What a weight from my heart ! But this is inconceivable—impossible ! Mr. Holmes, you are a wizard, a sorcerer ! How did you know it was there ? "

" Because I knew it was nowhere else."

" I cannot believe my eyes ! " He ran wildly to the door. " Where is my wife ? I must tell her that all is well. Hilda ! Hilda ! " we heard his voice on the stairs.

The Premier looked at Holmes with twinkling eyes.

" Come, sir," said he. " There is more in this than meets the eye. How came the letter back in the box ? "

Holmes turned away smiling from the keen scrutiny of those wonderful eyes.

" We also have our diplomatic secrets," said he, and picking up his hat he turned to the door.

THE PREMIER SNATCHED THE BLUE ENVELOPE FROM HIS HAND.

Illustration by Sidney Paget for the *Strand Magazine*, December, 1904.

Auctorial and Bibliographical Note. Of the twelve short stories on his "best" list, excluding those in the *Case-Book*, Conan Doyle ranked "The Adventure of the Second Stain" eighth. The original manuscript, 31 small folio leaves (5½ in another hand), white vellum, was auctioned in New York City on January 26, 1922, bringing $170. It was later listed in Scribner's Sherlock Holmes Catalogue at $450. It is presently owned by Haverford College, Haverford, Pennsylvania, the gift of the late Christopher Morley.

EDITORIAL OFFICE OF " THE STRAND MAGAZINE."

nothing but strict business — a bookcase, desks, chairs, and many papers.

To the left, on the next floor, stands the editorial office of THE STRAND MAGAZINE, wherein, before the central writing-table, sits Mr. H. Greenhough Smith, in whose charge lies the selection and arrangement of the literary matter—the editing, in fact, of course under the supervision of Mr. Newnes—of

this, by far the most widely-circulated monthly in the country. This room also, with its bookcase, its cabinets for the reception of proofs and MSS, its telephones, and its many loose papers, is unmistakably a room for work.

Just so is the adjoining room, occupied by Mr. W. H. J. Boot, the Art Editor. Like Mr. Greenhough Smith's room, it overlooks

EDITORIAL OFFICE OF THE "STRAND MAGAZINE"

Shown at his desk is the editor of the *Strand*, H. Greenhough Smith, friend of Conan Doyle. As the man responsible for the selection and arrangement of the *Strand*'s literary matter, he secured for his pages all the Sherlock Holmes short stories and the two later novels.

IV. FROM DR. WATSON'S FIRST MARRIAGE TO THE DEATH OF THE FIRST MRS. WATSON

[*circa* November 1, 1886 to late December, 1887, or early January, 1888]

"I should recommend you also to send a note . . .
to your wife to say that you have thrown in your lot with me."
—Sherlock Holmes to John H. Watson, M.D.,
"The Man with the Twisted Lip"

"A CERTAIN GRACIOUS LADY"

Victoria, Queen of Great Britain and Ireland (1837–1901) and Empress of India (1876–1901), she reigned over England during most of the Holmes-Watson period.

22

"NOW, WATSON, THE FAIR SEX IS
YOUR DEPARTMENT"

[Sherlock Holmes, "The Adventure of the Second Stain"]

Much has been written on the subject of Dr. Watson's marriages and wives—so much, indeed, that the late Dorothy L. Sayers was moved to say: "There is a conspiracy afoot to provide Watson with as many wives as Henry VIII," and the late Gavin Brend was forced to remind his fellow Holmsesians that we are dealing, not with Bluebeard, but with Dr. John H. Watson.

And yet it is absolutely essential for the student who seeks to reconstruct, not only Watson's career, but also that of Holmes, to try to determine with as much exactitude as possible just how often Watson married, and whom he married, and when.

This is because the proper dating of so many of the cases hinges upon correctly interpreting a Watsonian reference to "my marriage." The good doctor tells us, for example, that "The Adventure of the Noble Bachelor" took place "a few weeks before my own marriage." "The Stockbroker's Clerk" was "shortly after my marriage." Three more adventures ("The Naval Treaty," a "Second Stain," and the unrecorded "Tired Captain") happened during "the July which immediately succeeded my marriage." Still another adventure, that of "The Dying Detective," occurred in "the second year of my married life."

Few students of the Canon question Watson's union with Mary Morstan, whom he wooed and won during the adventure of *The Sign of the Four*[1]—and most, but by no means all, students are now agreed that the proper year of *The Sign of the Four* is 1888 (whether the month was April, July or September is quite another matter). Our own date for the Morstan-Watson nuptials is *circa* May 1, 1889; other commentators have dated it June or November, 1887, and the late Christopher Morley, in "Dr. Watson's Secret," made a valiant effort to untangle some of "the infuriating inconsistencies of Watsonian chronology" by supposing that Watson had contracted a *secret* marriage with Mary some time before the adventure of *The Sign of the Four*.

When Holmes returned from the dead in April, 1894 ("The Adventure of the Empty House"), Watson spoke of his "sad bereavement," and most students have interpreted this to mean that Mary Morstan Watson died in 1891, 1892, 1893, or early 1894.[2]

At some time in 1902, between June 27th ("The Adventure of the Three Garridebs") and September 3rd ("The

[1] One student who did question it was the late A. Carson Simpson, who expressed the view that Watson married, not Mary Morstan of *The Sign of the Four*, but the widowed Mrs. Cecil Forrester of the same adventure. See "It Must Have Been Two Other Fellows."

[2] Dr. Ebbe Curtis Hoff, in "The Adventure of John and Mary," has suggseted the second half of 1892 on the basis of the fact that there is "a gap from June to December of that year in the otherwise monthly publications of Watson's accounts in the *Strand Magazine* which may be accounted for by her decease."

3 But Mr. D. Martin Dakin rejects this marriage entirely on the grounds that "The Adventure of the Blanched Soldier" is fictitious. "The whole reference is probably the mistake of a misguided writer who wanted to account for Holmes writing the story himself and had not the wit to realize that [the marriage referred to in it] belonged to an earlier period" ("The Problem of the *Case-Book*").

Adventure of the Illustrious Client"), Watson moved to rooms in Queen Anne Street. He was undoubtedly contemplating matrimony at that time, although his marriage may not have taken place until shortly before "The Adventure of the Blanched Soldier" (January, 1903), in which Holmes himself writes: "The good Watson had at that time deserted me for a wife . . ."**3**

We may date this marriage late (October, November, or December) 1902.

It is probable that Watson returned at once to the practice of medicine, for, in September, 1902 ("The Adventure of the Illustrious Client") he mentions "some pressing professional business of my own"; and by the summer of 1903 ("The Adventure of the Mazarin Stone") he bears "every sign of the busy medical man, with calls on his every hour."

The identity of this Mrs. Watson remains an enigma. Mr. S. C. Roberts has conjectured, somewhat playfully, that she was the young and beautiful Miss Violet de Merville of "The Adventure of the Illustrious Client." But the late Elmer Davis wrote ("The Real Sherlock Holmes") that ". . . the evidence adduced to support [this theory] is mere inference, and the probabilities are powerfully against it. Miss de Merville, with the 'ethereal otherworld beauty of a fanatic,' and 'a will of iron' was hardly the woman to attract a prudent middle-aged widower; if Dr. Watson had really that 'experience of women extending over many nations and three separate continents' of which he boasts in *The Sign of the Four* . . . he must have known that she was more dangerous than dynamite, supremely the sort of woman to avoid. Moreover, so solidly conventional a late Victorian as Watson would have been unlikely to marry a woman who had 'doted upon' and 'been obsessed by' the infamous Gruner; nor, possibly, would he have been drawn to one who had enlisted the interest, however chivalrous and paternal, of his sovereign."

Mr. Davis also made the valid point that Watson had left Baker Street for the Queen Anne Street rooms *before* he met Miss de Merville—if indeed he ever met her at all; there is no evidence that he did in the story.

It seems we must discard Miss Violet de Merville as the Mrs. Watson of 1902.

Who else, then, could she have been?

Mr. Stuart Palmer once speculated ("The Adventure of the Marked Man") that this Mrs. Watson was Signora Emilia Lucca of "The Adventure of the Red Circle"; Mr. Richard W. Clarke surmised ("On the Nomenclature of Watson's Ships") that she was a Miss Alicia Cutter of New York City, whom Watson had met during the problem of "The Disappearance of Lady Frances Carfax"; and the late Christopher Morley wrote: "In brooding on the problem of [Watson's 1902] marriage one could be tempted to wish that the superb Grace Dunbar of 'The Problem of Thor Bridge' might have been [that] Mrs. Watson. But knowing Senator Neil Gibson, it is unlikely." Morley on another occasion ventured the opinion that the Mrs. Watson of 1902 was Lady Frances Carfax herself, and this suggestion has received the enthusiastic support of Mr. George Haynes in "The Last Mrs. Watson."

Whoever this Mrs. Watson was, she behaved very differently from Mary Morstan Watson. "Can it be doubted," Elmer Davis wrote, "that [she] put her foot down well in advance of the ceremony, and made it a condition precedent on her acceptance that her husband should have no more to do with the sort of people he knew before he was married— i.e., conspicuously with Sherlock Holmes? The probability is supported by Holmes' own words in 'The Adventure of the Blanched Soldier'—'The good Watson had at that time deserted me for a wife, *the only selfish action which I can recall in our association.*' This clearly refers to the [1902] marriage because Mary Morstan Watson, from indifference or complaisance, never objected when her husband went off with Holmes. The [last] Mrs. Watson, obviously, was made of sterner stuff. Further, it may be inferred that she had known [Mary Morstan Watson], and had observed at first-hand the doctor's frequent darting away from the fireside. Not a relative, for Mary Morstan had no relatives in England; but, considering the difference in ages, she might well have been one of the daughters of Mrs. Cecil Forrester to whom Mary was once the governess. Some one, at any rate, who knew the circumstances well enough to tell the amorous doctor, 'I don't intend to go through what poor Mary suffered'; or (on the alternative hypothesis that it was Mary Watson rather than John Watson whose love grew cold): 'I care enough for you to want you to stay home.' "

Indeed, Christopher Morley thought that the Mrs. Watson of 1902 was so intent on keeping Watson away from Holmes and busy with his practice that she herself wrote at least one of the later adventures for him.

There is, however, another school of thought: one that holds that the "sad bereavement" to which Watson referred in "The Adventure of the Empty House" was not bereavement by death but the fact that Mary and John had separated: "Watson's so-called [1902] marriage was when he and Mary decided to resume mutual bed and board," Christopher Morley wrote in "Watson à la Mode," recanting on his previous opinions on the last Mrs. Watson.

This is also the view of Professor H. W. Starr ("Some New Light on Watson"): "Mary Morstan had not died at all; she is the wife—and the only wife—referred to throughout the entire Canon."[4]

Professor Starr, in collaboration with Mr. T. B. Hunt, elaborated on this view in "What Happened to Mary Morstan": "Mary Morstan . . . fought courageously—and with the Doctor's self-sacrificing help—against the inroads of insanity. Again and again his love and medical skill pulled her back from the shadow of the asylum; to her he gave the closing years of his life, attending her in seclusion, saving her from the final horror of an institution. This is the 'sad bereavement.' "

We must now consider briefly the suggestion put forward by the late H. W. Bell—that still another marriage by Watson accounts for the "missing year" late 1895 to late 1896. As noted in Chapter 16, this suggestion has not survived careful examination. Nonetheless, we most heartily concur with Mr. Bell that Watson *was* married three times—although we hold that his "third" marriage was *chronologically his first.*

[4] Others who have expressed a similar point of view include Mr. Daniel L. Moriarty in his "The Woman Who Beat Sherlock Holmes"; Mr. Wingate H. Bett in a letter to "Wigmore Street Post-Bag" in the *Sherlock Holmes Journal;* and Mr. Jerry Neal Williamson in "In Defense of Scotland Yard."

This view is based on researches which demonstrate (conclusively to us, at least) that Watson married for the first time *circa* November 1, 1886. His wife must have died very suddenly in late December, 1887, or early January, 1888; Watson was married and living in his house in Kensington when he called to wish Holmes the greetings of the season on the second day after Christmas, 1887 ("The Adventure of the Blue Carbuncle"), but he was back in Baker Street, where he was to remain for sixteen months, when the adventure of *The Valley of Fear* began on the morning of January 7, 1888.

Who was this Mrs. Watson?

There can be no certainty—but it is interesting to speculate that she may have been Miss Helen Stoner of "The Adventure of the Speckled Band."

In his remarkable exegesis, "A Scandal in Baker Street," Mr. Nathan L. Bengis has shown that Watson knew Helen well in India; she had been his nurse at Peshawar—and we know many patients eventually marry their nurses.

We also know that Helen met an *untimely* death. As Mr. Bengis wrote: "Note the telling effect of the italicized word, which, in a man as tight-lipped as Watson was, expresses more than a casual regret at the passing of a woman about thirty-nine."

We also know that her death occurred *before* Watson chronicled "The Adventure of the Speckled Band"—which could hardly have been earlier than March, 1889. This released him from his promise not to reveal the facts about the death of Dr. Grimesby Roylott; if Helen Stoner was indeed the first Mrs. Watson, it released him also from his marriage to her and made it possible for him to propose to Mary Morstan in September, 1888, and marry her *circa* May 1, 1889.

But there is another possibility, and a strong one.

We have already had cause to refer to the unfinished manuscript, *Angels of Darkness,* penned by Watson's friend Dr. Conan Doyle. There, it will be recalled, Conan Doyle revealed that Watson had for a time practiced medicine in San Francisco, California, U.S.A. But more than that was revealed: as Mr. John Dickson Carr wrote in his *Life of Sir Arthur Conan Doyle* (italics ours): "*Either* [*Watson*] *had a wife before he wedded Mary Morstan,* or else he heartlessly jilted the poor girl whom he holds in his arms as the curtain falls on *Angels of Darkness.*"

From what we already know of Watson's character, it is unthinkable that he should have "jilted the poor girl," and your editor is firm in his belief that the *first* Mrs. Watson was an American, a girl from San Francisco who was a patient of Watson's when he briefly practiced medicine there.

Now, at least four times in his chronicles, Watson attempts to imply that *The Sign of the Four* took place *earlier* than it actually did, or, alternatively, that certain cases in which he appears in the married state took place *after* September, 1888, leading the reader to suppose that the wife in these cases was Mary, when, in reality, she was (in our view) the girl from San Francisco.

In "A Scandal in Bohemia," for example, Watson speaks of the "well-remembered door" of No. 221 Baker Street—an address, he is careful to tell us, that he would always associate with his wooing. This was the first case published by Watson after the appearance of *The Sign of the Four*, in which he had described his wooing of Mary. The contemporary reader would naturally assume that the wife of "A Scandal in Bohemia" was Mary—and we really cannot blame him, for this was Watson's intention.

Again, in "The Red-Headed League," the police official, Jones, is made to say: "Once or twice, as in that business of the Sholto murder and the Agra treasure . . ." That Jones should remember, in October, 1887, an event that did not take place until September, 1888, is remarkable. It becomes even more remarkable when one notes that Police Official Jones of "The Red-Headed League" and Inspector Jones of *The Sign of the Four* were *two different men*: it was *Peter* Jones in "The Red-Headed League," but it was *Athelney* Jones in *The Sign of the Four* (Jones is not an unusual name, and it is possible that the two police officers were brothers).

Again, in "A Case of Identity," Watson tells us that he looked back to "the weird business of *The Sign of the Four*" —and in "The Five Orange Pips" Holmes *supposedly* mentions *The Sign of the Four* as a possibly more fantastic case. It is also in "The Five Orange Pips" that Watson says he was a dweller for a few days in Baker Street once more because his wife was on a visit to her *aunt's*. But it was her *mother* she was visiting in the first publication of Watson's chronicle in the *Strand Magazine* for November, 1891—and *Mary*, of course, was an orphan.**5**

Indeed, it is equally incredible that *Mary* should have been visiting an *aunt:* as Dr. Ebbe Curtis Hoff wrote in "The Adventure of John and Mary": "When Mary came home from India as a child to go to school in Edinburgh, her mother was already dead, and she had no relative in England. As a schoolgirl of seventeen, she had to face decisions arising out of the disappearance of her father and with no advice except that of the manager of the Langham Hotel and the police. If Mary had had an aunt, she would have come forward at [this] time of crisis and need. There is no mention of an aunt at that time because there was no aunt. Mary . . . had no relative in England."

It is apparent that the Mrs. Watson of "The Five Orange Pips" and Mary Morstan Watson, like Peter Jones and Athelney Jones, *were two different people.* Watson, who wished to conceal this fact, hastily changed "mother" to "aunt" when "The Five Orange Pips appeared in *The Adventures of Sherlock Holmes*, not realizing at the time that he was making the matter no better.

It is not impossible that Watson went even beyond this— that the "1890s" in his account of "The Red-Headed League," for example, were neither slips of the memory nor slips of the pen nor mistakes by the typesetter, but *insertions deliberately intended to confound the chronologically minded contemporary reader*, as they have certainly confused many later chronologists.**6**

Does all this seem out of character?

We will later have cause to note the extremely subtle way in which Watson attempted to confound the chronologically minded contemporary reader in "The Adventure of Charles Augustus Milverton" (although, in that chronicle, he did

5 So was Helen Stoner—a point against the theory that she may have been the first Mrs. Watson.

6 "Watson wove a tangled web in his chronology because he was deliberately trying to deceive," the late Christopher Morley wrote in "Dr. Watson's Secret."

7 Three times during 1890 Watson returned to Baker Street for longer or for shorter periods.

8 We may be sure that Mary *would* see Watson's published writings. As the late Dorothy L. Sayers wrote in "Dr. Watson's Christian Name," "Tenderly devoted as [Mary Watson] was to her husband, she could not have failed to read his stories attentively on publication. . . . On such dull matters as dates and historical facts, the dear woman would offer no comment, but on any details affecting her domestic life she would pounce like a tigress."

9 We should remember here that the first Mrs. Watson was Watson's *patient* before she was Watson's *wife*. She obviously suffered from poor health, and her very sudden death should not be unexpected.

warn the reader that he would make every effort to attempt to conceal the date).

Let us also remember that "in Watson's character underlies certainly a very marked streak, not only of pawky humor, but also of *cunning* and his friend Sherlock Holmes was every now and then brought up against it in a rather unexpected way. ('I never get your limits, Watson. There are unexplained possibilities about you,' Holmes would remark; or, again, 'Your native cunning . . .'). Holmes evidently spoke in a humorous vein on these occasions, but none the less . . ." (Cornelis Helling, "The True Story of the Dancing Men").

But *why* did Watson deliberately attempt to mislead the reader in at least four of his early chronicles?

The answer leaps to the eye when one considers these *publication dates:*

1. "A Scandal in Bohemia"—July, 1891.
2. "The Red-Headed League"—August, 1891.
3. "A Case of Identity"—September, 1891.
4. "The Five Orange Pips"—November, 1891.

In July to November, 1891, Watson was married to and living with Mary Morstan Watson. How would she feel with such a constant reminder *in the public prints* that in Watson's affections she was always second to "that other"? (See *The Sign of the Four,* Note 170).

The state of Mary's health made Watson's married life with her difficult enough, we know;**7** he had no intention of making it more difficult still by reminding her, in so many of the chronicles published in the *Strand Magazine* during their married life together, that she was not the first but the second Mrs. Watson.**8**

Let us now summarize Watson's marriages as we see them:

1. *Circa* November 1, 1886, Watson married the girl from San Francisco he had met while practicing medicine there, during the period when he was called to America to attend his ailing brother. He almost at once purchased a small and never very successful practice in Kensington. The first Mrs. Watson died, probably in late December, 1887, but very possibly early in January, 1888, and Watson returned to Baker Street.**9**

2. *Circa* May 1, 1889, Watson married Mary Morstan, whom he had met during the adventure of *The Sign of the Four* in September, 1888. He soon bought a connection in the Paddington district from old Mr. Farquhar ("The Stockbroker's Clerk"). Unlike his Kensington practice, his Paddington practice "increased steadily" ("The Engineer's Thumb"). (It is probable, as we have seen, that Mary Morstan Watson died in June, 1892, or shortly thereafter.)

3. In early October, 1902, Dr. John H. Watson married for the third time. Soon after that he returned to the practice of medicine, this time in Queen Anne Street. This, too, was a highly successful practice; Watson tells us (in "The Adventure of the Creeping Man") that it was "not inconsiderable" by September, 1903.

Truly, as Sherlock Holmes said, "the fair sex is your department," Watson.

23

THE REIGATE SQUIRES

[Thursday, April 14, to Tuesday, April 26, 1887]

IT was some time before the health of my friend, Mr. Sherlock Holmes, recovered from the strain caused by his immense exertions in the spring of '87. The whole question of the Netherland-Sumatra Company and of the colossal schemes of Baron Maupertuis is too recent in the minds of the public, and too intimately concerned with politics and finance, to be a fitting subject for this series of sketches. It led, however, in an indirect fashion to a singular and complex problem, which gave my friend an opportunity of demonstrating the value of a fresh weapon among the many with which he waged his lifelong battle against crime.

On referring to my notes, I see that it was on the 14th of April that I received a telegram from Lyons, which **1-2** informed me that Holmes was lying ill in the Hotel Dulong. Within twenty-four hours I was in his sick- **3** room, and was relieved to find that there was nothing **4** formidable in his symptoms. His iron constitution, how- ever, had broken down under the strain of an investigation which had extended over two months, during which period he had never worked less than fifteen hours a day, and had more than once, as he assured me, kept to his task for five days at a stretch. The triumphant issue of his labours could not save him from reaction after so terrible an exertion, and at a time when Europe was ringing with his name, and when his room was literally ankle-deep with congratulatory telegrams, I found him a prey to the blackest depression. Even the knowledge that he had succeeded where the police of three countries had failed, and that he had outmanœuvred at every point the most accomplished swindler in Europe, was insuf- ficient to rouse him from his nervous prostration.

Three days later we were back in Baker Street together, **5** but it was evident that my friend would be much the better for a change, and the thought of a week of spring- time in the country was full of attractions to me also. My old friend Colonel Hayter, who had come under my professional care in Afghanistan, had now taken a house **6** near Reigate, in Surrey, and had frequently asked me to **7** come down to him upon a visit. On the last occasion he had remarked that if my friend would only come with me, he would be glad to extend his hospitality to him also. A little diplomacy was needed, but when Holmes understood that the establishment was a bachelor one, and that he would be allowed the fullest freedom, he fell in with my plans, and a week after our return from Lyons, we were

1 *the 14th of April.* The 14th of April, 1887, was a Thursday. Here, for the first time, all chronol- ogists are in complete agreement with Watson. The case ended on Tuesday, April 26, 1887.

2 *I received a telegram.* Although your editor seems to stand alone in his contention that Watson was both married and in practice in April, 1887, he has stated his case for this view in *The Chron- ological Holmes:* "1) Had Holmes and Watson been sharing the Baker Street rooms together at this time, Holmes would almost certainly have invited his 'intimate friend and associate' to accom- pany him on as lengthy and trying an investigation as that of the Netherland-Sumatra Company. . . . 2) Watson says: 'Three days later we were back in Baker Street together.' Note the significant omis- sion of the familiar *'our rooms in Baker Street,'* the stress on the *'together.'* 3) Watson seems to go out of his way to explain to us that 'a little diplomacy' was needed to get Holmes to Reigate, underlining that it was 'only when Holmes un- derstood that *the establishment was a bachelor one'* that he consented to go. Here Watson is clearly explaining why he did not invite Holmes to convalesce at his—Watson's—home: *his* home was *not* a bachelor establishment; the Master would not want the first Mrs. Watson fussing over him when he was in good health, much less when he was ailing. 4) Watson says that 'all my professional caution' was destined to be wasted; later he says, 'Speaking professionally, it was admirably done.' In few other cases do we find Watson so playing the medical man; clearly 'The Reigate Squires' came at a time when he was in *active* practice. 5) Finally, we have Holmes' closing quotation: *'Our quiet rest in the country has been a distinct suc- cess, and I shall certainly return, much invigorated, to Baker Street to-morrow.'* Watson, then, was *not* to return to Baker Street on the morrow, but to his home and practice, which he had neglected only to care for his old and intimate friend."

3 *the Hotel Dulong.* There was a Hotel *Dubost* at 19 Place Carnot.

4 *Within twenty-four hours I was in his sick- room.* Watson therefore arrived in Lyons on Fri- day, April 15, 1887.

5 *Three days later we were back in Baker Street together.* Bringing us to Monday, April 18, 1887.

6 *who had come under my professional care in Afghanistan.* "He evidently was not the Colonel of the 66th [Foot of the Berkshires], who was Galbraith, killed at Maiwand; nor do I think that Hayter could have been the Colonel of the Northumberland Fusiliers, who kept the Khyber Line," Mrs. Crighton Sellars wrote in "Dr. Watson and the British Army." "In the year 1880, however, Hayter may have been of some lower rank, and he might have been in either regiment, or in some other organziation stationed at Candahar."

"It would seem fairly safe to identify him with the Major Charles Hayter who was director of Kabul Transport in the Second Afghan War (Hanna: *The Second Afghan War*, pp. 470, 525)," Mr. S. C. Roberts wrote in *Doctor Watson.*

7 *Reigate, in Surrey.* A residential suburb, 22 miles from London, in the Vale, be it noted, of *Holmesdale.*

8 *we were under the Colonel's roof.* Holmes and Watson therefore arrived at Reigate on Monday, April 25, 1887.

9 *an odd volume of Pope's 'Homer.'* Alexander Pope, 1688–1744, English poet, quoted by Watson in *A Study in Scarlet* (see Note 21). In 1720 appeared Pope's translation of the *Iliad* and in 1725–1726 the *Odyssey*, both tremendous literary and financial successes.

10 *next morning.* The morning of Tuesday, April 26, 1887.

BUT I HELD UP A WARNING FINGER.

Illustration by Sidney Paget for the *Strand Magazine*, June, 1893.

8 under the Colonel's roof.   Hayter was a fine old soldier, who had seen much of the world, and he soon found, as I had expected, that Holmes and he had plenty in common.

On the evening of our arrival we were sitting in the Colonel's gun-room after dinner, Holmes stretched upon the sofa, while Hayter and I looked over his little armoury of firearms.

" By the way," said he, suddenly, " I'll take one of these pistols upstairs with me in case we have an alarm."

" An alarm ! " said I.

" Yes, we've had a scare in this part lately.   Old Acton, who is one of our county magnates, had his house broken into last Monday.   No great damage done, but the fellows are still at large."

" No clue ? " asked Holmes, cocking his eye at the Colonel.

" None as yet.   But the affair is a petty one, one of our little country crimes, which must seem too small for your attention, Mr. Holmes, after this great international affair."

Holmes waved away the compliment, though his smile showed that it had pleased him.

" Was there any feature of interest ? "

" I fancy not.   The thieves ransacked the library, and got very little for their pains.   The whole place was turned upside down, drawers burst open and presses ransacked, **9** with the result that an odd volume of Pope's ' Homer,' two plated candlesticks, an ivory letter-weight, a small oak barometer, and a ball of twine are all that have vanished."

" What an extraordinary assortment ! " I exclaimed.

" Oh, the fellows evidently grabbed hold of anything they could get."

Holmes grunted from the sofa.

" The county police ought to make something of that," said he.   " Why, it is surely obvious that——"

But I held up a warning finger.

" You are here for a rest, my dear fellow.   For Heaven's sake, don't get started on a new problem when your nerves are all in shreds."

Holmes shrugged his shoulders with a glance of comic resignation towards the Colonel, and the talk drifted away into less dangerous channels.

It was destined, however, that all my professional **10** caution should be wasted, for next morning the problem obtruded itself upon us in such a way that it was impossible to ignore it, and our country visit took a turn which neither of us could have anticipated.   We were at breakfast when the Colonel's butler rushed in with all his propriety shaken out of him.

" Have you heard the news, sir ? " he gasped.   " At the Cunninghams', sir ! "

" Burglary ? " cried the Colonel, with his coffee-cup in mid-air.

" Murder ! "

The Colonel whistled.   " By Jove ! " said he, " who's killed, then ?   The J.P. or his son ? "

" Neither, sir.   It was William, the coachman.   Shot through the heart, sir, and never spoke again."

" Who shot him, then ? "

" The burglar, sir. He was off like a shot and got clean away. He'd just broke in at the pantry window when William came on him and met his end in saving his master's property."

" What time ? "

" It was last night, sir, somewhere about twelve."

" Ah, then, we'll step over presently," said the Colonel, coolly settling down to his breakfast again. " It's a baddish business," he added, when the butler had gone. " He's our leading squire about here, is old Cunningham, and a very decent fellow, too.   He'll be cut up over this, for the man has been in his service for years, and was a good servant.   It's evidently the same villains who broke into Acton's."

" And stole that very singular collection ? " said Holmes, thoughtfully.

" Precisely."

" Hum ! It may prove the simplest matter in the world ; but, all the same, at first glance this is just a little curious, is it not ?   A gang of burglars acting in the country might be expected to vary the scene of their operations, and not to crack two cribs in the same district **11** within a few days.   When you spoke last night of taking precautions, I remember that it passed through my mind that this was probably the last parish in England to which the thief or thieves would be likely to turn their attention ; which shows that I have still much to learn."

" I fancy it's some local practitioner," said the Colonel. " In that case, of course, Acton's and Cunningham's are just the places he would go for, since they are far the largest about here."

" And richest ? "

" Well, they ought to be ; but they've had a law-suit for some years which has sucked the blood out of both of them, I fancy.   Old Acton has some claim on half Cunningham's estate, and the lawyers have been at it with both hands."

" If it's a local villain, there should not be much difficulty in running him down," said Holmes, with a yawn. " All right, Watson, I don't intend to meddle."

" Inspector Forrester, sir," said the butler, throwing open the door.

The official, a smart, keen-faced young fellow, stepped into the room. " Good morning, Colonel," said he.   " I hope I don't intrude, but we hear that Mr. Holmes, of Baker Street, is here."

The Colonel waved his hand towards my friend, and the Inspector bowed.

" We thought that perhaps you would care to step across, Mr. Holmes."

" The Fates are against you, Watson," said he, laughing. " We were chatting about the matter when you came in, Inspector. Perhaps you can let us have a few details."   As he leaned back in his chair in the familiar attitude, I knew that the case was hopeless.

" We had no clue in the Acton affair. But here we have plenty to go on, and there's no doubt it is the same party in each case. The man was seen."

" Ah ! "

" Yes, sir. But he was off like a deer after the shot

11 *to crack two cribs*. To "crack a crib" is thieves' slang—meaning to break into a house or store.

"INSPECTOR FORRESTER, SIR," SAID THE BUTLER, THROWING OPEN THE DOOR.

Illustration by Sidney Paget for the *Strand Magazine*, June, 1893.

that killed poor William Kirwan was fired. Mr. Cunningham saw him from the bedroom window, and Mr. Alec Cunningham saw him from the back passage. It was a quarter to twelve when the alarm broke out. Mr. Cunningham had just got into bed, and Mister Alec was smoking a pipe in his dressing-gown. They both heard William, the coachman, calling for help, and Mister Alec he ran down to see what was the matter. The back door was open, and as he came to the foot of the stairs he saw two men wrestling together outside. One of them fired a shot, the other dropped, and the murderer rushed across the garden and over the hedge. Mr. Cunningham, looking out of his bedroom window, saw the fellow as he gained the road, but lost sight of him at once. Mister Alec stopped to see if he could help the dying man, and so the villain got clean away. Beyond the fact that he was a middle-sized man, and dressed in some dark stuff, we have no personal clue, but we are making energetic inquiries, and if he is a stranger we shall soon find him out."

" What was this William doing there ? Did he say anything before he died ? "

" Not a word. He lives at the lodge with his mother, and as he was a very faithful fellow, we imagine that he walked up to the house with the intention of seeing that all was right there. Of course, this Acton business has put everyone on their guard. The robber must have just burst open the door—the lock has been forced—when William came upon him."

" Did William say anything to his mother before going out ? "

" She is very old and deaf, and we can get no information from her. The shock has made her half-witted, but I understand that she was never very bright. There is one very important circumstance, however. Look at this ! "

He took a small piece of torn paper from a notebook and spread it out upon his knee.

" This was found between the finger and thumb of the dead man. It appears to be a fragment torn from a larger sheet. You will observe that the hour mentioned upon it is the very time at which the poor fellow met his

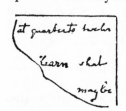

fate. You see that his murderer might have torn the rest of the sheet from him or he might have taken this fragment from the murderer. It reads almost as though it was an appointment."

Holmes took up the scrap of paper, a facsimile of which is here reproduced.

" Presuming that it is an appointment," continued the Inspector, " it is, of course, a conceivable theory that this William Kirwan, although he had the reputation of being an honest man, may have been in league with the thief. He may have met him there, may even have helped him to break in the door, and then they may have fallen out between themselves."

" This writing is of extraordinary interest," said

Holmes, who had been examining it with intense concentration. "These are much deeper waters than I had thought." He sank his head upon his hands, while the Inspector smiled at the effect which his case had had upon the famous London specialist.

"Your last remark," said Holmes, presently, "as to the possibility of there being an understanding between the burglar and the servant, and this being a note of appointment from one to the other, is an ingenious and not entirely an impossible supposition. But this writing opens up——" He sank his head into his hands again and remained for some minutes in the deepest thought. When he raised his face I was surprised to see that his cheek was tinged with colour, and his eyes as bright as before his illness. He sprang to his feet with all his old energy.

"I'll tell you what!" said he. "I should like to have a quiet little glance into the details of this case. There is something in it which fascinates me extremely. If you will permit me, Colonel, I will leave my friend, Watson, and you, and I will step round with the Inspector to test the truth of one or two little fancies of mine. I will be with you again in half an hour."

An hour and a half had elapsed before the Inspector returned alone.

"Mr. Holmes is walking up and down in the field outside," said he. "He wants us all four to go up to the house together."

"To Mr. Cunningham's?"

"Yes, sir."

"What for?"

The Inspector shrugged his shoulders. "I don't quite know, sir. Between ourselves, I think Mr. Holmes has not quite got over his illness yet. He's been behaving very queerly, and he is very much excited."

"I don't think you need alarm yourself," said I. "I have usually found that there was method in his madness."

"Some folk might say there was madness in his method," muttered the Inspector. "But he's all on fire to start, Colonel, so we had best go out, if you are ready."

We found Holmes pacing up and down in the field, his chin sunk upon his breast, and his hands thrust into his trouser pockets.

"The matter grows in interest," said he. "Watson, your country trip has been a distinct success. I have had a charming morning."

"You have been up to the scene of the crime, I understand?" said the Colonel.

"Yes; the Inspector and I have made quite a little reconnaissance together."

"Any success?"

"Well, we have seen some very interesting things. I'll tell you what we did as we walk. First of all we saw the body of this unfortunate man. He certainly died from a revolver wound, as reported."

"Had you doubted it, then?"

"Oh, it is as well to test everything. Our inspection was not wasted. We then had an interview with Mr. Cunningham and his son, who were able to point out the

... THE FINE OLD QUEEN ANNE HOUSE, WHICH BEARS
THE DATE OF MALPLAQUET UPON THE LINTEL OF THE
DOOR.

The reign of Queen Anne, first queen of Great
Britain, last Stuart ruler, 1665–1714, was marked by
the popularization of Palladian architecture (see
"The Adventure of the Abbey Grange," Note 4).
Malplaquet is the village in North France where,
in 1709, Marlborough and Eugene of Savoy defeated the French. Gatton Hall, near Reigate, is
one of several manorial houses in the district suspected of being "the fine old Queen Anne House."
Mr. Charles O. Merriman has also noted that The
Priory at Reigate (here illustrated, from *The Baker
Street Journal*, June, 1963) is "a building of note
. . . but does not bear the date of Malplaquet on
the lintel of the door."

12 "*Throw the door open, officer.*" Although
there is an inspector present, Holmes gives direct
orders to a constable, evidence of his increased
stature with the official police, not only in London,
but also in its suburbs.

exact spot where the murderer had broken through the
garden hedge in his flight. That was of great interest."
  " Naturally."
  " Then we had a look at this poor fellow's mother. We
could get no information from her, however, as she is very
old and feeble."
  " And what is the result of your investigations ? "
  " The conviction that the crime is a very peculiar one.
Perhaps our visit now may do something to make it less
obscure. I think that we are both agreed, Inspector,
that the fragment of paper in the dead man's hand, bearing, as it does, the very hour of his death written upon it,
is of extreme importance."
  " It should give a clue, Mr. Holmes."
  " It *does* give a clue. Whoever wrote that note was the
man who brought William Kirwan out of his bed at that
hour. But where is the rest of that sheet of paper ? "
  " I examined the ground carefully in the hope of finding it," said the Inspector.
  " It was torn out of the dead man's hand. Why was
someone so anxious to get possession of it ? Because it
incriminated him. And what would he do with it ?
Thrust it into his pocket most likely, never noticing that
a corner of it had been left in the grip of the corpse. If
we could get the rest of that sheet, it is obvious that we
should have gone a long way towards solving the mystery."
  " Yes, but how can we get at the criminal's pocket
before we catch the criminal."
  " Well, well, it was worth thinking over. Then there
is another obvious point. The note was sent to William.
The man who wrote it could not have taken it, otherwise
of course he might have delivered his own message by
word of mouth. Who brought the note, then ? Or did
it come through the post ? "
  " I have made inquiries," said the Inspector. " William received a letter by the afternoon post yesterday.
The envelope was destroyed by him."
  " Excellent ! " cried Holmes, clapping the Inspector on
the back. " You've seen the postman. It is a pleasure
to work with you. Well, here is the lodge, and if you will
come up, Colonel, I will show you the scene of the crime."
  We passed the pretty cottage where the murdered man
had lived, and walked up an oak-lined avenue to the fine
old Queen Anne house, which bears the date of Malplaquet upon the lintel of the door. Holmes and the
Inspector led us round it until we came to the side gate,
which is separated by a stretch of garden from the hedge
which lines the road. A constable was standing at the
kitchen door.
  12 " Throw the door open, officer," said Holmes. " Now
it was on those stairs that young Mr. Cunningham stood
and saw the two men struggling just where we are. Old
Mr. Cunningham was at that window—the second on the
left—and he saw the fellow get away just to the left of
that bush. So did the son. They are both sure of it
on account of the bush. Then Mister Alec ran out
and knelt beside the wounded man. The ground is
very hard, you see, and there are no marks to guide
us."

As he spoke two men came down the garden path, from round the angle of the house. The one was an elderly man, with a strong, deep-lined, heavy-eyed face; the other a dashing young fellow, whose bright, smiling expression and showy dress were in strange contrast with the business which had brought us there.

" Still at it, then ? " said he to Holmes. " I thought you Londoners were never at fault. You don't seem to be so very quick after all."

" Ah ! you must give us a little time," said Holmes, good-humouredly.

" You'll want it," said young Alec Cunningham. " Why, I don't see that we have any clue at all."

" There's only one," answered the Inspector. " We thought that if we could only find—— Good heavens ! Mr. Holmes, what is the matter ? "

My poor friend's face had suddenly assumed the most dreadful expression. His eyes rolled upwards, his features writhed in agony, and with a suppressed groan he dropped on his face upon the ground. Horrified at the suddenness and severity of the attack, we carried him into the kitchen, where he lay back in a large chair and breathed heavily for some minutes. Finally, with a shamefaced apology for his weakness, he rose once more.

" Watson would tell you that I have only just recovered from a severe illness," he explained. " I am liable to these sudden nervous attacks."

" Shall I send you home in my trap ? " asked old Cunningham.

" Well, since I am here there is one point on which I should like to feel sure. We can very easily verify it."

" What is it ? "

" Well, it seems to me that it is just possible that the arrival of this poor fellow William was not before but after the entrance of the burglar into the house. You appear to take it for granted that although the door was forced the robber never got in."

" I fancy that is quite obvious," said Mr. Cunningham, gravely. " Why, my son Alec had not yet gone to bed, and he would certainly have heard anyone moving about."

" Where was he sitting ? "

" I was sitting smoking in my dressing-room."

" Which window is that ? "

" The last on the left, next my father's."

" Both your lamps were lit, of course ? "

" Undoubtedly."

" There are some very singular points here," said Holmes, smiling. " Is it not extraordinary that a burglar —and a burglar who had had some previous experience —should deliberately break into a house at a time when he could see from the lights that two of the family were still afoot ? "

" He must have been a cool hand."

" Well, of course, if the case were not an odd one we should not have been driven to ask you for an explanation," said Mister Alec. " But as to your idea that the man had robbed the house before William tackled him, I think it a most absurd notion. Shouldn't we have

AS HE SPOKE TWO MEN CAME DOWN THE GARDEN PATH . . .

Illustration by William H. Hyde for *Harper's Weekly*, June 17, 1893.

"GOOD HEAVENS! MR. HOLMES, WHAT IS THE MATTER?"

Illustration by Sidney Paget for the *Strand Magazine*, June 1, 1893.

13 *Fifty pounds.* About $250.

14 *five hundred."* About $2,500.

found the place disarranged and missed the things which he had taken ? "

" It depends on what the things were," said Holmes. " You must remember that we are dealing with a burglar who is a very peculiar fellow, and who appears to work on lines of his own. Look, for example, at the queer lot of things which he took from Acton's—what was it ?—a ball of string, a letter-weight, and I don't know what other odds and ends ! "

" Well, we are quite in your hands, Mr. Holmes," said old Cunningham. " Anything which you or the Inspector may suggest will most certainly be done."

" In the first place," said Holmes, " I should like you to offer a reward—coming from yourself, for the officials may take a little time before they would agree upon the sum, and these things cannot be done too promptly. I have jotted down the form here, if you would not mind 13 signing it. Fifty pounds was quite enough, I thought." 14   " I would willingly give five hundred," said the J.P., taking the slip of paper and the pencil which Holmes handed to him. " This is not quite correct, however," he added, glancing over the document.

" I wrote it rather hurriedly."

" You see you begin : ' Whereas, at about a quarter to one on Tuesday morning, an attempt was made '—and so on. It was at a quarter to twelve, as a matter of fact."

I was pained at the mistake, for I knew how keenly Holmes would feel any slip of the kind. It was his speciality to be accurate as to fact, but his recent illness had shaken him, and this one little incident was enough to show me that he was still far from being himself. He was obviously embarrassed for an instant, while the Inspector raised his eyebrows and Alec Cunningham burst into a laugh. The old gentleman corrected the mistake, however, and handed the paper back to Holmes.

" Get it printed as soon as possible," he said. " I think your idea is an excellent one."

Holmes put the slip of paper carefully away in his pocket-book.

" And now," said he, " it would really be a good thing that we should all go over the house together, and make certain that this rather erratic burglar did not, after all, carry anything away with him."

Before entering, Holmes made an examination of the door which had been forced. It was evident that a chisel or strong knife had been thrust in, and the lock forced back with it. We could see the marks in the wood where it had been pushed in.

" You don't use bars, then ? " he asked.

" We have never found it necessary."

" You don't keep a dog ? "

" Yes ; but he is chained on the other side of the house."

" When do the servants go to bed ? '

" About ten."

" I understand that William was usually in bed also at that hour ? "

" Yes."

" It is singular that on this particular night he should

have been up. Now, I should be very glad if you would have the kindness to show us over the house, Mr. Cunningham."

A stone-flagged passage, with the kitchens branching away from it, led by a wooden staircase directly to the first floor of the house. It came out upon the landing opposite to a second more ornamental stair which led up from the front hall. Out of this landing opened the drawing-room and several bedrooms, including those of Mr. Cunningham and his son. Holmes walked slowly, taking keen note of the architecture of the house. I could tell from his expression that he was on a hot scent, and yet I could not in the least imagine in what direction his inferences were leading him.

"My good sir," said Mr. Cunningham, with some impatience, "this is surely very unnecessary. That is my room at the end of the stairs, and my son's is the one beyond it. I leave it to your judgment whether it was possible for the thief to have come up here without disturbing us."

"You must try round and get on a fresh scent, I fancy," said the son, with a rather malicious smile.

"Still, I must ask you to humour me a little further. I should like, for example, to see how far the windows of the bedrooms command the front. This, I understand, is your son's room "—he pushed open the door—" and that, I presume, is the dressing-room in which he sat smoking when the alarm was given. Where does the window of that look out to ? " He stepped across the bedroom, pushed open the door, and glanced round the other chamber.

"I hope you are satisfied now ? " said Mr. Cunningham, testily.

"Thank you ; I think I have seen all that I wished."

"Then, if it is really necessary, we can go into my room."

"If it is not too much trouble."

The J.P. shrugged his shoulders, and led the way into his own chamber, which was a plainly furnished and commonplace room. As we moved across it in the direction of the window, Holmes fell back until he and I were the last of the group. Near the foot of the bed was a small square table, on which stood a dish of oranges and a carafe of water. As we passed it, Holmes, to my unutterable astonishment, leaned over in front of me and deliberately knocked the whole thing over. The glass smashed into a thousand pieces, and the fruit rolled about into every corner of the room.

"You've done it now, Watson," said he, coolly. "A pretty mess you've made of the carpet."

I stooped in some confusion and began to pick up the fruit, understanding that for some reason my companion desired me to take the blame upon myself. The others did the same, and set the table on its legs again.

"Holloa ! " cried the Inspector, " where's he got to ? "

Holmes had disappeared.

"Wait here an instant," said young Alec Cunningham. "The fellow is off his head, in my opinion. Come with me, father, and see where he has got to ! "

HOLMES . . . LEANED OVER IN FRONT OF ME AND DELIBERATELY KNOCKED THE WHOLE THING OVER.

Illustration by Sidney Paget for the *Strand Magazine*, June, 1893.

THE TWO CUNNINGHAMS WERE BENDING OVER THE
PROSTRATE FIGURE OF SHERLOCK HOLMES . . .

Illustration by Sidney Paget for the *Strand Magazine*, June, 1893.

They rushed out of the room, leaving the Inspector,
the Colonel, and me, staring at each other.

" 'Pon my word, I am inclined to agree with Mister
Alec," said the official. " It may be the effect of this
illness, but it seems to me that——"

His words were cut short by a sudden scream of " Help !
Help ! Murder ! " With a thrill I recognized the voice
as that of my friend. I rushed madly from the room on
to the landing. The cries, which had sunk down into a
hoarse, inarticulate shouting, came from the room which
we had first visited. I dashed in, and on into the dressing-room beyond. The two Cunninghams were bending
over the prostrate figure of Sherlock Holmes, the younger
clutching his throat with both hands, while the elder
seemed to be twisting one of his wrists. In an instant
the three of us had torn them away from him, and
Holmes staggered to his feet, very pale, and evidently
greatly exhausted.

" Arrest these men, Inspector ! " he gasped.

" On what charge ? "

" That of murdering their coachman, William
Kirwan ! "

The Inspector stared about him in bewilderment.
" Oh, come now, Mr. Holmes," said he at last ; " I am
sure you don't really mean to——"

" Tut, man ; look at their faces ! " cried Holmes,
curtly.

Never, certainly, have I seen a plainer confession of
guilt upon human countenances. The older man seemed
numbed and dazed, with a heavy, sullen expression upon
his strongly marked face. The son, on the other hand,
had dropped all that jaunty, dashing style which had
characterized him, and the ferocity of a dangerous wild
beast gleamed in his dark eyes and distorted his handsome features. The Inspector said nothing, but, stepping to the door, he blew his whistle. Two of his
constables came at the call.

" I have no alternative, Mr. Cunningham," said he. " I
trust that this may all prove to be an absurd mistake ;
but you can see that—— Ah, would you ? Drop it ! "
He struck out with his hand, and a revolver, which the
younger man was in the act of cocking, clattered down
upon the floor.

" Keep that," said Holmes, quickly putting his foot
upon it. " You will find it useful at the trial. But this
is what we really wanted." He held up a little crumpled
piece of paper.

" The remainder of the sheet ? " cried the Inspector.

" Precisely."

" And where was it ? "

" Where I was sure it must be. I'll make the whole
matter clear to you presently. I think, Colonel, that you
and Watson might return now, and I will be with you
again in an hour at the furthest. The Inspector and I
must have a word with the prisoners ; but you will
certainly see me back at luncheon-time."

Sherlock Holmes was as good as his word, for about
one o'clock he rejoined us in the Colonel's smoking-room.
He was accompanied by a little, elderly gentleman, who

was introduced to me as the Mr. Acton whose house had been the scene of the original burglary.

"I wished Mr. Acton to be present while I demonstrated this small matter to you," said Holmes, "for it is natural that he should take a keen interest in the details. I am afraid, my dear Colonel, that you must regret the hour that you took in such a stormy petrel as I am."

"On the contrary," answered the Colonel, warmly, "I consider it the greatest privilege to have been permitted to study your methods of working. I confess that they quite surpass my expectations, and that I am utterly unable to account for your result. I have not yet seen the vestige of a clue."

"I am afraid that my explanation may disillusionize you, but it has always been my habit to hide none of my methods, either from my friend Watson or from anyone who might take an intelligent interest in them. But first, as I am rather shaken by the knocking about which I had in the dressing-room, I think that I shall help myself to a dash of your brandy, Colonel. My strength has been rather tried of late."

"I trust you had no more of those nervous attacks."

Sherlock Holmes laughed heartily. "We will come to that in its turn," said he. "I will lay an account of the case before you in its due order, showing you the various points which guided me in my decision. Pray interrupt me if there is any inference which is not perfectly clear to you.

"It is of the highest importance in the art of detection to be able to recognize out of a number of facts which are incidental and which vital. Otherwise your energy and **15** attention must be dissipated instead of being concentrated. Now, in this case there was not the slightest doubt in my mind from the first that the key of the whole matter must be looked for in the scrap of paper in the dead man's hand.

"Before going into this I would draw your attention to the fact that if Alec Cunningham's narrative were correct, and if the assailant after shooting William Kirwan had *instantly* fled, then it obviously could not be he who tore the paper from the dead man's hand. But if it was not he, it must have been Alec Cunningham himself, for by the time the old man had descended several servants were upon the scene. The point is a simple one, but the Inspector had overlooked it because he had started with the supposition that these county magnates had had nothing to do with the matter. Now, I make a point of never having any prejudices and of following docilely wherever fact may lead me, and so in the very first stage **16** of the investigation I found myself looking a little askance at the part which had been played by Mr. Alec Cunningham.

"And now I made a very careful examination of the corner of paper which the Inspector had submitted to us. It was at once clear to me that it formed part of a very remarkable document. Here it is. Do you not now observe something very suggestive about it?"

15 *which are incidental and which vital.* "No man, not even Holmes, could always be successful in this task," Mr. T. S. Blakeney wrote in *Sherlock Holmes: Fact or Fiction?*, "and he recognized the possibility of serious error, as in the remark: 'perhaps when a man has special knowledge and special powers like my own it rather encourages him to see a complex explanation when a simpler one is at hand' ["The Adventure of the Abbey Grange"]. Nevertheless, he was inclined to trust his intuitions rather than the surface impressions made by the data of a case—'there is nothing more deceptive than an obvious fact' ["The Boscombe Valley Mystery"]—and in a sarcastic phrase he observes, 'all my instincts are one way and all the facts are the other, and I much fear that British juries have not yet attained that pitch of intelligence when they will give the preference to my theories over Lestrade's facts' ["The Adventure of the Norwood Builder"]."

16 *wherever fact may lead me.* "Holmes keenly appreciated the great value of an open mind," Mr. George Simmons wrote in "Sherlock Holmes— The Inner Man," "and it seems that he was acquainted with [Thomas Henry] Huxley's ideas on the subject: 'Sit down before fact as a little child, be prepared to give up every preconceived notion, follow humbly and to whatever abysses nature leads, or you shall learn nothing.' "

"THE POINT IS A SIMPLE ONE . . ."

Illustration by Sidney Paget for the *Strand Magazine*, June, 1893.

17 *with tolerable confidence.* "The deduction of a man's age from his handwriting is certainly a very doubtful matter," Mr. Vernon Rendall wrote in "The Limitations of Sherlock Holmes." "I do not believe that 'in normal cases one can place a man in his true decade with tolerable confidence.' This statement is not confirmed by my experience with a host of contributors writing for two papers for many years. . . . The period at which a hand becomes fixed varies widely, but, once settled, it remains unchanged for many years, though ill-health or excitement may introduce marked changes. See R. L. Stevenson's *The Wrong Box*, ch. VI."

"By modern standards Holmes was mistaken in thinking that you can tell the age of adult writers," Mrs. Winifred Christie wrote in "Sherlock Holmes and Graphology." "But he concluded perfectly rightly that you can deduce the state of health. What he called the broken-backed appearance of the older man's writing presents two symptoms: tremulousness shows debility, and the broken up-strokes heart disease. Heart weakness is confirmed by the presence of irrelevant dots."

" It has a very irregular look," said the Colonel.

" My dear sir," cried Holmes, " there cannot be the least doubt in the world that it has been written by two persons doing alternate words. When I draw your attention to the strong t's of ' at ' and ' to ' and ask you to compare them with the weak ones of ' quarter ' and ' twelve,' you will instantly recognize the fact. A very brief analysis of those four words would enable you to say with the utmost confidence that the ' learn ' and the ' maybe ' are written in the stronger hand, and the ' what ' in the weaker."

" By Jove, it's as clear as day ! " cried the Colonel. " Why on earth should two men write a letter in such a fashion ? "

" Obviously the business was a bad one, and one of the men who distrusted the other was determined that, whatever was done, each should have an equal hand in it. Now, of the two men it is clear that the one who wrote the ' at ' and ' to ' was the ringleader."

" How do you get at that ? "

" We might deduce it from the mere character of the one hand as compared with the other. But we have more assured reasons than that for supposing it. If you examine this scrap with attention you will come to the conclusion that the man with the stronger hand wrote all his words first, leaving blanks for the other to fill up. These blanks were not always sufficient, and you can see that the second man had a squeeze to fit his ' quarter ' in between the ' at ' and the ' to,' showing that the latter were already written. The man who wrote all his words first is undoubtedly the man who planned this affair."

" Excellent ! " cried Mr. Acton.

" But very superficial," said Holmes. We come now, however, to a point which is of importance. You may not be aware that the deduction of a man's age from his writing is one which has been brought to considerable accuracy by experts. In normal cases one can place a **17** man in his true decade with tolerable confidence. I say normal cases, because ill-health and physical weakness reproduce the signs of old age, even when the invalid is a youth. In this case, looking at the bold, strong hand of

"THERE CANNOT BE THE LEAST DOUBT IN THE WORLD THAT IT HAS BEEN WRITTEN BY TWO PERSONS . . ."

Illustration by William H. Hyde for *Harper's Weekly*, June 17, 1893.

the one, and the rather broken-backed appearance of the other, which still retains its legibility, although the t's have begun to lose their crossings, we can say that the one was a young man, and the other was advanced in years without being positively decrepit."

" Excellent ! " cried Mr. Acton again.

" There is a further point, however, which is subtler and of greater interest. There is something in common between these hands. They belong to men who are blood-relatives. It may be most obvious to you in the Greek e's, but to me there are many small points which indicate **18** the same thing. I have no doubt at all that a family mannerism can be traced in these two specimens of writing. I am only, of course, giving you the leading results now of my examination of the paper. There were twenty-three other deductions which would be of more interest to experts than to you. They all tended to **19** deepen the impression upon my mind that the Cunninghams, father and son, had written this letter.

" Having got so far, my next step was, of course, to examine into the details of the crime and to see how far they would help us. I went up to the house with the Inspector, and saw all that was to be seen. The wound upon the dead man was, as I was able to determine with absolute confidence, caused by a shot from a revolver fired at a distance of something over four yards. There was no powder-blackening on the clothes. Evidently, therefore, Alec Cunningham had lied when he said that the two men were struggling when the shot was fired. Again, both father and son agreed as to the place where the man escaped into the road. At that point, however, as it happens, there is a broadish ditch, moist at the bottom. As there were no indications of boot-marks about this ditch, I was absolutely sure not only that the Cunninghams had again lied, but that there had never been any unknown man upon the scene at all.

" And now I had to consider the motive of this singular crime. To get at this I endeavoured first of all to solve the reason of the original burglary at Mr. Acton's. I understood from something which the Colonel told us that a lawsuit had been going on between you, Mr. Acton,

18 *It may be most obvious to you in the Greek e's.* "Mr. Holmes was right in detecting family mannerisms in the Greek e's," Mrs. Christie continued. "There are family writings as there are family walks and voices."

19 *which would be of more interest to experts.* That Holmes was not exaggerating in any way has been shown by Mr. John Ball, Jr., in his essay, "The Twenty-Three Deductions": "Here, then, are the twenty-three points which Sherlock Holmes noted and from which he further strengthened his case against the Cunninghams and satisfied himself completely of their guilt: 1. The quality of the paper—costly, average, or cheap. 2. The rag content of the paper, if any. 3. The probable source of the paper (from the above). 4. The quality of the ink. 5. The chemical nature of the ink. 6. The probable source of the ink (from the above). 7. The age of the writing. 8. The presence, or absence, of folds in the paper. 9. Whether the fragment had been torn from the whole, or the whole from the fragment. 10. The direction of the tear—up or down. 11. Whether the first penman was right- or left-handed. 12. Whether the second penman was right or left-handed. 13. The type of pen used. 14. Whether or not both penmen used the same writing point. 15. Whether the fragment came from a corner of a standard sheet, or was otherwise cut from a larger piece of paper. 16. The original use of the paper—notepaper, wrapping paper, or other. 17. The presence or absence of erasures. 18. The evidence, or lack of evidence, that the writing had been blotted after the first writing. 19. The evidence, or lack of evidence, that the writing had been blotted after the second writing. 20. Whether or not both penmen had used the identical ink supply. 21. The presence, or absence, of fingernail marks made by the hand which tore the paper. 22. Any evidence of scent still clinging to the paper. 23. The presence, or absence, of extraneous marks or stains on the paper. This would also include evidence of pocket-rubbing had the whole document been carried on anyone's person for any length of time."

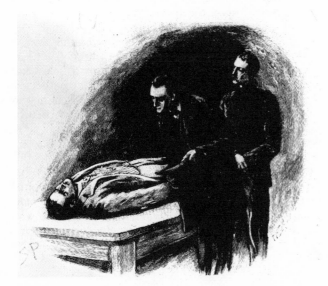

"THERE WAS NO POWDER-BLACKENING ON THE CLOTHES."

Illustration by Sidney Paget for the *Strand Magazine*, June, 1893.

and the Cunninghams. Of course, it instantly occurred to me that they had broken into your library with the intention of getting at some document which might be of importance in the case."

" Precisely so," said Mr. Acton ; " there can be no possible doubt as to their intentions. I have the clearest claim upon half their present estate, and if they could have found a single paper—which, fortunately, was in the strong box of my solicitors—they would undoubtedly have crippled our case."

" There you are ! " said Holmes, smiling. " It was a dangerous, reckless attempt, in which I seemed to trace the influence of young Alec. Having found nothing, they tried to divert suspicion by making it appear to be an ordinary burglary, to which end they carried off whatever they could lay their hands upon. That is all clear enough, but there was much that was still obscure. What I wanted above all was to get the missing part of that note. I was certain that Alec had torn it out of the dead man's hand, and almost certain that he must have thrust it into the pocket of his dressing-gown. Where else could he have put it ? The only question was whether it was still there. It was worth an effort to find out, and for that object we all went up to the house.

" The Cunninghams joined us, as you doubtless remember, outside the kitchen door. It was, of course, of the very first importance that they should not be reminded of the existence of this paper, otherwise they would naturally destroy it without delay. The Inspector was about to tell them the importance which was attached to it when, by the luckiest chance in the world, I tumbled down in a sort of fit and so changed the conversation."

" Good heavens ! " cried the Colonel, laughing. " Do you mean to say all our sympathy was wasted and your fit an imposture ? "

" Speaking professionally, it was admirably done," cried I, looking in amazement at this man who was for ever confounding me with some new phase of his astuteness.

" It is an art which is often useful," said he. " When I recovered I managed by a device, which had, perhaps, some little merit of ingenuity, to get old Cunningham to write the word ' twelve,' so that I might compare it with the ' twelve ' upon the paper."

" Oh, what an ass I have been ! " I exclaimed.

" I could see that you were commiserating with me over my weakness," said Holmes, laughing. " I was sorry to cause you the sympathetic pain which I know that you felt. We then went upstairs together, and having entered the room, and seen the dressing-gown hanging up behind the door, I contrived by upsetting a table to engage their attention for the moment and slipped back to examine the pockets. I had hardly got the paper, however, which was as I had expected, in one of them, when the two Cunninghams were on me, and would, I verily believe, have murdered me then and there but for your prompt and friendly aid. As it is, I feel that young man's grip on my throat now, and the father has twisted my wrist round in the effort to get the paper out of my hand.   They saw that I must know all about it, you see, and the sudden change from absolute security to complete despair made them perfectly desperate.

"I had a little talk with old Cunningham afterwards as to the motive of the crime.   He was tractable enough, though his son was a perfect demon, ready to blow out his own or anybody else's brains if he could have got to his revolver.   When Cunningham saw that the case against him was so strong he lost all heart, and made a clean breast of everything.   It seems that William had secretly followed his two masters on the night when they made their raid upon Mr. Acton's, and, having thus got them into his power, proceeded under threats of exposure to levy blackmail upon them.   Mister Alec, however, was a dangerous man to play games of that sort with.   It was a stroke of positive genius on his part to see in the burglary scare, which was convulsing the country-side, an opportunity of plausibly getting rid of the man whom he feared. William was decoyed up and shot ; and, had they only got the whole of the note, and paid a little more attention to detail in their accessories, it is very possible that suspicion might never have been aroused."

"And the note ?" I asked.

Sherlock Holmes placed the subjoined paper before us.

"It is very much the sort of thing that I expected," said he.   "Of course, we do not yet know what the relations may have been between Alec Cunningham, William Kirwan, and Annie Morrison.   The result shows that the trap was skilfully baited.   I am sure that you cannot fail to be delighted with the traces of heredity shown in the p's and in the tails of the g's.   The absence of the i-dots in the old man's writing is also most characteristic.   Watson, I think our quiet rest in the country has been a distinct success, and I shall certainly return, much invigorated, to Baker Street to-morrow."

Auctorial and Bibliographical Note: Conan Doyle ranked "The Reigate Squires" twelfth on his list of the "twelve best" Sherlock Holmes short stories (excluding those in the *Case-Book*).

The adventure has had a curious titular history, outlined by the late Edgar W. Smith in the second issue of the old *Baker Street Journal:* "Of all the many corruptions which make the American text of the Saga so markedly inferior to the text of the John Murray (London) editions, there is none more striking than the deliberate change of the *title* of one of the tales. Originally called 'The Adventure of the Reigate Squire' in the *Strand Magazine* for June, 1893, this story became, more appropriately, 'The Reigate Squires' in both the Newnes *Memoirs* (1894) and the Murray short-story omnibus (1928). But when it first appeared in the United States, also in June, 1893, the editors of *Harper's Weekly*, evidently fearful that the term 'squires' might affront the robust American democracy of those days, mutated the title to 'The Reigate Puzzle'—and this senseless nomenclature has been perpetuated in both the Harper *Memoirs* (1894) and the . . . Doubleday omnibus (1930)."

A small fragment of the manuscript of "The Reigate Squires" is in the possession of Mr. Adrian Conan Doyle.

24

A SCANDAL IN BOHEMIA

[Friday, May 20, to Sunday, May 22, 1887]

1 the *woman*. Many students of Holmes' life hold that Irene Adler above all other women was the one he might have loved, even *did* love. This view has been hotly contested by other students of the Canon who maintain that what Holmes actually said to Watson on this occasion was something more on the order of "She is the woman who is mixed up in this case."

2 *but admirably balanced mind*. "The truth is that emotions, however abhorrent to [Holmes] in theory, are definitely a part of him in practice," Dean Theodore C. Blegen wrote in "These Were Hidden Fires, Indeed!" "They fill much of his life. They dictate many of his characteristic actions. He is a far cry from intellect frozen in unemotional ice. . . . He is flesh and blood. He is a man of moods. He is a man of emotions."

3 *save with a gibe and a sneer*. Watson, an incurable romantic, is being a little hard on Holmes in this early description of the detective as a frigid misogynist. In many later adventures, Holmes demonstrates that his was "a great heart as well as . . . a great brain."

4 *the late Irene Adler*. Watson must have written this before July, 1891, when "A Scandal in Bohemia" appeared in the *Strand Magazine*, and many commentators have since expressed doubts that Irene Adler was "the late" at that time. On the other hand, Mr. Jerry Neal Williamson has written ("A Scandal in 'A Scandal in Bohemia' "): "The solution of Watson's reference . . . is simple. [The King of Bohemia], not trusting to Holmes' ability, and using the detective for an alibi, murdered *the* woman."

Mr. Manly Wade Wellman has concurred with this verdict ("A New Scandal in Bohemia"): "So young, so healthy, so much to live for—she could have died only by violence. Undoubtedly the ruffianly King of Bohemia, or his hired assassins, finally

I

1 TO Sherlock Holmes she is always *the* woman. I have seldom heard him mention her under any other name. In his eyes she eclipses and predominates the whole of her sex. It was not that he felt any emotion akin to love for Irene Adler. All emotions, and that one particularly, were abhorrent to his cold, **2** precise, but admirably balanced mind. He was, I take it, the most perfect reasoning and observing machine that the world has seen : but, as a lover, he would have placed himself in a false position. He never spoke of the softer **3** passions, save with a gibe and a sneer. They were admirable things for the observer—excellent for drawing the veil from men's motives and actions. But for the trained reasoner to admit such intrusions into his own delicate and finely adjusted temperament was to introduce a distracting factor which might throw a doubt upon all his mental results. Grit in a sensitive instrument, or a crack in one of his own high-power lenses, would not be more disturbing than a strong emotion in a nature such as his. And yet there was but one woman to him, and that woman **4** was the late Irene Adler, of dubious and questionable memory.

I had seen little of Holmes lately. My marriage had drifted us away from each other. My own complete happiness, and the home-centred interests which rise up around the man who first finds himself master of his own establishment, were sufficient to absorb all my attention ; **5** while Holmes, who loathed every form of society with his whole Bohemian soul, remained in our lodgings in Baker Street, buried among his old books, and alternating from week to week between cocaine and ambition, the drowsiness of the drug, and the fierce energy of his own keen nature. He was still, as ever, deeply attracted by the study of crime, and occupied his immense faculties and extraordinary powers of observation in following out those clues, and clearing up those mysteries, which had been abandoned as hopeless by the official police. From time to time I heard some vague account of his doings : of his summons to Odessa in the case of the Trepoff murder, **6** of his clearing up of the singular tragedy of the Atkinson brothers at Trincomalee, and finally of the mission which **7** he had accomplished so delicately and successfully for the reigning family of Holland. Beyond these signs of his **8** activity, however, which I merely shared with all the readers of the daily press, I knew little of my former friend and companion.

One night—it was on the 20th of March, 1888—I was **9** returning from a journey to a patient (for I had now returned to civil practice), when my way led me through **10** Baker Street. As I passed the well-remembered door, which must always be associated in my mind with my wooing, and with the dark incidents of the Study in Scarlet, I was seized with a keen desire to see Holmes again, and to know how he was employing his extraordinary powers. His rooms were brilliantly lit, and, even as I looked up, I saw his tall spare figure pass twice in a dark silhouette against the blind. He was pacing the room swiftly, eagerly, with his head sunk upon his chest, and his hands clasped behind him. To me, who knew his every mood and habit, his attitude and manner told their own story. He was at work again. He had risen out of his drug-created dreams, and was hot upon the scent of some new problem. I rang the bell, and was shown up to the chamber which had formerly been in part my own.

AS I PASSED THE WELL-REMEMBERED DOOR . . .

Watson tells us here that it "must be associated in my mind with my wooing," and some students of the Saga who believe that Watson was wedded and widowered before his meeting with Mary Morstan take this as in indication that the Mrs. Watson of the "Scandal" must have been one of Holmes' early clients. As we have seen, in Chapter 22, Miss Helen Stoner of "The Adventure of the Speckled Band," has been suggested. The photograph shown below (of No. 31, Baker Street) is from *Sherlock Holmes: A Biography*, by William S. Baring-Gould.

found and killed her for that compromising picture. Sherlock Holmes must have heard the news shortly before he slipped away unseen from the Reichenbach Fall, and we who know him cannot doubt his immediate decision to do something about it."

Perhaps this in some part accounts for the seeming relish with which Holmes referred to "the late King of Bohemia" in August, 1914 ("His Last Bow").

5 *loathed every form of society.* "The word *society* is poorly chosen," Mr. Vincent Starrett wrote in *The Private Life of Sherlock Holmes.* "What Watson—a careless writer—intended to convey was that social life offended the Bohemian soul of his companion." This is consistent with Holmes' "one of those unwelcome social summonses" in "The Adventure of the Noble Bachelor."

6 *the Trepoff murder.* For an account of this case, the reader is referred to "The Adventure of the Seven Clocks" in *The Exploits of Sherlock Holmes,* by Adrian M. Conan Doyle and John Dickson Carr.

Mr. Rolfe Boswell, browsing in the *Musgorysky Reader,* once ran across a reference to one Fyodor Fyodorovich Trepoff, 1803–1899, who was military policemaster of St. Petersburg. "I wonder," Mr. Boswell wrote, "what connection he may have had with Mr. Holmes' 'summons to Odessa in the case of the Trepoff murder'? Since Fyodor was alive after [the time] when the 'Scandal in Bohemia' was called to the Master's notice, he could not, of course, have been the *victim*—but other interpretations are possible."

7 *the singular tragedy of the Atkinson brothers at Trincomalee.* It seems highly unlikely that Holmes found it necessary to visit Ceylon, where Trincomalee was an important naval base. It is perhaps more probable that British diplomats at The Hague placed the facts before Holmes at the same time that he was accomplishing his mission for the reigning family of Holland (see below), and that Holmes cleared up the matter long-distance, making this an "armchair" case.

On the other hand, Mrs. Winifred M. Christie has noted ("On the Remarkable Explorations of Sigerson"), that Holmes in September, 1888 (*The Sign of the Four*), was a master of the subject of Buddhism in Ceylon. "We may surmise that from then onwards he felt urgently impelled to make an equally exhaustive study of Buddhism in Tibet," an urge that led him, in the years of the Great Hiatus, to indulge in the remarkable explorations of Sigerson.

Mr. George W. Welch ("The Terai Planter") is another who is sure that Holmes visited Ceylon at this time. Mr. Welch's theory is that the "Atkinson brothers" were really young Trevor and Beddoes of "The *Gloria Scott,*" and he explains many of the discrepancies in that adventure by suggesting that these two (with Trevor senior) were involved in a nefarious scheme. Holmes determined to bring the culprits to justice. "Having dealt with [the Trepoff murder at Odessa] Holmes moved East—perhaps by way of Bokhara and Samarkand—and so descended on the Terai district from the north. . . . [Young Trevor and Beddoes] eluded Holmes and fled south—throughout the length of India and then across the Palk Strait into Ceylon. . . . Holmes finally caught up with the Atkinson brothers at Trincomalee, and there settled the account between himself and two of the most cunning criminals of the nineteenth century."

8 *the reigning family of Holland.* The Dutch king was William III, 1817–1890. In 1879 he married Princess Emma of Waldeck-Pyrmont (born 1858). Wilhelmina, the only child of William and Emma, was born in 1880; ten years later she became queen on the death of her father. Emma died in 1934, forty-four years after her husband.

9 *the 20th of March 1888.* The 20th of March, 1888, was a Tuesday, and the case of "A Scandal in Bohemia," as we shall see, certainly did not open on a Tuesday. Watson's date is clearly in error, in whole or in part. Our own date for this case is *Friday, May 20, to Sunday, May 22, 1887.* However, Bell and many other commentators (Andrew, Heldenbrand, Hoff, Knox, Offord, Christopher Morley, and Wellman) accept Watson's 1888 as the year, while still others (Blakeney, Brend, Christ, Folsom, Harrison, Newton, Pattrick, Smith, and Zeisler) support 1889.

10 *I had now returned to civil practice.* How could Watson have "returned" to a type of practice which, by his own accounts, he had never engaged in before this time? His wording here is strong evidence for the San Francisco practice we have discussed earlier. The 1887 practice, as we learn in "The Red-Headed League," was in Kensington. But where in Kensington? The late Gavin Brend deduced from this adventure that it was within a two or three minutes' walk of South Kensington Station, and from "The Final Problem" he concluded that it was either 5, 6, or 8, Pelham Crescent. Miss Helen Simpson ("Medical Career and Capacities of Dr. J. H. Watson") thought that Watson would have paid "the usual price" for his Kensington practice—"three years' earnings, about £900 [$4,500] in all."

11 *threw across his case of cigars.* ". . . a smoker's act of desecration comparable with that of a wine drinker warming up his Château-Lafite in an aluminium saucepan," Colonel R. D. Sherbrooke-Walker, T.D., wrote in "Holmes, Watson and Tobacco."

12 *Just a trifle more, I fancy, Watson.* It is clear that some time has elapsed between Watson's marriage and the "Scandal." How long it takes a man to put on seven to eight pounds is a matter that varies tremendously with the individual. The change from living in Baker Street to being master of his own establishment must have been a considerable one for Watson, and it is possible that he added seven to eight pounds very quickly.

THEN HE STOOD BEFORE THE FIRE . . .

Sidney Paget's first illustration for a Sherlock Holmes story, from the *Strand Magazine*, July, 1891. Mr. Walter Klinefelter has written (*Sherlock Holmes in Portrait and Profile*) of Holmes as he appears here that "his chin is somewhat prominent; and his forehead is rather higher than the average, an effect that the artist no doubt found easy to reproduce because of the fact that the hair above Holmes' temples seems to have made a considerable recession by the time he was thirty-four, the age he had attained when he essayed to match his wits against those of *the* woman, Irene Adler. [In our view, Holmes was a year younger at the time— only thirty-three.] His cheekbones, too, are high, but his nose, though long and fairly large, has none of that beakiness which would suggest the Red Indian."

His manner was not effusive. It seldom was ; but he was glad, I think, to see me. With hardly a word spoken, but with a kindly eye, he waved me to an arm-chair, threw **11** across his case of cigars, and indicated a spirit case and a gasogene in the corner. Then he stood before the fire, and looked me over in his singular introspective fashion.

" Wedlock suits you," he remarked. " I think, Watson, that you have put on seven and a half pounds since I saw you."

" Seven," I answered.

" Indeed, I should have thought a little more. Just a **12** trifle more, I fancy, Watson. And in practice again, I observe. You did not tell me that you intended to go into **13** harness."

' Then, how do you know ? "

" I see it, I deduce it. How do I know that you have been getting yourself very wet lately, and that you have a most clumsy and careless servant girl ? "

" My dear Holmes," said I, " this is too much. You would certainly have been burned had you lived a few centuries ago. It is true that I had a country walk on Thursday and came home in a dreadful mess ; but, as I have changed my clothes, I can't imagine how you deduce **14** it. As to Mary Jane, she is incorrigible, and my wife has given her notice ; but there again I fail to see how you work it out."

He chuckled to himself and rubbed his long nervous hands together.

"It is simplicity itself," said he; "my eyes tell me that on the inside of your left shoe, just where the firelight strikes it, the leather is scored by six almost parallel cuts. Obviously they have been caused by some one who has very carelessly scraped round the edges of the sole in order to remove crusted mud from it. Hence, you see, my double deduction that you had been out in vile weather, and that you had a particularly malignant boot-slitting specimen of the London slavey. As to your practice, if a gentleman walks into my rooms smelling of iodoform, with a black mark of nitrate of silver upon his right forefinger, and a bulge on the side of his top hat to show where he has secreted his stethoscope, I must be dull indeed if I do not **15** pronounce him to be an active member of the medical profession."

I could not help laughing at the ease with which he explained his process of deduction. "When I hear you give your reasons," I remarked, "the thing always appears to me to be so ridiculously simple that I could easily do it myself, though at each successive instance of your reasoning I am baffled, until you explain your process. And yet I believe that my eyes are as good as yours."

"Quite so," he answered, lighting a cigarette, and throwing himself down into an arm-chair. "You see, but you do not observe. The distinction is clear. For example, you have frequently seen the steps which lead up from the hall to this room."

"Frequently."

"How often?"

"Well, some hundreds of times."

"Then how many are there?"

"How many! I don't know."

"Quite so! You have not observed. And yet you have seen. That is just my point. Now, I know that there are seventeen steps, because I have both seen and observed. By the way, since you are interested in these little problems, and since you are good enough to chronicle one or two of my trifling experiences, you may **16** be interested in this." He threw over a sheet of thick pink-tinted note-paper which had been lying open upon the table. "It came by the last post," said he. "Read **17** it aloud."

The note was undated, and without either signature or address.

"There will call upon you to-night, at a quarter to eight o'clock," it said, "a gentleman who desires to consult you upon a matter of the very deepest moment. Your recent services to one of the Royal Houses of Europe have shown that you are one who may safely be trusted with matters which are of an importance which can hardly be exaggerated. This account of you we have from all quarters received. Be in your chamber then at that hour, and do not take it amiss if your visitor wear a mask."

"This is indeed a mystery," I remarked. "What do you imagine that it means?"

"I have no data yet. It is a capital mistake to theorise before one has data. Insensibly one begins to twist facts

13 *You did not tell me that you intended to go into harness.*" Holmes could not possibly have made this statement at this time if "A Scandal in Bohemia" followed closely on the heels of "The Reigate Squires," as we believe that it did. It must be remembered that the "Scandal" was written *before* and not after "The Reigate Squires." Watson, having hitherto chronicled only *A Study in Scarlet* and *The Sign of the Four* naturally found it necessary to prepare his public for the fact that he was a married man at the time of the "Scandal." Hence the "wedlock suits you . . . seven and a half pounds since I saw you . . . you did not tell me that you intended to go into harness" passages are descriptions almost certainly recorded on an earlier occasion—in our view, in April, 1887, at the time of "The Reigate Squires."

14 *Mary Jane.* The implication is that the newly established Watson household could support only one servant at this time. We have seen ("The Musgrave Ritual") that Hurlstone required the services of eight maids, a cook, a butler, two footmen, and a boy. "The gardens and the stables, of course, have a separate staff." As recently as October 18, 1960, the *Financial Times* reckoned that a well-appointed English household should enjoy the services of a butler, two footmen, an odd man, a head housemaid, two other housemaids, a cook, a kitchen maid, a lady's maid, a chauffeur, and three "daily helps" (quoted from Anthony Sampson's *The Anatomy of Britain*).

15 *to show where he has secreted his stethoscope.* We must not picture Dr. Watson going with a *modern* binaural instrument in his top hat. The stethoscope of his day was monaural—simply a hollow tube of hard rubber or some similar substance, belled at one end and flanged at the other, about six inches long and weighing little more than an ounce.

16 *to chronicle one or two of my trifling experiences.* Holmes later adds: "I am lost without my Boswell." By the time of the "Scandal," then, Watson had certainly begun to *write up* some of Holmes' cases. We cannot say, however, that this limits the "Scandal" to a time later than December, 1887, when *A Study in Scarlet* was published in *Beeton's Christmas Annual*, for Watson's chronicles were certainly in manuscript form, perhaps for many months, before they were printed.

17 *"It came by the last post."* In downtown London, in Holmes' and Watson's day, there were as many as *twelve* postal deliveries a day, and in Baker Street there were six. There were no Sunday deliveries, however—if one wanted to send a message on the Sabbath, he found it necessary to hire a Commissionaire or some other special messenger.

I CAREFULLY EXAMINED THE WRITING . . .

Illustration by Sidney Paget for the *Strand Magazine*, July, 1891.

to suit theories, instead of theories to suit facts. But the note itself. What do you deduce from it ? "

I carefully examined the writing, and the paper upon which it was written.

" The man who wrote it was presumably well-to-do," I remarked, endeavouring to imitate my companion's processes. " Such paper could not be bought under half a crown a packet. It is peculiarly strong and stiff."

" Peculiar—that is the very word," said Holmes. " It is not an English paper at all. Hold it up to the light."

I did so, and saw a large *E* with a small *g*, a *P*, and a large *G* with a small *t* woven into the texture of the paper.

" What do you make of that ? " asked Holmes.

" The name of the maker, no doubt ; or his monogram, rather."

" Not at all. The *G* with the small *t* stands for ' Gesellschaft,' which is the German for ' Company.' It is a customary contraction like our ' Co.' *P*, of course, stands for ' Papier.' Now for the *Eg*. Let us glance at our

18 Continental Gazetteer." He took down a heavy brown volume from his shelves. " Eglow, Eglonitz—here we are,

19 Egria. It is in a German-speaking country—in Bohemia,

20 not far from Carlsbad. ' Remarkable as being the scene

21 of the death of Wallenstein, and for its numerous glass

22 factories and paper mills.' Ha, ha, my boy, what do you make of that ? " His eyes sparkled, and he sent up a great blue triumphant cloud from his cigarette.

---

18 *our Continental Gazetteer.* Holmes used his Continental Gazetteer again when he checked the Andaman Islands in connection with *The Sign of the Four.* It was probably the *Gazetteer of the World*, first published in 1885, a standard reference work of the time.

19 *a German-speaking country.* In point of fact, the inhabitants of Bohemia were then only about 35 percent German.

20 *not far from Carlsbad.* While "Eglow" and "Eglonitz" are not to be identified in modern reference works, Egria, more correctly, *Eger,* is undoubtedly a town in Bohemia not far from Carlsbad. Bohemia itself, a former kingdom of Europe, later a crownland of Austria, is today a province of Czechoslovakia.

21 *the death of Wallenstein.* Properly, Albrecht Wenzel Eusebius von Waldstein, 1583–1634, Duke of Friedland, Sagan, and Mecklenburg. A Bohemian general in the Thirty Years' War, he was suspected of treason and assassinated. He is the subject of a tragedy by Schiller.

22 *paper mills.'* "It takes a deal of search to find references to paper mills [in Bohemia]," the late Professor Jay Finley Christ commented in "Problems in 'A Scandal in Bohemia.' " "Maybe the king used the whole of the national output for his correspondence and other purposes."

13

"SUCH PAPER COULD NOT BE BOUGHT UNDER HALF A CROWN A PACKET."

13 in the illustration is the 1817 George III "bull-head" half-crown; *13a* the 1826 George IV half-crown, reverse only; *13b* the 1836 William IV half-crown, reverse only; *13c* the 1887 Victoria half-crown, reverse only. A half-crown, worth two shillings sixpence, or approximately 60¢ in U.S. currency at the time, would have been a considerable expenditure for writing paper in Holmes' and Watson's day. The late A. Carson Simpson, in *Numismatics in the Canon,* Part I (from which the illustrations above and right were taken), tells us that this coin "began as a gold-piece" and descended "from the quarter rose-noble, . . . known as a half-crown under Henry VIII, . . . last struck in gold by James I. It became a silver coin in 1551, contemporaneously with the silver crown, and was coined by all subsequent monarchs except Mary I and Philip and Mary." It has more Canonical references than the crown, of which perhaps the most noteworthy is the Master's anxious query in "The Adventure of the Dying Detective": "How many half-crowns?" he asks when he directs Watson to put them in his watch pocket to keep him in better balance.

"The paper was made in Bohemia," I said.

"Precisely. And the man who wrote the note is a German. Do you note the peculiar construction of the sentence—'This account of you we have from all quarters received.' A Frenchman or Russian could not have written that. It is the German who is so uncourteous to his verbs. It only remains, therefore, to discover what is wanted by this German who writes upon Bohemian paper, and prefers wearing a mask to showing his face. And here he comes, if I am not mistaken, to resolve all our doubts."

As he spoke there was the sharp sound of horses' hoofs and grating wheels against the kerb, followed by a sharp pull at the bell. Holmes whistled.

"A pair by the sound," said he. "Yes," he continued, glancing out of the window. "A nice little brougham and a pair of beauties. A hundred and fifty guineas apiece. **23** There's money in this case, Watson, if there is nothing else."

"I think that I had better go, Holmes."

"Not a bit, Doctor. Stay where you are. I am lost without my Boswell. And this promises to be interesting. **24** It would be a pity to miss it."

"But your client——"

"Never mind him. I may want your help, and so may he. Here he comes. Sit down in that arm-chair, Doctor, and give us your best attention."

A slow and heavy step, which had been heard upon the stairs and in the passage, paused immediately outside the door. Then there was a loud and authoritative tap.

"Come in!" said Holmes.

A man entered who could hardly have been less than six feet six inches in height, with the chest and limbs of a Hercules. His dress was rich with a richness which would, in England, be looked upon as akin to bad taste. Heavy bands of astrakhan were slashed across the sleeves and fronts of his double-breasted coat, while the deep blue cloak which was thrown over his shoulders was lined with flame-coloured silk, and secured at the neck with a brooch which consisted of a single flaming beryl. Boots which extended half-way up his calves, and which were trimmed at the tops with rich brown fur, completed the impression of barbaric opulence which was suggested by his whole appearance. He carried a broad-brimmed hat in his hand, while he wore across the upper part of his face, extending down past the cheek-bones, a black vizard mask, which he had apparently adjusted that very moment, for

A MAN ENTERED WHO COULD HARDLY HAVE BEEN LESS THAN SIX FEET SIX INCHES IN HEIGHT . . .

Illustration by Sidney Paget for the *Strand Magazine*, July, 1891.

23 *A hundred and fifty guineas apiece.* Say about $775 apiece in U.S. currency at the time.

24 *I am lost without my Boswell.* Holmes is of course being sarcastic at Watson's expense in this reference to James Boswell, 1740–1795, author of the *Life of Samuel Johnson*, one of the most celebrated biographies of all time. "You have degraded what should have been a course of lectures into a series of tales," Holmes complained to Watson in "The Adventure of the Copper Beeches." In "Mr. Sherlock Holmes and Dr. Samuel Johnson," Mr. Richard D. Altick has considered some of the many similarities between Johnson and Holmes, Boswell and Watson. He suggests that Watson read much in Boswell during the Afghan campaign.

13a   13b   13c

25 *"by binding you both to absolute secrecy for two years.* The case must have taken place before July, 1889, or Watson, a man of honor, could not have published his account of the "Scandal" in July, 1891.

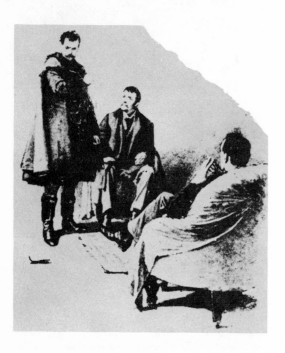

. . . WITH A GESTURE OF DESPERATION, HE TORE THE
MASK FROM HIS FACE . . .

Illustration by Sidney Paget for the *Strand Magazine*, July, 1891.

his hand was still raised to it as he entered. From the lower part of the face he appeared to be a man of strong character, with a thick, hanging lip, and a long straight chin, suggestive of resolution pushed to the length of obstinacy.

" You had my note ? " he asked, with a deep, harsh voice and a strongly marked German accent. " I told you that I would call." He looked from one to the other of us, as if uncertain which to address.

" Pray take a seat," said Holmes. " This is my friend and colleague, Dr. Watson, who is occasionally good enough to help me in my cases. Whom have I the honour to address ? "

" You may address me as the Count von Kramm, a Bohemian nobleman. I understand that this gentleman, your friend, is a man of honour and discretion, whom I may trust with a matter of the most extreme importance. If not, I should much prefer to communicate with you alone."

I rose to go, but Holmes caught me by the wrist and pushed me back into my chair. " It is both, or none," said he. " You may say before this gentleman anything which you may say to me."

The Count shrugged his broad shoulders. " Then I must begin," said he, " by binding you both to absolute **25** secrecy for two years, at the end of that time the matter will be of no importance. At present it is not too much to say that it is of such weight that it may have an influence upon European history."

" I promise," said Holmes.

" And I."

" You will excuse this mask," continued our strange visitor. " The august person who employs me wishes his agent to be unknown to you, and I may confess at once that the title by which I have just called myself is not exactly my own."

" I was aware of it," said Holmes dryly.

" The circumstances are of great delicacy, and every precaution has to be taken to quench what might grow to be an immense scandal and seriously compromise one of the reigning families of Europe. To speak plainly, the matter implicates the great House of Ormstein, hereditary kings of Bohemia."

" I was also aware of that," murmured Holmes, settling himself down in his arm-chair, and closing his eyes.

Our visitor glanced with some apparent surprise at the languid, lounging figure of the man who had been no doubt depicted to him as the most incisive reasoner, and most energetic agent in Europe. Holmes slowly re-opened his eyes, and looked impatiently at his gigantic client.

" If your Majesty would condescend to state your case," he remarked, " I should be better able to advise you."

The man sprang from his chair, and paced up and down the room in uncontrollable agitation. Then, with a gesture of desperation, he tore the mask from his face and hurled it upon the ground. " You are right," he cried, " I am the King. Why should I attempt to conceal it ? "

" Why, indeed ? " murmured Holmes. " Your Majesty had not spoken before I was aware that I was addressing

Wilhelm Gottsreich Sigismond von Ormstein, Grand Duke of Cassel-Falstein, and hereditary King of Bohemia."

"But you can understand," said our strange visitor, sitting down once more and passing his hand over his high, white forehead, "you can understand that I am not accustomed to doing such business in my own person. Yet the matter was so delicate that I could not confide it to an agent without putting myself in his power. I have come *incognito* from Prague for the purpose of consulting **26** you."

"Then, pray consult," said Holmes, shutting his eyes once more.

"The facts are briefly these: Some five years ago, during a lengthy visit to Warsaw, I made the acquaintance of the well-known adventuress Irene Adler. The name is no doubt familiar to you."

"Kindly look her up in my index, Doctor," murmured Holmes, without opening his eyes. For many years he had adopted a system of docketing all paragraphs concerning men and things, so that it was difficult to name a subject or a person on which he could not at once furnish information. In this case I found her biography sandwiched in between that of a Hebrew Rabbi and that of a **27** staff-commander who had written a monograph upon the deep-sea fishes.

26 incognito. Italian: unknown; under an assumed name, title, or character; not known or formally recognized, so as to avoid name and recognition; as a king traveling *incognito.*

27 *a Hebrew Rabbi.* Identified by Miss Ruth Berman ("On Docketing a Hebrew Rabbi") as Hermann Adler, Chief Rabbi of the United Congregations of the British Empire from 1891 to 1911, "a prominent figure in English public life."

". . . AND HEREDITARY KING OF BOHEMIA."

His coat-of-arms, shown here, is blazoned: Gules, a lion rampant queue fourchée, and renownée, argent, crowned or. The real "King of Bohemia" at the time of the "Scandal" was Franz Josef von Hapsburg, "Emperor of Austria and Apostolic King of Hungary," but it could not have been the aging (born 1830) Franz Josef who called on Holmes in Baker Street. Possibly it was his only son and heir, the Grand Duke Rudolf (he who died so mysteriously in the hunting lodge at Mayerling on January 30, 1889); this was the late Professor Jay Finley Christ's view, as it is that of Dr. Julian Wolff. Mr. T. S. Blakeney ("A Case for Identification—in Bohemia") prefers to identify Holmes' visitor as the Archduke Franz Ferdinand; Professor John B. Wolf ("Another Incubus in the Saddle") has put forward Crown Prince Wilhelm von Hohenzollern of Prussia, soon to become Wilhelm II of the German Empire; and the late Edgar W. Smith, as we have seen in Chapter 8, once made a strong case ("A Scandal in Identity") for the then Prince of Wales, Albert Edward, later King Edward VII. If Mr. Smith was correct in his identification, it is possible that Sherlock Holmes was of service to Albert Edward on no less than five occasions—in the affair of the Suicide Club, in the case of "A Scandal in Bohemia," in "The Adventure of the Beryl Coronet," at the time of *The Hound of the Baskervilles* ("At the present time, one of the most revered names in England is being besmirched by a blackmailer, and only I can stop a disastrous scandal") and in "The Adventure of the Illustrious Client." It is small wonder that Edward VII offered Holmes a knighthood ("The Adventure of the Three Garridebs").

28 *Born in New Jersey in the year 1858.* And who was the woman Dr. Watson called "Irene Adler"? Professor John B. Wolf ("Another Incubus in the Saddle") has noted that "A rumor . . . so strong . . . it cannot be denied tells us of an affair between Prince Wilhelm and an American opera singer. Since the lady's name was subsequently emblazoned in lights over the Metropolitan in New York and she was hailed as one of the first great American opera stars, good taste encourages me to hide her name even now from those who might make something of youthful indiscretions."

On the other hand, Dr. Julian Wolff ("The Adventuress of Sherlock Holmes"), noting that a celebrated actress known as "the Jersey Lily" was born in 1852 and married in 1889 (*The Columbia Encyclopedia*) or 1899 (*the Encyclopædia Britannica*), that her beauty "attracted the attention of the Prince of Wales," that she "had photographs of the Danish King and Queen" but that they had been lost or appropriated, has identified "Irene Adler" as the celebrated actress and noted beauty, Miss Lillie Langtry.

Many Sherlockians, however, would still prefer to believe that "Irene Adler" was the professional name taken by the late Clara Stephens of Trenton, New Jersey, the aunt of the late James Montgomery (for documentation, see his "Art in the Blood")":

> We never mention Aunt Clara,
> Her picture is turned to the wall,
> Though she lives on the French Riviera
> Mother says that she's dead to us all.

29 *this young person.* When one considers that Irene was at the most twenty-nine at this time, and that Holmes himself was a mere thirty-three, this superior attitude begins to look a trifle absurd.

30 *I am but thirty now."* The Grand Duke Rudolf was born in 1858; the Archduke Franz Ferdinand in 1863; Crown Prince Wilhelm von Hohenzollern in 1859; Albert Edward, the Prince of Wales, in 1841. By age alone, it should seem that the Grand Duke Rudolf comes closest to having been Holmes' visitor in May, 1887. (In fact, however, he had married in 1881.)

31 *Clotilde Lothman von Saxe-Meningen.* Professor Wolf, on his theory that the "King of Bohemia" was Crown Prince Wilhelm von Hohenzollern, points out that he was married to Princess Auguste-Victoria zu Schleswig-Holstein; Schleswig-Holstein being the *Danish* duchies of the second German reich.

"Let me see," said Holmes. "Hum! Born in New **28** Jersey in the year 1858. Contralto—hum! La Scala, hum! Prima donna Imperial Opera of Warsaw—Yes! Retired from operatic stage—ha! Living in London—quite so! Your Majesty, as I understand, became **29** entangled with this young person, wrote her some compromising letters, and is now desirous of getting those letters back."

"Precisely so. But how——"

"Was there a secret marriage?"

"None."

"No legal papers or certificates?"

"None."

"Then I fail to follow Your Majesty. If this young person should produce her letters for blackmailing or other purposes, how is she to prove their authenticity?"

"There is the writing."

"Pooh, pooh! Forgery."

"My private note-paper."

"Stolen."

"My own seal."

"Imitated."

"My photograph."

"Bought."

"We were both in the photograph."

"Oh, dear! That is very bad! Your Majesty has indeed committed an indiscretion."

"I was mad—insane."

"You have compromised yourself seriously."

"I was only Crown Prince then. I was young. I am **30** but thirty now."

"It must be recovered."

"We have tried and failed."

"Your Majesty must pay. It must be bought."

"She will not sell."

"Stolen, then."

"Five attempts have been made. Twice burglars in my pay ransacked her house. Once we diverted her luggage when she travelled. Twice she has been waylaid. There has been no result."

"No sign of it?"

"Absolutely none."

Holmes laughed. "It is quite a pretty little problem," said he.

"But a very serious one to me," returned the King, reproachfully.

"Very, indeed. And what does she propose to do with the photograph?"

"To ruin me."

"But how?"

"I am about to be married."

"So I have heard."

31 "To Clotilde Lothman von Saxe-Meningen, second daughter of the King of Scandinavia. You may know the strict principles of her family. She is herself the very soul of delicacy. A shadow of a doubt as to my conduct would bring the matter to an end."

"And Irene Adler?"

"Threatens to send them the photograph. And she will do it. I know that she will do it. You do not know her, but she has a soul of steel. She has the face of the most beautiful of women, and the mind of the most resolute of men. Rather than I should marry another woman, there are no lengths to which she would not go—none."

" You are sure that she has not sent it yet ? "

" I am sure."

" And why ? "

" Because she has said that she would send it on the day when the betrothal was publicly proclaimed. That will be next Monday."

" Oh, then, we have three days yet," said Holmes, with **32** a yawn. " That is very fortunate, as I have one or two matters of importance to look into just at present. Your Majesty will, of course, stay in London for the present ? "

" Certainly. You will find me at the Langham, under **33** the name of the Count von Kramm."

" Then I shall drop you a line to let you know how we progress."

" Pray do so. I shall be all anxiety."

" Then, as to money ? "

" You have *carte blanche*." **34**

" Absolutely ? "

" I tell you that I would give one of the provinces of my kingdom to have that photograph."

" And for present expenses ? "

The King took a heavy chamois leather bag from under his cloak, and laid it on the table.

" There are three hundred pounds in gold, and seven hundred in notes," he said.

Holmes scribbled a receipt upon a sheet of his notebook, and handed it to him.

" And mademoiselle's address ? " he asked.

" Is Briony Lodge, Serpentine Avenue, St. John's **35** Wood."

Holmes took a note of it. " One other question," said he. " Was the photograph a cabinet ? " **36**

" It was."

" Then, good night, Your Majesty, and I trust that we

"... THREE HUNDRED POUNDS IN GOLD, AND SEVEN HUNDRED IN NOTES ..."

A princely sum, equal to some $5,000 in U.S. currency at the time. The late A. Carson Simpson wrote that the "three hundred pounds in gold" may well have included the rarely seen five-pound piece (shown below)—"it would indeed have been a kingly gesture to tender sixty of these large, showy pieces."

32 *we have three days yet.*" Chronologists have found this sentence difficult to interpret: if Holmes excluded both Sunday and Monday as "working days," the interview with the King of Bohemia must have taken place on a Wednesday (Blakeney and Christ); if either, on a Thursday (Andrew, Bell, Folsom); if neither, on a Friday (Baring-Gould and Zeisler). In any case, it is difficult to see how Holmes could have made such a statement on a Tuesday (Watson and Christopher Morley). If the case began on a Wednesday or a Thursday, however, Watson's "country walk on Thursday" must have taken place as long as six or seven days before; certainly he would have "changed his clothes" in that time, and it would be far more natural for him to have said "last Thursday" or "a week ago." If, on the other hand, the case began on a Friday, Watson's walk must have taken place on the preceding day, and it would have been more natural for him to have said that he came home in a dreadful mess "yesterday." For the record, we note that Thursday, May 19, 1887, was a day on which the wind had increased "to a gale in almost all parts of our islands. . . . The weather is fine in Sweden and Germany, but squally and unsettled elsewhere. . . . Since yesterday morning rain has fallen generally. . . . Thunderstorms occurred . . . over the east of England. Temperature has fallen several degrees . . ." (weather report in the London *Times*).

33 *the Langham.* The Langham was the grandest of all London's hotels of the period: it had been visited by the Prince of Wales at its opening on June 12, 1865, and its foundation stone had been laid by the Earl of Shrewsbury on July 17, 1863. (It is now an office of the BBC.) ". . . the Langham . . . was designed by Messrs. Giles and Murray," Mr. William H. Gill wrote in "Some Notable Sherlockian Buildings." "It was built in a florid bastard Gothic and Renaissance mixture, and was by far the most magnificent hotel in the world. It covered an acre of ground, contained over 600 rooms, whilst the water supply came from an artesian well 300 feet below. Its huge dining room was packed with 2,000 diners on the day of its opening. Small wonder that it attracted the flashy King of Bohemia . . ." (It also attracted Captain Morstan, the father of Mary (*The Sign of the Four*) and the Honourable Philip Green ("The Disappearance of Lady Frances Carfax").)

34 carte blanche." French: unconditional authority or permission to do what one pleases in any given matter. From a blank paper, especially a blank form or order duly signed by one person and given to another person to fill up at his own discretion.

35 *St. John's Wood.* Then a vast colony of second-rate villas. "St. John's Wood" Mr. A. L. Shearn wrote in "The Street and the Detective," "was the one place beyond all others where gentlemen of discretion provided for their mistresses in a proper manner, establishing them in quiet villas surrounded by sheltered gardens and high walls."

36 *a cabinet?"* A photograph 3⅞" × 5½" in size, larger than the *carte de visite* and smaller than *boudoir* size. "These fancy terms do not mean anything except photograph-sizes, which the professional photographers dreamed up," Magistrate S. Tupper Bigelow commented in his *Irregular Anglo-American Glossary of More or Less Unfamiliar Words, Terms and Phrases in the Sherlock Holmes Saga.*

37 *the two crimes which I have elsewhere recorded.* Watson refers to *A Study in Scarlet* and *The Sign of the Four;* it must be remembered that the "Scandal" was his third *published* Holmes adventure.

38 *a bijou villa.* A bijou is a jewel or a trinket, but the word is also used figuratively, as here.

39 *Chubb lock.* A patented lock of English manufacture, with tumblers, the invention of Charles Chubb. The date of Chubb's birth is not known, but he died May 16, 1845.

"... A DRUNKEN-LOOKING GROOM, ILL-KEMPT AND SIDE-WHISKERED WITH AN INFLAMED FACE AND DISREPUTABLE CLOTHES, ..."

Illustration by Sidney Paget for the *Strand Magazine,* July, 1891.

shall soon have some good news for you. And good night, Watson," he added, as the wheels of the Royal brougham rolled down the street. "If you will be good enough to call to-morrow afternoon, at three o'clock, I should like to chat this little matter over with you."

II

At three o'clock precisely I was at Baker Street, but Holmes had not yet returned. The landlady informed me that he had left the house shortly after eight o'clock in the morning. I sat down beside the fire, however, with the intention of awaiting him, however long he might be. I was already deeply interested in his inquiry, for, though it was surrounded by none of the grim and strange features which were associated with the two crimes which **37** I have elsewhere recorded, still, the nature of the case and the exalted station of his client gave it a character of its own. Indeed, apart from the nature of the investigation which my friend had on hand, there was something in his masterly grasp of a situation, and his keen, incisive reasoning, which made it a pleasure to me to study his system of work, and to follow the quick, subtle methods by which he disentangled the most inextricable mysteries. So accustomed was I to his invariable success that the very possibility of his failing had ceased to enter into my head.

It was close upon four before the door opened, and a drunken-looking groom, ill-kempt and side-whiskered with an inflamed face and disreputable clothes, walked into the room. Accustomed as I was to my friend's amazing powers in the use of disguises, I had to look three times before I was certain that it was indeed he. With a nod he vanished into the bedroom, whence he emerged in five minutes tweed-suited and respectable, as of old. Putting his hands into his pockets, he stretched out his legs in front of the fire, and laughed heartily for some minutes.

"Well, really!" he cried, and then he choked; and laughed again until he was obliged to lie back, limp and helpless, in the chair.

"What is it?"

"It's quite too funny. I am sure you could never guess how I employed my morning, or what I ended by doing."

"I can't imagine. I suppose that you have been watching the habits, and perhaps the house, of Miss Irene Adler."

"Quite so, but the sequel was rather unusual. I will tell you, however. I left the house a little after eight o'clock this morning, in the character of a groom out of work. There is a wonderful sympathy and freemasonry among horsey men. Be one of them, and you will know all that there is to know. I soon found Briony Lodge. **38** It is a bijou villa, with a garden at the back, but built out **39** in front right up to the road, two stories. Chubb lock to the door. Large sitting-room on the right side, well furnished, with long windows almost to the floor, and those preposterous English window fasteners which a child could open. Behind there was nothing remarkable, save that the passage window could be reached from the top of the coach-house. I walked round it and examined it closely from every point of view, but without noting anything else of interest.

"I then lounged down the street, and found, as I expected, that there was a mews in a lane which runs down by one wall of the garden. I lent the ostlers a hand in rubbing down their horses, and I received in exchange twopence, a glass of half-and-half, two fills of shag tobacco **40-41** and as much information as I could desire about Miss Adler, to say nothing of half a dozen other people in the neighbourhood in whom I was not in the least interested, but whose biographies I was compelled to listen to."

"And what of Irene Adler ?" I asked.

"Oh, she has turned all the men's heads down in that part. She is the daintiest thing under a bonnet on this planet. So say the Serpentine Mews, to a man. She lives quietly, sings at concerts, drives out at five every day, and returns at seven sharp for dinner. Seldom goes out at other times, except when she sings. Has only one male

"SHE IS THE DAINTEST THING UNDER A BONNET ON THIS PLANET."

Bonnets and hats, 1848–1896, as drawn by Marjorie and C. H. B. Quennell for *A History of Everyday Things in England, Vol. IV, 1851 to 1914.*

40 *a glass of half-and-half.* A mixture of two malt liquors, usually porter and ale, but sometimes old and new ale. Holmes drank the glass of half-and-half in his character of "a drunken-looking groom," and again, in "The Adventure of the Blue Carbuncle," he drinks a glass of beer with the innkeeper Windigate; but he appears to have drunk malt liquors principally in the early years, and then only in situations which required it, not out of any special fondness.

41 *two fills of shag tobacco.* Says Joseph Fune in *A Paper: of Tobacco. Treating of the Rise, Progress, Pleasures, and Advantages of Smoking,* London: Chapman and Hall, 1839, p. 129: "Shag tobacco has obtained its distinctive name from its being so finely cut that the filaments appear like so much 'shag'—the old name for short and matted wool or hair. It is manufactured of the strongest and very worst kind of leaf, and is chiefly consumed by the poorer classes. Persons of a nervous temperament, who take little exercise, ought to particularly avoid smoking this kind of tobacco, as its frequent use is apt to induce paralytic afflictions. The present price of shag is fourpence [about 8¢ U.S. at the time of our adventure]."

Mr. John L. Hicks adds ("No Fire Without Some Smoke"): "It is reported that on one occasion when William Makepeace Thackeray visited his friend Alfred Tennyson, they smoked shag tobacco while praising Miss Barrett's poetry. . . . Great Victorians, both early and late, had a preference for shag as an aid to ratiocination." (It is thought by many Sherlockians that the detective acquired his lifelong liking for shag at this time.)

"... OF THE INNER TEMPLE."

The Inner and the Middle Temple (shown above in a photograph by G. F. Allen, from *The Second Country Life Picture Book of London;* London: Country Life, Ltd., 1953) belong respectively to legal societies of the same name and constitute two of the Inns of Court; they are buildings occupied by barristers and law students. Wrote the poet Spenser: "... Those bricky towers, / The which of Thames' broad aged back doe ride, / Where now the studious lawyers have their bowers, / There whilom went the Temple knights to ride, / Till they decayed through pride."

42 *'first to Gross and Hankey's.* Presumably a jewelry establishment, where Norton would buy the ring—although it is not listed in the directories of the day.

43 *the church of St. Monica in the Edgware Road.* A correspondent, Mr. T. L. A. Daintith of Coulsdon, Surrey, suggests that the marriage of Irene Adler to Godfrey Norton was a Catholic one: "To my mind, Holmes' whole description of the affair is that of an Anglican suddenly caught up in a nuptial Mass." He suggests that the ceremony took place in St. Agnes' Church, Cricklewood, just off the Edgware Road at the southern end:

visitor, but a good deal of him. He is dark, handsome, and dashing; never calls less than once a day, and often twice. He is a Mr. Godfrey Norton, of the Inner Temple. See the advantages of a cabman as a confidant. They had driven him home a dozen times from Serpentine Mews, and knew all about him. When I had listened to all that they had to tell, I began to walk up and down near Briony Lodge once more, and to think over my plan of campaign.

"This Godfrey Norton was evidently an important factor in the matter. He was a lawyer. That sounded ominous. What was the relation between them, and what the object of his repeated visits? Was she his client, his friend, or his mistress? If the former, she had probably transferred the photograph to his keeping. If the latter, it was less likely. On the issue of this question depended whether I should continue my work at Briony Lodge, or turn my attention to the gentleman's chambers in the Temple. It was a delicate point, and it widened the field of my inquiry. I fear that I bore you with these details, but I have to let you see my little difficulties, if you are to understand the situation."

"I am following you closely," I answered.

"I was still balancing the matter in my mind when a hansom cab drove up to Briony Lodge, and a gentleman sprang out. He was a remarkably handsome man, dark, aquiline, and moustached—evidently the man of whom I had heard. He appeared to be in a great hurry, shouted to the cabman to wait, and brushed past the maid who opened the door with the air of a man who was thoroughly at home.

"He was in the house about half an hour, and I could catch glimpses of him, in the windows of the sitting-room, pacing up and down, talking excitedly and waving his arms. Of her I could see nothing. Presently he emerged, looking even more flurried than before. As he stepped up to the cab, he pulled a gold watch from his pocket and looked at it earnestly. 'Drive like the devil,' **42** he shouted, 'first to Gross and Hankey's in Regent Street, and then to the church of St. Monica in the Edgware **43** Road. Half a guinea if you do it in twenty minutes!'

"Away they went, and I was just wondering whether I should not do well to follow them, when up the lane **44** came a neat little landau, the coachman with his coat only half buttoned, and his tie under his ear, while all the tags of his harness were sticking out of the buckles. It hadn't pulled up before she shot out of the hall door and into it. I only caught a glimpse of her at the moment, but she was a lovely woman, with a face that a man might die for.

"'The Church of St. Monica, John,' she cried, 'and half a sovereign if you reach it in twenty minutes.'

"This was quite too good to lose, Watson. I was just balancing whether I should run for it, or whether I should perch behind her landau, when a cab came through the street. The driver looked twice at such a shabby fare; but I jumped in before he could object. 'The Church of St. Monica,' said I, 'and half a sovereign if you reach it in twenty minutes.' It was twenty-five minutes to twelve, **45** and of course it was clear enough what was in the wind.

"My cabby drove fast. I don't think I ever drove faster, but the others were there before us. The cab and the landau with their steaming horses were in front of the door when I arrived. I paid the man and hurried into the church. There was not a soul there save the two whom I had followed, and a surpliced clergyman, who seemed to be expostulating with them. They were all three standing in a knot in front of the altar. I lounged up the side aisle like any other idler who has dropped into a church. Suddenly, to my surprise, the three at the altar faced round to me, and Godfrey Norton came running as hard as he could towards me.

"'Thank God!' he cried. 'You'll do. Come! Come!'

"'What then?' I asked.

"The only Catholic church actually *in* the Edgware Road is at the far end and no cab could possibly do the journey [to Regent Street and then to the far end of the Edgware Road] in twenty minutes. In any case the name St. Agnes is far more likely to be a disguise for St. Monica than is St. Anthony, the farther church."

The Edgware Road, embracing a part of the old Watling Street, runs diagonally from the Marble Arch to Cricklewood with scarcely a curve, and thence to Hendon, Edgware, and St. Albans. It is one of the broadest thoroughfares leading out of London, and has often been called "The Gateway to the Northwest."

44 *landau.* A two-seated, four-wheeled, covered vehicle with a top divided into two sections, the

" ' . . . IN REGENT STREET . . .' "

Regent Street, nearly a mile in length, leads to the north from Pall Mall. Built by John Nash between 1816 and 1820, it takes its name from the Prince Regent, afterward George IV. It was on Regent Street that Holmes and Watson essayed in vain to trail the trailers of Sir Henry Baskerville. Here, too, Holmes was severely beaten by the minions of the lustful Gruner ("The Adventure of the Illustrious Client").

" 'HALF A GUINEA IF YOU DO IT IN TWENTY MINUTES!' "

Shown here is the 1787 gold half-guinea ("spade") of George III. The half-guinea, worth ten shillings sixpence, or some $2.62 in U.S. currency at the time, is worth sixpence (12¢) more than the half-sovereign Irene Adler (and Sherlock Holmes) were later to pay for the drive to St. Monica's. Norton's trip, however, involved *two* stops—the first at Gross and Hankey's.

back section of which could be let down or thrown back, while the front section could be removed or left stationary; named for the German town in which it was first manufactured.

45 *it was clear enough what was in the wind.* Clear to Holmes, perhaps, but the first of a series of very puzzling statements, nonetheless. By English law, a marriage once had to be solemnized before noon. But in May, 1886—almost two years before Watson's date for the "Scandal"—the legal period had been extended from 8:00 A.M. to 3:00 P.M. Surely Godfrey Norton, as a lawyer, should have known this.

46 *in search of a best man.* The facts are these: in English law, two witnesses are always required, and neither of these makes, much less mumbles, any responses; marriage ceremonies in a Catholic church or a church of the Church of England are not over with in an instant; no clergyman would marry a spinister and a bachelor if there were any "informality" about the license. In addition, as the Reverend Otis R. Rice has pointed out in "Clergymen in the Canon," "since the banns had obviously not been published, as required by canon law, the only legal procedure would be a special license from the Archbishop of Canterbury at Lambeth Palace." The opportunities for speculation are abundant here, and students of the Saga

" ' Come, man, come, only three minutes, or it won't be legal.'

" I was half dragged up to the altar, and before I knew where I was, I found myself mumbling responses which were whispered in my ear, and vouching for things of which I knew nothing, and generally assisting in the secure tying up of Irene Adler, spinster, to Godfrey Norton, bachelor. It was all done in an instant, and there was the gentleman thanking me on the one side and the lady on the other, while the clergyman beamed on me in front. It was the most preposterous position in which I ever found myself in my life, and it was the thought of it that started me laughing just now. It seems that there had been some informality about their licence, that the clergyman absolutely refused to marry them without a witness of some sort, and that my lucky appearance saved the bridegroom from having to sally out into the streets in search **46** of a best man. The bride gave me a sovereign, and I mean to wear it on my watch-chain in memory of the occasion."

" This is a very unexpected turn of affairs," said I; " and what then ? "

" Well, I found my plans very seriously menaced. It looked as if the pair might take an immediate departure, and so necessitate very prompt and energetic measures on my part. At the church door, however, they separated, he driving back to the Temple, and she to her own house. **47** ' I shall drive out in the Park at five as usual,' she said as she left him. I heard no more. They drove away in

"THE BRIDE GAVE ME A SOVEREIGN . . ."

19 above is the 1871 sovereign of Victoria; *19a* the 1830 sovereign of George IV, reverse only. This standard gold coin of twenty shillings ($5.00) "had its origin as a large, thin hammered coin of Henry VII, which derived its name from the effigy of the enthroned ruler on its obverse. . . . It was struck by succeeding rulers until Charles I concentrated on the unit as his 20/–unit; the Commonwealth followed suit. Charles II introduced the guinea, the basic gold coin until George III's 1816 currency reform, which established the sovereign as the unit for as long as gold was regularly coined. The last sovereign regularly coined in London was in 1917, but colonial mints continued to strike them in later years. . . . Numismatists will all unite in the hope that [Holmes] neither had [the sovereign given to him by Irene] pierced nor had a loop soldered onto it . . . , but had a ring put around it with the loop attached to the ring, so as not to impair the coin."—A Carson Simpson, *Numismatics in the Canon*, Part I.

". . . BEFORE I KNEW WHERE I WAS, I FOUND MYSELF MUMBLING RESPONSES . . ."

Illustration by Sidney Paget for the *Strand Magazine*, July, 1891.

different directions, and I went off to make my own arrangements."

" Which are ? "

" Some cold beef and a glass of beer," he answered, ringing the bell. " I have been too busy to think of food, and I am likely to be busier still this evening. By the way, Doctor, I shall want your co-operation."

" I shall be delighted."

" You don't mind breaking the law ? "

" Not in the least."

" Nor running a chance of arrest ? "

" Not in a good cause."

" Oh, the cause is excellent ! "

" Then I am your man."

" I was sure that I might rely on you."

" But what is it you wish ? "

" When Mrs. Turner has brought in the tray I will make it clear to you. Now," he said, as he turned hungrily on the simple fare that our landlady had provided, " I must discuss it while I eat, for I have not much **48** time. It is nearly five now. In two hours we must be on the scene of action. Miss Irene, or Madame, rather, returns from her drive at seven. We must be at Briony Lodge to meet her."

" And what then ? "

" You must leave that to me. I have already arranged what is to occur. There is only one point on which I must insist. You must not interfere, come what may. You understand ? "

" I am to be neutral ? "

" To do nothing whatever. There will probably be some small unpleasantness. Do not join in it. It will end in my being conveyed into the house. Four or five minutes afterwards the sitting-room window will open. You are to station yourself close to that open window."

" Yes."

" You are to watch me, for I will be visible to you."

" Yes."

" And when I raise my hand—so—you will throw into the room what I give you to throw, and will, at the same time, raise the cry of fire. You quite follow me ? "

" Entirely."

" It is nothing very formidable," he said, taking a long cigar-shaped roll from his pocket. " It is an ordinary plumber's smoke rocket, fitted with a cap at either end to **49** make it self-lighting. Your task is confined to that. When you raise your cry of fire, it will be taken up by quite a number of people. You may then walk to the end of the street, and I will rejoin you in ten minutes. I hope that I have made myself clear ? "

" I am to remain neutral, to get near the window, to watch you, and, at the signal, to throw in this object, then to raise the cry of fire, and to await you at the corner of the street."

" Precisely."

" Then you may entirely rely on me."

" That is excellent. I think perhaps it is almost time that I prepared for the new rôle I have to play."

He disappeared into his bedroom, and returned in a

have taken full advantage of them. The late Page Heldenbrand, in "The Duplicity of Sherlock Holmes," has suggested that Norton was none other than Colonel Sebastian Moran, whom we shall meet in "The Adventure of the Empty House." And Dr. Ebbe C. and Mrs. Phoebe M. Hoff, in "The Affair at St. Monica's," have suggested that the "minister" was an imposter, as was "Godfrey Norton." The former was Shinwell Johnson, whom we shall meet in "The Adventure of the Illustrious Client," and the latter was an adventurer known in international circles as "Slick" or "The Gent." The entire affair had been arranged and paid for by the King of Bohemia's affianced, Clotilde.

47 *in the Park.* Possibly Hyde Park but more likely the nearer Regent's Park, on the road called the Outer Circle, surrounding the Inner Circle with its fine chestnut trees.

48 *the simple fare that our landlady had provided.* Another riddle for readers. In every other Holmes adventure, the name of the landlady, when it is given, is Mrs. *Hudson.* Did Mrs. Hudson, as landlady, provide the fare and Mrs. Turner—the maid, perhaps, or a crony of Mrs. Hudson's, or her sister—merely serve it? Or is this simple absent-mindedness or forgetfulness on the part of Holmes (thinking, perhaps, of the principal in another case he was following at the time) or Watson (thinking, perhaps, of a patient waiting in his consulting room)? A short-lived marriage between Mrs. Hudson and a Mr. Turner has also been postulated. And there have been other explanations: Mrs. Turner "was only substituting for her cousin," the late Page Heldenbrand wrote in "Another Bohemian Scandal," "and was quickly to disappear from the Baker Street scene when Martha Hudson returned from a short visit and resumed her reign over the premises"; she was, it seems, that same Martha Turner who met Jack the Ripper on the night of August 7, 1888, in front of George Yard Buildings, a group of squalid tenements just off High Street in Whitechapel. Mr. Russell McLauchlin, on the other hand, has suggested ("What Price Baker Street?") that Mrs. Turner presided over a house in Baker Street used by Holmes as an "accommodation address"—perhaps one of those "five small refuges" he mentions in "The Adventure of Black Peter"—while Holmes and Watson actually lived in Mrs. Hudson's house in Gloucester Place; one street west of Baker Street, it, too, runs north from Portman Square to the Marylebone Road.

49 *an ordinary plumber's smoke rocket.* Once used by plumbers to test for leaks in drains.

50 *Mr. John Hare*. John Hare, 1844–1921, knighted in 1907, was an eminent English actor and manager of the day, and a close friend of W. S. Gilbert's. At the St. James's Theater between 1879 and 1888 he established his popularity in "character" and "men of the world" roles.

HE . . . RETURNED IN A FEW MINUTES IN THE CHARACTER OF AN AMIABLE AND SIMPLE-MINDED NONCONFORMIST CLERGYMAN.

Illustration by Sidney Paget for the *Strand Magazine*, July, 1891. "Holmes' calculated choice of the role of the *Nonconformist* rather than that of an *Anglican* divine was beneath [his] usual standard of courage and forthrightness," the Reverend Otis R. Rice wrote in "Clergymen in the Canon." "For he well knew that to impersonate a minister of the Established Church was a legal offense. In passing, it is interesting to note that the uniform of the Nonconformist padre of the day was as distinctive as was the dog-collar and black rabat of an Anglican. . . . All in all, this is not one of Mr. Holmes,' most ethical performances, no matter how important the ends may have seemed to him. . . . Holmes turns up again impersonating a man of the cloth in 'The Final Problem.' "

few minutes in the character of an amiable and simple-minded Nonconformist clergyman. His broad black hat, his baggy trousers, his white tie, his sympathetic smile, and general look of peering and benevolent curiosity, were **50** such as Mr. John Hare alone could have equalled. It was not merely that Holmes changed his costume. His expression, his manner, his very soul seemed to vary with every fresh part that he assumed. The stage lost a fine actor, even as science lost an acute reasoner, when he became a specialist in crime.

It was a quarter past six when we left Baker Street, and it still wanted ten minutes to the hour when we found **51** ourselves in Serpentine Avenue. It was already dusk, and the lamps were just being lighted as we paced up and down in front of Briony Lodge, waiting for the coming of its occupant. The house was just such as I had pictured it from Sherlock Holmes's succinct description, but the locality appeared to be less private than I expected. On the contrary, for a small street in a quiet neighbourhood, it was remarkably animated. There was a group of shabbily-dressed men smoking and laughing in a corner, a scissors-grinder with his wheel, two guardsmen who were flirting with a nurse-girl, and several well-dressed young men who were lounging up and down with cigars in their mouths.

"You see," remarked Holmes, as we paced to and fro in front of the house, "this marriage rather simplifies matters. The photograph becomes a double-edged weapon now. The chances are that she would be as averse to its being seen by Mr. Godfrey Norton, as our client is to its coming to the eyes of his Princess. Now the question is—Where are we to find the photograph?"

"Where, indeed?"

"It is most unlikely that she carries it about with her. It is cabinet size. Too large for easy concealment about a woman's dress. She knows that the King is capable of having her waylaid and searched. Two attempts of the sort have already been made. We may take it then that she does not carry it about with her."

"Where, then?"

"Her banker or her lawyer. There is that double possibility. But I am inclined to think neither. Women are naturally secretive, and they like to do their own secreting. Why should she hand it over to anyone else? She could trust her own guardianship, but she could not tell what indirect or political influence might be brought to bear upon a business man. Besides, remember that she had resolved to use it within a few days. It must be where she can lay her hands upon it. It must be in her own house."

"But it has twice been burgled."

"Pshaw! They did not know how to look."

"But how will you look?"

"I will not look."

"What then?"

"I will get her to show me."

"But she will refuse."

"She will not be able to. But I hear the rumble of wheels. It is her carriage. Now carry out my orders to the letter."

As he spoke, the gleam of the sidelights of a carriage came round the curve of the avenue. It was a smart little landau which rattled up to the door of Briony Lodge. As it pulled up, one of the loafing men at the corner dashed forward to open the door in the hope of earning a copper, but was elbowed away by another loafer who had rushed up with the same intention. A fierce quarrel broke out, which was increased by the two guardsmen, who took sides with one of the loungers, and by the scissors-grinder, who was equally hot upon the other side. A blow was struck, and in an instant the lady, who had stepped from her carriage, was the centre of a little knot of flushed and struggling men who struck savagely at each other with their fists and sticks. Holmes dashed into the crowd to protect the lady ; but just as he reached her, he gave a cry and dropped to the ground, with the blood running freely down his face. At his fall the guardsmen took to their heels in one direction and the loungers in the other, while a number of better dressed people who had watched the scuffle without taking part in it, crowded in to help the lady and to attend to the injured man. Irene Adler, as I will still call her, had hurried up the steps ; but she stood at the top with her superb figure outlined against the lights of the hall, looking back into the street.

" Is the poor gentleman much hurt ? " she asked.

" He is dead," cried several voices.

" No, no, there's life in him," shouted another. " But he'll be gone before you can get him to hospital."

" He's a brave fellow," said a woman. " They would have had the lady's purse and watch if it hadn't been for him. They were a gang, and a rough one, too. Ah, he's breathing now."

" He can't lie in the street. May we bring him in, marm ? "

" Surely. Bring him into the sitting-room. There is a comfortable sofa. This way, please ! "

Slowly and solemnly he was borne into Briony Lodge, and laid out in the principal room, while I still observed the proceedings from my post by the window.. The lamps had been lit, but the blinds had not been drawn, so that I could see Holmes as he lay upon the couch. I do not know whether he was seized with compunction at that moment for the part he was playing, but I know that I never felt more heartily ashamed of myself in my life than when I saw the beautiful creature against whom I was conspiring, or the grace and kindliness with which she waited upon the injured man. And yet it would be the blackest treachery to Holmes to draw back now from the part which he had entrusted to me. I hardened my heart and took the smoke rocket from under my ulster. After all, I thought, we are not injuring her. We are but preventing her from injuring another.

Holmes had sat up upon the couch, and I saw him motion like a man who is in want of air. A maid rushed across and threw open the window. At the same instant I saw him raise his hand, and at the signal I tossed my rocket into the room with a cry of " Fire." The word was no sooner out of my mouth than the whole crowd of spectators, well dressed and ill—gentlemen, ostlers, and servant maids—joined in a general shriek of " Fire."

51 *It was already dusk.* In fairness to Watson's "March," this *does* sound like the latter part of that month, when sunset in London falls between 5:39 P.M. (on the 1st) and 6:30 P.M. (on the 31st). But the late Professor Jay Finley Christ long ago pointed out that this date, by Watson's account, would be March 21st, and that every March 21st on a weekday in any year falls within Lent, when the tradition of the Church frowns upon marriage, except in certain "emergencies, a subject upon which speculation is perilous." In our view, the adventure took place in *May;* in Watson's execrable handwriting, this word could easily be mistaken, by the typesetter, for "March."

. . . HE GAVE A CRY AND DROPPED TO THE GROUND . . .

Illustration by Sidney Paget for the *Strand Magazine,* July, 1891.

52 *Thick clouds of smoke curled through the room.* Despite Holmes' earlier gibes at Dupin in *A Study in Scarlet,* he was not above taking a leaf from the book of that "very inferior fellow" (see Edgar Allan Poe's "The Purloined Letter"). We have seen (*A Study in Scarlet,* Note 62) that Conan Doyle's own opinion of Poe was a high one. "As the creator I've praised to satiety / Poe's Monsieur Dupin, his skill and variety / . . . [Holmes], the created, would scoff and would sneer, / Where I, the creator, would bow and revere . . .", Conan Doyle once explained in a verse "To an Undiscerning Critic." "It is impossible to read [this passage in "A Scandal in Bohemia"], Mr. Vincent Starrett wrote in his *Private Life of Sherlock Holmes,* "without a bit of wonderment; what if the ingenious rocket had missed fire? Would not the whole planned sequence have gone agley? But Watson, although he may have faltered, never actually blundered. Holmes knew the qualities of his assistant. No case was ever lost by Watson's failure."

53 *They were all engaged for the evening.* It is apparent that even in these early days Holmes was able to summon up very quickly a large number of trained assistants. In our view, Holmes in this instance recruited his troupe from among his fellow-players in the days when he had been an actor in Shakespearean repertory.

54 *the Arnsworth Castle business.* For the account of a "Darlington Substitution Scandal," but hardly that mentioned by Holmes here, see "The Adventure of the Wax Gamblers," in *The Exploits of Sherlock Holmes.* For an account of "the Arnsworth Castle business," see "The Adventure of the Red Widow" in the same volume.

52 Thick clouds of smoke curled through the room, and out at the open window. I caught a glimpse of rushing figures, and a moment later the voice of Holmes from within, assuring them that it was a false alarm. Slipping through the shouting crowd I made my way to the corner of the street, and in ten minutes was rejoiced to find my friend's arm in mine, and to get away from the scene of the uproar. He walked swiftly and in silence for some few minutes, until we had turned down one of the quiet streets which lead towards the Edgware Road.

"You did it very nicely, Doctor," he remarked. "Nothing could have been better. It is all right."

"You have the photograph!"

"I know where it is."

"And how did you find out?"

"She showed me, as I told you that she would."

"I am still in the dark."

"I do not wish to make a mystery," said he, laughing. "The matter was perfectly simple. You, of course, saw that every one in the street was an accomplice. They were **53** all engaged for the evening."

"I guessed as much."

"Then, when the row broke out, I had a little moist red paint in the palm of my hand. I rushed forward, fell down, clapped my hand to my face, and became a piteous spectacle. It is an old trick."

"That also I could fathom."

"Then they carried me in. She was bound to have me in. What else could she do? And into her sitting-room which was the very room which I suspected. It lay between that and her bedroom, and I was determined to see which. They laid me on a couch, I motioned for air, they were compelled to open the window and you had your chance."

"How did that help you?"

"It was all-important. When a woman thinks that her house is on fire, her instinct is at once to rush to the thing which she values most. It is a perfectly overpowering impulse, and I have more than once taken advantage of it. In the case of the Darlington Substitution Scandal it was of use to me, and also in the Arnsworth Castle busi- **54** ness. A married woman grabs at her baby—an unmarried one reaches for her jewel box. Now it was clear to me that our lady of to-day had nothing in the house more precious to her than what we are in quest of. She would rush to secure it. The alarm of fire was admirably done. The smoke and shouting was enough to shake nerves of steel. She responded beautifully. The photograph is in a recess behind a sliding panel just above the right bell-pull. She was there in an instant, and I caught a glimpse of it as she half drew it out. When I cried out that it was a false alarm, she replaced it, glanced at the rocket, rushed from the room, and I have not seen her since. I rose, and, making my excuses, escaped from the house, I hesitated whether to attempt to secure the photograph at once; but the coachman had come in, and as he was watching me narrowly, it seemed safer to wait. A little over-precipitance may ruin all."

"And now?" I asked.

" Our quest is practically finished.   I shall call with the King to-morrow, and with you, if you care to come with us.   We will be shown into the sitting-room to wait for the lady, but it is probable that when she comes she may find neither us nor the photograph.   It might be a satisfaction to His Majesty to regain it with his own hands."

" And when will you call ? "

" At eight in the morning.   She will not be up, so that we shall have a clear field.   Besides, we must be prompt, for this marriage may mean a complete change in her life and habits.   I must wire to the King without delay."

We had reached Baker Street, and had stopped at the door.   He was searching his pockets for the key, when some one passing said :

" Good night, Mister Sherlock Holmes."

There were several people on the pavement at the time, but the greeting appeared to come from a slim youth in an ulster who had hurried by.

" I've heard that voice before," said Holmes, staring down the dimly lit street.   " Now, I wonder who the deuce that could have been."

III

I slept at Baker Street that night, and we were engaged upon our toast and coffee when the King of Bohemia rushed into the room.

" You have really got it ! " he cried, grasping Sherlock Holmes by either shoulder, and looking eagerly into his face.

" Not yet."

" But you have hopes ? "

" I have hopes."

" Then, come.   I am all impatience to be gone."

" We must have a cab."

" No, my brougham is waiting."

" Then that will simplify matters."

We descended, and started off once more for Briony Lodge.

" Irene Adler is married," remarked Holmes.

" Married ! When ? "

" Yesterday."

" But to whom ? "

" To an English lawyer named Norton."

" But she could not love him ? "

" I am in hopes that she does."

" And why in hopes ? "

" Because it would spare Your Majesty all fear of future annoyance.   If the lady loves her husband, she does not love Your Majesty.   If she does not love Your Majesty there is no reason why she should interfere with Your Majesty's plan."

" It is true.   And yet——! Well ! I wish she had been of my own station ! What a queen she would have made ! " He relapsed into a moody silence which was not broken until we drew up in Serpentine Avenue.

The door of Briony Lodge was open, and an elderly woman stood upon the steps.   She watched us with a sardonic eye as we stepped from the brougham.

" Mr. Sherlock Holmes, I believe ? " said she.

" I am Mr. Holmes," answered my companion, looking

"GOOD NIGHT, MISTER SHERLOCK HOLMES."

Illustration by Sidney Paget for the *Strand Magazine*, July, 1891. Mr. James Edward Holroyd has noted that the drawing "gives additional support to the majority view that 221B was on the west side of Baker Street. We know that Irene was walking from north to south, because she had followed [Holmes and Watson] from St. John's Wood. The house is shown on her right, or west, side."

55 *Male costume is nothing new to me.* We know that Irene Adler was an operatic soprano, and Mr. Guy Warrack, in *Sherlock Holmes and Music*, has correctly concluded that "It is therefore to the male-impersonation contralto roles that we must look in trying to reconstruct Irene Adler's operatic career." He cites several such roles: Gluck's *Orfeo*, Arsace in Rossini's *Sermiramide*, Maffo Orsini in Donizetti's *Lucrezia Borgia* and "the page Urbain in Meyerbeer's *Les Hugenots*," an opera Holmes attended after he had successfully concluded the adventure of *The Hound of the Baskervilles*. Mr. Anthony Boucher had added the roles of Siébel in Gounod's *Faust*, Stéphano in his *Roméo et Juliette*, and Pieretto in Donizetti's *Linda di Chamounix* ("The Records of Baker Street").

at her with a questioning and rather startled gaze.

" Indeed ! My mistress told me that you were likely to call. She left this morning with her husband, by the 5.15 train from Charing Cross, for the Continent."

" What ! " Sherlock Holmes staggered back, white with chagrin and surprise. " Do you mean that she has left England ? "

" Never to return."

" And the papers ? " asked the King hoarsely. " All is lost."

" We shall see." He pushed past the servant, and rushed into the drawing-room, followed by the King and myself. The furniture was scattered about in every direction, with dismantled shelves, and open drawers, as if the lady had hurriedly ransacked them before her flight. Holmes rushed at the bell-pull, tore back a small sliding shutter, and, plunging in his hand, pulled out a photograph and a letter. The photograph was of Irene Adler herself in evening dress, the letter was superscribed to " Sherlock Holmes, Esq. To be left till called for." My friend tore it open and we all three read it together. It was dated at midnight of the preceding night, and ran in this way :—

" MY DEAR MR. SHERLOCK HOLMES,—You really did it very well. You took me in completely. Until after the alarm of fire, I had not a suspicion. But then, when I found how I had betrayed myself, I began to think. I had been warned against you months ago. I had been told that if the King employed an agent, it would certainly be you. And your address had been given me. Yet, with all this, you made me reveal what you wanted to know. Even after I became suspicious, I found it hard to think evil of such a dear, kind old clergyman. But, you know, I have been trained as an actress myself. Male **55** costume is nothing new to me. I often take advantage of the freedom which it gives. I sent John, the coachman, to watch you, ran upstairs, got into my walking clothes, as I call them, and came down just as you departed.

" Well, I followed you to your door, and so made sure that I was really an object of interest to the celebrated Mr. Sherlock Holmes. Then I, rather imprudently, wished you good night, and started for the Temple to see my husband.

" We both thought the best resource was flight when pursued by so formidable an antagonist ; so you will find the nest empty when you call to-morrow. As to the photograph, your client may rest in peace. I love and am loved by a better man than he. The King may do what he will without hindrance from one whom he has cruelly wronged. I keep it only to safeguard myself, and to preserve a weapon which will always secure me from any steps which he might take in the future. I leave a photograph which he might care to possess ; and I remain, dear Mr. Sherlock Holmes, very truly yours,

" IRENE NORTON, *née* ADLER."

" What a woman—oh, what a woman ! " cried the King

of Bohemia, when we had all three read this epistle. "Did I not tell you how quick and resolute she was? Would she not have made an admirable queen? Is it not a pity she was not on my level?"

"From what I have seen of the lady, she seems, indeed, to be on a very different level to Your Majesty," said Holmes, coldly. "I am sorry that I have not been able to bring Your Majesty's business to a more successful conclusion."

"On the contrary, my dear sir," cried the King. "Nothing could be more successful. I know that her word is inviolate. The photograph is now as safe as if it were in the fire."

"I am glad to hear Your Majesty say so."

"I am immensely indebted to you. Pray tell me in what way I can reward you. This ring——" He slipped an emerald snake ring from his finger and held it out upon the palm of his hand.

56

"Your Majesty has something which I should value even more highly," said Holmes.

"You have but to name it."

"This photograph!"

The King stared at him in amazement.

"Irene's photograph!" he cried. "Certainly, if you wish it."

"I thank Your Majesty. Then there is no more to be done in the matter. I have the honour to wish you a very good morning." He bowed, and, turning away without observing the hand which the King had stretched out to him, he set off in my company for his chambers.

And that was how a great scandal threatened to affect the kingdom of Bohemia, and how the best plans of Mr. Sherlock Holmes were beaten by a woman's wit. He used to make merry over the cleverness of women, but I have not heard him do it of late. And when he speaks of Irene Adler, or when he refers to her photograph, it is always under the honourable title of *the* woman.

56 *held it out upon the palm of his hand.* Although the offer of the emerald snake ring met with a blunt refusal, Holmes later allowed himself to accept a snuff-box of old gold with a great amethyst in the center of the lid as a token of the King's appreciation ("A Case of Identity").

"THIS PHOTOGRAPH!"

Illustration by Sidney Paget for the *Strand Magazine,* July, 1891. "Those who are sentimentally inclined seize on the fact that Holmes asked the King of Bohemia for [Irene Adler's] photograph as evidence of attachment," Dr. Richard Asher wrote in "Holmes and the Fair Sex." "Is it not patently obvious that Holmes, having been deceived by her skill in disguising herself, wanted the photograph to add to his records to make sure that he would recognize her if she ever crossed his path again . . . ?"

Auctorial and Bibliographical Note: Conan Doyle ranked "A Scandal in Bohemia" fifth on his list of the "twelve best" short stories, excluding those in the *Case-Book;* the readers of the *Observer* ranked it sixth on their list of the best Sherlock Holmes short stories and novels. The original manuscript, consisting of thirty folio pages, the thirtieth of which is signed "A. Conan Doyle, 2 Upper Wimpole Street, London, W.", is now in the Library of the University of Texas at Austin, a presentation of Mr. Frederic A. Dannay. The first separate edition of this first of the short stories, a great rarity, is now thought to have been the small brochure illustrated here: No. 13 in the Handy Classic Series, published by the Optimus Printing Company of New York in 1895.

25

THE MAN WITH THE TWISTED LIP

[Saturday, June 18, to Sunday, June 19, 1887]

1 *the Theological College of St. George's.* Watson would naturally disguise the true name of a College whose principal had a brother "much addicted to opium." Could "St. George's" have been the Roman Catholic Missionary College of St. Joseph?

2 *De Quincey's.* Thomas de Quincey, 1785–1859, English essayist. The opium habit overcame him for a time and inspired his *Confessions of an English Opium-Eater*, first published in the *London Magazine* in 1821.

3 *June, '89.* Watson's "June" is accepted by all chronologists and commentators, his "'89" by all except your editor, who places the adventure in the June of 1887.

4 *like birds to a lighthouse.* Mr. John D. Beirle has pointed out ("The Curious Incident of the Drive Through Middlesex and Surrey") that this comment "surely does not agree with what we know to be the character of Mary Morstan Watson."

ISA WHITNEY, brother of the late Elias Whitney, **1** D.D., Principal of the Theological College of St. George's, was much addicted to opium. The habit grew upon him, as I understand, from some foolish freak **2** when he was at college, for having read De Quincey's description of his dreams and sensations, he had drenched his tobacco with laudanum in an attempt to produce the same effects. He found, as so many more have done, that the practice is easier to attain than to get rid of, and for many years he continued to be a slave to the drug, an object of mingled horror and pity to his friends and relatives. I can see him now, with yellow, pasty face, drooping lids and pin-point pupils, all huddled in a chair, the wreck and ruin of a noble man.

3 One night—it was in June, '89—there came a ring to my bell, about the hour when a man gives his first yawn, and glances at the clock. I sat up in my chair, and my wife laid her needlework down in her lap and made a little face of disappointment.

" A patient ! " said she. " You'll have to go out."

I groaned, for I was newly come back from a weary day.

We heard the door open, a few hurried words, and then quick steps upon the linoleum. Our own door flew open, and a lady, clad in some dark-coloured stuff with a black veil, entered the room.

" You will excuse my calling so late," she began, and then, suddenly losing her self-control, she ran forward, threw her arms about my wife's neck, and sobbed upon her shoulder. " Oh ! I'm in such trouble ! " she cried ; " I do so want a little help."

" Why," said my wife, pulling up her veil, " it is Kate Whitney. How you startled me, Kate ! I had not an idea who you were when you came in."

" I didn't know what to do, so I came straight to you." That was always the way. Folk who were in grief came **4** to my wife like birds to a lighthouse.

" It was very sweet of you to come. Now, you must have some wine and water, and sit here comfortably and tell us all about it. Or should you rather that I sent James **5** off to bed ? "

" Oh, no, no. I want the Doctor's advice and help too. It's about Isa. He has not been home for two days. I am so frightened about him ! "

It was not the first time that she had spoken to us of her husband's trouble, to me as a doctor, to my wife as an old friend and school companion. We soothed and comforted her by such words as we could find. Did she know where her husband was ? Was it possible that we could bring him back to her ?

It seemed that it was. She had the surest information that of late he had, when the fit was on him, made use of an opium den in the furthest east of the City. Hitherto his orgies had always been confined to one day, and he had come back, twitching and shattered, in the evening. But now the spell had been upon him eight-and-forty hours, and he lay there, doubtless, among the dregs of the docks, breathing in the poison or sleeping off the effects. There he was to be found, she was sure of it, at the " Bar of Gold," in Upper Swandam Lane. But what was she to do ? How could she, a young and timid woman, make her way into such a place, and pluck her husband out from among the ruffians who surrounded him ?

There was the case, and of course there was but one way out of it. Might I not escort her to this place ? And, then, as a second thought, why should she come at all ? I was Isa Whitney's medical adviser, and as such I had influence over him. I could manage it better if I were alone. I promised her on my word that I would send him home in a cab within two hours if he were indeed at the address which she had given me. And so in ten minutes I had left my arm-chair and cheery sitting-room behind me, and was speeding eastward in a hansom on a strange errand, as it seemed to me at the time, though the future only could show how strange it was to be.

But there was no great difficulty in the first stage of my adventure. Upper Swandam Lane is a vile alley lurking behind the high wharves which line the north side of the river to the east of London Bridge. Between a slop shop **6-7** and a gin shop, approached by a steep flight of steps leading down to a black gap like the mouth of a cave, I found the den of which I was in search. Ordering my cab to wait, I passed down the steps, worn hollow in the centre by the ceaseless tread of drunken feet, and by the light of a flickering oil lamp above the door I found the latch and made my way into a long, low room, thick and heavy with the brown opium smoke, and terraced with wooden berths, like the forecastle of an emigrant ship.

Through the gloom one could dimly catch a glimpse of bodies lying in strange fantastic poses, bowed shoulders, bent knees, heads thrown back and chins pointing upwards, with here and there a dark, lack-lustre eye turned upon the new-comer. Out of the black shadows there glimmered little red circles of light, now bright, now faint, as the burning poison waxed or waned in the bowls of the metal pipes. The most lay silent, but some muttered to

5 *James*. We have previously noted one explanation for John Watson's wife calling him "James": that his middle name was Hamish, the Gaelic for James. The late H. W. Bell dismissed "James" as a mere typographical error. Mr. John Ball, Jr., has suggested that Watson's scribbled "John" could be misread as "James" by the typographer ("Early Days in Baker Street"). Christopher Morley ascribed the James to forgetfulness on the part of Mrs. Watson and even went so far as to suggest that this slip may eventually have led to a separation of the Watsons ("Was Sherlock Holmes an American?"). Mr. Giles Playfair argued that Watson deliberately falsified the records by having his wife refer to him as "James" (to avoid a possible libel action), but later threw in the cabby's name "John" as a clue to the true authorship of the story ("John and James"). Said Mr. T. S. Blakeney: "Composite authorship may generally be attributed to historical writings, irrespective of whether the original record was the work of the putative author or of another person of the same name; and the suggestion arises that the 'James' Watson spoken of [here] may be one of these editors" (*Sherlock Holmes: Fact or Fiction?*). The possibility that Watson's name was really James, whereas he chose for some unspecified reason to write as John H. has been advanced by Mr. J. S. Coltart in "The Watsons." James was the name of Watson's bull pup, says Mr. Ralph A. Ashton ("The Fourth Occupant, or The Room with the Twisted Tongue"); "James" was Watson's stepson, a view that depends on the doctor's marriage to Mrs. Forrester rather than to Mary Watson, as well as dating "The Man with the Twisted Lip." *after The Sign of the Four* (A. Carson Simpson, "It Must Have Been Two Other Fellows"); James was a playful reference to Watson's role as Holmes' Boswell—James Boswell (Dr. Ebbe Curtis Hoff, "The Adventure of John and Mary"); "There must have been a former husband—James by name" (Arthur K. Akers, "Who Was Mrs. Watson's First Husband?"). Finally, a new and startling hypotheses to account for the confusion—that there were *two* Watsons, John and James; that John died prematurely (shortly after the adventure of "The Reigate Squires"); and that James, seizing a good opportunity, thereupon masqueraded as his elder brother—has been provided by Mr. Bliss Austin in "What Son Was Watson?" (When we recall that Conan Doyle named Watson for his friend James Watson, the slip of the pen is understandable.)

6 *to the east of London Bridge*. The structure Holmes and Watson knew is the bridge on which work started in March, 1824. The first stone was laid on June 15, 1825, the tenth anniversary of the battle of Waterloo. On August 1, 1831, the completed work was opened to the public by William IV and Queen Adelaide.

There is, or was, no "Upper Swandam Lane" in the great city of London, and there is no "vile alley" on the north side of the river, east of London Bridge, which would be accessible to Watson's cab (almost the whole of the area is taken up by the Billingsgate Fish Market). Most commentators have selected Lower Thames Street, which stretches parallel to the Thames from London Bridge to All Hallows by the Tower of London. Mr. C. E. C. Townsend, on the other hand, concluded in his essay, "The Bar of Gold," that the opium den was "situated somewhere in the 200 yards of Wapping High Street that lie between Wapping Station and the bend where it joins Garnet Street." Mr. Alan Wilson ("Where Was the 'Bar of Gold'?") discarded Watson's "east of London Bridge" entirely and settled on No. 22 *Upper* Thames Street, to the *west* of London Bridge. The late H. W. Bell ("Three Identifications") was forced to resort to *crossing the river*. There, on the Surrey side, to the east of London Bridge, he found Stoney Lane, an alley leading into Tooley Street, with houses at the lower end overlooking the river; this he identified as "Upper Swandam Lane."

7 *a slop shop.* A small store selling clothing and other articles to sailors.

8 *"Of Friday, June 19."* But June 19, 1889, was a *Wednesday* (as Isa Whitney thought it was), and the late Professor Jay Finley Christ accepted Wednesday, June 19, 1889, as the beginning of the case. Mr. Bell and Dr. Zeisler, however, both held that Watson's "Friday" was correct, and consequently were forced to discard his "19" (Bell for June 14th, Zeisler for June 21st). Another possible emendation would be to read "July" for "June," for in 1889 July 19th *did* fall on a Friday. Certainly Watson is in error about his "Friday": *or* his "June" *or* his "19" *or* his " '89." One or more of them *must* be wrong. In our view, the day was *Saturday, June 18, 1887.* Watson, in telling Whitney that it was "June 19" at "nearly eleven" on the Saturday night, made the not unnatural mistake of giving the next day's date.

themselves, and others talked together in a strange, low, monotonous voice, their conversation coming in gushes, and then suddenly tailing off into silence, each mumbling out his own thoughts, and paying little heed to the words of his neighbour. At the further end was a small brazier of burning charcoal, beside which on a three-legged wooden stool there sat a tall, thin old man, with his jaw resting upon his two fists, and his elbows upon his knees, staring into the fire.

As I entered, a sallow Malay attendant had hurried up with a pipe for me and a supply of the drug, beckoning me to an empty berth.

"Thank you, I have not come to stay," said I. "There is a friend of mine here, Mr. Isa Whitney, and I wish to speak with him."

There was a movement and an exclamation from my right, and, peering through the gloom, I saw Whitney, pale, haggard, and unkempt, staring out at me.

"My God! It's Watson," said he. He was in a pitiable state of reaction, with every nerve in a twitter. "I say, Watson, what o'clock is it?"

"Nearly eleven."

"Of what day?"

8   "Of Friday, June 19."

"Good heavens! I thought it was Wednesday. It *is* Wednesday. What d'you want to frighten a chap for?" He sank his face on to his arms, and began to sob in a high treble key.

"I tell you that it is Friday, man. Your wife has been waiting this two days for you. You should be ashamed of yourself!"

"So I am. But you've got mixed, Watson, for I have only been here a few hours, three pipes, four pipes—I forget how many. But I'll go home with you. I wouldn't frighten Kate—poor little Kate. Give me your hand! Have you a cab?"

"Yes, I have one waiting."

"Then I shall go in it. But I must owe something.

. . . THERE SAT A TALL, THIN OLD MAN, WITH HIS JAW RESTING UPON HIS TWO FISTS, AND HIS ELBOWS UPON HIS KNEES, STARING INTO THE FIRE.

Illustration by Sidney Paget for the *Strand Magazine*, December, 1891.

Find what I owe, Watson.   I am all off colour.   I can do nothing for myself."

I walked down the narrow passage between the double row of sleepers, holding my breath to keep out the vile, stupefying fumes of the drug, and looking about for the manager.   As I passed the tall man who sat by the brazier I felt a sudden pluck at my skirt, and a low voice whispered, " Walk past me, and then look back at me."   The words fell quite distinctly upon my ear.   I glanced down. They could only have come from the old man at my side, and yet he sat now as absorbed as ever, very thin, very wrinkled, bent with age, an opium pipe dangling down from between his knees, as though it had dropped in sheer lassitude from his fingers.   I took two steps forward and looked back.   It took all my self-control to prevent me from breaking out into a cry of astonishment.   He had turned his back so that none could see him but I.   His form had filled out, his wrinkles were gone, the dull eyes had regained their fire, and there, sitting by the fire, and grinning at my surprise, was none other than Sherlock Holmes.   He made a slight motion to me to approach him, and instantly, as he turned his face half round to the company once more, subsided into a doddering, loose-lipped senility.

" Holmes ! " I whispered, " what on earth are you doing in this den ? "

" As low as you can," he answered, " I have excellent ears.   If you would have the great kindness to get rid of that sottish friend of yours, I should be exceedingly glad to have a little talk with you."

" I have a cab outside."

" Then pray send him home in it.   You may safely trust him, for he appears to be too limp to get into any mischief.   I should recommend you also to send a note by the cabman to your wife to say that you have thrown in your lot with me.   If you will wait outside, I shall be with **9** you in five minutes."

It was difficult to refuse any of Sherlock Holmes' requests, for they were always so exceedingly definite, and put forward with such an air of mastery.   I felt, however, that when Whitney was once confined in the cab, my mission was practically accomplished ; and for the rest, I could not wish anything better than to be associated with my friend in one of those singular adventures which were the normal condition of his existence. In a few minutes I had written my note, paid Whitney's bill, led him out to the cab, and seen him driven through the darkness.   In a very short time a decrepit figure had emerged from the opium den, and I was walking down the street with Sherlock Holmes.   For two streets he shuffled along with a bent back and an uncertain foot.   Then, glancing quickly round, he straightened himself out and burst into a hearty fit of laughter.

" I suppose, Watson," said he, ' that you imagine that I have added opium-smoking to cocaine injections and all the other little weaknesses on which you have favoured me with your medical views."

" I was certainly surprised to find you there."

" But not more so than I to find you."

Illustration by Sidney Paget for the *Strand Magazine*, December, 1891.

9 *to say that you have thrown in your lot with me.* In the view of the late Clifton R. Andrew ("What Happened to Watson's Married Life After June 14, 1889?"), Watson's marriage to the Mrs. Watson of "The Man with the Twisted Lip" was ended, not by her death, but by divorce. ". . . if the treatment accorded Mrs. Watson by the doctor in deference to Holmes' cajolery . . . wasn't the straw that broke the camel's back, I am most badly mistaken. Mrs. Watson's self-respect was given too stiff a jolt that time. When Watson finally did return home from his expedition, I am afraid there was a scene. I suppose it was something like this: 'Well, John (or James)—and my heart is breaking when I say this—I think we have reached the parting of our ways. It is all too evident that your friendship with Mr. Sherlock Holmes transcends your love for me and your home. Last night was the climax. How could you run off with Mr. Holmes and leave me to care for Kate Whitney, alone? Poor dear, she was so distraught, and we were waiting for your return and then that cabman gave me your note. Yes, this is the end—I have seen it coming this last year or so. I can't take the place of Mr. Holmes and his strange adventures. Let's face it, James (or John) and go our separate ways. Maybe we'll both be happier. I'm sure *you* will!' "

10 *"Near Lee, in Kent.* Lee is a residential suburb seven miles' drive from London—as Watson later states—along the Old Kent Road. Lee is no longer in Kent: in 1906 it became a part of the metropolitan borough of Lewisham. At Lee, in Popham House, lived Mr. John Scott Eccles, whom we will meet in "The Adventure of Wisteria Lodge."

" I came to find a friend."

" And I to find an enemy ! "

" An enemy ? "

" Yes, one of my natural enemies, or, shall I say, my natural prey.   Briefly, Watson, I am in the midst of a very remarkable inquiry, and I have hoped to find a clue in the incoherent ramblings of these sots, as I have done before now.   Had I been recognized in that den my life would not have been worth an hour's purchase, for I have used it before now for my own purposes, and the rascally Lascar who runs it has sworn vengeance upon me.   There is a trap-door at the back of that building, near the corner of Paul's Wharf, which could tell some strange tales of what has passed through it upon the moonless nights."

" What ! You do not mean bodies ? "

" Aye, bodies, Watson.   We should be rich men if we had a thousand pounds for every poor devil who has been done to death in that den.   It is the vilest murder-trap on the whole river-side, and I fear Neville St. Clair has entered it never to leave it more.   But our trap should be here ! "   He put his two forefingers between his teeth and whistled shrilly, a signal which was answered by a similar whistle from the distance, followed shortly by the rattle of wheels and the clink of horse's hoofs.

" Now, Watson," said Holmes, as a tall dog-cart dashed up through the gloom, throwing out two golden tunnels of yellow light from its side-lanterns, " you'll come with me, won't you ? "

" If I can be of use."

" Oh, a trusty comrade is always of use.   And a chronicler still more so.   My room at the Cedars is a double-bedded one."

" The Cedars ? "

" Yes ; that is Mr. St. Clair's house.   I am staying there while I conduct the inquiry."

" Where is it, then ? "

10   " Near Lee, in Kent.   We have a seven-mile drive before us."

" But I am all in the dark."

"IT IS THE VILEST MURDER-TRAP ON THE WHOLE RIVER-SIDE . . ."

There is, in fact, a Paul's Wharf (*shown at right*) which lies *west* of London Bridge on the north side of the Thames about midway between Blackfriars and Southwark Bridges, and is therefore discarded as a clue to the location of the "Bar of Gold" by all except Mr. Alan Wilson, who writes: "Halfway down Upper Thames Street is a small alley called Trig Lane. Farther on is another called Paul's Pier Wharf, and yet farther on another entitled Castle Barnard's Wharf. Behind these, on the river, are Paul's Wharf and East Paul's Wharf. It follows, then, that since the Bar of Gold backed on to the corner of Paul's Wharf, and Paul's Wharf is found behind Upper Thames Street (Upper Swandam Lane), we should be able to find the opium den lying between Trig Lane and Castle Barnard Wharf."

" Of course you are. You'll know all about it presently. Jump up here ! All right, John, we shall not
need you. Here's half-a-crown. Look out for me to-
morrow about eleven. Give her her head ! So long,
then ! "

He flicked the horse with his whip, and we dashed away
through the endless succession of sombre and deserted
streets, which widened gradually, until we were flying
across a broad balustraded bridge, with the murky river
flowing sluggishly beneath us. Beyond lay another broad
wilderness of bricks and mortar, its silence broken only
by the heavy, regular footfall of the policeman, or the
songs and shouts of some belated party of revellers. A
dull wrack was drifting slowly across the sky, and a star
or two twinkled dimly here and there through the rifts of
the clouds. Holmes drove in silence, with his head
sunk upon his breast, and the air of a man who is lost in
thought, whilst I sat beside him curious to learn what this
new quest might be which seemed to tax his powers so
sorely, and yet afraid to break in upon the current of his
thoughts. We had driven several miles, and were beginning to get to the fringe of the belt of suburban villas,
when he shook himself, shrugged his shoulders, and lit
up his pipe with the air of a man who has satisfied himself
that he is acting for the best.

" You have a grand gift of silence, Watson," said he.
" It makes you quite invaluable as a companion. 'Pon
my word, it is a great thing for me to have someone to
talk to, for my own thoughts are not over-pleasant. I
was wondering what I should say to this dear little woman
to-night when she meets me at the door."

" You forget that I know nothing about it."

" I shall just have time to tell you the facts of the case
before we get to Lee. It seems absurdly simple, and yet,
somehow, I can get nothing to go upon. There's plenty
of thread, no doubt, but I can't get the end of it in my
hand. Now, I'll state the case clearly and concisely to
you, Watson, and maybe you may see a spark where all is
dark to me."

" Proceed, then."

" Some years ago—to be definite, in May, 1884—there
came to Lee a gentleman, Neville St. Clair by name, who
appeared to have plenty of money. He took a large villa,
laid out the grounds very nicely, and lived generally in
good style. By degrees he made friends in the neighbourhood, and in 1887 he married the daughter of a local
brewer, by whom he has now had two children. He had **11**
no occupation, but was interested in several companies,
and went into town as a rule in the morning, returning by
the 5.14 from Cannon Street every night. Mr. St. Clair **12**
is now 37 years of age, is a man of temperate habits, a
good husband, a very affectionate father, and a man who is
popular with all who know him. I may add that his
whole debts at the present moment, as far as we have been
able to ascertain, amount to £88 10s., while he has £220
standing to his credit in the Capital and Counties Bank. **13**
There is no reason, therefore, to think that money troubles
have been weighing upon his mind.

" Last Monday Mr. Neville St. Clair went into town

HE FLICKED THE HORSE WITH HIS WHIP . . .

Illustration by Sidney Paget for the *Strand Magazine*, December, 1891.

11 *by whom he has now had two children.* Here,
admittedly, is a statement which, if allowed to
stand, would date "The Man with the Twisted
Lip" in 1889, as Watson said. As the late Dr.
Ernest Bloomfield Zeisler pointed out, in his
Baker Street Chronology, if the "boy had been
conceived in accordance with the propriety of the
Victorian times in which it occurred, and had also
been born after the conventional period of gesta-
tion, he would have been about twenty and a half
months old [in 1889], an age at which [a gift of
small bricks—see below] would have been appropriate."

12 *Cannon Street.* Cannon Street Station, extending from Dowgate Hill nearly to Bush Lane, was
constructed between 1864 and 1866, when the
former South Eastern Railway extended its lines
from London Bridge to Cannon Street and on to
Charing Cross. The station was designed by Mr.
John Hawkshaw, F.R.S., assisted by Sir J. W.
Barry. No less than 27 million bricks were used in
the erection of the arches under the station, the
length of which is 687 feet, the width 202 feet, and
the total height 120 feet.

13 *£88 10s., while he has £220 standing to his
credit in the Capital and Counties Bank.* St. Clair
owed the equivalent of $442.50, had $1,100 in the
Capital and Counties Bank. This, as we learn in
"The Adventure of the Priory School," was
Holmes' own bank.

"... FRESNO STREET, WHICH BRANCHES OUT OF UPPER
SWANDAM LANE ..."

Fresno Street is another false name. But, if Mr.
Alan Wilson is correct in his identification of
"Upper Swandam Lane" as Upper Thames Street,
"Fresno Street ... must lead off Upper Thames
Street at the Blackfriars end. It must also have
been on the north side of the street as a band of
policemen were coming down it on the way to
their beat [see above]. Between Blackfriars and
Paul's Pier Wharf (our farthest limit) there is,
however, only one street, and that is the small road
called Bennett's Hill, which leads from Queen Victoria Street to Upper Thames Street. This narrow
road enters Upper Thames Street at a point almost
exactly opposite No. 22 [Mr. Wilson's choice for
the building that housed the Bar of Gold, shown in
the photograph above]. ... Mrs. St. Clair reached
the bottom of Bennett's Hill (Fresno Street) and
as she turned left into Upper Thames Street she
heard a cry and, looking up, saw her husband staring out of a second-floor window at No. 22 ..."
Mr. Bell (still on the Surrey side of the Thames)
identified "Fresno Street" as Pickle Herring Street
and its continuation, Shad Thames.

rather earlier than usual, remarking before he started that
he had two important commissions to perform, and that
he would bring his little boy home a box of bricks. Now,
by the merest chance his wife received a telegram upon
this same Monday, very shortly after his departure, to the
effect that a small parcel of considerable value which she
had been expecting was waiting for her at the offices of
14 the Aberdeen Shipping Company. Now, if you are well
up in your London, you will know that the office of the
company is in Fresno Street, which branches out of Upper
Swandam Lane, where you found me to-night. Mrs. St.
Clair had her lunch, started for the City, did some shopping, proceeded to the company's office, got her packet,
and found herself exactly at 4.35 walking through Swandam Lane on her way back to the station. Have you
followed me so far ? "

" It is very clear."

" If you remember, Monday was an exceedingly hot
15 day, and Mrs. St. Clair walked slowly, glancing about
in the hope of seeing a cab, as she did not like the neighbourhood in which she found herself. While she walked
in this way down Swandam Lane she suddenly heard an
ejaculation or cry, and was struck cold to see her husband
looking down at her, and, as it seemed to her, beckoning
to her from a second-floor window. The window was
open, and she distinctly saw his face, which she describes
as being terribly agitated. He waved his hands frantically to her, and then vanished from the window so suddenly
that it seemed to her that he had been plucked back by
some irresistible force from behind. One singular point
which struck her quick feminine eye was that, although
he wore some dark coat, such as he had started to town
in, he had on neither collar nor necktie.

" Convinced that something was amiss with him, she
rushed down the steps—for the house was none other
than the opium den in which you found me to-night—
and, running through the front room, she attempted to
ascend the stairs which led to the first floor. At the foot
of the stairs, however, she met this Lascar scoundrel, of
whom I have spoken, who thrust her back, and, aided by
a Dane, who acts as assistant there, pushed her out into
the street. Filled with the most maddening doubts and
fears, she rushed down the lane, and, by rare good fortune,
met, in Fresno Street, a number of constables with an
inspector, all on their way to their beat. The inspector
and two men accompanied her back, and, in spite of the
continued resistance of the proprietor, they made their
way to the room in which Mr. St. Clair had last been seen.
There was no sign of him there. In fact, in the whole of
that floor there was no one to be found, save a crippled
wretch of hideous aspect, who, it seems, made his home
there. Both he and the Lascar stoutly swore that no one
else had been in the front room during that afternoon.
So determined was their denial that the inspector was
staggered, and had almost come to believe that Mrs. St.
Clair had been deluded when, with a cry, she sprang at a
small deal box which lay upon the table, and tore the lid
from it. Out there fell a cascade of children's bricks. It
was the toy which he had promised to bring home.

" This discovery, and the evident confusion which the cripple showed, made the inspector realize that the matter was serious. The rooms were carefully examined, and results all pointed to an abominable crime. The front room was plainly furnished as a sitting-room, and led into a small bedroom, which looked out upon the back of one of the wharves. Between the wharf and the bedroom window is a narrow strip, which is dry at low tide, but is covered at high tide with at least four and a half feet of water. The bedroom window was a broad one, and opened from below. On examination traces of blood were to be seen upon the window-sill, and several scattered drops were visible upon the wooden floor of the bedroom. Thrust away behind a curtain in the front room were all the clothes of Mr. Neville St. Clair, with the exception of his coat. His boots, his socks, his hat, and his watch—all were there. There were no signs of violence upon any of these garments, and there were no other traces of Mr. Neville St. Clair. Out of the window he must apparently have gone, for no other exit could be discovered, and the ominous blood-stains upon the sill gave little promise that he could save himself by swimming, for the tide was at its very highest at the moment of the tragedy.   **16**

" And now as to the villains who seemed to be immediately implicated in the matter. The Lascar was known to be a man of the vilest antecedents, but as by Mrs. St. Clair's story he was known to have been at the foot of the stair within a few seconds of her husband's appearance at the window, he could hardly have been more than an accessory to the crime. His defence was one of absolute ignorance, and he protested that he had no knowledge as to the doings of Hugh Boone, his lodger, and that he could not account in any way for the presence of the missing gentleman's clothes.

14 *the Aberdeen Shipping Company.* "There was an Aberdeen Steam Navigation Company, with offices at No. 102, Queen Victoria Street," the late H. W. Bell wrote in "Three Identifications." "But unless we are prepared to accept the equation: Cannon Street + East Cheap = Upper Swandam Lane, that 'vile alley,' and we are able to credit Neville St. Clair with the notable fear of hurling his jacket from East Cheap over the tops of the intervening houses into the Thames [see below], a distance of over 200 yards, we must recognize the presence of [a] coincidence."

15 *Monday was an exceedingly hot day.* There was *no* exceedingly hot Monday in the June of 1889. In 1887, on the other hand, Monday, June 13th *was* "an exceedingly hot day." The *Times'* evening weather report noted that "In London, where the sky has been almost cloudless, temperature has risen to a maximum of 81 deg. . . . The amount of bright sunshine registered today at Westminster has been about 13 hours 40 minutes."

16 *for the tide was at its very highest at the moment of the tragedy.* It must be admitted that the tide was *not* at its very highest just east of London Bridge shortly after 4:35 P.M. on Monday, June 13, 1887. Either the typesetter misread Watson's handwriting again or Mrs. St. Clair was mistaken about the "exact" time at which she was walking through Upper Swandam Lane. Your editor would vastly prefer either of these explanation to believing that Holmes did not know when the water just east of London Bridge was at its very highest.

"AT THE FOOT OF THE STAIRS, HOWEVER, SHE MET THIS LASCAR SCOUNDREL . . ."

Illustration by Sidney Paget for the *Strand Magazine*, December, 1891.

"HE IS A PROFESSIONAL BEGGAR . . ."

Illustration by Sidney Paget for the *Strand Magazine*, December, 1891.

17 *Threadneedle Street.* Originally Three-Needle Street, the home of London's Merchant Tailors. Here stands the Bank of England, sometimes referred to as "The Old Lady of Threadneedle Street." Here, too, Alexander Holder, of the responsible firm of Holder and Stevenson, had his office ("The Adventure of the Beryl Coronet").

18 *I have watched this fellow more than once.* ". . . had [Holmes] been as adept in seeing through the disguises of others as he was in fooling others with his own, [he] would have solved this case practically at the start. . . . He [describes] the beggar's appearance in such vivid detail as to leave no doubt that he had at least several times scrutinized the mendicant at close range. Yet apparently at no time during these close contacts did it occur to him that the 'shock of orange hair' and the 'pale face disfigured by a horrible scar' were—or even might be—a disguise. If he had come to the case with even the faintest surmise as to this fact, he would undoubtedly have solved it almost at once, without benefit of shag." —Nathan L. Bengis, "Sherlock Stays After School."

19 *"Mrs. St. Clair had fainted at the sight of the blood upon the window.* Several pages later, however, Mrs. St. Clair notes that "I am not hysterical, nor given to fainting."

" So much for the Lascar manager. Now for the sinister cripple who lives upon the second floor of the opium den, and who was certainly the last human being whose eyes rested upon Neville St. Clair. His name is Hugh Boone, and his hideous face is one which is familiar to every man who goes much to the City. He is a professional beggar, though in order to avoid the police regulations he pretends to a small trade in wax vestas. Some **17** little distance down Threadneedle Street upon the left-hand side there is, as you may have remarked, a small angle in the wall. Here it is that the creature takes his daily seat, cross-legged, with his tiny stock of matches on his lap, and as he is a piteous spectacle a small rain of charity descends into the greasy leather cap which lies upon the pavement before him. I have watched this **18** fellow more than once, before ever I thought of making his professional acquaintance, and I have been surprised at the harvest which he has reaped in a short time. His appearance, you see, is so remarkable that no one can pass him without observing him. A shock of orange hair, a pale face disfigured by a horrible scar, which, by its contraction, has turned up the outer edge of his upper lip, a bull-dog chin, and a pair of very penetrating dark eyes, which present a singular contrast to the colour of his hair, all mark him out from amid the common crowd of mendicants, and so, too, does his wit, for he is ever ready with a reply to any piece of chaff which may be thrown at him by the passers-by. This is the man whom we now learn to have been the lodger at the opium den, and to have been the last man to see the gentleman of whom we are in quest."

" But a cripple ! " said I. " What could he have done single-handed against a man in the prime of life ? "

" He is a cripple in the sense that he walks with a limp ; but, in other respects, he appears to be a powerful and well-nurtured man. Surely your medical experience would tell you, Watson, that weakness in one limb is often compensated for by exceptional strength in the others."

" Pray continue your narrative."

" Mrs. St. Clair had fainted at the sight of the blood **19** upon the window, and she was escorted home in a cab by the police, as her presence could be of no help to them in their investigations. Inspector Barton, who had charge of the case, made a very careful examination of the premises, but without finding anything which threw any light upon the matter. One mistake had been made in not arresting Boone instantly, as he was allowed some few minutes during which he might have communicated with his friend the Lascar, but this fault was soon remedied, and he was seized and searched, without anything being found which could incriminate him. There were, it is true, some bloodstains upon his right shirt-sleeve, but he pointed to his ring finger, which had been cut near the nail, and explained that the bleeding came from there, adding that he had been to the window not long before, and that the stains which had been observed there came doubtless from the same source. He denied strenuously having ever seen Mr. Neville St. Clair, and swore that the presence of the clothes in his room was as much a mystery to him as to the police. As to Mrs. St. Clair's assertion, that she had **actually** seen her husband **at the** window, he declared that she must have been either mad or dreaming. He was removed, loudly protesting, to the police station, while the inspector remained upon the premises in the hope that the ebbing tide might afford some fresh clue.

"And it did, though they hardly found upon the mud-bank what they had feared to find. It was Neville St. Clair's coat, and not Neville St. Clair, which lay un-covered as the tide receded. And what do you think they found in the pockets?"

"I cannot imagine."

"No, I don't think you will guess. Every pocket stuffed with pennies and halfpennies—four hundred and twenty-one pennies, and two hundred and seventy half-pennies. It was no wonder that it had not been swept away by the tide. But a human body is a different matter. There is a fierce eddy between the wharf and the house. It seemed likely enough that the weighted coat had re-mained when the stripped body had been sucked away into the river."

"But I understand that all the other clothes were found in the room. Would the body be dressed in a coat alone?"

"No, sir, but the facts might be met speciously enough. Suppose that this man Boone had thrust Neville St. Clair through the window, there is no human eye which could have seen the deed. What would he do then? It would of course instantly strike him that he must get rid of the tell-tale garments. He would seize the coat then, and be in the act of throwing it out when it would occur to him that it would swim and not sink. He has little time, for he had heard the scuffle downstairs when the wife tried to force her way up, and perhaps he has already heard from his Lascar confederate that the police are hurrying up the street. There is not an instant to be lost. He rushes to some secret hoard, where he has accumulated the fruits of his beggary, and he stuffs all the coins upon which he can lay his hands into the pockets to make sure of the coat's sinking. He throws it out, and would have done the same with the other garments had not he heard the rush of steps below, and only just had time to close the window when the police appeared."

"It certainly sounds feasible."

"Well, we will take it as a working hypothesis for want of a better. Boone, as I have told you, was arrested and taken to the station, but it could not be shown that there had ever before been anything against him. He had for years been known as a professional beggar, but his life appeared to have been a very quiet and innocent one. There the matter stands at present, and the questions which have to be solved, what Neville St. Clair was doing in the opium den, what happened to him when there, where is he now, and what Hugh Boone had to do with his disappearance, are all as far from a solution as ever. I confess that I cannot recall any case within my experience which looked at the first glance so simple, and yet which presented such difficulties."

Whilst Sherlock Holmes had been detailing this singu-

"EVERY POCKET STUFFED WITH PENNIES AND HALF-PENNIES . . ."

"Before there was a distinct halfpenny coin, one (or rather two) could be made at home by anyone who possessed a pair of shears. The reverse of the penny of those days bore a *voided* cross, that is, one of which only the edges were raised. Since, like all hammered coins, these were quite thin, it was a simple matter to cut them in half, using the hol-low space between the raised edges of the cross as a guide. When Edward I struck a circular silver halfpenny, the voided cross on the penny was re-placed by a solid one: it extended to the edge, so that clipping could be easily detected."—A. Carson Simpson, *Numismatics in the Canon*, Part I. This is the only Canonical reference to the halfpenny (the 1863 bronze Victoria halfpenny is shown above). Mr. Simpson added that it is small wonder that the coat sunk, for the coins would have weighed about twelve pounds avoirdupois.

". . . AND HE STUFFS ALL THE COINS UPON WHICH HE CAN LAY HIS HANDS INTO THE POCKETS . . ."

Illustration by Sidney Paget for the *Strand Maga-zine*, December, 1891.

20 *and ending in Kent.* The reader who attempts to trace this route on a modern map should remember that it will show the county boundaries as they stand today. Before 1888 there was no County of London: north of the river London lay in Middlesex and south of the river in Surrey. The boundaries of these counties only withdrew to the suburbs when the County of London was created by Act of Parliament in 1888. "The correct conclusion from Holmes' statement," Mr. Michael Kaser once wrote to your editor, "is that the case took place, not in 1889, as Watson alleges, but at least a year earlier. . . . The present evidence supports the view that Watson mistook the year (or the typesetter misprinted it) in his account."

21 *mousseline-de-soie.* A soft thin silk fabric with a weave like that of muslin.

22 *a standing question.* "I fear she had designs on [Holmes]," Dr. Richard Asher wrote in "Holmes and the Fair Sex." ". . . she insisted on Holmes staying at her house in Kent, a seven-mile drive away [from London], far from the scene of his investigation. . . . When Watson drove down to her house she was not expecting Watson (it was only by chance that Holmes and Watson had met in an opium den). Was her attitude that of a bereaved wife or was she a designing woman? There she was, all decked out in . . . *mousseline-de-soie,* not to mention the pink chiffon. 'The door flew open and she stood with her figure outlined against the flood of light, one hand raised in eagerness, her body slightly bent, her head and face protruded, with eager eyes and parted lips, a standing question.' Surely as men of the world we can interpret that correctly. Watson goes on to record that when she saw there were two of them in the dog-cart she gave a cry which sank into a groan and Sherlock Holmes shook his head and shrugged his shoulders. . . . Is it not abundantly clear that Holmes had brought Watson with him as a chaperone? Anyway, that night Holmes got Watson to sleep in his room. Yet, even with his friend beside him, Holmes does not seem to have felt quite secure, for he sat up all night on a pile of cushions smoking shag and probably ruminating over his narrow escape."

lar series of events we had been whirling through the outskirts of the great town until the last straggling houses had been left behind, and we rattled along with a country hedge upon either side of us. Just as he finished, however, we drove through two scattered villages, where a few lights still glimmered in the windows.

"We are on the outskirts of Lee," said my companion. "We have touched on three English counties in our short drive, starting in Middlesex, passing over an angle of **20** Surrey, and ending in Kent. See that light among the trees ? That is the Cedars, and beside that lamp sits a woman whose anxious ears have already, I have little doubt, caught the clink of our horse's feet."

"But why are you not conducting the case from Baker Street ? " I asked.

"Because there are many inquiries which must be made out here. Mrs. St. Clair has most kindly put two rooms at my disposal, and you may rest assured that she will have nothing but a welcome for my friend and colleague. I hate to meet her, Watson, when I have no news of her husband. Here we are. Whoa, there, whoa ! "

We had pulled up in front of a large villa which stood within its own grounds. A stable-boy had run out to the horse's head, and, springing down, I followed Holmes up the small, winding gravel drive which led to the house. As we approached the door flew open, and a little blonde woman stood in the opening, clad in some sort of light **21** *mousseline-de-soie,* with a touch of fluffy pink chiffon at her neck and wrists. She stood with her figure outlined against the flood of light, one hand upon the door, one half raised in eagerness, her body slightly bent, her head and face protruded, with eager eyes and parted lips, a **22** standing question.

"Well ? " she cried, " well ? " And then, seeing that there were two of us, she gave a cry of hope which sank into a groan as she saw that my companion shook his head and shrugged his shoulders.

"No good news ? "

"None."

"No bad ? "

"No."

"Thank God for that. But come in. You must be weary, for you have had a long day."

"This is my friend, Dr. Watson. He has been of most vital use to me in several of my cases, and a lucky chance has made it possible for me to bring him out and associate him with this investigation."

"I am delighted to see you," said she, pressing my hand warmly. "You will, I am sure, forgive anything which may be wanting in our arrangements, when you consider the blow which has come so suddenly upon us."

"My dear madam," said I, " I am an old campaigner, and if I were not, I can very well see that no apology is needed. If I can be of any assistance, either to you or to my friend here, I shall be indeed happy."

"Now, Mr. Sherlock Holmes," said the lady as we entered a well-lit dining-room, upon the table of which a cold supper had been laid out. " I should very much like to ask you one or two plain questions, to which I beg that you will give a plain answer."

" Certainly, madam."

" Do not trouble about my feelings. I am not hysterical, nor given to fainting. I simply wish to hear your real, real opinion."

" Upon what point ? "

" In your heart of hearts, do you think that Neville is alive ? "

Sherlock Holmes seemed to be embarrassed by the question. " Frankly now ! " she repeated, standing upon the rug, and looking keenly down at him, as he leaned back in a basket chair.

" Frankly, then, madam, I do not."

" You think that he is dead ? "

" I do."

" Murdered ? "

" I don't say that. Perhaps."

" And on what day did he meet his death ? "

" On Monday."

" Then perhaps, Mr. Holmes, you will be good enough to explain how it is that I have received this letter from him to-day ? "

Sherlock Holmes sprang out of his chair as if he had been galvanized.

" What ! " he roared.

" Yes, to-day." She stood smiling, holding up a little slip of paper in the air.

" May I see it ? "

" Certainly."

He snatched it from her in his eagerness, and smoothing it out upon the table, he drew over the lamp, and examined it intently. I had left my chair, and was gazing at it over his shoulder. The envelope was a very coarse one, and was stamped with the Gravesend postmark, and with the **23** date of that very day, or rather of the day before, for it **24** was considerably after midnight.

" Coarse writing ! " murmured Holmes. " Surely this is not your husband's writing, madam."

" No, but the enclosure is."

" I perceive also that whoever addressed the envelope had to go and inquire as to the address."

" How can you tell that ? "

" The name, you see, is in perfectly black ink, which has dried itself. The rest is of the greyish colour which shows that blotting-paper has been used. If it had been written straight off, and then blotted, none would be of a deep black shade. This man has written the name, and there has then been a pause before he wrote the address, which can only mean that he was not familiar with it. It is, of course, a trifle, but there is nothing so important as trifles. Let us now see the letter ! Ha ! there has been **25** an enclosure here ! "

" Yes, there was a ring. His signet ring."

" And you are sure that this is your husband's hand ? "

" One of his hands."

" One ? "

" His hand when he wrote hurriedly. It is very unlike his usual writing, and yet I know it well."

" ' Dearest, do not be frightened. All will come well.

"FRANKLY NOW!" SHE REPEATED . . .

Illustration by Sidney Paget for the *Strand Magazine*, December, 1891.

23 *Gravesend*. An ancient and busy river port in Kent where vessels on their way up the Thames change their sea pilots for river pilots. Pocohontas is buried at Gravesend.

24 *or rather the day before*. The morning could not have been a Monday morning, for the letter could not have been received on a Sunday.

25 *there is nothing so important as trifles*. "It was the opinion of Michelangelo that 'Trifles make perfection, but perfection is no trifle,'" Mr. George Simmons wrote in "Sherlock Holmes— The Inner Man." "Perhaps Holmes acquired some of that dilettante's knowledge of art, about which Watson [later] ragged him, from reading of the great Italian Master."

There is a huge error which it may take some little time to rectify. Wait in patience.—Neville.' Written in pencil upon a fly-leaf of a book, octavo size, no watermark. Posted to-day in Gravesend by a man with a dirty thumb. Ha ! And the flap has been gummed, if I am not very much in error, by a person who had been chewing tobacco. And you have no doubt that it is your husband's hand, madam ? "

" None. Neville wrote those words."

" And they were posted to-day at Gravesend. Well, Mrs. St. Clair, the clouds lighten, though I should not venture to say that the danger is over."

" But he must be alive, Mr. Holmes."

" Unless this is a clever forgery to put us on the wrong scent. The ring, after all, proves nothing. It may have been taken from him."

" No, no ; it is, it is, it is his very own writing ! "

" Very well. It may, however, have been written on Monday, and only posted to-day."

" That is possible."

" If so, much may have happened between."

" Oh, you must not discourage me, Mr. Holmes. I know that all is well with him. There is so keen a sympathy between us that I should know if evil came upon him. On the very day that I saw him last he cut himself in the bedroom, and yet I in the dining-room rushed upstairs instantly with the utmost certainty that something had happened. Do you think that I would respond to such a trifle, and yet be ignorant of his death ? "

" I have seen too much not to know that the impression of a woman may be more valuable than the conclusion of an analytical reasoner. And in this letter you certainly have a very strong piece of evidence to corroborate your view. But if your husband is alive and able to write letters, why should he remain away from you ? "

" I cannot imagine. It is unthinkable."

" And on Monday he made no remarks before leaving you ? "

" No."

" And you were surprised to see him in Swandam Lane ? "

" Very much so."

" Was the window open ? "

" Yes."

" Then he might have called to you ? "

" He might."

" He only, as I understand, gave an inarticulate cry ? "

" Yes."

" A call for help, you thought ? "

" Yes. He waved his hands."

" But it might have been a cry of surprise. Astonishment at the unexpected sight of you might cause him to throw up his hands."

" It is possible."

" And you thought he was pulled back."

" He disappeared so suddenly."

" He might have leaped back. You did not see anyone else in the room."

" No, but this horrible man confessed to having been there, and the Lascar was at the foot of the stairs."

" Quite so.   Your husband, as far as you could see, had his ordinary clothes on ? "

" But without his collar or tie.   I distinctly saw his bare throat."

" Had he ever spoken of Swandam Lane ? "

" Never."

" Had he ever shown any signs of having taken opium ? "

" Never."

" Thank you, Mrs. St. Clair.   Those are the principal points about which I wished to be absolutely clear.   We shall now have a little supper and then retire, for we may have a very busy day to-morrow."

A large and comfortable double-bedded room had been placed at our disposal, and I was quickly between the sheets, for I was weary after my night of adventure. Sherlock Holmes was a man, however, who when he had an unsolved problem upon his mind would go for days, and even for a week, without rest, turning it over, rearranging his facts, looking at it from every point of view, until he had either fathomed it, or convinced himself that his data were insufficient.   It was soon evident to me that he was now preparing for an all-night sitting.   He took off his coat and waistcoat, put on a large blue dressing-gown, and then wandered about the room collecting **26** pillows from his bed, and cushions from the sofa and arm-chairs.   With these he constructed a sort of Eastern divan, upon which he perched himself cross-legged, with an ounce of shag tobacco and a box of matches laid out in front of him.   In the dim light of the lamp I saw him sitting there, an old brier pipe between his lips, his eyes fixed vacantly upon the corner of the ceiling, the blue smoke curling up from him, silent, motionless, with the light shining upon his strong-set aquiline features.   So he sat as I dropped off to sleep, and so he sat when a sudden ejaculation caused me to wake up, and I found the summer sun shining into the apartment.   The pipe was still between his lips, the smoke still curled upwards, and the room was full of a dense tobacco haze, but nothing remained of the heap of shag which I had seen upon the previous night.

26 *a large blue dressing-gown.* In "The Adventure of the Blue Carbuncle," we are told that Holmes wore a purple dressing gown; in "the Adventure of the Empty House" that his dressing gown was mouse-colored (this gown reappears in "The Adventure of the Bruce-Partington Plans"). Three dressing gowns or one? "Elementary," Christopher Morley wrote in "Was Sherlock Holmes an American?" "This particular gown was blue when new. . . . It had gone purple by the time of 'The Blue Carbuncle.' During the long absence 1891–1894, when Mrs. Hudson faithfully aired and sunned it in the backyard, it faded to mouse." (Morley liked to wear, to dinners of the Baker Street Irregulars, a hideous tie striped in blue, purple, and mouse.) Elsewhere (as a footnote to Mr. Humfrey Michell's essay on "The Sartorial Sherlock Holmes"), the Old Gasogene wrote: "It has long been on my mind to mention the fact that our beloved Freddie Steele . . . misled us in the matter of [Holmes' dressing-gown]. Probably he himself took the notion from William Gillette, who wore as Sherlock one of those robes with satin cuffs and long satin lapels (perhaps even padded or quilted with a kind of diagonal stitch). Bathrobes of this type are definitely American; I don't believe they have ever been seen in Britain. . . . I'm sure Holmes' gown was not like that. It was of substantial wool or wool-flanelette, severely cut, with plenty of pockets, and large horn buttons. Rather than a twisted cord-girdle it was tied round with a strip of the same material . . ." On the other hand, Mr. S. B. Blake ("Sherlock Holmes' Dressing Gown(s)") suggested that Holmes had two gowns, one blue, one purple, that were burned in the fire set by Moriarty's minions in April, 1891, and that Holmes acquired a third gown in Italy which he took with him during his travels in Tibet and elsewhere.

THE PIPE WAS STILL BETWEEN HIS LIPS . . .

Illustration by Sidney Paget for the *Strand Magazine*, December, 1891.

27 *It was twenty-five minutes past four.* Watson tells us that he awoke on the second day of the case shortly before "twenty-five minutes past four" and found "the summer sun shining into the apartment"; soon thereafter he walked "out into the bright morning sunshine." In June in England the sun rises at 3:50 A.M. on the 1st, at 3:49 A.M. on the 30th. June is certainly the likeliest month of the year for the case, although, by the sun alone, the latter part of May and the early part of July are possibilities.

28 *Charing Cross.* "Dr. Johnson said, 'I think the full tide of existence is at Charing Cross.' . . . In 1266 a village on this site was spoken of as Cherringe, where William of Radnor, Bishop of Landaff, asked permission of Henry III to take up his abode in a hermitage during his visits to London. This earlier mention of the name unfortunately renders it impossible to derive it, as has often been done, from *La Chère Reine*, Eleanor, wife of Edward I. . . . to whom her husband erected here the last of the nine crosses which marked the resting-places of the beloved corpse in 1291 on its way from Lincoln to Westminster. More probably the name is derived from the Saxon word *Charan*, to turn, both the road and the river making a bend here."—Augustus J. C. Hare, *Walks in London*, Vol. I.

Here, at Charing Cross, stood the hospital which put the "C. C. H." on Dr. Mortimer's stick (*The Hound of the Baskervilles*); here, too, were the vaults of the bank of Cox & Co. which once contained a travel-worn, battered dispatch box with the name of John H. Watson, M.D., painted upon the lid ("The Problem of Thor Bridge").

29 *Gladstone bag.* A long, light, narrow leather traveling bag opening very wide; named for Britain's celebrated Prime Minister.

30 *Waterloo Bridge Road.* Constructed at the same time as Waterloo Bridge, about 1816.

31 *Wellington Street.* Constructed as an approach to Waterloo Bridge in 1829–1830, to run from the Thames to the Strand. Here stood the office of *Household Words* when Dickens edited it; here stands the Lyceum Theatre, of which we will read in *The Sign of the Four*.

32 *"Inspector Bradstreet, sir."* We will meet Bradstreet again in "The Adventure of the Blue Carbuncle" and "The Adventure of the Engineer's Thumb."

"Awake, Watson?" he asked.

"Yes."

"Game for a morning drive?"

"Certainly."

"Then dress. No one is stirring yet, but I know where the stable-boy sleeps, and we shall soon have the trap out." He chuckled to himself as he spoke, his eyes twinkled, and he seemed a different man to the sombre thinker of the previous night.

As I dressed I glanced at my watch. It was no wonder that no one was stirring. It was twenty-five minutes past **27** four. I had hardly finished when Holmes returned with the news that the boy was putting in the horse.

"I want to test a little theory of mine," said he, pulling on his boots. "I think, Watson, that you are now standing in the presence of one of the most absolute fools in Europe. I deserve to be kicked from here to Charing **28** Cross. But I think I have the key of the affair now."

"And where is it?" I asked, smiling.

"In the bath-room," he answered. "Oh, yes, I am not joking," he continued, seeing my look of incredulity. "I have just been there, and I have taken it out, and I **29** have got it in this Gladstone bag. Come on, my boy, and we shall see whether it will not fit the lock."

We made our way downstairs as quickly as possible ; and out into the bright morning sunshine. In the road stood our horse and trap, with the half-clad stable-boy waiting at the head. We both sprang in, and away we dashed down the London road. A few country carts were stirring, bearing in vegetables to the metropolis, but the lines of villas on either side were as silent and lifeless as some city in a dream.

"It has been in some points a singular case," said Holmes, flicking the horse on into a gallop. "I confess that I have been as blind as a mole, but it is better to learn wisdom late, than never to learn it at all."

In town, the earliest risers were just beginning to look sleepily from their windows as we drove through the streets of the Surrey side. Passing down the Waterloo **30** Bridge Road we crossed over the river, and dashing up **31** Wellington Street wheeled sharply to the right, and found ourselves in Bow Street. Sherlock Holmes was well known to the Force, and the two constables at the door saluted him. One of them held the horse's head while the other led us in.

"Who is on duty?" asked Holmes.

32 "Inspector Bradstreet, sir."

"Ah, Bradstreet, how are you?" A tall, stout official had come down the stone-flagged passage, in a peaked cap and frogged jacket. "I wish to have a word with you, Bradstreet."

"Certainly, Mr. Holmes. Step into my room here."

It was a small office-like room, with a huge ledger upon the table, and a telephone projecting from the wall. The inspector sat down at his desk.

"What can I do for you, Mr. Holmes?"

"I called about that beggar-man, Boone—the one who was charged with being concerned in the disappearance of Mr. Neville St. Clair, of Lee."

" Yes. He was brought up and remanded for further inquiries."

" So I heard. You have him here ? "

" In the cells."

" Is he quiet ? "

" Oh, he gives no trouble. But he is a dirty scoundrel."

" Dirty ? "

" Yes, it is all we can do to make him wash his hands, and his face is as black as a tinker's. Well, when once his case has been settled he will have a regular prison bath ; and I think, if you saw him, you would agree with me that he needed it."

" I should like to see him very much."

" Would you ? That is easily done. Come this way. You can leave your bag."

" No, I think I'll take it."

" Very good. Come this way, if you please." He led us down a passage, opened a barred door, passed down a winding stair, and brought us to a whitewashed corridor with a line of doors on each side.

" The third on the right is his," said the inspector. " Here it is ! " He quietly shot back a panel in the upper part of the door, and glanced through.

" He is asleep," said he. " You can see him very well."

We both put our eyes to the grating. The prisoner lay with his face towards us, in a very deep sleep, breathing slowly and heavily. He was a middle-sized man, coarsely clad as became his calling, with a coloured shirt protruding through the rent in his tattered coat. He was, as the inspector had said, extremely dirty, but the

. . . AND FOUND OURSELVES IN BOW STREET.

Bow Street, on the east of Covent Garden, has been associated with the principal police courts of London for several centuries, and gave its name to the Bow Street Runners, the predecessors of Lestrade and Gregson. Fielding lived in Bow Street while writing *Tom Jones;* it contained Will's, known as the "Wits' Coffee House"; and it was at No. 8 Bow Street that Boswell first saw Dr. Johnson. The photograph is from *Baker Street By-ways,* by James Edward Holroyd.

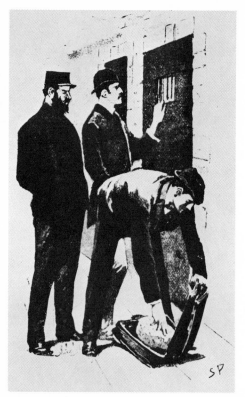

HE OPENED HIS GLADSTONE BAG AS HE SPOKE, AND TOOK
OUT, TO MY ASTONISHMENT, A VERY LARGE BATH SPONGE.

Illustration by Sidney Paget for the *Strand Magazine*, December, 1891.

. . . HE BROKE INTO A SCREAM . . .

Illustration by Sidney Paget for the *Strand Magazine*, December, 1891.

grime which covered his face could not conceal its repulsive ugliness. A broad weal from an old scar ran across it from eye to chin, and by its contraction had turned up one side of the upper lip, so that three teeth were exposed in a perpetual snarl. A shock of very bright red hair grew low over his eyes and forehead.

" He's a beauty, isn't he ? " said the inspector.

" He certainly needs a wash," remarked Holmes. ' I had an idea that he might, and I took the liberty of bringing the tools with me." He opened his Gladstone bag as he spoke, and took out, to my astonishment, a very large bath sponge.

" He ! he ! You are a funny one," chuckled the inspector.

" Now, if you will have the great goodness to open that door very quietly, we will soon make him cut a much more respectable figure."

" Well, I don't know why not," said the inspector. " He doesn't look a credit to the Bow Street cells, does he ? " He slipped his key into the lock, and we all very quietly entered the cell. The sleeper half turned, and then settled down once more into a deep slumber. Holmes stooped to the water jug, moistened his sponge, and then rubbed it twice vigorously across and down the prisoner's face.

" Let me introduce you," he shouted, " to Mr. Neville St. Clair, of Lee, in the county of Kent."

Never in my life have I seen such a sight. The man's face peeled off under the sponge like the bark from a tree. Gone was the coarse brown tint ! Gone, too, the horrid scar which had seamed it across, and the twisted lip which had given the repulsive sneer to the face ! A twitch brought away the tangled red hair, and there, sitting up in his bed, was a pale, sad-faced, refined-looking man, black-haired and smooth-skinned, rubbing his eyes, and staring about him with sleepy bewilderment. Then suddenly realizing the exposure, he broke into a scream, and threw himself down with his face to the pillow.

" Great heaven ! " cried the inspector, " it is, indeed, the missing man. I know him from the photograph."

The prisoner turned with the reckless air of a man who abandons himself to his destiny. " Be it so," said he. " And pray what am I charged with ? "

" With making away with Mr. Neville St.—— Oh, come, you can't be charged with that, unless they make a case of attempted suicide of it," said the inspector, with a grin. " Well, I have been twenty-seven years in the Force, but this really takes the cake."

" If I am Mr. Neville St. Clair, then it is obvious that no crime has been committed, and that, therefore, I am illegally detained."

" No crime, but a very great error has been committed," said Holmes. " You would have done better to have trusted your wife."

" It was not the wife, it was the children," groaned the prisoner. " God help me, I would not have them ashamed of their father. My God ! What an exposure ! What can I do ? "

Sherlock Holmes sat down beside him on the couch, and patted him kindly on the shoulder.

" If you leave it to a court of law to clear the matter up," said he, " of course you can hardly avoid publicity. On the other hand, if you convince the police authorities that there is no possible case against you, I do not know that there is any reason that the details should find their way into the papers. Inspector Bradstreet would, I am sure, make notes upon anything which you might tell us, and submit it to the proper authorities. The case would then never go into court at all."

" God bless you ! " cried the prisoner passionately. " I would have endured imprisonment, aye, even execution, rather than have left my miserable secret as a family blot to my children.

" You are the first who have ever heard my story. My father was a schoolmaster in Chesterfield, where I re- **33** ceived an excellent education. I travelled in my youth, took to the stage, and finally became a reporter on an evening paper in London. One day my editor wished to have a series of articles upon begging in the metropolis, and I volunteered to supply them. There was the point from which all my adventures started. It was only by trying begging as an amateur that I could get the facts upon which to base my articles. When an actor I had, of course, learned all the secrets of making up, and had been famous in the green-room for my skill. I took **34** advantage now of my attainments. I painted my face, and to make myself as pitiable as possible I made a good scar and fixed one side of my lip in a twist by the aid of a small slip of flesh-coloured plaster. Then with a red head of hair, and an appropriate dress, I took my station in the busiest part of the City, ostensibly as a match-seller, **35** but really as a beggar. For seven hours I plied my trade, and when I returned home in the evening I found, to my surprise, that I had received no less than twenty-six shillings and fourpence. **36**

" I wrote my articles, and thought little more of the matter until, some time later, I backed a bill for a friend, and had a writ served upon me for £25. I was at my **37** wits' end where to get the money, but a sudden idea came to me. I begged a fortnight's grace from the creditor, asked for a holiday from my employers, and spent the time in begging in the City under my disguise. In ten days I had the money, and had paid the debt.

" Well, you can imagine how hard it was to settle down to arduous work at two pounds a week, when I knew that I could earn as much in a day by smearing my face with a little paint, laying my cap on the ground, and sitting still. It was a long fight between my pride and the money, but the dollars won at last, and I threw up reporting, and sat **38** day after day in the corner which I had first chosen, inspiring pity by my ghastly face and filling my pockets with coppers. Only one man knew my secret. He was the keeper of a low den in which I used to lodge in Swandam Lane, where I could every morning emerge as a squalid beggar, and in the evenings transform myself into a well-dressed man about town. This fellow, a Lascar,

33 *Chesterfield.* A manufacturing town in Derbyshire, not far from the Priory School and Holdernesse Hall ("The Adventure of the Priory School").

34 *the green-room.* The common waiting room for performers in a theatre, so called because it was originally decorated in green.

35 *the City.* The business and financial district in the East End of London—the City of London as opposed to the West End, the City of Westminster.

36 *twenty-six shillings and fourpence.* About $6.58.

37 *£25.* $125.

38 *but the dollars won at last.* The late A. Carson Simpson pointed out (*Numismatics in the Canon,* Part I) that "dollar" is British slang for the crown, or 5-shilling piece. We must read "crowns" when a Canonical character whose background is purely British speaks of "dollars" (as James Browner does in "The Cardboard Box": "All was as bright as a new dollar").

". . . YOU CAN IMAGINE HOW HARD IT WAS TO SETTLE DOWN TO ARDUOUS WORK AT TWO POUNDS A WEEK . . ."

This may be a reference to that little-used coin, the two-pound piece (the double-sovereign of George IV is shown below), for Neville St. Clair made this remark at a time when many businesses customarily paid their employees in coin rather than in notes or by cheque; some used the largest denominations available, to simply the task of the paymasters.

39 *seven hundred pounds a year.* About $3,500.

was well paid by me for his rooms, so that I knew that my secret was safe in his possession.

"Well, very soon I found that I was saving considerable sums of money. I do not mean that any beggar in the **39** streets of London could earn seven hundred pounds a year—which is less than my average takings—but I had exceptional advantages in my power of making up, and also in a facility in repartee, which improved by practice, and made me quite a recognized character in the City. All day a stream of pennies, varied by silver, poured in upon me, and it was a very bad day upon which I failed to take two pounds.

"As I grew richer I grew more ambitious, took a house in the country, and eventually married, without anyone having a suspicion as to my real occupation. My dear wife knew that I had business in the City. She little knew what.

"Last Monday I had finished for the day, and was dressing in my room above the opium den, when I looked out of the window, and saw, to my horror and astonishment, that my wife was standing in the street, with her eyes fixed full upon me. I gave a cry of surprise, threw up my arms to cover my face, and rushing to my confidant, the Lascar, entreated him to prevent anyone from coming up to me. I heard her voice downstairs, but I knew that she could not ascend. Swiftly I threw off my clothes, pulled on those of a beggar, and put on my pigments and wig. Even a wife's eyes could not pierce so complete a disguise. But then it occurred to me that there might be a search in the room and that the clothes might betray me. I threw open the window, re-opening by my violence a small cut which I had inflicted upon myself in the bedroom that morning. Then I seized my coat, which was weighted by the coppers which I had just transferred to it from the leather bag in which I carried my takings. I hurled it out of the window, and it disappeared into the Thames. The other clothes would have followed, but at that moment there was a rush of constables up the stairs, and a few minutes after I found, rather, I confess, to my relief, that instead of being identified as Mr. Neville St. Clair, I was arrested as his murderer.

"I do not know that there is anything else for me to explain. I was determined to preserve my disguise as long as possible, and hence my preference for a dirty face. Knowing that my wife would be terribly anxious, I slipped off my ring, and confided it to the Lascar at a moment when no constable was watching me, together with a hurried scrawl, telling her that she had no cause to fear."

"That note only reached her yesterday," said Holmes.

"Good God! What a week she must have spent."

"The police have watched this Lascar," said Inspector Bradstreet, "and I can quite understand that he might find it difficult to post a letter unobserved. Probably he handed it to some sailor customer of his, who forgot all about it for some days."

"That was it," said Holmes, nodding approvingly, "I

have no doubt of it.   But have you never been prosecuted for begging ? "

" Many times ; but what was a fine to me ? "

" It must stop here, however," said Bradstreet.   " If the police are to hush this thing up, there must be no more of Hugh Boone."

" I have sworn it by the most solemn oaths which a man can take."

" In that case I think that it is probable that no further steps may be taken.   But if you are found again, then all **40** must come out.   I am sure, Mr. Holmes, that we are very much indebted to you for having cleared the matter up. I wish I knew how you reach your results."

" I reached this one," said my friend, " by sitting upon five pillows and consuming an ounce of shag.   I think, Watson, that if we drive to Baker Street we shall just be in time for breakfast."

40 *no further steps may be taken.* "Imagine . . . a superintendent of police being complaisant enough to overlook a systematic robbery of the public by a fraudulent beggar, and undertaking without demur not to prosecute," Mr. J. B. Mackenzie wrote in "Sherlock Holmes' Plots and Strategy."

A Note on the "Canonicity" of "The Man with the Twisted Lip." "Viewed objectively," Mr. John D. Beirle wrote in "The Curious Incident of the Drive Through Middlesex and Surrey," " 'The Man with the Twisted Lip' gives evidence of hasty and even careless composition by someone not familiar with Dr. Watson's family life. . . . The unfortunate conclusion to which we are forced is that this 'adventure' is not by Dr. John H. Watson, nor is it, actually a recollection of facts. Rather, we must conclude that it is a work of pure fiction . . ."

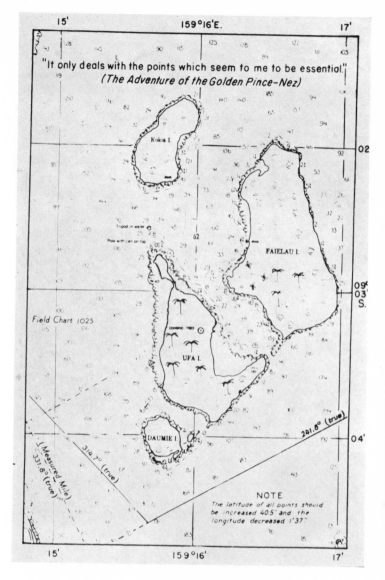

"It only deals with the points which seem to me to be essential."
(The Adventure of the Golden Pince-Nez)

Field Chart 1025

NOTE
The latitude of all points should be increased 40.5" and the longitude decreased 1'37"

. . . THE SINGULAR ADVENTURES OF THE GRICE PATERSONS IN THE ISLAND OF UFFA . . .

Mr. Page Heldenbrand, in his *Christmas Perennial*, has pointed out that "Paterson" should be read "Patteson"— "For in 1856, 'John Coleridge Patteson, afterwards bishop of Melanesia, had paid his first visit to the islands, and native teachers trained at the Melanesian mission college subsequently established themselves there' (*Encyclopædia Britannica*). So in 1887, then, we might expect to find missionary Grice Patteson carrying on his father's work in the Melanesia area . . ."

The arms of Patteson (*shown above*) are given by Dr. Wolff in his *Practical Handbook of Sherlockian Heraldry* as: Argent, on a fess indented between two mascles pale-wise sable, three fleurs-de-lys or. Crest: a pelican in her piety or, charged on the body with two fleurs-de-lys in fess sable between two roses gules barbed and seeded proper."

Dr. Wolff has also included in his *Sherlockian Atlas* a map of the island of Ufa ("Uffa") as charted by the U.S. Navy (H. O. Field Chart No. 1023, published December, 1943, on board U.S.S. *Pathfinder* under authority of the Secretary of the Navy; reprinted at the Hydrographic Office, February, 1944, showing a portion of the South Pacific Ocean, Solomon Islands, Russell Islands, Eastern Part, Sunlight Channel, and Renard Sound and Approaches)—reproduced above with embellishments by Dr. Wolff.

Mr. John Ball, Jr., in his "Practical Art of Baritsu," supports Dr. Wolff's identification, and suggests that solving the case called for Holmes to visit the South Pacific. It is probable, Mr. Ball thinks, that Holmes acquired his knowledge of baritsu ("The Adventure of the Empty House") at the Kodokan in Japan following this visit in the period April–December, 1887.

Needless to say, other commentators have held different views: Mr. Rolfe Boswell (" 'In Uffish Thought' ") has identified "the island of Uffa" with the great mound on which Norwich Castle stands, built by Uffa, King of the East Angles *circa* 580. The late Christopher Morley

carried this idea of an "inland island" a step further by suggesting that any region in East Anglia rising above the fens or meadows is often known as an island, and said that he "would be inclined to think that Market Hill in Woodbridge was the Island of Uffa"; there, in old time, the Saxon serfs built their dwellings around the conspicuous burial ground of their departed chief, King Uffa.

The late Professor Jay Finley Christ, on the other hand, held ("James Boswell and the Island of Uffa") that "Uffa" was a Watsonian combination of Ulva and Staffa, two tiny islands just off the western coast of Scotland. To this, Mrs. Crighton Sellars added: "Please pass along to [Professor Christ] that I am sure there is an island of the name between South Uist and Staffa. It gets its name from the Gaelic word *Uibhir* which is pronounced Ui-ver or Uffa (the Gaelic BH is sounded as a V), a word meaning equivalent or equal quantity; in this instance clearly meaning equally distant from both Uist and Staffa."

Again, Mr. Edmund T. Price ("The Singular Adventures of the Grice Patersons in the Island of Uffa and the Loss of the British Barque *Sophy Anderson*") has suggested that "*Ophir* instead of *Uffa* opens an entirely new horizon for the singular adventures . . ."

26

THE FIVE ORANGE PIPS

[Thursday, September 29, to Friday, September 30, 1887]

WHEN I glance over my notes and records of the Sherlock Holmes cases between the years '82 and '90, I am faced by so many which present **1** strange and interesting features, that it is no easy matter to know which to choose and which to leave. Some, however, have already gained publicity through the papers, and others have not offered a field for those peculiar qualities which my friend possessed in so high a degree, and which it is the object of these papers to illustrate. Some, too, have baffled his analytical skill, and would be, as narratives, beginnings without an ending, while others have been but partially cleared up, and have their explanations founded rather upon conjecture and surmise than on that absolute logical proof which was so dear to him. There is, however, one of these last which was so remarkable in its details and so startling in its results, that I am tempted to give some account of it, in spite of the fact that there are points in connection with it which never have been, and probably never will be, entirely cleared up.

The year '87 furnished us with a long series of cases of **2** greater or less interest, of which I retain the records. Among my headings under this one twelve months, I find an account of the adventure of the Paradol Chamber, **3** of the Amateur Mendicant Society, who held a luxurious club in the lower vault of a furniture warehouse, of the facts connected with the loss of the British barque *Sophy Anderson*, of the singular adventures of the Grice Patersons in the island of Uffa, and finally of the Camberwell poisoning case. In the latter, as may be remembered, **4** Sherlock Holmes was able, by winding up the dead man's watch, to prove that it had been wound up two hours ago, and that therefore the deceased had gone to bed within that time—a deduction which was of the greatest importance in clearing up the case. All these I may sketch out at some future date, but none of them present such singular features as the strange train of circumstances which I have now taken up my pen to describe.

It was in the latter days of September, and the equinoctial gales had set in with exceptional violence. All day

1 *between the years '82 and '90*. Why is '81 omitted? "Clearly because *A Study in Scarlet* was the only case [in the year 1881] of which [Watson] had any record," the late Gavin Brend wrote in *My Dear Holmes*. "After this case it was no longer necessary for him to make a discreet withdrawal to his bedroom when a client arrived to see Holmes, as had been his custom during the first few weeks. . . . But he probably took no further part in the proceedings, and above all, he kept no notes. The idea of a permanent partnership had not yet occurred to either man." Returning to this theme in his essay, "From Maiwand to Marylebone," Mr. Brend wrote: [Holmes and Watson] "were complete strangers when they first appeared in Baker Street. Probably therefore some time would elapse before either of them thought of the possibility of a complete record of all the cases. I [visualize] 1881 as a year in which Watson spent most of his time in writing his account of the one case in which he had been allowed to participate, *A Study in Scarlet*. He would know little, if anything, of any other case which occurred during that year and above all he kept no records. It was only at the beginning of 1882 that systemized records of the cases came into existence."

2 *The year '87*. Although Watson nowhere tells us specifically that "The Five Orange Pips" was one of the cases that took place in the year 1887, the implication is strong that it did; there would otherwise be little reason for Watson to preface his account with an extended listing of some of the important cases of that year. Knox and Morley agree with your editor that the adventure *did* take place in 1887; Andrew, Bell, Brend, Harrison, Hoff, and Roberts have all dated it in 1888; Blakeney, Christ, Folsom, Pattrick, Petersen, Smith, and Zeisler in 1889.

3 *the adventure of the Paradol Chamber*. For a pastiche by Mr. Alan Wilson stemming from this reference of Dr. Watson's, see the *Sherlock Holmes Journal*, Vol. V., No. 2, Spring, 1961, pp. 45–50, and Vol. V, No. 3, Winter, 1961, pp. 78–82.

There is also a playlet by Mr. John Dickson Carr (first published in Vol. II, No. 3 of the *Unicorn News*, reprinted in the February, 1950, issue of *Ellery Queen's Mystery Magazine*); this Holmesian horseplay climaxed the 1948 Annual Dinner of the Mystery Writers of America, with Clayton Rawson as Sherlock Holmes, Lawrence G. Blochman as Dr. Watson, Audrey Roos as Lady Imogene Ferrers, and John Dickson Carr as the Marquis de Paradol.

4 *the Camberwell poisoning case.* For a pastiche stemming from this reference of Dr. Watson's, see "The Adventure of the Gold Hunter," by John Dickson Carr, in *The Exploits of Sherlock Holmes.*

5 *the wind cried and sobbed like a child in the chimney.* "It is high time," Mr. Bliss Austin remarked in "What Son Was Watson?", "that someone investigated this matter of how a child in a chimney sobs."

6 *Clark Russell's fine sea stories.* "Is it only coincidence," Christopher Morley once asked, "that in the [*Strand Magazine*'s] issue of October '91 there was a sea story ('Three in Charge') by Clark Russell; and lo, in the very next number, November '91, we find the good Watson reading Clark Russell by the fire . . . ?"

William Clark Russell, 1844–1911, was hailed by Sir Edwin Arnold as "the prose Homer of the great ocean" and by Algernon Charles Swinburne as "the greatest master of the sea, living or dead." Between 1867 and 1905 he published 65 titles of

the wind had screamed and the rain had beaten against the windows, so that even here in the heart of great, hand-made London we were forced to raise our minds for the instant from the routine of life, and to recognize the presence of those great elemental forces which shriek at mankind through the bars of his civilization, like untamed beasts in a cage. As evening drew in the storm grew louder and louder, and the wind cried and sobbed **5** like a child in the chimney. Sherlock Holmes sat moodily at one side of the fireplace cross-indexing his records of crime, whilst I at the other was deep in one of Clark Rus- **6** sell's fine sea stories, until the howl of the gale from without seemed to blend with the text, and the splash of the rain to lengthen out into the long swash of the sea waves. My wife was on a visit to her aunt's, and for a few days I was a dweller once more in my old quarters at Baker Street.

" Why," said I, glancing up at my companion, " that was surely the bell ? Who could come to-night ? Some friend of yours, perhaps ? "

" Except yourself I have none," he answered. " I do not encourage visitors."

" A client, then ? "

" If so, it is a serious case. Nothing less would bring a man out on such a day, and at such an hour. But I take it that it is more likely to be some crony of the landlady's."

Sherlock Holmes was wrong in his conjecture, however, for there came a step in the passage, and a tapping at the door. He stretched out his long arm to turn the lamp away from himself and towards the vacant chair upon which a new-comer must sit. " Come in ! " said he.

The man who entered was young, some two-and-twenty **7** at the outside, well groomed and trimly clad, with something of refinement and delicacy in his bearing. The streaming umbrella which he held in his hand, and his long shining waterproof told of the fierce weather through which he had come. He looked about him anxiously in the glare of the lamp, and I could see that his face was pale and his eyes heavy, like those of a man who is weighed down with some great anxiety.

" I owe you an apology," he said, raising his golden pince-nez to his eyes. " I trust that I am not intruding. I fear that I have brought some traces of the storm and the rain into your snug chamber."

" Give me your coat and umbrella," said Holmes. " They may rest here on the hook, and will be dry presently. You have come up from the south-west, I see."
8 " Yes, from Horsham."

" That clay and chalk mixture which I see upon your **9** toe-caps is quite distinctive."

" I have come for advice."

" That is easily got."

" And help."

" That is not always so easy."

HE LOOKED ABOUT HIM ANXIOUSLY IN THE GLARE OF THE LAMP . . .

Illustration by Sidney Paget for the *Strand Magazine*, November, 1891.

W. CLARK RUSSELL.
BORN 1844.

MR. CLARK RUSSELL was born in New York of English parents. His literary taste is a natural gift, his mother being a niece of Charles Lloyd, the poet, and a cousin of Christopher Wordsworth, the late Bishop of Lincoln, and herself known as

From a]   AGE 5.   [Oil Painting.

a poetess, and the authoress, among other things, of "The Wife's Dream." Mr. Clark Russell went to sea as a middy before he was fourteen, and during the next eight years picked up the thorough knowledge of sea-faring life which he afterwards turned to such good use in his novels. His first book was "John Holdsworth," but it was his second story, "The Wreck of the Grosvenor," which he wrote in little more than two months and sold to a publisher for fifty pounds, which marked a new era in the evolution of the nautical novel. Since that time Mr. Clark Russell has had the sea to himself, and his

*From a]   AGE 17.   [Photograph.
As a Midshipman.*

descriptions of sea-scenery, and his pictures of real-life sailors, are not likely soon to find a rival. Mr. Clark Russell's latest story, "List, Ye Landsmen," one of his very best, is now appearing in *Tit-Bits.*

From a Photo. by   PRESENT DAY.   [Elliott & Fry.

. . . ONE OF CLARK RUSSELL'S FINE SEA-STORIES . . .

From "Portraits of Celebrities" in the *Strand Magazine,* issue of January, 1893.

fiction, most of them in three volumes, and 15 other titles as well. The book that Dr. Watson was reading, Christopher Morley suggested, was probably *Round the Galley Fire,* published in 1883: "This particular book had a special influence on [Conan Doyle]; so much so that he adapted its title for his own *Round the Red Lamp* some years later. Or I should like to think Watson's reading might have been that little masterpiece 'The Mystery of the Ocean Star'—first published in *Longman's Magazine* before '88 [and] included in a collection of stories imported to New York by Appleton in '88."

But Christopher Morley's brother Dr. Felix Morley thought it more likely that Watson was reading *A Sea Queen,* published by Harper's early in 1883 and containing the passage: ". . . and, above all, as I saw through the window, with masses of sulphur-colored scud sweeping along it, and the voices of the tempest, which shrieked like tortured children at the hall-door and the window-casements, and roared like the discharge of heavy ordnance in the chimneys" ("How the Child Got into the Chimney").

7 *some two-and-twenty at the outside.* Openshaw later says: "I was a youngster of twelve or so. That would be in 1878." The year cannot be later than 1888, and is more probably 1887.

8 *Horsham.* A town in Sussex, and one that Holmes and Watson were to visit in "The Adventure of the Sussex Vampire."

9 *quite distinctive.*" Said the editors of the Catalogue of the Sherlock Holmes Exhibition: "This conversation . . . seems to reveal a hiatus in Holmes' otherwise encyclopaedic knowledge . . . ; or it suggests either that Watson's notes were at fault when he mentions Horsham, or that Openshaw did not tell Holmes the whole truth about his movements. The (geological) map shows that Horsham stands on what are known as the Tunbridge Wells Sands (at the top of the Hastings Beds) and is closely surrounded on three sides by the Weald Clay. Apart from material deposited by builders or from some similar artificial source, it would have been quite impossible for Openshaw to get chalk on his toe-caps in or around Horsham. Sand and clay, perhaps; chalk and clay, no. . . . It will be observed, however, that somewhat to the north—on a line that passes through Dorking—there is a zone in which the traveller would pass rapidly through the Lower Greensand, Gault Clay, Upper Greensand (a very narrow strip) and the Chalk. . . . In this zone even a short walk could provide a mixture of chalk and clay. This condition is not confined to the southwest, but extends along a line to the southeast as far as Folkestone. Holmes' alleged statement that such a mixture implies a district to the southwest is simply not true; it seems more probable that Holmes said 'south,' and that Watson, with Horsham in mind, gratuitously improved on Holmes' statement when writing up his notes. However, the problem remains: how did Openshaw's boots come to bear traces of both clay and chalk? There seem to be three possibilities: 1) For 'Horsham' read, for example, 'Dorking'; Watson having through carelessness or from discretion altered the locale. 2) Openshaw had acquired the chalk on a previous journey and had simply omitted to clean his boots. This does not accord with the statement that he was 'well groomed and trimly clad.' 3) Openshaw broke his journey at Dorking to keep some appointment which he did not disclose to Holmes. Our preference is for solution 1), since Holmes would certainly have detected the deception implicit in 3)."

10 *He was wrongfully accused of cheating at cards."* Major Prendergast was fortunate that Holmes was able to clear his name, for the Tankerville Club must have borne an evil reputation: a fellow member of the Major's was none other than the notorious Colonel Sebastian Moran ("The Adventure of the Empty House").

11 *three times by men and once by a woman."* "That woman," the late H. W. Bell wrote in *Sherlock Holmes and Dr. Watson: The Chronology of Their Adventures*, "can only have been Irene Adler . . ." He, and many later commentators, consequently date "The Five Orange Pips" after "A Scandal in Bohemia." But the late Gavin Brend (*My Dear Holmes*) disagreed that the woman was Irene Adler: ". . . is there, in fact, any justification for this view? For a start, Holmes had a sincere respect and admiration for this attractive adventuress and was wont to eulogize her on the slightest provocation. To him she is always 'the woman.' But here we have not 'the woman' but 'a woman.' We should have expected something warmer—more appreciative. It might have been, for instance, 'a woman, but what a woman!' or 'a woman, the peerless Irene Adler!' As it stands it suggests some less exciting lady who defeated Holmes but failed to capture his imagination. As a candidate for this role we would like to advance the claims of Effie Munro of 'The Yellow Face.' This case . . . was one of Holmes' few failures. It was a problem set by a woman which defeated Holmes. Need we look any further?"

12 *Coventry.* A manufacturing town in Warwickshire, from which comes the phrase "sent to Coventry," meaning to ostracize socially. Coventry is also the home of Lady Godiva and Peeping Tom, whose legend, celebrated by Tennyson, was perpetuated until recently by pageants. Here, too, was the location of Cyril Morton's Midland Electric Company ("The Adventure of the Solitary Cyclist").

13 *Jackson's.* Thomas Jonathan Jackson, 1824–1863, next to Lee the Confederacy's greatest gen-

" I have heard of you, Mr. Holmes. I heard from Major Prendergast how you saved him in the Tankerville Club Scandal."

10 " Ah, of course. He was wrongfully accused of cheating at cards."

" He said that you could solve anything."

" He said too much."

" That you are never beaten."

11 " I have been beaten four times—three times by men and once by a woman."

" But what is that compared with the number of your successes ? "

" It is true that I have been generally successful."

" Then you may be so with me."

" I beg that you will draw your chair up to the fire, and favour me with some details as to your case."

" It is no ordinary one."

" None of those which come to me are. I am the last court of appeal."

" And yet I question, sir, whether, in all your experience, you have ever listened to a more mysterious and inexplicable chain of events than those which have happened in my own family."

" You fill me with interest," said Holmes. " Pray give us the essential facts from the commencement, and I can afterwards question you as to those details which seem to me to be most important."

The young man pulled his chair up, and pushed his wet feet out towards the blaze.

" My name," said he, " is John Openshaw, but my own affairs have, so far as I can understand it, little to do with this awful business. It is a hereditary matter, so in order to give you an idea of the facts, I must go back to the commencement of the affair.

" You must know that my grandfather had two sons— my uncle Elias and my father Joseph. My father had a **12** small factory at Coventry, which he enlarged at the time of the invention of bicycling. He was the patentee of the Openshaw unbreakable tire, and his business met with such success that he was able to sell it, and to retire upon a handsome competence.

" My uncle Elias emigrated to America when he was a young man, and became a planter in Florida, where he was reported to have done very well. At the time of the war **13-14** he fought in Jackson's army, and afterwards under Hood, **15** where he rose to be a colonel. When Lee laid down his arms my uncle returned to his plantation, where he re- **16** mained for three or four years. About 1869 or 1870 he came back to Europe, and took a small estate in Sussex, near Horsham. He had made a very considerable fortune in the States, and his reason for leaving them was his aversion to the negroes, and his dislike of the Republican policy in extending the franchise to them. He was a singular man, fierce and quick-tempered, very foul-mouthed when he was angry, and of a most retiring disposition. During all the years that he lived at Horsham I doubt if ever he set foot in the town. He had a garden and two or three fields round his house, and there he would take his exercise, though very often for weeks on end he would never leave his room. He drank a great deal of brandy, and smoked very heavily, but he would see no society, and did not want any friends, not even his own brother.

"He didn't mind me, in fact he took a fancy to me, for at the time when he saw me first I was a youngster of twelve or so. That would be in the year 1878, after he had been eight or nine years in England. He begged my father to let me live with him, and he was very kind [17] to me in his way. When he was sober he used to be fond of playing backgammon and draughts with me, and he would make me his representative both with the servants and with the tradespeople, so that by the time that I was sixteen I was quite master of the house. I kept all the keys, and could go where I liked and do what I liked, so long as I did not disturb him in his privacy. There was one singular exception, however, for he had a single room, a lumber-room up among the attics, which was invariably locked, and which he would never permit either me or anyone else to enter. With a boy's curiosity I have peeped through the keyhole, but I was never able to see more than such a collection of old trunks and bundles as would be expected in such a room.

"One day—it was in March, 1883—a letter with a foreign stamp lay upon the table in front of the Colonel's plate. It was not a common thing for him to receive letters, for his bills were all paid in ready money, and he had no friends of any sort. 'From India !' said he, as he took it up, 'Pondicherry postmark ! What can this be ?' Opening it hurriedly, out there jumped five little dried orange pips, which pattered down upon his plate. I began to laugh at this, but the laugh was struck from my lips at the sight of his face. His lip had fallen, his eyes were protruding, his skin the colour of putty, and he glared at the envelope which he still held in his trembling hand. 'K. K. K.,' he shrieked, and then : 'My God, my God, my sins have overtaken me.'

"'What is it, uncle ?' I cried.

"'Death,' said he, and rising from the table he retired to his room, leaving me palpitating with horror. I took up the envelope, and saw scrawled in red ink upon the inner flap, just above the gum, the letter K three times repeated. There was nothing else save the five dried pips. What could be the reason of his overpowering terror ? I left the breakfast-table, and as I ascended the stairs I met him coming down with an old rusty key, which must have belonged to the attic, in one hand, and a small brass box, like a cash box, in the other.

"'They may do what they like, but I'll checkmate them still,' said he, with an oath. 'Tell Mary that I shall want a fire in my room to-day, and send down to Fordham, the Horsham lawyer.'

"I did as he ordered, and when the lawyer arrived I was asked to step up to the room. The fire was burning brightly, and in the grate there was a mass of black, fluffy ashes, as of burned paper, while the brass box stood open and empty beside it. As I glanced at the box I noticed, with a start, that upon the lid were printed the treble K which I had read in the morning upon the envelope.

eral. At the first battle of Bull Run, he and his brigade won the sobriquet "Stonewall" by their stand. Jackson later won renown in the Shenandoah Valley campaign of 1862, and by his support of Lee in the Seven Days' Battles, by his generalship at the second battle of Bull Run and Fredericksburg. He was mortally wounded at Chancellorsville.

14 *Hood.* John Bell Hood, 1831–1879, Confederate general who commanded in the Atlanta campaign. His forces were virtually annhilated by G. H. Thomas at Nashville, and Hood resigned his command in January, 1865.

15 *Lee.* Robert Edward Lee, 1807–1870, general-in-chief of the Confederate armies in the Civil War; a great commander and a man of exalted character.

16 *where he remained for three or four years."* "One is tempted to identify . . . Openshaw with Captain F. M. Woodward, who commanded a scratch regiment of two Mississippi battalions under Hood at Nashville," Mr. Manly Wade Wellman wrote in "Two Southern Exposures of Sherlock Holmes"; "Woodward means a defended wood, and Openshaw an undefended one— wouldn't Watson handle the name problem just like that? Or Openshaw may be a sound-alike for the artillerist Bouanchaud, or for J. T. Holtzclaw, the infantry brigadier who was as savage as his surname. We cannot say for certain without more material."

17 *He begged my father to let me live with him.* "Elias led a solitary life in Horsham, so the desire for company in the house was understandable; but surely it was an oddly selfish request, calculated as it was to deprive a retired widower of his only child. (There is no mention of a Mrs. Openshaw, so presumably she was dead)," Mr. Benjamin Clark wrote in "The Horsham Fiasco." "Even odder, however, was the apparently ready acquiescence of the father to this arrangement. Joseph was a rich man so, as far as the present was concerned, the boy had nothing to gain materially by the change, which none the less he was perfectly willing to make without, apparently, any regrets. In short, all concerned, according to the record as we have it, saw nothing odd in this leaving of a solitary parent for an uncle who was a heavy drinker and who, from the account, had nothing better to offer his nephew in the way of education than an occasional game of backgammon or draughts (when he was sober), and the responsibilities incident to the running of a house. If—and this is the only probable explanation— Joseph consented to the arrangement to make sure of being Elias' heir, then his action for one already well off reveals a love of mammon that is almost indecent."

18 *and the lawyer took it away with him.* "I am not a lawyer," Mr. W. G. Daish wrote in "Ponderings and Pitfalls," "but I have sometimes wondered how far young Openshaw would have got with the will he witnessed . . . under which he was eventually to be a beneficiary and which, meanwhile, made his own father, his closest relative, the sole legatee."

19 *brought in a verdict of suicide.* ". . . surely an extraordinary verdict, under the circumstances, for who, drunk or sober, would ever attempt to end his life by lying face down in a two-feet-deep puddle?"—Benjamin Clark, "The Horsham Fiasco."

20 *some fourteen thousand pounds.* Some $70,000.

21 *March the 10th, 1883.* Openshaw tells us that his uncle came to England "about 1869 or 1870"— that by 1878 he had been "eight or nine years back"—that by the time he (John Openshaw) "was sixteen" he was "quite the master of the house"—and that it was shortly after this—to be precise, on "March the 10th, 1883" (a Saturday)— that his uncle was sent the pips. All of this is consistent with 1887 as the year of the case.

"WE FOUND HIM, WHEN WE WENT TO SEARCH FOR HIM, FACE DOWNWARDS IN A LITTLE GREEN-SCUMMED POOL . . ."

Illustration by Sidney Paget for the *Strand Magazine*, November, 1891.

" ' I wish you, John,' said my uncle, ' to witness my will. I leave my estate, with all its advantages and all its disadvantages to my brother, your father, whence it will, no doubt, descend to you. If you can enjoy it in peace, well and good ! If you find you cannot, take my advice, my boy, and leave it to your deadliest enemy. I am sorry to give you such a two-edged thing, but I can't say what turn things are going to take. Kindly sign the paper where Mr. Fordham shows you.'

" I signed the paper as directed, and the lawyer took it **18** away with him. The singular incident made, as you may think, the deepest impression upon me, and I pondered over it, and turned it every way in my mind without being able to make anything of it. Yet I could not shake off the vague feeling of dread which it left behind it, though the sensation grew less keen as the weeks passed, and nothing happened to disturb the usual routine of our lives. I could see a change in my uncle, however. He drank more than ever, and he was less inclined for any sort of society. Most of his time he would spend in his room, with the door locked upon the inside, but sometimes he would emerge in a sort of drunken frenzy and would burst out of the house and tear about the garden with a revolver in his hand, screaming out that he was afraid of no man, and that he was not to be cooped up, like a sheep in a pen, by man or devil. When these hot fits were over, however, he would rush tumultuously in at the door, and lock and bar it behind him, like a man who can brazen it out no longer against the terror which lies at the roots of his soul. At such times I have seen his face even on a cold day, glisten with moisture as though it were new raised from a basin.

" Well, to come to an end of the matter, Mr. Holmes, and not to abuse your patience, there came a night when he made one of those drunken sallies from which he never came back. We found him, when we went to search for him, face downwards in a little green-scummed pool, which lay at the foot of the garden. There was no sign of any violence, and the water was but two feet deep, so that the jury, having regard to his known eccentricity, **19** brought in a verdict of suicide. But I, who knew how he winced from the very thought of death, had much ado to persuade myself that he had gone out of his way to meet it. The matter passed, however, and my father entered into possession of the estate, and of some fourteen thou- **20** sand pounds, which lay to his credit at the bank."

" One moment," Holmes interposed. " Your statement is, I foresee, one of the most remarkable to which I have ever listened. Let me have the date of the reception by your uncle of the letter, and the date of his supposed suicide."

21 " The letter arrived on March the 10th, 1883. His death was seven weeks later, upon the night of the 2nd of May."

" Thank you. Pray proceed."

" When my father took over the Horsham property, he, at my request, made a careful examination of the attic, which had been always locked up. We found the brass box there, although its contents had been destroyed.

On the inside of the cover was a paper label, with the initials K. K. K. repeated upon it, and 'Letters, memoranda, receipts and a register' written beneath. These, we presume, indicated the nature of the papers which had been destroyed by Colonel Openshaw. For the rest, there was nothing of much importance in the attic, save a great many scattered papers and notebooks bearing upon my uncle's life in America. Some of them were of the war time, and showed that he had done his duty well, and had borne the repute of being a brave soldier. Others were of a date during the reconstruction of the Southern States, and were mostly concerned with politics, for he had evidently taken a strong part in opposing the carpet-bag politicians who had been sent down from the North. **22**

" Well, it was the beginning of '84, when my father came to live at Horsham, and all went as well as possible with us until the January of '85. On the fourth day after **23** the New Year I heard my father give a sharp cry of surprise as we sat together at the breakfast-table. There he was, sitting with a newly opened envelope in one hand and five dried orange pips in the outstretched palm of the other one. He had always laughed at what he called my cock-and-bull story about the Colonel, but he looked very puzzled and scared now that the same thing had come upon himself.

" ' Why, what on earth does this mean, John ? ' he stammered.

" My heart had turned to lead. ' It is K. K. K.,' said I.

" He looked inside the envelope. ' So it is,' he cried. ' Here are the very letters. But what is this written above them ? '

" ' Put the papers on the sundial,' I read, peeping over his shoulder.

" ' What papers ? What sundial ? ' he asked.

" ' The sundial in the garden. There is no other,' said I ; ' but the papers must be those that are destroyed.'

" ' Pooh ! ' said he, gripping hard at his courage. ' We are in a civilized land here, and we can't have tomfoolery of this kind. Where does the thing come from ? '

" ' From Dundee,' I answered, glancing at the postmark.

" ' Some preposterous practical joke,' said he. ' What have I to do with sundials and papers ? I shall take no notice of such nonsense.'

" ' I should certainly speak to the police,' I said.

" ' And be laughed at for my pains. Nothing of the sort.'

" ' Then let me do so.'

" ' No, I forbid you. I won't have a fuss made over such nonsense.'

" It was in vain to argue with him, for he was a very obstinate man. I went about, however, with a heart which was full of forebodings.

" On the third day after the coming of the letter my father went from home to visit an old friend of his, Major Freebody, who is in command of one of the forts upon Portsdown Hill. I was glad that he should go, for it seemed to me that he was farther from danger when he was away from home. In that, however, I was in error.

22 *the carpet-bag politicians.* Northern politicians who settled in the Southern states after the Civil War, so called from reckless speculating bankers of the West who often decamped with funds entrusted to them stowed in traveling bags made of carpeting.

23 *the January of '85.* ". . . it was almost two years later before the next Georgian expedition got under way. Surely a delay of that duration is all the more remarkable when one considers that while Colonel Openshaw was in possession of the papers he could not make public their contents without implicating himself, whereas his brother, if the records had still been in existence, ran no risk, and in fact might even, without being aware of their significance, have turned them over to the police, who in turn would have given them to the American authorities."—Benjamin Clark, "The Horsham Fiasco."

" 'WHY, WHAT ON EARTH DOES THIS MEAN, JOHN?' " HE STAMMERED.

Illustration by Sidney Paget for the *Strand Magazine*, November, 1891.

24 *Fareham.* Portsdown Hill is southwest of Fareham, a town in Hampshire northeast of Portsmouth and Southsea.

25 *two years and eight months have elapsed since then.* This statement would seem to prove conclusively that Openshaw visited Holmes in September, 1887.

26 *yesterday morning.* Since Openshaw's letter had been delivered "yesterday morning," the opening day of the case cannot have been a Monday.

27 *This is no time for despair.*" "Horace said it more tersely, 'Nil desperandum,' in *Odes*, Book I, 7," Morris Rosenblum wrote in "The Horatian Spirit in Holmes."

. . . HE SHOOK OUT . . . FIVE LITTLE DRIED ORANGE PIPS.

Illustration by Sidney Paget for the *Strand Magazine*, November, 1891.

Upon the second day of his absence I received a telegram from the Major, imploring me to come at once. My father had fallen over one of the deep chalk-pits which abound in the neighbourhood, and was lying senseless, with a shattered skull. I hurried to him, but he passed away without having ever recovered his consciousness.

24 He had, as it appears, been returning from Fareham in the twilight, and as the country was unknown to him, and the chalk-pit unfenced, the jury had no hesitation in bringing in a verdict of ' Death from accidental causes.' Carefully as I examined every fact connected with his death, I was unable to find anything which could suggest the idea of murder. There were no signs of violence, no footmarks, no robbery, no record of strangers having been seen upon the roads. And yet I need not tell you that my mind was far from at ease, and that I was wellnigh certain that some foul plot had been woven round him.

" In this sinister way I came into my inheritance. You will ask me why I did not dispose of it ? I answer because I was well convinced that our troubles were in some way dependent upon an incident in my uncle's life, and that the danger would be as pressing in one house as in another.

" It was in January, '85, that my poor father met his end, and two years and eight months have elapsed since

25 then. During that time I have lived happily at Horsham, and I had begun to hope that this curse had passed away from the family, and that it had ended with the last generation. I had begun to take comfort too soon, however ;

26 yesterday morning the blow fell in the very shape in which it had come upon my father."

The young man took from his waistcoat a crumpled envelope, and, turning to the table, he shook out upon it five little dried orange pips.

" This is the envelope," he continued. " The postmark is London—eastern division. Within are the very words which were upon my father's last message. ' K. K. K.'; and then ' Put the papers on the sundial.' "

" What have you done ? " asked Holmes.

" Nothing."

" Nothing ? "

" To tell the truth "—he sank his face into his thin, white hands—" I have felt helpless. I have felt like one of those poor rabbits when the snake is writhing towards it. I seem to be in the grasp of some resistless, inexorable evil, which no foresight and no precautions can guard against."

" Tut ! Tut ! " cried Sherlock Holmes. " You must act, man, or you are lost. Nothing but energy can save

27 you. This is no time for despair."

" I have seen the police."

" Ah ? "

" But they listened to my story with a smile. I am

28 convinced that the inspector has formed the opinion that the letters are all practical jokes, and that the deaths of my relations were really accidents, as the jury stated, and were not to be connected with the warnings."

Holmes shook his clenched hands in the air. " Incredible imbecility ! ' he cried.

" They have, however, allowed me a policeman, who

may remain in the house with me."

" Has he come with you to-night ? "

" No. His orders were to stay in the house."

Again Holmes raved in the air.

" Why did you come to me ? " he said ; " and, above all, why did you not come at once ? "

" I did not know. It was only to-day that I spoke to Major Prendergast about my trouble, and was advised by him to come to you."

" It is really two days since you had the letter. We should have acted before this. You have no further evidence, I suppose, than that which you have placed before us—no suggestive detail which might help us."

" There is one thing," said John Openshaw. He rummaged in his coat pocket, and drawing out a piece of discoloured, blue-tinted paper, he laid it out upon the table. " I have some remembrance," said he, " that on the day when my uncle burned the papers I observed that the small, unburned margins which lay amid the ashes were of this particular colour. I found this single sheet upon the floor of his room, and I am inclined to think that it may be one of the papers which had, perhaps, fluttered out from among the others, and in that way have escaped destruction. Beyond the mention of pips, I do not see that it helps us much. I think myself that it is a page from some private diary. The writing is undoubtedly my uncle's."

Holmes moved the lamp, and we both bent over the sheet of paper, which showed by its ragged edge that it had indeed been torn from a book. It was headed " March, 1869," and beneath were the following enigmatical notices :

" 4th. Hudson came. Same old platform.

" 7th. Set the pips on McCauley, Paramore, and Swain of St. Augustine.

" 9th. McCauley cleared.

" 10th. John Swain cleared.

" 12th. Visited Paramore. All well."

" Thank you ! " said Holmes, folding up the paper and returning it to our visitor. " And now you must on no account lose another instant. We cannot spare time even to discuss what you have told me. You must get home instantly, and act."

" What shall I do ? "

" There is but one thing to do. It must be done at once. You must put this piece of paper which you have shown us into the brass box which you have described. You must also put in a note to say that all the other papers were burned by your uncle, and that this is the only one which remains. You must assert that in such words as will carry conviction with them. Having done this, you must at once put the box out upon the sundial, as directed. Do you understand ? "

" Entirely."

" Do not think of revenge, or anything of the sort, at present. I think that we may gain that by means of the law ; but we have our web to weave, while theirs is already woven. The first consideration is to remove the pressing danger which threatens you. The second

28 *the inspector.* "Incredible as this seems," Miss N. Currier Dorian wrote in " ' A Bad Lot,' " "the figures show that of the eight cases (*A Study in Scarlet, The Sign of the Four,* 'The Adventure of the Noble Bachelor,' 'The Boscombe Valley Mystery,' 'The Five Orange Pips,' 'The Adventure of the Empty House,' 'The Adventure of the Norwood Builder,' 'The Adventure of the Three Gables') in which Holmes collided with the authorities or criticized them severely, five are cases in which Lestrade represented the professionals (one—the *Study*—in company with Gregson), and one is Athelney Jones (*The Sign of the Four*); the other two are exceptions. 'The Five Orange Pips,' the first of these exceptions, does not name any officer in charge: in the face of the figures given, it is surely a reasonable guess that the man who brought down Holmes' charge of 'imbecility' was Lestrade. . . . The prevalent idea that Holmes had no use for Scotland Yard or any of the professional forces is not in keeping with the facts."

is to clear up the mystery, and **to** punish the guilty parties."

" I thank you," said the young man, rising, and pulling on his overcoat. " You have given me fresh life and hope. I shall certainly do as you advise."

" Do not lose an instant. And, above all, take care of yourself in the meanwhile, for I do not think that there can be a doubt that you are threatened by a very real and imminent danger. How do you go back ? "

" By train from Waterloo."

" It is not yet nine. The streets will be crowded, so I trust that you may be in safety. And yet you cannot guard yourself too closely."

" I am armed."

" That is well. To-morrow I shall set to work upon your case."

" I shall see you at Horsham, then ? "

" No, your secret lies in London. It is there that I shall seek it."

" Then I shall call upon you in a day, or in two days. with news as to the box and the papers. I shall take your advice in every particular." He shook hands with us, and took his leave. Outside the wind still screamed, and the rain splashed and pattered against the windows. This strange, wild story seemed to have come to us from amid the mad elements—blown in upon us like a sheet of seaweed in a gale—and now to have been reabsorbed by them once more.

Sherlock Holmes sat for some time in silence with his head sunk forward, and his eyes bent upon the red glow of the fire. Then he lit his pipe, and leaning back in his chair he watched the blue smoke rings as they chased each other up to the ceiling.

" I think, Watson," he remarked at last, " that of all our cases we have had none more fantastic than this."

29 " Save, perhaps, the Sign of Four."

" Well, yes. Save, perhaps, that. And yet this John Openshaw seems to me to be walking amid even greater perils than did the Sholtos."

" But have you," I asked, " formed any definite conception as to what these perils are ? "

" There can be no question as to their nature," he answered.

" Then what are they ? Who is this K. K. K., and why does he pursue this unhappy family ? "

Sherlock Holmes closed his eyes, and placed his elbows upon the arms of his chair, with his finger-tips together. " The ideal reasoner," he remarked, " would, when he has once been shown a single fact in all its bearings, deduce from it not only all the chain of events which led up to it, but also all the results which would follow from it. As **30** Cuvier could correctly describe a whole animal by the contemplation of a single bone, so the observer who has thoroughly understood one link in a series of incidents, should be able accurately to state all the other ones, both before and after. We have not yet grasped the results which the reason alone can attain to. Problems may be solved in the study which have baffled all those who have sought a solution by the aid of their senses. To carry the

SHERLOCK HOLMES SAT FOR SOME TIME IN SILENCE WITH HIS HEAD SUNK FORWARD, AND HIS EYES BENT UPON THE RED GLOW OF THE FIRE.

Illustration by Sidney Paget for the *Strand Magazine*, November, 1891.

29 "*Save, perhaps, the Sign of the Four.*" See our remarks on this gratuitous insert of Watson's in our chapter, "Now, Watson, the Fair Sex Is Your Department."

30 *Cuvier.* Georges Léopold Chrétian Frédéric Dagobert, Baron Cuvier, 1769–1832, French naturalist, statesman, philosopher, founder of the science of comparative anatomy.

art, however, to its highest pitch, it is necessary that the reasoner should be able to utilize all the facts which have come to his knowledge, and this in itself implies, as you will readily see, a possession of all knowledge, which, even in these days of free education and encyclopædias, is a somewhat rare accomplishment.   It is not so impossible, however, that a man should possess all knowledge which is likely to be useful to him in his work, and this I have endeavoured in my case to do.   If I remember rightly, you on one occasion, in the early days of our friendship, defined my limits in a very precise fashion."

"Yes," I answered, laughing.   "It was a singular document.   Philosophy, astronomy, and politics were marked at zero, I remember.   Botany variable, geology profound as regards the mudstains from any region within fifty miles of town, chemistry eccentric, anatomy un-systematic, sensational literature and crime records unique, violin player, boxer, swordsman, lawyer, and self-poisoner by cocaine and tobacco.   Those, I think, were the main points of my analysis."

Holmes grinned at the last item.   "Well," he said, " I **31** say now, as I said then, that a man should keep his little brain attic stocked with all the furniture that he is likely to use, and the rest he can put away in the lumber-room of his library, where he can get it if he wants it.   Now, for such a case as the one which has been submitted to us to-night, we need certainly to muster all our resources. Kindly hand me down the letter K of the American Ency-clopædia which stands upon the shelf beside you.   Thank **32** you.   Now let us consider the situation, and see what may be deduced from it.   In the first place, we may start with a strong presumption that Colonel Openshaw had some very strong reason for leaving America.   Men at his time of life do not change all their habits, and exchange willingly the charming climate of Florida for the lonely life of an English provincial town.   His extreme love of solitude in England suggests the idea that he was in fear of someone or something, so we may assume as a working hypothesis that it was fear of someone or something which drove him from America.   As to what it was he feared, we can only deduce that by considering the formidable letters which were received by himself and his successors. Did you remark the postmarks of those letters ? "

"The first was from Pondicherry, the second from Dundee, and the third from London."

"From East London.   What do you deduce from that ? "

"They are all seaports.   That the writer was on board a ship."

"Excellent.   We have already a clue.   There can be no doubt that the probability—the strong probability—is that the writer was on board of a ship.   And now let us consider another point.   In the case of Pondicherry seven weeks elapsed between the threat and its fulfilment, in Dundee it was only some three or four days.   Does that suggest anything ? "

"A greater distance to travel."

"But the letter had also a greater distance to come."

"Then I do not see the point."

31 *Holmes grinned.* And small wonder. Watson in 1881 had made no reference to Holmes as a "self-poisoner by cocaine and tobacco," and he had called the detective's knowledge of chemis-try "profound."

32 *the American Encyclopædia.* Miss Madeleine B. Stern suggests ("Sherlock Holmes: Rare Book Collector") that "the *International Encyclopædia* (New York, 1885), which contains an article on the Klan . . . was possibly the work in question."

33 *obviously of vital importance.* "Just how one or even three men were able to subdue the pistol-packing, drink-crazed [Elias] Openshaw and place him face down in a pool without leaving a sign of their presence will forever remain a mystery. . . . The murderer or murderers then returned to London *but without making any attempt to regain those records* we are told were the *sine qua non* of peaceful repose for some of the South's first men. . . . The circumstances attending the death of John's father verge even closer to the incredible. First by train to Horsham. . . . Then to Portsdown Hill. . . . And yet, after Joseph's death, nobody appeared in any of these places to testify to being questioned recently by a Southern-accented American. Once again there is no attempt to get the records, so presumably there is no end to insomnia in Dixieland."—Benjamin Clark, "The Horsham Fiasco."

"There is at least a presumption that the vessel in which the man or men are is a sailing ship. It looks as if they always sent their singular warning or token before them when starting upon their mission. You see how quickly the deed followed the sign when it came from Dundee. If they had come from Pondicherry in a steamer they would have arrived almost as soon as their letter. But as a matter of fact seven weeks elapsed. I think that those seven weeks represented the difference between the mail boat which brought the letter, and the sailing vessel which brought the writer."

"It is possible."

"More than that. It is probable. And now you see the deadly urgency of this new case, and why I urged young Openshaw to caution. The blow has always fallen at the end of the time which it would take the senders to travel the distance. But this one comes from London, and therefore we cannot count upon delay."

"Good God!" I cried. "What can it mean, this relentless persecution?"

33 "The papers which Openshaw carried are obviously of vital importance to the person or persons in the sailing ship. I think that it is quite clear that there must be more than one of them. A single man could not have carried out two deaths in such a way as to deceive a coroner's jury. There must have been several in it, and they must have been men of resource and determination. Their papers they mean to have, be the holder of them who it may. In this way you see K. K. K. ceases to be the initials of an individual, and becomes the badge of a society."

"But of what society?"

"Have you never—" said Sherlock Holmes, bending forward and sinking his voice—" have you never heard of the Ku Klux Klan?"

"I never have."

Holmes turned over the leaves of the book upon his knee. " Here it is," said he presently, " ' Ku Klux Klan. A name derived from a fanciful resemblance to the sound produced by cocking a rifle. This terrible secret society was formed by some ex-Confederate soldiers in the Southern States after the Civil War, and it rapidly formed local branches in different parts of the country, notably in Tennessee, Louisiana, the Carolinas, Georgia, and Florida. Its power was used for political purposes, principally for the terrorizing of the negro voters, and the murdering or driving from the country of those who were opposed to its views. Its outrages were usually preceded by a warning sent to the marked man in some fantastic but generally recognized shape—a sprig of oak leaves in some parts, melon seeds or orange pips in others. On receiving this the victim might either openly abjure his former ways, or might fly from the country. If he braved the matter out, death would unfailingly come upon him, and usually in some strange and unforeseen manner. So perfect was the organization of the society, and so systematic its methods, that there is hardly a case upon record where any man succeeded in braving it with impunity, or in which any of its outrages were traced home to the perpetrators.   For some years the organization flourished, in spite of the efforts of the United States Government, and of the better classes of the community in the South. Eventually, in the year 1869, the movement rather suddenly collapsed, although there have been sporadic outbreaks of the same sort since that date.'   **34**

"You will observe," said Holmes, laying down the volume, " that the sudden breaking up of the society was coincident with the disappearance of Openshaw from America with their papers.   It may well have been cause and effect.   It is no wonder that he and his family have some of the more implacable spirits upon their track. You can understand that this register and diary may implicate some of the first men in the South, and that there may be many who will not sleep easy at night until it is recovered."

"Then the page which we have seen——"

" Is such as we might expect.   It ran, if I remember right, ' sent the pips to A, B, and C '—that is, sent the society's warning to them.   Then there are successive entries that A and B cleared, or left the country, and finally that C was visited, with, I fear, a sinister result for C.   Well, I think, Doctor, that we may let some light into this dark place, and I believe that the only chance young Openshaw has in the meantime is to do what I have told him.   There is nothing more to be said or to be done to-night, so hand me over my violin and let us try to forget for half an hour the miserable weather, and the still more miserable ways of our fellow-men."

It had cleared in the morning, and the sun was shining with a subdued brightness through the dim veil which hangs over the great city.   Sherlock Holmes was already at breakfast when I came down.

"You will excuse me for not waiting for you," said he ; " I have, I foresee, a very busy day before me in looking into this case of young Openshaw's."

"What steps will you take ? " I asked.

" It will very much depend upon the results of my first inquiries.   I may have to go down to Horsham after all."

"You will not go there first ? "

"No, I shall commence with the City.   Just ring the bell, and the maid will bring up your coffee."

As I waited, I lifted the unopened newspaper from the table and glanced my eye over it.   It rested upon a head- **35** ing which sent a chill to my heart.

"Holmes," I cried, "you are too late."

"Ah ! " said he, laying down his cup, " I feared as much.   How was it done ? "   He spoke calmly, but I could see that he was deeply moved.

" My eye caught the name of Openshaw, and the heading ' Tragedy near Waterloo Bridge.'   Here is the account : ' Between nine and ten last night Police-constable Cook, of the H Division, on duty near Waterloo Bridge, heard a cry for help and a splash in the water. The night, however, was extremely dark and stormy, so that, in spite of the help of several passers-by, it was quite impossible to effect a rescue.   The alarm, however, was given, and, by the aid of the water police, the body was

34 *since that date.* Mr. Manly Wade Wellman has noted ("Two Southern Exposures of Sherlock Holmes") that the original Ku Klux Klan was "broken up and disbanded" by its Grand Wizard, Bedford Forrest, by the end of 1868. But the more disreputable element kept its masks, and even as in more recent years, pirated the K.K.K. label for the perpetration of outrages. Still, preservation of Klan secrets was hardly a matter for killing men in far countries: John C. Lister, one of the Klan's original six founders, published a revealing history of the order in 1884, and he was neither ambushed nor threatened nor even blamed by his former fellows.

35 *I lifted the unopened newspaper from the table.* Showing that the second day could not have been a Sunday.

"HOLMES," I CRIED, "YOU ARE TOO LATE."

Illustration by Sidney Paget for the *Strand Magazine*, November, 1891.

36 *I should send him away to his death——!"*
"John Openshaw has the melancholy distinction of being one of the only two clients to be murdered after they had consulted Holmes, the other unfortunate being Hilton Cubitt of 'The Adventure of the Dancing Men,'" the late Gavin Brend wrote in *My Dear Holmes*.

37 *The Embankment*. This thoroughfare, extending from Blackfriars to Westminster Bridge, is one mile and a third in length and one hundred feet wide. It was formerly opened on July 13, 1870, by King Edward VII, then Prince of Wales, accompanied by Princess Louise. The first idea of embanking the Thames originated with Sir Christopher Wren upon the occasion of the rebuilding of London after the Great Fire of 1666.

38 *All day*. On the opening day of the case "the wind had screamed and the rain had beaten against the windows," according to Watson. The newspaper report of Openshaw's death called the night "extremely dark and stormy." The second day had "cleared in the morning and the sun was shining with a subdued brightness," again according to Watson. In the latter days of September, 1887, there are two days and two days only that answer this description: *Thursday the 29th and Friday the 30th*. In its Thursday morning report, the London *Times* noted rain falling "over the greater part of the British Islands . . . and the fall continues in many places. Thunderstorms have been prevalent." In its Thursday evening report, the *Times* noted "rain falling in London . . ." Said the *Times* in its report for the Friday morning: "Showers of rain have fallen very generally, and thunder and lightning have occurred in most places. The weather has since improved in many places." And in its evening report for the same day: "The weather is, on the whole, fair. . . . Thunder and lightning were again prevalent over our islands on Thursday night."

39 *Of these he took five*. The late Gavin Brend once wrote:

It takes me some time to get to grips
With this sinister business of orange pips.
So, kind Mr. Greengrocer, will you please wait
Whilst I get out a pencil and calculate?
There's five for McCauley and five for John Swain,
Five for Paramore, five again
For Uncle Elias and five for Dad
With five for young John though this makes me feel sad.
Then in case you should think I have ended too soon
Five more are required for Captain Calhoun.
So thirty-five pips, Mr. Greengrocer, please.
How many oranges needed for these?
Yes, I think at last I am coming to grips
With the mathematics of orange pips.

eventually recovered. It proved to be that of a young gentleman whose name, as it appears from an envelope which was found in his pocket, was John Openshaw, and whose residence is near Horsham. It is conjectured that he may have been hurrying down to catch the last train from Waterloo Station, and that in his haste and the extreme darkness, he missed his path, and walked over the edge of one of the small landing-places for river steamboats. The body exhibited no traces of violence, and there can be no doubt that the deceased had been the victim of an unfortunate accident, which should have the effect of calling the attention of the authorities to the condition of the riverside landing-stages.'"

We sat in silence for some minutes, Holmes more depressed and shaken than I had ever seen him.

" That hurts my pride, Watson," he said at last. " It is a petty feeling, no doubt, but it hurts my pride. It becomes a personal matter with me now, and, if God sends me health, I shall set my hand upon this gang. That he should come to me for help, and that I should send him

36 away to his death—— ! " He sprang from his chair, and paced about the room in uncontrollable agitation, with a flush upon his sallow cheeks, and a nervous clasping and unclasping of his long, thin hands.

" They must be cunning devils," he exclaimed at last. " How could they have decoyed him down there ? The

37 Embankment is not on the direct line to the station. The bridge, no doubt, was too crowded, even on such a night, for their purpose. Well, Watson, we shall see who will win in the long run. I am going out now ! "

" To the police ? "

" No ; I shall be my own police. When I have spun the web they may take the flies, but not before."

38 All day I was engaged in my professional work, and it was late in the evening before I returned to Baker Street. Sherlock Holmes had not come back yet. It was nearly ten o'clock before he entered, looking pale and worn. He walked up to the sideboard, and, tearing a piece from the loaf, he devoured it voraciously, washing it down with a long draught of water.

" You are hungry," I remarked.

" Starving. It had escaped my memory. I have had nothing since breakfast."

" Nothing ? "

" Not a bite. I had no time to think of it."

" And how have you succeeded ? "

" Well."

" You have a clue ? "

" I have them in the hollow of my hand. Young Openshaw shall not remain long unavenged. Why, Watson, let us put their own devilish trade-mark upon them. It is well thought of ! "

" What do you mean ? "

He took an orange from the cupboard, and tearing it to pieces, he squeezed out the pips upon the table. Of

39 these he took five, and thrust them into an envelope. On the inside of the flap he wrote, " S.H. for J.C." Then

40 he sealed it and addressed it to " Captain James Calhoun, Barque *Lone Star*, Savannah, Georgia."

"That will await him when he enters port," said he, chuckling. "It may give him a sleepless night. He will find it as sure a precursor of his fate as Openshaw did before him."

"And who is this Captain Calhoun?"

"The leader of the gang. I shall have the others, but he first."

"How did you trace it, then?"

He took a large sheet of paper from his pocket, all covered with dates and names.

"I have spent the whole day," said he, "over Lloyd's registers and the files of old papers, following the future **41** career of every vessel which touched at Pondicherry in January and in February in '83. There were thirty-six ships of fair tonnage which were reported there during those months. Of these, the *Lone Star* instantly attracted my attention, since, although it was reported as having cleared from London, the name is that which is given to one of the States of the Union."

"Texas, I think."

"I was not and am not sure which; but I knew that the ship must have an American origin."   **42**

"What then?"

"I searched the Dundee records, and when I found that the barque *Lone Star* was there in January, '85, my suspicion became a certainty. I then inquired as to vessels which lay at present in the port of London."

"Yes?"

"The *Lone Star* had arrived here last week. I went down to the Albert dock, and found that she had been **43** taken down the river by the early tide this morning, homeward bound to Savannah. I wired to Gravesend, and learned that she had passed some time ago, and as the wind is easterly, I have no doubt that she is now past the Goodwins, and not very far from the Isle of Wight." **44-45**

"What will you do, then?"

"Oh, I have my hand upon him. He and the two mates are, as I learn, the only native-born Americans in the ship. The others are Finns and Germans. I also know that they were all three away from the ship last night. I had it from the stevedore, who has been loading their cargo. By the time their sailing ship reaches Savannah the mail boat will have carried this letter, and the cable will have informed the police of Savannah that these three gentlemen are badly wanted here upon a charge of murder."

There is ever a flaw, however, in the best laid of human plans, and the murderers of John Openshaw were never to receive the orange pips which would show them that another, as cunning and as resolute as themselves, was upon their track. Very long and severe were the equinoctial gales that year. We waited long for news of the *Lone Star* of Savannah, but none ever reached us. We did at last hear that somewhere far out in the Atlantic a shattered sternpost of a boat was seen swinging in the trough of a wave, with the letters " L. S." carved upon it, **46** and that is all which we shall ever know of the fate of the *Lone Star.*

40 *"Captain James Calhoun.* "All three murders . . . carry Moriarty's signature," Mr. James Buchholtz wrote in "A Tremor at the Edge of the Web." "Here are three homicides dismissed by the authorities as suicide or accident. . . . [Holmes' reference to the gang he would set his hand upon] is clearly to the gang he *did* eliminate within the next few years. . . . With Holmes in such a mood, there can be little doubt as to who the true recipient of orange pips which he sent was. . . . It is here that the death struggle above the Reichenbach Falls begins."

That Moriarty was behind the affair of the Pips is also the view of Mr. Benjamin Clark ("The Horsham Fiasco"): "If the smokescreen of Klan persecution were eliminated, attention would logically be turned to the question of who, after John's death, inherited Elias' considerable fortune and Joseph's handsome competence. We have at least *prima facie* evidence suggesting that the love of money ran strong in the Openshaws. . . . Also consider the propensity to violence apparent in the Colonel. Is the assumption improbable that these strains were to be found commingled in less diluted form in the blood of a relative whose name was never made known to us. Could that unknown, an individual of genius-like cleverness and fiendish greed, have engineered the whole scheme. By any chance could he have been—'Dear me, Mr. Holmes, dear me!' "

41 *Lloyd's registers.* Holmes refers to Lloyd's Register of Shipping, not to be confused with Lloyd's Bank or "Lloyd's of London."

42 *an American origin."* It did, indeed. The barque *Lone Star*, a real ship, was "found in the Georgia register (owner—Johannsen Brothers of Savannah)," by Mr. Richard W. Clarke ("On the Nomenclature of Watson's Ships").

43 *the Albert dock.* See *The Sign of the Four,* Note 162.

44 *the Goodwins.* Dangerous shoals, about ten miles long, in the Straits of Dover, about five miles off the eastern coast of Kent.

45 *the Isle of Wight."* An island off Hampshire, 23 by 13 miles; it has cement manufactures, is a summer resort, yachting center, and favorite place of residence.

46 *with the letters "L. S." carved upon it.* "A ship's stern-post ordinarily bears the craft's name, not her initials," Mr. Rolfe Boswell noted in "A Connecticut Yankee in Support of Sir Arthur."

Auctorial Note: Conan Doyle placed "The Five Orange Pips" seventh on his list of the "twelve best" Sherlock Holmes short stories, excluding those in the *Case-Book.*

27

A CASE OF IDENTITY

[Tuesday, October 18, to Wednesday, October 19, 1887]

1 *throughout three continents.* The two continents other than Europe in which Holmes was unofficial adviser and helper to everybody absolutely puzzled is an interesting subject for speculation.

2 *I picked up the morning paper.* The day was therefore not a Sunday.

"MY dear fellow," said Sherlock Holmes, as we sat on either side of the fire in his lodgings at Baker Street, " life is infinitely stranger than anything which the mind of man could invent. We would not dare to conceive the things which are really mere commonplaces of existence. If we could fly out of that window hand in hand, hover over this great city, gently remove the roofs, and peep in at the queer things which are going on, the strange coincidences, the plannings, the cross-purposes, the wonderful chains of events, working through generations, and leading to the most *outré* results, it would make all fiction with its conventionalities and foreseen conclusions most stale and unprofitable."

" And yet I am not convinced of it," I answered. " The cases which come to light in the papers are, as a rule, bald enough, and vulgar enough. We have in our police reports realism pushed to its extreme limits, and yet the result is, it must be confessed, neither fascinating nor artistic."

" A certain selection and discretion must be used in producing a realistic effect," remarked Holmes. " This is wanting in the police report, where more stress is laid perhaps upon the platitudes of the magistrate than upon the details, which to an observer contain the vital essence of the whole matter. Depend upon it there is nothing so unnatural as the commonplace."

I smiled and shook my head. " I can quite understand you thinking so," I said. " Of course, in your position of unofficial adviser and helper to everybody who is absolutely puzzled, throughout three continents, you are brought in contact with all that is strange and bizarre. But here "—I picked up the morning paper from the ground—" let us put it to a practical test. Here is the first heading upon which I come. ' A husband's cruelty to his wife.' There is half a column of print, but I know without reading it that it is all perfectly familiar to me. There is, of course, the other woman, the drink, the push, the blow, the bruise, the sympathetic sister or landlady. The crudest of writers could invent nothing more crude."

" Indeed, your example is an unfortunate one for your argument," said Holmes, taking the paper, and glancing his eye down it. " This is the Dundas separation case, and, as it happens, I was engaged in clearing up some small points in connection with it. The husband was a teetotaller, there was no other woman, and the conduct complained of was that he had drifted into the habit of winding up every meal by taking out his false teeth and hurling them at his wife, which you will allow is not an **3** action likely to occur to the imagination of the average story-teller. Take a pinch of snuff, Doctor, and acknowledge that I have scored over you in your example."

He held out his snuff-box of old gold, with a great amethyst in the centre of the lid. Its splendour was in such contrast to his homely ways and simple life that I could not help commenting upon it.

" Ah," said he, " I forgot that I had not seen you for some weeks. It is a little souvenir from the King of Bohemia in return for my assistance in the case of the Irene Adler papers." **4**

" And the ring ? " I asked, glancing at a remarkable brilliant which sparkled upon his finger. **5**

" It was from the reigning family of Holland, though **6** the matter in which I served them was of such delicacy that I cannot confide it even to you, who have been good enough to chronicle one or two of my little problems."

" And have you any on hand just now ? " I asked with interest.

" Some ten or twelve, but none which presents any feature of interest. They are important, you understand, **7** without being interesting. Indeed, I have found that it is usually in unimportant matters that there is a field for observation, and for the quick analysis of cause and effect which gives the charm to an investigation. The larger crimes are apt to be the simpler, for the bigger the crime, the more obvious, as a rule, is the motive. In these cases, save for one rather intricate matter which has been referred to me from Marseilles, there is nothing which presents any features of interest. It is possible, however, that I may have something better before very many minutes are over, for this is one of my clients, or I am much mistaken."

HE HELD OUT HIS SNUFF-BOX OF OLD GOLD, WITH A GREAT AMETHYST IN THE CENTRE OF THE LID.

The snuffbox, shown here, is now in the collection of the Sherlock Holmes Tavern. It was undoubtedly, we feel, the work of a gifted Bohemian craftsman and had been especially commissioned by the King. The work would take some time—say four or five months —but we are surely safe in saying that "A Scandal in Bohemia" and "A Case of Identity" probably fall within a six months' period and certainly fall with a twelve months' span.

3 *taking out his false teeth and hurling them at his wife.* "This interesting case . . . involved a bit of leg-pulling, I'm afraid, for . . . even today, with all the skill of modern dental science, we cannot construct a set of artificial teeth that would withstand such violent and frequent abuse," Dr. Charles Goodman wrote in "The Dental Holmes."

4 *the Irene Adler papers.*" The "papers" is a little mysterious. There were the letters written to Irene by the King of Bohemia, but, as Holmes himself pointed out, "How is she to prove their authenticity?" There were "No legal papers or certificates"; Holmes' concern was entirely with the photograph.

5 *a remarkable brilliant.* Perhaps a diamond, perhaps some other gem cut in the classic form of a brilliant: a form resembling two cones placed base to base, the upper being truncated comparatively near its base and the lower having the apex only cut off.

6 *the reigning family of Holland.* Another indication that "A Case of Identity" was not long after "A Scandal in Bohemia."

7 *none which presents any feature of interest.* Holmes at this period was evidently not yet so well off that he could afford to rid himself entirely of handling a number of small fry, similar to those who called upon his services in the early months of 1881 (*A Study in Scarlet*).

"THIS IS THE DUNDAS SEPARATION CASE . . ."

"Perhaps there may be some reason to believe that the arms are: argent, a lion rampant gules, as shown under 'Downdas of that ilk,' in the facsimile of an old heraldic manuscript," Dr. Julian Wolff wrote in his *Practical Handbook of Sherlockian Heraldry.*

. . . A BROAD-BRIMMED HAT WHICH WAS TILTED IN A
COQUETTISH DUCHESS-OF-DEVONSHIRE FASHION OVER HER
EAR.

This is Gainsborough's portrait of the Duchess of
Devonshire, Georgiana Cavendish, 1757–1806, a
celebrated beauty and setter of fashions.

SHERLOCK HOLMES WELCOMED HER WITH THE EASY
COURTESY FOR WHICH HE WAS REMARKABLE . . .

Illustration by Sidney Paget for the *Strand Magazine*, September, 1891.

He had risen from his chair, and was standing between
the parted blinds, gazing down into the dull, neutral-
tinted London street. Looking over his shoulder I saw
that on the pavement opposite there stood a large woman
with a heavy fur boa round her neck, and a large curling
red feather in a broad-brimmed hat which was tilted in a
coquettish Duchess-of-Devonshire fashion over her ear.
From under this great panoply she peeped up in a nervous, hesitating fashion at our windows, while her body
oscillated backwards and forwards, and her fingers fidgeted
with her glove buttons. Suddenly, with a plunge, as of
the swimmer who leaves the bank, she hurried across the
road, and we heard the sharp clang of the bell.

" I have seen those symptoms before," said Holmes,
throwing his cigarette into the fire. " Oscillation upon
8 the pavement always means an *affaire du cœur*. She
would like advice, but is not sure that the matter is not
too delicate for communication. And yet even here we
may discriminate. When a woman has been seriously
wronged by a man she no longer oscillates, and the usual
symptom is a broken bell wire. Here we may take it
that there is a love matter, but that the maiden is not so
much angry as perplexed, or grieved. But here she
comes in person to resolve our doubts."

As he spoke there was a tap at the door, and the boy in
buttons entered to announce Miss Mary Sutherland, while
the lady herself loomed behind his small black figure like
a full-sailed merchantman behind a tiny pilot boat. Sherlock Holmes welcomed her with the easy courtesy for
which he was remarkable, and having closed the door,
and bowed her into an arm-chair, he looked over her in the
minute and yet abstracted fashion which was peculiar to
him.

" Do you not find," he said, " that with your short
sight it is a little trying to do so much typewriting ? "

" I did at first," she answered, " but now I know where
the letters are without looking." Then, suddenly realizing the full purport of his words, she gave a violent start,
and looked up with fear and astonishment upon her
broad, good-humoured face. " You've heard about me,
Mr. Holmes," she cried, " else how could you know all
that ? "

" Never mind," said Holmes, laughing, " it is my business to know things. Perhaps I have trained myself to
see what others overlook. If not, why should you come
to consult me ? "

" I came to you, sir, because I heard of you from Mrs.
Etherege, whose husband you found so easy when the
police and everyone had given him up for dead. Oh,
Mr. Holmes, I wish you would do as much for me. I'm
9 not rich, but still I have a hundred a year in my own right,
besides the little that I make by the machine, and I would
give it all to know what has become of Mr. Hosmer
Angel."

" Why did you come away to consult me in such a
hurry ? " asked Sherlock Holmes, with his finger-tips
together, and his eyes to the ceiling.

Again a startled look came over the somewhat vacuous
face of Miss Mary Sutherland. " Yes, I did bang out of

the house," she said, " for it made me angry to see the easy way in which Mr. Windibank—that is, my father—took it all.   He would not go to the police, and he would not go to you, and so at last, as he would do nothing, and kept on saying that there was no harm done, it made me mad, and I just on with my things and came right away to you."

" Your father ? " said Holmes.   " Your stepfather, surely, since the name is different ? "

" Yes, my stepfather.   I call him father, though it sounds funny, too, for he is only five years and two months older than myself."

" And your mother is alive ? "

" Oh, yes, mother is alive and well.   I wasn't best pleased, Mr. Holmes, when she married again so soon after father's death, and a man who was nearly fifteen years younger than herself.   Father was a plumber in the Tottenham Court Road, and he left a tidy business **10** behind him, which mother carried on with Mr. Hardy, the foreman, but when Mr. Windibank came he made her sell the business, for he was very superior, being a traveller in wines.   They got four thousand seven hundred for **11** the goodwill and interest, which wasn't near as much as father could have got if he had been alive."

I had expected to see Sherlock Holmes impatient under this rambling and inconsequential narrative, but, on the contrary, he had listened with the greatest concentration of attention.

" Your own little income," he asked, " does it come out of the business ? "

" Oh, no, sir, it is quite separate, and was left me by my Uncle Ned in Auckland.   It is in New Zealand Stock, paying $4\frac{1}{2}$ per cent.   Two thousand five hundred pounds was the amount, but I can only touch the interest." **12**

" You interest me extremely," said Holmes.   " And since you draw so large a sum as a hundred a year, with what you earn into the bargain, you no doubt travel a little and indulge yourself in every way.   I believe that a single lady can get on very nicely upon an income of about sixty pounds." **13**

" I could do with much less than that, Mr. Holmes, but you understand that as long as I live at home I don't wish to be a burden to them, and so they have the use of the money just while I am staying with them.   Of course that is only just for the time.   Mr. Windibank draws my interest every quarter, and pays it over to mother, and I find that I can do pretty well with what I earn at type-writing.   It brings me twopence a sheet, and I can often do from fifteen to twenty sheets in a day."

"IT BRINGS ME TWOPENCE A SHEET . . ."

"The twopence coin deserves some separate mention," the late A. Carson Simpson wrote in *Numismatics in the Canon*, Part I, "since it is the modern form of the old half-groat, a silver piece first struck by Edward III in 1351, when England finally found it needed a silver coin larger than the penny, and the groat and half-groat were added to the monetary system. It was struck regularly until it became an exclusively Maundy coin—even when the groat itself was dropped temporarily (from early in the reign of Elizabeth I through the Commonwealth) . . ." Shown here is the 1824 George IV Maundy twopence.

8 *an* affaire du cœur. French: a love affair.

9 *a hundred a year.* A hundred pounds; about $500 a year U.S. at the time.

10 *the Tottenham Court Road.* "The Tottenham Court Road," Mr. Harold P. Clunn wrote in *The Face of London*, "was a favourite resort of Londoners in the early part of the seventeenth century, because it led to the old Manor House of Totham Court. It was then a country road with hawthorn hedges and containing good pastures and meadows on both sides, but occasionally rowdiness and disorders occurred in this locality. Here booths were erected and gaming and prize-fighting were indulged in, which culminated in riots and other offences calculated to create a breach of the peace. Tottenham Court Road was mostly built between 1770 and 1800 and until the concluding years of the nineteenth century was a shabby street, but to-day it is the great centre of the London furnishing establishments and nearly the whole of the east side has been rebuilt in the past fifty years."

It was in Tottenham Court Road that Holmes found the broker who sold him a Stradivarius for only fifty-five shillings ("The Cardboard Box"). Here, too, was Morton and Waylight's, where the knocked-about Mr. Warren was timekeeper ("The Adventure of the Red Circle"). And it was at the corner of Tottenham Court Road and Goodge Street that a fracas occurred during which Mr. Henry Baker lost a goose ("The Adventure of the Blue Carbuncle").

11 *four thousand seven hundred.* About $23,500.

12 *Two thousand five hundred pounds.* About $12,500.

13 *about sixty pounds.* A highly revealing statement on the cost of living in Britain in the 1880's. A single lady could then get on very nicely upon an income of about sixty pounds—about $300—a year. Since Mary Sutherland had an income of one hundred pounds ($500) and an earned income of £37/18 (about $189.50—see below—assuming an average output of seventeen and a half sheets a day, a five-day week and no holidays) it is not surprising that she could dress in such finery.

"I MET HIM FIRST AT THE GASFITTERS' BALL . . ."

Illustration by Sidney Paget for the *Strand Magazine*, September, 1891.

"You have made your position very clear to me," said Holmes. "This is my friend, Dr. Watson, before whom you can speak as freely as before myself. Kindly tell us now all about your connection with Mr. Hosmer Angel."

A flush stole over Miss Sutherland's face, and she picked nervously at the fringe of her jacket. "I met him first at the gasfitters' ball," she said. "They used to send father tickets when he was alive, and then afterwards they remembered us, and sent them to mother. Mr. Windibank did not wish us to go. He never did wish us to go anywhere. He would get quite mad if I wanted so much as to join a Sunday school treat. But this time I was set on going, and I would go, for what right had he to prevent? He said the folk were not fit for us to know, when all father's friends were to be there. And he said that I had nothing fit to wear, when I had my purple plush that I had never so much as taken out of the drawer. At last, when nothing else would do, he went off to France upon the business of the firm, but we went, mother and I, with Mr. Hardy, who used to be our foreman, and it was there I met Mr. Hosmer Angel."

"I suppose," said Holmes, "that when Mr. Windibank came back from France, he was very annoyed at your having gone to the ball."

"Oh, well, he was very good about it. He laughed, I remembered, and shrugged his shoulders, and said there was no use denying anything to a woman, for she would have her way."

"I see. Then at the gasfitters' ball you met, as I understand, a gentleman called Mr. Hosmer Angel."

"Yes, sir. I met him that night, and he called next day to ask if we had got home all safe, and after that we met him—that is to say, Mr. Holmes, I met him twice for walks, but after that father came back again, and Mr. Hosmer Angel could not come to the house any more."

"No?"

"Well, you know, father didn't like anything of the sort. He wouldn't have any visitors if he could help it, and he used to say that a woman should be happy in her own family circle. But then, as I used to say to mother, a woman wants her own circle to begin with, and I had not got mine yet."

"But how about Mr. Hosmer Angel? Did he make no attempt to see you?"

"Well, father was going off to France again in a week, and Hosmer wrote and said that it would be safer and better not to see each other until he had gone. We could write in the meantime, and he used to write every day. I took the letters in in the morning so there was no need for father to know."

"Were you engaged to the gentleman at this time?"

"Oh yes, Mr. Holmes. We were engaged after the first walk that we took. Hosmer—Mr. Angel—was a 14 cashier in an office in Leadenhall Street—and——"

"What office?"

"That's the worst of it, Mr. Holmes, I don't know."

"Where did he live then?"

"He slept on the premises."

" And you don't know his address ? "

" No—except that it was Leadenhall Street."

" Where did you address your letters, then ? "

" To the Leadenhall Street Post Office, to be left till called for. He said that if they were sent to the office he would be chaffed by all the other clerks about having letters from a lady, so I offered to typewrite them, like he did his, but he wouldn't have that, for he said that when I wrote them they seemed to come from me but when they were typewritten he always felt that the machine had come between us. That will just show you how fond he was of me, Mr. Holmes, and the little things that he would think of."

" It was most suggestive," said Holmes. " It has long been an axiom of mine that the little things are infinitely the most important. Can you remember any other little things about Mr. Hosmer Angel ? "

" He was a very shy man, Mr. Holmes. He would rather walk with me in the evening than in the daylight, for he said that he hated to be conspicuous. Very retiring and gentlemanly he was. Even his voice was gentle. He'd had the quinsy and swollen glands when he was young, he told me, and it had left him with a weak throat, and a hesitating, whispering fashion of speech. He was always well-dressed, very neat and plain, but his eyes were weak, just as mine are, and he wore tinted glasses against the glare."

" Well, and what happened when Mr. Windibank, your stepfather, returned to France ? "

" Mr. Hosmer Angel came to the house again, and proposed that we should marry before father came back. He was in dreadful earnest, and made me swear, with my hands on the Testament, that whatever happened I would always be true to him. Mother said he was quite right to make me swear, and that it was a sign of his passion. Mother was all in his favour from the first, and was even fonder of him than I was. Then, when they talked of marrying within the week, I began to ask about father ; but they both said never to mind about father, but just to tell him afterwards, and mother said she would make it all right with him. I didn't quite like that, Mr. Holmes. It seemed funny that I should ask his leave, as he was only a few years older than me ; but I didn't want to do anything on the sly, so I wrote to father at Bordeaux, where the Company has its French offices, but the letter came back to me on the very morning of the wedding."

" It missed him then ? "

" Yes, sir, for he had started to England just before it arrived."

" Ha ! that was unfortunate. Your wedding was arranged, then, for the Friday. Was it to be in church ? "

" Yes, sir, but very quietly. It was to be at St. Saviour's, near King's Cross, and we were to have break-**15** fast afterwards at the St. Pancras Hotel. Hosmer came **16** for us in a hansom, but as there were two of us, he put us both into it, and stepped himself into a four-wheeler which happened to be the only other cab in the street. We got to the church first, and when the four-wheeler drove up we waited for him to step out, but he never did, and when the cabman got down from the box and looked,

15 *King's Cross.* This neighborhood, Mr. Harold P. Clunn wrote in *The Face of London*, "was formerly known as Battlebridge and underwent a great transformation about 125 years ago. Before 1820 it had been a filthy and dangerous neighbourhood, and here the dustcarts of London used to be emptied. Afterwards all the mean hovels were removed and decent houses erected in their place. Battlebridge was renamed King's Cross after George IV and is supposed to have been the spot where King Alfred fought the Danes."

16 *St. Pancras Hotel.* St. Saviour's, or Southwark Cathedral, which stands at the south end of London Bridge, seems a most unlikely place for Miss Sutherland's wedding. Since she tells us that the wedding breakfast was to be celebrated at the St. Pancras Hotel, it is suggested that she confused St. Pancras Old Church, which *is* close to King's Cross, with the hotel at which the breakfast was to have been served.

" . . . WHEN THE CABMAN GOT DOWN FROM THE BOX AND LOOKED, THERE WAS NO ONE THERE!"

Illustration by Sidney Paget for the *Strand Magazine*, September, 1891.

17 *That was last Friday.* Holmes says to Mary Sutherland: "Your wedding was arranged, then, for Friday . . ." and Mary answers: "That was last Friday, Mr. Holmes." The case therefore took place before the Friday of the following week, or Holmes and Mary would have said "a week ago today" rather than "the Friday" and "last Friday."

18 *last Saturday's* Chronicle." "Experience suggests that neither the bride nor the advertising department would proceed at this speed," the late Gavin Brend wrote in *My Dear Holmes.*

there was no one there ! The cabman said he could not imagine what had become of him, for he had seen him get **17** in with his own eyes. That was last Friday, Mr. Holmes, and I have never seen or heard anything since then to throw any light upon what became of him."

" It seems to me that you have been very shamefully treated," said Holmes.

"Oh no, sir ! He was too good and kind to leave me so. Why, all the morning he was saying to me that, whatever happened, I was to be true ; and that even if something quite unforeseen occurred to separate us, I was always to remember that I was pledged to him, and that he would claim his pledge sooner or later. It seemed strange talk for a wedding morning, but what has happened since gives a meaning to it."

" Most certainly it does. Your own opinion is, then, that some unforeseen catastrophe has occurred to him ? "

" Yes, sir. I believe that he foresaw some danger, or else he would not have talked so. And then I think that what he foresaw happened."

" But you have no notion as to what it could have been ? "

" None."

" One more question. How did your mother take the matter ? "

" She was angry, and said that I was never to speak of the matter again."

" And your father ? Did you tell him ? "

" Yes, and he seemed to think, with me, that something had happened, and that I should hear of Hosmer again. As he said, what interest could anyone have in bringing me to the doors of the church, and then leaving me ? Now, if he had borrowed my money, or if he had married me and got my money settled on him, there might be some reason ; but Hosmer was very independent about money, and never would look at a shilling of mine. And yet what could have happened ? And why could he not write ? Oh, it drives me half mad to think of it ! and I can't sleep a wink at night." She pulled a little handkerchief out of her muff, and began to sob heavily into it.

" I shall glance into the case for you," said Holmes, rising, " and I have no doubt that we shall reach some definite result. Let the weight of the matter rest upon me now, and do not let your mind dwell upon it further. Above all, try to let Mr. Hosmer Angel vanish from your memory, as he has done from your life."

" Then you don't think I'll see him again ? "

" I fear not."

" Then what has happened to him ? "

" You will leave that question in my hands. I should like an accurate description of him, and any letters of his which you can spare."

18 " I advertised for him in last Saturday's *Chronicle*," said she. " Here is the slip, and here are four letters from him."

" Thank you. And your address ? "

" 31 Lyon Place, Camberwell."

" Mr. Angel's address you never had, I understand. Where is your father's place of business ? "

" He travels for Westhouse & Marbank, the great claret

importers of Fenchurch Street." **19**

" Thank you. You have made your statement **very** clearly. You will leave the papers here, and remember the advice which I have given you. Let the whole incident be a sealed book, and do not allow it to affect your life."

You are very kind, Mr. Holmes, but I cannot do that. I shall be true to Hosmer. He shall find me ready when he comes back."

For all the preposterous hat and the vacuous face, there was something noble in the simple faith of our visitor which compelled our respect. She laid her little bundle of papers upon the table, and went her way, with a promise to come again whenever she might be summoned.

Sherlock Holmes sat silent for a few minutes with his finger-tips still pressed together, his legs stretched out in front of him, and his gaze directed upwards to the ceiling. Then he took down from the rack the old and oily clay pipe, which was to him as a counsellor, and, having lit it he leaned back in his chair, with the thick blue cloud-wreaths spinning up from him, and a look of infinite languor in his face.

" Quite an interesting study, that maiden," he observed. " I found her more interesting than her little problem, which, by the way, is rather a trite one. You will find parallel cases, if you consult my index, in Andover in '77, **20** and there was something of the sort at The Hague last year. Old as is the idea, however, there were one or two details which were new to me. But the maiden herself was most instructive."

" You appeared to read a good deal upon her which was quite invisible to me," I remarked.

" Not invisible, but unnoticed, Watson. You did not know where to look, and so you missed all that was important. I can never bring you to realize the importance of sleeves, the suggestiveness of thumb-nails, or the great issues that may hang from a bootlace. Now what did you gather from that woman's appearance ? Describe it."

" Well, she had a slate-coloured, broad-brimmed straw hat, with a feather of a brickish red. Her jacket was black, with black beads sewn upon it, and a fringe of little black jet ornaments. Her dress was brown, rather darker than coffee colour, with a little purple plush at the neck and sleeves. Her gloves were greyish, and were worn through at the right forefinger. Her boots I didn't observe. She had small, round, hanging gold ear-rings, and a general air of being fairly well to do, in a vulgar, comfortable, easy-going way."

Sherlock Holmes clapped his hands softly together and chuckled.

" 'Pon my word, Watson, you are coming along wonderfully. You have really done very well indeed. It is true that you have missed everything of importance, but you have hit upon the method, and you have a quick eye for colour. Never trust to general impressions, my boy, but concentrate yourself upon details. My first glance is always at a woman's sleeve. In a man it is perhaps better first to take the knee of the trouser. As you observe, this woman had plush upon her sleeves, which is a most use-

SHE LAID HER LITTLE BUNDLE OF PAPERS UPON THE
TABLE . . .

Illustration by Sidney Paget for the *Strand Magazine*, September, 1891.

19 *Fenchurch Street*." "From Lombard Street, Fenchurch Street leads to Aldgate, taking its name from the fenny ground caused by the overflowings of the Lang Bourne, a clear brook of sweet water which ran down Fen Church Street and Lombard Street as far as St. Mary Woolnoth, where it broke into several small rills which flowed southward to the Thames," Augustus J. C. Hare wrote in *Walks in London*, Vol. I. "Many of the buildings in this street bear a date immediately after the Great Fire, in which it was consumed. Pepys saw 'Fanchurch Street, Gracious Street, and Lombard Street all in dust.' "

20 *Andover*. A municipal borough in Hampshire.

21 *on the morning of the 14th.* Since Mr. Hosmer Angel disappeared on the day set for the wedding, and this day was "last Friday," we can now say with some assurance that "A Case of Identity" took place after a Friday the 14th and a Saturday the 15th and before a Friday the 21st. In what years between March, 1881, and August, 1890, can we find such a Friday and Saturday? We can find them in 1883 and 1888, when the 14th and 15th of *September* were a Friday and Saturday, and we can find them in 1881 and 1887, when the 14th and 15th of *October* were a Friday and Saturday. Evidence from *The Sign of the Four*, "A Scandal in Bohemia" and "The Red-Headed League" will eliminate for us 1881, 1883, and 1888. The Friday on which Hosmer Angel disappeared is clearly Friday, October 14, 1887, and the Saturday on which Mary's advertisement appeared Saturday, October 15, 1887.

22 *Balzac.* Honoré de Balzac, 1799–1850, French novelist, whose greatest work is his many-volumed *La Comédie humaine.*

ful material for showing traces. The double line a little above the wrist, where the typewritist presses against the table, was beautifully defined. The sewing-machine, of the hand type, leaves a similar mark, but only on the left arm, and on the side of it farthest from the thumb, instead of being right across the broadest part, as this was. I then glanced at her face, and observing the dint of a pince-nez at either side of her nose, I ventured a remark upon short sight and typewriting, which seemed to surprise her."

" It surprised me."

" But, surely, it was very obvious. I was then much surprised and interested on glancing down to observe that, though the boots which she was wearing were not unlike each other, they were really odd ones, the one having a slightly decorated toe-cap, and the other a plain one. One was buttoned only in the two lower buttons out of five, and the other at the first, third, and fifth. Now, when you see that a young lady, otherwise neatly dressed, has come away from home with odd boots, half buttoned, it is no great deduction to say that she came away in a hurry."

" And what else ? " I asked, keenly interested, as I always was, by my friend's incisive reasoning.

" I noted, in passing, that she had written a note before leaving home, but after being fully dressed. You observed that her right glove was torn at the forefinger, but you did not apparently see that both glove and finger were stained with violet ink. She had written in a hurry, and dipped her pen too deep. It must have been this morning, or the mark would not remain clear upon the finger. All this is amusing, though rather elementary, but I must go back to business, Watson. Would you mind reading me the advertised description of Mr. Hosmer Angel ? "

I held the little printed slip to the light. " Missing,"
21 it said, " on the morning of the 14th, a gentleman named Hosmer Angel. About 5ft. 7in. in height ; strongly built, sallow complexion, black hair, a little bald in the centre, bushy black side whiskers and moustache ; tinted glasses, slight infirmity of speech. Was dressed, when last seen, in black frock-coat faced with silk, black waistcoat, gold Albert chain, and grey Harris tweed trousers, with brown gaiters over elastic-sided boots. Known to have been employed in an office in Leadenhall Street. Anybody bringing," etc. etc.

" That will do," said Holmes. " As to the letters," he continued glancing over them, " they are very commonplace. Absolutely no clue in them to Mr. Angel,
22 save that he quotes Balzac once. There is one remarkable point, however, which will no doubt strike you."

" They are typewritten," I remarked.

" Not only that, but the signature is typewritten. Look at the neat little ' Hosmer Angel ' at the bottom. There is a date you see, but no superscription, except Leadenhall Street, which is rather vague. The point about the signature is very suggestive—in fact, we may call it conclusive."

" Of what ? "

" My dear fellow, is it possible you do not see how strongly it bears upon the case."

" I cannot say that I do, unless it were that he wished to be able to deny his signature if an action for breach of promise were instituted."

" No, that was not the point. However, I shall write two letters which should settle the matter. One is to a firm in the City, the other is to the young lady's stepfather, Mr. Windibank, asking him whether he could meet us here at six o'clock to-morrow evening. It is just as well that we should do business with the male relatives. And now, Doctor, we can do nothing until the answers to those letters come, so we may put our little problem upon the shelf for the interim."

I had had so many reasons to believe in my friend's subtle powers of reasoning, and extraordinary energy in action, that I felt that he must have some solid grounds for the assured and easy demeanour with which he treated the singular mystery which he had been called upon to fathom. Only once had I known him to fail, in the case of the King of Bohemia and of the Irene Adler photograph, but when I looked back to the weird business of the Sign of Four, and the extraordinary circumstances **23** connected with the Study in Scarlet, I felt that it would be a strange tangle indeed which he could not unravel.

I left him then, still puffing at his black clay pipe, with the conviction that when I came again on the next evening I would find that he held in his hands all the clues which would lead up to the identity of the disappearing bridegroom of Miss Mary Sutherland.

A professional case of great gravity was engaging my own attention at the time, and the whole of next day I was busy at the bedside of the sufferer. It was not until close upon six o'clock that I found myself free, and was able to spring into a hansom and drive to Baker Street, half afraid that I might be too late to assist at the *dénouement* of the little mystery. I found Sherlock Holmes **24** alone, however, half asleep, with his long, thin form curled up in the recesses of his arm-chair. A formidable array of bottles and test-tubes, with the pungent cleanly smell of hydrochloric acid, told me that he had spent his day in the chemical work which was so dear to him.

" Well, have you solved it ? " I asked as I entered.

" Yes. It was the bisulphate of baryta." **25**

" No, no, the mystery ! " I cried.

" Oh, that ! I thought of the salt that I have been working upon. There was never any mystery in the matter, though, as I said yesterday, some of the details are of interest. The only drawback is that there is no law, I fear, that can touch the scoundrel."

" Who was he, then, and what was his object in deserting Miss Sutherland ? "

The question was hardly out of my mouth, and Holmes had not yet opened his lips to reply, when we heard a heavy footfall in the passage, and a tap at the door.

" This is the girl's stepfather, Mr. James Windibank," said Holmes. " He has written to me to say that he **26** would be here at six. Come in ! "

The man who entered was a sturdy middle-sized fellow, some thirty years of age, clean shaven, and sallow skinned, with a bland, insinuating manner, and a pair of wonder-

23 *when I looked back to the weird business of the Sign of Four.* See our remarks on this statement of Watson's in the chapter titled "Now, Watson the Fair Sex Is Your Department."

24 dénouement. French: the final revelation or occurrence which clarifies the nature and outcome of a plot.

25 *the bisulphate of baryta."* ". . . barium bisulfate does not exist . . . ," Professor Remsen Ten Eyck Schenck wrote in "Baker Street Fables."

But Mr. L. S. Holstein replied (" '7. Knowledge of Chemistry—Profound' "): "Although Dr. Schenck says barium bisulphate does not exist, a reference to Mellors' *Inorganic Chemistry* (Vol. III, p. 784) —a universally recognized authority—will elicit the information that the bisulphate does exist; and, in addition, Mellor states its known properties . . ."

The editors of the Catalogue of the Sherlock Holmes Exhibition wrote: "Barium Hydrogen Sulphate (Bisulphate of baryta) [is a] substance . . . first prepared by J. J. Berzelius in 1843. . . . It is decomposed by water. . . . Apart from some doubt as to its precise structure, the compound is of little interest, and has never been more than a chemical curiosity; it has certainly never been an article of commercial supply. The only source of such a compound would be from a private collection. It seems probable that a sealed tube of the substance which had lost its label was found by one of Holmes' friends in a University laboratory; and

I FOUND SHERLOCK HOLMES ALONE, . . . HALF ASLEEP, WITH HIS LONG, THIN FORM CURLED UP IN THE RECESSES OF HIS ARM-CHAIR.

Illustration by Sidney Paget for the *Strand Magazine*, September, 1891.

the finder, knowing that Holmes made something of a hobby of routine chemical analysis, asked him to identify it."

More recently, Mr. D. A. Redmond ("Some Chemical Problems in the Canon") has noted that the hexasulphide of barium, $BaS_6O_6.3H_2O$, may be precipitated by acetone. ("I had better postpone my analysis of the acetones."—Holmes in "The Adventure of the Copper Beeches.") Mr. Redmond suggests that this "points to a consistent pattern of investigation by the Master, lasting for an extended time. Stemming from his original investigation on blood, dating from his days at Bart's, he pursued a line of biochemical research singularly neglected by later workers."

26 *He has written to me.* Holmes later tells us that he had also received a letter by the same post from Westhouse & Marbank. The second day of the adventure was therefore not a Sunday.

27 *dropped his gloves.* Mary Sutherland came to Baker Street with a large, heavy fur boa around her neck, with a broad-brimmed straw hat with a large, curling feather, with button gloves and with a jacket. The next afternoon Mr. Windibank came to Baker Street wearing a top hat with gloves, but there is no mention of an overcoat or an umbrella. We must therefore look for two warm, clear days in the period Monday, October 17, through Thursday, October 20, 1887: 1) Monday, October 17th, was "fair but cold and hazy." 2) On Tuesday, October 18th, the "weather was milder generally than of late" and "except in the North and Northwest" the weather was dry. 3) On Wednesday, October 19th, the weather was "fair on the whole." There were "light breezes from the west, with a

"WHAT! WHERE?" SHOUTED MR. WINDIBANK, TURNING WHITE TO THE LIPS, AND GLANCING ABOUT HIM LIKE A RAT IN A TRAP.

Illustration by Sidney Paget for the *Strand Magazine*, September, 1891.

fully sharp and penetrating grey eyes. He shot a questioning glance at each of us, placed his shiny top-hat upon the sideboard, and, with a slight bow, sidled down into the nearest chair.

"Good evening, Mr. James Windibank," said Holmes. "I think that this typewritten letter is from you, in which you made an appointment with me for six o'clock!"

"Yes, sir. I am afraid that I am a little late, but I am not quite my own master, you know. I am sorry that Miss Sutherland has troubled you about this little matter, for I think it is far better not to wash linen of this sort in public. It was quite against my wishes that she came, but she is a very excitable, impulsive girl, as you may have noticed, and she is not easily controlled when she has made up her mind on a point. Of course, I do not mind you so much, as you are not connected with the official police, but it is not pleasant to have a family misfortune like this noised abroad. Besides, it is a useless expense, for how could you possibly find this Hosmer Angel?"

"On the contrary," said Holmes quietly; "I have every reason to believe that I will succeed in discovering Mr. Hosmer Angel."

Mr. Windibank gave a violent start, and dropped his **27** gloves. "I am delighted to hear it," he said.

"It is a curious thing," remarked Holmes, "that a typewriter has really quite as much individuality as a man's handwriting. Unless they are quite new, no two of them write exactly alike. Some letters get more worn than others, and some wear only on one side. Now, you remark in this note of yours, Mr. Windibank, that in every case there is some little slurring over of the ' e,' and a slight defect in the tail of the ' r.' There are fourteen other characteristics, but those are the more obvious."

"We do all our correspondence with this machine at the office, and no doubt it is a little worn," our visitor answered, glancing keenly at Holmes with his bright little eyes.

"And now I will show you what is really a very interesting study, Mr. Windibank," Holmes continued. "I think of writing another little monograph some of these **28** days on the typewriter and its relation to crime. It is a subject to which I have devoted some little attention. I have here four letters which purport to come from the missing man. They are all typewritten. In each case, not only are the ' e's ' slurred and the ' r's ' tailless, but you will observe, if you care to use my magnifying lens, that the fourteen other characteristics to which I have alluded are there as well."

Mr. Windibank sprang out of his chair, and picked up his hat. "I cannot waste time over this sort of fantastic talk, Mr. Holmes," he said. "If you can catch the man, catch him, and let me know when you have done it."

"Certainly," said Holmes, stepping over and turning the key in the door. "I let you know, then, that I have caught him!"

"What! where?" shouted Mr. Windibank, turning white to his lips, and glancing about him like a rat in a trap.

"Oh, it won't do—really it won't," said Holmes suavely. "There is no possible getting out of it, Mr. Windibank. It is quite too transparent, and it was a very bad compliment when you said it was impossible for me to solve so simple a question. That's right! Sit down, and let us talk it over."

Our visitor collapsed into a chair with a ghastly face and a glitter of moisture on his brow. "It—it's not actionable," he stammered.

"I am very much afraid that it is not. But between ourselves, Windibank, it was as cruel, and selfish, and heartless a trick in a petty way as ever came before me. Now, let me just run over the course of events, and you will contradict me if I go wrong."

The man sat huddled up in his chair, with his head sunk upon his breast, like one who is utterly crushed. Holmes stuck his feet up on the corner of the mantelpiece, and leaning back with his hands in his pockets, began talking, rather to himself, as it seemed, than to us.

"The man married a woman very much older than himself for her money," said he, "and he enjoyed the use of the money of the daughter as long as she lived with them. It was a considerable sum for people in their position, and the loss of it would have made a serious difference. It was worth an effort to preserve it. The daughter was of a good, amiable disposition, but affectionate and warm-hearted in her ways, so that it was evident that with her fair personal advantages, and her little income, she would not be allowed to remain single long. Now her marriage would mean, of course, the loss of a hundred a year, so what does her stepfather do to prevent it? He takes the obvious course of keeping her at home, and forbidding her to seek the company of people of her own age. But soon he found that that would not answer for ever. She became restive, insisted upon her rights, and finally announced her positive intention of going to a certain ball. What does her clever stepfather do then? He conceives an idea more creditable to his head than to his heart. With the connivance and assistance of his wife he disguised himself, covered those keen eyes with tinted glasses, masked the face with a moustache and a pair of bushy whiskers, sunk that clear voice into an insinuating whisper, and, doubly secure on account of the girl's short sight, he appears as Mr. Hosmer Angel, and keeps off other lovers by making love himself."

"It was only a joke at first," groaned our visitor. "We never thought that she would have been so carried away."

"Very likely not. However that may be, the young lady was very decidedly carried away, and having quite made up her mind that her stepfather was in France, the suspicion of treachery never for an instant entered her mind. She was flattered by the gentleman's attentions, and the effect was increased by the loudly expressed admiration of her mother. Then Mr. Angel began to call, for it was obvious that the matter should be pushed as far as it would go, if a real effect were to be produced. There were meetings, and an engagement, which would finally secure the girl's affections from turning towards anyone else. But the deception could not be kept up for

clear or partially clear sky in many places." 4) On Thursday, October 20th, however, colder weather settled in "over the whole United Kingdom." It was foggy in the Southeast of England, with no sunshine whatever registered at Westminster. Clearly, Mary Sutherland visited Holmes on *Tuesday, October 18, 1887*; Mr. Windibank called, and the case ended, the next day—*Wednesday, October 19, 1887.*

28 *on the typewriter and its relation to crime.* "In . . . the *Journal of Criminal Law and Criminology* (November–December, 1947) there appears a review of an article in the *Police Journal,* the title of which is 'Identification of Typewriting,' reputedly by one George McLean," Mr. Archibald Hart wrote in "The Effects of Trades Upon Hands." "Is it not apparent that some hoarder of the only existent copies of all of Holmes' brochures is now releasing them one by one under false authorships? 'McLean' urges us to note the peculiarities of each typed character, the vertical and horizontal alignment, the side impressions of each character, and the shortening of the serifs in P, D, B, and H, and the diacritic in the letter T."

HE TOOK TWO SWIFT STEPS TO THE WHIP . . .

Illustration by Sidney Paget for the *Strand Magazine*, September, 1891.

ever. These pretended journeys to France were rather cumbrous. The thing to do was clearly to bring the business to an end in such a dramatic manner that it would leave a permanent impression upon the young lady's mind, and prevent her from looking upon any other suitor for some time to come. Hence those vows of fidelity exacted upon a Testament, and hence also the allusions to a possibility of something happening on the very morning of the wedding. James Windibank wished Miss Sutherland to be so bound to Hosmer Angel, and so uncertain as to his fate, that for ten years to come, at any rate, she would not listen to another man. As far as the church door he brought her, and then, as he could go no further, he conveniently vanished away by the old trick of stepping in at one door of a four-wheeler, and out at the other. I think that that was the chain of events, Mr. Windibank!"

Our visitor had recovered something of his assurance while Holmes had been talking, and he rose from his chair now with a cold sneer upon his pale face.

" It may be so, or it may not, Mr. Holmes," said he, " but if you are so very sharp you ought to be sharp enough to know that it is you who are breaking the law now, and not me. I have done nothing actionable from the first, but as long as you keep that door locked you lay yourself open to an action for assault and illegal constraint."

" The law cannot, as you say, touch you," said Holmes, unlocking and throwing open the door, " yet there never was a man who deserved punishment more. If the young lady has a brother or a friend he ought to lay a whip across your shoulders. By Jove! " he continued, flushing up at the sight of the bitter sneer upon the man's face, " it is not part of my duties to my client, but here's a hunting-crop handy, and I think I shall just treat myself to——" He took two swift steps to the whip, but before he could grasp it there was a wild clatter of steps upon the stairs, the heavy hall door banged, and from the window we could see Mr. James Windibank running at the top of his speed down the road.

" There's a cold-blooded scoundrel! " said Holmes, laughing, as he threw himself down into his chair once more. " That fellow will rise from crime to crime until he does something very bad, and ends on a gallows. The case has, in some respects, been not entirely devoid of interest."

" I cannot now entirely see all the steps of your reasoning," I remarked.

" Well, of course it was obvious from the first that this Mr. Hosmer Angel must have some strong object for his curious conduct, and it was equally clear that the only man who really profited by the incident, as far as we could see, was the stepfather. Then the fact that the two men were never together, but that the one always appeared when the other was away, was suggestive. So were the tinted spectacles and the curious voice, which both hinted at a disguise, as did the bushy whiskers. My suspicions were all confirmed by his peculiar action in typewriting his signature, which of course inferred that his handwriting was so familiar to her that she would recognize even the smallest sample of it. You see all these isolated facts, together with many minor ones, all pointed in the same direction."

" And how did you verify them ? "

" Having once spotted my man, it was easy to get corroboration. I knew the firm for which this man worked. Having taken the printed description, I eliminated everything from it which could be the result of a disguise—the whiskers, the glasses, the voice, and I sent it to the firm, with a request that they would inform me whether it answered the description of any of their travellers. I had already noticed the peculiarities of the typewriter, and I wrote to the man himself at his business address, asking him if he would come here. As I expected, his reply was typewritten, and revealed the same trivial but characteristic defects. The same post brought me a letter from Westhouse & Marbank, of Fenchurch Street, to say that the description tallied in every respect with that of their employé, James Windibank. *Voilà tout !* "   **29**

" And Miss Sutherland ? "

" If I tell her she will not believe me. You may remember the old Persian saying, ' There is danger for him who taketh the tiger cub, and danger also for whoso snatches a delusion from a woman.' There is as much **30** sense in Hafiz as in Horace, and as much knowledge of the **31** world."

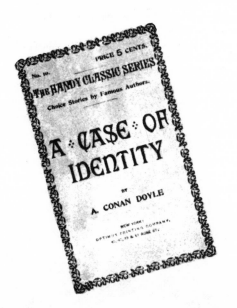

29 Voilà tout!" French: there, that is all; that is the whole of it.

30 *a delusion from a woman.*' "My own search through all accessible translations of Persian, Iranian, and other Oriental sayings has failed to turn up such a maxim," Mr. Morris Rosenblum wrote in "Foreign Language Quotations in the Canon." "In the very next sentence Holmes referred to Hafiz —but please note that very cleverly he did not say directly that Hafiz was the author of the expression. Nevertheless, I looked through the complete works of Hafiz in translation without coming across anything resembling the idea of the woman, tiger cubs, and delusions."

To this Mr. Bliss Austin added (*A Baker Street Christmas Stocking,* 1955) ". . . all efforts by a number of the Faithful to find this proverb in Hafiz have led to naught. . . . Among other sources, I consulted two authorities on Persia and its literature who were not only unacquainted with it but even expressed open doubt that it was genuine. . . . But apparently the stumbling block was the misleading reference to Hafiz. Thus I recently came across a book by Selwyn Garney Champion, M.D., entitled *Racial Proverbs, A Selection of the World's Proverbs, Arranged Linguistically* (New York: The Macmillan Company, 1938)—and there on page 469 as No. 216 of the Persian proverbs, I found: 'There is danger for whoso snatches a delusion from a woman.' So it seems that at least part of Holmes' quotation is authentic . . ."

31 *in Hafiz as in Horace.* Since the *Dîwan* of the fourteenth century Persian poet Hafiz (the popular name for Shams ed-Din Mohammed), was not translated in its entirety into English prose until 1891, Miss Madeleine B. Stern has suggested ("Sherlock Holmes: Rare Book Collector") that "we must assume that Holmes' copy was either of the 1800 Hindley edition of the *Persian Lyrics* printed in Persian and English with verse and prose paraphrases and a catalogue of the Gazels, or of the fine 1875 edition containing a verse rendering of the principal poems by Bicknell." As to Holmes' copy of Horace, it was "doubtless, because of Holmes' interest in printing types, the Parma edition published by Bodoni . . ."

Bibliographical Note: The first separate edition of "A Case of Identity"—a great rarity—is now thought to have been the small brochure illustrated here, No. 10 in the Handy Classic Series, published by the Optimus Printing Company of New York in 1895.

28

THE RED-HEADED LEAGUE

[Saturday, October 29, to Sunday, October 30, 1887]

1 *one day*. Holmes thrice gives us the day on which the adventure of "The Red-Headed League" took place: "To-day is Saturday"; "To-day being Saturday rather complicates matters"; "Saturday would suit them better than any other day . . ." And Mr. Merryweather says: "It is the first Saturday night for seven-and-twenty years that I have not had my rubber."

2 *the autumn*. Both Mr. Rolfe Boswell ("A Rare Day in June") and Mr. Raymond A. de Groat ("The Guilty Pawnbroker, or The Lost Summer of 1890") insist that the month was not in "the autumn" but in June; Mr. Boswell dates the case June 17, 1890; Mr. de Groat June 21, 1890. But Watson's "autumn" would seem to be confirmed by the "October" of the sign and the fact that Mr. Jabez Wilson wore "a faded brown overcoat."

3 *last year*. Since "The Red-Headed League" was published in August, 1891, we might at first think that this indicated the autumn of 1890. But Watson's chronicles were in manuscript form long before they were published; his statement here means only that "The Red-Headed League" took place in the autumn before he chronicled the story.

4 *in the next room*." Watson presumably means Holmes' bedroom.

1-2-3 I HAD called upon my friend, Mr. Sherlock Holmes, one day in the autumn of last year, and found him in deep conversation with a very stout, florid-faced, elderly gentleman, with fiery red hair. With an apology for my intrusion, I was about to withdraw, when Holmes pulled me abruptly into the room, and closed the door behind me.

"You could not possibly have come at a better time, my dear Watson," he said cordially.

"I was afraid that you were engaged."

"So I am. Very much so."

4 "Then I can wait in the next room."

"Not at all. This gentleman, Mr. Wilson, has been my partner and helper in many of my most successful cases, and I have no doubt that he will be of the utmost use to me in yours also."

The stout gentleman half rose from his chair, and gave a bob of greeting, with a quick little questioning glance from his small, fat-encircled eyes.

"Try the settee," said Holmes, relapsing into his arm-chair, and putting his finger-tips together, as was his custom when in judicial moods. "I know, my dear Watson, that you share my love of all that is bizarre and outside the conventions and humdrum routine of every-day life. You have shown your relish for it by the enthusiasm which has prompted you to chronicle, and, if you will excuse my saying so, somewhat to embellish so many of my own little adventures."

"Your cases have indeed been of the greatest interest to me," I observed.

. . . A VERY STOUT, FLORID-FACED, ELDERLY GENTLEMAN, WITH FIERY RED HAIR.

Portrait of Jabez Wilson by Sidney Paget, for the *Strand Magazine*, August, 1891. "How old was Mr. Wilson?" Mr. Thomas L. Stix asked in "Concerning 'The Red-Headed League.'" Watson regarded him as "an elderly gentleman—which would mean 60, perhaps. At 60 one does not possess fiery red hair. Indeed, at 50 the pigmentation has changed."

" You will remember that I remarked the other day, just before we went into the very simple problem presented by Miss Mary Sutherland, that for strange effects **5** and extraordinary combinations we must go to life itself, which is always far more daring than any effort of the imagination."

" A proposition which I took the liberty of doubting."

" You did, Doctor, but none the less you must come round to my view, for otherwise I shall keep piling fact upon fact on you, until your reason breaks down under them and acknowledges me to be right. Now, Mr. Jabez Wilson here has been good enough to call upon me this morning, and to begin a narrative which promises to be one of the most singular which I have listened to for some time. You have heard me remark that the strangest and most unique things are very often connected not with the larger but with the smaller crimes, and occasionally, indeed, where there is room for doubt whether any positive crime has been committed. As far as I have heard, it is impossible for me to say whether the present case is an instance of crime or not, but the course of events is certainly among the most singular that I have ever listened to. Perhaps, Mr. Wilson, you would have the great kindness to recommence your narrative. I ask you not merely because my friend Dr. Watson has not heard the opening part, but also because the peculiar nature of the story makes me anxious to have every possible detail from your lips. As a rule, when I have heard some slight indication of the course of events I am able to guide myself by the thousands of other similar cases which occur to my memory. In the present instance I am forced to admit that the facts are, to the best of my belief, unique."

The portly client puffed out his chest with an appearance of some little pride, and pulled a dirty and wrinkled newspaper from the inside pocket of his greatcoat. As he glanced down the advertisement column, with his head thrust forward, and the paper flattened out upon his knee, I took a good look at the man, and endeavoured after the fashion of my companion to read the indications which might be presented by his dress or appearance.

I did not gain very much, however, by my inspection. Our visitor bore every mark of being an average commonplace British tradesman, obese, pompous, and slow. He wore rather baggy grey shepherds' check trousers, a not over-clean black frock-coat, unbuttoned in the front, and a drab waistcoat with a heavy brassy Albert chain, and a square pierced bit of metal dangling down as an ornament. A frayed top-hat, and a faded brown overcoat with a wrinkled velvet collar lay upon a chair beside him. Altogether, look as I would, there was nothing remarkable about the man save his blazing red head, and the expression of extreme chagrin and discontent upon his features.

Sherlock Holmes's quick eye took in my occupation and he shook his head with a smile as he noticed my questioning glances. " Beyond the obvious facts that he has at some time done manual labour, that he takes snuff, that he is a Freemason, that he has been in China, and that he **6** has done a considerable amount of writing lately, I can deduce nothing else."

5 *the very simple problem presented by Miss Mary Sutherland.* "The Red-Headed League" is later than "A Case of Identity," but only a little later, as shown by Holmes' "the other day."

6 *a Freemason.* A member of a widespread and celebrated secret society (called more fully the Free and Accepted Masons) consisting of persons who are united for fraternal purposes.

7 *"I won't insult your intelligence by telling you how I read that.* "As for us, gentlemen," Mr. Thomas L. Stix wrote in "Concerning 'The Red-Headed League,'" "we wish to have our intelligence insulted. How did Holmes know about the snuff? He didn't. But it sounded good, and he thought he could get away with it—and did . . ."

8 *and have even contributed to the literature of the subject.* Miss Madeleine B. Stern has noted ("Sherlock Holmes: Rare Book Collector") that "most of the works on tattooing, corporal marking and ethnic mutilation follow rather than precede Holmes." And Mr. Ernest C. Burnham, Jr., has added ("The Tattooed Fish in 'The Red-Headed League'") that "It is noteworthy that in our present enlightened age, there are only two major works (W. D. Hambly, *History of Tattooing*, Macmillan, 1927; H. Ebenstein, *Pierced Hearts and True Love*, D. Verschoyle, 1953) on the subject of tattooing . . ."

9 *quite peculiar to China.* Mr. Burnham has also pointed out that "China is conspicuous by its absence from the rolls of practitioners of tattooing, as the Chinese abhorred and condemned tattooing as barbarous, and they accordingly only used tattooing to mark criminals. . . . Furthermore, the usual designs used in all places were human figures and flowers, not fishes or animals . . ." Mr. Burnham has also noted that the right wrist is a most unusual part of the body to have tattooed, and that "staining" is a most peculiar way to refer to the technique of tattooing: "nothing is stained in tattoos . . . the colouring is introduced below the skin and not on the surface . . ." Mr. Burnham concluded that Jabez Wilson was tattooed in Japan and that Holmes mistook the coin worn by Mr. Wilson for a Chinese coin.

"WHEN, IN ADDITION, I SEE A CHINESE COIN HANGING FROM YOUR WATCH-CHAIN . . ."

Watson has called the coin "a square pierced bit of metal." Did he mean a "square, pierced, bit" or a "square-pierced bit"? Not the former, surely, for, as Mr. Martin J. Swanson has pointed out: "Nowhere can I find any mention of China having issued square coins at any time (the Chinese trademark was a round coin with a square hole), while Japan almost exclusively issued squared, pierced coins. We now see that Wilson surely received both tattoo and coin while in Japan, not China . . ."

The late A. Carson Simpson, on the other hand, has interpreted Watson's phrase to mean a "square-pierced bit." In his great work, *Numismatics in the Canon*, Part II, he pointed out that only one Chinese coin was "legal tender for all debts, public and private, irrespective of amount, until the end of the nineteenth century. It began in 618 A.D., when General Li Yüan became Emperor Kao Tsu, first of the T'ang Dynasty. He at once issued the new coin, known as 'current money of the newest beginning.' Called by the Chinese a 'tsien,' it was round, about an inch in diameter, with a square hole in the centre and a raised edge. It was generally a cast (not struck) coin and the material used ranged from high-grade brass to varying mixtures of copper, zinc, tin, lead and iron.

Mr. Jabez Wilson started up in his chair, with his forefinger upon the paper, but his eyes upon my companion.

"How, in the name of good fortune, did you know all that, Mr. Holmes?" he asked. "How did you know, for example, that I did manual labour? It's as true as gospel, and I began as a ship's carpenter."

"Your hands, my dear sir. Your right hand is quite a size larger than your left. You have worked with it, and the muscles are more developed."

"Well, the snuff, then, and the Freemasonry?"

7 "I won't insult your intelligence by telling you how I read that, especially as, rather against the strict rules of your order, you use an arc and compass breastpin."

"Ah, of course, I forgot that. But the writing?"

"What else can be indicated by that right cuff so very shiny for five inches, and the left one with the smooth patch near the elbow where you rest it upon the desk."

"Well, but China?"

"The fish which you have tattooed immediately above your right wrist could only have been done in China. I have made a small study of tattoo marks, and have even **8** contributed to the literature of the subject. That trick of staining the fishes' scales of a delicate pink is quite **9** peculiar to China. When, in addition, I see a Chinese coin hanging from your watch-chain, the matter becomes even more simple."

"The classic design was a simple one, bearing on one side ideographs representing the name of the reigning emperor, the date and the words 'precious circulating medium.' The reverse was generally blank, though some dynasties put the date there, in regnal years, and others the name of the mint. Some have simply a short arc at the top of the reverse, which has an interesting history. When a wax impression of the coin, with its revised legends (incorporating the new imperial name and date) was submitted to the Emperor Wen Teh for approval, one of his fashionably-long fingernails made a small curved gouge in the wax. The mintmasters, of course, realized that the approved design was that of the wax model in the condition in which it was handed back to them, and proceeded to strike the coin accordingly, nail-mark and all; one is shown on our plate.

"By now the reader will have realized that the coin in question is the one known to foreigners as the 'cash,' worth between $\frac{1}{6}$ and $\frac{1}{7}$ of a cent. It seems inconceivable that this very minor coin should have been the only legal tender of the vast Chinese Empire—the first country in the world to strike coins—for almost thirteen centuries, but such was the case, perhaps because the emperors, as 'sons of heaven,' felt themselves to be above giving even a thought to the meaner uses of trade. Whatever the reason, the humble brass 'cash' would go well with Jabez Wilson's 'brassy Albert chain' and we may fairly conclude that this was the coin which he wore."

Mr. Jabez Wilson laughed heavily. " Well, I never ! " said he. " I thought at first you had done something clever, but I see that there was nothing in it after all."

" I begin to think, Watson," said Holmes, " that I make a mistake in explaining. ' Omne ignotum pro magnifico,' you know, and my poor little reputation, such **10** as it is, will suffer shipwreck if I am so candid. Can you not find the advertisement, Mr. Wilson ? "

" Yes, I have got it now," he answered, with his thick, red finger planted half-way down the column. " Here it is. This is what began it all. You just read it for yourself, sir."

I took the paper from him and read as follows :—

" TO THE RED-HEADED LEAGUE.—On account of the bequest of the late Ezekiah Hopkins, of Lebanon, Penn., U.S.A., there is now another vacancy open which entitles a member of the League to a salary of four pounds a week **11** for purely nominal services. All red-headed men who are sound in body and mind, and above the age of twenty-one years, are eligible. Apply in person on Monday, at **12** eleven o'clock, to Duncan Ross, at the offices of the League, 7 Pope's Court, Fleet Street." **13**

" What on earth does this mean ? " I ejaculated, after I had twice read over the extraordinary announcement.

Holmes chuckled, and wriggled in his chair, as was his habit when in high spirits. " It is a little off the beaten track, isn't it ? " said he. " And now, Mr. Wilson, off you go at scratch, and tell us all about yourself, **14** your household, and the effect which this advertisement had upon your fortunes. You will first make a note, Doctor, of the paper and the date."

" It is *The Morning Chronicle*, of April 27, 1890. Just two months ago." **15**

10 '*Omne ignotum pro magnifico.*' "Although Holmes was no dilettante in Latin, he resorted to a full quotation from the Roman authors only [this] once," Mr. Morris Rosenblum noted in "Some Latin Byways in the Canon." Elsewhere ("Foreign Language Quotations in the Canon") Mr. Rosenblum wrote: "This is taken from the *Agricola* (*The Life and Character of Julius Agricola*), Chapter 30, Section 4, by Publius Cornelius Tacitus, written about 98 A.D. Translated as 'Everything unknown passes for something splendid,' this is one of the best known epigrams of Tacitus, and is often quoted to characterize the mystery and appeal of the unknown."

11 *four pounds a week*. About $20.

12 *Apply in person on Monday*. We shortly learn that Spaulding, Wilson's assistant, brought the paper to Wilson "*just this day* eight weeks" ago—and therefore on a Saturday. We shall see that Wilson was in error in saying "eight weeks" (*nine* weeks had passed), but there is no reason to believe he was mistaken about the day of the week. But Wilson also says that he ordered Spaulding "to put up the shutters for the day, and to come right away with me." Watson, then, would appear to have misquoted the advertisement to us: it must have read "Apply in person *today*."

13 *Pope's Court*. "It is probable," the late H. W. Bell wrote in "Three Identifications," "that 'Pope's Court' is a transparent alias for Mitre Court, which connects Fleet Street with the Temple." But Mr. Michael Harrison wrote (*In the Footsteps of Sherlock Holmes*): "I had to go back to Rocque's map of London (1745) to find that [Pope's Court] was a court which lay between Bell Yard and Chancery Lane, being joined by two narrow alleys to each. It is shown (though not named) on Colonel Bayly's Ordnance Survey Map of 1874, and the Chancery Lane entrance to the eastern alley is still there: now closed by the door on the extreme left of the late eighteenth or early nineteenth century premises of Messrs. Jordan, the law-stationers. The alley now is merely a hall-way of the building— but it still exists."

14 *off you go at scratch*. The line from which contestants start a race. Holmes is saying, "Begin at the beginning."

"WHAT ON EARTH DOES THIS MEAN?" I EJACULATED . . .

Illustration by Sidney Paget for the *Strand Magazine*, August, 1891.

15 *April 27, 1890. Just two months ago.*" There is clearly something wrong here, since April 27, 1890, was a Sunday, a day on which newspapers would not have been published in Victorian London. "Just two months ago" would put the time of Wilson's interview with Holmes and Watson at about June 27th, making nonsense of Watson's "autumn." In addition, the *Morning Chronicle*, on which both Dickens and his father worked, had long been defunct. We suggest that the advertisement appeared on Saturday, August 27, 1887. Watson, we believe, was wrong about the year but perfectly correct about the date of the month— and it is easy to misread "August" as "April."

16 *a girl of fourteen.* She does not appear again —at least in "The Red-Headed League." But Magistrate S. Tupper Bigelow has suggested ("Two Canonical Problems Solved") that she was Patience Moran, whom we will meet in "The Boscombe Valley Mystery"—and a niece, he says, of Colonel Sebastian Moran of "The Adventure of the Empty House."

17 *a nice little crib.* In addition to beling thieves' cant for a house, store, shop, or the like ("to crack a crib"), *crib* is English slang for a berth or a job.

" Very good.   Now, Mr. Wilson ? "

" Well, it is just as I have been telling you, Mr. Sherlock Holmes," said Jabez Wilson, mopping his forehead, " I have a small pawnbroker's business at Coburg Square, near the City. It's not a very large affair, and of late years it has not done more than just give me a living. I used to be able to keep two assistants, but now I only keep one ; and I would have a job to pay him, but that he is willing to come for half wages, so as to learn the business."

" What is the name of this obliging youth ? " asked Sherlock Holmes.

" His name is Vincent Spaulding, and he's not such a youth either. It's hard to say his age. I should not wish a smarter assistant, Mr. Holmes ; and I know very well that he could better himself, and earn twice what I am able to give him.   But after all, if he is satisfied, why should I put ideas in his head ? "

" Why, indeed ? You seem most fortunate in having an employé who comes under the full market price. It is not a common experience among employers in this age. I don't know that your assistant is not as remarkable as your advertisement."

" Oh, he has his faults, too," said Mr. Wilson. " Never was such a fellow for photography. Snapping away with a camera when he ought to be improving his mind, and then diving down into the cellar like a rabbit into its hole to develop his pictures. That is his main fault ; but on the whole, he's a good worker. There's no vice in him."

" He is still with you, I presume ? "

16 " Yes, sir. He and a girl of fourteen, who does a bit of simple cooking, and keeps the place clean—that's all I have in the house, for I am a widower, and never had any family. We live very quietly, sir, the three of us ; and we keep a roof over our heads, and pay our debts, if we do nothing more.

" The first thing that put us out was that advertisement. Spaulding, he came down into the office just this day eight weeks with this very paper in his hand, and he says :

" ' I wish to the Lord, Mr. Wilson, that I was a red-headed man.'

" ' Why that ? ' I asks.

" ' Why,' says he, ' here's another vacancy on the League of the Red-headed Men. It's worth quite a little fortune to any man who gets it, and I understand that there are more vacancies than there are men, so that the trustees are at their wits' end what to do with the money. If my hair would only change colour, here's a nice little **17** crib all ready for me to step into.'

" ' Why, what is it, then ? ' I asked. You see, Mr. Holmes, I am a very stay-at-home man, and, as my business came to me instead of my having to go to it, I was often weeks on end without putting my foot over the door-mat. In that way I didn't know much of what was going on outside, and I was always glad of a bit of news.

" ' Have you never heard of the League of the Red-headed Men ? ' he asked, with his eyes open.

" ' Never.'

" ' Why, I wonder at that, for you are eligible yourself for one of the vacancies.'

" ' And what are they worth ? ' I asked.

" ' Oh, merely a couple of hundred a year, but the work is slight, and it need not interfere much with one's other occupations.'

" Well, you can easily think that that made me prick up my ears, for the business has not been over good for some years, and an extra couple of hundred would have been very handy.

" ' Tell me all about it,' said I.

" ' Well,' said he, showing me the advertisement, ' you can see for yourself that the League has a vacancy, and there is the address where you should apply for particulars. As far as I can make out, the League was founded by an American millionaire, Ezekiah Hopkins, who was very peculiar in his ways. He was himself red-headed, and he had a great sympathy for all red-headed men ; so, when he died, it was found that he had left his enormous fortune in the hands of trustees, with instructions to apply the interest to the providing of easy berths to men whose hair is of that colour. From all I hear it is splendid pay, and very little to do.'

" ' But,' said I, ' there would be millions of red-headed men who would apply.'

" ' Not so many as you might think,' he answered. ' You see, it is really confined to Londoners, and to grown men. This American had started from London when he was young, and he wanted to do the old town a good turn. Then, again, I have heard it is no use your applying if your hair is light red, or dark red, or anything but real, bright, blazing, fiery red. Now, if you cared to apply, Mr. Wilson, you would just walk in ; but perhaps it would hardly be worth your while to put yourself out of the way for the sake of a few hundred pounds.'

" Now, it is a fact, gentlemen, as you may see for yourselves, that my hair is of a very full and rich tint, so that it seemed to me that, if there was to be any competition in the matter, I stood as good a chance as any man that I had ever met. Vincent Spaulding seemed to know so much about it that I thought he might prove useful, so I just ordered him to put up the shutters for the day, and to come right away with me. He was very willing to have a holiday, so we shut the business up, and started off for the address that was given us in the advertisement.

" I never hope to see such a sight as that again, Mr. Holmes. From north, south, east, and west every man who had a shade of red in his hair had tramped into the City to answer the advertisement. Fleet Street was choked with red-headed folk, and Pope's Court looked like **18** a coster's orange barrow. I should not have thought **19** there were so many in the whole country as were brought together by that single advertisement. Every shade of colour they were—straw, lemon, orange, brick, Irish-setter, liver, clay ; but, as Spaulding said, there were not many who had the real vivid flame-coloured tint. When I saw how many were waiting, I would have given it up in despair ; but Spaulding would not hear of it. How he did it I could not imagine, but he pushed and pulled and butted until he got me through the crowd, and right up to the steps which led to the office. There was a double stream upon the stair, some going up in hope, and some

. . . " ' YOU CAN SEE FOR YOURSELF THAT THE LEAGUE HAS A VACANCY . . . ' "

Illustration by Sidney Paget for the *Strand Magazine*, August, 1891.

18 *Fleet Street was choked with red-headed folk.* Fleet Street, as we have seen, was the heart of London's newspaper industry, "yet no single newspaper reported this amazing spectacle. How came Fleet Street to miss this scoop right on its own doorstep?" (" 'The Red-Headed League' Reviewed").

19 *a coster's.* Short for costermonger: an apple seller; a hawker of fruit or vegetables from a street stand, barrow, or cart.

"THEN SUDDENLY HE PLUNGED FORWARD, WRUNG MY HAND, AND CONGRATULATED ME WARMLY ON MY SUCCESS."

Illustration by Sidney Paget for the *Strand Magazine*, August, 1891.

coming back dejected; but we wedged in as well as we could, and soon found ourselves in the office."

" Your experience has been a most entertaining one," remarked Holmes, as his client paused and refreshed his memory with a huge pinch of snuff. " Pray continue your very interesting statement."

" There was nothing in the office but a couple of wooden chairs and a deal table, behind which sat a small man, with a head that was even redder than mine. He said a few words to each candidate as he came up, and then he always managed to find some fault in them which would disqualify them. Getting a vacancy did not seem to be such a very easy matter after all. However, when our turn came, the little man was more favourable to me than to any of the others, and he closed the door as we entered, so that he might have a private word with us.

" ' This is Mr. Jabez Wilson,' said my assistant, ' and he is willing to fill a vacancy in the League.'

" ' And he is admirably suited for it,' the other answered. ' He has every requirement. I cannot recall when I have seen anything so fine.' He took a step backwards, cocked his head on one side, and gazed at my hair until I felt quite bashful. Then suddenly he plunged forward, wrung my hand, and congratulated me warmly on my success.

" ' It would be injustice to hesitate,' said he. ' You will, however, I am sure, excuse me for taking an obvious precaution.' With that he seized my hair in both his hands, and tugged until I yelled with the pain. ' There is water in your eyes,' said he, as he released me. ' I perceive that all is as it should be. But we have to be careful, for we have twice been deceived by wigs and once by paint. I could tell you tales of cobbler's wax which would disgust you with human nature.' He stepped over to the window, and shouted through it at the top of his voice that the vacancy was filled. A groan of disappointment came up from below, and the folk all trooped away in different directions, until there was not a red head to be seen except my own and that of the manager.

" ' My name,' said he, ' is Mr. Duncan Ross, and I am myself one of the pensioners upon the fund left by our noble benefactor. Are you a married man, Mr. Wilson? Have you a family?'

" I answered that I had not.

" His face fell immediately.

" ' Dear me!' he said gravely, ' that is very serious indeed! I am sorry to hear you say that. The fund was, of course, for the propagation and spread of the red-heads as well as for their maintenance. It is exceedingly unfortunate that you should be a bachelor.'

" My face lengthened at this, Mr. Holmes, for I thought that I was not to have the vacancy after all; but after thinking it over for a few minutes, he said that it would be all right.

" ' In the case of another,' said he, ' the objection might be fatal, but we must stretch a point in favour of a man with such a head of hair as yours. When shall you be able to enter upon your new duties?'

"'Well, it is a little awkward, for I have a business already,' said I.

"'Oh, never mind about that, Mr. Wilson!' said Vincent Spaulding. 'I shall be able to look after that for you.'

"'What would be the hours?' I asked.

"'Ten to two.'

"Now a pawnbroker's business is mostly done of an evening, Mr. Holmes, especially Thursday and Friday evening, which is just before pay-day; so it would suit me very well to earn a little in the mornings. Besides, I knew that my assistant was a good man, and that he would see to anything that turned up.

"'That would suit me very well,' said I. 'And the pay?'

"'Is four pounds a week.'

"'And the work?'

"'Is purely nominal.'

"'What do you call purely nominal?'

"'Well, you have to be in the office, or at least in the building, the whole time. If you leave, you forfeit your whole position for ever. The will is very clear upon that point. You don't comply with the conditions if you budge from the office during that time.'

"'It's only four hours a day, and I should not think of leaving,' said I.

"'No excuse will avail,' said Mr. Duncan Ross, 'neither sickness, nor business, nor anything else. There you must stay, or you lose your billet.'

"'And the work?'

"'Is to copy out the *Encyclopædia Britannica*. There is the first volume of it in that press. You must find **20** your own ink, pens, and blotting-paper, but we provide **21** this table and chair. Will you be ready to-morrow?' **22**

"'Certainly,' I answered.

"'Then, good-bye, Mr. Jabez Wilson, and let me congratulate you once more on the important position which you have been fortunate enough to gain.' He bowed me out of the room, and I went home with my assistant, hardly knowing what to say or do, I was so pleased at my own good fortune.

"'Well, I thought over the matter all day, and by evening I was in low spirits again; for I had quite persuaded myself that the whole affair must be some great hoax or fraud, though what its object might be I could not imagine. It seemed altogether past belief that anyone could make such a will, or that they would pay such a sum for doing anything so simple as copying out the *Encyclopædia Britannica*. Vincent Spaulding did what he could to cheer me up, but by bedtime I had reasoned myself out of the whole thing. However, in the morning I determined to have a look at it anyhow, so I bought a penny bottle of ink, and with a quill pen, and seven sheets of foolscap **23** paper, I started off for Pope's Court.

"Well, to my surprise and delight everything was as right as possible. The table was set out ready for me, and Mr. Duncan Ross was there to see that I got fairly to work. He started me off upon the letter A, and then he left me; but he would drop in from time to time to see that all was right with me. At two o'clock he bade me

20 *press.* An upright case or cupboard for the keeping of articles.

21 *You must find your own ink, pens, and blotting-paper.* "Is that a likely statement from the man who is the manager for the late Ezekiah Hopkins, philanthropist of Lebanon, Pennsylvania, U.S.A.? Would a man who paid four pounds a week for purely nominal services boggle at pen, ink, and blotting-paper?" Mr. Thomas L. Stix asked in "Concerning 'The Red-Headed League.'"

22 *Will you be ready to-morrow?'* If the advertisement appeared on Saturday and was answered on Saturday, as we believe, Jabez Wilson was being asked to report for his first day's work on a Sunday. This is certainly highly unusual—and yet Wilson later tells us that "*Every* morning I was there at ten . . ." and Holmes himself speaks of Wilson's "absence *every* morning in the week . . ."

23 *foolscap.* Paper in sheets measuring approximately 13 by 16 or 17 inches—so called because the watermark of a fool's cap and bells was used by the old papermakers.

24 *might get on to the B's before very long.* As Mr. Thomas L. Stix has pointed out ("Concerning 'The Red-Headed League'"): "The *Encyclopædia Britannica*—the 1875 edition, which is the one that must have been used—has 928 pages in Volume One, and doesn't reach the article on Attica until page 794 of Volume Two. Now, the average page of the *Britannica* has 3,728 words. The calculation is simple. The pawnbroker says that he copied 6,419,616 words in eight weeks, working only four hours a day. That, gentlemen, is at the rate of 33,435 words per hour, or 557.25 words per minute. That is manifestly impossible. If he had copied at the rate of one page an hour—a prodigious amount to accomplish—Mr. Wilson would be just beginning to write about Ab-Ul-Mejid, 1823–1861—the Sultan of Turkey."

And the late Gavin Brend wrote:

> Archery, Abbots, Africa, Asia,
> Archimedes and Australasia,
> Alps, Architecture, Apes, Antiques:
> This could go on for weeks and weeks.
>
> How I look forward to the day
> That frees me from this monstrous "A"!
> "Copy out letter 'A,' " he said—
> And all because my hair is red!

25 *"THE RED-HEADED LEAGUE IS DISSOLVED.* Why did the League give notice to the unfortunate Mr. Wilson before it had accomplished its purpose? Why not pay him another four pounds? As Mr. Thomas L. Stix has observed ("Concerning 'The Red-Headed League'"), the posting of the notice "gave Mr. Wilson the opportunity—an opportunity that he seized brilliantly—to call in Mr. Sherlock Holmes."

good day, complimented me upon the amount that I had written, and locked the door of the office after me.

"This went on day after day, Mr. Holmes, and on Saturday the manager came in and planked down four golden sovereigns for my week's work. It was the same next week, and the same the week after. Every morning I was there at ten, and every afternoon I left at two. By degrees Mr. Duncan Ross took to coming in only once of a morning, and then, after a time, he did not come in at all. Still, of course, I never dared to leave the room for an instant, for I was not sure when he might come, and the billet was such a good one, and suited me so well, that I would not risk the loss of it.

24 "Eight weeks passed away like this, and I had written about Abbots, and Archery, and Armour, and Architecture, and Attica, and hoped with diligence that I might get on to the B's before very long. It cost me something in foolscap, and I had pretty nearly filled a shelf with my writings. And then suddenly the whole business came to an end."

"To an end?"

"Yes, sir. And no later than this morning. I went to my work as usual at ten o'clock, but the door was shut and locked, with a little square of cardboard hammered on to the middle of the panel with a tack. Here it is, and you can read for yourself."

He held up a piece of white cardboard, about the size of a sheet of note-paper. It read in this fashion :—

25
26   " THE RED-HEADED LEAGUE IS DISSOLVED.
OCT. 9, 1890."

Sherlock Holmes and I surveyed this curt announcement and the rueful face behind it, until the comical side of the affair so completely over-topped every other consideration that we both burst out into a roar of laughter.

" I cannot see that there is anything very funny," cried our client, flushing up to the roots of his flaming head. " If you can do nothing better than laugh at me, I can go elsewhere."

"No, no," cried Holmes, shoving him back into the chair from which he had half risen. " I really wouldn't miss your case for the world. It is most refreshingly unusual. But there is, if you will excuse me saying so, something just a little funny about it. Pray what steps did you take when you found the card upon the door ? "

" I was staggered, sir. I did not know what to do. Then I called at the offices round, but none of them seemed to know anything about it. Finally, I went to the landlord, who is an accountant living on the ground floor, and I asked him if he could tell me what had become of the Red-headed League. He said that he had never heard of any such body. Then I asked him who Mr. Duncan Ross was. He answered that the name was new to him.

". . . BUT THE DOOR WAS SHUT AND LOCKED . . ."

Illustration by Sidney Paget for the *Strand Magazine*, August, 1891.

" ' Well, said I, the gentleman at No. 4.' **27**

" ' What, the red-headed man ? '

" ' Yes.'

" ' Oh,' said he, ' his name was William Morris. He was a solicitor, and was using my room as a temporary **28** convenience until his new premises were ready. He moved out yesterday.'

" ' Where could I find him ? '

" ' Oh, at his new offices. He did tell me the address. Yes, 17 King Edward Street, near St. Paul's.' **29-30**

" I started off, Mr. Holmes, but when I got to that address it was a manufactory of artificial knee-caps, and no one in it had ever heard of either Mr. William Morris, or Mr. Duncan Ross."

" And what did you do then ? " asked Holmes.

" I went home to Saxe-Coburg Square, and I took the advice of my assistant. But he could not help me in any way. He could only say that if I waited I should hear by post. But that was not quite good enough, Mr. Holmes. I did not wish to lose such a place without a struggle, so, as I had heard that you were good enough to give advice to poor folk who were in need of it, I came right away to you."

" And you did very wisely," said Holmes. " Your case is an exceedingly remarkable one, and I shall be happy to look into it. From what you have told me I think that it is possible that graver issues hang from it than might at first sight appear."

" Grave enough ! " said Mr. Jabez Wilson. " Why, I have lost four pounds a week."

" As far as you are personally concerned," remarked Holmes, " I do not see that you have any grievance against this extraordinary league. On the contrary, you are, as I understand, richer by some thirty pounds, to say nothing of the minute knowledge which you have gained on every subject which comes under the letter A. You have lost nothing by them."

" No, sir. But I want to find out about them, and who they are, and what their object was in playing this prank —if it was a prank—upon me. It was a pretty expensive joke for them, for it cost them two-and-thirty pounds," **31**

" We shall endeavour to clear up these points for you. And, first, one or two questions, Mr. Wilson. This assistant of yours who first called your attention to the advertisement—how long had he been with you ? "

" About a month then."

" How did he come ? "

" In answer to an advertisement."

" Was he the only applicant ? "

" No, I had a dozen."

" Why did you pick him ? "

" Because he was handy, and would come cheap."

" At half wages, in fact."

" Yes."

" What is he like, this Vincent Spaulding ? "

" Small, stout-built, very quick in his ways, no hair on his face, though he's not short of thirty. Has a white splash of acid upon his forehead."

Holmes sat up in his chair in considerable excitement.

26 *Oct. 9, 1890."* Here, too, something seems to be wrong: October 9, 1890, was not a Saturday but a *Thursday*. Still, as the late Gavin Brend wrote in *My Dear Holmes:* "There is no reason why the notice should bear the same date on which it was read by Wilson." The late Robert R. Pattrick agreed: "I see no reason to doubt that the sign was dated 'Oct. 9, 1890,' and was intended —deliberately and confusingly—to refer to Thursday [October 9, 1890]." In our view, the case opened on *Saturday, October 29, 1887.* (Holmes was thus perfectly correct in saying that he went into the problem of Miss Mary Sutherland just "the other day"; less than two weeks had elapsed between the two cases.) Watson was wrong on the year, but he was right on the month, and it is again charitable to believe that his "29" was mis-read by the typesetter as "9." It must be admitted that this is not a popular view: virtually all commentators date "The Red-Headed League" 1890. Three others who do not are Knox (1888), Folsom, and Zeisler (1889).

27 *'the gentleman at No. 4.'* As Mr. Colin Prestige seems to have been the first to point out: "From the advertisement in *The Morning Chronicle* of April 27, 1890, we read: "Apply . . . at the offices of the League, 7 Pope's Court.' But Jabez Wilson, on being told . . . that the name Duncan Ross was new to the landlord, quotes himself as saying, 'Well, the gentleman at No. 4.' "

28 *a solicitor.* One who represents a client in a court of justice; an attorney; formerly, in England, a practitioner in chancery only. In England solicitors prepare causes for the barristers, but have not the right to appear as advocates before the higher courts.

29 *King Edward Street.* Once called Stinking Lane because of the filth which used to accumulate there from the neighboring Newgate and Smithfield markets.

30 *St. Paul's.'* The great cathedral built by Christopher Wren, begun June 21, 1675, and finished thirty-five years later at a cost of £747,954 2s. 9d., all of which was raised by imposing a tax on every cauldron of coal brought into the port of London. Augustus J. C. Hare (*Walks in London,* Vol. I) wrote of St. Paul's: "When you are near it, the mighty dome is lost, but you have always an inward all-pervading impression of its existence, as you have seen it a thousand times rising in dark majesty over the city; or, as lighted up by the sun, it is sometimes visible from the river, when all minor objects are obliterated in mist. And, apart from the dome, the noble proportions of every pillar and cornice of the great church cannot fail to strike those who linger to look at them, while even the soot-begrimed garlands, which would be offensive were they clean, have here an indescribable stateliness."

HE CURLED HIMSELF UP IN HIS CHAIR . . .

Illustration by Sidney Paget for the *Strand Magazine*, August, 1891.

31 *it cost them two-and-thirty pounds.*" About $160. Since Wilson was *not* paid on the Saturday on which he called on Holmes, it follows that he had been paid on the eight preceding Saturdays. Thus he is incorrect in saying: "Spaulding . . . came down to the office just this day *eight weeks* with this very paper in his hand," but he is correct in saying that "the manager . . . planked down four golden sovereigns" as pay for his first week's work and that "eight weeks passed away *like this.*"

32 *for fifty minutes.*" "Three pipes of shag in fifty minutes!" Colonel R. D. Sherbrooke-Walker, T.D., wrote in "Holmes, Watson and Tobacco." "It was not a feat—it was a monstrous abuse of the membrane of the nose and throat!"

33 *more to my taste than Italian or French.* "This is not to be taken too literally," Mr. Benjamin Grosbayne wrote in "Sherlock Holmes—Musician," "for in *The Hound of the Baskervilles* [Holmes invites Watson to hear *Les Huguenots*]. Surely, if he chose an opera by Meyerbeer, he must have liked French music also, though he may have gone only to hear the lyric cast of the evening regardless of the musical fare. And he may have felt that, after all, Meyerbeer was German born."

34 *Aldersgate.* Presumably, then, this station of the Metropolitan Line was the nearest to the mysterious Saxe-Coburg Square, and an important clue to its true location. The street in which the station

"I thought as much," said he. "Have you ever observed that his ears are pierced for ear-rings?"

"Yes, sir. He told me that a gipsy had done it for him when he was a lad."

"Hum!" said Holmes, sinking back in deep thought. "He is still with you?"

"Oh, yes, sir; I have only just left him."

"And has your business been attended to in your absence?"

"Nothing to complain of, sir. There's never very much to do of a morning."

"That will do, Mr. Wilson. I shall be happy to give you an opinion upon the subject in the course of a day or two. To-day is Saturday, and I hope that by Monday we may come to a conclusion."

"Well, Watson," said Holmes, when our visitor had left us, "what do you make of it all?"

"I make nothing of it," I answered, frankly. "It is a most mysterious business."

"As a rule," said Holmes, "the more bizarre a thing is the less mysterious it proves to be. It is your commonplace, featureless crimes which are really puzzling, just as a commonplace face is the most difficult to identify. But I must be prompt over this matter."

"What are you going to do then?" I asked.

"To smoke," he answered. "It is quite a three-pipe problem, and I beg that you won't speak to me for fifty **32** minutes." He curled himself up in his chair, with his thin knees drawn up to his hawk-like nose, and there he sat with his eyes closed and his black clay pipe thrusting out like the bill of some strange bird. I had come to the conclusion that he had dropped asleep, and indeed was nodding myself, when he suddenly sprang out of his chair with the gesture of a man who had made up his mind, and put his pipe down upon the mantelpiece.

"Sarasate plays at the St. James's Hall this afternoon," he remarked. "What do you think, Watson? Could your patients spare you for a few hours?"

"I have nothing to do to-day. My practice is never very absorbing."

"Then put on your hat, and come. I am going through the City first, and we can have some lunch on the way. I observe that there is a good deal of German music on the programme, which is rather more to my taste **33** than Italian or French. It is introspective, and I want to introspect. Come along!"

34 We travelled by the Underground as far as Aldersgate; and a short walk took us to Saxe-Coburg Square, the scene of the singular story which we had listened to in the morning. It was a pokey, little, shabby-genteel place, where four lines of dingy two-storied brick houses looked **35** out into a small railed-in enclosure, where a lawn of weedy grass and a few clumps of faded laurel bushes made a hard fight against a smoke-laden and uncongenial atmo- **36** sphere. Three gilt balls and a brown board with "Jabez Wilson" in white letters, upon a corner house, announced the place where our red-headed client carried on his business. Sherlock Holmes stopped in front of it

"SARASATE PLAYS AT THE ST. JAMES'S HALL THIS AFTERNOON". . .

Pablo Martin Melitón Sarasate y Navascues was born at Pamplona, Spain, on March 10, 1844, and died at Biarritz on September 20, 1908. Sarasate studied in France, entering the Paris Conservatoire in 1856, and playing all over Europe before making his first London appearance at the Crystal Palace in 1861. In the same year, he made his first appearance at the St. James's Hall, with which he was to be associated for the rest of his life. Mr. Benjamin Grosbayne wrote of him (in "Sherlock Holmes—Musician"): "His beauty of tone, aristocracy of style, grace of delivery, subtlety of rhythm and amazing dexterity with both hands made him a supreme favorite in every musical center of the world. With what delight Holmes must have heard the Iberian play his own *Gypsy Airs, Caprice Basque, Zapateado* and Bruch's *Scottish Fantasy,* still war-horses on present-day programs; and MacKenzie's *Pibroch Suite,* the last two dedicated to Sarasate himself. A record of the *Gypsy Airs* by the violinist-composer, made near the turn of the century when recording was in its infancy, is occasionally found in collectors' hands." From the chronological point of view, it is interesting to note that Sarasate did *not* play in London in October, 1890. As Mr. Rolfe Boswell wrote in "Sarasate, Sherlock and Shaw": "early that month Sarasate was giving a series of five brilliant concerts at Barcelona, before returning to England to play no fewer than twenty-eight times in London and the provinces, then going on to Germany for December." The St. James's Hall, we may add, no longer exists: it was demolished in 1905, and the Piccadilly Hotel now stands on its site. It opened in 1858, at a cost of £60,000. Charles Dickens gave readings there, and it also housed the early Moore and Burgess "Christy Minstrel" shows. There were three separate halls, one large, two small. As Mr. William H. Gill wrote in "Some Notable Sherlockian Buildings": "Our friends, who enjoyed its concerts, may not have appreciated its Moorish-style elevation designed by Owen Jones . . . nor its lofty Large Hall, flanked by two smaller music rooms. One can imagine Holmes and Watson in the front row of the Large Hall, and they must have supped in the spacious dining rooms added in 1875, before taking a hansom cab back to Baker Street."

stands was named for the northern gate of the City, the name of which (some say) is derived from the personal name "Ealdred" or "Aldred" and (others say) from the alder-trees which once grew around the gate. In Holmes' and Watson's day, Aldersgate was a shabby thoroughfare indeed, but during our own century it has greatly increased in importance.

35 *looked out into a small railed-in enclosure.* The late H. W. Bell long ago pointed out ("Three Identifications") that there are only two squares in the neighborhood of Aldersgate, one of which, Charterhouse Square, he eliminated by its extent, shape, and lack of seclusion. He found that the other—Bridgewater Square—satisfied "almost all the requirements . . ." Since Jabez Wilson's was a corner house, Mr. Bell cast his vote for No. 5, Bridgewater Square. On the other hand, Mr. W. J. Barnes, banking on Watson's later clue of Farringdon Street, has written ("Saxe-Coburg Square—A New Identification") that he prefers Northampton Square "with four wedge-shaped blocks adjacent. Two of these blocks each has a side on a main artery of sufficient length to include the five business establishments mentioned. . . . We reject the western block on St. John's Street in favour of the easterly block on Goswell Road. . . . Upper Ashby Street forms the north side of this block and Sebastian Street (formerly Upper Charles Street) the south side." And there are other views: Mr. N. P. Metcalfe at a meeting of the Sherlock Holmes

. . . A SHORT WALK TOOK US TO SAXE-COBURG SQUARE . . .

Illustration by Joseph Camana from *Cases of Sherlock Holmes,* St. Louis: Webster Publishing Company, 1947.

Society of London once favored a site backing on to Farringdon Street just north of the Holborn Viaduct, while the late Mr. Bill McGowan at the same meeting preferred Brooke Market at the back of Gray's Inn Road. Still another candidate—Charles Square—has been proposed by Mr. Michael Harrison in his book, *In the Footsteps of Sherlock Holmes.*

36 *Three gilt balls.* The ancient sign of a pawnbroker, originally the arms of the Medici family of Lombardy, the Lombards being widely known as moneylenders.

37 *thumped vigorously upon the pavement with his stick.* This is one of the two Canonical adventures in which Holmes carries a walking stick; the other is "The Adventure of the Illustrious Client," in which Holmes carries a stick to enable him to ward off the blows of his assailants in an anticipated attack.

38 *"Third right, fourth left."* These directions do not lead into the Strand from any square in London, the late H. W. Bell noted in "Three Identifications." "We do not know whether Spaulding made the first answer that came into his head, in order to save time and return to his excavating, or whether Watson has inadvertently misquoted him in his notes. But it is a fact that, if we alter the phrase to 'third left, fourth right,' we do obtain a route by which anyone not wholly deficient in a sense of direction could readily get to the Strand..."

39 *I have known something of him before."* "Would not the fourth smartest man in London have known what Sherlock Holmes looked like? He was famous enough even then," Mr. Thomas L. Stix commented in "Concerning 'The Red-Headed League.'"

And the late Robert R. Pattrick wrote ("Moriarty Was There"): "The 'fourth smartest man in London' would not be a freelance. It is even possible that the scheme of 'The Red-Headed League' was originated by Moriarty himself.... The capture of Clay ["Spaulding"] ... was probably Holmes' greatest triumph in the long war. Clay, ranking just below Moriarty in cleverness, and second only to Colonel Moran in daring, would be a key man in the organization ..."

with his head on one side and looked it all over, with his eyes shining brightly between puckered lids. Then he walked slowly up the street and then down again to the corner, still looking keenly at the houses. Finally he returned to the pawnbroker's, and, having thumped

37 vigorously upon the pavement with his stick two or three times, he went up to the door and knocked. It was instantly opened by a bright-looking, clean-shaven young fellow, who asked him to step in.

"Thank you," said Holmes, "I only wished to ask you how you would go from here to the Strand."

38 "Third right, fourth left," answered the assistant promptly, closing the door.

"Smart fellow, that," observed Holmes as we walked away. "He is, in my judgment, the fourth smartest man in London, and for daring I am not sure that he has not a claim to be third. I have known something of him be-

39 fore."

"Evidently," said I, "Mr. Wilson's assistant counts for a good deal in this mystery of the Red-headed League. I am sure that you inquired your way merely in order that you might see him."

"Not him."

"What then?"

"The knees of his trousers."

"And what did you see?"

"What I expected to see."

"Why did you beat the pavement?"

"My dear Doctor, this is a time for observation, not for talk. We are spies in an enemy's country. We know something of Saxe-Coburg Square. Let us now explore the paths which lie behind it."

The road in which we found ourselves as we turned round the corner from the retired Saxe-Coburg Square presented as great a contrast to it as the front of a picture

40 does to the back. It was one of the main arteries which convey the traffic of the City to the north and west. The roadway was blocked with the immense stream of com-

IT WAS INSTANTLY OPENED BY A BRIGHT-LOOKING, CLEAN-SHAVEN YOUNG FELLOW ...

Illustration by Sidney Paget for the *Strand Magazine*, August, 1891.

merce flowing in a double tide inwards and outwards, while the footpaths were black with the hurrying swarm of pedestrians. It was difficult to realize as we looked at the line of fine shops and stately business premises that they really abutted on the other side upon the faded and stagnant square which we had just quitted.

"Let me see," said Holmes, standing at the corner, and glancing along the line, "I should like just to remember the order of the houses here. It is a hobby of mine to have an exact knowledge of London. There is Mortimer's, the tobacconist, the little newspaper shop, the Coburg branch of the City and Suburban Bank, the Vegetarian Restaurant, and McFarlane's carriage-building depôt. That carries us right on to the other block. And now, Doctor, we've done our work, so it's time we had some play. A sandwich, and a cup of coffee, and then off to violin land, where all is sweetness, and delicacy, and harmony, and there are no red-headed clients to vex us with their conundrums."

My friend was an enthusiastic musician, being himself not only a very capable performer, but a composer of no ordinary merit. All the afternoon he sat in the stalls wrapped in the most perfect happiness, gently waving his long thin fingers in time to the music, while his gently smiling face and his languid, dreamy eyes were as unlike those of Holmes the sleuth-hound, Holmes the relentless, keen-witted, ready-handed criminal agent, as it was possible to conceive. In his singular character the dual **11** nature alternately asserted itself, and his extreme exactness and astuteness represented, as I have often thought, the reaction against the poetic and contemplative mood which occasionally predominated in him. The swing of his nature took him from extreme languor to devouring energy; and, as I knew well, he was never so truly formidable as when, for days on end, he had been lounging in his arm-chair amid his improvisations and his black-letter editions. Then it was that the lust of the chase would suddenly come upon him, and that his brilliant reasoning power would rise to the level of intuition, until those who were unacquainted with his methods would look askance at him as on a man whose knowledge was not that of other mortals. When I saw him that afternoon so enwrapped in the music at St. James's Hall I felt that an evil time might be coming upon those whom he had set himself to hunt down.

"You want to go home, no doubt, Doctor," he remarked, as we emerged.

"Yes, it would be as well."

"And I have some business to do which will take some hours. This business at Coburg Square is serious."

"Why serious ?"

"A considerable crime is in contemplation. I have every reason to believe that we shall be in time to stop it. But to-day being Saturday rather complicates matters. I shall want your help to-night."

"At what time ?"

"Ten will be early enough."

"I shall be at Baker Street at ten."

"Very well. And, I say, Doctor ! there may be some little danger, so kindly put your army revolver in your

40 *It was one of the main arteries.* This was Aldersgate Street, presumably, or perhaps its continuation, Goswell Road. But Mr. Frank V. Morley has pointed out ("I Am puzzled About Saxe-Coburg Square") that the Goswell Road "is more Pickwick than the sort of Oxford Street described by Watson."

41 *as it was possible to conceive.* ". . . observe another great detective, Lord Peter Wimsey, in a similar situation: 'He was wrapped in the motionless austerity with which all genuine musicians listen to genuine music. Harriet was musican enough to respect this aloofness; she knew well enough that the ecstatic rapture on the face of the man opposite meant only that he was hoping to be thought musical, and that the elderly lady over the way, waving her fingers to the beat, was a musical moron (Dorothy L. Sayers, *Gaudy Night*, New York: Harcourt, Brace & Co., 1936, p. 467).'"—Professor Remsen Ten Eyck Schenck, "Baker Street Fables."

ALL THE AFTERNOON HE SAT IN THE STALLS WRAPPED IN THE MOST PERFECT HAPPINESS . . .

Illustration by Sidney Paget for the *Strand Magazine*, August, 1891.

42 *Kensington.* A metropolitan borough distinguished as the "Royal Borough" by grant of Edward VII in 1901. It extends from the northwest part of the county boundary, where it adjoins the Middlesex borough of Willesden, for nearly four miles to Chelsea on its southeast, and it has an average breadth, northeast to southwest, of about one and a half miles. The borough includes about half of Kensington Gardens, including Kensington Palace. Kensington has long been a haunt of literary and artistic people. Kensington is also famous for its museums.

43 *as in that business of the Sholto murder and the Agra treasure.* See our remarks in "Now, Watson, the Fair Sex Is Your Department."

44 *some thirty thousand pounds.* Some $1,500,000.

pocket." He waved his hand, turned on his heel, and disappeared in an instant among the crowd.

I trust that I am not more dense than my neighbours, but I was always oppressed with a sense of my own stupidity in my dealings with Sherlock Holmes. Here I had heard what he had heard, I had seen what he had seen, and yet from his words it was evident that he saw clearly not only what had happened, but what was about to happen, while to me the whole business was still confused and **42** grotesque. As I drove home to my house in Kensington I thought over it all, from the extraordinary story of the red-headed copier of the *Encyclopædia* down to the visit to Saxe-Coburg Square, and the ominous words with which he had parted from me. What was this nocturnal expedition, and why should I go armed ? Where were we going, and what were we to do ? I had the hint from Holmes that this smooth-faced pawnbroker's assistant was a formidable man—a man who might play a deep game. I tried to puzzle it out, but gave it up in despair, and set the matter aside until night should bring an explanation.

It was a quarter past nine when I started from home and made my way across the Park, and so through Oxford Street to Baker Street. Two hansoms were standing at the door, and, as I entered the passage, I heard the sound of voices from above. On entering his room, I found Holmes in animated conversation with two men, one of whom I recognized as Peter Jones, the official police agent ; while the other was a long, thin, sad-faced man, with a very shiny hat and oppressively respectable frock-coat.

" Ha ! our party is complete," said Holmes, buttoning up his pea-jacket, and taking his heavy hunting-crop from the rack. " Watson, I think you know Mr. Jones, of Scotland Yard ? Let me introduce you to Mr. Merryweather, who is to be our companion in to-night's adventure."

" We're hunting in couples again, Doctor, you see," said Jones in his consequential way. " Our friend here is a wonderful man for starting a chase. All he wants is an old dog to help him to do the running down."

" I hope a wild goose may not prove to be the end of our chase," observed Mr. Merryweather gloomily.

" You may place considerable confidence in Mr. Holmes, sir," said the police agent loftily. " He has his own little methods, which are, if he won't mind my saying so, just a little too theoretical and fantastic, but he has the makings of a detective in him. It is not too much to say that once or twice, as in that business of the Sholto **43** murder and the Agra treasure, he has been more nearly correct than the official force."

" Oh, if you say so, Mr. Jones, it is all right ! " said the stranger, with deference. " Still, I confess that I miss my rubber. It is the first Saturday night for seven-and-twenty years that I have not had my rubber."

" I think you will find," said Sherlock Holmes, " that you will play for a higher stake to-night than you have ever done yet, and that the play will be more exciting. For you, Mr. Merryweather, the stake will be some **44** thirty thousand pounds ; and for you, Jones, it will be the man upon whom you wish to lay your hands."

" John Clay, the murderer, thief, smasher, and forger. He's a young man, Mr. Merryweather, but he is at the head of his profession, and I would rather have my brace-lets on him than on any criminal in London. He's a remarkable man, is young John Clay. His grandfather was a Royal Duke, and he himself has been to Eton and **45** Oxford. His brain is as cunning as his fingers, and though we meet signs of him at every turn, we never know where to find the man himself. He'll crack a crib in Scotland one week, and be raising money to build an orphanage in Cornwall the next. I've been on his track **46** for years, and have never set eyes on him yet."

" I hope that I may have the pleasure of introducing you to-night. I've had one or two little turns also with Mr. John Clay, and I agree with you that he is at the head of his profession. It is past ten, however, and quite time that we started. If you two will take the first han-som, Watson and I will follow in the second."

Sherlock Holmes was not very communicative during the long drive, and lay back in the cab humming the tunes which he had heard in the afternoon. We rattled through an endless labyrinth of gas-lit streets until we emerged into Farringdon Street. **47**

" We are close there now," my friend remarked. " This fellow Merryweather is a bank director and person-ally interested in the matter. I thought it as well to have Jones with us also. He is not a bad fellow, though an absolute imbecile in his profession. He has one positive virtue. He is as brave as a bulldog, and as tenacious as a lobster if he gets his claws upon anyone. Here we are, and they are waiting for us."

We had reached the same crowded thoroughfare in which we had found ourselves in the morning. Our cabs were dismissed, and, following the guidance of Mr. Merryweather, we passed down a narrow passage, and through a side door, which he opened for us. Within there was a small corridor, which ended in a very massive iron gate. This also was opened, and led down a flight of winding stone steps, which terminated at another formidable gate. Mr. Merryweather stopped to light a lantern, and then conducted us down a dark, earth-smell-ing passage, and so, after opening a third door, into a huge vault or cellar, which was piled all round with crates and massive boxes.

" You are not very vulnerable from above," Holmes remarked, as he held up the lantern and gazed about him.

" Nor from below," said Mr. Merryweather, striking his stick upon the flags which lined the floor. " Why, dear me, it sounds quite hollow ! " he remarked, looking up in surprise.

" I must really ask you to be a little more quiet," said Holmes severely. " You have already imperilled the whole success of our expedition. Might I beg that you would have the goodness to sit down upon one of those boxes, and not to interfere ? "

The solemn Mr. Merryweather perched himself upon a crate, with a very injured expression upon his face, while Holmes fell upon his knees upon the floor, and, with the lantern and a magnifying lens, began to examine minutely the cracks between the stones. A few seconds sufficed

45 *His grandfather was a Royal Duke.* "It is gen-erally agreed that John Clay's grandfather was one of the seven sons of George III because they were the Royal Dukes who were in action during the epoch that his link with royalty was forged," Dr. Julian Wolff wrote in *Practical Handbook of Sher-lockian Heraldry.* Mr. Carl T. Erickson has made a case ("Royal Blood and Feet of Clay") for the third son, the Duke of Clarence, who later became William IV, and Mr. N. P. Metcalfe, at a meeting of the Sherlock Holmes Society of London, once eliminated six of the sons until only the Duke of Sussex remained. However, as Dr. Wolff concluded: "The truth is that there are too many suspects, none of them impossible—or even improbable."

46 *Cornwall.* A maritime county in the southwest of England, a peninsula ending in the promontory called Land's End. Cornwall is a county of low-lying plateaus with market and dairy farms in fertile valleys. It is a great fishing center, and its climate and picturesque coast towns make it popu-lar with tourists.

47 *Farringdon Street.* The late H. W. Bell dis-missed Farringdon *Street* as a slip of the pen, be-lieving that Watson intended to refer to Farring-don *Road.* On the other hand, Mr. Barnes, as we have seen, found this clue "quite acceptable." The question remains: with Aldersgate Station only "a short walk" from Saxe-Coburg Square, why did Holmes and party endure a "long drive" through "an endless labyrinth of gas-lit streets"?

MR. MERRYWEATHER STOPPED TO LIGHT A LANTERN . . .

Illustration by Sidney Paget for the *Strand Maga-zine,* August, 1891.

to satisfy him, for he sprang to his feet again, and put his glass in his pocket.

"We have at least an hour before us," he remarked, "for they can hardly take any steps until the good pawn-broker is safely in bed. Then they will not lose a minute, for the sooner they do their work the longer time they will have for their escape. We are at present, Doctor—as no doubt you have divined—in the cellar of the City branch of one of the principal London banks. Mr. Merryweather is the chairman of directors, and he will explain to you that there are reasons why the more daring criminals of London should take a considerable interest in this cellar at present."

"It is our French gold," whispered the director. "We have had several warnings that an attempt might be made upon it."

"Your French gold?"

"Yes. We had occasion some months ago to strengthen our resources, and borrowed, for that purpose, thirty thousand napoleons from the Bank of France. It has become known that we have never had occasion to unpack the money, and that it is still lying in our cellar. The crate upon which I sit contains two thousand napoleons packed between layers of lead foil. Our reserve of bullion is much larger at present than is usually kept in a single branch office, and the directors have had mis-**48** givings upon the subject."

"... THIRTY THOUSAND NAPOLEONS FROM THE BANK OF FRANCE."

The late A. Carson Simpson, our specialist in the numismatics of the Canon, tells us in "A Very Treasury of Divers Realms" that "there can be no doubt that a 'napoleon' is a French 20-franc goldpiece." It is true that Holmes is said to have valued the shipment at "some £30,000." The 20-franc piece being worth about $3.86 and the pound close to $5.00, the value of 30,000 of the former would be closer to £20,000. This is almost certainly another of Watson's errors. The French gold napoleons shown above include: 38, Louis XVIII, uniformed bust; 38a, Bonaparte, First Consul, obverse only; 38b, Napoleon I, obverse only; 39, Louis XVIII, bare head, Perpignan mint; 39a, Charles X, obverse only; 40, Louis-Philippe; 40a, Second Republic, Ceres head, obverse only; 41, Napoleon III, Strasbourg mint; 42, Third Republic, angel type.

" Which were very well justified," observed Holmes. " And now it is time that we arranged our little plans. I expect that within an hour matters will come to a head. In the meantime, Mr. Merryweather, we must put the screen over that dark lantern."

" And sit in the dark ? "

" I am afraid so. I had brought a pack of cards in my pocket, and I thought that, as we were a *partie carrée*, you **49-50** might have your rubber after all. But I see that the enemy's preparations have gone so far that we cannot risk the presence of a light. And, first of all, we must choose our positions. These are daring men, and, though we shall take them at a disadvantage they may do us some harm, unless we are careful. I shall stand behind this crate, and do you conceal yourself behind those. Then, when I flash a light upon them, close in swiftly. If they fire, Watson, have no compunction about shooting them down."

I placed my revolver, cocked, upon the top of the wooden case behind which I crouched. Holmes shot the slide across the front of his lantern, and left us in pitch darkness—such an absolute darkness as I have never **51** before experienced. The smell of hot metal remained to assure us that the light was still there, ready to flash out at a moment's notice. To me, with my nerves worked up to a pitch of expectancy, there was something depressing and subduing in the sudden gloom, and in the cold, dank air of the vault.

" They have but one retreat," whispered Holmes. " That is back through the house into Saxe-Coburg Square. I hope that you have done what I asked you, Jones ? "

" I have an inspector and two officers waiting at the front door."

" Then we have stopped all the holes. And now we must be silent and wait."

What a time it seemed ! From comparing notes afterwards it was but an hour and a quarter, yet it appeared to me that the night must have almost gone, and the dawn be breaking above us. My limbs were weary and stiff, for I feared to change my position, yet my nerves were worked up to the highest pitch of tension, and my hearing was so acute that I could not only hear the gentle breathing of my companions, but I could distinguish the deeper, heavier in-breath of the bulky Jones from the thin sighing note of the bank director. From my position I could look over the case in the direction of the floor. Suddenly my eyes caught the glint of a light.

At first it was but a lurid spark upon the stone pavement. Then it lengthened out until it became a yellow line, and then, without any warning or sound, a gash seemed to open and a hand appeared, a white, almost womanly hand, which felt about in the centre of the little area of light. For a minute or more the hand, with its writhing fingers, protruded out of the floor. Then it was withdrawn as suddenly as it appeared, and all was dark again save the single lurid spark, which marked a chink between the stones.

Its disappearance, however, was but momentary.

48 *the directors have had misgivings upon the subject.*" "Mr. [G. B.] Newton, who is a retired bank manager, confessed to astonishment at the singular way in which the directors of the City and Suburban Bank conducted their business. The 30,000 napoleons (not, incidentally, a very substantial sum with which to allay the possible anxieties of depositors) had been stored, not at the Bank of England, as would have been the normal procedure, nor even at the C. & S. Bank's own head office strong room, but in an apparently not very impregnable cellar below its Coburg branch. It had moreover 'become known' that the bullion was unpacked and lying in the cellar—a most reprehensible leakage of top-secret information for which no-one in particular seems to have been responsible. No wonder the directors had 'misgivings.' Yet, notwithstanding that 'they had had several warnings that an attempt might be made upon it,' they took no special precautions but apparently just hoped for the best. The keys giving access to this rather doubtful stronghold were apparently in the sole possession of Mr. Merryweather and Clay could have saved himself a good deal of trouble if he had knocked him on the head and stolen them."—" 'The Red-Headed League' Reviewed."

49 *I had brought a pack of cards in my pocket.* "Without a doubt," Mr. L. A. Morrow wrote in "The Game Is . . .", "Holmes' game was whist . . ." Whist was the famous card game from which modern bridge developed. The name is said to be derived from "Whist!" meaning to be silent, a reproach still applicable to those who are talkative at the card table. The game of whist was famous as far back as the eighteenth century, and Edmond Hoyle's *Treatise on Whist*, published in 1742, codified the rules. This book became the classic of card lore, hence the phrase "According to Hoyle."

Holmes' devotion to whist must have been exceedingly great; "taking a deck of cards instead of a gun when going after a desperate bank robber is hardly the action of one whose interest in cards is casual," as Mr. Morrow wrote. As Mr. Morrow and others have shown, Holmes studded his conversation with terms taken from the lexicon of a card enthusiast: "At present it must be admitted that the odd trick is in his possession, and, as you are aware, Watson, it is not my habit to leave the game in that condition," Holmes said in "The Adventure of the Missing Three-Quarter." "You see that we hold all the cards . . . ," he said in "The Greek Interpreter." "He will hold a card back for years in order to play it at the moment when the stake is best worth winning," Holmes said of Charles Augustus Milverton. "We have added one card to our hand, Watson, but it needs careful playing all the same," he said in "The Adventure of Shoscombe Old Place," and, in that same adventure: "We are getting some cards in our hands. . . . It's not an easy one to play . . ." "Now, Count, you are a card-player. When the other fellow has all the trumps, it saves time to throw down your hand,"

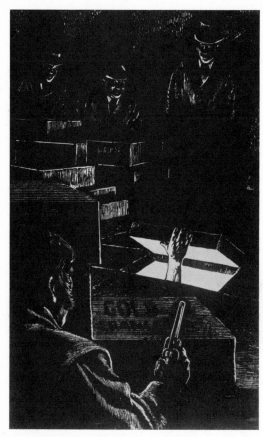

. . . A HAND APPEARED, A WHITE, ALMOST WOMANLY
HAND, WHICH FELT ABOUT IN THE CENTRE OF THE
LITTLE AREA OF LIGHT.

Illustration by Joseph Camana for *Cases of Sherlock Holmes*, St. Louis: Webster Publishing Company, 1947.

he warned in "The Adventure of the Mazarin
Stone." "I see the fall of the cards," he said in "The
Adventure of the Bruce-Partington Plans." And
in *The Hound of the Baskervilles*, Holmes said:
"We must see what further cards we have in our
hands, and play them with decision."

50 *a* partie carrée. French: a party of four, more
usually applied to a party of two men and two
women.

51 *The smell of hot metal.* "Mr. Guy Warrack:
'How was it that Clay, who probably had a very
sensitive nose, was not warned of the presence of
Holmes and his party in the vault by the smell of
their oil lamp?' "—'The Red-Headed League'
Reviewed."

52 *Jump, Archie, jump.* Mr. Jerry Neal William-
son has speculated ("The Sad Case of Young Stam-
ford") that this Archie was the same Archie
Stamford, the forger, later taken by Holmes and
Watson near Farnham, on the borders of Surrey
("The Adventure of the Solitary Cyclist").

With a rending, tearing sound, one of the broad, white
stones turned over upon its side, and left a square, gaping
hole, through which streamed the light of a lantern.
Over the edge there peeped a clean-cut, boyish face, which
looked keenly about it, and then, with a hand on either
side of the aperture, drew itself shoulder high and waist
high, until one knee rested upon the edge. In another
instant he stood at the side of the hole, and was hauling
after him a companion, lithe and small like himself, with
a pale face and a shock of very red hair.

"It's all clear," he whispered. "Have you the chisel,
52 and the bags. Great Scott! Jump, Archie, jump, and
53 I'll swing for it!"

Sherlock Holmes had sprung out and seized the intruder by the collar. The other dived down the hole,
and I heard the sound of rending cloth as Jones clutched
at his skirts. The light flashed upon the barrel of a
revolver, but Holmes's hunting-crop came down on the
54 man's wrist, and the pistol clinked upon the stone floor.

"It's no use, John Clay," said Holmes blandly; "you
have no chance at all."

"So I see," the other answered with the utmost coolness. "I fancy that my pal is all right, though I see you
have got his coat-tails."

"There are three men waiting for him at the door,"
said Holmes.

"Oh, indeed. You seem to have done the thing very
completely. I must compliment you."

"And I you," Holmes answered. "Your red-headed
idea was very new and effective."

"You'll see your pal again presently," said Jones.
"He's quicker at climbing down holes than I am. Just
55 hold out while I fix the derbies."

"I beg that you will not touch me with your filthy
hands," remarked our prisoner, as the handcuffs clattered
upon his wrists. "You may not be aware that I have
royal blood in my veins. Have the goodness also when
you address me always to say 'sir' and 'please.'"

"All right," said Jones, with a stare and a snigger.
"Well, would you please, sir, march upstairs, where
we can get a cab to carry your highness to the police
station."

"That is better," said John Clay serenely. He made
a sweeping bow to the three of us, and walked quietly off
in the custody of the detective.

"Really, Mr. Holmes," said Mr. Merryweather, as
we followed them from the cellar, "I do not know how
the bank can thank you or repay you. There is no doubt
that you have detected and defeated in the most complete
manner one of the most determined attempts at bank
robbery that have ever come within my experience."

"I have had one or two little scores of my own to settle
with Mr. John Clay," said Holmes. "I have been at
some small expense over this matter, which I shall expect
the bank to refund, but beyond that I am amply repaid
by having had an experience which is in many ways
unique, and by hearing the very remarkable narrative of
the Red-headed League."

"You see, Watson," he explained in the early hours

of the morning, as we sat over a glass of whisky-and-soda in Baker Street, "it was perfectly obvious from the first that the only possible object of this rather fantastic business of the advertisement of the League, and the copying of the *Encyclopædia*, must be to get this not over-bright pawnbroker out of the way for a number of hours every day. It was a curious way of managing it, but really it would be difficult to suggest a better. The method was no doubt suggested to Clay's ingenious mind by the colour of his accomplice's hair. The four pounds a week was a lure which must draw him, and what was it to them, who were playing for thousands? They put in the advertisement; one rogue has the temporary office, the other rogue incites the man to apply for it, and together they manage to secure his absence every morning in the week. From the time that I heard of the assistant having come for half-wages, it was obvious to me that he had some strong motive for securing the situation."

"But how could you guess what the motive was?"

"Had there been women in the house, I should have suspected a mere vulgar intrigue. That, however, was out of the question. The man's business was a small one, and there was nothing in his house which could account for such elaborate preparations and such an expenditure as they were at. It must then be something out of the house. What could it be? I thought of the assistant's fondness for photography, and his trick of vanishing into the cellar. The cellar! There was the end of this tangled clue. Then I made inquiries as to this mysterious assistant, and found that I had to deal with one of the coolest and most daring criminals in London. He was doing something in the cellar—something which took many hours a day for months on end. What could it be, once more? I could think of nothing save that he was running a tunnel to some other building.

"So far I had got when we went to visit the scene of action. I surprised you by beating upon the pavement with my stick. I was ascertaining whether the cellar stretched out in front or behind. It was not in front. Then I rang the bell, and, as I hoped, the assistant answered it. We have had some skirmishes, but we had never set eyes on each other before. I hardly looked at his face. His knees were what I wished to see. You must yourself have remarked how worn, wrinkled and stained they were. They spoke of those hours of burrowing. The only remaining point was what they were burrowing for. I walked round the corner, saw that the **56** City and Suburban Bank abutted on our friend's premises, and felt that I had solved my problem. When you drove home after the concert I called upon Scotland Yard, and upon the chairman of the bank directors, with the result that you have seen."

"And how could you tell that they would make their attempt to-night?" I asked.

"Well, when they closed their League offices that was a sign that they cared no longer about Mr. Jabez Wilson's presence; in other words, that they had completed their tunnel. But it was essential that they should use it soon, as it might be discovered, or the bullion might be removed.

53 *and I'll swing for it!*" Did this merely mean that Clay would swing back through the trapdoor or was he anticipating that he would be hanged? "This must have been thieves' jargon," Magistrate S. Tupper Bigelow wrote in "Two Canonical Problems Solved," "or Dr. Watson didn't hear . . . correctly, because John Clay knew as well as anyone that in England of those days, only traitors (like Sir Roger Casement) and murderers were hanged . . ."

54 *Holmes' hunting-crop came down on the man's wrist.* "This adventure, if I am not mistaken, is the only one in which Holmes used his famous hunting-crop as a weapon. . . . Watson tells us in after years that a hunting-crop was Holmes' favorite weapon but I can't find any other instance of its use in offence or defence."—The late Clifton R. Andrew in a footnote to "'The Red-Headed League' Reviewed."

55 *the derbies.*" The handcuffs.

56 *The only remaining point was what they were burrowing for.* Another remaining point is: What was done with the excavated earth? "How could it possibly have been disposed of?" Mr. Nathan L. Bengis wrote in "Sherlock Stays After School." "The amount of earth excavated in the digging of the tunnel . . . must have been prodigious. The dirt could not have been allowed to accumulate in the cellar, even if conceivably the

"IT'S NO USE, JOHN CLAY," SAID HOLMES BLANDLY . . .

Illustration by Sidney Paget for the *Strand Magazine*, August, 1891.

cellar was large enough to receive it, as a gigantic pile would have been too conspicuous to avoid detection should Wilson ever have taken it into his head to descend into the basement for a minute. The debris could not have been taken out into the street, as the risk of detection would have been too great between the hours of ten and two, when Wilson was away from his shop. Altogether, it is a neat puzzle . . ."

"The area underlying the footpath was the repository of the dirt," Mr. W. J. Barnes suggested. "John Clay had merely transported the excavated earth from one side of the cellar to the other . . ."

And Magistrate S. Tupper Bigelow suggested ("Two Canonical Problems Solved") that the earth was loaded into large empty cardboard boxes which were then taken away by a dray which delivered more cardboard boxes.

Also: how did the criminals hope to remove the bullion, the weight of which must have been enormous? "The task of lowering 15 crates into the tunnel, along it and up again would have been a herculean one for two men. And if this were achieved what were they going to do next? Loading it into a cart outside a pawnbroker's shop on a Sunday morning might well provoke some awkward questions and you cannot just go gadding about the countryside with large quantities of bullion in tow without attracting some attention" ("'The Red-Headed League' Reviewed").

To this question Mr. Charles Scholefield suggested that the criminals would use a carriage from McFarlane's Depot; probably the tunnel connected not only Wilson's but also McFarlane's with the bank.

57 *as it would give them two days for their escape.* But "two days" the robbers could *not* have had unless the Monday following the robbery on Sunday morning was a Bank Holiday, and no Bank Holiday falls during the autumn of the year.

58 *as Gustave Flaubert wrote to George Sand.* "The correct wording," Mr. Morris Rosenblum wrote in "Foreign Language Quotations in the Canon," "is 'L'homme n'est rien, l'œuvre tout.' . . . The quotation occurs in the letter dated December, 1875, pages 272–3 of *Lettres de Gustave Flaubert à George Sand*, Charpentier, Paris, 188?. The translation, 'The man is nothing, the work is everything,' is found on page 348, Letter CCCI of the English edition, *The George Sand-Gustave Flaubert Letters*, by Aimee L. McKenzie, Boni and Liveright, New York, 1921."

Saturday would suit them better than any other day, as it **57** would give them two days for their escape. For all these reasons I expected them to come to-night."

"You reasoned it out beautifully," I exclaimed in unfeigned admiration. "It is so long a chain, and yet every link rings true."

"It saved me from ennui," he answered, yawning. "Alas, I already feel it closing in upon me! My life is spent in one long effort to escape from the commonplaces of existence. These little problems help me to do so."

"And you are a benefactor of the race," said I.

He shrugged his shoulders. "Well, perhaps, after all, it is of some little use," he remarked. "'*L'homme c'est rien—l'œuvre c'est tout*,' as Gustave Flaubert wrote to **58** George Sand."

Auctorial and Bibliographical Note: Conan Doyle's own opinion of "The Red-Headed League" was a high one: he rated it in second position in his "twelve best" list of the short stories (excluding those in the *Case-Book*). It also rated high —No. 5—with the readers of the *Observer*, who considered both the short stories and the novels.

According to Mr. David A. Randall, "The Red-Headed League" was first published in book form in an unauthorized edition of Conan Doyle's short stories titled *The Doings of Raffles Haw*; New York: Lovell, Coryell and Company, August, 1892, as "Number Five in the Belmore Series."

29

THE ADVENTURE OF THE DYING DETECTIVE

[Saturday, November 19, 1887]

MRS. HUDSON, the landlady of Sherlock Holmes, was a long-suffering woman. Not only was her first-floor flat invaded at all hours by **1** throngs of singular and often undesirable characters, but her remarkable lodger showed an eccentricity and irregularity in his life which must have sorely tried her patience. His incredible untidiness, his addiction to music at strange hours, his occasional revolver practice within doors, his weird and often malodorous scientific experiments, and the atmosphere of violence and danger which hung around him made him the very worst tenant in London. On the other hand, his payments were princely. I have no doubt that **2** the house might have been purchased at the price which Holmes paid for his rooms during the years that I was with him.

The landlady stood in the deepest awe of him, and never dared to interfere with him, however outrageous his proceedings might seem. She was fond of him, too, for he had a remarkable gentleness and courtesy in his dealings with women. He disliked and distrusted the sex, but he was always a chivalrous opponent. Knowing how genuine was her regard for him, I listened earnestly to her story when she came to my rooms in the second year of my **3** married life and told me of the sad condition to which my poor friend was reduced.

" He's dying, Dr. Watson," said she. " For three days he has been sinking, and I doubt if he will last the day. **4** He would not let me get a doctor. This morning when I saw his bones sticking out of his face and his great bright eyes looking at me I could stand no more of it. ' With your leave or without it, Mr. Holmes, I am going for a doctor this very hour,' said I. ' Let it be Watson, then,' said he. I wouldn't waste an hour in coming to him, sir, or you may not see him alive."

I was horrified, for I had heard nothing of his illness. I need not say that I rushed for my coat and my hat. As we drove back I asked for the details.

" There is little I can tell you, sir. He has been working at a case down at Rotherhithe, in an alley near the **5** river, and he has brought this illness back with him. He took to his bed on Wednesday afternoon and has never

1 *her first-floor flat.* Watson of course uses "first-floor" in the English sense; an American would say "second-floor."

2 *his payments were princely.* There can be no doubt that Holmes by this time could easily afford the rent of the Baker Street suite without assistance—but "the impecunious Watson was no judge of what was princely," as Mr. Vincent Starrett wrote in "The Singular Adventures of Martha Hudson."

3 *in the second year of my married life.* Although Watson certainly married for a second (or a third) time in late 1902, most commentators are agreed that Holmes retired in 1903. It is therefore generally conceded that "The Adventure of the Dying Detective" did not take place in the November (*see below*) of that year. The date assigned to the adventure by the various commentators thus hinges on the date that each assigns to Watson's first marriage, and the consensus (Blakeney, Christ, Folsom, Pattrick, Petersen, Smith, and Zeisler) favors 1890. Messrs. Bell, Boucher, and Starrett chose 1888, Messrs. Andrew, Brend, and Harrison 1889. Your editor would again seem to stand alone in his selection of *1887*.

4 *"For three days he has been sinking.* The late Dr. Ernest Bloomfield Zeisler (*Baker Street Chronology*) well summed up the case for dating this adventure on a *Saturday:* "Mrs. Hudson says that the Master took to his bed on Wednesday afternoon, that 'for three days he has been sinking' and that 'for these three days neither food nor drink has passed his lips.' Watson tells Culverton Smith that the Master had been ill 'about three days.' Smith recalls to the Master that the poisoned box 'came on Wednesday.' Watson goes to the Master at once, and shortly after his arrival it is four o'clock. Since Wednesday afternoon to Saturday afternoon is three days there is no doubt that the story begins on a Saturday . . ."

5 *Rotherhithe.* A section of London, long popularly known as Redriff, which includes the Surrey docks and is mainly inhabited by dock and waterside workers. The name may come from *rethra*, a mariner, and *hythe*, a haven.

6 *a foggy November day.* Our choice of the Saturday in November of 1887 on which this adventure took place is dictated by the weather reports in the London *Times*. In the Saturday–Sunday reports published in the Monday editions of that newspaper for November, 1887, fog is mentioned only once: in the report for *Saturday, November 19, 1887.*

. . . BUT IT WAS THAT GAUNT, WASTED FACE STARING AT ME FROM THE BED WHICH SENT A CHILL TO MY HEART.

Illustration by Frederic Dorr Steele for *Collier's Magazine*, November 22, 1913.

moved since.   For these three days neither food nor drink has passed his lips."

" Good God ! Why did you not call in a doctor ? "

" He wouldn't have it, sir. You know how masterful he is. I didn't dare to disobey him. But he's not long for this world, as you'll see for yourself the moment that you set eyes on him."

He was indeed a deplorable spectacle.   In the dim light **6** of a foggy November day the sick-room was a gloomy spot, but it was that gaunt, wasted face staring at me from the bed which sent a chill to my heart.   His eyes had the brightness of fever, there was a hectic flush upon either cheek, and dark crusts clung to his lips ; the thin hands upon the coverlet twitched incessantly, his voice was croaking and spasmodic.   He lay listlessly as I entered the room, but the sight of me brought a gleam of recognition to his eyes.

" Well, Watson, we seem to have fallen upon evil days," said he, in a feeble voice, but with something of his old carelessness of manner.

" My dear fellow ! " I cried, approaching him.

" Stand back ! Stand right back ! " said he, with the sharp imperiousness which I had associated only with moments of crisis. " If you approach me, Watson, I shall order you out of the house."

" But why ? "

" Because it is my desire. Is that not enough ? "

Yes, Mrs. Hudson was right. He was more masterful than ever. It was pitiful, however, to see his exhaustion.

" I only wished to help," I explained.

" Exactly ! You will help best by doing what you are told."

" Certainly, Holmes."

He relaxed the austerity of his manner.

" You are not angry ? " he asked, gasping for breath.

Poor devil, how could I be angry when I saw him lying in such a plight before me ?

" It's for your own sake, Watson," he croaked.

" For *my* sake ? "

" I know what is the matter with me. It is a coolie disease from Sumatra—a thing that the Dutch know more about than we, though they have made little of it up to date. One thing only is certain. It is infallibly deadly, and it is horribly contagious."

He spoke now with a feverish energy, the long hands twitching and jerking as he motioned me away.

" Contagious by touch, Watson—that's it, by touch. Keep your distance and all is well."

" Good heavens, Holmes ! Do you suppose that such a consideration weighs with me for an instant ? It would not affect me in the case of a stranger. Do you imagine it would prevent me from doing my duty to so old a friend ? "

Again I advanced, but he repulsed me with a look of furious anger.

" If you will stand there I will talk. If you do not you must leave the room."

I have so deep a respect for the extraordinary qualities

of Holmes that I have always deferred to his wishes, even when I least understood them. But now all my professional instincts were aroused. Let him be my master elsewhere, I at least was his in a sick-room.

"Holmes," said I, "you are not yourself. A sick man is but a child, and so I will treat you. Whether you like it or not, I will examine your symptoms and treat you for them."

He looked at me with venomous eyes.

"If I am to have a doctor whether I will or not, let me at least have someone in whom I have confidence," said he.

"Then you have none in me?"

"In your friendship, certainly. But facts are facts, Watson, and after all you are only a general practitioner with very limited experience and mediocre qualifications. It is painful to have to say these things, but you leave me no choice."

I was bitterly hurt.

"Such a remark is unworthy of you, Holmes. It shows me very clearly the state of your own nerves. But if you have no confidence in me I would not intrude my services. Let me bring Sir Jasper Meek or Penrose Fisher, or any of the best men in London. But someone you *must* have, and that is final. If you think that I am going to stand here and see you die without either helping you myself or bringing anyone else to help you, then you have mistaken your man."

"You mean well, Watson," said the sick man, with something between a sob and a groan. "Shall I demonstrate your own ignorance? What do you know, pray, of Tapanuli fever? What do you know of the black Formosa corruption?" **7**

"I have never heard of either."

"There are many problems of disease, many strange pathological possibilities, in the East, Watson." He paused after each sentence to collect his failing strength. "I have learned so much during some recent researches which have a medico-criminal aspect. It was in the **8** course of them that I contracted this complaint. You can do nothing."

"Possibly not. But I happen to know that Dr. Ainstree, the greatest living authority upon tropical disease, is now in London. All remonstrance is useless, Holmes. I am going this instant to fetch him." I turned resolutely to the door.

Never have I had such a shock! In an instant, with a tiger-spring, the dying man had intercepted me. I heard the sharp snap of a twisted key. The next moment he had staggered back to his bed, exhausted and panting after his one tremendous outflame of energy.

"You won't take the key from me by force, Watson. I've got you, my friend. Here you are, and here you will stay until I will otherwise. But I'll humour you." (All this in little gasps, with terrible struggles for breath between.) "You've only my own good at heart. Of course I know that very well. You shall have your way, but give me time to get my strength. Not now, Watson, not now. It's four o'clock. At six you can go."

I HEARD THE SHARP SNAP OF A TWISTED KEY.

Illustration by Walter Paget for the *Strand Magazine*, December, 1913.

7 *the black Formosa corruption?"* It has long been supposed that "Tapanuli fever" and "the black Formosa corruption" were nonexistent diseases, but research by Mr. Hugh L'Etang suggests that they exist and that they are in fact one and the same disease: tsutsugamushi fever, or scrub typhus. "This is an infectious disease transmitted by mites and found, among other places, in Japan, Formosa, the Pescadores, Sumatra, New Guinea, Northern Australia and the Philippines. . . . Tsutsugamushi disease is characterized in its early stages by the skin lesion where the mite has bitten the surface. First there is a red area, then an ulcer with a striking black crust. The commonest sites for this black ulcer are the neck, armpit, upper arm, groin, calf and ankle. The neighbouring lymph glands are enlarged. At the same time there is headache, chilliness, fever, weakness and generalized aches and pains. From the fifth to the eighth day a rash appears mainly on the trunk. The rash is dull red in colour, and when it fades leaves a brownish stain. During the second week the illness reaches a peak, the patient becomes apathetic and even delirious, and involvement of lungs and heart may be found. In some types of typhus, the face develops a blue-brown colour. However, I suggest that it is due to the characteristic black scar, rather than from the dark rash on the skin, that [the] name, the 'black Formosa corruption' may have been derived. The mortality in Formosa is 12%. . . . If . . . the existence of Formosa cannot be denied, the name Tapanuli sounds decidedly spurious. Yet, there is a place called Tapanuli. . . . It is a residency of 15,084 square miles on the North West Coast of Sumatra, and the population is just over one million. Tapanuli is a mountainous area with many peaks above 6,000 feet. In the northeast, there is a lake called Toba, the largest of the mountain lakes of Sumatra. Cultivation is confined to the valleys and flat coastal strips where maize, rice, coconuts, coffee, nutmegs and rubber are grown. . . ." ("Some Observations on the Black Formosa Corruption and Tapanuli Fever").

8 *some recent researches which have a medico-criminal aspect.* "Can there be any doubt," Miss Madeleine B. Stern wrote in "Sherlock Holmes: Rare Book Collector," "that those 'researches' included visits to the rare and secondhand bookshops of London? There was a wealth of related material from which Holmes could choose, all the way from Codronchi's *Methodus Testificandi* (Frankfurt, 1597), the first important work on

"This is insanity, Holmes."

"Only two hours, Watson. I promise you will go at six. Are you content to wait?"

"I seem to have no choice."

"None in the world, Watson. Thank you, I need no help in arranging the clothes. You will please keep your distance. Now, Watson, there is one other condition that I would make. You will seek help, not from the man you mention, but from the one that I choose."

"By all means."

"The first three sensible words that you have uttered since you entered this room, Watson. You will find some books over there. I am somewhat exhausted; I wonder how a battery feels when it pours electricity into a non-conductor? At six, Watson, we resume our conversation."

But it was destined to be resumed long before that hour, and in circumstances which gave me a shock hardly second to that caused by his spring to the door. I had stood for some minutes looking at the silent figure in the bed. His face was almost covered by the clothes and he appeared to be asleep. Then, unable to settle down to reading, I walked slowly round the room, examining the pictures of celebrated criminals with which every wall was adorned. Finally, in my aimless perambulation, I came to the mantelpiece. A litter of pipes, tobacco-pouches, syringes, pen-knives, revolver cartridges, and other *débris* was scattered over it. In the midst of these was a small black and white ivory box with a sliding lid. It was a neat little thing, and I had stretched out my hand to examine it more closely, when——

It was a dreadful cry that he gave—a yell which might have been heard down the street. My skin went cold and my hair bristled at that horrible scream. As I turned I caught a glimpse of a convulsed face and frantic eyes. I stood paralysed, with the little box in my hand.

"Put it down! Down, this instant, Watson—this instant, I say!" His head sank back upon the pillow and he gave a deep sigh of relief as I replaced the box upon the mantelpiece. "I hate to have my things touched, Wat-

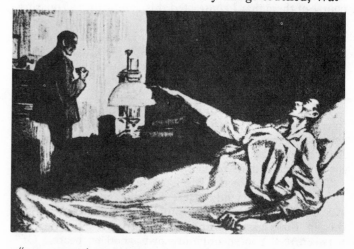

"PUT IT DOWN! DOWN, THIS INSTANT, WATSON—THIS INSTANT, I SAY!"

How two artists illustrated the same scene: *right,* Frederic Dorr Steele for *Collier's Magazine,* November 22, 1913; *left,* Walter Paget for the *Strand Magazine,* December, 1913.

son. You know that I hate it. You fidget me beyond endurance. You, a doctor—you are enough to drive a patient into an asylum. Sit down, man, and let me have my rest!"

The incident left a most unpleasant impression upon my mind. The violent and causeless excitement, followed by this brutality of speech, so far removed from his usual suavity, showed me how deep was the disorganization of his mind. Of all ruins, that of a noble mind is the most deplorable. I sat in silent dejection until the stipulated time had passed. He seemed to have been watching the clock as well as I, for it was hardly six before he began to talk with the same feverish animation as before.

" Now, Watson," said he. " Have you any change in your pocket?"

" Yes."

" Any silver?"

" A good deal."

" How many half-crowns?"

" I have five."

" Ah, too few! Too few! How very unfortunate, Watson! However, such as they are you can put them in your watch-pocket. And all the rest of your money in your left trouser-pocket. Thank you. It will balance you so much better like that."

This was raving insanity. He shuddered, and again made a sound between a cough and a sob.

" You will now light the gas, Watson, but you will be very careful that not for one instant shall it be more than half on. I implore you to be careful. Watson. Thank you, that is excellent. No, you need not draw the blind. Now you will have the kindness to place some letters and papers upon this table within my reach. Thank you. Now some of that litter from the mantelpiece. Excellent, Watson! There is a sugar-tongs there. Kindly raise that small ivory box with its assistance. Place it here among the papers. Good! You can now go and fetch Mr. Culverton Smith, of 13 Lower Burke Street."

To tell the truth, my desire to fetch a doctor had somewhat weakened, for poor Holmes was so obviously delirious that it seemed dangerous to leave him. However, he was as eager now to consult the person named as he had been obstinate in refusing.

" I never heard the name," said I.

" Possibly not, my good Watson. It may surprise you to know that the man upon earth who is best versed in this disease is not a medical man, but a planter. Mr. Culverton Smith is a well-known resident of Sumatra, now visiting London. An outbreak of the disease upon his plantation, which was distant from medical aid, caused him to study it himself, with some rather far-reaching consequences. He is a very methodical person, and I did not desire you to start before six because I was well aware that you would not find him in his study. If you could persuade him to come here and give us the benefit of his unique experience of this disease, the investigation of which has been his dearest hobby, I cannot doubt that he could help me."

I give Holmes's remarks as a consecutive whole, and will not attempt to indicate how they were interrupted by

forensic medicine, to the latest researches in that delectable field. Holmes never could have resisted Antoine Louis' *Mémoire sur une Question Anatomique relative à la Jurisprudence* (Paris, 1763) in which the author weighed the differential signs of murder and suicide in cases of hanging. The articles of Hunter 'On the Uncertainty of the Signs of Murder, in the Case of Bastard Children' (London, 1784) and of Gross 'On Manual Strangulation' (Cincinnati, 1836) must have made an immediate appeal, while Bertillion's great work *Les Signalments Anthropométriques* (Paris, 1886), which introduced to the world the 'Bertillonage' method of identifying persons by selected measurements, must surely have been added to the medico-criminal bookshelf of Sherlock Holmes."

gaspings for breath and those clutchings of his hands which indicated the pain from which he was suffering. His appearance had changed for the worse during the few hours that I had been with him. Those hectic spots were more pronounced, the eyes shone more brightly out of darker hollows, and a cold sweat glimmered upon his brow. He still retained, however, the jaunty gallantry of his speech. To the last gasp he would always be the master.

" You will tell him exactly how you have left me," said he. " You will convey the very impression which is in your own mind—a dying man—a dying and delirious man. Indeed, I cannot think why the whole bed of the ocean is not one solid mass of oysters, so prolific the creatures seem. Ah, I am wandering ! Strange how the brain controls the brain. What was I saying, Watson ? "

" My directions for Mr. Culverton Smith."

" Ah, yes, I remember. My life depends upon it. Plead with him, Watson. There is no good feeling between us. His nephew, Watson—I had suspicions of foul play and I allowed him to see it. The boy died horribly. He has a grudge against me. You will soften him, Watson. Beg him, pray him, get him here by any means. He can save me—only he ! "

" I will bring him in a cab, if I have to carry him down to it."

" You will do nothing of the sort. You will persuade him to come. And then you will return in front of him. Make any excuse so as not to come with him. Don't forget, Watson. You won't fail me. You never did fail me. No doubt there are natural enemies which limit the increase of the creatures. You and I, Watson, we have done our part. Shall the world, then, be overrun by oysters ? No, no ; horrible ! You'll convey all that is in your mind."

I left him, full of the image of this magnificent intellect babbling like a foolish child. He had handed me the key, and with a happy thought I took it with me lest he should lock himself in. Mrs. Hudson was waiting, trembling and weeping, in the passage. Behind me as I passed from the flat I heard Holmes's high, thin voice in some delirious chant. Below, as I stood whistling for a cab, a man came on me through the fog.

" How is Mr. Holmes, sir ? " he asked.

It was an old acquaintance, Inspector Morton, of Scotland Yard, dressed in unofficial tweeds.

" He is very ill," I answered.

He looked at me in a most singular fashion. Had it not been too fiendish, I could have imagined that the gleam of the fanlight showed exultation in his face.

" I heard some rumour of it," said he.

The cab had driven up, and I left him.

Lower Burke Street proved to be a line of fine houses
9 lying in the vague borderland between Notting Hill and Kensington. The particular one at which my cabman pulled up had an air of smug and demure respectability in its old-fashioned iron railings, its massive folding-door, and its shining brasswork. All was in keeping with a solemn butler who appeared framed in the pink radiance
10 of a tinted electric light behind him.

9 *Notting Hill.* Notting Hill, or Kensington Park, as it is sometimes called, is a handsome quarter of the Royal Borough of Kensington, filled with broad streets, squares and crescents.

10 *a tinted electric light.* Since this is Watson's first mention of electric lighting, the reader may have some interest in the position in regard to electricity in England at that time. In a letter to your editor, the late Gavin Brend wrote: "It would have been theoretically possible [to find a private building lighted by electricity] at any time after 1880 but in practice it was most unlikely, for the original legislation was most restrictive and the first supply companies found it practically impossible to function. Only later in the eighties were the restrictions removed."

" Yes, Mr. Culverton Smith is in.   Dr. Watson !   Very good, sir, I will take up your card."

My humble name and title did not appear to impress Mr. Culverton Smith.   Through the half-open door I heard a high, petulant, penetrating voice.

" Who is this person ?   What does he want ?   Dear me, Staples, how often have I said that I am not to be disturbed in my hours of study ? "

There came a gentle flow of soothing explanation from the butler.

" Well, I won't see him, Staples.   I can't have my work interrupted like this.   I am not at home.   Say so. Tell him to come in the morning if he really must see me."

Again the gentle murmur.

" Well, well, give him that message.   He can come in the morning, or he can stay away.   My work must not be hindered."

I thought of Holmes tossing upon his bed of sickness, and counting the minutes, perhaps, until I could bring help to him.   It was not a time to stand upon ceremony. His life depended upon my promptness.   Before the apologetic butler had delivered his message I had pushed past him and was in the room.

With a shrill cry of anger a man rose from a reclining chair beside the fire.   I saw a great yellow face, coarse-grained and greasy, with heavy double-chin, and two sullen, menacing grey eyes which glared at me from under tufted and sandy brows.   A high bald head had a small velvet smoking-cap poised coquettishly upon one side of its pink curve.   The skull was of enormous capacity, and yet, as I looked down I saw to my amazement that the figure of the man was small and frail, twisted in the shoulders and back like one who has suffered from rickets in his childhood.

" What's this ? " he cried, in a high, screaming voice. " What is the meaning of this intrusion ?   Didn't I send you word that I would see you to-morrow morning ? "

" I am sorry," said I, " but the matter cannot be delayed. Mr. Sherlock Holmes——"

The mention of my friend's name had an extraordinary effect upon the little man.   The look of anger passed in an instant from his face.   His features became tense and alert.

" Have you come from Holmes ? " he asked.

" I have just left him."

" What about Holmes ?   How is he ? "

" He is desperately ill.   That is why I have come."

The man motioned me to a chair, and turned to resume his own.   As he did so I caught a glimpse of his face in the mirror over the mantelpiece.   I could have sworn that it was set in a malicious and abominable smile.   Yet I persuaded myself that it must have been some nervous contraction which I had surprised, for he turned to me an instant later with genuine concern upon his features.

" I am sorry to hear this," said he.   " I only know Mr. Holmes through some business dealings which we have had, but I have every respect for his talents and his character.   He is an amateur of crime, as I am of disease. For him the villain, for me the microbe.   There are my

"WHAT'S THIS?" HE CRIED, IN A HIGH, SCREAMING VOICE. "WHAT IS THE MEANING OF THIS INTRUSION?"

Illustration by Walter Paget for the *Strand Magazine*, December, 1913.

prisons," he continued, pointing to a row of bottles and jars which stood upon a side table. " Among those gelatine cultivations some of the very worst offenders in the world are now doing time."

" It was on account of your special knowledge that Mr. Holmes desired to see you. He has a high opinion of you, and thought that you were the one man in London who could help him."

The little man started, and the jaunty smoking-cap slid to the floor.

" Why ? " he asked. " Why should Mr. Holmes think that I could help him in his trouble ? "

" Because of your knowledge of Eastern diseases."

" But why should he think that this disease which he has contracted is Eastern ? "

" Because, in some professional inquiry, he has been working among Chinese sailors down in the docks."

Mr. Culverton Smith smiled pleasantly and picked up his smoking-cap.

" Oh, that's it—is it ? " said he. " I trust the matter is not so grave as you suppose. How long has he been ill ? "

" About three days."

" Is he delirious ? "

" Occasionally."

" Tut, tut ! This sounds serious. It would be inhuman not to answer his call. I very much resent any interruption to my work, Dr. Watson, but this case is certainly exceptional. I will come with you at once."

I remembered Holmes's injunction.

" I have another appointment," said I.

" Very good. I will go alone. I have a note of Mr. Holmes's address. You can rely upon my being there within half an hour at most."

It was with a sinking heart that I re-entered Holmes's bedroom. For all that I knew the worst might have happened in my absence. To my enormous relief, he had improved greatly in the interval. His appearance was as ghastly as ever, but all trace of delirium had left him and he spoke in a feeble voice, it is true, but with even more than his usual crispness and lucidity.

" Well, did you see him, Watson ? "

" Yes ; he is coming."

" Admirable, Watson ! Admirable ! You are the best of messengers."

" He wished to return with me."

" That would never do, Watson. That would be obviously impossible. Did he ask what ailed me ? "

" I told him about the Chinese in the East End."

" Exactly ! Well, Watson, you have done all that a good friend could. You can now disappear from the scene."

" I must wait and hear his opinion, Holmes."

" Of course you must. But I have reasons to suppose that this opinion would be very much more frank and valuable if he imagines that we are alone. There is just room behind the head of my bed, Watson."

" My dear Holmes ! "

" I fear there is no alternative, Watson. The room does not lend itself to concealment, which is as well, as it is the less likely to arouse suspicion.   But just there, Watson, I fancy that it could be done."   Suddenly he sat up with a rigid intentness upon his haggard face.   " There are the wheels, Watson.   Quick, man, if you love me !   And don't budge, whatever happens—whatever happens, do you hear ?   Don't speak !   Don't move !   Just listen with all your ears."   Then in an instant his sudden access of strength departed, and his masterful, purposeful talk droned away into the low, vague murmurings of a semi-delirious man.

From the hiding-place into which I had been so swiftly hustled I heard the footfalls upon the stair, with the opening and the closing of the bedroom door.   Then, to my surprise, there came a long silence, broken only by the heavy breathings and gaspings of the sick man.   I could imagine that our visitor was standing by the bedside and looking down at the sufferer.   At last that strange hush was broken.

" Holmes ! " he cried.   ' Holmes ! " in the insistent tone of one who awakens a sleeper.   " Can't you hear me, Holmes ? "   There was a rustling, as if he had shaken the sick man roughly by the shoulder.

" Is that you, Mr. Smith ? " Holmes whispered.   " I hardly dared hope that you would come."

The other laughed.

" I should imagine not," he said.   " And yet, you see, I am here.   Coals of fire, Holmes—coals of fire ! "

" It is very good of you—very noble of you.   I appreciate your special knowledge."

Our visitor sniggered.

" You do.   You are, fortunately, the only man in London who does.   Do you know what is the matter with you ? "

" The same," said Holmes.

" Ah !   You recognize the symptoms ? "

" Only too well."

" Well, I shouldn't be surprised, Holmes.   I shouldn't be surprised if it *were* the same.   A bad look-out for you if it is.   Poor Victor was a dead man on the fourth day—a strong, hearty young fellow.   It was certainly, as you said, very surprising that he should have contracted an out-of-the-way Asiatic disease in the heart of London—a disease, too, of which I had made such a very special study.   Singular coincidence, Holmes.   Very smart of you to notice it, but rather uncharitable to suggest that it was cause and effect."

" I knew that you did it."

" Oh, you did, did you ?   Well, you couldn't prove it, anyhow.   But what do you think of yourself spreading reports about me like that, and then crawling to me for help the moment you are in trouble ?   What sort of a game is that—eh ? "

I heard the rasping, laboured breathing of the sick man.   " Give me the water ! " he gasped.

" You're precious near your end, my friend, but I don't want you to go till I have had a word with you.   That's why I give you water.   There, don't slop it about !   That's right.   Can you understand what I say ? "

Holmes groaned.

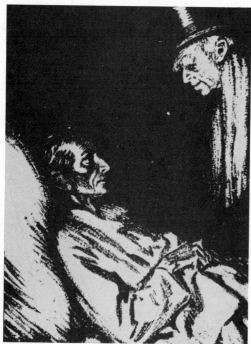

"I DON'T SEE YOU IN THE WITNESS-BOX. QUITE ANOTHER SHAPED BOX, MY GOOD HOLMES, I ASSURE YOU."

Illustration by Frederic Dorr Steele for *Collier's Magazine*, November 22, 1913.

11 *It drew blood.* Dr. George B. Koelle has suggested ("The Poisons of the Canon") that Culverton Smith's weapon was in fact the plague bacillus. "It is of considerable interest to note that the first account of the isolation of the etiologic agent of oriental plague, *Pastuerella pestis*, was [not] published [until] 1894. . . . Thus, Smith's unpublished studies, performed at his Sumatran plantation, preceded the recognized work by several years, but his pioneering efforts have escaped notice outside the Canon. . . . It will be recalled that Leora Arrowsmith, a character of fiction, was fatally infected by a cigarette which she inadvertently allowed to come into contact with a spilled culture of plague bacilli."

On the other hand, Mr. Hugh L'Etang ("Some Observations on the Black Formosa Corruption and Tapanuli Fever") holds that: ". . . snake venom would be a most convenient poison with which to load the box. The fang may well have been modelled on a snake's fang and hollowed, or grooved, to transmit the poison. . . . It seems likely that Victor Savage was killed by a neurotoxic or nerve poison. This could certainly be produced by the King Cobra of Malaya and the East Indies."

" Do what you can for me. Let bygones be bygones," he whispered. " I'll put the words out of my head—I swear I will. Only cure me, and I'll forget it."

" Forget what ? "

" Well, about Victor Savage's death. You as good as admitted just now that you had done it. I'll forget it."

" You can forget it or remember it, just as you like. I don't see you in the witness-box. Quite another shaped box, my good Holmes, I assure you. It matters nothing to me that you should know how my nephew died. It's not him we are talking about. It's you."

" Yes, yes."

" The fellow who came for me—I've forgotten his name —said that you contracted it down in the East End among the sailors."

" I could only account for it so."

" You are proud of your brains, Holmes, are you not ? Think yourself smart, don't you ? You came across someone who was smarter this time. Now cast your mind back, Holmes. Can you think of no other way you could have got this thing ? "

" I can't think. My mind is gone. For Heaven's sake help me ! "

" Yes, I will help you. I'll help you to understand just where you are and how you got there. I'd like you to know before you die."

" Give me something to ease my pain."

" Painful, is it ? Yes, the coolies used to do some squealing towards the end. Takes you as cramp, I fancy."

" Yes, yes ; it is cramp."

" Well, you can hear what I say, anyhow. Listen now ! Can you remember any unusual incident in your life just about the time your symptoms began ? "

" No, no ; nothing."

" Think again."

" I'm too ill to think."

" Well, then, I'll help you. Did anything come by post ? "

" By post ? "

" A box by chance ? "

" I'm fainting—I'm gone ! "

" Listen, Holmes ! " There was a sound as if he was shaking the dying man, and it was all that I could do to hold myself quiet in my hiding-place. " You must hear me. You *shall* hear me. Do you remember a box—an ivory box ? It came on Wednesday. You opened it—do you remember ? "

" Yes, yes, I opened it. There was a sharp spring inside it. Some joke——"

" It was no joke, as you will find to your cost. You fool, you would have it and you have got it. Who asked you to cross my path ? If you had left me alone I would not have hurt you."

" I remember," Holmes gasped. " The spring ! It **11** drew blood. This box—this on the table."

" The very one, by George ! And it may as well leave the room in my pocket. There goes your last shred of evidence. But you have the truth now, Holmes, and you can die with the knowledge that I killed you. You knew too much of the fate of Victor Savage, so I have sent you to share it. You are very near your end, Holmes. I will sit here and I will watch you die."

Holmes's voice had sunk to an almost inaudible whisper.

" What is that ? " said Smith. " Turn up the gas ? Ah, the shadows begin to fall, do they ? Yes, I will turn it up, that I may see you the better." He crossed the room and the light suddenly brightened. " Is there any other little service that I can do you, my friend ? "

" A match and a cigarette."

I nearly called out in my joy and my amazement. He was speaking in his natural voice—a little weak, perhaps, but the very voice I knew. There was a long pause, and I felt that Culverton Smith was standing in silent amazement looking down at his companion.

" What's the meaning of this ? " I heard him say at last, in a dry, rasping tone.

" The best way of successfully acting a part is to be it," said Holmes. " I give you my word that for three days I have tasted neither food nor drink until you were good enough to pour me out that glass of water. But it is the tobacco which I find most irksome. Ah, here *are* some cigarettes." I heard the striking of a match. " That is very much better. Halloa ! halloa ! Do I hear the step of a friend ? "

There were footfalls outside, the door opened, and Inspector Morton appeared.

" All is in order and this is your man," said Holmes. The officer gave the usual cautions.   **12**

" I arrest you on the charge of the murder of one Victor Savage," he concluded.

" And you might add the attempted murder of one Sherlock Holmes," remarked my friend with a chuckle. " To save an invalid trouble, inspector, Mr. Culverton Smith was good enough to give our signal by turning up the gas. By the way, the prisoner has a small box in the right-hand pocket of his coat which it would be as well to remove. Thank you. I would handle it gingerly if I were you. Put it down here. It may play its part in the trial."

There was a sudden rush and a scuffle, followed by the clash of iron and a cry of pain.

" You'll only get yourself hurt," said the inspector. " Stand still, will you ? " There was the click of the closing handcuffs.

" A nice trap ! " cried the high, snarling voice. " It will bring *you* into the dock, Holmes, not me. He asked me to come here to cure him. I was sorry for him and I came. Now he will pretend, no doubt, that I have said anything which he may invent which will corroborate his insane suspicions. You can lie as you like, Holmes. My word is always as good as yours."

" Good heavens ! " cried Holmes. " I had totally forgotten him. My dear Watson, I owe you a thousand apologies. To think that I should have overlooked you ! I need not introduce you to Mr. Culverton Smith, since I understand that you met somewhat earlier in the evening Have you the cab below ? I will follow you when I am dressed, for I may be of some use at the station."

12 *The officer gave the usual cautions.* Under the law it is the duty of a police officer making an arrest to warn the person taken into custody that anything he says may be taken down and used as evidence.

"YOU'LL ONLY GET YOURSELF HURT," SAID THE INSPECTOR. "STAND STILL, WILL YOU?"

Illustration by Walter Paget for the *Strand Magazine*, December, 1913.

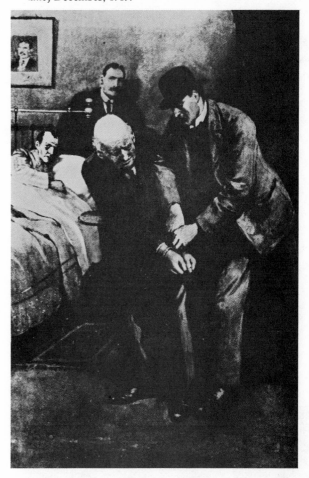

13 *vaseline*. Your editor once insisted that Holmes, at the time of this adventure, would have used the term "petroleum jelly." He has since been corrected by that erudite scholar, Mr. Morris Rosenblum, who accurately pointed out that the word "vaseline" was introduced as a proprietary term by R. A. Chesebrough as long ago as 1872. "It is found in British publications in 1874 and 1876."

14 *upon which I have sometimes thought of writing a monograph*. It is doubtful that this projected work was ever undertaken, although the subject may have been intended to form a chapter in Holmes' contemplated textbook on the whole art of detection ("The Adventure of the Abbey Grange").

15 *a reversion*. In law, the returning of an estate to the grantor or his heirs, by operation of law, after the grant has terminated; hence, the residue of an estate left in the proprietor or owner thereof, to take effect in possession, by operation of law, after the termination of a limited or less estate carved out of it and conveyed to him. Holmes' use of the precise term is another indication of his practical knowledge of British law.

Bibliographical Note:

This is the cover of the *Strand* magazine for December, 1913, in which "The Adventure of the Dying Detective" made its first English appearance (it had previously appeared in the November 22, 1913, issue of *Collier's Magazine* in America). The story made its first appearance in book form in 1913 in a little (4″ by 5½″) volume published by the P. F. Collier Company of New York. The original manuscript of "The Adventure of the Dying Detective," with eighteen pages signed by Sir Arthur Conan Doyle at Crowborough, Sussex, July 27, 1923, was loaned by the late Denis P. S. Conan Doyle to the Sherlock Holmes Exhibition of 1951. In a letter to your editor dated January 20, 1966, Mr. Adrian M. Conan Doyle does not include it in the list of original manuscripts now in his possession.

" I never needed it more," said Holmes, as he refreshed himself with a glass of claret and some biscuits in the intervals of his toilet. " However, as you know, my habits are irregular, and such a feat means less to me than to most men. It was very essential that I should impress Mrs. Hudson with the reality of my condition, since she was to convey it to you, and you in turn to him. You won't be offended, Watson ? You will realize that among your many talents dissimulation finds no place, and that if you had shared my secret you would never have been able to impress Smith with the urgent necessity of his presence, which was the vital point of the whole scheme. Knowing his vindictive nature, I was perfectly certain that he would come to look upon his handiwork."

" But your appearance, Holmes—your ghastly face ? "

" Three days of absolute fast does not improve one's beauty, Watson. For the rest, there is nothing which a

13 sponge may not cure. With vaseline upon one's forehead, belladonna in one's eyes, rouge over the cheek-bones, and crusts of beeswax round one's lips, a very satisfying effect can be produced. Malingering is a subject upon which I

14 have sometimes thought of writing a monograph. A little occasional talk about half-crowns, oysters, or any other extraneous subject produces a pleasing effect of delirium."

" But why would you not let me near you, since there was in truth no infection ? "

" Can you ask, my dear Watson ? Do you imagine that I have no respect for your medical talents ? Could I fancy that your astute judgment would pass a dying man who, however weak, had no rise of pulse or temperature ? At four yards, I could deceive you. If I failed to do so, who would bring my Smith within my grasp ? No, Watson, I would not touch that box. You can just see if you look at it sideways where the sharp spring like a viper's tooth emerges as you open it. I dare say it was by some such device that poor Savage, who stood between this monster

15 and a reversion, was done to death. My correspondence, however, is, as you know, a varied one, and I am somewhat upon my guard against any packages which reach me. It was clear to me, however, that by pretending that he had really succeeded in his design I might surprise a confession. That pretence I have carried out with the thoroughness of the true artist. Thank you, Watson, you must help me on with my coat. When we have finished at the police-station I think that something nutritious at Simpson's would not be out of place."

" . . . I THINK THAT SOMETHING NUTRITIOUS AT SIMPSON'S WOULD NOT BE OUT OF PLACE."

Simpson's Tavern and Divan, as it looked before it was rebuilt in 1903–1904 when the Strand was widened at this point. Wrote Mr. Michael Harrison, from whose book, *In the Footsteps of Sherlock Holmes*, this photograph was taken: "A dinner from the joint was to be had for 2s. 6d. [about 61¢], and a fish dinner of 2s. 9d. [about 67¢] was served from 12:30 P.M. to 8:30 P.M." Simpson's-in-the-Strand was evidently one of Holmes' favorite London restaurants: he and Watson dined there *twice* during "The Adventure of the Illustrious Client."

30

THE ADVENTURE OF THE BLUE CARBUNCLE

[Tuesday, December 27, 1887]

I HAD called upon my friend Sherlock Holmes upon the second morning after Christmas, with the intention of wishing him the compliments of the season. **1** He was lounging upon the sofa in a purple dressing-gown, a pipe-rack within his reach upon the right, and a pile of crumpled morning papers, evidently newly studied, near **2** at hand. Beside the couch was a wooden chair, and on the angle of the back hung a very seedy and disreputable hard felt hat, much the worse for wear, and cracked in several places. A lens and a forceps lying upon the seat of the chair suggested that the hat had been suspended in this manner for the purpose of examination.

"You are engaged," said I; "perhaps I interrupt you."

"Not at all. I am glad to have a friend with whom I can discuss my results. The matter is a perfectly trivial one" (he jerked his thumb in the direction of the old hat), "but there are points in connection with it which are not entirely devoid of interest, and even of instruction."

I seated myself in his arm-chair, and warmed my hands before his crackling fire, for a sharp frost had set in, and the windows were thick with the ice crystals. "I suppose," I remarked, "that, homely as it looks, this thing has some deadly story linked on to it—that it is the clue which will guide you in the solution of some mystery, and the punishment of some crime."

"No, no. No crime," said Sherlock Holmes, laughing. "Only one of those whimsical little incidents which will happen when you have four million human beings all jostling each other within the space of a few square miles. Amid the action and reaction of so dense a swarm of humanity, every possible combination of events may be expected to take place, and many a little problem will be presented which may be striking and bizarre without being criminal. We have already had experience of such."

"So much so," I remarked, "that, of the last six cases which I have added to my notes, three have been entirely free of any legal crime." **3**

"Precisely. You allude to my attempt to recover the Irene Adler papers, to the singular case of Miss Mary

---

1 *upon the second morning after Christmas.* Watson's belatedness was most probably caused by the serious illness of his first wife; by January 7th of the following year, 1888, he was back in Baker Street. While 1889 is the favored year for this adventure (Andrew, Bell, Blakeney, Brend, Folsom, Knox, Pattrick, Smith, and Zeisler), a hardy minority (Christ, Kimball, Morley, and Petersen) has chosen 1890. Your editor would seem to stand alone once more in dating the adventure 1887.

2 *crumpled morning papers, evidently newly studied.* The day was obviously not a Sunday.

. . . ON THE ANGLE OF THE BACK HUNG A VERY SEEDY AND DISREPUTABLE HARD FELT HAT . . .

Illustration by Sidney Paget for the *Strand Magazine*, January, 1892.

3 *three have been entirely free of any legal crime.*" "In fifteen [of Holmes' recorded cases]," the late Fletcher Pratt wrote in "Very Little Murder," "or one quarter of the total, *no crime took place*. In nine of these cases, there was no legal crime. . . . In six . . . no crime took place because Holmes prevented the felonious act. These cases in which there was no legal crime outnumber all other classifications. There are also four cases of acts within the purview of the law, although non-criminal: the three cases of justifiable homicide and the one of death by misadventure."

4 *the man with the twisted lip.* "The Adventure of the Blue Carbuncle was therefore later, but not much later, than "A Scandal in Bohemia," "A Case of Identity," and "The Man with the Twisted Lip." Lawyer Irving M. Fenton, with Watson's phrasing "entirely free of legal crime" in mind, wrote ("An Analysis of the Crimes and Near-Crimes at Appledore Towers in the Light of the English Criminal Law"): "Apparently [Watson] considered throwing a smoke-bomb into a house and creating a near-riot, just as a prank. A magistrate would call it disorderly conduct. So, too, to wash a man's face against his will is a technical assault."

5 *billycock.* Usually, a round, low-crowned soft felt hat, but sometimes a stiff felt hat, or bowler.

6 *Goodge Street.* A London street that retains much of its original appearance (shabby) and has so far been little invaded by modern buildings.

7 *a row broke out.* The late Gavin Brend, who traced "The Route of the Blue Carbuncle," felt sure that it was the south corner on which the row took place. The tallish man, he wrote, "is clearly proceeding northwards along Tottenham Court Road. Now, if the roughs are coming out of Goodge Street on the south side, neither party will see the other until they run into each other on the south side corner. On the other hand if the collision occurs on the north corner, no matter what direction the roughs approach each party is visible to the other and has no opportunity of avoiding the other if so desired. It is possible that both parties were in a belligerent mood and that neither made any attempt to avoid the crash. Yet I would like to think that the original cause was accidental. After all it was 'the season of forgiveness' and I would like to reduce all unpleasantness to a minimum . . ."

8 *the initials 'H. B.' are legible upon the lining of this hat.* Sherlockian commentators have been harsh on Holmes for his deductions from this hat. Magistrate S. Tupper Bigelow wrote ("The Blue Enigma"): "Holmes deduced . . . that the owner of the hat was Henry Baker and that the owner of the hat and the intended recipient of the bird were husband and wife. Such deductions are pure

Sutherland, and to the adventure of the man with the **4** twisted lip. Well, I have no doubt that this small matter will fall into the same innocent category. You know Peterson, the commissionaire ? "

" Yes. '

' It is to him that this trophy belongs."

" It is his hat."

" No, no ; he found it. Its owner is unknown. I beg **5** that you will look upon it, not as a battered billycock, but as an intellectual problem. And, first as to how it came here. It arrived upon Christmas morning, in company with a good fat goose, which is, I have no doubt, roasting at this moment in front of Peterson's fire. The facts are these. About four o'clock on Christmas morning, Peterson, who, as you know, is a very honest fellow, was returning from some small jollification, and was making his way homewards down Tottenham Court Road. In front of him he saw, in the gaslight, a tallish man, walking with a slight stagger, and carrying a white goose slung over his **6** shoulder. As he reached the corner of Goodge Street a **7** row broke out between this stranger and a little knot of roughs. One of the latter knocked off the man's hat, on which he raised his stick to defend himself, and, swinging it over his head, smashed the shop window behind him. Peterson had rushed forward to protect the stranger from his assailants, but the man, shocked at having broken the window and seeing an official-looking person in uniform rushing towards him, dropped his goose, took to his heels, and vanished amid the labyrinth of small streets which lie at the back of Tottenham Court Road. The roughs had also fled at the appearance of Peterson, so that he was left in possession of the field of battle, and also of the spoils of victory in the shape of this battered hat and a most unimpeachable Christmas goose."

" Which surely he restored to their owner ? "

" My dear fellow, there lies the problem. It is true that ' For Mrs. Henry Baker ' was printed upon a small card which was tied to the bird's left leg, and it is also true that the initials ' H. B.' are legible upon the lining of **8** this hat ; but, as there are some thousands of Bakers, and **9** some hundreds of Henry Bakers in this city of ours, it is not easy to restore lost property to any one of them."

THE ROUGHS HAD ALSO FLED AT THE APPEARANCE OF PETERSON . . .

Illustration by Sidney Paget for the *Strand Magazine*, January 1892.

" What, then, did Peterson do ? "

" He brought round both hat and goose to me on Christmas morning, knowing that even the smallest problems are of interest to me. The goose we retained until this morning, when there were signs that, in spite of the slight frost, it would be well that it should be eaten without unnecessary delay. Its finder has carried it off therefore to fulfil the ultimate destiny of a goose, while I continue to retain the hat of the unknown gentleman who lost his Christmas dinner."

" Did he not advertise ?

" No."

" Then, what clue could you have as to his identity ? "

" Only as much as we can deduce.·'

" From his hat ? "

" Precisely."

" But you are joking. What can you gather from this old battered felt ? "

" Here is my lens. You know my methods. What can you gather yourself as to the individuality of the man who has worn this article ? "

I took the tattered object in my hands, and turned it over rather ruefully. It was a very ordinary black hat of the usual round shape, hard and much the worse for wear. The lining had been of red silk, but was a good deal discoloured. There was no maker's name ; but, as Holmes had remarked, the initials " H. B." were scrawled upon one side. It was pierced in the brim for a hat-securer, but the elastic was missing. For the rest, it was cracked, exceedingly dusty, and spotted in several places, although there seemed to have been some attempt to hide the discoloured patches by smearing them with ink.

" I can see nothing," said I, handing it back to my friend.

" On the contrary, Watson, you can see everything. You fail, however, to reason from what you see. You are too timid in drawing your inferences."

" Then, pray tell me what it is that you can infer from this hat ? "

He picked it up, and gazed at it in the peculiar introspective fashion which was characteristic of him. " It is perhaps less suggestive than it might have been," he remarked, " and yet there are a few inferences which are very distinct, and a few others which represent at least a strong balance of probability. That the man was highly intellectual is of course obvious upon the face of it, and also that he was fairly well-to-do within the last three years, although he has now fallen upon evil days. He had foresight, but has less now than formerly, pointing to a moral retrogression, which, when taken with the decline of his fortunes, seems to indicate some evil influence, probably drink, at work upon him. This may account also for the obvious fact that his wife has ceased to love him."

" My dear Holmes ! "

" He has, however, retained some degree of self-respect," he continued, disregarding my remonstrance. " He is a man who leads a sedentary life, goes out little, is out of training entirely, is middle-aged, has grizzled hair which he has had cut within the last few days, and

assumption. If 'H. B.' stood for 'Henry Baker,' which is by no means conclusive, it is just as logical to assume that Mrs. Henry Baker and Henry Baker were mother and son or daughter-in-law and father as husband and wife; Watson, indeed, suggested that the owner of the hat might have been a bachelor, and why not? The bird might have been intended for Mrs. Henry Baker, but 'H. B.' could stand for anything."

And Mr. Thomas L. Stix wrote ("Un-Christmas-like Thoughts on 'The Blue Carbuncle'"): "If we are to quibble, and we will, we should suggest the possibility that 'H. B.' in the hat and the card on the goose, 'For Mrs. Henry Baker,' do not necessarily prove that the 'H. B.' in the hat indicated Henry Baker. Even the casual student of the Sacred Writings will follow my meaning. The tobacco pouch found in the cabin of Black Peter Carey with the initials 'P. C.' did not belong to Peter Carey at all, but to Patrick Cairns. And again, in 'The Adventure of the Noble Bachelor,' the note which confused Lestrade . . . was from Francis Moulton, not Flora Miller . . .'"

9 *some hundreds of Henry Bakers*. "A search of the Los Angeles County telephone books reveals but 16 Henry Bakers in a population of more than four million," the late Robert R. Pattrick once wrote. "Greater London [at this time] had a population of somewhat over five million. This would indicate that there could have been only about 20 Henry Bakers. Holmes, I fear, was guilty of gross exaggeration . . ."

The late Mr. Pattrick was correct: Magistrate S. Tupper Bigelow, in "The Blue Enigma," has noted that the London Post Office Directory of 1890 listed a paltry seven Henry Bakers; only 139 Bakers were listed altogether.

10 *"a man with so large a brain must have some-thing in it."* "The 'big head, big brain; big brain, great mind' syllogism had many believers [in the nineteenth century], and the phrenologists were always weighing the brains of deceased murderers and madmen and comparing them in size with those of statesmen and writers . . .", Mr. Thomas M. McDade wrote in "Heads and Holmes."

But modern experts "do not believe that a large head necessarily indicates unusual brainpower," as Mr. Vernon Rendall wrote in "The Limitations of Sherlock Holmes." "I remember an old friend who had an abnormally big hat, and a big brain under-neath it, saying that the biggest head he knew belonged to a singularly stupid man."

11 *then he has assuredly gone down in the world."* "Admitting the hat was three years old and that it was of the best quality, what justification is there for assuming that Baker could not still afford to buy an expensive hat or that it was the only one he had?" Magistrate S. Tupper Bigelow asked in "The Blue Enigma." "Men are notoriously fond of old hats. . . . On the basis of these data, Baker might well have had a battery of expensive hats at home, and chose to wear the billycock on that particular evening. So there is no evidence what-ever that he had assuredly gone down in the world."

12 *which is a distinct proof of a weakening nature.* "By what kind of ratiocination Holmes concluded that moral rather than mental retrogression, whether from undue addiction to alcohol or otherwise, causes foresight to deteriorate is obscure. One is foresighted or one is not. As for reading foresight into the purchase of a hat-securer, it is equally attributable to the efficiency of a high-pressure salesman who sold Baker the hat; if the shop stocked hat-securers, the salesman, selling an ex-pensive hat to a customer, would certainly make an effort to sell him one, and that he succeeded has nothing whatever to do with Baker's foresight but perhaps something to do with his susceptibil-ity to suggestion. And why would Baker replace it, anyhow? They are not very practical gadgets, for one thing; they are a nuisance to wear, for another . . ."—Magistrate S. Tupper Bigelow, "The Blue Enigma."

13 *hardly be in the best of training.* "This, of course, is 'ineffable twaddle' and 'unmitigated bleat' at their best. There cannot be a three-year-old hat in the world, now or then, whether worn by the finest Olympic athlete or a skid-row bum, that does not have evidence of perspiration on its inside or on its inner band. Everybody perspires in given circumstances."—Magistrate S. Tupper Bigelow, "The Blue Enigma."

which he anoints with lime-cream. These are the more patent facts which are to be deduced from his hat. Also, by the way, that it is extremely improbable that he has gas laid on in his house."

" You are certainly joking, Holmes."

" Not in the least. Is it possible that even now when I give you these results you are unable to see how they are attained ? "

" I have no doubt that I am very stupid ; but I must confess that I am unable to follow you. For example, how did you deduce that this man was intellectual ? "

For answer Holmes clapped the hat upon his head. It came right over the forehead and settled upon the bridge of his nose. " It is a question of cubic capacity," said he : " a man with so large a brain must have something **10** in it."

" The decline of his fortunes, then ? "

" This hat is three years old. These flat brims curled at the edge came in then. It is a hat of the very best quality. Look at the band of ribbed silk, and the excel-lent lining. If this man could afford to buy so expensive a hat three years ago, and has had no hat since, then he **11** has assuredly gone down in the world."

" Well, that is clear enough, certainly. But how about the foresight, and the moral retrogression ? "

Sherlock Holmes laughed. " Here is the foresight," said he, putting his finger upon the little disc and loop of the hat-securer. " They are never sold upon hats. If this man ordered one, it is a sign of a certain amount of foresight, since he went out of his way to take this pre-caution against the wind. But since we see that he has broken the elastic, and has not troubled to replace it, it is obvious that he has less foresight now than formerly, **12** which is a distinct proof of a weakening nature. On the other hand, he has endeavoured to conceal some of these stains upon the felt by daubing them with ink, which is a sign that he has not entirely lost his self-respect."

" Your reasoning is certainly plausible."

" The further points, that he is middle-aged, that his hair is grizzled, that it has been recently cut, and that he uses lime-cream, are all to be gathered from a close examination of the lower part of the lining. The lens discloses a large number of hair-ends, clean cut by the scissors of the barber. They all appear to be adhesive, and there is a distinct odour of lime-cream. This dust, you will observe, is not the gritty, grey dust of the street, but the fluffy brown dust of the house, showing that it has been hung up indoors most of the time ; while the marks of moisture upon the inside are proof positive that the wearer perspired very freely, and could, therefore, **13** hardly be in the best of training."

" But his wife—you said that she had ceased to love him."

" This hat has not been brushed for weeks. When I see you, my dear Watson, with a week's accumulation of dust upon your hat, and when your wife allows you to go out in such a state, I shall fear that you also have been **14** unfortunate enough to lose your wife's affection."

" But he might be a bachelor."

" Nay, he was bringing home the goose as a peace-offering to his wife.   Remember the card upon the bird's leg."

" You have an answer to everything.   But how on earth do you deduce that the gas is not laid on in the house ? "

" One tallow stain, or even two, might come by chance ; but, when I see no less than five, I think that there can be little doubt that the individual must be brought into frequent contact with burning tallow—walks upstairs at night probably with his hat in one hand and a guttering candle in the other.   Anyhow, he never got tallow stains **15** from a gas jet.   Are you satisfied ? "

" Well, it is very ingenious," said I, laughing ; " but since, as you said just now, there has been no crime committed, and no harm done save the loss of a goose, all this seems to be rather a waste of energy."

Sherlock Holmes had opened his mouth to reply, when the door flew open, and Peterson the commissionaire rushed into the compartment with flushed cheeks and the face of a man who is dazed with astonishment.

" The goose, Mr. Holmes ! The goose, sir ! " he gasped.

" Eh ! What of it, then ? Has it returned to life, and flapped off through the kitchen window ? " Holmes twisted himself round upon the sofa to get a fairer view of the man's excited face.

" See here, sir ! See what my wife found in its crop ! " He held out his hand, and displayed upon the centre of the palm a brilliantly scintillating blue stone, rather smaller than a bean in size, but of such purity and radiance that it twinkled like an electric point in the dark hollow of his hand.

Sherlock Holmes sat up with a whistle. " By Jove, Peterson," said he, " this is treasure-trove indeed ! I suppose you know what you have got ? "

" A diamond, sir ! A precious stone ! It cuts into glass as though it were putty." **16**

" It's more than a precious stone. It's *the* precious stone."

" Not the Countess of Morcar's blue carbuncle ? " I **17** ejaculated.

"SEE WHAT MY WIFE FOUND IN ITS CROP!"

Illustration by Sidney Paget for the *Strand Magazine*, January, 1892.

But: ". . . a goose has no crop," Miss Mildred Sammons wrote in a letter to the "Line o'Type or Two" column of the *Chicago Tribune*, December 26, 1946.

Her letter started a controversy which has not died down to this day. The late Professor Jay Finley Christ wrote that Sherlock Holmes had made "an alimentary error . . ."

Dr. Rupert Coles, Chief Poultry Adviser of Britain's Ministry of Agriculture and Fish, as well as members of the Department of Ornithology at the Natural History Museum of Chicago later confirmed the statement.

But the Goose-Does-So-Have-a-Crop School has stout defenders, one of the stoutest of which was the late Dr. Ernest Bloomfield Zeisler, who called on experts in the poultry department of the Agricultural School of the University of New Hampshire to support his statement that "the crop of a goose is not as prominent or as easily seen as in a turkey but apparently all barnyard fowl possess crops" ("A Pigment of the Imagination").

14 *you also have been unfortunate enough to lose your wife's affection."* "Englishmen, or so I have heard it said, do not ask their wives for permission to go out until the wives have carefully inspected them and their hats, and many wives, English and others, don't know anything at all about their husbands' hats or even care; they may even be abed when the master leaves for work in the morning; or possibly they dawdle over another cup of coffee while their beloveds rush for the 7:35. They may, indeed, even be slatterns, so that dusty hats on their husbands would be the last thing in the world they would notice; and all such may nevertheless be deeply in love with their husbands."— Magistrate S. Tupper Bigelow, "The Blue Enigma."

15 *and a guttering candle in the other.* "But why take his hat upstairs at all," Mr. J. B. Mackenzie asked in "Sherlock Holmes' Plots and Strategy," "or—if he were in the habit of performing this out-of-the-way detail—why put it elsewhere than upon his head? Then, how would grease from the candle, held in one hand, fall on the hat, carried in the other?"

16 *It cuts into glass as though it were putty."* "This is a most unreliable method of testing gem stones," Mr. Philip Kasson wrote in "The True Blue: A Case of Identification." "Glass is relatively soft compared to most gems. Hardness means scratching ability, and a stone can be scratched by another of equal or greater hardness. Diamonds, rubies, sapphires, garnets, aquamarines, beryls, etc., etc., are all harder and will cut glass. Even glass will cut glass. Peterson's test proved nothing."

17 *the Countess of Morcar's blue carbuncle?"* "A carbuncle is a garnet, cut *en cabochon* (with a domed top). . . . Garnets come in many colours: white, yellow, green, red, orange, brown, purple, and black, but no blue garnet has ever been found." —Philip Kasson, "The True Blue."

18 *not within a twentieth part of the market price.*" "This would put the value of the blue stone at about £20,000, or $100,000, which is almost the amount Henry Hope spent for the [famous Hope diamond]."—Philip Kasson, "The True Blue."

19 *the Hotel Cosmopolitan.*" "I take the Cosmopolitan to be Claridge's," the late Gavin Brend wrote in "The Route of the Blue Carbuncle." "There are, no doubt, some other possible selections, but I believe they are fewer than might be supposed. The Ritz, the Carlton, the Berkeley and the Cecil all came into existence after 1889 though some of them were built on the sites of earlier hotels. The Savoy opened in October of that year but it is unlikely (I hope) that within a couple of months a bedroom grate would already be in need of repair."

20 *the Assizes.* The periodical sessions of the judges of the superior courts in every county of England for the purpose of administering justice in the trial and determination of civil and criminal cases.

21 *solder the second bar of the grate.* Aside from the fact that grates are not normally soldered, we may point to the fact that the 22nd of December could not have been a Sunday, or Horner would not have been at work. December 22, 1889, *was* a Sunday, which would seem to us to eliminate that year from consideration.

" Precisely so. I ought to know its size and shape, seeing that I have read the advertisement about it in *The Times* every day lately. It is absolutely unique, and its value can only be conjectured, but the reward offered of a thousand pounds is certainly not within a twentieth part **18** of the market price."

" A thousand pounds ! Great Lord of mercy ! " The commissionaire plumped down into a chair, and stared from one to the other of us.

" That is the reward, and I have reason to know that there are sentimental considerations in the background which would induce the Countess to part with half of her fortune if she could but recover the gem."

" It was lost, if I remember aright, at the Hotel Cos- **19** mopolitan," I remarked.

" Precisely so, on the twenty-second of December, just five days ago. John Horner, a plumber, was accused of having abstracted it from the lady's jewel-case. The evidence against him was so strong that the case has been **20** referred to the Assizes. I have some account of the matter here, I believe." He rummaged amid his newspapers, glancing over the dates, until at last he smoothed one out, doubled it over, and read the following paragraph :

" Hotel Cosmopolitan Jewel Robbery. John Horner, 26, plumber, was brought up upon the charge of having upon the 22nd inst., abstracted from the jewel-case of the Countess of Morcar the valuable gem known as the blue carbuncle. James Ryder, upper-attendant at the hotel, gave his evidence to the effect that he had shown Horner up to the dressing-room of the Countess of Morcar upon the day of the robbery, in order that he might solder the **21** second bar of the grate, which was loose. He had remained with Horner some little time but had finally been called away. On returning he found that Horner had disappeared, that the bureau had been forced open, and that the small morocco casket in which, as it afterwards transpired, the Countess was accustomed to keep her jewel, was lying empty upon the dressing-table. Ryder instantly gave the alarm, and Horner was arrested the same evening ; but the stone could not be found either upon his person or in his rooms. Catherine Cusack, maid to the Countess, deposed to having heard Ryder's cry of dismay on discovering the robbery, and to having rushed into the room, where she found matters were as described by the last witness. Inspector Bradstreet, B Division, gave evidence as to the arrest of Horner, who struggled frantically, and protested his innocence in the strongest terms. Evidence of a previous conviction for robbery having been given against the prisoner, the magistrate refused to deal summarily with the offence, but referred it to the Assizes. Horner, who had shown signs of intense emotion during the proceedings, fainted away at the conclusion, and was carried out of court."

" Hum ! So much for the police-court," said Holmes thoughtfully, tossing aside his paper. " The question for us now to solve is the sequence of events leading from a rifled jewel-case at one end to the crop of a goose in Tottenham Court Road at the other. You see, Watson, our little deductions have suddenly assumed a much more important and less innocent aspect. Here is the stone ; the stone came from the goose, and the goose came from Mr. Henry Baker, the gentleman with the bad hat and all the other characteristics with which I have bored you. So now we must set ourselves very seriously to finding this gentleman, and ascertaining what part he has played in this little mystery. To do this, we must try the simplest means first, and these lie undoubtedly in an advertisement in all the evening papers. If this fail, I shall **22** have recourse to other methods."

"What will you say ?"

" Give me a pencil, and that slip of paper. Now, then : ' Found at the corner of Goodge Street, a goose and a black felt hat. Mr. Henry Baker can have the same by applying at 6.30 this evening at 221B Baker Street.' That is clear and concise."

"Very. But will he see it ?"

" Well, he is sure to keep an eye on the papers, since, to a poor man, the loss was a heavy one. He was clearly so scared by his mischance in breaking the window, and by the approach of Peterson, that he thought of nothing but flight ; but since then he must have bitterly regretted the impulse which caused him to drop his bird. Then, again, the introduction of his name will cause him to see it, for every one who knows him will direct his attention to it. Here you are, Peterson, run down to the advertising agency, and have this put in the evening papers." **23**

" In which, sir ?"

" Oh, in the *Globe, Star, Pall Mall, St. James's Gazette, Evening News, Standard, Echo*, and any others that occur to you." **24**

" Very well, sir. And this stone ?"

" Ah, yes, I shall keep the stone. Thank you. And, I say, Peterson, just buy a goose on your way back, and leave it here with me, for we must have one to give to this gentleman in place of the one which your family is now devouring."

When the commissionaire had gone, Holmes took up the stone and held it against the light. " It's a bonny thing," said he. " Just see how it glints and sparkles. Of course it is a nucleus and focus of crime. Every good stone is. They are the devil's pet baits. In the larger and older jewels every facet may stand for a bloody deed. This stone is not yet twenty years old. It was found in the banks of the Amoy River in Southern China, and is **25** remarkable in having every characteristic of the carbuncle, save that it is blue in shade, instead of ruby red. In spite of its youth, it has already a sinister history. There have been two murders, a vitriol-throwing, a suicide, and several robberies brought about for the sake of this forty-grain weight of crystallized charcoal. Who would think **26-27** that so pretty a toy would be a purveyor to the gallows and the prison ? I'll lock it up in my strong-box now, and drop a line to the Countess to say that we have it."

" Do you think this man Horner is innocent ?"

" I cannot tell."

" Well, then, do you imagine that this other one, Henry Baker, had anything to do with the matter ?"

22 *an advertisement in all the evening papers.* Additional evidence that this day was not a Sunday. But how did Holmes get advertisements into all the evening papers when it was already mid-morning?

23 *run down to the advertising agency.* A persistent rumor has it that when the first *Strands* containing "The Adventure of the Blue Carbuncle" appeared on the stalls, the story here read: "run down to Willing's . . ." The *Strand*'s editors, catching the fact that Willing's Advertising Agency was being given a free advertisement, quietly changed the line to read "run down to the advertising agency." If issues of the *Strand* containing the original wording do exist, they are certainly a collector's item—and one which no collector to our knowledge admits having.

24 *and any others that occur to you."* Holmes "was not really allowing the commissionaire a very free hand," Mr. James Edward Holroyd wrote. "In Dickens' *Dictionary of London*, 1889, I find that there were only three other evenings and all were specialized. The *Evening Corn Trade List* (£5 15s per annum) and the *Shipping and Mercantile Gazette* (5d. against the ½d. and 1d. charge of [the seven papers Holmes named]) were both commercial and probably prohibitive; while the remaining paper, the *Evening Post and Daily Recorder*, was a financial journal. None of the three would be likely to occur to the commissionaire, nor were they the kind of paper that a poor man like H. B. would be 'sure to keep an eye on.'"

25 *the Amoy River in Southern China.* ". . . no garnet has ever been found in China, let alone on the banks of the Amoy River for the very good reason that there is no Amoy River in China, nor ever was," Magistrate S. Tupper Bigelow wrote in "The Blue Enigma." "Amoy is a city in southern China, but the Kiulung River, not the Amoy, flows into Amoy."

26 *this forty-grain weight.* Holmes "did not seem to know that gems are weighed in carats, not just in England, but everywhere, then and now. It is true that the precise weight of a carat in grains differed from country to country, but an English carat of [that time] was 3.163 troy grains, which would make the weight of the blue carbuncle 12.62 English carats. Such a gem would not be 'rather smaller than a bean in size'; it would be the size of a well-nourished lima bean, if we must use beans as a comparative basis."—Magistrate S. Tupper Bigelow, "The Blue Enigma."

27 *of crystallized charcoal.* Charcoal is a rather pure form of carbon, and crystallized carbon is a diamond, not a carbuncle. The chemical composition of the carbuncle is "a combination of the elements of magnesium, calcium, manganese or ferrous iron, together with any of the elements of aluminum, ferric iron, or chromium . . ."—Philip Kasson, "The True Blue."

Mr. Doyle W. Beckmeyer has suggested in "Valuable Sherlockian Hunting-Ground" that the blue "carbuncle" was in fact a star sapphire, but a sapphire is chemically aluminum oxide.

In Mr. Kasson's view, however, "the blue carbuncle" was a blue diamond—a view stoutly supported by Mr. D. A. Redmond in "Some Chemical Problems in the Canon." Here Mr. Redmond made the interesting suggestion that: "one name for massive black diamond is 'carbonado.' A gemstone discovered in a mass of carbonado, which would be a rare occurrence, might well have originally been called the 'Blue Carbonado.' In the course of the extensive travels . . . of the stone, this would readily be corrupted to a more familiar word: the 'Blue Carbuncle.'"

But perhaps Magistrate S. Tupper Bigelow sized up the situation most cogently when he wrote in "The Blue Enigma" that ". . . no gem discovered up to now can possibly satisfy the 'blue carbuncle' on all accounts."

28 *a Scotch bonnet.* A tam-o'-shanter; a soft woolen bonnet or cap with a flat circular crown, the circumference of which is about twice that of the head.

29 *It is a cold night.* December 27, 1887, was a Tuesday and a cold one. Said the *Times'* morning report: "Temperature has fallen generally. . . . Some frost prevails. . . . Over the greater part of England and Ireland . . . very cold, dry weather seems likely." And in its report for the evening of the same day: "Cold weather is reported generally, the maximum readings of the thermometer over England today being only . . . 33 deg. . . . in London."

"It is, I think, much more likely that Henry Baker is an absolutely innocent man, who had no idea that the bird which he was carrying was of considerably more value than if it were made of solid gold. That, however, I shall determine by a very simple test, if we have an answer to our advertisement."

"And you can do nothing until then?"

"Nothing."

"In that case I shall continue my professional round. But I shall come back in the evening at the hour you have mentioned, for I should like to see the solution of so tangled a business."

"Very glad to see you. I dine at seven. There is a woodcock, I believe. By the way, in view of recent occurrences, perhaps I ought to ask Mrs. Hudson to examine its crop."

I had been delayed at a case, and it was a little after half-past six when I found myself in Baker Street once more. As I approached the house I saw a tall man in a **28** Scotch bonnet, with a coat which was buttoned up to his chin, waiting outside in the bright semicircle which was thrown from the fanlight. Just as I arrived, the door was opened, and we were shown up together to Holmes' room.

"Mr. Henry Baker, I believe," said he, rising from his arm-chair, and greeting his visitor with the easy air of geniality which he could so readily assume. "Pray take **29** this chair by the fire, Mr. Baker. It is a cold night, and I observe that your circulation is more adapted for summer than for winter. Ah, Watson, you have just come at the right time. Is that your hat, Mr. Baker?"

"Yes, sir, that is undoubtedly my hat."

He was a large man, with rounded shoulders, a massive head, and a broad, intelligent face, sloping down to a pointed beard of grizzled brown. A touch of red in nose and cheeks, with a slight tremor of his extended hand, recalled Holmes' surmise as to his habits. His rusty black frock-coat was buttoned right up in front, with the collar turned up, and his lank wrists protruded from his sleeves without a sign of cuff or shirt. He spoke in a low staccato fashion, choosing his words with care, and gave the impression generally of a man of learning and letters who had had ill-usage at the hands of fortune.

"We have retained these things for some days," said Holmes, "because we expected to see an advertisement from you giving your address. I am at a loss to know now why you did not advertise."

Our visitor gave a rather shamefaced laugh. "Shillings have not been so plentiful with me as they once were," he remarked. "I had no doubt that the gang of roughs who assaulted me had carried off both my hat and the bird. I did not care to spend more money in a hopeless attempt at recovering them."

"Very naturally. By the way, about the bird—we were compelled to eat it."

"To eat it!" Our visitor half rose from his chair in his excitement.

"Yes; it would have been no use to anyone had we not done so. But I presume that this other goose upon the sideboard, which is about the same weight and perfectly fresh, will answer your purpose equally well?"

" Oh, certainly, certainly ! " answered Mr. Baker, with a sigh of relief.

" Of course, we still have the feathers, legs, crop, and so on of your own bird, if you so wish——"

The man burst into a hearty laugh. " They might be useful to me as relics of my adventure," said he, " but beyond that I can hardly see what use the *disjecta membra* **30** of my late acquaintance are going to be to me.   No, sir, I think that, with your permission, I will confine my attentions to the excellent bird which I perceive upon the sideboard."

Sherlock Holmes glanced sharply across at me with a slight shrug of his shoulders.

" There is your hat, then, and there your bird," said he. " By the way, would it bore you to tell me where you got the other one from ?   I am somewhat of a fowl fancier, and I have seldom seen a better-grown goose."

" Certainly, sir," said Baker, who had risen and tucked his newly gained property under his arm.   " There are a few of us who frequent the Alpha Inn near the Museum— we are to be found in the Museum itself during the day, you understand.   This year our good host, Windigate by name, instituted a goose-club, by which, on consideration of some few pence every week, we were to receive a bird at Christmas.   My pence were duly paid, and the rest is **31** familiar to you.   I am much indebted to you, sir, for a Scotch bonnet is fitted neither to my years nor my gravity."   With a comical pomposity of manner he bowed solemnly to both of us, and strode off upon his way.

" So much for Mr. Henry Baker," said Holmes, when he had closed the door behind him.   " It is quite certain that he knows nothing whatever about the matter.   Are you hungry, Watson ? "

" Not particularly."

" Then I suggest that we turn our dinner into a supper, and follow up this clue while it is still hot."

" By all means."

It was a bitter night, so we drew on our ulsters and wrapped cravats about our throats.   Outside, the stars were shining coldly in a cloudless sky, and the breath of the passers-by blew out into smoke like so many pistol shots.   Our footfalls rang out crisply and loudly as we swung through the doctors' quarter, Wimpole Street, **32** Harley Street, and so through Wigmore Street into Oxford **33** Street.   In a quarter of an hour we were in Bloomsbury **34-35** at the Alpha Inn, which is a small public-house at the corner of one of the streets which runs down into Holborn.   Holmes pushed open the door of the private bar, and ordered two glasses of beer from the ruddy-faced, white-aproned landlord.

" Your beer should be excellent if it is as good as your geese," he said.

" My geese ! "   The man seemed surprised.

" Yes.   I was speaking only half an hour ago to Mr. Henry Baker, who was a member of your goose-club."

" Ah ! yes, I see.   But you see, sir, them's not *our* geese."

" Indeed !   Whose, then ? "

" Well, I get the two dozen from a salesman in Covent Garden."   **36**

30 *the* disjecta membra. "The *disjecta membra* [scattered limbs] are an adaptation of a phrase in one of Horace's *Satires* (I, 4, line 62): 'Invenias disjecti membra poetae' ('You would still find the limbs of the dismembered poet').   Horace referred to the discernible traces of the poet whose works had been stripped of their original qualities by a transliteration   or   paraphrase."—Morris Rosenblum, "Some Latin Byways in the Canon."

31 *we were to receive a bird at Christmas.* The pleasant custom of an Alpha Inn Christmas Goose Club was revived by the Sherlock Holmes Society of London in 1959. Tickets were printed in "a deliciously Victorian style," and the draw was held at the Sherlock Holmes Tavern on December 23, 1959.

32 *Wimpole Street.* So named after Wimpole on the borders of Hertfordshire and Cambridgeshire, originally the country seat of the Harleys, Earls of Oxford. Wimpole Street and Harley Street (see "The Resident Patient," Note 21) run parallel.

33 *Wigmore Street.* Wigmore Street, now a smart shopping thoroughfare, extends from Cavendish Square to Portman Square. Like Wimpole Street, it derives its name from a country estate, Wigmore in Hertfordshire, whence Robert Harley took his title as Earl of Oxford, Earl Mortimer, and Lord Harley of Wigmore Castle.

34 *In a quarter of an hour.* The late H. W. Bell pointed out in "A Note on Dr. Watson's Wound" that, "Since the distance covered was about one mile and five-eighths, the rate was a mile in less than 9½ minutes."

WITH A COMICAL POMPOSITY OF MANNER HE BOWED
SOLEMNLY TO BOTH OF US . . .

Illustration by Sidney Paget for the *Strand Magazine*, January, 1892.

... AT THE ALPHA INN, WHICH IS A SMALL PUBLIC-
HOUSE AT THE CORNER OF ONE OF THE STREETS WHICH
RUNS DOWN INTO HOLBORN.

The late Christopher Morley once expressed the view that "the Alpha Inn" was the Museum Tavern. "This fulfills all the necessary conditions," the late Gavin Brend wrote in "A Sherlock Holmes Anniversary," "but so too does the Plough, a corner [Little Russell Street] building in Museum Street, and my vote is for this house on the grounds that the stars in the constellation the Plough are named after the Greek letters and Alpha is the biggest and brightest of them all." Holborn was originally called after the "Hole-Bourne," as the upper course of the Fleet River was known, from its running through a deep hollow. Holborn is known for its diamond trade. It is the smallest of the metropolitan boroughs; Bloomsbury is a part of it.

35 *Bloomsbury.* Bloomsbury is the district bounded by New Oxford Street and High Holborn on the south, Tottenham Court Road on the west, Euston Road on the north, and Southampton Row on the east. A district of wide streets and spacious squares, it is an excellent example of early town planning. It is today a region largely made up of boardinghouses and hotels, but it also, today, has many publishers' offices.

36 *Covent Garden."* Covent Garden Market is meant. But Covent Garden Market was never a poultry market; it was—and is—a flower, fruit, and vegetable market. "How, then, did Watson come to confuse Covent Garden with what clearly must have been Leadenhall Market, some two miles away in the heart of the City of London?" Mr. Ian M. Leslie asked in "Dr. Watson's Christmas Party of 1889."

37 *Endell Street.* A northward continuation of Bow Street, leading to New Oxford Street. It was opened in 1845.

38 *to-morrow morning."* The 28th of December in the year in which this adventure took place was therefore not a Sunday (as it was in 1890).

"Indeed! I know some of them. Which was it?"
"Breckinridge is his name."
"Ah! I don't know him. Well, here's your good health, landlord, and prosperity to your house. Good night."

"Now for Mr. Breckinridge," he continued, buttoning up his coat, as we came out into the frosty air. "Remember, Watson, that though we have so homely a thing as a goose at one end of this chain, we have at the other a man who will certainly get seven years' penal servitude, unless we can establish his innocence. It is possible that our inquiry may but confirm his guilt; but, in any case, we have a line of investigation which has been missed by the police, and which a singular chance has placed in our hands. Let us follow it out to the bitter end. Faces to the south, then, and quick march!"

37 We passed across Holborn, down Endell Street, and so through a zigzag of slums to Covent Garden Market. One of the largest stalls bore the name of Breckinridge upon it, and the proprietor, a horsy-looking man, with a sharp face and trim side-whiskers, was helping a boy to put up the shutters.

"Good evening. It's a cold night," said Holmes.

The salesman nodded, and shot a questioning glance at my companion.

"Sold out of geese, I see," continued Holmes, pointing at the bare slabs of marble.

38 "Let you have five hundred to-morrow morning."
"That's no good."
"Well, there are some on the stall with the gas flare."
"Ah, but I was recommended to you."
"Who by?"
"The landlord of the 'Alpha.'"
"Ah, yes; I sent him a couple of dozen."
"Fine birds they were, too. Now where did you get them from?"

To my surprise the question provoked a burst of anger from the salesman.

" Now then, mister," said he, with his head cocked and his arms akimbo, " what are you driving at ?   Let's have it straight, now."

" It is straight enough.   I should like to know who sold you the geese which you supplied to the ' Alpha.' "

" Well, then, I shan't tell you.   So now ! "

" Oh, it is a matter of no importance ; but I don't know why you should be so warm over such a trifle."

" Warm !   You'd be as warm, maybe, if you were as pestered as I am.   When I pay good money for a good article there should be an end of the business ; but it's ' Where are the geese ? ' and ' Who did you sell the geese to ? ' and ' What will you take for the geese ? '   One would think they were the only geese in the world, to hear the fuss that is made over them."

" Well, I have no connection with any other people who have been making inquiries," said Holmes carelessly. " If you won't tell us the bet is off, that is all.   But I'm always ready to back my opinion on a matter of fowls, and I have a fiver on it that the bird I ate is country bred."

" Well, then, you've lost your fiver, for it's town bred," snapped the salesman.

" It's nothing of the kind."

" I say it is."

" I don't believe you."

" D'you think you know more about fowls than I, who have handled them ever since I was a nipper ?   I tell you, all those birds that went to the ' Alpha ' were town bred."

" You'll never persuade me to believe that."

" Will you bet, then ? "

" It's merely taking your money, for I know that I am right.   But I'll have a sovereign on with you, just to teach you not to be obstinate."

The salesman chuckled grimly.   " Bring me the books, Bill," said he.

The small boy brought round a small thin volume and a great greasy-backed one, laying them out together beneath the hanging lamp.

" Now then, Mr. Cocksure," said the salesman, " I thought that I was out of geese, but before I finish you'll find that there is still one left in my shop.   You see this little book ? "

" Well ? "

" That's the list of the folk from whom I buy.   D'you see ?   Well, then, here on this page are the country folk, and the numbers after their names are where their accounts are in the big ledger.   Now, then !   You see this other page in red ink ?   Well, that is a list of my town suppliers. Now, look at that third name.   Just read it out to me."

" Mrs. Oakshott, 117 Brixton Road—249," read Holmes.

" Quite so.   Now turn that up in the ledger."

Holmes turned to the page indicated.   " Here you are, ' Mrs. Oakshott, 117 Brixton Road, egg and poultry supplier.' "

" Now, then, what's the last entry ? "

" ' December 22.   Twenty-four geese at 7s. 6d.' "   **39**

" Quite so.   There you are.   And underneath ? "

39 *7s. 6d.*' " About $1.87.

"JUST READ IT OUT TO ME."

Illustration by Sidney Paget for the *Strand Magazine*, January, 1892.

40 *12s.'*" $3.00

41 *the 'Pink 'Un'* A sporting journal, printed on pink paper, not unlike the American *Police Gazette.*

"WELL, YOU CAN ASK THE KING OF PROOSIA, FOR ALL I CARE."

"The King of Proosia" was Wilhelm II, 1859–1941, by all chronologies except your editor's; Wilhelm I, 1797–1888, by his. In either case, the coat of arms of "the King of Proosia" is shown here, from Dr. Julian Wolff's *Practical Handbook of Sherlockian Heraldry.*

40   " ' Sold to Mr. Windigate of the " Alpha " at *12s.*' "
" What have you to say now ? "

Sherlock Holmes looked deeply chagrined. He drew a sovereign from his pocket and threw it down upon the slab, turning away with the air of a man whose disgust is too deep for words. A few yards off he stopped under a lamp-post, and laughed in the hearty, noiseless fashion which was peculiar to him.

41   " When you see a man with whiskers of that cut and the ' Pink 'Un ' protruding out of his pocket, you can always draw him by a bet," said he. " I dare say that if I had put a hundred pounds down in front of him that man would not have given me such complete information as was drawn from him by the idea that he was doing me on a wager. Well, Watson, we are, I fancy, nearing the end of our quest, and the only point which remains to be determined is whether we should go on to this Mrs. Oakshott to-night, or whether we should reserve it for to-morrow. It is clear from what that surly fellow said that there are others besides ourselves who are anxious about the matter, and I should——"

His remarks were suddenly cut short by a loud hubbub which broke out from the stall which we had just left. Turning round we saw a little rat-faced fellow standing in the centre of the circle of yellow light which was thrown by the swinging lamp, while Breckinridge the salesman, framed in the door of his stall, was shaking his fists fiercely at the cringing figure.

" I've had enough of you and your geese," he shouted. " I wish you were all at the devil together. If you come pestering me any more with your silly talk I'll set the dog at you. You bring Mrs. Oakshott here and I'll answer her, but what have you to do with it ? Did I buy the geese off you ? "

" No ; but one of them was mine all the same," whined the little man.

" Well, then, ask Mrs. Oakshott for it."

" She told me to ask you."

" Well, you can ask the King of Proosia, for all I care. I've had enough of it. Get out of this ! " He rushed fiercely forward, and the inquirer flitted away into the darkness.

" Ha, this may save us a visit to Brixton Road," whispered Holmes. " Come with me, and we will see what is to be made of this fellow." Striding through the scattered knots of people who lounged round the flaring stalls, my companion speedily overtook the little man and touched him upon the shoulder. He sprang round, and I could see in the gaslight that every vestige of colour had been driven from his face.

" Who are you, then ? What do you want ? " he asked in a quavering voice.

" You will excuse me," said Holmes blandly, " but I could not help overhearing the questions which you put to the salesman just now. I think that I could be of assistance to you."

" You ? Who are you ? How could you know anything of the matter ? "

" My name is Sherlock Holmes. It is my business to know what other people don't know."

" But you can know nothing of this ? "

" Excuse me, I know everything of it. You are endeavouring to trace some geese which were sold by Mrs. Oakshott, of Brixton Road, to a salesman named Breckinridge, by him in turn to Mr. Windigate, of the ' Alpha,' and by him to his club, of which Mr. Henry Baker is a member."

" Oh, sir, you are the very man whom I have longed to meet," cried the little fellow, with outstretched hands and quivering fingers. " I can hardly explain to you how interested I am in this matter."

Sherlock Holmes hailed a four-wheeler which was passing. " In that case we had better discuss it in a cosy room rather than in this wind-swept market-place," said he. " But pray tell me, before we go further, who it is that I have the pleasure of assisting."

The man hesitated for an instant. " My name is John Robinson," he answered, with a sidelong glance.

" No, no ; the real name," said Holmes sweetly. " It is always awkward doing business with an *alias*."

A flush sprang to the white cheeks of the stranger. " Well, then," said he, " my real name is James Ryder."

" Precisely so. Head attendant at the Hotel Cosmopolitan. Pray step into the cab, and I shall soon be able to tell you everything which you would wish to know."

The little man stood glancing from one to the other of us with half-frightened, half-hopeful eyes, as one who is not sure whether he is on the verge of a windfall or of a catastrophe. Then he stepped into the cab, and in half an hour we were back in the sitting-room at Baker Street. Nothing had been said during our drive, but the high, thin breathings of our new companion, and the claspings and unclaspings of his hands, spoke of the nervous tension within him.

" Here we are ! " said Holmes cheerily, as we filed into the room. " The fire looks very seasonable in this weather. You look cold, Mr. Ryder. Pray take the basket chair. I will just put on my slippers before we settle this little matter of yours. Now, then ! You want to know what became of those geese ? "

" Yes, sir."

" Or rather, I fancy, of that goose. It was one bird, I imagine, in which you were interested—white, with a black bar across the tail." **42**

Ryder quivered with emotion. " Oh, sir," he cried, " can you tell me where it went to ? "

" It came here."

" Here ? "

" Yes, and a most remarkable bird it proved. I don't wonder that you should take an interest in it. It laid an egg after it was dead—the bonniest, brightest little blue egg that ever was seen. I have it here in my museum."

Our visitor staggered to his feet, and clutched the mantelpiece with his right hand. Holmes unlocked his strong-box, and held up the blue carbuncle, which shone out like a star, with a cold, brilliant, many-pointed radiance. Ryder stood glaring with a drawn face, uncertain whether to claim or to disown it.

" The game's up, Ryder," said Holmes quietly. " Hold up, man, or you'll be into the fire. Give him an arm back into his chair, Watson. He's not got blood enough to go

"OH, SIR, YOU ARE THE VERY MAN WHOM I HAVE
LONGED TO MEET."

Illustration by Sidney Paget for the *Strand Magazine*, January, 1892.

42 *white, with a black bar across the tail.*" As Magistrate S. Tupper Bigelow has pointed out in his essay, "Barred-Tail Geese," there is no such thing as a *white* barred-tail goose, although the Pinkfooted Goose, which breeds in Greenland and Iceland, produces a barred-tail gosling "in the proportion of about one in 10,000."

"FOR GOD'S SAKE HAVE MERCY!" HE SHRIEKED.

Illustration by Sidney Paget for the *Strand Magazine*, January, 1892.

43 *for all that it was a cold night.* December 22, 1887, was a Thursday—and a cold one. Said the London *Times:* "The weather over the United Kingdom is . . . changing . . . to a period of cold and frost. Temperature was . . . 32 deg. in London."

in for felony with impunity. Give him a dash of brandy. So! Now he looks a little more human. What a shrimp it is, to be sure!"

For a moment he had staggered and nearly fallen, but the brandy brought a tinge of colour into his cheeks, and he sat staring with frightened eyes at his accuser.

"I have almost every link in my hands, and all the proofs which I could possibly need, so there is little which you need tell me. Still, that little may as well be cleared up to make the case complete. You had heard, Ryder, of this blue stone of the Countess of Morcar's?"

"It was Catherine Cusack who told me of it," said he, in a crackling voice.

"I see. Her ladyship's waiting-maid. Well, the temptation of sudden wealth so easily acquired was too much for you, as it has been for better men before you; but you were not very scrupulous in the means you used. It seems to me, Ryder, that there is the making of a very pretty villain in you. You knew that this man Horner, the plumber, had been concerned in some such matter before, and that suspicion would rest the more readily upon him. What did you do, then? You made some small job in my lady's room—you and your confederate Cusack—and you managed that he should be the man sent for. Then, when he had left, you rifled the jewel-case, raised the alarm, and had this unfortunate man arrested. You then——"

Ryder threw himself down suddenly upon the rug, and clutched at my companion's knees. "For God's sake, have mercy!" he shrieked. "Think of my father! Of my mother! It would break their hearts. I never went wrong before! I never will again. I swear it. I'll swear it on a Bible. Oh, don't bring it into court! For Christ's sake, don't!"

"Get back into your chair!" said Holmes sternly. "It is very well to cringe and crawl now, but you thought little enough of this poor Horner in the dock for a crime of which he knew nothing."

"I will fly, Mr. Holmes. I will leave the country, sir. Then the charge against him will break down."

"Hum! We will talk about that. And now let us hear a true account of the next act. How came the stone into the goose, and how came the goose into the open market? Tell us the truth, for there lies your only hope of safety."

Ryder passed his tongue over his parched lips. "I will tell you it just as it happened, sir," said he. "When Horner had been arrested, it seemed to me that it would be best for me to get away with the stone at once, for I did not know at what moment the police might not take it into their heads to search me and my room. There was no place about the hotel where it would be safe. I went out, as if on some commission, and I made for my sister's house. She had married a man named Oakshott, and lived in Brixton Road, where she fattened fowls for the market. All the way there every man I met seemed to me to be a policeman or a detective, and for all that it was a cold **43** night, the sweat was pouring down my face before I came to the Brixton Road. My sister asked me what was the matter, and why I was so pale; but I told her that I had been upset by the jewel robbery at the hotel. Then I went into the back-yard, and smoked a pipe, and wondered what it would be best to do.

"I had a friend once called Maudsley, who went to the bad, and has just been serving his time in Pentonville. **44** One day he had met me, and fell into talk about the ways of thieves and how they could get rid of what they stole. I knew that he would be true to me, for I knew one or two things about him, so I made up my mind to go right on to Kilburn, where he lived, and take him into my confidence. **45** He would show me how to turn the stone into money. But how to get to him in safety? I thought of the agonies I had gone through in coming from the hotel. I might at any moment be seized and searched, and there would be the stone in my waistcoat pocket. I was leaning against the wall at the time, and looking at the geese which were waddling about round my feet, and suddenly an idea came into my head which showed me how I could beat the best detective that ever lived.

"My sister had told me some weeks before that I might have the pick of her geese for a Christmas present, and I knew that she was always as good as her word. I would take my goose now, and in it I would carry my stone to Kilburn. There was a little shed in the yard, and behind **46** this I drove one of the birds, a fine big one, white, with a barred tail. I caught it and, prising its bill open, I thrust the stone down its throat as far as my finger could reach. The bird gave a gulp, and I felt the stone pass along its gullet and down into its crop. But the creature flapped **47** and struggled, and out came my sister to know what was the matter. As I turned to speak to her the brute broke loose, and fluttered off among the others.

44 *Pentonville.* Pentonville Prison, on Caledonian Road, was erected 1840–1842, on the "separate and silent system." It was called "a model prison," and was the one satirically treated by Dickens in the closing pages of *David Copperfield.* It occupies an area of 6¾ acres.

45 *Kilburn.* The district to the north of Maida Vale, once famous for a spring of mineral water belonging to a drinking house called Kilbourn Wells. Kilburn today is one of the most lively shopping centers of semisuburban London.

46 *carry my stone to Kilburn.* "An interesting parallel . . . has come to my notice while reading *Studies in Social History,* edited by Dr. J. H. Plumb," Mr. T. S. Blakeney wrote in "Some Disjecta Membra." "On page 193 one learns that Sir Robert Walpole's steward, John Wrott, used to secrete the rents he collected and sent to his master, inside geese, in order to hoodwink highwaymen, who in those days (early eighteenth century) infested the roads from Norfolk to London."

47 *I felt the stone pass along its gullet.* "The gem which was seen was small as a bean, / Yet hark to the quivering Ryder: / The jittery clown said he *felt* it pass down / As the bird took the jewel inside her."—Professor Jay Finley Christ, "Sherlock Backs a Turkey."

"BUT THE CREATURE FLAPPED AND STRUGGLED . . ."

"Let us pause for a minute at Mrs. Oakshott's residence," the late Gavin Brend wrote in "The Route of the Blue Carbuncle." "Suppose in its efforts to escape Ryder the goose had scrambled over the north garden wall of No. 117, where do you imagine that it would be? The answer is—believe it or not—that it would be in Baker Street! No. 117 [the photograph is by Mr. Alan Wilson of the Sherlock Holmes Society of London] stands at the corner of Brixton Road and a side street which since 1937 has been called Blackwell Street but which before that bore the name of Baker Street. If we were dealing with a work of fiction we might wonder whether this was a mere coincidence or whether the author selected 117 Brixton Road as a private joke of his own simply because he knew that it was adjacent to Baker Street, Brixton."

"The original No. 117 still stands, and is on a corner site, the side running along Blackwell Street," Mr. Colin Prestige wrote in "South London Adventures." "(As Gavin Brend recently pointed out, this Blackwell Street used to be known as Baker Street! The old name is still faintly visible, painted on the brickwork in washed-out colours.) The garden to No. 117 is very small. It is now covered with grass."

" ' Whatever were you doing with that bird, Jem ? ' says she.

" ' Well,' said I, ' you said you'd give me one for Christmas, and I was feeling which was the fattest.'

" ' Oh,' says she, ' we've set yours aside for you.   Jem's bird, we call it.   It's the big, white one over yonder. There's twenty-six of them, which makes one for you, and one for us, and two dozen for the market.'

" ' Thank you, Maggie,' says I ; ' but if it is all the same to you I'd rather have that one I was handling just now.'

" ' The other is a good three pound heavier,' she said, ' and we fattened it expressly for you.'

" ' Never mind.   I'll have the other, and I'll take it now,' said I.

" ' Oh, just as you like,' said she, a little huffed.   ' Which is it you want, then ? '

" ' That white one, with the barred tail, right in the middle of the flock.'

" ' Oh, very well.   Kill it and take it with you.'

" Well, I did what she said, Mr. Holmes, and I carried the bird all the way to Kilburn.   I told my pal what I had done, for he was a man that it was easy to tell a thing like that to.   He laughed until he choked, and we got a knife and opened the goose.   My heart turned to water, for there was no sign of the stone, and I knew that some terrible mistake had occurred.   I left the bird, rushed back to my sister's, and hurried into the back-yard.   There was not a bird to be seen there.

" ' Where are they all, Maggie ? ' I cried.

" ' Gone to the dealer's.'

" ' Which dealer's ? '

" ' Breckinridge, of Covent Garden.'

" ' But was there another with a barred tail ? ' I asked, ' the same as the one I chose ? '

" ' Yes, Jem, there were two barred-tailed ones, and I could never tell them apart.'

" Well, then, of course, I saw it all, and I ran off as hard as my feet would carry me to this man Breckinridge ; but he had sold the lot at once, and not one word would he tell me as to where they had gone.   You heard him yourselves to-night.   Well, he has always answered me like that. My sister thinks that I am going mad.   Sometimes I think that I am myself.   And now—and now I am myself a branded thief, without ever having touched the wealth for which I sold my character.   God help me !   God help me ! "   He burst into convulsive sobbing, with his face buried in his hands.

There was a long silence, broken only by his heavy breathing, and by the measured tapping of Sherlock Holmes' finger-tips upon the edge of the table.   Then my friend rose, and threw open the door.

" Get out ! " said he.

" What, sir !   Oh, Heaven bless you ! "

" No more words.   Get out ! "

And no more words were needed.   There was a rush, a clatter upon the stairs, the bang of a door, and the crisp rattle of running footfalls from the street.

" After all, Watson," said Holmes, reaching up his hand for his clay pipe, " I am not retained by the police to supply their deficiencies.   If Horner were in danger it would be another thing, but this fellow will not appear against him, and the case must collapse.   I suppose that I am commuting a felony, but it is just possible that I am saving a soul. **48** This fellow will not go wrong again.   He is too terribly frightened.   Send him to gaol now, and you make him a gaolbird for life.   Besides, it is the season of forgiveness. **49** Chance has put in our way a most singular and whimsical problem, and its solution is its own reward.   If you will **50** have the goodness to touch the bell, Doctor, we will begin another investigation, in which also a bird will be the chief feature.''

HE BURST INTO CONVULSIVE SOBBING,
WITH HIS FACE BURIED IN HIS HANDS.

Illustration by Sidney Paget for the *Strand Magazine*, January, 1892.

48 *I suppose that I am commuting a felony*. In "The Adventure of the Priory School," Holmes accuses the Duke of Holdernesse of *condoning* a felony; in "The Adventure of the Mazarin Stone," Holmes agrees to *compound* a felony; and in "The Adventure of the Three Gables," he says: "Well, well, I suppose I shall have to *compound* a felony as usual." Is *commuting* here a confusion with *committing*, *condoning*, or *compounding*? Surely not: Holmes' knowledge of British law, as we have seen, was too profound for him to have made such an elementary mistake; nor was Holmes committing or compounding a felony in the strict legal sense of those words in England. He must therefore have meant *commute*, one meaning of which is "to exchange, especially one form of punishment for another, such as the exchanging of the death penalty for one of banishment." But this raises another question: as British Counsel E. J. C., writing in the *Baker Street Journal*, once pointed out, in England the power to commute an offense is *a prerogative of the Crown and may not be delegated to a mere subject*. Is Holmes by any chance hinting here that he—like John Clay—had royal blood in his veins? These are deep waters, indeed . . .

49 *and you make him a gaolbird for life*. "Holmes' habit of letting off criminals is by now, of course, notorious," Mr. Robert Keith Leavitt wrote in "Nummi in Arca or The Fiscal Holmes." "In the 60 cases of record in the Writings, there are 37 definite felonies where the criminal was known to Mr. Sherlock Holmes. In no less than 14 of these cases did the celebrated detective take the law into his own hands and free the guilty person. In 23 cases the offender was taken by the police. In 7 cases justice was balked by suicide, by death at sea or by other acts of God. In 12 cases no crime was involved. And in 4 cases the criminal or criminals got away uncaught."

50 *its solution is its own reward*. "Yes—plus a little matter of a thousand pounds [reward], which [Holmes] quite evidently wasn't going to spilt with anyone," Mr. James C. Iraldi wrote in "The Other Geese."

Bibliographical Note: The first separate edition of "The Adventure of the Blue Carbuncle" was sponsored by the Baker Street Irregulars, Inc. It was published in New York in 1948, with an Introduction by the late Christopher Morley, a Bibliographical Note by the late Edgar W. Smith, and two of Sidney Paget's illustrations from the *Strand Magazine*.

A Day with Dr. Conan Doyle.

By Harry How.

From a Photo, by]   DR. CONAN DOYLE AND MRS. CONAN DOYLE.   *[Elliott & Fry.*

ETECTIVISM up to date—that is what Dr. Conan Doyle has given us. We were fast becoming weary of the representative of the old school; he was, at his best, a very ordinary mortal, and, with the palpable clues placed in his path, the average individual could have easily cornered the "wanted" one without calling in the police or the private inquiry agent. Sherlock Holmes entered the criminal arena. He started on the track. A clever fellow; a cool, calculating fellow, this Holmes. He could see the clue to a murder in a ball of worsted, and certain conviction in a saucer of milk. The little things we regarded as nothings were all and everything to Holmes. He was an artful fellow, too; and though he knew "all about it" from the first, he ingeniously contrived to hold his secret until we got to the very last line in

CONAN DOYLE IN THE "STRAND"

"A Day with Dr. Conan Doyle," interview in the August, 1892, issue.
Strand readers were as interested in the creator as in his creations.

V. FROM DR. WATSON'S RETURN
TO BAKER STREET
TO HIS MARRIAGE TO MARY MORSTAN

[Late December, 1887, or early January, 1888, *circa* May 1, 1889]

"Don't go, doctor. I should prefer that you remain."
—Sherlock Holmes, *The Sign of the Four*.

According to the late H. W. Bell
(The Moated House at Brambletye,
        from an 1890 etching)

**"THE ANCIENT MANOR HOUSE OF BIRLSTONE,"
SCENE OF THE CRIME IN *THE VALLEY OF FEAR***

"It is evident," the late H. W. Bell wrote in "Three Identifications," "that Birlstone Manor must be sought for on or near the road connecting Tunbridge Wells, in Kent, with East Grinstead, in Sussex; and it is a fact that until some years ago there existed a house near Forest Row which fulfilled all the requirements of the story." (It may be noted that Conan Doyle himself lived for some years in the neighborhood of Forest Row.) "Forest Row," Mr. Bell continued, "lies twelve miles and six furlongs from Tunbridge Wells. Half a mile to the west are the remains of Brambletye House and Brambletye Manor . . ." It is Brambletye Manor, also called "The Moated House of Brambletye," that Mr. Bell would identify with "Birlstone Manor." Brambletye Manor, abandoned about 1631, was reoccupied before the end of the seventeenth century. An etching, dated 1809, shows that by the beginning of the nineteenth century the drawbridge had been abolished and replaced by a permanent construction in masonry. However, by 1892, at the latest, the original arrangement had been restored. After Douglas' death the drawbridge was once more replaced by a bridge of stone, which is, in fact, all that now remains of the building. Mr. Bell pointed out that the "ramping lion" on the ancient stone pillars at the entrance to the drive, which Watson attributed to "Capus of Birlstone" (*see p. 483*) was actually the crest of the last known occupant of the long-since ruined Brambletye *House*, Sir Richard James, Bart., in the reign of Charles II.

Indeed, Mr. Bell's identification of the Moated House of Brambletye as "Birlstone Manor" "does not bear cross-examination," as Mr. C. O. Merriman wrote in "A Case of Identity—No. 2." Mr. Merriman pointed out that: "1) the building certainly did not exist at the date when Holmes and Watson undertook the case of *The Valley of Fear;* 2) there is grave doubt about the double-moat and in addition many of the other means of identification in the Saga are not available; 3) the etching by Laetitia Byrne clearly shows no window was at a closer range than ten to twelve feet of the water in the moat . . ."

In a detailed examination, Mr. Merriman thereupon supported the late James Montgomery's identification of "Birlstone Manor" as Groombridge House (*A Case of Identity*).

According to the late James Montgomery and Mr. C. O. Merriman.

(Groombridge House, Groombridge Kent. Note door, right, giving facilities for umbrella-fishing by Sherlock Holmes.)

31

THE VALLEY OF FEAR

[Saturday, January 7, to Sunday, January 8, 1888]

PART I

The Tragedy of Birlstone

I ◆ THE WARNING

'I am inclined to think——' said I.   **1**

'I should do so,' Sherlock Holmes remarked, impatiently. **2**

I believe that I am one of the most long-suffering of mortals, but I admit that I was annoyed at the sardonic interruption.

'Really, Holmes,' said I, severely, 'you are a little trying at times.'

He was too much absorbed with his own thoughts to give any immediate answer to my remonstrance. He leaned upon his hand, with his untasted breakfast before him, and he stared at the slip of paper which he had just drawn from its envelope. Then he took the envelope itself, held it up to the light, and very carefully studied both the exterior and the flap.

'It is Porlock's writing,' said he, thoughtfully. 'I can hardly **3** doubt that it is Porlock's writing, though I have only seen it twice before. The Greek "e" with the peculiar top flourish is distinctive. But if it is from Porlock, then it must be something of the very first importance.'

He was speaking to himself rather than to me, but my vexation disappeared in the interest which the words awakened.

'Who, then, is Porlock?' I asked.

'Porlock, Watson, is a *nom de plume*, a mere identification **4** mark, but behind it lies a shifty and evasive personality. In **5** a former letter he frankly informed me that the name was not his own, and defied me ever to trace him among the teeming millions of this great city. Porlock is important, not for himself, but for the great man with whom he is in touch. Picture to yourself the pilot-fish with the shark, the jackal with the lion—anything that is insignificant in companionship with what is formidable. Not only formidable, Watson, but sinister—in the highest degree sinister. That is where he comes within my purview. You have heard me speak of Professor Moriarty?'

'The famous scientific criminal, as famous among crooks as——'

'My blushes, Watson,' Holmes murmured, in a deprecating voice.

'I was about to say "as he is unknown to the public." '

1 *'I am inclined to think—' said I.* Conan Doyle did not, at first, have any intention of making Dr. Watson the narrator of this adventure. The original manuscript (176 folio pages with many deletions, corrections, and additions in the author's hand) shows that such expressions as "said Dr. Watson" and "said he" are crossed out and the direct "said I" substituted. The manuscript was auctioned in New York City on January 30, 1923, bringing $275. It was later listed in Scribner's Sherlock Holmes Catalogue at $900. Except for its short "Epilogue" (which is lost or missing), it is owned today by old Irregular J. Bliss Austin of Pittsburgh.

2 *Sherlock Holmes remarked, impatiently.* Mr. Anthony Boucher has written, in his Introduction to *The Final Adventures of Sherlock Holmes*, Volume I, "This is a ripe, mature Holmes, free from external eccentricities, his hand unburdened by either the cocaine needle or the violin's bow. Here is Holmes as the perfect thinking mind, in cryptanalysis, in observation, in deduction. And here, more than in any other Canonical story that comes to mind, is Holmes at his most completely charming, whether playfully dangling the cryptically obvious before his colleagues (whom for once he respects) or ruefully admitting 'a distinct touch' from Watson's pawky humor. There is, in fact, more overt humor here than is usual in the Canon; there is a certain fey quality in this Holmes, 'his eyes sparkling with mischief.' Like the superb episodes from the memoirs of Etienne Gerard, the story manages at once to be deftly amusing and intensely exciting; and . . . we can only be deeply grateful to Dr. Watson for having served it up so magnificently." For these and other reasons, as we shall shortly see, many commentators prefer to place *The Valley of Fear* late in Holmes' career.

3 *'It is Porlock's writing.'* "'A person on business from Porlock' interrupted forever the highest flight of the genius of Samuel Taylor Coleridge; a letter from Porlock provoked one of the greatest displays of the genius of Sherlock Holmes," Mr. Boucher continued in his Introduction. "I feel that some deeper meaning is latent here, but cannot define it—any more than I can understand how the comparison was omitted from the charming essay, 'Persons from Porlock,' by that noblest Holmesian of them all, Vincent Starrett [in *Bookman's Holiday*; New York: Random House, 1942]."

4 *a* nom de plume. French: a pen name; a writer's assumed name.

5 *a shifty and evasive personality.* "Although the thing cannot be proved, I am strongly of the opinion that Mycroft [Holmes, Sherlock's elder brother] was in fact the 'Fred Porlock' who acted as his brother's informer in *The Valley of Fear*," Monsignor Ronald A. Knox wrote in "The Mystery of Mycroft." There are, as shall see, many mysteries about Mycroft.

6 *libel in the eyes of the law.* "If we wonder why Watson forebore to publish *The Valley of Fear* at the time of the occurrence, the answer is found in the chronicle itself: 'In calling Moriarty a criminal you are uttering libel in the eyes of the law.' After Moriarty's death [in 1891] and when Holmes' return had released Watson from his vow of silence, the matter could finally be made public. And Watson, being Watson, waited a good long time."—Dr. John Dardess, "On the Dating of *The Valley of Fear*."

7 *solatium.* In law, compensation for injury to the feelings, as distinguished from compensation for pecuniary loss or physical injury. As always, when it is a question of the law, Holmes chooses the precise word.

8 *apocrypha.* From the Greek: hidden things; secrets.

'A touch—a distinct touch!' cried Holmes. 'You are developing a certain unexpected vein of pawky humour, Watson, against which I must learn to guard myself. But in calling Moriarty a criminal you are uttering libel in the eyes **6** of the law, and there lies the glory and the wonder of it. The greatest schemer of all time, the organizer of every devilry, the controlling brain of the underworld—a brain which might have made or marred the destiny of nations. That's the man. But so aloof is he from general suspicion—so immune from criticism—so admirable in his management and self-effacement, that for those very words that you have uttered he could hale you to a court and emerge with your year's **7** pension as a solatium for his wounded character. Is he not the celebrated author of *The Dynamics of an Asteroid*—a book which ascends to such rarefied heights of pure mathematics that it is said that there was no man in the scientific press capable of criticizing it? Is this a man to traduce? Foul-mouthed doctor and slandered professor—such would be your respective rôles. That's genius, Watson. But if I am spared by lesser men our day will surely come.'

'May I be there to see!' I exclaimed, devoutly. 'But you were speaking of this man Porlock.'

'Ah, yes—the so-called Porlock is a link in the chain some little way from its great attachment. Porlock is not quite a sound link, between ourselves. He is the only flaw in that chain so far as I have been able to test it.'

'But no chain is stronger than its weakest link.'

'Exactly, my dear Watson. Hence the extreme importance of Porlock. Led on by some rudimentary aspirations towards right, and encouraged by the judicious stimulation of an occasional ten-pound note sent to him by devious methods, he has once or twice given me advance information which has been of value—that highest value which anticipates and prevents rather than avenges crime. I cannot doubt that if we had the cipher we should find that this communication is of the nature that I indicate.'

Again Holmes flattened out the paper upon his unused plate. I rose and, leaning over him, stared down at the curious inscription, which ran as follows:

```
534 C2 13 127 36 31 4 17 21 41
DOUGLAS 109 293 5 37 BIRLSTONE
26 BIRLSTONE 9 127 171
```

'What do you make of it, Holmes?'

'It is obviously an attempt to convey secret information.'

'But what is the use of a cipher message without the cipher?'

'In this instance, none at all.'

'Why do you say "in this instance"?'

'Because there are many ciphers which I would read as **8** easily as I do the apocrypha of the agony column. Such crude devices amuse the intelligence without fatiguing it. But this is different. It is clearly a reference to the words in a page of some book. Until I am told which page and which book I am powerless.'

'But why "Douglas" and "Birlstone"?'

'Clearly because those are words which were not contained in the page in question.'

'Then why has he not indicated the book?'

'Your native shrewdness, my dear Watson, that innate cunning which is the delight of your friends, would surely prevent you from enclosing cipher and message in the same envelope. Should it miscarry you are undone. As it is, both have to go wrong before any harm comes from it. Our second post is now overdue, and I shall be surprised if it does not bring us either a further letter of explanation or, as is more probable, the very volume to which these figures refer.'

Holmes's calculation was fulfilled within a very few minutes by the appearance of Billy, the page, with the very letter which we were expecting.

'The same writing,' remarked Holmes, as he opened the envelope, 'and actually signed,' he added, in an exultant voice, as he unfolded the epistle. 'Come, we are getting on, Watson.'

His brow clouded, however, as he glanced over the contents.

'Dear me, this is very disappointing! I fear, Watson, that all our expectations come to nothing. I trust that the man Porlock will come to no harm.

' "Dear Mr Holmes," he says, "I will go no further in this matter. It is too dangerous. He suspects me. I can see that he suspects me. He came to me quite unexpectedly after I had actually addressed this envelope with the intention of sending you the key to the cipher. I was able to cover it up. If he had seen it, it would have gone hard with me. But I read suspicion in his eyes. Please burn the cipher message, which can now be of no use to you.—FRED PORLOCK." '

Holmes sat for some little time twisting this letter between his fingers, and frowning, as he stared into the fire.

'After all,' he said at last, 'there may be nothing in it. It may be only his guilty conscience. Knowing himself to be a traitor, he may have read the accusation in the other's eyes.'

'The other being, I presume, Professor Moriarty?'

'No less. When any of that party talk about "he," you know whom they mean. There is one predominant "he" for all of them.'

'But what can he do?'

'Hum! That's a large question. When you have one of the first brains of Europe up against you and all the powers of darkness at his back, there are infinite possibilities. Anyhow, friend Porlock is evidently scared out of his senses. Kindly compare the writing in the note with that upon its envelope, which was done, he tells us, before this ill-omened visit. The one is clear and firm; the other hardly legible.'

'Why did he write at all? Why did he not simply drop it?'

'Because he feared I would make some inquiry after him in that case, and possibly bring trouble on him.'

'No doubt,' said I. 'Of course'—I had picked up the original cipher message and was bending my brows over it—'it's pretty maddening to think that an important secret may lie here on this slip of paper, and that it is beyond human power to penetrate it.'

Sherlock Holmes had pushed away his untasted breakfast and lit the unsavoury pipe which was the companion of his deepest meditations.

'I wonder!' said he, leaning back and staring at the ceiling. 'Perhaps there are points which have escaped your Machiavellian intellect. Let us consider the problem in the light of pure **9** reason. This man's reference is to a book. That is our point of departure.'

'A somewhat vague one.'

9 *Machiavellian.* Holmes refers to Niccolo Machiavelli, 1469–1527, Italian author and statesman. His most famous book, *The Prince*, was the first objective, scientific analysis of the methods by which political power is obtained and kept.

"WHAT DO YOU MAKE OF IT, HOLMES?"

This illustration by Frank Wiles, captioned "The Cipher—and the man who solved it," appeared as the frontispiece to the first installment of *The Valley of Fear* when it appeared in the *Strand Magazine*, September, 1914. Of this illustration, the late James Montgomery wrote (*A Study in Pictures*): "This striking close-up of the Master surely ranks with the best and most famous of all his portrayals, from Paget to Steele." And he added: "Wiles of course adheres to the accepted authentic mood, but without sacrificing any of that magic he develops a wealth of detail far exceeding any previous artist." And Walter Klinefelter has written of this frontispiece (*Sherlock Holmes in Portrait and Profile*): "If Wiles had not made another drawing for *The Valley of Fear*, he would still have to be given credit for a notable contribution to the portraiture of Sherlock Holmes."

10 *Even if I accepted the compliment for my-self.* "Surely . . . Holmes had a copy of the Bible —not of any inferior edition, either, but, aware as we are of his philological interest and his pre-occupation with 'Chaldee' ["The Adventure of the Devil's Foot"], of none other than the cele-brated Complutensian Polyglot Bible edited under the auspices of Cardinal Ximenes between 1514 and 1517, and printed in Hebrew, Chaldee, Greek and Latin—the earliest, indeed, of the great Poly-glots. Yes, Holmes had probably acquired a treasure . . . [but a treasure which would] have proved of no aid in deciphering Porlock's message."— Madeleine B. Stern, "Sherlock Holmes: Rare Book Collector."

11 ' "*Bradshaw*"!' Bradshaw's, now, alas, no more, was the guide to British railways conceived by George Bradshaw, 1801–1853, an engraver of maps and plans of towns. The first issues of a northern and southern Bradshaw were published on Octo-ber 19, 1839, followed in January, 1840, by a unit-ing of the two. Of Bradshaw, R. J. Cruikshank wrote in *Roaring Century:* ". . . the creation of a Quaker who offered it as a piece of much-needed public service. For at least a hundred years it was to follow the Quaker custom of naming the months, First Month for January, Second Month for Feb-ruary and so on. At a time when scores of inde-pendent [railway] lines were sprouting, with great gaps between connections, the production of a guide was a miracle of patience. . . . The humorous journalists could not have taken greater delight in its obscurity of style and its esoteric allusiveness. . . . The hands, daggers and other printing devices in which Bradshaw indulged suggested the warn-ings of a secret society. . . . Comic Bradshaws were brought out to the further confusion of innocent minds. The gentle philanthropist must have been mildly puzzled at the Press he got—but Bradshaw survived to be an honoured British institution."

12 *inadmissible for the same reason.* Mr. Robert Winthrop Adams has suggested ("John H. Wat-son, M.D., Characterologist") that this "British Webster" was the *Comprehensive English Diction-ary;* London, Edinburgh, and Glasgow, 1868, by John Ogilvie, LL.D., Scottish lexicographer. But it is surprising, as Mr. Howard R. Schorin pointed out in his essay on "Cryptography in the Canon," that Holmes eliminated the dictionary: "it is pre-cisely this book which has been used for such mes-sages since the Revolutionary and Napoleonic wars, when the numbered-source code was most popular and in use. Fletcher Pratt, in *Secret and Urgent,* sums up the matter: 'Theoretically, any book will do, but as one must have access imme-diately to any word he wishes to use, only the dic-tionary will serve his purpose.'"

'Let us see, then, if we can narrow it down. As I focus my mind upon it, it seems rather less impenetrable. What indica-tions have we as to this book?'

'None.'

'Well, well, it is surely not quite so bad as that. The cipher message begins with a large 534, does it not? We may take it as a working hypothesis that 534 is the particular page to which the cipher refers. So our book has already become a *large* book, which is surely something gained. What other indications have we as to the nature of this large book? The next sign is C2. What do you make of that, Watson?'

'Chapter the second, no doubt.'

'Hardly that, Watson. You will, I am sure, agree with me that if the page be given the number of the chapter is im-material. Also that if page 534 only finds us in the second chapter, the length of the first one must have been really intolerable.'

'Column!' I cried.

'Brilliant, Watson. You are scintillating this morning. If it is not column, then I am very much deceived. So now, you see, we begin to visualize a large book, printed in double columns, which are each of a considerable length, since one of the words is numbered in the document as the two hundred and ninety-third. Have we reached the limits of what reason can supply?'

'I fear that we have.'

'Surely you do yourself an injustice. One more coruscation, my dear Watson. Yet another brain-wave. Had the volume been an unusual one he would have sent it to me. Instead of that he had intended, before his plans were nipped, to send me the clue in this envelope. He says so in his note. This would seem to indicate that the book is one which he thought that I would have no difficulty in finding for myself. He had it, and he imagined that I would have it too. In short, Watson, it is a very common book.'

'What you say certainly sounds plausible.'

'So we have contracted our field of search to a large book, printed in double columns and in common use.'

'The Bible!' I cried, triumphantly.

'Good, Watson, good! But not, if I may say so, quite good **10** enough. Even if I accepted the compliment for myself, I could hardly name any volume which would be less likely to lie at the elbow of one of Moriarty's associates. Besides, the editions of Holy Writ are so numerous that he could hardly suppose that two copies would have the same pagination. This is clearly a book which is standardized. He knows for certain that his page 534 will exactly agree with my page 534.'

'But very few books would correspond with that.'

'Exactly. Therein lies our salvation. Our search is narrowed down to standardized books which anyone may be supposed to possess.'

11 ' "Bradshaw"!'

'There are difficulties, Watson. The vocabulary of "Brad-shaw" is nervous and terse, but limited. The selection of words would hardly lend itself to the sending of general messages. We will eliminate "Bradshaw." The dictionary is, **12** I fear, inadmissible for the same reason. What, then, is left?'

'An almanack.'

'Excellent, Watson! I am very much mistaken if you have not touched the spot. An almanack! Let us consider the claims of *Whitaker's Almanack*. It is in common use. It has the **13** requisite number of pages. It is in double column. Though reserved in its earlier vocabulary, it becomes, if I remember right, quite garrulous towards the end.' He picked the volume from his desk. 'Here is page 534, column two, a substantial block of print dealing, I perceive, with the trade and resources of British India. Jot down the words, Watson. Number thirteen is "Mahratta." Not, I fear, a very auspicious beginning. **14** Number one hundred and twenty-seven is "Government," which at least makes sense, though somewhat irrelevant to ourselves and Professor Moriarty. Now let us try again. What does the Mahratta Government do? Alas! the next word is "pigs'-bristles." We are undone, my good Watson! It is finished.'

He had spoken in jesting vein, but the twitching of his bushy eyebrows bespoke his disappointment and irritation. **15** I sat helpless and unhappy, staring into the fire. A long silence was broken by a sudden exclamation from Holmes, who dashed at a cupboard, from which he emerged with a second yellow-covered volume in his hand.

'We pay the price, Watson, for being too up-to-date,' he cried. 'We are before our time, and suffer the usual penalties. Being the seventh of January, we have very properly laid in **16** the new almanack. It is more than likely that Porlock took his message from the old one. No doubt he would have told us so had his letter of explanation been written. Now let us see what page 534 has in store for us. Number thirteen is "There," which is much more promising. Number one hundred and twenty-seven is "is"—"There is"'—Holmes's eyes were gleaming with excitement, and his thin, nervous fingers twitched as he counted the words—'"danger." Ha! ha! Capital! Put that down, Watson. "There is danger—may—come—very—soon—one." Then we have the name "Douglas" —"rich—country—now—at—Birlstone—House—Birlstone —confidence—is—pressing." There, Watson! what do you think of pure reason and its fruits? If the greengrocer had such a thing as a laurel-wreath I should send Billy round for it.'

I was staring at the strange message which I had scrawled, as he deciphered it, upon a sheet of foolscap on my knee.

'What a queer, scrambling way of expressing his meaning!' said I.

'On the contrary, he has done quite remarkably well,' said Holmes. 'When you search a single column for words with which to express your meaning, you can hardly expect to get everything you want. You are bound to leave something to the intelligence of your correspondent. The purport is perfectly clear. Some devilry is intended against one Douglas, whoever he may be, residing as stated, a rich country gentleman. He is sure—"confidence" was as near as he could get to "confident"—that it is pressing. There is our result, and a very workmanlike little bit of analysis it was.'

Holmes had the impersonal joy of the true artist in his better work, even as he mourned darkly when it fell below the high level to which he aspired. He was still chuckling over his success when Billy swung open the door and Inspector MacDonald of Scotland Yard was ushered into the room.

Those were the early days at the end of the 'eighties, when **17**

13 Whitaker's Almanack. Britain's best-known almanac, similar to the *World Almanac* in the United States, originally compiled by Joseph Whitaker, 1820–1895.

14 "*Mahratta*." A confederation of chieftains in central India, broken up by the British in 1818.

15 *his bushy eyebrows*. A detail which adds to our picture of Holmes.

16 *the seventh of January*. A Saturday in 1888, our year for the adventure of *The Valley of Fear*.

17 *Those were the early days at the end of the 'eighties*. Eighteen-eighty-nine would appear to be the latest possible date for the adventure, if we are to credit Watson's statement. Of the chronologists who do accept it (and we shall see that there is a school which does not) Bell, Smith, and Starrett say 1887; Baring-Gould, Folsom, Pattrick, Stephens, and Zeisler say 1888; Christ and Morley say 1889.

18 *Aberdonian.* Relating to or characteristic of Aberdeen, Scotland.

19 *helped him to attain success.* It is a great pity that Watson did not see fit to chronicle either of these cases. Perhaps they included some of the unrecorded cases mentioned by Watson—the Camberwell poisoning case ("The Five Orange Pips"), for example; Porlock posted his cipher message to Holmes from Camberwell.

20 *this morning.'* Although Inspector MacDonald states that Douglas was murdered "this morning" (that is, on the morning of the seventh of January), we are told in the next chapter that the first alarm of murder went out "at eleven-forty-five" on the preceding night, the sixth.

Alec MacDonald was far from having attained the national fame which he has now achieved. He was a young but trusted member of the detective force, who had distinguished himself in several cases which had been entrusted to him. His tall, bony figure gave promise of exceptional physical strength, while his great cranium and deep-set, lustrous eyes spoke no less clearly of the keen intelligence which twinkled out from behind his bushy eyebrows. He was a silent, precise man, with

18 a dour nature and a hard Aberdonian accent. Twice already
19 in his career had Holmes helped him to attain success, his own sole reward being the intellectual joy of the problem. For this reason the affection and respect of the Scotchman for his amateur colleague were profound, and he showed them by the frankness with which he consulted Holmes in every difficulty. Mediocrity knows nothing higher than itself, but talent instantly recognizes genius, and MacDonald had talent enough for his profession to enable him to perceive that there was no humiliation in seeking the assistance of one who already stood alone in Europe, both in his gifts and in his experience. Holmes was not prone to friendship, but he was tolerant of the big Scotchman, and smiled at the sight of him.

'You are an early bird, Mr Mac,' said he. 'I wish you luck with your worm. I fear this means that there is some mischief afoot.'

'If you said "hope" instead of "fear" it would be nearer the truth, I'm thinking, Mr Holmes,' the inspector answered, with a knowing grin. 'Well, maybe a wee nip would keep out the raw morning chill. No, I won't smoke, I thank you. I'll have to be pushing on my way, for the early hours of a case are the precious ones, as no man knows better than your own self. But—but——'

The inspector had stopped suddenly, and was staring with a look of absolute amazement at a paper upon the table. It was the sheet upon which I had scrawled the enigmatic message.

'Douglas!' he stammered. 'Birlstone! What's this, Mr Holmes? Man, it's witchcraft! Where in the name of all that is wonderful did you get those names?'

'It is a cipher that Dr Watson and I have had occasion to solve. But why—what's amiss with the names?'

The inspector looked from one to the other of us in dazed astonishment.

'Just this,' said he, 'that Mr Douglas, of Birlstone Manor
20 House, was horribly murdered this morning.'

"WHAT'S THIS, MR. HOLMES? MAN, IT'S WITCHCRAFT!"

This is one of the twelve illustrations drawn by Arthur I. Keller for Associated Sunday Magazines, in which *The Valley of Fear* appeared in the United States between September 20 and November 22, 1914. Keller here exaggerates Watson's slowness of mentality (as compared to the swiftness of mentality of Holmes) into almost moronic proportions—aptly described by the late Edmund Pearson as "boobus Britannicus" ("Sherlock Holmes Among the Illustrators"). The late James Montgomery wrote of Keller (*A Study in Pictures*): His "pictures vary in quality, some being excellent, although none of the five depicting the English phase of the tale succeed in capturing the subtle Sherlockian mood. It is when the story shifts to America that he is most successful. There he is not hampered by the need for English flavor, and his portrayal of the rough men and primitive conditions in Vermissa Valley becomes very realistic indeed." Frank Wiles illustrated this same scene for the *Strand Magazine*, September, 1914.

It was one of those dramatic moments for which my friend existed. It would be an over-statement to say that he was shocked or even excited by the amazing announcement. Without having a tinge of cruelty in his singular composition, he was undoubtedly callous from long over-stimulation. Yet, if his emotions were dulled, his intellectual perceptions were exceedingly active. There was no trace then of the horror which I had myself felt at this curt declaration, but his face showed rather the quiet and interested composure of the chemist who sees the crystals falling into position from his over-saturated solution.

'Remarkable!' said he; 'remarkable!'

'You don't seem surprised.'

'Interested, Mr Mac, but hardly surprised. Why should I be surprised? I receive an anonymous communication from a quarter which I know to be important, warning me that danger threatens a certain person. Within an hour I learn that this danger has actually materialized, and that the person is dead. I am interested, but, as you observe, I am not surprised.'

In a few short sentences he explained to the inspector the facts about the letter and the cipher. MacDonald sat with his chin on his hands, and his great sandy eyebrows bunched into a yellow tangle.

'I was going down to Birlstone this morning,' said he. 'I had come to ask you if you cared to come with me—you and your friend here. But from what you say we might perhaps be doing better work in London.'

'I rather think not,' said Holmes.

'Hang it all, Mr Holmes!' cried the inspector. 'The papers will be full of the Birlstone Mystery in a day or two, but where's the mystery if there is a man in London who prophesied the crime before ever it occurred? We have only to lay our hands on that man and the rest will follow.'

'No doubt, Mr Mac. But how did you propose to lay your hands on the so-called Porlock?'

MacDonald turned over the letter which Holmes had handed him.

'Posted in Camberwell—that doesn't help us much. Name, you say, is assumed. Not much to go on, certainly. Didn't you say that you have sent him money?'

'Twice.'

'And how?'

'In notes to Camberwell post-office.'

'Did you never trouble to see who called for them?'

'No.'

The inspector looked surprised and a little shocked.

'Why not?'

'Because I always keep faith. I had promised when he first wrote that I would not try to trace him.'

'You think there is someone behind him?'

'I *know* there is.'

'This Professor that I have heard you mention?'

'Exactly.'

Inspector MacDonald smiled, and his eyelid quivered as he glanced towards me.

21 *the C.I.D.* The Criminal Investigation Department of Scotland Yard.

22 *Jean Baptiste Greuze.*' French genre and portrait painter, 1725–1805.

"YES, I SAW THE PICTURE—A YOUNG WOMAN WITH HER HEAD ON HER HANDS, PEEKING AT YOU SIDEWAYS."

This would seem to be the painting now in the National Galleries of Scotland (Catalogue No. NG437) described as *Girl with Arms Folded*.

'I won't conceal from you, Mr Holmes, that we think in the **21** C.I.D. that you have a weê bit of a bee in your bonnet over this Professor. I made some inquiries myself about the matter. He seems to be a very respectable, learned, and talented sort of man.'

'I'm glad you've got as far as to recognize the talent.'

'Man, you can't but recognize it. After I heard your view, I made it my business to see him. I had a chat with him on eclipses—how the talk got that way I canna think—but he had out a reflector lantern and a globe and made it all clear in a minute. He lent me a book, but I don't mind saying that it was a bit above my head, though I had a good Aberdeen upbringing. He'd have made a grand meenister, with his thin face and grey hair and solemn-like way of talking. When he put his hand on my shoulder as we were parting, it was like a father's blessing before you go out into the cold, cruel world.'

Holmes chuckled, and rubbed his hands.

'Great!' he said; 'great! Tell me, friend MacDonald; this pleasing and touching interview was, I suppose, in the Professor's study?'

'That's so.'

'A fine room, is it not?'

'Very fine—very handsome indeed, Mr Holmes.'

'You sat in front of his writing-desk?'

'Just so.'

'Sun in your eyes and his face in the shadow?'

'Well, it was evening, but I mind that the lamp was turned on my face.'

'It would be. Did you happen to observe a picture over the Professor's head?'

'I don't miss much, Mr Holmes. Maybe I learned that from you. Yes, I saw the picture—a young woman with her head on her hands, keeking at you sideways.'

'That painting was by Jean Baptiste Greuze.'

The inspector endeavoured to look interested.

22 'Jean Baptiste Greuze,' Holmes continued, joining his finger-tips and leaning well back in his chair, 'was a French artist who flourished between the years 1750 and 1800. I allude, of course, to his working career. Modern criticism has more than endorsed the high opinion formed of him by his contemporaries.'

The inspector's eyes grew abstracted.

'Hadn't we better——' he said.

'We are doing so,' Holmes interrupted. 'All that I am saying has a very direct and vital bearing upon what you have called the Birlstone Mystery. In fact, it may in a sense be called the very centre of it.'

MacDonald smiled feebly, and looked appealingly to me.

'Your thoughts move a bit too quick for me. Mr Holmes. You leave out a link or two, and I can't get over the gap. What in the whole wide world can be the connection between this dead painting man and the affair at Birlstone?'

'All knowledge comes useful to the detective,' remarked Holmes. 'Even the trivial fact that in the year 1865 a picture by Greuze, entitled "La Jeune Fille à l'agneau," fetched not **23** less than four thousand pounds—at the Portalis sale, may start a train of reflection in your mind.'

It was clear that it did. The inspector looked honestly interested.

'I may remind you,' Holmes continued, 'that the Professor's salary can be ascertained in several trustworthy books of reference. It is seven hundred a year.'   **24**

'Then how could he buy——'

'Quite so. How could he?'

'Aye, that's remarkable,' said the inspector, thoughtfully. 'Talk away, Mr Holmes. I'm just loving it. It's fine.'

Holmes smiled. He was always warmed by genuine admiration—the characteristic of the real artist.

'What about Birlstone?' he asked.

'We've time yet,' said the inspector, glancing at his watch. 'I've a cab at the door, and it won't take us twenty minutes to Victoria. But about this picture—I thought you **25** told me once, Mr Holmes, that you had never met Professor Moriarty.'

'No, I never have.'

'Then how do you know about his rooms?'

'Ah, that's another matter. I have been three times in his rooms, twice waiting for him under different pretexts and leaving before he came. Once—well, I can hardly tell about the once to an official detective. It was on the last occasion that I took the liberty of running over his papers, with the most unexpected results.'

'You found something compromising?'

'Absolutely nothing. That was what amazed me. However, you have now seen the point of the picture. It shows him to be a very wealthy man. How did he acquire wealth? He is unmarried. His younger brother is a station-master in the West of England. His chair is worth seven hundred a year. And he owns a Greuze.'

'Well?'

'Surely the inference is plain.'

'You mean that he has a great income, and that he must earn it in an illegal fashion?'

'Exactly. Of course, I have other reasons for thinking so—dozens of exiguous threads which lead vaguely up towards the centre of the web where the poisonous motionless creature is lurking. I only mention the Greuze because it brings the matter within the range of your own observation.'

'Well, Mr Holmes, I admit that what you say is interesting. It's more than interesting—it's just wonderful. But let us have it a little clearer if you can. Is it forgery, coining, burglary? Where does the money come from?'

'Have you ever read of Jonathan Wild?'   **26**

'Well, the name has a familiar sound. Someone in a novel, was he not? I don't take much stock of detectives in novels—chaps that do things and never let you see how they do them. That's just inspiration, not business.'

'Jonathan Wild wasn't a detective, and he wasn't in a novel. He was a master criminal, and he lived last century—1750 or thereabouts.'

'Then he's no use to me. I'm a practical man.'

'Mr Mac, the most practical thing that ever you did in your life would be to shut yourself up for three months and read twelve hours a day at the annals of crime. Everything comes in circles, even Professor Moriarty. Jonathan Wild was the hidden force of the London criminals, to whom he sold his brains and his organization on a fifteen per cent. commission. The old wheel turns and the same spoke comes up. It's all

23 *at the Portalis sale.* In the manuscript, the *Strand Magazine*, the first American edition of *The Valley of Fear* and the Doubleday omnibus, the painting fetched "one million and two hundred thousand francs—more than forty thousand pounds."

In fact, according to the *Times* of London (Literary Supplement, July 1, 1960) "the sale-room price of a Greuze has never exceeded the 129,000 francs given for *Les Oeufs Cassées* at the Demidoff sale in 1870."

Let us say that *La Jeune Fille à l'agneau* sold for some $20,000 U.S.

Greuze would seem to have painted at least five different pictures of a young girl with a lamb: 1) *L'Amitié* from the Marion Davis collection in the Los Angeles County Museum; 2) *L'Amitié* in the Mary Frick Jacobs collection of the Baltimore Art Museum; 3) a painting in the Wallace collection in London; 4) a painting in the National Art Gallery in London; 5) a painting in the Walters Art Gallery in Baltimore. According to Mr. Thomas L. Stix ("Who's Afraid of the Big Bad Moriarty") a picture, supposedly by Greuze, of a girl and a lamb was actually sold to Benjamin Disraeli for £1,800 at the Portalis sale of 1865. The picture proved to be a forgery; Portalis refunded the £1,800 to Disraeli and the picture "after Greuze" was subsequently sold "as is" for £45.

24 *seven hundred a year.'* About $3,500.

25 *Victoria.* The old Victoria Station of the London, Brighton and South Coast Railway and the London, Chatham and Dover Railway, first opened to the public on October 1, 1860. The original station cost £675,000 and covered eleven acres.

26 *Jonathan Wild?'* English artisan, fence, and informer. Holmes was mistaken in saying that Wild lived about 1750: he was hanged on May 24, 1725. Holmes was also mistaken in saying that Wild "wasn't in a novel": Wild was the subject of a satire by Fielding and a romance by Defoe.

27 '*Six thousand a year*. About $30,000.

been done before and will be again. I'll tell you one or two things about Moriarty which may interest you.'

'You'll interest me right enough.'

'I happen to know who is the first link in his chain—a chain with this Napoleon-gone-wrong at one end and a hundred broken fighting men, pickpockets, blackmailers, and card-sharpers at the other, with every sort of crime in between. His chief of the staff is Colonel Sebastian Moran, as aloof and guarded and inaccessible to the law as himself. What do you think he pays him?'

'I'd like to hear.'

27   'Six thousand a year. That's paying for brains, you see— the American business principle. I learned that detail quite by chance. It's more than the Prime Minister gets. That gives you an idea of Moriarty's gains and of the scale on which he works. Another point. I made it my business to hunt down some of Moriarty's cheques lately—just common innocent cheques that he pays his household bills with. They were drawn on six different banks. Does that make any impression on your mind?'

'Queer, certainly. But what do you gather from it?'

'That he wanted no gossip about his wealth. No single man should know what he had. I have no doubt that he has twenty banking accounts—the bulk of his fortune abroad in the Deutsche Bank or the Crédit Lyonnais as likely as not. Some time when you have a year or two to spare I commend to you the study of Professor Moriarty.'

Inspector MacDonald had grown steadily more impressed as the conversation proceeded. He had lost himself in his interest. Now his practical Scotch intelligence brought him back with a snap to the matter in hand.

'He can keep, anyhow,' said he. 'You've got us side-tracked with your interesting anecdotes, Mr Holmes. What really counts is your remark that there is some connection between the Professor and the crime. That you get from the warning received through the man Porlock. Can we for our present practical needs get any farther than that?'

'We may form some conception as to the motives of the crime. It is, as I gather from your original remarks, an in-explicable, or at least an unexplained, murder. Now, pre-suming that the source of the crime is as we suspect it to be, there might be two different motives. In the first place, I may tell you that Moriarty rules with a rod of iron over his people. His discipline is tremendous. There is only one punishment in his code. It is death. Now, we might suppose that this mur-dered man—this Douglas, whose approaching fate was known by one of the arch-criminal's subordinates—had in some way betrayed the chief. His punishment followed and would be known to all, if only to put the fear of death into them.'

'Well, that is one suggestion, Mr Holmes.'

'The other is that it has been engineered by Moriarty in the ordinary course of business. Was there any robbery?'

'I have not heard.'

'If so it would, of course, be against the first hypothesis and in favour of the second. Moriarty may have been engaged to engineer it on a promise of part spoils, or he may have been paid so much down to manage it. Either is possible. But, whichever it may be, or if it is some third combination, it is down at Birlstone that we must seek the solution. I know our man too well to suppose that he has left anything up here which may lead us to him.'

'Then to Birlstone we must go!' cried MacDonald, jumping from his chair. 'My word! it's later than I thought. I can give you gentlemen five minutes for preparation, and that is all.'

'And ample for us both,' said Holmes, as he sprang up and hastened to change from his dressing-gown to his coat. 'While we are on our way, Mr Mac, I will ask you to be good enough to tell me all about it.'

'All about it,' proved to be disappointingly little, and yet there was enough to assure us that the case before us might well be worthy of the expert's closest attention. He brightened and rubbed his thin hands together as he listened to the meagre but remarkable details. A long series of sterile weeks lay behind us, and here, at last, there was a fitting **28** object for those remarkable powers which, like all special gifts, become irksome to their owner when they are not in use. That razor brain blunted and rusted with inaction. Sherlock Holmes's eyes glistened, his pale cheeks took a warmer hue, and his whole eager face shone with an inward light when the call for work reached him. Leaning forward in the cab, he listened intently to MacDonald's short sketch of the problem which awaited us in Sussex. The inspector was himself dependent, as he explained to us, upon a scribbled account forwarded to him by the milk train in the early hours of the morning. White Mason, the local officer, was a personal friend, and hence MacDonald had been notified very much more promptly than is usual at Scotland Yard when provincials need their assistance. It is a very cold scent upon which the Metropolitan expert is generally asked to run.

'Dear Inspector MacDonald,' said the letter which he read to us, 'official requisition for your services is in separate envelope. This is for your private eye. Wire me what train in the morning you can get for Birlstone, and I will meet it— or have it met if I am too occupied. This case is a snorter. Don't waste a moment in getting started. If you can bring Mr Holmes, please do so, for he will find something after his own heart. You would think the whole thing had been fixed up for theatrical effect, if there wasn't a dead man in the middle of it. My word, it *is* a snorter!'

'Your friend seems to be no fool,' remarked Holmes.

'No, sir; White Mason is a very live man, if I am any judge.'

'Well, have you anything more?'

'Only that he will give us every detail when we meet.'

'Then how did you get at Mr Douglas and the fact that he had been horribly murdered?'

'That was in the enclosed official report. It didn't say "horrible." That's not a recognized official term. It gave the name John Douglas. It mentioned that his injuries had been in the head, from the discharge of a shot-gun. It also mentioned the hour of the alarm, which was close on to midnight last night. It added that the case was undoubtedly one of murder, but that no arrest had been made, and that the case was one which presented some very perplexing and extraordinary features. That's absolutely all we have at present, Mr Holmes.'

'Then, with your permission, we will leave it at that, Mr Mac. The temptation to form premature theories upon in-

28 *A long series of sterile weeks lay behind us.* "The probability . . . is that an editorial hand has touched up (not very successfully) *The Valley of Fear*," Mr. T. S. Blakeney wrote in *Sherlock Holmes: Fact or Fiction?*, "for we find Watson saying that 'a long series of sterile weeks' lay behind this adventure, which is clearly untrue, as 'The Adventure of the Blue Carbuncle' was less than a fortnight before . . ."

LEANING FORWARD IN THE CAB, HE LISTENED INTENTLY TO MACDONALD'S SHORT SKETCH OF THE PROBLEM WHICH AWAITED US IN SUSSEX.

Illustration by Frank Wiles for the *Strand Magazine*, September, 1914.

29 *Weald*. A district in Kent, Sussex, and Surrey, extending along the coast from near Dover to Beachy Head, and reaching inward across the Downs to the east part of Hampshire.

30 *Tunbridge Wells*. A municipal borough in Kent. It became fashionable after chalybeate springs were discovered there in 1606.

31 *the time of the first Crusade*. 1095–1099.

32 *Hugo de Capus*. Mr. Bell found the mention of this name "the only really puzzling feature of the narrative." "The name," he wrote in "Three Identifications," "seems not to have existed in England, or, indeed anywhere nearer than the province of Carniola in the present kingdom of Yugoslavia."

To this Dr. Julian Wolff added (*Practical Handbook of Sherlockian Heraldry*): "Burke's *Visitations* mentions 'Hugo comes,' a nephew and companion of William the Conqueror. (Descent from Hugh Capet, King of France, may account for the de Capus.) Hugo's father, the half brother of William, was awarded seven hundred manors and it is not unlikely that the Red King, William Rufus, the Conqueror's son, granted Birlstone to Hugo who built a fortalice there. Eleventh-century heraldry is obscure, but Watson seemed to be familiar with the lion of de Capus—or perhaps he confused it with 'the rampant' lion of Des Champs, which came from France in 1746, not 1066."

sufficient data is the bane of our profession. I can only see two things for certain at present: a great brain in London and a dead man in Sussex. It's the chain between that we are going to trace.'

◆

3 ◆ THE TRAGEDY OF BIRLSTONE
◆

And now for a moment I will ask leave to remove my own insignificant personality and to describe events which occurred before we arrived upon the scene by the light of knowledge which came to us afterwards. Only in this way can I make the reader appreciate the people concerned and the strange setting in which their fate was cast.

The village of Birlstone is a small and very ancient cluster of half-timbered cottages on the northern border of the county of Sussex. For centuries it had remained unchanged, but within the last few years its picturesque appearance and situation have attracted a number of well-to-do residents, whose villas peep out from the woods around. These woods are locally supposed to be the extreme fringe of the great **29** Weald forest, which thins away until it reaches the northern chalk downs. A number of small shops have come into being to meet the wants of the increased population, so that there seems some prospect that Birlstone may soon grow from an ancient village into a modern town. It is the centre for a con- **30** siderable area of country, since Tunbridge Wells, the nearest place of importance, is ten or twelve miles to the eastward, over the borders of Kent.

About half a mile from the town, standing in an old park famous for its huge beech trees, is the ancient Manor House of Birlstone. Part of this venerable building dates back to the **31-32** time of the first Crusade, when Hugo de Capus built a fortalice in the centre of the estate, which had been granted to him by the Red King. This was destroyed by fire in 1543, and some of its smoke-blackened corner-stones were used when, in

THE LATE JAMES MONTGOMERY'S MAP OF GROOMBRIDGE PLACE

The late James Montgomery based his identification of "Birlstone Manor" as Groombridge House on a presentation copy of *The Valley of Fear* in which Conan Doyle wrote: "With all kind of remembrance from Arthur Conan Doyle who hopes you have pleasant memories of Groombridge House which is the old house herein described. June 22/21." Said Mr. Montgomery: "The village of Groombridge, situated on the northerly slopes of Ashdown Forest, once famous as a royal hunting ground, is only about three miles from Tunbridge Wells. . . . The village is located in two counties, the newer half (known today as the New Town) being in Sussex, and the older part (the Old Town), including Groombridge Place itself, lying in Kent. . . . We learn from the short account (*St. John the Evangelist, Groombridge, Kent*, by B. W. Shepherd-Walwyn) purchasable for sixpence . . . from the local tobacconist (now one L. V. Narramore) that a Saxon noble named Gromen built a castle here and surrounded it with a moat. . . . The castle was equipped with a drawbridge, which may have given rise to the name 'Groombridge.'"

Jacobean times, a brick country house rose upon the ruins **33** of the feudal castle. The Manor House, with its many gables and its small, diamond-paned windows, was still much as the builder had left it in the early seventeenth century. Of the double moats which had guarded its more warlike predecessor the outer had been allowed to dry up, and served the humble function of a kitchen garden. The inner one was still there, and lay, forty feet in breadth, though now only a few feet in depth, round the whole house. A small stream fed it and continued beyond it, so that the sheet of water, though turbid, was never ditch-like or unhealthy. The ground-floor windows were within a foot of the surface of the water. The only approach to the house was over a drawbridge, the chains and windlass of which had long been rusted and broken. The latest tenants of the Manor House had, however, with characteristic energy, set this right, and the drawbridge was not only capable of being raised, but actually was raised every evening and lowered every morning. By thus renewing the custom of the old feudal days the Manor House was converted into an island during the night—a fact which had a very direct bearing upon the mystery which was soon to engage the attention of all England.

The house had been untenanted for some years, and was threatening to moulder into a picturesque decay when the Douglases took possession of it. This family consisted of only two individuals, John Douglas and his wife. Douglas was a remarkable man both in character and in person; in age he may have been about fifty, with a strong-jawed, rugged face, a grizzling moustache, peculiarly keen grey eyes, and a wiry, vigorous figure which had lost nothing of the strength and activity of youth. He was cheery and genial to all, but somewhat offhand in his manners, giving the impression that he had seen life in social strata on some far lower horizon than the county society of Sussex. Yet, though looked at with some curiosity and reserve by his more cultivated neighbours he soon acquired a great popularity among the villagers, subscribing handsomely to all local objects, and attending their smoking concerts and other functions, where, having a remarkably rich tenor voice, he was always ready to oblige with an excellent song. He appeared to have plenty of money, which was said to have been gained in the Californian gold-

33 *in Jacobean times.* In the reign of James I of England (1603–1625) and sometimes of James II (1685–1688).

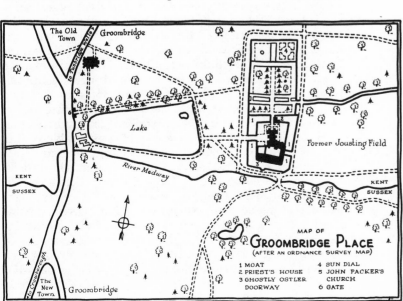

MAP OF
GROOMBRIDGE PLACE
(AFTER AN ORDNANCE SURVEY MAP)

1 MOAT   4 SUN DIAL
2 PRIEST'S HOUSE   5 JOHN PACKER'S
3 GHOSTLY OSTLER   CHURCH
  DOORWAY   6 GATE

34 *Hampstead.* A metropolitan borough four miles northwest of the City. It stands upon one of the highest hills around London. The town occupies its southern slopes, the Heath its summit—it is 443 miles above sea level. The name is clearly derived from *ham or hame*, a home, and *steede*, a place, and has consequently the same meaning as "homestead." For a Holmes and Watson adventure that took place in Hampstead, see "Charles Augustus Milverton."

fields, and it was clear from his own talk and that of his wife that he had spent a part of his life in America. The good impression which had been produced by his generosity and by his democratic manners was increased by a reputation gained for utter indifference to danger. Though a wretched rider, he turned out at every meet, and took the most amazing falls in his determination to hold his own with the best. When the vicarage caught fire he distinguished himself also by the fearlessness with which he re-entered the building to save property, after the local fire brigade had given it up as impossible. Thus it came about that John Douglas, of the Manor House, had within five years won himself quite a reputation in Birlstone.

His wife, too, was popular with those who had made her acquaintance, though, after the English fashion, the callers upon a stranger who settled in the county without introductions were few and far between. This mattered the less to her as she was retiring by disposition and very much absorbed, to all appearance, in her husband and her domestic duties. It was known that she was an English lady who had met Mr Douglas in London, he being at that time a widower. She was a beautiful woman, tall, dark, and slender, some twenty years younger than her husband, a disparity which seemed in no wise to mar the contentment of their family life. It was remarked sometimes, however, by those who knew them best that the confidence between the two did not appear to be complete, since the wife was either very reticent about her husband's past life or else, as seemed more likely, was very imperfectly informed about it. It had also been noted and commented upon by a few observant people that there were signs sometimes of some nerve-strain upon the part of Mrs Douglas, and that she would display acute uneasiness if her absent husband should ever be particularly late in his return. On a quiet countryside, where all gossip is welcome, this weakness of the lady of the Manor House did not pass without remark, and it bulked larger upon people's memory when the events arose which gave it a very special significance.

There was yet another individual whose residence under that roof was, it is true, only an intermittent one, but whose presence at the time of the strange happenings which will now be narrated brought his name prominently before the public. This was Cecil James Barker, of Hales Lodge, Hamp-**34** stead. Cecil Barker's tall, loose-jointed figure was a familiar one in the main street of Birlstone village, for he was a frequent and welcome visitor at the Manor House. He was the more noticed as being the only friend of the past unknown life of Mr Douglas who was ever seen in his new English surroundings. Barker was himself an undoubted Englishman, but by his remarks it was clear that he had first known Douglas in America, and had there lived on intimate terms with him. He appeared to be a man of considerable wealth, and was reputed to be a bachelor. In age he was rather younger than Douglas, forty-five at the most, a tall, straight, broad-chested fellow, with a clean-shaven prizefighter face, thick, strong, black eyebrows, and a pair of masterful black eyes which might, even without the aid of his very capable hands, clear a way for him through a hostile crowd. He neither rode nor shot, but spent his days in wandering round the old village with his pipe in his mouth, or in driving with his host, or in his absence with his hostess, over the beautiful countryside. 'An easy-going, free-handed gentleman,' said Ames, the butler. 'But, my word, I had rather not be the man that crossed him.' He was cordial and intimate with Douglas, and he was no less friendly with his wife, a friendship which more than once seemed to cause some irritation to the husband, so that even the servants were able to perceive his annoyance. Such was the third person who was one of the family when the catastrophe occurred. As to the other denizens of the old building, it will suffice out of a large household to mention the prim, respectable, and capable Ames and Mrs Allen, a buxom and cheerful person, who relieved the lady of some of her household cares. The other six servants in the house bear no relation to the events of the night of January 6th.

It was at eleven-forty-five that the first alarm reached the small local police-station in the charge of Sergeant Wilson, of the Sussex Constabulary. Mr Cecil Barker, much excited, had rushed up to the door and pealed furiously upon the bell. A terrible tragedy had occurred at the Manor House, and Mr John Douglas had been murdered. That was the breathless burden of his message. He had hurried back to the house, followed within a few minutes by the police-sergeant, who arrived at the scene of the crime a little past twelve o'clock, after taking prompt steps to warn the county authorities that something serious was afoot.

On reaching the Manor House the sergeant had found the drawbridge down, the windows lighted up, and the whole household in a state of wild confusion and alarm. The white-faced servants were huddling together in the hall, with the frightened butler wringing his hands in the doorway. Only Cecil Barker seemed to be master of himself and his emotions. He had opened the door which was nearest to the entrance, and had beckoned to the sergeant to follow him. At that moment there arrived Dr Wood, a brisk and capable general practitioner from the village. The three men entered the fatal room together, while the horror-stricken butler followed at their heels, closing the door behind him to shut out the terrible scene from the maid-servants.

The dead man lay upon his back, sprawling with outstretched limbs in the centre of the room. He was clad only in a pink dressing-gown, which covered his night clothes. There were carpet slippers upon his bare feet. The doctor knelt beside him, and held down the hand-lamp which had stood on the table. One glance at the victim was enough to show the healer that his presence could be dispensed with. The man had been horribly injured. Lying across his chest was a curious weapon, a shot-gun with the barrel sawn off a foot in front of the triggers. It was clear that this had been fired at close range, and that he had received the whole charge in the face, blowing his head almost to pieces. The triggers had been wired together, so as to make the simultaneous discharge more destructive.

The country policeman was unnerved and troubled by the tremendous responsibility which had come so suddenly upon him.

'We will touch nothing until my superiors arrive,' he said, in a hushed voice, staring in horror at the dreadful head.

'Nothing has been touched up to now,' said Cecil Barker. 'I'll answer for that. You see it all exactly as I found it.'

'When was that?' The sergeant had drawn out his notebook.

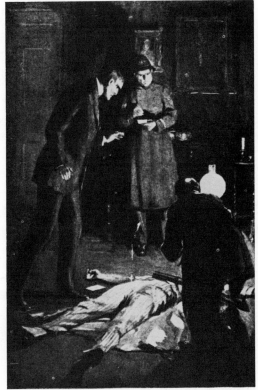

THE DOCTOR KNELT BESIDE HIM, AND HELD DOWN THE HAND-LAMP WHICH HAD STOOD ON THE TABLE.

Illustration by Frank Wiles for the *Strand Magazine*, October, 1914.

35 *nearer half-past four than six at this time of year.* "Sergeant Wilson says . . . that on the day of the tragedy sunset was nearer 4:30 than 6:00, and Inspector MacDonald says it was dusk by 4:30 P.M. Now sunset on January 6th is at 4:04 in London and is at most one minute earlier in Tunbridge Wells, and this fits very well with dusk at 4:40."—Dr. Ernest Bloomfield Zeisler, *Baker Street Chronology.*

'It was just half-past eleven. I had not begun to undress, and I was sitting by the fire in my bedroom, when I heard the report. It was not very loud—it seemed to be muffled. I rushed down. I don't suppose it was thirty seconds before I was in the room.'

'Was the door open?'

'Yes, it was open. Poor Douglas was lying as you see him. His bedroom candle was burning on the table. It was I who lit the lamp some minutes afterwards.'

'Did you see no one?'

'No. I heard Mrs Douglas coming down the stair behind me, and I rushed out to prevent her from seeing this dreadful sight. Mrs Allen, the housekeeper, came and took her away. Ames had arrived, and we ran back into the room once more.'

'But surely I have heard that the drawbridge is kept up all night.'

'Yes, it was up until I lowered it.'

'Then how could any murderer have got away? It is out of the question. Mr Douglas must have shot himself.'

'That was our first idea. But see.' Barker drew aside the curtain, and showed that the long, diamond-paned window was open to its full extent. 'And look at this!' He held the lamp down and illuminated a smudge of blood like the mark of a boot-sole upon the wooden sill. 'Someone has stood there in getting out.'

'You mean that someone waded across the moat?'

'Exactly.'

'Then, if you were in the room within half a minute of the crime, he must have been in the water at that very moment.'

'I have not a doubt of it. I wish to Heaven that I had rushed to the window. But the curtain screened it, as you can see, and so it never occurred to me. Then I heard the step of Mrs Douglas, and I could not let her enter the room. It would have been too horrible.'

'Horrible enough!' said the doctor, looking at the shattered head and the terrible marks which surrounded it. 'I've never seen such injuries since the Birlstone railway smash.'

'But, I say,' remarked the police-sergeant, whose slow, bucolic common sense was still pondering over the open window. 'It's all very well your saying that a man escaped by wading this moat, but what I ask you is—how did he ever get into the house at all if the bridge was up?'

'Ah, that's the question,' said Barker.

'At what o'clock was it raised?'

'It was nearly six o'clock,' said Ames, the butler.

'I've heard,' said the sergeant, 'that it was usually raised at sunset. That would be nearer half-past four than six at this **35** time of year.'

'Mrs Douglas had visitors to tea,' said Ames. 'I couldn't raise it until they went. Then I wound it up myself.'

'Then it comes to this,' said the sergeant. 'If anyone came from outside—*if* they did—they must have got in across the bridge before six and been in hiding ever since, until Mr Douglas came into the room after eleven.'

'That is so. Mr Douglas went round the house every night the last thing before he turned in to see that the lights were right. That brought him in here. The man was waiting, and shot him. Then he got away through the window and left his gun behind him. That's how I read it—for nothing else will fit the facts.'

The sergeant picked up a card which lay beside the dead man upon the floor. The initials V. V., and under it the number 341, were rudely scrawled in ink upon it.

'What's this?' he asked, holding it up.

Barker looked at it with curiosity.

'I never noticed it before,' he said. 'The murderer must have left it behind him.'

'V. V. 341. I can make no sense of that.'

'What's V. V.? Somebody's initials, maybe. What have you got there, Dr Wood?'

It was a good-sized hammer which had been lying upon the rug in front of the fireplace—a substantial, workmanlike hammer. Cecil Barker pointed to a box of brass-headed nails upon the mantelpiece.

'Mr Douglas was altering the pictures yesterday,' he said. 'I saw him myself standing upon that chair and fixing the big picture above it. That accounts for the hammer.'

'We'd best put it back on the rug where we found it,' said the sergeant, scratching his puzzled head in his perplexity. 'It will want the best brains in the force to get to the bottom of this thing. It will be a London job before it is finished.' He raised the hand-lamp and walked slowly round the room. 'Halloa!' he cried, excitedly, drawing the window curtain to one side. 'What o'clock were those curtains drawn?'

'When the lamps were lit,' said the butler. 'It would be shortly after four.'

'Someone has been hiding here, sure enough.' He held down the light, and the marks of muddy boots were very visible in the corner. 'I'm bound to say this bears out your theory, Mr Barker. It looks as if the man got into the house after four, when the curtains were drawn, and before six, when the bridge was raised. He slipped into this room because it was the first that he saw. There was no other place where he could hide, so he popped in behind this curtain. That all seems clear enough. It is likely that his main idea was to burgle the house, but Mr Douglas chanced to come upon him, so he murdered him and escaped.'

'That's how I read it,' said Barker. 'But, I say, aren't we wasting precious time? Couldn't we start out and scour the country before the fellow gets away?'

The sergeant considered for a moment.

'There are no trains before six in the morning, so he can't get away by rail. If he goes by road with his legs all dripping, it's odds that someone will notice him. Anyhow, I can't leave here myself until I am relieved. But I think none of you should go until we see more clearly how we all stand.'

The doctor had taken the lamp and was narrowly scrutinizing the body.

'What's this mark?' he asked. 'Could this have any connection with the crime?'

The dead man's right arm was thrust out from his dressing-gown and exposed as high as the elbow. About half-way up the forearm was a curious brown design, a triangle inside a circle, standing out in vivid relief upon the lard-coloured skin.

'It's not tattooed,' said the doctor, peering through his glasses. 'I never saw anything like it. The man has been branded at some time, as they brand cattle. What is the meaning of this?'

'I don't profess to know the meaning of it,' said Cecil Barker; 'but I've seen the mark on Douglas any time this last ten years.'

'And so have I,' said the butler. 'Many a time when the master has rolled up his sleeves I have noticed that very mark. I've often wondered what it could be.'

'Then it has nothing to do with the crime, anyhow,' said the sergeant. 'But it's a rum thing all the same. Everything about this case is rum. Well, what is it now?'

The butler had given an exclamation of astonishment, and was pointing at the dead man's outstretched hand.

'They've taken his wedding-ring!' he gasped.

'What!'

'Yes, indeed! Master always wore his plain gold wedding-ring on the little finger of his left hand. That ring with the rough nugget on it was above it, and the twisted snake-ring on the third finger. There's the nugget and there's the snake, but the wedding-ring is gone.'

'He's right,' said Barker.

'Do you tell me,' said the sergeant, 'that the wedding-ring was *below* the other?'

'Always!'

'Then the murderer, or whoever it was, first took off this ring you call the nugget-ring, then the wedding-ring, and afterwards put the nugget-ring back again.'

'That is so.'

The worthy country policeman shook his head.

'Seems to me the sooner we get London on to this case the better,' said he. 'White Mason is a smart man. No local job has ever been too much for White Mason. It won't be long now before he is here to help us. But I expect we'll have to look to London before we are through. Anyhow, I'm not ashamed to say that it is a deal too thick for the likes of me.''

4 ❖ DARKNESS

At three in the morning the chief Sussex detective, obeying the urgent call from Sergeant Wilson, of Birlstone, arrived from headquarters in a light dog-cart behind a breathless trotter. By the five-forty train in the morning he had sent his message to Scotland Yard, and he was at the Birlstone station at twelve o'clock to welcome us. Mr White Mason was a quiet, comfortable-looking person, in a loose tweed suit, with a clean-shaven, ruddy face, a stoutish body and powerful bandy legs adorned with gaiters, looking like a small farmer, a retired gamekeeper, or anything upon earth except a very favourable specimen of the provincial criminal officer.

'A real downright snorter, Mr MacDonald,' he kept repeat-**36** ing. 'We'll have the pressmen down like flies when they understand it. I'm hoping we will get our work done before they get poking their noses into it and messing up all the trails.

36 *pressmen*. Reporters.

There has been nothing like this that I can remember. There are some bits that will come home to you, Mr Holmes, or I am mistaken. And you also, Dr Watson, for the medicos will have a word to say before we finish. Your room is at the Westville Arms. There's no other place, but I hear that it is clean and good. The man will carry your bags. This way, gentlemen, if *you* please.'

He was a very bustling and genial person, this Sussex detective. In ten minutes we had all found our quarters. In ten more we were seated in the parlour of the inn and being treated to a rapid sketch of those events which have been outlined in the previous chapter. MacDonald made an occasional note, while Holmes sat absorbed with the expression of surprised and reverent admiration with which the botanist surveys the rare and precious bloom.

'Remarkable!' he said, when the story was unfolded. 'Most remarkable! I can hardly recall any case where the features have been more peculiar.'

'I thought you would say so, Mr Holmes,' said White Mason, in great delight. 'We're well up with the times in Sussex. I've told you now how matters were, up to the time when I took over from Sergeant Wilson between three and four this morning. My word, I made the old mare go! But I need not have been in such a hurry as it turned out, for there was nothing immediate that I could do. Sergeant Wilson had all the facts. I checked them and considered them, and maybe added a few on my own.'

'What were they?' asked Holmes, eagerly.

'Well, I first had the hammer examined. There was Dr Wood there to help me. We found no signs of violence upon it. I was hoping that, if Mr Douglas defended himself with the hammer, he might have left his mark upon the murderer before he dropped it on the mat. But there was no stain.'

'That, of course, proves nothing at all,' remarked Inspector MacDonald. 'There has been many a hammer murder and no trace on the hammer.'

'Quite so. It doesn't prove it wasn't used. But there might have been stains, and that would have helped us. As a matter of fact, there were none. Then I examined the gun. They were buck-shot cartridges, and, as Sergeant Wilson pointed out, the triggers were wired together so that if you pulled on the hinder one both barrels were discharged. Whoever fixed that up had made up his mind that he was going to take no chances of missing his man. The sawn gun was not more than two feet long; one could carry it easily under one's coat. There was no complete maker's name, but the printed letters "PEN" were on the fluting between the barrels, and the rest of the name had been cut off by the saw.'

'A big "P" with a flourish above it—"E" and "N" smaller?' asked Holmes.

'Exactly.'

'Pennsylvania Small Arm Company—well-known American firm,' said Holmes.   **37**

White Mason gazed at my friend as the little village practitioner looks at the Harley Street specialist who by a word can solve the difficulties that perplex him.

'That is very helpful, Mr Holmes. No doubt you are right. Wonderful—wonderful! Do you carry the names of all the gunmakers in the world in your memory?'

37 *well-known American firm.'* Commentators have pointed to this remark, and to Holmes' earlier remark that "paying for brains" is "the American business principle" as evidence that Holmes was born in America or at least had spent some of his earlier years there.

38 *five years ago.* By our dating, then, Douglas would have taken the Manor House in 1883.

"TEN YEARS WITH SIR CHARLES CHANDOS—"

"Sir Charles does not play a prominent role in *The Valley of Fear*," Dr. Julian Wolff wrote in his *Practical Handbook of Sherlockian Heraldry.* "He is merely mentioned as the former employer of Ames, the butler . . . But Sir John Chandos, his ancestor, was the right-hand man of the Black Prince and appears prominently in chronicles of English chivalry. To all Canonical scholars, however, his greatest fame derives from the fact that his squire was a certain Nigel Loring.

"It is a surprise to find that there is any question about the arms of such a famous family. Yet in *The White Company* the arms are described as a scarlet wedge upon a silver field, while in *Sir Nigel* a red wedge upon a golden field is mentioned. Major T. G. Woolley's article, 'Three Interesting Seals' (*The Coat of Arms*, 3. no. 19, July, 1954) blazons them as 'Arg a pile gu.' In a letter to the editor of that magazine (3, no. 21, January, 1955) it is noted by George Walker that the modern Chandos families use a field of or. Robson's *British Herald* gives one with or, one argent and, to make the problem more complicated, another with ermine. In any event, the arms are as illustrated here and are blazoned: or (or argent, or ermine) a pile gules.''

Holmes dismissed the subject with a wave.

'No doubt it is an American shot-gun,' White Mason continued. 'I seem to have read that a sawed-off shot-gun is a weapon used in some parts of America. Apart from the name upon the barrel, the idea had occurred to me. There is some evidence, then, that this man who entered the house and killed its master was an American.'

MacDonald shook his head. 'Man, you are surely travelling over-fast,' said he. 'I have heard no evidence yet that any stranger was ever in the house at all.'

'The open window, the blood on the sill, the queer card, marks of boots in the corner, the gun.'

'Nothing there that could not have been arranged. Mr Douglas was an American, or had lived long in America. So had Mr Barker. You don't need to import an American from outside in order to account for American doings.'

'Ames, the butler——'

'What about him? Is he reliable?'

'Ten years with Sir Charles Chandos—as solid as a rock. He has been with Douglas ever since he took the Manor **38** House five years ago. He has never seen a gun of this sort in the house.'

'The gun was made to conceal. That's why the barrels were sawn. It would fit into any box. How could he swear there was no such gun in the house?'

'Well, anyhow, he had never seen one.'

MacDonald shook his obstinate Scotch head. 'I'm not convinced yet that there was ever anyone in the house,' said he. 'I'm asking you to conseedar'—his accent became more Aberdonian as he lost himself in his argument. 'I'm asking you to conseedar what it involves if you suppose that this gun was ever brought into the house and that all these strange things were done by a person from outside. Oh, man, it's just inconceivable! It's clean against common sense. I put it to you, Mr Holmes, judging it by what we have heard.'

'Well, state your case, Mr Mac,' said Holmes, in his most judicial style.

'The man is not a burglar, supposing that he ever existed. The ring business and the card point to premeditated murder for some private reason. Very good. Here is a man who slips into a house with the deliberate intention of committing murder. He knows, if he knows anything, that he will have a deeficulty in making his escape, as the house is surrounded with water. What weapon would he choose? You would say the most silent in the world. Then he could hope, when the deed was done, to slip quickly from the window, to wade the moat, and to get away at his leisure. That's understandable. But is it understandable that he should go out of his way to bring with him the most noisy weapon he could select, knowing well that it will fetch every human being in the house to the spot as quick as they can run, and that it is all odds that he will be seen before he can get across the moat? Is that credible, Mr Holmes?'

'Well, you put the case strongly,' my friend replied, thoughtfully. 'It certainly needs a good deal of justification. May I ask, Mr White Mason, whether you examined the farther side of the moat at once, to see if there were any signs of the man having climbed out from the water?'

'There were no signs, Mr Holmes. But it is a stone ledge,

and one could hardly expect them.'

'No tracks or marks?'

'None.'

'Ha! Would there be any objection, Mr White Mason, to our going down to the house at once? There may possibly be some small point which might be suggestive.'

'I was going to propose it, Mr Holmes, but I thought it well to put you in touch with all the facts before we go. I suppose, if anything should strike you——' White Mason looked doubtfully at the amateur.

'I have worked with Mr Holmes before,' said Inspector MacDonald. 'He plays the game.'

'My own idea of the game, at any rate,' said Holmes, with a smile. 'I go into a case to help the ends of justice and the work of the police. If ever I have separated myself from the official force, it is because they have first separated themselves from me. I have no wish ever to score at their expense. At the same time, Mr White Mason, I claim the right to work in my own way and give my results at my own time—complete, rather than in stages.'

'I am sure we are honoured by your presence and to show you all we know,' said White Mason, cordially. 'Come along, Dr Watson, and when the time comes we'll all hope for a place in your book.' **39**

We walked down the quaint village street with a row of pollarded elms on either side of it. Just beyond were two **40** ancient stone pillars, weather-stained and lichen-blotched, bearing upon their summits a shapeless something which had once been the ramping lion of Capus of Birlstone. A short walk along the winding drive, with such sward and oaks around it as one only sees in rural England; then a sudden turn, and the long, low, Jacobean house of dingy, liver-coloured brick lay before us, with an old-fashioned garden of cut yews on either side of it. As we approached it there were the wooden drawbridge and the beautiful broad moat, as still and luminous as quicksilver in the cold winter sunshine. Three centuries had flowed past the old Manor House, centuries of births and of home-comings, of country dances and of the meetings of fox-hunters. Strange that now in its old age this dark business should have cast its shadow upon the venerable walls. And yet those strange peaked roofs and quaint over-hung gables were a fitting covering to grim and terrible intrigue. As I looked at the deep-set windows and the long sweep of the dull-coloured, water-lapped front I felt that no more fitting scene could be set for such a tragedy.

'That's the window,' said White Mason; 'that one on the immediate right of the drawbridge. It's open just as it was found last night.'

'It looks rather narrow for a man to pass.'

'Well, it wasn't a fat man, anyhow. We don't need your deductions, Mr Holmes, to tell us that. But you or I could squeeze through all right.'

Holmes walked to the edge of the moat and looked across. Then he examined the stone ledge and the grass border beyond it.

'I've had a good look, Mr Holmes,' said White Mason. 'There is nothing there; no sign that anyone has landed. But why should he leave any sign?'

'Exactly. Why should he? Is the water always turbid?'

. . . A SHAPELESS SOMETHING WHICH HAD ONCE BEEN THE RAMPING LION OF CAPUS OF BIRLSTONE.

The "ramping lion" as shown in Dr. Julian Wolff's *Practical Handbook of Sherlockian Heraldry.*

THEN HE EXAMINED THE STONE LEDGE AND THE GRASS BORDER BEYOND IT.

Illustration by Frank Wiles for the *Strand Magazine*, October, 1914.

39 *all hope for a place in your book.*' Since White Mason knows Watson as Holmes' biographer, it would seem to place the adventure of *The Valley of Fear* no earlier than January, 1888, after the appearance of *A Study in Scarlet* in *Beeton's Christmas Annual* in December, 1887.

40 *pollarded elms.* A pollarded tree is one that is shorn at the top so that it will produce a thick growth of slender shoots.

'Generally about this colour. The stream brings down the clay.'

'How deep is it?'

'About two feet at each side and three in the middle.'

'So we can put aside all idea of the man having been drowned in crossing?'

'No; a child could not be drowned in it.'

We walked across the drawbridge, and were admitted by a quaint, gnarled, dried-up person who was the butler— Ames. The poor old fellow was white and quivering from the shock. The village sergeant, a tall, formal, melancholy man, still held his vigil in the room of fate. The doctor had departed.

'Anything fresh, Sergeant Wilson?' asked White Mason.

'No, sir.'

'Then you can go home. You've had enough. We can send for you if we want you. The butler had better wait outside. Tell him to warn Mr Cecil Barker, Mrs Douglas, and the housekeeper that we may want a word with them presently. Now, gentlemen, perhaps you will allow me to give you the views I have formed first, and then you will be able to arrive at your own.'

He impressed me, this country specialist. He had a solid grip of fact and a cool, clear, common-sense brain, which should take him some way in his profession. Holmes listened to him intently, with no sign of that impatience which the official exponent too often produced.

'Is it suicide or is it murder—that's our first question, gentlemen, is it not? If it were suicide, then we have to believe that this man began by taking off his wedding-ring and concealing it; that he then came down here in his dressing-gown, trampled mud into a corner behind the curtain in order to give the idea someone had waited for him, opened the window, put blood on the——'

'We can surely dismiss that,' said MacDonald.

'So I think. Suicide is out of the question. Then a murder has been done. What we have to determine is whether it was done by someone outside or inside the house.'

'Well, let's hear the argument.'

'There are considerable difficulties both ways, and yet one or the other it must be. We will suppose first that some person or persons inside the house did the crime. They got this man down here at a time when everything was still, and yet no one was asleep. They then did the deed with the queerest and noisiest weapon in the world, so as to tell everyone what had happened—a weapon that was never seen in the house before. That does not seem a very likely start, does it?'

'No, it does not.'

'Well, then, everyone is agreed that after the alarm was given only a minute at the most had passed before the whole household—not Mr Cecil Barker alone, though he claims to have been the first, but Ames and all of them—were on the spot. Do you tell me that in that time the guilty person managed to make footmarks in the corner, open the window, mark the sill with blood, take the wedding-ring off the dead man's finger, and all the rest of it? It's impossible!'

'You put it very clearly,' said Holmes. 'I am inclined to agree with you.'

'Well, then, we are driven back to the theory that it was done by someone from outside. We are still faced with some big difficulties, but, anyhow, they have ceased to be impossibilities. The man got into the house between four-thirty and six—that is to say, between dusk and the time when the bridge was raised. There had been some visitors, and the door was open, so there was nothing to prevent him. He may have been a common burglar, or he may have had some private grudge against Mr Douglas. Since Mr Douglas has spent most of his life in America, and this shot-gun seems to be an American weapon, it would seem that the private grudge is the more likely theory. He slipped into this room because it was the first he came to, and he hid behind the curtain. There he remained until past eleven at night. At that time Mr Douglas entered the room. It was a short interview, if there were any interview at all, for Mrs Douglas declares that her husband had not left her more than a few minutes when she heard the shot.'

'The candle shows that,' said Holmes.

'Exactly. The candle, which was a new one, is not burned more than half an inch. He must have placed it on the table before he was attacked, otherwise, of course, it would have fallen when he fell. This shows that he was not attacked the instant that he entered the room. When Mr Barker arrived the lamp was lit and the candle put out.'

'That's all clear enough.'

'Well, now, we can reconstruct things on those lines. Mr Douglas enters the room. He puts down the candle. A man appears from behind the curtain. He is armed with this gun. He demands the wedding-ring—Heaven only knows why, but so it must have been. Mr Douglas gave it up. Then either in cold blood or in the course of a struggle—Douglas may have gripped the hammer that was found upon the mat—he shot Douglas in this horrible way. He dropped his gun and also, it would seem, this queer card, "V. V. 341," whatever that may mean, and he made his escape through the window and across the moat at the very moment when Cecil Barker was discovering the crime. How's that, Mr Holmes?'

'Very interesting, but just a little unconvincing.'

'Man, it would be absolute nonsense, if it wasn't that anything else is even worse,' cried MacDonald. 'Somebody killed the man, and whoever it was I could clearly prove to you that he should have done it some other way. What does he mean by allowing his retreat to be cut off like that? What does he mean by using a shot-gun when silence was his one chance of escape? Come, Mr Holmes, it's up to you to give us a lead, since you say Mr White Mason's theory is unconvincing.'

Holmes had sat intently observant during this long discussion, missing no word that was said, with his keen eyes darting to right and to left, and his forehead wrinkled with speculation.

'I should like a few more facts before I get so far as a theory, Mr Mac,' said he, kneeling down beside the body. 'Dear me! these injuries are really appalling. Can we have the butler in for a moment? . . . Ames, I understand that you have often seen this very unusual mark, a branded triangle inside a circle, upon Mr Douglas's forearm?'

'Frequently, sir.'

'You never heard any speculation as to what it meant?'

'No, sir.'

'It must have caused great pain when it was inflicted. It is undoubtedly a burn. Now, I observe, Ames, that there is a small piece of plaster at the angle of Mr Douglas's jaw. Did

HOLMES HAD GONE TO THE WINDOW AND WAS
EXAMINING WITH HIS LENS THE BLOOD-MARK
UPON THE SILL.

Illustration by Frank Wiles for the *Strand Maga-zine*, October, 1914.

you observe that in life?'

'Yes, sir; he cut himself in shaving yesterday morning.'

'Did you ever know him cut himself in shaving before?'

'Not for a very long time, sir.'

'Suggestive!' said Holmes. 'It may, of course, be a mere coincidence, or it may point to some nervousness which would indicate that he had reason to apprehend danger. Had you noticed anything unusual in his conduct yesterday, Ames?'

'It struck me that he was a little restless and excited, sir.'

'Ha! The attack may not have been entirely unexpected. We do seem to make a little progress, do we not? Perhaps you would rather do the questioning, Mr Mac?'

'No, Mr Holmes; it's in better hands.'

'Well, then, we will pass to this card—"V. V. 341." It is rough cardboard. Have you any of the sort in the house?'

'I don't think so.'

Holmes walked across to the desk and dabbed a little ink from each bottle on to the blotting-paper. 'It has not been printed in this room,' he said; 'this is black ink, and the other purplish. It has been done by a thick pen, and these are fine. No, it has been done elsewhere, I should say. Can you make anything of the inscription, Ames?'

'No, sir, nothing.'

'What do you think, Mr Mac?'

'It gives me the impression of a secret society of some sort. The same with this badge upon the forearm.'

'That's my idea, too,' said White Mason.

'Well, we can adopt it as a working hypothesis, and then see how far our difficulties disappear. An agent from such a society makes his way into the house, waits for Mr Douglas, blows his head nearly off with this weapon, and escapes by wading the moat, after leaving a card beside the dead man which will, when mentioned in the papers, tell other members of the society that vengeance has been done. That all hangs together. But why this gun, of all weapons?'

'Exactly.'

'And why the missing ring?'

'Quite so.'

'And why no arrest? It's past two now. I take it for granted that since dawn every constable within forty miles has been looking out for a wet stranger?'

'That is so, Mr Holmes.'

'Well, unless he has a burrow close by, or a change of clothes ready, they can hardly miss him. And yet they *have* missed him up to now.' Holmes had gone to the window and was examining with his lens the blood-mark upon the sill. 'It is clearly the tread of a shoe. It is remarkably broad—a splay foot, one would say. Curious, because, so far as one can trace any footmark in this mud-stained corner, one would say it was a more shapely sole. However, they are certainly very indistinct. What's this under the side table?'

'Mr Douglas's dumb-bells,' said Ames.

'Dumb-bell—there's only one. Where's the other?'

'I don't know, Mr Holmes. There may have been only one. I have not noticed them for months.'

'One dumb-bell——' Holmes said, seriously, but his remarks were interrupted by a sharp knock at the door. A tall, sunburned, capable-looking, clean-shaven man looked in at us. I had no difficulty in guessing that it was the Cecil Barker of whom I had heard. His masterful eyes travelled quickly with a questioning glance from face to face.

'Sorry to interrupt your consultation,' said he, 'but you should hear the latest.'

'An arrest?'

'No such luck. But they've found his bicycle. The fellow left his bicycle behind him. Come and have a look. It is within a hundred yards of the hall door.'

We found three or four grooms and idlers standing in the drive inspecting a bicycle which had been drawn out from a clump of evergreens in which it had been concealed. It was a well-used Rudge-Whitworth, splashed as from a considerable journey. There was a saddle-bag with spanner and oil-can, but no clue as to the owner.

'It would be a grand help to the police,' said the inspector, 'if these things were numbered and registered. But we must be thankful for what we've got. If we can't find where he went to, at least we are likely to get where he came from. But what in the name of all that is wonderful made the fellow leave it behind? And how in the world has he got away without it? We don't seem to get a gleam of light in the case, Mr Holmes.'

'Don't we?' my friend answered, thoughtfully. 'I wonder!'

5 • THE PEOPLE OF THE DRAMA

'Have you seen all you want of the study?' asked White Mason as we re-entered the house.

'For the time,' said the inspector; and Holmes nodded.

'Then perhaps you would now like to hear the evidence of some of the people in the house? We could use the dining-room, Ames. Please come yourself first and tell us what you know.'

The butler's account was a simple and a clear one, and he gave a convincing impression of sincerity. He had been engaged five years ago when Mr Douglas first came to Birlstone. He understood that Mr Douglas was a rich gentleman who had made his money in America. He had been a kind and considerate employer—not quite what Ames was used to, perhaps, but one can't have everything. He never saw any signs of apprehension in Mr Douglas—on the contrary, he was the most fearless man he had ever known. He ordered the drawbridge to be pulled up every night because it was the ancient custom of the old house, and he liked to keep the old ways up. Mr Douglas seldom went to London or left the village, but on the day before the crime he had been shopping at Tunbridge Wells. He, Ames, had observed some restlessness and excitement on the part of Mr Douglas upon that day, for he had seemed impatient and irritable, which was unusual with him. He had not gone to bed that night, but was in the pantry at the back of the house, putting away the silver, when he heard the bell ring violently. He heard no shot, but it was hardly possible he should, as the pantry and kitchens were at the very back of the house and there were several closed doors and a long passage between. The housekeeper had come out of her room, attracted by the violent ringing of the bell. They had gone to the front of the house together. As they reached the bottom of the stair he had seen Mrs Douglas coming down it. No, she was not hurrying—it did not seem to him that she was particularly agitated. Just as she reached the bottom of the stair Mr Barker had rushed out of the study. He had stopped Mrs Douglas and begged her to go back.

'For God's sake, go back to your room!' he cried. 'Poor Jack is dead. You can do nothing. For God's sake, go back!'

After some persuasion upon the stairs Mrs Douglas had gone back. She did not scream. She made no outcry whatever. Mrs Allen, the housekeeper, had taken her upstairs and stayed with her in the bedroom. Ames and Mr Barker had then returned to the study, where they had found everything exactly as the police had seen it. The candle was not lit at that time, but the lamp was burning. They had looked out of the window, but the night was very dark and nothing could be seen or heard. They had then rushed out into the hall, where Ames had turned the windlass which lowered the drawbridge. Mr Barker had then hurried off to get the police.

Such, in its essentials, was the evidence of the butler.

The account of Mrs Allen, the housekeeper, was, so far as it went, a corroboration of that of her fellow-servant. The housekeeper's room was rather nearer to the front of the house than the pantry in which Ames had been working. She was preparing to go to bed when the loud ringing of the bell had attracted her attention. She was a little hard of hearing. Perhaps that was why she had not heard the sound of the shot, but in any case the study was a long way off. She remembered hearing some sound which she imagined to be the slamming of a door. That was a good deal earlier—half an hour at least before the ringing of the bell. When Mr Ames ran to the front she went with him. She saw Mr Barker, very pale and excited, come out of the study. He intercepted Mrs Douglas who was coming down the stairs. He entreated her to go back, and she answered him, but what she said could not be heard.

'Take her up. Stay with her!' he had said to Mrs Allen.

She had therefore taken her to the bedroom and endeavoured to soothe her. She was greatly excited, trembling all over, but made no other attempt to go downstairs. She just sat in her dressing-gown by her bedroom fire with her head sunk in her hands. Mrs Allen stayed with her most of the night. As to the other servants, they had all gone to bed, and the alarm did not reach them until just before the police arrived. They slept at the extreme back of the house, and could not possibly have heard anything.

So far the housekeeper—who could add nothing on cross-examination save lamentations and expressions of amazement.

Mr Cecil Barker succeeded Mrs Allen as a witness. As to the occurrences of the night before, he had very little to add to what he had already told the police. Personally, he was convinced that the murderer had escaped by the window. The blood-stain was conclusive, in his opinion, upon that point. Besides, as the bridge was up there was no other possible way of escaping. He could not explain what had become of the assassin, or why he had not taken his bicycle, if it were indeed his. He could not possibly have been drowned in the moat, which was at no place more than three feet deep.

In his own mind he had a very definite theory about the murder. Douglas was a reticent man, and there were some chapters in his life of which he never spoke. He had emigrated to America from Ireland when he was a very young man. He had prospered well, and Barker had first met him in California, where they had become partners in a successful mining claim at a place called Benito Canyon. They had done very well, but Douglas had suddenly sold out and started for England. He was a widower at that time. Barker had afterwards realized his money and come to live in London. Thus they had renewed their friendship. Douglas had given him the impression that some danger was hanging over his head, and he had always looked upon his sudden departure from California, and also his renting a house in so quiet a place in England, as being connected with this peril. He imagined that some secret society, some implacable organization, was on Douglas's track which would never rest until it killed him. Some remarks of his had given him this idea, though he had never told him what the society was, nor how he had come to offend it. He could only suppose that the legend upon the placard had some reference to this secret society.

'How long were you with Douglas in California?' asked Inspector MacDonald.

'Five years altogether.'

'He was a bachelor, you say?'

'A widower.'

'Have you ever heard where his first wife came from?'

'No; I remember his saying that she was of Swedish extraction, and I have seen her portrait. She was a very beautiful woman. She died of typhoid the year before I met him.'

'You don't associate his past with any particular part of America?'

'I have heard him talk of Chicago. He knew that city well and had worked there. I have heard him talk of the coal and iron districts. He had travelled a good deal in his time.'

'Was he a politician? Had this secret society to do with politics?'

'No; he cared nothing about politics.'

'You have no reason to think it was criminal?'

'On the contrary, I never met a straighter man in my life.'

'Was there anything curious about his life in California?'

'He liked best to stay and to work at our claim in the mountains. He would never go where other men were if he could help it. That's why I first thought that someone was after him. Then when he left so suddenly for Europe I made sure that it was so. I believe that he had a warning of some sort. Within a week of his leaving half a dozen men were inquiring for him.'

'What sort of men?'

'Well, they were a mighty hard-looking crowd. They came up to the claim and wanted to know where he was. I told them that he was gone to Europe and that I did not know where to find him. They meant him no good—it was easy to see that.'

'Were these men Americans—Californians?'

'Well, I don't know about Californians. They were Americans all right. But they were not miners. I don't know what they were, and was very glad to see their backs.'

'That was six years ago?'

41 *this business dates back not less than eleven years at the least?'* We later learn that the events at Vermissa Valley began on "the fourth of February in the year 1875." Douglas was there some three months, bringing us to May, 1875. Douglas married Ettie Shafter in Chicago and went to California after two attempts on his life. After Ettie's death, Douglas met Barker and they "were together five years in California." It is clear that the adventure of *The Valley of Fear* could not have taken place before January, 1886, and is probably some years after that.

'Nearer seven.'

'And then you were together five years in California, so that **41** this business dates back not less than eleven years at the least?'

'That is so.'

'It must be a very serious feud that would be kept up with such earnestness for as long as that. It would be no light thing that would give rise to it.'

'I think it shadowed his whole life. It was never quite out of his mind.'

'But if a man had a danger hanging over him, and knew what it was, don't you think he would turn to the police for protection?'

'Maybe it was some danger that he could not be protected against. There's one thing you should know. He always went about armed. His revolver was never out of his pocket. But, by bad luck, he was in his dressing-gown and had left it in the bedroom last night. Once the bridge was up I guess he thought he was safe.'

'I should like these dates a little clearer,' said MacDonald. 'It is quite six years since Douglas left California. You followed him next year, did you not?'

'That is so.'

'And he has been married five years. You must have returned about the time of his marriage.'

'About a month before. I was his best man.'

'Did you know Mrs Douglas before her marriage?'

'No, I did not. I had been away from England for ten years.'

'But you have seen a good deal of her since?'

Barker looked sternly at the detective.

'I have seen a good deal of *him* since,' he answered. 'If I have seen her, it is because you cannot visit a man without knowing his wife. If you imagine there is any connection——'

'I imagine nothing, Mr Barker. I am bound to make every inquiry which can bear upon the case. But I mean no offence.'

'Some inquiries are offensive,' Barker answered, angrily.

'It's only the facts that we want. It is in your interest and everyone's interests that they should be cleared up. Did Mr Douglas entirely approve your friendship with his wife?'

Barker grew paler, and his great strong hands were clasped convulsively together.

'You have no right to ask such questions!' he cried. 'What has this to do with the matter you are investigating?'

'I must repeat the question.'

'Well, I refuse to answer.'

'You can refuse to answer, but you must be aware that your refusal is in itself an answer, for you would not refuse if you had not something to conceal.'

Barker stood for a moment, with his face set grimly and his strong, black eyebrows drawn low in intense thought. Then he looked up with a smile.

'Well, I guess you gentlemen are only doing your clear duty, after all, and that I have no right to stand in the way of it. I'd only ask you not to worry Mrs Douglas over this matter, for she has enough upon her just now. I may tell you that poor Douglas had just one fault in the world, and that was his jealousy. He was fond of me—no man could be fonder of a friend. And he was devoted to his wife. He loved me to come here and was for ever sending for me. And yet if his wife and I talked together or there seemed any sympathy between us, a kind of wave of jealousy would pass over him and he would be off the handle and saying the wildest things in a moment. More than once I've sworn off coming for that reason, and then he would write me such penitent, imploring letters that I just had to. But you can take it from me, gentlemen, if it was my last word, that no man ever had a more loving, faithful wife—and I can say, also, no friend could be more loyal than I.'

It was spoken with fervour and feeling, and yet Inspector MacDonald could not dismiss the subject.

'You are aware,' said he, 'that the dead man's wedding-ring has been taken from his finger?'

'So it appears,' said Barker.

'What do you mean by "appears"? You know it as a fact.'

The man seemed confused and undecided.

'When I said "appears," I meant that it was conceivable that he had himself taken off the ring.'

'The mere fact that the ring should be absent, whoever may have removed it, would suggest to anyone's mind, would it not, that the marriage and the tragedy were connected?'

Barker shrugged his broad shoulders.

'I can't profess to say what it suggests,' he answered. 'But if you mean to hint that it could reflect in any way upon this lady's honour'—his eyes blazed for an instant, and then with an evident effort he got a grip upon his own emotions—'well, you are on the wrong track, that's all.'

'I don't know that I've anything else to ask you at present,' said MacDonald, coldly.

'There was one small point,' remarked Sherlock Holmes. 'When you entered the room there was only a candle lighted upon the table, was there not?'

'Yes, that was so.'

'By its light you saw that some terrible incident had occurred?'

'Exactly.'

'You at once rang for help?'

'Yes.'

'And it arrived very speedily?'

'Within a minute or so.'

'And yet when they arrived they found that the candle was out and that the lamp had been lighted. That seems very remarkable.'

Again Barker showed some signs of indecision.

'I don't see that it was remarkable, Mr Holmes,' he answered, after a pause. 'The candle threw a very bad light. My first thought was to get a better one. The lamp was on the table, so I lit it.'

'And blew out the candle?'

'Exactly.'

Holmes asked no further question, and Barker, with a deliberate look from one to the other of us, which had, as it seemed to me, something of defiance in it, turned and left the room.

Inspector MacDonald had sent up a note to the effect that he would wait upon Mrs Douglas in her room, but she had replied that she would meet us in the dining-room. She entered now, a tall and beautiful woman of thirty, reserved and self-possessed to a remarkable degree, very different from the tragic and distracted figure that I had pictured. It is true that her face was pale and drawn, like that of one who has endured a great shock, but her manner was composed, and the finely moulded hand which she rested upon the edge of the table was as steady as my own. Her sad, appealing eyes travelled from one to the other of us with a curiously inquisitive expression. That questioning gaze transformed itself suddenly into abrupt speech.

'Have you found out anything yet?' she asked.

Was it my imagination that there was an undertone of fear rather than of hope in the question?

'We have taken every possible step, Mrs Douglas,' said the inspector. 'You may rest assured that nothing will be neglected.'

'Spare no money,' she said, in a dead, even tone. 'It is my desire that every possible effort should be made.'

'Perhaps you can tell us something which may throw some light upon the matter.'

'I fear not, but all I know is at your service.'

'We have heard from Mr Cecil Barker that you did not actually see—that you were never in the room where the tragedy occurred?'

'No; he turned me back upon the stairs. He begged me to return to my room.'

'Quite so. You had heard the shot and you had at once come down.'

'I put on my dressing-gown and then came down.'

'How long was it after hearing the shot that you were stopped on the stair by Mr Barker?'

'It may have been a couple of minutes. It is so hard to reckon time at such a moment. He implored me not to go on. He assured me that I could do nothing. Then Mrs Allen, the housekeeper, led me upstairs again. It was all like some dreadful dream.'

'Can you give us any idea how long your husband had been downstairs before you heard the shot?'

'No, I cannot say. He went from his dressing-room and I did not hear him go. He did the round of the house every night, for he was nervous of fire. It is the only thing that I have ever known him nervous of.'

'That is just the point which I want to come to, Mrs Douglas. You have only known your husband in England, have you not?'

'Yes. We have been married five years.'

'Have you heard him speak of anything which occurred in America and which might bring some danger upon him?'

Mrs Douglas thought earnestly before she answered.

'Yes,' she said at last. 'I have always felt that there was a danger hanging over him. He refused to discuss it with me. It was not from want of confidence in me—there was the most complete love and confidence between us—but it was out of his desire to keep all alarm away from me. He thought I should brood over it if I knew all, and so he was silent.'

'How did you know it, then?'

Mrs Douglas's face lit with a quick smile.

'Can a husband ever carry about a secret all his life and a woman who loves him have no suspicion of it? I knew it in many ways. I knew it by his refusal to talk about some episodes in his American life. I knew it by certain precautions he took. I knew it by certain words he let fall. I knew it by the way he looked at unexpected strangers. I was perfectly certain that he had some powerful enemies, that he believed they were on his track and that he was always on his guard against them. I was so sure of it that for years I have been terrified if ever he came home later than was expected.'

'Might I ask,' said Holmes, 'what the words were which attracted your attention?'

' "The Valley of Fear," ' the lady answered. 'That was an expression he has used when I questioned him. "I have been in the Valley of Fear. I am not out of it yet." "Are we never to get out of the Valley of Fear?" I have asked him, when I have seen him more serious than usual. "Sometimes I think that we never shall," he has answered.'

'Surely you asked him what he meant by the Valley of Fear?'

'I did; but his face would become very grave and he would shake his head. "It is bad enough that one of us should have been in its shadow," he said. "Please God it shall never fall upon you." It was some real valley in which he had lived and in which something terrible had occurred to him—of that I am certain—but I can tell you no more.'

'And he never mentioned any names?'

'Yes; he was delirious with fever once when he had his hunting accident three years ago. Then I remember that there was a name that came continually to his lips. He spoke it with anger and a sort of horror. McGinty was the name—Bodymaster McGinty. I asked him, when he recovered, who Bodymaster McGinty was, and whose body he was master of. "Never of mine, thank God!" he answered, with a laugh and that was all I could get from him. But there is a connection between Bodymaster McGinty and the Valley of Fear.'

'There is one other point,' said Inspector MacDonald. 'You met Mr Douglas in a boarding-house in London, did you not, and became engaged to him there? Was there any romance, anything secret or mysterious, about the wedding?'

'There was romance. There is always romance. There was nothing mysterious.'

'He had no rival?'

'No; I was quite free.'

'You have heard, no doubt, that his wedding-ring has been taken. Does that suggest anything to you? Suppose that some enemy of his old life had tracked him down and committed this crime, what possible reason could he have for taking his wedding-ring?'

For an instant I could have sworn that the faintest shadow of a smile flickered over the woman's lips.

'I really cannot tell,' she answered. 'It is certainly a most extraordinary thing.'

'Well, we will not detain you any longer, and we are sorry to have put you to this trouble at such a time,' said the inspector. 'There are some other points, no doubt, but we can refer to you as they arise.'

She rose, and I was again conscious of that quick, questioning glance with which she had just surveyed us: 'What impression has my evidence made upon you?' The question might as well have been spoken. Then, with a bow, she swept from the room.

'She's a beautiful woman—a very beautiful woman,' said MacDonald, thoughtfully, after the door had closed behind her. 'This man Barker has certainly been down here a good deal. He is a man who might be attractive to a woman. He admits that the dead man was jealous, and maybe he knew best himself what cause he had for jealousy. Then there's that wedding-ring. You can't get past that. The man who tears a wedding-ring off a dead man's—— What do you say to it, Mr Holmes?'

My friend had sat with his head upon his hands, sunk in the deepest thought. Now he rose and rang the bell.

'Ames,' he said, when the butler entered, 'where is Mr Cecil Barker now?'

'I'll see, sir.'

He came back in a moment to say that Mr Barker was in the garden.

'Can you remember, Ames, what Mr Barker had upon his feet last night when you joined him in the study?'

'Yes, Mr Holmes. He had a pair of bedroom slippers. I brought him his boots when he went for the police.'

'Where are the slippers now?'

'They are still under the chair in the hall.'

'Very good, Ames. It is, of course, important for us to know which tracks may be Mr Barker's and which from outside.'

'Yes, sir. I may say that I noticed that the slippers were stained with blood, so, indeed, were my own.'

'That is natural enough, considering the condition of the room. Very good, Ames. We will ring if we want you.'

A few minutes later we were in the study. Holmes had brought with him the carpet slippers from the hall. As Ames had observed, the soles of both were dark with blood.

'Strange!' murmured Holmes, as he stood in the light of the window and examined them minutely. 'Very strange indeed!'

Stooping with one of his quick, feline pounces he placed the slipper upon the blood-mark on the sill. It exactly corresponded. He smiled in silence at his colleagues.

The inspector was transfigured with excitement. His native accent rattled like a stick upon railings.

'Man!' he cried, 'there's not a doubt of it! Barker has just marked the window himself. It's a good deal broader than any boot-mark. I mind that you said it was a splay foot, and here's the explanation. But what's the game, Mr Holmes—what's the game?'

'Aye, what's the game?' my friend repeated, thoughtfully.

White Mason chuckled and rubbed his fat hands together in his professional satisfaction.

'I said it was a snorter!' he cried. 'And a real snorter it is!'

. . . HE PLACED THE SLIPPER UPON THE BLOOD-MARK
ON THE SILL.

Illustration by Frank Wiles for the *Strand Magazine*, November, 1914.

6 ❖ A DAWNING LIGHT

The three detectives had many matters of detail into which to inquire, so I returned alone to our modest quarters at the village inn; but before doing so I took a stroll in the curious, old-world garden which flanked the house. Rows of very ancient yew trees, cut into strange designs, girded it round. Inside was a beautiful stretch of lawn with an old sundial in the middle, the whole effect so soothing and restful that it was welcome to my somewhat jangled nerves. In that deeply peaceful atmosphere one could forget or remember only as some fantastic nightmare that darkened study with the sprawling, blood-stained figure upon the floor. And yet as I strolled round it and tried to steep my soul in its gentle balm, a strange incident occurred which brought me back to the tragedy and left a sinister impression in my mind.

I have said that a decoration of yew trees circled the garden. At the end which was farthest from the house they thickened into a continuous hedge. On the other side of this hedge, concealed from the eyes of anyone approaching from the direction of the house, there was a stone seat. As I approached the spot I was aware of voices, some remark in the deep tones of a man, answered by a little ripple of feminine laughter. An instant later I had come round the end of the hedge, and my eyes lit upon Mrs Douglas and the man Barker before they were aware of my presence. Her appearance gave me a shock. In the dining-room she had been demure and discreet. Now all pretence of grief had passed away from her. Her eyes shone with the joy of living, and her face still quivered with amusement at some remark of her companion. He sat forward, his hands clasped and his forearms on his knees, with an answering smile upon his bold, handsome face. In an instant—but it was just one instant too late—they resumed their solemn masks as my figure came into view. A hurried word or two passed between them, and then Barker rose and came towards me.

'Excuse me, sir,' said he, 'but am I addressing Dr Watson?'

I bowed with a coldness which showed, I dare say, very plainly the impression which had been produced upon my mind.

'We thought that it was probably you, as your friendship with Mr Sherlock Holmes is so well known. Would you mind coming over and speaking to Mrs Douglas for one instant?'

I followed him with a dour face. Very clearly I could see in my mind's eye that shattered figure upon the floor. Here within a few hours of the tragedy were his wife and his nearest friend laughing together behind a bush in the garden which had been his. I greeted the lady with reserve. I had grieved with her grief in the dining-room. Now I met her appealing gaze with an unresponsive eye.

'I fear that you think me callous and hard-hearted?' said she.

I shrugged my shoulders.

'It is no business of mine,' said I.

'Perhaps some day you will do me justice. If you only realized——'

'There is no need why Dr Watson should realize,' said Barker, quickly. 'As he has himself said, it is no possible business of his.'

'Exactly,' said I, 'and so I will beg leave to resume my walk.'

'One moment, Dr Watson,' cried the woman, in a pleading voice. 'There is one question which you can answer with more authority than anyone else in the world, and it may make a very great difference to me. You know Mr Holmes and his relations with the police better than anyone else can do. Supposing that a matter were brought confidentially to his knowledge, is it absolutely necessary that he should pass it on to the detectives?'

'Yes, that's it,' said Barker, eagerly. 'Is he on his own or is he entirely in with them?'

42 débonnaire. French: having affable or courteous bearing or manner; affable; complaisant; winsome; cheery.

43 *Shocking, Watson, shocking!*' Holmes, in a *débonnaire* frame of mind, "does not tell the whole story. The single dumb-bell which worried him could have been used alternately by the right and left arm and thus unilateral development prevented. Watson knew this, but like a good soldier he let Holmes have his fun and made no reply."—Dr. Edward J. Van Liere, "Sherlock Holmes and Doctor Watson, Perennial Athletes."

'I really don't know that I should be justified in discussing such a point.'

'I beg—I implore that you will, Dr Watson, I assure you that you will be helping us—helping me greatly if you will guide us on that point.'

There was such a ring of sincerity in the woman's voice that for the instant I forgot all about her levity and was moved only to do her will.

'Mr Holmes is an independent investigator,' I said. 'He is his own master, and would act as his own judgment directed. At the same time he would naturally feel loyalty towards the officials who were working on the same case, and he would not conceal from them anything which would help them in bringing a criminal to justice. Beyond this I can say nothing, and I would refer you to Mr Holmes himself if you want fuller information.'

So saying I raised my hat and went upon my way, leaving them still seated behind that concealing hedge. I looked back as I rounded the far end of it, and saw that they were still talking very earnestly together, and, as they were gazing after me, it was clear that it was our interview that was the subject of their debate.

'I wish none of their confidences,' said Holmes, when I reported to him what had occurred. He had spent the whole afternoon at the Manor House in consultation with his two colleagues, and returned about five with a ravenous appetite for a high tea which I had ordered for him. 'No confidences, Watson, for they are mighty awkward if it comes to an arrest for conspiracy and murder.'

'You think it will come to that?'

42   He was in his most cheerful and *débonnaire* humour.

'My dear Watson, when I have exterminated that fourth egg I will be ready to put you in touch with the whole situation. I don't say that we have fathomed it—far from it—but when we have traced the missing dumb-bell——'

'The dumb-bell!'

'Dear me, Watson, is it possible that you have not penetrated the fact that the case hangs upon the missing dumb-bell? Well, well, you need not be downcast, for, between ourselves, I don't think that either Inspector Mac or the excellent local practitioner has grasped the overwhelming importance of this incident. One dumb-bell, Watson! Consider an athlete with one dumb-bell. Picture to yourself the unilateral development—the imminent danger of a spinal **43** curvature. Shocking, Watson; shocking!'

He sat with his mouth full of toast and his eyes sparkling with mischief, watching my intellectual entanglement. The mere sight of his excellent appetite was an assurance of success, for I had very clear recollections of days and nights without a thought of food, when his baffled mind had chafed before some problem whilst his thin, eager features became more attenuated with the asceticism of complete mental concentration. Finally he lit his pipe, and, sitting in the inglenook of the old village inn, he talked slowly and at random about his case, rather as one who thinks aloud than as one who makes a considered statement.

'A lie, Watson—a great big, thumping, obtrusive, uncompromising lie—that's what meets us on the threshold. There is our starting-point. The whole story told by Barker is a lie.

But Barker's story is corroborated by Mrs Douglas. Therefore she is lying also. They are both lying and in a conspiracy. So now we have the clear problem—why are they lying, and what is the truth which they are trying so hard to conceal? Let us try, Watson, you and I, if we can get behind the lie and reconstruct the truth.

'How do I know that they are lying? Because it is a clumsy fabrication which simply *could* not be true. Consider! According to the story given to us the assassin had less than a minute after the murder had been committed to take that ring, which was under another ring, from the dead man's finger, to replace the other ring—a thing which he would surely never have done—and to put that singular card beside his victim. I say that this was obviously impossible. You may argue—but I have too much respect for your judgment, Watson, to think that you will do so—that the ring may have been taken before the man was killed. The fact that the candle had only been lit a short time shows that there had been no lengthy interview. Was Douglas, from what we hear of his fearless character, a man who would be likely to give up his wedding-ring at such short notice, or could we conceive of his giving it up at all? No, no, Watson, the assassin was alone with the dead man for some time with the lamp lit. Of that I have no doubt at all. But the gunshot was apparently the cause of death. Therefore the gunshot must have been fired some time earlier than we are told. But there could be no mistake about such a matter as that. We are in the presence, therefore, of a deliberate conspiracy upon the part of the two people who heard the gunshot—of the man Barker and of the woman Douglas. When on the top of this I am able to show that the blood-mark upon the window-sill was deliberately placed there by Barker in order to give a false clue to the police, you will admit that the case grows dark against him.

'Now we have to ask ourselves at what hour the murder actually did occur. Up to half-past ten the servants were moving about the house, so it was certainly not before that time. At a quarter to eleven they had all gone to their rooms with the exception of Ames, who was in the pantry. I have been trying some experiments after you left us this afternoon, and I find that no noise which MacDonald can make in the study can penetrate to me in the pantry when the doors are all shut. It is otherwise, however, from the housekeeper's room. It is not so far down the corridor, and from it I could vaguely hear a voice when it was very loudly raised. The sound from a shot-gun is to some extent muffled when the discharge is at very close range, as it undoubtedly was in this instance. It would not be very loud, and yet in the silence of the night it should have easily penetrated to Mrs Allen's room. She is, as she has told us, somewhat deaf, but none the less she mentioned in her evidence that she did hear something like a door slamming half an hour before the alarm was given. Half an hour before the alarm was given would be a quarter to eleven. I have no doubt that what she heard was the report of the gun, and that was the real instant of the murder. If this is so, we have now to determine what Mr Barker and Mrs Douglas, presuming that they are not the actual murderers, could have been doing from a quarter to eleven when the sound of the gun-shot brought them down, until a quarter-past eleven, when they rang the bell and summoned the servants. What were they doing, and why did they not instantly give the alarm? That is the question which faces us, and when it has been answered we will surely have gone some way to solve our problem.'

'I am convinced myself,' said I, 'that there is an understanding between those two people. She must be a heartless creature to sit laughing at some jest within a few hours of her husband's murder.'

'Exactly. She does not shine as a wife even in her own account of what occurred. I am not a whole-souled admirer of womankind, as you are aware, Watson, but my experience of life has taught me that there are few wives having any regard for their husbands who would let any man's spoken word stand between them and that husband's dead body. Should I ever marry, Watson, I should hope to inspire my wife with some feeling which would prevent her from being walked off by a housekeeper when my corpse was lying within a few yards of her. It was badly stage-managed, for even the rawest of investigators must be struck by the absence of the usual feminine ululation. If there had been nothing else, this incident alone would have suggested a pre-arranged conspiracy to my mind.'

'You think, then, definitely, that Barker and Mrs Douglas are guilty of the murder?'

'There is an appalling directness about your questions, Watson,' said Holmes, shaking his pipe at me. 'They come at me like bullets. If you put it that Mrs Douglas and Barker know the truth about the murder and are conspiring to conceal it, then I can give you a whole-souled answer. I am sure they do. But your more deadly proposition is not so clear. Let us for a moment consider the difficulties which stand in the way.

'We will suppose that this couple are united by the bonds of a guilty love and that they have determined to get rid of the man who stands between them. It is a large supposition, for discreet inquiry among servants and others has failed to corroborate it in any way. On the contrary, there is a good deal of evidence that the Douglases were very attached to each other.'

'That I am sure cannot be true,' said I, thinking of the beautiful, smiling face in the garden.

'Well, at least they gave that impression. However, we will suppose that they are an extraordinarily astute couple, who deceive everyone upon this point and who conspire to murder the husband. He happens to be a man over whose head some danger hangs——'

'We have only their word for that.'

Holmes looked thoughtful.

'I see, Watson. You are sketching out a theory by which everything they say from the beginning is false. According to your idea, there was never any hidden menace or secret society or Valley of Fear or Boss McSomebody or anything else. Well, that is a good, sweeping generalization. Let us see what that brings us to. They invent this theory to account for the crime. They then play up to the idea by leaving this bicycle in the park as a proof of the existence of some outsider. The stain on the window-sill conveys the same idea. So does the card upon the body, which might have been prepared in the house. That all fits into your hypothesis, Watson. But now we come on the nasty angular, uncompromising bits which won't slip into their places. Why a cut-off shot-gun of all weapons—and an American one at that? How could they be so sure that the sound of it would not bring someone on to them? It's a mere chance, as it is, that Mrs Allen did not start out to inquire for the slamming door. Why did your guilty couple do all this, Watson?'

'I confess that I can't explain it.'

'Then, again, if a woman and her lover conspire to murder a husband, are they going to advertise their guilt by ostentatiously removing his wedding-ring after his death? Does that strike you as very probable, Watson?'

'No, it does not.'

'And once again, if the thought of leaving a bicycle concealed had occurred to you, would it really have seemed worth doing when the dullest detective would naturally say this is an obvious blind, as the bicycle is the first thing which the fugitive needed in order to make his escape?'

'I can conceive of no explanation.'

'And yet there should be no combination of events for which the wit of man cannot conceive an explanation. Simply as a mental exercise, without any assertion that it is true, let me indicate a possible line of thought. It is, I admit, mere imagination, but how often is imagination the mother of truth? **44**

'We will suppose that there *was* a guilty secret, a really shameful secret, in the life of this man Douglas. This leads to his murder by someone who is, we will suppose, an avenger —someone from outside. This avenger, for some reason which I confess I am still at a loss to explain, took the dead man's wedding-ring. The vendetta might conceivably date back to the man's first marriage and the ring be taken for some such reason. Before this avenger got away Barker and the wife had reached the room. The assassin convinced them that any attempt to arrest him would lead to the publication of some hideous scandal. They were converted to this idea and preferred to let him go. For this purpose they probably lowered the bridge, which can be done quite noiselessly, and then raised it again. He made his escape, and for some reason thought that he could do so more safely on foot than on the bicycle. He therefore left his machine where it would not be discovered until he had got safely away. So far we are within the bounds of possibility, are we not?'

'Well, it is possible, no doubt,' said I, with some reserve.

'We have to remember, Watson, that whatever occurred is certainly something very extraordinary. Well now, to continue our supposititious case, the couple—not necessarily a guilty couple—realize after the murderer is gone that they have placed themselves in a position in which it may be difficult for them to prove that they did not themselves either do the deed or connive at it. They rapidly and rather clumsily met the situation. The mark was put by Barker's blood-stained slipper upon the window-sill to suggest how the fugitive got away. They obviously were the two who must have heard the sound of the gun, so they gave the alarm exactly as they would have done, but a good half-hour after the event.'

'And how do you propose to prove all this?'

'Well, if there were an outsider he may be traced and taken. That would be the most effective of all proofs. But if not— well, the resources of science are far from being exhausted.

44 *how often is imagination the mother of truth?* Joseph Conrad, 1857–1924, in *A Personal Record* (1912) called imagination "the supreme master of art as of life."

45 *the* genius loci. A beneficient spirit or demon thought by the ancient Romans to haunt a particular place.

I think that an evening alone in that study would help me much.'

'An evening alone!'

'I propose to go up there presently. I have arranged it with the estimable Ames, who is by no means whole-hearted about Barker. I shall sit in that room and see if its atmosphere brings **45** me inspiration. I'm a believer in the *genius loci*. You smile, friend Watson. Well, we shall see. By the way, you have that big umbrella of yours, have you not?'

'It is here.'

'Well, I'll borrow that, if I may.'

'Certainly—but what a wretched weapon! If there is danger——'

'Nothing serious, my dear Watson, or I should certainly ask for your assistance. But I'll take the umbrella. At present I am only awaiting the return of our colleagues from Tunbridge Wells, where they are at present engaged in trying for a likely owner to the bicycle.'

It was nightfall before Inspector MacDonald and White Mason came back from their expedition, and they arrived exultant, reporting a great advance in our investigation.

'Man, I'll admeet that I had my doubts if there was ever an outsider,' said MacDonald, 'but that's all past now. We've had the bicycle identified, and we have a description of our man, so that's a long step on our journey.'

'It sounds to me like the beginning of the end,' said Holmes; 'I'm sure I congratulate you both with all my heart.'

'Well, I started from the fact that Mr Douglas had seemed disturbed since the day before, when he had been at Tunbridge Wells. It was at Tunbridge Wells, then, that he had become conscious of some danger. It was clear, therefore, that if a man had come over with a bicycle it was from Tunbridge Wells that he might be expected to have come. We took the bicycle over with us and showed it at the hotels. It was identified at once by the manager of the Eagle Commercial as belonging to a man named Hargrave who had taken a room there two days before. This bicycle and a small valise were his whole belongings. He had registered his name as coming from London, but had given no address. The valise was London-made and the contents were British, but the man himself was undoubtedly an American.'

'Well, well,' said Holmes, gleefully, 'you have indeed done some solid work whilst I have been sitting spinning theories with my friend. It's a lesson in being practical, Mr Mac.'

'Aye, it's just that, Mr Holmes,' said the inspector with satisfaction.

'But this may all fit in with your theories,' I remarked.

'That may or may not be. But let us hear the end, Mr Mac. Was there nothing to identify this man?'

'So little that it was evident he had carefully guarded himself against identification. There were no papers or letters and no marking upon the clothes. A cycle-map of the county lay upon his bedroom table. He had left the hotel after breakfast yesterday morning upon his bicycle, and no more was heard of him until our inquiries.'

'That's what puzzles me, Mr Holmes,' said White Mason. 'If the fellow did not want the hue and cry raised over him, one would imagine that he would have returned and remained at the hotel as an inoffensive tourist. As it is, he must know that he will be reported to the police by the hotel manager, and that his disappearance will be connected with the murder.'

'So one would imagine. Still he has been justified of his wisdom up to date at any rate, since he has not been taken. But his description—what of that?'

MacDonald referred to his note-book.

'Here we have it so far as they could give it. They don't seem to have taken any very particular stock of him, but still the porter, the clerk, and the chambermaid are all agreed that this about covers the points. He was a man about five foot nine in height, fifty or so years of age, his hair slightly grizzled, a greyish moustache, a curved nose, and a face which all of them described as fierce and forbidding.'

'Well, bar the expression, that might almost be a description of Douglas himself,' said Holmes. 'He is just over fifty, with grizzled hair and moustache and about the same height. Did you get anything else?'

'He was dressed in a heavy grey suit with a reefer jacket, and he wore a short, yellow overcoat and a soft cap.'

'What about the shot-gun?'

'It is less than two feet long. It could very well have fitted into his valise. He could have carried it inside his overcoat without difficulty.'

'And how do you consider that all this bears upon the general case?'

'Well, Mr Holmes,' said MacDonald, 'when we have got our man—and you may be sure that I had his description on the wires within five minutes of hearing it—we shall be better able to judge. But even as it stands, we have surely gone a long way. We know that an American calling himself Hargrave came to Tunbridge Wells two days ago with bicycle and valise. In the latter was a sawn-off shot-gun, so he came with the deliberate purpose of crime. Yesterday morning he set off for this place upon his bicycle with his gun concealed in his overcoat. No one saw him arrive, so far as we can learn, but he need not pass through the village to reach the park gates, and there are many cyclists upon the road. Presumably he at once concealed his cycle among the laurels, where it was found, and possibly lurked there himself, with his eye on the house waiting for Mr Douglas to come out. The shot-gun is a strange weapon to use inside a house, but he had intended to use it outside, and then it has very obvious advantages, as it would be impossible to miss with it, and the sound of shots is so common in an English sporting neighbourhood that no particular notice would be taken.'

'That is all very clear!' said Holmes.

'Well, Mr Douglas did not appear. What was he to do next? He left his bicycle and approached the house in the twilight. He found the bridge down and no one about. He took his chance, intending, no doubt, to make some excuse if he met anyone. He met no one. He slipped into the first room that he saw and concealed himself behind the curtain. From thence he could see the drawbridge go up and he knew that his only escape was through the moat. He waited until a quarter-past eleven, when Mr Douglas, upon his usual nightly round, came into the room. He shot him and escaped, as arranged. He was aware that the bicycle would be described by the hotel people and be a clue against him, so he left it there and made

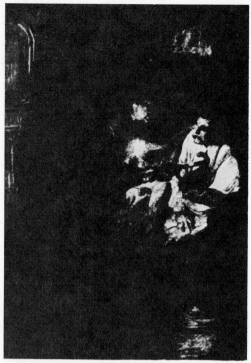

"I SAY, WATSON," HE WHISPERED, "WOULD YOU BE AFRAID TO SLEEP IN THE SAME ROOM AS A LUNATIC . . . ?"

Illustration by Arthur I. Keller for Associated Sunday Magazines, 1914. Frank Wiles illustrated the same scene (*Below*) for the *Strand Magazine*, December, 1914.

his way by some other means to London or to some safe hiding-place which he had already arranged. How is that, Mr Holmes?'

'Well, Mr Mac, it is very good and very clear so far as it goes. That is your end of the story. My end is that the crime was committed half an hour earlier than reported; that Mrs Douglas and Mr Barker are both in a conspiracy to conceal something; that they aided the murderer's escape—or at least, that they reached the room before he escaped—and that they fabricated evidence of his escape through the window, whereas in all probability they had themselves let him go by lowering the bridge. That's *my* reading of the first half.'

The two detectives shook their heads.

'Well, Mr Holmes, if this is true we only tumble out of one mystery into another,' said the London inspector.

'And in some ways a worse one,' added White Mason. 'The lady has never been in America in her life. What possible connection could she have with an American assassin which would cause her to shelter him?'

'I freely admit the difficulties,' said Holmes. 'I propose to make a little investigation of my own tonight, and it is just possible that it may contribute something to the common cause.'

'Can we help you, Mr Holmes?'

'No, no! Darkness and Dr Watson's umbrella. My wants are simple. And Ames—the faithful Ames—no doubt he will stretch a point for me. All my lines of thought lead me back invariably to the one basic question—why should an athletic man develop his frame upon so unnatural an instrument as a single dumb-bell?'

It was late that night when Holmes returned from his solitary excursion. We slept in a double-bedded room, which was the best that the little country inn could do for us. I was already asleep when I was partly awakened by his entrance.

'Well, Holmes,' I murmured, 'have you found out anything?'

He stood beside me in silence, his candle in his hand. Then the tall, lean figure inclined towards me.

'I say, Watson,' he whispered, 'would you be afraid to sleep in the same room as a lunatic, a man with softening of the brain, an idiot whose mind has lost its grip?'

'Not in the least,' I answered in astonishment.

'Ah, that's lucky,' he said, and not another word would he utter that night.

7 ◆ THE SOLUTION

Next morning, after breakfast, we found Inspector Mac-Donald and Mr White Mason seated in close consultation in the small parlour of the local police-sergeant. Upon the table in front of them were piled a number of letters and telegrams, which they were carefully sorting and docketing. Three had been placed upon one side.

'Still on the track of the elusive bicyclist?' Holmes asked, cheerfully. 'What is the latest news of the ruffian?'

MacDonald pointed ruefully to his heap of correspondence.

'He is at present reported from Leicester, Nottingham, Southampton, Derby, East Ham, Richmond, and fourteen other places. In three of them—East Ham, Leicester, and Liverpool—there is a clear case against him and he has actually been arrested. The country seems to be full of fugitives with yellow coats.'

'Dear me!' said Holmes, sympathetically. 'Now, Mr Mac, and you, Mr White Mason, I wish to give you a very earnest piece of advice. When I went into this case with you I bargained, as you will no doubt remember, that I should not present you with half-proved theories, but that I should retain and work out my own ideas until I had satisfied myself that they were correct. For this reason I am not at the present moment telling you all that is in my mind. On the other hand, I said that I would play the game fairly by you, and I do not think it is a fair game to allow you for one unnecessary moment to waste your energies upon a profitless task. Therefore I am here to advise you this morning, and my advice to you is summed up in three words: Abandon the case.'

MacDonald and White Mason stared in amazement at their celebrated colleague.

'You consider it hopeless?' cried the inspector.

'I consider *your* case to be hopeless. I do not consider that it is hopeless to arrive at the truth.'

'But this cyclist. He is not an invention. We have his description, his valise, his bicycle. The fellow must be somewhere. Why should we not get him?'

'Yes, yes; no doubt he is somewhere, and no doubt we shall get him, but I would not have you waste your energies in East Ham or Liverpool. I am sure that we can find some shorter cut to a result.'

'You are holding something back. It's hardly fair of you, Mr Holmes.' The inspector was annoyed.

'You know my methods of work, Mr Mac. But I will hold it back for the shortest time possible. I only wish to verify my details in one way, which can very readily be done, and then I make my bow and return to London, leaving my results entirely at your service. I owe you too much to act otherwise, for in all my experience I cannot recall any more singular and interesting study.'

'This is clean beyond me, Mr Holmes. We saw you when we returned from Tunbridge Wells last night, and you were in general agreement with our results. What has happened since then to give you a completely new idea of the case?'

'Well, since you ask me, I spent, as I told you that I would, some hours last night at the Manor House.'

'Well, what happened?'

'Ah! I can only give you a very general answer to that for the moment. By the way, I have been reading a short, but clear and interesting, account of the old building, purchasable at the modest sum of one penny from the local tobacconist.' Here Holmes drew a small tract, embellished with a rude **46** engraving of the ancient Manor House, from his waistcoat

46 *a small tract.* Identified, as we have seen, by the late James Montgomery, as the account written by B. W. Shepherd-Walwyn.

47 *the second George.* George II, George Augustus, 1683–1760, was king 1726–1760. He was the last British king to lead troops in person, in the War of the Austrian Succession.

48 *often of extraordinary interest.* "We see in 'The Adventure of the Lion's Mane' an example of how Holmes could bring his out-of-the-way knowledge to bear on a problem, and he has a number of interesting remarks on this point in 'The Five Orange Pips,'" Mr. T. S. Blakeney wrote in *Sherlock Holmes: Fact or Fiction?*

pocket. 'It immensely adds to the zest of an investigation, my dear Mr Mac, when one is in conscious sympathy with the historical atmosphere of one's surroundings. Don't look so impatient, for I assure you that even so bald an account as this raises some sort of picture of the past in one's mind. Permit me to give you a sample. "Erected in the fifth year of the reign of James I., and standing upon the site of a much older building, the Manor House of Birlstone presents one of the finest surviving examples of the moated Jacobean residence——" '

'You are making fools of us, Mr Holmes.'

'Tut, tut, Mr Mac!—the first sign of temper I have detected in you. Well, I won't read it verbatim, since you feel so strongly upon the subject. But when I tell you that there is some account of the taking of the place by a Parliamentary colonel in 1644, of the concealment of Charles for several days in the course of the Civil War, and finally of a visit there **47** by the second George, you will admit that there are various associations of interest connected with this ancient house.'

'I don't doubt it, Mr Holmes, but that is no business of ours.'

'Is it not? Is it not? Breadth of view, my dear Mr Mac, is one of the essentials of our profession. The interplay of ideas and the oblique uses of knowledge are often of extraordinary **48** interest. You will excuse these remarks from one who, though a mere connoisseur of crime, is still rather older and perhaps more experienced than yourself.'

'I'm the first to admit that,' said the detective, heartily. 'You get to your point, I admit, but you have such a deuced round-the-corner way of doing it.'

'Well, well, I'll drop past history and get down to present-day facts. I called last night, as I have already said, at the Manor House. I did not see either Mr Barker or Mrs Douglas. I saw no necessity to disturb them, but I was pleased to hear that the lady was not visibly pining and that she had partaken of an excellent dinner. My visit was specially made to the good Mr Ames, with whom I exchanged some amiabilities which culminated in his allowing me, without reference to anyone else, to sit alone for a time in the study.'

'What! With that!' I ejaculated.

'No, no; everything is now in order. You gave permission for that, Mr Mac, as I am informed. The room was in its normal state, and in it I passed an instructive quarter of an hour.'

'What were you doing?'

'Well, not to make a mystery of so simple a matter, I was looking for the missing dumb-bell. It has always bulked rather large in my estimate of the case. I ended by finding it.'

'Where?'

'Ah! There we come to the edge of the unexplored. Let me go a little farther, a very little farther, and I will promise that you shall share everything that I know.'

'Well, we're bound to take you on your own terms,' said the inspector; 'but when it comes to telling us to abandon the case—— Why, in the name of goodness, should we abandon the case?'

'For the simple reason, my dear Mr Mac, that you have not got the first idea what it is that you are investigating.'

'We are investigating the murder of Mr John Douglas, of Birlstone Manor.'

'Yes, yes; so you are. But don't trouble to trace the mysterious gentleman upon the bicycle. I assure you that it won't help you.'

'Then what do you suggest that we do?'

'I will tell you exactly what to do, if you will do it.'

'Well, I'm bound to say I've always found you had reason behind all your queer ways. I'll do what you advise.'

'And you, Mr White Mason?'

The country detective looked helplessly from one to the other. Mr Holmes and his methods were new to him.

'Well, if it is good enough for the inspector it is good enough for me!' he said, at last.

'Capital' said Holmes. 'Well, then I should recommend a nice, cheery, country walk for both of you. They tell me that the views from Birlstone Ridge over the Weald are very remarkable. No doubt lunch could be got at some suitable hostelry, though my ignorance of the country prevents me from recommending one. In the evening, tired but happy——'

'Man, this is getting past a joke!' cried MacDonald, rising angrily from his chair.

'Well, well, spend the day as you like,' said Holmes, patting him cheerfully upon the shoulder. 'Do what you like and go where you will, but meet me here before dusk without fail—without fail, Mr Mac.'

'That sounds more like sanity.'

'All of it was excellent advice, but I don't insist, so long as you are here when I need you. But now, before we part, I want you to write a note to Mr Barker.'

'Well?'

'I'll dictate it, if you like. Ready?

'DEAR SIR,—It has struck me that it is our duty to drain the moat, in the hope that we may find some——'

'It's impossible,' said the inspector; 'I've made inquiry.'

'Tut, tut, my dear sir! Do, please, do what I ask you.'

'Well, go on.'

'——in the hope that we may find something which may bear upon our investigation. I have made arrangements, and the workmen will be at work early tomorrow morning diverting the **49** stream——'

'Impossible!'

'——diverting the stream, so I thought it best to explain matters beforehand.

Now sign that, and send it by hand about four o'clock. At that hour we shall meet again in this room. Until then we can each do what we like, for I can assure you that this inquiry has come to a definite pause.'

Evening was drawing in when we reassembled. Holmes was very serious in his manner, myself curious, and the detectives obviously critical and annoyed.

'Well, gentlemen,' said my friend, gravely, 'I am asking you now to put everything to the test with me, and you will judge for yourselves whether the observations which I have made justify the conclusions to which I have come. It is a chill evening, and I do not know how long our expedition may last, so I beg that you will wear your warmest coats. It is of the first importance that we should be in our places before it grows dark, so, with your permission, we will get started at once.'

49 *early tomorrow morning*. The third day of adventure (in fact, it ended on the second day) could not therefore have been a Sunday, and the first day, then, was not a Friday.

50 *'Possess our souls in patience.* "In your patience possess ye your souls."—Luke, 21:19. We shall see that this was a favorite expression of Holmes': "We can only possess our souls in patience," he says in "The Adventure of Wisteria Lodge," and "We can but possess our souls in patience" he says again in "The Adventure of the Three Garridebs."

51 *the pride and the justification of our life's work?* "This art was one of Holmes' strongest assets as a detective—he called it the scientific use of the imagination, 'the region where we balance probabilities and choose the most likely' (*The Hound of the Baskervilles*)," Mr. T. S. Blakeney wrote in *Sherlock Holmes: Fact or Fiction?*

We passed along the outer bounds of the Manor House park until we came to a place where there was a gap in the rails which fenced it. Through this we slipped, and then, in the gathering gloom, we followed Holmes until we had reached a shrubbery which lies nearly opposite to the main door and the drawbridge. The latter had not been raised. Holmes crouched down behind the screen of laurels, and we all three followed his example.

'Well, what are we to do now?' asked MacDonald, with some gruffness.

50   'Possess our souls in patience and make as little noise as possible,' Holmes answered.

'What are we here for at all? I really think that you might treat us with more frankness.'

Holmes laughed.

'Watson insists that I am the dramatist in real life,' said he. 'Some touch of the artist wells up within me and calls insistently for a well-staged performance. Surely our profession, Mr Mac, would be a drab and sordid one if we did not sometimes set the scene so as to glorify our results. The blunt accusation, the brutal tap upon the shoulder—what can one make of such a *dénouement*? But the quick inference, the subtle trap, the clever forecast of coming events, the triumphant vindication of bold theories—are these not the pride

51 and the justification of our life's work? At the present moment you thrill with the glamour of the situation and the anticipation of the hunter. Where would be that thrill if I had been as definite as a time-table? I only ask a little patience, Mr Mac, and all will be clear to you.'

'Well, I hope the pride and justification and the rest of it will come before we all get our death of cold,' said the London detective, with comic resignation.

We all had good reason to join in the aspiration, for our vigil was a long and bitter one. Slowly the shadows darkened over the long, sombre face of the old house. A cold, damp reek from the moat chilled us to the bones and set our teeth chattering. There was a single lamp over the gateway and a steady globe of light in the fatal study. Everything else was dark and still.

'How long is this to last?' asked the inspector, suddenly. 'And what is it we are watching for?'

'I have no more notion than you how long it is to last,' Holmes answered with some asperity. 'If criminals would always schedule their movements like railway trains it would certainly be more convenient for all of us. As to what it is we—— Well, *that's* what we are watching for.'

As he spoke the bright yellow light in the study was obscured by somebody passing to and fro before it. The laurels among which we lay were immediately opposite the window and not more than a hundred feet from it. Presently it was thrown open with a whining of hinges, and we could dimly see the dark outline of a man's head and shoulders looking out into the gloom. For some minutes he peered forth, in a furtive, stealthy fashion, as one who wishes to be assured that he is unobserved. Then he leaned forward, and in the intense silence we were aware of the soft lapping of agitated water. He seemed to be stirring up the moat with something which he held in his hand. Then suddenly he hauled something in as a fisherman lands a fish—some large, round object which obscured the light as it was dragged through the open casement.

'Now!' cried Holmes. 'Now!'

We were all upon our feet, staggering after him with our stiffened limbs, whilst he, with one of those outflames of nervous energy which could make him on occasion both the most active and the strongest man that I have ever known, ran swiftly across the bridge and rang violently at the bell. There was the rasping of bolts from the other side, and the amazed Ames stood in the entrance. Holmes brushed him aside without a word and, followed by all of us, rushed into the room which had been occupied by the man whom we had been watching.

The oil lamp on the table represented the glow which we had seen from outside. It was now in the hand of Cecil Barker, who held it towards us as we entered. Its light shone upon his strong, resolute, clean-shaven face and his menacing eyes.

'What the devil is the meaning of all this?' he cried. 'What are you after, anyhow?'

Holmes took a swift glance round and then pounced upon a sodden bundle tied together with cord which lay where it had been thrust under the writing-table.

'This is what we are after, Mr Barker. This bundle, weighted with a dumb-bell, which you have just raised from the bottom of the moat.'

Barker stared at Holmes with amazement in his face.

'How in thunder came you to know anything about it?' he asked.

'Simply that I put it there.'

'You put it there! You!'

'Perhaps I should have said "replaced it there," ' said Holmes. 'You will remember, Inspector MacDonald, that I was somewhat struck by the absence of a dumb-bell. I drew your attention to it, but with the pressure of other events you had hardly the time to give it the consideration which would have enabled you to draw deductions from it. When water is near and a weight is missing it is not a very far-fetched supposition that something has been sunk in the water. The idea was at least worth testing, so with the help of Ames, who admitted me to the room, and the crook of Dr Watson's umbrella, I was able last night to fish up and inspect this bundle. It was of the first importance, however, that we should be able to prove who placed it there. This we accomplished by the very obvious device of announcing that the moat would be dried tomorrow, which had, of course, the effect that whoever had hidden the bundle would most certainly withdraw it the moment that darkness enabled him to do so. We have no fewer than four witnesses as to who it was who took advantage of the opportunity, and so, Mr Barker, I think the word lies now with you.'

Sherlock Holmes put the sopping bundle upon the table beside the lamp and undid the cord which bound it. From within he extracted a dumb-bell, which he tossed down to its fellow in the corner. Next he drew forth a pair of boots. 'American, as you perceive,' he remarked, pointing to the toes. Then he laid upon the table a long, deadly, sheathed knife. Finally he unravelled a bundle of clothing, comprising a complete set of underclothes, socks, a grey tweed suit, and a short yellow overcoat.

'The clothes are commonplace,' remarked Holmes, 'save

THEN SUDDENLY HE HAULED SOMETHING IN AS A
FISHERMAN LANDS A FISH . . .

Illustration by Frank Wiles for the *Strand Magazine*, January, 1915. We should note here that—while cold weather is clearly indicated throughout the action of the adventure—the temperature was *not below freezing* on either the 8th or the 6th of January: on the 6th the bundle was lowered into the moat; on the 8th it was fished out. The late Dr. Ernest Bloomfield Zeisler has shown that 1889 will not answer this requirement: on January 6th of that year the temperature ranged from a low of 19.8 degrees to a high of 29.5 degrees. Dr. Zeisler also showed that a dark night was required on the 6th, for the tragedy, and the 8th, for the vigil. Eighteen-eighty-nine is ruled out once more: the moon was full on January 6th; it set at 9:53 P.M. on that day, but not until midnight on January 8th. Only 1888 meets the requirements: from the 6th to the 8th, according to the London *Times*, the minimum temperature reached was 38 degrees. As for the moon, it was at last quarter on the 6th, and did not rise before midnight on either the 6th or the 8th.

52 *Vermissa, U.S.A.* The town of "Vermissa," where Neale had his men's toggery, is most probably Pottsville, near the Schuykill anthracite region.

53 *Vermissa Valley.* Watsonese for the Shenandoah Valley.

54 peine forte et dure. French: heavy and harsh punishment.

only the overcoat, which is full of suggestive touches.' He held it tenderly towards the light, whilst his long, thin fingers flickered over it. 'Here, as you perceive, is the inner pocket prolonged into the lining in such a fashion as to give ample space for the truncated fowling-piece. The tailor's tab is on **52** the neck—Neale, Outfitter, Vermissa, U.S.A. I have spent an instructive afternoon in the rector's library, and have enlarged my knowledge by adding the fact that Vermissa is a flourishing little town at the head of one of the best-known coal and iron valleys in the United States. I have some recollection, Mr Barker, that you associated the coal districts with Mr Douglas's first wife, and it would surely not be too far-fetched an inference that the V. V. upon the card by the dead **53** body might stand for Vermissa Valley, or that this very valley, which sends forth emissaries of murder, may be that Valley of Fear of which we have heard. So much is fairly clear. And now, Mr Barker, I seem to be standing rather in the way of your explanation.'

It was a sight to see Cecil Barker's expressive face during this exposition of the great detective. Anger, amazement, consternation, and indecision swept over it in turn. Finally he took refuge in a somewhat acid irony.

'You know such a lot, Mr Holmes, perhaps you had better tell us some more,' he sneered.

'I have no doubt that I could tell you a great deal more, Mr Barker, but it would come with a better grace from you.'

'Oh, you think so, do you? Well, all I can say is that if there's any secret here it is not my secret, and I am not the man to give it away.'

'Well, if you take that line, Mr Barker,' said the inspector, quietly, 'we must just keep you in sight until we have the warrant and can hold you.'

'You can do what you damn please about that,' said Barker, defiantly.

The proceedings seemed to have come to a definite end so far as he was concerned, for one had only to look at that **54** granite face to realize that no *peine forte et dure* would ever force him to plead against his will. The deadlock was broken, however, by a woman's voice. Mrs Douglas had been standing listening at the half-opened door, and now she entered the room.

'You have done enough for us, Cecil,' said she. 'Whatever comes of it in the future, you have done enough.'

'Enough and more than enough,' remarked Sherlock Holmes, gravely. 'I have every sympathy with you, madam, and I should strongly urge you to have some confidence in the common sense of our jurisdiction and to take the police voluntarily into your complete confidence. It may be that I am myself at fault for not following up the hint which you conveyed to me through my friend, Dr Watson, but at that time I had every reason to believe that you were directly concerned in the crime. Now I am assured that this is not so. At the same time, there is much that is unexplained, and I should strongly recommend that you ask *Mr Douglas* to tell us his own story.'

Mrs Douglas gave a cry of astonishment at Holmes's words. The detectives and I must have echoed it, when we were aware of a man who seemed to have emerged from the wall, and who advanced now from the gloom of the corner in which he had appeared. Mrs Douglas turned, and in an instant her arms were round him. Barker had seized his outstretched hand.

'It's best this way, Jack,' his wife repeated. 'I am sure that it is best.'

'Indeed, yes, Mr Douglas,' said Sherlock Holmes. 'I am sure that you will find it best.'

The man stood blinking at us with the dazed look of one who comes from the dark into the light. It was a remarkable face—bold grey eyes, a strong, short-clipped, grizzled moustache, a square, projecting chin, and a humorous mouth. He took a good look at us all, and then, to my amazement, he advanced to me and handed me a bundle of paper.

'I've heard of you,' said he, in a voice which was not quite English and not quite American, but was altogether mellow and pleasing. 'You are the historian of this bunch. Well, Dr Watson, you've never had such a story as that pass through your hands before, and I'd lay my last dollar on that. Tell it your own way, but there are the facts, and you can't miss the public so long as you have those. I've been cooped up two days, and I've spent the daylight hours—as much daylight as I could get in that rat-trap—in putting the thing into words. You're welcome to them—you and your public. There's the story of the Valley of Fear.'

'That's the past, Mr Douglas,' said Sherlock Holmes, quietly. 'What we desire now is to hear your story of the present.'

'You'll have it, sir,' said Douglas. 'Can I smoke as I talk? Well, thank you, Mr Holmes; you're a smoker yourself, if I remember right, and you'll guess what it is to be sitting for two days with tobacco in your pocket and afraid that the smell will give you away.' He leaned against the mantelpiece and sucked at the cigar which Holmes had handed him. 'I've heard of you, Mr Holmes; I never guessed that I would meet you. But before you are through with that'—he nodded at my papers—'you will say I've brought you something fresh.'

Inspector MacDonald had been staring at the new-comer with the greatest amazement.

'Well, this fairly beats me!' he cried at last. 'If you are Mr John Douglas, of Birlstone Manor, then whose death have we been investigating for these two days, and where in the world have you sprung from now? You seemed to me to come out of the floor like a Jack-in-a-box.'

'Ah, Mr Mac,' said Holmes, shaking a reproving forefinger, 'you would not read that excellent local compilation which described the concealment of King Charles. People did not hide in those days without reliable hiding-places, and the hiding-place that has once been used may be again. I had persuaded myself that we should find Mr Douglas under this roof.'

'And how long have you been playing this trick upon us, Mr Holmes?' said the inspector angrily. 'How long have you allowed us to waste ourselves upon a search that you knew to be an absurd one?'

'Not one instant, my dear Mr Mac. Only last night did I form my views of the case. As they could not be put to the proof until this evening, I invited you and your colleague to take a holiday for the day. Pray, what more could I do? When I found the suit of clothes in the moat it at once became apparent to me that the body we had found could not have been the body of Mr John Douglas at all, but must be that of the bicyclist from Tunbridge Wells. No other conclusion was possible. Therefore I had to determine where Mr John Douglas himself could be, and the balance of probability was that, with the connivance of his wife and his friend, he was concealed in a house which had such conveniences for a fugitive, and awaiting quieter times, when he could make his final escape.'

'Well, you figured it out about right,' said Mr Douglas, approvingly. 'I thought I'd dodge your British law, for I was not sure how I stood under it, and also I saw my chance to throw these hounds once for all off my track. Mind you, from first to last I have done nothing to be ashamed of, and nothing that I would not do again, but you'll judge that for yourselves when I tell you my story. Never mind warning me, inspector; I'm ready to stand pat upon the truth.

'I'm not going to begin at the beginning. That's all there' —he indicated my bundle of papers—'and a mighty queer yarn you'll find it. It all comes down to this: that there are some men that have good cause to hate me and would give their last dollar to know that they had got me. So long as I am alive and they are alive, there is no safety in this world for me. They hunted me from Chicago to California; then they chased me out of America; but when I married and settled down in this quiet spot I thought my last years were going to be peaceable. I never explained to my wife how things were. Why should I pull her into it? She would never have a quiet moment again, but would be always imagining trouble. I fancy she knew something, for I may have dropped a word here or a word there—but until yesterday, after you gentlemen had seen her, she never knew the rights of the matter. She told you all she knew, and so did Barker here, for on the night when this thing happened there was mighty little time for explanations. She knows everything now, and I would have been a wiser man if I had told her sooner. But it was a hard question, dear'—he took her hand for an instant in his own—'and I acted for the best.

'Well, gentlemen, the day before these happenings I was over in Tunbridge Wells and I got a glimpse of a man in the street. It was only a glimpse, but I have a quick eye for these things, and I never doubted who it was. It was the worst enemy I had among them all—one who has been after me like a hungry wolf after a caribou all these years. I knew there was trouble coming, and I came home and made ready for it. I guessed I'd fight through it all right on my own. There was a time when my luck was the talk of the whole United States. I never doubted that it would be with me still.

'I was on my guard all that next day and never went out into the park. It's as well, or he'd have had the drop on me with that buckshot gun of his before ever I could draw on him. After the bridge was up—my mind was always more restful when that bridge was up in the evenings—I put the thing clear out of my head. I never figured on his getting into the house and waiting for me. But when I made my round in my dressing-gown, as my habit was, I had no sooner entered the study than I scented danger. I guess when a man has had dangers in his life—and I've had more than most in my time —there is a kind of sixth sense that waves the red flag. I saw the signal clear enough, and yet I couldn't tell you why. Next

instant I spotted a boot under the window curtain, and then
I saw why plain enough.

'I'd just the one candle that was in my hand, but there was
a good light from the hall-lamp through the open door. I
put down the candle and jumped for a hammer that I'd left
on the mantel. At the same moment he sprang at me. I saw
the glint of a knife and I lashed at him with the hammer. I
got him somewhere, for the knife tinkled down on the floor.
He dodged round the table as quick as an eel, and a moment
later he'd got his gun from under his coat. I heard him cock
it, but I had got hold of it before he could fire. I had it by
the barrel, and we wrestled for it all ends up for a minute or
more. It was death to the man that lost his grip. He never
lost his grip, but he got it butt downwards for a moment too
long. Maybe it was I that pulled the trigger. Maybe we just
jolted it off between us. Anyhow, he got both barrels in the
face, and there I was, staring down at all that was left of Ted
Baldwin. I'd recognized him in the township and again when
he sprang for me, but his own mother wouldn't recognize him
as I saw him then. I'm used to rough work, but I fairly turned
sick at the sight of him.

'I was hanging on to the side of the table when Barker came
hurrying down. I heard my wife coming, and I ran to the
door and stopped her. It was no sight for a woman. I promised I'd come to her soon. I said a word or two to Barker—he
took it all in at a glance—and we waited for the rest to come
along. But there was no sign of them. Then we understood
that they could hear nothing, and that all that had happened
was only known to ourselves.

'It was at that instant that the idea came to me. I was fairly
dazzled by the brilliancy of it. The man's sleeve had slipped
up and there was the branded mark of the Lodge upon his
forearm. See here.'

The man whom we knew as Douglas turned up his own coat
and cuff to show a brown triangle within a circle exactly like
that which we had seen upon the dead man.

'It was the sight of that which started me on to it. I seemed
to see it all clear at a glance. There was his height and hair
and figure about the same as my own. No one could swear to
his face, poor devil! I brought down this suit of clothes, and
in a quarter of an hour Barker and I had put my dressing-
gown on him and he lay as you found him. We tied all his
things into a bundle, and I weighted them with the only
weight I could find and slung them through the window. The
card he had meant to lay upon my body was lying beside his
own. My rings were put on his finger, but when it came to
the wedding-ring'—he held out his muscular hand—'you can
see for yourselves that I had struck my limit. I have not moved
it since the day I was married, and it would have taken a file
to get it off. I don't know, anyhow, that I would have cared
to part with it, but if I had wanted to I couldn't. So we just
had to leave that detail to take care of itself. On the other
hand, I brought a bit of plaster down and put it where I am
wearing one myself at this instant. You slipped up there, Mr
Holmes, clever as you are, for if you had chanced to take
off that plaster you would have found no cut underneath
it.

'Well, that was the situation. If I could lie low for a while
and then get away where I would be joined by my wife, we

I HEARD HIM COCK IT, BUT I HAD GOT HOLD OF IT
BEFORE HE COULD FIRE.

Illustration by Frank Wiles for the *Strand Magazine*, January, 1915.

55 *back some twenty years in time.* The story of "The Scowrers," which immediately follows, begins: "It was the fourth of February in the years 1875." If, as Watson says, this was a "journey back" of "some twenty years" it would seem that the adventure of *The Valley of Fear* took place *circa* 1895. There is a case, and a good case, for dating *The Valley of Fear* at the end of the 'nineties rather than at the end of the 'eighties: 1) When Birdy Edwards, in February, 1875, traveled through the gorges of the Gilmerton Mountains from Stagville to Vermissa, he was "not far from his thirtieth year"; 2) he spent three months in the Valley, and at the end of that time he arrested the famous gang of Scowrers; 3) the date of the trial of the Scowrers may reasonably be assigned to the autumn of 1875; McGinty went to the scaffold and Ted Baldwin went to the penitentiary for ten years; 4) it was presumably in 1886, then, that Birdy Edwards was driven from Chicago to California, where he remained for five years; it could not have been, therefore, earlier than the end of 1892 that Edwards packed up and came to England; 5) this, we are told, was "nearer seven years than six" before the date of the killing at Birlstone; this would place the date of the killing not earlier than the January of 1899, and this would correspond both with Dr. Watson's estimate that Douglas (Edwards) "may have been about fifty" and his statement that the events at Birlstone were "some twenty years" after the events in the Vermissa Valley.

For these and other reasons, many commentators *have* dated *The Valley of Fear* at the end of the 'nineties; 1890.

But these commentators are faced with the embarrassing fact that Professor James Moriarty, who died, Watson tells us, on May 4, 1891, is very much alive at the time of The *Valley of Fear.* Thus the late Gavin Brend (*My Dear Holmes*) is driven to postulate a *second* Moriarty, arising phoenix-like out of the ashes of the first. And Mr. Anthony Boucher holds that "the case did take place some time shortly before Holmes' retirement . . . and did *not* involve Moriarty. Watson wrote it up as the two novelettes: a completely self-contained non-Moriarty story. Then he began brooding along these lines: 'The public likes Moriarty, but, hang it, the only really good case involving him was that Reichenbach business. Of course there was that stunning piece of work Holmes did in deciphering that letter from Porlock; but once he'd deciphered it, it led us into a very routine affair with no plot-value at all. And that time that he explained Moriarty to Inspector Mac, but that case was even worse . . . nothing but men in it. . . . *I know!* Let's use those two episodes as a prologue and blame the whole Birlstone business on Moriarty.'"

"The justification for . . . any date [at the end of the 'eighties] requires that Baldwin got out before his full term of ten years," Mr. T. S. Blakeney wrote in *Sherlock Holmes: Fact or Fiction?*, "and there is nothing unlikely about that. If such a murderous villain could escape the death penalty there would be nothing improbable in his managing to

would have a chance at last of living at peace for the rest of our lives. These devils would give me no rest so long as I was above ground, but if they saw in the papers that Baldwin had got his man there would be an end of all my troubles. I hadn't much time to make it clear to Barker and to my wife, but they understood enough to be able to help me. I knew all about this hiding-place, so did Ames, but it never entered his head to connect it with the matter. I retired into it, and it was up to Barker to do the rest.

'I guess you can fill in for yourselves what he did. He opened the window and made the mark on the sill to give an idea of how the murderer escaped. It was a tall order, that, but as the bridge was up there was no other way. Then, when everything was fixed, he rang the bell for all he was worth. What happened afterwards you know—and so, gentlemen, you can do what you please, but I've told you the truth and the whole truth, so help me, God! What I ask you now is, how do I stand by the English law?'

There was a silence, which was broken by Sherlock Holmes.

'The English law is, in the main, a just law. You will get no worse than your deserts from it. But I would ask you how did this man know that you lived here, or how to get into your house, or where to hide to get you?'

'I know nothing of this.'

Holmes's face was very white and grave.

'The story is not over yet, I fear,' said he. 'You may find worse dangers than the English law, or even than your enemies from America. I see trouble before you; Mr Douglas. You'll take my advice and still be on your guard.'

And now, my long-suffering readers, I will ask you to come away with me for a time, far from the Sussex Manor House of Birlstone, and far also from the year of grace in which we made our eventful journey which ended with the strange story of the man who had been known as John Douglas. I **55** wish you to journey back some twenty years in time, and westward some thousands of miles in space, that I may lay before you a singular and a terrible narrative—so singular and so terrible that you may find it hard to believe that, even as I tell it, even so did it occur. Do not think that I intrude one story before another is finished. As you read on you will find that this is not so. And when I have detailed those distant events and you have solved this mystery of the past we shall meet once more in those rooms in Baker Street where this, like so many other wonderful happenings, will find its end.

get out of prison before his time, whether by good conduct or by bribery."

More recent chronologist prefer to hold that it was *not* Baldwin who drove Douglas-Edwards from Chicago. As the late Dr. Ernest Bloomfield Zeisler wrote (in "Concerning *The Valley of Fear*"): 'it was most unlikely that the Scowrers would wait until Ted Baldwin's release from the penitentiary to make their attempt to drive Edwards from Chicago." We suggest that Dr. Watson sat down to chronicle the adventure of *The Valley of Fear* in the Missing Year 1895–1896; thus his "twenty years in time" dates, not from the tragedy at Birlstone, but from his *writing* of his chronicle.

PART II

The Scowrers   **56**

8 • THE MAN

It was the fourth of February in the year 1875. It had been a severe winter, and the snow lay deep in the gorges of the Gilmerton Mountains. The steam plough had, however, kept the rail-track open, and the evening train which connects the long line of coal-mining and iron-working settlements was slowly groaning its way up the steep gradients which lead from Stagville on the plain to Vermissa, the central township which lies at the head of the Vermissa Valley. From this point the track sweeps downwards to Barton's Crossing, Helmdale, and the purely agricultural county of Merton. It was a single-track railroad, but at every siding, and they were numerous, long lines of trucks piled with coal and with iron ore told of the hidden wealth which had brought a rude population and a bustling life to this most desolate corner of the United States of America.

For desolate it was. Little could the first pioneer who had traversed it have ever imagined that the fairest prairies and the most lush water-pastures were valueless compared with this gloomy land of black crag and tangled forest. Above the dark and often scarcely penetrable woods upon their sides, the high, bare crowns of the mountains, white snow and jagged rock, towered upon either flank, leaving a long, winding, tortuous valley in the centre. Up this the little train was slowly crawling.

The oil-lamps had just been lit in the leading passenger-car, a long, bare carriage in which some twenty or thirty people were seated. The greater number of these were work-men returning from their day's toil in the lower portion of the valley. At least a dozen, by their grimed faces and the safety lanterns which they carried, proclaimed themselves as miners. These sat smoking in a group, and conversed in low voices, glancing occasionally at two men on the opposite side of the car, whose uniform and badges showed them to be policemen. Several women of the labouring class, and one or two travellers who might have been small local storekeepers, made up the rest of the company, with the exception of one young man in a corner by himself. It is with this man that we are concerned. Take a good look at him, for he is worth it.

He is a fresh-complexioned, middle-sized young man, not far, one would guess, from his thirtieth year. He has large, shrewd, humorous grey eyes which twinkle inquiringly from time to time as he looks round through his spectacles at the people about him. It is easy to see that he is of a sociable and possibly simple disposition, anxious to be friendly to all men. Anyone could pick him at once as gregarious in his habits and communicative in his nature, with a quick wit and a ready smile. And yet the man who studied him more closely might discern a certain firmness of jaw and grim tightness about the lips which would warn him that there were depths beyond and that this pleasant, brown-haired young Irishman might conceivably leave his mark for good or evil upon any society to which he was introduced.

Having made one or two tentative remarks to the nearest miner, and received only short gruff replies, the traveller resigned himself to uncongenial silence, staring moodily out of the window at the fading landscape. It was not a cheering prospect. Through the growing gloom there pulsed the red glow of the furnaces on the sides of the hills. Great heaps of slag and dumps of cinders loomed up on each side, with the high shafts of the collieries towering above them. Huddled groups of mean wooden houses, the windows of which were beginning to outline themselves in light, were scattered here and there along the line, and the frequent halting-places were crowded with their swarthy inhabitants. The iron and coal valleys of the Vermissa district were no resorts for the leisured or the cultured. Everywhere there were stern signs of the crudest battle of life, the rude work to be done, and the rude, strong workers who did it.

The young traveller gazed out into this dismal country with a face of mingled repulsion and interest, which showed that the scene was new to him. At intervals he drew from his pocket a bulky letter to which he referred, and on the margins of which he scribbled some notes. Once from the back of his waist he produced something which one would hardly have expected to find in the possession of so mild-mannered a man. It was a navy revolver of the largest size. As he turned it slantwise to the light, the glint upon the rims of the copper shells within the drum showed that it was fully loaded. He quickly restored it to his secret pocket, but not before it had been observed by a working man who had seated himself upon the adjoining bench.

'Halloa, mate!' said he. 'You seem heeled and ready.'

The young man smiled with an air of embarrassment.

'Yes,' said he; 'we need them sometimes in the place I come from.'

'And where may that be?'

'I'm last from Chicago.'

'A stranger in these parts?'

'Yes.'

'You may find you need it here,' said the workman.

'Ah! Is that so?' The young man seemed interested.

'Have you heard nothing of doings hereabouts?'

'Nothing out of the way.'

'Why, I thought the country was full of it. You'll hear quick enough. What made you come here?'

'I heard there was always work for a willing man.'

'Are you one of the Labour Union?'

'Sure.'

'Then you'll get your job, I guess. Have you any friends?'

'Not yet, but I have the means of making them.'

'How's that, then?'

'I am one of the Ancient Order of Freemen. There's no town without a lodge, and where there is a lodge I'll find my friends.'

The remark had a singular effect upon his companion. He glanced round suspiciously at the others in the car. The miners were still whispering among themselves. The two police officers were dozing. He came across, seated himself close to the young traveller, and held out his hand.

'Put it there,' he said.

A hand-grip passed between the two.

'I see you speak the truth. But it's well to make certain.'

He raised his right hand to his right eyebrow. The traveller at once raised his left hand to his left eyebrow.

'Dark nights are unpleasant,' said the workman.

'Yes, for strangers to travel,' the other answered.

'That's good enough. I'm Brother Scanlan, Lodge 341, Vermissa Valley. Glad to see you in these parts.'

'Thank you. I'm Brother John McMurdo, Lodge 29, Chicago. Bodymaster, J. H. Scott. But I am in luck to meet a brother so early.'

'Well, there are plenty of us about. You won't find the Order more flourishing anywhere in the States than right here in Vermissa Valley. But we could do with some lads like you. I can't understand a spry man of the Labour Union finding no work to do in Chicago.'

'I found plenty of work to do,' said McMurdo.

'Then why did you leave?'

McMurdo nodded towards the policemen and smiled.

'I guess those chaps would be glad to know,' he said.

Scanlan groaned sympathetically.

'In trouble?' he asked, in a whisper.

'Deep.'

'A penitentiary job?'

'And the rest.'

'Not a killing?'

'It's early days to talk of such things,' said McMurdo, with the air of a man who had been surprised into saying more than he intended. 'I've my own good reason for leaving Chicago, and let that be enough for you. Who are you that you should take it on yourself to ask such things?'

His grey eyes gleamed with sudden and dangerous anger from behind his glasses.

'All right, mate. No offence meant. The boys will think none the worse of you whatever you may have done. Where are you bound for now?'

'To Vermissa.'

'That's the third halt down the line. Where are you staying?'

McMurdo took out an envelope and held it close to the murky oil-lamp.

'Here is the address—Jacob Shafter, Sheridan Street. It's a boarding-house that was recommended by a man I knew in Chicago.'

'Well, I don't know it, but Vermissa is out of my beat. I live at Hobson's Patch, and that's here where we are drawing **57** up. But, say, there's one bit of advice I'll give you before we part. If you're in trouble in Vermissa, go straight to the Union House and see Boss McGinty. He is the bodymaster of Vermissa Lodge, and nothing can happen in these parts unless Black Jack McGinty wants it. So long, mate. Maybe we'll meet in Lodge one of these evenings. But mind my words; if you are in trouble go to Boss McGinty.'

Scanlan descended, and McMurdo was left once again to his thoughts. Night had now fallen, and the flames of the frequent furnaces were roaring and leaping in the darkness. Against their lurid background dark figures were bending and straining, twisting, and turning, with the motion of winch or of windlass, to the rhythm of an eternal clank and roar.

57 *Hobson's Patch.* "It does not require a very active imagination to identify Craig's Patch with the 'Hobson's Patch' of the Story," the late James Montgomery wrote in "Paging Birdy Edwards."

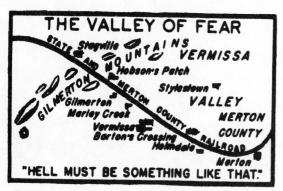

"I GUESS HELL MUST LOOK SOMETHING LIKE THAT . . ."

Dr. Julian Wolff's map of *The Valley of Fear.*

'I guess hell must look something like that,' said a voice.

McMurdo turned and saw that one of the policemen had shifted in his seat and was staring out into the fiery waste.

'For that matter,' said the other policeman, 'I allow that hell must *be* something like that. If there are worse devils down yonder than some we could name, it's more than I'd expect. I guess you are new to this part, young man?'

'Well, what if I am?' McMurdo answered, in a surly voice.

'Just this, mister; that I should advise you to be careful in choosing your friends. I don't think I'd begin with Mike Scanlan or his gang if I were you.'

'What in thunder is it to you who are my friends?' roared McMurdo, in a voice which brought every head in the carriage round to witness the altercation. 'Did I ask you for your advice, or did you think me such a sucker that I couldn't move without it? You speak when you are spoken to, and by the Lord you'd have to wait a long time if it was me!'

He thrust out his face, and grinned at the patrolmen like a snarling dog.

The two policemen, heavy, good-natured men, were taken aback by the extraordinary vehemence with which their friendly advances had been rejected.

'No offence, stranger,' said one. 'It was a warning for your own good, seeing that you are, by your own showing, new to the place.'

'I'm new to the place, but I'm not new to you and your kind,' cried McMurdo, in a cold fury. 'I guess you're the same in all places, shoving your advice in when nobody asks for it.'

'Maybe we'll see more of you before very long,' said one of the patrolmen, with a grin. 'You're a real hand-picked one, if I am a judge.'

'I was thinking the same,' remarked the other. 'I guess we may meet again.'

'I'm not afraid of you, and don't you think it,' cried McMurdo. 'My name's Jack McMurdo—see? If you want me you'll find me at Jacob Shafter's, at Sheridan Street, Vermissa, so I'm not hiding from you, am I? Day or night I dare to look the like of you in the face. Don't make any mistake about that.'

There was a murmur of sympathy and admiration from the miners at the dauntless demeanour of the new-comer, while the two policemen shrugged their shoulders and renewed a conversation between themselves. A few minutes later the train ran into the ill-lit depot and there was a general clearing, for Vermissa was far the largest township on the line. McMurdo picked up his leather grip-sack, and was about to start off into the darkness when one of the miners accosted him.

'By gosh, mate, you know how to speak to the cops,' he said, in a voice of awe. 'It was grand to hear you. Let me carry your grip-sack and show you the road. I'm passing Shafter's on the way to my own shack.'

There was a chorus of friendly 'Good nights' from the other miners as they passed from the platform. Before ever he had set foot in it, McMurdo the turbulent had become a character in Vermissa.

The country had been a place of terror, but the township was in its way even more depressing. Down that long valley there was at least a certain gloomy grandeur in the huge fires and the clouds of drifting smoke, while the strength and industry of man found fitting monuments in the hills which he had spilled by the side of his monstrous excavations. But the town showed a dead level of mean ugliness and squalor. The broad street was churned up by the traffic into a horrible rutted paste of muddy snow. The sidewalks were narrow and uneven. The numerous gas-lamps served only to show more clearly a long line of wooden houses, each with its verandah facing the street, unkempt and dirty. As they approached the centre of the town the scene was brightened by a row of well-lit stores, and even more by a cluster of liquor saloons and gaming-houses, in which the miners spent their hard-earned but generous wages.

'That's the Union House,' said the guide, pointing to one saloon which rose almost to the dignity of being an hotel. 'Jack McGinty is the Boss there.'

'What sort of a man is he?' asked McMurdo.

'What! Have you never heard of the Boss?'

'How could I have heard of him when you know that I am a stranger in these parts?'

'Well, I thought his name was known right across the Union. It's been in the papers often enough.'

'What for?'

'Well'—the miner lowered his voice—'over the affairs.'

'What affairs?'

'Good Lord, mister, you are queer goods, if I may say it without offence. There's only one set of affairs that you'll hear of in these parts, and that's the affairs of the Scowrers.'

'Why, I seem to have read of the Scowrers in Chicago. A gang of murderers, are they not?'

'Hush, on your life!' cried the miner, standing still in his alarm, and gazing in amazement at his companion. 'Man, you won't live long in these parts if you speak in the open street like that. Many a man has had the life beaten out of him for less.'

'Well, I know nothing about them. It's only what I have read.'

'And I'm not saying that you have not read the truth.' The man looked nervously round him as he spoke, peering into the shadows as if he feared to see some lurking danger. 'If killing is murder, then God knows there is murder and to spare. But don't you dare to breathe the name of Jack McGinty in connection with it, stranger, for every whisper goes back to him, and he is not one that is likely to let it pass. Now, that's the house you're after—that one standing back from the street. You'll find old Jacob Shafter that runs it as honest a man as lives in this township.'

'I thank you,' said McMurdo, and shaking hands with his new acquaintance he plodded, his grip-sack in his hand, up the path which led to the dwelling-house, at the door of which he gave a resounding knock. It was opened at once by some-one very different from what he had expected.

It was a woman, young and singularly beautiful. She was of the Swedish type, blonde and fair-haired, with the piquant **58** contrast of a pair of beautiful dark eyes, with which she surveyed the stranger with surprise and a pleasing embarrass-ment which brought a wave of colour over her pale face. Framed in the bright light of the open doorway, it seemed to McMurdo that he had never seen a more beautiful picture, the more attractive for its contrast with the sordid and gloomy

58 *of the Swedish type.* The Shafters, originally Germans, became Swedish in the English editions because it was impossible, in 1914–1915, to depict any German as a kindly character in an English publication.

"HUSH, ON YOUR LIFE!" CRIED THE MINER . . .

Illustration by Frank Wiles for the *Strand Magazine*, January, 1915.

surroundings. A lovely violet growing upon one of those black slagheaps of the mines would not have seemed more surprising. So entranced was he that he stood staring without a word, and it was she who broke the silence.

'I thought it was father,' said she, with a pleasing little touch of a Swedish accent. 'Did you come to see him? He is down town. I expect him back every minute.'

McMurdo continued to gaze at her in open admiration until her eyes dropped in confusion before this masterful visitor.

'No, miss,' he said at last; 'I'm in no hurry to see him. But your house was recommended to me for board. I thought it might suit me, and now I know it will.'

'You are quick to make up your mind,' said she, with a smile.

'Anyone but a blind man could do as much,' the other answered.

She laughed at the compliment.

'Come right in, sir,' she said. 'I'm Miss Ettie Shafter, Mr Shafter's daughter. My mother's dead, and I run the house. You can sit down by the stove in the front room until father comes along. Ah, here he is; so you can fix things with him right away.'

A heavy, elderly man came plodding up the path. In a few words McMurdo explained his business. A man of the name of Murphy had given him the address in Chicago. He in turn had had it from someone else. Old Shafter was quite ready. The stranger made no bones about terms, agreed at once to every condition, and was apparently fairly flush of money. For twelve dollars a week, paid in advance, he was to have board and lodging. So it was that McMurdo, the self-confessed fugitive from justice, took up his abode under the roof of the Shafters, the first step which was to lead to so long and dark a train of events, ending in a far-distant land.

9 ✦ THE BODYMASTER

McMurdo was a man who made his mark quickly. Wherever he was the folk around soon knew it. Within a week he had become infinitely the most important person at Shafter's. There were ten or a dozen boarders there, but they were honest foremen or commonplace clerks from the stores, of a very different calibre to the young Irishman. Of an evening when they gathered together his joke was always the readiest, his conversation the brightest, and his song the best. He was a born boon companion, with a magnetism which drew good humour from all around him.

And yet he showed again and again, as he had shown in the railway-carriage, a capacity for sudden, fierce anger which compelled the respect and even fear of those who met him. For the law, too, and all connected with it, he exhibited a bitter contempt which delighted some and alarmed others of his fellow-boarders.

From the first he made it evident, by his open admiration, that the daughter of the house had won his heart from the instant that he had set eyes upon her beauty and her grace. He was no backward suitor. On the second day he told her that he loved her, and from then onwards he repeated the same story with an absolute disregard of what she might say to discourage him.

'Someone else!' he would cry. 'Well, the worse luck for someone else! Let him look out for himself! Am I to lose my life's chance and all my heart's desire for someone else? You can keep on saying "No," Ettie! The day will come when you will say "Yes," and I'm young enough to wait.'

He was a dangerous suitor, with his glib Irish tongue and his pretty, coaxing ways. There was about him also that glamour of experience and of mystery which attracts a woman's interest and finally her love. He could talk of the sweet valleys of County Monaghan from which he came, of the lovely distant island, the low hills and green meadows of which seemed the more beautiful when imagination viewed them from this place of grime and snow. Then he was versed in the life of the cities of the North, of Detroit and the lumber-camps of Michigan, of Buffalo, and finally of Chicago, where he had worked in a saw-mill. And afterwards came the hint of romance, the feeling that strange things had happened to him in that great city, so strange and so intimate that they might not be spoken of. He spoke wistfully of a sudden leaving, a breaking of old ties, a flight into a strange world ending in this dreary valley, and Ettie listened, her dark eyes gleaming with pity and with sympathy—those two qualities which may turn so rapidly and so naturally to love.

McMurdo had obtained a temporary job as a book-keeper, for he was a well-educated man. This kept him out most of the day, and he had not found occasion yet to report himself to the head of the Lodge of the Ancient Order of Freemen. He was reminded of his omission, however, by a visit one evening from Mike Scanlan, the fellow-member whom he had met in the train. Scanlan, a small, sharp-faced, nervous, black-eyed man, seemed glad to see him once more. After a glass or two of whisky, he broached the object of his visit.

'Say, McMurdo,' said he, 'I remembered your address, so I made bold to call. I'm surprised that you've not reported to the bodymaster. What's amiss that you've not seen Boss McGinty yet?'

'Well, I had to find a job. I have been busy.'

'You must find time for him if you have none for anything else. Good Lord, man, you're mad not to have been down to the Union House and registered your name the first morning after you came here! If you fall foul of him—well, you *mustn't*—that's all.'

McMurdo showed mild surprise.

'I've been a member of Lodge for over two years, Scanlan, but I never heard that duties were so pressing as all that.'

'Maybe not in Chicago!'

'Well, it's the same society here.'

'Is it?' Scanlan looked at him long and fixedly. There was something sinister in his eyes.

'Is it not?'

'You'll tell me that in a month's time. I hear you had a talk with the patrolmen after I left the train.'

'How did you know that?'

'Oh, it got about—things do get about for good and for bad in this district.'

'Well, yes. I told the hounds what I thought of them.'

'By the Lord, you'll be a man after McGinty's heart!'

'What—does he hate the police, too?'

Scanlan burst out laughing.

'You go and see him, my lad,' said he, as he took his leave. 'It's not the police, but you, that he'll hate if you don't! Now, take a friend's advice and go at once!'

It chanced that on the same evening McMurdo had another more pressing interview which urged him in the same direction. It may have been that his attentions to Ettie had been more evident than before, or that they had gradually obtruded themselves into the slow mind of his good Swedish host; but, whatever the cause, the boarding-house keeper beckoned the young man into his private room and started on to the subject without any circumlocution.

'It seems to me, mister,' said he, 'dat you are gettin' set on my Ettie. Ain't dat so, or am I wrong?'

'Yes, that is so,' the young man answered.

'Well, I vant to tell you right now dat it ain't no manner of use. There's someone slipped in afore you.'

'She told me so.'

'Well, you can lay dat she told you truth! But did she tell you who it vas?'

'No; I asked her, but she would not tell.'

'I dare say not, the leetle baggage. Perhaps she did not vish to vrighten you avay.'

'Frighten!' McMurdo was on fire in a moment.

'Ah yes, my vriend! You need not be ashamed to be vrightened of him. It is Teddy Baldwin.'

'And who the devil is he?'

'He is a Boss of Scowrers.'

'Scowrers! I've heard of them before. It's Scowrers here and Scowrers there, and always in a whisper! What are you all afraid of? Who *are* the Scowrers?'

The boarding-house keeper instinctively sank his voice, as everyone did who talked about that terrible society.

'The Scowrers,' said he, 'are the Ancient Order of Freemen.'

The young man started.

'Why, I am a member of that Order myself.'

'You! I would never have had you in my house if I had known it—not if you vere to pay me a hundred dollar a veek.'

'What's amiss with the Order? It's for charity and good-fellowship. The rules say so.'

'Maybe in some places. Not here!'

'What is it here?'

'It's a murder society, dat's vat it is.'

McMurdo laughed incredulously.

'How do you prove that?' he asked.

'Prove it! Are there not vifty murders to prove it? Vat about Milman and Van Shorst, and the Nicholson vamily, and old Mr Hyam, and little Billy James, and the others? Prove it! Is dere a man or a voman in dis valley dat does not know it?'

'See here!' said McMurdo, earnestly. 'I want you to take back what you've said or else to make it good. One or the other you must do before I quit this room. Put yourself in my place. Here am I, a stranger in the town. I belong to a society that I know only as an innocent one. You'll find it through the length and breadth of the States, but always as an innocent one. Now, when I am counting upon joining it here, you tell me that it is the same as a murder society called the "Scowrers." I guess you owe me either an apology or else an explanation, Mr Shafter.'

'I can but tell you vat the whole vorld knows, mister. The bosses of the one are the bosses of the other. If you offend the one, it is the other dat vill strike you. We have proved it too often.'

'That's just gossip! I want proof!' said McMurdo.

'If you live here long you vill get your proof. But I vorget dat you are yourself one of dem. You vill soon be as bad as the rest. But you will find other lodgings, mister. I cannot have you here. Is it not bad enough dat one of these people come courting my Ettie, and dat I dare not turn him down, but dat I should have another for my boarder? Yes, indeed, you shall not sleep here after tonight!'

So McMurdo found himself under sentence of banishment both from his comfortable quarters and from the girl whom he loved. He found her alone in the sitting-room that same evening, and he poured his troubles into her ear.

'Sure, your father is after giving me notice,' he said. 'It's little I would care if it was just my room; but indeed, Ettie, though it's only a week that I've known you, you are the very breath of life to me, and I can't live without you.'

'Oh, hush, Mr McMurdo! Don't speak so!' said the girl. 'I have told you, have I not, that you are too late? There is another, and if I have not promised to marry him at once, at least I can promise no one else.'

'Suppose I had been first, Ettie, would I have had a chance?'

The girl sank her face into her hands.

'I wish to Heaven that you *had* been first,' she sobbed.

McMurdo was down on his knees before her in an instant.

'For God's sake, Ettie, let it stand at that!' he cried. 'Will you ruin your life and my own for the sake of this promise? Follow your heart, acushla! 'Tis a safer guide than any promise given before you knew what it was that you were saying.'

He had seized Ettie's white hand between his own strong brown ones.

'Say that you will be mine and we will face it out together.'

'Not here?'

'Yes, here.'

'No, no, Jack!' His arms were round her now. 'It could not be here. Could you take me away?'

A struggle passed for a moment over McMurdo's face, but it ended by setting like granite.

'No, here,' he said. 'I'll hold you against the world, Ettie, right here where we are!'

'Why should we not leave together?'

'No, Ettie, I can't leave here.'

'But why?'

'I'd never hold my head up again if I felt that I had been driven out. Besides, what is there to be afraid of? Are we not free folk in a free country? If you love me and I love you, who will dare to come between?'

'You don't know, Jack. You've been here too short a time. You don't know this Baldwin. You don't know McGinty and his Scowrers.'

'No, I don't know them, and I don't fear them, and I don't believe in them!' said McMurdo. 'I've lived among rough men, my darling, and instead of fearing them it has always ended that they have feared me—always, Ettie. It's mad on the face of it! If these men, as your father says, have done crime after crime, in the valley, and if everyone knows them by name, how comes it that none are brought to justice? You answer me that, Ettie!'

'Because no witness dares to appear against them. He would not live a month if he did. Also because they have always their own men to swear that the accused one was far from the scene of the crime. But surely, Jack, you must have read all this! I had understood that every paper in the States was writing about it.'

'Well, I have read something, it is true, but I had thought it was a story. Maybe these men have some reason in what they do. Maybe they are wronged and have no other way to help themselves.'

'Oh, Jack, don't let me hear you speak so! That is how he speaks—the other one!'

'Baldwin—he speaks like that, does he?'

'And that is why I loathe him so. Oh, Jack, now I can tell you the truth, I loathe him with all my heart; but I fear him also. I fear him for myself, but, above all, I fear him for father. I know that some great sorrow would come upon us if I dared to say what I really felt. That is why I have put him off with half-promises. It was in real truth our only hope. But if you would fly with me, Jack, we could take father with us and live for ever far from the power of these wicked men.'

Again there was the struggle upon McMurdo's face, and again it set like granite.

'No harm shall come to you, Ettie—nor to your father either. As to wicked men, I expect you may find that I am as bad as the worst of them before we're through.'

'No, no, Jack! I would trust you anywhere.'

McMurdo laughed bitterly.

'Good Lord, how little you know of me! Your innocent soul, my darling, could not even guess what is passing in mine. But, halloa, who's the visitor?'

The door had opened suddenly and a young fellow came swaggering in with the air of one who is the master. He was a handsome, dashing young man of about the same age and build as McMurdo himself. Under his broad-brimmed black felt hat, which he had not troubled to remove, a handsome face, with fierce, domineering eyes and a curved, hawkbill of a nose, looked savagely at the pair who sat by the stove.

Ettie had jumped to her feet, full of confusion and alarm.

'I'm glad to see you, Mr Baldwin,' said she. 'You're earlier than I had thought. Come and sit down.'

Baldwin stood with his hands on his hips looking at McMurdo.

'Who is this?' he asked, curtly.

'It's a friend of mine, Mr Baldwin—a new boarder here. Mr McMurdo, can I introduce you to Mr Baldwin?'

The young men nodded in a surly fashion to each other.

'Maybe Miss Ettie has told you how it is with us?' said Baldwin.

'I didn't understand that there was any relation between you.'

'Did you not? Well, you can understand it now. You can take it from me that this young lady is mine, and you'll find it a very fine evening for a walk.'

'Thank you, I am in no humour for a walk.'

'Are you not?' The man's savage eyes were blazing with anger. 'Maybe you are in a humour for a fight, Mr Boarder?'

'That I am,' cried McMurdo, springing to his feet. 'You never said a more welcome word.'

'For God's sake, Jack! Oh, for God's sake!' cried poor, distracted Ettie. 'Oh, Jack, Jack, he will do you a mischief!'

'Oh, it's "Jack," is it?' said Baldwin, with an oath. 'You've come to that already, have you?'

'Oh, Ted, be reasonable—be kind! For my sake, Ted, if ever you loved me, be great-hearted and forgiving!'

'I think, Ettie, that if you were to leave us alone we could get this thing settled,' said McMurdo, quietly. 'Or maybe, Mr Baldwin, you will take a turn down the street with me. It's a fine evening, and there's some open ground beyond the next block.'

'I'll get even with you without needing to dirty my hands,' said his enemy. 'You'll wish you had never set foot in this house before I am through with you.'

'No time like the present,' cried McMurdo.

'I'll choose my own time, mister. You can leave the time to me. See here!' He suddenly rolled up his sleeve and showed upon his forearm a peculiar sign which appeared to have been branded there. It was a circle with a triangle within it. 'D'you know what that means?'

'I neither know nor care!'

'Well, you will know. I'll promise you that. You won't be much older either. Perhaps Miss Ettie can tell you something about it. As to you, Ettie, you'll come back to me on your knees. D'ye hear, girl? On your knees! And then I'll tell you what your punishment may be. You've sowed—and, by the Lord, I'll see that you reap!' He glared at them both in fury. Then he turned upon his heel, and an instant later the outer door had banged behind him.

For a few moments McMurdo and the girl stood in silence. Then she threw her arms around him.

'Oh, Jack, how brave you were! But it is no use—you must fly! Tonight—Jack—tonight! It's your only hope. He will have your life. I read it in his horrible eyes. What chance have you against a dozen of them, with Boss McGinty and all the power of the Lodge behind them?'

McMurdo disengaged her hands, kissed her, and gently pushed her back into a chair.

'There, acushla, there! Don't be disturbed or fear for me. I'm a Freeman myself. I'm after telling your father about it. Maybe I am no better than the others, so don't make a saint of me. Perhaps you hate me, too, now that I've told you as much.'

'Hate you, Jack! While life lasts I could never do that. I've heard that there is no harm in being a Freeman anywhere but here, so why should I think the worse of you for that? But if you are a Freeman, Jack, why should you not go down and make a friend of Boss McGinty? Oh, hasten, Jack, hasten! Get your word in first, or the hounds will be on your trail.'

'I was thinking the same thing,' said McMurdo. 'I'll go right now and fix it. You can tell your father that I'll sleep here tonight and find some other quarters in the morning.'

The bar of McGinty's saloon was crowded as usual, for it was the favourite lounge of all the rougher elements of the town. The man was popular, for he had a rough, jovial disposition which formed a mask, covering a great deal which lay behind it. But, apart from this popularity, the fear in which he was held throughout the township, and, indeed, down the whole thirty miles of the valley and past the mountains upon either side of it, was enough in itself to fill his bar, for none could afford to neglect his goodwill.

Besides those secret powers which it was universally believed that he exercised in so pitiless a fashion, he was a high public official, a municipal councillor, and a commissioner for roads, elected to the office through the votes of the ruffians who in turn expected to receive favours at his hands. Rates and taxes were enormous, the public works were notoriously neglected, the accounts were slurred over by bribed auditors, and the decent citizen was terrorized into paying public blackmail, and holding his tongue lest some worse thing befall him. Thus it was that, year by year, Boss McGinty's diamond pins became more obtrusive, his gold chains more weighty across a more gorgeous vest, and his saloon stretched farther and farther, until it threatened to absorb one whole side of the Market Square.

McMurdo pushed open the swinging door of the saloon and made his way amid the crowd of men within, through an atmosphere which was blurred with tobacco smoke and heavy with the smell of spirits. The place was brilliantly lighted, and the huge, heavily gilt mirrors upon every wall reflected and multiplied the garish illumination. There were several bar-tenders in their shirt-sleeves hard at work, mixing drinks for the loungers who fringed the broad, heavily metalled counter. At the far end, with his body resting upon the bar, and a cigar stuck at an acute angle from the corner of his mouth, there stood a tall, strong, heavily built man, who could be none other than the famous McGinty himself. He was a black-maned giant, bearded to the cheek-bones, and with a shock of raven hair which fell to his collar. His complexion was as swarthy as that of an Italian, and his eyes were of a strange dead black, which, combined with a slight squint, gave them a particularly sinister appearance. All else in the man, his noble proportions, his fine features, and his frank bearing, fitted in with that jovial man-to-man manner which he affected. Here, one would say, is a bluff, honest fellow, whose heart would be sound, however rude his outspoken words might seem. It was only when those dead dark eyes, deep and remorseless, were turned upon a man that he shrank within himself, feeling that he was face to face with an infinite possibility of latent evil, with a strength and courage and cunning behind it which made it a thousand times more deadly.

Having had a good look at his man, McMurdo elbowed his way forward with his usual careless audacity, and pushed himself through the little group of courtiers who were fawning upon the powerful Boss, laughing uproariously at the smallest of his jokes. The young stranger's bold grey eyes looked back fearlessly through their glasses at the deadly black ones which turned sharply upon him.

'Well, young man, I can't call your face to mind.'

'I'm new here, Mr McGinty.'

'You are not so new that you can't give a gentleman his proper title.'

"WELL, YOUNG MAN, I CAN'T CALL YOUR FACE TO MIND."

Illustration by Frank Wiles for the *Strand Magazine*, February, 1915.

'He's Councillor McGinty, young man,' said a voice from the group.

'I'm sorry, Councillor. I'm strange to the ways of the place. But I was advised to see you.'

'Well, you see me. This is all there is. What d'you think of me?'

'Well, it's early days. If your heart is as big as your body, and your soul as fine as your face, then I'd ask for nothing better,' said McMurdo.

'By gosh, you've got an Irish tongue in your head, anyhow,' cried the saloon-keeper, not quite certain whether to humour this audacious visitor or to stand upon his dignity. 'So you are good enough to pass my appearance?'

'Sure,' said McMurdo.

'And you were told to see me?'

'I was.'

'And who told you?'

'Brother Scanlan, of Lodge 341, Vermissa. I drink your health, Councillor, and to our better acquaintance.' He raised a glass with which he had been served to his lips and elevated his little finger as he drank it.

McGinty, who had been watching him narrowly, raised his thick black eyebrows.

'Oh, it's like that, is it?' said he. 'I'll have to look a bit closer into this, Mister——'

'McMurdo.'

'A bit closer, Mr McMurdo, for we don't take folk on trust in these parts, nor believe all we're told neither. Come in here for a moment, behind the bar.'

There was a small room there lined round with barrels. McGinty carefully closed the door, and then seated himself on one of them, biting thoughtfully on his cigar, and surveying his companion with those disquieting eyes. For a couple of minutes he sat in complete silence.

McMurdo bore the inspection cheerfully, one hand in his coat-pocket, the other twisting his brown moustache. Suddenly McGinty stooped and produced a wicked-looking revolver.

'See here, my joker,' said he; 'if I thought you were playing any game on us, it would be a short shrift for you.'

'This is a strange welcome,' McMurdo answered, with some dignity, 'for the bodymaster of a Lodge of Freemen to give to a stranger brother.'

'Aye, but it's just that same that you have to prove,' said McGinty, 'and God help you if you fail. Where were you made?'

'Lodge 29, Chicago.'

'When?'

'June 24th, 1872.'

'What bodymaster?'

'James H. Scott.'

'Who is your district ruler?'

'Bartholomew Wilson.'

'Hum! You seem glib enough in your tests. What are you doing here?'

'Working, the same as you, but a poorer job.'

'You have your back answer quick enough.'

'Yes, I was always quick of speech.'

'Are you quick of action?'

'I have had that name among those who knew me best.'

'Well, we may try you sooner than you think. Have you heard anything of the Lodge in these parts?'

'I've heard that it takes a man to be a brother.'

'True for you, Mr McMurdo. Why did you leave Chicago?'

'I'm hanged if I tell you that.'

McGinty opened his eyes. He was not used to being answered in such fashion, and it amused him.

'Why won't you tell me?'

'Because no brother may tell another a lie.'

'Then the truth is too bad to tell?'

'You can put it that way if you like.'

'See here, mister; you can't expect me, as bodymaster, to pass into the Lodge a man for whose past he can't answer.'

McMurdo looked puzzled. Then he took a worn newspaper-cutting from an inner pocket.

'You wouldn't squeal on a fellow?' said he.

'I'll wipe my hand across your face if you say such words to me,' cried McGinty, hotly.

'You are right, Councillor,' said McMurdo, meekly. 'I should apologize. I spoke without thought. Well, I know that I am safe in your hands. Look at that cutting.'

McGinty glanced his eyes over the account of the shooting of one Jonas Pinto, in the Lake Saloon, Market Street, Chicago, in the New Year week of '74.

'Your work?' he asked, as he handed back the paper.

McMurdo nodded.

'Why did you shoot him?'

'I was helping Uncle Sam to make dollars. Maybe mine were not as good gold as his, but they looked as well and were cheaper to make. This man Pinto helped me to shove the queer——'

'To do what?'

'Well, it means to pass the dollars out into circulation. Then he said he would split. Maybe he did split. I didn't wait to see. I just killed him and lighted out for the coal country.'

'Why the coal country?'

''Cause I'd read in the papers that they weren't too particular in those parts.'

McGinty laughed.

'You were first a coiner and then a murderer, and you came to these parts because you thought you'd be welcome?'

'That's about the size of it,' McMurdo answered.

'Well, I guess you'll go far. Say, can you make those dollars yet?'

McMurdo took half a dozen from his pocket. 'Those never passed the Washington mint,' said he.

'You don't say!' McGinty held them to the light in his enormous hand, which was as hairy as a gorilla's. 'I can see no difference! Gosh, you'll be a mighty useful brother, I'm thinking. We can do with a bad man or two amongst us, friend McMurdo, for there are times when we have to take our own part. We'd soon be against the wall if we didn't shove back at those that were pushing us.'

'Well, I guess I'll do my share of shoving with the rest of the boys.'

'You seem to have a good nerve. You didn't flinch when I put this pistol on you.'

'It was not me that was in danger.'

'Who, then?'

'It was you, Councillor.' McMurdo drew a cocked pistol from the side-pocket of his pea-jacket. 'I was covering you all the time. I guess my shot would have been as quick as yours.'

McGinty flushed an angry red and then burst into a roar of laughter.

'By gosh!' said he. 'Say, we've had no such holy terror come to hand this many a year. I reckon the Lodge will learn to be proud of you. Well, what the deuce do you want? And can't I speak alone with a gentleman for five minutes but you must butt in upon us?'

The bar-tender stood abashed.

'I'm sorry, Councillor, but it's Mr Ted Baldwin. He says he must see you this very minute.'

The message was unnecessary, for the set, cruel face of the man himself was looking over the servant's shoulder. He pushed the bar-tender out and closed the door on him.

'So,' said he, with a furious glance at McMurdo, 'you got here first, did you? I've a word to say to you, Councillor, about this man.'

'Then say it here and now, before my face,' cried McMurdo.

'I'll say it at my own time, in my own way.'

'Tut, tut!' said McGinty, getting off his barrel. 'This will never do. We have a new brother here, Baldwin, and it's not for us to greet him in such a fashion. Hold out your hand, man, and make it up.'

'Never!' cried Baldwin, in a fury.

'I've offered to fight him if he thinks I have wronged him,' said McMurdo. 'I'll fight him with fists, or, if that won't satisfy him, I'll fight him any other way he chooses. Now I'll leave it to you, Councillor, to judge between us as a bodymaster should.'

'What is it, then?'

'A young lady. She's free to choose for herself.'

'Is she?' cried Baldwin.

'As between two brothers of the Lodge, I should say that she was,' said the Boss.

'Oh, that's your ruling, is it?'

'Yes, it is, Ted Baldwin,' said McGinty, with a wicked stare. 'Is it you that would dispute it?'

'You would throw over one that has stood by you this five years in favour of a man that you never saw before in your life? You're not bodymaster for life, Jack McGinty, and, by God, when next it comes to a vote——'

The Councillor sprang at him like a tiger. His hand closed round the other's neck and he hurled him back across one of the barrels. In his mad fury he would have squeezed the life out of him if McMurdo had not interfered.

'Easy, Councillor! For Heaven's sake, go easy!' he cried, as he dragged him back.

McGinty released his hold, and Baldwin, cowed and shaken, gasping for breath, and shivering in every limb, as one who has looked over the very edge of death, sat up on the barrel over which he had been hurled.

'You've been asking for it this many a day, Ted Baldwin. Now you've got it,' cried McGinty, his huge chest rising and falling. 'Maybe you think if I were voted down from body-master you would find yourself in my shoes. It's for the Lodge to say that. But so long as I am the chief, I'll have no man lift his voice against me or my rulings.'

'I have nothing against you,' mumbled Baldwin, feeling his throat.

'Well, then,' cried the other, relapsing in a moment into a bluff joviality, 'we are all good friends again, and there's an end of the matter.'

He took a bottle of champagne down from the shelf and twisted out the cork.

'See now,' he continued, as he filled three high glasses, 'let us drink the quarrelling toast of the Lodge. After that, as you know, there can be no bad blood between us. Now, then, the left hand on the apple of my throat, I say to you, Ted Baldwin, what is the offence, sir?'

'The clouds are heavy,' answered Baldwin.

'But they will for ever brighten.'

'And this I swear.'

The men drank their wine, and the same ceremony was performed between Baldwin and McMurdo.

'There,' cried McGinty, rubbing his hands, 'that's the end of the black blood. You come under Lodge discipline if it goes farther, and that's a heavy hand in these parts, as Brother Baldwin knows, and as you will very soon find out, Brother McMurdo, if you ask for trouble.'

'Faith, I'd be slow to do that,' said McMurdo. He held out his hand to Baldwin. 'I'm quick to quarrel and quick to forgive. It's my hot Irish blood, they tell me. But it's over for me, and I bear no grudge.'

Baldwin had to take the proffered hand, for the baleful eye of the terrible Boss was upon him. But his sullen face showed how little the words of the other had moved him.

McGinty clapped them both on the shoulders.

'Tut! These girls, these girls!' he cried. 'To think that the same petticoats should come between two of my boys. It's the devil's own luck. Well, it's the colleen inside of them that must settle the question, for it's outside the jurisdiction of a bodymaster, and the Lord be praised for that. We have enough on us, without the women as well. You'll have to be affiliated to Lodge 341, Brother McMurdo. We have our own ways and methods, different to Chicago. Saturday night is our meeting, and if you come then we'll make you free for ever of the Vermissa Valley.'

10 • LODGE 341, VERMISSA

On the day following the evening which had contained so many exciting events McMurdo moved his lodgings from old Jacob Shafter's and took up his quarters at the Widow Mac-Namara's, on the extreme outskirts of the town. Scanlan, his original acquaintance aboard the train, had occasion, shortly afterwards, to move into Vermissa, and the two lodged to-gether. There was no other boarder, and the hostess was an easy-going old Irishwoman who left them to themselves, so that they had a freedom for speech and action welcome to men who had secrets in common. Shafter had relented to the extent of letting McMurdo come to his meals there when he liked, so that his intercourse with Ettie was by no means broken. On the contrary, it drew closer and more intimate as the weeks went by. In his bedroom at his new abode Mc-Murdo felt it to be safe to take out the coining moulds, and under many a pledge of secrecy a number of the brothers from the Lodge were allowed to come in and see them, each of them carrying away in his pocket some examples of the false money, so cunningly struck that there was never the slightest difficulty or danger in passing it. Why, with such a wonderful art at his command, McMurdo should condescend to work at all was a perpetual mystery to his companions, though he made it clear to anyone who asked him that if he lived without any visible means it would very quickly bring the police upon his track.

One policeman was, indeed, after him already, but the incident, as luck would have it, did the adventurer a great deal more good than harm. After the first introduction there were few evenings when he did not find his way to McGinty's saloon, there to make closer acquaintance with 'the boys,' which was the jovial title by which the dangerous gang who infested the place were known to each other. His dashing manner and fearlessness of speech made him a favourite with them all, while the rapid and scientific way in which he polished off his antagonist in an 'all in' bar-room scrap earned the respect of that rough community. Another incident, however, raised him even higher in their estimation.

Just at the crowded hour one night the door opened and a man entered with the quiet blue uniform and peaked cap of the Coal and Iron Police. This was a special body raised by the railways and colliery owners to supplement the efforts of the ordinary civil police, who were perfectly helpless in the face of the organized ruffianism which terrorized the district. There was a hush as he entered, and many a curious glance was cast at him, but the relations between policemen and criminals are peculiar in the States, and McGinty himself, standing behind the counter, showed no surprise when the inspector enrolled himself among his customers.

'A straight whisky, for the night is bitter,' said the police-officer. 'I don't think we have met before, Councillor?'

'You'll be the new captain?' said McGinty.

'That's so. We're looking to you, Councillor, and to the other leading citizens, to help us in upholding law and order in this township. Captain Marvin is my name—of the Coal and Iron.'

'We'd do better without you, Captain Marvin,' said McGinty, coldly. 'For we have our own police of the township, and no need for any imported goods. What are you but the paid tool of the men of capital, hired by them to club or to shoot your poorer fellow-citizens?'

'Well, well, we won't argue about that,' said the police-officer, good-humouredly. 'I expect we all do our duty same as we see it, but we can't all see it the same.' He had drunk off his glass and had turned to go, when his eyes fell upon the face of Jack McMurdo, who was scowling at his elbow. 'Halloa! halloa!' he cried, looking him up and down. 'Here's an old acquaintance.'

McMurdo shrank away from him.

'I was never a friend to you nor any other cursed copper in my life,' said he.

'An acquaintance isn't always a friend,' said the police-captain, grinning. 'You're Jack McMurdo of Chicago, right enough, and don't you deny it.'

McMurdo shrugged his shoulders.

'I'm not denying it,' said he. 'D'ye think I'm ashamed of my own name?'

'You've got good cause to be, anyhow.'

'What the devil d'you mean by that?' he roared, with his fists clenched.

'No, no, Jack; bluster won't do with me. I was an officer in Chicago before ever I came to this darned coal-bunker, and I know a Chicago crook when I see one.'

McMurdo's face fell.

'Don't tell me that you're Marvin of the Chicago Central!' he cried.

'Just that same old Teddy Marvin at your service. We haven't forgotten the shooting of Jonas Pinto up there.'

'I never shot him.'

'Did you not? That's good impartial evidence, ain't it? Well, his death came in uncommon handy for you, or they would have had you for shoving the queer. Well, we can let that be bygones, for, between you and me—and perhaps I'm going farther than my duty in saying it—they could get no clear case against you, and Chicago's open to you tomorrow.'

'I'm very well where I am.'

'Well, I've given you the office, and you're a sulky dog not to thank me for it.'

'Well, I suppose you mean well, and I do thank you,' said McMurdo, in no very gracious manner.

'It's mum with me so long as I see you living on the straight,' said the captain. 'But, by gum, if you get off on the cross after this it's another story! So good night to you—and good night, Councillor.'

He left the bar-room, but not before he had created a local hero. McMurdo's deeds in far Chicago had been whispered before. He had put off all questions with a smile as one who did not wish to have greatness thrust upon him. But now the thing was officially confirmed. The bar-loafers crowded round him and shook him heartily by the hand. He was free of the community from that time on. He could drink hard and show little trace of it, but that evening, had his mate Scanlan not been at hand to lead him home, the fêted hero would surely have spent his night under the bar.

On a Saturday night McMurdo was introduced to the Lodge. He had thought to pass in without ceremony as being an initiate of Chicago; but there were particular rites in Vermissa of which they were proud, and these had to be undergone by every postulant. The assembly met in a large room reserved for such purposes at the Union House. Some sixty members assembled at Vermissa, but that by no means represented the full strength of the organization, for there were several other lodges in the valley, and others across the mountains on either side, who exchanged members when any serious business was afoot, so that a crime might be done by men who were strangers to the locality. Altogether there were not fewer than five hundred scattered over the coal district.

In the bare assembly room the men were gathered round a long table. At the side was a second one laden with bottles and glasses, on which some members of the company were already turning their eyes. McGinty sat at the head with a flat black velvet cap upon his shock of tangled, black hair and a coloured, purple stole round his neck, so that he seemed to be a priest presiding over some diabolical ritual. To right and left of him were the higher Lodge officials, the cruel, handsome face of Ted Baldwin among them. Each of these wore some scarf or medallion as emblem of his office. They were, for the most part, men of mature age, but the rest of the company consisted of young fellows from eighteen to twenty-five, the ready and capable agents who carried out the commands of their seniors. Among the older men were many whose features showed the tigerish, lawless souls within, but looking at the rank and file it was difficult to believe that these eager and open-faced young fellows were in very truth a dangerous gang of murderers, whose minds had suffered such complete moral perversion that they took a horrible pride in their proficiency at the business, and looked with the deepest respect at the man who had the reputation for making what they called a 'clean job.' To their contorted natures it had become a spirited and chivalrous thing to volunteer for service against some man who had never injured them, and whom, in many cases, they had never seen in their lives. The crime committed, they quarrelled as to who had actually struck the fatal blow, and amused each other and the company by describing the cries and contortions of the murdered man. At first they had shown some secrecy in their arrangements, but at the time which this narrative describes their proceedings were extraordinarily open, for the repeated failures of the law had proved to them that, on the one hand, no one would dare to witness against them, and, on the other, they had an unlimited number of staunch witnesses upon whom they could call, and a well-filled treasure chest from which they could draw the funds to engage the best legal talent in the State. In ten long years of outrage there had been no single conviction, and the only danger that ever threatened the Scowrers lay in the victim himself, who, however out-numbered and taken by surprise, might, and occasionally did, leave his mark upon his assailants.

McMurdo had been warned that some ordeal lay before him, but no one would tell him in what it consisted. He was led now into an outer room by two solemn brothers. Through the plank partition he could hear the murmur of many voices from the assembly within. Once or twice he caught the sound of his own name, and he knew that they were discussing his candidature. Then there entered an inner guard, with a green and gold sash across his chest.

'The bodymaster orders that he shall be trussed, blinded, and entered,' said he. The three of them then removed his coat, turned up the sleeve of his right arm and finally passed a rope round above the elbows and made it fast. They next placed a thick, black cap right over his head and the upper part of his face, so that he could see nothing. He was then led into the assembly hall.

It was pitch-dark and very oppressive under his hood. He heard the rustle and murmur of the people round him, and then the voice of McGinty sounded, dull and distant, through the covering of his ears.

'John McMurdo,' said the voice, 'are you already a member of the Ancient Order of Freemen?'

He bowed in assent.

'Is your lodge No. 29, Chicago?'

He bowed again.

'Dark nights are unpleasant,' said the voice.

'Yes, for strangers to travel,' he answered.

'The clouds are heavy.'

'Yes; a storm is approaching.'

'Are the brethren satisfied?' asked the bodymaster.

There was a general murmur of assent.

'We know, brother, by your sign and by your countersign, that you are indeed one of us,' said McGinty. 'We would have you know, however, that in this county and in other counties of these parts we have certain rites, and also certain duties of our own, which call for good men. Are you ready to be tested?'

'I am.'

'Are you of stout heart?'

'I am.'

'Take a stride forward to prove it.'

As the words were said he felt two hard points in front of his eyes, pressing upon them so that it appeared as if he could not move forward without a danger of losing them. None the less, he nerved himself to step resolutely out, and as he did so the pressure melted away. There was a low murmur of applause.

'He is of stout heart,' said the voice. 'Can you bear pain?'

'As well as another,' he answered.

'Test him!'

It was all he could do to keep himself from screaming out, for an agonizing pain shot through his forearm. He nearly fainted at the sudden shock of it, but he bit his lip and clenched his hands to hide his agony.

'I can take more than that,' said he.

This time there was loud applause. A finer first appearance had never been made in the Lodge. Hands clapped him on the back, and the hood was plucked from his head. He stood blinking and smiling amid the congratulations of the brothers.

'One last word, Brother McMurdo,' said McGinty. 'You have already sworn the oath of secrecy and fidelity, and you are aware that the punishment for any breach of it is instant and inevitable death?'

'I am,' said McMurdo.

'And you accept the rule of the bodymaster for the time being under all circumstances?'

'I do.'

'Then, in the name of Lodge 341, Vermissa, I welcome you to its privileges and debates. You will put the liquor on the table, Brother Scanlan, and we will drink to our worthy brother.'

McMurdo's coat had been brought to him, but before putting it on he examined his right arm, which still smarted heavily. There, on the flesh of the forearm, was a clear-cut circle with a triangle within it, deep and red, as the branding-iron had left it. One or two of his neighbours pulled up their sleeves and showed their own Lodge marks.

'We've all had it,' said one, 'but not all as brave as you over it.'

'Tut! It was nothing,' said he; but it burned and ached all the same.

When the drinks which followed the ceremony of initiation had all been disposed of, the business of the Lodge proceeded.

IT WAS ALL HE COULD DO TO KEEP HIMSELF FROM SCREAMING OUT . . .

Illustration by Arthur I. Keller for Associated Sunday Magazines, 1914. Frank Wiles illustrated the same scene for the *Strand Magazine*, March, 1915.

McMurdo, accustomed only to the prosaic performances of Chicago, listened with open ears, and more surprise than he ventured to show, to what followed.

'The first business on the agenda paper,' said McGinty, 'is to read the following letter from Division Master Windle, of Merton County, Lodge 249. He says:

DEAR SIR,

There is a job to be done on Andrew Rae, of Rae and Sturmash, coal-owners near this place. You will remember that your Lodge owes us a return, having had the services of two brethren in the matter of the patrolman last fall. If you will send two good men they will be taken charge of by Treasurer Higgins of this Lodge, whose address you know. He will show them when to act, and where.—Yours in freedom.

J. W. WINDLE, D.M.A.O.F.

'Windle has never refused us when we have had occasion to ask for the loan of a man or two, and it is not for us to refuse him.' McGinty paused and looked round the room with his dull, malevolent eyes. 'Who will volunteer for the job?'

Several young fellows held up their hands. The bodymaster looked at them with an approving smile.

'You'll do, Tiger Cormac. If you handle it as well as you did the last you won't be amiss. And you, Wilson.'

'I've no pistol,' said the volunteer, a mere boy in his teens.

'It's your first, is it not? Well, you have to be blooded some time. It will be a great start for you. As to the pistol, you'll find it waiting for you, or I'm mistaken. If you report yourselves on Monday it will be time enough. You'll get a great welcome when you return.'

'Any reward this time?' asked Cormac, a thick-set, dark-faced, brutal-looking young man, whose ferocity had earned him the nickname of 'Tiger.'

'Never mind the reward. You just do it for the honour of the thing. Maybe when it is done there will be a few odd dollars at the bottom of the box.'

'What has the man done?' asked young Wilson.

'Sure, it's not for the likes of you to ask what the man has done. He has been judged over there. That's no business of ours. All we have to do is to carry it out for them, same as they would for us. Speaking of that, two brothers from the Merton Lodge are coming over to us next week to do some business in this quarter.'

'Who are they?' asked someone.

'Faith, it is wiser not to ask. If you know nothing you can testify nothing, and no trouble can come of it. But they are men who will make a clean job when they are about it.'

'And time, too!' cried Ted Baldwin. 'Folk are getting out of hand in these parts. It was only last week that three of our men were turned off by Foreman Blaker. It's been owing him a long time, and he'll get it full and proper.'

'Get what?' McMurdo whispered to his neighbour.

'The business end of a buck-shot cartridge,' cried the man, with a loud laugh. 'What think you of our ways, brother?'

McMurdo's criminal soul seemed to have already absorbed the spirit of the vile association of which he was now a member.

'I like it well,' said he. ' 'Tis a proper place for a lad of mettle.'

Several of those who sat around heard his words and applauded them.

'What's that?' cried the black-maned bodymaster, from the end of the table.

' 'Tis our new brother, sir, who finds our ways to his taste.'

McMurdo rose to his feet for an instant.

'I would say, Worshipful Master, that if a man should be wanted I should take it as an honour to be chosen to help the Lodge.'

There was great applause at this. It was felt that a new sun was pushing its rim above the horizon. To some of the elders it seemed that the progress was a little too rapid.

'I would move,' said the secretary, Harraway, a vulture-faced old greybeard who sat near the chairman, 'that Brother McMurdo should wait until it is the good pleasure of the Lodge to employ him.'

'Sure, that was what I meant. I'm in your hands,' said McMurdo.

'Your time will come, brother,' said the chairman. 'We have marked you down as a willing man, and we believe that you will do good work in these parts. There is a small matter to-night in which you may take a hand, if it so please you.'

'I will wait for something that is worth while.'

'You can come tonight, anyhow, and it will help you to know what we stand for in this community. I will make the announcement later. Meanwhile'—he glanced at his agenda paper—'I have one or two more points to bring before the meeting. First of all, I will ask the treasurer as to our bank balance. There is the pension to Jim Carnaway's widow. He was struck down doing the work of the Lodge, and it is for us to see that she is not the loser.'

'Jim was shot last month when they tried to kill Chester Wilcox, of Marley Creek,' McMurdo's neighbour informed him.

'The funds are good at the moment,' said the treasurer, with the bank-book in front of him. 'The firms have been generous of late. Max Linder and Co. paid five hundred to be left alone. Walker Brothers sent in a hundred, but I took it on myself to return it and ask for five. If I do not hear by Wednesday their winding gear may get out of order. We had to burn their breaker last year before they became reasonable. Then the West Section Coaling Company has paid its annual contribution. We have enough in hand to meet any obligations.'

'What about Archie Swindon?' asked a brother.

'He has sold out and left the district. The old devil left a note for us to say that he had rather be a free crossing-sweeper in New York than a large mine-owner under the power of a ring of blackmailers. By gosh, it was as well that he made a break for it before the note reached us! I guess he dare not show his face in this valley again.'

An elderly, clean-shaven man, with a kindly face and a good brow, rose from the end of the table which faced the chairman.

'Mr Treasurer,' he asked, 'may I ask who has bought the property of this man that we have driven out of the district?'

'Yes, Brother Morris. It has been bought by the State and Merton County Railroad Company.'

'And who bought the mines of Todman and of Lee that came into the market in the same way last year?'

'The same company, Brother Morris.'

'And who bought the ironworks of Manson and of Shuman and of Van Deher and of Atwood, which have all been given up of late?'

'They were all bought by the West Wilmerton General Mining Company.'

'I don't see, Brother Morris,' said the chairman, 'that it matters a nickel to us who buys them, since they can't carry them out of the district.'

'With all respect to you, Worshipful Master, I think that it may matter very much to us. This process has been going on now for ten long years. We are gradually driving all the small men out of trade. What is the result? We find in their places great companies like the Railroad or the General Iron, who have their directors in New York or Philadelphia, and care nothing for our threats. We can take it out of their local bosses, but it only means that others will be sent in their stead. And we are making it dangerous for ourselves. The small men could not harm us. They had not the money nor the power. So long as we did not squeeze them too dry, they would stay on under our power. But if these big companies find that we stand between them and their profits, they will spare no pains and no expense to hunt us down and bring us to court.'

There was a hush at these ominous words, and every face darkened as gloomy looks were exchanged. So omnipotent and unchallenged had they been that the very thought that there was possible retribution in the background had been banished from their minds. And yet the idea struck a chill to the most reckless of them.

'It is my advice,' the speaker continued, 'that we bear less heavily upon the small men. On the day that they have all been driven out the power of this society will have been broken.'

Unwelcome truths are not popular. There were angry cries as the speaker resumed his seat. McGinty rose with gloom upon his brow.

'Brother Morris,' said he, 'you were always a croaker. So long as the members of the Lodge stand together there is no power in this United States that can touch them. Sure, have we not tried it often enough in the law courts? I expect the big companies will find it easier to pay than to fight, same as the little companies do. And now, brethren'—McGinty took off his black velvet cap and his stole as he spoke—'this Lodge has finished its business for the evening, save for one small matter which may be mentioned when we are parting. The time has now come for fraternal refreshment and for harmony.'

Strange indeed is human nature. Here were these men to whom murder was familiar, who again and again had struck down the father of the family, some man against whom they had no personal feeling, without one thought of compunction or of compassion for his weeping wife or helpless children, and yet the tender or pathetic in music could move them to tears. McMurdo had a fine tenor voice, and if he had failed to gain the goodwill of the Lodge before, it could no longer have been withheld after he had thrilled them with 'I'm Sitting on the Stile, Mary,' and 'On the Banks of Allan Water.' In his very first night the new recruit had made himself one of the most popular of the brethren, marked already for advancement and high office. There were other qualities needed, however, besides those of good fellowship, to make a worthy Freeman, and of these he was given an example before the evening was over. The whisky bottle had passed round many times, and the men were flushed and ripe for mischief, when their bodymaster rose once more to address them.

'Boys,' said he, 'there's one man in this town that wants trimming up, and it's for you to see that he gets it. I'm speaking of James Stanger, of the *Herald*. You've seen how he's been opening his mouth against us again?'

There was a murmur of assent, with many a muttered oath. McGinty took a slip of paper from his waistcoat pocket.

'"Law and Order!" That's how he heads it. "Reign of Terror in the Coal and Iron District. Twelve years have now elapsed since the first assassinations which proved the existence of a criminal organization in our midst. From that day these outrages have never ceased, until now they have reached a pitch which makes us the opprobrium of the civilized world. Is it for such results as this that our great country welcomes to its bosom the alien who flies from the despotisms of Europe? Is it that they shall themselves become tyrants over the very men who have given them shelter, and that a state of terrorism and lawlessness should be established under the very shadow of the sacred folds of the starry flag of freedom which would raise horror in our minds if we read of it as existing under the most effete monarchy of the East? The men are known. The organization is patent and public. How long are we to endure it? Can we for ever live——" Sure, I've read enough of the slush!' cried the chairman, tossing the paper down upon the table. 'That's what he says of us. The question I'm asking you is, What shall we say to him?'

'Kill him!' cried a dozen fierce voices.

'I protest against that,' said Brother Morris, the man of the good brow and shaven face. 'I tell you, brethren, that our hand is too heavy in this valley, and that there will come a point where, in self-defence, every man will unite to crush us out. James Stanger is an old man. He is respected in the township and the district. His paper stands for all that is solid in the valley. If that man is struck down, there will be a stir through this State that will only end with our destruction.'

'And how would they bring about our destruction, Mister Stand-back?' cried McGinty. 'Is it by the police? Sure, half of them are in our pay and half of them afraid of us. Or is it by the law courts and the judge? Haven't we tried that before now, and whatever came of it?'

'There is a Judge Lynch that might try the case,' said Brother Morris.

A general shout of anger greeted the suggestion.

'I have but to raise my finger,' cried McGinty, 'and I could put two hundred men into this town that would clear it out from end to end.' Then, suddenly raising his voice and bending his huge black brows into a terrible frown: 'See here, Brother Morris, I have my eye on you, and have had for some time. You've no heart yourself, and you try to take the heart out of others. It will be an ill day for you, Brother Morris, when your own name comes on our agenda paper, and I'm thinking that it's just there that I ought to place it.'

Morris had turned deadly pale and his knees seemed to give way under him as he fell back into his chair. He raised his glass in his trembling hand and drank before he could answer.

'I apologize, Worshipful Master, to you and to every brother in this Lodge if I have said more than I should. I am a faithful member—you all know that—and it is my fear lest evil come to the Lodge which makes me speak in anxious words. But I have greater trust in your judgment than in my own, Worshipful Master, and I promise you that I will not offend again.'

The bodymaster's scowl relaxed as he listened to the humble words.

'Very good, Brother Morris. It's myself that would be sorry if it were needful to give you a lesson. But so long as I am in this chair we shall be a united Lodge in word and in deed. And now, boys,' he continued, looking round at the company, 'I'll say this much—that if Stanger got his full deserts there would be more trouble than we need ask for. These editors hang together, and every journal in the State would be crying out for police and troops. But I guess you can give him a pretty severe warning. Will you fix it, Brother Baldwin?'

'Sure!' said the young man, eagerly.

'How many will you take?'

'Half a dozen, and two to guard the door. You'll come, Gower, and you, Mansel, and you, Scanlan, and the two Willabys.'

'I promised the new brother he should go,' said the chairman.

Ted Baldwin looked at McMurdo with eyes which showed that he had not forgotten nor forgiven.

'Well, he can come if he wants,' he said, in a surly voice. 'That's enough. The sooner we get to work the better.'

The company broke up with shouts and yells and snatches of drunken song. The bar was still crowded with revellers, and many of the brethren remained there. The little band who had been told off for duty passed out into the street, proceeding in twos and threes along the sidewalk so as not to provoke attention. It was a bitterly cold night, with a half-moon shining brilliantly in a frosty, star-spangled sky. The men stopped and gathered in a yard which faced a high building. The words 'Vermissa Herald' were printed in gold lettering between the brightly-lit windows. From within came the clanking of the printing-press.

'Here, you,' said Baldwin to McMurdo; 'you can stand below at the door and see that the road is kept open for us. Arthur Willaby can stay with you. You others come with me. Have no fear, boys, for we have a dozen witnesses that we are in the Union bar at this very moment.'

It was nearly midnight, and the street was deserted save for one or two revellers upon their way home. The party crossed the road and, pushing open the door of the newspaper office, Baldwin and his men rushed in and up the stair which faced them. McMurdo and another remained below. From the room above came a shout, a cry for help, and then the sound of trampling feet and of falling chairs. An instant later a grey-haired man rushed out on to the landing. He was seized before he could get farther, and his spectacles came tinkling down to McMurdo's feet. There was a thud and a groan. He was on his face and half a dozen sticks were clattering together as they fell upon him. He writhed, and his long, thin limbs quivered under the blows. The others ceased at last, but Baldwin, his cruel face set in an infernal smile, was hacking at the man's head, which he vainly endeavoured to defend with his arms. His white hair was dabbled with patches of blood. Baldwin was still stooping over his victim, putting in a short, vicious blow whenever he could see a part exposed, when McMurdo dashed up the stair and pushed him back.

'You'll kill the man,' said he. 'Drop it!'

Baldwin looked at him in amazement.

'Curse you!' he cried. 'Who are you to interfere—you that are new to the Lodge? Stand back!' He raised his stick, but McMurdo had whipped his pistol out of his hip-pocket.

'Stand back yourself!' he cried. 'I'll blow your face in if you lay a hand on me. As to the Lodge, wasn't it the order of the bodymaster that the man was not to be killed, and what are you doing but killing him?'

'It's truth he says,' remarked one of the men.

'By gosh, you'd best hurry yourselves!' cried the man below. 'The windows are all lighting up and you'll have the whole township on your back inside of five minutes.'

There was indeed the sound of shouting in the street, and a little group of compositors and typesetters was forming in the hall below and nerving itself to action. Leaving the limp and motionless body of the editor at the head of the stair, the criminals rushed down and made their way swiftly along the street. Having reached the Union House, some of them mixed with the crowd in McGinty's saloon, whispering across the bar to the Boss that the job had been well carried through. Others, and among them McMurdo, broke away into side-streets, and so by devious paths to their own homes.

"STAND BACK YOURSELF!" HE CRIED.

Illustration by Frank Wiles for the *Strand Magazine*, March, 1915.

II ◆ THE VALLEY OF FEAR

When McMurdo awoke next morning he had good reason to remember his initiation into the Lodge. His head ached with the effect of the drink, and his arm, where he had been branded, was hot and swollen. Having his own peculiar source of income, he was irregular in his attendance at his work, so he had a late breakfast and remained at home for the morning, writing a long letter to a friend. Afterwards he read the *Daily Herald*. In a special column, put in at the last moment, he read, 'Outrage at the *Herald* Office. Editor seriously injured.' It was a short account of the facts with which he was himself more familiar than the writer could have been. It ended with the statement:

The matter is now in the hands of the police, but it can hardly be hoped that their exertions will be attended by any better results than in the past. Some of the men were recognized, and there is hope that a conviction may be obtained. The source of the outrage was, it need hardly be said, that infamous society which has held this community in bondage for so long a period, and against which the *Herald* has taken so uncompromising a stand. Mr Stanger's many friends will rejoice to hear that, though he has been cruelly and brutally beaten and has sustained severe injuries about the head, there is no immediate danger to his life.

Below, it stated that a guard of Coal and Iron Police, armed with Winchester rifles, had been requisitioned for the defence of the office.

McMurdo had laid down the paper, and was lighting his pipe with a hand which was shaky from the excesses of the previous evening, when there was a knock outside, and his landlady brought to him a note which had just been handed in by a lad. It was unsigned, and ran thus:

> I should wish to speak to you, but had rather not do so in your house. You will find me beside the flagstaff upon Miller Hill. If you will come there now I have something which it is important for you to hear and for me to say.

McMurdo read the note twice with the utmost surprise, for he could not imagine what it meant or who was the author of it. Had it been in a feminine hand he might have imagined that it was the beginning of one of those adventures which had been familiar enough in his past life. But it was the writing of a man, and of a well-educated one, too. Finally, after some hesitation, he determined to see the matter through.

Miller Hill is an ill-kept public park in the very centre of the town. In summer it is a favourite resort of the people, but in winter it is desolate enough. From the top of it one has a view not only of the whole grimy, straggling town, but of the winding valley beneath, with its scattered mines and factories blackening the snow on either side of it, and of the wooded and white-capped ranges which flank it. McMurdo strolled up the winding path hedged in with evergreen until he reached the deserted restaurant which forms the centre of summer gaiety. Beside it was a bare flagstaff, and underneath it a man, his hat drawn down and the collar of his overcoat raised up. When he turned his face McMurdo saw that it was Brother Morris, he who had incurred the anger of the bodymaster the night before. The Lodge sign was given and exchanged as they met.

'I wanted to have a word with you, Mister McMurdo,' said the older man, speaking with a hesitation which showed that he was on delicate ground. 'It was kind of you to come.'

'Why did you not put your name to the note?'

'One has to be cautious, mister. One never knows in times like these how a thing may come back to one. One never knows either who to trust or who not to trust.'

'Surely one may trust brothers of the Lodge?'

'No, no; not always,' cried Morris, with vehemence. 'Whatever we say, even what we think, seems to go back to that man, McGinty.'

'Look here,' said McMurdo, sternly; 'it was only last night, as you know well, that I swore good faith to our bodymaster. Would you be asking me to break my oath?'

'If that is the view you take,' said Morris, sadly, 'I can only say that I am sorry I gave you the trouble to come to meet me. Things have come to a bad pass when two free citizens cannot speak their thoughts to each other.'

McMurdo, who had been watching his companion very narrowly, relaxed somewhat in his bearing.

'Sure, I spoke for myself only,' said he. 'I am a new-comer, as you know, and I am strange to it all. It is not for me to open my mouth, Mr Morris, and if you think well to say anything to me I am here to hear it.'

'And to take it back to Boss McGinty,' said Morris, bitterly.

'Indeed, then, you do me injustice there,' cried McMurdo. 'For myself I am loyal to the Lodge, and so I tell you straight, but I would be a poor creature if I were to repeat to any other what you might say to me in confidence. It will go no further than me, though I warn you that you may get neither help nor sympathy.'

'I have given up looking for either the one or the other,' said Morris. 'I may be putting my very life in your hands by what I say, but, bad as you are—and it seemed to me last night that you were shaping to be as bad as the worst—still you are new to it, and your conscience cannot yet be as hardened as theirs. That was why I thought to speak with you.'

'Well, what have you to say?'

'If you give me away, may a curse be on you!'

'Sure, I said I would not.'

'I would ask you, then, when you joined the Freemen's Society in Chicago, and swore vows of charity and fidelity, did ever it cross your mind that you might find it would lead you to crime?'

'If you call it crime,' McMurdo answered.

'Call it crime!' cried Morris, his voice vibrating with passion. 'You have seen little of it if you can call it anything else. Was it crime last night when a man, old enough to be your father, was beaten till the blood dripped from his white hairs? Was that crime—or what else would you call it?'

'There are some would say it was war,' said McMurdo. 'A war of two classes with all in, so that each struck as best it could.'

'Well, did you think of such a thing when you joined the Freemen's Society at Chicago?'

'No, I'm bound to say I did not.'

'Nor did I when I joined it at Philadelphia. It was just a benefit club and a meeting-place for one's fellows. Then I heard of this place—curse the hour that the name first fell upon my ears!—and I came to better myself. My God, to better myself! My wife and three children came with me. I started a dry goods store in Market Square, and I prospered well. The word had gone round that I was a Freeman, and I was forced to join the local Lodge, same as you did last night. I've the badge of shame on my forearm, and something worse branded on my heart. I found that I was under the orders of a black villain, and caught in a meshwork of crime. What could I do? Every word I said to make things better was taken as treason, same as it was last night. I can't get away, for all I have in the world is in my store. If I leave the society, I know well that it means murder to me, and God knows what to my wife and children. Oh, man, it is awful—awful!' He put his hands to his face, and his body shook with convulsive sobs.

McMurdo shrugged his shoulders.

'You were too soft for the job,' said he. 'You are the wrong sort for such work.'

'I had a conscience and a religion, but they made me a criminal among them. I was chosen for a job. If I backed down I knew well what would come to me. Maybe I'm a coward. Maybe it's the thought of my poor little woman and the children that makes me one. Anyhow, I went. I guess it will haunt me for ever. It was a lonely house, twenty miles from here, over the range yonder. I was told off for the door, same as you were last night. They could not trust me with the job. The others went in. When they came out their hands were crimson to the wrists. As we turned away a child was screaming out of the house behind us. It was a boy of five who had seen his father murdered. I nearly fainted with the horror of it, and yet I had to keep a bold and smiling face, for well I knew that if I did not it would be out of my house that they would come next with their bloody hands, and it would be my little Fred that would be screaming for his father. But I was a criminal then—part sharer in a murder, lost for ever in this world, and lost also in the next. I am a good Catholic, but the priest would have no word with me when he heard I was a Scowrer, and I am excommunicated from my faith. That's how it stands with me. And I see you going down the same road, and I ask you what the end is to be? Are you ready to be a cold-blooded murderer also, or can we do anything to stop it?'

'What would you do?' asked McMurdo abruptly. 'You would inform?'

'God forbid!' cried Morris. 'Sure, the very thought would cost me my life.'

'That's well,' said McMurdo. 'I'm thinking that you are a weak man, and that you make too much of the matter.'

'Too much! Wait till you have lived here longer. Look down the valley. See the cloud of a hundred chimneys that overshadows it. I tell you that the cloud of murder hangs thicker and lower than that over the heads of the people. It is the Valley of Fear—the Valley of Death. The terror is in the hearts of the people from the dusk to the dawn. Wait, young man, and you will learn for yourself.'

'Well, I'll let you know what I think when I have seen more,' said McMurdo, carelessly. 'What is very clear is that you are not the man for the place, and that the sooner you sell out—if you only get a dime a dollar for what the business is worth—the better it will be for you. What you have said is safe with me, but, by gosh! if I thought you were an informer——'

'No, no!' cried Morris, piteously.

'Well, let it rest at that. I'll bear what you have said in mind, and maybe some day I'll come back to it. I expect you meant kindly by speaking to me like this. Now I'll be getting home.'

'One word before you go,' said Morris. 'We may have been seen together. They may want to know what we have spoken about.'

'Ah, that's well thought of.'

'I offer you a clerkship in my store.'

'And I refuse it. That's our business. Well, so long, Brother Morris, and may you find things go better with you in the future.'

That same afternoon, as McMurdo sat smoking, lost in thought, beside the stove of his sitting-room, the door swung open, and its framework was filled with the huge figure of Boss McGinty. He passed the sign, and then, seating himself opposite to the young man, he looked at him steadily for some time, a look which was as steadily returned.

'I'm not much of a visitor, Brother McMurdo,' he said, at last. 'I guess I am too busy over the folk that visit me. But I thought I'd stretch a point and drop down to see you in your own house.'

'I'm proud to see you here, Councillor,' McMurdo answered, heartily, bringing his whisky bottle out of the cupboard. 'It's an honour that I had not expected.'

'How's the arm?' asked the Boss.

McMurdo made a wry face.

'Well, I'm not forgetting it,' he said. 'But it's worth it.'

'Yes, it's worth it,' the other answered, 'to those that are loyal, and go through with it, and are a help to the Lodge. What were you speaking to Brother Morris about on Miller Hill this morning?'

The question came so suddenly that it was well that he had his answer prepared. He burst into a hearty laugh.

'Morris didn't know I could earn a living here at home. He shan't know either, for he has got too much conscience for the likes of me. But he's a good-hearted old chap. It was his idea that I was at a loose end, and that he would do me a good turn by offering me a clerkship in a dry goods store.'

'Oh, that was it?'

'Yes, that was it.'

'And you refused it?'

'Sure. Couldn't I earn ten times as much in my own bedroom with four hours' work?'

'That's so. But I wouldn't get about too much with Morris.'

'Why not?'

'Well, I guess because I tell you not. That's enough for most folk in these parts.'

'It may be enough for most folks, but it ain't enough for me, Councillor,' said McMurdo, boldly. 'If you are a judge of men you'll know that.'

The swarthy giant glared at him, and his hairy paw closed for an instant round the glass as though he would hurl it at the head of his companion. Then he laughed in his loud, boisterous, insincere fashion.

'You're a queer card, for sure,' said he. 'Well, if you want reasons I'll give them. Did Morris say nothing to you against the Lodge?'

'No.'

'Nor against me?'

'No.'

'Well, that's because he daren't trust you. But in his heart he is not a loyal brother. We know that well, so we watch him, and we wait for the time to admonish him. I'm thinking that the time is drawing near. There's no room for scabby sheep in our pen. But if you keep company with a disloyal man, we might think that you were disloyal, too. See?'

'There's no chance of my keeping company with him, for I dislike the man,' McMurdo answered. 'As to being disloyal, if it was any man but you, he would not use the word to me twice.'

'Well, that's enough,' said McGinty, draining off his glass. 'I came down to give you a word in season, and you've had it.'

'I'd like to know,' said McMurdo, 'how you ever came to learn that I had spoken with Morris at all.'

McGinty laughed.

'It's my business to know what goes on in this township,' said he. 'I guess you'd best reckon on my hearing all that passes. Well, time's up, and I'll just say——'

But his leave-taking was cut short in a very unexpected fashion. With a sudden crash the door flew open, and three frowning, intent faces glared in at them from under the peaks of police caps. McMurdo sprang to his feet and half drew his revolver, but his arm stopped midway as he became conscious that two Winchester rifles were levelled at his head. A man in uniform advanced into the room, a six-shooter in his hand.

WITH A SUDDEN CRASH THE DOOR FLEW OPEN . . .

Illustration by Frank Wiles for the *Strand Magazine*, April, 1915.

It was Captain Marvin, once of Chicago, and now of the Coal and Iron Constabulary. He shook his head with a half smile at McMurdo.

'I thought you'd be getting into trouble, Mr Crooked McMurdo, of Chicago,' said he. 'Can't keep out of it, can you? Take your hat and come along with us.'

'I guess you'll pay for this, Captain Marvin,' said McGinty. 'Who are you, I'd like to know, to break into a house in this fashion, and molest honest, law-abiding men?'

'You're standing out in this deal, Councillor McGinty,' said the police-captain. 'We are not out after you, but after this man McMurdo. It is for you to help, not to hinder us in our duty.'

'He is a friend of mine, and I'll answer for his conduct,' said the Boss.

'By all accounts, Mr McGinty, you may have to answer for your own conduct some of these days,' the police captain answered. 'This man McMurdo was a crook before ever he came here, and he's a crook still. Cover him, patrolman, while I disarm him.'

'There's my pistol,' said McMurdo, coolly. 'Maybe, Captain Marvin, if you and I were alone and face to face, you would not take me so easily.'

'Where's your warrant?' asked McGinty. 'By gosh! a man might as well live in Russia as in Vermissa while folk like you are running the police. It's a capitalist outrage, and you'll hear more of it, I reckon.'

'You do what you think is your duty the best way you can, Councillor. We'll look after ours.'

'What am I accused of?' asked McMurdo.

'Of being concerned in the beating of old Editor Stanger at the *Herald* office. It wasn't your fault that it isn't a murder charge.'

'Well, if that's all you have against him,' cried McGinty, with a laugh, 'you can save yourself a deal of trouble by dropping it right now. This man was with me in my saloon playing poker up to midnight, and I can bring a dozen to prove it.'

'That's your affair, and I guess you can settle it in court to-morrow. Meanwhile, come on, McMurdo, and come quietly if you don't want a gun-butt across your head. You stand wide, Mr McGinty, for I warn you I will brook no resistance when I am on duty.'

So determined was the appearance of the captain that both McMurdo and his Boss were forced to accept the situation. The latter managed to have a few whispered words with the prisoner before they parted.

'What about——' he jerked his thumb upwards to signify the coining plant.

'All right,' whispered McMurdo, who had devised a safe hiding-place under the floor.

'I'll bid you good-bye,' said the Boss, shaking hands. 'I'll see Reilly, the lawyer, and take the defence upon myself. Take my word for it that they won't be able to hold you.'

'I wouldn't bet on that. Guard the prisoner, you two, and shoot him if he tries any games. I'll search the house before I leave.'

Marvin did so, but apparently found no trace of the concealed plant. When he had descended he and his men escorted McMurdo to the headquarters. Darkness had fallen and a keen blizzard was blowing, so that the streets were nearly deserted, but a few loiterers followed the group, and, emboldened by invisibility, shouted imprecations at the prisoner.

'Lynch the cursed Scowrer!' they cried. 'Lynch him!' They laughed and jeered as he was pushed into the police depot. After a short formal examination from the inspector-in-charge, he was handed on to the common cell. Here he found Baldwin and three other criminals of the night before, all arrested that afternoon, and waiting their trial next morning.

But even within this inner fortress of the law the long arm of the Freemen was able to extend. Late at night there came a jailer with a straw bundle for their bedding, out of which he extracted two bottles of whisky, some glasses, and a pack of cards. They spent an hilarious night without an anxious thought as to the ordeal of the morning.

Nor had they cause, as the result was to show. The magistrate could not possibly, on the evidence, have brought in the sentence which would have carried the matter to a higher court. On the one hand, the compositors and pressmen were forced to admit that the light was uncertain, that they were themselves much perturbed, and that it was difficult for them to absolutely swear to the identity of the assailants, although they believed that the accused were among them. Cross-examined by the clever attorney who had been engaged by McGinty, they were even more nebulous in their evidence. The injured man had already deposed that he was so taken by surprise by the suddenness of the attack that he could state nothing beyond the fact that the first man who struck him wore a moustache. He added that he knew them to be Scowrers, since no one else in the community could possibly have any enmity to him, and he had long been threatened on account of his outspoken editorials. On the other hand, it was clearly shown by the united and unfaltering evidence of six citizens, including that high municipal official, Councillor McGinty, that the men had been at a card party at the Union House until an hour very much later than the commission of the outrage. Needless to say that they were discharged with something very near to an apology from the Bench for the inconvenience to which they had been put, together with an implied censure of Captain Marvin and the police for their officious zeal.

The verdict was greeted with loud applause by a court in which McMurdo saw many familiar faces. Brothers of the Lodge smiled and waved. But there were others who sat with compressed lips and brooding eyes as the men filed out of the dock. One of them, a little, dark-bearded, resolute fellow, put the thoughts of himself and comrades into words as the ex-prisoners passed him.

'You damned murderers!' he said. 'We'll fix you yet.'

◆

12 ◆ THE DARKEST HOUR
◆

If anything had been needed to give an impetus to Jack McMurdo's popularity among his fellows, it would have been his arrest and acquittal. That a man on the very night of joining the Lodge should have done something which brought him before the magistrate was a new record in the annals of the society. Already he had earned the reputation of a good boon companion, a cheery reveller, and withal a man of high temper, who would not take an insult even from the all-powerful Boss himself. But, in addition to this, he impressed his comrades with the idea that among them all there was not one whose brain was so ready to devise a bloodthirsty scheme, or whose hand would be more capable of carrying it out. 'He'll be the boy for the clean job,' said the oldsters to each other, and waited their time until they could set him to his work. McGinty had instruments enough already, but he recognized that this was a supremely able one. He felt like a man holding a fierce bloodhound in leash. There were curs to do the smaller work, but some day he would slip this creature upon its prey. A few members of the Lodge, Ted Baldwin among them, resented the rapid rise of the stranger, and hated him for it, but they kept clear of him, for he was as ready to fight as to laugh.

But if he gained favour with his fellows, there was another quarter, one which had become even more vital to him, in which he lost it. Ettie Shafter's father would have nothing more to do with him, nor would he allow him to enter the house. Ettie herself was too deeply in love to give him up altogether, and yet her own good sense warned her of what would come from a marriage with a man who was regarded as a criminal. One morning after a sleepless night she determined to see him, possibly for the last time, and make one strong endeavour to draw him from those evil influences which were sucking him down. She went to his house, as he had often begged her to do, and made her way into the room which he used as his sitting-room. He was seated at a table with his back turned and a letter in front of him. A sudden spirit of girlish mischief came over her—she was still only nineteen. He had not heard her when she pushed open the door. Now she tip-toed forward, and laid her hand lightly upon his bended shoulders.

If she had expected to startle him, she certainly succeeded, but only in turn to be startled herself. With a tiger spring he turned on her, and his right hand was feeling for her throat. At the same instant, with the other hand he crumpled up the paper that lay before him. For a moment he stood glaring. Then astonishment and joy took the place of the ferocity which had convulsed his features—a ferocity which had sent her shrinking back in horror as from something which had never before intruded into her gentle life.

'It's you!' said he, mopping his brow. 'And to think that you should come to me, heart of my hearts, and I should find nothing better to do than to want to strangle you! Come then, darling,' and he held out his arms. 'Let me make it up to you.'

But she had not recovered from that sudden glimpse of guilty fear which she had read in the man's face. All her woman's instinct told her that it was not the mere fright of a man who is startled. Guilt—that was it—guilt and fear.

'What's come over you, Jack?' she cried. 'Why were you so scared of me? Oh, Jack, if your conscience was at ease, you would not have looked at me like that.'

'Sure, I was thinking of other things, and when you came tripping so lightly on those fairy feet of yours——'

"GIVE IT UP, JACK! FOR MY SAKE—FOR GOD'S SAKE, GIVE IT UP!"

Illustration by Arthur I. Keller for Associated Sunday Magazines, 1914. Frank Wiles illustrated the same scene for the *Strand Magazine*, April, 1915.

'No, no; it was more than that, Jack.' Then a sudden suspicion seized her. 'Let me see that letter you were writing.'

'Ah, Ettie, I couldn't do that.'

Her suspicions became certainties.

'It's to another woman!' she cried. 'I know it. Why else should you hold it from me? Was it to your wife that you were writing? How am I to know that you are not a married man —you, a stranger, that nobody knows?'

'I am not married, Ettie. See now, I swear it. You're the only woman on earth to me. By the Cross of Christ, I swear it!'

He was so white with passionate earnestness that she could not but believe him.

'Well, then,' she cried, 'why will you not show me the letter?'

'I'll tell you, acushla,' said he. 'I'm under oath not to show it, and just as I wouldn't break my word to you, so I would keep it to those who hold my promise. It's the business of the Lodge, and even to you it's secret. And if I was scared when a hand fell on me, can't you understand it when it might have been the hand of a detective?'

She felt that he was telling the truth. He gathered her into his arms, and kissed away her fears and doubts.

'Sit here by me, then. It's a queer throne for such a queen, but it's the best your poor lover can find. He'll do better for you some of these days, I'm thinking. Now your mind is easy once again, is it not?'

'How can it ever be at ease, Jack, when I know that you are a criminal among criminals—when I never know the day that I may hear that you are in the dock for murder? McMurdo the Scowrer—that was what one of our boarders called you yesterday. It went through my heart like a knife.'

'Sure, hard words break no bones.'

'But they were true.'

'Well, dear, it's not as bad as you think. We are but poor men that are trying in our own way to get our rights.'

Ettie threw her arms round her lover's neck.

'Give it up, Jack! For my sake—for God's sake, give it up! It was to ask you that I came here today. Oh, Jack, see, I beg it of you on my bended knees. Kneeling here before you, I implore you to give it up.'

He raised her, and soothed her with her head against his breast.

'Sure, my darlin', you don't know what it is you are asking. How could I give it up when it would be to break my oath and to desert my comrades? If you could see how things stand with me, you could never ask it of me. Besides, if I wanted to, how could I do it? You don't suppose that the Lodge would let a man go free with all its secrets?'

'I've thought of that, Jack. I've planned it all. Father has saved some money. He is weary of this place, where the fear of these people darkens our lives. He is ready to go. We would fly together to Philadelphia or New York, where we should be safe from them.'

McMurdo laughed.

'The Lodge has a long arm. Do you think it could not stretch from here to Philadelphia or New York?'

'Well, then, to the West, or to England, or to Sweden, whence father came. Anywhere to get away from this Valley of Fear.'

McMurdo thought of old Brother Morris.

'Sure, it is the second time I have heard the valley so

named,' said he. 'The shadow does indeed seem to lie heavy on some of you.'

'It darkens every moment of our lives. Do you suppose that Ted Baldwin has ever forgiven us? If it were not that he fears you, what do you suppose that our chances would be? If you saw the look in those dark, hungry eyes of his when they fall on me!'

'By gosh! I'd teach him better manners if I caught him at it. But see here, little girl. I can't leave here. I can't. Take that from me once and for all. But if you will leave me to find my own way, I will try to prepare a way of getting honourably out of it.'

'There is no honour in such a matter.'

'Well, well, it's just how you look at it. But if you'll give me six months I'll work it so as I can leave without being ashamed to look others in the face.'

The girl laughed with joy.

'Six months!' she cried. 'Is it a promise?'

'Well, it may be seven or eight. But within a year at the farthest we will leave the valley behind us.'

It was most that Ettie could obtain, and yet it was something. There was this distant light to illuminate the gloom of the immediate future. She returned to her father's house more light-hearted than she had ever been since Jack McMurdo had come into her life.

It might be thought that as a member all the doings of the society would be told to him, but he was soon to discover that the organization was wider and more complex than the simple Lodge. Even Boss McGinty was ignorant as to many things, for there was an official named the county delegate living at Hobson's Patch, farther down the line, who had power over several different Lodges, which he wielded in a sudden and arbitrary way. Only once did McMurdo see him, a sly little grey-haired rat of a man with a slinking gait and a sidelong glance which was charged with malice. Evans Pott was his name, and even the great Boss of Vermissa felt towards him something of the repulsion and fear which the huge Danton may have felt for the puny but dangerous Robespierre. **59**

One day Scanlan, who was McMurdo's fellow-boarder, received a note from McGinty, enclosing one from Evans Pott, which informed him that he was sending over two good men, Lawler and Andrews, who had instructions to act in the neighbourhood, though it was best for the cause that no particulars as to their objects should be given. Would the bodymaster see to it that suitable arrangements be made for their lodgings and comfort until the time for action should arrive? McGinty added that it was impossible for anyone to remain secret at the Union House, and that, therefore, he would be obliged if McMurdo and Scanlan would put the strangers up for a few days in their boarding-house.

The same evening the two men arrived, each carrying his grip-sack. Lawler was an elderly man, shrewd, silent, and self-contained, clad in an old black frock-coat, which, with his soft felt hat and ragged, grizzled beard, gave him a general resemblance to an itinerant preacher. His companion, Andrews, was little more than a boy, frank-faced and cheerful, with the breezy manner of one who is out for a holiday, and means to enjoy every minute of it. Both of the men were total abstainers, and behaved in all ways as exemplary members of

59 *the huge Danton may have felt for the puny but dangerous Robespierre.* Georges Jacques Danton, 1759–1794, French revolutionist, was a lawyer who won immense popularity through his powerful oratory. As a leader of the Cordeliers, he championed the extreme left in the National Assembly and was instrumental in the overthrow of the monarchy in 1792. The rise of the extremists led by Maximillien Robespierre, 1758–1794, led Danton to seek a relatively moderate course. But Danton gradually lost his influence; early in 1794 he was arrested on a charge of conspiracy and, after a mock trial, guillotined.

society, with the one single exception that they were assassins who had often proved themselves to be most capable instruments for this Association of murder. Lawler had already carried out fourteen commissions of the kind, and Andrews three.

They were, as McMurdo found, quite ready to converse about their deeds in the past, which they recounted with the half-bashful pride of men who had done good and unselfish service for the community. They were reticent, however, as to the immediate job in hand.

'They chose us because neither I nor the boy here drink,' Lawler explained. 'They can count on us saying no more than we should. You must not take it amiss, but it is the orders of the county delegate that we obey.'

'Sure, we are all in it together,' said Scanlan, McMurdo's mate, as the four sat together at supper.

'That's true enough, and we'll talk till the cows come home of the killing of Charlie Williams, or of Simon Bird, or any other job in the past. But till the work is done we say nothing.'

'There are half a dozen about here that I have a word to say to,' said McMurdo, with an oath. 'I suppose it isn't Jack Knox, of Ironhill, that you are after? I'd go some way to see him get his deserts.'

'No; it's not him yet.'

'Or Herman Strauss?'

'No, nor him either.'

'Well, if you won't tell us, we can't make you, but I'd be glad to know.'

Lawler smiled, and shook his head. He was not to be drawn.

In spite of the reticence of their guests, Scanlan and McMurdo were quite determined to be present at what they called the 'fun.' When, therefore, at an early hour one morning McMurdo heard them creeping down the stairs, he awakened Scanlan, and the two hurried on their clothes. When they were dressed they found that the others had stolen out, leaving the door open behind them. It was not yet dawn, and by the light of the lamps they could see the two men some distance down the street. They followed them warily, treading noiselessly in the deep snow.

The boarding-house was near the edge of the township, and soon they were at the cross-roads which are beyond its boundary. Here three men were waiting, with whom Lawler and Andrews held a short, eager conversation. Then they all moved on together. It was clearly some notable job which needed numbers. At this point there are several trails which lead to various mines. The strangers took that which led to the Crow Hill, a huge business which was in strong hands, who had been able, thanks to their energetic and fearless New England manager, Josiah H. Dunn, to keep some order and discipline during the long reign of terror.

Day was breaking now, and a line of workmen were slowly making their way, singly and in groups, along the blackened path.

McMurdo and Scanlan strolled on with the others, keeping in sight of the men whom they followed. A thick mist lay over them, and from the heart of it there came the sudden scream of a steam whistle. It was the ten-minute signal before the cages descended and the day's labour began.

When they reached the open space round the mine-shaft there were a hundred miners waiting, stamping their feet and blowing on their fingers, for it was bitterly cold. The strangers stood in a little group under the shadow of the engine-house. Scanlan and McMurdo climbed a heap of slag, from which the whole scene lay before them. They saw the mine engineer, a great bearded Scotsman named Menzies, come out of the engine-house and blow his whistle for the cages to be lowered. At the same instant a tall, loose-framed young man, with a clean-shaven, earnest face, advanced eagerly towards the pit-head. As he came forward his eyes fell upon the group, silent and motionless, under the engine-house. The men had drawn down their hats and turned up their collars to screen their faces. For a moment the presentiment of death laid its cold hand upon the manager's heart. At the next he had shaken it off and saw only his duty towards intrusive strangers.

'Who are you?' he asked, as he advanced. 'What are you loitering there for?'

There was no answer, but the lad Andrews stepped forward and shot him in the stomach. The hundred waiting miners stood as motionless and helpless as if they were paralysed. The manager clapped his two hands to the wound and doubled himself up. Then he staggered away, but another of the assassins fired, and he went down sideways, kicking and clawing among a heap of clinkers. Menzies, the Scotsman, gave a roar of rage at the sight, and rushed with an iron spanner at the murderers, but was met by two balls in the face, which dropped him dead at their very feet. There was a surge forward of some of the miners, and an inarticulate cry of pity and of anger, but a couple of the strangers emptied their six-shooters over the heads of the crowd, and they broke and scattered, some of them rushing wildly back to their homes in Vermissa. When a few of the bravest had rallied, and there was a return to the mine, the murderous gang had vanished in the mists of the morning without a single witness being able to swear to the identity of these men who in front of a hundred spectators had wrought this double crime.

Scanlan and McMurdo made their way back, Scanlan somewhat subdued, for it was the first murder job that he had seen with his own eyes, and it appeared less funny than he had been led to believe. The horrible screams of the dead manager's wife pursued them as they hurried to the town. McMurdo was absorbed and silent, but he showed no sympathy for the weakening of his companion.

'Sure, it is like a war,' he repeated. 'What is it but a war between us and them, and we hit back where we best can?'

There was high revel in the Lodge room at the Union House that night, not only over the killing of the manager and engineer of the Crow Hill mine, which would bring this organization into line with the other blackmailed and terror-stricken companies of the district, but also over a distant triumph which had been wrought by the hands of the Lodge itself. It would appear that when the county delegate had sent over five good men to strike a blow in Vermissa, he had demanded that, in return, three Vermissa men should be secretly selected and sent across to kill William Hales, of Stake Royal, one of the best-known and most popular mine-owners in the Gilmerton district, a man who was believed not to have an enemy in the world, for he was in all ways a pattern employer. He had insisted, however, upon efficiency in the work, and had therefore paid off certain drunken and idle *employés* who were members of the all-powerful society.

60 contretemps. French: an unexpected embarrassing occurrence; an awkward incident.

Coffin notices hung outside his door had not weakened his resolution, and so in a free, civilized country he found himself condemned to death.

The execution had now been duly carried out. Ted Baldwin, who sprawled in the seat of honour beside the bodymaster, had been the chief of the party. His flushed face and glazed, bloodshot eyes told of sleeplessness and drink. He and his two comrades had spent the night before among the mountains. They were unkempt and weather-stained. But no heroes, returning from a forlorn hope, could have had a warmer welcome from their comrades. The story was told and retold amid cries of delight and shouts of laughter. They had waited for their man as he drove home at nightfall, taking their station at the top of a steep hill, where his horse must be at a walk. He was so furred to keep out the cold that he could not lay his hand on his pistol. They had pulled him out and shot him again and again.

None of them knew the man, but there is eternal drama in a killing, and they had shown the Scowrers of Gilmerton that the Vermissa men were to be relied upon. There had been one **60** *contretemps*, for a man and his wife had driven up while they were still emptying their revolvers into the silent body. It had been suggested that they should shoot them both, but they were harmless folk who were not connected with the mines, so they were sternly bidden to drive on and keep silent, lest a worse thing befall them. And so the blood-mottled figure had been left as a warning to all such hard-hearted employers, and the three noble avengers had hurried off into the mountains, where unbroken Nature comes down to the very edge of the furnaces and the slag-heaps.

It had been a great day for the Scowrers. The shadow had fallen even darker over the valley. But as the wise general chooses the moment of victory in which to redouble his efforts, so that his foes may have no time to steady themselves after disaster, so Boss McGinty, looking out upon the scene of his operations with brooding and malicious eyes, had devised a new attack upon those who opposed him. That very night, as the half-drunken company broke up, he touched McMurdo on the arm and led him aside into that inner room where they had their first interview.

'See here, my lad,' said he, 'I've got a job that's worthy of you at last. You'll have the doing of it in your own hands.'

'Proud I am to hear it,' McMurdo answered.

'You can take two men with you—Manders and Reilly. They have been warned for service. We'll never be right in this district until Chester Wilcox has been settled, and you'll have the thanks of every Lodge in the coalfields if you can down him.'

'I'll do my best, anyhow. Who is he, and where shall I find him?'

McGinty took his eternal half-chewed, half-smoked cigar from the corner of his mouth, and proceeded to draw a rough diagram on a page torn from his note-book.

'He's the chief foreman of the Iron Dyke Company. He's a hard citizen, an old colour-sergeant of the war, all scars and grizzle. We've had two tries at him, but had no luck, and Jim Carnaway lost his life over it. Now it's for you to take it over. That's the house, all alone at the Iron Dyke cross-road, same as you see here in the map, without another within earshot. It's no good by day. He's armed, and shoots quick and straight, with no questions asked. But at night—well, there he is, with his wife, three children, and a hired help. You can't pick or choose. It's all or none. If you could get a bag of blasting powder at the front door with a slow match to it——'

'What's the man done?'

'Didn't I tell you he shot Jim Carnaway?'

'Why did he shoot him?'

'What in thunder has that to do with you? Carnaway was about his house at night, and he shot him. That's enough for me and you. You've got to set the thing right.'

'There's these two women and the children. Do they go up, too?'

'They have to, else how can we get him?'

'It seems hard on them, for they've done nothing amiss.'

'What sort of talk is this? Do you stand back from it?'

'Easy, Councillor, easy. What have I ever said or done that you should think I would be after standing back from an order of the bodymaster of my own Lodge? If it's right or if it's wrong it's for you to decide.'

'You'll do it, then?'

'Of course I will do it.'

'When?'

'Well, you had best give me a night or two that I may see the house and make my plans. Then——'

'Very good,' said McGinty, shaking him by the hand. 'I leave it with you. It will be a great day when you bring us the news. It's just the last stroke that will bring them all to their knees.'

McMurdo thought long and deeply over the commission which had been so suddenly placed in his hands. The isolated house in which Chester Wilcox lived was about five miles off in an adjacent valley. That very night he started off all alone to prepare for the attempt. It was daylight before he returned from his reconnaissance. Next day he interviewed his two subordinates, Manders and Reilly, reckless youngsters, who were as elated as if it were a deer hunt. Two nights later they met outside the town, all three armed, and one of them carrying a sack stuffed with the powder which was used in the quarries. It was two in the morning before they came to the lonely house. The night was a windy one, with broken clouds drifting swiftly across the face of a three-quarter moon. They had been warned to be on their guard against bloodhounds, so they moved forward cautiously, with their pistols cocked in their hands. But there was no sound save the howling of the wind and no movement but the swaying branches above them. McMurdo listened at the door of the lonely house, but all was still within. Then he leaned the powder bag against it, ripped a hole in it with his knife, and attached the fuse. When it was well alight, he and his two companions took to their heels, and were some distance off, safe and snug in a sheltering ditch, before the shattering roar of the explosion, with the low, deep rumble of the collapsing building, told them that their work was done. No cleaner job had ever been carried out in the bloodstained annals of the society. But, alas that work so well organized and boldly conceived should all have gone for nothing! Warned by the fate of the various victims, and knowing that he was marked down for destruction, Chester Wilcox had moved himself and his family only the day before to some safer and less known quarters, where a guard of police should watch over them. It was an empty house which had been torn down by the gunpowder, and the grim old colour-sergeant of the war was still teaching discipline to the miners of Iron Dyke.

'Leave him to me,' said McMurdo. 'He's my man, and I'll get him sure, if I have to wait a year for him.'

A vote of thanks and confidence was passed in full Lodge, and so for the time the matter ended. When a few weeks later it was reported in the papers that Wilcox had been shot at from an ambuscade, it was an open secret that McMurdo was still at work upon his unfinished job.

Such were the methods of the Society of Freemen, and such were the deeds of the Scowrers by which they spread their rule of fear over the great and rich district which was for so long a period haunted by their terrible presence. Why should these pages be stained by further crimes? Have I not said enough to show the men and their methods? These deeds are written in history, and there are records wherein one may read the details of them. There one may learn of the shooting of Policemen Hunt and Evans because they had ventured to arrest two members of the society—a double outrage planned at the Vermissa Lodge, and carried out in cold blood upon two helpless and disarmed men. There also one may read of the shooting of Mrs Larbey whilst she was nursing her husband, who had been beaten almost to death by orders of Boss McGinty. The killing of the elder Jenkins, shortly followed by that of his brother, the mutilation of James Murdoch, the blowing-up of the Staphouse family, and the murder of the Stendals all followed hard upon each other in the same terrible winter. Darkly the shadow lay upon the Valley of Fear. The spring had come with running brooks and blossoming trees. There was hope for all Nature, bound so long in an iron grip; but nowhere was there any hope for the men and women who lived under the yoke of the terror. Never had the cloud above them been so dark and hopeless as in the early summer of the year '75.

13 ✦ DANGER

It was the height of the reign of terror. McMurdo, who had already been appointed inner Deacon, with every prospect of some day succeeding McGinty as bodymaster, was now so necessary to the councils of his comrades that nothing was done without his help and advice. The more popular he became, however, with the Freemen, the blacker were the scowls which greeted him as he passed along the streets of Vermissa. In spite of their terror the citizens were taking heart to bind themselves together against their oppressors. Rumours had reached the Lodge of secret gatherings in the *Herald* office and of distribution of firearms among the law-abiding people. But McGinty and his men were undisturbed by such reports. They were numerous, resolute, and well armed. Their opponents were scattered and powerless. It would all end, as it had done in the past, in aimless talk, and possibly in important arrests. So said McGinty, McMurdo, and all the bolder spirits.

It was a Saturday evening in May. Saturday was always the Lodge night, and McMurdo was leaving his house to attend it, when Morris, the weaker of the Order, came to see him. His brow was creased with care and his kindly face was drawn and haggard.

'Can I speak with you freely, Mr McMurdo?'

'Sure.'

'I can't forget that I spoke my heart to you once, and that you kept it to yourself, even though the Boss himself came to ask you about it.'

'What else could I do if you trusted me? It wasn't that I agreed with what you said.'

'I know that well. But you are the one that I can speak to and be safe. I've a secret here'—he put his hand to his breast —'and it is just burning the life out of me. I wish it had come to any one of you but me. If I tell it, it will mean murder, for sure. If I don't, it may bring the end of us all. God help me, but I am near out of my wits over it!'

McMurdo looked at the man earnestly. He was trembling in every limb. He poured some whisky into a glass and handed it to him.

'That's the physic for the likes of you,' said he. 'Now let me hear of it.'

Morris drank, and his white face took a tinge of colour.

'I can tell it you all in one sentence,' said he. 'There's a detective on our trail.'

McMurdo stared at him in astonishment.

'Why, man, you're crazy!' he said. 'Isn't the place full of police and detectives, and what harm did they ever do us?'

'No, no; it's no man of the district. As you say, we know them, and it is little that they can do. But you've heard of Pinkerton's?'   **61**

'I've read of some folk of that name.'

'Well, you can take it from me you've no show when they are on your trail. It's not a take-it-or-miss-it Government concern. It's a dead earnest business proposition that's out for results, and keeps out till, by hook or by crook, it gets them. If a Pinkerton man is deep in this business we are all destroyed.'

'We must kill him.'

'Ah, it's the first thought that came to you! So it will be up at the Lodge. Didn't I say to you that it would end in murder?'

'Sure, what is murder? Isn't it common enough in these parts?'

'It is indeed, but it's not for me to point out the man that is to be murdered. I'd never rest easy again. And yet it's our own necks that may be at stake. In God's name what shall I do?' He rocked to and fro in his agony of indecision.

But his words had moved McMurdo deeply. It was easy to see that he shared the other's opinion as to the danger, and the need for meeting it. He gripped Morris's shoulder and shook him in his earnestness.

'See here, man,' he cried, and he almost screeched the words in his excitement, 'you won't gain anything by sitting keening like an old wife at a wake. Let's have the facts. Who is the fellow? Where is he? How did you hear of him? Why did you come to me?'

61 *Pinkerton's?'* The Pinkerton National Detective Agency, founded by Allan Pinkerton, 1819–1884. In addition to breaking up the Molly Maguires, Pinkerton's solved train robberies, acted as a Union spy service during the Civil War, and was active in the 1892 Homestead strike. As we have seen, its methods, particularly in the use of labor spies, were bitterly attacked by the trade unions.

'I came to you, for you are the one man that would advise me. I told you that I had a store in the East before I came here. I left good friends behind me, and one of them is in the telegraph service. Here's a letter that I had from him yesterday. It's this part from the top of the page. You can read it for yourself.'

This was what McMurdo read:

'How are the Scowrers getting on in your parts? We read plenty of them in the papers. Between you and me I expect to hear news from you before long. Five big corporations and the two railroads have taken the thing up in dead earnest. They mean it, and you can bet they'll get there. They are right deep down into it. Pinkerton has taken hold under their orders, and his best man, Birdy Edwards, is operating. The thing has got to be stopped right now.'

'Now read the postscript.'

'Of course, what I give you is what I learned in business, so it goes no further. It's a queer cipher that you handle by the yard every day and can get no meaning from.'

McMurdo sat in silence for some time with the letter in his restless hands. The mist had lifted for a moment, and there was the abyss before him.

'Does anyone else know of this?' he asked.

'I have told no one else.'

'But this man—your friend—has he any other person that he would be likely to write to?'

'Well, I dare say he knows one or two more.'

'Of the Lodge?'

'It's likely enough.'

'I was asking because it is likely that he may have given some description of this fellow, Birdy Edwards. Then we could get on his trail.'

'Well, it's possible. But I should not think he knew him. He is just telling me the news that came to him by way of business. How would he know this Pinkerton man?'

McMurdo gave a violent start.

'By gosh!' he cried, 'I've got him. What a fool I was not to know it! Lord, but we're in luck! We will fix him before he can do any harm. See here, Morris; will you leave this thing in my hands?'

'Sure, if you will only take it off mine!'

'I'll do that. You can stand right back and let me run it. Even your name need not be mentioned. I'll take it all on myself as if it were to me that this letter has come. Will that content you?'

'It's just what I would ask.'

'Then leave it at that and keep your head shut. Now I'll get down to the Lodge, and we'll soon make old man Pinkerton sorry for himself.'

'You wouldn't kill this man?'

'The less you know, friend Morris, the easier your conscience will be and the better you will sleep. Ask no questions, and let things settle themselves. I have hold of it now.'

Morris shook his head sadly as he left.

'I feel that his blood is on my hands,' he groaned.

'Self-protection is no murder, anyhow,' said McMurdo, smiling grimly. 'It's him or us. I guess this man would destroy us all if we left him long in the valley. Why, Brother Morris, we'll have to elect you bodymaster yet, for you've surely saved the Lodge.'

And yet it was clear from his actions that he thought more seriously of this new intrusion than his words would show. It may have been his guilty conscience; it may have been the reputation of the Pinkerton organization; it may have been the knowledge that great rich corporations had set themselves the task of clearing out the Scowrers; but, whatever his reason, his actions were those of a man who is preparing for the worst. Every paper which could incriminate him was destroyed before he left the house. After that he gave a long sigh of satisfaction, for it seemed to him that he was safe; and yet the danger must still have pressed somewhat upon him, for on his way to the Lodge he stopped at old Shafter's. The house was forbidden him, but when he tapped at the window Ettie came out to him. The dancing Irish devilry had gone from her lover's eyes. She read his danger in his earnest face.

'Something has happened!' she cried. 'Oh, Jack, you are in danger!'

'Sure, it is not very bad, my sweetheart. And yet it may be wise that we make a move before it is worse.'

'Make a move!'

'I promised you once that I would go some day. I think the time is coming. I had news tonight—bad news—and I see trouble coming.'

'The police?'

'Well, a Pinkerton. But, sure, you wouldn't know what that is, acushla, nor what it may mean to the likes of me. I'm too deep in this thing, and I may have to get out of it quick. You said you would come with me if I went.'

'Oh, Jack, it would be the saving of you.'

'I'm an honest man in some things, Ettie. I wouldn't hurt a hair of your bonnie head for all that the world can give, nor ever pull you down one inch from the golden throne above the clouds where I always see you. Would you trust me?'

She put her hand in his without a word.

'Well, then, listen to what I say and do as I order you, for indeed it's the only way for us. Things are going to happen in this valley. I feel it in my bones. There may be many of us that will have to look out for ourselves. I'm one, anyhow. If I go, by day or night, it's you that must come with me!'

'I'd come after you, Jack.'

'No, no; you shall come *with* me. If this valley is closed to me and I can never come back, how can I leave you behind, and me perhaps in hiding from the police with never a chance of a message? It's with me you must come. I know a good woman in the place I come from, and it's there I'd leave you till we can get married. Will you come?'

'Yes, Jack, I will come.'

'God bless you for your trust in me. It's a fiend out of hell that I should be if I abused it. Now, mark you, Ettie, it will be just a word to you, and when it reaches you you will drop everything and come right down to the waiting-hall at the depot and stay there till I come for you.'

'Day or night, I'll come at the word, Jack.'

Somewhat eased in mind now that his own preparations for escape had been begun, McMurdo went on to the Lodge. It had already assembled, and only by complicated signs and countersigns could he pass through the outer guard and inner guard who close-tiled it. A buzz of pleasure and welcome greeted him as he entered. The long room was crowded, and through the haze of tobacco smoke he saw the tangled black mane of the bodymaster, the cruel, unfriendly features of Baldwin, the vulture face of Harraway, the secretary, and a dozen more who were among the leaders of the Lodge. He rejoiced that they should all be there to take counsel over his news.

'Indeed, it's glad we are to see you, brother!' cried the chairman. 'There's business here that wants a Solomon in judgment to set it right.'

'It's Lander and Egan,' explained his neighbour, as he took his seat. 'They both claim the head-money given by the Lodge for the shooting of old man Crabbe over at Stylestown, and who's to say which fired the bullet?'

McMurdo rose in his place and raised his hand. The expression of his face froze the attention of the audience. There was a dead hush of expectation.

'Worshipful Master,' he said, in a solemn voice, 'I claim urgency.'

'Brother McMurdo claims urgency,' said McGinty. 'It's a claim that by the rules of this Lodge takes precedence. Now, brother, we attend you.'

McMurdo took the letter from his pocket.

'Worshipful Master and brethren,' he said, 'I am the bearer of ill news this day, but it is better that it should be known and discussed than that a blow should fall upon us without warning which would destroy us all. I have information that the most powerful and richest organizations in this State have bound themselves together for our destruction, and that at this very moment there is a Pinkerton detective, one Birdy Edwards, at work in the valley collecting the evidence which may put a rope round the neck of many of us, and send every man in this room into a felon's cell. That is the situation for the discussion of which I have made a claim of urgency.'

There was a dead silence in the room. It was broken by the chairman.

'What is your evidence for this, Brother McMurdo?' he asked.

'It is in this letter which has come into my hands,' said McMurdo. He read the passage aloud. 'It is a matter of honour with me that I can give no further particulars about the letter, nor put it into your hands, but I assure you that there is nothing else in it which can affect the interests of the Lodge. I put the case before you as it has reached me.'

'Let me say, Mr Chairman,' said one of the older brethren, 'that I have heard of Birdy Edwards, and that he has the name of being the best man in the Pinkerton service.'

'Does anyone know him by sight?' asked McGinty.

'Yes,' said McMurdo, 'I do.'

There was a murmur of astonishment through the hall.

'I believe we hold him in the hollow of our hands,' he continued, with an exulting smile upon his face. 'If we act quickly and wisely we can cut this thing short. If I have your confidence and your help it is little that we have to fear.'

'What have we to fear anyhow? What can he know of our affairs?'

'You might say so if all were as staunch as you, Councillor. But this man has all the millions of the capitalists at his back. Do you think there is no weaker brother among all our Lodges that could not be bought? He will get at our secrets—maybe has got them already. There's only one sure cure.'

'That he never leaves the valley,' said Baldwin.

McMurdo nodded.

'Good for you, Brother Baldwin,' he said. 'You and I have had our differences, but you have said the true word tonight.'

'Where is he, then? How shall we know him?'

'Worshipful Master,' said McMurdo, earnestly, 'I would put it to you that this is too vital a thing for us to discuss in open Lodge. God forbid that I should throw a doubt on any-one here, but if so much as a word of gossip got to the ears of this man there would be an end of any chance of our getting him. I would ask the Lodge to choose a trusty committee, Mr Chairman—yourself, if I might suggest it, and Brother Bald-win here, and five more. Then I can talk freely of what I know and of what I would advise should be done.'

The proposition was at once adopted and the committee chosen. Besides the chairman and Baldwin, there were the vulture-faced secretary, Harraway; Tiger Cormac, the brutal young assassin; Carter, the treasurer; and the brothers Willaby, who were fearless and desperate men who would stick at nothing.

The usual revelry of the Lodge was short and subdued, for there was a cloud upon the men's spirits, and many there for the first time began to see the cloud of avenging Law drifting up in that serene sky under which they had dwelt so long. The horrors which they had dealt out to others had been so much a part of their settled lives that the thought of retribu-tion had become a remote one, and so seemed the more start-ling now that it came so closely upon them. They broke up early and left their leaders to their council.

'Now, McMurdo,' said McGinty, when they were alone. The seven men sat frozen in their seats.

'I said just now that I knew Birdy Edwards,' McMurdo explained. 'I need not tell you that he is not here under that name. He's a brave man, I dare bet, but not a crazy one. He passes under the name of Steve Wilson, and he is lodging at Hobson's Patch.'

'How do you know this?'

'Because I fell into talk with him. I thought little of it at the time, nor would have given it a second thought but for this letter, but now I'm sure it's the man. I met him on the cars when I went down the line on Wednesday—a hard case if ever there was one. He said he was a pressman. I believed it for the moment. Wanted to know all he could get about the Scowrers and what he called "the outrages" for the *New York Press*. Asked me every kind of question so as to get some-thing for his paper. You bet I was giving nothing away. "I'd pay for it, and pay well," said he, "if I could get some stuff that would suit my editor." I said what I thought would please him best, and he handed me a twenty-dollar bill for my information. "There's ten times that for you," said he, "if you can find me all that I want." '

'What did you tell him, then?'

'Any stuff I could make up.'

'How do you know he wasn't a newspaper man?'

'I'll tell you. He got out at Hobson's Patch, and so did I. I chanced into the telegraph bureau, and he was leaving it.

' "See here," said the operator, after he'd gone out, "I guess we should charge double rates for this." "I guess you should," said I. He had filled the form with stuff that might have been Chinese for all we could make of it. "He fires a sheet of this off every day," said the clerk. "Yes," said I; "it's special news for his paper, and he's scared that the others should tap it." That was what the operator thought and what I thought at the time, but I think different now.'

'By gosh, I believe you are right!' said McGinty. 'But what do you allow that we should do about it?'

'Why not go right down now and fix him?' someone suggested.

'Aye, the sooner the better.'

'I'd start this next minute if I knew where we could find him,' said McMurdo. 'He's in Hobson's Patch, but I don't know the house. I've got a plan, though, if you'll only take my advice.'

'Well, what is it?'

'I'll go to the Patch tomorrow morning. I'll find him through the operator. He can locate him, I guess. Well, then, I'll tell him that I'm a Freeman myself. I'll offer him all the secrets of the Lodge for a price. You bet he'll tumble to it. I'll tell him the papers are at my house, and that it's as much as my life would be worth to let him come while folk were about. He'll see that that's horse sense. Let him come at ten o'clock at night, and he shall see everything. That will fetch him, sure.'

'Well?'

'You can plan the rest for yourselves. Widow MacNamara's is a lonely house. She's as true as steel and as deaf as a post. There's only Scanlan and me in the house. If I get his promise —and I'll let you know if I do—I'd have the whole seven of you come to me by nine o'clock. We'll get him in. If ever he gets out alive—well, he can talk of Birdy Edwards's luck for the rest of his days.'

'There's going to be a vacancy at Pinkerton's or I'm mistaken,' said McGinty. 'Leave it at that, McMurdo. At nine tomorrow we shall be with you. You once get the door shut behind him, and you can leave the rest with us.'

I4 · THE TRAPPING OF BIRDY EDWARDS

As McMurdo had said, the house in which he lived was a lonely one and very well suited for such a crime as they had planned. It was on the extreme fringe of the town, and stood well back from the road. In any other case the conspirators would have simply called out their man, as they had many a time before, and emptied their pistols into his body; but in this instance it was very necessary to find out how much he knew, how he knew it, and what had been passed on to his employers. It was possible that they were already too late and that the work had been done. If that were indeed so, they could at least have their revenge upon the man who had done it. But they were hopeful that nothing of great importance had yet come to the detective's knowledge, as otherwise, they argued, he would not have troubled to write down and forward such trivial information as McMurdo claimed to have given him. However, all this they would learn from his own lips. Once in their power they would find a way to make him speak. It was not the first time that they had handled an unwilling witness.

McMurdo went to Hobson's Patch as agreed. The police seemed to take a particular interest in him that morning, and Captain Marvin—he who had claimed the old acquaintance with him at Chicago—actually addressed him as he waited at the depot. McMurdo turned away and refused to speak with him. He was back from his mission in the afternoon, and saw McGinty at the Union House.

'He is coming,' he said.

'Good!' said McGinty. The giant was in his shirt-sleeves, with chains and seals gleaming athwart his ample waistcoat and a diamond twinkling through the fringe of his bristling beard. Drink and politics had made the Boss a very rich as well as powerful man. The more terrible, therefore, seemed that glimpse of the prison or the gallows which had risen before him the night before.

'Do you reckon he knows much?' he asked, anxiously.

McMurdo shook his head gloomily.

'He's been here some time—six weeks at the least. I guess he didn't come into these parts to look at the prospect. If he has been working among us all that time with the railroad money at his back, I should expect that he has got results, and that he has passed them on.'

'There's not a weak man in the Lodge,' cried McGinty. 'True as steel, every man of them. And yet, by the Lord, there is that skunk Morris. What about him? If any man gives us away it would be he. I've a mind to send a couple of the boys round before evening to give him a beating up and see what they can get from him.'

'Well, there would be no harm in that,' McMurdo answered. 'I won't deny that I have a liking for Morris and would be sorry to see him come to harm. He has spoken to me once or twice over Lodge matters, and though he may not see them the same as you or I, he never seemed the sort that squeals. But still, it is not for me to stand between him and you.'

'I'll fix the old devil,' said McGinty, with an oath. 'I've had my eye on him this year past.'

'Well, you know best about that,' McMurdo answered. 'But whatever you do must be tomorrow, for we must lie low until the Pinkerton affair is settled up. We can't afford to set the police buzzing today of all days.'

'True for you,' said McGinty. 'And we'll learn from Birdy Edwards himself where he got his news, if we have to cut his heart out first. Did he seem to scent a trap?'

McMurdo laughed.

'I guess I took him on his weak point,' he said. 'If he could get on a good trail of the Scowrers he's ready to follow it home. I took his money,' McMurdo grinned as he produced a wad of dollar notes, 'and as much more when he has seen all my papers.'

'What papers?'

'Well, there are no papers. But I filled him up about constitutions and books of rules and forms of membership. He expects to get right down to the end of everything before he leaves.'

'Faith, he's right there,' said McGinty, grimly. 'Didn't he ask you why you didn't bring him the papers?'

'As if I would carry such things, and me a suspected man, and Captain Marvin after speaking to me this very day at the depot!'

'Aye, I heard of that,' said McGinty. 'I guess the heavy end of this business is coming on to you. We could put him down an old shaft when we've done with him, but however we work it we can't get past the man living at Hobson's Patch and you being there today.'

McMurdo shrugged his shoulders.

'If we handle it right they can never prove the killing,' said he. 'No one can see him come to the house after dark, and I'll lay to it that no one will see him go. Now, see here, Councillor. I'll show you my plan, and I'll ask you to fit the others into it. You will all come in good time. Very well. He comes at ten. He is to tap three times, and me to open the door for him. Then I'll get behind him and shut it. He's our man then.'

'That's all easy and plain.'

'Yes, but the next step wants considering. He's a hard proposition. He's heavily armed. I've fooled him proper, and yet he is likely to be on his guard. Suppose I show him right into a room with seven men in it where he expected to find me alone. There is going to be shooting and somebody is going to be hurt.'

'That's so.'

'And the noise is going to bring every blamed copper in the township on to the top of us.'

'I guess you are right.'

'This is how I should work it. You will all be in the big room—same as you saw when you had a chat with me. I'll open the door for him, show him into the parlour beside the door, and leave him there while I get the papers. That will give me the chance of telling you how things are shaping. Then I will go back to him with some faked papers. As he is reading them I will jump for him and get my grip on his pistol arm. You'll hear me call, and in you will rush. The quicker the better, for he is as strong a man as I, and I may have more than I can manage. But I allow that I can hold him till you come.'

'It's a good plan,' said McGinty. 'The Lodge will owe you a debt for this. I guess when I move out of the chair I can put a name to the man that's coming after me.'

'Sure, Councillor, I am little more than a recruit,' said McMurdo, but his face showed what he thought of the great man's compliment.

When he had returned home he made his own preparations for the grim evening in front of him. First he cleaned, oiled and loaded his Smith and Wesson revolver. Then he surveyed the room in which the detective was to be trapped. It was a large apartment, with a long deal table in the centre and the big stove at one end. At each of the other sides were windows. There were no shutters to these—only light curtains which drew across. McMurdo examined these attentively. No doubt it must have struck him that the apartment was very exposed for so secret a matter. Yet its distance from the road made it of less consequence. Finally he discussed the matter with his fellow-lodger. Scanlan, though a Scowrer, was an inoffensive little man who was too weak to stand against the opinion of his comrades, but was secretly horrified by the deeds of blood at which he had sometimes been forced to assist. McMurdo told him shortly what was intended.

'And if I were you, Mike Scanlan, I would take a night off and keep clear of it. There will be bloody work here before morning.'

'Well, indeed, then, Mac,' Scanlan answered, 'it's not the will but the nerve that is wanting in me. When I saw Manager Dunn go down at the colliery yonder it was just more than I could stand. I'm not made for it, same as you or McGinty. If the Lodge will think none the worse of me, I'll just do as you advise, and leave you to yourselves for the evening.'

The men came in good time as arranged. They were outwardly respectable citizens, well-clad and cleanly, but a judge of faces would have read little hope for Birdy Edwards in those hard mouths and remorseless eyes. There was not a man in the room whose hands had not been reddened a dozen times before. They were as hardened to human murder as a butcher to sheep. Foremost, of course, both in appearance and in guilt, was the formidable Boss. Harraway, the secretary, was a lean, bitter man, with a long, scraggy neck and nervous jerky limbs—a man of incorruptible fidelity where the finances of the Order were concerned, and with no notion of justice or honesty to anyone beyond. The treasurer, Carter, was a middle-aged man with an impassive, rather sulky expression and a yellow parchment skin. He was a capable organizer, and the actual details of nearly every outrage had sprung from his plotting brain. The two Willabys were men of action, tall, lithe young fellows with determined faces, while their companion, Tiger Cormac, a heavy, dark youth, was feared even by his own comrades for the ferocity of his disposition. These were the men who assembled that night under the roof of McMurdo for the killing of the Pinkerton detective.

Their host had placed whisky upon the table, and they had hastened to prime themselves for the work before them. Baldwin and Cormac were already half drunk, and the liquor had brought out all their ferocity. Cormac placed his hands on the stove for an instant—it had been lighted, for the spring nights were still cold.

'That will do,' said he, with an oath.

'Aye,' said Baldwin, catching his meaning. 'If he is strapped to that we will have the truth out of him.'

'We'll have the truth out of him, never fear,' said McMurdo. He had nerves of steel, this man, for, though the whole weight of the affair was on him, his manner was as cool and unconcerned as ever. The others marked it and applauded.

'You are the one to handle him,' said the Boss, approvingly. 'Not a warning will he get till your hand is on his throat. It's a pity there are no shutters to your windows.'

McMurdo went from one to the other and drew the curtain tighter.

'Sure, no one can spy upon us now. It's close upon the hour.'

'Maybe he won't come. Maybe he'll get a sniff of danger,' said the secretary.

'He'll come, never fear,' McMurdo answered. 'He is as eager to come as you can be to see him. Hark to that!'

They all sat like wax figures, some with their glasses arrested half-way to their lips. Three loud knocks had sounded at the door.

'Hush!'

McMurdo raised his hand in caution. An exulting glance went round the circle and hands were laid upon hidden weapons.

'Not a sound for your lives!' McMurdo whispered, as he went from the room, closing the door carefully behind him.

With strained ears the murderers waited. They counted the steps of their comrade down the passage. Then they heard him open the outer door. There were a few words as of greeting. Then they were aware of a strange step inside and of an unfamiliar voice. An instant later came the slam of the door and the turning of the key in the lock. Their prey was safe within the trap. Tiger Cormac laughed horribly, and Boss McGinty clapped his great hand across his mouth.

'Be quiet, you fool!' he whispered. 'You'll be the undoing of us yet.'

There was a mutter of conversation from the next room. It seemed interminable. Then the door opened and McMurdo appeared, his finger upon his lip.

He came to the end of the table and looked round at them. A subtle change had come over him. His manner was as of one who has great work to do. His face had set into granite firmness. His eyes shone with a fierce excitement behind his spectacles. He had become a visible leader of men. They stared at him with eager interest, but he said nothing. Still with the same singular gaze, he looked from man to man.

'Well,' cried Boss McGinty at last, 'is he here? Is Birdy Edwards here?'

'Yes,' McMurdo answered slowly. 'Birdy Edwards is here. I am Birdy Edwards!'

There were ten seconds after that brief speech during which the room might have been empty, so profound was the silence. The hissing of a kettle upon the stove rose sharp

"NOT A SOUND FOR YOUR LIVES!" MCMURDO
WHISPERED . . .

Illustration by Arthur I. Keller for Associated Sunday Magazines, 1914.

and strident to the ear. Seven white faces, all turned upwards to this man who dominated them, were set motionless with utter terror. Then, with a sudden shivering of glass, a bristle of glistening rifle-barrels broke through each window, whilst the curtains were torn from their hangings. At the sight Boss McGinty gave the roar of a wounded bear and plunged for the half-opened door. A levelled revolver met him there, with the stern blue eyes of Captain Marvin of the Coal and Iron Police gleaming behind the sights. The Boss recoiled and fell back into his chair.

'You're safer there, Councillor,' said the man whom they had known as McMurdo. 'And you, Baldwin, if you don't take your hand off your gun you'll cheat the hangman yet. Pull it out, or, by the Lord that made me—— There, that will do. There are forty armed men round this house, and you can figure it out for yourselves what chance you have. Take their guns, Marvin!'

There was no possible resistance under the menace of those rifles. The men were disarmed. Sulky, sheepish, and very amazed, they still sat round the table.

'I'd like to say a word to you before we separate,' said the man who had trapped them. 'I guess we may not meet again until you see me on the stand in the court-house. I'll give you something to think over betwixt now and then. You know me now for what I am. At last I can put my cards on the table. I am Birdy Edwards, of Pinkerton's. I was chosen to break up your gang. I had a hard and a dangerous game to play. Not a soul, not one soul, not my nearest and dearest knew that I was playing it, except Captain Marvin here and my employers. But it's over tonight, thank God, and I am the winner!'

The seven pale, rigid faces looked up at him. There was an unappeasable hatred in their eyes. He read the relentless threat.

'Maybe you think that the game is not over yet. Well, I take my chance on that. Anyhow, some of you will take no further hand, and there are sixty more besides yourselves that will see a jail this night. I'll tell you this, that when I was put upon this job I never believed there was such a society as yours. I thought it was paper talk, and that I would prove it so. They told me it was to do with the Freemen, so I went to Chicago and was made one. Then I was surer than ever that it was just paper talk, for I found no harm in the society, but a deal of good. Still, I had to carry out my job, and I came for the coal valleys. When I reached this place I learned that I was wrong and that it wasn't a dime novel after all. So I stayed to look after it. I never killed a man in Chicago. I never minted a dollar in my life. Those I gave you were as good as any others, but I never spent money better. I knew the way into your good wishes, and so I pretended to you that the law was after me. It all worked just as I thought.

'So I joined your infernal Lodge and I took my share in your councils. Maybe they will say that I was as bad as you. They can say what they like, so long as I get you. But what is the truth? The night I joined you beat up old man Stanger. I could not warn him, for there was no time, but I held your hand, Baldwin, when you would have killed him. If ever I have suggested things, so as to keep my place among you, they were things which I knew that I could prevent. I could not save Dunn and Menzies, for I did not know enough, but I will see that their murderers are hanged. I gave Chester Wilcox warning, so that when I blew his house in he and his folk were in hiding. There was many a crime that I could not stop, but if you look back and think how often your man came home the other road, or was down in town when you went for him, or stayed indoors when you thought that he would come out, you'll see my work.'

'You blasted traitor!' hissed McGinty, through his closed teeth.

'Aye, John McGinty, you may call me that if it eases your smart. You and your like have been the enemy of God and man in these parts. It took a man to get between you and the poor devils of men and women that you held under your grip. There was just one way of doing it, and I did it. You call me a "traitor," but I guess there's many a thousand will call me a "deliverer" that went down into hell to save them. I've had three months of it. I wouldn't have three such months again if they let me loose in the Treasury at Washington for it. I had to stay till I had it all, every man and every secret, right here in this hand. I'd have waited a little longer if it hadn't come to my knowledge that my secret was coming out. A letter had come into the town that would have set you wise to it all. Then I had to act, and act quickly. I've nothing more to say to you, except that when my time comes I'll die easier when I think of the work I have done in this valley. Now, Marvin, I'll keep you no more. Have them in and get it over.'

There is little more to tell. Scanlan had been given a sealed note to be left at the address of Miss Ettie Shafter—a mission which he had accepted with a wink and a knowing smile. In the early hours of the morning a beautiful woman and a much-muffled man boarded a special train which had been sent by the railroad company, and made a swift, unbroken journey out of the land of danger. It was the last time that ever either Ettie or her lover set foot in the Valley of Fear. Ten days later they were married in Chicago, with old Jacob Shafter as witness of the wedding.

The trial of the Scowrers was held far from the place where their adherents might have terrified the guardians of the law. In vain they struggled. In vain the money of the Lodge— money squeezed by blackmail out of the whole country-side —was spent like water in the attempt to save them. That cold, clear, unimpassioned statement from one who knew every detail of their lives, their organization, and their crimes was unshaken by all the wiles of their defenders. At last, after so many years, they were broken and scattered. The cloud was lifted for ever from the valley. McGinty met his fate upon the scaffold, cringing and whining when the last hour came. Eight of his chief followers shared his fate. Fifty odd had various degrees of imprisonment. The work of Birdy Edwards was complete.

And yet, as he had guessed, the game was not over yet. There was another hand to be played, and yet another and another. Ted Baldwin, for one, had escaped the scaffold; so had the Willabys; so had several other of the fiercest spirits of the gang. For ten years they were out of the world, and then came a day when they were free once more—a day which Edwards, who knew his men, was very sure would be an end of his life of peace. They had sworn an oath on all that they thought holy to have his blood as a vengeance for their comrades. And well they strove to keep their vow. From Chicago he was chased, after two attempts so near to success that it was sure that the third would get him. From Chicago he went, under a changed name, to California, and it was there that the light went for a time out of his life when Ettie Edwards died. Once again he was nearly killed, and once again, under the name of Douglas, he worked in a lonely canyon, where, with an English partner named Barker, he amassed a fortune. At last there came a warning to him that the bloodhounds were on his track once more, and he cleared—only just in time—for England. And here came the John Douglas who for a second time married a worthy mate and lived for five years as a Sussex country gentleman—a life which ended with the strange happenings of which we have heard.

◆
◆ EPILOGUE
◆

The police-court proceedings had passed, in which the case of John Douglas was referred to a higher court. So had the Assizes, at which he was acquitted as having acted in self-defence. 'Get him out of England at any cost,' wrote Holmes to the wife. 'There are forces here which may be more dangerous than those he has escaped. There is no safety for your husband in England.'

Two months had gone by, and the case had to some extent passed from our minds. Then one morning there came an enigmatic note slipped into our letter-box. 'Dear me, Mr Holmes! Dear me!' said this singular epistle. There was neither superscription nor signature. I laughed at the quaint message, but Holmes showed an unwonted seriousness.

'Devilry, Watson!' he remarked, and sat long with a clouded brow.

Late that night Mrs Hudson, our landlady, brought up a message that a gentleman wished to see Holmes, and that the matter was of the utmost importance. Close at the heels of his messenger came Mr Cecil Barker, our friend of the moated Manor House. His face was drawn and haggard.

'I've had bad news—terrible news, Mr Holmes,' said he.

'I feared as much,' said Holmes.

'You have not had a cable, have you?'

'I have had a note from someone who has.'

'It's poor Douglas. They tell me his name is Edwards, but he will always be Jack Douglas of Benito Canyon to me. I told you that they started together for South Africa in the *Palmyra* three weeks ago.'

'Exactly.'

'The ship reached Cape Town last night. I received this cable from Mrs Douglas this morning:

'Jack has been lost overboard in gale off St Helena. No one knows how accident occurred—IVY DOUGLAS.'

'Ha! It came like that, did it?' said Holmes, thoughtfully. 'Well, I've no doubt it was well stage-managed.'

"I'VE HAD BAD NEWS—TERRIBLE NEWS, MR. HOLMES," SAID HE.

Illustration by Frank Wiles for the *Strand Magazine*, May, 1915.

'You mean that you think there was no accident?'

'None in the world.'

'He was murdered?'

'Surely!'

'So I think also. These infernal Scowrers, this cursed vindictive nest of criminals——'

'No, no, my good sir,' said Holmes. 'There is a master hand here. It is no case of sawed-off shot-guns and clumsy six-shooters. You can tell an old master by the sweep of his brush. I can tell a Moriarty when I see one. This crime is from London, not from America.'

'But for what motive?'

'Because it is done by a man who cannot afford to fail—one whose whole unique position depends upon the fact that all he does must succeed. A great brain and a huge organization have been turned to the extinction of one man. It is crushing the nut with the hammer—an absurd extravagance of energy—but the nut is very effectually crushed all the same.'

'How came this man to have anything to do with it?'

'I can only say that the first word that ever came to us of the business was from one of his lieutenants. These Americans were well advised. Having an English job to do, they took into partnership, as any foreign criminal could do, this great consultant in crime. From that moment their man was doomed. At first he would content himself by using his machinery in order to find their victim. Then he would indicate how the matter might be treated. Finally, when he read in the reports of the failure of this agent, he would step in himself with a master touch. You heard me warn this man at Birlstone Manor House that the coming danger was greater than the past. Was I right?'

Barker beat his head with his clenched fist in his impotent anger.

'Do you tell me that we have to sit down under this? Do you say that no one can ever get level with this king-devil?'

'No, I don't say that,' said Holmes, and his eyes seemed to be looking far into the future. 'I don't say that he can't be beat. But you must give me time—you must give me time!'

We all sat in silence for some minutes, while those fateful eyes still strained to pierce the veil.

32

THE YELLOW FACE

[Saturday, April 7, 1888]

IN publishing these short sketches, based upon the numerous cases which my companion's singular gifts have made me the listener to, and eventually the actor in some strange drama, it is only natural that I should dwell rather upon his successes than upon his failures. And this is not so much for the sake of his reputation, for indeed it was when he was at his wits' end that his energy and his versatility were most admirable, but because where he failed it happened so often that no one else succeeded, and that the tale was left for ever without a conclusion. Now and again, however, it chanced that even when he erred the truth was still discovered. I have notes of some half-dozen cases of the kind, of which the affair of the second stain, and that which I am now about **1** to recount are the two which present the strongest features of interest.

Sherlock Holmes was a man who seldom took exercise for exercise's sake. Few men were capable of greater muscular effort, and he was undoubtedly one of the finest boxers of his weight that I have ever seen ; but he looked **2** upon aimless bodily exertion as a waste of energy, and he seldom bestirred himself save where there was some professional object to be served. Then he was absolutely untiring and indefatigable. That he should have kept himself in training under such circumstances is remark- **3** able, but his diet was usually of the sparest, and his habits were simple to the verge of austerity. Save for the occasional use of cocaine he had no vices, and he only turned to the drug as a protest against the monotony of existence when cases were scanty and the papers uninteresting.

One day in early spring he had so far relaxed as to go for a walk with me in the Park, where the first faint shoots of green were breaking out upon the elms, and the sticky spearheads of the chestnuts were just beginning to burst into their five-fold leaves. For two hours we **4** rambled about together, in silence for the most part, as befits two men who know each other intimately. It was **5** nearly five before we were back in Baker Street once more.

" Beg pardon, sir," said our page-boy, as he opened the door ; " there's been a gentleman here asking for you, sir."

1 *the affair of the second stain.* Whether or not Holmes can be said to have "erred" in the adventure published as "The Second Stain" is a point still debated by commentators. Most hold that Holmes did *not* err in that adventure, and that Watson must therefore have kept notes of more than one adventure which he associated with a "second stain." A minority, however, holds that the adventure referred to here and the published adventure are one and the same. Thus Mr. Anthony Boucher has written that: "[It is true that Holmes erred] if one views the published adventure from the aspect of the murder of Eduardo Lucas, which was solved by chance, quite without the efforts of Holmes. By shifting the point of view to the recovery of the papers and making the murder irrelevant, Watson contrived, when he published the case, to make it appear a triumph." And Dr. Felix Morley has written ("The Significance of the Second Stain"): "Thinking he had completely solved the mystery [Holmes] says to Watson, 'You will be relieved to hear that there will be no war, that the Right Honourable Trelawney Hope will suffer no setback in his brilliant career . . . that the Prime Minister will have no European complication to deal with . . .' Can it be said, comparing that boast with the situation [that developed in England and on the Continent] that Holmes did not err, even though, in old Watson's truthful words, 'the truth was still discovered'?" The Doubleday omnibus refers here, not to "the second stain," but to "The Musgrave Ritual"—an emendation that scarcely helps matters, since "The Musgrave Ritual" was certainly not one of Holmes' failures.

2 *one of the finest boxers of his weight.* This was "a real compliment," Dr. Edward J. Van Liere wrote in "Sherlock Holmes and Doctor Watson, Perennial Athletes," "for Watson was a keen sportsman, who probably had had occasion to see many boxing matches and knew a good boxer when he saw one."

But what *was* Holmes' weight? "Presumably about the same as McMurdo [*The Sign of the*

Four]." the late H. T. Webster wrote in "Observations on Sherlock Holmes As an Athlete and Sportsman"; "and McMurdo, described as short and deep chested, sounds like a typical middle-weight. Holmes was six feet tall, according to his own word ["The Adventure of the Three Students"], and probably weighed about 11 stone [154 pounds], which would make him resemble the celebrated Bob Fitzsimmons in build."

3 *That he should have kept himself in training.* "How did Holmes and Watson keep themselves in good physical condition?" Dr. Van Liere asked. "This will always be a mystery. Search as we will, we can find no evidence that either Holmes or Watson kept themselves in training. This seems remarkable since there were times when they needed their strength and stamina in order to put their foes out of commission, and indeed there were occasions when their very lives depended upon it. . . . I, for one, am ready to believe that they did not lead such sedentary lives as Doctor Watson would have us think."

4 *just beginning to burst into their five-fold leaves.* "From the description, the early part of April is indicated," the late H. W. Bell wrote in *Sherlock Holmes and Dr. Watson: The Chronology of Their Adventures,* and he added in a note: "Mr. E. H. M. Cox, editor of the *New Flora and Silva,* writes me that in the average year the description of the text would indicate 'about April 10th.'"

5 *two men who know each other intimately.* As early as April, 1883, Holmes referred to Watson as his "intimate friend and associate" ("The Adventure of the Speckled Band"), so by itself this statement means little in dating the case. At the least, however, it tends to indicate a later rather than an earlier relationship. Your editor and the Reverend Henry T. Folsom have settled on 1888, but many other years have their champions: 1882: Bell, Brend, Newton, Petersen, Starrett, Wellman; 1883: Christ and Smith; 1885 or 1886: Pattrick and Zeisler; 1887: Dr. Felix Morley. Holmes' "occasional use of cocaine" and the presence of a page boy at Baker Street are other clues that point to the end of the 'eighties.

6 *I was badly in need of a case.* Even in the years when Holmes was most successful, there must have been stagnant periods in the practice. In any event, however, the adventure of "The Yellow Face" could not have taken place in a late March or early April when Holmes was demonstrably at work on a case.

7 *seven-and-sixpence.* About $1.87.

Holmes glanced reproachfully at me. "So much for afternoon walks!" said he. "Has this gentleman gone, then?"

"Yes, sir."

"Didn't you ask him in?"

"Yes, sir; he came in."

"How long did he wait?"

"Half an hour, sir. He was a very restless gentleman, sir, a-walkin' and a-stampin' all the time he was here. I was waitin' outside the door, sir, and I could hear him. At last he goes out into the passage and he cries: 'Is that man never goin' to come?' Those were his very words, sir. 'You'll only need to wait a little longer,' says I. 'Then I'll wait in the open air, for I feel half choked,' says he. 'I'll be back before long,' and with that he ups and he outs, and all I could say wouldn't hold him back."

"Well, well, you did your best," said Holmes, as we walked into our room. "It's very annoying though, **6** Watson. I was badly in need of a case, and this looks, from the man's impatience, as if it were of importance. Halloa! that's not your pipe on the table! He must have left his behind him. A nice old briar, with a good long stem of what the tobacconists call amber. I wonder how many real amber mouthpieces there are in London. Some people think a fly in it is a sign. Why, it is quite a branch of trade, the putting of sham flies into the sham amber. Well, he must have been disturbed in his mind to leave a pipe behind him which he evidently values highly."

"How do you know that he values it highly?" I asked.

"Well, I should put the original cost of the pipe at **7** seven-and-sixpence. Now it has, you see, been twice mended: once in the wooden stem and once in the amber. Each of these mends, done, as you observe, with silver bands, must have cost more than the pipe did originally. The man must value the pipe highly when he prefers to patch it up rather than buy a new one with the same money."

"Anything else?" I asked, for Holmes was turning the pipe about in his hand and staring at it in his peculiar pensive way.

He held it up and tapped on it with his long, thin forefinger as a professor might who was lecturing on a bone.

"Pipes are occasionally of extraordinary interest," said he. "Nothing has more individuality save, perhaps, watches and bootlaces. The indications here, however, are neither very marked nor very important. The owner is obviously a muscular man, left-handed, with an excellent set of teeth, careless in his habits, and with no need to practise economy."

My friend threw out the information in a very off-hand way, but I saw that he cocked his eye at me to see if I had followed his reasoning.

" You think a man must be well-to-do if he smokes a seven-shilling pipe ? " said I.

" This is Grosvenor mixture at eightpence an ounce," **8** Holmes answered, knocking a little out on his palm. " As he might get an excellent smoke for half the price, he has no need to practise economy."

" And the other points ? "

" He has been in the habit of lighting his pipe at lamps and gas-jets. You can see that it is quite charred all **9** down one side. Of course, a match could not have done that. Why should a man hold a match to the side of his pipe ? But you cannot light it at a lamp without getting the bowl charred. And it is on the right side of the pipe. From that I gather that he is a left-handed man. You hold your own pipe to the lamp, and see how naturally you, being right-handed, hold the left side to the flame. You might do it once the other way, but not as a constancy. This has always been held so. Then he has bitten through his amber. It takes a muscular, energetic fellow, and one with a good set of teeth, to do that. But if I am not mistaken I hear him upon the stair, so we shall have something more interesting than his pipe to study."

An instant later our door opened, and a tall young man entered the room. He was well but quietly dressed in a dark-grey suit, and carried a brown wide-awake in his **10** hand. I should have put him at about thirty, though he was really some years older.

8 *eightpence.* About 16¢.

9 *"He has been in the habit of lighting his pipe at lamps and gas-jets.* A habit Holmes' client would seem to have shared with Holmes himself; see "The Adventure of Charles Augustus Milverton."

10 *a brown wide-awake.* A soft broad-brimmed felt hat.

"PIPES ARE OCCASIONALLY OF EXTRAORDINARY INTEREST," SAID HE.

How two artists imagined Sherlock Holmes in the same deductive moment. *Right*, William H. Hyde for *Harper's Weekly*, February 11, 1893. *Below*, Sidney Paget for the *Strand Magazine*, February, 1893.

" I beg your pardon," said he, with some embarrassment ; " I suppose I should have knocked. Yes, of course I should have knocked. The fact is that I am a little upset, and you must put it all down to that." He passed his hand over his forehead like a man who is half dazed, and then fell, rather than sat, down upon a chair.

" I can see that you have not slept for a night or two," said Holmes, in his easy, genial way. " That tries a man's nerves more than work, and more even than pleasure. May I ask how I can help you ? "

" I wanted your advice, sir. I don't know what to do, and my whole life seems to have gone to pieces."

" You wish to employ me as a consulting detective ? "

" Not that only. I want your opinion as a judicious man—as a man of the world. I want to know what I ought to do next. I hope to God you'll be able to tell me."

He spoke in little, sharp, jerky outbursts, and it seemed to me that to speak at all was very painful to him, and that his will all through was overriding his inclinations.

" It's a very delicate thing," said he. " One does not like to speak of one's domestic affairs to strangers. It seems dreadful to discuss the conduct of one's wife with two men whom I have never seen before. It's horrible to have to do it. But I've got to the end of my tether, and I must have advice."

" My dear Mr. Grant Munro——" began Holmes.

Our visitor sprang from his chair. " What ! " he cried. " You know my name ? "

" If you wish to preserve your *incognito*," said Holmes, smiling, " I should suggest that you cease to write your name upon the lining of your hat, or else that you turn the crown towards the person whom you are addressing. I was about to say that my friend and I have listened to many strange secrets in this room, and that we have had the good fortune to bring peace to many troubled souls. I trust that we may do as much for you. Might I beg you, as time may prove to be of importance, to furnish me with the facts of your case without further delay ? "

Our visitor again passed his hand over his forehead as if he found it bitterly hard. From every gesture and expression I could see that he was a reserved, self-contained man, with a dash of pride in his nature, more likely to hide his wounds than to expose them. Then suddenly, with a fierce gesture of his closed hand, like one who throws reserve to the winds, he began.

" The facts are these, Mr. Holmes," said he. " I am a married man, and have been so for three years. During that time my wife and I have loved each other as fondly, and lived as happily, as any two that ever were joined.

We have not had a difference, not one, in thought, or word, or deed. And now, since last Monday, there has suddenly sprung up a barrier between us, and I find that there is something in her life and in her thoughts of which I know as little as if she were the woman who brushes by me in the street. We are estranged, and I want to know why.

" Now there is one thing I want to impress upon you before I go any further, Mr. Holmes : Effie loves me. Don't let there be any mistake about that. She loves me with her whole heart and soul, and never more than now. I know it, I feel it. I don't want to argue about that. A man can tell easily enough when a woman loves him. But there's this secret between us, and we can never be the same until it is cleared."

" Kindly let me have the facts, Mr. Munro," said Holmes, with some impatience.

" I'll tell you what I know about Effie's history. She was a widow when I met her first, though quite young— only twenty-five. Her name then was Mrs. Hebron. She went out to America when she was young and lived in the town of Atlanta, where she married this Hebron, who was a lawyer with a good practice. They had one child, but the yellow fever broke out badly in the place, and both **11** husband and child died of it. I have seen his death cer- **12** tificate. This sickened her of America, and she came back to live with a maiden aunt at Pinner, in Middlesex. **13** I may mention that her husband had left her comfortably off, and that she had a capital of about four thousand five hundred pounds, which had been so well invested by him **14** that it returned an average of 7 per cent. She had only been six months at Pinner when I met her ; we fell in love with each other, and we married a few weeks after- wards.

" I am a hop merchant myself, and as I have an income of seven or eight hundred, we found ourselves comfortably off, and took a nice eighty-pound-a-year villa at Norbury. **15-16** Our little place was very countrified, considering that it is so close to town. We had an inn and two houses a little above us, and a single cottage at the other side of the field which faces us, and except those there were no houses until you get half-way to the station. My business took me into town at certain seasons, but in summer I had less to do, and then in our country home my wife and I were just as happy as could be wished. I tell you that there never was a shadow between us until this accursed affair began.

" There's one thing I ought to tell you before I go further. When we married, my wife made over all her property to me—rather against my will, for I saw how awkward it would be if my business affairs went wrong. However, she would have it so, and it was done. Well, about six weeks ago she came to me.

" ' Jack,' said she, ' when you took my money you said **17** that if ever I wanted any I was to ask you for it.'

" ' Certainly,' said I, ' it's all your own.'

" ' Well,' said she, ' I want a hundred pounds.' **18**

" I was a bit staggered at this, for I had imagined it was simply a new dress or something of the kind that she was after.

11 *the yellow fever broke out badly in the place.* Mr. Bell thought that John Hebron's death "undoubtedly took place during an epidemic of almost unprecedented malignity [which] visited a portion of the Southern states" in the summer and autumn of 1878 (according to Appleton's *Annual Cyclopaedia and Register of Important Events of the Year 1878*, New York, 1879, pp. 315 ff. "But now a very different problem arises," he wrote. "In the first place, there has never been, so far as we have been able to ascertain, any outbreak of yellow fever in Atlanta; and, as the city lies at an altitude of over 1,000 feet, and the climate is not of the damp, subtropical kind in which the disease flourishes, the occurrence of it there would be most unlikely. It is more probable that Hebron became infected elsewhere [New Orleans?], and returned to die in Atlanta."

12 *I have seen his death certificate.* But Mr. Stuart C. Rand has pointed out ("What Sherlock Didn't Know") that neither the state of Georgia nor the city of Atlanta issued death certificates until they were provided for by an Act of 1914.

13 *Pinner.* Pinner gets its name from a small stream called the Pin, a tributary of the River Colne. The old village consists principally of one broad main street sloping down to the stream. Pinner is now joined to Harrow-on-the-Hill, two and three-quarter miles away, by a continuous line of houses and shops along the main London and Rickmansworth Road.

14 *four thousand five hundred pounds.* About $22,500. But to have such a sum return "an average of 7 per cent" would be "an impossibility with any degree of safety," as Mr. R. M. McLaren pointed out in "Doctor Watson—Punter or Speculator?"

15 *eighty-pound-a-year villa.* Munro's annual income was at most $4,000, and he considered himself "comfortably well off." He paid about $400 a year rental for a "nice" villa. This is another of the statements in the Canon that throws a revealing light on the economics of the times in which Holmes and Watson lived.

16 *Norbury.* Now part of the County Borough of Croydon, Norbury in Holmes' and Watson's day was merely a hamlet on the fringe of London, with a railway station and a golf club.

17 *"Jack,' said she.* Since Munro's Christian name, so far as we know, was *Grant*, we must presume "Jack" to be a nick- or pet-name used by his wife.

18 *a hundred pounds.'* About $500.

" 'WHAT MAY YOU BE WANTIN'?' SHE ASKED . . ."

Illustration by Sidney Paget for the *Strand Magazine*, February, 1893.

" ' What on earth for ? ' I asked.

" ' Oh,' said she, in her playful way, ' you said that you were only my banker, and bankers never ask questions, you know.'

" ' If you really mean it, of course you shall have the money,' said I.

" ' Oh, yes, I really mean it.'

" ' And you won't tell me what you want it for ? '

" ' Some day, perhaps, but not just at present, Jack.'.

" So I had to be content with that, though it was the first time that there had ever been any secret between us. I gave her a cheque, and I never thought any more of the matter. It may have nothing to do with what came afterwards, but I thought it only right to mention it.

" Well, I told you just now that there is a cottage not far from our house. There is just a field between us, but to reach it you have to go along the road and then turn down a lane. Just beyond it is a nice little grove of Scotch firs, and I used to be very fond of strolling down there, for trees are always neighbourly kinds of things. The cottage had been standing empty this eight months, and it was a pity, for it was a pretty two-storied place, with an old-fashioned porch and honeysuckle about it. I have stood many a time and thought what a neat little homestead it would make.

" Well, last Monday evening I was taking a stroll down that way, when I met an empty van coming up the lane, and saw a pile of carpets and things lying about on the grass-plot beside the porch. It was clear that the cottage had at last been let. I walked past it, and then stopping, as an idle man might, I ran my eye over it, and wondered what sort of folk they were who had come to live so near us. And as I looked I suddenly became aware that a face was watching me out of one of the upper windows.

" I don't know what there was about that face, Mr. Holmes, but it seemed to send a chill right down my back. I was some little way off, so that I could not make out the features, but there was something unnatural and inhuman about the face. That was the impression I had, and I moved quickly forwards to get a nearer view of the person who was watching me. But as I did so the face suddenly disappeared, so suddenly that it seemed to have been plucked away into the darkness of the room. I stood for five minutes thinking the business over, and trying to analyse my impressions. I could not tell if the face was that of a man or a woman. But the colour was what impressed me most. It was of a livid dead yellow, and with something set and rigid about it, which was shockingly unnatural. So disturbed was I, that I determined to see a little more of the new inmates of the cottage. I approached and knocked at the door, which was instantly opened by a tall, gaunt woman, with a harsh, forbidding face.

" ' What may you be wantin' ? ' she asked, in a northern accent.

" ' I am your neighbour over yonder,' said I, nodding towards my house. ' I see that you have only just moved in, so I thought that if I could be of any help to you in any——'

" ' Aye, we'll just ask ye when we want ye,' said she, and shut the door in my face. Annoyed at the churlish rebuff, I turned my back and walked home. All the evening, though I tried to think of other things, my mind would still turn to the apparition at the window and the rudeness of the woman. I determined to say nothing about the former to my wife, for she is a nervous, highly strung woman, and I had no wish that she should share the unpleasant impression which had been produced upon myself. I remarked to her, however, before I fell asleep that the cottage was now occupied, to which she returned no reply.

" I am usually an extremely sound sleeper. It has been a standing jest in the family that nothing could ever wake me during the night ; and yet somehow on that particular night, whether it may have been the slight excitement produced by my little adventure or not, I know not, but I slept much more lightly than usual. Half in my dreams I was dimly conscious that something was going on in the room, and gradually became aware that my wife had dressed herself and was slipping on her mantle and her bonnet. My lips were parted to murmur out some sleepy words of surprise or remonstrance at this untimely preparation, when suddenly my half-opened eyes fell upon her face, illuminated by the candle-light, and astonishment held me dumb. She wore an expression such as I had never seen before—such as I should have thought her incapable of assuming. She was deadly pale, and breathing fast, glancing furtively towards the bed, as she fastened her mantle, to see if she had disturbed me. Then, thinking that I was still asleep, she slipped noiselessly from the room, and an instant later I heard a sharp creaking, which could only come from the hinges of the front door. I sat up in bed and rapped my knuckles against the rail to make certain that I was truly awake. Then I took my watch from under the pillow. It was three in the morning. What on this earth could my wife be doing out on the country road at three in the morning ?

" I had sat for about twenty minutes turning the thing over in my mind and trying to find some possible explanation. The more I thought the more extraordinary and inexplicable did it appear. I was still puzzling over it when I heard the door gently close again and her footsteps coming up the stairs.

" ' Where in the world have you been, Effie ? ' I asked, as she entered.

" She gave a violent start and a kind of gasping cry when I spoke, and that cry and start troubled me more than all the rest, for there was something indescribably guilty about them. My wife had always been a woman of a frank, open nature, and it gave me a chill to see her slinking into her own room, and crying out and wincing when her own husband spoke to her.

" ' You awake, Jack ? ' she cried, with a nervous laugh. ' Why, I thought that nothing could awaken you.'

" ' Where have you been ? ' I asked, more sternly.

" ' I don't wonder that you are surprised,' said she, and I could see that her fingers were trembling as she undid

19 *that day.* That is, Tuesday, since Munro has told us that it was "last Monday evening" on which his troubles began.

20 *the Crystal Palace.* John Paxton, one of the owners of *Punch*, started life as gardener to the Duke of Devonshire. "In the supreme undertaking of his life," says R. J. Cruikshank in *Roaring Century*, "the building of the Crystal Palace for the Great Exhibition of 1851, Paxton displayed the originality and courage of genius. In an age bemused by bogus Gothic, he produced a design that was unlike anything else the Victorians had seen. Employing ideas of construction first worked out in building the conservatory at Chatsworth to house the giant Victoria Regina lily, Paxton gave this age the high temple of its pride. Rising in glittering bubbles of glass above the trees of Hyde Park, it looked as dream-like as the stately pleasure dome which Kubla Khan decreed in Xanadu. It seemed so frail that many people were sure the first hailstorm would shatter it. . . . The design of iron and glass, combining airy grace with massive strength, was so far ahead of its time that it was sixty years and more before architecture caught up with it." The Crystal Palace was removed from Hyde Park and re-erected at Sydenham (where Grant Munro walked to it) in 1854; it was torn down in 1941 because it served as a guide for enemy air raiders.

the fastenings of her mantle. 'Why, I never remember having done such a thing in my life before. The fact is, that I felt as though I were choking, and had a perfect longing for a breath of fresh air. I really think that I should have fainted if I had not gone out. I stood at the door for a few minutes, and now I am quite myself again.'

"All the time that she was telling me this story she never once looked in my direction, and her voice was quite unlike her usual tones. It was evident to me that she was saying what was false. I said nothing in reply, but turned my face to the wall, sick at heart, with my mind filled with a thousand venomous doubts and suspicions. What was it that my wife was concealing from me? Where had she been during that strange expedition? I felt that I should have no peace until I knew, and yet I shrank from asking her again after once she had told me what was false. All the rest of the night I tossed and tumbled, framing theory after theory, each more unlikely than the last.

19 "I should have gone to the City that day, but I was too perturbed in my mind to be able to pay attention to business matters. My wife seemed to be as upset as myself, and I could see from the little questioning glances which she kept shooting at me, that she understood that I disbelieved her statement, and that she was at her wits' ends what to do. We hardly exchanged a word during breakfast, and immediately afterwards I went out for a walk, that I might think the matter over in the fresh morning air.

20 "I went as far as the Crystal Palace, spent an hour in the grounds, and was back in Norbury by one o'clock. It happened that my way took me past the cottage, and I stopped for an instant to look at the windows and to see if I could catch a glimpse of the strange face which had stared out at me on the day before. As I stood there imagine my surprise, Mr. Holmes, when the door suddenly opened and my wife walked out!

"I was struck dumb with astonishment at the sight of her, but my emotions were nothing to those which showed themselves upon her face when our eyes met. She seemed for an instant to wish to shrink back inside the house again, and then, seeing how useless all concealment must be, she came forward with a very white face and frightened eyes which belied the smile upon her lips.

" 'Oh, Jack!' she said, 'I have just been in to see if I can be of any assistance to our new neighbours. Why do you look at me like that, Jack? You are not angry with me?'

" 'So,' said I, 'this is where you went during the night?'

" 'What do you mean?' she cried.

" 'You came here. I am sure of it. Who are these people that you should visit them at such an hour?'

" 'I have not been here before.'

" 'How can you tell me what you know is false?' I cried. 'Your very voice changes as you speak. When have I ever had a secret from you? I shall enter that cottage, and I shall probe the matter to the bottom.'

" 'No, no, Jack, for God's sake!' she gasped, in incontrollable emotion. Then as I approached the door, she seized my sleeve and pulled me back with convulsive strength.

" ' I implore you not to do this, Jack,' she cried. ' I swear that I will tell you everything some day, but nothing but misery can come of it if you enter that cottage.' Then, as I tried to shake her off, she clung to me in a frenzy of entreaty.

" ' Trust me, Jack ! ' she cried. ' Trust me only this once. You will never have cause to regret it. You know that I would not have a secret from you if it were not for your own sake. Our whole lives are at stake on this. If you come home with me all will be well. If you force your way into that cottage, all is over between us.'

" There was such earnestness, such despair, in her manner that her words arrested me, and I stood irresolute before the door.

" ' I will trust you on one condition, and on one condition only,' said I at last. ' It is that this mystery comes to an end from now. You are at liberty to preserve your secret, but you must promise me that there shall be no more nightly visits, no more doings which are kept from my knowledge. I am willing to forget those which are passed if you will promise that there shall be no more in the future.'

" ' I was sure that you would trust me,' she cried, with a great sigh of relief. ' It shall be just as you wish. Come away, oh, come away up to the house ! ' Still plucking at my sleeve she led me away from the cottage. As we went I glanced back, and there was that yellow, livid face watching us out of the upper window. What link could there be between that creature and my wife ? Or how could the coarse, rough woman whom I had seen the day before be connected with her ? It was a strange puzzle, and yet I knew that my mind could never know ease again until I had solved it.

" For two days after this I stayed at home, and my wife **21** appeared to abide loyally by our engagement, for, as far as I know, she never stirred out of the house. On the third day, however, I had ample evidence that her solemn prom- **22** ise was not enough to hold her back from this secret influence which drew her away from her husband and her duty.

" I had gone into town on that day, but I returned by the 2.40 instead of the 3.36, which is my usual train. As **23** I entered the house the maid ran into the hall with a startled face.

" ' Where is your mistress ? ' I asked.

" ' I think that she has gone out for a walk,' she answered.

" My mind was instantly filled with suspicion. I rushed upstairs to make sure that she was not in the house. As I did so I happened to glance out of one of the upper windows, and saw the maid with whom I had just been speaking running across the field in the direction of the cottage. Then, of course, I saw exactly what it all meant. My wife had gone over there and had asked the servant to call her if I should return. Tingling with anger, I rushed down and strode across, determined to

. . . SHE SEIZED MY SLEEVE AND PULLED ME BACK WITH CONVULSIVE STRENGTH.

Illustration by William H. Hyde for *Harper's Weekly*, February 11, 1893. Sidney Paget illustrated much the same scene for the *Strand Magazine*, February, 1893.

21 *"For two days after this*. That is, Wednesday and Thursday.

22 *On the third day*. That is, on Friday.

23 *the 2.40 instead of the 3.36*. Unfortunately, neither train appears to have existed in Holmes' and Watson's day.

24 *That was yesterday.* Mr. Grant Munro therefore called upon Mr. Sherlock Holmes on a Saturday.

" 'TELL ME EVERYTHING, THEN,' SAID I."

Illustration by Sidney Paget for the *Strand Magazine*, February, 1893.

end the matter once and for ever. I saw my wife and the maid hurrying back together along the lane, but I did not stop to speak with them. In the cottage lay the secret which was casting a shadow over my life. I vowed that, come what might, it should be a secret no longer. I did not even knock when I reached it, but turned the handle and rushed into the passage.

" It was all still and quiet upon the ground-floor. In the kitchen a kettle was singing on the fire, and a large black cat lay coiled up in a basket, but there was no sign of the woman whom I had seen before. I ran into the other room, but it was equally deserted. Then I rushed up the stairs, but only to find two other rooms empty and deserted at the top. There was no one at all in the whole house. The furniture and pictures were of the most common and vulgar description, save in the one chamber at the window of which I had seen the strange face. That was comfortable and elegant, and all my suspicions rose into a fierce, bitter blaze when I saw that on the mantelpiece stood a full-length photograph of my wife, which had been taken at my request only three months ago.

" I stayed long enough to make certain that the house was absolutely empty. Then I left it, feeling a weight at my heart such as I had never had before. My wife came out into the hall as I entered my house, but I was too hurt and angry to speak with her, and pushing past her I made my way into my study. She followed me, however, before I could close the door.

" ' I am sorry that I broke my promise, Jack,' said she, ' but if you knew all the circumstances I am sure you would forgive me.'

" ' Tell me everything, then,' said I.

" ' I cannot, Jack, I cannot ! ' she cried.

" ' Until you tell me who it is that has been living in that cottage, and who it is to whom you have given that photograph, there can never be any confidence between us,' said I, and breaking away from her I left the house.

24 That was yesterday, Mr. Holmes, and I have not seen her since, nor do I know anything more about this strange business. It is the first shadow that has come between us, and it has so shaken me that I do not know what I should do for the best. Suddenly this morning it occurred to me that you were the man to advise me, so I have hurried to you now, and I place myself unreservedly in your hands. If there is any point which I have not made clear, pray question me about it. But above all tell me quickly what I have to do, for this misery is more than I can bear."

Holmes and I had listened with the utmost interest to this extraordinary statement, which had been delivered in the jerky, broken fashion of a man who is under the influence of extreme emotion. My companion sat silent now for some time, with his chin upon his hand, lost in thought.

" Tell me," said he at last, " could you swear that this was a man's face which you saw at the window ? "

" Each time that I saw it I was some distance away from it, so that it is impossible for me to say."

" You appear, however, to have been disagreeably impressed by it."

" It seemed to be of an unnatural colour, and to have a strange rigidity about the features. When I approached, it vanished with a jerk."

" How long is it since your wife asked you for a hundred pounds ? "

" Nearly two months."

" Have you ever seen a photograph of her first husband ? "

" No ; there was a great fire at Atlanta very shortly after his death, and all her papers were destroyed." **25**

" And yet she had a certificate of death. You say that you saw it ? "

" Yes, she got a duplicate after the fire."

" Did you ever meet anyone who knew her in America ? "

" No."

" Did she ever talk of revisiting the place ? '

" No."

" Or get letters from it ? "

" Not to my knowledge."

" Thank you. I should like to think over the matter a little now. If the cottage is permanently deserted we may have some difficulty ; if on the other hand, as I fancy is more likely, the inmates were warned of your coming, and left before you entered yesterday, then they may be back now, and we should clear it all up easily. Let me advise you, then, to return to Norbury and to examine the windows of the cottage again. If you have reason to believe that it is inhabited do not force your way in, but send a wire to my friend and me. We shall be with you within an hour of receiving it, and we shall then very soon get to the bottom of the business."

" And if it is still empty ? "

" In that case I shall come out to-morrow and talk it over with you. Good-bye, and above all things do not fret until you know that you really have a cause for it."

" I am afraid that this is a bad business, Watson," said my companion, as he returned after accompanying Mr. Grant Munro to the door. " What do you make of it ? "

" It had an ugly sound," I answered.

" Yes. There's blackmail in it, or I am much mistaken."

" And who is the blackmailer ? "

" Well, it must be this creature who lives in the only comfortable room in the place, and has her photograph above his fireplace. Upon my word, Watson, there is something very attractive about that livid face at the window, and I would not have missed the case for worlds."

" You have a theory ? "

" Yes, a provisional one. But I shall be surprised if it does not turn out to be correct. This woman's first husband is in that cottage."

" Why do you think so ? "

" How else can we explain her frenzied anxiety that her second one should not enter it ? The facts, as I read them, are something like this : This woman was married in America. Her husband developed some hateful qualities, or, shall we say, that he contracted some loathsome disease, and became a leper or an imbecile. She fled

25 *there was a great fire at Atlanta very shortly after his death.* There has been no great fire in Atlanta since the time of William Tecumseh Sherman's visit to that city. For the record, however, the city of *Augusta*, Georgia, *has* suffered both a yellow fever epidemic and a great fire—but not in years that support any known Holmesian chronology.

from him at last, returned to England, changed her name, and started her life, as she thought, afresh. She had been married three years, and believed that her position was quite secure—having shown her husband the death certificate of some man whose name she had assumed—when suddenly her whereabouts was discovered by her first husband, or, we may suppose, by some unscrupulous woman who had attached herself to the invalid. They write to the wife and threaten to come and expose her. She asks for a hundred pounds and endeavours to buy them off. They come in spite of it, and when the husband mentions casually to the wife that there are new-comers in the cottage, she knows in some way that they are her pursuers. She waits until her husband is asleep, and then she rushes down to endeavour to persuade them to leave her in peace. Having no success, she goes again next morning, and her husband meets her, as he has told us, as she came out. She promises him then not to go there again, but two days afterwards, the hope of getting rid of those dreadful neighbours is too strong for her, and she makes another attempt, taking down with her the photograph which had probably been demanded from her. In the midst of this interview the maid rushes in to say that the master has come home, on which the wife, knowing that he would come straight down to the cottage, hurries the inmates out at the back door, into that grove of fir trees probably which was mentioned as standing near. In this way he finds the place deserted. I shall be very much surprised, however, if it is still so when he reconnoitres it this evening. What do you think of my theory ? "

" It is all surmise."

" But at least it covers all the facts. When new facts come to our knowledge which cannot be covered by it, it will be time enough to reconsider it. At present we can do nothing until we have a fresh message from our friend at Norbury."

But we had not very long to wait. It came just as we had finished our tea. " The cottage is still tenanted," it said. " Have seen the face again at the window. I'll **26** meet the seven o'clock train, and take no steps until you arrive."

He was waiting on the platform when we stepped out, and we could see in the light of the station lamps that he was very pale, and quivering with agitation.

" They are still there, Mr. Holmes," said he, laying his hand upon my friend's sleeve. " I saw lights in the cottage as I came down. We shall settle it now, once and for all."

" What is your plan, then ? " asked Holmes, as we walked down the dark, tree-lined road.

" I am going to force my way in and see for myself who is in the house. I wish you both to be there as witnesses."

" You are quite determined to do this, in spite of your wife's warning that it is better that you should not solve the mystery ? "

" Yes, I am determined."

" Well, I think that you are in the right. Any truth

26 *the seven o'clock train.* Again, there was no such train.

is better than indefinite doubt. We had better go up at once. Of course, legally, we are putting ourselves hopelessly in the wrong, but I think that it is worth it."

It was a very dark night and a thin rain began to fall **27** as we turned from the high-road into a narrow lane, deeply rutted, with edges on either side. Mr. Grant Munro pushed impatiently forward, however, and we stumbled after him as best we could.

"There are the lights of my house," he murmured, pointing to a glimmer among the trees, "and here is the cottage which I am going to enter."

We turned a corner in the lane as he spoke, and there was the building close beside us. A yellow bar falling across the black foreground showed that the door was not quite closed, and one window in the upper story was brightly illuminated. As we looked we saw a dark blur moving across the blind.

"There is that creature," cried Grant Munro; "you can see for yourselves that someone is there. Now follow me, and we shall soon know all."

We approached the door, but suddenly a woman appeared out of the shadow and stood in the golden track of the lamp-light. I could not see her face in the darkness, but her arms were thrown out in an attitude of entreaty.

"For God's sake, don't, Jack!" she cried. "I had a presentiment that you would come this evening. Think better of it, dear! Trust me again, and you will never have cause to regret it."

"I have trusted you too long, Effie!" he cried, sternly. "Leave go of me! I must pass you. My friends and I are going to settle this matter once and for ever." He pushed her to one side and we followed closely after him. As he threw the door open an elderly woman ran out in front of him and tried to bar his passage, but he thrust her back, and an instant afterwards we were all upon the stairs. Grant Munro rushed into the lighted room at the top, and we entered it at his heels.

It was a cosy, well-furnished apartment, with two candles burning upon the table and two upon the mantelpiece. In the corner, stooping over a desk, there sat what appeared to be a little girl. Her face was turned away as we entered, but we could see that she was dressed in a red frock, and that she had long white gloves on. As she whisked round to us I gave a cry of surprise and horror. The face which she turned towards us was of the strangest livid tint, and the features were absolutely devoid of any expression. An instant later the mystery was explained. Holmes, with a laugh, passed his hand behind the child's ear, a mask peeled off from her countenance, and there was a little coal-black negress with all her white teeth flashing in amusement at our amazed faces. I burst out laughing out of sympathy with her merriment, but Grant Munro stood staring, with his hand clutching at his throat.

"My God!" he cried, "what can be the meaning of this?"

"I will tell you the meaning of it," cried the lady, sweeping into the room with a proud, set face. "You

27 *It was a very dark night and a thin rain began to fall.* "Very dark" shortly after seven o'clock in Norbury and "a thin rain" would both seem to corroborate a date in early April.

. . . AND THERE WAS A LITTLE COAL-BLACK NEGRESS . . .

Illustration by Sidney Paget for the *Strand Magazine*, February, 1893.

But: "One glance at Lucy's coal-black complexion, after [Holmes] had literally unmasked her, should have told him that she could not be Effie Munro's child. Any anthropologist could have reminded him that the child of a mixed racial marriage has pigmentation approximately halfway between that of the parents."—Edward Quayle, "Suffer the Little Children . . ."

28 *I cut myself off from my race in order to wed him.* "The insuperable difficulty," the late H. W. Bell wrote in *Sherlock Holmes and Dr. Watson: The Chronology of Their Adventures*, "lies in the impossibility of any marriage between a coloured man and a white woman. According to the Constitution of the State of Georgia, adopted in 1865 [and retained in the revised Constitution adopted in 1878]: 'The marriage relation between white persons and persons of African descent is forever prohibited, and such marriages shall be null and void' (Art. 5, Sect. 1, par. 9). Moreover, further legislation provides that any officer issuing a license for marriage between two persons, one of whom is of African descent and the other white, shall be penalised by fine and imprisonment or both, while in the case of anyone performing such a marriage, the penalties are doubled. . . . Even on the theory that [Mrs. Munro and John Hebron] were married in some State in which such unions were permitted, their marriage upon their return to Atlanta, would have come to an abrupt and sanguinary end."

In reply to this, Mr. Manly Wade Wellman has written ("Two Southern Exposures of Sherlock Holmes"): "Laws against . . . mixed marriages, both in ante-bellum Georgia and in more modern times, have been cited with an air of settling the matter as mere romance. But other laws, that obtained here during the Reconstruction years when carpetbagger and scalawag leaders marshalled numerous Negro legislators and set up behaviors that have not obtained before or since, may . . . explain the seeming impossibility."

And Mr. Robert H. Schutz has written ("Some Problems in 'The Yellow Face' "): "Referring to one book on the subject of Negroes in the professional fields [C. G. Woodson, *The Negro Professional Man and the Community, with Special Emphasis on the Physician and Lawyer*], we find that as early as 1850 there were several Negro lawyers in New York City. Furthermore, there is an Atlanta in New York State (also in other northern states), and the New York State laws in 1880 did not prohibit inter-racial marriages."

29 *little Lucy is darker far than ever her father was.* Again, by the information given, this could not be anthropologically correct.

30 *what is to become of us, my child and me?"* "Seeing that every point in [Mrs. Munro's] story which we have been able to check is wholly false," Mr. Bell wrote, "we are driven to the conclusion that John Hebron was a white man; that in the course of a journey, perhaps in Alabama, in July, 1878, he became infected with yellow fever; that Mrs. Hebron had been engaged in a criminal intrigue with a Negro, whose name has not survived, and that her child's birth, following the death of her husband, was the reason for her flight. Her paramour was doubtless adequately dealt with.

have forced me against my own judgment to tell you, and now we must both make the best of it. My husband died at Atlanta. My child survived."

" Your child ! "

She drew a large silver locket from her bosom. " You have never seen this open."

" I understood that it did not open."

She touched a spring, and the front hinged back. There was a portrait within of a man, strikingly handsome and intelligent, but bearing unmistakable signs upon his features of his African descent.

" That is John Hebron, of Atlanta," said the lady, " and a nobler man never walked the earth. I cut myself off **28** from my race in order to wed him ; but never once while he lived did I for one instant regret it. It was our misfortune that our only child took after his people rather than mine. It is often so in such matches, and little Lucy **29** is darker far than ever her father was. But, dark or fair, she is my own dear little girlie, and her mother's pet." The little creature ran across at the words and nestled up against the lady's dress.

" When I left her in America," she continued, " it was only because her health was weak, and the change might have done her harm. She was given to the care of a faithful Scotchwoman who had once been our servant. Never for an instant did I dream of disowning her as my child. But when chance threw you in my way, Jack, and I learned to love you, I feared to tell you about my child. God forgive me, I feared that I should lose you, and I had not the courage to tell you. I had to choose between you, and in my weakness I turned away from my own little girl. For three years I have kept her existence a secret from you, but I heard from the nurse, and I knew that all was well with her. At last, however, there came an overwhelming desire to see the child once more. I struggled against it, but in vain. Though I knew the danger I determined to have the child over, if it were but for a few weeks. I sent a hundred pounds to the nurse, and I gave her instructions about this cottage, so that she might come as a neighbour without my appearing to be in any way connected with her. I pushed my precautions so far as to order her to keep the child in the house during the daytime, and to cover up her little face and hands, so that even those who might see her at the window should not gossip about there being a black child in the neighbourhood. If I had been less cautious I might have been more wise, but I was half crazy with fear lest you should learn the truth.

" It was you who told me first that the cottage was occupied. I should have waited for the morning, but I could not sleep for excitement, and so at last I slipped out, knowing how difficult it is to awaken you. But you saw me go, and that was the beginning of my troubles. Next day you had my secret at your mercy, but you nobly refrained from pursuing your advantage. Three days later, however, the nurse and child only just escaped from the back door as you rushed in at the front one. And now to-night you at last know all, and I ask you what is to **30** become of us, my child and me ? " She clasped her hands and waited for an answer.

It was a long two minutes before Grant Munro broke the silence, and when his answer came it was one of which I love to think. He lifted the little child, kissed her, and then, still carrying her, he held his other hand out to his wife, and turned towards the door.

"We can talk it over more comfortably at home," said he. "I am not a very good man, Effie, but I think that I am a better one than you have given me credit for being."

Holmes and I followed them down to the lane, and my friend plucked at my sleeve as we came out. "I think," said he, "that we shall be of more use in London than in Norbury."

Not another word did he say of the case until late that night when he was turning away, with his lighted candle, for his bedroom.

"Watson," said he, "if it should ever strike you that I am getting a little over-confident in my powers, or giving less pains to a case than it deserves, kindly whisper 'Norbury' in my ear, and I shall be infinitely obliged to you."

She preserved his portrait in her locket, and at last, when forced to give some sort of explanation to the infatuated Munro, carried the situation with a high hand and 'a proud, set face.' She was an actress of parts, and an accomplished liar; but her greatest distinction is that she deceived Sherlock Holmes."

HE LIFTED THE LITTLE CHILD . . .

Illustration by Sidney Paget for the *Strand Magazine*, February, 1893.

33

THE GREEK INTERPRETER

[*Wednesday, September 12, 1888*]

1 *my long and intimate acquaintance*. A later rather than an earlier year in the partnership is certainly indicated. Your editor favors 1888—as do Messrs. Christ, Folsom, Petersen, and Zeisler. Brend chose 1882, Newton 1883, Andrew 1886, Pattrick 1889, and Bell, Smith, and Sayers 1890.

2 *after tea*. Holmes would have been no true-born Englishman had he not wanted his tea occasionally. He accepts a 5:30 cup from Watson in *The Sign of the Four*, helps himself to a cup on another occasion ("The Adventure of the Beryl Coronet"), consumes hot tea before embarking on a journey to Kent ("The Adventure of the Abbey Grange"). At the Hereford arms in Ross, Holmes, Watson, and Lestrade sat over a cup of tea ("The Boscombe Valley Mystery"), and Holmes took his tea at an inn again in "The Naval Treaty."

3 *a summer evening*. We shortly learn that it was also a Wednesday evening.

4 *golf clubs*. That Holmes was then and is today a keen golfer is the theory held by Mr. Webster Evans, who notes (in "Sherlock Holmes and Sport") that in "The Adventure of Wisteria Lodge" Watson records the fact that Holmes "spent his days in long and often solitary walks" in the country. "Holmes murmured some excuse about it being very pleasant to see "the first green shoots upon the hedges and the catkins on the hazels.' But that word green—I wonder if he was really only walking. After all, golf is a game that would suit a man of Holmes' temperament. And as Professor Moriarty wrote *The Dynamics of an Asteroid*, why should not Holmes have written *The Dynamics of a Spheroid*—a book which, like Moriarty's, would certainly be likely to ascend to such rarefied heights of pure mathematics that there could be no man in the scientific press capable of criticising it!"

1 DURING my long and intimate acquaintance with Mr. Sherlock Holmes I had never heard him refer to his relations, and hardly ever to his own early life. This reticence upon his part had increased the somewhat inhuman effect which he produced upon me, until sometimes I found myself regarding him as an isolated phenomenon, a brain without a heart, as deficient in human sympathy as he was pre-eminent in intelligence. His aversion to women, and his disinclination to form new friendships, were both typical of his unemotional character, but not more so than his complete suppression of every reference to his own people. I had come to believe that he was an orphan with no relatives living, but one day, to my very great surprise, he began to talk to me about his brother.

2-3 It was after tea on a summer evening, and the conversation, which had roamed in a desultory, spasmodic **4** fashion from golf clubs to the causes of the change in the **5** obliquity of the ecliptic, came round at last to the question **6** of atavism and hereditary aptitudes. The point under discussion was how far any singular gift in an individual was due to his ancestry, and how far to his own early training.

"In your own case," said I, " from all that you have told me it seems obvious that your faculty of observation and your peculiar facility for deduction are due to your own systematic training."

"To some extent," he answered, thoughtfully. "My ancestors were country squires, who appear to have led much the same life as is natural to their class. But, none the less, my turn that way is in my veins, and may have come with my grandmother, who was the sister of Vernet, the French artist. Art in the blood is liable to take the strangest forms."

"But how do you know that it is hereditary?"

"Because my brother Mycroft possesses it in a larger degree than I do."

This was news to me, indeed. If there were another man with such singular powers in England, how was it that neither police nor public had heard of him? I put the question, with a hint that it was my companion's modesty which made him acknowledge his brother as his superior.   Holmes laughed at my suggestion.

"My dear Watson," said he.   "I cannot agree with those who rank modesty among the virtues.   To the logician all things should be seen exactly as they are, and to under-estimate oneself is as much a departure from truth as to exaggerate one's own powers.   When I say, therefore, that Mycroft has better powers of observation than I, you may take it that I am speaking the exact and literal truth."

"Is he your junior?"

"Seven years my senior."

"How comes it that he is unknown?"

"Oh, he is very well known in his own circle."

"Where, then?"

"Well, in the Diogenes Club, for example."

I had never heard of the institution, and my face must have proclaimed as much, for Sherlock Holmes pulled out his watch.

"The Diogenes Club is the queerest club in London, **7** and Mycroft one of the queerest men.   He's always there **8** from a quarter to five till twenty to eight.   It's six now, so if you care for a stroll this beautiful evening I shall be very happy to introduce you to two curiosities."

Five minutes later we were in the street, walking towards Regent Circus.   **9**

"You wonder," said my companion, "why it is that Mycroft does not use his powers for detective work.   He is incapable of it."

"But I thought you said——!"

"I said that he was my superior in observation and deduction.   If the art of the detective began and ended in reasoning from an arm-chair, my brother would be the

. . . SHERLOCK HOLMES PULLED OUT HIS WATCH.

Illustration by Sidney Paget for the *Strand Magazine*, September, 1893.

5 *the change in the obliquity of the ecliptic.* The angle between the planes of the earth's equator and orbit (ecliptic) diminishes at the rate of 0″.47 per year. Scientists say this rate of decrease will gradually slacken, and, after many thousands of years, the obliquity will be about 22½° and will begin to increase.

6 *atavism.* The recurrence, in a descendant, of characteristics of a remote ancestor, instead of those of an immediate ancestor—"reversion to the primitive."

7 *the queerest club in London.* Lord Donegall, the editor of the *Sherlock Holmes Journal*, has suggested that the Diogenes is "only an alias" for the Athenaeum. This famous London club was founded in 1824 ". . . for the association of individuals known for their scientific and literary attainments, artists of eminence in any class of the fine arts and noblemen and gentlemen distinguished as liberal patrons of science, literature, or the arts." Theodore Hook wrote of it:

> There's first the Athenaeum Club; so wise
>   there's not a man of it
> That has not sense enough for six—in fact
>   that is the plan of it;
> The very waiters answer you with eloquence
>   Socratical,
> And always place the knives and forks in
>   order mathematical.

The Athenaeum did not permit smoking until 1862, and it was one of the last clubs in London to install a bar.

8 *and Mycroft one of the queerest men.* As we have noted before, there are mysteries about Mycroft. Mr. Wilbur K. McKee has even gone so far as to suggest ("The Son of a Certain Gracious Lady") that "Mycroft Holmes was not actually the brother of Sherlock" at all but was really Albert Edward, Prince of Wales, later King Edward VII.

A less sensational suggestion has been made by Mr. J. Randolph Cox ("Mycroft Holmes: Private Detective"); in Mr. Cox's view, Mycroft Holmes, in earlier days, had himself been a consulting detective who chose to be known as *Martin Hewitt.* Shortly before the Bruce-Partington affair (November, 1895) Mycroft gave his old friend Brett, a journalist, permission to publish the reminiscences of his earlier exploits as *Martin Hewitt, Investigator,* as by Arthur Morrison; London: Ward, Lock & Bowden, 1894. This was followed, in 1895, by *Chronicles of Martin Hewitt;* in 1896 by *Adventures of Martin Hewitt;* in 1903 by *The Red Triangle.*

The late Monsignor Ronald A. Knox had a very different view of Mycroft ("The Mystery of Mycroft"): "Mycroft was, at this period of his life, in the service and in the pay of the ex-Professor [James Moriarty]."

9 *Regent Circus.* Possibly Oxford Circus, possibly Piccadilly Circus. As Mr. Michael Harrison explains (*In the Footsteps of Sherlock Holmes*): "When Nash was planning his new thoroughfare, to connect Langham Place with Pall Mall, he arranged for two 'piazzas,' one at the point where Oxford Street crossed the 'new'—'Regent'—Street, and the other at the junction of Coventry Street and Piccadilly. Yet both these piazzas were called, at the beginning, 'Regent Circus'; the one at the end of Piccadilly being known as 'the first Regent Circus,' and the one at Oxford Street being called 'the second Regent Circus.' It was not so very long before, in popular usage, 'the first Regent Circus' became 'Piccadilly Circus' [and the second "Oxford Circus"]; and it is somewhat extraordinary that Watson should have stuck to the old name, long before all but pedants and map-makers and officials of the Metropolitan Board of Works had given up the old, confusing name."

greatest criminal agent that ever lived. But he has no ambition and no energy. He would not even go out of his way to verify his own solutions, and would rather be considered wrong than take the trouble to prove himself right. Again and again I have taken a problem to him and have received an explanation which has afterwards proved to be the correct one. And yet he was absolutely incapable of working out the practical points which must be gone into before a case could be laid before a judge or jury."

" It is not his profession, then ? "

" By no means. What is to me a means of livelihood is to him the merest hobby of a dilettante. He has an extraordinary faculty for figures, and audits the books in **10** some of the Government departments. Mycroft lodges in Pall Mall, and he walks round the corner into White- **11** hall every morning and back every evening. From year's end to year's end he takes no other exercise, and is seen nowhere else, except only in the Diogenes Club, which is just opposite his rooms."

"MYCROFT LODGES IN PALL MALL . . ."

"From Trafalgar Square, Pall Mall, the handsomest street in London, leads to the west. Its name is a record of its having been the place where the game of Palle-malle was played—a game popular in the deserted streets of old sleepy Italian cities, and deriving its name from *Palla*, a ball, and *Maglia*, a mallet. It was introduced into England in the reign of James I, who . . . recommended his son Prince Henry to play it. Charles II, who was passionately fond of the game, removed the site for it to St. James's Park. . . . The street was not enclosed till about 1690, when it was at first called Catherine Street, in honour of Catherine of Braganza, and it still continued to be a fashionable promenade rather than a highway for carriage traffic. . . . Club-houses are the characteristic of the street, though none of the existing buildings dates beyond the [nineteenth] century. In the

[eighteenth] century their place was filled by taverns where various literary and convivial societies held their meetings: Pepys in 1660 was frequently at one of these, 'Wood's at the Pell-Mell.' The first trial of street gas in London was made here in 1807, in a row of lamps, on the King's birthday, before the colonnade of Carlton House. Amid all the changes of the town, London-lovers have continued to give their best affections to Pall Mall, and how many there are who agree with the lines of Charles Morris—'In town let me live, then, in town let me die; / For in truth I can't relish the country, not I. / If one must have a villa in summer to dwell, / Oh! give me the sweet shady side of Pall Mall.' "—Augustus J. C. Hare, *Walks in London*, Vol. II. Our photograph, from James Edward Holroyd's *Baker Street By-ways*, shows Pall Mall, looking east, with a hansom cab turning into Lower Regent Street.

"I cannot recall the name."

"Very likely not. There are many men in London, you know, who, some from shyness, some from misanthropy have no wish for the company of their fellows. Yet they are not averse to comfortable chairs and the latest periodicals. It is for the convenience of these that the Diogenes Club was started, and it now contains the most unsociable and unclubbable men in town. No member is permitted to take the least notice of any other one. Save in the Strangers' Room, no talking is, under any circumstances, permitted, and three offences, if brought to the notice of the committee, render the talker liable to expulsion. My brother was one of the founders, and I have myself found it a very soothing atmosphere."

We had reached Pall Mall as we talked, and were walking down it from the St. James's end. Sherlock Holmes **12** stopped at a door some little distance from the Carlton, **13** and, cautioning me not to speak, he led the way into the hall. Through the glass panelling I caught a glimpse of a large and luxurious room in which a considerable number of men were sitting about and reading papers, each in his own little nook. Holmes showed me into a small chamber which looked out on to Pall Mall, and then, leaving me for a minute, he came back with a companion who I knew could only be his brother.

Mycroft Holmes was a much larger and stouter man than Sherlock. His body was absolutely corpulent, but his face, though massive, had preserved something of the

MYCROFT HOLMES WAS A MUCH LARGER AND STOUTER
MAN THAN SHERLOCK.

Portrait of Mycroft Holmes by Sidney Paget for the *Strand Magazine*, September, 1893.

It is also extraordinary that Watson should mention "Regent Circus" here at all, for he tells us shortly that he and Holmes walked down Pall Mall "from the St. James's end." To approach Pall Mall from Baker Street, via St. James's, they would hardly go by way of "Regent Circus"—whether Watson meant Piccadilly Circus or Oxford Circus.

10 *audits the books in some of the Government departments.* "It is difficult to believe," Mr. S. C. Roberts has written, "that . . . Mycroft could have attained to such a position if he had not had an expensive public school and university education behind him."

And Mr. C. O. Merriman has added ("Unfair to Mycroft"): "I do not know if the rival claims of the Institute of Chartered Accountants of England and Wales and that of the Institute of Scottish Chartered Accountants have ever been registered on the score of Mycroft's early education but I think that perhaps I may take this opportunity of recording the fact that my first researches show clearly that Mycroft was a member of the English Institute. An examination of the Charter of Incorporation shows that a Mr. W. Holmes was an Associate Member. The upending of the 'M' can only be ascribed to a temperamental printer."

11 *Whitehall.* Running from Charing Cross to Parliament Street, Whitehall is the home of Britain's government offices and the Cenotaph (war memorial). Here was once the palace of the archbishops of York, in which Henry VIII and Cromwell died and outside which Charles I was executed.

12 *St. James's.* "From St. James's Palace, St. James's Street, built in 1670, and at first called Long Street, leads to Piccadilly. From its earliest days it has been popular. 'The Campus Martius of St. James's Street, / Where the beaux cavalry pace to and fro, / Before they take the field in Rotten Row.'—Sheridan."—Augustus J. C. Hare, *Walks in London*, Vol. II.

13 *the Carlton.* The Carlton *Hotel* was not erected until between 1897 and 1899; so Watson must refer here to the Carlton *Club* (then located in Pall Mall), founded at the Thatched House Tavern in 1832 to fight the supporters of the Reform Bill and to serve as a rallying point for the Tories after their wholesale defeat in the elections. Sir James Damery, of "The Adventure of the Illustrious Client," was a member of the Carlton.

14 "*I hear of Sherlock everywhere since you became his chronicler.* The adventure is therefore to be dated after the publication of *A Study in Scarlet* in December, 1887.

15 *that Manor House case.* If the adventure of "The Greek Interpreter" took place in September, 1888, as your editor believes that it did, it is curious that Sherlock and Mycroft on this occasion should not at least have mentioned the Jack the Ripper killings, the second of which took place on the night of August 7th, the third on August 31st, and the fourth on September 8th. The omission is especially curious in the light of the late Page Heldenbrand's comment in "Another Bohemian Scandal": "In view of the sensation caused by [Jack the] Ripper's contretemps, the utter despair of Scotland Yard, and the renown enjoyed by Holmes in 1888, we can be absolutely certain that he took a hand in attempting to discourage wayward Jack's cutting-up." This is also your editor's view, and he has attempted to reconstruct Holmes' part in the capture of Jack the Ripper in Chapter XV, "Jack the Harlot Killer," of *Sherlock Holmes of Baker Street.* We should also note here that Mr. Gordon Neitzke, in "Sherlock Holmes and Jack the Ripper," has voiced the alarming speculation that *Watson* was the Ripper.

16 *a sapper.* A member of a military engineer unit organized, trained, and equipped primarily for trench-digging and other field fortification work.

17 *He is in the artillery.*" "One could wish that they had gone a little further and told us whether the man belonged to the Royal Horse Artillery of the Field or Garrison branch," Mrs. Crighton Sellars wrote in "Dr. Watson and the British Army." "For my part, I deduce that the ex-Sergeant belonged to the Garrison Artillery, because he did not have the cavalry stride and because of his weight, which precluded too much riding and activity."

18 *there is another child to be thought of.*" Compare the above with a diagnosis once made by Dr. Joseph Bell: "Well, my man, you've served in the army." "Aye, sir." "Not long discharged?" "No, sir." "A Highland regiment?" "Aye, sir." "A non-com. officer?" "Aye, sir." "Stationed at Barbados?" "Aye, sir." "You see, gentlemen," Bell explained to his students, "the man was respectful but did not remove his hat. They do not in the army, but he would have learned civilian ways had he been long discharged. He has an air of authority and he is obviously Scottish. As to Barbados, his complaint is elephantiasis, which is West Indian and not British."

sharpness of expression which was so remarkable in that of his brother. His eyes, which were of a peculiarly light watery grey, seemed to always retain that far-away, introspective look which I had only observed in Sherlock's when he was exerting his full powers.

" I am glad to meet you, sir," said he, putting out a broad, flat hand, like the flipper of a seal. " I hear of **14** Sherlock everywhere since you became his chronicler. By the way, Sherlock, I expected to see you round last **15** week to consult me over that Manor House case. I thought you might be a little out of your depth."

" No, I solved it," said my friend, smiling.

" It was Adams, of course ? "

" Yes, it was Adams."

" I was sure of it from the first." The two sat down together in the bow-window of the club. " To anyone who wishes to study mankind this is the spot," said Mycroft. " Look at the magnificent types ! Look at these two men who are coming towards us, for example."

" The billiard-marker and the other ? "

" Precisely. What do you make of the other ? "

The two men had stopped opposite the window. Some chalk marks over the waistcoat pocket were the only signs of billiards which I could see in one of them. The other was a very small, dark fellow, with his hat pushed back and several packages under his arm.

" An old soldier, I perceive," said Sherlock.

" And very recently discharged," remarked the brother.

" Served in India, I see."

" And a non-commissioned officer."

" Royal Artillery, I fancy," said Sherlock.

" And a widower."

' But with a child."

" Children, my dear boy, children."

" Come," said I, laughing, " this is a little too much."

" Surely," answered Holmes, " it is not hard to say that a man with that bearing, expression of authority, and sun-baked skin is a soldier, is more than a private, and is not long from India."

" That he has not left the service long is shown by his still wearing his ' ammunition boots,' as they are called," observed Mycroft.

" He has not the cavalry stride, yet he wore his hat on one side, as is shown by the lighter skin on that side of **16** his brow. His weight is against his being a sapper. He **17** is in the artillery."

" Then, of course, his complete mourning shows that he has lost someone very dear. The fact that he is doing his own shopping looks as though it were his wife. He has been buying things for children, you perceive. There is a rattle, which shows that one of them is very young. The wife probably died in child-bed. The fact that he has a picture-book under his arm shows that there is another **18** child to be thought of."

I began to understand what my friend meant when he said that his brother possessed even keener faculties than he did himself. He glanced across at me and smiled. Mycroft took snuff from a tortoiseshell box and brushed away the wandering grains from his coat with a large, red silk handkerchief.

"By the way, Sherlock," said he, "I have had something quite after your own heart—a most singular problem —submitted to my judgment. I really had not the energy to follow it up, save in a very incomplete fashion, but it gave me a basis for some very pleasing speculations. If you would care to hear the facts——"

"My dear Mycroft, I should be delighted."

The brother scribbled a note upon a leaf of his pocket-book, and, ringing the bell, he handed it to the waiter.

"I have asked Mr. Melas to step across," said he. "He lodges on the floor above me, and I have some slight acquaintance with him, which led him to come to me in his perplexity. Mr. Melas is a Greek by extraction, as I understand, and he is a remarkable linguist. He earns his living partly as interpreter in the law courts, partly by acting as guide to any wealthy Orientals who may visit the Northumberland Avenue hotels. I think I will leave him to tell his own very remarkable experience in his own fashion."

A few minutes later we were joined by a short, stout man, whose olive face and coal-black hair proclaimed his Southern origin, though his speech was that of an educated Englishman. He shook hands eagerly with Sherlock Holmes, and his dark eyes sparkled with pleasure when he understood that the specialist was anxious to hear his story.

"I do not believe that the police credit me—on my word I do not," said he, in a wailing voice. "Just because they have never heard of it before, they think that such a thing cannot be. But I know that I shall never be easy in my mind until I know what has become of my poor man with the sticking-plaster upon his face."

"I am all attention," said Sherlock Holmes.

"This is Wednesday evening," said Mr. Melas; "well, then it was on Monday night—only two days ago, you understand—that all this happened. I am an interpreter, as, perhaps, my neighbour there has told you. I interpret all languages—or nearly all—but as I am a Greek by birth, and with a Grecian name, it is with that particular tongue that I am principally associated. For many years I have been the chief Greek interpreter in London, and my name is very well known in the hotels.

"It happens, not unfrequently, that I am sent for at strange hours, by foreigners who get into difficulties, or by travellers who arrive late and wish my services. I was not surprised, therefore on Monday night when a Mr. Latimer, a very fashionably dressed young man, came up to my rooms and asked me to accompany him in a cab, which was waiting at the door. A Greek friend had come to see him upon business, he said, and, as he could speak nothing but his own tongue, the services of an interpreter were indispensable. He gave me to understand that his house was some little distance off, in Kensington, and he seemed to be in a great hurry, bustling me rapidly into the cab when we had descended into the street.

"I say into the cab, but I soon became doubtful as to whether it was not a carriage in which I found myself.

19 *Shaftesbury Avenue*. The adventure must certainly have taken place after 1886, since Shaftesbury Avenue was not opened to traffic until that year. It was a widening of the former King and Dudley streets, except for the portion between Piccadilly Circus and Rupert Street. Today it is a street of theatres, dressmakers' and milliners' shops.

It was certainly more roomy than the ordinary four-wheeled disgrace to London, and the fittings, though frayed, were of rich quality. Mr. Latimer seated himself opposite to me, and we started off through Charing Cross

19 and up the Shaftesbury Avenue. We had come out upon Oxford Street, and I had ventured some remark as to this being a roundabout way to Kensington, when my words were arrested by the extraordinary conduct of my companion.

"He began by drawing a most formidable-looking bludgeon loaded with lead from his pocket, and switched it backwards and forwards several times, as if to test its weight and strength. Then he placed it, without a word, upon the seat beside him. Having done this, he drew up the windows on each side, and I found to my astonishment that they were covered with paper so as to prevent my seeing through them.

" ' I am sorry to cut off your view, Mr. Melas,' said he. ' The fact is that I have no intention that you should see what the place is to which we are driving. It might possibly be inconvenient to me if you could find your way there again.'

" As you can imagine, I was utterly taken aback by such an address. My companion was a powerful, broad-shouldered young fellow, and, apart from the weapon, I should not have had the slightest chance in a struggle with him.

" ' This is very extraordinary conduct, Mr. Latimer,' I stammered. ' You must be aware that what you are doing is quite illegal.'

" ' It is somewhat of a liberty, no doubt,' said he, ' but we'll make it up to you. But I must warn you, however, Mr. Melas, that if at any time to-night you attempt to raise an alarm or do anything which is against my interests, you will find it a very serious thing. I beg you to remember that no one knows where you are, and that whether you are in this carriage or in my house, you are equally in my power.'

" His words were quiet, but he had a rasping way of saying them which was very menacing. I sat in silence, wondering what on earth could be his reason for kidnapping me in this extraordinary fashion. Whatever it might be, it was perfectly clear that there was no possible use in my resisting, and that I could only wait to see what might befall.

" For nearly two hours we drove without my having the least clue as to where we were going. Sometimes the rattle of the stones told of a paved causeway, and at others our smooth, silent course suggested asphalt, but save this variation in sound there was nothing at all which could in the remotest way help me to form a guess as to where we were. The paper over each window was impenetrable to light, and a blue curtain was drawn across the glass-work in front. It was a quarter past seven when we left Pall Mall, and my watch showed me that it was ten minutes to nine when we at last came to a standstill. My companion let down the window and I caught a glimpse of a low, arched doorway with a lamp burning above it. As I was hurried from the carriage it swung open, and I found myself inside the house, with a vague impression of a

" . . . HE DREW UP THE WINDOWS ON EACH SIDE . . . "

Illustration by Sidney Paget for the *Strand Magazine*, September, 1893.

lawn and trees on each side of me as I entered. Whether these were private grounds, however, or *bona-fide* country **20** was more than I could possibly venture to say.

"There was a coloured gas-lamp inside, which was turned so low that I could see little save that the hall was of some size and hung with pictures. In the dim light I could make out that the person who had opened the door was a small, mean-looking, middle-aged man with rounded shoulders. As he turned towards us the glint of the light showed me that he was wearing glasses.

"'Is this Mr. Melas, Harold?' said he.

"'Yes.'

"'Well done! Well done! No ill-will, Mr. Melas, I hope, but we could not get on without you. If you deal fair with us you'll not regret it; but if you try any tricks, God help you!'

"He spoke in a jerky, nervous fashion, and with some giggling laughs in between, but somehow he impressed me with fear more than the other.

"'What do you want with me?' I asked.

"'Only to ask a few questions of a Greek gentleman who is visiting us, and to let us have the answers. But say no more than you are told to say, or '—here came the nervous giggle again—'you had better never have been born.'

"As he spoke he opened a door and showed the way into a room which appeared to be very richly furnished— but again the only light was afforded by a single lamp half turned down. The chamber was certainly large, and the way in which my feet sank into the carpet as I stepped across it told me of its richness. I caught glimpses of velvet chairs, a high, white marble mantelpiece, and what seemed to be a suit of Japanese armour at one side of it. There was a chair just under the lamp, and the elderly man motioned that I should sit in it. The younger had left us, but he suddenly returned through another door, leading with him a gentleman clad in some sort of loose dressing-gown, who moved slowly towards us. As he came into the circle of dim light which enabled me to see him more clearly, I was thrilled with horror at his appearance. He was deadly pale and terribly emaciated, with the protruding, brilliant eyes of a man whose spirit is greater than his strength. But what shocked me more than any signs of physical weakness was that his face was grotesquely criss-crossed with sticking-plaster, and that one large pad of it was fastened over his mouth.

"'Have you the slate, Harold?' cried the older man, as this strange being fell rather than sat down into a chair. 'Are his hands loose? Now then, give him the pencil. You are to ask the questions, Mr. Melas, and he will write the answers. Ask him first of all whether he is prepared to sign the papers.'

"The man's eyes flashed fire.

"'Never,' he wrote in Greek upon the slate.

"'On no conditions?' I asked at the bidding of our tyrant.

"'Only if I see her married in my presence by a Greek priest whom I know.'

"The man giggled in his venomous way.

". . . I WAS THRILLED BY HORROR AT HIS APPEARANCE."

Illustration by Sidney Paget for the *Strand Magazine*, September, 1893.

" ' You know what awaits you, then ? '

" ' I care nothing for myself.'

" These are samples of the questions and answers which made up our strange, half-spoken, half-written conversation. Again and again I had to ask him whether he would give in and sign the document. Again and again I had the same indignant reply. But soon a happy thought came to me. I took to adding on little sentences of my own to each question—innocent ones at first, to test whether either of our companions knew anything of the matter, and then, as I found that they showed no sign, I played a more dangerous game. Our conversation ran something like this :

" ' You can do no good by this obstinacy. *Who are you ?* '

" ' I care not. *I am a stranger in London.* '

" ' Your fate will be on your own head. *How long have you been here ?* '

" ' Let it be so. *Three weeks.* '

" ' The property can never be yours. *What ails you ?* '

" ' It shall not go to villains. *They are starving me.* '

" ' You shall go free if you sign. *What house is this ?* '

" ' I will never sign. *I do not know.* '

" ' You are not doing her any service. *What is your name ?* '

" ' Let me hear her say so. *Kratides.* '

" ' You shall see her if you sign. *Where are you from ?* '

" ' Then I shall never see her. *Athens.* '

" Another five minutes, Mr. Holmes, and I should have wormed out the whole story under their very noses. My very next question might have cleared the matter up, but at that instant the door opened and a woman stepped into the room. I could not see her clearly enough to know more than that she was tall and graceful, with black hair, and clad in some sort of loose white gown.

" ' Harold ! ' said she, speaking English with a broken accent, ' I could not stay away longer. It is so lonely up there with only—oh, my God, it is Paul ! '

" These last words were in Greek, and at the same instant the man, with a convulsive effort, tore the plaster from his lips, and screaming out ' Sophy ! Sophy !'

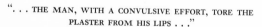

" . . . THE MAN, WITH A CONVULSIVE EFFORT, TORE THE PLASTER FROM HIS LIPS . . ."

Illustration by William H. Hyde for *Harper's Weekly*, September 16, 1893. Sidney Paget illustrated the same scene for the *Strand Magazine*, September, 1893.

rushed into the woman's arms. Their embrace was but for an instant, however, for the younger man seized the woman and pushed her out of the room, while the elder easily overpowered his emaciated victim, and dragged him away through the other door. For a moment I was left alone in the room, and I sprang to my feet with some vague idea that I might in some way get a clue to what this house was in which I found myself. Fortunately, however, I took no steps, for, looking up, I saw that the older man was standing in the doorway, with his eyes fixed upon me.

" ' That will do, Mr. Melas,' said he. ' You perceive that we have taken you into our confidence over some very private business. We should not have troubled you only that our friend who speaks Greek and who began these negotiations has been forced to return to the East. It was quite necessary for us to find someone to take his place, and we were fortunate in hearing of your powers.'

" I bowed.

" ' There are five sovereigns here,' said he, walking up **21** to me, ' which will, I hope, be a sufficient fee. But remember,' he added, tapping me lightly on the chest and giggling, ' if you speak to a human soul about this —one human soul mind—well, may God have mercy upon your soul ! '

" I cannot tell you the loathing and horror with which this insignificant-looking man inspired me. I could see him better now as the lamp-light shone upon him. His features were peeky and sallow, and his little, pointed beard was thready and ill-nourished. He pushed his face forward as he spoke, and his lips and eyelids were continually twitching, like a man with St. Vitus's dance. **22** I could not help thinking that his strange, catchy little laugh was also a symptom of some nervous malady. The terror of his face lay in his eyes, however, steel grey, and glistening coldly, with a malignant, inexorable cruelty in their depths.

" ' We shall know if you speak of this,' said he. ' We have our own means of information. Now, you will find the carriage waiting, and my friend will see you on your way.'

" I was hurried through the hall, and into the vehicle, again obtaining that momentary glimpse of trees and a garden. Mr. Latimer followed closely at my heels, and took his place opposite to me without a word. In silence we again drove for an interminable distance, with the windows raised, until at last, just after midnight, the carriage pulled up.

" ' You will get down here, Mr. Melas,' said my companion. ' I am sorry to leave you so far from your house, but there is no alternative. Any attempt upon your part to follow the carriage can only end in injury to yourself.'

" He opened the door as he spoke, and I had hardly time to spring out when the coachman lashed the horse, and the carriage rattled away. I looked round me in astonishment. I was on some sort of a heathy common, mottled over with dark clumps of furze bushes. Far away stretched a line of houses, with a light here and there in the upper windows. On the other side I saw the red

21 *five sovereigns.* About $25.

22 *St. Vitus's dance.* "The term St. Vitus's dance is seldom used nowadays; it is presently called acute chorea," Dr. Edward J. Van Liere wrote in "Dr. Watson and Nervous Maladies." "This condition is characterized by irregular involuntary contractions of the muscles and is associated with a variable amount of psychic disturbance. The name 'St. Vitus's dance' has been handed down from the Middle Ages. Epidemics characterized by excitement, gesticulations, and dancing, brought about mainly by religious fervor, were in those days not uncommon. When these symptoms became excessive the people in the Rhenish provinces frequently made pilgrimages to the Chapel of St. Vitus in Zebern."

". . . I SAW SOMEONE COMING TOWARDS ME IN THE DARKNESS."

Illustration by Sidney Paget for the *Strand Magazine*, September, 1893.

signal lamps of a railway.

" The carriage which had brought me was already out of sight. I stood gazing round and wondering where on earth I might be, when I saw someone coming towards me in the darkness. As he came up to me I made out that it was a railway porter.

" ' Can you tell me what place this is ? ' I asked.

23 " ' Wandsworth Common,' said he.

" ' Can I get a train into town ? '

24 " ' If you walk on a mile or so, to Clapham Junction,' said he, ' you'll just be in time for the last to Victoria.'

" So that was the end of my adventure, Mr. Holmes. I do not know where I was nor whom I spoke with, nor anything, save what I have told you. But I know that there is foul play going on, and I want to help that unhappy man if I can. I told the whole story to Mr. Mycroft Holmes next morning, and, subsequently, to the police."

We all sat in silence for some little time after listening to this extraordinary narrative. Then Sherlock looked across at his brother.

" Any steps ? " he asked.

Mycroft picked up the *Daily News*, which was lying on a side-table.

" ' Anybody supplying any information as to the whereabouts of a Greek gentleman named Paul Kratides, from Athens, who is unable to speak English, will be rewarded. A similar reward paid to anyone giving information about a Greek lady whose first name is Sophy. X 2473.' That was in all the dailies. No answer."

" How about the Greek Legation ? "

" I have inquired. They know nothing."

" A wire to the head of the Athens police, then."

" Sherlock has all the energy of the family," said Mycroft, turning to me. " Well, you take up the case by all means, and let me know if you do any good."

" Certainly," answered my friend, rising from his chair. " I'll let you know, and Mr. Melas also. In the meantime, Mr. Melas, I should certainly be on my guard if I were you, for, of course, they must know through these advertisements that you have betrayed them."

As we walked home together Holmes stopped at a telegraph office and sent off several wires.

" You see, Watson," he remarked, " our evening has been by no means wasted. Some of my most interesting cases have come to me in this way through Mycroft. The problem which we have just listened to, although it can admit of but one explanation, has still some distinguishing features."

" You have hopes of solving it ? "

" Well, knowing as much as we do, it will be singular indeed if we fail to discover the rest. You must yourself have formed some theory which will explain the facts to which we have listened."

" In a vague way, yes."

" What was your idea, then ? "

" It seemed to me to be obvious that this Greek girl had been carried off by the young Englishman named Harold Latimer."

23 " ' *Wandsworth Common.* ' Wandsworth ("Wendel's farm") is the largest borough in the county of London, intersected by the small river Wandle. Its common, once the resort of gypsies, is today a beautiful pleasure ground well planted with trees, which contains a lake where fishing is allowed, a teahouse, and bowling greens.

24 *Clapham Junction.* An important railway junction about four miles from Central London.

"Carried off from where?"

"Athens, perhaps."

Sherlock Holmes shook his head. "This young man could not talk a word of Greek. The lady could talk English fairly well. Inference, that she had been in England some little time, but he had not been in Greece."

"Well, then, we will presume that she had come on a visit to England, and that this Harold had persuaded her to fly with him."

"That is the more probable."

"Then the brother—for that, I fancy, must be the relationship—comes over from Greece to interfere. He imprudently puts himself into the power of the young man and his older associate. They seize him and use violence towards him in order to make him sign some papers to make over the girl's fortune—of which he may be trustee—to them. This he refuses to do. In order to negotiate with him, they have to get an interpreter, and they pitch upon this Mr. Melas, having used some other one before. The girl is not told of the arrival of her brother, and finds it out by the merest accident."

"Excellent, Watson," cried Holmes. "I really fancy that you are not far from the truth. You see that we hold all the cards, and we have only to fear some sudden act of violence on their part. If they give us time we must have them."

"But how can we find where this house lies?"

"Well, if our conjecture is correct, and the girl's name is, or was, Sophy Kratides, we should have no difficulty in tracing her. That must be our main hope, for the brother, of course, is a complete stranger. It is clear that some time has elapsed since this Harold established these relations with the girl—some weeks at any rate—since the brother in Greece has had time to hear of it, and come across. If they have been living in the same place during this time, it is probable that we shall have some answer to Mycroft's advertisement."

We had reached our house in Baker Street whilst we had been talking, Holmes ascended the stairs first, and as he opened the door of our room he gave a start of surprise. Looking over his shoulder I was equally astonished. His brother Mycroft was sitting smoking in the arm-chair.

"Come in, Sherlock! Come in, sir," said he, blandly, smiling at our surprised faces. "You don't expect such energy from me, do you, Sherlock? But somehow this case attracts me."

"How did you get here?"

"I passed you in a hansom."

"There has been some new development?"

"I had an answer to my advertisement."

"Ah!"

"Yes; it came within a few minutes of your leaving."

"And to what effect?"

Mycroft Holmes took out a sheet of paper.

"Here it is," said he, "written with a J pen on royal cream paper by a middle-aged man with a weak constitution. 'Sir,' he says, 'in answer to your advertisement of to-day's date, I beg to inform you that I know the young

"COME IN, SHERLOCK! COME IN, SIR,"
SAID HE, BLANDLY . . .

Illustration by Sidney Paget for the *Strand Magazine*, September, 1893.

25 *Beckenham.* An urban district in Kent.

26 *Lower Brixton."* A district of London now much favored by minor actors.

27 *It was almost dark.* Mycroft was always to be found at the Diogenes Club "from a quarter to five till twenty to eight," according to Holmes. On this Wednesday evening he took a hansom to Baker Street, passing Holmes and Watson on their walk home. After a brief conversation, the three ordered the four-wheeler and drove directly to Mr. Melas' lodgings in Pall Mall. "It was almost dark" at the time they arrived, according to Watson. Mycroft, leaving the Diogenes Club by hansom at 7:40 P.M., must have arrived at Baker Street shortly after 8:00 P.M., Holmes and Watson at about the same time. Their conversation would have taken a few minutes at most, their drive to Mr. Melas' lodgings (which we know were just opposite the Diogenes Club) no longer than Mycroft's drive from the Diogenes Club to Baker Street. The three would therefore have reached Mr. Melas' lodgings about 8:20 P.M. It cannot have been much earlier than that, as we have shown; it can hardly have been later; Mycroft, Sherlock, and Watson then drove from Pall Mall to Scotland Yard, waited "more than an hour" for Gregson, and reached London Bridge at "a quarter to ten." We must therefore find a Wednesday in the summer of 1888 when twilight ended at approximately 8:20 P.M. There can be only one choice: on Wednesday, September 5th, twilight ended at approximately 8:41 P.M.—too late for it to have been "almost dark" at 8:20 P.M.; on Wednesday, September 19th, twilight ended at approximately 8:04 P.M.—too early for it to have been "almost dark" at 8:20 P.M. The case therefore took place on *Wednesday, September 12, 1888* —a day on which twilight ended and darkness began at approximately 8:23 P.M. Holmes called the evening on which the case began a "beautiful evening," and he was perfectly correct in doing so: the London *Times'* report for Wednesday, September 12th, noted that "Fine weather . . . has become general over the British Isles. . . . with low night temperatures but mild days. The wind has been light or moderate in force."

lady in question very well. If you should care to call upon me, I could give you some particulars as to her painful history. She is living at present at The Myrtles, **25** Beckenham.—Yours faithfully, J. DAVENPORT.'

26 "He writes from Lower Brixton," said Mycroft Holmes. "Do you not think that we might drive to him now, Sherlock, and learn these particulars?"

"My dear Mycroft, the brother's life is more valuable than the sister's story. I think we should call at Scotland Yard for Inspector Gregson, and go straight out to Beckenham. We know that a man is being done to death, and every hour may be vital."

"Better pick up Mr. Melas upon our way," I suggested; "we may need an interpreter."

"Excellent!" said Sherlock Holmes. "Send the boy for a four-wheeler, and we shall be off at once." He opened the table-drawer as he spoke, and I noticed that he slipped his revolver into his pocket. "Yes," said he, in answer to my glance, "I should say from what we have heard that we are dealing with a particularly dangerous gang."

27 It was almost dark before we found ourselves in Pall Mall, at the rooms of Mr. Melas. A gentleman had just called for him, and he was gone.

"Can you tell me where?" asked Mycroft Holmes.

"I don't know, sir," answered the woman who had opened the door. "I only know that he drove away with the gentleman in a carriage."

"Did the gentleman give a name?"

"No, sir."

"He wasn't a tall, handsome, dark young man?"

"Oh, no, sir; he was a little gentleman, with glasses, thin in the face, but very pleasant in his ways, for he was laughing all the time that he was talking."

"Come along!" cried Sherlock Holmes, abruptly. "This grows serious!" he observed, as we drove to Scotland Yard. "These men have got hold of Melas again.

. . . HE SLIPPED HIS REVOLVER INTO HIS POCKET.

"Holmes' revolver was unsuited in his hands to any other than muzzle-to-gizzard shooting," Mr. Robert Keith Leavitt wrote in "Annie Oakley in Baker Street." "It was the Webley Metropolitan Police Model—the same which Inspector Lestrade gaily said he carried whenever he had his pants on [*The Hound of the Baskervilles*]. This arm had the short 2½" barrel required for hip-pocket (or dressing-gown-pocket) wear, but on account of its short sight-radius, it was difficult for anybody but a past master to shoot with accuracy. It may be objected that two passages show Holmes *did* have confidence in this piece. In *The Sign of the Four* he loaded it with two and only two cartridges. This, however, indicated confidence rather in Tonga's than in his own accuracy. He knew he would have time for only two shots at best. In 'The Adventure of the Three Garridebs' he referred to his revolver as 'my old favourite,' but it must be obvious to the close student that he did so with a wry sneer."

He is a man of no physical courage, as they are well aware from their experience the other night. This villain was able to terrorize him the instant that he got into his presence. No doubt they want his professional services ; but, having used him, they may be inclined to punish him for what they will regard as his treachery."

Our hope was that by taking train we might get to Beckenham as soon as, or sooner than, the carriage. On reaching Scotland Yard, however, it was more than an hour before we could get Inspector Gregson and comply with the legal formalities which would enable us to enter the house. It was a quarter to ten before we reached London Bridge, and half-past before the four of us alighted on the Beckenham platform. A drive of half a mile brought us to The Myrtles—a large, dark house, standing back from the road in its own grounds. Here we dismissed our cab, and made our way up the drive together.

" The windows are all dark," remarked the Inspector. " The house seems deserted."

" Our birds are flown and the nest empty," said Holmes.

" Why do you say so ? "

" A carriage heavily loaded with luggage has passed out during the last hour."

The Inspector laughed. " I saw the wheel-tracks in the light of the gate-lamp, but where does the luggage come in ? "

" You may have observed the same wheel-tracks going the other way. But the outward-bound ones were very much deeper—so much so that we can say for a certainty that there was a very considerable weight on the carriage."

" You get a trifle beyond me there," said the Inspector, shrugging his shoulders. " It will not be an easy door to force. But we will try if we cannot make someone hear us."

He hammered loudly at the knocker and pulled at the bell, but without any success. Holmes had slipped away, but he came back in a few minutes.

" I have a window open," said he.

" It is a mercy that you are on the side of the Force, and not against it, Mr. Holmes," remarked the Inspector, as he noted the clever way in which my friend had forced back the catch. " Well, I think that, under the circumstances, we may enter without waiting for an invitation."

One after the other we made our way into a large apartment, which was evidently that in which Mr. Melas had found himself. The Inspector had lit his lantern, and by its light we could see the two doors, the curtain, the lamp and the suit of Japanese mail as he had described them. On the table stood two glasses, an empty brandy bottle, and the remains of a meal.

" What is that ? " asked Holmes, suddenly.

We all stood still and listened. A low, moaning sound was coming from somewhere above our heads. Holmes rushed to the door and out into the hall. The dismal noise came from upstairs. He dashed up, the Inspector and I at his heels, while his brother, Mycroft, followed as quickly as his great bulk would permit.

"IT'S CHARCOAL!" HE CRIED.

Illustration by Sidney Paget for the *Strand Magazine*, September, 1893.

Three doors faced us upon the second floor, and it was from the central of these that the sinister sounds were issuing, sinking sometimes into a dull mumble and rising again into a shrill whine. It was locked, but the key was on the outside. Holmes flung open the door and rushed in, but he was out again in an instant with his hand to his throat.

" It's charcoal ! " he cried. " Give it time. It will clear."

Peering in, we could see that the only light in the room came from a dull, blue flame, which flickered from a small brass tripod in the centre. It threw a livid, unnatural circle upon the floor, while in the shadows beyond, we saw the vague loom of two figures, which crouched against the wall. From the open door there reeked a horrible, poisonous exhalation, which set us gasping and coughing. Holmes rushed to the top of the stairs to draw in the fresh air, and then, dashing into the room, he threw up the window and hurled the brazen tripod out into the garden.

" We can enter in a minute," he gasped, darting out again. " Where is a candle ? I doubt if we could strike a match in that atmosphere. Hold the light at the door and we shall get them out, Mycroft. Now ! "

With a rush we got to the poisoned men and dragged them out on to the landing. Both of them were blue-lipped and insensible, with swollen, congested faces and protruding eyes. Indeed, so distorted were their features that, save for his black beard and stout figure, we might have failed to recognize in one of them the Greek interpreter who had parted from us only a few hours before at the Diogenes Club. His hands and feet were securely strapped together and he bore over one eye the mark of a violent blow. The other, who was secured in a similar fashion, was a tall man in the last stage of emaciation, with several strips of sticking-plaster arranged in a grotesque pattern over his face. He had ceased to moan as we laid him down, and a glance showed me that for him, at least, our aid had come too late. Mr. Melas, however, still lived, and in less than an hour, with the aid of ammonia and brandy, I had the satisfaction of seeing him open his eyes, and of knowing that my hand had drawn him back from the dark valley in which all paths meet.

It was a simple story which he had to tell, and one which did but confirm our own deductions. His visitor **28** on entering his rooms had drawn a life-preserver from his sleeve, and had so impressed him with the fear of instant and inevitable death, that he had kidnapped him for the second time. Indeed, it was almost mesmeric the effect which this giggling ruffian had produced upon the unfortunate linguist, for he could not speak of him save with trembling hands and a blanched cheek. He had been taken swiftly to Beckenham, and had acted as interpreter in a second interview, even more dramatic than the first, in which the two Englishmen had menaced their prisoner with instant death if he did not comply with their demands. Finally, finding him proof against every threat, they had hurled him back into his prison, and after reproaching Melas with his treachery, which

28 *a life-preserver*. A short bludgeon, usually of flexible cane, whalebone, or the like, loaded with lead at one end.

appeared from the newspaper advertisements, they had stunned him with a blow from a stick, and he remembered nothing more until he found us bending over him.

And this was the singular case of the Grecian Interpreter, the explanation of which is still involved in some mystery. We were able to find out, by communicating with the gentleman who had answered the advertisement, that the unfortunate young lady came of a wealthy Grecian family, and that she had been on a visit to some friends in England. While there she had met a young man named Harold Latimer, who had acquired an ascendancy over her, and had eventually persuaded her to fly with him. Her friends, shocked at the event, had contented themselves with informing her brother at Athens, and had then washed their hands of the matter. The brother, on his arrival in England, had imprudently placed himself in the power of Latimer and of his associate, whose name was Wilson Kemp—a man of the foulest antecedents. These two, finding, that through his ignorance of the language, he was helpless in their hands, had kept him a prisoner, and had endeavoured, by cruelty and starvation, to make him sign away his own and his sister's property. They had kept him in the house without the girl's knowledge, and the plaster over the face had been for the purpose of making recognition difficult in case she should ever catch a glimpse of him. Her feminine perceptions, however, had instantly seen through the disguise when, on the occasion of the interpreter's first visit, she had seen him for the first time. The poor girl, however, was herself a prisoner, for there was no one about the house except the man who acted as coachman and his wife, both of whom were tools of the conspirators. Finding that their secret was out and that their prisoner was not to be coerced, the two villains, with the girl, had fled away at a few hours' notice from the furnished house which they had hired, having first, as they thought, taken vengeance both upon the man who had defied and the one who had betrayed them.

Months afterwards a curious newspaper cutting reached us from Buda-Pesth. It told how two Englishmen who had been travelling with a woman had met with a tragic end. They had each been stabbed, it seems, and the Hungarian police were of opinion that they had quarrelled and had inflicted mortal injuries upon each other. Holmes, however, is, I fancy, of a different way of thinking, and he holds to this day that if one could find the Grecian girl one might learn how the wrongs of herself and her brother came to be avenged.

IT THREW A LIVID, UNNATURAL CIRCLE UPON THE FLOOR . . .

Illustration by William H. Hyde for *Harper's Weekly*, September 16, 1893.

Bibliographical Note: On December 19, 1964, *The New York Times* reported from London that: "The manuscript of 'The Adventure of the Greek Interpreter'. . . was purchased today [December 18th] at auction for $12,600 by the author's son, Adrian Conan Doyle. . . . The manuscript . . . appears to be the only complete one from *The Memoirs* that has been sold on the open market. The 34-page manuscript was sold by a New York woman, according to Christie's. . . ." According to Mr. Lew D. Feldman of "The House of El Dieff," who exhibited the manuscript at the dinner of the Baker Street Irregulars on January 8, 1965, $12,600 is not only the highest price ever paid for a Sherlock Holmes manuscript or any other manuscript by Conan Doyle but also the highest price ever paid for a manuscript written in English by an author who lived during the twentieth century.

34

"YOUR HAND STOLE TOWARDS
YOUR OLD WOUND ..."

[Sherlock Holmes to John H. Watson, M.D., "The Cardboard Box"]

On the twenty-seventh day of July in the year 1880, John H. Watson, M.D., was doing his duty as Assistant Surgeon to the Berkshires (66th Foot) at the fatal battle of Maiwand when he was struck on the shoulder by a Jezail bullet, which shattered the bone and grazed the subclavian artery.

Few statements could be clearer or more circumstantial.

And yet, eight years later, in September, 1888, at the time of *The Sign of the Four,* Dr. Watson tells us that he sat nursing his wounded *leg.* "I had had a Jezail bullet through it some time before," he writes, "and though it did not prevent me from walking it ached wearily at every change in the weather."

"An army surgeon with a weak leg," was how he then described himself.

"Are you game for a six-mile trudge, Watson? . . . Your leg will stand it?" Holmes asks him solicitously—and later refers to "a six-mile limp for a half-pay officer with a damaged *tendo Achillis.*"

Let us examine, first, the wound Dr. Watson tells us he suffered at the "fatal battle."

Expert medical testimony (the late Dr. Roland Hammond, in "The Surgeon Probes Doctor Watson's Wound") notes first that "the shoulder is broadly defined as that portion of the trunk between the upper portion of the arm and the base of the neck, especially the curved upper surfaces of this, and often including the part of the back between the two. It is the part of the body on which burdens are carried. On the other hand, the medical man in speaking of the shoulder, limits his definition to the articulation by which the arm is connected to the trunk." Watson's wound, Dr. Hammond thought, "may have been located nearer to the base of the neck than in the shoulder region."

The wound was on Watson's left side, we know, for Holmes in *A Study in Scarlet* says: "His [Watson's] left arm has been injured. He holds it in a stiff and unnatural manner."

The bullet shattered the bone, and Dr. Hammond—with Dr. John Dardess concurring ("The Maiwand-Criterion Hiatus")—held that this bone could only have been the clavicle or collarbone. Dr. J. W. Sovine ("The Singular Bullet") thought that it might have been one of three others—the left humerus, the left scapula, or the left rib—but Dr. Hammond was of the opinion that "an injury to the first rib . . . would have resulted in uncontrollable hemorrhage from the subclavian vein and artery and irreparable damage to the great nerve cable known as the brachial plexus lying directly behind the blood vessels."

The subclavian artery—which Watson tells us that the bullet "grazed" but not that it *severed*—ascends on the left side vertically from the arch of the aorta to the inner border of the scalenus anterior muscle. Passing behind this muscle, it curves over the first rib to its lower border where is passes beneath the clavicle and becomes the axillary artery. "It is evident," Dr. Hammond wrote, "that [this] artery could be grazed only where it lies on the first rib. . . . We must finally conclude that a bullet producing the damage described *might* avoid injury to important structures but it would be touch and go at best. The fracture of the clavicle must have been extensive with many loose chips of bone to knit into place. Although this bone repairs more readily than any other bone in the body, a compound fracture of the clavicle often leaves an unsightly deformity associated with pain and stiffness of the shoulder and arm. We are assured that Watson's recovery was complete, which is a tribute to a healthy constitution and skillful surgical care."

Here, then, is a healthy, young medico (Watson, according to the best authorities was twenty-eight at the time of the battle), who sustains a compound fracture of the clavicle 'from a bullet which grazes but *does not sever* the subclavian artery.

Why, then, was it necessary for Watson's orderly, Murray, to "throw him across a pack-horse" in order to bring him safely to "the British lines"?

Dr. Sovine suggests that "the Jezail bullet struck Dr. Watson just above and missing the left clavicle, while he was bent over a wounded patient; that it grazed the left subclavian artery and shattered the left scapula, then ricocheted, passing to the left and downward, describing a spiral curve deep under the skin of the chest and abdomen, thence downward into the left leg, coming to rest in the calf muscles. . . . The shoulder was still bothersome in 1881, but healed and forgotten by the fall of 1887; while the bullet in the leg would be forgotten most of the time, but quite painful during weather changes. . . . Apparently when the weather was decent [Watson's] leg was quite serviceable."

This is also the view of Mr. R. M. McLaren ("Doctor Watson—Punter or Speculator?"): "The wound sustained by Watson in Afghanistan was an extraordinary one, the bullet having entered his shoulder and emerged from his leg . . ."

The views expressed above may, perhaps, be summed up as the One Singular Wound at Maiwand School.

Other commentators are of the opinion that Watson was wounded *twice* at Maiwand, first in the shoulder, then in the leg. Dr. Reginald Fitz, for example, in his "A Belated Eulogy: to John H. Watson, M.D.", wrote: "Dr. Watson had a busy day at the front—until he copped two bullets, one in the leg and one in the shoulder." Dr. Dardess felt the same: "I think there can be little doubt . . . that Watson was wounded *twice* at Maiwand."

But, if this was the case, why did Watson, so precise about his shoulder wound, never mention a leg wound at Maiwand?

He did not mention it, still another school of commentators holds, because the wound was not properly in his "leg" at all, but in a part of his anatomy which his modesty and delicacy forbade his mentioning.

"A man 'thrown across a packhorse' ", the late James Keddie, Sr., mused in "The Mystery of the Second Wound," "presents a singularly enticing target. His head and arms hang down one side . . . his legs dangle on the other."

"Dr. Watson was painfully and honorably wounded on the left buttock while serving his country and comrades on the open field of battle," Mr. John Ball, Jr., wrote in "The Jezail Bullet." "He was, in all probability, bending over a fallen comrade, ministering to him when he was himself hit. He was serving with utter disregard for his own safety; any suggestion of cowardice in that he was not 'facing the foe' is an unwarranted slander. This is the one and only wound which he received. . . . He was never at any time shot in the shoulder, nor did he believe himself to have been so injured. He deliberately misrepresented his area of injury . . ."

That Watson's wound was indeed "of a fundamental nature" is also the opinion of Mr. G. W. Welch (" 'No Mention of That Local Hunt, Watson' ").

This Unmentionable Wound was what made it so difficult for Watson in later life to resist any female allurement, in the opinion of Mr. Belden Wigglesworth (" 'Many Nations and Three Separate Continents' "): "His extraordinary incontinence may really have been due to the continued irritation of the old scar in his perineum."

Dr. Julian Wolff, on the other hand, has cast aspersions on Watson's masculinity by suggesting ("That Was No Lady") that Watson's one wound at Maiwand was in the groin.

And Dr. Samuel R. Meaker, writing in "Watson Medicus," says: "I do not wish to be indelicate, but, after all, prudery has no place in scientific deliberations. So I would simply call attention to the fact that all three of Watson's marriages were childless."

Still another school of thought holds that Watson was wounded once at Maiwand (in the shoulder) and again, at some later date, in the leg.

"On the journey by pack-horse," Dr. Vernon Pennell wrote in "A Resumé of the Medical Life of John H. Watson, M.D., Late of the Army Medical Department," Watson "must have received one, or possibly two, more wounds, both by Jezail bullets."

And Lieutenant Colonel L. V. S. Blacker has suggested ("Dr. Watson's Wound(s)") that Watson "was taken up the Indus on the upper deck of [a] paddle steamer. After some days of voyaging upstream, the steamer would pass close under high banks where the frontier mountains close in upon it. In those days Wazir, Mahsud and other tribesmen ranged these mountains, rifle in fist. I suggest that one of these marauders took pot-shot at the steamer and his bullet struck the already wounded John Watson in the leg."

The Reverend Henry T. Folsom, on the other hand, holds that Watson acquired his second wound during a *second* hitch in the Army from the summer of 1881 to early 1883. "At that time, while apparently encountering some Ghazi guerrilla in a border incident, he caught a *second* Jezail, this time in the leg" ("Seventeen Out of Twenty-Three").

Still, Watson makes no mention whatsoever of a leg wound in any of the numerous 1887 cases, and it is somewhat difficult to believe that he received his second wound until sometime after early April, 1888 ("The Yellow Face").

Holmes' solicitude for Watson at the time of the adventure of *The Sign of the Four* suggests that Watson suffered his second wound while assisting Holmes on a case (compare Holmes' reaction to the wound received by Watson in 1902 during "The Adventure of the Three Garridebs").

Watson's second wound did not prevent him from walking, and we know that he walked for some distance in "The Greek Interpreter," which took place in the same month as *The Sign of the Four* (September, 1888), and just preceding that adventure.

Most probably, we think, Watson sustained his second wound in late April or early May, 1888, which would accord with his "some time before" in *The Sign of the Four*. It is of course curious that he was wounded for the second time by a Jezail bullet.

Happily, Watson seems to have made a swift and complete recovery. Only a month after *The Sign of the Four* he was able to say, in *The Hound of the Baskervilles*, "I am reckoned fleet of foot."

35

THE SIGN OF THE FOUR

[Tuesday, September 18, to Friday, September 21, 1888]

1 *hypodermic syringe.* Dr. Kohki Naganuma has questioned ("Sherlock Holmes and Cocaine") Holmes' use of cocaine by hypodermic injection at this time since "Karl Ludwig Schleich, of Berlin, [was] the first surgeon to use cocaine solution in hypodermic injection [in 1891]." But Dr. Julian Wolff has replied ("A Narcotic Monograph") that "although Schleich is usually given credit for priority in the use of cocaine by injection, actually the credit should go to a great American surgeon. The first such use of cocaine was not in 1891 by Schleich, as is generally supposed, but in 1884, by Dr. William S. Halsted. . . . 1884 was early enough so that it was no anachronism for Holmes to be taking cocaine injections when Watson said he was."

It should be pointed out that, at this time, there was no popular prejudice against drugs or drug-takers. As Mr. Michael Harrison has written (*In the Footsteps of Sherlock Holmes*): "In Holmes' day, not only was the purchase of most 'Schedule IV' drugs legal; Madeleine Smith and Mrs. Maybrick bought their arsenic; De Quincey and Dickens and Robert Louis Stevenson, their laudanum; with no more trouble than that with which they purchased their tooth-powder. No 'Dangerous Drug Act' had been passed, in its original form, when Holmes bought and took his cocaine in doses that Watson's description of the typical cocaine-addiction syndromes indicate to have been heavy ones. (Holmes probably purchased his supplies from either John Taylor, Chemist, at the corner of George Street and Baker Street—east side—or of Curtis and Company, No. 44, on the west side) . . ."

2 *the Beaune.* Beaune is a rather potent red wine from Burgundy, too strong a drink for lunch. The late Christopher Morley in "Dr. Watson's Secret" expressed his view that Watson was fortifying himself because, unknown to Holmes, he had married Mary Morstan some months before and knew that she would be calling on Holmes as a client that very afternoon.

3 *'morphine.* This is the only occasion in the entire Saga in which we find even the suggestion that Holmes ever took morphine.

Sherlock Holmes took his bottle from the corner of the **1** mantelpiece, and his hypodermic syringe from its neat morocco case. With his long, white, nervous fingers he adjusted the delicate needle, and rolled back his left shirt-cuff. For some little time his eyes rested thoughtfully upon the sinewy forearm and wrist, all dotted and scarred with innumerable puncture-marks. Finally, he thrust the sharp point home, pressed down the tiny piston, and sank back into the velvet-lined arm-chair with a long sigh of satisfaction.

Three times a day for many months I had witnessed this performance, but custom had not reconciled my mind to it. On the contrary, from day to day I had become more irritable at the sight, and my conscience swelled nightly within me at the thought that I had lacked the courage to protest. Again and again I had registered a vow that I should deliver my soul upon the subject; but there was that in the cool, nonchalant air of my companion which made him the last man with whom one would care to take anything approaching to a liberty. His great powers, his masterly manner, and the experience which I had had of his many extraordinary qualities, all made me diffident and backward in crossing him.

2 Yet upon that afternoon, whether it was the Beaune which I had taken with my lunch, or the additional exasperation produced by the extreme deliberation of his manner, I suddenly felt that I could hold out no longer.

3 'Which is it today,' I asked, 'morphine or cocaine?'

He raised his eyes languidly from the old black-letter volume which he had opened.

4 'It is cocaine,' he said, 'a seven-per-cent. solution. Would you care to try it?'

'No, indeed,' I answered, brusquely. 'My constitution has not got over the Afghan campaign yet. I cannot afford to throw any extra strain upon it.'

He smiled at my vehemence. 'Perhaps you are right, Watson,' he said. 'I suppose that its influence is physically a bad one. I find it, however, so transcendently stimulating and clarifying to the mind that its secondary action is a matter of small moment.'

'But consider!' I said, earnestly. 'Count the cost! Your brain may, as you say, be roused and excited, but it is a pathological and morbid process, which involves increased tissue-change, and may at last leave a permanent weakness. You know, too, **5** what a black reaction comes upon you. Surely the game is hardly worth the candle. Why should you, for a mere passing pleasure, risk the loss of those great powers with which you have been endowed? Remember that I speak not only as one comrade to another, but as a medical man to one for whose constitution he is to some extent answerable.'

He did not seem offended. On the contrary, he put his finger-tips together, and leaned his elbows on the arms of his chair, like one who has a relish for conversation.

'My mind,' he said, 'rebels at stagnation. Give me problems, give me work, give me the most abstruse cryptogram, or the most intricate analysis, and I am in my own proper atmosphere. I can dispense then with artificial stimulants. But I abhor the dull routine of existence. I crave for mental exaltation. That is why I have chosen my own particular profession, or rather created it, for I am the only one in the world.'

'The only unofficial detective?' I said, raising my eyebrows.

'The only unofficial consulting detective,' he answered. 'I am the last and highest court of appeal in detection. When Gregson, or Lestrade, or Athelney Jones are out of their depths—which, by the way, is their normal state—the matter is laid before me. I examine the data, as an expert, and pronounce a specialist's opinion. I claim no credit in such cases. My name figures in no newspaper. The work itself, the pleasure of finding a field for my peculiar powers, is my highest reward. But you have yourself had some experience of my methods of work in the Jefferson Hope case.'

'Yes, indeed,' said I, cordially. 'I was never so struck by anything in my life. I even embodied it in a small brochure, with the somewhat fantastic title of "A Study in Scarlet."'   **6**

He shook his head sadly.

'I glanced over it,' said he. 'Honestly, I cannot congratulate you upon it. Detection is, or ought to be, an exact science, and should be treated in the same cold and unemotional manner. You have attempted to tinge it with romanticism, **7** which produces much the same effect as if you worked a love-story or an elopement into the fifth proposition of Euclid.' **8**

'But the romance was there,' I remonstrated. 'I could not tamper with the facts.'

'Some facts should be suppressed, or, at least, a just sense of proportion should be observed in treating them. The only point in the case which deserved mention was the curious analytical reasoning from effects to causes, by which I succeeded in unravelling it.'

I was annoyed at this criticism of a work which had been specially designed to please him. I confess, too, that I was irritated by the egotism which seemed to demand that every line of my pamphlet should be devoted to his own special doings. More than once during the years that I had lived with him in Baker Street I had observed that a small vanity underlay my companion's quiet and didactic manner. I made no remark, however, but sat nursing my wounded leg. I had had a Jezail bullet through it some time before, and, though it did not prevent me from walking, it ached wearily at every change of the weather.

his article "Devilish Drugs, Part I." "The strength of *injecto cocainae hypodermica*," he says, "became official in the B. P. in 1898 at ten per cent. May it not be presumed that, at least, Holmes was trying to 'cut down'? His occasional indiscretions, however, were still being recorded by Watson ten years later. One wonders, when they ceased, whether Holmes had found satisfactory treatment for his addictions in heroin, introduced from Germany about this time as a 'cure for the morphia habit,' and not condemned as such until a *B.M.J.* editorial in 1906 discussed the pharmacology of diamorphine."

5 *what a black reaction comes upon you.* "'Cocaine is stuff that starts off making you feel just grand and with everything in the garden lovely. It peps you up and makes you feel you can do twice as much as you usually do. Take too much of it and you get violent mental excitement, delusions and delirium,'"—Agatha Christie, "The Case of the Drug Peddler" in *The Labors of Hercule.*

A more recent statement on the use of cocaine comes from Mr. Walter Modell of the Department of Pharmacology of Cornell University Medical College. In "Mass Drug Catastrophes and the Roles of Science and Technology," *Science*, 21 April, 1967, Vol. 156, No. 3773, Mr. Modell writes: "Although habit-forming, cocaine is not tenaciously so, and, since it is not physiologically addictive, strong personalities like Freud and Sherlock Holmes had no trouble in controlling the habit." However, he goes on to warn the reader that "Cocaine acts as a potent and sometimes unpredictable central stimulant, and rash and violent behavior have been attributed directly to its action; it is clearly anti-social. It is also highly toxic and, because of irregular and sometimes unanticipatedly rapid absorption, occasionally fatal."

6 *"A Study in Scarlet."'* Most commentators have taken this as a reference to *Beeton's Christmas Annual,* and have therefore insisted that *The Sign of the Four* must be dated after December, 1887—a view buttressed by Holmes' later remark that the criminal classes were coming to know him well, especially since Watson had taken to publishing "some" of his cases. On the other hand, Mr. H. B. Williams has suggested that it was the *original* publication of Watson's reminiscences (see *A Study in Scarlet,* Note 1) that Watson referred to here as "a small brochure" and "my pamphlet."

7 *to tinge it with romanticism.* It was probably the interlude with the Mormons that Holmes found tiresome.

8 *the fifth proposition of Euclid.'* "The Master here referred to the fifth proposition merely to illustrate his point," the late Dr. Ernest Bloomfield Zeisler wrote in "A Chronological *Study in Scarlet*," "for careful research has failed to reveal why any other proposition of Euclid would not have done as well."

4 *'a seven-per-cent. solution.* The fact that Holmes was resorting to cocaine injections "Three times a day" at this time is disturbing, but "a seven-per-cent. solution" is not in itself an extraordinarily heavy dose, according to F. A. Allen, M.P.S., in

9 *François le Villard.* "... a gentleman who may be identified as the son of Francisque Le Villard, author of works on the Paris theater," Miss Madeleine B. Stern wrote in "Sherlock Holmes: Rare Book Collector.'"

10 *this morning.* The chronologically minded reader will note that the day was therefore not a Sunday.

11 *'coup-de-maîtres.'* French: master strokes.

12 *'Oh, didn't you know?'* Of course Watson knew. Holmes had mentioned his monograph on cigar ashes in *A Study in Scarlet.*

13 *with coloured plates.* This phrase has suggested to Mr. Poul Anderson ("Art in the Blood") that Holmes "must certainly have been able to draw and even paint in fine detail, for ... surely he would not have entrusted the preparation of [these coloured plates] to anyone else. Likewise, in such adventures as 'The Norwood Builder,' he revealed considerable architectural acumen."

14 *lunkah.* Like the Trichonopoly, the lunkah is a thin cigar, open at both ends.

15 *bird's-eye.* A kind of pipe tobacco cut in small circular slices.

16 *as a preserver of impresses.* "Apropos of this monograph, it will be recalled that after his solution of the Priory School case in 1901 Holmes had material for an interesting note on the subject of faking the prints made by animals, with special reference to the devices employed by some of the robber Barons of Holdernesse during the Middle Ages to disguise the tracks of their horses," Mr. Walter Klinefelter wrote in "The Writings of Mr. Sherlock Holmes."

And Miss Madeleine B. Stern has added ("Sherlock Holmes: Rare Book Collector"): "Holmes' work . . . antedates most of the researches in this field. While much attention had been given before that time to fossil footprints, it was not until Holmes led the way that André Fréçon (*Des Empreintes en Général et de Leur Application dans . . . la Médecine Judiciaire*, Lyons, 1889) in France and Anton Prant ('Ueber das Aufsuchen von Fuss-spuren und Handebrucken und ihre Identifcrung,' *Arcgiv. f. Kriminal-Anthropologie*, Leipzig, 1899) in Germany could produce their works on the more modern variety of footprint. Some material on gypsum or plaster of Paris was, however, available to Holmes, who surely acquired for his work a copy of Richard Peters' *Agricultural Enquiries on Plaster of Paris* (Philadelphia, 1797) as well as Mathijsen's *De Bandage Platre* (Liège, 1654), a treatise which, incidentally, introduced the modern plaster-of-Paris bandage."

17 *upon the influence of a trade upon the form of the hand.* "For his study of the influence of a

'My practice has extended recently to the Continent,' said Holmes, after awhile, filling up his old briar-root pipe. 'I was **9** consulted last week by François le Villard, who, as you probably know, has come rather to the front lately in the French detective service. He has all the Celtic power of quick intuition, but he is deficient in the wide range of exact knowledge which is essential to the higher developments of his art. The case was concerned with a will, and possessed some features of interest. I was able to refer him to two parallel cases, the one at Riga in 1857, and the other at St Louis in 1871, which have suggested to him the true solution. Here is **10** the letter which I had this morning acknowledging my assistance.'

He tossed over, as he spoke, a crumpled sheet of foreign note-paper. I glanced my eyes down it, catching a profusion of notes of admiration, with stray *'magnifiques,'* *'coup-de-* **11** *maîtres,'* and *'tours-de-force,'* all testifying to the ardent admiration of the Frenchman.

'He speaks as a pupil to his master,' said I.

'Oh, he rates my assistance too highly,' said Sherlock Holmes, lightly. 'He has considerable gifts himself. He possesses two out of the three qualities necessary for the ideal detective. He has the power of observation and that of deduction. He is only wanting in knowledge, and that may come in time. He is now translating my small works into French.'

'Your works?'

12 'Oh, didn't you know?' he cried, laughing. 'Yes, I have been guilty of several monographs. They are all upon technical subjects. Here, for example, is one "Upon the Distinction Between the Ashes of the Various Tobaccos." In it I enumerate a hundred and forty forms of cigar, cigarette, and pipe **13** tobacco, with coloured plates illustrating the difference in the ash. It is a point which is continually turning up in criminal trials, and which is sometimes of supreme importance as a clue. If you can say definitely, for example, that some murder had been done by a man who was smoking an Indian **14** lunkah, it obviously narrows your field of search. To the trained eye there is as much difference between the black ash **15** of a Trichinopoly and the white fluff of bird's-eye as there is between a cabbage and a potato.'

'You have an extraordinary genius for minutiæ,' I remarked.

'I appreciate their importance. Here is my monograph upon the tracing of footsteps, with some remarks upon the **16** uses of plaster of Paris as a preserver of impresses. Here, too, is a curious little work upon the influence of a trade upon **17-18** the form of the hand, with lithotypes of the hands of slaters, **19-20** sailors, cork-cutters, compositors, weavers, and diamond- **21-22** polishers. That is a matter of great practical interest to the **23** scientific detective—especially in cases of unclaimed bodies, **24** or in discovering the antecedents of criminals. But I weary you with my hobby.'

'Not at all,' I answered, earnestly. 'It is of the greatest interest to me, especially since I have had the opportunity of observing your practical application of it. But you spoke just now of observation and deduction. Surely the one to some extent implies the other.'

'Why, hardly,' he answered, leaning back luxuriously in his armchair, and sending up thick blue wreaths from his pipe.

"... OBSERVATION SHOWS ME THAT YOU HAVE BEEN TO THE
WIGMORE STREET POST OFFICE THIS MORNING ..."

At the time of this adventure, Wigmore Street was known as
Upper Seymour Street, and Holmes so refers to its Post Office in
early editions of *The Sign of the Four.* But why Watson went to
this Post Office at all is a small mystery: there was a Post Office
at No. 66 Baker Street, just across King Street from "No. 221,"
only six doors away.

'For example, observation shows me that you have been to
the Wigmore Street Post Office this morning, but deduction
lets me know that when there you dispatched a telegram.'

'Right!' said I. 'Right on both points! But I confess that I
don't see how you arrived at it. It was a sudden impulse upon
my part, and I have mentioned it to no one.'

'It is simplicity itself,' he remarked, chuckling at my surprise—'so absurdly simple that an explanation is superfluous;
and yet it may serve to define the limits of observation and
of deduction. Observation tells me that you have a little
reddish mould adhering to your instep. Just opposite the
Wigmore Street Office they have taken up the pavement and
thrown up some earth, which lies in such a way that it is
difficult to avoid treading in it in entering. The earth is of
this peculiar reddish tint which is found, as far as I know,
nowhere else in the neighbourhood. So much is observation.
The rest is deduction.'

'How, then, did you deduce the telegram?'

'Why, of course I knew that you had not written a letter,
since I sat opposite to you all morning. I see also in your open
desk there that you have a sheet of stamps and a thick bundle
of postcards. What could you go into the post office for, then,
but to send a wire? Eliminate all other factors, and the one **25**
which remains must be the truth.' **26**

'In this case it certainly is so,' I replied, after a little
thought. 'The thing, however, is, as you say, of the simplest.
Would you think me impertinent if I were to put your
theories to a more severe test?'

'On the contrary,' he answered; 'it would prevent me from
taking a second dose of cocaine. I should be delighted to look
into any problem which you might submit to me.'

'I have heard you say that it is difficult for a man to have
any object in daily use without leaving the impress of his individuality upon it in such a way that a trained observer might
read it. Now, I have here a watch which has recently come into

trade upon the form of the hand," Miss Stern
continued, Holmes "must have acquired, for his
medico-anatomical shelf, a copy of Ramazzini's
De Morbis Artificium Diatriba of 1670, the first
account of occupational diseases."

Mr. Archibald Hart has noted ("The Effects of
Trades Upon Hands") that "Gilbert Forbes (a
transparent alias) has reprinted Holmes' work
under the title of 'Some Observations on Occupational Markings.' This little article, brilliantly illustrated with twenty-five photographs and drawings (lithotypes) first appeared in the *Police
Journal*, London, England, October–December,
1946. It has been reprinted in the United States in
the *Journal of Criminal Law and Criminology*,
November–December, 1957."

And Professor Remsen Ten Eyck Schenck has
written ("The Effect of Trades Upon the Body"):
"A recent book of Rancesco Ronchese, M.D., entitled *Occupation Marks*, Grune & Stratton, New
York, 1948, will prove of interest to Irregulars.
Such a monograph might well have been developed
from Holmes' 'curious little work,' had only Watson's admiration for his colleague's methods been
sufficient to inspire closer to observation of his
patients, thus greatly extending the scope of the
study and permitting a collaboration which must
necessarily have constituted an advance in forensic
medicine."

18 *slaters.* "The marks probably included the fin-
gertips of the left hand worn smooth by handling
the stone, as seen also in masons and bricklayers
. . . , and calluses across the right palm from
gripping the hammer," Professor Schenck wrote.
"It is also reasonable that callosities of the knees
would be prominent . . . , since roofing is done
chiefly in a kneeling position."

19 *sailors.* "It is incredible that a sailor should
be thus distinguishable from a variety of other
possibilities," Professor Schenck continued. "A distinctive occupational mark arises from the perpetual
repetition of the same act in the same way, and
while a sailor's life is hard, it is extremely varied.
It would be at once apparent from a mariner's
hands that he did hard manual labor, and with
both hands instead of only with the right, but
there are surely a dozen trades to which this applies equally well."

20 *cork-cutters.* "The hand of the cork-cutter is
another phenomenon which has been banished from
the contemporary scene by modern machinery.
One can speculate that calluses were produced on
the thumb and first two fingers of the left hand by
grasping the cork, and similarly on the thumb and
across the inside of all four fingers of the right by
the handle of the knife . . ." (Schenck).

21 *compositors.* See "The Adventure of the Copper Beeches," Note 10.

22 *weavers.* "There is, unfortunately, no way at this date to establish just what constituted for Holmes the unmistakable manual stigma of the weaver," Professor Schenck continued. "A wide variety of calluses peculiar to the textile trades is described by [Rancesco Ronchese], but these differ with the particular assignment of the worker at the machine—the doffer, the quiller, the hooker, the mule spinner, etc.—and none of them could have been created by hand-looming. It is likely that the marks to which Holmes referred were calluses on the right hand from handling the shuttle, and perhaps on the left from the heddles . . ."

23 *diamond-polishers.* "Some clues [to the hand of the diamond-polisher] are available: jewelry polishers have nails worn smooth and stained red by the rouge . . . , lens polishers show certain nails worn down from picking the glass from its pitch bed . . . , and those who polish metal jewelry wear calluses from holding the metal parts against the wheel. . . . Since diamonds are polished in a pitch bed at the end of a 'dop stick' any or all of the three marks described might appear in a lapidary doing much hand work" (Schenck).

24 *the antecedents of criminals.* In four of his own cases—"A Case of Identity," "The Red-Headed League," "The Adventure of the Copper Beeches," and "The Adventure of the Solitary Cyclist"—Holmes demonstrates his personal proficiency in estimating the effects of various trades upon hands.

25 *but to send a wire?* "Equally well [Watson] might have gone for a money order or a postal order, to inquire the cost of sending a parcel to India or Australia, or to buy stamps of a different value to those contained in his sheet," Mr. Vernon Rendall commented in "The Limitations of Sherlock Holmes."

26 *the one which remains must be the truth.'* "This is the most famous maxim of Holmes, and it was a great favourite with him," Mr. T. S. Blakeney wrote in *Sherlock Holmes: Fact of Fiction?* "It is twice uttered in *The Sign of the Four* [". . . when you have eliminated the impossible, whatever remains, *however improbable*, must be the truth"], and we find it repeated almost identically in 'The Adventure of the Beryl Coronet,' 'The Adventure of the Bruce-Partington Plans' and 'The Adventure of the Blanched Soldier.' With it may be compared the remark to Watson in 'The Adventure of the Priory School': 'it *is* impossible as I state it, and therefore I must in some respect have stated it wrong.' "

my possession. Would you have the kindness to let me have an opinion upon the character or habits of the late owner?'

I handed him over the watch with some slight feeling of amusement in my heart, for the test was, as I thought, an impossible one, and I intended it as a lesson against the somewhat dogmatic tone which he occasionally assumed. He balanced the watch in his hand, gazed hard at the dial, opened the back, and examined the works, first with his naked eyes and then with a powerful convex lens. I could hardly keep from smiling at his crestfallen face when he finally snapped the case to and handed it back.

'There are hardly any data,' he remarked. 'The watch has been recently cleaned, which robs me of my most suggestive facts.'

'You are right,' I answered. 'It was cleaned before being sent to me.'

In my heart I accused my companion of putting forward a most lame and impotent excuse to cover his failure. What data could he expect from an uncleaned watch?

'Though unsatisfactory, my research has not been entirely barren,' he observed, staring up at the ceiling with dreamy, lack-lustre eyes. 'Subject to your correction, I should judge that the watch belonged to your elder brother, who inherited it from your father.'

'That you gather, no doubt, from the H. W. upon the back?'

'Quite so. The W. suggests your own name. The date of the watch is nearly fifty years back and the initials are as old as the watch; so it was made for the last generation. Jewellery usually descends to the eldest son, and he is most likely to have the same name as the father. Your father has, if I remember right, been dead many years. It has, therefore, been in the hands of your eldest brother.'

'Right, so far,' said I. 'Anything else?'

'He was a man of untidy habits—very untidy and careless. He was left with good prospects, but he threw away his chances, lived for some time in poverty with occasional short intervals of prosperity, and, finally, taking to drink, he died. That is all I can gather.'

I sprang from my chair and limped impatiently about the room with considerable bitterness in my heart.

'This is unworthy of you, Holmes,' I said. 'I could not have believed that you would have descended to this. You have made inquiries into the history of my unhappy brother, and you now pretend to deduce this knowledge in some fanciful way. You cannot expect me to believe that you have read all this from his old watch! It is unkind, and, to speak plainly, has a touch of charlatanism in it.'

'My dear Doctor,' said he, kindly, 'pray accept my apologies. Viewing the matter as an abstract problem, I had forgotten how personal and painful a thing it might be to you. I assure you, however, that I never even knew that you had a brother until you handed me the watch.'

'Then how in the name of all that is wonderful did you get these facts? They are absolutely correct in every particular.'

'Ah, that is good luck. I could only say what was the balance of probability. I did not at all expect to be accurate.'

'But it was not mere guesswork?'

'No, no: I never guess. It is a shocking habit—destructive to the logical faculty. What seems strange to you is only so because you do not follow my train of thought or observe the small facts upon which large inferences may depend. For example, I began by stating that your brother was careless. When you observe the lower part of that watch-case you notice that it is not only dinted in two places, but it is cut and marked all over from the habit of keeping other hard objects, such as coins or keys, in the same pocket. Surely it is no great feat to assume that a man who treats a fifty-guinea watch so cavalierly must be a careless man. Neither is it a **27** very far-fetched inference that a man who inherits one article of such value is pretty well provided for in other respects.'

I nodded, to show that I followed his reasoning.

'It is very customary for pawnbrokers in England, when they take a watch, to scratch the number of the ticket with a pin-point upon the inside of the case. It is more handy than a label, as there is no risk of the number being lost or transposed. There are no less than four such numbers visible to my lens on the inside of this case. Inference—that your brother was often at low water. Secondary inference—that he had occasional bursts of prosperity, or he could not have redeemed the pledge. Finally, I ask you to look at the inner plate, which contains the keyhole. Look at the thousands of **28** scratches all round the hole—marks where the key has slipped. What sober man's key could have scored those grooves? But you will never see a drunkard's watch without them. He winds it at night, and he leaves these traces of his unsteady hand. Where is the mystery in all this?'

'It is as clear as daylight,' I answered. 'I regret the injustice which I did you. I should have had more faith in your marvellous faculty. May I ask whether you have any professional inquiry on foot at present?'

'None. Hence the cocaine. I cannot live without brainwork. What else is there to live for? Stand at the window here. Was ever such a dreary, dismal, unprofitable world? See how the yellow fog swirls down the street and drifts across the dun- **29** coloured houses. What could be more hopelessly prosaic and material? What is the use of having powers, Doctor, when one has no field upon which to exert them? Crime is commonplace, existence is commonplace, and no qualities save those which are commonplace have any function upon earth.'

I had opened my mouth to reply to this tirade, when, with a crisp knock, our landlady entered, bearing a card upon the brass salver.

'A young lady for you, sir,' she said, addressing my companion.

'Miss Mary Morstan,' he read. 'Hum! I have no recollection of the name. Ask the young lady to step up, Mrs Hudson. Don't go, doctor. I should prefer that you remain.'

27 *a fifty-guinea watch.* Holmes valued the watch at being worth the equivalent of about $262.50 U.S. at that time.

28 *the keyhole.* The stem-winding watch had been developed by 1840 but the key-wind was cheaper and more trouble-free. The owner of a key-winding watch usually kept the key on his watch chain; the Phi Beta Kappa key coveted by students was originally designed as a watch key.

29 *the yellow fog.* We are later told that "A dense drizzly fog lay low upon the great city," that "We plunged away at a furious pace through the foggy streets," and that "we had left the damp fog of the city behind us . . ." Although most commentators (Andrew, Ashton, Baring-Gould, Blakeney, Christ, Folsom, Knox, Pattrick, Petersen, Roberts, Smith, Starrett, and Zeisler) are today agreed that the adventure of *The Sign of the Four* took place in 1888, a strong minority (Austin, Bell, Brend, Bristowe, Harrison, Hoff, MacCarthy, McCleary, Montgomery, Christopher Morley, Offord, and Wellman) date the case 1887. But the month also is in dispute: April, June, July, and September all have their supporters. At this time, let us note only that fog would have been a phenomenon in June and July, at least.

MISS MORSTAN ENTERED THE ROOM WITH A FIRM STEP . . .

An illustration by an artist as yet unidentified. It comes from *Stories of Sherlock Holmes*, Vol. I, New York: Harper & Brothers, 1904.

2 • THE STATEMENT OF THE CASE

Miss Morstan entered the room with a firm step and an outward composure of manner. She was a blonde young lady,

30 *a little domestic complication.* Mr. Robert Keith Leavitt has suggested (in "Who Was Cecil Forrester?") that *Mr.* Cecil Forrester, Farintosh of "The Adventure of the Speckled Band," Woodhouse of "The Adventure of the Bruce-Partington Plans," and Colonel Upwood of *The Hound of the Baskervilles* were all one and the same man— "former friend of Captain Morstan and probably of the none-too-scrupulous Major Sholto, sometime husband of Mary Morstan's employer, party hanger-on, card-sharp and all-too-dubious hero of the strange adventure·of the politician, the lighthouse and the trained cormorant ["The Adventure of the Veiled Lodger"]."

And Mrs. Ruth Douglass, in "The Camberwell Poisoner," has advanced the speculation that the "little domestic complication" in Mrs. Forrester's household was the Camberwell Poisoning; that the poisoner was Mrs. Forrester; that she escaped justice and used Mary first as bait (for Watson) and then as a tool (in order to obtain poison, through Mary, from Watson's medical cabinet). She finally killed Mary.

31 *In the year 1878.* Mary Morstan was therefore born in 1861.

32 *a choking sob cut short the sentence.* "This is rather excessive emotion to be exhibited by an Englishwoman of the upper classes when speaking of an event which occurred ten years before and of a person she has long believed dead," Messrs. T. B. Hunt and H. W. Starr observed in "What Happened to Mary Morstan?" "She is subject to similar collapses whenever Captain Morstan's death is mentioned. How else can this be explained save by the existence of a marked Oedipus complex?"

small, dainty, well gloved, and dressed in the most perfect taste. There was, however, a plainness and simplicity about her costume which bore with it a suggestion of limited means. The dress was a sombre greyish beige, untrimmed and unbraided, and she wore a small turban of the same dull hue, relieved only by a suspicion of white feather in the side. Her face had neither regularity of feature nor beauty of complexion, but her expression was sweet and amiable, and her large blue eyes were singularly spiritual and sympathetic. In an experience of women which extends over many nations and three separate continents, I have never looked upon a face which gave a clearer promise of a refined and sensitive nature. I could not but observe that, as she took the seat which Sherlock Holmes placed for her, her lip trembled, her hand quivered, and she showed every sign of intense inward agitation.

'I have come to you, Mr Holmes,' she said, 'because you once enabled my employer, Mrs Cecil Forrester, to unravel **30** a little domestic complication. She was much impressed by your kindness and skill.'

'Mrs Cecil Forrester,' he repeated, thoughtfully. 'I believe that I was of some slight service to her. The case, however, as I remember it, was a very simple one.'

'She did not think so. But at least you cannot say the same of mine. I can hardly imagine anything more strange, more utterly inexplicable, than the situation in which I find myself.'

Holmes rubbed his hands, and his eyes glistened. He leaned forward in his chair with an expression of extraordinary concentration upon his clear-cut, hawk-like features.

'State your case,' said he, in brisk, business tones.

I felt that my position was an embarrassing one.

'You will, I am sure, excuse me,' I said, rising from my chair.

To my surprise, the young lady held up her gloved hand to detain me.

'If your friend,' she said, 'would be good enough to stop, he might be of inestimable service to me.'

I relapsed into my chair.

'Briefly,' she continued, 'the facts are these. My father was an officer in an Indian regiment, who sent me home when I was quite a child. My mother was dead, and I had no relative in England. I was placed, however, in a comfortable boarding establishment at Edinburgh, and there I remained until I was **31** seventeen years of age. In the year 1878 my father, who was senior captain of his regiment, obtained twelve months' leave and came home. He telegraphed to me from London that he had arrived all safe, and directed me to come down at once, giving the Langham Hotel as his address. His message, as I remember, was full of kindness and love. On reaching London I drove to the Langham, and was informed that Captain Morstan was staying there, but that he had gone out the night before and had not returned. I waited all day without news of him. That night, on the advice of the manager of the hotel, I communicated with the police, and next morning we advertised in all the papers. Our inquiries led to no result; and from that day to this no word has ever been heard of my unfortunate father. He came home with his heart full of hope, to find some peace, some comfort, and instead——'

She put her hand to her throat, and a choking sob cut short the sentence. **32**

'The date?' asked Holmes, opening his note-book.

'He disappeared upon the 3rd of December, 1878—nearly ten years ago.' **33**

'His luggage?'

'Remained at the hotel. There was nothing in it to suggest a clue—some clothes, some books, and a considerable number of curiosities from the Andaman Islands. He had been one **34** of the officers in charge of the convict guard there.'

'Had he any friends in town?'

'Only one that we know of—Major Sholto, of his own regiment, the 34th Bombay Infantry. The Major had retired **35** some little time before, and lived at Upper Norwood. We **36** communicated with him, of course, but he did not even know that his brother officer was in England.'

'A singular case,' remarked Holmes.

'I have not yet described to you the most singular part. About six years ago—to be exact, upon the 4th of May, 1882 **37** —an advertisement appeared in *The Times* asking for the address of Miss Mary Morstan, and stating that it would be to her advantage to come forward. There was no name or address appended. I had at that time just entered the family of Mrs Cecil Forrester in the capacity of governess. By her advice I published my address in the advertisement column. The same day there arrived through the post a small cardboard box addressed to me, which I found to contain a very large and lustrous pearl. No word of writing was enclosed. Since then every year upon the same date there has always appeared a similar box, containing a similar pearl, without any clue as to the sender. They have been pronounced by an expert to be of a rare variety and of considerable value. You can see for yourselves that they are very handsome.'

She opened a flat box as she spoke, and showed me six of the finest pearls that I had ever seen. **38**

'Your statement is most interesting,' said Sherlock Holmes. 'Has anything else occurred to you?'

'Yes, and no later than today. That is why I have come to you. This morning I received this letter, which you will per- **39** haps read for yourself.'

'Thank you,' said Holmes. 'The envelope, too, please. Post-mark, London, S.W. Date, July 7. Hum! Man's thumb- **40–41** mark on corner—probably postman. Best quality paper. Envelopes at sixpence a packet. Particular man in his stationery.

33 *nearly ten years ago.'* A statement that would seem to point to the period between June and early December, 1888, for the time of the adventure.

34 *the Andaman Islands.* In the Bay of Bengal, about 800 miles from the nearest part of India. They were occupied by the Japanese in 1942.

35 *the 34th Bombay Infantry.* "At the period of the Mutiny, when the events relating to Morstan and Sholto began, the regimental numbers of the Bombay Infantry of the Indian Army appear to have gone no higher than Thirty," Mrs. Crighton Sellars wrote in "Dr. Watson and the British Army." "I take it that this is one of the occasions on which Dr. Watson chose to create a fictional regiment in which to put his reprehensible characters. But there was a *Bengal 38th Infantry* known as 'The Agra Regiment' to which I make a guess that Captain Morstan and Major Sholto really belonged."

36 *Upper Norwood.* A suburb of London, part of the county borough of Croydon. Noted for its bracing air, it contained and still contains some good private hotels, such as the old-established Queen's Hotel in Church Road.

37 *the 4th of May, 1882.* A statement that would seem to point roughly to the period between early February and early August, 1888, for the time of the adventure.

38 *six of the finest pearls that I had ever seen.* The advertisement in the *Times* appeared on May 4, 1882. Miss Morstan's reply could not have appeared until the next day, and on that day she received the first pearl. The other pearls were received "every year upon the same date," that is, on May 5th, and she now has six pearls in all. Therefore her visit to Baker Street would seem to have been made after May 5, 1887, and before May 5, 1888. Students who argue for the June, July, or September of 1888 as the date of this adventure must therefore explain why Mary failed to produce *seven* pearls. It has been said that this was a note-taking error on Watson's part; that he wrote the two dates (1882 and 1888) and calculated

'. . . ENVELOPES AT SIXPENCE A PACKET . . .'

In U.S. currency at the time, the envelopes cost about 12¢ a packet. (We recall that the King of Bohemia paid about 60¢ U.S. for his writing paper.) "The sixpence," the late A. Carson Simpson wrote in *Numismatics in the Canon*, Part I, "was first struck in 1550 by Edward VI, omitted by Mary I, called a 'half-shilling' under William & Mary, then coined under its old name by all succeeding monarchs. The silver shortage caused George III to issue them in only one year (1787) between his accession and the 1816 currency reform." The sixpence is mentioned in the Canon three times.

' "BE AT THE THIRD PILLAR FROM THE LEFT OUTSIDE
THE LYCEUM THEATRE AT SEVEN O'CLOCK." '

The Lyceum Theatre was first built as an opera
house in 1794 by Dr. Samuel Arnold, the great-
grandfather of Edgar Allan Poe. It was destroyed
by fire and rebuilt in 1834. From 1878 to 1904 it
was managed by Sir Henry Irving and then became for a time a music hall. It still exists, as a
dance hall, at the corner of Exeter Street and
Wellington Street, the Strand.

the number of pearls he had seen by subtracting.
Mr. T. S. Blakeney has suggested that Mary "may
have had the first pearl she received made up into
a brooch or pendant, as she would not be expecting any more; but naturally, on finding pearls
came in every year, she would keep the remaining six together." And the late Professor Jay
Finley Christ thought that Mary might well have
sold the first pearl. The most probable explanation
on the whole would seem to be that Mary Morstan
produced seven pearls and seven box tops and
that Watson simply miscounted them; otherwise,
as the late Dr. Ernest Bloomfield Zeisler pointed
out, Holmes or his client would certainly have
commented on the situation.

39 *This morning.* We later learn that "This
morning" was a Tuesday morning.

40 *S.W.* South West—indicating the postal district of London from which the letter had been
mailed.

41 *July* 7. Thaddeus Sholto's letter to Mary Morstan had to arrive on the morning on which the
adventure began in order to arrange for the appointment for "tonight," but it might have been
mailed either late Monday night or early Tuesday
morning. Unfortunately for the 1887 School, July
7, 1887, was neither a Monday nor a Tuesday, but
a Saturday. What speaks for July, other than the
postmark on the letter? There is Thaddeus Sholto,
venturing forth "in a very long befrogged top-
coat" which "he buttoned tightly up in spite of
the closeness of the night." There is "a warm
wind" which "blew from the westward." There
are barefoot Irregulars, and there is Mary, late at
night, "seated by an open window, dressed in some
sort of white diaphanous material." All of these
might be interpreted as pointing towards July,
if it were not for the fact that we are later told
that it was "very hot *for the time of the year.*"

No address. "Be at the third pillar from the left outside the
Lyceum Theatre tonight at seven o'clock. If you are distrustful bring two friends. You are a wronged woman, and shall
have justice. Do not bring police. If you do, all will be in vain.
Your unknown friend." Well, really, this is a very pretty little
mystery! What do you intend to do, Miss Morstan?'

'That is exactly what I want to ask you.'

'Then we shall most certainly go—you and I and—yes, why,
Dr Watson is the very man. Your correspondent says two
friends. He and I have worked together before.'

'But would he come?' she asked, with something appealing
in her voice and expression.

'I shall be proud and happy,' said I, fervently, 'if I can be
of any service.'

'You are both very kind,' she answered. 'I have led a retired
life, and have no friends whom I could appeal to. If I am here
at six it will do, I suppose?'

'You must not be later,' said Holmes. 'There is one other
point, however. Is this handwriting the same as that upon
the pearl-box addresses?'

'I have them here,' she answered, producing half-a-dozen
pieces of paper.

'You are certainly a model client. You have the correct intuition. Let us see, now.' He spread out the papers upon the table, and gave little, darting glances from one to the other. 'They are disguised hands, except the letter,' he said, presently; 'but there can be no question as to the authorship. See how the irrepressible Greek *e* will break out, and see the twirl of the final *s*. They are undoubtedly by the same person. I should not like to suggest false hopes, Miss Morstan, but is there any resemblance between this hand and that of your father?'

'Nothing could be more unlike.'

'I expected to hear you say so. We shall look out for you, then, at six. Pray allow me to keep the papers. I may look into the matter before then. It is only half-past three. *Au revoir*, then.'

'*Au revoir*,' said our visitor; and with a bright, kindly glance from one to the other of us, she replaced her pearl-box in her bosom and hurried away.

Standing at the window, I watched her walking briskly down the street, until the grey turban and white feather were but a speck in the sombre crowd.

'What a very attractive woman!' I exclaimed, turning to my companion.

He had lit his pipe again, and was leaning back with drooping eyelids. 'Is she?' he said, languidly; 'I did not observe.' **42**

'You really are an automaton—a calculating machine,' I cried. 'There is something positively inhuman in you at times.'

He smiled gently.

'It is of the first importance,' he said, 'not to allow your judgment to be biased by personal qualities. A client is to me a mere unit, a factor in a problem. The emotional qualities are antagonistic to clear reasoning. I assure you that the most winning woman I ever knew was hanged for poisoning three little children for their insurance-money, and the most repellent man of my acquaintance is a philanthropist who has spent nearly a quarter of a million upon the London poor.' **43**

'In this case, however——'

'I never make exceptions. An exception disproves the rule. Have you ever had occasion to study character in handwriting? What do you make of this fellow's scribble?'

'It is legible and regular,' I answered. 'A man of business habits and some force of character.'

Holmes shook his head.

'Look at his long letters,' he said. 'They hardly rise above the common herd. That *d* might be an *a*, and that *l* an *e*. Men of character always differentiate their long letters, however illegibly they may write. There is vacillation in his *k*'s and self-esteem in his capitals. I am going out now. I have some few references to make. Let me recommend this book—one of the most remarkable ever penned. It is Winwood Reade's *Martyrdom of Man*. I shall be back in an hour.' **44**

I sat in the window with the volume in my hand, but my thoughts were far from the daring speculations of the writer. My mind ran upon our late visitor—her smiles, the deep, rich tones of her voice, the strange mystery which overhung her life. If she were seventeen at the time of her father's disappearance she must be seven-and-twenty now—a sweet **45**

In your editor's view, Thaddeus Sholto's letter was mailed late on *Monday, September 17, 1888*. Watson's no doubt carelessly written 'S 17' was misread, by himself or by the typesetter, as "Jl 7."

42 '*I did not observe.*' "It is possible that a man so observant that he would even notice the depth to which parsley had sunk into the butter on a hot day could fail to notice that Mary Morstan was attractive?" Dr. Richard Asher asked in "Holmes and the Fair Sex." "No; Holmes was aware of her charms and on guard against them. As he later said, 'A client is to me a mere unit, a factor in a problem. The emotional qualities are antagonistic to clear reasoning.' It seems that from this very point Holmes purposely did not allow any emotional feelings toward Miss Morstan to rise in himself. Not only because it would have been antagonistic to clear reasoning but because he saw that Watson, already deeply smitten, was musing upon her smiles and the deep rich tones of her voice until such dangerous thoughts came into his head that he plunged furiously into the latest treatise on pathology."

43 *three little children for their insurance-money.* "Who this woman was who attracted Holmes so strongly and came to such a dreadful end, we do not know," Dr. Asher continued. "She may have been Mrs. Morgan, for a poisoner called Morgan occupied a place of honour in his index among other distinguished M's ["The Adventure of the Empty House"]. Whoever she was, this woman seems to have left her mark upon Holmes."

44 *Winwood Reade's* Martyrdom of Man. William Winwood Reade, 1838–1875, traveler, novelist, and controversalist, was a nephew of Charles Reade. His *Martyrdom of Man* was published in London in 1872 by Trübner and Company of Paternoster Row. The book became so popular that by 1884 it had reached an eighth edition. Mr. S. C. Roberts ("The Personality of Sherlock Holmes") has written that the book was "one of the most popular monuments of nineteenth century rationalism. Holmes, with his social moodiness, his artistic temperament and his queer intellectual interests, had no doubt reacted against the conventional beliefs of his squirearchical family and Winwood Reade's book was exactly the work that would catch him on the rebound. It is a sad work and its conclusions may well have depressed a contemporary of Sherlock Holmes: 'A season of mental anguish is at hand and through this we must pass in order that our posterity may rise. The soul must be sacrificed; the hope in immortality must die.' "

45 *she must be seven-and-twenty now.* Since Captain Morstan came home in 1878, when Mary was seventeen, this is still another indication that 1888 was the year of the case.

46 *the 28th of April, 1882.'* Corroborating Mary's statement that the advertisement seeking her out appeared "upon the 4th of May, 1882"—"about six years ago."

47 *Four years later.* Corroborating Mary's statement that Captain Morstan returned to England and disappeared in 1878, which was "nearly ten years ago."

48 *rather than six years ago?* And Holmes later tells us that the Sholtos were six years searching for the treasure. As the date of Sholto's death cannot be in doubt, we again reach 1888 as the year of *The Sign of the Four.*

age, when youth has lost its self-consciousness and become a little sobered by experience. So I sat and mused, until such dangerous thoughts came into my head that I hurried away to my desk and plunged furiously into the latest treatise upon pathology. What was I, an Army surgeon with a weak leg and a weaker banking account, that I should dare to think of such things? She was a unit, a factor—nothing more. If my future were black, it was better surely to face it like a man than to attempt to brighten it by mere will-o'-the-wisps of the imagination.

3 • IN QUEST OF A SOLUTION

It was half-past five before Holmes returned. He was bright, eager, and in excellent spirits, a mood which in his case alternated with fits of the blackest depression.

'There is no great mystery in this matter,' he said, taking the cup of tea which I had poured out for him; 'the facts appear to admit of only one explanation.'

'What! you have solved it already?'

'Well, that would be too much to say. I have discovered a suggestive fact, that is all. It is, however, *very* suggestive. The details are still to be added. I have just found, on consulting the back files of *The Times*, that Major Sholto, of Upper Norwood, late of the 34th Bombay Infantry, died upon the
46 28th of April, 1882.'

'I may be very obtuse, Holmes, but I fail to see what this suggests.'

'No? You surprise me. Look at it in this way, then. Captain Morstan disappears. The only person in London whom he could have visited is Major Sholto. Major Sholto denies
47 having heard that he was in London. Four years later Sholto dies. *Within a week of his death* Captain Morstan's daughter receives a valuable present, which is repeated from year to year, and now culminates in a letter which describes her as a wronged woman. What wrong can it refer to except this deprivation of her father? And why should the presents begin immediately after Sholto's death, unless it is that Sholto's heir knows something of the mystery and desires to make compensation? Have you any alternative theory which will meet the facts?'

'But what a strange compensation! And how strangely made! Why, too, should he write a letter now, rather than six
48 years ago? Again, the letter speaks of giving her justice. What justice can she have? It is too much to suppose that her father is still alive. There is no other injustice in her case that you know of.'

'There are difficulties; there are certainly difficulties,' said Sherlock Holmes, pensively; 'but your expedition of tonight will solve them all. Ah, here is a four-wheeler, and Miss Morstan inside. Are you all ready? Then we had better go down, for it is a little past the hour.'

I picked up my hat and my heaviest stick, but I observed that Holmes took his revolver from his drawer and slipped it into his pocket. It was clear that he thought that our night's work might be a serious one.

Miss Morstan was muffled in a dark cloak, and her sensitive face was composed, but pale. She must have been more than woman if she did not feel some uneasiness at the strange enterprise upon which we were embarking, yet her self-control was perfect, and she readily answered the few additional questions which Sherlock Holmes put to her.

'Major Sholto was a very particular friend of papa's,' she said. 'His letters were full of allusions to the Major. He and papa were in command of the troops at the Andaman Islands, so they were thrown a great deal together. By the way, a curious paper was found in papa's desk which no one could understand. I don't suppose that it is of the slightest importance, but I thought you might care to see it, so I brought it with me. It is here.'

Holmes unfolded the paper carefully and smoothed it out upon his knee. He then very methodically examined it all over with his double lens.

'It is paper of native Indian manufacture,' he remarked. 'It has at some time been pinned to a board. The diagram upon it appears to be a plan of part of a large building with numerous halls, corridors, and passages. At one point is a small cross done in red ink, and above it is "3.37 from left," in faded pencil-writing. In the left-hand corner is a curious hieroglyphic like four crosses in a line with their arms touching. Beside it is written, in very rough and coarse characters, "The sign of the four—Jonathan Small, Mahomet Singh, Abdullah Khan, Dost Akbar." No, I confess that I do not see how this bears upon the matter. Yet it is evidently a document of importance. It has been kept carefully in a pocket-book; for the one side is as clean as the other.'

'It was in his pocket-book that we found it.'

'Preserve it carefully, then, Miss Morstan, for it may prove to be of use to us. I begin to suspect that this matter may turn out to be much deeper and more subtle than I at first supposed. I must reconsider my ideas.'

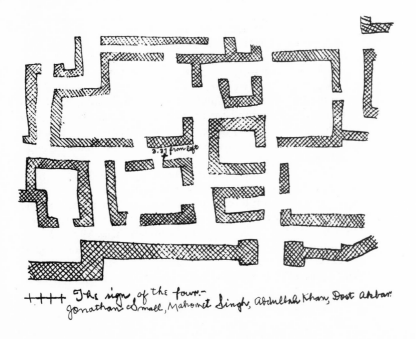

"YET IT IS EVIDENTLY A DOCUMENT OF IMPORTANCE."

Dr. Julian Wolff's reconstruction of the "plan of part of a large building with numerous halls, corridors, and passages."

49 *It was a September evening.* The late Clifton R. Andrew once wrote ("On the Dating of *The Sign of the Four*"): "Watson was speaking of the weather. . . . That evening in July, 1888, was so pleasantly cool and balmy—or perhaps blowing with such exceptional equinoctial violence—that it seemed to him not like an evening in July at all, but like an evening in September." The September School again points to the fog, which can only be otherwise explained by a combination of Beaune on the part of Watson and cocaine on the part of Holmes.

50 *a dense drizzly fog lay low upon the great city.* In fact, Tuesday, September 18, 1888, *was* a day on which the *Times* of London reported "fog and mist." No sunshine whatsoever was recorded on that day at Westminster.

51 *the crowds were already thick at the side-entrances.* "They were probably playing Shakespeare at the time of the rendezvous, which would account for the crowd of devotees," the late Christopher Morley wrote in *Sherlock Holmes and Dr. Watson: A Textbook of Friendship;* "though seven o'clock is surely too early for the carriage trade to be arriving. The 'side-entrances' would be to the gallery and the pit, where in the English custom seats are not reserved and the crowd 'queues up' to wait for the doors to open. By happy coincidence the play *Sherlock Holmes*, dramatized and starred by William Gillette, was first performed [in London] at the Lyceum Theatre, September 2, 1901."

He leaned back in the cab, and I could see by his drawn brow and his vacant eye that he was thinking intently. Miss Morstan and I chatted in an undertone about our present expedition and its possible outcome, but our companion maintained his impenetrable reserve until the end of our journey.

49 It was a September evening, and not yet seven o'clock, but the day had been a dreary one, and a dense drizzly fog lay **50** low upon the great city. Mud-coloured clouds drooped sadly over the muddy streets. Down the Strand the lamps were but misty splotches of diffused light, which threw a feeble circular glimmer upon the slimy pavement. The yellow glare from the shop-windows streamed out into the steamy, vaporous air, and threw a murky, shifting radiance across the crowded thoroughfare. There was, to my mind, something eerie and ghost-like in the endless procession of faces which flitted across these narrow bars of light—sad faces and glad, haggard and merry. Like all human kind, they flitted from the gloom into the light, and so back into the gloom once more. I am not subject to impressions, but the dull, heavy evening, with the strange business upon which we were engaged, combined to make me nervous and depressed. I could see from Miss Morstan's manner that she was suffering from the same feeling. Holmes alone could rise superior to petty influences. He held his open note-book upon his knee, and from time to time he jotted down figures and memoranda in the light of his pocket-lantern.

At the Lyceum Theatre the crowds were already thick at **51** the side-entrances. In front a continuous stream of hansoms and four-wheelers were rattling up, discharging their cargoes of shirt-fronted men and beshawled, bediamonded women. We had hardly reached the third pillar, which was our rendezvous, before a small, dark, brisk man in the dress of a coachman accosted us.

'Are you the parties who come with Miss Morstan?' he asked.

'I am Miss Morstan, and these two gentlemen are my friends,' said she.

He bent a pair of wonderfully penetrating and questioning eyes upon us.

'You will excuse me, miss,' he said, with a certain dogged manner, 'but I was to ask you to give me your word that neither of your companions is a police-officer.'

'I give you my word on that,' she answered.

He gave a shrill whistle, on which a street arab led across a four-wheeler and opened the door. The man who had addressed us mounted to the box, while we took our places inside. We had hardly done so before the driver whipped up his horse, and we plunged away at a furious pace through the foggy streets.

The situation was a curious one. We were driving to an unknown place, on an unknown errand. Yet our invitation was either a complete hoax—which was an inconceivable hypothesis—or else we had good reason to think that important issues might hang upon our journey. Miss Morstan's demeanour was as resolute and collected as ever. I endeavoured to cheer and amuse her by reminiscences of my adventures in Afghanistan; but, to tell the truth, I was myself so excited at our situation, and so curious as to our destination, that my stories were slightly involved. To this day she declares that I told her one moving anecdote as to how a musket looked into my tent at the dead of night, and how I fired a double-barrelled tiger cub at it. At first I had some idea as to the **52** direction in which we were driving; but soon, what with our pace, the fog, and my own limited knowledge of London, I lost my bearings, and knew nothing, save that we seemed to be going a very long way. Sherlock Holmes was never at fault, however, and he muttered the names as the cab rattled **53** through squares and in and out by tortuous by-streets.

'Rochester Row,' said he. 'Now Vincent Square. Now we **54-55** come out on the Vauxhall Bridge Road. We are making for **56** the Surrey side, apparently. Yes, I thought so. Now we are **57** on the bridge. You can catch glimpses of the river.' **58**

We did indeed get a fleeting view of a stretch of the Thames, with the lamps shining upon the broad, silent water; **59** but our cab dashed on, and was soon involved in a labyrinth of streets upon the other side.

'Wandsworth Road,' said my companion. 'Priory Road. **60-61** Larkhall Lane. Stockwell Place. Robert Street. Coldharbour **62-63** Lane. Our quest does not appear to take us to very fashionable **64-65** regions.'

We had indeed reached a questionable and forbidding neighbourhood. Long lines of dull brick houses were only relieved by the coarse glare and tawdry brilliancy of public-houses at the corners. Then came rows of two-storied villas, each with a fronting of miniature garden, and then again interminable lines of new, staring brick buildings—the mon-

"OUR QUEST DOES NOT APPEAR TO TAKE US TO VERY FASHIONABLE REGIONS."

This sketch map accompanied the late Robert R. Pattrick's article, "The Oasis in the Howling Desert," when it appeared in *The Sherlock Holmes Journal*, Spring, 1960.

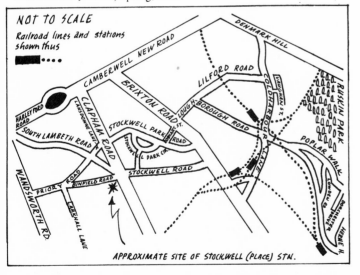

APPROXIMATE SITE OF STOCKWELL (PLACE) STN.

52 *a double-barrelled tiger cub.* "The celebrated 'double-barrelled' tiger cub must, I think, have been a snow leopard," Mr. T. S. Blakeney wrote in "Thoughts on *The Sign of the Four*." "According to Ellerman and Morrison-Scott, *Checklist of Palaearctic and Indian Mammals* (British Museum of Natural History, 1951), tigers do not inhabit the region of South Afghanistan or North West Frontier of India, so neither in the Kandahar/Maiwand region, nor in that of Peshawar, would Watson have found one."

53 *Sherlock Holmes was never at fault, however.* "It is a hobby of mine to have an exact knowledge of London," Holmes said in "The Red-Headed League." And in "The Adventure of the Empty House," Watson wrote: "Holmes' knowledge of the byways of London was extraordinary . . ."

54 *'Rochester Row.'* Rochester Row, leading to Horseferry Road, is about halfway along the Vauxhall Bridge Road on the east side. Its notable features include the Greycoat School, founded in 1698; St. Stephen's Church, founded in 1847; and the district police court, opened in 1846.

55 *Vincent Square.* Just south of Rochester Row is the old-fashioned Vincent Square, now used as a playground by the boys of the Westminster School.

56 *the Vauxhall Bridge Road.* Built about 1816, at the time of the erection of Vauxhall Bridge, the Vauxhall Bridge Road provides direct communication between Hyde Park Corner and Grosvenor Place and the south of London. It divides old Westminster from the quarter of Pimlico and South Belgravia.

57 *the Surrey side.* The south side of the Thames, which now forms the northern boundary of the county of Surrey.

58 *the bridge.* Holmes and Watson crossed on the bridge constructed in 1811–1816. The present span, an iron and steel structure 759 feet long and 80 feet wide, designed by Maurice Fitzmaurice, was not opened until 1906.

59 *the Thames.* The Thames, rising among the Cotswold Hills in Gloucestershire and running for 209 miles to the North Sea, is the principal river of England. The Thames flows through London and its suburbs for a distance of some 25 miles and attains a width of 750 feet at London Bridge.

60 *'Wandsworth Road.'* Which some editions of the Canon erroneously call "Wordsworth Road."

This has compounded confusion where confusion already exists, for there is a Wordsworth Road in London, miles away in another direction entirely. *Wandsworth* Road, on the other hand, is a right-handed turn at the south side of Vauxhall Bridge.

61 '*Priory Road.* There is, unhappily, no Priory Road in this part of London *today*. But, as the late Robert R. Pattrick pointed out in "The Oasis in the Howling Desert," "the street known today as 'Lansdowne Way' was then divided into two parts. The entire section between Wandsworth Road and Larkhall Lane was Priory Road."

62 *Larkhall Lane.* As Professor Stephen F. Crocker has said ("Louder, Holmes! and Stop Muttering!"): "They just came to it; of course they did not follow it. It would have taken them in the wrong direction and brought them out farther away on Wandsworth Road again."

63 *Stockwell Place.* There is, or was, no street of that name. But there was a Stockwell *Road*, a Stockwell *Park Road*, and a Stockwell *Park Circle* (*see sketch map*). Professor Crocker has logically suggested that "The word *place* can, of course, refer to a short street or court, a private residence terrace, or some similar variation from the ordinary street; but the word can also refer to a place, open space, or square, in a city or town. In this sense, the whole area could easily be referred to as 'Stockwell Place.'" Whether they proceeded north (via Stockwell Park Road) or south (via Binfield Road, Stockwell Road, and Stockwell Park Circle) they came next to Robert (Robsart) Street.

64 *Robert Street.* Then, and now, *Robsart* Street. But it had been *Robert* Street until April 30, 1880, when it was combined with Park Street to form the present Robsart Street.

65 *Coldharbour Lane.* The probable route was along Loughborough Road to Lilford Road and thence to Coldharbour Lane (*see map*).

66 *sahib.* Hindu term of courtesy for a European gentleman.

67 *khitmutgar.* Hindu for butler or manservant.

68 *like a mountain-peak from fir-trees.* "It is of interest to find that Sholto's noteworthy cranium had its parallel elsewhere," Mr. T. S. Blakeney wrote in "Thoughts on *The Sign of the Four*." "Compare the description by the late Sir Arthur

AT LAST THE CAB DREW UP AT THE THIRD HOUSE IN A NEW TERRACE.

This photograph of No. 3, Milkwood Road—S.E. 24—the possible residence of Thaddeus Sholto—was taken by Mr. Humphrey Morton of the Sherlock Holmes Society of London. On the other hand, the late Robert R. Pattrick suggested that the house might have stood on the street known today as Dorchester Drive.

ster tentacles which the giant city was throwing out into the country. At last the cab drew up at the third house in a new terrace. None of the other houses were inhabited, and that at which we stopped was as dark as its neighbours, save for a single glimmer in the kitchen-window. On our knocking, however, the door was instantly thrown open by a Hindu servant, clad in a yellow turban, white, loose-fitting clothes, and a yellow sash. There was something strangely incongruous in this Oriental figure framed in the commonplace doorway of a third-rate suburban dwelling-house.

66   'The sahib awaits you,' said he, and even as he spoke there came a high, piping voice from some inner room.

67   'Show them in to me, khitmutgar,' it cried. 'Show them straight in to me.'

4 • THE STORY OF THE BALD-HEADED MAN

We followed the Indian down a sordid and common passage, ill-lit and worse furnished, until he came to a door upon the right, which he threw open. A blaze of yellow light streamed out upon us, and in the centre of the glare there stood a small man with a very high head, a bristle of red hair all round the fringe of it, and a bald, shining scalp which shot out from **68** among it like a mountain-peak from fir-trees. He writhed his hands together as he stood, and his features were in a perpetual jerk—now smiling, now scowling, but never for an instant in repose. Nature had given him a pendulous lip, and a too visible line of yellow and irregular teeth, which he strove feebly to conceal by constantly passing his hand over the lower part of his face. In spite of his obtrusive baldness, he gave the impression of youth. In point of fact, he had just turned his thirtieth year.

'Your servant, Miss Morstan,' he kept repeating, in a thin, high voice. 'Your servant, gentlemen. Pray step into my little sanctum. A small place, Miss, but furnished to my own liking. An oasis of art in the howling desert of South London.'

We were all astonished by the appearance of the apartment into which he invited us. In that sorry house it looked as out-of-place as a diamond of the first water in a setting of brass. The richest and glossiest of curtains and tapestries draped the walls, looped back here and there to expose some richly-mounted painting or Oriental vase. The carpet was of amber and black, so soft and so thick that the foot sank pleasantly into it, as into a bed of moss. Two great tiger-skins thrown athwart it increased the suggestion of Eastern luxury, as did a huge hookah which stood upon a mat in the corner. A lamp **69** in the fashion of a silver dove was hung from an almost invisible golden wire in the centre of the room. As it burned it filled the air with a subtle and aromatic odour.

'Mr Thaddeus Sholto,' said the little man, still jerking and smiling. 'That is my name. You are Miss Morstan, of course. And these gentlemen——'

'This is Mr Sherlock Holmes, and this Dr Watson.'

'A doctor, eh?' cried he, much excited. 'Have you your stethoscope? Might I ask you—would you have the kindness? I have grave doubts as to my mitral valve, if you would be so **70** very good. The aortic I may rely upon, but I should value **71** your opinion upon the mitral.'

I listened to his heart, as requested, but was unable to find anything amiss, save, indeed, that he was in an ecstasy of fear, for he shivered from head to foot.

'It appears to be normal,' I said. 'You have no cause for uneasiness.'

Conan Doyle (*Conan Doyle Stories*, 'The Leather Funnel,' p. 466) of Lionel Dacre, who had a 'huge, dome-like skull, which curved upward from amongst his thinning locks, *like a snow-peak above its fringe of fir-trees*.' I draw no conclusion from this resemblance of heads—I merely call attention to it.''

69 *hookah*. "Arabic word," the late Christopher Morley wrote in *Sherlock Holmes and Dr. Watson: A Textbook of Friendship*. "A tobacco pipe in which the smoke is inhaled through a long flexible tube which draws it through a bowl of perfumed water. Among Tenniel's famous illustrations in *Alice in Wonderland* (Chapter V) is a drawing of the Caterpillar smoking a hookah."

70 *mitral valve*. In the heart, the valve which guards the opening between the left auricle and the left ventricle, and prevents the blood in the ventricle from returning to the auricle.

71 *The aortic*. The valve which separates the left ventricle from the aorta, the great arterial trunk which carries blood from the heart to practically all parts of the body.

'MR. THADDEUS SHOLTO,' SAID THE LITTLE MAN . . .

Wrote Dr. Julian Wolff in his *Practical Handbook of Sherlockian Heraldry*: "In *The Private Life of Sherlock Holmes*, Vincent Starrett has a note that Watson's description of Thaddeus Sholto's house and conversation was the result of a meeting with Oscar Wilde. While no one will seriously state that Sholto was Wilde, himself, it does seem likely that he was very close to him. Students will immediately think of one Lord Alfred Douglas whose father was the eighth Marquess of Queensberry, John Sholto Douglas. It is not very difficult to deduce that Major John Sholto and his two sons may have been related to the Douglases and that they had similar arms, or the very same ones differenced.

"From *Burke's Peerage*: Quarterly: 1st and 4th, arg., a human heart, gu., imperially crowned, ppr.; on a chief, azure, three bullets of the field; 2nd and 3rd, az., a bend, between six cross-crosslets fitchée, or; all within a bordure, of the last, charged with the double tressure of Scotland. (The present illustration is taken from a facsimile of an old manuscript and shows a border engrailed gules instead of the one described—which pertains to the peerage, and would not be used by the major's family.)"

72 *I keep no other wines.* Chianti is a wine from the region of the Chianti Mountains in Tuscany, especially a dry red variety; Tokay is a moderately strong wine of a topaz color, produced in the vicinity of Tokay, in Hungary. The combination of the two is curious, as Mr. Cyrus Durgin pointed out in "The Speckled Band": "That, surely, is a strange combination of wines for household use, as occasional, social beverages. Chianti, which is a dry table wine, and does not keep well once the bottle is opened, is not likely to be found in Anglo-Saxon homes, up from the cellar and ready for drinking. . . . With Tokay, a sweeter and sometimes fortified wine, the matter is different. That could be a casual beverage for social amenity. I suppose the only conclusion is that a person who would keep only Tokay and Chianti—two wines very different in every respect—would necessarily be an eccentric person. I think we are entitled to assume, from the evidence of the narrative, that Mr. Thaddeus Sholto was indeed peculiar."

73 *a genuine Corot.* Jean Baptiste Camille Corot, 1796–1875, French landscape painter of the Barbizon School. Many of his paintings depict the misty hours before dawn, using mainly silvery grays and greens to create a very poetic effect.

74 *the Salvator Rosa.* Neapolitan painter, 1615–1673, famous for vigorous landscapes and spirited battle scenes.

75 *the Bourguereau.* Adolphe William Bouguereau, 1825–1905, French academic and sentimental painter. "This French painter was especially esteemed in the eighties and nineties," the late Christopher Morley wrote in *Sherlock Holmes and Dr. Watson: A Textbook of Friendship.* "His favorite subjects were religious and mythological; Mr. Sholto, as a man of refined tastes, would have been grieved to know that Bouguereau's *Nymphs and Faun* was for many years the most famous barroom painting in New York, at the old Hoffman House on Fifth Avenue."

76 *the modern French school.*' Sholto's statement, in terms of the artists he mentions, is somewhat questionable in the year 1888, fourteen years after the Impressionists had first shown in Paris. Mr. Ben Wolf ("Zero Wolf Meets Sherlock Holmes") has suggested that "Thaddeus would seem to have permitted his subscription to the *Gazette des Beaux Arts* to lapse some years earlier."

'You will excuse my anxiety, Miss Morstan,' he remarked, airily. 'I am a great sufferer, and I have long had suspicions as to that valve. I am delighted to hear that they are unwarranted. Had your father, Miss Morstan, refrained from throwing a strain upon his heart, he might have been alive now.'

I could have struck the man across the face, so hot was I at this callous and off-hand reference to so delicate a matter. Miss Morstan sat down, and her face grew white to the lips.

'I knew in my heart that he was dead,' said she.

'I can give you every information,' said he; 'and what is more, I can do you justice; and I will, too, whatever Brother Bartholomew may say. I am so glad to have your friends here, not only as an escort to you, but also as witnesses to what I am about to do and say. The three of us can show a bold front to Brother Bartholomew. But let us have no outsiders—no police or officials. We can settle everything satisfactorily among ourselves, without any interference. Nothing would annoy Brother Bartholomew more than any publicity.'

He sat down upon a low settee, and blinked at us inquiringly with his weak, watery blue eyes.

'For my part,' said Holmes, 'whatever you may choose to say will go no farther.'

I nodded to show my agreement.

'That is well! That is well!' said he. 'May I offer you a glass of Chianti, Miss Morstan? Or of Tokay? I keep no other **72** wines. Shall I open a flask? No? Well, then, I trust that you have no objection to tobacco smoke, to the balsamic odour of the Eastern tobacco. I am a little nervous, and I find my hookah an invaluable sedative.'

He applied a taper to the great bowl, and the smoke bubbled merrily through the rosewater. We sat all three in a semi-circle, with our heads advanced and our chins upon our hands, while the strange, jerky little fellow, with his high, shining head, puffed uneasily in the centre.

'When I first determined to make this communication to you,' said he, 'I might have given you my address; but I feared that you might disregard my request and bring unpleasant people with you. I took the liberty, therefore, of making an appointment in such a way that my man Williams might be able to see you first. I have complete confidence in his discretion, and he had orders, if he were dissatisfied, to proceed no further in the matter. You will excuse these precautions, but I am a man of somewhat retiring, and I might even say refined, tastes, and there is nothing more unæsthetic than a policeman. I have a natural shrinking from all forms of rough materialism. I seldom come in contact with the rough crowd. I live, as you see, with some little atmosphere of elegance around me. I may call myself a patron of the arts. **73** It is my weakness. The landscape is a genuine Corot, and, though a connoisseur might perhaps throw a doubt **74** upon that Salvator Rosa, there cannot be the least question **75** about the Bouguereau. I am partial to the modern French **76** school.'

'You will excuse me, Mr Sholto,' said Miss Morstan, 'but I am here at your request to learn something which you desire to tell me. It is very late, and I should desire the interview to be as short as possible.'

'At the best, it must take some time,' he answered; 'for we

shall certainly have to go to Norwood and see Brother Bartholomew. We shall all go and try if we can get the better of Brother Bartholomew. He is very angry with me for taking the course which has seemed right to me. I had quite high words with him last night. You cannot imagine what a terrible fellow he is when he is angry.'

'If we are to go to Norwood, it would perhaps be as well to start at once,' I ventured to remark.

He laughed until his ears were quite red.

'That would hardly do,' he cried. 'I don't know what he would say if I brought you in that sudden way. No, I must prepare you by showing you how we all stand to each other. In the first place, I must tell you that there are several points in the story of which I am myself ignorant. I can only lay the facts before you as far as I know them myself.

'My father was, as you may have guessed, Major John Sholto, once of the Indian Army. He retired some eleven years ago, and came to live at Pondicherry Lodge, in Upper Norwood. **77** He had prospered in India, and brought back with him a considerable sum of money, a large collection of valuable curiosities, and a staff of native servants. With these advantages he bought himself a house, and lived in great luxury. My twin-brother Bartholomew and I were the only children.

'I very well remember the sensation which was caused by the disappearance of Captain Morstan. We read the details in the papers, and knowing that he had been a friend of our father's, we discussed the case freely in his presence. He used to join in our speculations as to what could have happened. Never for an instant did we suspect that he had the whole secret hidden in his own breast, that of all men he alone knew the fate of Arthur Morstan.

'We did know, however, that some mystery, some positive danger, overhung our father. He was very fearful of going out alone, and he always employed two prize-fighters to act as porters at Pondicherry Lodge. Williams, who drove you to-night, was one of them. He was once light-weight champion of England. Our father would never tell us what it was he feared, but he had a most marked aversion to men with wooden legs. On one occasion he actually fired his revolver at a wooden-legged man, who proved to be a harmless tradesman canvassing for orders. We had to pay a large sum to hush the matter up. My brother and I used to think this a mere whim of my father's; but events have since led us to change our opinion.

'Early in 1882 my father received a letter from India which was a great shock to him. He nearly fainted at the breakfast-table when he opened it, and from that day he sickened to his death. What was in the letter we could never discover, but I could see as he held it that it was short and written in a scrawling hand. He had suffered for years from an enlarged spleen, but he now became rapidly worse, and towards the end of April we were informed that he was beyond all hope, **78** and that he wished to make a last communication to us.

'When we entered his room he was propped up with pillows and breathing heavily. He besought us to lock the door and to come upon either side of the bed. Then, grasping our hands, he made a remarkable statement to us, in a voice which was broken as much by emotion as by pain. I shall try and give it to you in his own very words.

77 *some eleven years ago*. Corroborating Mary's statement that Major Sholto "had retired some little time before" her father's death.

78 *towards the end of April*. Further evidence of the date of Sholto's decease.

79 *at this supreme moment.* "The standard of rectitude of the British (or Indian) Army officer in Holmes' day was regrettably low, judged by the types who flit across the screen," Mr. T. S. Blakeney wrote in "Thoughts on *The Sign of the Four*." Major Sholto "felt no compunction at being false to his charge as an officer commanding troops at Port Blair, though he had not only gambled himself to the verge of ruin, but had been ready to assist in the escape of four murderers in his care, only to double-cross them, and his confederate, Captain Morstan, in the end. Even his regrets about Miss Morstan were lip-service only—he urged his sons to do nothing for her in his life-time. He must have had a hardened conscience indeed! He is fit to run Milverton close as being the worst man in London. Incidentally, one would like to know how Captain Morstan managed about his debts. He had had 'a nasty facer,' and he never, apparently, had a convenient uncle to leave him a fortune, as Sholto did. It is of interest to note, also, that neither Miss Morstan nor Watson were in the least troubled at the idea of taking the best part of a quarter of a million pounds' worth of jewels, though she had not the slightest right to them."

' "I have only one thing," he said, "which weighs upon my **79** mind at this supreme moment. It is my treatment of poor Morstan's orphan. The cursed greed which has been my besetting sin through life has withheld from her the treasure, half at least of which should have been hers. And yet I have made no use of it myself, so blind and foolish a thing is avarice. The mere feeling of possession has been so dear to me that I could not bear to share it with another. See that chaplet tipped with pearls beside the quinine-bottle? Even that I could not bear to part with, although I had got it out with the design of sending it to her. You, my sons, will give her a fair share of the Agra treasure. But send her nothing—not even the chaplet—until I am gone. After all, men have been as bad as this and have recovered.

' "I will tell you how Morstan died," he continued. "He had suffered for years from a weak heart, but he concealed it from everyone. I alone knew it. When in India, he and I, through a remarkable chain of circumstances, came into possession of a considerable treasure. I brought it over to England, and on the night of Morstan's arrival he came straight over here to claim his share. He walked over from the station, and was admitted by my faithful old Lal Chowdar, who is now dead. Morstan and I had a difference of opinion as to the division of the treasure, and we came to heated words. Morstan had sprung out of his chair in a paroxysm of anger, when he suddenly pressed his hand to his side, his face turned a dusky hue, and he fell backwards, cutting his head against the corner of the treasure-chest. When I stooped over him I found, to my horror, that he was dead.

' "For a long time I sat half distracted, wondering what I should do. My first impulse was, of course, to call for assistance; but I could not but recognize that there was every chance that I would be accused of his murder. His death at the moment of a quarrel, and the gash in his head, would be black against me. Again, an official inquiry could not be made without bringing out some facts about the treasure, which I was particularly anxious to keep secret. He had told me that no soul upon earth knew where he had gone. There seemed to be no necessity why any soul ever should know.

' "I was still pondering over the matter, when, looking up, I saw my servant, Lal Chowdar, in the doorway. He stole in and bolted the door behind him. 'Do not fear, sahib,' he said; 'no one need know that you have killed him. Let us hide him away, and who is the wiser?' 'I did not kill him,' said I. Lal Chowdar shook his head and smiled. 'I heard it all, sahib,' said he; 'I heard you quarrel, and I heard the blow. But my lips are sealed. All are asleep in the house. Let us put him away together.' That was enough to decide me. If my own servant could not believe my innocence, how could I hope to make it good before twelve foolish tradesmen in a jury-box? Lal Chowdar and I disposed of the body that night, and within a few days the London papers were full of the mysterious disappearance of Captain Morstan. You will see from what I say that I can hardly be blamed in the matter. My fault lies in the fact that we concealed not only the body, but also the treasure, and that I have clung to Morstan's share as well as to my own. I wish you, therefore, to make restitution. Put your ears down to my mouth. The treasure is hidden in——"

'At this instant a horrible change came over his expression; his eyes stared wildly, his jaw dropped, and he yelled, in a voice which I can never forget, "Keep him out! For Christ's sake, keep him out!" We both stared round at the window behind us upon which his gaze was fixed. A face was looking in at us out of the darkness. We could see the whitening of the nose where it was pressed against the glass. It was a bearded, hairy face, with wild, cruel eyes and an expression of concentrated malevolence. My brother and I rushed towards the window, but the man was gone. When we returned to my father, his head had dropped and his pulse had ceased to beat.

'We searched the garden that night, but found no sign of the intruder, save that just under the window a single footmark was visible in the flower-bed. But for that one trace, we might have thought that our imaginations had conjured up that wild, fierce face. We soon, however, had another and a more striking proof that there were secret agencies at work all round us. The window of my father's room was found open in the morning, his cupboards and boxes had been rifled, and upon his chest was fixed a torn piece of paper, with the words, "The sign of the four," scrawled across it. What the phrase meant, or who our secret visitor may have been, we never knew. As far as we can judge, none of my father's property had been actually stolen, though everything had been turned out. My brother and I naturally associated this peculiar incident with the fear which haunted my father during his life; but it is still a complete mystery to us.'

The little man stopped to relight his hookah, and puffed thoughtfully for a few moments. We had all sat absorbed, listening to his extraordinary narrative. At the short account of her father's death Miss Morstan had turned deadly white, and for a moment I feared that she was about to faint. She rallied, however, on drinking a glass of water which I quietly poured out for her from a Venetian carafe upon the side-table. Sherlock Holmes leaned back in his chair with an abstracted expression and the lids drawn low over his glittering eyes. As I glanced at him I could not but think how, on that very day, he had complained bitterly of the commonplaceness of life. Here at least was a problem which would tax his sagacity to the utmost. Mr Thaddeus Sholto looked from one to the other of us with an obvious pride at the effect which his story had produced, and then continued, between the puffs of his overgrown pipe.

'My brother and I,' said he, 'were, as you may imagine, much excited as to the treasure which my father had spoken of. For weeks and for months we dug and delved in every part of the garden without discovering its whereabouts. It was maddening to think that the hiding-place was on his very lips at the moment that he died. We could judge the splendour of the missing riches by the chaplet which he had taken out. Over this chaplet my Brother Bartholomew and I had some little discussion. The pearls were evidently of great value, and he was averse to part with them, for, between friends, my brother was himself a little inclined to my father's fault. He thought, too, that if we parted with the chaplet it might give rise to gossip, and finally bring us into trouble. It was all that I could do to persuade him to let me find out Miss Morstan's address and send her a detached pearl at fixed intervals, so that at least she might never feel destitute.'

80 "Le mauvais goût mène au crime." "Bad taste leads to crime." The expression was coined by Le Baron de Mareste but was immortalized by Stendal (Henri Beyle, 1783–1842).

81 *a valetudinarian*.' A person of feeble or delicate health or constitution; an invalid; one subject to frequent illness.

82 *half a million sterling*.' £500,000, or about $2,500,000. Sterling, as applied to money values, means of standard mint and fineness.

'It was a kindly thought,' said our companion, earnestly; 'it was extremely good of you.'

The little man waved his hand deprecatingly.

'We were your trustees,' he said; 'that was the view which I took of it, though Brother Bartholomew could not altogether see it in that light. We had plenty of money ourselves. I desired no more. Besides, it would have been such bad taste to have treated a young lady in so scurvy a fashion. *"Le mau-* **80** *vais goût mène au crime."* The French have a very neat way of putting these things. Our difference of opinion on this subject went so far that I thought it best to set up rooms for myself; so I left Pondicherry Lodge, taking the old khitmutgar and Williams with me. Yesterday, however, I learn that an event of extreme importance has occurred. The treasure has been discovered. I instantly communicated with Miss Morstan, and it only remains for us to drive out to Norwood and demand our share. I explained my views last night to Brother Bartholomew, so we shall be expected, if not welcome, visitors.'

Mr Thaddeus Sholto ceased, and sat twitching on his luxurious settee. We all remained silent, with our thoughts upon the new development which the mysterious business had taken. Holmes was the first to spring to his feet.

'You have done well, sir, from first to last,' said he. 'It is possible that we may be able to make you some small return by throwing some light upon that which is still dark to you. But, as Miss Morstan remarked just now, it is late, and we had best put the matter through without delay.'

Our new acquaintance very deliberately coiled up the tube of his hookah, and produced from behind a curtain a very long, befrogged top-coat with astrakhan collar and cuffs. This he buttoned tightly up, in spite of the extreme closeness of the night, and finished his attire by putting on a rabbit-skin cap with hanging lappets which covered the ears, so that no part of him was visible save his mobile and peaky face.

'My health is somewhat fragile,' he remarked, as he led the way down the passage. 'I am compelled to be a valetudi- **81** narian.'

Our cab was awaiting us outside, and our programme was evidently prearranged, for the driver started off at once at a rapid pace. Thaddeus Sholto talked incessantly, in a voice which rose high above the rattle of the wheels.

'Bartholomew is a clever fellow,' said he. 'How do you think he found out where the treasure was? He had come to the conclusion that it was somewhere indoors: so he worked out all the cubic space of the house, and made measurements everywhere, so that not one inch should be unaccounted for. Among other things, he found that the height of the building was seventy-four feet, but on adding together the heights of all the separate rooms, and making every allowance for the space between, which he ascertained by borings, he could not bring the total to more than seventy feet. There were four feet unaccounted for. These could only be at the top of the building. He knocked a hole, therefore, in the lath and plaster ceiling of the highest room, and there, sure enough, he came upon another little garret above it, which had been sealed up and was known to no one. In the centre stood the treasure-chest, resting upon two rafters. He lowered it through the hole, and there it lies. He computes the value of the jewels **82** at not less than half a million sterling.'

At the mention of this gigantic sum we all stared at one another open-eyed. Miss Morstan, could we secure her rights, would change from a needy governess to the richest heiress in England. Surely it was the place of a loyal friend to rejoice at such news; yet I am ashamed to say that selfishness took me by the soul, and that my heart turned as heavy as lead within me. I stammered out some few halting words of congratulation, and then sat downcast, with my head drooped, deaf to the babble of our new acquaintance. He was clearly a confirmed hypochondriac, and I was dreamily conscious that he was pouring forth interminable trains of symptoms, and imploring information as to the composition and action of innumerable quack nostrums, some of which he bore about in a leather case in his pocket. I trust that he may not remember any of the answers which I gave him that night. Holmes declares that he overheard me caution him against the great danger of taking more than two drops of castor-oil, while I recommended strychnine in large doses as a sedative. How- **83** ever that may be, I was certainly relieved when our cab pulled up with a jerk and the coachman sprang down to open the door.

'This, Miss Morstan, is Pondicherry Lodge,' said Mr Thaddeus Sholto, as he handed her out.

5 • THE TRAGEDY OF PONDICHERRY LODGE

It was nearly eleven o'clock when we reached this final stage of our night's adventures. We had left the damp fog of the great city behind us, and the night was fairly fine. A warm wind blew from the westward, and heavy clouds moved slowly across the sky, with half a moon peeping occasionally through **84** the rifts. It was clear enough to see for some distance, but Thaddeus Sholto took down one of the side-lamps from the carriage to give us a better light upon our way.

Pondicherry Lodge stood in its own grounds, and was girt round with a very high stone wall topped with broken glass. A single narrow iron-clamped door formed the only means of entrance. On this our guide knocked with a peculiar postman-like rat-tat. **85**

'Who is there?' cried a gruff voice from within.

'It is I, McMurdo. You surely know my knock by this time.'

There was a grumbling sound and a clanking and jarring of keys. The door swung heavily back, and a short, deep-chested man stood in the opening, with the yellow light of the lantern shining upon his protruded face and twinkling, distrustful eyes.

'That you, Mr Thaddeus? But who are the others? I had no orders about them from the master.'

'No, McMurdo? You surprise me! I told my brother last night that I should bring some friends.'

'He hain't been out o' his room today, Mr Thaddeus, and I have no orders. You know very well that I must stick to regulations. I can let you in, but your friends they must just stop where they are.'

'THIS, MISS MORSTAN, IS PONDICHERRY LODGE' . . .

It must have been a house very similar to The Rookery, Streatham Common, shown here in an illustration from Michael Harrison's *In the Footsteps of Sherlock Holmes.*

83 *strychnine in large doses as a sedative.* Whether due to the Beaune or to the presence of Mary Morstan, it is quite clear that Watson on this Tuesday was far from his normal self.

84 *half a moon.* Further on, Watson says, "a moonbeam struck one corner and glimmered in a garret window," and Sholto says, "That is Bartholomew's window up there where the moonshine strikes." And later, when Watson is looking through the keyhole into the dead man's room, he says, "Moonlight was streaming into the room." A little later Watson says, "The moon still shone brightly on that angle of the house." There can, therefore, not be the least doubt that there was a moon visible in the London sky around 11:00 P.M. on the first night. But the words "streaming" and "brightly" make us doubt Watson's *half* a moon. For the record, the moon on Tuesday, September 18, 1888, was two days before the full; it rose at 5:55 P.M. and set at 3:12 A.M.

85 *postman-like rat-tat.* "The postman's double knock was traditional," the late Christopher Morley wrote in *Sherlock Holmes and Dr. Watson: A Textbook of Friendship:* "when the bells took the place of the old knocker it became a double ring. Hence James M. Cain's title, *The Postman Always Rings Twice.*"

86 *four ·years back?'* "It is a little difficult to accept this date," Mr. T. S. Blakeney wrote in *Sherlock Holmes: Fact or Fiction?*, "for if McMurdo joined Major Sholto's household as one of his two pugilist protectors, it must have been earlier than 1882, the year of Sholto's death. Bartholomew Sholto would hardly have engaged him, as he had no need for a protector, though naturally he would take over his father's servants, which accounts for McMurdo's presence at Pondicherry Lodge in 1888. The latter's benefit night (presumably when he retired from the ring) would have been just prior to his being engaged by Major Sholto on the latter's retirement from the Army—about 1877."

This was an unexpected obstacle. Thaddeus Sholto looked about him in a perplexed and helpless manner.

'This is too bad of you, McMurdo!' he said. 'If I guarantee them, that is enough for you. There is the young lady, too· She cannot wait on the public road at this hour.'

'Very sorry, Mr Thaddeus,' said the porter, inexorably. 'Folk may be friends o' yours, and yet no friends o' the master's. He pays me well to do my duty, and my duty I'll do. I don't know none o' your friends.'

'Oh, yes, you do, McMurdo,' cried Sherlock Holmes, genially. 'I don't think you can have forgotten me. Don't you remember the amateur who fought three rounds with you at **86** Alison's rooms on the night of your benefit four years back?'

'Not Mr Sherlock Holmes!' roared the prizefighter. 'God's truth! how could I have mistook you? If instead o' standin' there so quiet you had just stepped up and given me that cross-hit of yours under the jaw, I'd ha' known you without a question. Ah, you're one that has wasted your gifts, you have! You might have aimed high, if you had joined the fancy.'

'You see, Watson, if all else fails me, I have still one of the scientific professions open to me,' said Holmes, laughing. 'Our friend won't keep us out in the cold now, I am sure.'

'In you come, sir, in you come—you and your friends,' he answered. 'Very sorry, Mr Thaddeus, but orders are very strict. Had to be certain of your friends before I let them in.'

Inside, a gravel path wound through desolate grounds to a huge clump of a house, square and prosaic, all plunged in shadow save where a moonbeam struck one corner and glimmered in a garret window. The vast size of the building, with

"... THAT CROSS-HIT OF YOURS UNDER THE JAW ..."

"The right cross," the late H. T. Webster wrote in "Observations on Sherlock Holmes as an Athlete and Sportsman," "is . . . the characteristic Sunday punch of the tall rangy type of boxer. . . . This punch, to the head or body, is delivered straight from the shoulder but with a slight pivoting motion of the body which gives it something of the character of a hook. It is called a cross, because it must cross either over or under the opponent's left arm to land. It is the natural counter to a left jab, and unskilled boxers commonly leave themselves open to it when they begin to carry their lefts too far forward to serve as an effective guard. The fact that McMurdo says nothing about Holmes' left does not indicate that it was not a good one, but simply that in three rounds it had not yet given him much trouble. Very few left jabs in the history of the ring have been powerful enough to conquer rugged and skilled opposition in a few rounds. On the other hand, Holmes' left proved sufficiently formidable when applied to the features of a mere slogging ruffian like Roaring Jack Woodley ["The Adventure of the Solitary Cyclist"], who . . . had to be carried home in a cart. In general, then, we can reconstruct Holmes' boxing style as somewhat like that of Jem Mace, Jim Corbett, and Mike Gibbons. . . . He stood up straight in the classic style, used his extraordinary speed of foot to avoid the infighting which is likely to be troublesome to a man with a lightly armored body, staggered his opponent with a straight left, which was punishing but not lethal, and finished him with that powerful right cross."

its gloom and its deathly silence, struck a chill to the heart. Even Thaddeus Sholto seemed ill at ease, and the lantern quivered and rattled in his hand.

'I cannot understand it,' he said. 'There must be some mistake. I distinctly told Bartholomew that we should be here, and yet there is no light in his window. I do not know what to make of it.'

'Does he always guard the premises in this way?' asked Holmes.

'Yes, he has followed my father's custom. He was the favourite son, you know, and I sometimes think that my father may have told him more than he ever told me. That is Bartholomew's window up there where the moonshine strikes. It is quite bright, but there is no light from within, I think.'

'None,' said Holmes. 'But I see the glint of a light in that little window beside the door.'

'Ah, that is the housekeeper's room. That is where old Mrs Bernstone sits. She can tell us all about it. But perhaps you would not mind waiting here for a minute or two, for if we all go in together, and she has had no word of our coming, she may be alarmed. But, hush! what is that?'

He held up the lantern, and his hand shook until the circles of light flickered and wavered all round us. Miss Morstan seized my wrist, and we all stood, with thumping hearts, straining our ears. From the great black house there sounded through the silent night the saddest and most pitiful of sounds —the shrill, broken whimpering of a frightened woman.

'It is Mrs Bernstone,' said Sholto. 'She is the only woman in the house. Wait here. I shall be back in a moment.'

He hurried for the door, and knocked in his peculiar way. We could see a tall old woman admit him, and sway with pleasure at the very sight of him.

'Oh, Mr Thaddeus, sir, I am so glad you have come! I am so glad you have come, Mr Thaddeus, sir!'

We heard her reiterated rejoicings until the door was closed and her voice died away into a muffled monotone.

Our guide had left us the lantern. Holmes swung it slowly round, and peered keenly at the house, and at the great rubbish-heaps which cumbered the grounds. Miss Morstan and I stood together, and her hand was in mine. A wondrous subtle thing is love, for here were we two, who had never seen each other before that day, between whom no word or even look of affection had ever passed, and yet now in an hour of trouble our hands instinctively sought for each other. I have marvelled at it since, but at the time it seemed the most natural thing that I should go out to her so, and, as she has often told me, there was in her also the instinct to turn to me for comfort and protection. So we stood hand-in-hand, like two children, and there was peace in our hearts for all the dark things that surrounded us.

'What a strange place!' she said, looking round.

'It looks as though all the moles in England had been let loose in it. I have seen something of the sort on the side of a hill near Ballarat, where the prospectors had been at work.'

'And from the same cause,' said Holmes. 'These are the traces of the treasure-seekers. You must remember that they were six years looking for it. No wonder that the grounds **87** look like a gravel-pit.'

87 *six years looking for it*. Additional evidence that the year of *The Sign of the Four* is 1888, since Thaddeus and Bartholomew had been looking for the Agra treasure since the death of their father in April, 1882.

At that moment the door of the house burst open, and Thaddeus Sholto came running out, with his hands thrown forward and terror in his eyes.

'There is something amiss with Bartholomew!' he cried. 'I am frightened! My nerves cannot stand it.'

He was, indeed, half blubbering with fear, and his twitching, feeble face peeping out from the great astrakhan collar had the helpless, appealing expression of a terrified child.

'Come into the house,' said Holmes, in his crisp, firm way.

'Yes, do!' pleaded Thaddeus Sholto. 'I really do not feel equal to giving directions.'

We all followed him into the housekeeper's room, which stood upon the left-hand side of the passage. The old woman was pacing up and down with a scared look and restless, picking fingers, but the sight of Miss Morstan appeared to have a soothing effect upon her.

'God bless your sweet, calm face!' she cried, with an hysterical sob. 'It does me good to see you. Oh, but I have been sorely tried this day!'

Our companion patted her thin, work-worn hand, and murmured some few words of kindly, womanly comfort, which brought the colour back into the other's bloodless cheeks.

'Master has locked himself in, and will not answer me,' she explained. 'All day I have waited to hear from him, for he often likes to be alone; but an hour ago I feared that something was amiss, so I went up and peeped through the keyhole. You must go up, Mr Thaddeus—you must go up and look for yourself. I have seen Mr Bartholomew Sholto, in joy and in sorrow for ten long years, but I never saw him with such a face on him as that.'

Sherlock Holmes took the lamp and led the way, for Thaddeus Sholto's teeth were chattering in his head. So shaken was he that I had to pass my hand under his arm as we went up the stairs, for his knees were trembling under him. Twice as we ascended Holmes whipped his lens out of his pocket and carefully examined marks which appeared to me to be mere shapeless smudges of dust upon the coco-nut-matting which served as a stair-carpet. He walked slowly from step to step, holding the lamp low, and shooting keen glances to right and left. Miss Morstan had remained behind with the frightened housekeeper.

The third flight of stairs ended in a straight passage of some length, with a great picture in Indian tapestry upon the right of it and three doors upon the left. Holmes advanced along it in the same slow and methodical way, while we kept close at his heels, with our long, black shadows streaming backwards down the corridor. The third door was that which we were seeking. Holmes knocked without receiving any answer, and then tried to turn the handle and force it open. It was locked on the inside, however, and by a broad and powerful bolt, as we could see when we set our lamp up against it. The key being turned, however, the hole was not entirely closed. Sherlock Holmes bent down to it, and instantly rose again with a sharp intaking of the breath.

'There is something devilish in this, Watson,' said he, more moved than I had ever before seen him. 'What do you make of it?'

I stooped to the hole, and recoiled in horror. Moonlight

was streaming into the room, and it was bright with a vague and shifty radiance. Looking straight at me, and suspended, as it were, in the air, for all beneath was in shadow, there hung a face—the very face of our companion Thaddeus. There was the same high, shining head, the same circular bristle of red hair, the same bloodless countenance. The features were set, **88** however, in a horrible smile, a fixed and unnatural grin, which in that still and moonlit room was more jarring to the nerves than any scowl or contortion. So like was the face to that of our little friend that I looked round at him to make sure that he was indeed with us. Then I recalled to mind that he had mentioned to us that his brother and he were twins.

'This is terrible!' I said to Holmes. 'What is to be done?'

'The door must come down,' he answered, and, springing against it, he put all his weight upon the lock.

It creaked and groaned, but did not yield. Together we flung ourselves upon it once more, and this time it gave way with a sudden snap, and we found ourselves within Bartholomew Sholto's chamber.

It appeared to have been fitted up as a chemical laboratory. A double line of glass-stoppered bottles was drawn up upon the wall opposite the door, and the table was littered over with Bunsen burners, test-tubes, and retorts. In the corners stood carboys of acid in wicker baskets. One of these appeared to leak or to have been broken, for a stream of dark-coloured liquid had trickled out from it, and the air was heavy with a peculiarly pungent, tar-like odour. A set of steps stood at one side of the room, in the midst of a litter of lath and plaster, and above them there was an opening in the ceiling large enough for a man to pass through. At the foot of the steps a long coil of rope was thrown carelessly together.

By the table, in a wooden arm-chair, the master of the house was seated all in a heap, with his head sunk upon his left shoulder, and that ghastly, inscrutable smile upon his face. He was stiff and cold, and had clearly been dead many hours. It seemed to me that not only his features, but all his limbs, were twisted and turned in the most fantastic fashion. By his hand upon the table there lay a peculiar instrument—a brown, close-grained stick, with a stone head like a hammer, rudely lashed on with coarse twine. Beside it was a torn sheet of note-paper with some words scrawled upon it. Holmes glanced at it, and then handed it to me.

'You see,' he said, with a significant raising of the eyebrows.

In the light of the lantern I read, with a thrill of horror, 'The sign of the four.'

'In God's name, what does it all mean?' I asked.

'It means murder,' said he, stooping over the dead man. 'Ah! I expected it. Look here!'

He pointed to what looked like a long, dark thorn stuck in the skin just above the ear.

'It looks like a thorn,' said I.

'It is a thorn. You may pick it out. But be careful, for it is poisoned.'

I took it up between my finger and thumb. It came away from the skin so readily that hardly any mark was left behind. One tiny speck of blood showed where the puncture had been.

'This is all an insoluble mystery to me,' said I. 'It grows darker instead of clearer.'

'On the contrary,' he answered, 'it clears every instant. I

88 *the same circular bristle of red hair.* "This was an amazing identification," the late Professor Jay Finley Christ wrote in *An Irregular Chronology*. "The reader is invited to try to distinguish red hair from brown or even from black, by the light of a half-moon, while the observer is peering through a partially stopped key-hole. Let him try it in the open, too, if he likes."

BY THE TABLE, IN A WOODEN ARM-CHAIR, THE MASTER
OF THE HOUSE WAS SEATED . . .

Illustration by J. Watson Davis for *Tales of Sherlock Holmes*, New York: A. L. Burt Company, 1906.

IN THE LIGHT OF THE LANTERN I READ, WITH A THRILL OF HORROR, THE SIGN OF THE FOUR.

(*Above*) This pen-and-ink drawing by an unknown artist illustrated the first Dutch translation of *The Sign of the Four*, published some seventy years ago. (*Below*) Frontispiece by Charles Kerr for *The Sign of the Four*, London: Spencer Blackett, 1890. Of this illustration, the late James Montgomery wrote (*A Study in Pictures*) that it "presents Holmes and Watson to us, but one wishes that it didn't. . . . Watson's terrified face rivals that of the corpse, while the black smudge of a mustache under Holmes' . . . nose completes our disillusionment." Of this illustration, Mr. Vincent Starrett wrote in *The Private Life of Sherlock Holmes*: ". . . a competent but uninspired interpretation of the episode. . . . Just possibly the blot upon our Sherlock's lip is intended to indicate the shade cast by his prodigious nose; it looks, however, like a touch of a moustache. For the rest, there is something statuelike and dauntless in the carriage of the famous head; the legs are statesmanlike in their determined stance; and all in all—what with the somewhat epileptic corpse, and Watson—the picture is a trifle comic."

CHARLES KERR.

only require a few missing links to have an entirely connected case.'

We had almost forgotten our companion's presence since we entered the chamber. He was still standing in the doorway, the very picture of terror, wringing his hands and moaning to himself. Suddenly, however, he broke out into a sharp, querulous cry.

'The treasure is gone!' he said. 'They have robbed him of the treasure! There is the hole through which we lowered it. I helped him to do it! I was the last person who saw him! I left him here last night, and I heard him lock the door as I came downstairs.'

'What time was that?'

'It was ten o'clock. And now he is dead, and the police will be called in, and I shall be suspected of having had a hand in it. Oh, yes, I am sure I shall. But you don't think so, gentlemen? Surely, you don't think that it was I? Is it likely that I would have brought you here if it were I? Oh, dear! oh, dear! I know that I shall go mad!'

He jerked his arms and stamped his feet in a kind of convulsive frenzy.

'You have no reason for fear, Mr Sholto,' said Holmes, kindly, putting his hand upon his shoulder; 'take my advice, and drive down to the station to report the matter to the police. Offer to assist them in every way. We shall wait here until your return.'

The little man obeyed in a half-stupefied fashion, and we heard him stumbling down the stairs in the dark.

6 SHERLOCK HOLMES GIVES
   A DEMONSTRATION

'Now, Watson,' said Holmes, rubbing his hands, 'we have half an hour to ourselves. Let us make good use of it. My case is, as I have told you, almost complete; but we must not err on the side of over-confidence. Simple as the case seems now, there may be something deeper underlying it.'

'Simple!' I ejaculated.

'Surely,' said he, with something of the air of a clinical professor expounding to his class. 'Just sit in the corner there, that your footprints may not complicate matters. Now to work! In the first place, how did these folk come, and how did they go? The door has not been opened since last night. How of the window?' He carried the lamp across to it, muttering his observations aloud the while, but addressing them to himself rather than to me. 'Window is snibbed on the inner **89** side. Framework is solid. No hinges at the side. Let us open it. No water-pipe near. Roof quite out of reach. Yet a man has mounted by the window. It rained a little last night. Here is the print of a foot in mould upon the sill. And here is a circular muddy mark, and here again upon the floor, and here again by the table. See here, Watson! This is really a very pretty demonstration.'

I looked at the round, well-defined muddy disks.

'That is not a footmark,' said I.

'It is something much more valuable to us. It is the impression of a wooden stump. You see here on the sill is the boot-mark, a heavy boot with a broad metal heel, and beside it is the mark of the timber-toe.'

'It is the wooden-legged man.'

'Quite so. But there has been someone else—a very able and efficient ally. Could you scale that wall, doctor?'

I looked out of the open window. The moon still shone brightly on that angle of the house. We were a good sixty feet from the ground, and, look where I would, I could see no foothold, nor as much as a crevice in the brickwork.

'It is absolutely impossible,' I answered.

'Without aid it is so. But suppose you had a friend up here who lowered you this good stout rope which I see in the corner, securing one end of it to this great hook in the wall. Then, I think, if you were an active man, you might swarm up, wooden leg and all. You would depart, of course, in the same fashion, and your ally would draw up the rope, untie it from the hook, shut the window, snib it on the inside, and get away in the way that he originally came. As a minor point, it may be noted,' he continued, fingering the rope, 'that our wooden-legged friend, though a fair climber, was not a professional sailor. His hands were far from horny. My lens discloses more than one blood-mark, especially towards the end of the rope, from which I gather that he slipped down with such velocity that he took the skin off his hand.'

'This is all very well,' said I; 'but the thing becomes more unintelligible than ever. How about this mysterious ally? How came he into the room?'

'Yes, the ally!' repeated Holmes, pensively. 'There are features of interest about this ally. He lifts the case from the regions of the commonplace. I fancy that this ally breaks

89 *snibbed*. Fastened; bolted.

fresh ground in the annals of crime in this country—though parallel cases suggest themselves from India, and, if my memory serves me, from Senegambia.'

'How came he, then?' I reiterated. 'The door is locked; the window is inaccessible. Was it through the chimney?'

'The grate is much too small,' he answered. 'I had already considered that possibility.'

'How, then?' I persisted.

'You will not apply my precept,' he said, shaking his head. 'How often have I said to you that when you have eliminated the impossible, whatever remains, *however improbable,* must be the truth? We know that he did not come through the door, the window, or the chimney. We also know that he could not have been concealed in the room, as there is no concealment possible. Whence, then, did he come?'

'He came through the hole in the roof!' I cried.

'Of course he did. He must have done so. If you will have the kindness to hold the lamp for me, we shall now extend our researches to the room above—the secret room in which the treasure was found.'

He mounted the steps, and, seizing a rafter with either hand, he swung himself up into the garret. Then, lying on his face, he reached down for the lamp, and held it while I followed him.

The chamber in which we found ourselves was about ten feet one way and six the other. The floor was formed by the rafters, with thin lath and plaster between, so that in walking one had to step from beam to beam. The roof ran up to an apex, and was evidently the inner shell of the true roof to the house. There was no furniture of any sort, and the accumulated dust of years lay thick upon the floor.

'Here you are, you see,' said Sherlock Holmes, putting his hand against the sloping wall. 'This is a trap-door which leads out on to the roof. I can press it back, and here is the roof itself, sloping at a gentle angle. This, then, is the way by which Number One entered. Let us see if we can find some other traces of his individuality.'

He held down the lamp to the floor, and as he did so I saw for the second time that night a startled, surprised look come over his face. For myself, as I followed his gaze, my skin was cold under my clothes. The floor was covered thickly with the prints of a naked foot—clear, well-defined, perfectly formed, but scarce half the size of those of an ordinary man.

'Holmes,' I said, in a whisper, 'a child has done this horrid thing.'

He had recovered his self-possession in an instant.

'I was staggered for the moment,' he said, 'but the thing is quite natural. My memory failed me, or I should have been able to foretell it. There is nothing more to be learned here. Let us go down.'

'What is your theory, then, as to those footmarks?' I asked, eagerly, when we had regained the lower room once more.

'My dear Watson, try a little analysis yourself,' said he, with a touch of impatience. 'You know my methods. Apply them, and it will be instructive to compare results.'

'I cannot conceive anything which will cover the facts,' I answered.

'It will be clear enough to you soon,' he said, in an offhand way. 'I think that there is nothing else of importance here, but I will look.'

He whipped out his lens and a tape measure, and hurried about the room on his knees, measuring, comparing examining, with his long, thin nose only a few inches from the planks, and his beady eyes gleaming and deep-set like those of a bird. So swift, silent, and furtive were his movements, like those of a trained bloodhound picking out a scent, that I could not but think what a terrible criminal he would have made had he turned his energy and sagacity against the law instead of exerting them in its defence. As he hunted about he kept muttering to himself, and finally he broke out into a loud crow of delight.

'We are certainly in luck,' said he. 'We ought to have very little trouble now. Number One has had the misfortune to tread in the creosote. You can see the outline of the edge of his small foot here at the side of this evil-smelling mess. The carboy has been cracked, you see, and the stuff has leaked out.'

'What then?' I asked.

'Why, we have got him, that's all,' said he. 'I know a dog that would follow that scent to the world's end. If a pack can track a trailed herring across a shire, how far can a specially-trained hound follow so pungent a smell as this? It sounds like a sum in the rule of three. The answer should give us the **90** —— But, halloa! here are the accredited representatives of the law.'

Heavy steps and the clamour of loud voices were audible from below, and the hall door shut with a loud crash.

'Before they come,' said Holmes, 'just put your hand here on this poor fellow's arm, and here on his leg. What do you feel?'

'The muscles are as hard as a board,' I answered.

'Quite so. They are in a state of extreme contraction, far exceeding the usual *rigor mortis*. Coupled with this distortion of the face, this Hippocratic smile, or '*risus sardonicus*,' as the **91** old writers called it, what conclusion would it suggest to your mind?'

'Death from some powerful vegetable alkaloid,' I answered, 'some strychnine-like substance which would produce **92** tetanus.'

'That was the idea which occurred to me the instant I saw the drawn muscles of the face. On getting into the room I at once looked for the means by which the poison had entered the system. As you saw, I discovered a thorn which had been driven or shot with no great force into the scalp. You observe that the part struck was that which would be turned towards the hole in the ceiling if the man were erect in his chair. Now examine this thorn.'

I took it up gingerly and held it in the light of the lantern. It was long, sharp, and black, with a glazed look near the point as though some gummy substance had dried upon it. The blunt end had been trimmed and rounded off with a knife.

'Is that an English thorn?' he asked.

'No, it certainly is not.'

'With all these data you should be able to draw some just inference. But here are the regulars; so the auxiliary forces may beat a retreat.'

As he spoke, the steps which had been coming nearer sounded loudly on the passage, and a very stout, portly man in a grey suit strode heavily into the room. He was red-faced,

90 *the rule of three.* "I don't know whether the old name Rule of Three is still used in arithmetic," the late Christopher Morley wrote in *Sherlock Holmes and Dr. Watson: A Textbook of Friendship.* "It was applied to the principle that if three quantities of a proportion are known, the fourth can be determined; since the product of the means equals the product of the extremes. *Viz.*, if a:b::c:d, then ad $=$ bc, and a $= \dfrac{bc}{d}$."

91 *Hippocratic smile.* From Hippocrates, ancient Greek physician, *c.* 460–*c.* 370 B.C., who made the earliest recorded notes of many symptoms of disease and death.

92 '*some strychnine-like substance.* A remarkable example of Dr. Watson's quick ability to make an accurate diagnosis. As Dr. George B. Koelle has written in "The Poisons of the Canon": "The possibilities which suggest themselves include stophanthin (a cardiac drug similar to digitalis) and two central nervous system stimulants, picrotoxin and strychnine. The last mentioned drug is the more reasonable choice. It is a highly potent agent which is obtained from the fruit of a tree indigenous to Australia. It would be rapidly absorbed from a wound. Following a series of violent convulsions, it produces death by tonic respiratory paralysis. One of its most striking features is the *risus sardonicus*, or sardonic grin, which may remain on the face of the victim. This was dramatically exhibited to our friends when they discovered the corpse of . . . Sholto."

93 *Bishopgate*. Properly, *Bishopsgate*, a district in the City of London. The name may have been due to the liability of the Bishop of London in medieval times, to make the hinges of Bishopsgate, in return for which he was allowed to receive one stick from every cart laden with wood as it entered the City through the gate.

burly, and plethoric, with a pair of very small, twinkling eyes, which looked keenly out from between swollen and puffy pouches. He was closely followed by an inspector in uniform, and by the still palpitating Thaddeus Sholto.

'Here's a business!' he said, in a muffled, husky voice. 'Here's a pretty business! But who are all these? Why, the house seems to be as full as a rabbit-warren!'

'I think you must recollect me, Mr Athelney Jones,' said Holmes, quietly.

'Why, of course I do!' he wheezed. 'It's Mr Sherlock Holmes, the theorist. Remember you! I'll never forget how you lectured us all on causes and inferences and effects in the Bishop-
93 gate jewel case. It's true you set us on the right track; but you'll own now that it was more by good luck than good guidance.'

'It was a piece of very simple reasoning.'

'Oh, come, now, come! Never be ashamed to own up. But what is all this? Bad business! Bad business! Stern facts here —no room for theories. How lucky that I happened to be out at Norwood over another case! I was at the station when the message arrived. What d'you think the man died of?'

'Oh, this is hardly a case for me to theorize over,' said Holmes, drily.

'No, no. Still, we can't deny that you hit the nail on the head sometimes. Dear me! Door locked, I understand. Jewels worth half a million missing. How was the window?'

'Fastened; but there are steps on the sill.'

'Well, well, if it was fastened the steps could have nothing to do with the matter. That's common-sense. Man might have died in a fit; but then the jewels are missing. Ha! I have a theory. These flashes come upon me at times. Just step outside, sergeant, and you, Mr Sholto. Your friend can remain. What do you think of this, Holmes? Sholto was, on his own confession, with his brother last night. The brother died in a fit, on which Sholto walked off with the treasure! How's that?'

'On which the dead man very considerately got up and locked the door on the inside.'

'Hum! There's a flaw there. Let us apply common-sense to the matter. This Thaddeus Sholto *was* with his brother; there *was* a quarrel: so much we know. The brother is dead and the jewels are gone. So much also we know. No one saw the brother from the time Thaddeus left him. His bed had not been slept in. Thaddeus is evidently in a most disturbed state of mind. His appearance is—well, not attractive. You see that I am weaving my web round Thaddeus. The net begins to close upon him.'

'You are not quite in possession of the facts yet,' said Holmes. 'This splinter of wood, which I have every reason to believe to be poisoned, was in the man's scalp where you still see the mark; this card, inscribed as you see it, was on the table, and beside it lay this rather curious stone-headed instrument. How does all that fit into your theory?'

'Confirms it in every respect,' said the fat detective, pompously. 'House is full of Indian curiosities. Thaddeus brought this up, and if this splinter be poisonous, Thaddeus may as well have made murderous use of it as any other man. The card is some hocus-pocus—a blind, as like as not. The only question is, how did he depart? Ah, of course, here is a hole in the roof.'

With great activity, considering his bulk, he sprang up the steps and squeezed through into the garret, and immediately afterwards we heard his exulting voice proclaiming that he had found the trap-door.

'He can find something,' remarked Holmes, shrugging his shoulders; 'he has occasional glimmerings of reason. *Il n'y a pas des sots si incommodes que ceux qui ont de l'esprit!*' **94**

'You see!' said Athelney Jones, reappearing down the steps again; 'facts are better than theories, after all. My view of the case is confirmed. There is a trap-door communicating with the roof, and it is partly open.'

'It was I who opened it.'

'Oh, indeed! You did notice it, then?' He seemed a little crestfallen at the discovery. 'Well, whoever noticed it, it shows how our gentleman got away. Inspector!'

'Yes, sir,' from the passage.

'Ask Mr Sholto to step this way.—Mr Sholto, it is my duty to inform you that anything which you may say will be used against you. I arrest you in the Queen's name as being concerned in the death of your brother.'

'There, now! Didn't I tell you?' cried the poor little man, throwing out his hands, and looking from one to the other of us.

'Don't trouble yourself about it, Mr Sholto,' said Holmes; 'I think that I can engage to clear you of the charge.'

'Don't promise too much, Mr Theorist, don't promise too much!' snapped the detective. 'You may find it a harder matter than you think.'

'Not only will I clear him, Mr Jones, but I will make you a free present of the name and description of one of the two people who were in this room last night. His name, I have every reason to believe, is Jonathan Small. He is a poorly educated man, small, active, with his right leg off, and wearing a wooden stump which is worn away upon the inner side. His left boot has a coarse, square-toed sole, with an iron band round the heel. He is a middle-aged man, much sunburned, and has been a convict. These few indications may be of some assistance to you, coupled with the fact that there is a good deal of skin missing from the palm of his hand. The other man——'

'Ah! the other man?' asked Athelney Jones, in a sneering voice, but impressed none the less, as I could easily see, by the precision of the other's manner.

'Is a rather curious person,' said Sherlock Holmes, turning upon his heel. 'I hope before very long to be able to introduce you to the pair of them. A word with you, Watson.'

He led me out to the head of the stair.

'This unexpected occurrence,' he said, 'has caused us rather to lose sight of the original purpose of our journey.'

'I have just been thinking so,' I answered; 'it is not right that Miss Morstan should remain in this stricken house.'

'No. You must escort her home. She lives with Mrs Cecil Forrester, in Lower Camberwell, so it is not very far. I will wait for you here if you will drive out again. Or perhaps you are too tired?'

'By no means. I don't think I could rest until I know more of this fantastic business. I have seen something of the rough side of life, but I give you my word that this quick succession of strange surprises tonight has shaken my nerve completely.

94 Il n'y a pas des sots si incommodes que ceux qui ont de l'esprit. "This is Number 451 of *Les Maximes* by François Duc de la Rochefoucauld, 1613–1680," Mr. Morris Rosenblum wrote in "Foreign Language Quotations in the Canon." "Holmes made one minor change which does not affect the meaning: the original has *point* instead of *pas*. The usual translation is, 'There are no fools so troublesome as those who have some wit.'"

95 *Lambeth.* "On crossing Westminster Bridge we are in Lambeth, originally a swamp, traversed by the great Roman road to Newhaven, now densely populated, and covered with a labyrinth of featureless streets and poverty-stricken courts," Augustus J. C. Hare wrote in *Walks in London*, Vol. II. "The name, by doubtful etymology, is derived from Lamb-hithe, a landing-place for sheep."

96 "Wir sind gewohnt dass die Menschen verhöhnen was sie nicht verstehen." "Bayard Taylor's translation is, 'We are used to see that Man despises what he never comprehends,'" Mr. Morris Rosenblum wrote in "Foreign Language Quotations in the Canon." "The quotation is taken from *Faust, Part I*, and is found in the monologue by Faust when he addresses the Poodle in the Study-Room. Watson or his printers were at fault in not setting up the lines in their original poetic form:

Wir sind gewohnt, dass die Menschen verhöhnen
Was sie nicht verstehen."

97 *Goethe.* Johann Wolfgan von Goethe, 1749–1832, German poet, dramatist, novelist, scientist. "Is it not permissible to conclude that a set of Goethe's *Poetische and Prosaische Werke* (Stuttgart & Tübingen, 1836–1873) stood [on the Holmes bookshelf]?" Miss Madeleine B. Stern asked in "Sherlock Holmes: Rare Book Collector."

I should like, however, to see the matter through with you, now that I have got so far.'

'Your presence will be of great service to me,' he answered. 'We shall work the case out independently, and leave this fellow Jones to exult over any mare's-nest which he may choose to construct. When you have dropped Miss Morstan, I wish you to go to No. 3, Pinchin Lane, down near the water's **95** edge at Lambeth. The third house on the right-hand side is a bird-stuffer's; Sherman is the name. You will see a weasel holding a young rabbit in the window. Knock old Sherman up, and tell him, with my compliments, that I want Toby at once. You will bring Toby back in the cab with you.'

'A dog, I suppose?'

'Yes, a queer mongrel, with a most amazing power of scent. I would rather have Toby's help than that of the whole detective force of London.'

'I shall bring him then,' said I. 'It is one now. I ought to be back before three, if I can get a fresh horse.'

'And I,' said Holmes, 'shall see what I can learn from Mrs Bernstone, and from the Indian servant, who, Mr Thaddeus tells me, sleeps in the next garret. Then I shall study the great Jones's methods and listen to his not too delicate sarcasms. *"Wir sind gewohnt dass die Menschen verhöhnen was sie* **96 – 97** *nicht verstehen."* Goethe is always pithy.'

◆
7 ◆ THE EPISODE OF THE BARREL
◆

The police had brought a cab with them, and in this I escorted Miss Morstan back to her home. After the angelic fashion of women, she had borne trouble with a calm face as long as there was someone weaker than herself to support, and I had found her bright and placid by the side of the frightened housekeeper. In the cab, however, she first turned faint, and then burst into a passion of weeping—so sorely had she been tried by the adventures of the night. She has told me since that she thought me cold and distant upon that journey. She little guessed the struggle within my breast, or the effort of self-restraint which held me back. My sympathies and my love went out to her, even as my hand had in the garden. I felt that years of the conventionalities of life could not teach me to know her sweet, brave nature as had this one day of strange experiences. Yet there were two thoughts which sealed the words of affection upon my lips. She was weak and helpless, shaken in mind and nerve. It was to take her at a disadvantage to obtrude love upon her at such a time. Worse still, she was rich. If Holmes's researches were successful, she would be an heiress. Was it fair, was it honourable, that a half-pay surgeon should take such advantage of an intimacy which chance had brought about? Might she not look upon me as a mere vulgar fortune-seeker? I could not bear to risk that such a thought should cross her mind. This Agra treasure intervened like an impassable barrier between us.

It was nearly two o'clock when we reached Mrs Cecil Forrester's. The servants had retired hours ago, but Mrs Forrester had been so interested by the strange message which Miss Morstan had received that she had sat up in the hope of her return. She opened the door herself, a middle-aged, graceful woman, and it gave me joy to see how tenderly her arm stole round the other's waist, and how motherly was the voice in which she greeted her. She was clearly no mere paid dependent, but an honoured friend. I was introduced, and Mrs Forrester earnestly begged me to step in and to tell her our adventures. I explained, however, the importance of my errand, and promised faithfully to call and report any progress which we might make with the case. As we drove away I stole a glance back, and I still seem to see that little group on the step—the two graceful, clinging figures, the half-opened door, the hall-light shining through stained glass, the barometer, and the bright stair-rods. It was soothing to **98** catch even that passing glimpse of a tranquil English home **99** in the midst of the wild, dark business which had absorbed us.

And the more I thought of what had happened, the wilder and darker it grew. I reviewed the whole extraordinary sequence of events as I rattled on through the silent, gas-lit streets. There was the original problem: that, at least, was pretty clear now. The death of Captain Morstan, the sending of the pearls, the advertisement, the letter—we had had light upon all those events. They had only led us, however, to a deeper and far more tragic mystery. The Indian treasure, the curious plan found among Morstan's baggage, the strange scene at Major Sholto's death, the rediscovery of the treasure immediately followed by the murder of the discoverer, the very singular accompaniments to the crime, the footsteps, the remarkable weapons, the words upon the card, corresponding with those upon Captain Morstan's chart—here was, indeed, a labyrinth in which a man less singularly endowed than my fellow-lodger might well despair of ever finding the clue.

Pinchin Lane was a row of shabby, two-storied brick houses in the lower quarter of Lambeth. I had to knock for some time at No. 3 before I could make any impression. At last, however, there was the glint of a candle behind the blind, and a face looked out at the upper window.

'Go on, you drunken vagabond,' said the face. 'If you kick up any more row, I'll open the kennels and let out forty-three dogs upon you.'

'If you'll let one out, it's just what I have come for,' said I.

'Go on!' yelled the voice. 'So help me gracious, I have a wiper in this bag, an' I'll drop it on your 'ead if you don't hook it!'

'But I want a dog,' I cried.

'I won't be argued with!' shouted Mr Sherman. 'Now, stand clear; for when I say "Three," down goes the wiper.'

'Mr Sherlock Holmes——' I began; but the words had a most magical effect, for the window instantly slammed down, and within a minute the door was unbarred and open. Mr Sherman was a lanky, lean old man, with stooping shoulders, a stringy neck, and blue-tinted glasses.

'A friend of Mr Sherlock is always welcome,' said he. 'Step **100** in, sir. Keep clear of the badger, for he bites. Ah, naughty, naughty! would you take a nip at the gentleman?' This to a

98 *the bright stair-rods.* These were not handrails, as some Americans might think, but the brass rods designed to hold the stair carpet in place; still found in many English homes.

99 *a tranquil English home.* "I like to think," the late Christopher Morley wrote in "Dr. Watson's Secret," "that Mrs. Forrester's 'tranquil English home,' with the stained glass in the front door, the barometer and the bright stair-rods, was in Knatchbull Road, Camberwell, for which Boucicault named the villain in *After Dark.*"

100 '*A friend of Mr. Sherlock.* Mr. Sherman's "claim to our attention lies in the fact that, with the exception of brother Mycroft, he is the only person ever to refer to Holmes by his Christian name, albeit prefixed by the respectful 'Mister,'" Mr. Bernard Davies wrote in "Was Holmes a Londoner?" "In the eighties there was an animal dealer in Lower Kensington Lane, very close to the water's edge and within a stone's throw of Knight's Place, who might easily be the original of Mr. Sherman . . ." Your editor and other commentators have taken this as additional evidence that Sherlock Holmes spent at least a part of his boyhood in the South of London: "We can picture him now, a thin, eager youth helping the old man with the skinning, making impressions of bird and animal tracks in plaster of Paris, bursting with questions about the poisonous effects of vipers and swamp adders" (*Sherlock Holmes of Baker Street*). Clearly Charles Dickens also knew old Sherman well, for he used him as the basis for Mr. Venus in *Our Mutual Friend* which began to appear in serial form at just about this time.

101 *half spaniel and half lurcher.* "The lurcher being a cross between a collie and a greyhound, there are actually three 'halves' involved here," Mr. Stuart Palmer wrote in his "Notes on Certain Evidences of Caniphobia in Mr. Sherlock Holmes and His Associates." The lurcher is usually classified with the sporting group of dogs, whose forte is to lie in wait for and seize game, and not with the hounds, whose forte is tracking. "Toby's abilities are [therefore] very unusual, and must be attributed to the excellent training given him by his owner, Sherman, the bird-stuffer," Mrs. Eleanor S. Cole wrote in "Holmes, Watson and the K-9's."

102 *a lump of sugar.* "Surely proving that the good doctor (and the old naturalist, evidently) knew nothing of what sugar does to a dog's teeth and stomach," Mr. Palmer added.

103 *the Palace clock.* What Watson evidently thought he heard was the clock on the *Crystal* Palace, which, until it burned down, stood on Sydenham Hill. But Watson was in error, as Mr. Humfrey Michell pointed out in "The Palace Clock," "since there was no chiming clock at the 'Palace.' What he undoubtedly heard was the clock on the tower of the School for the Blind in Upper Norwood, which, for the benefit of those who could not see, struck the quarters, halves and hours in very resonant tones audible over a wide area."

104 *your bull's-eye.* Holmes is asking for the loan of the sergeant's lantern.

105 *this bit of card.* For "card" read "cord." This typographical error has persisted through many printings of the Saga.

stoat, which thrust its wicked head and red eyes between the bars of its cage. 'Don't mind that, sir; it's only a slow-worm. It hain't got no fangs, so I gives it the run o' the room, for it keeps the beetles down. You must not mind my bein' just a little short wi' you at first, for I'm guyed at by the children, and there's many a one just comes down this lane to knock me up. What was it that Mr Sherlock Holmes wanted, sir?'

'He wanted a dog of yours.'

'Ah! that would be Toby.'

'Yes, "Toby" was the name.'

'Toby lives at No. 7 on the left here.'

He moved slowly forward with his candle among the queer animal family which he had gathered round him. In the uncertain, shadowy light I could see dimly that there were glancing, glimmering eyes peeping down at us from every cranny and corner. Even the rafters above our heads were lined by solemn fowls, who lazily shifted their weight from one leg to the other as our voices disturbed their slumbers.

Toby proved to be an ugly, long-haired, lop-eared creature, **101** half spaniel and half lurcher, brown and white in colour, with a very clumsy, waddling gait. It accepted, after some **102** hesitation, a lump of sugar which the old naturalist handed to me, and, having thus sealed an alliance, it followed me to the cab, and made no difficulties about accompanying me. It **103** had just struck three on the Palace clock when I found myself back once more at Pondicherry Lodge. The ex-prizefighter McMurdo had, I found, been arrested as an accessory, and both he and Mr Sholto had been marched off to the station. Two constables guarded the narrow gate, but they allowed me to pass with the dog on my mentioning the detective's name.

Holmes was standing on the doorstep, with his hands in his pockets, smoking his pipe.

'Ah, you have him there!' said he. 'Good dog, then! Athelney Jones has gone. We have had an immense display of energy since you left. He has arrested not only friend Thaddeus, but the gatekeeper, the housekeeper, and the Indian servant. We have the place to ourselves, but for a sergeant upstairs. Leave the dog here and come up.'

We tied Toby to the hall table, and reascended the stairs. The room was as we had left it, save that a sheet had been draped over the central figure. A weary-looking police-sergeant reclined in the corner.

104 'Lend me your bull's-eye, sergeant,' said my companion.
105 'Now tie this bit of card round my neck, so as to hang it in front of me. Thank you. Now I must kick off my boots and stockings. Just you carry them down with you, Watson. I am going to do a little climbing. And dip my handkerchief into the creosote. That will do. Now come up into the garret with me for a moment.'

We clambered up through the hole. Holmes turned his light once more upon the footsteps in the dust.

'I wish you particularly to notice these footmarks,' he said. 'Do you observe anything noteworthy about them?'

'They belong,' I said, 'to a child or a small woman.'

'Apart from their size, though. Is there nothing else?'

'They appear to be much as other footmarks.'

'Not at all. Look here! This is the print of a right foot in the dust. Now I make one with my naked foot beside it. What is the chief difference?'

'Your toes are all cramped together. The other print has each toe distinctly divided.'

'Quite so. That is the point. Bear that in mind. Now, would you kindly step over to that flap-window and smell the edge of the wood-work? I shall stay over here, as I have this handkerchief in my hand.'

I did as he directed, and was instantly conscious of a strong tarry smell.

'That is where he put his foot in getting out. If *you* can trace him, I should think that Toby will have no difficulty. Now run downstairs, loose the dog, and look out for Blondin.' **106**

By the time that I got out into the grounds Sherlock Holmes was on the roof, and I could see him like an enormous glow-worm crawling very slowly along the ridge. I lost sight of him behind a stack of chimneys, but he presently reappeared, and then vanished once more upon the opposite side. When I made my way round there I found him seated at one of the corner eaves.

'That you, Watson?' he cried.

'Yes.'

'This is the place. What is that black thing down there?'

'A water-barrel.'

'Top on it?'

'Yes.'

'No sign of a ladder?'

'No.'

'Confound the fellow! It's a most breakneck place. I ought to be able to come down where he could climb up. The water-pipe feels pretty firm. Here goes, anyhow.'

There was a scuffling of feet, and the lantern began to come steadily down the side of the wall. Then with a light spring he came on to the barrel, and from there to the earth.

'It was easy to follow him,' he said, drawing on his stockings and boots. 'Tiles were loosened the whole way along, and in his hurry he had dropped this. It confirms my diagnosis, as you doctors express it.'

The object which he held up to me was a small pocket or pouch woven out of coloured grasses, and with a few tawdry beads strung round it. In shape and size it was not unlike a cigarette-case. Inside were half-a-dozen spines of dark wood, sharp at one end and rounded at the other, like that which had struck Bartholomew Sholto.

'They are hellish things,' said he. 'Look out that you don't prick yourself. I'm delighted to have them, for the chances are that they are all he has. There is the less fear of you or me finding one in our skin before long. I would sooner face a Martini bullet myself. Are you game for a six-mile trudge, **107** Watson?'

'Certainly,' I answered.

'Your leg will stand it?'

'Oh, yes.'

'Here you are, doggy! Good old Toby! Smell it, Toby, smell it!' He pushed the creosote handkerchief under the dog's nose, while the creature stood with its fluffy legs separated, and with a most comical cock to its head, like a connoisseur sniffing the *bouquet* of a famous vintage. Holmes then threw the handkerchief to a distance, fastened a stout cord to the mongrel's collar, and led him to the foot of the water-barrel.

106 *Blondin.*' Holmes compares himself to Charles Blondin, 1824–1897, the French acrobat who crossed Niagara Falls on a tightrope in 1855, 1859, and 1860. His real name was Jean François Gravelet.

107 *a Martini bullet.* A bullet from a type of rifle used at that time by the British Army.

108 *The east had been gradually whitening.* A statement of Watson's used by many chronologists to refute the "July" of the postmark on Thaddeus Sholto's letter to Mary Morstan. In July there is no real night in England until after the 20th of the month. In September, on the other hand, day breaks at 3:09 A.M. on the first, at approximately 3:37 A.M. on the fifteenth, and a few minutes after 4:00 A.M. on the thirtieth.

109 *eight-and-twenty hours' start.'* Jonathan Small had a wooden leg. He was "utterly unable to reach the lofty room of Bartholomew Sholto." But he was an active, healthy man of fifty or thereabouts who had led "a hard, open-air life." He scaled the wall bounding Pondicherry Lodge; he later "sprang" out of the *Aurora* when she buried her bow in a mudbank. A six-mile walk in two hours would have been well within the capabilities of such a man, desperately anxious to reach his destination. Small and his companion would therefore have left Pondicherry Lodge around one o'clock Tuesday morning, since we are later told that they reached their destination "about three." It is apparent, then, that they could not have left Pondicherry Lodge later than 1:00 A.M. on the Tuesday morning. Holmes and Watson therefore left Pondicherry Lodge around five o'clock on the Wednesday morning.

The creature instantly broke into a succession of high, tremulous yelps, and, with his nose on the ground, and his tail in the air, pattered off upon the trail at a pace which strained his leash and kept us at the top of our speed.

108 The east had been gradually whitening, and we could now see some distance in the cold, grey light. The square, massive house, with its black, empty windows and high, bare walls, towered up, sad and forlorn, behind us. Our course led right across the grounds, in and out among the trenches and pits with which they were scarred and intersected. The whole place, with its scattered dirt-heaps and ill-grown shrubs, had a blighted, ill-omened look which harmonized with the black tragedy which hung over it.

On reaching the boundary wall Toby ran along, whining eagerly, underneath its shadow, and stopped finally in a corner screened by a young beech. Where the two walls joined, several bricks had been loosened, and the crevices left were worn down and rounded upon the lower side, as though they had frequently been used as a ladder. Holmes clambered up, and, taking the dog from me, he dropped it over upon the other side.

'There's the print of wooden-leg's hand,' he remarked, as I mounted up beside him. 'You see the slight smudge of blood upon the white plaster. What a lucky thing it is that we have had no very heavy rain since yesterday! The scent will lie upon the road in spite of their eight-and-twenty hours' **109** start.'

I confess that I had my doubts myself when I reflected upon the great traffic which had passed along the London road in the interval. My fears were soon appeased, however. Toby never hesitated or swerved, but waddled on in his peculiar rolling fashion. Clearly, the pungent smell of the creosote rose high above all other contending scents.

'Do not imagine,' said Holmes, 'that I depend for my success in this case upon the mere chance of one of these fellows having put his foot in the chemical. I have knowledge now which would enable me to trace them in many different ways. This, however, is the readiest, and, since fortune has put it into our hands, I should be culpable if I neglected it. It has, however, prevented the case from becoming the pretty little intellectual problem which it at one time promised to be. There might have been some credit to be gained out of it, but for this too palpable clue.'

'There is credit, and to spare,' said I. 'I assure you, Holmes, that I marvel at the means by which you obtain your results in this case, even more than I did in the Jefferson Hope murder. The thing seems to me to be deeper and more inexplicable. How, for example, could you describe with such confidence the wooden-legged man?'

'Pshaw, my dear boy! it was simplicity itself. I don't wish to be theatrical. It is all patent and above-board. Two officers who are in command of a convict guard learn an important secret as to buried treasure. A map is drawn for them by an Englishman named Jonathan Small. You remember that we saw the name upon the chart in Captain Morstan's possession. He had signed it in behalf of himself and his associates—the sign of the four, as he somewhat dramatically called it. Aided by this chart, the officers—or one of them—gets the treasure and brings it to England, leaving, we will suppose, some condition under which he received it unfulfilled. Now, then, why did not Jonathan Small get the treasure himself? The answer is obvious. The chart is dated at a time when Morstan was brought into close association with convicts. Jonathan Small did not get the treasure because he and his associates were themselves convicts and could not get away.'

'But this is mere speculation,' said I.

'It is more than that. It is the only hypothesis which covers the facts. Let us see how it fits in with the sequel. Major Sholto remains at peace for some years, happy in the possession of his treasure. Then he receives a letter from India which gives him a great fright. What was that?'

'A letter to say that the men whom he had wronged had been set free.'

'Or had escaped. That is much more likely, for he would have known what their term of imprisonment was. It would not have been a surprise to him. What does he do then? He guards himself against a wooden-legged man—a white man, mark you, for he mistakes a white tradesman for him, and actually fires a pistol at him. Now, only one white man's name is on the chart. The others are Hindus or Mohammedans. There is no other white man. Therefore, we may say with confidence that the wooden-legged man is identical with Jonathan Small. Does the reasoning strike you as being faulty?'

'No: it is clear and concise.'

'Well, now, let us put ourselves in the place of Jonathan Small. Let us look at it from his point of view. He comes to England with the double idea of regaining what he would consider to be his rights, and of having his revenge upon the man who had wronged him. He found out where Sholto lived, and very possibly he established communications with someone inside the house. There is this butler, Lal Rao, whom we have not seen. Mrs Bernstone gives him far from a good character. Small could not find out, however, where the treasure was hid, for no one ever knew, save the major and one faithful servant who had died. Suddenly, Small learns that the major is on his death-bed. In a frenzy lest the secret of the treasure die with him, he runs the gauntlet of the guards, makes his way to the dying man's window, and is only deterred from entering by the presence of his two sons. Mad with hate, however, against the dead man, he enters the room that night, searches his private papers in the hope of discovering some memorandum relating to the treasure, and finally leaves a memento of his visit in the short inscription upon the card. He had doubtless planned beforehand that, should he slay the major, he would leave some such record upon the body as a sign that it was not a common murder, but, from the point of view of the four associates, something in the nature of an act of justice. Whimsical and bizarre conceits of this kind are common enough in the annals of crime, and usually afford valuable indications as to the criminal. Do you follow all this?'

'Very clearly.'

'Now, what could Jonathan Small do? He could only continue to keep a secret watch upon the efforts made to find the treasure. Possibly he leaves England and only comes back at intervals. Then comes the discovery of the garret, and he is instantly informed of it. We again trace the presence of some

110 *a damaged* tendo Achillis.' Or heel cord, lying immediately under the skin. As the late Dr. Roland Hammond pointed out in "The Attempted Mayhem of 'Silver Blaze,'" this tissue is formed by the conjoined tendons of the gastrocnemius and soleus muscles which form the calf of the leg.

111 *Now the red rim of the sun pushes itself over the London cloud-bank.* Holmes and Watson left Pondicherry Lodge around five o'clock on the Wednesday morning, as we have seen; within an hour at most of their leave-taking the sun rose. The sun on this Wednesday morning therefore rose between 5:30 and 6:00 A.M. The Wednesday we know was a fine, clear day, as evidenced by Holmes' "one little cloud floats like a pink feather . . ." On Wednesday, September 19, 1888, the weather, according to the London *Times*, was "fine generally. . . . Fair weather has prevailed today in all districts." Day broke at 3:45 A.M.; the sun rose at 5:44 A.M.

112 *Jean Paul?'* The pseudonym of J. P. F. Richter, 1763–1825, a German writer who had a great vogue in the early nineteenth century. The association with Carlyle is obvious: it was Carlyle who introduced Jean Paul's works to English readers. "Is it not permissible to conclude," Miss Madeleine B. Stern wrote in "Sherlock Holmes: Rare Book Collector," "that . . . Jean Paul's *Herbst-Blumine* (Tübingen, 1810–1820) [stood] on the Holmes' bookshelf? . . . It is likely that Holmes also owned a copy of the London 1867 edition of De Quincey's *Confessions of an English Opium-Eater*—an edition to which are added *Analects of Jean Paul Richter*. Among the analects is one on 'The Grandeur of Man in His Littleness,' a concept to which Holmes referred during his work on *The Sign of the Four*."

113 *having loaded two of the chambers.* "Thus it is demonstrable that [Holmes] fancies himself an obvious past-master with a handgun," Mr. Ralph A. Ashton wrote in "The Secret Weapons of 221B Baker Street." As we have already seen, Mr. Robert Keith Leavitt held that this "indicated confidence rather in Tonga's than in his own accuracy. He knew he would have time for only two shots at best."

confederate in the household. Jonathan, with his wooden leg, is utterly unable to reach the lofty room of Bartholomew Sholto. He takes with him, however, a rather curious associate, who gets over this difficulty, but dips his naked foot into creosote, whence come Toby, and a six-mile limp for a half-
110 pay officer with a damaged *tendo Achillis*.'

'But it was the associate, and not Jonathan, who committed the crime.'

'Quite so. And rather to Jonathan's disgust, to judge by the way he stamped about when he got into the room. He bore no grudge against Bartholomew Sholto, and would have preferred if he could have been simply bound and gagged. He did not wish to put his head in a halter. There was no help for it, however: the savage instincts of his companion had broken out, and the poison had done its work: so Jonathan Small left his record, lowered the treasure-box to the ground, and followed it himself. That was the train of events as far as I can decipher them. Of course, as to his personal appearance he must be middle-aged, and must be sunburned after serving his time in such an oven as the Andamans. His height is readily calculated from the length of his stride, and we know that he was bearded. His hairiness was the one point which impressed itself upon Thaddeus Sholto when he saw him at the window. I don't know that there is anything else.'

'The associate?'

'Ah, well, there is no great mystery in that. But you will know all about it soon enough. How sweet the morning air is! See how that one little cloud floats like a pink feather from some gigantic flamingo. Now the red rim of the sun pushes
111 itself over the London cloud-bank. It shines on a good many folk, but on none, I dare bet, who are on a stranger errand than you and I. How small we feel, with our petty ambitions and strivings, in the presence of the great elemental forces of
112 Nature! Are you well up in your Jean Paul?'

'Fairly so. I worked back to him through Carlyle.'

'That was like following the brook to the parent lake. He makes one curious but profound remark. It is that the chief proof of man's real greatness lies in his perception of his own smallness. It argues, you see, a power of comparison and of appreciation which is in itself a proof of nobility. There is much food for thought in Richter. You have not a pistol, have you?'

'I have my stick.'

'It is just possible that we may need something of the sort if we get to their lair. Jonathan I shall leave to you, but if the other turns nasty I shall shoot him dead.'

He took out his revolver as he spoke, and, having loaded
113 two of the chambers, he put it back into the right-hand pocket of his jacket.

We had during this time been following the guidance of Toby down the half-rural villa-lined roads which lead to the Metropolis. Now, however, we were beginning to come among continuous streets, where labourers and dockmen were already astir, and slatternly women were taking down shutters and brushing door-steps. At the square-topped corner public-houses business was just beginning, and rough-looking men were emerging, rubbing their sleeves across their beards after their morning wet. Strange dogs sauntered up and stared wonderingly at us as we passed, but our inimitable Toby looked neither to the right nor to the left, but trotted on-wards with his nose to the ground and an occasional eager whine which spoke of a hot scent.

We had traversed Streatham, Brixton, Camberwell, and **114** now found ourselves in Kennington Lane, having borne away through the side-streets to the east of the Oval. The men **115** whom we pursued seemed to have taken a curiously zig-zag road, with the idea probably of escaping observation. They had never kept to the main road if a parallel side-street would serve their turn. At the foot of Kennington Lane they had edged away to the left through Bond Street and Miles Street. **116** Where the latter street turns into Knight's Place, Toby ceased **117** to advance, but began to run backwards and forwards with one ear cocked and the other drooping, the very picture of canine indecision. Then he waddled round in circles, looking up to us from time to time, as if to ask for sympathy in his embarrassment.

'What the deuce is the matter with the dog?' growled Holmes. 'They surely would not take a cab, or go off in a balloon.'

'Perhaps they stood here for some time,' I suggested.

'Ah! it's all right. He's off again,' said my companion, in a tone of relief.

He was indeed off, for after sniffing round again he sud-denly made up his mind, and darted away with an energy and determination such as he had not yet shown. The scent appeared to be much hotter than before, for he had not even to put his nose on the ground, but tugged at his leash and tried to break into a run. I could see by the gleam in Holmes's eyes that he thought we were nearing the end of our journey.

Our course now ran down Nine Elms until we came to Broderick and Nelson's large timber-yard, just past the White Eagle tavern. Here the dog, frantic with excitement, turned **118** down through the side gate into the enclosure, where the sawyers were already at work. On the dog raced through saw-dust and shavings, down an alley, round a passage, between two wood-piles, and finally, with a triumphant yelp, sprang upon a large barrel which still stood upon the hand-trolley on which it had been brought. With lolling tongue and blinking eyes, Toby stood upon the cask, looking from one to the other of us for some sign of appreciation. The staves of the barrel and the wheels of the trolley were smeared with a dark liquid, and the whole air was heavy with the smell of creosote.

Sherlock Holmes and I looked blankly at each other, and then burst simultaneously into an uncontrollable fit of laughter.

114 *Streatham*. Another London suburb now much favored by the minor lights of the acting profession. William Blake, poet and artist, 1757–1827, spent most of his life in this part of London, and Dr. Sam Johnson was almost domesticated at Streatham Park, the home of Henry Thrale.

115 *the Oval*. Kennington Oval, the ground of the Surrey County Cricket Club.

116 *Bond Street*. Now Bond Way.

117 *Knight's Place*. ". . . Knight's Place was . . . a terrace of houses in Wandsworth Road, on the left as one emerges from Miles Street, the crumbling remains of which may still be seen," Mr. Bernard Davies wrote in "Was Holmes a Londoner?"

118 *the White Eagle Tavern*. "I spent an afternoon and evening recently in attempt to find Mordecai Smith's landing-stage but without much success," Mr. Charles O. Merriman wrote in "Tar Derivatives Not Wanted." "I certainly passed the Southampton Arms, the Nine Elms Brewery and other hosteleries but of the White Eagle Tavern, there was no sign."

8 ❖ THE BAKER STREET IRREGULARS

'What now?' I asked. 'Toby has lost his character for infalli-bility.'

'He acted according to his lights,' said Holmes, lifting him

119 *Broad Street.* ". . . of Belmont Place, Prince's Street and Broad Street there was no trace," Mr. Merriman continued. Prince's Street, Mr. Davies explained in "Was Holmes a Londoner?" "survives as the eastern half of Black Prince Road, Lambeth, but Belmont Place is, alas, no more. It was, however, a similar row of buildings opposite Knight's Place at the corner of Nine Elms Lane, long since rebuilt. Obviously there is a typical Watsonian lacuna between Belmont Place, which the correct trail evidently passed, and 'Prince's Street,' involving the recrossing of Kennington Lane and then a detour, possibly via Tyers Street, until the riverside pier was reached 'at the end of Broad Street' (now Black Prince Road, West)."

down from the barrel and walking him out of the timber-yard. 'If you consider how much creosote is carted about London in one day, it is no great wonder that our trail should have been crossed. It is much used now, especially for the seasoning of wood. Poor Toby is not to blame.'

'We must get on the main scent again, I suppose.'

'Yes. And, fortunately, we have no distance to go. Evidently what puzzled the dog at the corner of Knight's Place was that there were two different trails running in opposite directions. We took the wrong one. It only remains to follow the other.'

There was no difficulty about this. On leading Toby to the place where he had committed his fault, he cast about in a wide circle and finally dashed off in a fresh direction.

'We must take care that he does not now bring us to the place where the creosote-barrel came from,' I observed.

'I had thought of that. But you notice that he keeps on the pavement, whereas the barrel passed down the roadway. No, we are on the true scent now.'

It tended down towards the river-side, running through **119** Belmont Place and Prince's Street. At the end of Broad Street it ran right down to the water's edge, where there was a small wooden wharf. Toby led us to the very edge of this, and there stood whining, looking out on the dark current beyond.

'We are out of luck,' said Holmes. 'They have taken to a boat here.'

Several small punts and skiffs were lying about in the water and on the edge of the wharf. We took Toby round to each in turn, but, though he sniffed earnestly, he made no sign.

Close to the rude landing-stage was a small brick house, with a wooden placard slung out through the second window. 'Mordecai Smith' was printed across it in large letters, and underneath, 'Boats to hire by the hour or day.' A second inscription above the door informed us that a steam launch was kept—a statement which was confirmed by a great pile of coke upon the jetty. Sherlock Holmes looked slowly round, and his face assumed an ominous expression.

'This looks bad,' said he. 'These fellows are sharper than I expected. They seem to have covered their tracks. There has, I fear, been preconcerted management here.'

He was approaching the door of the house, when it opened, and a little curly-headed lad of six came running out, followed by a stoutish, red-faced woman with a large sponge in her hand.

'You come back and be washed, Jack,' she shouted. 'Come back, you young imp; for if your father comes home and finds you like that, he'll let us hear of it.'

'Dear little chap!' cried Holmes, strategically. 'What a rosy-cheeked young rascal! Now, Jack, is there anything you would like?'

The youth pondered for a moment.

'I'd like a shillin',' said he.

'Nothing you would like better?'

'I'd like two shillin' better,' the prodigy answered, after some thought.

'Here you are, then! Catch!—A fine child, Mrs Smith!'

'Lor' bless you, sir, he is that, and forward. He gets a'most too much for me to manage, 'specially when my man is away days at a time.'

'Away, is he?' said Holmes, in a disappointed voice. 'I am sorry for that, for I wanted to speak to Mr Smith.'

'He's been away since yesterday mornin', sir, and, truth to tell, I am beginning to feel frightened about him. But if it was about a boat, sir, maybe I could serve as well.'

'I wanted to hire his steam launch.'

'Why, bless you, sir, it is in the steam launch that he has gone. That's what puzzles me; for I know there ain't more coals in her than would take her to about Woolwich and back. **120** If he'd been away in the barge I'd ha' thought nothin'; for many a time a job has taken him as far as Gravesend, and then if there was much doin' there he might ha' stayed over. But what good is a steam launch without coals?'

'He might have bought some at a wharf down the river.'

'He might, sir, but it weren't his way. Many a time I've heard him call out at the prices they charge for a few odd bags. Besides, I don't like that wooden-legged man, wi' his ugly face and outlandish talk. What did he want always knockin' about here for?'

'A wooden-legged man?' said Holmes, with bland surprise.

'Yes, sir, a brown, monkey-faced chap that's called more'n once for my old man. It was him that roused him up yester-night, and, what's more, my man knew he was comin', for he had steam up in the launch. I tell you straight, sir, I don't feel easy in my mind about it.'

'But, my dear Mrs Smith,' said Holmes, shrugging his shoulders, 'you are frightening yourself about nothing. How could you possibly tell that it was the wooden-legged man who came in the night? I don't quite understand how you can be so sure.'

'His voice, sir. I knew his voice, which is kind o' thick and foggy. He tapped at the winder—about three it would be. "Show a leg, matey," says he: "time to turn out guard." My old man woke up Jim—that's my eldest—and away they went, without so much as a word to me. I could hear the wooden leg clackin' on the stones.'

'And was this wooden-legged man alone?'

'Couldn't say, I am sure, sir. I didn't hear no one else.'

'I am sorry, Mrs Smith, for I wanted a steam launch, and I have heard good reports of the—— Let me see, what is her name?'

'The *Aurora*, sir.'

'Ah! She's not that old green launch with a yellow line, very broad in the beam?'

'No, indeed. She's as trim a little thing as any on the river. She's been fresh painted, black with two red streaks.'

'Thanks. I hope that you will hear soon from Mr Smith. I am going down the river, and if I should see anything of the *Aurora* I shall let him know that you are uneasy. A black funnel, you say?'

'No, sir. Black with a white band.'

'Ah, of course. It was the sides which were black. Good morning, Mrs Smith. There is a boatman here with a wherry, **121** Watson. We shall take it and cross the river.'

'The main thing with people of that sort,' said Holmes, as we sat in the sheets of the wherry, 'is never to let them think that their information can be of the slightest importance to you. If you do, they will instantly shut up like an oyster. If you listen to them under protest, as it were, you are very likely to get what you want.'

'Our course now seems pretty clear,' said I.

'What would you do, then?'

120 *Woolwich.* An unattractive garrison town and metropolitan borough, the site of Woolwich Dockyard and Woolwich Arsenal.

121 *a wherry.* A long, light rowboat, sharp at both ends.

122 *Greenwich.* A metropolitan borough lying on the south bank of the Thames, noted for its whitebait. Britain's Cabinet Ministers used to celebrate the close of the Parliamentary session with a "Whitebait Dinner" at Greenwich, but the custom was given up about 1880. Holmes surely had in his files a description of a ghastly murder that was committed at Greenwich on the night of February 7, 1818, when Mr. Bird, a retired tradesman, aged eighty-four, and Mary Symonds, his housekeeper, both had their skulls driven in by a large hammer. The house was plundered, and the discovery of the stolen property led to the conviction of the murderer, who was afterward executed on Pennenden Heath, near Maidstone.

123 *wharfingers?'* Wharf owners.

124 *Millbank Penitentiary.* A model prison built from designs of Jeremy Bentham (d. 1832). The prison was taken down in 1893, and the west part of the site is now covered by large blocks of workmen's dwellings, while the east portion, nearest the river, is occupied by the Tate Gallery, flanked on the north by Queen Alexandra's Military Hospital and on the south by the Royal Army Medical College.

'I would engage a launch and go down the river on the track of the *Aurora*.'

'My dear fellow, it would be a colossal task. She may have touched at any wharf on either side of the stream between **122** here and Greenwich. Below the bridge there is a perfect labyrinth of landing-places for miles. It would take you days and days to exhaust them, if you set about it alone.'

'Employ the police, then.'

'No. I shall probably call Athelney Jones in at the last moment. He is not a bad fellow, and I should not like to do anything which would injure him professionally. But I have a fancy for working it out myself, now that we have gone so far.'

'Could we advertise, then, asking for information from **123** wharfingers?'

'Worse and worse! Our men would know that the chase was hot at their heels, and they would be off out of the country. As it is, they are likely enough to leave, but as long as they think they are perfectly safe they will be in no hurry. Jones's energy will be of use to us there, for his view of the case is sure to push itself into the daily Press, and the runaways will think that everyone is off on the wrong scent.'

'What are we to do, then?' I asked, as we landed near Mill- **124** bank Penitentiary.

'Take this hansom, drive home, have some breakfast, and get an hour's sleep. It is quite on the cards that we may be afoot tonight again. Stop at a telegraph office, cabby! We will keep Toby, for he may be of use to us yet.'

We pulled up at the Great Peter Street post-office, and Holmes dispatched his wire.

'Whom do you think that is to?' he asked, as we resumed our journey.

'I am sure I don't know.'

'You remember the Baker Street division of the detective police force whom I employed in the Jefferson Hope case?'

'Well?' said I, laughing.

'This is just the case where they might be invaluable. If they fail, I have other resources; but I shall try them first. That wire was to my dirty little lieutenant, Wiggins, and I expect that he and his gang will be with us before we have finished our breakfast.'

It was between eight and nine o'clock now, and I was conscious of a strong reaction after the successive excitements of the night. I was limp and weary, befogged in mind and fatigued in body. I had not the professional enthusiasm which carried my companion on, nor could I look at the matter as a mere abstract intellectual problem. As far as the death of Bartholomew Sholto went, I had heard little good of him, and could feel no intense antipathy to his murderers. The treasure, however, was a different matter. That, or part of it, belonged rightfully to Miss Morstan. While there was a chance of recovering it I was ready to devote my life to the one object. True, if I found it, it would probably put her for ever beyond my reach. Yet it would be a petty and selfish love which would be influenced by such a thought as that. If Holmes could work to find the criminals, I had a tenfold stronger reason to urge me on to find the treasure.

A bath at Baker Street and a complete change freshened me up wonderfully. When I came down to our room I found the breakfast laid and Holmes pouring out the coffee.

'Here it is,' said he, laughing and pointing to an open newspaper. 'The energetic Jones and the ubiquitous reporter have fixed it up between them. But you have had enough of the case. Better have your ham and eggs first.'

I took the paper from him and read the short notice, which was headed, 'Mysterious Business at Upper Norwood.'

About twelve o'clock last night [said the *Standard*], Mr Bartholomew Sholto, of Pondicherry Lodge, Upper Norwood, was found dead in his room under circumstances which point to foul play. As far as we can learn, no actual traces of violence were found upon Mr Sholto's person, but a valuable collection of Indian gems which the deceased gentleman had inherited from his father has been carried off. The discovery was first made by Mr Sherlock Holmes and Dr Watson, who had called at the house with Mr Thaddeus Sholto, brother of the deceased. By a singular piece of good fortune, Mr Athelney Jones, the well-known member of the detective police force, happened to be at the Norwood Police Station, and was on the ground within half an hour of the first alarm. His trained and experienced faculties were at once directed towards the detection of the criminals, with the gratifying result that the brother, Thaddeus Sholto, has already been arrested, together with the housekeeper, Mrs Bernstone, an Indian butler named Lal Rao, and a porter, or gatekeeper, named McMurdo. It is quite certain that the thief or thieves were well acquainted with the house, for Mr Jones's well-known technical knowledge and his powers of minute observation have enabled him to prove conclusively that the miscreants could not have entered by the door or by the window, but must have made their way across the roof of the building, and so through a trap-door into a room which communicated with that in which the body was found. This fact, which has been very clearly made out, proves conclusively that it was no mere haphazard burglary. The prompt and energetic action of the officers of the law shows the great advantage of the presence on such occasions of a single vigorous and masterful mind. We cannot but think that it supplies an argument to those who would wish to see our detectives more decentralized, and so brought into closer and more effective touch with the cases which it is their duty to investigate.

'Isn't it gorgeous?' said Holmes, grinning over his coffee cup. 'What do you think of it?'

'I think that we have had a close shave ourselves of being arrested for the crime.'

'So do I. I wouldn't answer for our safety now, if he should happen to have another of his attacks of energy.'

At this moment there was a loud ring at the bell, and I could hear Mrs Hudson, our landlady, raising her voice in a wail of expostulation and dismay.

'By heavens, Holmes,' said I, half rising, 'I believe that they are really after us.'

'No, it's not quite so bad as that. It is the unofficial force—the Baker Street irregulars.'

As he spoke, there came a swift pattering of naked feet upon the stairs, a clatter of high voices, and in rushed a dozen dirty and ragged little street arabs. There was some show of discipline among them, despite their tumultuous entry, for they instantly drew up in line and stood facing us with expectant faces. One of their number, taller and older than the others, stood forward with an air of lounging superiority which was very funny in such a disreputable little scarecrow.

'Got your message, sir,' said he, 'and brought 'em on sharp. Three bob and a tanner for tickets.'

125

125 *Three bob and a tanner.* Slang for three shillings and sixpence (about 87¢). The boys had come from some distance if their tickets by bus or Underground cost threepence each.

'Here you are,' said Holmes, producing some silver. 'In future they can report to you, Wiggins, and you to me. I cannot have the house invaded in this way. However, it is just as well that you should all hear the instructions. I want to find the whereabouts of a steam launch called the *Aurora*, owner Mordecai Smith, black with two red streaks, funnel black with a white band. She is down the river somewhere. I want one boy to be at Mordecai Smith's landing-stage opposite Millbank to say if the boat comes back. You must divide it out among yourselves, and do both banks thoroughly. Let me know the moment you have news. Is that all clear?'

'Yes, guv'nor,' said Wiggins.

'The old scale of pay, and a guinea to the boy who finds the boat. Here's a day in advance. Now, off you go!'

He handed them a shilling each, and away they buzzed down the stairs, and I saw them a moment later streaming down the street.

'If the launch is above water they will find her,' said Holmes, as he rose from the table and lit his pipe. 'They can go everywhere, see everything, overhear everyone. I expect to hear before evening that they have spotted her. In the meanwhile, we can do nothing but await results. We cannot pick up the broken trail until we find either the *Aurora* or Mr Mordecai Smith.'

'Toby could eat these scraps, I dare say. Are you going to bed, Holmes?'

'No; I am not tired. I have a curious constitution. I never remember feeling tired by work, though idleness exhausts me completely. I am going to smoke and to think over this queer business to which my fair client has introduced us. If ever man had an easy task, this of ours ought to be. Wooden-legged men are not so common, but the other man must, I should think, be absolutely unique.'

'That other man again!'

'I have no wish to make a mystery of him to you, anyway. But you must have formed your own opinion. Now, do consider the data. Diminutive footmarks, toes never fettered by boots, naked feet, stone-headed wooden mace, great agility, small poisoned darts. What do you make of all this?'

'A savage!' I exclaimed. 'Perhaps one of those Indians who were the associates of Jonathan Small.'

'Hardly that,' said he. 'When first I saw signs of strange weapons, I was inclined to think so; but the remarkable character of the footmarks caused me to reconsider my views. Some of the inhabitants of the Indian Peninsula are small men, but none could have left such marks as that. The Hindu proper has long and thin feet. The sandal-wearing Mohammedan has the great toe well separated from the others, because the thong is commonly passed between. These little darts, too, could only be shot in one way. They are from a blowpipe. Now, then, where are we to find our savage?'

'South American,' I hazarded.

He stretched his hand up, and took down a bulky volume from the shelf.

'This is the first volume of a gazetteer which is now being published. It may be looked upon as the very latest authority. What have we here? "Andaman Islands, situated 340 miles to the north of Sumatra, in the Bay of Bengal." Hum! hum! What's all this? Moist climate, coral reefs, sharks, Port Blair, convict barracks, Rutland Island, cottonwoods—— Ah, here we are! "The aborigines of the Andaman Islands may perhaps claim the distinction of being the smallest race upon this earth, though some anthropologists prefer the Bushmen of Africa, the Digger Indians of America, and the Tierra del Fuegians. The average height is rather below four feet, although many full-grown adults may be found who are very much smaller than this. They are a fierce, morose, and intractable people, though capable of forming most devoted friendships when their confidence has once been gained." Mark that, Watson. Now, then, listen to this. "They are naturally hideous, having large, misshapen heads, small, fierce eyes, and distorted features. Their feet and hands, however, are remarkably small. So intractable and fierce are they, that all the efforts of the British officials have failed to win them over in any degree. They have always been a terror to shipwrecked crews, braining the survivors with their stone-headed clubs, or shooting them with their poisoned arrows. These massacres are invariably concluded by a cannibal feast." Nice, amiable people, Watson! If this fellow had **126** been left to his own unaided devices, this affair might have taken an even more ghastly turn. I fancy that, even as it is, Jonathan Small would give a good deal not to have employed him.'

'But how came he to have so singular a companion?'

'Ah, that is more than I can tell. Since, however, we had already determined that Small had come from the Andamans, it is not so very wonderful that this islander should be with him. No doubt we shall know all about it in time. Look here, Watson; you look regularly done. Lie down there on the sofa, and see if I can put you to sleep.'

He took up his violin from the corner, and as I stretched myself out he began to play some low, dreamy, melodious air —his own, no doubt, for he had a remarkable gift for improvisation. I have a vague remembrance of his gaunt limbs, his earnest face, and the rise and fall of his bow. Then I seemed to be floated peacefully away upon a soft sea of sound, until I found myself in dreamland, with the sweet face of Mary Morstan looking down upon me.

9 ❖ A BREAK IN THE CHAIN

It was late in the afternoon before I woke, strengthened and refreshed. Sherlock Holmes still sat exactly as I had left him, save that he had laid aside his violin and was deep in a book. He looked across at me as I stirred, and I noticed that his face was dark and troubled.

'You have slept soundly,' he said. 'I feared that our talk would wake you.'

'I heard nothing,' I answered. 'Have you had fresh news, then?'

126 *Nice, amiable people, Watson!* As Mr. Roger Lancelyn Green pointed out in his article, "Dr. Watson's First Critic," Andrew Lang, writing in the *Quarterly Review*, July, 1904, was one of the earliest critics to catch Holmes out in this description of the Andaman Islanders. The Andamanese, Lang declared, "have neither the malignant qualities, nor the heads like mops, nor the customs, with which they are credited by Sherlock." In fact, they shave their heads, have an average height of four feet ten and a half inches, do not use blow-pipes or poisoned arrows, and show no traces of cannibalism. To this Mr. T. S. Blakeney added ("Thoughts on *The Sign of the Four*"): "What was the Gazetteer to which Holmes referred for information on the Andamanese? Not, one feels, a wholly reliable one, for the aboriginies 1) are *not* cannibals—I was told in 1936, while on a visit to the Andaman Islands, by the Chief Commissioner, that when the aboriginies had been questioned about this practice, they expressed horror at the idea; 2) are not naturally hideous (some of the Nicobarese Islanders have unpleasing features, particularly their mouths); 3) their average height is more like 4 ft. 9 in. to 5 ft. than under 4 ft. Holmes' gazetteer gave a very untrue picture of the Andamanese; they were rather attractive little people, whose treatment at the hands of the Government of India was nothing less than tragic."

'Unfortunately, no. I confess that I am surprised and disappointed. I expected something definite by this time. Wiggins has just been up to report. He says that no trace can be found of the launch. It is a provoking check, for every hour is of importance.'

'Can I do anything? I am perfectly fresh now, and quite ready for another night's outing.'

'No; we can do nothing. We can only wait. If we go ourselves, the message might come in our absence, and delay be caused. You can do what you will, but I must remain on guard.'

'Then I shall run over to Camberwell and call upon Mrs Cecil Forrester. She asked me to, yesterday.'

'On Mrs Cecil Forrester?' asked Holmes with the twinkle of a smile in his eyes.

'Well, of course, on Miss Morstan too. They were anxious to hear what happened.'

'I would not tell them too much,' said Holmes. 'Women are never to be entirely trusted—not the best of them.'

I did not pause to argue over this atrocious sentiment.

'I shall be back in an hour or two,' I remarked.

'All right! Good luck! But, I say, if you are crossing the water you may as well return Toby, for I don't think it is at all likely that we shall have any use for him now.'

I took our mongrel accordingly, and left him, together with a half-sovereign, at the old naturalist's in Pinchin Lane. At Camberwell I found Miss Morstan a little weary after her night's adventures, but very eager to hear the news. Mrs Forrester, too, was full of curiosity. I told them all that we had done, suppressing, however, the more dreadful parts of the tragedy. Thus, although I spoke of Mr Sholto's death, I said nothing of the exact manner and method of it. With all my omissions, however, there was enough to startle and amaze them.

'It is a romance!' cried Mrs Forrester. 'An injured lady, half a million in treasure, a black cannibal, and a wooden-legged ruffian. They take the place of the conventional dragon or wicked earl.'

'And two knight-errants to the rescue,' added Miss Morstan, with a bright glance at me.

'Why, Mary, your fortune depends upon the issue of this search. I don't think that you are nearly excited enough. Just imagine what it must be to be so rich, and to have the world at your feet!'

It sent a little thrill of joy to my heart to notice that she showed no sign of elation at the prospect. On the contrary, she gave a toss of her proud head, as though the matter were one in which she took small interest.

'It is for Mr Thaddeus Sholto that I am anxious,' she said. 'Nothing else is of any consequence; but I think that he has behaved most kindly and honourably throughout. It is our duty to clear him of this dreadful and unfounded charge.'

It was evening before I left Camberwell, and quite dark by the time I reached home. My companion's book and pipe lay by his chair, but he had disappeared. I looked about in the hope of seeing a note, but there was none.

'I suppose that Mr Sherlock Holmes has gone out?' I said to Mrs Hudson as she came up to lower the blinds.

'No, sir. He has gone to his room, sir. Do you know, sir,'

sinking her voice into an impressive whisper, 'I am afraid for his health?'

'Why so, Mrs Hudson?'

'Well, he's that strange, sir. After you was gone he walked and he walked, up and down, and up and down, until I was weary of the sound of his footstep. Then I heard him talking to himself and muttering, and every time the bell rang out he came on the stair-head, with "What is that, Mrs Hudson?" And now he has slammed off to his room, but I can hear him walking away the same as ever. I hope he's not going to be ill, sir. I ventured to say something to him about cooling medicine, but he turned on me, sir, with such a look that I don't know however I got out of the room.'

'I don't think that you have any cause to be uneasy, Mrs Hudson,' I answered. 'I have seen him like this before. He has some small matter upon his mind which makes him restless.'

I tried to speak lightly to our worthy landlady, but I was myself somewhat uneasy when through the long night I still from time to time heard the dull sound of his tread, and knew how his keen spirit was chafing against this involuntary inaction.

At breakfast-time he looked worn and haggard, with a little **127** fleck of feverish colour upon either cheek.

'You are knocking yourself up, old man,' I remarked. 'I heard you marching about in the night.'

'No, I could not sleep,' he answered. 'This infernal problem is consuming me. It is too much to be baulked by so petty an obstacle, when all else had been overcome. I know the men, the launch, everything; and yet I can get no news. I have set other agencies at work, and used every means at my disposal. The whole river has been searched on either side, but there is no news, nor has Mrs Smith heard of her husband. I shall come to the conclusion soon that they have scuttled the craft. But there are objections to that.'

'Or that Mrs Smith has put us on a wrong scent.'

'No, I think that may be dismissed. I had inquiries made, and there is a launch of that description.'

'Could it have gone up the river?'

'I have considered that possibility too, and there is a search-party who will work up as far as Richmond. If no news comes **128** today, I shall start off myself tomorrow, and go for the men rather than the boat. But surely, surely, we shall hear something.'

We did not, however. Not a word came to us either from Wiggins or from the other agencies. There were articles in most of the papers upon the Norwood tragedy. They all appeared to be rather hostile to the unfortunate Thaddeus Sholto. No fresh details were to be found, however, in any of them, save that an inquest was to be held upon the following day. I walked over to Camberwell in the evening to report our ill-success to the ladies, and on my return I found Holmes dejected and somewhat morose. He would hardly reply to my questions, and busied himself all the evening in an abstruse chemical analysis which involved much heating of retorts and distilling of vapours, ending at last in a smell which fairly drove me out of the apartment. Up to the small hours of the morning I could hear the clinking of his test-tubes, which told me that he was still engaged in his malodorous experiment.

127 *At breakfast-time.* This would be Thursday morning, since the adventure began on a Tuesday (see Note 130).

128 *Richmond.* A municipal borough in Surrey, on the Thames. It is the site of the Palace of Sheen, where many sovereigns lived, a large deer park, and Kew Observatory. Here also was the Inn of the Star and Garter, which figures in Scott's works; it was torn down in 1919.

129 *In the early dawn.* Of the Friday morning.

130 *last Tuesday morning.* Of the four days covered by the action, the first is clearly Tuesday.

131 *the natural anxiety of a wife for her missing husband.* "What a pity," Mr. Charles B. Stephens wrote in "Holmes' Longest Shot?", "that Watson missed so completely this opportunity to applaud one of the longest shots his companion ever played. Consider the circumstances at the time when Holmes ordered this advertisement inserted, obviously no later than the preceding evening. The indefatigable Irregulars had drawn a blank in their search for the *Aurora*, and every lead seemed to run to a dead end. Holmes had only a slender, untested chain of reasoning on which to base his next move. He had to find the *Aurora* before he could spring his trap. With supreme confidence in his own reasoning and ability to succeed where others had failed, he deliberately inserted in the *Standard* the very advertisement that he felt reasonably certain would flush his quarry on the next evening. To make doubly certain of this effect on the fugitives, he added his Baker Street address to the copy. . . . The evidence seems clear and convincing that Holmes had this purpose in mind, and that he was looking to his own activities, not any possible answers to his advertisement, to turn up the missing *Aurora*. The reward was fantastic, the Baker Street address was wholly inconsistent with Watson's interpretation, and Holmes did nothing to prepare Watson for any possible visitors who might come in answer to the paragraph. It is true that had he not located the *Aurora* in time, Holmes could still have covered the flight of the criminals by alerting the police along the lower Thames. The fact remains that the gamble came off as he planned it . . ."

129 In the early dawn I woke with a start, and was surprised to find him standing by my bedside, clad in a rude sailor dress with a pea-jacket, and a coarse red scarf round his neck.

'I am off down the river, Watson,' said he. 'I have been turning it over in my mind, and I can see only one way out of it. It is worth trying, at all events.'

'Surely I can come with you, then?' said I.

'No; you can be much more useful if you will remain here as my representative. I am loth to go, for it is quite on the cards that some message may come during the day, though Wiggins was despondent about it last night. I want you to open all notes and telegrams, and to act on your own judgment if any news should come. Can I rely upon you?'

'Most certainly.'

'I am afraid that you will not be able to wire to me, for I can hardly tell yet where I may find myself. If I am in luck, however, I may not be gone so very long. I shall have news of some sort or other before I get back.'

I had heard nothing of him by breakfast-time. On opening the *Standard*, however, I found that there was a fresh allusion to the business.

> With reference to the Upper Norwood tragedy [it remarked], we have reason to believe that the matter promises to be even more complex and mysterious than was originally supposed. Fresh evidence has shown that it is quite impossible that Mr Thaddeus Sholto could have been in any way concerned in the matter. He and the housekeeper, Mrs Bernstone, were both released yesterday evening. It is believed, however, that the police have a clue as to the real culprits, and that it is being prosecuted by Mr Athelney Jones, of Scotland Yard, with all his well-known energy and sagacity. Further arrests may be expected at any moment.

'That is satisfactory so far as it goes,' thought I. 'Friend Sholto is safe, at any rate. I wonder what the fresh clue may be, though it seems to be a stereotyped form whenever the police have made a blunder.'

I tossed the paper down upon the table, but at that moment my eye caught an advertisement in the agony column. It ran in this way:

> LOST.—Whereas Mordecai Smith, boatman, and his son Jim, left Smith's Wharf at or about three o'clock last Tuesday morning in the steam launch *Aurora*, black with two red stripes, funnel black with a white band, the sum of five pounds will be paid to anyone who can give information to Mrs Smith, at Smith's Wharf, or at 221*b*, Baker Street, as to the whereabouts of the said Mordecai Smith and the launch *Aurora*.

130

This was clearly Holmes's doing. The Baker Street address was enough to prove that. It struck me as rather ingenious, because it might be read by the fugitives without their seeing in it more than the natural anxiety of a wife for her missing husband.

131

It was a long day. Every time that a knock came to the door, or a sharp step passed in the street, I imagined that it was either Holmes returning or an answer to his advertisement. I tried to read, but my thoughts would wander oft to our strange quest and to the ill-assorted and villainous pair whom we were pursuing. Could there be, I wondered, some radical flaw in my companion's reasoning? Might he not be suffering from some huge self-deception? Was it not possible that his nimble and speculative mind had built up this wild theory upon faulty premises? I had never known him to be wrong, and yet the keenest reasoner may occasionally be deceived. He was likely, I thought, to fall into error through the over-refinement of his logic—his preference for a subtle and bizarre explanation when a plainer and more commonplace one lay ready to his hand. Yet, on the other hand, I had myself seen the evidence, and I had heard the reasons for his deductions. When I looked back on the long chain of curious circumstances, many of them trivial in themselves, but all tending in the same direction, I could not disguise from myself that even if Holmes's explanation were incorrect the true theory must be equally *outré* and startling.

At three o'clock in the afternoon there was a loud peal at the bell, an authoritative voice in the hall, and, to my surprise, no less a person than Mr Athelney Jones was shown up to me. Very different was he, however, from the brusque and masterful professor of common-sense who had taken over the case so confidently at Upper Norwood. His expression was downcast, and his bearing meek and even apologetic.

'Good-day, sir; good-day,' said he. 'Mr Sherlock Holmes is out, I understand?'

'Yes, and I cannot be sure when he will be back. But perhaps you would care to wait. Take that chair and try one of these cigars.'

'Thank you; I don't mind if I do,' said he, mopping his face with a red bandanna handkerchief.

'And a whisky and soda?'

'Well, half a glass. It is very hot for the time of year; and **132** I have had a good deal to worry and try me. You know my theory about this Norwood case?'

'I remember that you expressed one.'

'Well, I have been obliged to reconsider it. I had my net drawn tightly round Mr Sholto, sir, when pop he went through a hole in the middle of it. He was able to prove an alibi which could not be shaken. From the time that he left his brother's room he was never out of sight of someone or other. So it could not be he who climbed over roofs and through trap-doors. It's a very dark case, and my professional credit is at stake. I should be very glad of a little assistance.'

'We all need help sometimes,' said I.

'Your friend Mr Sherlock Holmes is a wonderful man, sir,' said he, in a husky and confidential voice. 'He's a man who is not to be beat. I have known that young man go into a good many cases, but I never saw the case yet that he could not throw a light upon. He is irregular in his methods, and a little quick perhaps in jumping at theories; but, on the whole, I think he would have made a most promising officer and I don't care who knows it. I have had a wire from him this morning, by which I understand that he has got some clue to this Sholto business. Here is his message.'

He took the telegram out of his pocket, and handed it to me. It was dated from Poplar at twelve o'clock. 'Go to Baker **133** Street at once,' it said. 'If I have not returned, wait for me. I am close on the track of the Sholto gang. You can come with us tonight if you want to be in at the finish.'

'This sounds well. He has evidently picked up the scent again,' said I.

'Ah, then he has been at fault too,' exclaimed Jones, with

132 *It is very hot for the time of year.* "This is hardly a comment appropriate to July, when even a hot spell would be considered seasonable, but quite an acceptable comment in September, when drizzle, fog, close nights, warm west winds, or heat, may be expected to follow in close succession in London," Dr. Ebbe Curtis Hoff wrote in "The Adventure of John and Mary." For the record, the thermometer registered 65° in London at noon on Friday, September 21, 1888.

133 *Poplar.* A metropolitan borough in the East of London, taking its name from the trees which once flourished there.

134 *some of my cases.* It is possible that Holmes here confused the one *published* case with the number of cases Watson had undoubtedly *chronicled* by this time.

135 *I can step across the road and telephone.* "In September, 1879, there was an Exchange [in London] serving 10 subscribers," Colonel E. Ennalls Berl wrote in "Sherlock Holmes and the Telephone." "There was a company in Liverpool before 1883, and in 1883 the telephone was in operation in many cities. . . . In 1884 there was a public trunk line from London to Brighton, 40 or 50 miles, and as early as 1891 the Channel had been bridged, and Paris-London telephone service was inaugurated. . . . Naturally, as it was necessary for Jones to step across the road, it is clear that at that time there was no telephone at 221B Baker Street. But, according to Christopher Pulling, senior assistant secretary of Scotland Yard, there *was* one at the Yard, from 1887 on."

136 *I have oysters and a brace of grouse.* Grouse and oysters belong to September rather than to July, the first by law, the second by custom. The late Christopher Morley ("Was Sherlock Holmes an American?") always held that since Holmes had a liking for oysters he must have acquired his taste for them in their native habitat, otherwise Baltimore—additional evidence that he had traveled in America. This is borne out by the late Fletcher Pratt, writing in "The Gastronomic Holmes": "The English oysters, with their strong flavor of copper, are not the best preparation for a meal, but they were the best the market afforded and an excellent prelude to grouse. As for the grouse themselves, there is clearly no question as to how they were served. One brace of grouse would be insufficient for three men, one of whom was Watson, who did nothing to preserve his figure. Therefore there must have been three brace, one to each of the eaters; and if that is the case, they could only have been served in the classic manner prescribed by both Brillat-Savarin and Escoffier—roasted with the breasts only served, accompanied by a bread sauce, potato chips and a gravy made from the unused portions of the birds."

Readers who might like to serve a dinner *à la* Holmes are invited to try these recipes, prepared by Mr. Poul Ib Liebe ("Sherlock's Delights"), to which he has added an apricot pie: "Out of modesty—or possibly because of sheer forgetful-

evident satisfaction. 'Even the best of us are thrown off sometimes. Of course this may prove to be a false alarm; but it is my duty as an officer of the law to allow no chance to slip. But there is someone at the door. Perhaps this is he.'

A heavy step was heard ascending the stair, with a great wheezing and rattling as from a man who was sorely put to it for breath. Once or twice he stopped, as though the climb were too much for him, but at last he made his way to our door and entered. His appearance corresponded to the sounds which we had heard. He was an aged man, clad in seafaring garb, with an old pea-jacket buttoned up to his throat. His back was bowed, his knees were shaky, and his breathing was painfully asthmatic. As he leaned upon a thick oaken cudgel his shoulders heaved in the effort to draw the air into his lungs. He had a coloured scarf round his chin, and I could see little of his face save a pair of keen dark eyes, overhung by bushy white brows, and long grey side-whiskers. Altogether he gave me the impression of a respectable master mariner who had fallen into years and poverty.

'What is it, my man?' I asked.

He looked about him in the slow methodical fashion of old age.

'Is Mr Sherlock Holmes here?' said he.

'No; but I am acting for him. You can tell me any message you have for him.'

'It was to him himself I was to tell it,' said he.

'But I tell you I am acting for him. Was it about Mordecai Smith's boat?'

'Yes. I knows well where it is. An' I knows where the men he is after are. An' I knows where the treasure is. I knows all about it.'

'Then tell me, and I shall let him know.'

'It was to him I was to tell it,' he repeated, with the petulant obstinacy of a very old man.

'Well, you must wait for him.'

'No, no; I ain't goin' to lose a whole day to please no one. If Mr Holmes ain't here, then Mr Holmes must find it all out for himself. I don't care about the look of either of you, and I won't tell a word.'

He shuffled towards the door, but Athelney Jones got in front of him.

'Wait a bit, my friend,' said he. 'You have important information, and you must not walk off. We shall keep you, whether you like or not, until our friend returns.'

The old man made a little run towards the door, but, as Athelney Jones put his broad back up against it, he recognized the uselessness of resistance.

'Pretty sort o' treatment this!' he cried, stamping his stick. 'I come here to see a gentleman, and you two, who I never saw in my life, seize me and treat me in this fashion!'

'You will be none the worse,' I said. 'We shall recompense you for the loss of your time. Sit over here on the sofa, and you will not have long to wait.'

He came across sullenly enough, and seated himself with his face resting on his hands. Jones and I resumed our cigars and our talk. Suddenly, however, Holmes's voice broke in upon us.

'I think that you might offer me a cigar too,' he said.

We both started in our chairs. There was Holmes sitting close to us with an air of quiet amusement.

'Holmes!' I exclaimed. 'You here! But where is the old man?'

'Here is the old man,' said he, holding out a heap of white hair. 'Here he is—wig, whiskers, eyebrows, and all. I thought my disguise was pretty good, but I hardly expected that it would stand that test.'

'Ah, you rogue!' cried Jones, highly delighted. 'You would have made an actor, and a rare one. You had the proper work-house cough, and those weak legs of yours are worth ten pounds a week. I thought I knew the glint of your eye, though. You didn't get away from us so easily, you see.'

'I have been working in that get-up all day,' said he, lighting his cigar. 'You see, a good many of the criminal classes begin to know me—especially since our friend here took to publishing some of my cases: so I can only go on the war-path **134** under some simple disguise like this. You got my wire?'

'Yes; that was what brought me here.'

'How has your case prospered?'

'It has all come to nothing. I have had to release two of my prisoners, and there is no evidence against the other two.'

'Never mind. We shall give you two others in the place of them. But you must put yourself under my orders. You are welcome to all the official credit, but you must act on the lines that I point out. Is that agreed?'

'Entirely, if you will help me to the men.'

'Well, then, in the first place I shall want a fast police-boat —a steam launch—to be at the Westminster Stairs at seven o'clock.'

'That is easily managed. There is always one about there; but I can step across the road and telephone to make sure.' **135**

'Then I shall want two stanch men, in case of resistance.'

'There will be two or three in the boat. What else?'

'When we secure the men we shall get the treasure. I think that it would be a pleasure to my friend here to take the box round to the young lady to whom half of it rightfully belongs. Let her be the first to open it. Eh, Watson?'

'It would be a great pleasure to me.'

'Rather an irregular proceeding,' said Jones, shaking his head. 'However, the whole thing is irregular, and I suppose we must wink at it. The treasure must afterwards be handed over to the authorities until after the official investigation.'

'Certainly. That is easily managed. One other point. I should much like to have a few details about this matter from the lips of Jonathan Small himself. You know I like to work the details of my cases out. There is no objection to my having an unofficial interview with him, either here in my rooms or elsewhere, as long as he is efficiently guarded?'

'Well, you are master of the situation. I have had no proof yet of the existence of this Jonathan Small. However, if you can catch him, I don't see how I can refuse you an interview with him.'

'That is understood, then?'

'Perfectly. Is there anything else?'

'Only that I insist upon your dining with us. It will be ready in half an hour. I have oysters and a brace of grouse, **136** with something a little choice in white wines. Watson, you **137** have never yet recognized my merits as a housekeeper.'

ness—Holmes omits to inform us of the dessert, which might well have been apricot pie, a favorite Victorian sweet."

I. Oyster Special
   18 oysters
   1 lemon
   1 egg
   Flour
   Breadcrumbs
   ½ pound of lard.

   Each of the fresh oysters must be removed from the shells, soaked in lemon juice, rolled in flour, smeared with egg (slightly whipped), dipped into the crumbs, and finally boiled in the lard. A real delicacy!

II. Grouse *à la* Holmes
    3 grouse
    3 thin slices of bacon
    2 tsp. salt
    a little pepper

    Ingredients for frying:

    3 tsp. of butter
    2 cups of broth
    ½ cup of cream

    Sauce:

    2 cups of gravy (from the frying juice)
    ½ cup of cream
    a little salt
    1 tsp. of currant jelly

    Having skinned and cleansed the grouse, wings and legs are removed, the birds are rubbed with salt and pepper, and the breast-pieces are wrapped in bacon. The birds are then fried (first in the butter alone for a moment; then in the mixture of butter and broth) for about an hour, with occasional drippings of cream. Taste the gravy with salt, current jelly and cream *ad libitum*, and serve the ready dish with browned potatoes and mushrooms.

III. Apricot Pie
     1 pound of dried apricots
     6 eggs
     Sugar
     Vanilla

     The apricots are cooked and pressed through a sieve. The whites of the eggs are whipped (they must be quite stiff) to be mixed with the sweetened apricot mash and the whole mixture is then baked in the oven for about 20 minutes. The 6 egg yolks are whipped with sugar and vanilla to be served (cold) together with the (hot) pie.

     The recipes are intended for six persons.

137 *something a little choice in white wines.* Messrs. Morley and Pratt both suggested a Montrachet; Mr. Jorgen Cøld thought that it might have been a Steinberger Kabinett.

138 *on mediæval pottery.* Holmes' interest in many facets of the Middle Ages is suggested again in the adventures of "The Bruce-Partington Plans" and "The Three Students."

139 *on the Buddhism of Ceylon.* In his fascinating work, *Sherlock Holmes' Wanderjahre,* the late A. Carson Simpson demonstrated that Holmes during his stay in Tibet (1891–1893) "was assiduous in his study of Lamaistic Buddhism and eventually became an adept."

140 *bon vivant.* French: a lover of good living, especially of the table; a gourmet.

141 *filled up three glasses with port.* "It is to be noted," the late Fletcher Pratt wrote in "The Gastronomic Holmes," "that Holmes poured [the port] himself; another sign of the true gourmet, who would rather let a gorilla handle his sister than a waiter touch his port."

142 *a change of work is the best rest.* Holmes is referring to an aphorism usually credited to William Ewart Gladstone, 1809–1898, Prime Minister of England, 1868–1874, 1880–1885, 1886, 1892–1894. But, as Mr. T. S. Blakeney asked in "Thoughts on *The Sign of the Four,*" "can anyone say when and where he made this remark, and quote the authority for it?"

143 *succeeded in dissolving the hydrocarbon.* "It is inconceivable that dissolving a hydrocarbon should be a problem, even momentarily, to a chemist," Professor Remsen Ten Eyck Schenck wrote in "Baker Street Fables." "Holmes might as well have said 'when I had succeeded in tying my boot-lace,' with the air of having triumphed over great obstacles after days of heroic effort."

With this view, Dr. John D. Clark is in complete agreement ("A Chemist's View of Canonical Chemistry"): "There is rarely any difficulty in dissolving a hydrocarbon . . . All you have to do is apply a lighter liquid hydrocarbon, and *voilà!,* you have your solution. If you have ever removed a glob of tar from a fender with a gasoline-soaked rag, you know what I mean."

But Mr. Leon S. Holstein has written ("7. Knowledge of Chemistry—Profound'"): ". . . it is my understanding, from those versed in the art, that one method of examining unknown organic compounds is to first determine physical properties, one of which is the solubility or insolubility

Our meal was a merry one. Holmes could talk exceedingly well when he chose, and that night he did choose. He appeared to be in a state of nervous exaltation. I have never known him so brilliant. He spoke on a quick succession **138** of subjects—on miracle plays, on mediæval pottery, on **139** Stradivarius violins, on the Buddhism of Ceylon, and on the warships of the future—handling each as though he had made a special study of it. His bright humour marked the reaction from his black depression of the preceding days. Athelney Jones proved to be a sociable soul in his hours of relaxation, **140** and faced his dinner with the air of a *bon vivant.* For myself, I felt elated at the thought that we were nearing the end of our task, and I caught something of Holmes's gaiety. None of us alluded during dinner to the cause which had brought us together.

When the cloth was cleared, Holmes glanced at his watch, **141** and filled up three glasses with port.

'One bumper,' said he, 'to the success of our little expedition. And now it is high time we were off. Have you a pistol, Watson?'

'I have my old service-revolver in my desk.'

'You had best take it, then. It is well to be prepared. I see that the cab is at the door. I ordered it for half-past six.'

It was a little past seven before we reached the Westminster Wharf, and found our launch awaiting us. Holmes eyed it critically.

'Is there anything to mark it as a police-boat?'

'Yes; that green lamp at the side.'

'Then take it off.'

The small change was made, we stepped on board, and the ropes were cast off. Jones, Holmes, and I sat in the stern. There was one man at the rudder, one to tend the engines, and two burly police-inspectors forward.

'Where to?' asked Jones.

'To the Tower. Tell them to stop opposite to Jacobson's Yard.'

Our craft was evidently a very fast one. We shot past the long lines of loaded barges as though they were stationary. Holmes smiled with satisfaction as we overhauled a river steamer and left her behind us.

'We ought to be able to catch anything on the river,' he said.

'Well, hardly that. But there are not many launches to beat us.'

'We shall have to catch the *Aurora,* and she has a name for being a clipper. I will tell you how the land lies, Watson. You recollect how annoyed I was at being baulked by so small a thing?'

'Yes.'

'Well, I gave my mind a thorough rest by plunging into a chemical analysis. One of our greatest statesmen has said that **142** a change of work is the best rest. So it is. When I had suc- **143** ceeded in dissolving the hydrocarbon which I was at work at, I came back to the problem of the Sholtos, and thought the **whole matter out again.** My boys had been up the river and down the river without result. The launch was not at any landing-stage or wharf, nor had it returned. Yet it could hardly have been scuttled to hide their traces, though that always remained as a possible hypothesis if all else failed. I knew that this man Small had a certain degree of low cunning, but I did not think him capable of anything in the nature of delicate finesse. That is usually a product of higher education. I then reflected that since he had certainly been in London some time—as we had evidence that he maintained a continual watch over Pondicherry Lodge—he could hardly leave at a moment's notice, but would need some little time, if it were only a day, to arrange his affairs. That was the balance of probability, at any rate.'

'It seems to me to be a little weak,' said I: 'it is more probable that he had arranged his affairs before ever he set out upon his expedition.'

'No, I hardly think so. This lair of his would be too valuable a retreat in case of need for him to give it up until he was sure that he could do without it. But a second consideration struck me. Jonathan Small must have felt that the peculiar appearance of his companion, however much he may have top-coated him, would give rise to gossip, and possibly be associated with this Norwood tragedy. He was quite sharp enough to see that. They had started from their head-quarters under cover of darkness, and he would wish to get back before it was broad light. Now, it was past three o'clock, according to Mrs Smith, when they got the boat. It would be quite bright, and people would be about in an hour or so. There-**144** fore, I argued, they did not go very far. They paid Smith well to hold his tongue, reserved his launch for the final escape, and hurried to their lodgings with the treasure-box. In a

in various reagents. The remark in question was merely to convey that whatever compound or admixture he was working on, Holmes had determined that it was soluble in some standard reagent."

144 *in an hour or so.* It would therefore be quite bright, and people would be about, a little past four o'clock on the Tuesday morning. Again, this is a meaningless statement in July. To sum up what we know about this Tuesday: there was fog, according to both Holmes and Watson, and it was a steamy, vaporous day, according to Watson. A half-moon (Watson says) rose well before 11:00 P.M. There was no rain on this day, according to Holmes, and it was a day on which it would have been "quite bright" shortly after 4:00 A.M. For the record, on Tuesday, September 18, 1888, "fog and mist" were "reported locally." No sunshine whatsoever was recorded at Westminster. The moon was two days before the full; it rose at 5:55 P.M. and set at 3:12 A.M. Day broke at 3:43 A.M., so it would certainly have been "quite bright" by 4:00 A.M.

"TO THE TOWER."

The Tower of London, from South Bank, as photographed by G. F. Allen for the *Second Country Life Picture Book of London*, London: Country Life, Ltd., 1953. The turreted and massive White Tower is the oldest part of the fortress. It was begun in the reign of William the Conquerer on a site that the Roman legionaries had used before him.

145 *the Downs*. The anchorage for ships inside the Goodwin Sands just south of the Thames Estuary.

couple of nights, when they had time to see what view the papers took, and whether there was any suspicion, they would make their way under cover of darkness to some ship at **145** Gravesend or in the Downs, where no doubt they had already arranged for passages to America or the Colonies.'

'But the launch? They could not have taken that to their lodgings.'

'Quite so. I argued that the launch must be no great way off, in spite of its invisibility. I then put myself in the place of Small, and looked at it as a man of his capacity would. He would probably consider that to send back the launch or to keep it at a wharf would make pursuit easy if the police did happen to get on his track. How, then, could he conceal the launch and yet have her at hand when wanted? I wondered what I should do myself if I were in his shoes. I could only think of one way of doing it. I might hand the launch over to some boat-builder or repairer, with directions to make a trifling change in her. She would then be removed to his shed or yard, and so be effectually concealed, while at the same time I could have her at a few hours' notice.'

'That seems simple enough.'

'It is just these very simple things which are extremely liable to be overlooked. However, I determined to act on the idea. I started at once in this harmless seaman's rig, and inquired at all the yards down the river. I drew blank at fifteen, but at the sixteenth—Jacobson's— I learned that the *Aurora* had been handed over to them two days ago by a wooden-legged man, with some trivial directions as to her rudder. "There ain't naught amiss with her rudder," said the foreman. "There she lies, with the red streaks." At that moment who should come down but Mordecai Smith, the missing owner! He was rather the worse for liquor. I should not, of course, have known him, but he bellowed out his name and the name of his launch. "I want her tonight at eight o'clock," said he—"eight o'clock sharp, mind, for I have two gentlemen who won't be kept waiting." They had evidently paid him well, for he was very flush of money, chucking shillings about to the men. I followed him some distance, but he subsided into an ale-house; so I went back to the yard, and, happening to pick up one of my boys on the way, I stationed him as a sentry over the launch. He is to stand at the water's edge and wave his handkerchief to us when they start. We shall be lying off in the stream, and it will be a strange thing if we do not take men, treasure and all.'

'You have planned it all very neatly, whether they are the right men or not,' said Jones; 'but if the affair were in my hands I should have had a body of police in Jacobson's Yard, and arrested them when they came down.'

'Which would have been never. This man Small is a pretty shrewd fellow. He would send a scout on ahead, and if anything made him suspicious he would lie snug for another week.'

'But you might have stuck to Mordecai Smith, and so been led to their hiding-place,' said I.

'In that case I should have wasted my day. I think that it is a hundred to one against Smith knowing where they live. As long as he has liquor and good pay, why should he ask questions? They send him messages what to do. No, I thought over every possible course, and this is the best.'

While this conversation had been proceeding, we had been

Our photograph, by G. F. Allen, is from the *Second Country Life Picture Book of London*, London: Country Life, Ltd., 1953. Watson's statement here is the one statement in the entire chronicle which casts any doubt whatsoever upon September: on the Friday that ended the case, sunset—Watson tells us—came a few minutes after seven. On September 1st, sunset would come at 6:44 P.M.; on September 15th it would come at 5:13 P.M.; on September 30th the time would be 5:38 P.M. No one can doubt that Holmes and Watson boarded the police launch "a little past seven" as Watson tells us they did: Holmes says he ordered the cab for half-past six and the launch "to be ready at the Westminster Stairs at seven o'clock." And Holmes tells us that Mordecai Smith ordered *his* launch to be ready "at eight o'clock sharp, mind . . ." In brief, we have only Watson's uncorroborated statement that sunset came shortly after seven o'clock, and not considerably earlier, on that Friday evening; such evidence cannot be allowed to outweigh the heavy Holmesian evidence that the sun rose sometime after five o'clock on the preceding Wednesday morning—before six, surely, and probably, from the conversation recorded by Watson, around 5:45.

shooting the long series of bridges which span the Thames. As we passed the City the last rays of the sun were gilding the cross upon the summit of St Paul's. It was twilight before we reached the Tower.

'That is Jacobson's Yard,' said Holmes, pointing to a bristle of masts and rigging on the Surrey side. 'Cruise gently up and down here under cover of this string of lighters.' He took a pair of night-glasses from his pocket and gazed some time at the shore. 'I see my sentry at his post,' he remarked, 'but no sign of a handketchief.'

'Suppose we go downstream a short way and lie in wait for them,' said Jones, eagerly.

We were all eager by this time, even the policemen and stokers, who had a very vague idea of what was going forward.

'We have no right to take anything for granted,' Holmes answered. 'It is certainly ten to one that they go downstream, but we cannot be certain. From this point we can see the entrance of the yard, and they can hardly see us. It will be a clear night and plenty of light. We must stay where we are. **146** See how the folk swarm over yonder in the gaslight.'

'They are coming from work in the yard.'

'Dirty-looking rascals, but I suppose everyone has some little immortal spark concealed about him. You would not think it, to look at them. There is no *a priori* probability **147** about it. A strange enigma is man!'

146 *It will be a clear night and plenty of light.* Watson speaks later of the "moon glimmering on the marshland." For the record, the moon on the night of Friday, September 21, 1888, was one day past the full; it rose at 6:57 P.M.

147 a priori. Latin: from the first.

148 *So says the statistician.* "Now, for purposes of comparison, consider exactly what Reade did say," Professor Stephen F. Crocker wrote in "Sherlock Holmes Recommends Winwood Reade":

> All the events which occur upon the earth result from Law: even those actions which are entirely dependent on the caprices of the memory, or the impulse of the passions, are shown by statistics to be, when taken in the gross, entirely independent of the human will. As a single atom, man is an enigma; as a whole, he is a mathematical problem. As an individual, he is a free agent; as a species, the offspring of necessity.

"This passage is clearly the one Holmes had in mind because it is the only one in *The Martyrdom of Man* which resembles the one in *The Sign of the Four*. . . . But a comparison of the Holmes passage with that of Reade shows not only striking resemblances, but also significant differences."

149 *the Pool.* The name given to that part of the Thames between London Bridge and Cuckolds Point.

150 *the West India Docks.* The oldest enclosed docks in London, opened in 1802, the West India Docks lie between Limehouse and Blackwall, to the north of the Isle of Dogs. The three principal basins, the Import Dock, the Export Dock, and the South Dock, are stored principally with frozen mutton, rum, sugar, hops, grain, and hardwood timbers.

151 *the long Deptford Reach.* About a mile long, from the end of Limehouse Reach to Greenwich Ferry.

152 *the Isle of Dogs.* On the left bank of the Thames opposite Greenwich. "An uninviting title euphemistically derived from 'Isle of Ducks,' and applied to what was till lately about the best imitation on a small scale of the Great Dismal Swamp to be found in England. The place, it may be observed *en passant*, was not until late years an island at all, but simply a peninsula jutting out into the river between Limehouse and Blackwall. Just at the beginning of the [nineteenth] century, however, the Corporation, which had long been exercised by the demands of enterprising engineers for permission to cut the river straight and take possession of its old Scamandering bed for docks, took heart of grace, and cut a canal through the neck of the 'unlucky Isle of Doggs,' as Master Pepys hath it, and so opened a short cut for ships bound up and down the river. Apparently, however, the new road was not found satisfactory, for it has long since been closed and sold to the West India Dock Company, who now use it as a timber dock."—*Dickens' Dictionary of the Thames from Its Source to the Nore: An Unconventional Handbook.*

'Someone calls him a soul concealed in an animal,' I suggested.

'Winwood Reade is good upon the subject,' said Holmes. 'He remarks that, while the individual man is an insoluble puzzle, in the aggregate he becomes a mathematical certainty. You can, for example, never foretell what any one man will do, but you can say with precision what an average number will be up to. Individuals vary, but percentages remain con- **148** stant. So says the statistician. But do I see a handkerchief? Surely there is a white flutter over yonder.'

'Yes, it is your boy,' I cried. 'I can see him plainly.'

'And there is the *Aurora*,' exclaimed Holmes, 'and going like the devil! Full speed ahead, engineer. Make after that launch with the yellow light. By Heaven, I shall never forgive myself if she proves to have the heels of us!'

She had slipped unseen through the yard-entrance and passed behind two or three small craft, so that she had fairly got her speed up before we saw her. Now she was flying down the stream, near in to the shore, going at a tremendous rate. Jones looked gravely at her and shook his head.

'She is very fast,' he said. 'I doubt if we shall catch her.'

'We *must* catch her!' cried Holmes, between his teeth. 'Heap it on, stokers! Make her do all she can! If we burn the boat we must have them!'

We were fairly after her now. The furnaces roared, and the powerful engines whizzed and clanked, like a great metallic heart. Her sharp, steep prow cut through the still river-water and sent two rolling waves to right and to left of us. With every throb of the engines we sprang and quivered like a living thing. One great yellow lantern in our bows threw a long, flickering funnel of light in front of us. Right ahead a dark blur upon the water showed where the *Aurora* lay, and the swirl of white foam behind her spoke of the pace at which she was going. We flashed past barges, steamers, merchant-vessels, in and out, behind this one and round the other. Voices hailed us out of the darkness, but still the *Aurora* thundered on, and still we followed close upon her track.

'Pile it on, men, pile it on!' cried Holmes, looking down into the engine-room, while the fierce glow from below beat upon his eager, aquiline face. 'Get every pound of steam you can.'

'I think we gain a little,' said Jones, with his eyes on the *Aurora*.

'I am sure of it,' said I. 'We shall be up with her in a very few minutes.'

At that moment, however, as our evil fate would have it, a tug with three barges in tow blundered in between us. It was only by putting our helm hard down that we avoided a collision, and before we could round them and recover our way the *Aurora* had gained a good two hundred yards. She was still, however, well in view, and the murky, uncertain twilight was settling into a clear starlit night. Our boilers were strained to their utmost, and the frail shell vibrated and creaked with the fierce energy which was driving us along. **149–150** We had shot through the Pool, past the West India Docks, **151** down the long Deptford Reach, and up again after rounding **152** the Isle of Dogs. The dull blur in front of us resolved itself now clearly enough into the dainty *Aurora*. Jones turned our searchlight upon her, so that we could plainly see the figures upon her deck. One man sat by the stern, with something black between his knees, over which he stooped. Beside him lay a dark mass, which looked like a Newfoundland dog. The boy held the tiller, while against the red glare of the furnace I could see old Smith, stripped to the waist, and shovelling coals for dear life. They may have had some doubt at first as to whether we were really pursuing them, but now as we followed every winding and turning which they took there could no longer be any question about it. At Greenwich we were about three hundred paces behind them. At Blackwall **153** we could not have been more than two hundred and fifty. I have coursed many creatures in many countries during my **154** chequered career, but never did sport give me such a wild thrill as this mad, flying man-hunt down the Thames. Steadily we drew in upon them, yard by yard. In the silence of the night we could hear the panting and clanking of their machinery. The man in the stern still crouched upon the deck, and his arms were moving as though he were busy, while every now and then he would look up and measure with a glance the distance which still separated us. Nearer we came and nearer. Jones yelled to them to stop. We were not more than four boat's lengths behind them, both boats flying at a tremendous pace. It was a clear reach of the river, with Barking Level **155** upon one side and the melancholy Plumstead Marshes upon **156** the other. At our hail the man in the stern sprang up from the deck and shook his two clenched fists at us, cursing the while in a high, cracked voice. He was a good-sized, powerful man, and as he stood poising himself with legs astride, I could see that, from the thigh downwards, there was but a wooden stump upon the right side. At the sound of his strident, angry cries, there was a movement in the huddled bundle upon the deck. It straightened itself into a little black man—the smallest I have ever seen—with a great, misshapen head and a shock of tangled dishevelled hair. Holmes had already drawn his revolver, and I whipped out mine at the sight of this savage, distorted creature. He was wrapped in some sort of a dark ulster or blanket, which left only his face exposed; but that face was enough to give a man a sleepless night. Never have I seen features so deeply marked with all bestiality and cruelty. His small eyes glowed and burned with a sombre light, and his thick lips were writhed back from his teeth, which grinned and chattered at us with half-animal fury.

'Fire if he raises his hand,' said Holmes quietly.

We were within a boat's-length by this time, and almost within touch of our quarry. I can see the two of them now as they stood: the white man with his legs far apart, shrieking out curses, and the unhallowed dwarf with his hideous face, and his strong, yellow teeth gnashing at us in the light of our lantern.

It was well that we had so clear a view of him. Even as we looked he plucked out from under his covering a short, round piece of wood, like a school-ruler, and clapped it to his lips. Our pistols rang out together. He whirled round, threw up his arms, and, with a kind of choking cough, fell sideways into the stream. I caught one glimpse of his venomous, menacing eyes amid the white swirl of the waters. At the same moment the wooden-legged man threw himself upon the rudder and put it hard down, so that his boat made straight in for the southern bank, while we shot past her stern, only

153 *Blackwall.* On the left bank of the Thames from Orchard Wharf to the Isle of Dogs. "Here are the East India Docks, where the principal sailing ships trading with the port of London load and discharge. The visitor to these docks may still inspect some remaining few of the China tea-clippers—now [1892] almost run off the line by fast steamers—and the fine passenger ships trading to the Australasian ports. Adjoining the docks is the spacious ship-building yard of Messrs. Green, and farther down the river are the Trinity House head-quarters, beyond which again are the Royal Victoria and Albert Docks."—*Dickens' Dictionary of the Thames.*

154 *I have coursed many creatures in many countries.* One of the many passages in the Canon which show Watson's keen interest in hunting, as Mr. G. W. Welch has demonstrated in " 'No Mention of the Local Hunt, Watson.' "

155 *Barking Level.* On the left (Essex) bank of the Thames, at the northwest of Barking, more commonly called Tripcock Reach.

156 *Plumpstead Marshes.* Taking their name from the parish of Plumstead, a southeastern suburb of London. Until the middle of the nineteenth century the marshes formed a great alluvial deposit containing many thousands acres of land, five miles in length and one and a half miles wide, a hotbed of malaria.

clearing her by a few feet. We were round after her in an instant, but she was already nearly at the bank. It was a wild and desolate place, where the moon glimmered upon a wide expanse of marsh-land, with pools of stagnant water and beds of decaying vegetation. The launch, with a dull thud, ran up upon the mud-bank, with her bow in the air and her stern flush with the water. The fugitive sprang out, but his stump instantly sank its whole length into the sodden soil. In vain he struggled and writhed. Not one step could he possibly take either forwards or backwards. He yelled in impotent rage, and kicked frantically into the mud with his other foot; but his struggles only bored his wooden pin the deeper into the sticky bank. When we brought our launch alongside he was so firmly anchored that it was only by throwing the end of a rope over his shoulders that we were able to haul him out, and, to drag him, like some evil fish over our side. The two Smiths, father and son, sat sullenly in their launch, but came aboard meekly enough when commanded. The *Aurora* herself we hauled off and made fast to our stern. A solid iron chest of Indian workmanship stood upon the deck. This, there could be no question, was the same that had contained the ill-omened treasure of the Sholtos. There was no key, but it was of considerable weight, so we transferred it carefully to our own little cabin. As we steamed slowly upstream again, we flashed our searchlight in every direction, but there was no sign of the Islander. Somewhere in the dark ooze at the bottom of the Thames lie the bones of that strange visitor to our shores.

'See here,' said Holmes, pointing to the wooden hatchway. 'We were hardly quick enough with our pistols.' There, sure enough, just behind where we had been standing, stuck one of those murderous darts which we knew so well. It must have whizzed between us at the instant we fired. Holmes smiled at it and shrugged his shoulders in his easy fashion, but I confess that it turned me sick to think of the horrible death which had passed so close to us that night.

◆

I I ◆ THE GREAT AGRA TREASURE

◆

Our captive sat in the cabin opposite to the iron box which he had done so much and waited so long to gain. He was a sunburned, reckless-eyed fellow, with a network of lines and wrinkles all over his mahogany features, which told of a hard, open-air life. There was a singular prominence about his bearded chin which marked a man who was not to be easily turned from his purpose. His age may have been fifty or there-abouts, for his black, curly hair was thickly shot with grey. His face in repose was not an unpleasing one, though his heavy brows and aggressive chin gave him, as I had lately seen, a terrible expression when moved to anger. He sat now with his handcuffed hands upon his lap, and his head sunk upon his breast, while he looked with his keen, twinkling eyes at the box which had been the cause of his ill-doings. It seemed to me that there was more sorrow than anger in his rigid and contained countenance. Once he looked up at me with a gleam of something like humour in his eyes.

'Well, Jonathan Small,' said Holmes, lighting a cigar, 'I am sorry that it has come to this.'

'And so am I, sir,' he answered, frankly. 'I don't believe that I can swing over the job. I give you my word on the Book that I never raised hand against Mr Sholto. It was that little hell-hound Tonga who shot one of his cursed darts into him. I had no part in it, sir. I was as grieved as if it had been my blood-relation. I welted the little devil with the slack end of the rope for it, but it was done, and I could not undo it again.'

'Have a cigar,' said Holmes; 'and you had best take a pull out of my flask, for you are very wet. How could you expect so small and weak a man as this black fellow to overpower Mr Sholto and hold him while you were climbing the rope?'

'You seem to know as much about it as if you were there, sir. The truth is that I hoped to find the room clear. I knew the habits of the house pretty well, and it was the time when Mr Sholto usually went down to his supper. I shall make no secret of the business. The best defence that I can make is just the simple truth. Now, if it had been the old major I would have swung for him with a light heart. I would have thought no more of knifing him than of smoking this cigar. But it's cursed hard that I should be lagged over this young Sholto, with whom I had no quarrel whatever.'

'You are under the charge of Mr Athelney Jones, of Scotland Yard. He is going to bring you up to my rooms, and I shall ask you for a true account of the matter. You must make a clean breast of it, for if you do I hope that I may be of use to you. I think I can prove that the poison acts so quickly that the man was dead before ever you reached the room.'

'That he was, sir. I never got such a turn in my life as when I saw him grinning at me with his head on his shoulder as I climbed through the window. It fairly shook me, sir. I'd have half killed Tonga for it if he had not scrambled off. That was how he came to leave his club, and some of his darts, too, as he tells me, which I dare say helped to put you on our track; though how you kept on it is more than I can tell. I don't feel no malice against you for it. But it does seem a queer thing,' he added, with a bitter smile, 'that I, who have a fair claim to half a million of money, should spend the first half of my life building a breakwater in the Andamans, and am like to spend the other half digging drains at Dartmoor. It **157** was an evil day for me when first I clapped eyes upon the merchant Achmet and had to do with the Agra treasure, which never brought anything but a curse yet upon the man who owned it. To him, it brought murder, to Major Sholto it brought fear and guilt, to me it has meant slavery for life.'

At this moment Athelney Jones thrust his face and shoulders into the tiny cabin.

'Quite a family party,' he remarked. 'I think I shall have a pull at that flask, Holmes. Well, I think we may all congratulate each other. Pity we didn't take the other alive; but there was no choice. I say, Holmes, you must confess that you cut it rather fine. It was all we could do to overhaul her.'

"IT WAS THAT LITTLE HELL-HOUND TONGA WHO SHOT ONE OF HIS CURSED DARTS INTO HIM."

One of the eight superb pictures drawn by F. H. Townsend for the "Souvenir Edition" of *The Sign of the Four* published by George Newnes in 1903.

157 *Dartmoor*. That is, at Princetown Prison, in the wild upland country of South Devon. The prison was first built in 1809 to receive French prisoners captured in the Napoleonic Wars. (Conan Doyle has his Napoleonic D'Artagnan, the Brigadier Etienne Gerard, escape from Princetown Prison in the short story called "How the King Held the Brigadier" in *Exploits of Gerard*.) There are exciting allusions to Princetown Prison in our next adventure, *The Hound of the Baskervilles*.

158 *Vauxhall Bridge.* An iron structure of nine spans, built in 1811–1816 to connect Kennington with Pimlico.

159 *the obliging inspector.* "An obliging inspector indeed!," Mr. Ronald S. Bonn wrote in his prize-winning essay, "The Problem of the Postulated Doctor." "Would any inspector in London so have obliged any civilian in the world than this one—the one man alive whose conduct bore the imprimatur of Sherlock Holmes' friendship? And what must that obliging inspector's feelings have been, some time later—quite a long time later, Watson admits—when the doctor reappeared and cooly showed him an empty box?"

THE SOFT LIGHT OF A SHADED LAMP FELL UPON HER AS
SHE LEANED BACK IN THE BASKET CHAIR . . .

One of the very few existing portraits of Miss Mary Morstan, by an as-yet-unidentified artist, from *Stories of Sherlock Holmes*, Vol. I, New York: Harper & Brothers, 1904.

'All is well that ends well,' said Holmes. 'But I certainly did not know that the *Aurora* was such a clipper.'

'Smith says she is one of the fastest launches on the river, and that if he had had another man to help him with the engines we should never have caught her. He swears he knew nothing of this Norwood business.'

'Neither he did,' cried our prisoner—'not a word. I chose his launch because I heard that she was a flier. We told him nothing; but we paid him well, and he was to get something handsome if we reached our vessel, the *Esmeralda*, at Gravesend, outward bound for the Brazils.'

'Well, if he has done no wrong we shall see that no wrong comes to him. If we are pretty quick in catching our men, we are not so quick in condemning them.' It was amusing to notice how the consequential Jones was already beginning to give himself airs on the strength of the capture. From the slight smile which played over Sherlock Holmes's face, I could see that the speech had not been lost upon him.

158 'We will be at Vauxhall Bridge presently,' said Jones, ' and shall land you, Dr Watson, with the treasure-box. I need hardly tell you that I am taking a very grave responsibility upon myself in doing this. It is most irregular; but of course an agreement is an agreement. I must, however, as a matter of duty, send an inspector with you, since you have so valuable a charge. You will drive, no doubt?'

'Yes, I shall drive.'

'It is a pity there is no key, that we may make an inventory first. You will have to break it open. Where is the key, my man?'

'At the bottom of the river,' said Small shortly.

'Hum! There was no use your giving this unnecessary trouble. We have had work enough already through· you. However, doctor, I need not warn you to be careful. Bring the box back with you to the Baker Street rooms. You will find us there, on our way to the station.'

They landed me at Vauxhall, with my heavy iron box, and with a bluff, genial inspector as my companion. A quarter of an hour's drive brought us to Mrs Cecil Forrester's. The servant seemed surprised at so late a visitor. Mrs Cecil Forrester was out for the evening, she explained, and likely to be very late. Miss Morstan, however, was in the drawing-room; so to the drawing-room I went, box in hand, leaving the obliging

159 inspector in the cab.

She was seated by the open window, dressed in some sort of white diaphanous material, with a little touch of scarlet at the neck and waist. The soft light of a shaded lamp fell upon her as she leaned back in the basket chair, playing over her sweet, grave face, and tinting with a dull, metallic sparkle the rich coils of her luxuriant hair. One white arm and hand drooped over the side of the chair, and her whole pose and figure spoke of an absorbing melancholy. At the sound of my footfall she sprang to her feet, however, and a bright flush of surprise and of pleasure coloured her pale cheeks.

'I heard a cab drive up,' she said. 'I thought that Mrs Forrester had come back very early, but I never dreamed that it might be you. What news have you brought me?'

'I have brought something better than news,' said I, putting down the box upon the table and speaking jovially and boisterously, though my heart was heavy within me. 'I have brought you something which is worth all the news in the world. I have brought you a fortune.'

She glanced at the iron box.

'Is that the treasure, then?' she asked, coolly enough.

'Yes, this is the great Agra treasure. Half of it is yours and half is Thaddeus Sholto's. You will have a couple of hundred thousand each. Think of that! an annuity of ten thousand pounds. There will be few richer young ladies in England. Is it not glorious?'

I think that I must have been rather overacting my delight, and that she detected a hollow ring in my congratulations, for I saw her eyebrows rise a little, and she glanced at me curiously.

'If I have it,' said she, 'I owe it to you.'

'No, no,' I answered, 'not to me, but to my friend Sherlock Holmes. With all the will in the world, I could never have followed up a clue which has taxed even his analytical genius. As it was, we very nearly lost it at the last moment.'

'Pray sit down and tell me all about it, Dr Watson,' said she.

I narrated briefly what had occurred since I had seen her last. Holmes's new method of search, the discovery of the *Aurora,* the appearance of Athelney Jones, our expedition in the evening, and the wild chase down the Thames. She listened with parted lips and shining eyes to my recital of our adventures. When I spoke of the dart which had so narrowly missed us, she turned so white that I feared that she was about to faint.

'It is nothing,' she said, as I hastened to pour her out some water. 'I am all right again. It was a shock to me to hear that I had placed my friends in such horrible peril.'

'That is all over,' I answered. 'It was nothing. I will tell you no more gloomy details. Let us turn to something brighter. There is the treasure. What could be brighter than that? I got leave to bring it with me, thinking that it would interest you to be the first to see it.'

'It would be of the greatest interest to me,' she said. There was no eagerness in her voice, however. It had struck her, doubtless, that it might seem ungracious upon her part to be indifferent to a prize which had cost so much to win.

'What a pretty box!' she said, stooping over it. 'This is Indian work, I suppose?'

'Yes; it is Benares metal-work.'

'And so heavy!' she exclaimed, trying to raise it. 'The box alone must be of some value. Where is the key?'

'Small threw it into the Thames,' I answered. 'I must borrow Mrs Forrester's poker.'

There was in the front a thick and broad hasp, wrought in the image of a sitting Buddha. Under this I thrust the end of the poker and twisted it outward as a lever. The hasp sprang open with a loud snap. With trembling fingers I flung back the lid. We both stood gazing in astonishment. The box was empty!

No wonder that it was heavy. The iron-work was two-thirds of an inch thick all round. It was massive, well made, and solid, like a chest constructed to carry things of great price, but not one shred or crumb of metal or jewellery lay within it. It was absolutely and completely empty.

'The treasure is lost,' said Miss Morstan, calmly.

As I listened to the words and realized what they meant, a great shadow seemed to pass from my soul. I did not know

160 *as truly as ever a man loved a woman.* "Note the restraint of [this] avowal," Mr. Nathan L. Bengis wrote in "A Scandal in Baker Street." Watson "would not commit himself to say what we can easily imagine him to have declared to [an earlier love]: 'No man ever loved a woman as I love you.' . . . It is easy to see now that [Mary Morstan], jealous as she was, must have felt that in Watson's affections she was always second to 'that other.'"

43   44

44a   45

'THERE ARE NO RUPEES FOR YOU THIS JOURNEY.'

From A. Carson Simpson's *Numismatics in the Canon*, Part II, we show the four types of rupee in circulation up to the time of *The Sign of the Four*: *43* is the East India Company Surat mint sicca (no date); *44* is the East India Company William IV rupee of 1834; *44a* is the East India Company Victoria, bare head rupee of 1849, obverse only; *45* is the East India Company Victoria, crowned head rupee of 1862.

how this Agra treasure had weighed me down, until now that it was finally removed. It was selfish, no doubt, disloyal, wrong, but I could realize nothing save that the golden barrier was gone from between us.

'Thank God!' I ejaculated from my very heart.

She looked at me with a quick, questioning smile.

'Why do you say that?' she asked.

'Because you are within my reach again,' I said, taking her hand. She did not withdraw it. 'Because I love you, Mary, as **160** truly as ever a man loved a woman. Because this treasure, these riches, sealed my lips. Now that they are gone I can tell you how I love you. That is why I said, "Thank God."'

'Then I say "Thank God," too,' she whispered, as I drew her to my side.

Whoever had lost a treasure, I knew that night that I had gained one.

12 ❖ THE STRANGE STORY OF ❖ JONATHAN SMALL

A very patient man was that inspector in the cab, for it was a weary time before I rejoined him. His face clouded over when I showed him the empty box.

'There goes the reward!' said he, gloomily. 'Where there is no money there is no pay. This night's work would have been worth a tenner each to Sam Brown and me if the treasure had been there.'

'Mr Thaddeus Sholto is a rich man,' I said; 'he will see that you are rewarded, treasure or no.'

The inspector shook his head despondently, however.

'It's a bad job,' he repeated; 'and so Mr Athelney Jones will think.'

His forecast proved to be correct, for the detective looked blank enough when I got to Baker Street and showed him the empty box. They had only just arrived, Holmes, the prisoner, and he, for they had changed their plans so far as to report themselves at a station upon the way. My companion lounged in his arm-chair with his usual listless expression, while Small sat stolidly opposite to him with his wooden leg cocked over his sound one. As I exhibited the empty box he leaned back in his chair and laughed aloud.

'This is your doing, Small,' said Athelney Jones, angrily.

'Yes, I have put it away where you shall never lay hand on it,' he cried, exultantly. 'It is my treasure, and if I can't have the loot I'll take darned good care that no one else does. I tell you that no living man has any right to it, unless it is three men who are in the Andaman convict-barracks and myself. I know now that I cannot have the use of it, and I know that they cannot. I have acted all through for them as much as for myself. It's been the sign of four with us always. Well, I know that they would have had me do just what I have done, and throw the treasure into the Thames rather than let it go to kith or kin of Sholto or Morstan. It was not to make them rich that we did for Achmet. You'll find the treasure where the key is, and where little Tonga is. When I saw that your launch must catch us, I put the loot away in a safe place. There are no rupees for you this journey.'

'You are deceiving us, Small,' said Athelney Jones, sternly. 'If you had wished to throw the treasure into the Thames, it would have been easier for you to have thrown box and all.'

'Easier for me to throw, and easier for you to recover,' he answered, with a shrewd, side-long look. 'The man that was clever enough to hunt me down is clever enough to pick an iron box from the bottom of a river. Now that they are scattered over five miles or so, it may be a harder job. It went to my heart to do it, though. I was half mad when you came up with us. However, there's no good grieving over it. I've had ups in my life, and I've had downs, but I've learned not to cry over spilled milk.'

'This is a very serious matter, Small,' said the detective. 'If you had helped justice, instead of thwarting it in this way, you would have had a better chance at your trial.'

'Justice!' snarled the ex-convict. 'A pretty justice! Whose loot is this, if it is not ours? Where is the justice that I should give it up to those who have never earned it? Look how I have earned it! Twenty long years in that fever-ridden swamp, all **161** day at work under the mangrove-tree, all night chained up in the filthy convict-huts, bitten by mosquitoes, racked with ague, bullied by every cursed black-faced policeman who loved to take it out of a white man. That was how I earned the Agra treasure, and you talk to me of justice because I cannot bear to feel that I have paid this price only that another may enjoy it! I would rather swing a score of times, or have one of Tonga's darts in my hide, than live in a convict's cell and feel that another man is at his ease in a palace with the money that should be mine.'

Small had dropped his mask of stoicism, and all this came out in a wild whirl of words, while his eyes blazed and the handcuffs clanked together with the impassioned movement of his hands. I could understand, as I saw the fury and the passion of the man, that it was no groundless or unnatural terror which had possessed Major Sholto when he first learned that the injured convict was upon his track.

'You forget that we know nothing of all this,' said Holmes, quietly. 'We have not heard your story, and we cannot tell how far justice may originally have been on your side.'

'Well, sir, you have been very fair-spoken to me, though I can see that I have you to thank that I have these bracelets upon my wrists. Still, I bear no grudge for that. It is all fair and above-board. If you want to hear my story, I have no wish to hold it back. What I say to you is God's truth, every word of it. Thank you, you can put the glass beside me here, and I'll put my lips to it if I am dry.

'I am a Worcestershire man myself, born near Pershore. I **162** dare say you would find a heap of Smalls living there now if you were to look. I have often thought of taking a look round there, but the truth is that I was never much of a credit to the family, and I doubt if they would be so very glad to see me. They were all steady, chapel-going folk, small farmers, well known and respected over the country-side, while I was always a bit of a rover. At last, however, when I was about eighteen, I gave them no more trouble, for I got into a mess over a girl,

161 *Twenty long years in that fever-ridden swamp.* "The relief of Agra by Greathed was, as a matter of history, on 10th October, 1857, and as the Mutiny was virtually over before Small was arrested, his trial was certainly not much earlier than 1858," Mr. T. S. Blakeney wrote in *Sherlock Holmes: Fact or Fiction?* "He was in prison first in Agra, then Madras, before he proceeded to the Andamans, where he would arrive about 1860. Add his twenty years, plus the considerable time on his journey to England (as described), plus the time taken in locating Major Sholto, and we can see that the spring of 1882 as the date of the latter's death is just about right. It is true Small speaks of arriving in England 'some three or four years ago,' but he is not attempting chronological accuracy."

162 *Pershore.* Worcestershire is a county in West Central England; mostly hilly, it has famous orchards and much sheep pasturage. There are rich iron and coal deposits in the northern part. Its city of Worcester is the home of the world-famous "Worcestershire sauce." Pershore, Small's home town, is an ancient market village.

163 *taking the Queen's shilling.* The pay of Tommy Atkins at that time was a shilling a day:

> Jolly good pay
> Lucky to touch it
> A shilling a day.

164 *the 3rd Buffs.* "This is a real and very famous regiment," Mrs. Crighton Sellars wrote in "Dr. Watson and the British Army," "officially known as the Buffs (East Kent Regiment) consisting of the Third Foot. It is one of the oldest in the British Army, having its origin at the time of Queen Elizabeth [I]. . . . It is hard to believe that [Small] really belonged to this regiment, because it was sent to the Crimea in 1855—too late for Balaklava and Inkerman, but in time for the famous assault on the Redan—and stayed there until the Mutiny in India was over. The Buffs' previous service in India was under General Grey at Punniar against the Mahrattas in 1843, and I doubt if Small went there with them at that date, particularly as they had not been in England before that, but went to India from New South Wales."

165 *John Holder.* Mr. T. S. Blakeney, in "Thoughts on *The Sign of the Four*," suggests that John Holder "was a younger brother of Alexander Holder, the banker in 'The Adventure of the Beryl Coronet.' John Holder was, perhaps, the black sheep of a rather odd family, for not only was Alexander Holder temperamental till it could verge on madness . . . , but his son was a ne'er-do-well, and his niece's taste in men friends left a lot to be desired. I seem to see John Holder as the prototype of Kipling's Gentleman Ranker." And he added: "If this association between the cases of *The Sign of the Four* and 'The Beryl Coronet' is correct, it may not be the only one. I owe to our lamented friend, Gavin Brend, the excellent suggestion that the wooden-legged tradesman at whom Major Sholto once fired a revolver was none other than Francis Prosper, the fiancé of Lucy Parr, the maid at Fairbank, Streatham, the home of Alexander Holder. Streatham and Norwood are adjacent suburbs of London."

166 *the great mutiny.* "The Sepoy rebellion against British administration in India, 1857–1859," the late Christopher Morley wrote in *Sherlock Holmes and Dr. Watson: A Textbook of Friendship.* "Sepoys were native Indian troops. General McLeod Innes, V.C., in his history *The Sepoy Revolt* (1897) includes among immediate causes of the mutiny: 1) reduction of the British garrisons on account of the Crimean War; 2) an alleged prophecy, widely spread among superstitious natives, that British rule would come to an end in 100 years from Clive's conquest of Bengal in 1757; 3) equally superstitious dread of the railways and telegraphs being built; and 4) injudicious disregard of Hindu religious tenets. For instance,

163–164 and could only get out of it again by taking the Queen's shilling and joining the 3rd Buffs, which was just starting for India.

'I wasn't destined to do much soldiering, however. I had just got past the goose-step, and learned to handle my musket, when I was fool enough to go swimming in the Ganges. **165** Luckily for me, my company sergeant, John Holder, was in the water at the same time, and he was one of the finest swimmers in the Service. A crocodile took me, just as I was half-way across, and nipped off my right leg as clean as a surgeon could have done it, just above the knee. What with the shock and the loss of blood, I fainted, and should have been drowned if Holder had not caught hold of me and paddled for the bank. I was five months in hospital over it, and when at last I was able to limp out of it with this timber toe strapped to my stump I found myself invalided out of the army and unfitted for any active occupation.

'I was, as you can imagine, pretty down on my luck at this time, for I was a useless cripple, though not yet in my twentieth year. However, my misfortune soon proved to be a blessing in disguise. A man named Abel White, who had come out there as an indigo-planter, wanted an overseer to look after his coolies and keep them up to their work. He happened to be a friend of our colonel's who had taken an interest in me since the accident. To make a long story short, the colonel recommended me strongly for the post, and, as the work was mostly to be done on horseback, my leg was no great obstacle, for I had enough knee left to keep a good grip on the saddle. What I had to do was to ride over the plantation, to keep an eye on the men as they worked, and to report the idlers. The pay was fair, I had comfortable quarters, and altogether I was content to spend the remainder of my life in indigo-planting. Mr Abel White was a kind man, and he would often drop into my little shanty and smoke a pipe with me, for white folk out there feel their hearts warm to each other as they never do here at home.

'Well, I was never in luck's way long. Suddenly, without a **166** note of warning, the great mutiny broke upon us. One month India lay as still and peaceful, to all appearance, as Surrey or Kent; the next there were two hundred thousand black devils let loose, and the country was a perfect hell. Of course you know all about it, gentlemen—a deal more than I do, very like, since reading is not in my line. I only know what I saw with my own eyes. Our plantation was at a place called Muttra, near the border of the North-west Provinces. Night after night the whole sky was alight with the burning bungalows, and day after day we had small companies of Europeans passing through our estate with their wives and children, on their way to Agra, where were the nearest troops. Mr. Abel White was an obstinate man. He had it in his head that the affair had been exaggerated, and that it would blow over as suddenly as it had sprung up. There he sat on his **167** verandah, drinking whisky-pegs and smoking cheroots, while the country was in a blaze about him. Of course, we stuck by him, I and Dawson, who, with his wife, used to do the bookwork and the managing. Well, one fine day the crash came. I had been away on a distant plantation, and was riding slowly home in the evening, when my eye fell upon something **168** all huddled together at the bottom of a steep nullah. I rode down to see what it was, and the cold struck through my heart when I found it was Dawson's wife, all cut into ribbons and half-eaten by jackals and native dogs. A little farther up the road Dawson himself was lying on his face, quite dead, with an empty revolver in his hand, and four Sepoys lying across each other in front of him. I reined up my horse, wondering which way I should turn; but at that moment I saw thick smoke curling up from Abel White's bungalow, and the flames beginning to burst through the roof. I knew then that I could do my employer no good, but would only throw my own life away if I meddled in the matter. From where I stood I could see hundreds of the black fiends, with their red coats still on their backs dancing and howling round the burning house. Some of them pointed at me, and a couple of bullets sang past my head: so I broke away across the paddy-fields, **169** and found myself late at night safe within the walls at Agra.

'As it proved, however, there was no great safety here, either. The whole country was up like a swarm of bees. Wherever the English could collect in little bands, they held just the ground that their guns commanded. Everywhere else they were helpless fugitives. It was a fight of the millions against the hundreds; and the cruellest part of it was that these men that we fought against, foot, horse, and gunners, were our own picked troops, whom we had taught and trained, handling our own weapons and blowing our own bugle-calls. At Agra there were the 3rd Bengal Fusiliers, some **170** Sikhs, two troops of horse, and a battery of artillery. A volunteer corps of clerks and merchants had been formed, and this I joined, wooden leg and all. We went out to meet the rebels at Shahgunge early in July, and we beat them back for a time, but **171** our powder gave out, and we had to fall back upon the city.

'Nothing but the worst news came to us from every side—which is not to be wondered at, for if you look at the map you will see that we were right in the heart of it. Lucknow is rather better than a hundred miles to the east, and Cawnpore about as far to the south. From every point on the compass there was nothing but torture and murder and outrage.

'The city of Agra is a great place, swarming with fanatics and fierce devil-worshippers of all sorts. Our handful of men were lost among the narrow, winding streets. Our leader moved across the river, therefore, and took up his position in the old fort of Agra. I don't know if any of you gentlemen have ever read or heard anything of that old fort. It is a very queer place—the queerest that ever I was in, and I have been in some rum corners, too. First of all, it is enormous in size. I should think that the enclosure must be acres and acres. There is a modern part, which took all our garrison, women, children, stores, and everything else, with plenty of room over. But the modern part is nothing like the size of the old quarter, where nobody goes, and which is given over to the scorpions and the centipedes. It is all full of great, deserted halls, and winding passages, and long corridors twisting in and out, so that it is easy enough for folk to get lost in it. For this reason it was seldom that anyone went into it, though now and again a party with torches might go exploring.

'The river washes along the front of the old fort, and so protects it, but on the sides and behind there are many doors, and these had to be guarded, of course, in the old quarter as well as in that which was actually held by our troops. We were

a new rifle cartridge was introduced which was lubricated with animal grease; the cartridge cap had to be bitten off by the soldiers and this meant contamination to Hindus and Mohammedans. Also a new Enlistment Act was rumored to make it necessary for native troops to cross the ocean, which they called the Black Water and regarded with horror. The tragic massacre of European civilians at Cawnpore, the desperate defenses of Delhi and Lucknow, have become legendary. Most boys of my generation first read of them in the long series of historical juveniles written by good old G. A. Henty, 1832–1902.''

167 *whisky-pegs*. Anglo-Indian slang for a high-ball; whisky or brandy with soda. The usual explanation for the name is that each drink is a peg in your coffin.

168 *nullah*. Hindu word for a ravine or valley.

169 *paddy-fields*. Rice-fields, from *padi*, a Malayan word for rice.

170 *the 3rd Bengal Fusiliers*. "By which," Mrs. Crighton Sellars wrote in "Dr. Watson and the British Army," Small "probably meant (or else Watson deliberately misquotes him) the Third Bengal Infantry—the famous *Guttrieka-pultan*—which stood firm and loyal during the Mutiny."

171 *Shahgunge*. Between Lucknow and Cawnpore.

172 *Punjaubees.* Small evidently used—and Watson accepted—"Punjaubee" (Punjabi) and "Sikh" as interchangeable terms, which of course they are not.

173 *Chilian Wallah.* This battle, fought January 13, 1849, won for Britain the territory of the Punjab.

174 *bhang.* Indian hemp, smoked or chewed as a narcotic.

short-handed, with hardly men enough to man the angles of the building and to serve the guns. It was impossible for us, therefore, to station a strong guard at every one of the innumerable gates. What we did was to organize a central guard-house in the middle of the fort, and to leave each gate under the charge of one white man and two or three natives. I was selected to take charge during certain hours of the night of a small isolated door upon the south-west side of the building. Two Sikh troopers were placed under my command, and I was instructed if anything went wrong to fire my musket, when I might rely upon help coming at once from the central guard. As the guard was a good two hundred paces away, however, and as the space between was cut up into a labyrinth of passages and corridors, I had great doubts as to whether they could arrive in time to be of any use in case of an actual attack.

'Well, I was pretty proud at having this small command given me, since I was a raw recruit, and a game-legged one at
172 that. For two nights I kept the watch with my Punjaubees. They were tall, fierce-looking chaps, Mahomet Singh and Abdullah Khan by name, both old fighting-men, who had
173 borne arms against us at Chilian Wallah. They could talk English pretty well, but I could get little out of them. They preferred to stand together and jabber all night in their queer Sikh lingo. For myself, I used to stand outside the gateway looking down on the broad, winding river and on the twinkling lights of the great city. The beating of drums, the rattle of tom-toms, and the yells and howls of the rebels, drunk with
174 opium and with bhang, were enough to remind us all night of our dangerous neighbours across the stream. Every two hours the officer of the night used to come round to all the posts, to make sure that all was well.

'The third night of my watch was dark and dirty, with a small, driving rain. It was dreary work standing in the gateway hour after hour in such weather. I tried again and again to make my Sikhs talk, but without much success. At two in the morning the rounds passed, and broke for a moment the weariness of the night. Finding that my companions would not be led into conversation, I took out my pipe, and laid down my musket to strike a match. In an instant the two Sikhs were upon me. One of them snatched my firelock up and levelled it at my head, while the other held a great knife to my throat and swore between his teeth that he would plunge it into me if I moved a step.

'My first thought was that these fellows were in league with the rebels, and that this was the beginning of an assault. If our door were in the hands of the Sepoys the place must fall, and the women and children be treated as they were in Cawnpore. Maybe you gentlemen think that I am just making out a case for myself, but I give you my word that when I thought of that, though I felt the point of the knife at my throat, I opened my mouth with the intention of giving a scream, if it was my last one, which might alarm the main guard. The man who held me seemed to know my thoughts; for, even as I braced myself to it, he whispered: "Don't make a noise. The fort is safe enough. There are no rebel dogs on this side of the river." There was the ring of truth in what he said, and I knew that if I raised my voice I was a dead man. I could read it in the fellow's brown eyes. I waited, therefore, in silence, to see what it was that they wanted from me.

' "Listen to me, sahib," said the taller and fiercer of the pair, the one whom they called Abdullah Khan. "You must either be with us now, or you must be silenced for ever. The thing is too great a one for us to hesitate. Either you are heart and soul with us on your oath on the cross of the Christians, or your body this night shall be thrown into the ditch, and we shall pass over to our brothers in the rebel army. There is no middle way. Which is it to be—death or life? We can only give you three minutes to decide, for the time is passing, and all must be done before the rounds come again."

' "How can I decide?" said I. "You have not told me what you want of me. But I tell you now that if it is anything against the safety of the fort I will have no truck with it, so you can drive home your knife, and welcome."

' "It is nothing against the fort," said he. "We only ask you to do that which your countrymen come to this land for. We ask you to be rich. If you will be one of us this night, we will swear to you upon the naked knife, and by the threefold oath, which no Sikh was ever known to break, that you shall have your fair share of the loot. A quarter of the treasure shall be yours. We can say no fairer."

' "But what is the treasure, then?" I asked. "I am as ready to be rich as you can be, if you will but show me how it can be done."

' "You will swear, then," said he, "by the bones of your father, by the honour of your mother, by the cross of your faith, to raise no hand and speak no word against us, either now or afterwards?"

' "I will swear it," I answered, "provided that the fort is not endangered."

' "Then, my comrade and I will swear that you shall have a quarter of the treasure, which shall be equally divided among the four of us."

' "There are but three," said I.

' "No; Dost Akbar must have his share. We can tell the **175** tale to you while we await them. Do you stand at the gate, Mahomet Singh, and give notice of their coming. The thing stands thus, sahib, and I tell it to you because I know that an oath is binding upon a Feringhee, and that we may trust you. **176** Had you been a lying Hindoo, though you had sworn by all the gods in their false temples, your blood would have been upon the knife and your body in the water. But the Sikh knows the Englishman, and the Englishman knows the Sikh. Hearken, then, to what I have to say.

' "There is a rajah in the northern provinces who has much wealth, though his lands are small. Much has come to him from his father, and more still he has set by himself, for he is of a low nature, and hoards his gold rather than spend it. When the troubles broke out he would be friends both with the lion and the tiger—with the Sepoy and with the Company's Raj. Soon, however, it seemed to him that the white men's day was come, for through all the land he could hear of nothing but of their death and their overthrow. Yet, being a careful man, he made such plans that, come what might, half at least of his treasure should be left to him. That which was in gold and silver he kept by him in the vaults of his palace; but the most precious stones and the choicest pearls that he had he put in an iron box, and sent it by a trusty servant, who, under the guise of a merchant, should take it to

175 *Dost Akbar.* "What sort of Sikhs were these . . . who rejoiced in such names as Mahomet Singh, Dost Akbar and Abdullah Khan?" Mr. T. S. Blakeney asked in "Thoughts on *The Sign of the Four.*" "Do Sikhs sport such Mohammedan names? The name 'Singh' is the only admissable one of the lot. Moreover, just as we have seen a curious parallel between the heads of Thaddeus Sholto and a practitioner of black magic known to the late Sir Arthur Conan Doyle, so I may point to the odd fact that, just as these three Sikhs have names that Sikhs would not own, so in Conan Doyle's 'The Mystery of Cloomber' there are three Buddhists—Ram Singh, Lal Hoomi and Mowdar Khan--who have names that assuredly no Buddhist priests would possess."

And Dr. Andrew Boyd has added ("Dr. Watson's Dupe"): "Two Mohammedan names and one bizarre Mohammedan-Sikh hybrid. No educated man with years of service in the Indian Army could possibly have recorded them, even if he was recording another man's garbled narrative, without comment. For those who are not familiar with the way that Indian personal names are strictly related to religion, one may explain that Watson might as well have claimed a knowledge of Scotland and then set down a tale about three simple Highland soldiers named Venizelos, Vasco de Gama, and Voroshilov."

176 *Feringhee* Indian term for a European; said to be the native mispronunciation of the name "Frank."

the fort at Agra, there to lie until the land is at peace. Thus, if the rebels won he would have his money; but if the Company conquered, his jewels would be saved to him. Having thus divided his hoard, he threw himself into the cause of the Sepoys, since they were strong upon his borders. By his doing this, mark you, sahib, his property becomes the due of those who have been true to their salt.

' "This pretended merchant, who travels under the name of Achmet, is now in the city of Agra, and desires to gain his way into the fort. He has with him as travelling-companion my foster-brother, Dost Akbar, who knows his secret. Dost Akbar has promised this night to lead him to a side-postern of the fort, and has chosen this one for his purpose. Here he will come presently and here he will find Mahomet Singh and myself awaiting him. The place is lonely, and none shall know of his coming. The world shall know of the merchant, Achmet, no more, but the great treasure of the rajah shall be divided among us. What say you to it, sahib?"

'In Worcestershire the life of a man seems a great and sacred thing; but it is very different when there is fire and blood all round you, and you have been used to meeting death at every turn. Whether Achmet, the merchant, lived or died was a thing as light as air to me, but at the talk about the treasure my heart turned to it, and I thought of what I might do in the old country with it, and how my folk would stare when they saw their ne'er-do-well coming back with his pockets full of gold moidores. I had, therefore, already made up my mind. Abdullah Khan, however, thinking that I hesitated, pressed the matter more closely.

' "Consider, sabib," said he, "that if this man is taken by the commandant he will be hung or shot, and his jewels taken by the Government, so that no man will be a rupee the better for them. Now, since we do the taking of him, why should we not do the rest as well? The jewels will be as well with us as in the Company's coffers. There will be enough to make every one of us rich men and great chiefs. No one can know about the matter, for here we are cut off from all men. What could be better for the purpose? Say again, then, sahib, whether you are with us, or if we must look upon you as an enemy."

' "I am with you heart and soul," said I.

' "It is well," he answered, handing me back my firelock. "You see that we trust you, for your word, like ours, is not to be broken. We have now only to wait for my brother and the merchant."

' "Does your brother know, then, of what you will do?" I asked.

' "The plan is his. He has devised it. We will go to the gate and share the watch with Mahomet Singh."

'The rain was still falling steadily, for it was just the beginning of the wet season. Brown, heavy clouds were drifting across the sky, and it was hard to see more than a stone-cast. A deep moat lay in front of our door, but the water was in places nearly dried up, and it could easily be crossed. It was strange to me to be standing there with those two wild Punjaubees waiting for the man who was coming to his death.

'Suddenly my eye caught the glint of a shaded lantern at the other side of the moat. It vanished among the mound-heaps, and then appeared again coming slowly in our direction.

"... WITH HIS POCKETS FULL OF GOLD MOIDORES ..."

"Undoubtedly it was . . .. Brazilian moidores with which Small became familiar in India," the late A. Carson Simpson wrote in *Numismatics in the Canon*, Part II. Shown here are: *46*, the 1816 João, Prince Regent; *46a*, the 1822 João VI, reverse only; *47*, the 1826 Pedro I, Bahia mint; *47a*, the 1833 Pedro II, Rio de Janeiro mint, obverse only.

' "Here they are!" I exclaimed.

' "You will challenge him, sahib, as usual," whispered Abdullah. "Give him no cause for fear. Send us in with him, and we shall do the rest while you stay here on guard. Have the lantern ready to uncover, that we may be sure that it is indeed the man."

'The light had flickered onwards, now stopping and now advancing, until I could see two dark figures upon the other side of the moat. I let them scramble down the sloping bank, splash through the mire, and climb half-way up to the gate, before I challenged them.

' "Who goes there?" said I, in a subdued voice.

' "Friends," came the answer. I uncovered my lantern and threw a flood of light upon them. The first was an enormous Sikh, with a black beard which swept nearly down to his cummerbund. Outside of a show I have never seen so tall a man. **177** The other was a little, fat, round fellow, with a great yellow turban, and a bundle in his hand, done up in a shawl. He seemed to be all in a quiver with fear, for his hands twitched as if he had the ague, and his head kept turning to left and right with two bright little twinkling eyes, like a mouse when he ventures out from his hole. It gave me the chills to think of killing him, but I thought of the treasure, and my heart set as hard as a flint within me. When he saw my white face he gave a little chirrup of joy, and came running up towards me.

' "Your protection, sahib," he panted; "your protection for the unhappy merchant Achmet. I have travelled across Rajpootana that I might seek the shelter of the fort at Agra. **178** I have been robbed and beaten and abused because I have been the friend of the Company. It is a blessed night this when I am once more in safety—I and my poor possessions."

' "What have you in the bundle?" I asked.

' "An iron box," he answered, "which contains one or two little family matters which are of no value to others, but which I should be sorry to lose. Yet I am not a beggar; and I shall reward you, young sahib, and your governor also, if he will give me the shelter I ask."

'I could not trust myself to speak longer with the man. The more I looked at his fat, frightened face, the harder did it seem that we should slay him in cold blood. It was best to get it over.

' "Take him to the main guard," said I. The two Sikhs closed in upon him on each side, and the giant walked behind, while they marched in through the dark gateway. Never was a man so compassed round with death. I remained at the gateway with the lantern.

'I could hear the measured tramp of their footsteps sounding through the lonely corridors. Suddenly it ceased, and I heard voices, and a scuffle, with the sound of blows. A moment later there came, to my horror, a rush of footsteps coming in my direction, with a loud breathing of a running man. I turned my lantern down the long, straight passage, and there was the fat man, running like the wind, with a smear of blood across his face, and close at his heels, bounding like a tiger, the great, black-bearded Sikh, with a knife flashing in his hand. I have never seen a man run so fast as that little merchant. He was gaining on the Sikh, and I could see that if he once passed me and got to the open air he would save himself yet. My heart softened to him, but again the thought of

177 *cummerbund.* Anglo-Indian form of the Hindu *kamar-band,* a loin cloth or sash worn around the waist.

178 *Rajpootana.* A region settled in the seventh century by the Rajputs, later an affiliation of 21 Indian states.

' ". . . I SHALL REWARD YOU, YOUNG SAHIB . . ." '

Frontispiece by "H.D." for *Lippincott's Monthly Magazine,* February, 1890.

his treasure turned me hard and bitter. I cast my firelock between his legs as he raced past, and he rolled twice over like a shot rabbit. Ere he could stagger to his feet the Sikh was upon him, and buried his knife twice in his side. The man never uttered moan nor moved muscle, but lay where he had fallen. I think myself that he may have broken his neck with the fall. You see, gentlemen, that I am keeping my promise. I am telling you every word of the business just exactly as it happened, whether it is in my favour or not.'

He stopped, and held out his manacled hands for the whisky-and-water which Holmes had brewed for him. For myself, I confess that I had now conceived the utmost horror of the man, not only for this cold-blooded business in which he had been concerned, but even more for the somewhat flippant and careless way in which he narrated it. Whatever punishment was in store for him, I felt that he might expect no sympathy from me. Sherlock Holmes and Jones sat with their hands upon their knees, deeply interested in the story, but with the same disgust written upon their faces. He may have observed it, for there was a touch of defiance in his voice and manner as he proceeded.

'It was all very bad, no doubt,' said he. 'I should like to know how many fellows in my shoes would have refused a share of this loot when they knew that they would have their throats cut for their pains. Besides, it was my life or his when once he was in the fort. If he had got out, the whole business would come to light, and I should have been court-martialled and shot as likely as not; for people were not very lenient at a time like that.'

'Go on with your story,' said Holmes, shortly.

'Well, we carried him in, Abdullah, Akbar and I. A fine weight he was, too, for all that he was so short. Mahomet Singh was left to guard the door. We took him to a place which the Sikhs had already prepared. It was some distance off, where a winding passage leads to a great empty hall, the brick walls of which were all crumbling to pieces. The earth floor had sunk in at one place, making a natural grave, so we left Achmet the merchant there, having first covered him over with loose bricks. This done, we all went back to the treasure.

'It lay where he had dropped it when he was first attacked. The box was the same which now lies open upon your table. A key was hung by a silken cord to that carved handle upon the top. We opened it, and the light of the lantern gleamed upon a collection of gems such as I have read of and thought about when I was a little lad at Pershore. It was blinding to look upon them. When we had feasted our eyes we took them all out and made a list of them. There were one hundred and forty-three diamonds of the first water, including one which **179** has been called, I believe, "the Great Mogul," and is said to be the second largest stone in existence. Then there were ninety-seven very fine emeralds, and one hundred and seventy rubies, some of which, however, were small. There were forty carbuncles, two hundred and ten sapphires, sixty-one agates, and a great quantity of beryls, onyxes, cats'-eyes, turquoises, and other stones, the very names of which I did not know at the time, though I have become more familiar with them since. Besides this, there were nearly three hundred very fine pearls, twelve of which were set in a gold coronet. By the

179 *"the Great Mogul."* There is in fact a celebrated Golconda diamond called "The Great Mogul," said to have weighed 787 carats before cutting. It was found in 1650 or earlier, and belonged to the Great Mogul until the capture of Delhi in 1739, since which time it has not been traced. Does it lie at the bottom of the Thames?

way, these last had been taken out of the chest, and were not there when I recovered it.

'After we had counted our treasures we put them back into the chest and carried them to the gateway to show them to Mahomet Singh. Then we solemnly renewed our oath to stand by each other and be true to our secret. We agreed to conceal our loot in a safe place until the country should be at peace again, and then to divide it equally among ourselves. There was no use dividing it at present, for if gems of such value were found upon us it would cause suspicion, and there was no privacy in the fort nor any place where we could keep them. We carried the box, therefore, into the same hall where we had buried the body, and there, under certain bricks in the best-preserved wall, we made a hollow and put our treasure. We made careful note of the place, and next day I drew four plans, one for each of us, and put the sign of the four of us at the bottom, for we had sworn that we should each always act for all, so that none might take advantage. That is an oath that I can put my hand to my heart and swear that I have never broken.

'Well, there's no use my telling you gentlemen what came of the Indian Mutiny. After Wilson took Delhi and Sir Colin **180–181** relieved Lucknow the back of the business was broken. Fresh troops came pouring in, and Nana Sahib made himself scarce **182** over the frontier. A flying column under Colonel Greathed **183** came round to Agra and cleared the Pandies away from it. **184** Peace seemed to be settling upon the country, and we four were beginning to hope that the time was at hand when we might safely go off with our share of the plunder. In a moment, however, our hopes were shattered by our being arrested as the murderers of Achmet.

'It came about in this way. When the rajah put his jewels into the hands of Achmet, he did it because he knew that he was a trusty man. They are suspicious folk in the East, however; so what does this rajah do but take a second even more trusty servant and set him to play the spy upon the first? The second man was ordered never to let Achmet out of his sight, and he followed him like his shadow. He went after him that night, and saw him pass through the doorway. Of course, he thought he had taken refuge in the fort, and applied for admission there himself next day, but could find no trace of Achmet. This seemed to him so strange that he spoke about it to a sergeant of guides, who brought it to the ears of the commandant. A thorough search was quickly made and the body was discovered. Thus at the very moment that we thought that all was safe we were all four seized and brought to trial on a charge of murder—three of us because we had held the gate that night, and the fourth because he was known to have been in the company of the murdered man. Not a word about the jewels came out at the trial, for the rajah had been deposed and driven out of India; so no one had any particular interest in them. The murder, however, was clearly made out, and it was certain that we must all have been concerned in it. The three Sikhs got penal servitude for life, and I was condemned to death, though my sentence was afterwards commuted into the same as the others.

'It was rather a queer position that we found ourselves in then. There we were all four tied by the leg and with precious little chance of ever getting out again, while we each held a

180 *Wilson*. Brigadier-General Archdale Wilson, 1803–1874, commander of the Bengal artillery when the Mutiny broke out.

181 *Sir Colin*. Sir Colin Campbell, 1792–1863, one of the outstanding British leaders in the campaign.

182 *Nana Sahib*. One of the native leaders of the rebellion.

183 *Colonel Greathed*. Colonel William Wilberforce Harris Greathed, 1826–1878.

184 *Pandies*. Nickname for the mutineers, from the name of one Pande, a ringleader at the beginning of the trouble.

secret which might have put each of us in a palace if we could only have made use of it. It was enough to make a man eat his heart out to have to stand the kick and the cuff of every petty jack-in-office, to have rice to eat and water to drink, when that gorgeous fortune was ready for him outside, just waiting to be picked up. It might have driven me mad; but I was always a pretty stubborn one, so I just held on and bided my time.

'At last it seemed to me to have come. I was changed from Agra to Madras, and from there to Blair Island in the Andamans. There are very few white convicts at this settlement, and, as I had behaved well from the first, I soon found myself a sort of privileged person. I was given a hut in Hope Town, which is a small place, on the slopes of Mount Harriet, and I was left pretty much to myself. It is a dreary, fever-stricken place, and all beyond our little clearings was infested with wild cannibal natives, who were ready enough to blow a poisoned dart at us if they saw a chance. There was digging and ditching and yam-planting, and a dozen other things to be done, so we were busy enough all day; though in the evening we had a little time to ourselves. Among other things, I learned to dispense drugs for the surgeon, and picked up a smattering of his knowledge. All the time I was on the lookout for a chance of escape; but it is hundreds of miles from any other land, and there is little or no wind in those seas: so it was a terribly difficult job to get away.

'The surgeon, Dr Somerton, was a fast, sporting young chap, and the other young officers would meet in his rooms of an evening and play cards. The surgery, where I used to make up my drugs, was next to his sitting-room, with a small window between us. Often, if I felt lonesome, I used to turn out the lamp in the surgery, and then, standing there. I could hear their talk and watch their play. I am fond of a hand at cards myself, and it was almost as good as having one to watch the others. There was Major Sholto, Captain Morstan, and Lieutenant Bromley Brown, who were in command of the native troops, and there was the surgeon himself, and two or three prison-officials, crafty old hands who played a nice, sly, safe game. A very snug little party they used to make.

'Well, there was one thing which very soon struck me, and that was that the soldiers used always to lose and the civilians to win. Mind, I don't say there was anything unfair, but so it was. These prison-chaps had done little else than play cards ever since they had been at the Andamans, and they knew each other's game to a point, while the others just played to pass the time and threw their cards down anyhow. Night after night the soldiers got up poorer men, and the poorer they got the more keen they were to play. Major Sholto was the hardest hit. He used to pay in notes and gold at first, but soon it came to notes of hand and for big sums. He sometimes would win for a few deals, just to give him heart, and then the luck would set in against him worse than ever. All day he would wander about as black as thunder, and he took to drinking a deal more than was good for him.

'One night he lost even more heavily than usual. I was sitting in my hut when he and Captain Morstan came stumbling along on the way to their quarters. They were bosom friends, those two, and never far apart. The Major was raving about his losses.

' "It's all up, Morstan," he was saying, as they passed my hut. "I shall have to send in my papers. I am a ruined man."

' "Nonsense, old chap!" said the other, slapping him upon the shoulder. "I've had a nasty facer myself, but——" That was all I could hear, but it was enough to set me thinking.

'A couple of days later Major Sholto was strolling on the beach: so I took the chance of speaking to him.

' "I wish to have your advice, Major," said I.

' "Well, Small, what is it?" he asked, taking his cheroot from his lips.

' "I wanted to ask you, sir," said I, "who is the proper person to whom hidden treasure should be handed over. I know where half a million worth lies, and, as I cannot use it myself, I thought perhaps the best thing that I could do would be to hand it over to the proper authorities, and then perhaps they would get my sentence shortened for me."

' "Half a million, Small?" he gasped, looking hard at me to see if I was in earnest.

' "Quite that, sir—in jewels and pearls. It lies there ready for anyone. And the queer thing about it is that the real owner is outlawed and cannot hold property, so that it belongs to the first comer."

' "To Government, Small," he stammered, "to Government." But he said it in a halting fashion, and I knew in my heart that I had got him.

' "You think, then, sir, that I should give the information to the Governor-General?" said I, quietly.

' "Well, well, you must not do anything rash, or that you might repent. Let me hear all about it, Small. Give me the facts."

'I told him the whole story, with small changes, so that he could not identify the places. When I had finished he stood stock-still and full of thought. I could see by the twitch of his lip that there was a struggle going on within him.

' "This is a very important matter, Small," he said at last. "You must not say a word to anyone about it, and I shall see you again soon."

'Two nights later he and his friend, Captain Morstan, came to my hut in the dead of the night with a lantern.

' "I want you just to let Captain Morstan hear that story from your own lips, Small," said he.

'I repeated it as I had told it before.

' "It rings true, eh?" said he. "It's good enough to act upon?"

'Captain Morstan nodded.

' "Look here, Small," said the Major. 'We have been talking it over, my friend here and I, and we have come to the conclusion that this secret of yours is hardly a Government matter, after all, but is a private concern of your own, which, of course, you have the power of disposing of as you think best. Now the question is: What price would you ask for it? We might be inclined to take it up, and at least look into it, if we could agree as to terms." He tried to speak in a cool, careless way, but his eyes were shining with excitement and greed.

' "Why, as to that, gentlemen," I answered, trying also to be cool, but feeling as excited as he did, "there is only one bargain which a man in my position can make, I shall want you to help me to my freedom, and to help my three companions to theirs. We shall then take you into partnership, and give you a fifth share to divide between you."

' "Hum!" said he. "A fifth share! That is not very tempting."

' "It would come to fifty thousand apiece," said I.

' "But how can we gain your freedom? You know very well that you ask an impossibility."

' "Nothing of the sort," I answered. "I have thought it all out to the last detail. The only bar to our escape is that we can get no boat fit for the voyage, and no provisions to last us for so long a time. There are plenty of little yachts and yawls at Calcutta or Madras which would serve our turn well. Do you bring one over. We shall engage to get aboard her by night, and if you will drop us on any part of the Indian coast you will have done your part of the bargain."

' "If there were only one," he said.

' "None or all," I answered. "We have sworn it. The four of us must always act together."

' "You see, Morstan," said he, "Small is a man of his word. He does not flinch from his friends. I think we may very well trust him."

' "It's a dirty business," the other answered. "Yet, as you say, the money will save our commissions handsomely."

' "Well, Small," said the Major, "we must, I suppose, try and meet you. We must first, of course, test the truth of your story. Tell me where the box is hid, and I shall get leave of absence and go back to India in the monthly relief-boat to inquire into the affair."

' "Not so fast," said I, growing colder as he got hot. "I must have the consent of my three comrades. I tell you that it is four or none with us."

' "Nonsense!" he broke in. "What have three black fellows to do with our agreement?"

' "Black or blue," said I, "they are in with me, and we all go together."

'Well, the matter ended by a second meeting, at which Mahomet Singh, Abdullah Khan, and Dost Akbar were all present. We talked the matter over again, and at last we came to an arrangement. We were to provide both the officers with charts of the part of the Agra fort, and mark the place in the wall where the treasure was hid. Major Sholto was to go to India to test our story. If he found the box he was to leave it there, to send out a small yacht provisioned for a voyage, which was to lie off Rutland Island, and to which we were to make our way, and finally to return to his duties. Captain Morstan was then to apply for leave of absence, to meet us at Agra, and there we were to have a final division of the treasure, he taking the Major's share as well as his own. All this we sealed by the most solemn oaths that the mind could think or the lips utter. I sat up all night with paper and ink, and by the morning I had the two charts all ready, signed with the sign of four—that is, of Abdullah, Akbar, Mahomet, and myself.

'Well, gentlemen, I weary you with my long story, and I know that my friend Mr Jones is impatient to get me safely **185** stowed in chokey. I'll make it as short as I can. The villain Sholto went off to India, but he never came back again. Captain Morstan showed me his name among a list of passengers in one of the mail-boats very shortly afterwards. His uncle had died, leaving him a fortune, and he had left the army; yet he could stoop to treat five men as he had treated us. Morstan went over to Agra shortly afterwards, and found, as we expected, that the treasure was indeed gone. The scoundrel had

185 *chokey*. Anglo-Indian slang for jail or prison, from the Hindu *chauki*, meaning a four-sided place or building.

stolen it all, without carrying out one of the conditions on which we had sold him the secret. From that day I lived only for vengeance. I thought of it by day and I nursed it by night. It became an overpowering, absorbing passion with me. I cared nothing for the law—nothing for the gallows. To escape, to track down Sholto, to have my hand upon his throat—that was my one thought. Even the Agra treasure had come to be a smaller thing in my mind than the slaying of Sholto.

'Well, I have set my mind on many things in this life, and never one which I did not carry out. But it was weary years before my time came. I have told you that I had picked up something of medicine. One day when Dr Somerton was down with a fever a little Andaman Islander was picked up by a convict-gang in the woods. He was sick to death, and had gone to a lonely place to die. I took him in hand, though he was as venomous as a young snake, and after a couple of months I got him all right and able to walk. He took a kind of fancy to me then, and would hardly go back to his woods, but was always hanging about my hut. I learned a little of his lingo from him, and this made him all the fonder of me.

'Tonga—for that was his name—was a fine boatman, and owned a big, roomy canoe of his own. When I found that he was devoted to me and would do anything to serve me, I saw my chance of escape. I talked it over with him. He was to bring his boat round on a certain night to an old wharf which was never guarded, and there he was to pick me up. I gave him directions to have several gourds of water and a lot of yams, coco-nuts, and sweet potatoes.

'He was stanch and true, was little Tonga. No man ever had a more faithful mate. On the night named he had his boat at the wharf. As it chanced, however, there was one of the convict-guard down there—a vile Pathan who had never **186** missed a chance of insulting and injuring me. I had always vowed vengeance, and now I had my chance. It was as if fate had placed him in my way that I might pay my debt before I left the island. He stood on the bank with his back to me, and his carbine on his shoulder. I looked about for a stone to beat out his brains with, but none could I see.

'Then a queer thought came into my head, and showed me where I could lay my hand on a weapon. I sat down in the darkness and unstrapped my wooden leg. With three long hops I was on him. He put his carbine to his shoulder, but I struck him full, and knocked the whole front of his skull in. You can see the split in the wood now where I hit him. We both went down together, for I could not keep my balance; but when I got up I found him lying quiet enough. I made for the boat, and in an hour we were well out at sea. Tonga had brought all his earthly possessions with him, his arms and his gods. Among other things, he had a long bamboo spear, and some Andaman coco-nut matting, with which I made a sort of a sail. For ten days we were beating about, trusting to luck, and on the eleventh we were picked up by a trader which was going from Singapore to Jiddah with a cargo of Malay pilgrims. They were a rum crowd, and Tonga and I soon managed to settle down among them. They had one very good quality: they let you alone and asked no questions.

'Well, if I were to tell you all the adventures that my little chum and I went through, you would not thank me, for I

186 *Pathan*. A member of the principal race of Afghanistan. Many are still employed in the British Army, especially in the cavalry. They are counted among the bravest warriors in the East.

would have you here until the sun was shining. Here and there we drifted about the world, something always turning up to keep us from London. All the time, however, I never lost sight of my purpose. I would dream of Sholto at night. A hundred times I have killed him in my sleep. At last, however, some three or four years ago, we found ourselves in England. I had no great difficulty in finding where Sholto lived, and I set to work to discover whether he had realized the treasure, or if he still had it. I made friends with someone **187** who could help me—I name no names, for I don't want to get anyone else in a hole—and I soon found that he still had the jewels. Then I tried to get at him in many ways; but he was pretty sly, and had always two prizefighters, besides his sons and his khitmutgar on guard over him.

'One day, however, I got word that he was dying. I hurried at once to the garden, mad that he should slip out of my clutches like that, and, looking through the window, I saw him lying in his bed, with his sons on each side of him. I'd have come through and taken my chance with the three of them, only even as I looked at him his jaw dropped, and I knew that he was gone. I got into his room the same night, though, and I searched his papers to see if there was any record of where he had hidden our jewels. There was not a line, however, so I came away, bitter and savage as a man could be. Before I left I bethought me that if I ever met my Sikh friends again it would be a satisfaction to know that I had left some mark of our hatred; so I scrawled down the sign of the four of us, as it had been on the chart, and I pinned it on his bosom. It was too much that he should be taken to the grave without some token from the men whom he had robbed and befooled.

'We earned a living at this time by my exhibiting poor Tonga at fairs and other such places as the black cannibal. He would eat raw meat and dance his war-dance: so we always had a hatful of pennies after a day's work. I still heard all the news from Pondicherry Lodge, and for some years there was no news to hear, except that they were hunting for the treasure. At last, however, came what we had waited for so long. The treasure had been found. It was up at the top of the house, in Mr Bartholomew Sholto's chemical laboratory. I came at once and had a look at the place, but I could not see how, with my wooden leg, I was to make my way up to it. I learned, however, about a trap-door in the roof, and also about Mr Sholto's supper-hour. It seemed to me that I could manage the thing easily through Tonga. I brought him out with me with a long rope wound round his waist. He could climb like a cat, and he soon made his way through the roof, but, as ill-luck would have it, Bartholomew Sholto was still in the room, to his cost. Tonga thought he had done something very clever in killing him, for when I came up by the rope I found him strutting about as proud as a peacock. Very much surprised was he when I made at him with the rope's end and cursed him for a little, bloodthirsty imp. I took the treasure box and let it down, and then slid down myself, having first left the sign of the four upon the table, to show that the jewels had come back at last to those who had most right to them. Tonga then pulled up the rope, closed the window, and made off the way that he had come.

'I don't know that I have anything else to tell you. I had

---

187 *someone who could help me.* Professor James Moriarty, in the view of the late Robert R. Pattrick (*see below*).

188 *and was to give him a big sum.* "Queer strangers do not hire fast steam launches," the late Robert R. Pattrick wrote in "Moriarty Was There," "and have them stand in readiness for a day or two, on the basis of a promise. Something more tangible is required, and Small as yet had nothing to prove his story of 'a big sum.' . . . Moriarty, by means which we shall never know, apparently satisfied himself as to the truth of Small's story, made the plans, and advanced the money for the boat hire. Small, after obtaining the treasure, returned with it to the hideout which had been provided for him. The boat hire, and the additional 15% fee for Moriarty, was then paid from the treasure."

189 *the gentleman at the Andaman Isles.'* "Mr. Nathan Bengis has . . . stigmatized Small as a blackguard of the deepest dye," Mr. T. S. Blakeney wrote in "Thoughts on *The Sign of the Four*," "and we know that Holmes, Watson and Athelney Jones openly showed repugnance at Small's story. But I suggest that there is quite a lot to be said in defence of Small. It is not only that he took his defeat by Holmes in a very sporting fashion, though he might well have felt sore at missing by

heard a waterman speak of the speed of Smith's launch, the *Aurora*, so I thought she would be a handy craft for our escape. I engaged with old Smith, and was to give him a big sum if he got us safe to our ship. He knew, no doubt, that **188** there was some screw loose, but he was not in our secrets. All this is the truth, and if I tell it to you, gentlemen, it is not to amuse you—for you have not done me a very good turn— but it is because I believe the best defence I can make is just to hold back nothing, but let all the world know how badly I have myself been served by Major Sholto, and how innocent I am of the death of his son.'

'A very remarkable account,' said Sherlock Holmes. 'A fitting wind-up to an extremely interesting case. There is nothing at all new to me in the latter part of your narrative, except that you brought your own rope. That I did not know. By the way, I had hoped that Tonga had lost all his darts; yet he managed to shoot one at us in the boat.'

'He had lost them all, sir, except the one which was in his blow-pipe at the time.'

'Ah, of course,' said Holmes. 'I had not thought of that.'

'Is there any other point which you would like to ask about?' asked the convict, affably.

'I think not, thank you,' my companion answered.

'Well, Holmes,' said Athelney Jones, 'you are a man to be humoured, and we all know that you are a connoisseur of crime; but duty is duty, and I have gone rather far in doing what you and your friend asked me. I shall feel more at ease when we have our story-teller here safe under lock and key. The cab still waits, and there are two inspectors downstairs. I am much obliged to you both for your assistance. Of course, you will be wanted at the trial. Good night to you.'

'Good night, gentlemen both,' said Jonathan Small.

'You first, Small,' remarked the wary Jones as they left the room. 'I'll take particular care that you don't club me with your wooden leg, whatever you may have done to the gentle- man at the Andaman Isles.' **189**

'Well, and there is the end of our little drama,' I remarked, after we had sat some time smoking in silence. 'I fear that it may be the last investigation in which I shall have the chance of studying your methods. Miss Morstan has done me the honour to accept me as a husband in prospective.'

He gave a most dismal groan.

'I feared as much,' said he. 'I really cannot congratulate you.' **190**

I was a little hurt.

'Have you any reason to be dissatisfied with my choice?' I asked.

'Not at all. I think she is one of the most charming young ladies I ever met, and might have been most useful in such work as we have been doing. She had a decided genius that way; witness the way in which she preserved that Agra plan from all the other papers of her father. But love is an emo- tional thing, and whatever is emotional is opposed to that true, cold reason which I place above all things. I should **191** never marry myself, lest I bias my judgment.' **192**

'I trust,' said I, laughing, 'that my judgment may survive the ordeal. But you look weary.'

'Yes, the reaction is already upon me. I shall be as limp as a rag for a week.'

so narrow a margin his escape with the loot. But there were, I think, many extenuating circum- stances in the story of the killing of Achmet. . . . I urge, therefore, that Jonathan Small be judged with more leniency; he was placed in an impos- sible situation where whatever he did was likely to bring misfortune to someone."

190 *'I really cannot congratulate you.'* "And why couldn't Holmes congratulate Watson?" Mr. Jerry Neal Williamson asked in "'The Latest Treatise Upon Pathology.'" "Because Holmes knew that Watson had shared an affair, and other things, with a certain well-known woman and had become entangled with her; and he feared that Watson would wound Mary, 'one of the most charming young ladies' Holmes had ever met. In Holmes' usual candid honesty, he could not ex- press happiness over his companion's betrothal, for he did not feel it. Holmes was worried: for Watson, for Mary, and for Watson's mistress. . . . Dr. John H. Watson enjoyed a sporadic affair with none other than Irene Adler, during the years 1886 to 1888!"

There are, needless to say, other views: Dr. Ebbe Curtis Hoff, for example, in "The Adven- ture of John and Mary," has suggested that Holmes could not congratulate Watson because: 1) he lost a potential colleague in Mary; 2) he lost his Boswell; and 3) he saw ahead a tragic bereavement for his friend: when Mary first came to Baker Street "Holmes noticed . . . a thickening of the nails. . . . Holmes knew, of course, that this 'clubbing' of the fingers is pathognomic of a num- ber of illnesses caused by faulty oxygenation of the blood, such as mitral stenosis or pulmonary tuberculosis."

191 *whatever is emotional is opposed to that true, cold reason which I place above all things.* "This is impressive enough," Dean Theodore C. Blegen wrote in "These Were Hidden Fires, In- deed!", "but we might remember that in 'The Adventure of the Abbey Grange' warm kindness rather than cold reason leads Mr. Holmes to play the role of judge, with Dr. Watson as jury, and Captain Crocker escapes the law. 'I had rather play tricks with the law of England than with my own conscience,' says Mr. Holmes, and we ap- plaud him, for we want Crocker to go free and we sentimentally hope he will marry the lady in the case."

192 *I should never marry myself,* "There is no evidence . . . that Sherlock Holmes never had mar- ried," Miss Esther Longfellow wrote in "The Distaff Side of Baker Street." "He does not so say. He merely indicates that he never *should* . . . and that the state is distasteful to him because it would interfere with his work, to which he is now wedded. It is plain that Mr. Holmes knows exactly what effect marriage would have upon him. How would he know this if he had never married?"

193 *Shelman der Stoff.* "Credit is due to young Schiller also," Mr. Morris Rosenblum wrote in "Foreign Language Quotations in the Canon," "since the lines come from the *Xenian,* a collection written by Goethe and Schiller in 1796. . . . The use of *Mensch* is a departure from the original *Menschen.* The translation runs, 'Nature, alas, made only one being out of you although there was material for a good man and a rogue.'"

Mr. Bliss Austin has added ("Two Bibliographical Footnotes") that ". . . the Canonical version of this quotation omits the comma after *Schade.* This is clearly Watson's doing. Holmes, who—like Goethe—was always pithy, would hardly have recited this couplet complete with punctuation, and it probably never occurred to Watson that there should be a comma at this particular place."

Bibliographical Note: The readers of the *Observer* ranked *The Sign of the Four* No. 3 on their list of favorite Sherlock Holmes stories. The original manuscript, consisting of 160 leaves, folio, was auctioned in New York City on December 9, 1909, bringing $105. "Persistent rumor places this manuscript in Chicago, but diligent inquiry has failed to uncover its lucky possessor," Professor David A. Randall wrote in his scholarly bibliographical notes on *The Sign of the Four* in the *Baker Street Journal.* One folio sheet of the manuscript, about 220 words, the beginning of the story, with corrections in the author's hand as well as several printer's notations in ink, shown at right, was auctioned in New York City on November 22, 1929, bringing $50. In 1946 it was owned by Mr. Carroll A. Wilson; it was later (1954) in the possession of Mr. Ed Morris of Philadelphia. By far the most extensive and the most scholarly bibliography of *The Sign of the Four* is *The "Signs" of our Times* by Mr. Nathan L. Bengis; New York: Privately printed, June, 1956.

'Strange,' said I, 'how terms of what in another man I should call laziness alternate with your fits of splendid energy and vigour.'

'Yes,' he answered, 'there are in me the makings of a very fine loafer, and also of a pretty spry sort of a fellow. I often think of those lines of old Goethe:

193
Schade dass die Natur nur *einen* Mensch aus dir schuf,
Denn zum würdigen Mann war und zum Schelmen der Stoff.

By the way, apropos of this Norwood business, you see that they had, as I surmised, a confederate in the house, who could be none other than Lal Rao, the butler: so Jones actually has the undivided honour of having caught one fish in his great haul.'

'The division seems rather unfair,' I remarked. 'You have done all the work in this business. I get a wife out of it, Jones gets the credit; pray what remains for you?'

'For me,' said Sherlock Holmes, 'there still remains the cocaine-bottle.' And he stretched his long, white hand up for it.

The Sign of the Four.

Chapter I.
The Science of deduction.

Sherlock Holmes took his bottle from the corner of the mantelpiece and his hypodermic syringe from its neat Morocco case. With his long, white, nervous fingers he adjusted the delicate needle, and rolled back his left shirt cuff. For some little time his eyes rested thoughtfully upon the sinewy fore arm and wrist all dotted and scarred with innumerable puncture-marks. Finally he thrust the sharp point home, pressed down the tiny piston, and sank back into the velvet-lined armchair with a long sigh of satisfaction.

Three times a day for many months I had witnessed this performance, but custom had not reconciled my mind to it. On the contrary, from day to day I had become more irritable at the sight, and my conscience swelled nightly within me at the thought that I had lacked the courage to protest. Again and again I had registered a vow that I should deliver my soul upon the subject, but there was that in the cool nonchalant air of my companion which made him the last man with whom one would care to take anything approaching to a liberty. His great powers, his masterly manner, and the experience which I had had of his many

May Day

oLeeds
Bradford
YORK
LANCASHIRE
Tarleton

New Brighton oLiverpool
THE PEAK
LOWER GILL MOOR
Mackleton HALLAMSHIRE Ch

oBangor
Crewe o
Derbyo

53

0 5 10 15 20 25 30 35 40 45
MILES.

N

Walsall
Aston
oBirmingham
Covo
WORCESTER-SHIRE
HEREFORDSHIRE Pershore
Hereford o
BOSCOMBE VALLEY
Ross o
Gloucester OXF
52
Abergavenny STROUD VALLEY
Swindon o B
SA
Cren
RIVER SEVERN Bristol o

A T L A N T I C
Andove
Wilton o Winc
THOR MERE
S
51
O C E A N
Fordingbridge
NEW FOR
D E V O N S H I R E
Folkestone Court
oExeter
GRIMPEN
MIRE
King's Pyland
Tavistock THORSLEY
PARISH Grimpen
Princetown Fernworthy
DART- PORTLAND
LONG DOWN Coombe Tracey
Plymouth MOOR
HIGH BARROW
PARISH
ENGLISH CHA
St. Ives oRedruth
Tredannick BEAUCHAMP ARRIANCE
Wollas
Falmouth
POLDHU BAY MOUNTS Helston
BAY
Gloria Scott
50

5 4 3 2

ENGLAND

"I KNOW THAT COUNTRY, HOLMES."
The Adventure of the Sussex Vampire.

JULIAN
WOLFF
1940

The Adventure
of the
Sussex Vampire

The
Problem of
Thor Bridge

The Case
of
Isadora Persano

The Adventure
of the
Speckled Band

The Adventure
of the
Cardboard Box

The Adventure
of the
Engineer's
Thumb

The Adventure
of the
Bruce Partington
Plans

The Famous
Card Scandal
of the
Non-Pareil Club

The
Disappearance
of Lady
Frances Carfax

The Politician
the Lighthouse
and the Trained
Cormorant

HARROW WEALD

PINNER

MIDDLESEX

HARROW

WILLESDEN

KIL

NOTT

Kensi

KENS

Gloucester

HAMMERSMITH

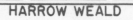

0   1   MILES   3   4

SCALE

CHISWICK

H

OLD
DEER
PARK

RICHMOND

WIMBLED

KINGSTON

MOLESEY

ESHER

OXSHOTT

LONDON

"I NATURALLY GRAVITATED TO LONDON"

A Study in Scarlet

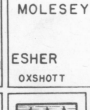

The Adventure
of the
Three Students

The Adventure
of the
Noble Bachelor

The Adventure
of the Dying
Detective

The Giant Rat
of
Sumatra

Wilson
the Notorious
Canary Trainer